ANITA BURGH
Three Great Novels

Also by Anita Burgh

Anita Burgh

Three Great Novels

Distinctions of Class
Advances
Breeders

ORION

Distinction of Class Copyright © Anita Burgh 1997
Advances Copyright © Anita Burgh 1997
Breeders Copyright © Anita Burgh 1996

This omnibus edition first published in Great Britain in 2005 by Orion,
an imprint of the Orion Publishing Group Ltd.

A CIP catalogue record for this book is
available from the British Library.

ISBN 0 75286 928 0 (trade paperback)

Typeset by SetSystems Ltd,
Saffron Walden, Essex

Set in Minion

Printed in Great Britain by
Clays Ltd, St Ives plc

The Orion Publishing Group Ltd
Orion House
5 Upper Saint Martin's Lane
London, WC2H 9EA

Contents

Distinctions
of Class

Billy and Pete
for different reasons
with equal love

Prologue

Jane Reed sat alone at the back of the plane. Jane always sat alone as the engines revved to a screaming intensity and the fuselage began to shudder with the strain. She needed to be isolated with her fear; the confidence, the banter of the others only fuelled her terror. She was better by herself.

The great machine began to roll. This was the point when she always intended to change her mind, to stand up and insist on getting off, but never did. The force, as the plane began its headlong catapulting down the runway, pressed her back into her seat. She closed her eyes so as not to see the terrifying speed she could feel, the knuckles of her hands showing white as she clenched them tightly together.

We're just like suicidal lemmings, sitting here, she thought as the plane hurtled towards its point of no return.

Jane had tried everything – hypnosis, Valium, gin, even pot – but there was no drug, no treatment known to man, that could calm this otherwise confident woman into acceptance of air travel.

The large, chintz-covered armchair in which she sat accentuated her smallness. She was dressed casually for travel in a well-cut tracksuit made of the finest silk and not intended for the running track. The grey of the fabric matched exactly the grey of the large eyes hidden now by the firmly shut eyelids. The handmade shoes, the Hermès scarf draped about her shoulders, the cascade of gold chains around her neck, proclaimed her wealth before one even noticed the large diamond rings sparkling on the manicured hands.

Had she not been so famous it would have been impossible to be certain of her age. Her skin was clear and still had the bloom of a much younger woman. The few fine lines around her eyes seemed only to emphasize their size and beauty, as if they had been applied by an expert beautician. Her mouth was full and generous. The high cheekbones and the firm chin were as nature had made them, unhelped by surgeons' skills. The small, light body gave an impression of fragility that disguised the toughness of which Jane was capable. People always wanted to help and protect her, and Jane had learned to use this fact to her advantage. But she was famous, and wherever her name appeared, there in brackets beside it, for all the world to see, was her age. Not that Jane minded, for with her looks, being in her forties seemed irrelevant.

'You can open your eyes, undo your seatbelt, have a fag. We're safely up!'

Jane heard the patient humour in Fran's voice. Gingerly she opened her eyes and grinned at the woman who stood opposite her.

'Silly, aren't I?'

'Damn silly when you think how often you fly.'

'Safer than crossing the road?'

'Exactly. Safest form of travel there is.'

'But I always feel as if I'm stepping into my own coffin when I get into this thing.'

'I know.'

'You know?'

'I should do.' Fran laughed. 'We have this inane conversation every time we take off.'

'Do we?'

'Yes, dear Jane, word for word!' Fran flopped down in the opposite chair. 'Drink?'

Jane nodded agreement and Fran pressed the bell to summon the steward-ess. With her unvaried smile the stewardess placed the already poured drinks before them.

Jane watched the girl undulate back up the plane. Her tartan uniform looked ridiculous. It just didn't suit the decor. Jane knew it was her own fault. The chintz seat covers, slubbed silk walls and matching curtains had been intended to make the interior look like a drawing room, to delude Jane into thinking she was not airborne. It had failed. Chintzy aeroplanes did not look right. That epicene young designer, stamping his Gucci shoes with rage at her suggestions, had been right all along. She would have to have it changed.

'Cashmere! Green cashmere, that's the answer.'

'What for?' Fran looked up from the papers she was working on.

'This plane. Just look at it, like a flying bordello. It's dreadful. I want it changed immediately we get back. The stewardess's uniform as well. Some-thing Scottish, but not bloody tartan, and get rid of all this chintz.'

'I agree about the chintz – shame about the tartan.'

'But it always looks so out of place outside Scotland, like refugees from *Brigadoon*!'

'Light or dark?'

'Light.'

'I'll get on to Campbells of Beauly.' Fran made a note in the huge notepad that she always carried.

'You know, Fran, I can't think why we don't manufacture it ourselves. We've the tweeds, wool, silk – why not cashmere? We must find out if it needs special looms or whatever.' She looked at the now offending chintz. 'Do you think you can upholster in it?'

'Shouldn't think so. Wouldn't stand up to my huge arse for long, if you did.' Fran snorted.

Jane frowned. 'Don't put yourself down, Fran.'

'It's true, I do have a huge arse.'

'There's no need to keep harping on it,' Jane said sharply. She hated the way that Fran disparaged herself. Fran's shape was certainly unique – square face, which seemed to melt, chinless, into an equally square neck above her solid trunk, which ended in a pair of stocky legs. After all these years, Jane was only aware of Fran's shape when Fran chose to mention it. But Fran, within seconds of greeting a stranger, would make some remark about her size. She claimed she did it to get in first, but Jane felt it was done out of embarrassment for her unfashionable bulk. While it upset Jane to imagine what pain and insecurity must lurk in Fran, it also had the uncomfortable effect of reminding Jane of the agonies and insecurities she herself had suffered in the past and which she liked to imagine she had buried.

'Irritates you, does it?'

'A bit.' Jane smiled apologetically, already regretting snapping at her friend.

'It's all right for skin-and-bone fashion plates like you.'

'Skin and bone! Me? You must be joking. My boobs are far too big.'

'So you can say your boobs are too big but I'm not allowed to comment on the memorable size of my arse?'

'Touché!' Jane offered Fran a cigarette from her heavy, gold cigarette case, decorated in sapphires with initials which had once been hers.

'You looked lovely the other night at Max Shielberg's party.' Jane smiled.

'Bah! I looked like a Bedouin's tent, more like!'

'I haven't always looked like this. It took years of practice. And the money helps.'

'All the money in the world wouldn't make me look any different.'

'I love you as you are.'

'I don't know if that's a compliment or not.' But Fran smiled broadly at her.

'God, I feel tired,' sighed Jane, stretching her hands over her head.

'You don't look it – as usual.' Fran looked at her friend. 'I quite expected you to pop in last night for a natter.'

'I would have, Fran, but it was so late. I didn't want to wake you.'

'Official receptions don't usually go on that late.' There was a teasing note in Fran's voice.

'It didn't, it ended at ten, I went on . . .'

'Anywhere interesting?'

'Anyone, you mean.' Jane laughed at her friend. 'No . . . not the way you're thinking! But a very interesting man. He's a Brazilian diplomat – wanted to talk about the trust and the possibility of setting one up in Brazil, so there!'

'Affairs have to start somewhere.'

'Fran, you're impossible! Worse than a mother! A couple of drinks and you think I'm having an affair.'

'I wish you would, Jane,' Fran said, suddenly serious. 'You don't have nearly enough fun for a woman who's still as attractive as you are.'

'My dear friend, the idea of starting an affair, at my age, is too daunting. Getting to know a stranger, all that agonizing waiting for the phone to ring – "Will he, won't he?" – Quite honestly, I couldn't be bothered.'

'Then don't have an affair with a stranger – have one with an old friend.'

Jane looked up sharply. 'And what exactly do you mean by that?'

'What I say . . .'

'One can't go back. It never works, Fran.'

'You know what? I think you're scared to try. I never thought I would think of you as a coward.'

'Well, you learn something new every day, don't you?' Jane said lightly.

Jane saw that Fran was settling herself for a long talk, but Jane kicked her shoes off and curled up in the large armchair.

'You going to sleep?' The disappointment in Fran's voice was blatant.

'Just a little snooze. Wake me up for dinner.' She lay back, her eyes closed. There were times when she thought that Fran could bore into her mind. It was almost if she knew about the letter.

Her hand rested protectively on her handbag. Now and again she would pat it, as if it were a pet dog, and a gentle smile hovered about her mouth. Inside lay a letter, creased from constant reading; a letter that years ago she would have had no problem in answering. But now? She was thankful to have these moments, above the Atlantic, to think. Jane Reed had a decision to make: one that could change her extraordinary life, once again.

One
1951–55

1

It had been a noisy childhood. The traffic rumbled a pavement's width from their front door; trains shunted monotonously in the sidings two streets away; the piercing shouts of children playing in the street continued from morning to night; the neighbours bickered endlessly beyond the paper-thin walls. At regular intervals the mournful wail of the factory hooter, summoning the various shifts to work, punctuated this tapestry of noise.

Jane lay in her narrow bed. The bed had to be narrow because the room was so small that the bedside table, low bookcase, and child's desk and chair filled it to capacity. A dingy, black-and-brown peg-rag rug lay on the linoleum floor which had once been patterned in blue and pink but was now faded from continual polishing to a dull beige. The unused gas bracket loomed above her bed, capped off but full of gas, a constant source of nightmares for Jane. The walls were distempered, the brushmarks clearly visible on the surface. As the paint flaked constantly, it was renewed every year so that, with each application, the colour darkened. Now the original pale pink colour had become a lurid salmon pink. The green curtains at the small sash window did not complement the pink walls, nor did the blue, flowered material hanging across the alcove which served as a wardrobe.

As the factory hooter pealed out its first summons, Jane stirred and lay waiting for the next significant noise of her morning. Through the flimsy wall she heard the shrill ringing of her neighbour's alarm clock. He swore as he attempted to stop the bell and sent the clock crashing to the floor. The bed springs twanged as he heaved himself up. She could imagine him flicking his greasy, black hair out of his eyes as he fumbled for his heavy boots. Two loud steps and the sash window was raised. She closed her eyes as if, by not seeing, she could blot out the sound she dreaded and which she heard every waking morning, except Sunday. On Sundays, when he lay in, she was spared the hawking and gobbing noises as he cleared the phlegm from his lungs, the globules of sputum rattling onto the corrugated iron roof of the shed beneath his window. Later, his mother would come with a bucket of disinfected water and sluice the slime away, so that always about Jane's room hung the institutional smell of disinfectant. The very sight of him filled her with disgust.

7

She knew the neighbours thought her stuck-up but she could never bring herself to speak to him.

Beneath her, in the kitchen, she heard her father stirring the sugar in the teacups. Apart from scrubbing the yard once a week, it was the only thing she had ever seen him do about the house. She was surprised that after last night's row, he should even bother. A door slammed, and then the heavy footsteps on the stairs. Her door opened – how nice, she thought, if, just once, he would knock. He placed the cup on the green painted tea chest that served as a bedside table. He grunted. He always grunted in the mornings, rarely spoke. She did not look at him. Silently he turned and shuffled along the landing to her mother's room.

She sipped the sweet, orange-coloured tea and wished that she need not remember last night, but the memory kept slinking into her consciousness. There had been no warning, but that was not unusual. In this house, rows and violence flared up with depressing regularity, from nowhere and frequently about nothing.

They had been sitting around the table eating their tea – fishcakes for Friday.

'I've spoken to the foreman, Jane. You can start work next month,' her father announced.

'Pardon?'

'You heard.'

'I heard, but I didn't understand.'

'Oh, didn't you? Then let me explain,' her father said in a sarcastic tone. 'You're over fourteen. It's time you quit school and got a job and started paying your way, like everyone has to.'

'Charlie! Don't talk such rubbish!' her mother interjected.

'I'm not talking rubbish. Fourteen is school-leaving age, so why hasn't she left?'

'Fourteen is for those who didn't pass the scholarship, and well you know it. I want Jane to stay on into the sixth form. Then she'll get a proper job and all the expense will have been worthwhile.'

'Sixth form!' he snorted. 'Now who's talking rubbish, woman?' He glared at his wife.

'But, Dad, they're putting up the school-leaving age to fifteen.'

'Exactly! So now's the time for you to leave, before they do.'

'But I haven't finished, I'd leave with no qualifications. It would all have been a waste.'

'I always said it would be a waste. But, that aside, truth is, young woman, I've had enough of supporting you. I'm fed up to the back teeth, working my fingers to the bone, seeing you lolling about on your fat arse doing nothing. I'm not paying out a penny more.'

'You bastard!' her mother shouted. 'You "work your fingers to the bone", that'll be the day! No, you're up to something, you rotten sod! You're doing this to spite me, aren't you?'

'Don't talk so bloody silly. I said why I'm doing it.'

'No, there's more to this.' Her mother stared hard at her husband. 'There's something else. You never wanted her to go to the Grammar, never. And now she's there, you want to ruin everything. Have you no pride in her?'

'Pride? In that?' her father sneered at her. 'Stuck-up little cow, that's all she's become with her fancy education. And thinking she's superior to me all the time.'

'Dad, that's not fair . . .'

'Jealous!' her mother interrupted triumphantly. 'You pathetic creature, you're jealous of your own daughter. Jealous, 'cause she's getting the chance you never had.'

Jane looked sharply at her father. She had heard the story so many times – how her father had won a scholarship to the grammar school, and how his own father had refused to let him go. Could that really be the reason for his actions? She looked at the once handsome face now marred by bitterness and her anger began to fade. She felt sorry for him. Tentatively she put out her hand to him.

'Dad, I'm so sorry. I didn't think . . .'

'Don't talk bloody stupid, girl! I don't know what rubbish your mother is going on about. Jealous? Why should I be jealous of you? I work hard for my money and I've decided I don't want to spend any more on you. It's as simple as that, you see . . .' He smiled at her but the smile was full of malice.

'Boozing!' Her mother had not finished with him yet. 'So you can have more money to go down the bloody boozer, that's your reason, you selfish bugger!'

'I spend my money how I bloody well want and if you don't shut your face, Maeve, you won't see a penny more of it either.'

Both parents purposefully lit cigarettes, inhaled deeply, and, in unison, pushed the plates in front of them to one side, as if clearing a space for combat. Like boxers flexing their muscles they faced each other across the table. The snarling and sniping continued, each cutting the other a little deeper with every remark. There was no longer any place for Jane in this argument, her parents had taken it entirely to themselves and, ignoring her, concentrated with practised ease on the task of destroying each other.

It was a familiar enough scene and Jane knew there was no point in her staying. She collected the plates, washed them up, put them neatly away and slipped up to the haven of her room.

It was Friday, too, she thought sadly. All her life Friday had been different. When she was a child, it had meant bath night. The water-filled copper was lit, two huge saucepans bubbled on the gas stove. The tin bath was taken from its rusty hook in the yard and placed in front of the banked-up fire, and she would sit in the water and enjoy the warmth and the pretty colour of the firelight glistening on her skin. Her mother would shampoo her hair and rinse it with jugs full of water that cascaded over her face as if she were sitting in her own private waterfall. She would be lifted out and wrapped in a heated towel and then allowed to spend the rest of the evening in her pyjamas, ready warmed on the hearth, listening to the wireless. As she grew older and her body began to develop, she was not allowed to bath in front of the fire any more but had to endure the chill of the kitchen. However, alone in the kitchen, she could cut her nails on Fridays, something her mother had never allowed, declaring it an invitation for the devil to enter her body.

And, once a month, Friday meant a trip across town to see her aunt. Her uncle owned a shop and they lived on a hill, in a house which had bay windows and a door with stained glass in it, and a little garden in front. It was her mother's dream to live in such a road with a front garden separating them from the traffic.

The main reason for the visit was that her aunt owned a television set. They certainly did not go there for the conversation. As soon as they arrived, they would sit down in front of the magical machine and, when the screen went blank, they left. If she was very lucky, her aunt would invite her to stay the night. Then she had the luxury of a bath in a real bathroom with shiny tiles on the wall and endless hot water from the giant geyser that wheezed and sighed above the bath.

She lay on her bed and longed to sleep but the row progressed with increased ferocity. She wondered where they got the energy from. The sound of crashing glass made her sit bolt upright. She leaped from her bed and rushed downstairs. In the living room both parents stood in frozen attitudes, looking at a smashed glass bowl, its pieces lying in the hearth and on the fireside rug.

'Mum! Dad! For God's sake stop this!'

Slowly her mother turned to face her. Jane was shocked by the ravaged, tear-stained face, the eyes blazing with anger, the mouth contorted by her inner bitterness.

'Look at that! Look at that! The one lovely thing I possessed. The only thing . . .' and the woman started to cry with a harsh wailing noise which sounded more animal than human.

'Dad, how could you? Mum loved that bowl!'

'That's right, blame me. I didn't break the bloody thing. The silly cow did it herself!' he shouted back.

Jane stepped forward and gingerly began to pick up the sharp fragments of glass.

'Maybe we can mend it,' she said hopefully.

'Don't be so stupid. It's gone.' Suddenly her mother pushed her. Jane looked at her with surprise. Her mother pushed her again, harder, her fingers prodding painfully into Jane's flesh. 'See what you've done? See my glass bowl?'

'But, Mum, I wasn't even here, I didn't touch it.'

'It's your fault! It's because of you it's all broken. If it wasn't for you, we wouldn't have been arguing in the first place. Oh, Christ! Why were you ever born . . .?'

Jane stood shocked and speechless. The sentence seemed to hang suspended in the air between them. Her parents both looked as surprised as she. Her first instinct was to cry but a sudden swell of anger doused all feelings of self pity.

'I never asked to be born, certainly not into this hellhole!' she screamed. She turned from them and rushed blindly out of the door and up the stairs to her room. There, with the door safely shut, she allowed the tears of anger and pain to flow.

2

Now it was morning. There had been other mornings after other rows when life had simply gone on as usual, but this time Jane could not see how anything could be the same again.

It was fairly common, after a row with her husband, for Jane's mother to say to her child, 'If it wasn't for you, I'd be off . . .' But she had never gone. Jane had always assumed that she had stayed because of love for her. Consequently, Jane could not remember a time when she had not felt guilt for her mother's unhappiness, seeing herself as the trap which had prevented the woman from finding a better, happier life. But now . . . 'Why were you ever born?' How could you love someone if you wished she had never been born, and, from wishing that, how big a step was it to wishing her dead?

Jane knew that her father did not like her – she could hardly have escaped the fact since he frequently told her so. But she was certain it had not always been that way. She could just remember a time, during the war, when she had sat on his lap, enjoying the smell of his tobacco, her head on his chest, her cheek against the rough serge of his uniform, his voice rumbling deeply against her ear as he read her the story of Jane Squirrel from the only book that he had bought her and signed 'with love'. She still had the book but she did not know, or understand, what had changed his attitude to her. It all seemed so long ago. Of course, there had been the incident of the bird. Maybe that was it.

A neighbour had given her a kitten, and she was overjoyed when her mother said she could keep it. She lavished love on the little animal, delighting in its purring contentment. Two weeks after the cat had come into her life, he strayed into a garden at the bottom of the alley. The old woman who lived there had hurled a brick at the cat, shattering the tiny creature's spine. Jane had found him, blood spewing from his mouth, writhing in agony. She scooped him into her arms and tried to love him better as he died. Her grief had been such that her mother had said she could never again have a pet. So she was surprised when on her birthday her father had appeared with a budgerigar in a cage. Her father was angered by her lack of enthusiasm. She had tried to explain that she was frightened to have another pet in case it, too, died. Nor did she want to own a poor creature locked up in a cage. Perhaps her explanations had been clumsy, for he had hit her hard, declaring her an ungrateful bitch, and stormed off to the pub. He looked after the bird himself and, secretly, she would watch him stroking its green and yellow feathers, looking at it with tenderness. She felt herself wishing that she was the little bird and that he would look at her and touch her like that. But she could not remember how soon after the book the bird had come, or even if it was her attitude to the bird that had made him dislike her.

She slipped out of bed. In the kitchen her father sat with a cup of tea, studiously reading his *Daily Mirror*. He ignored her. She washed her face and hands, wishing as always that there were somewhere more private. She poured herself some tea and, sitting down, noted with distaste the chamber pot, placed by the back door to be emptied – she turned her back on it.

'Dad, can we talk?' she asked nervously.

'There's nothing to talk about.'

'But school, it means so much to me.'

'I expect it does, but there's one important lesson to learn in life and that is that you can't always have what you want. The sooner you learn that the better.'

'But –'

'The subject is closed. I'm going to my allotment.' He struggled into his jacket and made for the door. 'Empty the piss pot for me,' he said as he clattered out into the yard in his heavy boots. She heard the scrape of his bicycle as he dragged it out of the shed. He had asked her to do that to humiliate her. He knew how she loathed the chamber pot, how for years she had refused one of her own, preferring to brave the cold and the dark, and to pick her way, torch in hand, to the outside lavatory. With an expression of distaste she picked up the pot and carefully carried it down the yard, fearful that she might be seen with her shameful burden. The yeasty smell of the urine hit her nostrils as she hurriedly threw it down the lavatory and pulled the chain. Back in the kitchen, she boiled the kettle to scald the chamber pot, and afterwards scrubbed her hands vigorously with the 'Lifebuoy' soap.

She went into the small living room and cleared the grate, carefully picking up the remaining pieces of broken glass, putting them to one side in the vain hope that something could be done with them. She looked around the tiny room, at the moquette-covered settee, her father's worn, imitation-leather armchair, the dining table with its ugly, bulbous legs which seemed to attract the dust spewed out daily from the factory. She straightened the picture of camels striding across the Sahara Desert, and wondered why it always depressed her. She looked at herself in the mirror – 'bevelled-edged' her mother would declare with pride – and she hated this tiny house, and this ugly room with the dado starting to peel from the walls. She hated this life where neighbours gobbed out of windows, and chamber pots had to be emptied, and knew with a heart-sinking certainty that if she could not stay at school there would be no escape for her, ever.

Her life had changed dramatically the day she had passed the exam that had given her a place at the local grammar school. She had rushed home with the news, bursting with pride and excitement, slipping around the back way to avoid the local women gossiping on their doorsteps. And the news tumbled out of her in breathless excitement.

'My God, think of the cost of the uniform!' was her mother's reaction.

'Right!' her father agreed for once. 'We can't afford it. And anyhow, it's a ridiculous waste of money. What's the point of educating a girl? She'll only land up at the kitchen sink.'

For Jane, his reaction was the best thing that could have happened. Had her father been happy for her to go to the school, then her mother would inevitably have objected, so deep was her distrust of him. But, by declaring that he would never sign the necessary papers, her father inadvertently secured Jane's future.

Going to the new school, she became alienated from her friends in the street who went to the secondary modern school where they learned to hate all grammar-school kids, including herself. She would cycle miles out of her way to avoid passing them, for she was likely to be met with a hail of abuse and occasionally with stones. The gulf which had opened up between herself and her friends saddened and puzzled her. She was still the same person, a uniform couldn't change that. They had all had the same chance – it wasn't her fault that she had passed while they had failed. Now she had no one to play with, for the resentments continued long after school was out.

But at school there were wonderful compensations. She discovered that some people thought reading was a thing to be encouraged, not, as her mother saw it, a waste of time, and unhealthy too. She had not been allowed to join the library because her mother thought that the books were dirty and full of germs, so she had to make do with the few books in the house. By the age of ten she had read all the works of Dickens from the matching set which her father had won in a raffle, and the *Complete Home Doctor*. She saved all her pocket money for books, which worried her mother who confided to Aunt Vi that she thought Jane was odd in the head.

For the first time she learned that there was music which, when you listened to it, washed through your brain and could make you sad when you were happy, and happy when you were sad: music which made her feel that anything in her young life was possible.

She discovered paintings, in prints on the walls, and in the large books in the library, which could lift her soul as the music had done. She learned poems which explained emotions she knew but had been unable to express.

At first she was shy of the other girls in her class. Not only did they speak with a different accent from hers, but there was an ease of manner about them and a confidence in their own ability which she lacked, and which puzzled her. She wondered where it came from. Having until now moved only within her own class, she had not given the existence of any other a thought. Now, faced with it, she felt uncomfortable and retreated behind a shield of shyness.

There she might have remained had not one of the girls, Sylvia, invited her home for tea one day. Not only did she find a friend but her whole view of her life was subtly changed.

She had watched, amazed at first, then envious, at the easy, affectionate relationship between Sylvia and her parents. She was speechless with surprise when they had asked her how her school work was going, what her plans for the future were. She listened to this family chatting to each other and realised for the first time that at home she was lonely. Until now she had accepted the hours spent alone, the silence of parents who, in any case, barely spoke to each other. How could she have known she was lonely when she had nothing with which to compare her state? Now she recognized it and wished her relationship with her parents could be different. But, think as she might, she could see no way of changing things.

Instead she spent as much time with her new friend as possible. Jane observed intently how her friends behaved, their manners, their rituals, the way they spoke. Should the mother tell her daughter to sit up, to take her elbows off the table, to pass the cream and help herself last, it was Jane who absorbed the instructions. The niceties of which way to hold a soup spoon, the difference between breaking and cutting a roll, were of no importance in Jane's house. At home there were only two rules. The first, and probably the most important, was to do nothing that would make the neighbours talk. The second was never to let any man 'mess about with you'. What this meant Jane was not quite sure, but instinctively she felt that the two were somehow connected.

Now, with her father's ultimatum, all her dreams were at risk. And they had been such modest dreams, too. She would have liked to go to university but had rejected that idea as being too costly. What she wanted most was a home of her own, a home like Sylvia's, and a husband. The only way she could hope to achieve her dream was by continuing her education. If she went to work in the factory, she knew that she would end up like her mother, married to someone like her father. Then she could forget her fine hopes of a husband who wore a suit each day, of china that matched, of bookcases full of books, of records of Bach and Beethoven.

It was not true what her father had said: she did not look down on them, did not feel superior, even though daily she knew more than they did. The ever widening gap between her and them was not of her making. Wasn't it natural that having been shown a more pleasant way of life she should want it for herself? There was so much that she would have loved to share with them, but of what use was poetry and art to them? The more she learned, the more they became strangers to her.

3

Jane had been right. This morning everything had changed. She had changed. She saw that she must fight for herself and her dreams.

The memory of her mother's remark returned. But she must not allow herself to show resentment: she could not afford to alienate her mother. Her best weapon was her mother's hatred of her father. He would not change; his mind once made up remained constant.

She felt, with the sadness, a strange lightness, as if the knowledge that her mother wished she had never been born relieved her of the guilt which had dogged her whole life.

But there was an emptiness within her at the recognition that her mother did not love her.

Hearing her mother stir she put the kettle on, and quickly finished the last of the clearing-up – at least that would please her. Her mother entered the room, and glowered at her, on her guard for any onslaught from Jane.

'I've put the kettle on, Mum, do you want anything to eat?'

'Just tea,' her mother replied, visibly relaxing. 'Where's your father?'

'Gone to the allotment.'

'Good, maybe he'll fall down a bloody big hole and not get out again! Miserable sod!' She sipped her tea. 'You'll never know what I've had to put up with from that bastard, Jane. How much I hate him for all the happiness he's deprived me of.'

'I know, Mum.' Jane tried to interject sympathy she was not feeling into her voice.

'God, I wish I could leave him!'

'Why don't you?'

'Don't be bloody daft! How would we manage?'

'I could get a job in the factory – after all he's arranged one for me – and then I could help you with money,' she replied with a mixture of guilt and satisfaction at her own deviousness.

'Not on your nelly!' her mother exclaimed excitedly. 'And have that bastard win? You'll finish at that school if it's the last thing I do.'

'But how? I suppose I could see if there are any grants going, but that wouldn't mean much – you have to be a war orphan to get any real help.'

'The bugger couldn't even get himself killed either, which would have been a help.'

'Mother!'

'Well, if I think like that he's only himself to blame for making me,' she said defensively and continued noisily sipping the tea, deep in thought. 'I don't know how yet, but I'll work something out. The bastard needn't think he's won this one.'

Jane felt she could begin to relax a little, certain her mother would resolve the problem and now convinced in her mind that whatever she did it was not for love of Jane but for hatred of her husband.

'Shall we go to the pictures tonight? There's a new Bette Davis at the Plaza.'

'Why not? We'll get the shopping in, go and have tea at Lever's and then go to the pictures. Sod him, let him get his own bloody tea for a change.'

'Remember what happened last time we saw a Bette Davis film there?'

'No, what?'

'That man fainted two rows in front of us, remember? Right in the middle of that scene when Bette Davis wouldn't give her dying husband his pills. Really messed it up, all the noise and fuss!'

'Lor', yes, I remember. And you were all disappointed he hadn't got a knife stuck in him, and that we would be witness to a murder.' Her mother laughed at the memory and how she had scolded Jane for her overactive imagination.

A death in the cinema would have had a certain element of glamour about it, which was more than could be said for Jane's only experiences of real death – death near to her, death in her street, death in the family. Terrifying experiences – for it was customary, and expected, that neighbours should pay their last respects to the deceased. This custom included children as well as everyone else in the street. She would be dragged, protesting, into the darkened, curtained front room and by the flickering lights of candles forced to stare at the waxen corpse in the coffin, hear the crying of the bereaved relatives. She would never for the rest of her life be able to look at violets with pleasure, not since the day she had been held over the corpse of her grandfather in his coffin, and been forced, screaming, to kiss his ice-cold, rigid face goodbye. The perfume of the sweet violets pinned to his lace-frilled pillowcase permeated the room and flooded her brain for ever with remembrance of death.

So they went to the cinema and they sat in the one-and-nines and ate a box of chocolates. An uneasy truce was established.

And her mother did solve the problem by getting a job herself in the factory, the very one destined for Jane. But Jane, despite telling herself that she didn't care any more, found the old guilt returning, and as she saw her mother's tiredness, her guilt increased.

Her father rarely spoke to either of them now. In some ways this was a good thing for it made the rows less frequent. He spent more time in the local pub, just as her mother had predicted, and he kept to his word not to spend another penny on Jane. Their life settled back into its former rigid routine – if it was stew it must be Wednesday.

Because her mother worked, one of the great banes of Jane's life, the ritual Monday washday, was no more. In the past, Monday had been her least favourite day of the week, the day when the large copper which dominated the kitchen came into its own. The fire was lit beneath it and the clothes piled in. To the smell of her mother's dreadful cooking was added the dank, sickly-sweet smell of the boiling clothes. Sometimes, when the wind was particularly strong, her mother would decide to wash the blankets. When she was small, Jane was lifted into the tin bath to tramp up and down on the washing. Her mother seemed to think it was fun for her, but she loathed it, hated the slimy feel of the soda-filled water, and she was frightened to see her little pink feet turning white, the flesh becoming swollen, bloated and crinkled. She was terrified that her feet would never return to normal. Mondays meant that her mother would be in a foul mood from morning to night. Even when it rained the washing ritual had to be observed, as though her mother regarded the washing as a religious rite that if not performed invited catastrophe to the tribe. On wet days the living room would be festooned with wet washing, the steam rising off it in white tendrils, the dampness permeating the whole house. But now her mother hired a washing machine, which was delivered each Saturday morning. The washing was done in a quarter of the time, and her mother was less bad-tempered and moody about washing day.

The visits to her aunt's house continued. And, even better, since her uncle had bought a caravan they now enjoyed odd weekends at the seaside. He paid extra rental for his site because it was on the edge of the field packed with caravans, as close to the sea as possible. Jane loved to lie in her bunk at night, listening to the gentle hiss of the Calor Gas lamps and the endless sound of the sea pounding onto the shingle beach. She would listen to the scrabbling, hissing, sliding noise of the shingle as it struggled with the might of the sea, imagining the tiny shards of shell being thrown carelessly from one wave to another, rather as she saw herself sometimes when she had become embroiled helplessly in one of her parents' rows.

Always in shapeless black or maroon dresses worn in an unsuccessful attempt to camouflage her enormous bulk, Aunt Vi was the kindest and funniest person Jane had ever known. With such layers of fat, her face should have been a featureless blob, but instead it was lit by dark-brown eyes which glinted constantly with merriment. The warmth and strength of her character transcended her appearance. Jane was fascinated by her aunt's mouth. The lips were large and soft and when her aunt ate a chocolate they closed around the sweet with a pleasure so sensual that it was possible to envy the chocolate its caress. There was no television in the caravan to dampen conversation, so Jane was to learn for the first time what a quick wit her aunt possessed, the particular joy she took in the ridiculous. Anything to do with bodily functions would reduce her aunt to tears of laughter. No matter which orifice was involved, Aunt Vi would find something funny to say about it. There were many times when Jane wished that she were her mother, but then she would feel pangs of guilt at her own disloyalty.

Her aunt had discovered a new interest, and when not at the seaside, she would collect Jane and her mother and together they would join a coach party to visit one of the large houses newly opened to the public. Neither of the two older women seemed the least bit interested in the treasures on show, but reserved their scrutiny for worn curtains, threadbare carpets, or dust on the

Chippendale. The success of the trip for them depended, it seemed to Jane, on the value of the tea and the cleanliness of the lavatories. But Jane loved these outings, trying, as she walked around with the parties, to imagine the rooms a hundred years ago, lit by candles, with women in long dresses working at their needlepoint.

The weekends, and the trips they took, were to prove the happiest times of her childhood and Jane would always remain grateful to Aunt Vi. In her sister-in-law's company even her mother became relaxed, a different person, catching some of the lightness and joy in life which Aunt Vi possessed in abundance. Jane would watch her mother laughing and catch a glimpse of the carefree person she must once have been. On these weekends the bitterness would leave her face, and her lips, usually set in a thin, intransigent line, would relax and even smile. But by Sunday evening and the return home, her good humour was wiped away, her eyes were hooded again with suspicion, her mouth reset in its mean line.

As her childhood slipped away, Jane felt more and more like two people: the one at school who could laugh and joke and was full of ideas, and the girl at home, the moody one, as her mother called her.

Her mother despaired of Jane's looks. Mrs Reed's ideal was a cousin of Jane's with blonde hair, a pert pretty nose and the vacuous expression of a china doll. Since both Jane's parents had brown eyes, her mother regarded the grey of Jane's with suspicion, as if she thought her daughter a changeling. As a small child Jane's dark, straight hair had been twisted with rags each night. The resulting bobbing ringlets were at total variance with her strong-featured face. Her mother had finally tired of her attempts to coax curls where curls were not intended and eventually Jane's hair was cut unbecomingly short with a fringe. So it remained until at fourteen Jane decided to grow both hair and fringe and made no attempt to wave it.

It came therefore as something of a surprise to her, at sixteen, to find that boys did not agree with her mother's assessment of her looks.

She became part of a large group of teenagers who eddied from tennis club to youth-club dance, who cycled to the coast, rambled the downs, drank copious cups of coffee, put the world to rights, and flirted mildly with each other. A couple of times, attracted by a boy's looks and a strange feeling in her stomach that had nothing to do with food, she had gone out alone with him. She would set out on the date full of excitement and anticipation, only to return perplexed and irritated by his clumsy kisses and fumbling at her body. Sweaty palms and awkward attempts at lovemaking quenched that strange feeling within her, and certainly did not lift her to the heights of passion that the poets spoke of.

Her school days drew to an end. She rejected her mother's offer of help to send her to university. She knew that she could no longer deal with her guilt about her mother's having to work to support her: there was guilt enough without adding to it. Nearly eighteen, she did not know what she was to do.

The only firm resolve she had was not to work in an office. It was one of her teachers who suggested that she might like to become a nurse. She had never thought about it, but there were certain advantages – she would be paid while she trained, she would meet interesting people, she would be in London, she would get away from home. So, with no sense of vocation, just a need to find an escape, she began to plan on a nursing career.

4

Knowing nothing of London hospitals, she applied to the only one she had heard of – St Thomas's. When the application form arrived, demanding that one of her referees be a minister of the church, she tore it up. Her churchgoing had been restricted to her baptism and a short spell at the local Methodist chapel, which she had attended, not from any religious zeal, but because they had the best Sunday-school outings. She worried that perhaps the blessing of the church would be required by all the hospitals.

'Here, look at this.' Her mother handed her the daily paper. 'If it's good enough for her, it'll do you!'

Jane scanned the report which said it was rumoured that a foreign princess was to enter a London teaching hospital to train as a nurse.

'It will probably be like the other one and want a vicar's reference.'

'Go on, try it, you don't know. Fancy, you could be hobnobbing with royalty!' Her mother seemed amused at this idea.

'It's only a rumour, Mum. Still, it's the name of another hospital, and if she's going there, it must be a good one.'

'I don't understand why it has to be a London hospital. A nasty place, London – you could get into all sorts of trouble there. What's wrong with the local hospital? I could keep an eye on you then.'

'I want the best, Mum.' It wasn't strictly true. It was logical to try for the best training, but the main reason was her longing to get away from home, and she could hardly tell her mother that. She was encouraged, when the form arrived, to see that this hospital was not interested in what the church thought of her. She applied and two months later, with money earned as a part-time waitress, Jane bought a ticket and took the train to London for her interview.

Since she had only drifted into the idea of nursing, she was not in the least bit nervous as she entered the ornate Victorian building, smelling for the first time that combination of boiled cabbage, disinfectant and polish peculiar to hospitals.

The waiting room into which she was shown was already crowded with girls. There was no vacant seat, so she leaned against the wall. There was an oppressive atmosphere and Jane noticed that none of the girls could sit still. They twisted in their seats, picked imaginary flecks from their clothes, patted their hair and tortured their handkerchiefs. There was a constant clicking of handbag clasps as mirrors were produced and anxious faces were scrutinized. The tension was catching and Jane soon found herself straightening her skirt and fiddling with her hair.

The door opened and a girl appeared, her face gaunt with strain. The others leaped up.

'What was it like?' several asked.

'It was dreadful.' The girl slumped on a chair offered her solicitously by one of the others. 'She's terrifying! Absolutely terrifying!'

'What did she ask you?' one demanded.

'I can't remember! I'm sorry, I can't remember a thing.' She put her hands to her face.

A name was called, and cries of 'good luck' followed the next girl as she disappeared through a door with 'Matron' stencilled on it.

A buzz of conversation started but, instead of lessening, the tension increased as the more knowledgeable among them trotted out statistics concerning numbers of candidates and the shortage of places. Jane began to regret wasting train-fare money on what was obviously a fool's errand.

By the time it was her turn she had been completely infected by the nervousness of the others, and felt her palms clammy with perspiration, her stomach churning with fear.

She noticed nothing of the room she entered for she found herself in the presence of a person whose aura of absolute authority made the back of her throat dry so suddenly that she feared speech would be an impossibility. All she noticed was how white the collar and cuffs were against the navy-blue uniform of the thin woman, whose upright posture made Jane involuntarily straighten her shoulders.

'Be seated,' a firm and surprisingly deep voice told her. Jane sat and found herself being surveyed from the other side of the desk by a pair of blue eyes with no hint of warmth in them. They scrutinized her, as if seeing through the stuff of her clothes and checking whether her underwear was clean. Embarrassed by the stare, Jane studiously examined her hands.

'Why nursing?' the voice rapped out at her.

'I . . .' Jane coughed. 'I can't afford to go to university, miss.'

'What employment is your father in?'

'He's a storeman in a factory. My mother works in the same factory, on the assembly line. They make nuts and bolts and things . . .' Her voice lamely tailed off, as the woman scribbled on the pad in front of her. She finished writing and again stared at Jane with her unblinking eyes. Jane felt that more was expected of her. 'You see, miss, I don't want my mother to work any more, it's too much for her. It's time I started supporting myself, really.' She studied her hands again, unable to think of what else to say.

'There is slightly more to nursing than the pay packet at the end of the month.'

'Oh, I know, miss.'

'Do you feel you have a vocation?'

It was a question Jane should have had the sense to anticipate, but she had not. In fact she had not really given any thought to what questions she might be asked. Now she began to regret her lack of preparation.

'What? Like a nun . . .?' Jane giggled nervously, desperately playing for time as she tried to think what the right answer might be. The woman's eyes did not waver. 'I'm sorry, miss. It's a serious question, isn't it?'

'All my questions are serious, Miss Reed.'

'Well, if I'm honest, no. I applied because I didn't know what else I could do, and I don't want to work in an office.'

'Hardly a reason to attempt a career in nursing.'

'No, miss. But I have thought about it, and I think nursing will be interesting work and it will exercise my mind. And I like meeting people. I think it will be a satisfying career . . . miss.' She watched wretchedly as the matron made further notes. Undoubtedly it had been a stupid answer to give but it was the only one possible. She knew that she could not have lied: those ice-cold eyes that seemed to bore into her made lying impossible.

'Tell me, Miss Reed, what would be your reaction when dressing the wound of a postoperative colostomy? A colostomy, Miss Reed, is a surgically made opening into the surface of the abdomen through which evil-smelling, liquid faeces are evacuated,' the matron explained. It must have been the woman's matter-of-fact tone that made contemplation of such a horrifying prospect possible.

'I think, miss, the most important thing would be not to allow the patient to see any feelings of disgust that one might have at the sight and the smell. He would certainly be in a very sensitive state of mind.'

'I see.' More notes were made. 'What qualities do you think a nurse should have?'

Pleased with her answer to the previous question, Jane relaxed for a second. 'Good feet?' Flustered, she coughed. 'I mean, she should be strong,' she added quickly. 'And level-headed. She must like people and have a sense of humour,' Jane finished in a rush, feeling now that everything was pointless and wishing she could get out of this room.

'Do you think you have these qualities?'

'Yes,' Jane answered promptly.

'Kindly stand up. Come round here, Miss Reed. Would you lift your skirts?'

Jane did as she was asked, feeling very puzzled and foolish as the woman carefully studied her legs.

'It's a bit like auditioning for the chorus line, isn't it, miss?' she joked weakly, more to cover her embarrassment than to make anybody laugh.

'Your legs are very important. They have to be strong, you will be spending long hours on them. By the way, you call me "Matron" not "miss", I'm not a schoolteacher.'

'Sorry, Matron.'

'Thank you, Miss Reed. There is a tour of the hospital at the end of these interviews. I shall inform you within the week of my decision.' The woman returned her attention to her notepad, and Jane miserably picked up her handbag from the floor, turned, opened a door, and walked into a cupboard. For a wild, hysterical moment she thought to close the door and hide, hoping that Matron had not seen her.

'The door is to your left, Miss Reed,' the humourless voice announced.

Back in the waiting room the others clustered about her, plying her with questions.

'Don't ask me anything! It was dreadful. I said I had no vocation and I walked into a bloody cupboard!'

She did not need the others to tell her she had made a complete mess of it all. She put on her coat and left the hospital, not even waiting for the hospital tour.

A week later the letter from the hospital arrived. She could not believe the contents. She had been accepted. In some mysterious way her answers had been the right ones. She had yet to learn that the last thing a nurse needed was a burning sense of vocation, that such types soon fell by the wayside. Neither did she realize that her weak little jokes had shown a sense of humour despite her nerves, nor that strong legs and a strong back would be her greatest allies. And in her answers, most importantly, she had put the patient first. She had also yet to learn that Matron was no fool and could read a character with one glance of her cold, blue eyes.

Jane was ecstatic. Suddenly nursing was the only thing in the whole world that she wanted to do.

Six months later, she and her mother stood on the platform of the station, waiting for the London train to pull in.

'You'll write?'

'Of course I'll write. Bet you don't answer!'

'Don't get into any mischief!'

'No, Mum.'

'You know, don't let any dirty bugger mess about with you.'

'No, Mum.'

'And keep your underwear clean.'

'Yes, Mum, "in case of accidents", I know, Mum.' She grinned.

They stood now in an awkward silence. Not knowing what to say to each other, both wanted the train to come.

At last the train drew in and Jane made for an empty compartment.

'No, Jane, the middle. Always travel in the middle of the train.'

'Why? What's wrong with the front?'

'In case of an accident, of course! You're less likely to get killed travelling in the middle.'

'Mum, your world is full of possible accidents.'

'It makes sense to take precautions. You can never tell when that bastard up there might drop something on you.' Jane laughed at her mother's irreverent remark and resignedly allowed herself to be loaded into the middle of the train. 'And,' her mother continued, 'always travel in a coach with other women.'

'I know, I know, so I won't be raped! Oh, Mum, stop worrying, do, I'm only going to London.'

Her mother looked unconvinced that her warnings would be heeded. She climbed back onto the platform and stood looking up at Jane who, leaning out of the window, was taken aback by how small and vulnerable her mother looked standing on the platform, and how lonely she suddenly seemed.

'Don't worry, Mum, I'll be all right.'

'Worry? Me? I'm not going to worry about a big lump like you.' But she did not laugh, instead her voice sounded strained, as if it was difficult for her to speak. She looked dejected.

'Mum, don't be sad, please.'

'I'm not sad. Glad to wash my hands of you, more like,' and her mother smiled, but the smile crumpled and seemed to slide off her face like melting wax.

'Mum . . .!' A great cloud of steam gushed out from the engine and raced down the platform towards them, enveloping her mother. 'Mum . . .' but the train began to pull away, making speech impossible. She hung from the window and blew a kiss, but doubted if her mother saw it through the steam.

The rows of terraced houses of her home town slipped by as the train gathered speed. Streets in which she had played all her life, streets where she knew the people, streets where she felt safe.

She was surprised to feel sad. Hadn't she waited impatiently for the day when she could get away from her home and her parents? Yet, back there on the platform, she was certain that if her mother had said, 'Don't go,' she would have leaped off the train. In those moments she had been closer to her mother, and felt more affection from her, than she had ever experienced before. Nothing had been said: it was only a feeling. Should she trust such a feeling? She was puzzled by the emotion, for she thought she had constructed solid barriers, that she no longer cared. Yet here she was, full of joy that her mother did care, that under the layers of bitterness and nagging there remained some affection for her.

And now? London! The prospect excited her. At eighteen, she had not yet learned to be afraid of the unknown. Her future filled her only with anticipation.

5

It was warm for September as she struggled with her heavy suitcase up the long road towards the Nurses' Home. She was hot – her suit was too thick for this weather, the skirt too tight for easy walking, even without a case. Her stiletto-heeled shoes, which she had bought to celebrate her new liberty, were still unfamiliar, and she wobbled about the pavement as she fought to keep her balance. Her outfit and the pretty little skullcap, decorated with blue flowers, had looked so right in the mirror at home. But now the sight of the other girls, in simple skirts and blouses, flatties, and without hats, made her feel overdressed.

'Gosh, just like first day back at boarding school after the hols, isn't it?' a cheerful girl gushed at her.

'I wouldn't know,' Jane said abruptly, as she battled her way through the throng and up the steps of the building.

The hallway was bedlam. The high, piercing shrieks of overexcited girls mingled with the deep-voiced banter of red-faced fathers who struggled valiantly with the ever-increasing piles of luggage. Tearful mothers could be heard giving last-minute instructions to inattentive daughters. A phone rang continuously in a small porter's lodge, but no one answered it. A short woman in blue overalls checked each girl in and issued her with a room number. The lift doors clanged at regular intervals and its mechanism creaked and groaned as it carried load after load of girls, with their parents, to the rooms above.

Jane found her room. Hanging out of the window she could see a landscape of roofs and chimneys, and could hear the muted rumble of the traffic seven floors below. Twice the size of her room at home and with basin, cupboard, desk and bookcase, the room was perfect.

Looking at herself in the full-length mirror, Jane was irritated at how wrong she looked. The suit and lace blouse, which had cost weeks of work as a part-time waitress, at home had seemed the most beautiful garments she had ever possessed. Suddenly, she hated them, and felt stiff and gauche. She opened her case – to her mother and to her, London meant dressing up and so she had not packed any clothes which could be regarded as casual. She found a navy-blue jumper, hastily discarded her blouse and jacket, draped a scarf about her shoulders, and threw the hat to the back of the cupboard shelf. That would have to do.

The noise of fifty young women, chattering excitedly, made it easy to find the right lecture room. Jane went to the back and sat at a desk, silently watching and listening. Many of the others bounded about the room, noisily introducing themselves or emitting sudden shrieks as they recognized one another from some long-forgotten interschool hockey match, or realized that they had friends in common. She watched them, admiringly, as effortlessly they made friends. Everything about them – their voices, their clothes, the noisy confidence – made her feel isolated.

'Grim lot, aren't they?' The voice made Jane jump. Swinging round she found a dark-haired, plump girl was sitting beside her. 'Right stuck-up crowd, if you ask me.' She smiled and two large dimples appeared on either side of her mouth.

'They do seem very confident.' Jane smiled back, relieved at last to have someone to talk to.

'Bleeding dreadful! "Oh golly!" "I say!", "Samantha, darling, how's Nigel?"' Expertly the girl imitated the accents all around them, making Jane laugh. 'I'm Sandra Evans, not from Wales, from Battersea.' She held out her hand, and Jane grasped it.

'Jane Reed, from Kent.'

'I gather Kent's quite posh.'

'Not the part I come from,' she said hurriedly. 'Do you think they're all like this? I mean, they all seem to know each other.'

'No, I shouldn't think so, there must be some other normal people about. All the big hospitals take a quota of grammar-school girls each year. We can't be the only two.'

'Really? I didn't know that.'

'Oh yes, it's true. But this princess business has probably made matters worse. I expect some of this lot hope they'll meet and marry her brother and become royal. Otherwise they would probably have chosen St Thomas's.'

'Is she coming?'

'No! A laugh, isn't it? Now they're stuck here instead of swanning about Tommie's in frilly caps!' The girl laughed loudly.

'I thought all London hospitals were the same.'

'Not likely!' She warmed to her theme, delighted to find such a willing audience. 'Only five of the London hospitals are acceptable to this lot. St Thomas's is the tops. They wouldn't be seen dead in a place like the Westminster –'

A noisy scraping of chairs heralded the arrival of a tall, stout woman in the uniform of a sister. The woman waited for the chattering to cease. So imposing was her manner that silence was immediate. Her gimlet eyes scanned the room as if inspecting each girl in turn.

'I'm Home Sister,' a deep voice rumbled at them.

'More like Home Brother with a voice like that,' Sandra whispered, making Jane choke as she fought to suppress a giggle, her face turning red with the effort.

'Silence!' Sister raised herself to her full height, her ample breasts heaving as she shouted, making the pleats of her apron bib open and shut from the strain forced upon them.

'Crikey, she's got tits like an accordion!' Sandra whispered again and Jane choked loudly.

'What is the problem, Nurse?' Sister's voice boomed across the lecture room. Jane continued to fight the laughter that was rippling up within her, her face growing puce with the effort. 'Your name, Nurse?' Everyone in the room turned to stare at Jane. 'Nurse, I asked for your name, kindly have the courtesy to answer!'

'I think she wants to know your name, Jane.' A straight-faced Sandra nudged her.

'Me? But I'm not a nurse,' Jane whispered.

'You are now, matey!' The dimples flashed at her.

Confused, Jane stood up. 'Did you mean me, Sister?'

'Of course I meant you. No one else is disrupting this talk. Your name?'

'Jane Reed,' she spluttered.

'I'm not interested in your Christian name, Reed. What's wrong with you? I do hope you haven't arrived here carrying nasty germs. That would never do!'

'No, no, Sister. I seem to have a tickle in my throat.'

'Someone give her a drink of water.' A glass of water appeared from the front row. 'Now, perhaps Nurse Reed will give me permission to continue?' Blushing with confusion, Jane sat down. 'I must emphasize,' the deep voice boomed on, 'that we will not have illness in the Nurses' Home. Your duty to your patients is to remain healthy. You will remain healthy by having an adequate amount of sleep, eating sensibly, taking your vitamins. Clean living, nurses, clean in body and mind!'

'Spoken in the true Flo Nightingale spirit!' Sandra sighed exaggeratedly.

'Sandra, shut up, you'll get me going again!' Jane pleaded.

Her reward was another glare from Home Sister, who continued pointedly. 'As I was saying, I am your home sister. I am responsible for your wellbeing. I stand for no nonsense. Understood?' A murmur of assent rippled around the room. 'Your rooms will be inspected daily. I will not tolerate untidiness. You are to be neat in your appearance – hair is to be worn off the face, none on your collar. No ponytails . . .' Several hands, nervously, patted offending ponytails. 'You will wear no make-up or perfume when on duty. Understood?'

'Why?' Jane whispered to Sandra who shrugged her shoulders.

'You have a question, Nurse Reed?'

'I was just wondering why no make-up or perfume, Sister.'

'We do not permit perfume because the last thing an ill patient wants to smell is cloying scent – it could make them nauseous. And no make-up, Nurse, because you are not a shopgirl or secretary, and in any case it could prove a distraction to your male patients. To continue. You are Set 128 – remember that number, you will use it frequently. You are not to fraternize with nurses in sets above or below you – it is bad for discipline. Likewise you will refer to each other by surname only, no Christian names are allowed. Do you understand?' The girls began to shuffle uncomfortably in their seats. The sister held aloft a large book. 'This is the Book. When you leave the Home you will sign out, and when you return you will sign in again. Failure to do so means instant report to Matron.' Others apart from Jane and Sandra began to whisper. 'While in preliminary training school, PTS for short, you will sign in by ten at night. T-E-N.' The whispering was louder. 'What is worrying you, Nurse?' she asked at random of a girl in the front row.

'It seems frightfully early, Sister.'

'You have hard work to do, my girl. It's quite late enough.'

'But when we are out of PTS, Sister, what then?'

'Midnight, Nurse. And before you ask, in your first year you are permitted three late passes until 2 a.m. You apply to me for them, and I warn you now, I shall require to know where you are going and with whom before I issue them.'

For another half-hour the sister droned on with an endless succession of rules that Jane knew she would never remember.

'Christ, it's like a bleeding nunnery!' sighed Sandra.

'And I thought I had found freedom,' Jane said with a rueful smile.

In batches of six they trooped down to the basement to be issued with their uniform. A harassed supervisor gave every girl a neat pile of clothes, each item of which had to be signed for. Then the girls had to parade in uniform dress and apron in front of Home Sister.

'You two bend over,' she ordered Jane and Sandra. The two girls bowed to her. 'Stupid girls! Turn around and bend over.' Proffering their rear ends to the sister was too much for them and they both began to giggle uncontrollably. 'And what do you find so funny, Nurses?'

'Why are we bending over, Sister?' Sandra gasped between her laughter.

'This is no laughing matter, Nurse. Control yourself, at once. I am checking that when you bend there is no sight of your suspenders.'

'No, Sister.' Sandra struggled to reply. 'But . . .'

Jane stuffed a handkerchief into her mouth.

'But what, Nurse Evans?'

'But, Sister, the dresses are so long, surely no one could glimpse anything.'

'I like to check for my own satisfaction, Nurse. It would not be fair to our poor, sick, male patients, now would it?'

'No, Sister,' they chorused in muffled voices, both now with handkerchiefs clutched to their mouths.

Once outside the room they collapsed in helpless laughter against the wall.

'Do you really think the wards are full of sex-crazed men?' asked Jane.

'I do hope so. Yummy!' shrieked Sandra. 'Imagine rows and rows of frustrated men waiting for a flash of our stockingtops!' Two other girls in the room looked with undisguised dismay at her.

'I can't imagine any man wanting us looking like this,' Jane pointed out as she looked at her reflection in the mirror. The long, thick dress reached to below midcalf. The undarted bodice flattened her breasts, and the stiff, starched apron embraced her like a large chastity belt.

Sandra flung the short red cape about her shoulders.

'Well, this is bloody daft. Look where it comes to. Right bum-freezer and no mistake.'

'Do you have to be so vulgar?' one of the other girls snapped.

'That's not vulgarity, that's fact. Mark my words, your bum will freeze just as fast as mine, come winter!' Sandra replied, laughing.

'God, the types they let in these days,' the girl drawled to her friend, exaggeratedly rolling her eyes.

'You can say that again, Miss Bumless. I wonder what she sits on if she hasn't got a bum?' Sandra aped the drawling voice. 'Come on, Jane, let's get out of here. Stuck-up cows!' Still giggling they rushed from the room and spent the rest of the afternoon in Sandra's room attempting to make their caps up, failing miserably at every attempt, and laughing uncontrollably at every failure.

The next day lectures started in earnest. It was easy to slip into the routine; it was just like being back at school, with homework to do and tests to revise for. The only difference was the uniform and having to get used to being called Nurse. Without a patient in sight, Nurse Reed felt a fraud.

Gradually Set 128 split into four distinct groups. There was what Sandra christened the Bible Belt, serious-faced girls who bustled about like eager novices trying to interest the others in Bible and prayer meetings.

'Put me on one more prayer list,' glowered Sandra at a small mouselike creature, 'and I'll shove your head down the lav and pull the chain!'

'She means well,' pleaded Jane as the frightened girl scuttled away.

'I'll pray when I want, not when some smug, self-satisfied do-gooder tells me to! They won't last. All vocation and no guts.'

'San-Evans!'

'You're sometimes too bleeding reasonable for your own good, Reed,' Sandra said with mock severity.

Then there were the quiet studious ones, always with anxious expressions. Every spare moment was devoted to study, testing each other, even practising bandaging on each other. They had been labelled the keenies.

'Sisters in the making,' groaned Sandra. 'They'll be hell on the wards.'

'At least they're certain to pass out of PTS,' said Jane, conscious that she spent far too much time gossiping and slipping out to the Cat's Whisker coffee bar with her own gang.

The third group was Sandra's particular *bête noire* – the ones who had originally earned her scorn – the Deb Brigade.

'Joined to snare doctor husbands, that lot, depriving some poor girl of a chance to be here,' was Sandra's studied opinion of them. They kept very much to themselves, never inviting any of the others to their frequent sherry parties; they received the most phone calls, were always away at weekends and were the first to make contact with the medical school next door. 'See,' Sandra said smugly.

Sandra made no secret of her loathing and the group studiously ignored her, inspiring Sandra to greater heights of verbal abuse. But they fascinated Jane who admired not only their clothes, their hair and their social life, but especially the way they did not seem to give a damn about anybody, including the dreaded home sister. They even managed to look attractive in the dreadful uniform.

'They've had them doctored,' announced Sandra as they debated this phenomenon.

'What do you mean?' Jane demanded.

'Mummy's little dressmaker put the odd tuck in here and there, shortened it, that sort of thing.'

'You're kidding!' Jane exclaimed, too nervous of Home Sister even to wear her cap at anything but the regulation angle.

'No, I'm not. Campbell-Grant's dress is definitely shorter than it was last week. You look.'

This fact only increased Jane's awe at such daring.

The Deb Brigade seemed to have fun, too, and Jane would have liked to be friends but the few overtures she plucked up courage to make were ignored.

'You're wasting your time, Jane. They only want to know their own sort.'

'But I had all sorts of friends at school. My best friend's dad was an army officer,' she said with pride.

'What was she doing in a grammar, then?'

'I don't know. I never asked.'

'Probably skint – father came up through the ranks, I shouldn't wonder. They wouldn't have wanted to know your friend either.'

'You're so cynical!'

'No, I'm not. I'm a realist. Stick with your own kind, it's safer.'

'You sound just like my father. In any case, you don't help to make friends, always sniping at them. They probably think I feel the same way.'

'You're free to choose, Reed. You don't have to kick around with the rest of us if you don't want to. Go and join the others, it's no skin off my nose!'

'Oh, Evans, you can be such a bitch at times.'

'Well, shut up about the others then.' Sandra grinned at her, knowing from the start that Jane would never desert the tight-knit group made up of the grammar-school intake, who went everywhere together and with whom Jane was relaxed and felt at home.

6

At the end of the first month, with her small savings and first pay packet, Jane went shopping. She knew exactly what she was going to buy. Within an hour she was the proud possessor of a red, circular felt skirt, a tight-fitting jumper, two frilled petticoats which made the skirt stand out in a most satisfying way, and the longed-for flat leather pumps. At last, she would look like the others. With what was left, she went home for the weekend.

'Good God, girl! How much did that lot cost?' her mother greeted her. Jane twirled around, the petticoats flashing beneath the skirt.

'It's what all the girls are wearing, Mum.'

'More suitable for a square dance than walking around the street in. What with all those frills, you look like the rear end of an ostrich!'

'You've never seen an ostrich in your life.'

'I've got imagination, haven't I?' Irritably her mother put the kettle on. 'What happened to that nice suit and smart shoes you spent all that money on? Thought that was what everyone was wearing.'

'I still wear it, it's just that casual clothes are all the rage now.'

'I should hope you bloody well do still wear it. I hope you're not going to fritter all your money away like this.' Aggressively she spooned the tea into the pot.

'I felt like treating myself, Mum. I was excited getting my first wage packet,' Jane answered, annoyed that she should feel guilty.

'It's all right for some, I suppose.' Her mother sniffed, pouring the boiling water onto the tea. 'Seen any stiffs yet?' she suddenly asked.

'Lord, no. I haven't even seen a live patient, let alone a dead one.' Jane was relieved that the inquisition on her clothes appeared to be over.

'What do you do all day then, buy clothes?'

'No, Mum.' Jane sighed. 'We go to school, have lessons in anatomy and things and we do practicals on dummies or each other.'

'I thought you learned all that as you went along. Sounds boring. I thought you'd have all sorts of interesting cases to tell me about.'

'Sorry, Mum,' Jane said apologetically.

Her mother sipped her tea, gazing blankly out of the window at the wall outside, where the galvanized tin bath hung. 'Bath's sprung a leak. Christ knows when I shall be able to afford another.'

Jane looked down at her skirt, her pleasure in it finally destroyed. 'I'm sorry, Mum. I didn't think.'

'Didn't think what?'

'I should have given you some of my money, instead of buying all this.'

'Did I ask for anything?' her mother snapped. 'No, I never ask for nothing. If you want to spend your money on rubbish like that, that's your affair.'

'No, Mum,' said Jane mechanically.

'In any case, it's too late now, isn't it? All gone, I presume.' She smiled a tight-lipped smile that had no humour in it. She stood up. 'I promised Mrs Green I'd pop in this evening. Didn't know you were coming home.'

'I thought I might go up to the Palais.'

'Yes, you do that, nice for you.'

Jane sat alone, angry with herself that she hadn't thought to buy her mother something – flowers, chocolates. It probably wouldn't have made much difference, though: her mother would still have disapproved. That fleeting moment of intimacy on the station platform four weeks ago was past. Perhaps, in her overexcited state, she had imagined it in the first place.

She went to the local dance but none of her friends were there. Like her they had moved on; already girls junior to her in school had taken their places. As she noticed their shy, sly glances she felt as though she were trespassing on their territory. It was extraordinary how quickly she felt she did not belong in her home town.

The next morning, she lied and said she had to be back in the hospital by lunchtime. There seemed little point in staying longer or, for that matter, returning for some time.

Weekends at the Nurses' Home dragged. Most of the girls, making the most of the free weekends in PTS, went home. Jane caught up on work that never seemed to get done when Sandra was about, and used the time to wander around the museums and art galleries, exploring London as she did so. It would have been more fun with someone else. When Sandra invited her home for the weekend, she accepted gratefully.

Sandra's home in Battersea was in a road just like her own. The only differences were that it had one more room and half the garden was taken up with an extension containing a brand-new bathroom. Even with the extra room it was a squeeze. Sandra was the eldest of six, and the only one to have left home.

The house was in chaos when they let themselves in. Piles of damp clothes adorned every surface, papers and magazines lay where they had been dropped and there were toys everywhere. Sandra scrabbled among the dirty crockery to find two cups, kicked a fat sleeping cat off a chair and dumped the washing from another chair onto the floor.

'Shirley, get down here!' Sandra shouted up the stairs. 'We've an hour till Mum gets back. Lazy bitch,' she said, settling back to her cup of tea. 'Now I've left she's supposed to supervise the others and make sure they straighten up for Mum.'

'What's everyone called?'

'There's Shirley, she's seventeen, Sharon's fifteen, Sherry's twelve, Sheena's eight and Sean's six.'

'So many Ss!'

'That's one of Mum's little economies, saves on the Cash's name tapes, see? S. Evans does us all.'

'Do you like being part of a large family?'

'Varies from bliss to sheer hell.' Sandra laughed. 'We never have enough money for anything. And how I hate sharing! You'll never know the paradise it is, having my own room at the hospital. On the other hand, you're never lonely. And if you've a problem, there's always someone to listen . . . that sort of thing. I guess I wouldn't have it any other way.'

'Sounds lovely to me. I mean, never being alone. But, are you Roman Catholics?'

'No. Everyone asks that, I suppose it's the only way they can understand such a large family. I don't think my parents planned it that way – it just happened. As Mum says, my dad was born oversexed and he always seems to know when she's got her knickers off!'

'Your mother said that to you?' Jane sat bolt upright in amazement. 'She talks about sex with you? Jokes about it?'

'Nothing odd in that, is there?'

'It's the most extraordinary thing I've ever heard.'

'Why? Doesn't your mother talk about it?'

'My mother doesn't even think about it, let alone talk about it. And she certainly doesn't do it.' Jane laughed at the very idea.

'Come off it, all husbands and wives do it.'

'I'm pretty certain mine don't. They don't even sleep together.'

'I'd hate twin beds.'

'I mean they have separate rooms,' Jane explained.

'Crikey, how grand! Have they always had separate rooms?'

'No. I can just remember when Dad came back from the war, they slept together then. I should remember: I had to get out of my mother's bed – how I hated him for kicking me out. But I don't think it was for long, 'cause he moved into the other back bedroom and I went back to sleeping with Mum.'

'How sad!'

'Oh, I don't think so. I think my mother was relieved. All she ever said to me about sex was that it was disgusting, and something a woman would have to put up with in marriage. It was the price we paid.'

'Poor woman, think of all the fun she's been missing! My mum doesn't think like that. She enjoys it. You should hear them at it some nights.'

Jane was out of her depth and could only smile, wide-eyed with amusement.

'Have you ever thought, perhaps that's why your father doesn't like you?' Sandra went on, undeterred. 'He blames you for taking his wife away from him – back from the war and you in his bed, that sort of thing. Poor man, he must be dreadfully lonely and frustrated. More tea, Reed?'

Jane was stunned. Silently she held her cup out for Sandra to fill. How could she have been so insensitive and blind? If Sandra was right, so much made sense. With her mother's emphatic views that sex was disgusting, it had never struck Jane that it could be anything else. She had a natural curiosity about the subject, but had presumed that her mother's attitude was perfectly normal. But if Mrs Evans enjoyed it, why didn't her mother? Was her mother different? Or was her father a bad lover? Since she had never given the subject much thought, the very idea of her parents making love seemed too ludicrous to contemplate.

'You've gone quiet, Reed.'

'You've given me a lot to think about, that's why. Shouldn't we start clearing up for your mum?' As Jane spoke, Shirley, a mirror image of Sandra, appeared, yawning exaggeratedly.

'About bloody time. Tired, are we?' Sandra sneered.

'Shut up! Two minutes in the house and you start,' her sister retorted. While the two sisters argued about who was the lazier, Jane began to do the washing-up. An hour later, once the sisters had formed a truce, all was tidy, the vegetables were peeled, and the kettle was on again as Mrs Evans, a short, fat woman, as wide as she was tall, bustled in. She gave Jane an expansive welcome and busied herself preparing the supper.

'Sit down, Mum. We'll do that. You look tired out.'

'Tired, me? Nonsense. But a cup of tea would be nice.'

She sat, sipping her tea with relish and, although she never seemed to stop talking, within ten minutes she knew what Jane thought about the hospital, her mother, her father, the government, even stiletto heels.

'And how's your week been, Sandra?' She turned to her daughter.

'Fine. Reed and I came top in the tests again. That put the noses of the snooty lot out of joint, I can tell you.'

'Still not made friends with them, then?'

'No. And I don't want to either. They're so stuck-up, Mum. I reckon if I fell down in a dead faint at their feet they'd step over me.'

'Sounds to me as if you're getting a nasty chip on your shoulder. You're as good as anyone, both of you, and don't ever forget it.'

'But, Mum, it's difficult not to let them get you down.'

'Nonsense! That's life, my girl. Don't think it's just St Cuthbert's. You'll find people everywhere who think they're a cut above you and want to put you down. You just have to learn to live with it and prove them wrong. And being rude to them isn't the way, Sandra.'

'Well, I'm not having anything to do with them, and that's that,' announced Sandra.

'It's difficult, Mrs Evans,' said Jane. 'I know what Sandra means, but I do wish we could all be friends. It all seems so silly.'

'Traitor!'

'Let her finish, Sandra, don't be so bossy.'

'Well, it's easier for Sandra, she seems to see everything so clearly in black and white, whereas . . . oh, I don't know, I don't think it's as simple as that.'

'Piffle! In any case, I didn't come home to spend the weekend talking about that lot.'

'All right, we'll drop it. God, my feet ache! Any more tea in that pot?' Mrs Evans asked, kicking off her shoes and vigorously rubbing her toes. 'Do you know, we had six post-ops today, a Saturday, I ask you.'

'Sandra told me you were a nurse, Mrs Evans,' Jane said with interest.

'A private nursing home isn't the same, is it, Mum?' Sandra butted in. 'Full of moaning women having hysterectomies!'

'Don't you listen to her, Jane. I like it there. I can't seem to stop. I've left once or twice, but I always go back.' The little woman spoke in quick staccato sentences, each word coming out in a rush, as if she were making the most of the short time she had to sit down and talk to them.

'But how on earth do you manage? I mean, all the family and everything,' Jane asked.

'It all gets done sooner or later, and what doesn't get done wasn't worth doing in the first place.'

Jane looked with admiration at this woman who must do the work of six and yet seemed so happy and contented. And she was so easy to talk to. Even when she disagreed she didn't hector them. It was difficult not to compare her with her own mother, whose endless moaning and nagging was still a sharp, guilty memory.

Sandra's father arrived. Tall and thin, a complete contrast to his wife – like the Sprats, Jane thought. She was immediately on her guard, wishing he had not returned to spoil the pleasant evening. And then he smiled at Jane, welcoming her to his house with gentle charm. There would be no shouting in this house from him, that was obvious. Instead he joined in their chatter as he mended his son's toy. By the end of the evening, Jane felt as if she had known this warm and welcoming family all her life. As she lay in bed, it was difficult not to envy Sandra her family.

The following day, as they were about to leave, Mrs Evans took Jane to one side.

'You're always welcome here, Jane. If ever you want someone to talk to, you come to me. It's hard when you first leave home, it's good to have a second mum to turn to.'

'Thank you, Mrs Evans, you're very kind.'

Jane was thoughtful after the visit. She felt Sandra was wrong to be so intransigent about the other girls. By being so bigoted, wasn't Sandra risking being as selective as the others? Maybe it just needed time. Certainly she would never be able to confess to Sandra how she envied the others and secretly longed to be like them. She was preoccupied, too, by her new insight into her parents' behaviour. It explained so much – the bitterness, the nagging and the rows, their general air of unhappiness. The resentment that had built up within began to soften into sadness and even sympathy for them.

7

No amount of time in the training school could have prepared Jane for the shock of the wards. The ordered routine of the practical nursing in the demonstration room, performed on life-size dummies, fell apart when real flesh-and-blood patients were the object of her care. The dummies in the school felt no pain, they did not curse her, nor did they smell.

She had presumed that her patients would be grateful; instead the majority were cantankerous and never ceased complaining. There were times when she felt that they seemed to be blaming her personally for whatever was wrong with them.

Jane seemed to live in a sea of urine. As soon as one bedpan round was complete and she had scrubbed and scoured the sluice room, it was time for the next. When she was not issuing bedpans, she was testing or measuring their contents. Her whole life seemed to be filled with specimens. She felt as if the patients did not exist, only their urine. To think how she used to object to her father's chamber pot. If he could see her now, he would have the last laugh.

The sister's voice could be heard from the start of duty to the end. The mere sound of it sparked terror in the student nurses' hearts. Sister seemed incapable of being satisfied with anything. What difference could it possibly make to the patients whether the bed wheels were all at the same angle, or whether the sheets were turned down exactly 15 inches? Or that the bath plugs were set in a particular position and the bath soap in another? It could not have been of any interest to them – they probably did not even notice such minutiae – but to the nurses it was a constant source of worry and irritation.

Everything was so drab: the buildings, and the endless corridors painted in dull, institutional green. The long wards painted the same green stretched noisily into the distance, with ugly bedsteads standing like iron sentries at measured distances. Everywhere Jane thought she could smell the sickly-sweet stench of death and decay, of the cancers eating away at so many of the wretched souls in those ugly beds in the noisy wards; and everywhere there was the never-ending, depressing green. It seemed incredible that people could recover in such surroundings.

She always felt tired. No matter how many early nights she had, she could never completely shake off the exhaustion. It was not just physical fatigue, though that was real enough, it was mental tiredness too. Fatigue induced by fear, fear that she might do something wrong, fear of being shouted at, fear of instant dismissal.

She was relieved that she did not have any sense of vocation for, if she had, the reality would have come as a heartbreaking shock. Jane felt she was totally unnecessary to anyone's recovery.

'What the hell are we here for, Evans?' she asked her friend as they lay on her bed, lazily smoking and resting their aching feet.

'It'll get better. Once we sign on, they'll let us do more interesting things, like dressings and injections.'

'Dressings! Injections! Don't make me laugh! I'm not even allowed to give a blanket bath!'

'I've heard Sister Field is a bit eccentric.'

'I hate it. I can't take it – the boredom, the yelling, the smells, the bloody patients. I hate it!' she shouted loudly.

'Love, don't give up. Wait until you've been somewhere interesting – then decide. I mean, to give up after one ward seems a bit silly, doesn't it? You might feel completely different about the next one. The men on my ward are lovely, and so appreciative that it makes it all worthwhile.'

'Great for you! You should try my moaning women.'

'They say that Gynae is one of the worst.'

'It's true, I can tell you! Half of them are moaning because they're not pregnant, and the other half are in because they were and they tried to get rid of it. It's crazy. So on top of their moans, the "want-to-be-pregnant brigade" hate the guts of the "get-rid-of-it-by-any-means brigade". And me? I loathe them all!'

'Oh dear, you are fed up.' Sandra smiled at her friend.

'And when you come off duty, what is there? The food's atrocious. Why do you think they give us all those vitamin pills?' Jane angrily lit another cigarette. 'Look at our raw, rough hands. And this bloody uniform – look at us, we look like drabs! It's sexless, it's uncomfortable, and I can never pleat this bloody cap right.' Petulantly she threw the cap she had given up folding across the room. Sandra retrieved it and started neatly folding it for her. 'And no one's died yet!' she said, almost as an afterthought.

'How remiss of them!' Sandra grinned at Jane's pink face, noticing with amusement that the colour did not make it any less attractive, the grey eyes glinting in rage at the whole system.

'Shut up! I'm not joking. I want a death to see if I can cope with it. If I can't, I might just as well give up now and save everyone a lot of trouble and money.'

'Make sure you don't use someone dying as an excuse to get out. It's never pleasant, my mum says. She says it doesn't matter how many you've laid out, it's always upsetting.'

'Your mum's a proper nurse. I'll never be one, I know that now.'

'Don't talk so bloody daft. A minute ago you were complaining that you didn't have enough contact with the patients. So how do you know that you aren't going to make it? Wait until you're on a decent ward, or Theatres.'

'God, I dread Theatres! I'd drop everything, I know I would. As it is, everything breaks if I go anywhere near it – I broke the sterilizer today. I just looked at it and it exploded. Sister was furious and we had to borrow one from the ward next door,' Jane said in a woebegone voice.

'You can't break a sterilizer by looking at it.'

'You tell Sister Field that. She says I did, the miserable old cow!'

'Is she as bad as they say?'

'Bad! She's evil! She's a bad-tempered, sexually frustrated old shrew. Do you know she made Tyler-Smith stand on a stool in the middle of the ward today? She'd dropped a dressing tray, and the old bitch made her stand on this flaming stool, just like an orphan out of *Jane Eyre*. And, what's more, she made her stay there while the Prof did his round with that gawping gaggle he calls students.'

'That woman Field can't be normal. There must be something wrong with her head, if you ask me.'

'I hate it all. And those bitches with their superior airs, I hate them too. Have you noticed how they all have double-barrelled names – that's another thing that gets on my nerves.'

Sandra laughed at her outburst.

'What's so funny?'

'I thought it was you wanted to be friends with them. Sounds as if you've changed your mind – dramatically.'

'I hate being made to feel inferior. Why should I? I'm as good as them. Honest, I didn't know such snobbery existed!' She flopped back onto her pillow, lapsing at last into a sullen silence.

Sandra wandered over to the window and peered out at the soot-laden, yellow fog swirling thickly against the panes.

'Great! There's a right peasouper building up out there.'

Jane glanced without interest at the window. 'What's good about that?'

'The bronchitics will be pouring in, snuffing it left, right and centre. That will please my dad.'

'Why on earth should a rush of bronchitics please your father?'

'Didn't you know? He makes coffins!'

Jane shrieked with laughter, her anger with everything evaporating. 'You're making it up to make me laugh. You told me your dad was a carpenter.'

'He is. What do you think coffins are made of, clot? This is his busy season, a good load of stiffs now sets him up nicely for the summer and then he can do what he really likes doing, making furniture. He'd like to do that all the time, but the coffins pay well.' She watched Jane rolling on the bed with uncontrollable laughter. 'He's very good!' she said defensively.

'Oh, Sandra, I'm sure he is. It's just the idea of someone listening to the weather forecast and hearing it all in terms of how many corpses he could count on – it's so funny!'

'Well, at least you're laughing.' Sandra sat down again on the bed. 'You know what you want? Get you out of this doom – a man.'

'Fat chance we have of meeting anyone.'

'There's loads of lovely blokes about. You're so busy moaning that you don't notice them. And with your looks you shouldn't have a problem.'

'Where are all these men?' asked Jane sitting up with interest.

'For a start, there's the doctors, the medical students, the – '

'Doctors! They're so grand they don't even know we exist. Same with the medics: they only talk to the seniors. Where are we supposed to meet anyone? This place is like a nunnery.'

'There's the Cat's Whisker.'

'I'm sick to death of cappuccino. In any case the students there are as skint as we are.'

'There are some yummy porters. Have you seen the one in Casualty?'

'A hospital porter isn't my idea of romance.'

'And who are you, Nurse Reed, to be so high and mighty? Don't tell me you're turning into a snob!' Sandra laughed.

'You know what I mean. I can't imagine anything remotely romantic happening in this place.'

'I suppose the love of your life will come charging in on a coal-black stallion.'

'That would be nice!' Jane smiled.

Sandra took her hand, her expression suddenly serious. 'Don't give up, Jane. It'll get better, honest it will. If you went, I'd miss you dreadfully.'

'It's probably out of my hands, Sandra. I expect the hospital will politely ask me to get lost after this three months' probation, which would solve everything.'

Jane survived her three months on the ward full of moaning women. It was with mixed feelings that she approached Matron's office to be told whether the hospital was willing to train her. Part of her was certain that she was wasting her time and everyone else's; part of her was afraid – what else could she do? It was the perennial question to which there seemed to be no answer. A very small part of her felt she would be sad to go, that perhaps things would get better.

She entered Matron's room. Nothing seemed to have changed since she had last been here at her interview. It was as if the woman hadn't moved from her position behind the desk.

'Nurse Reed, sit, please.' As before, there was no welcoming smile to help Jane read the woman's mind. Jane sat silently as Matron read her ward report.

'I think we should have a talk, Nurse Reed, don't you?'

'Yes, Matron,' a very subdued Jane replied.

'Nurse Reed, your appearance is a disgrace. Just look at your shoes! They are filthy and appear to be falling apart.' Jane looked guiltily at her shoes and attempted to twine them around the legs of her chair to hide them. 'Your stockings are laddered, and inking in the ladders with black ink fools no one, especially not me. Your apron has a black mark on it. Ink? And your cap is a mess! What have you to say, Nurse Reed?'

'I'm sorry about my shoes, Matron. It's the water in the sluices – they're always wet, and they were cheap to start with. I snagged my stockings as I was changing to come to see you and I didn't have another pair, and I hoped you wouldn't notice. And I have a dreadful time with the cap, I can never get it right, I do try ... but each time I screw it up into an unholy mess!' she finished breathlessly.

'Save up for better shoes. Always have a spare pair of stockings. Ask a friend to help you with your cap.'

'Yes, Matron,' Jane replied dejectedly.

'Apart from that, Nurse Reed, your ward report is excellent. Sister Field is pleased both with your work and your willingness and keenness to learn, also your cheerfulness in what, after all, is not one of the easiest wards in this hospital.'

Jane could feel her mouth opening in disbelief. 'I am pleased to inform you that the hospital will be willing to enter into a contract with you, should you wish to join us, for the rest of your training.'

'Oh yes, please, Matron. Thank you.'

Matron dismissed her and as she stood to go, she smiled at Jane. 'You will find, Nurse Reed, that nail varnish remover is quite good for getting ink stains off flesh.'

'Thank you, Matron.'

'And by the way, Nurse Reed, the door is to your left!' To her astonishment, Jane saw that Matron was grinning broadly.

Two
1956–57

1

Jane had been nursing for a year. In that time she had come to terms with the pettinesses of their small, enclosed world. She had learned to ignore the snobbery. On the ward she performed, without arguing, tasks which previously she had thought pointless. She did not get so tired. She was more tolerant of her patients, realizing that often their bad temper and depression were caused by fear. Finally she had to face death for the first time, with every pore of her body crawling with terror. But as she held the wasted, pain-racked body of the frightened old man, comforted him and helped to ease his fear, she conquered some of her own. As the last breath left the emaciated figure, she placed his hands on his chest and bent and kissed him on the forehead. It seemed the right thing to do. Then she ran into the sluice room and, among the bedpans and urine bottles, sobbed her grief for the old man she hardly knew. She knew now that Sandra's mother had been right, that death would never become a routine occupational hazard.

Now, as a second-year nurse, she had a different-coloured belt, two additional late passes, five shillings extra a week and far more confidence.

She was on her second tour of night duty. Last night on Male Surgical had been terrible. The ward was available for casualties, which meant that some beds had to be kept free for the victims that the city would damage and spew up each night.

It was a rare night that the beds were not all filled and this was no exception. A multiple pile-up in the Edgware Road, two knifings from Soho, and an Irishman who had decided to climb some scaffolding only to fall four storeys and live, despite two broken legs, a broken back and concussion so severe that it was doubtful if they would ever know what had possessed him to climb it in the first place. Two regular patients, of whom Jane had grown fond, chose that night, amid the noise and chaos, to give up the struggle and die, quietly and unnoticed.

It was the sort of night that really summed up Jane's fragmented feelings about being a nurse, when she felt there was no better job. It was also the sort of night when she felt she could not cope, was totally inadequate to the task in hand and too young to bear the responsibility of all that pain and anguish.

She went off duty exhausted. Fully dressed she lay on her bed, meaning to wash and change, but instead she fell rapidly into a deep sleep, happy in the knowledge that she had four nights off and could sleep as long as she liked.

An insistent banging on her door punctured this sleep. She stirred restlessly. The banging persisted.

'Reed! Reed? I know you're in there.'

'Go away,' she mumbled, putting her pillow over her head. The knocking continued. 'Go away, Evans!' she shouted, irritable now.

Instead the door was thrown open and Sandra burst into the room.

'I knew you were in here,' Sandra exclaimed triumphantly. 'You're on nights off, aren't you?' Blearily Jane nodded. 'Good. Then get up! Come on.'

'Go away, please. I want to sleep.'

Sandra sat herself down firmly on Jane's bed. 'You are bad-tempered! Come on, cheer up! We're going to a lovely party, so get up.'

'You might be going, but I'm sleeping for days.'

'God, you're wet! You've had hours already. Come on, wake up!'

'My feet are killing me,' Jane moaned.

'Then you need something to take your mind off them. A party!'

Sandra leaped up and, opening Jane's wardrobe, began to riffle through her clothes.

'Now, what will you wear?' She held up dresses, considering each for a second and then, rejecting them, threw them in a heap on the floor and burrowed back into the wardrobe. Jane watched the systematic destruction of her orderly room. 'Come on, misery, don't just sit there mooning. Take an interest, do. What are you going to wear? Not that it matters. You always look stunning, whatever you wear.'

'Is there any point in my repeating that I am not going to this bloody party?' Jane asked, sitting up wearily.

'None whatsoever. It'll do you good to get out and meet some new people. In any case I can't go on my own, now can I?'

'Ask someone else.'

'I don't want to go with anyone else, I want to go with you.'

Jane looked at the large brown eyes, and knew that she would go. It had been a foregone conclusion the minute that Sandra had come into the room. She could never resist her friend, and her objections had merely been a form of ritual.

'Whose party is it?'

'There, I knew you'd come. I don't know who's giving it, but it's sure to be super. You know those two Cambridge students working on Casualty as porters? Well, it's a friend of theirs. They're super, not the least bit stuck-up.' She picked out a blue dress. 'You've half an hour to have a bath, OK? You don't mind if I borrow this, do you?'

'Yes, I do mind. If I'm going, I want to wear that dress!' But it was too late, Sandra was already scurrying along the corridor to her own room, triumphantly holding Jane's dress aloft.

Half an hour later, she entered the hall of the Nurses' Home. As usual, at this time of the evening, it was crowded with off-duty nurses. Some were waiting for their dates to appear, others had no dates and nothing better to do than to watch what was going on and who was going out with whom.

Jane had been too well tutored by her mother's disappointment in her looks to regard herself as beautiful. Sandra's compliments she interpreted as acts of friendship. The admiring glances she received from the other girls' dates were, she thought, the stares of curiosity. She stood looking around the hall, in her red felt skirt and black jumper, her long dark hair tied back with a red ribbon, totally oblivious of how lovely she looked.

Across the room she saw Sandra in animated conversation with a young man Jane remembered seeing around the hospital, but he looked different in his sports jacket.

'He can't go like that!' Jane heard Sandra say angrily.

'Why not?' the young man asked.

'Don't be bloody daft, he looks as if he's dying!'

'No, he's not, he's just had a bad day.'

Jane noticed another man slumped on the settee. His face was grey, his eyes were glassy, and he was sweating profusely.

'What's the problem? Is he ill?' Jane interrupted, concerned.

'Bad day, my foot! He's drunk,' hissed Sandra. 'Just look at him.' Suddenly she noticed Jane. 'John, this is Jane. She's supposed to be this slob's partner,' Sandra said angrily.

'Jane, hullo. I'm dreadfully sorry, but I don't think David will be coming to the party, do you?' he said apologetically, turning to look at his friend with a perplexed expression. 'I really don't know what we can to.'

'We get him out of here and to his bed, that's what we do!' Sandra snapped, her dark eyes blazing with fury. Together they began to manhandle David from the settee. Suddenly he came to life and swiftly swung round, hung over the back of the settee and, with heaving shoulders, vomited.

'Oh, Christ!' said John.

'Bloody hell!' exclaimed Sandra, looking nervously around the room. They were lucky, the room was so crowded and the noise level so high that miraculously no one had noticed. 'Quick,' ordered Sandra, 'push that flaming settee back against the wall. Get him out of here, quick!' Surreptitiously they edged the settee back against the wall.

'How do I get him out?'

'God, you're impossible! Frogmarch him. Carry him. I don't care, but just get him out of here, fast. We can't risk the portress seeing us with you. We'll meet you outside.'

John supported his swaying friend and sheepishly led him past the portress's lodge. The woman leaped up and eyed them suspiciously as they stumbled past.

'The heat . . .' they heard John mumble in explanation.

Sandra and Jane waited a minute until the portress was busy with a crowd about her window and then slipped past. Mrs Grant, the portress, was one of the banes of their lives. She sat her life away in her pigeonhole of an office, behind a little window which opened and shut with a crack, like the jaws of a predatory animal. Each morning a queue of girls hoping for mail would form outside the window. At the appointed time, not a minute early or late, the window would snap open and Mrs Grant would reluctantly hand out mail. The Nurses' Home was her world, and very little escaped her sharp eyes. But tonight they were in luck, and they managed to get outside without her seeing.

They found David leaning at an angle against the railings and, on the corner, they saw John looking for a taxi.

'This evening is going to be a disaster. I'm not coming,' Jane declared. 'Oh, hell!' Her hand shot up to her mouth. 'The bloody Book – we forgot to sign out.'

'Stop flapping, Reed. I've arranged all that. Sykes is signing us out and in. And, yes, you are coming. Look, we'll dump David back at his digs. You can hardly let me go on my own, after this!'

'Well, how about neither of us going?'

'Damn that! We're all dressed up now. Come on, Jane, it still might be fun.'

Against her better judgement, Jane climbed into the taxi. The driver was none too keen to take them.

'I don't take drunks! Who'll clear it up if he's sick?'

'My good man . . .' started David, only to collapse back into the seat, winded by a vicious jab from Sandra's elbow.

'He's not drunk, driver. He has this dreadful collapsing illness, and we must get him to his bed quickly,' Sandra lied, giving the driver one of her largest smiles. 'It's not infectious, and we are nurses,' she reassured him. Sandra's smile did the trick and the taxi sped off towards David's lodgings. As he disembarked unsteadily from the taxi, David bowed low to both of them.

'I come from haunts of coot and hern . . .' he began cryptically, then buckled at the knees. The girls waited, sitting stiff-backed with indignation, while John deposited his friend in bed.

'Look, girls, I'm so sorry about this,' John said, climbing back into the taxi. 'He's always doing it. He can't drink, you see, it always makes him throw up.'

'Why does he do it then?' Sandra asked in a frigid voice.

'Habit, I suppose.' John gave them a weak grin. 'I promise you the rest of the evening won't be like this, honestly. It was much worse last time, he was sick in the Ritz.'

'"Coot" is right!' said Jane. The two girls looked at each other and started to laugh.

'You are coming then?' They nodded. 'Fabulous!'

A little later, the taxi pulled up in front of a small house in Fulham. As John paid it off, Jane stood on the pavement and looked through the open windows at the silhouetted shapes of a large crowd. Even from the street the noise was deafening; the very walls of the house seemed to bulge in time to the rock and roll that was bellowing out. She shouldn't have come, she thought. She never knew what to say to people at parties and this looked larger than any party she had ever been to. If they were all Cambridge types, they were likely to be arrogant, very intelligent, and she would have nothing in common with anyone.

'Evans, I don't want to go!'

'Lor', don't start that! We're here now. What's the matter with you? You've hardly said a word all the way.'

'I don't know. I've got this horrid floaty sort of feeling in my stomach and it makes me nervous, as if it's warning me.'

'Hell, you are a clot! That's excitement.' Jane did not look convinced. 'Stop behaving like an old woman! It'll be fine, I promise you. This is our chance to broaden our horizons. If we play our cards right we might even get an invitation to Cambridge.' She grabbed Jane confidently by the arm and eagerly followed John up the steps to the front door.

Inside, the crush was unbelievable. John had to push a path for them through the crowd. There did not appear to be anywhere to hang coats and reluctantly they threw theirs onto a large pile on the floor.

'Where's the booze?' John asked of a young man making his way with difficulty in the opposite direction, holding aloft two glasses of wine which slopped in all directions.

'Kitchen. Back.' He indicated with a jerk of his head.

The surfaces in the kitchen were covered with bottles of every shape and size. The floor was awash with spilled wine. A beer barrel stood on a table in the centre of the room; beneath it lay a young man apparently asleep, but with his mouth open so that the drips from the tap trickled down his gullet.

'I do hope he doesn't drown!' Jane tried to joke. The other two peered at him. As John gently prodded him with his foot, one eye opened and winked at them.

'I thought he'd be all right. And if not, what a way to go!' laughed John loudly. Jane did not laugh. She had seen too many drunken brawls in her street. She could understand that her father and his cronies needed to drink – for them it was an escape – but what on earth could this fortunate young man possibly need to escape from?

She followed the others back through the crush to the front room where the crowd was even denser. She need not have worried about making conversation with strangers: the crashing music made talking impossible. To her pleased surprise, one young man after another asked her to dance, and all she had to do was to smile as they valiantly tried to talk to her. The crowd seemed good-natured enough, but she could not put out of her mind that at any moment it might erupt in violence.

By three o'clock, and after a visit from the police requesting that they turn the volume down, things began to quieten. Softer music was put on. People began to sprawl on the floor. Jane searched for Sandra but could not find her among so many bodies. In a sudden lull, tiredness began to creep up on her. Sinking to a large cushion on the floor, she leaned her back against the wall and gratefully closed her eyes.

'Hullo.'

Jane looked up, shading her eyes to try to make out the tall figure standing over her.

'I'm sorry. You'll have to forgive me, I can't dance another step.' She laughed apologetically.

'I wasn't going to ask you to dance, I wanted to talk to you. May I?' He indicated the big cushion and she moved over to make room for him. He sank down beside her, elegantly jackknifing his tall frame.

'Alistair Redland,' he introduced himself.

'Jane Reed.'

They solemnly shook hands and smiled at each other. She thought he looked handsome, almost Nordic with his blond hair, but it could be a trick of the light, she thought. She smiled again, shyly.

'Are you enjoying the party?' he asked.

'Not much,' she replied.

'I'm sorry.' He laughed. 'What's wrong with it?'

'It's too crowded, and with so many drunks around, it's bound to end in a fight.'

'Really? Are you sure?' Again he laughed.

'Yes. It always does, doesn't it – drink, I mean?' She turned to him and for the first time he saw the real fear in her beautiful grey eyes.

'Jane, I don't think you need worry. They're just having a good time, you know, letting their hair down. I've never seen a real fight break out, not with this lot.' He sounded incredulous. 'I'm sorry you don't like my party, though.'

'I didn't realize it was your party.'

'Obviously, otherwise you wouldn't have told me you didn't like it.'

'Yes, I would,' she replied. 'There wouldn't be much point in lying, would there?'

'Well, no, I suppose not. It's just . . . well, usually people aren't quite so honest. Do you like my house?'

'It seems very nice. Do you share it with anyone?'

'No.'

'It's a bit big just for one person, isn't it?'

'I don't think so, it only has two bedrooms.'

'Only!' She laughed.

'Why are you laughing?'

'Just that my friend Sandra's family of eight live in a three-bedroomed house.'

'Oh, I see.' He looked thoughtful. 'Cigarette?' As she took the cigarette, she noticed what beautiful, strong hands he had. So many men were spoiled by ugly hands, but she liked his. 'Are you a student?'

'A student nurse at St Cuthbert's.'

'Do you like it?'

'Not much. I'm not a very good nurse, you see. I can't remember things. I mean, the other day I assisted a doctor with a blood transfusion and I'd forgotten to put the blood on the trolley; he wasn't amused. And I drop everything and break things.'

He smiled. 'It sounds dreadful. Couldn't you do something else?'

'Not really. I'd hate to work in an office and I couldn't work in a bank – I can't add up!'

He laughed. It was a good, open, honest laugh – nothing polite about it, she thought.

'And you?' she asked.

'I'm at Cambridge doing estate management. Not nearly as lively as nursing.'

'You don't sound as if you're at Cambridge.'

'What does that mean?'

'You talk normally, not as if you're strangling to death half the time.'

'Jane, you are funny!'

'Well, you know what I mean.' She grinned at him. 'Our hospital is full of them, and really sometimes it's difficult to understand what they're saying. But you, you have a beautiful voice, I could listen to you for hours.'

'I'm relieved to hear it. Let's hope you will.'

Jane found herself blushing.

'You blush, too! I don't believe it!'

They were too engrossed in each other to notice John and Sandra approaching.

'We thought of going on to a club. Coming, Alistair?'

'No, thanks, John, not tonight.'

'Coming, Jane?' Sandra asked her. Jane discovered to her surprise that suddenly she did not want to leave at all. Reluctantly she began to get to her feet.

Alistair's hand restrained her. With delight she heard him say softly, 'Stay here with me, Jay, please.'

'I think I'll stay here, Sandra.'

It was the easiest decision of her whole life.

2

The light shining down on their cushion was the only one in the room. Jane felt as if they were sitting on an isolated island, the sleeping bodies around them like large rocks in a dark sea. Alistair fetched a bottle of wine prudently hidden before the party.

Talking to him was easy. He seemed genuinely interested in her, and what she thought and felt about things.

As dawn began to filter into the room, her feeling of isolation began to fade. In the daylight, the romantic rocks became again the crumpled shapes of sleeping guests, the darkened sea the bare floorboards littered with glasses, bottles and cigarette ends. Alistair shuddered at the sight.

'Let's walk down to the river,' he suggested. They left the sleepers, the upturned bottles and the smoke-laden air. As they walked along the deserted street, he suddenly took her hand in his. It was a warm handclasp, and it felt right and comfortable. She looked at him shyly and he smiled, and in the full light of day she could see that he was handsome. It had not been a trick of the light, after all. A good foot taller than she, he was slim but muscular. His hair was the Nordic blonde she had thought it to be. It was straight with a hank that continually fell across his forehead. He had a habit of running his hands through it, flicking it back into place. His eyes, unusually in someone so blonde, were brown and flecked with gold. When he smiled fine lines appeared around them, as if he smiled a great deal. He walked with a long-legged stride so that Jane found herself almost running to keep up.

'Sorry.' He grinned at her, slowing down. 'I always forget that not everyone walks as fast as I do.'

They reached the wall of the Embankment and leaned against it, watching the greenish-brown water of the Thames sluggishly slip by. Two swans swam majestically towards them, inclining their heads elegantly in their direction, as if bidding them 'good day'. They laughed with pleasure and both solemnly called, 'Good morning!' to the passing birds. She squealed with horror as a large sleek rat slipped from the deck of a houseboat but they watched with fascination as it walked the mooring rope with the grace of a tightrope walker, manoeuvring intelligently around the cowls put there to baulk its progress. They applauded with delight as the rat safely reached the shore, but they regretted the noise they had made when it turned bright eyes on them and, startled, slunk away.

Although they stood apart as they leaned against the parapet, Jane was as aware of his body as if he were touching her. She wished he would. He talked about Turner. She tried to listen but found herself planning to move her hand, unnoticed, so that it would brush against his. She moved slightly to the left, but as she did, he turned around, widening the gap between them, and he talked of Wordsworth. Instead of listening, she watched his mouth. It was a generous mouth with full, fleshy lips. A mouth she would like to kiss. But then perhaps he didn't want to kiss her, otherwise surely he would have done so by now. He began to talk of Browning . . .

'Oh, to hell with the lot of them!' He stepped forward and, awkwardly, took her into his arms and was kissing her. She was so surprised her wish had been granted that she stood rigidly, her mouth passive against his. 'I'm sorry, I shouldn't have done that. I apologize, I don't know what got into me. You looked so pretty.'

'Don't apologize! I wanted you to kiss me. I didn't think you would and it took me by surprise.' She laughed with delight, unaware how ingenuous she sounded.

'Really? I mean, we've only just met.'

'I know. Silly, isn't it?'

'Shall we try again?'

'Yes, please.'

Gently his mouth brushed against hers. His arms tightened about her. The pressure of his lips upon hers strengthened. Involuntarily her lips parted and his tongue caressed the inside of her mouth. She felt as if he were drawing her into his own body. Nerves within her, dormant until now, kindled into life, sending rapid messages all over her. A dull ache consumed her, an aching she had never felt before. To Jane's disappointment, the kiss ended.

They broke apart. Cupping her face in his hands, he looked at her for a long, silent moment. His expression made Jane feel weak; there was a look of longing in his eyes which was new to her, but which excited her.

'Now,' he said, 'I'm starving! Let's get something to eat.' Jane began to laugh.

'What's funny?' he asked.

'It's not exactly what I wanted to hear.'

'Oh? What should I have said?'

'Something romantic, like "Come with me to Sidi Barani".'

'Where's Sidi Barani?'

'I don't know, but it sounds romantic.'

'My sincere apologies,' he teased her. 'As an alternative, might I suggest we go to this fantastic, intimate, exclusive transport café round the corner?'

'That's better.' She laughed.

The café was full. They sat at the only free table, oblivious of the slopped tea, the fat congealing on the plates, the ribald comments of the lorry drivers, and grinned at each other.

'It's not the Ritz,' he said apologetically.

'It doesn't have to be,' she answered happily. 'In fact I prefer it here, especially if your friend David has been there recently.' She told him about David's disgrace the night before.

'Good Lord, I'm sorry. He's famous for that but no one told me about last night. No wonder you were so edgy about the drinking.'

A harassed waitress quickly cleared the rickety table, took their order and within minutes their breakfast arrived. They ate the huge fried breakfast with relish and with no thought of diet or digestion. They lingered over their tea, smoking cigarettes, talking, and in the crowded café managed to find again an isolation.

Finally they wandered back to the house. One or two of the bodies remained asleep, others were sitting like rag dolls, propped against the walls, staring with glazed eyes into space.

'Don't think they're going to be much help,' said Alistair good-naturedly.

'I'll help you clear up,' Jane volunteered.

'Would you? That would be marvellous. I'll buy you lunch if you do.'

'That won't be necessary. I want to help,' she said stiffly.

'Jane, don't be so prickly! I said that because I would like to buy you lunch, not as a payment.'

'Sorry. Am I prickly?'

'Yes.'

'I don't want to be, not with you. I'm afraid lunch is out, though. I have to get back to the hospital. If there's been a row about David, poor Sandra will be having to cope with the thunder on her own. It wouldn't be fair, would it?'

'Dinner, then?'

'That would be lovely, thank you.'

'That's better,' he said and kissed her on the forehead. They found some cardboard boxes and began to collect the empty bottles and glasses, opening all the windows to clear the fug which had settled in all the rooms. By the time they returned to the kitchen with their boxes of rubbish, there was barely room to move. The young man had gone from under the beer barrel and in his place there was a large puddle of beer. The sickly, sour smell of it hung in the air.

'You hang on here,' Alistair ordered. 'I'll pop round the corner and get some tea towels and things.' He banged noisily out of the house. Jane found a bucket under the sink and an old rag; the water was hot and she started to mop up the offending puddle of beer.

'Who are you?' a voice demanded.

Startled, Jane looked up to see standing over her a girl of her own age. There the similarity ended, for every inch of this young woman was groomed to perfection. Perched jauntily on her curled blonde hair was a neat little white hat. Not a wrinkle marred the pencil-slim skirt of her suit. No dust spoiled the pristine whiteness of her gloves. The gloss of her high-heeled shoes was so bright that Jane was fascinated to see her own face reflected in them as she knelt on the floor, peering up at this elegant creature. The girl stood, one hand on hip, her feet elegantly positioned like the feet of a ballet dancer or model.

'I said, who are you?' she repeated imperiously.

Flustered, Jane got to her feet, conscious of her lack of make-up and her untidy hair. In her confusion she knocked the bucket and some of the water spilled on her skirt, which now flapped damply against the backs of her legs.

'I'm a friend of Alistair's,' she explained.

'I don't know you,' was the brusque reply.

'No, but I am all the same.' She felt anger welling up in her.

'Where is he?'

'Out.'

'I realize that. Where?' the other girl snapped.

'I said, out.'

'You needn't make a state secret of it!'

'You can leave a message with me, if you like.'

'I'd rather deliver my message personally. That way, I'll know he's received it,' she said unpleasantly. 'Don't let me stop your work.' She indicated the bucket.

Jane felt her antagonism increasing. She had no intention whatsoever of getting back on her hands and knees in front of this creature. Pointedly she pushed the bucket to one side with her foot. Leaning against the sink, arms folded, she glared belligerently across the small room at this girl who epitomized everything she secretly longed to be, smoothly, expensively sleek and confident.

'Could you move these?' The girl indicated the only chair in the room, on which there was a tray of glasses. Used to being ordered, Jane automatically did as she was asked and dusted the seat with the only towel in the room. Suddenly realizing what she was doing, she swiped the towel viciously across the chair, angry with herself for reacting like a servant. Again she took up her position by the sink. The girl looked suspiciously at the chair and gingerly sat on it. Snapping open her handbag she took out a cigarette but did not offer one to Jane.

'Is there any coffee?'

'No.' Jane did not know if there was or not, but she had no intention of looking and took a perverse pleasure in not being helpful, relishing the small sense of power it gave her. The feeling did not last long, for as she glanced surreptitiously at the other girl, she saw that she was very pretty and, but for the arrogant expression on her face, could have been lovely, despite the heavy make-up. She longed to know who she was but was not going to risk being rebuffed again by asking. She feared that perhaps she was a girlfriend and found the thought made her feel strangely cold inside.

She began to fret that Alistair had not returned. This girl's arrival made his absence seem interminable. At last, with relief, she heard the front door slam and Alistair appeared in the doorway weighed down with parcels.

'Sorry I was so long. I thought I'd better get some supplies in and I've got a fridge coming, too. At least we'll be able to keep the gin cool!' Stepping into the kitchen he saw the girl. 'Hullo, Clar, I didn't think it would take too long before you came snooping around.'

'If you must know, I didn't want to come. Mother sent me. Your telephone isn't working.'

'It is.'

'Not this morning it isn't,' she said tersely. Alistair went out into the hall.

'Some fool knocked the receiver off the hook,' he explained. 'You two met?'

'Hardly,' the girl drawled.

'This is Jane Reed, isn't she the most beautiful creature you ever saw?'

Alistair said proudly. The girl looked hard at Jane but said nothing. Jane stood, feeling astonishment, as for the first time in her life she heard a man describe her as beautiful. 'Jane, this is my sister, Clar.'

'Clarissa Cotham, actually. How do you do?' Jane found herself offered a very limp hand. She took it, relieved that she was his sister but puzzled that she had a different name.

'I see you had a party last night. So kind of you to invite me, Alistair!' she said sarcastically.

'I didn't for one moment think you'd like to come. You're always at pains to tell me you don't like my friends.'

'Is it so surprising? They're always so vulgar!' She looked straight at Jane.

'Clarissa, shut up, do. You're not impressing either of us. You're too childish for words. Why are you here?'

'Mother wants you to come to dinner tonight,' she said shortly. She did not seem capable of normal speech, Jane thought: everything was either said with a sneer or a snap.

'I can't come, I'm taking Jane out to dinner.'

'Well, you can tell her, Alistair, not me. She's got Fortescue coming round and wants everyone there. That's an order.' She stood up, brushed imaginary dirt from her suit, and picked up her handbag.

'You off? I thought perhaps you'd come to help.' It was Alistair's turn to be sarcastic.

'Me!' She snorted rather than laughed. 'I should get your little friend here to help you. She looks the capable sort,' and she swept from the room.

'Heavens!' exclaimed Jane.

'Dreadful, isn't she? She likes to think she's being sophisticated. In fact she's just bloody rude. I can't stand her myself.'

'Really?' She was curious. 'I always thought it would be marvellous to have a brother or sister. Someone to confide in.'

'Confide in? Confide in Clarissa! You're joking! If you're an only child, I envy you.'

'It can be very lonely being an only child.'

'It's a loneliness I could do with.' He laughed.

'No, really. I was always very lonely.'

'Poor Jay.' He crossed the room to her. 'I won't let you be lonely any more.' He kissed her with great gentleness. 'I'd much rather kiss you but I had better telephone Mother.'

Jane began to wash up the piles of glasses. She could not hear what he was saying on the phone, but from the tone of his voice it sounded as if he was arguing. He returned to the kitchen looking angry.

'Bloody family! I buy this house to get away from them for a bit and still they bother me. Jane, I'm sorry, I so wanted to take you out tonight but I have to go to this family dinner.'

'It's all right, I don't mind. I've got another three nights off duty after this.'

'Look, tell you what, it shouldn't go on too late. If I give you a key you could come here and I'll get back as soon as possible and we can go out for a drink. What do you think?'

'That would be lovely.'

'Great!' He had switched moods and the arrival of the new refrigerator completed his change in temper. He took a boyish pleasure in supervising the delivery and installation of the machine. Then they put the shopping away. It was an enormous fridge and the pack of butter, the pound of bacon and the six eggs looked lost in it.

'Why so big?'

'To get lots of bottles in, of course.'

'Alistair, we're off now, thanks for a super party.' A young man appeared in the doorway. Jane jumped with surprise at the sound of his voice. She had forgotten that there were still others in the house. She was so wrapped up in being with Alistair that it was as if life only existed in the room they were in.

'Right, Simon, I'll see you,' said Alistair. 'I wonder how many others are left, I'd quite forgotten they were here.'

Jane felt quietly satisfied that he felt the same. 'Perhaps you'll still be finding guests in three weeks' time.' She laughed.

'Let's check.'

They wandered around the house but everyone else had gone. In the dark of last night she had not realized what a pretty house it was. There were two large bedrooms and a third that had been turned into a bathroom. Last night she had not noticed that the sitting room had large double doors opening into an equally large room beyond it. There was a basement that opened into a small, well-stocked garden.

'I want to turn the whole of this basement into a kitchen-dining-room,' he explained. 'You see, it'll open straight into the garden,' and he opened a glass door to show her. 'I don't want a formal dining room, it'll be more fun to eat down here.'

'What will you do with the dining room upstairs?'

'Those doors fold back into the wall. It'll make a terrific, roomy drawing-room.'

'And the kitchen that's there already?'

'That's going to be my study.'

'A study! I thought you didn't like work very much?'

'I don't, but a chap's got to have a room to make his phone calls and read his letters, hasn't he?'

'If you say so,' but she didn't sound too sure. 'It's going to be very expensive to furnish, isn't it?'

'Not if I scour the junk shops. Furnish it bit by bit.' He looked at the stains on the floor. 'It was certainly a good idea to have the party before I started furnishing it, wasn't it?' Remembering the chaos of the morning, she laughingly agreed.

He tried to dissuade her from returning to the hospital, suggesting that she join him on a shopping expedition to find things for the house. She wanted more than anything to go with him, but, as she explained, there was Sandra to think of. Not only that, she was beginning to feel very tired and knew she should get some sleep.

'No, I'd better get back.'

'You promise you'll be here tonight?'

'I promise.'

He drove her back to the hospital in the dark green MG he obviously doted on and which he had christened Flo. She noticed with smug satisfaction the envious stares of the nurses who happened to be around as they screeched to a halt in front of the Nurses' Home. He slipped her a key and kissed her cheek. Guiltily creeping past the portress's lodge she was only too aware that her creased skirt could only mean that she had been up all night. Luckily she managed to get to her bedroom without meeting anyone in authority and, with relief, got out of her clothes and into a long, relaxing bath.

3

The warm water relaxed her tired body, but it did nothing to calm her mind. She could almost feel her thoughts, tumbling about in chaotic confusion, banging one against the other.

It had happened, she was sure it had, just as she had always known that one day it would. It had not been exactly as she had dreamed it would be – when she had met him no voice within her shouted, 'He's here!' The heavens had not tumbled. Instead she had thought he was 'nice'. Hardly the stuff of poetry. A bit disappointing, she thought, and giggled to herself. But something had happened by the river, no doubt of that. That longing to be kissed, the way he had looked at her, and that weird aching feeling she had experienced. And now something new – she was missing him. She had only just met him, he had not yet become part of her life, so what was there to miss? She examined this thought and spun every facet of it in her mind. Did it matter why? She missed him; that was enough. She smiled and lay back contentedly in the water. And what was it he had called her? J or maybe Jay? She hugged herself with pleasure; no one had ever given her a pet name before.

She stepped out of the bath and looked critically at her reflection in the mirror. She had been planning to cut her hair, having grown tired of putting it up in a bun. Now she wondered what to do with it. She shook her head, the black hair falling about her face. She had read that men preferred long hair; maybe she should wait before cutting it, maybe she would ask his opinion. She looked at her white body, wishing she was not so pale. He would be brown all over, she was certain of that, but the English summers were never long enough to turn her into the tawny creature she would have liked to be. She touched herself. She had good skin. She had learned that from handling patients, so many of whom had rough skins while hers was very smooth, she thought with satisfaction.

It was not that she never looked at her body – she often did – but now she was looking at it and trying to see it with his eyes. Could it please him, would he like it? She wished her breasts were smaller. At least her waist was small, but then the trouble with a small waist was that, irritatingly, it seemed to make her hips look inches bigger than they really were. She wondered what it would feel like, having a man touch her naked body. She closed her eyes and ran her hands down her body, she caressed her breasts, teased at her nipples – pretending her hands were his. It was as if these hands had a life of their own as they slipped, sensuously, across her flat belly and between her legs. An unfamiliar sensation, an intense feeling of excitement, jolted her body. Her eyes opened, and she looked at her reflection with surprise, shocked by the excited sparkle in her eyes. She shook herself, laughed at the girl in the mirror and swung the towel about her. What would her mother say if she could read her daughter's thoughts?

In her room she found Sandra lying on her bed. 'There you are!' Sandra exclaimed. 'I've lost count of the number of times I've trekked along here to see if you were back. Where on earth have you been all night?'

'If you must know, it seemed safer to stay there than to climb back in. And for your information, we sat and talked and then went for a walk, had breakfast, and we spent this morning clearing up the mess. So there!'

'Did he kiss you?'

'Mind your own business!'

'Ha! He did. Seeing him again?'

'Yes, tonight.'

'Fast work. Look.' Sandra pointed to Jane's basin, in which was a large bouquet of flowers.

'Who the hell . . .?'

'David. I got one too. He wants to take us out tonight.'

'That was sweet. Was anything said about the mess in the hall?'

'Not a dicky bird. Seems no one has discovered the puke yet. Mind you, the standard of cleaning in this dump, it'll probably still be there in fifty years. You coming out with us, then?'

'No, I told you, I'm seeing Alistair.'

'Perhaps we could get someone else and go out in a sixsome.'

'Thanks, I'd rather not.' Jane felt herself blushing.

'So! What have we here? Serious, is it?'

'Very. But then I always knew it should happen like this.'

'What?'

'Falling in love.'

'You've only just met him!'

'I know. Daft, isn't it?'

'Romantic but, yes, daft too. Don't you go doing anything silly, Jane,'

Sandra said, suddenly serious, and lapsing back into the Christian names which they had learned never to use. 'You wouldn't, would you?'

'Yes, Sandra, I would. It's him, I just know it is. There doesn't seem much point in waiting.'

Sandra sat up on the bed looking at her friend anxiously. 'You mean sleep with him? Don't be bloody daft, Jane – you can't sleep with him, not on a first date! What the hell would he think of you? For heaven's sake, look at the hours we've spent debating whether we should allow a bloke to kiss on a first date. Now this!' Agitatedly she lit a cigarette. 'You've gone stark staring bonkers, that's what's happened.'

'It must seem odd, but you weren't there, you didn't see the way he looked at me.'

'You can't have thought this through, Jane. What if he sleeps with you and then ditches you? It happens. And what if you get pregnant? You can say goodbye to your career then.'

'I'll have to risk it. If I'm wrong about how he feels it doesn't alter how I feel. He could ditch me without my having slept with him, and then I would never know what it would be like to sleep with the man I love. So, you see, I can't wait, can I? I can't take that risk, can I?'

'I've never heard such balderdash in my life. He won't be the only man you fall in love with.'

'Yes, he is. I'll never feel like this again.'

'Christ, you risk losing everything. If he loves you he won't mind waiting, will he?'

'But if he loves me too, then why wait?'

'I suppose there's logic in there somewhere. But how can you be so sure?'

'You don't understand. I never wanted to sleep with anyone ever before, never, never! Now I do. So this has to be different. I didn't really know myself until just now, lying in the bath, and thinking I just wanted to be with him, and to make love to him.'

'Dangerous places, baths!' Sandra grinned at her. 'But aren't you scared?'

'Terrified. But all bubbly as well. I think I'll get a little bit drunk, I'm sure that will make it easier.'

'You are a rotten moo; I always wanted to be the first. There you've been guarding your virginity, going on about the right man coming along, and there have I been trying to get rid of the bloody thing and no one wants mine.'

'And you've been lecturing me! Sandra, you're a fool. You make it sound like some dreadful impediment.'

'It is an impediment to being a complete woman, and I want to be a woman. Every man I meet, though, is either too gentlemanly, too scared or too drunk.' She pulled a wry face. Jane laughed despite herself.

'What about John? He seemed really taken with you, and he's very nice. Anything likely to happen with him?'

'He's no good. Too fond of his booze. I suppose I might be lucky and catch him one afternoon before he gets his nose in a glass.'

'I don't mean to sleep with, fool! I meant how did you get on with him?'

'Fine,' Sandra said airily. 'Judging by the way he necks, I should think he'd be pretty good in bed. But he's not likely to be the love of my life. He's fun but he'd run a mile at anything serious. Anyhow, if you're going out on this heavy date, you're going to need some sleep. I'm going. But you promise, if you do it you will tell me all?'

'Maybe.' Jane laughed as Sandra left her alone. With her thoughts in such confusion, she had not expected to sleep, so she was surprised when her alarm bell woke her to find that it was eight in the evening.

Excitedly, she dressed. Hurriedly she packed a small overnight bag. For a second she thought of her mother's horror if she knew what her daughter was doing, and just as quickly she put the thought to the back of her mind. She ran downstairs, too impatient to wait for the lift. As she signed herself out in the Book, she wondered, if she did sleep with Alistair, would she look different when she returned? Would it show on her face? Would people guess?

'Good evening, Nurse Reed. Nights off?'

Jane swung round to find the enormous bulk of Home Sister blocking her way. She felt a wave of guilt, terrified that the woman could read her thoughts and would stop her.

'Yes, Sister.'

'Going home?'

'Yes, Sister,' she lied.

'I hope you have a nice time.' Jane looked astonished at the sister's words; the woman had never spoken to her pleasantly before. It made Jane feel worse about lying and, feeling herself begin to blush, she bent down and fumbled with her case on the floor, relieved to see the sister's sturdy legs move away, as she mumbled, 'Thank you.'

She was too deep in thought to notice the bus journey across London. Arriving in Fulham, she hurried along the road to the little house. She let herself in and felt her way along the unfamiliar hall, stumbling over rolls of carpet as she searched the walls for a light switch.

A new carpet had been laid in the sitting room, from wall to wall. New curtains hung at the windows, the pelmets ornate and fringed. There was a chintz-covered sofa, its covers worn and faded. Beside it stood an intricately carved Indian coffee table, on which glowed an old bottle, converted into a lamp. A single abstract painting hung on the wall. Jane turned her head from side to side, studying it, in the hope of understanding it. She gave up the effort. Packing cases littered the floor and other paintings were stacked against the walls, waiting to be hung.

In the kitchen the greasy old gas cooker had been replaced by a gleaming new machine, covered with clocks and shining dials. In the corner the new fridge gurgled. She opened the door. It was now full of bottles of wine and some gin.

On the kitchen table stood a collection of shorter, sturdier bottles with unfamiliar, exotic names. A bright-green one looked fun but she settled for a familiar brandy. Her mother always had a small bottle in the medicine chest ready for the first twinge of toothache, when a brandy-soaked ball of cotton wool would be placed on her gum. Jane poured a glass, took a sip of the dark, golden drink, and immediately began to choke as the burning liquid touched the back of her throat. She found a bottle of lemonade, added that to her brandy and sipped the mixture nervously. She was pleased with the taste.

Clutching her glass she returned to the sitting room. One tea chest was full of books which she began to unpack and arrange on the empty alcove shelves. The majority were dull, about estate management, but at the bottom she found a pile of tattered and well-read children's books. Like her, Alistair had saved his books from his childhood.

Alistair found her in the kitchen, mixing herself another drink. She smiled with delight as he entered the room.

'I hope you don't mind my helping myself to a drink?'

'Of course not. I'll join you. Here, let me, what are you drinking?'

'Brandy and lemonade.'

'What?' he exclaimed, laughing. 'It sounds disgusting!'

'It's quite nice really. It was disgusting without the lemonade.'

'Don't ever tell my father what you've been doing with his best Napoleon brandy. He'd have apoplexy!' He continued to laugh but, seeing a shadow of confusion flicker across her face, he added hurriedly, 'Jay, drink whatever concoctions you want. But would you rather go out for a drink?'

'I'd rather stay here.'

'Fine. Then I have a treat for us.' He opened the fridge door and, like a magician, produced a bottle of champagne. 'Do you like champers?'

'I don't know. I never had it before.'

'Never had champagne? What an extraordinarily deprived life you've had!' He started to laugh but stopped himself. 'That was rather a stupid remark to make, wasn't it? Sorry.'

'I don't mind. It's true. After all, there isn't much call for champagne at the Railway Arms,' she replied easily. Alistair opened the bottle carefully, and she was disappointed that the cork did not pop. 'It always pops in the films,' she complained.

'That's because they're not opening it properly, it shouldn't really. There, try that.'

Gingerly she took a sip, and smiled broadly. 'Oh yes, I like that. Very much!' and with greater confidence she took another larger sip.

'Brandy and champagne. I thought you didn't like to drink?'

'I don't mind drinking, it's when people get drunk that I get frightened. In any case, I'm boosting my confidence.'

'Really? Might I ask why?'

'I want to be relaxed. I want you to – ' She stopped abruptly. 'Oh, I don't know. I'm feeling shy, I suppose.' She looked earnestly at her glass.

'Shy? Of me?'

'No. Yes.' She shook her head in confusion, wishing convention were different and that she could be honest and tell him she was building up her confidence to go to bed with him.

'You funny creature!' He put his arm about her shoulder and kissed her, but this time gently. Just as in the morning, Jane felt great waves of excitement flood through her body and she clung to him with an intensity that puzzled but pleased him. 'Let's go and sit somewhere more comfortable,' he said softly and, taking her by the hand, led her into the drawing room.

She hoped he was going to kiss her again, but instead he returned to the kitchen for the champagne. 'Whose case is that in the hall?' he asked, coming back with the bottle.

'Mine,' she replied, blushing furiously.

'Oh, I see. Are you planning to stay the night?' he asked with an attempt at nonchalance, as he refilled the glasses.

'If you don't mind.' Her blush intensified.

'I've only got one bed. But I don't mind sleeping on the sofa.'

'Oh no! I wouldn't dream of putting you out. In any case you're far too tall. There'd be nowhere for your feet. I'll sleep on the settee,' she said quickly, regretting as she did so the turn the conversation was taking, the fact that he was misunderstanding her intentions.

'We'll toss for it.' He grinned at her.

They sat side by side on his new sofa which, he proudly told her, had cost him a pound in the King's Road.

'It's lovely,' she said, disappointed that still he was not kissing her but appeared to prefer to talk. 'Can I have more champagne?' she asked, proffering her glass.

'What about the rest of the room? Bet you were surprised how much got done while you were away,' he said, refilling her glass.

'It's amazing. The men must have worked like greased lightning.'

'They did. Plus a little bribe from me to stay on and finish this room. I wanted somewhere halfway furnished for us. So what's your verdict?'

'I'm sorry, but I don't like those curtains. They're too fussy.'

'Pretty ghastly, aren't they? That's Mother. "Leave the curtains to me," she said. I didn't realize she'd produce those things.'

'The carpet's nice, though.' She hiccoughed discreetly.

'We had a row about that. She said wall-to-wall carpeting was vulgar.'

'What's vulgar about it?'

'Search me. She says it should be bare boards and rugs. But I won, I thought it would be easier to keep clean.'

'Bare boards! Fancy having bare boards if you can afford lovely carpets like this. It's just like being in a cinema.' With surprise she discovered that her glass was empty.

'Do you like my picture?' He poured more champagne.

'No, I think it's horrible. Really ... horrible!' She searched for another word but her brain seemed to be slowing down.

'What's wrong with it?'

'I don't like the colours and the shapes are silly, really ... silly.' Where had all the words gone? she wondered. 'I can't get excited about a green egg on a wobbly frying pan.' She shook her head slowly from side to side.

'It's a Picasso,' he said, watching her closely.

'Is it? He must have been feeling ill when he painted it then. Sorry, Mr Picasso, I think your picture – stinks,' she said with exaggerated care.

'That painting is a good test of how genuine people are. You have no idea, the number of people who suddenly change their minds when they know who the artist is.'

She turned sharply and looked angrily at him. 'I think that's horrible. Testing! Can't you trust yourself to judge people?'

'You're being prickly again, Jane.'

'I'm not surprised. Who the hell do you think you are, going around setting traps for people? What do you think I am, a liar?'

'No, Jane.' He laughed. 'That's one thing I'm certain you're not. Oh, come on. I didn't expect you to get het up about it. I only meant it's a sort of game. It's fun. Don't be cross with me.' He took hold of her and kissed her gently, and her anger melted away. In fact she could not remember what had made her angry in the first place.

'Do you always say exactly what you think?'

'Yes. Don't you?'

'No, not always.'

'Why not?'

'Well, sometimes it's more diplomatic not to.'

'You mean you lie?'

'No, Jane.' He laughed. 'I mean sometimes I try to be tactful.'

'I don't think I'd be any good at that.' She giggled, peering at him through her fingers.

'I agree. I don't somehow think you would either,' he said, kissing the nape of her neck.

'Would you like more champagne?' He took her glass.

'I'd rather you kissed me properly!'

'My pleasure.' Jane felt as if she were floating, conscious only of the closeness of their bodies, and the almost intolerable need for him that was building within her.

'I'm sorry,' he said, suddenly breaking away from her. 'I'm rushing things. But you looked so lovely and ... Oh, Christ, it's hard to sit here and not touch you, and try to talk about bloody curtains and paintings.'

'It was lovely, Alistair. I don't mind you rushing it at all. I thought it was super. More, please ...' She pursed her lips at him. 'Please ...'

'Sweetheart, look, I think I'd better take you home.'

'No!' she shouted, sitting up so suddenly that she spilled her drink. 'No! That's what I am afraid of, that you'll take me home and not want to see me again.'

'Jane, darling, don't be silly, of course I'd want to see you again. It's just ... sweetie, you're getting so drunk ... it wouldn't be right, don't you see? I'm only human and I'm afraid if you stay here, well, if you stay, I don't know what will happen.'

'Oh, lovely!' she said brightly, busily mopping up the champagne.

'Jane, you are going to get into awful trouble if you persist like this.' He smiled fondly at her.

'No, I won't. I wouldn't behave like this with anyone else.' She leaned towards him, her face a mere inch from his. 'I feel safe with you, you see. I trust you,' she said earnestly.

Alistair put his head into his hands. She watched anxiously, not quite sure what the problem was: she kept forgetting what they were talking about, which made understanding difficult. He looked up at her, an expression of mild exasperation on his face.

'OK,' he said, as if he had made a decision. 'Let's both get drunk!'

'Oh yes, what a good idea! I'd like to get drunk, that's what I wanted to do all along ...' She laughed at this idea as Alistair went to fetch another bottle of champagne.

They settled on the sofa, he in reach of the bottle, she with her head on his lap. 'Don't you think that tid – Oh Lor', I can't say it, even.' Alistair laughed helplessly. 'It's even too funny to say!'

'Try again,' advised Jane seriously.

'Don't you think the funniest word you ever heard is ...' He paused dramatically and then, taking another deep breath, declared triumphantly, 'tiddlywinks!'

They slipped from the sofa on to the floor, laughing until they ached.

'What about – winkle?'

'Hippopotamus!' They both shrieked at their own cleverness, and word followed word.

Suddenly Jane could not think of any more words and her head slumped forward.

'Come on, Jay, my love,' he said as he lifted her gently from the floor. 'Time for bed.'

'Yes, please,' she said dreamily. He carried her unsteadily to the staircase.

'Up the wooden stairs to bed we go. With a tiny candle for ...' she crooned to herself.

In the bedroom he placed her on the bed. She sat, still humming the little tune, studying her stockinged feet intently.

'You can borrow a pair of my pyjamas, that is, if I could find them.' He started to rummage through the cases that were scattered about the room.

'Doesn't matter. Doesn't matter a damn!' she said airily, flopping back on the bed fully dressed. She felt him cover her with the eiderdown.

'Alistair.' She groped with her hand for his. 'Alistair, don't go. Stay with me.'

She heard his shoes fall to the floor and she felt the bedsprings give as he slid in beside her. Beneath the warm eiderdown she settled contentedly into the crook of his arm. There was something she wanted to say to him, but she just could not remember what it was, as sleep overcame her.

4

She woke up, lifted her head and felt dreadful. It was as if, in the night, someone had placed in her head two large glass marbles with broken edges which were relentlessly rolling about inside her skull, rubbing one against the other to create a pain that seemed to break her head in two. She had a moment of total panic, when she thought she was dying, before she remembered the night before, and the cause of her bad head.

'Oh dear,' she sighed. 'What a fiasco!' She looked around the unfamiliar room. Cases were strewn about the bare floorboards, their contents spewing out as if they had burst. A sheet was pinned to the window in place of a curtain. The only furniture in the room was the double bed in which she lay, alone. What had happened? She shook her head, wincing with pain as the recalcitrant marbles rolled around within her skull. If only she could remember! Despite the pain in her head she slowly sat up, flicked back the eiderdown and, with nervous fingers, ran her hands over the bedding. It was dry. She lifted her skirt, her pants were in place. With relief she sank back on the pillows. It would have been dreadful if the most important moment of her life so far had passed by without her knowing. But even as she thought this, she knew she was also disappointed. Trouble with you, Jane Reed, she said to herself severely, you don't bloody well know what you do want. But what if it had happened? He could have put her pants back on, he could have used a Durex. But surely she would be sore? Surely she would feel different? Surely she would know?

Slowly she swung her legs over the side of the bed. Standing made the pounding in her head worse. Never again, she vowed vehemently, as, finding a hairbrush, she feebly dragged it through her hair. She longed for a toothbrush.

She found Alistair in the kitchen, concentrating so hard on cooking the breakfast that he was not aware of her standing in the doorway, shyly watching him.

'Hullo. How long have you been there?' He smiled at her.

'Not long. How long have you been up?'

'Ages. I can't lie in bed, never have been able to. You spoiled my surprise, I wanted to bring you breakfast in bed.'

'I don't like breakfast in bed, it always reminds me of illness. And I get crumbs everywhere!'

'Just as well you woke up, then.'

'Alistair?'

'Yes?'

She still stood in the doorway, wondering if she looked as awkward as she felt, as he went on with his cooking.

'Yes?' he repeated, looking up at her.

'Alistair? I . . .' She did not know how to ask him the question uppermost in her mind. It was such a silly-sounding question to ask.

'The answer's no, Jane. We didn't. We slept as innocently as babes.'

'Oh! I see. I thought not.' Wondering, at the same time, why he had not. One unwelcome conclusion was that perhaps he had not wanted to. God, she was in such a muddle! Did everyone get as confused as she did?

'What are you thinking?' he asked.

'I was thinking what an indecisive fool I am.' She smiled apologetically.

'That's not exactly the word I would use to describe you,' he said gently. Then, briskly breaking an egg into the pan, he changed the subject. 'Come on, sit down and have your breakfast.'

'I couldn't eat a thing, really. I feel dreadful.'

Alistair laughed at her woebegone face. 'Then you must make yourself eat. It'll make you feel a new woman, I promise. Best thing for a hangover is food. I should know, I'm the expert on the subject.'

'But you look fine.'

'It takes more than we had last night to affect me. You mixed the drink, that's why you're feeling so dreadful. Lesson number one, one spirit drink only, then stick to the wine. I know, from experience.' He laughed loudly, making her wince. 'Oh, my poor love, I'm sorry.' He crossed the kitchen and softly kissed her.

'Alistair. I am sorry about last night.'

'There's nothing to be sorry about.'

'No, really, I was stupid. I didn't think it through. I just crashed in presuming all sorts of things I hadn't the right to presume.'

'Like what?'

'Well . . . that you'd even want me,' she said in a small voice.

'Of course I wanted you. Too much.'

'Then why didn't you take advantage of me?'

' "Take advantage of me"!' He shouted with laughter. 'What a wonderfully archaic expression! Where on earth did you get that from? No, Jane, you really don't understand about sex. You would have to enjoy it, too, for it to work. And last night, well, last night you weren't in any state to enjoy anything.'

'I think you're right. I don't understand much about sex.'

'Then I'll teach you.' He smiled at her, but it was not like an ordinary smile: there was an intimacy to it which made a strange shiver snake down Jane's spine. 'Now eat! And then we'll go shopping,' he said, mock-sternly. The little moment of intimacy passed and Jane wondered if she had imagined it.

Their breakfast finished, they went out on what was to be the first of many shopping safaris for the house. Together they delved into the junk shops, shouting with delight as they found a lamp that took their fancy, or a chair that would be fine with a new cover. To her delight Jane found that they seemed to have the same taste, and agreed on everything.

Alistair stopped at an Italian restaurant, suggesting lunch. Reluctantly she followed him in.

'But I hate Heinz spaghetti!' she confided in a whisper. She was flustered when Alistair laughed out loud. 'Please!' she pleaded.

'I'm sorry.' He took her hand and leaned across the table, lowering his voice. 'Darling Jane, that's not Italian food. Let me order for you. I promise you, you'll love it.'

For Jane, who until now had eaten simply to stay alive and had never enjoyed eating for its own sake, the meal was a revelation. She gorged herself on the delicious food and wine.

'I'll take you to Italy one day,' he announced. 'The food is even better there. We'll sit in the sun and peel fresh figs, drink Frascati and make love all day.'

'That sounds like paradise. I've never been abroad.'

'You're the most wonderful girl to know. You've not done anything! May I be your Svengali?'

'I thought Svengali was a baddy.'

'I'll be a good one.' He laughed happily over his glass. He laughed so much and so often that she wondered if he was ever sad or depressed. It was difficult to imagine it. She could only think that she would always be happy when she was with him.

'Where's your home?' she asked.

'In the West Country. And yours?'

She told him and he pulled a face. 'Yes, it's pretty horrible, I agree. The funny thing is, I didn't realize it was until I left, and when I went back I was shocked at how drab and dirty it looked. I've only been away a year and already I feel I don't belong any more.'

'I couldn't imagine belonging anywhere else but my home. I was born there and I expect to die there too.'

'Has your family lived there long, then?'

'Ages.'

'That must be nice. But when you had dinner with your family last night, you didn't go home. It would have been too far.'

'They have a house in London, too.'

'How grand!'

'Is it? I suppose it is, if you think about it. It's always been there, so I never do.'

'What does your father do?'

'He farms.'

'I think I'd like him. Farmers are such jolly people, aren't they?'

Alistair snorted with laughter. 'I don't know which farmers you've met. Most of them moan like hell. I say he's a farmer, but he doesn't exactly dig the land.' He smiled to himself. 'You would like him, though, I'm certain of that. He's the most honest person I know. I'd like to be like him.'

'You love him a lot, don't you?'

'Yes, if I think about it, I do.'

'That's what I envy so much in people like you and Sandra – you never ever have to think about it.' Before Alistair could ask her what she meant, she continued, 'And your mother?'

'Ah! That's more difficult. She means well, but she will interfere in my life. She doesn't seem to realize that I've grown up. Last night's summons was typical: it wasn't really essential for me to be there. She seems to think that I don't have other things to do.'

'It must be difficult to accept that your children have grown up, especially if you love them.'

'If? Don't all parents love their children?'

'No,' she replied simply. 'Are your parents divorced?'

'No. What made you ask that?'

'Just that you and your sister have different names.'

'Oh, that. We're one of those odd families where everyone has a different name.' He smiled. 'Come on, if we're going to be back at the house when that furniture arrives, we'd better get going. Shall we come here for dinner tonight?'

'Dinner! You're joking. After that enormous meal, I couldn't eat another thing. And the expense, Alistair!'

'I think I can afford the odd dinner out, but, if you don't want to, we can get some stuff in and cook at home.' He spoke seriously but somehow Jane felt he was laughing.

They paid the bill and walked quickly down the King's Road, stopping to buy food for supper. They arrived back at the house just as the lorry with their treasures drew up outside.

The afternoon passed in a flurry of cleaning and polishing and deciding where to put the furniture they had bought. By the evening they were exhausted. Alistair mixed them two gins and tonics, and Jane found another drink to add to her repertoire. She settled at the kitchen table with her drink and watched with admiration as Alistair expertly prepared a meal. The evening was chilly. Alistair found some kindling and coal and lit a fire. They sat on the floor in front of it to eat their dinner, sipping claret, and Jane had her first lesson in wine.

She lay back on the large cushion, the firelight playing upon her. The wine, food and the warmth of the fire made her feel totally relaxed. Alistair stroked her hair, and she stretched languorously, feeling as she imagined a contented cat would feel. He kissed the nape of her neck. His tongue traced the outline of her ear. Tentatively his hand slipped open the buttons of her blouse, and as she made no objection, it slid with more confidence to fondle her breast. Her body began to stir beneath his gentle caressing; she moved closer to him and lay, eyes closed, enjoying and relishing these new sensations. Suddenly he removed his hand and she felt a moment's disappointment. Then feverishly he removed her blouse, cursing softly as he struggled to release her brassiere, and then to her joy he was sucking her breast and she was holding his head to her. This was what she had waited for, this was what she had lived for – this man's hands and mouth to be on her. Suddenly it was not enough, she wanted his hands where the ache and longing was intolerable. Her body curved towards him as if to tell him what it wanted, just as if she no longer had control over it.

He knelt above her, quickly removing his own clothes. She watched him, excitement sparkling in her eyes, and wondered if perhaps she should have done that for him. And what about her own skirt and stockings? Was she supposed to take them off, or would that be too forward? Oh, dear, what would he think of her? He began to remove her skirt. Gingerly she moved towards him, a great longing to feel him propelling her hand. She loved the velvet feel of his hardness.

'Good girl,' he said in a strange voice as if he had difficulty in speaking. She smiled at him, happy that she was pleasing him, but there was a strange faraway look in his eyes, as if he did not see her, which frightened her. The sound of his breathing grew faster. 'Oh, Jane!' he cried. She liked the feel of his weight on her but she could not help feeling disappointed that he had stopped kissing and caressing her. There was some resistance as he guided himself into her. He began to thrust harder. She had expected it to hurt more than it did; only a small cry escaped her lips. His pounding of her body intensified, his breath coming in great gulps. She felt buffeted by the great strength of this man, suffocated by him. She had lost complete control and for a second sheer terror filled her.

'Alistair!' She screamed arching her back with all her strength to get him off her.

'Jane!' he bellowed and, instead of stopping, his penetration of her increased in its ferocity. She felt it was going on for ever. 'Jane!' Again he shouted her name, his body looming above her as he lifted his weight momentarily from her. A great groan escaped from him and he collapsed on her, sweat pouring from him, forming in little pools on her own flesh.

She thought he had fainted, he lay so still, but slowly he began to move, gently kissing her, licking the sweat from her, and back to her body came the flickers of enjoyment, the shivery feeling down her spine.

He rolled away from her and smiled tenderly at her.

'You were marvellous,' he said.

'Was I?' She sounded surprised.

'Absolutely marvellous!' He laid his head against hers. 'You know, it's never been that good for me before! So together, so total.' He relaxed contentedly, stretching in the firelight. He cupped her face in his hands. 'Jane, darling, you should have told me you were a virgin, I would have been more gentle. Did I hurt you?'

'No, not much,' she said, covering her legs with her skirt to hide the streaks of blood. 'I thought you realized, you see. It's odd, though, I – ' she began and then stopped.

'What, my darling?'

'Oh, nothing.' She smiled back and curled up in the firelight with him. She realized that he had slipped into a light sleep, and she lay thinking. How could it have been as he said, when, at the moment which should have been the most precious, she had not really felt anything but afraid? And yet it had all started so beautifully – and ended that way too. Perhaps she was doing something wrong. She laughed quietly to herself: she always had preferred starters and puds.

That night, in bed, he took her twice more. Each time, as he climaxed, she did not feel afraid any more but she cried out his name, for it seemed to be expected of her. Really, after all the build-up, the debating with Sandra, the fearful anticipation, it was all rather disappointing.

5

Alistair's long vacation passed by in a haze of parties, dinners, exhibitions and an endless stream of his friends calling.

Jane's time was spent in scheming for changes in the duty rosters, to fit in with Alistair's plans. On the wards she watched the clock constantly; she became expert at split-second changing in and out of uniform, and rushing for buses – buses to take her to Alistair and early morning buses bringing her back to the Nurses' Home to face the heart-thumping terror of sneaking back in, unseen. She should have been tired but, miraculously, she was not. It was as if her love for him acted as a stimulant and gave her boundless energy.

But, finally, it was a tearful Jane who stood on the platform at Liverpool Street Station and watched the Fenman pull out, carrying Alistair and their carefree summer back to university.

Now she was tired again. Off duty all she wanted to do was sleep, as if only then could she escape the dreadful loneliness of life without him. But she dared not sleep in case the phone rang for her and she missed his call. She would not go to the Cat's Whisker coffee bar with the other nurses. Instead she lay daydreaming on her bed until ten o'clock and the certainty that no more calls would be accepted by the portress, when she would sink into the longed-for escape of sleep.

Each day it was an agitated Jane who joined the long queue of nurses waiting hopefully for mail. She wrote each day but Alistair replied only spasmodically. She hated the portress with a vehemence that surprised her when no letter had arrived, as if it were the woman's fault he had not written.

Near Christmas he returned and they spent two precious days in his house in Fulham. He had told no one he was there and so the phone never rang and no one called. They ate, drank, made love and talked. They hardly seemed to sleep. Apart from the budgerigar, Jane had only ever received practical presents; she gave Alistair a bright-red jumper. He gave her a leather-bound, gold-tooled edition of the metaphysical poets. Holding the beautiful book in her hands, she regretted the jumper and wished she had thought harder about a gift for him or at least had knitted it herself, but he seemed overjoyed with the sweater.

Then it was Paddington station on which Jane found herself, saying another tearful goodbye as he took the train to the West Country for Christmas with his family. She began to feel she was always saying goodbye on dirty, crowded station platforms.

She had to work through Christmas, having swapped her day off to have the earlier two days with Alistair. She had dreaded Christmas, fearing that she would be swamped with miserable longing for him. Instead the next few days passed at hectic speed as she was swept along on the tide of the hospital's festivities. When he phoned, she could tell him with conviction that she was fine and happy.

But then she was back to the waiting – the waiting for letters, phone calls, and for time to pass. Sometimes she was ashamed at the careless way she longed for the days to fly, knowing that on the wards there were patients whose lives were numbered by the very days that she nonchalantly wished away.

At the end of January she had a week's holiday and went for the first time to Cambridge.

It was a mystery to her how any studying was done. Alistair's life seemed to consist of sprawling in chairs, drinking coffee and talking all morning. At lunchtime they went to the local, the Pickerel, for beer, food, darts and more talking. They would return to his room in Magdalene College, overlooking Benson Court. He would sport his oak, shutting the second door to his rooms, which by tradition meant that under no circumstances was he to be disturbed and that, as far as the authorities were concerned, he was working. It was a useful university tradition for lovers. They would emerge for tea. Tea in Cambridge was a sacred ritual and there appeared to be an unwritten roster of whose turn it was to provide it, as each day they went to different rooms and each day the same crowd was there. This way, Jane sampled every cake that Fitzbillies bakery produced, and consumed so many crumpets she felt she never wanted to eat another.

In the evening he would leave her at the Pickerel, in the care of the landlady, Muriel, while he slipped across the street to dine in Hall. Muriel was used to looking after young ladies waiting for their lovers to return and she would make certain Jane had enough to eat and that no one bothered her. She had a soft spot for nurses and always piled Jane's plate with too much food.

'Got to keep your strength up, girl,' she would say and wink at a blushing Jane, her fat, jolly face creasing into a hundred laughter lines.

When the students returned, the drinking would start in earnest, the talk became louder and the little pub began to disappear in a haze of cigarette smoke. Sometimes the talk became too abstruse for Jane and she felt out of her depth, but often she thought that they were deliberately using long words and complicated arguments to show off to her. Frequently she had serious doubts whether they really knew what they were talking about. She would listen amused as they heatedly postulated the problems of the real world, and what they would personally do to solve those problems. She, however, was well aware that none of them had ever experienced the reality of that world. Cambridge was an unreal place, a delightful never-never land, she decided.

Alistair took a great risk by having Jane live in his rooms with him. Had he been found out, he would have been sent down immediately. Each night at ten they would play a charade of her leaving, loudly saying goodnight outside the porter's lodge; then she would either slip in quickly by a side gate before it was locked for the night, or much later Alistair would haul her up over the wall at the back of his court, while she suppressed her giggles as best she could, and laddered innumerable stockings. In the morning they would rise early, hiding away all evidence of Jane's belongings, and she would crouch in the wardrobe while his bedder cleaned the rooms. Shut up in the darkness, she was convinced that a sneeze was imminent or that the heavy thudding of her heart must be audible to the amiable, chatty bedder who did her chores so slowly.

Saturday was party night. They went to four parties, each larger and louder than the previous one, and finally ended up in the cellars of the Union building, where the noisiest gathering of them all was taking place, with a trad band making conversation impossible. As the evening progressed, Jane watched, alarmed, as everyone became increasingly drunk.

'God, Jane, what's got into you? You're being such a wet blanket,' Alistair shouted at her above the noise of the party.

'They're all drinking so much. It's no fun,' she shouted back.

'As far as I remember, madam, you quite like the stuff yourself. It seems it's all right if you get drunk when you want, but it's not all right for other people.' He glared at her, rocking back and forth on his feet. 'Oh, come on, Jane, have a drink. Cheer up, for Christ's sake!'

'No, thanks. You enjoy yourself. I'm fine here,' she replied through clenched teeth.

'Oh, hell, sod you then! Sulk on your bloody own,' he yelled angrily, and made his way through the swaying mob to the other side of the room.

How could he ruin everything? Jane asked herself desperately. She had to leave tomorrow: she had wanted this evening to be perfect and romantic. Instead, it threatened to turn into a drunken mêlée.

The sound of glass shattering silenced even the trumpet in the band. A great cheer went up from a crowd gathered around the door. Instinctively she knew that the crashing glass had something to do with Alistair. Elbowing her way through the throng, she reached the door around which a curious group still stood. The cold East Anglian wind whipped in through the gaping hole where the plate glass had been. Dangerous shards of glass glinted viciously in the muted light.

'What happened?' she asked anxiously, but everyone was talking at once and no one paid attention. 'Please, tell me, what's happened?' She tugged the sleeve of a man standing beside her.

'That mad bugger Redland just walked through the door.'

'He did what?'

'Someone bet him he couldn't and he did,' another voice told her, full of admiration.

Jane's hand flew to her mouth to suppress a horrified groan. She looked at the cruel, razor-sharp glass still hanging precariously in the door. 'Let me out!' she screamed.

Someone opened the door and the last of the glass crashed to the floor, shattering into small splinters, and the crowd leaped backwards, laughing, as they avoided the splinters flying everywhere. Jane pushed her way through them and emerged, coatless, into the bitter, dark night. Of Alistair there was no sign.

She hung over the wall of the Round Church shouting his name. Silence. There was only the noise of the party, muted now. In Bridge Street, the white snow accentuating their indecent redness, drops of blood littered the pavement. Sobbing, she followed the trail of blood, racing, skidding on the snow. On the apex of Magdalene Bridge, he must have stopped: there was blood on the parapet as well as on the pavement. She hung over the bridge, her eyes desperately searching the swirling, black water, vainly calling his name. Peering up the road she was relieved to see the neat spots of blood, like an obscene visiting card, trailing up to the gate of Benson Court.

She raced up the street, around the back, and began laboriously to climb the wall. Without Alistair there to bunk her over she had to search for foot and finger holds, shivering now with the extreme cold. It took ten minutes before, with torn skirt and ruined blouse, she was racing across the forbidden grass, uncaring of college regulations, and pell-mell up the stairs to his rooms.

In the middle of the floor, flat on his back, lay Alistair, a happy smile on his face, and blood caking his skin as it coagulated.

Quickly she fetched a bowl of water, tore a handkerchief into strips and began gently to clean his face, finding with relief that the cuts were superficial. A deeper one in his hand still oozed blood. She would have liked to get him to hospital – she was certain his hand needed stitches – but, however hard she shook him, she could not wake Alistair, and she could not risk adding to his troubles by raising the porter. She bound the hand tightly, and put a cushion under his head which she turned to one side in case he was sick. Then she covered him with the eiderdown. Taking off her ruined clothes, she sank onto the bed, leaving the light on in the sitting room and the door open so that she could keep an eye on him where he lay on the floor.

She meant to stay awake but at some point fell into a restless sleep.

'Ah, there you are. Move over.' Her fuddled brain heard Alistair's voice. Roughly he pushed her across the bed, up against the cold wall.

'You all right, darling?' she whispered.

'I will be in a minute when I've fucked you.'

She did not have time to react to the way he spoke before he was upon her, his knee prising her legs apart, and forcing himself into her. She lay rigid with fear. This very immobility seemed to infuriate him and goad him into thrusting at her more violently.

Mercifully it was soon over. He slumped from her and within moments was snoring in his sleep. But Jane could not sleep. She lay wide-eyed, looking at the darkness, afraid to move for fear of disturbing him, with tears rolling down her cheeks unheeded. Wishing it were all a terrible dream that she could wake from, she wept for the Alistair she loved and who seemed lost to her. What had happened, she wondered, to make him change like this? Not until the weak wintry dawn filtered into the room did she, in turn, sleep.

'Morning, Jay, my sweet.' She awoke to Alistair kissing her. She shrank from him. 'Here, what's the matter . . .?' He lifted himself from the bed. He moaned. 'Christ, my head, what the hell happened to my head? Oh, darling, what the hell was I up to? Kiss me better, there's a love.'

Suspiciously she looked at him, at the multitude of scratches and the large bruise that was already black on the side of his face. The kind expression was back in his eyes. 'I think I was a bad boy last night!' He grinned his little-boy grin at her. She gently kissed the cuts and bruises, softly massaged his temple. 'Ah, that's lovely, that's better, much better,' he sighed. He turned to her and began to make love to her as she was used to him making love to her. Only the soreness of her body told her that the previous night had not been merely the nightmare she had hoped it was.

Alistair stood naked in front of the mirror, inspecting his cuts and bruises. 'Christ, what did I do?'

'You walked through a plate-glass door. A bet or something.'

'I did what? Christ, there'll be hell to pay. I could get sent down for this. Oh, Lord! Why didn't you stop me?'

'I wasn't there, you told me to "sod off". I followed the trail of your blood back here.'

'Darling, I'm sorry. Your last night, too. I am an oaf! Will you ever forgive me?'

'It could have been worse.' Relief made her lenient. She managed to smile at him, knowing that despite last night she loved him, and always would.

'It's the whisky. I don't know what it is but I go berserk on the bloody stuff if I don't watch out. I can't remember a thing!'

'Don't drink it, then,' she said as reasonably as she could.

'I don't, normally, but John had a big bottle and, oh, I don't know, it just seemed like a good idea at the time!' He grinned sheepishly at her. 'You're a brick, Jane, not nagging me or anything when I was obviously a bloody pain. But promise me, the next time you see me with a Scotch in my hands, take the glass away.'

'I will, darling, I promise I will,' she said with feeling.

He crossed the room, opened the door and closed the outer one. 'Right, Sunday, no bedder. And no interruptions. I want you all to myself . . .' He leaped back into the bed with her and cradled her in his arms. She determined to put the incident to the back of her mind. It had not been the real Alistair who had come to her last night.

6

When she thought about it, Jane was well satisfied with the way her life had turned out.

She had an interesting and rewarding job. Sandra had been right: the more senior Jane became and the more responsibility she was given, the more involved she became in her work.

Her friendship with Sandra was stronger than ever. There was a patience and tolerance in their relationship that enabled them to weather the odd bouts of irritation they felt for each other. There was an openness that allowed them to air causes for such irritation. She loved her friend.

There was Sandra's family who welcomed her on her frequent visits, making her feel that their home was truly hers too, if she wanted it. And she did. In return, she gave them her time, helping with household chores, baby-sitting, anything that could, in any small way, thank them for the warmth they showered on her. There were days when she felt she belonged with them, that these people were her real family.

Having, at last, adjusted to Alistair's absence in Cambridge, she filled her days with new interests. She joined a library and read voraciously. She took advantage of the free tickets given by theatre managements to the nurses, and she went to plays, saw her first ballet, heard her first opera. With her free tickets she sat in rapt wonder listening to a full-sized symphony orchestra playing music she had until now only heard on records. She prowled through art galleries and museums. Without realizing it, Jane was educating herself.

At the centre of her life was Alistair. She had pined for love, planned for it, waited patiently for it. She was not to be disappointed in the reality and all the suppressed love within her overflowed. She adored him. She never questioned what he might think of her way of loving him. Had she been more experienced with men, she might have wondered if, at first, he might be perplexed and possibly afraid of her intensity. But, as the months went by and she asked nothing of him, only to be allowed to love him, she would have seen, had she been looking for it, that he began to relax in his attitude to her.

Alistair's friends saw a change in him. No one was sure if it was Jane's love that changed him, or the fact that he had been gated for the rest of the term after the incident of the glass door. But now he was working harder, drinking little, and writing to her often. Before Jane had come into his life he had rattled from one affair to another. Now suddenly he stopped, as if he no longer needed these inconsequential adventures.

The only cloud, for Jane, was that after months of love, she still did not enjoy the climax of their lovemaking. She lied to Sandra, pretended that everything was fantastic, that she was totally fulfilled. This was not strictly untrue – she did feel fulfilled in a sense, her love for him fulfilled her. Physically she did not mind; it did not bother her. The cloud, and it was really quite a small one, was her nagging worry that this was not how it should be. If making love had consisted only of foreplay, she could honestly have said she enjoyed it. She was certain that Alistair did not know how she felt: relishing his lovemaking up to that point, she found it easy to fake the rest.

She did not think of the future and what she would do when this love affair was over. She was convinced that she would never cease to love him as long as she lived. Sometimes, alone in the dark, she feared that he would tire of her. But, with the emptiness of her past, she could not contemplate an empty future – it would have destroyed her. So she lived for the present and never thought of the time beyond her next meeting with Alistair.

She rarely went home now. Her friends from her school days had dispersed. The gulf between her and her parents seemed even greater. They were totally engrossed in their loathing for each other and her visits seemed only to be unwelcome intrusions on their hatred. She tried to tell her mother of her love for Alistair, but her mother, having no faith in the existence of love, lectured her on the dangers of lust. And so, since she could not talk about him when she was home, she went there less and less often. For when she was not with him, she liked to talk of Alistair, to say his name, to hear it said. On her days off, when she could not see him, she would go to Sandra's home where she was free to speak of him with pride. She wrote to her parents, but they never replied. She did not really expect any reply.

Nearly a year after their first meeting, Jane had two weeks' holiday. She arranged this holiday to coincide with Alistair's coming down from Cambridge for good. They planned to spend it in the Fulham house. Two weeks of nights together and long leisurely breakfasts instead of having to get up at dawn to get back to the hospital. She wrote to her mother explaining that friends had invited her to join them for the holiday, and consoled herself that it was only half a lie.

With two heavy suitcases she indulged in a taxi to take her to the house. She found Alistair already there, in the kitchen, preparing their evening meal. As they chatted and argued good-naturedly about what they should do during these two weeks of holiday, the phone rang.

'Jane, answer that, please, my hands are greasy.'

'Flaxman 2433,' she said into the receiver.

'Oh! Did you say 2433?' a surprised-sounding female voice asked.

'Yes, 2433.'

'May I speak to Lord Redland, please?'

'Who?' Jane asked incredulously.

'Alistair Redland.' The voice sounded exasperated.

'Sorry. Yes.' She placed the receiver carefully on the table. 'It's for you, Alistair,' she said, her voice sounding unnaturally formal.

'Who is it?'

'I forgot to ask.'

'Clot!' Alistair playfully patted her behind as he went to pick up the phone.

'Hullo?' He signalled to Jane to get him a cigarette. 'Yes, Mother,' she heard him say. There was a pause, 'Jane, Jane Reed.' Another pause. 'A nurse, Mother, at St Cuthbert's.' He pulled a wry face at Jane. 'R-E-E-D!' He was grinning widely as he listened. 'Jane, my mother wants to know if you are related to the Fenton-Reeds of Plympton?'

'Of course I'm not.' The exasperation she felt at hearing herself explain to his mother was clear in her tone.

'No, Mother, she's not related to them.' He rolled his eyes with impatience, and smiled at Jane as she returned to setting the table.

'Yes, Mother. No, Mother. Three bags full, Mother,' he said, returning to his cooking. Jane continued to lay the table. They had bought candles and she noticed as she lit them that her hand was shaking. She felt sick and ice cold inside. How could he not have told her, she thought angrily.

'Right, darling. Table ready? Great, sit down, the food's going to be marvellous.' He was too busy collecting the dishes and putting them on the table to notice that she sat silent, a sad expression on her face. 'Now, the wine. This is a very special one, to celebrate our holiday.' He lifted his glass to her. 'You look lovely, Jane, even more beautiful in the candlelight.' She did not look up but stared steadfastly at her plate. 'Jane, what's the matter?'

'Nothing.'

'Why so moody then?'

'It's nothing.'

'I hate people who sulk.'

'I'm not sulking.'

'It's a bloody good imitation then. If you're not sulking, then why have you gone so silent?'

'Because everything is different now.' She could feel tears begin to prick her eyes, felt the skin of her face go stiff as she fought not to cry. She could hear the strain in her voice.

'Different? What's different?' he demanded irritably.

'You could have told me you were a bloody lord!' she blurted out.

'Oh, for heaven's sake, is that all?' He laughed.

'I don't think it's funny! You should have told me. It's ruined everything!'

'What the hell do you mean? Don't be so melodramatic. Look, I'm sorry you're upset. I didn't think. Maybe I should have told you, but when? How? I don't make a habit of going around saying, "Oh, by the way, I'm a lord." That would be daft.' He roared with laughter at the very idea.

'Don't laugh! It's changed everything.'

'Jane, don't be so bloody silly.'

'I am not being bloody silly!' she shouted. 'It has changed everything. You've been keeping it secret, laughing at me behind my back.'

He laid down his knife and fork and took her hand. 'Jane, listen to me.' She turned her head away from him. 'Jane.' He turned her face to him, but she would not look up at him. 'OK, don't look at me, then, but at least listen to me. I can't help being a lord. I was a lord when I met you. Nothing is different about me.'

'You could have told me at the beginning.'

'What? And have you react like this then?'

'No, I wouldn't have.'

'You would have, everybody does. It happens all the time. People react to a title, they're either all over one or they back away. It can take ages to cement a friendship if you're lumbered with one. I should know.' She said nothing. 'Christ! I know exactly what you're thinking. You think I'm playing with you, using the poor working-class girl. That I'll drop you when I've tired of you. Hell, it sounds like a Victorian melodrama.'

'It could happen. I think it's a reasonable assumption.'

'Reasonable! What the hell is reasonable about it? Just because I've got a stupid title doesn't mean I'm automatically a bastard, for God's sake!' He was shouting with anger at her. She studied her hands intently as she always did when nervous. 'You're a snob!' he yelled. 'A sodding snob!'

'Me?' She reacted angrily. 'Me, a snob? You're being ridiculous!'

'Yes, you are! You're rejecting me because of who I am. You're an inverted snob. Don't you realize I don't give a damn about you and your background? It's not *who* you are, it's *what* you are that matters. I like you for being Jane, my straightforward Jane. That's what attracted me to you in the first place. I was fed up with silly women playing games with me, and lying. You were the complete opposite. When I saw you, my guts turned over and I wanted to hold you and make love to you and make you mine and look after you. I can do that just as well as a lord, as I could as a plain bloody mister!' There was anger in his face but mixed now with an expression of sadness.

Jane began to cry. 'Do you really feel like that about me?' she mumbled through her tears.

'Yes, of course, I wouldn't have said it otherwise.'

'It's just it was such a shock when your mother asked to speak to you. It meant I didn't know who you were, and I thought we knew everything about each other. I mean, what else don't I know?'

'There's nothing else to know. You know all the important things. This title business, it's nothing.'

'I'm always so afraid of losing you.' She dried her eyes. 'I've never met a lord before,' she said, almost shyly.

Slowly he grinned at her. 'Don't make a habit of it, will you? They tend to be a randy lot!'

She did not laugh. 'I feel such a fool, Alistair, not knowing, and everyone else knowing.'

'Not everyone does, I don't advertise it. My friends at Cambridge are used to it and couldn't give a damn. I don't mix in the circles where it matters.' He smiled at her. 'Perhaps I should have said something. I'm sorry. But we get on so well and, oh, I don't know, perhaps it did become a bit of a game, after a while, wondering how long it would be before you found out my dreadful secret.'

'But you never suggested I meet any of your family. And you've obviously never mentioned me to them. Is not wanting me to know your secret the only reason?' she asked, pretending a calm she did not feel.

'I don't like the implication behind that question. Are you implying I'm ashamed of you?' His voice rose angrily. 'I've not taken you home simply because everything has been so perfect I didn't want interfering families involved. That's all. And, while we're on the subject, you've never once suggested you take me to meet your parents.'

'That's different.'

'Balls! It's no different at all. Are you ashamed of me, then?'

'Don't be silly. I didn't want them interfering either.'

'There you are, then.'

But it wasn't as simple as that. She had not suggested it because she knew that her parents would not understand, and her father in particular would have objected to Alistair simply because he was not one of them. Now, it would be impossible ever to take him home, for within her father lurked a dark and bitter hatred for the upper classes, and a deep resentment of those with titles. She knew she was not being totally honest with Alistair. And if she could deceive him in this matter, was it not probable that he was doing the same, lying to protect her feelings?

'You OK now?' he asked anxiously.

'Still feeling very stupid. I think my pride is hurt the most!' She managed to laugh.

'Thank God you're laughing. Now if all that is settled, can we get on with our dinner before it's ruined?' he asked practically.

Their dinner finished, the awkward incident past, they were lying on their cushion listening to their favourite piece of music, Sibelius's Fifth Symphony, when the phone rang again. Alistair was gone a long time. Jane dreamily lay back on the large paisley-covered cushion. The cushion was a joke, really, it did not match anything in the room, but they felt sentimental about it, since they could honestly claim it was where they had first met. So it stayed, in nonharmonizing splendour, and they would often lie on it together listening to music, as they had tonight. She watched the sun as it slid behind the rooftops opposite. She thought of Alistair being a lord, and decided that she might quite like the idea once she got used to it. It was definitely romantic. And different. How she would love some of those snobs at the hospital to know – they would strangle her with jealousy. She smiled to herself.

'The great debate whether or not you meet my family seems to have been decided for us. That was my mother again. She wants us to go home for the weekend. She wants to meet you.'

'Alistair, I couldn't!' Jane said, her voice shaking at the very idea.

'Jane, they aren't monsters. It's time you met them, really. She asked me if our relationship was serious. I said it was and so it's only natural that they should want to meet you.'

'But our holiday?'

'It's only for the weekend. They have no one staying this weekend, and it's the only one for months. I didn't think you would want to go if the house was full of people.'

'It's all too much!' she said, with rising panic in her voice.

'Darling, I'd like us to go,' Alistair said, his voice very serious.

'Will you be angry with me if I say no?'

'Extremely.'

'Then I suppose we have to go. But I think your parents are going to be very disappointed in me.'

'Don't talk daft. They'll love you. Have you got a long frock?'

'Good God, no, why?'

'We always dress for dinner. We'll have to buy you one tomorrow.'

'Alistair, I can't afford a dress! I've got £14 in the whole world.'

'I'll buy it for you.'

'I couldn't possibly let you. Hell, what would my mother say?'

'What would she say?'

'She told me never to accept clothing from a man. He would take it as his right to remove it!'

'Wise woman, your mother.' He grinned at her. 'Bit late, though. Come here, I want to make love to you. And stop worrying!'

But she could not. And long after he was asleep, she lay in the darkness, fearful of the ordeal before her, afraid of what his family might think of her, and afraid that, by meeting them, her relationship with Alistair would in some way be changed. If they let the outside world into their little personal paradise, Jane feared that it would be tarnished.

Alistair seemed so confident about the weekend, but Jane had an animal instinct which told her that trouble lay ahead.

7

The next morning, despite her protestations that she 'couldn't possibly', 'the expense' and 'what would people think?' He insisted on buying her not one but two dresses.

They hurried back to the car, adding the dress boxes to their other luggage. As they left London behind, the excitement she had felt at buying the new clothes slipped away as rapidly as the miles that separated them from the dear, familiar house in Fulham.

Apprehension began to seep through her, pierced with shafts of fear. Like building bricks, these emotions piled one on another, until she was filled with trepidation. For once she was glad that the car was too noisy for conversation. She did not want Alistair to know how fearful she was becoming. They were his family, and he loved them, she could not expect him to understand her terror at the idea of meeting them.

Why hadn't she had the courage to refuse? That was what she should have done: she should have explained to him reasonably that it was silly for her to go, that it would only cause trouble, that she and his family would have nothing in common. What if they were all like Clarissa? Far better to have left things as they were, persuaded him to live his life in separate boxes. Then why had she not? Curiosity? Perhaps, a bit. Not wishing to hurt him? No, that was a stupid idea. By going, she was much more likely to cause him hurt. Pride, she finally decided, that was why she was here – because of her stupid pride. Look where her insistence that she was as good as anybody, and to hell with the rest, had got her. That worked at the hospital, but now, she would be alone in totally alien surroundings. What havoc could his family wreak on their relationship? Once Alistair had seen her in the environment of his home, among those he loved, would he not see how pointless it was? Silly pride, too, knowing that when she got back to the Nurses' Home she would let it be known where she had been just so that she could see the expression on the faces of the Deb Brigade. Oh, God, what a fool she was!

They left the green meadowlands where fat cows grazed. They began to climb and soon the countryside had changed into a bleak and barren moor, the scrubland stretching as far as the eye could see. Large outcrops of rock loomed menacingly against the skyline. The desolation of the landscape matched the hopelessness and fear that she felt within her.

The car stopped in front of a pair of large, intricately wrought iron gates. To the summons of the car's horn, an old woman came out to heave the huge gates open. As the car slid through, she bobbed; Alistair waved and drove on. Jane turned round to see the woman swinging the gates shut.

'She's closing the gates again.'

'Of course. Don't worry, it's not a prison. You can get out any time.' He seemed amused by the astonished expression on her face.

'But she's old. Those gates are so heavy.'

'I wouldn't let Mrs Trevinick hear you say that, she wouldn't be at all pleased with you. She's done that job for forty years, to my knowledge. In any case, the gates are well oiled,' he added defensively.

'But why not keep them open? Seems silly to keep opening and shutting such huge things.'

'Good God, those gates have been kept shut for centuries; you can't change tradition like that. Then what would the old girl do?' He manoeuvred the car over a cattle grid. 'In any case it keeps snoopers out.'

She began to think she had dreamed the wild, fearful moorland, for suddenly here was a parkland of idyllic lushness. Large trees swayed in the gentle breeze, each obviously planted according to an overall design, to carry the eye forward across the land. They drove past a herd of deer, so tame they merely stopped cropping the grass for a second and with benign curiosity watched them pass by. The drive wound seemingly endlessly through this landscape which was like something in an eighteenth-century painting. Passing through a copse of beech, Alistair stopped the car and pointed to the valley below.

'There you are, darling, Respryn!'

'Bloody hell!' she exclaimed breathlessly.

Set against a wooded hill, which curved around and held it protectively in its folds, stood a house. It was of such age and beauty that it seemed to have grown there from the rock itself, as if it were an inspiration of nature and not of man. A hundred windows glinted in the sunshine. A battalion of chimneys, ornately decorated and twisted like sticks of rock, made it look more like a village than a house. Creepers grew abundantly on the grey stone walls, softening them so that no sharp angles disturbed the eye. In front of the house, the garden was surrounded by a low grey wall of the same stone. Clipped box hedges, planted in intricate geometric patterns between the smooth lawns, were guarded by several dozen tall, neatly trimmed ornamental conifers which marched like soldiers across the bright-green grass.

'Alistair, it's unbelievable. It can't be real, it's too beautiful!'

'It's a bit nice, isn't it?' He grinned proudly.

'Don't be so blasé!' She hit him playfully. 'It's fantastic! Almost too good to be true, like the lid of a biscuit tin or a jigsaw. Heavens! And you live there?' He nodded. 'Crikey, you never think of people living in places like that. It's the sort of place you pay your half-a-crown to visit, not to live in.'

'Gracious! We haven't come to that yet!' He smiled as he slid the car into gear and they carried on down the drive past a turreted gatehouse.

'We used to play in that as children, used it as a glorified playhouse.'

'But it's as big as a house!'

'Yes, but small when you compare it with the real house, isn't it?'

As they drove nearer, the size of the house became truly apparent. They passed under another gatehouse into the stable yard, where a large, gilt stable clock chimed the hour as they came to a halt. Several horses' heads appeared inquisitively over the stable doors. Taking her hand, Alistair led her towards an oak side door over which was cut a large stone crest.

'Anyone home?' he yelled as they entered a surprisingly small, oak-panelled hall. His call echoed through the corridor, then there was silence again, interrupted only by the ticking of a grandfather clock. From the wall a stuffed badger in a glass cage gazed glumly down at them. A tall, rather sombre man, dressed in immaculate, thinly striped trousers, moved silently and smoothly towards them.

'Anyone here, Banks?' asked Alistair.

'Her ladyship and Lady Clarissa are out to tea and his lordship is in the library,' the measured tones informed them.

'Splendid! Which room has my mother put Miss Reed in?'

Hearing her name mentioned, Jane stepped forward and, extending her hand, said brightly, 'How do you do?' The man looked at her hand, at her, then glanced at Alistair. Finally, and almost suspiciously, it seemed, he took her hand and inclined his head.

'The Rose Room, Lord Redland.'

'Fine. See to the cases in the car, will you, Banks? Thank you. Come on, Jane, let's find father.'

Alistair led her along a perplexing number of red-carpeted corridors so rapidly that she could only glimpse the pictures on the walls as they sped by.

'Alistair.' She pulled at his jacket and he slowed down, turning questioningly to her. 'Who was that?' she whispered.

'Back there? That was the butler, Banks. Been with us as long as I can remember.'

'Oh, gosh! Should I have shaken his hand?'

'Darling, do whatever you want.'

'I don't think you're supposed to shake hands. With butlers, I mean. Sorry!'

'Jane, you are a clown. It doesn't matter a fig. If you want to shake the butler's hand, then shake it. No need to apologize. It probably made a pleasant change for him; he spends his life being taken for granted.'

They set off again at the same speed, and crossed the main hall, their heels clattering on the mosaic tiles. She had only seconds to take in the glowing tapestries on the walls, the faded standards hanging from the ceiling. Briefly she glimpsed a large oak staircase sweeping up to the floors above, and then they were racing along yet more long, red-carpeted corridors. At last they stopped, and Alistair opened a linenfold panelled door.

She looked in wonder at the beautiful room. The long walls were covered in bookcases, the light from the tall casement windows glinting on the gold of the bindings, enhancing the rich colours of the leather covers. The sun shimmered through a stained-glass window, scattering the jewel-like colours onto the pale oak floor in rainbow-coloured puddles of light. On large tables about the room, maps were strewn in a random jumble. An enormous terrestrial globe, its surface sepia with age, stood to one side of a stone fireplace which reached the ceiling and was decorated with an intricately carved coat of arms. A fire burned in the grate but the room was so vast that it could never possibly heat it. Comfortable leather chairs were placed at random about the room and the air was heavy with the scent of books and leather.

'Hullo!' a voice called from the far end of the room and only then did Jane notice a tall, slender man with silver-grey hair standing on the top of a pair of library steps. He climbed down and Jane felt a nervous constriction in her throat. He had a natural elegance about him that triumphed over his bizarre choice of clothes. His well-worn trousers, neatly pressed, were of a grey and yellow check. His jacket with large leather elbow pads was equally worn and was of a different check and colour. His bright yellow shirt clashed alarmingly with the red polka-dotted scarf about his neck. Only a man of supreme confidence could have got away with such a collection of colours and patterns, Jane thought.

'Alistair, how lovely to see you,' he said, and the two men embraced warmly.

'Pa, I'd like you to meet a friend of mine, Jane Reed. Darling, this is my father, Lord Upnor.'

'Miss Reed, how kind of you to visit us.' Jane looked at him shyly. The blue eyes were surrounded by lines which could only have been caused by laughter, so gentle was his expression. The fine bones of his face showed beneath the tanned skin which set off the bright silver of his hair. She felt a warm, strong hand clasp hers. 'Did you have a good drive down?'

'Thank you,' she whispered, frowning with puzzlement that he too had a different name.

'I do hope you are not too tired, Miss Reed?'

'No, thank you, I'm fine.'

'Jane, why are you whispering?' Alistair laughingly asked.

'Was I?' She giggled nervously. 'Well, it's a bit overpowering, isn't it? A bit like being in church.' Still she whispered. The two men looked at her quizzically.

'Of course, the stained-glass window! Yes, I suppose it is a bit,' Lord Upnor said kindly. 'We have to blame my Victorian ancestor for that, the purists complain he ruined this room.'

'Oh, I like it. It's pretty.'

'I tend to agree with you, my dear, especially when the sun shines through it as now. A drink! Would you care for a drink, Miss Reed?'

'No, thank you.' She was regaining control of her voice, she realized with relief.

'Too early?' he enquired.

'Yes, Father, much too early, I'm afraid.' Alistair laughed.

'Pity,' the older man replied.

Jane stood awkwardly clutching her handbag in front of her so tightly that her knuckles gleamed whitely against the red chapped skin of her hands.

'Are you interested in books, Miss Reed?'

'Oh yes, I love them. Are these all yours?'

Lord Upnor laughed. 'Well, yes. Mind you, I tend to think I'm only looking after them, that they belong to the house, really. Would you like to see some of our treasures?'

'Yes, please.' She stepped forward eagerly, tripped over a rug and knocked against a table, sending a pile of books tumbling to the floor with a crash. 'Oh, bugger!' she exclaimed in her confusion, blushing red as she dropped her handbag in her haste to kneel down and pick up the books. 'Oh, dear, I'm sorry, these lovely books! I shouldn't have sworn like that either, I . . .'

'My dear Miss Reed, I don't think there is any risk that I will faint from shock.' Lord Upnor laughed with delight and both men helped her replace the books. 'Now, what shall we show her, Alistair?'

'What about the Book of Hours?'

'Splendid choice!' The older man crossed the room and, taking a large bunch of keys, opened a tall bookcase. He selected a small book and laid it reverently upon the table. 'Come, Miss Reed,' he beckoned her. He opened the book and the brilliant golds, vermilions and blues of the illustrations seemed to jump from the page, surely as bright as the day they were painted.

'How beautiful!' she exclaimed, her hands instinctively moving towards it. Then quickly she put them behind her back.

'Please. Please, you may hold it if you wish.' Lord Upnor handed her the book. Gently she turned the pages, her eyes devouring the pictures, hardly believing that she could be holding anything so old and precious.

'It's so beautiful, it makes me want to cry.' She looked up and the tears glinting in her eyes emphasized their excited sparkle.

'Ah, Alistair, we have another enthusiast here,' Lord Upnor said, pleasure at her care and interest evident in his voice. 'Then perhaps you would like to see my collection of botanical books?'

One beautiful book after another was produced to her exclamations of delight. She was fascinated by his large collection of ancient maps; they laughed over the strange spellings of the place names, admired the unbeliev-able accuracy. He had begun to catalogue the maps, he told her, they were his most prized possessions. The time flew by as the three of them sat, heads close together, studying the treasures. A loud gong sounded far away in the house.

'Good God! Is that the time?' Lord Upnor exclaimed. 'I'll get us all shot!'

Alistair showed her to her room and told her she had an hour in which to dress for dinner. He closed the door and left her alone.

8

Jane looked around her bedroom with awe. It was dominated by an intricately carved four-poster bed, whose rose-coloured curtains matched exactly the bowl of roses on the oak dressing table in front of the window. The window itself looked out on a flower garden from which, as the evening drew in, the sweet smell of roses and lavender mingled with the headier scent of night-scented stock. The floor was highly polished and scattered across it were rugs whose colours glowed even in the dim light.

An open door led into the bathroom. The large bath, its massive bulk encased in shining mahogany, sat splendidly on a raised dais. The taps were of gleaming brass; a huge rod of equally shiny brass slipped into the plug hole with ease. Turning on the taps, she jumped at the ominous gurgling they emitted before the water came gushing out. She undressed hurriedly, throwing her clothes about the room in her haste. She chose some jasmine bath oil by Floris from a collection beside the bath, then lowered herself into the huge tub. The bath was too long for her to lie down comfortably so she sat up, barely able to see over its rim, to examine the room. It was more like a sitting room than a bathroom, with its patterned wallpaper, paintings, armchairs – not a ceramic tile to be seen. There was even a fire laid in the pretty fireplace. But there was no lavatory. What was one supposed to do?

It was a bath for lingering in, but Alistair had said she had only an hour. Reluctantly she hauled herself out and, taking a soft, thick towel from the pile provided, she found she could wrap it twice around herself and still it trailed on the floor. Hearing noises from her bedroom, she peered cautiously around the door to see, to her consternation, a young maid tidying her clothes away.

'Please! Oh, gracious! I'll do that,' she said in some confusion.

'Good evening, miss. Did you find everything you needed? I came earlier to run your bath, but you were still downstairs,' the girl said in the soft tones of the West Country.

'Thank you, it's all lovely.'

'I wasn't sure which evening dress you would be wanting, miss, so I pressed them both to be on the safe side.'

'Gracious, you shouldn't have bothered. Perhaps you can help me decide which one to wear tonight?'

The girl crossed to the wardrobe and with only a second's hesitation said,

'The green one, miss. There's a big dinner tomorrow and I think the black would be a little more formal, don't you?' Gently she smoothed the folds of the dress. 'It is lovely, such good quality,' she said longingly.

'It's gorgeous. I . . .' Standing now beside the maid, Jane saw her other clothes neatly pressed and hanging in the wardrobe. This girl had unpacked her case! It was a horrible idea, this stranger touching her things, like being burgled, she thought angrily. 'But you . . .' She stopped as the girl turned and smiled at her pleasantly, waiting to hear what she had to say. It was not her fault: she was no doubt only doing what she had been ordered to do. 'It's the bath plug, I can't move it to let my bathwater out,' she said instead.

'They be horrible old-fashioned things, miss. You have to learn the knack of them. I'll see to it.' She bustled off into the bathroom and within seconds Jane heard the water sloshing about. Following her, she found the maid busily scouring the bath.

'You musn't do that, please. I can clean my own bath!' Jane said, appalled.

'Gracious, miss! That would never do. It's my job, you'll be getting me the sack.' The girl laughed good-naturedly, and continued with her cleaning. It was so wrong, thought Jane, a girl of her own age cleaning up after her, as if she were some sort of invalid.

'I'd prefer it if you didn't do it again. I promise I won't tell anyone. It's just, well, I don't like you doing it.'

'Very well, miss.' The girl looked puzzled and Jane was afraid that she had hurt her feelings.

'You see, I don't like being waited on like this.'

'Yes, miss. Whatever you say, miss,' the maid said stiffly. They had been getting on so well, thought Jane sadly, and now she had offended her and she would go. Jane did not want to be left alone, not yet. All the time she was talking to this girl she did not have to think of the ordeal ahead. She must think of something to delay her going, she thought, as she saw the girl moving towards the door.

'Can you tell me where the toilet is?'

The maid crossed to the corner of the room and, with a flourish, opened what Jane had taken to be a cupboard.

'There you are, miss,' she said, giggling.

Looking round the door Jane saw, in a room no bigger than the cupboard she had thought it was, a magnificent, polished mahogany lavatory, enthroned on a small dais. Jane laughed out loud. 'I've never seen a toilet like that, ever,' she snorted.

'It is grand, isn't it? Fit for a queen. We've never had a queen use it, not in my time, but we have had several duchesses!'

'Heavens! Are they all like this?'

'Only in the best rooms along this floor. Mind you, I wouldn't use it, I'd get all claustrophobic in there,' and the two young women collapsed in giggles together. The girl glanced at her watch. 'Gracious, the time, miss! You'll be late. Would you be wanting any help?'

'What with?'

'Dressing, miss.'

'No, thanks, I think I can manage that after all these years.' She grinned broadly and the maid laughed with her. 'What's your name?'

'May, miss.'

'Mine's Jane.'

The young girl stopped laughing and looked uncomfortably at her feet, and began to shuffle them. A heavy silence fell between them. Jane, realizing her mistake, did not know what to say. 'Will that be all, miss . . . Miss Jane?'

'Yes. Thank you. And thanks for pressing my dress.'

'It was a pleasure, miss.' Quietly the girl let herself out of the room and Jane sat despondently at the dressing table. Absent-mindedly she toyed with the silver dressing-table set, not seeing the fine engraved crest on the handles, oblivious to everything but her own confusion. She was never going to get things right. First the butler and now the maid. If she could not behave properly with her own kind, how the hell was she going to manage with the others? That was the problem, she was no different from the butler or May, so why should she be expected to behave differently?

With little enthusiasm she made up her face, brushed her hair so that it fell loose about her face, and only cheered up a little when she caught sight of her reflection in the cheval glass. She had not been sure of the dress in the shop, but Alistair had insisted they buy it. Now she was glad that they had for, as she twisted from side to side, she was pleased with the way the fine, dark-green jersey wool seemed to mould to her body, accentuating its curves. It was a feminine sort of dress, one she would never have dared to choose for herself. She stood on tiptoe – like most short women, she had a dream of growing at least another six inches in the night. It was odd, though, how the clinging lines of this dress made her seem taller, she was sure. If only she were blonde, she sighed. Conditioned by years of her mother's admiration for the blonde, baby-faced cousin, Jane was still unaware of how striking she looked with her dark hair, pale skin and haunting grey eyes.

From far away she heard another gong sound. She presumed that she should respond to it, but since no one had told her where to go she thought it safer to stay where she was. She sat on her bed and investigated the contents of her bedside table. There was fruit, a tin of biscuits, a jar of boiled sweets and a bottle of French mineral water, a pretty pin cushion, needle and thread, hankies – the list was endless. She could survive a siege in here, and she managed to smile to herself. Idly she inspected the books. They had obviously been chosen with her in mind, for she was amused to see a couple of hospital romances and a book on Burke and Hare. She got up and wandered about the room, looking at the paintings – a pastel of a child, a rather sombre oil of a Madonna and child. She studied the carving on the chimneypiece, smelled the roses, hung out of the window and worried about what she should do if Alistair did not appear.

There was a loud knock on the door.

'Come in,' she said nervously. To her relief it was Alistair. 'Oh, you look so handsome!' She smiled at him in his dinner jacket. She had never seen him dressed like that before.

'And you look wonderful. I was right about that frock. Come on, you're late, everyone is waiting for you.'

'I'm sorry, I didn't know where to go. I was frightened of getting lost.'

'My fault, I forgot to explain. That second gong is to tell everyone my mother is down and drinks are being served. We'd better hurry or you won't have time for even a tiny one.' Taking her hand he raced down the staircase with her, and it was with a thudding heart that Jane was led to a door behind which she could hear a babble of voices. As they entered the room the chatter stopped and to Jane's horror she saw that there was a crowd, when she had expected only Alistair's parents. Her heart sank as she saw his sister across the room.

'Miss Reed, at last!' A dark-blonde, tall and upright woman approached her with outstretched hand. Alistair introduced his mother. The woman's elegance was emphasized by her thinness. She had a pale complexion but her fair skin had the dryness to which so many English women fall prey, so that her make-up seemed to sit uncomfortably on top of her skin. But this was the only flaw that Jane could see. Although now faded, she had once been beautiful. 'We thought you were lost.'

'I'm sorry, I didn't know what the gong meant, or where to go.'

'Silly Alistair. However, you're here now. I do hope you find your room comfortable?'

'Yes, thank you, It's lovely, thank you. My room is lovely.' Too late she realized how repetitive her mumblings were, and how gauche she must sound.

'Let me introduce you to everyone. I gather you have met my husband.' Lady Upnor put her hand under Jane's elbow and expertly propelled her across the room to join the others. 'May I introduce my sister-in-law, Lady Honor Calem?'

Jane looked up shyly to see a face of the most extraordinary loveliness smiling at her. No matter how long this woman lived, people would never say of her, 'She must have been beautiful, once.' It was not just the creamy, clear skin, virtually unlined and covering fine bones, nor the large generous mouth smiling in welcome at Jane, nor even the mane of golden red hair which she shook unselfconsciously as she took Jane's hand. Her true beauty lay in the kindness, joy and vitality that shone in her large, expressive eyes. There was a warm vibrance to the woman, an inner charm, which would keep her beautiful.

'My daughter, Clarissa,' Lady Upnor continued.

'We've met,' Clarissa's clipped voice announced. 'I met her charring for Alistair.'

'Really? Did you help Alistair? How kind of you,' Clarissa's mother said smoothly. 'Perhaps you have met Clarissa's friends, too? No?' Jane found herself shaking hands with a young girl, Amanda Duckworth, whose prettiness was marred by a sulky expression. James Standard was a pleasant, rather red-faced young man, who looked as if he might be fat one day. 'And lastly, my friend, Roderick Plane.' Lady Upnor introduced her to a small rotund man in his late forties, who took Jane's hand in a damp, limp grasp. His mouth was large and slack, and he had the ruddy complexion and broken veins of a heavy drinker. His cheeks were like two large pouches, which gave the odd impression that his face was slipping off his skull. As he greeted her, Jane noticed that he was not looking at her but at a point over her left shoulder, as though she did not exist for him.

'There, now you know everyone.' Alistair's mother smiled at her but, with a chill feeling, Jane saw that it was with her lips only. There was no warmth in her eyes.

Jane was given a drink, and with her gin and tonic in her hand she moved over to a large window seat which set her outside the circle of the others as the conversations resumed. She admired the self-assured way the talk was batted back and forth across the room. There never seemed to be an awkward silence. She was struck by how loudly they talked and laughed and with what confidence they stated their opinions, as if the idea that they might be wrong had never crossed their minds.

'You look out of things over there, Miss Reed.' Alistair's mother smiled graciously at her.

'I'm fine, thank you, Lady Upnor.'

'Tell me, Miss Reed, do you like monkey-puzzle trees?'

'Yes, I do.'

'Rupert, you monster!' Lady Upnor shrieked, playfully tapping her husband's hand. 'You got to her first. Admit it! You are not to be trusted for one moment. It's true, Miss Reed, isn't it? He persuaded you to say that?'

'No. I really do like monkey-puzzle trees,' Jane insisted, angry with herself as she began to blush.

'Well, I agree with you, Lady Upnor,' Roderick Plane lisped. 'Ugly trees, should all be cut down.' Everyone began to argue, without explaining to Jane what the problem was.

'We will ask Miss Reed's opinion,' Lady Upnor said eventually. 'Miss Reed, tell me, don't you think my husband is being unreasonable? He knows I hate the trees and they are totally out of keeping with the period of the house. Since it pains me to look at them, don't you think he should cut them down?'

Everyone turned and looked at Jane expectantly. She wanted to say something bright – like 'It would probably pain the trees more to be cut down' – but, as she saw all the faces turned in her direction, she found her mouth was dry and the words would not form.

'I don't know,' she said lamely and hated herself for her lack of courage. Oddly, she felt as if she had failed a test, and sat miserably looking at her hands as the argument continued unabated. She looked up as she felt someone sit beside her. It was Alistair's aunt.

'At last we meet Alistair's mysterious lady! We knew something was up –

he's never home these days – and Blanche was convinced it was a young woman. We have all been agog to meet you,' she said with a low, gentle laugh.

'Meet me? Gracious, how embarrassing!'

'Not at all. A beautiful young woman like you should have oodles of attention.'

'Beautiful, me?' she said ingenuously.

'Certainly. Hasn't Alistair told you? With your lovely hair and those grey eyes – it's a ravishing combination. Are you Scottish, perhaps?'

'No, I'm English. Yes, Alistair says I'm beautiful but that doesn't count, does it? When you're fond of someone you see them differently.'

'Ah ha. So he loves you, you mean! Oh, what fun!' She laughed again with that soft, throaty chuckle.

'I didn't say he loved me,' Jane countered hurriedly.

'Of course you didn't. Silly boy, if he hasn't told you, but I assure you he does. "Fond of" for Alistair, that is being in love.' Although Jane liked what the woman was saying, it embarrassed her and she quickly changed the subject.

'If we're talking about beauty, Lady Calem, I think you are beautiful, in fact I think you're the most beautiful person I've ever seen.'

'Sweet of you to say so,' Lady Honor said, with the ease of one used to a lifetime of such compliments. 'I adore it when a woman says something nice to me. Their comments are so much more reliable, and such a rare commodity.' She leaned across and whispered in her husky voice, 'By the way, Jane, you call me Lady Honor. Calem was only a mister.'

'Crikey! I'm sorry. It's so confusing. Everybody seems to have a different name. I mean, Alistair's is different from his parents' and his sister's – where I come from that would only mean one thing – ' Aware of what she was about to say, she stopped abruptly and put her hand in front of her mouth.

'And what would that be?' Lady Honor's eyes twinkled in such a merry way that Jane heard herself saying:

'Why, that they were illegitimate.'

'Oh, of course!' Lady Honor laughed loudly. 'What a wonderful idea! How I should love to tell Blanche, but I don't think I had better.' She smiled broadly at Jane. 'The name bit is really quite simple. Our family name is Cotham, you see, but our titles are different. Rupert's is Upnor, and Alistair takes the lesser title of Viscount Redland. And Clarissa and I, being daughters of earls, use our Christian names, which shows the title is our own. Do you see?'

'Yes,' answered Jane so doubtfully that Lady Honor pealed with laughter again.

'Poor sweet! You'll catch on. It's really quite unimportant but I thought it might make you more comfortable if you got it right.'

'Might I hear the joke?' Roderick Plane had sidled up. Jane's heart jumped.

It was odd that she should feel completely at ease with Lady Honor and free to say whatever came into her head; but with this man . . . never.

'No, you can't, Roddie. It was far too naughty for your delicate ears,' the older woman teased him.

'I gather you're at St Cuthbert's?' he asked Jane. 'Do you know Sir Peter Willoughby or Sir Alexander Disney?'

'Hardly,' Jane answered with a smile. 'They're like gods, and they don't talk to mere mortals under the rank of staff nurse.'

'I see,' Roderick said without interest and drifted off.

'That's you finished for Roderick,' Lady Honor said cheerfully. 'He only speaks to people with titles, who are important, or who he thinks might become important, or might know people who are important.'

'How daft! Think of all the interesting people he never meets, then. What does he do?'

'Shrouded in mystery, my dear. He never says, but it's bound to be something shady. I have never understood what Blanche sees in him.'

'Tell me, Lady Honor, what was all that argument about the monkey-puzzles?'

'My dear, it is so boring. They have been arguing about those damn trees ever since the day they got married. My sister-in-law thinks they are out of place and my brother loves them and refuses to cut them down. Every new person she meets gets the same quizzing. I have a theory that she then only bothers with those who agree with her.' She laughed as she said it, but the information made Jane's heart sink even further.

'But the whole garden is Victorian, isn't it, so they aren't out of place. I mean, you would have to dig the whole garden up for it to be truly in keeping with the house.'

'Did I hear you discussing my garden?' Lady Upnor called to Jane across the room.

'Well, yes.'

'And what were you saying?'

'I was just asking Lady Honor . . .' She could feel herself blushing again. 'I was just saying that since the whole garden is a Victorian one, it would seem a shame to exclude the monkey-puzzles since they are so much part of a Victorian garden,' she answered with a courage she was far from feeling.

'I see. And are you an expert on the subject of Victorian gardens?' Lady Upnor asked.

'No. It's just that I've visited a lot and, well, you get used to what's in them, and I rather like them . . .' she trailed off.

'So you frequently stay in houses like this, then? I suppose you would have to, to be such an expert.'

'Oh no, I didn't mean that. I never stayed anywhere like this before. I meant houses where the public can visit, I've been to a lot of those.'

'God preserve us from such a fate!' Lady Upnor said feelingly. Jane felt

Lady Honor gently squeeze her hand. She wished she could disappear and sat waiting miserably for Lady Upnor to quiz her further. She was rescued, however, by the butler, who came to announce that dinner was served. Jane stood up.

'Are you going somewhere, Miss Reed?' Lady Upnor asked imperiously. Jane, blushing bright red, hurriedly sat down again, aware of Clarissa and her friend in the corner smirking at her. Alistair crossed the room to her side.

'How are you getting on?'

'Terrified!'

'You silly goose, you're doing fine.'

'Alistair, I think you have found a dear girl here,' she heard Lady Honor saying to him.

'She's an absolute cracker, isn't she?' Alistair said proudly and, as his mother stood up, he took Jane's arm to lead her in to dinner.

9

She was getting used to large rooms now, for everything in this house seemed to be on a monumental scale, but even so she was amazed at the size of the dining table that stretched for yards down the centre of the cavernous room. She sat with Alistair and his father on either side of her, but, because of the size of the table, they were some distance from her. There was no chance of intimate conversation here, which perhaps explained why they all talked so loudly.

The battalions of cutlery and lines of cut glass promised a feast. Candlelight glowed from enormous silver candelabra, placed at measured intervals. The whole table was a blaze of light as the candles reflected on the highly polished glasses and silver. Each piece of the individual place settings – cutlery, cigarette box, ashtray, pepper pot and salt cellar – was heavily engraved with a crest. The cutlery at the hospital was engraved and she knew for certain that this was to stop the staff stealing it. Were they frightened their staff or even their guests would walk off with the silver here? Perhaps it was to remind them that it was theirs or even who they were.

The butler and the footmen began to serve the food. The butler's glance was everywhere, checking and rechecking that all was well, that no one lacked or needed anything. Plates were smoothly removed and replaced. Wine glasses were unobtrusively refilled. The men worked quickly and quietly, seeing all but appearing not to listen. It gave them the air of assiduous robots.

The stage had been set for a banquet and Jane was astonished and disappointed at how unappetizing the food was. It was lukewarm and bland, the vegetables as overcooked as her mother's. Everything was covered with a sticky white sauce which tasted of nothing. Lord Upnor ate with noisy relish.

Jane toyed gingerly with her food: even if it had not been so repulsive, she was far too nervous to eat.

The wines, however, were wonderful and as they seeped into her bloodstream she could feel a little confidence returning. Alistair's father, and his aunt who sat opposite, were both attentive and coaxed her to talk. She started to enjoy herself.

'It's a ludicrous waste of money, James!' they heard Roderick Plane exclaim from the other end of the table.

'What's a waste of money, Roddie?' Lord Upnor asked with interest.

'Money spent on education, Lord Upnor. James and I cannot agree on the subject.'

'We would be in a fine old pickle if people weren't educated, Roddie. I mean doctors and bankers and vets especially, useful chappies like that,' Lord Upnor reasoned.

'Lord Upnor, I did not make myself clear. I do apologize to you,' Roderick Plane continued obsequiously. 'I'm not against education, provided you pay for it yourself. I'm against educating the masses. That's where the money is wasted. Our money, yours and mine!'

'And what do you mean by "masses", Mr Plane?' Alistair asked with what, to Jane's surprise, sounded like amusement.

'I mean the working classes. Mind you, I think the phrase "working class" is a misnomer – none of the bastards know what work is. I apologize for my language, Lady Upnor, but it is something I feel strongly about.' Lady Upnor inclined her head graciously to him.

Jane had read about people saying they heard warning bells in their heads. Now she knew what it felt like. As her anger rose, the noises in her head were almost deafening.

'Daddy would agree with you,' Amanda added helpfully. 'He has dreadful trouble with the beastly unions. He says we might as well be living in Russia.'

'Salt of the earth, more like scum of the earth!' her incredulous ears heard Roderick Plane blubber. Her anger was concrete, like a hard lump inside her. It rose into her throat until she felt she would choke. She noted the footmen standing impassively by and felt anger for them as well as for herself. Her face began to redden but from fury this time. She glanced across the table. Clarissa smiled coldly at her and, with a blinding certainty, Jane was convinced that Clarissa had in some way engineered this whole conversation.

'But surely, if what you say is true, and I don't for one minute think it is, by not educating them you would make them even more idle, take all ambition away from them?' Alistair argued reasonably. How could he be so calm and polite to this dreadful man? Jane fumed inwardly.

'My dear young man, you miss the point entirely. When they were not educated we never had any trouble with them, they knew their place and were content to live there and their children after them. Now, with education, you fill their empty heads with unnecessary information when all they are going to do is empty dustbins – a complete waste, you see.'

'But Roddie, not everybody becomes a dustman,' Lord Upnor interrupted.

'No, and the ones who don't get heads full of dangerous learning so that they begin to question the order of things. That is the path we are travelling, and we face disaster if we don't stop.'

'Daddy says it's cruel, really, educating them,' Amanda chipped in. 'He says that we send them to lovely schools, like the new ones the government is putting up, costing thousands, with plate-glass windows and afrormosia floors, and then at night they have to go back to their dreadful slums. Daddy thinks it can only lead to discontent.'

'How right your father is,' remarked Roderick unctuously.

'Balderdash!' The word exploded from Jane.

There was a moment's silence round the table.

'Are you an expert on education as well as gardens, Miss Reed?' asked Lady Upnor in a pleasant tone of voice which completely disguised the sarcasm of her question.

'No, Lady Upnor, but I know about state education and the need for it and the desire that people have for it – '

'I have not noticed a burning desire in my maid to improve her education. However, servants are certainly a lot more difficult these days than their fathers and mothers were and I think that education must take the blame for that. I think there is a lot of truth in what Roderick says.'

Lady Upnor had interrupted her, but anger gave Jane courage.

'If your argument were valid, Lady Upnor, then we would all have stayed in the trees.'

'Pity some didn't,' drawled Clarissa.

'And you keep talking about "them" as if "they" were some sort of different species to yourself. We are not, we are human just as you are and we have the right to the same opportunities in life.'

'Good gracious, Miss Reed, are you a Communist? How dreadful!' Lady Upnor smiled her cold smile at Jane.

'No, I'm not a Communist. But I do believe that everyone should be given a chance. If they don't take it, that is their mistake. But to say that such a large proportion of the population shouldn't even be given a chance is both malicious and stupid.'

'Do you have to be quite so rude?' demanded Clarissa.

'I think calling the working classes "scum" is pretty offensive!' replied Jane with an equal snap to her voice.

'Such a silly expression, "working class". After all what does it mean, someone who works. Well, if someone works he's got to be educated, Roddie. Far better not to educate old drones like ourselves,' Lord Upnor broke in, in an attempt to take the tension out of the situation.

'Jane really is the only person at this table who can speak with any authority on the subject. After all, she is the only one of us who does any work, isn't she?' Lady Honor asked, smiling sweetly at Roderick. 'That is unless you work, Roddie? Tell me, do you work?' She smiled mischievously at him.

'If people are going to become offensive then I think it is better that we ladies withdraw,' Lady Upnor said, getting to her feet.

'I don't think Jane was being offensive, Mother. She was defending her point of view,' Alistair said hurriedly.

'Don't you, darling?' Again she smiled that cold smile. How could something as pleasant as a smile become so fearsome? thought Jane. It was unfortunate that this had happened, but there had been no alternative. She would never have forgiven herself if she had not spoken up – even if, as she thought, it had been an elaborate trap set by Clarissa and her cronies. If she was never invited again it did not really matter, she did not want to know people who could talk and think like that, Jane consoled herself. She would be sad if she never saw Lady Honor and Alistair's father, but she could not change her opinions just to suit her ladyship.

As the women moved from the room, Jane continued to sit in her seat. Alistair leaned over to her. 'Darling, you go with the ladies,' he whispered.

'I want to wait for you.'

'No, darling, you can't. I'll be along later.'

Miserably she followed the other women, trailing behind them as they slowly mounted the wide oak staircase to the drawing room.

She sat and watched the others as they fluttered about Lady Upnor, who was pouring coffee. She was struck yet again by their unselfconscious elegance. They were all so tall and slender that every movement they made looked graceful. They sat entwining their legs one around the other, as only very tall women can. Their heads were poised on long slender necks and, as they talked and turned from side to side, she was reminded of a group of ballet dancers in repose. She felt awkward beside them. The smallness and rounded curves that delighted Alistair precluded her, she realized, from ever being as truly elegant as they were.

Lady Upnor was assiduous in caring for Jane, pointing out the best chocolates in the silver basket she offered her. She seemed a different woman from the one in the dining room. Jane smiled gratefully, confused by the woman's sudden swing of mood. Everyone by now had coffee and Lady Upnor took the chair closest to Jane.

'Tell me, Miss Reed, where did you manage to meet my son?'

'He gave a housewarming party. Some friends of his who were working at my hospital invited me. It was a lovely party.'

'Which friends?'

'John and David, I don't know their surnames.'

'Oh, those friends. Dreadful, vulgar young men!'

'I like them,' Jane said loyally.

'What's Alistair's house like?' asked Lady Honor. 'I must pay him a visit.'

'It's a horrible, poky little thing. Why on earth he insisted on buying it, I shall never understand – with all the room we have in the London house. He wouldn't listen to me, but then he never does.'

'It's natural, Blanche, that he should want a home of his own, surely?' Lady Honor argued.

'One realizes why now,' Lady Upnor said, looking pointedly at Jane, who looked quickly down at her hands. Compared with the elegant white hands of the other women, hers appeared even more red and chapped than usual. Despite copious use of hand cream, they never seemed to improve. She felt Clarissa staring at her hands, too, and quickly placed them at her side, wishing she could sit on them and hide them away. 'My dear Honor, you should see inside. It is simply ghastly. I offered him whatever he wanted to furnish it, but no, he had to buy piles of the most awful, evil-smelling junk. Quite ridiculous of him.'

'But his furniture is lovely. Really, Lady Honor, it's super and it doesn't smell!' Jane leaped to the defence of the Fulham house. Lady Honor smiled understandingly; Lady Upnor stared coldly at Jane.

'I gather you have known my son for a year?'

'Nearly, not quite.'

'I see,' said his mother. 'But your nursing, I presume you are not qualified yet?'

'No, I have another year, after August, to finish.'

'A year? I see. And of course you want to qualify?'

'Some days I do, other days I could quite happily walk out.'

'You mustn't do that!' Lady Upnor said hurriedly. 'It would be such a waste, if you did.'

'Yes, I suppose so.'

'Ghastly profession,' interjected Clarissa. 'Digging around in other people's orifices. Ruination to the hands!'

'Cla-ris-sa!' her mother enunciated. 'Don't be so vulgar!'

'It's true, Mummy. That's all it is, really, quite disgusting. What on earth made you choose it?' she asked Jane unpleasantly.

'It chose me. I needed to earn some money.'

'Couldn't you have worked in a shop or something?' Clarissa waved her hand vaguely.

'It's probably more interesting than working in a shop. And at least I'm using my brains.'

'Really?' Clarissa arched her brows. 'I wouldn't have thought it took much brainpower to give someone a bedpan.' Amanda giggled in the background.

'Clarissa, you go too far sometimes. In fact, the exams are terribly hard, I hear,' Lady Honor said, turning to Jane. 'Isn't that so, Jane?'

'Well, my hospital won't accept you without A levels.'

'Ha! Well, that cuts you out, Clarissa!' her aunt declared triumphantly.

'I suppose you could always marry a doctor. That's why people take up nursing, isn't it?' Clarissa said, ignoring her aunt's taunt.

'Not me, I don't like the medical students and have nothing to do with them, if I can help it.' Jane preferred to think she had not heard Clarissa say, 'More's the pity.'

'And what does your father do?' Lady Upnor continued.

'He works as a storeman in a factory.'

'I see. How interesting,' Lady Upnor said in an icy tone. Jane wished she would not keep saying 'I see' like that. What did she see? It was obvious that she was drawing conclusions from Jane's answers, but what conclusions?

'Fancy a game of backgammon, anyone?' She was relieved to hear Clarissa change the subject and presumed that she was at last bored with baiting her. 'How about you, Jane?'

'I'm sorry, I don't know how to play.'

'You can't play backgammon? But everybody plays backgammon,' her tormentor continued.

'Not everyone. I don't.' It was Jane's turn to snap.

'Do you ride?'

'No.'

'Play tennis?'

'Badly.'

'Heavens, what are we going to do with you all weekend?'

'Don't worry about me. I'm quite capable of looking after myself,' Jane replied.

'Evidently.' Clarissa smirked. Jane could feel tears of frustration pricking her eyes. How she longed to be back in Fulham, not here with this bitch baiting her at every turn. If only they were on their own, she could tell her exactly what she thought of her, but that was probably what she wanted. With relief she heard the men's voices and looked eagerly for Alistair, who came immediately and sat on the arm of her chair, stroking her hair.

'Alistair, you look most uncomfortable there. Sit on a chair properly,' his mother ordered him.

'I'm fine, Mother.'

'No, you're not. You will break the chair,' she said with irritation in her voice. Reluctantly, he got up and moved away.

'Drinks?' Lord Upnor asked and there was a bustle while drinks were arranged. 'Miss Reed?' He smiled at her.

'Might I have a gin and tonic, please?'

'A *gin and tonic*!' Roderick Plane bellowed. 'Good God, I never heard anyone order a gin and tonic after dinner in my life.' He roared with laughter, opening his mouth wide, exposing his bad teeth and spraying those nearest him with spittle.

'It's the only drink I like,' a bright-red Jane explained.

'If Miss Reed wants a gin and tonic I can't think why she shouldn't have one. In fact I think it's a very good idea, it's damned hot tonight. Make that two, Banks,' ordered Lord Upnor.

'Three, Banks,' Alistair added loyally.

'Ice, Miss Reed?' the butler asked imperturbably.

Until midnight, when people began to drift away, Jane sat silently, nursing her drink. She had decided it was safer if she kept her mouth shut. So she listened as they talked. The talk was fairly general, mainly about the estate and the farm, until Lord Upnor excused himself and retired. Then the tone changed completely. Roderick was obviously the master of ceremonies and was soon talking cruelly about their friends, and tearing their characters to pieces. She thought he was despicable but everybody else was shrieking with laughter.

All the adults had gone to bed and only the young remained. It was with them that she felt most uncomfortable. Their self-confidence and loud assurance made her feel inadequate and at the same time angry that she should feel like this. They seemed such a closely knit group, with their own jokes and private vocabulary. Alistair was a part of it. She was an outsider and realized that, no matter how long she knew them, she would always remain one.

When someone suggested a game of billiards, she used the game as an excuse to go to bed. Lying alone in the dark, listening to the unfamiliar noises of the old house, she longed for Alistair to be with her and, as if in answer to her wish, the door opened and Alistair crept in.

'Christ! What a route march I've had to get here,' he said, chuckling. 'My bloody mother's put us as far apart as possible. My room's in the other wing.'

He climbed in beside her. It was wonderful to feel his familiar arms about her.

'Where's your mother's room?'

'Along the corridor, miles away. Don't worry, she can't hear through these thick walls. Come here,' he said as he took her in his arms and began to make love to her. But Jane found it impossible to relax: she lay in his arms as unfeeling as a piece of wood.

'What's the matter?' he asked concerned.

'I don't know, I think it's because I feel it's wrong in your mother's house.'

'It's my father's, too, and he wouldn't mind for one minute!' he replied jokingly. 'Well, if it's going to be like this, remind me not to come here often!' he said, snuggling against her.

10

Jane awoke, disappointed to find that Alistair had gone. He must have crept stealthily away at first light as he had come to her in the darkness. She rolled onto his side of the bed, burying her face in the indentation he had made in the pillow, breathing deeply, searching for his smell which might still linger on the linen. If only it were just the two of them here, how happy she could be! The memory of last night made her shiver. How awkward, how gauche she must have seemed! The unnerving feeling of not belonging and the knowledge that she never would swept over her again. She was angry that she had been so tongue-tied, unable even to argue her case well. But then, how could she with that ice-cold hag smiling at her with her dead fish eyes?

Last night after dinner she had been interrogated. The questions had not been posed out of interest, but rather to analyse and place her; not to investigate her as a person but to find out where she fitted in the structure of their lives. Of course, she had not fitted into any approved slot.

It had all been so coldly performed that Jane began to appreciate that her suitability in human terms counted for nothing. She had proved herself socially inferior and that was the issue which counted. Her rejection was not personal. Those little sparks of irritation which she had seen in Lady Upnor were not directed at her personally but were caused by the older woman's discomfort at the position in which she found herself – of having to contemplate a social inferior as a guest. Had Jane met her simply as a patient, no doubt Lady Upnor would have been charm personified.

Jane began to feel afraid, afraid that Alistair would be prevailed upon to see her as his mother did, that she might deliberately make Jane look stupid so that he would himself become aware of her unsuitability. She felt as if by coming here she had stepped into the Victorian era petrified in its strict social codes. The injustice of it, the unfairness, the stupidity that distinctions of class should still be regarded as important, made her sad and then, with mounting emotion, angry.

How dare that woman stand in judgement? Why should she not be Alistair's friend if he so chose? Her underprivileged background did not alter her character. It was ludicrous that one's rightness and standing should depend on an accident of birth. It was as ridiculous as her father's precon-ceived ideas about class. Social behaviour could be learned. She had known which knife and fork to use, how to eat her soup; she had learned a lot over the years and she was quite capable of learning a hell of a lot more. Why should she be made to feel ashamed of her background? At least she was achieving something in her life, unlike Clarissa who, having had everything from birth, appeared to do nothing, thought less, and yet expected respect. When Jane was with Alistair she did not feel inadequate, so what was wrong with her, allowing that woman to make her feel like this?

A soft knock at the door brought her back to the day ahead. It was May with a tray of tea. A single red rose in a tiny crystal glass was reflected in the silver teapot.

'Good morning, miss,' May said as she pulled the curtains and bright sunshine flooded into the room. 'It's a lovely day, miss – it's going to be a really hot one.' She settled Jane with the tray. 'Lord Redland says to tell you he's gone riding and will be back about ten. He gave me the rose for you.' She began to giggle. 'Real romantic, isn't it?'

'It's a lovely rose,' Jane replied, unaware of her dignity in not commenting further.

'Yes, miss, sorry, miss,' the maid replied, far more aware than Jane of the limitations that bound her. 'Shall I run your bath?'

'If you must.' Jane smiled at the girl. 'But remember you mustn't expect to clean it out!'

'Yes, miss. You win!' Laughing, May went to run the bath. Jane sat in the large canopied bed, sipping her tea and gazing dreamily at her red rose. At least the rose showed that Alistair had not been affected by last night's bickering or her inability to make love to him. She was relieved that he had not expected her to go riding. Like a true city girl, she was terrified of horses.

'May,' she called, and the maid appeared in the doorway. 'May, tell me, what am I supposed to do? I've never stayed anywhere like this in my life and I'm completely at sea.'

'It's the mealtimes you really have to watch out for. Her ladyship's a real stickler for punctuality and she gets ever so cross if people are late. It doesn't matter who it is, I've seen her tell a cabinet minister off before now,' she said admiringly. 'Breakfast doesn't matter – most of the ladies have theirs in bed – but Lord Redland said as you didn't like to eat in bed.'

'Oh no, I hate it, all the crumbs!'

'Wish all the ladies felt like you.' The maid warmed to her subject. 'A right mess some of them make! Crumbs, spill their tea, marmalade on the sheets. And sometimes it's lunchtime before we can get into their rooms to straighten them!'

Jane tutted in sympathy at the maids' plight. 'And after breakfast?' she asked.

'I expect Lord Redland has plans for the morning. Lunch is at one. Dinner at eight. Tea is served at four, but you don't have to have that if you don't want.'

'What do people do all day?'

'Eat, it seems to me!' She giggled. 'Oh, they walk in the gardens, some ride, write letters, that sort of thing.' From the tone of her voice it was easy to see that May thought the regime very boring. 'There's a swimming pool, up past the rose garden. If the weather is nice, they might have a swim. But really, I think that's all they do. Most of the ladies have a rest in the afternoon, but God knows why!' She laughed.

'Would you come for a walk with me, if Lord Redland has other plans?' Jane asked. The girl looked at her, puzzled. 'I mean, you could show me where the rose garden is.'

'Good God, miss! That would mean instant dismissal.'

'If you went for a walk?' Jane asked incredulously.

'I can go for a walk. But not in the rose garden or anywhere I would be seen. Gracious, no.'

'Seen by whom?'

'Her ladyship, of course, miss. She won't even have the gardeners about when she's in the garden. Many a time they have to jump into a bush if she suddenly appears.'

'But that's Victorian! I never heard of such a thing! And you don't mind?'
'It's always been like that.'

Jane couldn't think what to add. The girl lived in a different world from hers. It was none of her business, after all.

'I was thinking, miss, that big dinner tonight. Would you like me to do your hair?'

'My hair?' Jane questioningly fingered the ends of her hair. 'What could you do with it?'

'I thought it would look lovely done up in a big chignon. You've such lovely long hair, so shiny too.'

'Do you really think so? Anything that gives me confidence, May, anything!' She grinned. 'Yes, let's.'

'Oh, miss, thank you. You'll look lovely, I promise. I want to be a lady's maid, you see, but I hardly ever get a chance to practise – most of the ladies who come here to stay, they bring their own. But your bath, miss, the water will be getting cold.'

Her bath finished, Jane cleaned it. Back in the bedroom she had to laugh at May. Not only was the bed made, but everything had been neatly folded and put away. Dressed, she followed May's directions to the breakfast room.

She was relieved to find the room empty. She ignored the rows of heated silver chafing dishes, containing everything from fried eggs to kippers and kedgeree, and helped herself to coffee. On another side table was a pile of newspapers. She would have liked to read one but they were aligned in such pristine order that she did not like to touch them, remembering how angry her father became if anyone read his *Daily Mirror* before him.

The door opened and Banks sidled into the room. She had noticed last night that the butler did not appear to walk but rather glided across the floor as if on casters.

'Good morning, Miss Reed.'

'Good morning, Mr Banks.' The butler gave her one of his rare smiles. He noticed her empty plate.

'Have you everything you need, miss? Perhaps I could fetch you something else that you would prefer to eat?' he asked with concern.

'Oh no, thank you, Mr Banks. It all looks lovely, I'm just not hungry. The coffee is delicious,' she added hurriedly, hoping to prevent him feeling hurt by her refusal. She stood up, uncertain of which of the two doors facing her was the correct one. Noticing her dilemma, the butler smoothly opened one of the doors for her.

'Might I suggest, Miss Reed, that the Long Gallery is particularly beautiful at this time of day?'

'A long gallery, I'd like to see that. If you could point me in the right direction.' She giggled.

'Allow me,' and the butler escorted her silently through the long corridors. Eventually they stopped before double doors which Banks opened with a dramatic flourish.

'There, Miss Reed, the Long Gallery!'

Jane gasped. She had thought the library grand, but it had not prepared her for this. At the foot of a small flight of steps stretched a long room which appeared narrow only because of its extraordinary length. Long windows let in a flood of light which reflected dazzlingly on the white plaster ceiling and the large pair of matching marble fireplaces. The oak-plank floor gleamed, reflecting more pools of light. The room was so shining and bright that it was like stepping into a long prism of glass.

'What a lovely room!' Involuntarily she clapped her hands with pleasure.

'It is 116 feet long, miss. In winter there are curtains at all the windows but in summer we take them down and then, I think, the room looks its best.'

'Oh yes, Mr Banks, I can see that. It's as though it were made of crystal, not wood and plaster.'

'Exactly.' The butler warmed to her appreciation of this room, which he obviously held dear. 'Note the ceiling, miss.' She craned her neck to look up. The plasterwork was so ornate and heavy it seemed to be defying gravity with its weight and intricacy. 'Italian plasterers came especially to do the work. They lived here for years, I gather. If you walk down the window side, Miss Reed, and up the other side you will see that each panel is a scene from the Bible.' Sure enough, there were Adam and Eve and the serpent.

'It is used for dancing, Mr Banks?'

'Very occasionally. Originally it was designed as a place for the ladies of the house to walk and take exercise when it was raining.' Far away in the depths of the house a telephone rang. Reluctantly excusing himself, Banks went to answer the phone, leaving her alone.

She soon discovered that the room was a museum, with some cases containing letters, none of which she could decipher. One case held embroidered gloves and stockings, a note in copperplate writing explaining that they had belonged to Queen Victoria and Elizabeth I. What strange people queens were, she thought. In many of the houses she had visited on coach trips were bits of clothing left by these two monarchs. Did they lose them, forget them, or give them? she wondered. She could not resist turning the key on a large clockwork china doll. Slowly the doll's small hands rose and moved across the miniature keyboard of a tiny piano and the room was filled with tinkling music.

It was possible, moving down the room, to see the interests that had amused the earls down the centuries. One had obviously had a passion for clocks. Another for Africa. Here was India's case, with jewel-encrusted knives, an ivory Taj Mahal. There were mementoes of war. And endless cases of silver spades and forks used for planting trees, laying foundation stones. Upper-crust bric-à-brac, she decided.

Finally she came to the end of the room and sat in a window embrasure on a beautiful tapestried cushion and surveyed the whole gallery. It was easy to imagine it full of graceful women in their sweeping dresses promenading about, laughing and gossiping, perhaps playing with a ball, a small dog joining in, fat babies rolling and sliding on the polished floor. It would not have been a museum then but full of noise and activity. This room must remember those days with longing.

That was true of the whole house, really, she thought. It had been built to house scores and now only a handful lived here. The walls must long for the fun to start again. Until then it seemed as if it were waiting.

Beneath her in the garden a man was hoeing a flowerbed, years of practice making his body move in a perfect flowing action. Gardeners had stood in that same place doing that same rhythmic hoeing through the ages. Across the park she saw Alistair and his father approaching on fine black horses. How many women had sat here waiting for their menfolk to ride across that parkland? It seemed that wherever she looked, the people and the scenery made a timeless tableau. The house would always be here, the situations would always be the same, only the people and their clothes had altered down the centuries.

She ran back down the long room, skidding on the highly polished floor, raced down the stairs and, after trying two doors, finally found the one that led into the stable yard as Alistair and his father clattered under the clock tower.

'Darling!' Alistair called, slipping from his horse. As he came towards her, leading the animal, she backed away nervously. 'Darling, I want to kiss you!' Alistair laughed at her.

'Does it bite?' she enquired anxiously.

'Of course he doesn't. See.' He kissed the horse on its muzzle. 'Major here wouldn't hurt a fly!'

'Trouble is,' she said with an apologetic laugh, 'I'm not a fly!'

'Good morning, Miss Reed.' Lord Upnor approached. 'How pretty you look!' He beamed at her.

'Isn't she a lovely sight to come back to, Pa?' Alistair asked proudly.

'She certainly is. I must say, it's a real pleasure to see a young woman without her face covered in goo.'

'Where's everyone else?' Jane asked quickly to cover her delighted amusement.

'In bed, probably,' Alistair explained.

'But last night Clarissa said something about riding . . .'

'That's as far as Clarissa's riding goes, talking about it, eh, Pa?' Alistair said dismissively. 'They've all got hangovers, I expect. They stayed up long after us.' He started towards the stable. 'Don't go away, Jane. Just let me get Major settled, then I want to show you something.'

'Not bothering with coffee, Alistair?'

'No, thanks, Pa. I want to show Trinick to Jane.'

'A good idea. See you both at luncheon, then.' The older man left his horse to a groom but Jane waited while Alistair rubbed down and watered Major.

11

They drove across the park for nearly a mile and then passed through gateposts from the top of which benign stone bears looked down on them. They followed a short shrub-lined drive and came to the front of a granite-built house, its walls covered completely in climbing plants. Virginia creeper swarmed over most of the façade, entwined with climbing roses and clematis. The walls of the house were a riot of colour. It appeared small, but this was only in contrast to the vast size of the main house.

Taking her hand, Alistair led her through the open front door into a flagged hall, where an elegant, curving staircase swept up to the floor above, and light filtered through a large creeper-covered window on the half landing.

Admiring each room in turn, she followed him through the pretty house. Upstairs they stood in the largest of the five bedrooms, where a large bow window seemed to fill the whole of one wall. Jane exclaimed, 'Oh! This is my favourite.'

'What do you think of it?'

'Alistair, it's gorgeous. Whose is it?'

'It's mine. I shall live here now I've finished at Cambridge. I've got to get it decorated, of course, and find some furniture. It won't take long, and Pa says I can take whatever I want from the attics at Respryn.'

He rattled on about his plans for the house, but Jane felt a coldness growing within her as she thought of him so far away from London, and from her. As she had never looked to the future, she had never paused to think what his plans might be. She had been stupid; of course his time at Cambridge had to come to an end, she had known that. So why could she not have had the sense to think ahead and to wonder what his plans might be? She could have asked and then she would have been forewarned, instead of finding out like this. How on earth was she to exist without him? How was she to get through all those days which now stretched bleakly before her? 'But your house in Fulham?' she eventually managed to ask.

'I'll keep that on, can't bury myself away down here all the time.' So she would see him sometimes; she wasn't to be cut entirely out of his life. 'Come here!' He dragged her down on to the bare floor.

'Alistair, someone might come!' she protested.

'No, they won't, and what if they do?' he asked, feverishly unbuttoning her blouse, searching for the softness of her breasts. She tried to resist but at his touch the familiar warmth flooded through her and she knew that it was too late.

'I've dreamed of making love to you here,' he whispered, his voice taking on the huskiness it always did when he wanted to make love. The sun, filtering through the greenery at the window, bathed their bodies. Oblivious to the bare boards and the dust, Jane responded to his caresses with a passion fired by fear of the future and anguish that this might be the last time, and further fuelled by anger at his mother's disapproval. She lay in the morning sunshine, Alistair's hands and mouth upon her. That woman could say what she wanted – it was Jane's breast in his mouth now, it was Jane's body he was about to enter. His mother had no control over his passion for her. For this moment, that was Jane's precious possession. Therein lay her power.

'I just knew that it would be perfect here in this room,' he said with satisfaction as he lit two cigarettes and handed her one. He propped himself against the wall, unselfconscious in his nakedness, his blonde hair hanging damp and dark on his forehead. When Jane went to pick up her clothes, he put out his hand to restrain her. 'Leave them, please. I want to look at you naked, here in this room.'

She settled down beside him, resting her head on his chest, listening to the beat of his heart as his pulse began to slow down. 'Well, what do you think of it?' he asked.

'Of what?'

'This house, Trinick, of course.'

'I told you, I think it's lovely. You're very lucky.'

'Do you think you'd like to live here?'

'I should think anyone would love to live here.'

'I'm not interested in "anyone". I want to know if you would like to live here?' Gently he lifted her chin so that he was gazing at her. 'You silly thing, Jay, I'm asking you to marry me.' He laughed as her mouth dropped open in astonishment. 'Don't look so surprised. What do you say? Yes or no?'

'Alistair, it's such a shock. I never thought about marriage, never allowed myself to. Heavens!' was all she could think to say.

'So, are you saying yes?'

'I don't know. It's all so sudden. I mean, your parents, what will they say?'

'I don't give a damn what my parents say, I'm not marrying my parents.' Agitatedly he lit another cigarette. 'I didn't realize it was to be such a difficult decision for you. I thought you'd say yes right away,' he said, a hint of petulance in his voice.

'Oh, my darling, I want to say yes, I really do.'

'Good, so that's settled.' He stubbed out his unfinished cigarette. He looked longingly at her full breasts, gently stroking them. He began to pull her towards him again.

'No, Alistair, we have to talk.'

'No?' he said, disappointed. Resting his elbow on the floor, he looked at her. 'What's there to talk about? It's settled and now I want to make love to you again, to celebrate,' he said with a triumphant laugh.

She moved away from him. 'It's not as simple as all that,' she insisted. Her concern removed any embarrassment she might feel at the ludicrousness of sitting naked, in midmorning, talking earnestly on the floor of an unfurnished room.

'It is.'

'No, darling, it isn't. For a start, you've never told me that you love me. I can't marry you if you don't love me.'

'That goes without saying.'

'It doesn't.'

'I'd hardly ask you to marry me if I didn't.'

'OK, then, say it.'

'All right! I love you!' He grinned sheepishly. 'Now can I make love to you?'

'No, I want to talk. I don't think you've thought this through.'

Alistair sighed and, seeming to resign himself to her refusal, propped himself back against the wall again.

'What haven't I thought through?'

'Your parents, for a start. What are they going to say?'

'I should think they'll be pleased. They both think it's time I got married.'

'Married, yes, but not to someone like me.'

'Why, what's wrong with you? Have you a past that I don't know about? Are you a reformed prostitute or do you have a criminal record?' He laughed at his own joke.

'Alistair, please, I'm being serious. Look, until this weekend I'd no idea how you lived outside Cambridge and Fulham. I'd no idea it was so frighteningly grand. They're expecting you to find someone more suitable than me, someone who won't be terrified by all this.'

'Good Lord, girl, if that's all that's bothering you? My father's as fit as a fiddle, I shan't inherit for years. Meanwhile, we live here, I learn to run the estate and you'll be learning a different life style. Simple, nothing to it,' he concluded, satisfied with the logic of his argument.

'But I could never be like your mother.'

'Maybe I don't want a wife like my mother.'

'Or Clarissa or Amanda. They know instinctively how to do things, they know what's what, they've been trained for it.'

'Heaven save me from someone like Clarissa!' He took her hand. 'Look, Jane, they like you, my father told me so this morning.'

'Yes, I think your father likes me, but that doesn't mean that he would want me as your wife. Of course your mother is going to say she does, or at least pretend she does. To do otherwise is to risk your running straight into my arms – any woman knows that. No, she doesn't like me, I sense it.'

'Rubbish!'

'It's true, she'll be disappointed in me.'

'Well, that's her problem. It's me you're marrying, and I can't see any problems that can't be surmounted. OK, so it's all very strange at the moment but you're intelligent. You'll soon learn and adjust, I know you will.'

'But at dinner last night. That argument about education – you could see then the chasm between me and them. Even then I let myself down by arguing so feebly. There was so much more I wanted to say but the little I did say did not amuse your mother.'

'Jane, you were splendid last night, I was proud of you. My mother will have respected you for standing up for what you believe. She likes a good argument and she'd regard that as a successful dinner. Had you sat and said nothing, then she would have been disappointed in you.'

'Oh, Alistair, you don't see, do you? You're so nice, you just don't realize.'

'Realize what?'

'It doesn't matter what I'm like, it matters who I am. That my dad works in a factory, that I'm working-class. They don't want that for you.'

'My parents aren't like that,' he protested. 'I've always been allowed to have what friends I want. For years my best friend here was the farm manager's son. No, they're not snobs, darling.'

'Friends are one thing, a wife is something entirely different.'

'Rubbish, you don't know them.'

'But last night, Alistair, I felt so out of everything. It's difficult to describe but I felt all the time that I was a spectator. You all seem to have a way, a code, even a language of your own and I haven't been given the dictionary.'

'Jane, my darling, sometimes I think you're bloody paranoid. I love you – there, I said it again. I like you, which is probably even more important than love in the long term. I need you, yes, I need you in my life. I want you to be the mother of my son. I don't give a damn about anyone else, I really don't.'

Jane felt a lump form in her throat at his words. 'Alistair, I love you. I would so like to marry you. I just don't see it happening, though.'

'Then you will? Thank God,' he said. 'You worry too much. We'll work it out. In a couple of years no one will know you weren't born to this life. Now can I make love to you?'

'What did you do last night after I went to bed?' she asked, coiling away from his outstretched arm.

'Hell, what's that got to do with this? You know what I did, I sat talking to Clarissa and Co for a while and then I sneaked along to you, and a right disaster that was.'

'Did you talk about me with Clarissa?'

'No,' he said, but his eyes did not meet hers.

'You're lying, Alistair. What was said?'

'Nothing, really . . . Oh hell, you know Clarissa.'

'I can imagine, then.'

'So, she's snooty about you. I don't see what that's got to do with you and me.'

'You rowed about me,' Jane said, nodding sagely. 'It could have a lot to do with us. Perhaps you feel sorry for me, perhaps that's what's made you suddenly propose.'

'Christ! How insulting can you be? How the hell could you think like that about me, after all this time?'

'It seems odd to me.'

'Glory be, you are a paranoid. Listen Jay, I love you. I want to marry you. I don't give a damn what my bloody sister says or does. I've been thinking about this for some time. I just wanted it to be here, in this house. Romantic, that's me.' She could never resist his boyish smile.

'Oh, Alistair . . . I'm sorry.'

'I should bloody well think so. Now, can we make love again?'

'Please!' She clung to him.

Later, as they lay relaxed in each other's arms, she said, 'Alistair, there are a couple of things.'

'Yes?' he mumbled drowsily.

'If we get married, it's for ever for me. I couldn't bear it if you were unfaithful to me. I could never share you.'

'Married to you, my darling, is it likely that I would even want to look at another woman?' he replied, stretching contentedly. She leaned over and kissed him.

'The other thing is, can we keep it a secret for now? Let your mother get used to me first?'

'Sod! No!' He sat up, suddenly wide awake. 'I want to tell the whole world.'

'It would be best, Alistair.'

'No. We've decided. I'm sure you're wrong about my mother. She's a bit stiff and formal, that's all. Oh, crikey, don't let's go over all that again. Please!' He looked at his watch. 'Hell! The time! We'll be late for bloody luncheon, then she most definitely won't approve.' He laughed. 'Come on!'

Hastily they dressed, desperately dusting each other down. 'I guess it's pretty obvious what we've been up to,' he said happily. 'Let's race back. We might just be in time for a shower.'

12

Luck was with them and they were able to slip up to their rooms without being seen. Jane quickly washed and changed out of her dusty clothes and she and Alistair arrived simultaneously in the morning room at five minutes to one. Holding her hand, he led her in.

'Alistair, you are almost late,' his mother admonished him.

'Almost, but not quite!' He grinned goodnaturedly back.

Lunch was a simpler affair than dinner had been but, for all that, it was still formally served and lengthy. Jane tried hard to concentrate on the conversation as it eddied around her but it was difficult; she could not seem to focus her mind. She wanted to curl away in a quiet corner and blanket herself around with happy thoughts. If she and Alistair loved each other, everything could be resolved, their love would make sure of that . . .

'I'm sorry, Lady Upnor, I didn't hear what you said,' she apologized nervously.

'I asked if you had passed a pleasant morning?'

'Lovely, thank you,' Jane replied. Alistair grinned from ear to ear.

'Alistair, why are you grinning like a Cheshire cat?' his mother asked him pleasantly.

'I'll tell you later, Mother,' Alistair said, still grinning widely.

'I'll look forward to that. Meanwhile I'd be obliged if you would take that asinine expression off your face. It's preventing me from enjoying my luncheon,' she teased.

Jane looked around at the happy faces, laughing at Alistair and his mother. Maybe he was right and she was being paranoid? Did she worry and think too much, as he said? It could be that her problems were of her own making. After all, her uncle loved an argument, she'd heard him change his opinions just to get an argument going. Arguing was not necessarily quarrelling, she must try and remember that. At last lunch was over. Alistair spoke quietly to his mother.

'Come on, Jane,' he called across to her. 'Let's go for a walk.' He led her out. 'We're to meet my parents at four, they're both busy until then.'

For the next two hours Alistair took her around the grounds of the house, showing her his favourite childhood haunts. They walked quickly through the formal gardens, which would have held no interest for a little boy, to a summer house in a copse, built like a woodman's cottage and looking as if it were made of gingerbread. They crossed a patch of wild ground where weeds, some flowering, grew in profusion among the bushes and under the trees. It was in dramatic but still beautiful contrast to the formal gardens.

'This is called the wilderness,' Alistair explained. 'When I was a child this place used to terrify me. I was convinced it was the wilderness in the Bible, you know, forty days and all that. I always expected to bump into the devil himself here!' He laughed at the memory. Beyond the wilderness, they came to a long brick wall. Alistair opened a small green gate and led her into the huge kitchen garden. The high walls seemed to trap the smells of the herbs and ripening fruit in a heady and concentrated essence. She touched the walls, which were warm from years of sun. The buzzing of the bees filled the air. This was another place of timelessness. These gardens must have looked, smelled and sounded like this for centuries. The idea made it a comforting place to be. Alistair picked a peach for her.

'It's no fun any more,' he said sadly. 'When we used to pinch them from under the gardeners' noses, that was fun. Now I'm allowed to pick what I want the fun's gone out of it and I swear they don't taste nearly as good.'

She would have liked to linger, but he insisted they press on, he wanted her to see his favourite place on the whole estate. They walked through a pretty wood which in spring, he told her, was a carpet of bluebells. They passed an ancient swing, suspended from the branch of an old beech, the rope now frayed and rotting from the weather. She could hear water cascading and around the next bend in the path was a small waterfall tumbling over rocks and down into the dark-green, limpid pool. Trees inclined themselves over the sides, their branches trailing in the water like slender fingers.

'Alistair, it's a magic place.' She found herself whispering.

'Pretty, isn't it?' he said with a satisfied expression. 'If things are going wrong, half an hour here watching and listening to the water and I'm fine again.' They sat on a flat rock. 'We used to play ghosts here in these woods. We had a pantry boy called Henry, he'd cover himself with a sheet, pop a torch in his mouth and jump out at us from behind the trees. It was the most exquisite terror. I wonder what happened to Henry – he went off to the war. I must ask Pa.'

'Are the public ever allowed in here?'

'The gardens are open a couple of days a year – some pet charity of my mother's.'

'It seems such a shame more people can't see and enjoy it.'

'Heavens, mother would never allow that. "People will make it look untidy!" I can just hear her.' He imitated his mother's voice.

'But the house, it seems wrong that it can't be seen and appreciated.'

'Good God, Mother would have a fit! She has the proletariat in the garden twice a year on painful sufferance. I mean, she goes out for the whole day when it happens. Can you imagine what she would think of people crashing about in her house?'

'I think things should be shared.'

'This is subversive talk, Miss Reed, I don't think it would go down too well with my mother.' He laughed and kissed her teasingly.

They sat a while in silence, listening to the sound of the waterfall. She wished that the water would work its magic on her, but as the time drew closer and closer to four o'clock and their appointment with Alistair's parents, she could feel the now familiar constriction of her throat, the quickening of her heartbeat.

'Come on, sweetheart, time to go.' Alistair helped her to her feet.

She was so nervous that she did not take in the attractive proportions of the room they entered, nor did she notice Alistair's father standing by the fireplace. She was conscious only of the older woman sitting rigidly upright at her desk and she noted the studied way with which she slowly and deliberately capped her pen, straightened the letter she had been writing, and patted her immaculate hairstyle. Only then did she turn to face them.

'Well, and what is the big secret, Alistair?' she asked. Alistair was beaming from ear to ear.

'I've asked Jane to marry me and I still can't believe it but she accepted. Isn't it marvellous? Of course we wanted you two to be the first to know.'

The silence that followed seemed to Jane to last for ever, though in reality it lasted only a fraction of a second. But within that time, as if watching a film in slow motion, Jane saw with horrified fascination that Lady Upnor's back became even more rigid, she noticed the almost imperceptible lift of the older woman's head, noticed how she closed her eyes as if in silent prayer or pain.

'This is splendid news!' It was Alistair's father who spoke. 'My dears, I am so pleased for you both.' He took their hands and smiled at Jane. 'Alistair, I think you've made a very wise choice. And now I may call you Jane,' he said, and bent forward to kiss her cheek.

'This is a surprise,' Lady Upnor said eventually. 'You might have given us some warning, Alistair. That was very naughty! Champagne, Rupert, we should have champagne.' Lord Upnor picked up the house phone.

'There you are, darling, it's all right,' Alistair said to Jane. 'She seemed to have some nutty idea that you wouldn't approve, Mother.'

'Really?' said Lady Upnor in a glacial voice. 'What on earth gave you that idea?' She looked calmly at Jane but there was no warmth in her eyes and Jane knew for certain that she had been right.

The champagne arrived and Lord Upnor proposed a toast. 'Welcome to our family, Jane. We wish you both the best luck in the world and every happiness.' The toast was drunk but from the corner of her eye Jane saw that Lady Upnor said nothing and, although she raised her glass to her lips, did not drink.

'But what about your nursing? I thought you said only last night that you hoped to qualify?'

'I did, Lady Upnor, but that was before Alistair proposed to me. I think I'd rather be his wife than finish my training.' She tried to laugh but without success.

'And how do you think you will adjust to living in the country? I gather you are a city girl from what you were saying. Do you think you will settle? Alistair will have to spend a lot of time here away from the bright lights of the city. There's not much to do in the country. How will you like that?'

'I think I can adapt, Lady Upnor. I have never been one for the bright lights. I just want to be with Alistair, and so long as I'm with him I'd be happy down a mine shaft.'

Lord Upnor beamed at her response. 'When is the wedding to be?' he asked.

'As soon as possible.' Alistair was grinning again, he seemed unable to stop.

'I presume you will want a quiet wedding?' his mother asked.

'Why?' Alistair asked.

'Yes, I think that would be best,' answered Jane, and for once the two women looked at each other with mutual understanding.

'Well,' the older woman continued relentlessly, 'I hope that you know each other well enough. Marriage is a big step, Alistair, and one not to be taken lightly.'

'Yes, Mother, I know. But Jane and I have spent a lot of time together this past year, I think we know each other pretty well,' Alistair said seriously, the grin momentarily disappearing.

'You're a fine one to talk, Blanche. We decided to get married a week after we met.'

'That was different,' his wife said curtly, and, as if aware that her guard was slipping, quickly added, 'We were older.'

'Jane seems a sensible girl to me, very grown-up for her years.' He turned to Jane. 'You must arrange for us to meet your parents, my dear.'

'Thank you,' she answered, feeling only dread at the prospect.

'Have you spoken to her parents, Alistair?' his mother asked.

'Not yet, but I will, of course. I've never even met them, I think she's ashamed of me,' he said laughing.

'Don't be so ridiculous, Alistair,' said his mother, not joining in the joke. 'In that case I hope you won't mind my suggesting that we shouldn't say anything about this to anyone until you have spoken to them. It would hardly be fair, would it?'

'I suppose not,' Alistair replied, disappointment in his voice.

'That was a surprise!' said Lady Upnor, and with a complete change of subject, as if washing her hands of the matter, added, 'I suggest we all get changed for dinner early tonight. I want everyone down on the dot of seven, in case people arrive early. It is so difficult for people who live in the country and who have to travel long distances to arrive punctually.' It was obvious that they had been dismissed and the subject was closed.

Later, sitting alone in her room, Jane felt it had been a very unsatisfactory interview. She was certain she would have felt better had the woman voiced her objections outright, said honestly what she was thinking. Then at least they could have put their case. Instead, the woman had said nothing, expressed no pleasure, no displeasure. Jane was aware that she had witnessed someone exerting a great deal of self-control and she admired Lady Upnor for that. Had Alistair noticed that his mother had refrained from calling her by name, had not kissed them, had not drunk her champagne? She felt that Lord Upnor's reaction was one of genuine pleasure. If he could accept her . . .? But that was a riddle to which there seemed to be no answer.

She had been proved right, but there was no satisfaction in being right on this occasion. Alistair loved her, that was the important point. She must try not to be so sensitive. She must watch and learn and, given time, maybe even his mother would begin to learn to like her.

13

As promised, May presented herself in plenty of time to do Jane's hair.

'Oh, miss, isn't it exciting,' she babbled.

'What, May?'

'Why, you and Lord Redland getting engaged. I think it's all so romantic.' The young girl giggled.

'But how do you know?' Jane asked astonished.

'You can't keep anything from us below stairs, miss! We thought something was in the wind. Lord Redland's never brought a young lady here before, and then the champagne.'

'But you can't jump to conclusions every time the family have champagne, May.'

'Yes, we can. His lordship hates the stuff, so it's only drunk on very important occasions – you see? Everyone wants to know what you're like, and I'm the only one that knows,' she said with pride.

Jane laughed at the girl's obvious excitement but made her promise, no matter how much people pestered her, to keep it a secret. Reluctantly, May promised, and started to do Jane's hair.

'I thought, miss, if we pulled it back like this, off your face, it would look ever so sophisticated. See?'

'Won't it look too severe?' Jane asked, studying her image in the dressing-table mirror.

'Oh no, miss, it'll look lovely. It'll show off your face something proper. And then I'll twist the rest into a super chignon.' Silence descended as May, frowning and with great concentration, brushed, combed, teased and coaxed Jane's hair into place, entwining it with small white rosebuds she had picked. 'There!' she eventually proclaimed, holding up a hand mirror so that Jane could see the back.

'May, it looks fabulous! The best hairdresser in London couldn't have done better.'

May beamed proudly at Jane's praise. 'Now the dress.' Gingerly she lowered the dress over Jane's head, taking care not to disturb her hair. 'Oh, miss, you look a treat!' May clasped her hands together with pleasure at her handiwork.

Excitedly, Jane twirled in front of the looking glass. The heavy folds of the black crepe dress, with scooped neckline and tight, wrist-length sleeves, made her look taller, an elegant stranger. 'Come in,' she called happily to the knock at the door.

'Wow! Jane, you look stunning,' Alistair exclaimed.

'Thanks to May. What do you think of my hair like this?'

'Fantastic. It makes your eyes look even larger – if that's possible. Haven't you any jewellery? Is it a bit plain?'

'Oh, Lord Redland, Miss Jane is perfect like that. It's more dramatic with no jewellery. Don't you think, M'Lord?'

Alistair studied Jane. 'Yes, May, you're right.'

'In any case, darling, I could never compete with the other women's jewels, could I?'

'Suppose not. But, I tell you, they're going to have one hell of a problem competing with your beauty,' he said proudly, while May beamed at them as if she had created this handsome pair single-handed.

As on the previous evening they all met for drinks, but the house party had grown to include two elderly couples whose names Jane did not catch. Four more friends of Clarissa's had arrived, including two girls who shook her hand casually and then swooped upon Alistair, making a great fuss of him. Tonight Jane could afford to be amused by their obvious flirtation with Alistair. She hugged the secret to her. He was not the available and highly prized bachelor they thought. Alistair winked at her across the room, and from his grin she felt certain that he was thinking exactly the same.

James Standard came over with a drink for her.

'Gin and tonic, isn't it?' he asked.

'Yes.' She laughed. 'Is anyone ever likely to forget?'

'You look really super, Jane,' he announced shyly.

'Thank you, James,' she replied, for once not blushing.

'I was wondering if you would like to have dinner with me one night back in London?'

'That would be lovely. I'm sure Alistair would enjoy that very much.'

'Ah, yes, well,' the young man muttered abashed, 'we must arrange something.'

Lady Upnor's fears were confirmed by the early arrival of some guests full of flustered apologies and obviously aware of her ladyship's views on punctuality. The room began to fill up. From the hearty greetings it seemed that they all knew one another. It still puzzled Jane why these people were so loud and why they had to shout. At school, she had always been taught that it was bad manners to make too much noise in company, and yet this group brayed and bellowed at each other with no such inhibitions.

'How do you do?' A strident voice made her jump. 'I'm Linda Talbot.' A tall, angular woman stood before Jane. Her wild grey hair looked as stiff as wire wool, and sharp intelligent eyes shone like a bird's in her lined face. She proffered her hand.

'Jane Reed,' she said, shaking the hand, surprised by the force of the grasp and the roughness of the skin.

'You dinner or house guest?'

'House. I'm a friend of Alistair's.'

'Splendid!' the loud voice proclaimed. 'He always had a good eye for the ladies. Bertie!' she bellowed. An equally tall and angular man responded to her call and approached, glass firmly clutched in hand. He had large spectacles that kept slipping down his nose and which he pushed back with the regularity of a metronome. 'Bertie, come and meet Jane Reed here, friend of Alistair's from London.'

'How do you do?' He stood back and peered at her through his spectacles. 'And what a fine filly you are, plenty of heart room and good quarters!' he said appreciatively.

Jane had never been compared to a horse before but from his smile presumed he was being complimentary.

'Bertie, you'll embarrass the poor girl, stop it. Do you hunt?' Linda Talbot asked Jane.

'No.'

'Pity.'

'Actually, I'm afraid of horses,' Jane confided.

'Afraid of horses, good Lord, did you hear that, Bertie, she's afraid of horses?' They both shook their heads in disbelief. Alistair joined their little group.

'Hello, Linda, Bertie, see you've met my Jane?' He kissed Linda on her weather-beaten cheek.

'Glad to see you've taken my advice, boy. Choose your women as you'd choose your horse!' Bertie guffawed.

'She doesn't hunt, though,' Linda said, astonishment still lingering in her voice.

'No, but she'll learn,' said Alistair, taking Jane's hand protectively.

Banks announced that dinner was served. Jane was fascinated at how smoothly the men paired off with women to take them in to dinner.

'How do they do that?' Jane asked Alistair, as the crocodile formed. 'How do they know who they are with?'

'Organization. Each man is told as he arrives who his dinner partner is to be. You see, never man and wife together.'

She noted and stored the information away. Tonight there must have been over thirty people dining. The table was longer than the night before, with even more silver on its immaculate damask. More flowers stood in frozen arrangements. More candles blazed, reflecting the women's jewels, making the diamonds flash in answer to the candles' glow. At least the spaces between the guests were not so wide tonight and normal conversation should be possible.

'Who is everyone?' she whispered. Alistair identified various people around the table.

'That pretty woman on the right of my father, she's the Duchess of Wessex: she's a good sport. On the other side is the Lord Lieutenant's wife – she's rather dull.'

'Where's your aunt?'

'Down there, see?' He indicated Lady Honor further down the table, already in animated conversation with a young man. 'He's an actor. Mother always sits Honor beside the artistic types, she's good with them. Have you met Admiral Sir Percy Wing?' Jane found herself being introduced to the guest on her right who looked like an illustration of an admiral, large, with a brown face and piercing blue eyes.

As the meal started and the babble of talk increased, she felt she should say something to the man beside her.

'My dad was in the navy,' she told the admiral.

'Really, my dear? How interesting. What was he?'

'A stoker.'

'Ah now, there's a fine breed of men. Without them the war at sea would certainly have been lost.' He warmed to his theme. 'In action I always felt for them, down below in the dark and heat, not knowing what was going on topside, just hearing the fearful noise. In many ways it was easier for us seeing the hell of it all. Splendid fellows!' he repeated with enthusiasm.

'Who are splendid fellows?' the Duchess asked from across the table.

'Stokers. This young lady's father was one.'

'Really? How awful for him,' the Duchess said with sympathy. 'One of my gardeners was a stoker, it was dreadful, he told me. Do you know that sometimes the only way they could keep those poor souls down in the stoke hole was for an officer to pull a gun on them? Dreadful.' She clucked.

'I didn't know your father was in the navy,' Lord Upnor joined in. 'Where did he see action?' The Duchess and the admiral as well as Alistair's father leaned forward with interest. Jane told them what she knew, apologizing that it was so little because her father rarely spoke of his war to anyone.

'Poor fellow,' the Duchess said sympathetically. 'He probably had a bad time. It would be better for him if he could talk, get it out of his system,' she advised Jane kindly.

'The Russian convoys were some of the worst,' and the admiral began to tell them of his war.

At least tonight she was enjoying the company, but still the meal seemed endless. The food was a little better, the white sauce was less in evidence, and the dishes were more imaginative. However, with so many guests to be served, the food tonight was not lukewarm but stone cold, since everyone had to wait until the last person had been served before starting. The meal ended, and with sinking heart Jane rose with the other ladies to retire to the drawing room.

As was becoming her habit she found a window seat and gazed out on the park below. To her surprise the Duchess chose to come and sit beside her. Jane decided that duchesses were easy people to talk to as she chattered away, answering the woman's questions about everything under the sun.

'May I ask you a question?' Jane asked.

'I doubt if I'll know the answer, I'm terribly thick.' The Duchess twinkled back at her.

'Why do the men stay behind in the dining room after we have left?'

The Duchess laughed. 'Irritating, isn't it? It started, I suppose, when men used to pee in pots kept in the sideboard.' She laughed even louder at Jane's shocked expression. 'Then, after they'd stopped their filthy habit, liking the custom, they continued it. Then, it was alleged, they discussed politics and important affairs deemed far too boring and difficult for our shell-like ears.' She snorted. 'It also gave us gals a chance to go to the loo and powder our noses so that the men could continue to think that we never sank to such basic functions. Now, of course, it just gives them a chance to drink more than we do, gossip, and tell dreadful stories.' Jane roared with delight. 'You've given me an idea. It is an antiquated notion. At my next dinner party, I shall have the men leave the room, and we gals will down the port! Yes, I shall. What fun! What's more – ' but the Duchess was interrupted by Lady Upnor.

'Constance, my dear, I do want you to meet Mrs Griggs, whose husband has just bought the old Frangers place. I think she might be a good committee woman for you.'

'Excuse me, my dear,' the Duchess said, 'I'll be back for more interesting social discussions with you. Duty calls.' She sighed and, to Jane's astonished amusement, winked at her. She had somehow imagined that a duchess would never wink. It seemed here, in this company, that all the rules of her childhood were being turned upside down. As the Duchess moved away, Lady Honor came to join her on the window seat.

'Jane, my dear, I've been let into the secret, I'm thrilled to bits.' She took Jane's hand.

'Thank you, Lady Honor,' Jane said with relief. 'Who told you?'

'My brother. He's very chuffed. I think it's all too divine. Clever Alistair, I'm so thrilled for him. You're so right for him – sensitive yet practical – you'll be a great help to him. He never fitted into the 'young man about town' image like Clarissa and her friends. He had more sense! I love him dearly, you know.'

Jane felt tears of gratitude prick her eyes. Lady Honor squeezed her hand again.

'Don't you worry, my dear. It will all be fine.' She smiled her beautiful smile and for a sweet moment Jane could not even begin to think what it was that threatened her. They watched the throng of women.

'Isn't the Duchess lovely?' Jane asked.

'Duchesses always are. Dukes being so important and so rich and so thin on the ground, they get the pick of the bunch.'

'Then why aren't you a duchess?' asked Jane.

'Sweet little Jane! That's a long story, I'll tell you one day.'

A number of women drifted over and Lady Honor introduced them to Jane. Jane found that they seemed to fall into two categories: those who asked her if she hunted and moved away when she said no, and those who asked her if she played bridge and also moved off at the same answer. She confided her findings to Alistair's aunt.

'That's rural life in England for you. Why do you think I spend most of the year abroad?'

'Do you?'

'Yes, mainly in Italy, I have a villa there.'

'So you're that aunt. Alistair told me about your house.'

'Yes, he loves it there. It's gorgeous and I find the company more amusing. And it's easier to be naughty abroad!' She laughed.

The men began to filter back into the room. Jane watched anxiously for Alistair, but he was one of the last. He was in deep conversation with his father, the older man's arm about his shoulder. Seeing her, they came straight over.

'My dear Jane, such a sparkle in your eyes, it's a wonder that people have not guessed your secret.' Lord Upnor smiled at her.

'Yes, Rupert,' said Lady Honor, 'I think all this secrecy is very stupid. It would have been such fun to announce it tonight.'

'It would have been fun, Honor, but Blanche is right: we should not say anything until Jane's parents know. It would not be fair.'

'Well, telephone them, Alistair, and ask them,' Lady Honor suggested practically.

'They're not on the telephone,' Jane explained.

'Of course not, how silly of me,' said Lady Honor. 'How about sending them a telegram?' she added brightly.

'Heaven forbid! They would think I was dead or something. It would give them a terrible shock,' Jane protested with a laugh.

'It is possible for people to survive without that infernal machine and telegrams, Honor, although we realize you couldn't,' Lord Upnor teased his sister affectionately. They moved away, leaving Alistair and Jane alone at last.

'Enjoying yourself?' he asked.

'Yes, I am. The Duchess is a poppet and people aren't nearly as scary as I thought.'

'See, no need to worry. God, Jane, you look so beautiful tonight, I wish we could slip away,' he said with longing.

'Alistair, help with drinks, there's a dear.' It was his mother. For the rest of the evening, every time Alistair managed to sit with Jane, his mother would come to drag him away.

Some of the younger guests clattered noisily off to a party. Alistair declined and Jane was surprised that Clarissa, pleading tiredness, did not go either.

The evening was a long one and it was not until well past one that the other members of the house party had gone to bed and Alistair's parents returned from seeing off their last guests.

'Let's have a last snort. Just the family,' Lord Upnor suggested, pouring the drinks himself for he had dismissed the servants. 'That was a very successful evening, Blanche, very successful.'

'I'm glad that you think so. I was mortified.'

'Mortified, what on earth happened?' her husband asked, concerned. Lady Upnor swung round to Jane, her face blazing with anger.

'Was it absolutely necessary to tell everyone that your father was a stoker?' She spat the last word out with vehemence.

'I was asked,' Jane replied, her voice already beginning to tremble. Alistair crossed the room and stood protectively at her side.

'You could have just said he was in the navy. It was not necessary to be quite so specific.'

'The admiral asked me what he was.'

'Blanche,' – Lord Upnor put a restraining hand on his wife's arm – 'I think you are going too far.'

Lady Upnor wrenched her arm away from his hold. 'You might not mind, Rupert, with your wishy-washy liberal ideas. I mind very much – that the whole county should know just how working-class my future daughter-in-law is.'

'Future daughter-in-law!' Clarissa exclaimed, looking with dismay from Jane to Alistair. 'You bloody fool, Alistair, you can't marry her. Sleep with her if you must, but for Christ's sake don't be such a bloody fool as to marry her. God, what are people going to say? Marrying that! How could you?'

Jane stood rooted to the spot with shock. Alistair, his father and aunt all began to defend her loudly at the same time.

'Clarissa, you will apologize,' Jane heard Lord Upnor say.

'I won't, Father! Never! I've nothing to be ashamed of. He's the one who should be doing the apologizing. I knew she was a scheming little tart the first time I met her,' she screeched. 'Hell, the only thing acceptable about her is her name, for Christ's sake.'

'You little bitch!' Lady Honor said with quiet vehemence.

'My name?' Jane asked, perplexed.

'If you have to marry a peasant, the least you could have done was choose a foreign one – at least her accent wouldn't give her away then,' Clarissa said spitefully.

'My name, what about my name?' Jane persisted, but no one seemed to hear her.

'I will not have my future wife spoken to like this,' Alistair stormed.

Lady Upnor sank on to the settee; her cast-iron self-control had completely disappeared and her hands shook as she turned angrily on her husband.

'This is all your fault, Rupert. You and your woolly ideas. You've filled that boy's head with your liberal rubbish. This would never have happened had he gone to Eton, as I wanted. Now you've ruined his life,' she concluded dramatically.

'Blanche, stop talking such utter rot.'

'Imagine, the future mistress of Respryn – it doesn't bear thinking about. How on earth do you think she'll manage?'

'I can learn,' Jane said weakly. She, too, was shaking.

'Learn? Don't be so stupid, girl. One is born to this position, you can't learn how to behave.' The babble around Jane was dreadful as everyone began arguing at once.

'Please, shut up!' She put her hands over her ears, trying to shut out the fearful sound.

'Don't you speak to me like that, young woman! This is my house. I shall say what I like in it!'

'My house, Blanche, and I object to Jane being treated in this way.'

'Rupert, I despise you,' Lady Upnor hissed at her husband.

'Oh, please, will everyone stop arguing about me?' Jane broke in desperately. 'Please, I can't stand it!' Alistair put his arm round her and Honor gently took her hand. 'I don't understand this hatred. We love each other, how can you spoil it all? And what the hell has my name got to do with all this?' She felt obsessed with the conundrum of her name.

'I meant at least your name is acceptable, even if nothing else is. You could have been called something unutterably awful like Sherry or Dawn,' Clarissa finally explained.

Jane began to laugh, a dangerous shrill laugh. 'You can't be a real person, Clarissa. You judge people by their names, their names! You're mad!' She was angry now, angry at such stupidity, angry at their rejection. Her eyes glinted with fury as she shook off Alistair's and Honor's touch. 'Who the hell do you think you are? How dare you? Why do you keep talking about me as if I'm some terrible virus? I'm a human being with pride, too! I'm not going to apologise to you, Lady Upnor, for being me – why should I? And how can you expect me to deny my father? I'm proud of what he did in the war. I'm proud of me.' She gulped desperately for breath. 'I'm sorry if I'm the cause of a family row. I don't want to cause any trouble, but I would like to point out, Lady Upnor, that I was invited here as a guest, even if you have decided not to treat me as one.' Flushed with her anger she turned to Alistair. 'I want to go to bed now, I can't cope with scenes like this . . .' She turned on her heel and, with head held very high, went to the door. Her hand on the doorknob, she paused, turned and faced them. 'And, Lady Upnor, if the truth is known, I'm not too sure if I want to be a member of this family!' She slammed the door shut behind her, but the noise of their argument mounted in a crescendo which she could still hear despite the thickness of the wood.

Alone in her room she allowed herself to cry. She lay on her bed, her body racked with long sobs, the tears pouring down her face and dampening the pillow. This should have been the happiest day of her life, but her worst fears had been realized.

She must have cried herself to sleep with exhaustion for she awoke, with a start, as her door burst open and Alistair stormed in.

'Pack,' he commanded. 'We're leaving.'

'But, Alistair – '

'No buts. Come on, I'll give you a hand.'

Within minutes she had collected her few possessions together and, still in her evening dress, her pretty hairstyle dishevelled and falling about her ears, she miserably followed Alistair down the stairs. His father stood in the hall.

'My dear Jane, I am so sorry. I cannot apologize to you enough.' He took her arm and looked with concern at her tear-stained face.

'Lord Upnor, I'm sorry too. I never wanted to be the cause of trouble between Alistair and his family.'

'My dear sweet girl, you must not blame yourself for one moment. What Alistair is doing is the right thing. You are to be his wife: his duty and loyalty must lie with you.' He kissed her gently on the cheek. 'Drive carefully, Alistair,' he said.

The car roared across the park, its headlights picked out the faces of the startled deer. In his anger Alistair crashed the gears and the little car protested. She huddled low in her seat, shivering more from misery than cold, as Alistair headed the car towards London.

She would always remember the wretchedness that she felt on that journey, the myriad emotions that engulfed her. Fury at being so insulted. Humiliation and shame at what she had endured. Pain at the rejection; and surprise at the realization that, after all that had happened, she felt a fierce pride in her father and her background. Puzzlement that she should be treated as if she had some dreadful disease just because she was working-class. And a gut-freezing fear that his mother might win and that she would lose Alistair.

Near Winchester, Alistair turned to her and said, 'I love you.' Those were the only words he spoke on the entire journey, hunched as he was over the steering wheel, driving far too fast, his mouth set in an angry line. For once Jane did not mind the speed, felt no fear. She was too far down her pit of misery even to notice.

14

They let themselves into the house as dawn tinged the London sky. Without consulting each other, they headed wordlessly for the bedroom. Miserably Jane sat on the side of the bed, her whole body slumped in dejection.

'Jane,' he said, and put his arms about her. She leaned against him. He sat stroking her hair, gently caressing her until, like a child, she slept in his arms. She would never know that he sat for hours holding her, watching her, guarding her. She would have feared nothing if she could have seen the expression of tenderness on his face as he sat the creeping dawn away and resolved what to do. Eventually he laid her gently on the bed and covered her; in her exhaustion she did not even stir. He bathed and changed and then went downstairs, for he had a lot to do.

The sound of church bells woke her. She lay for a while listening to the familiar sound. She loved Sundays in London: they would often walk for miles through the deserted streets . . . Then she remembered.

'Oh no!' she wailed to herself. 'Why couldn't I have stayed asleep?'

She heard noises from the kitchen and crept down. Alistair was making breakfast for them as he so often did. She stood watching him, memorizing the way he moved, the shape of his head, the way his hair fell forward as he bent intently to his cooking. She stored away the picture in her mind so that in the future she would easily be able to recall him.

'Good morning, Jay.' He smiled at her. 'You look a right old mess, you know.'

She looked down at her lovely black dress, now all crumpled, and became aware, for the first time, of her tangled hair and the fact that her face must be swollen from crying.

'I wanted to see you,' she said simply, holding her arms out to him. He came over, took her in his arms and kissed her swollen face tenderly.

'It will be all right, darling, I promise.' Gently he led her to the stairs. 'Now, you go up and get washed and I'll finish our breakfast.'

In the bathroom she was shocked at what she saw in the mirror. What a wreck she looked! She sponged her face and the ice-cold water began to reduce the puffiness about her eyes as it washed away the salty streaks which had made her skin feel stiff as parchment.

'That's better,' he said later when she returned to the kitchen. 'Here.' He set a plate of bacon and eggs before her.

'Alistair, I can't eat.'

'Yes, you can, you need it. I insist. You've had an exhausting night; you'll feel better for something to eat.'

She forced the food into her mouth but it seemed to taste of nothing, as if she were chewing cardboard. She managed only half her food but drank, almost with desperation, large mugs of sweetened tea. He had said that everything would be all right but her fear remained, as they ate in silence.

'Jane.' He spoke eventually. 'I must apologize for last night. I really had no idea that my mother and sister thought like that. I can't explain to you how ashamed I feel. You were right all along.' He looked despondent, his dark eyes reflecting his concern for her.

'It's all right, really. I'll get over it. At least I expected it. I won't say "I told you so"!' She tried to laugh but it failed.

She looked at her hands, studying them carefully. She knew what she had to say, but feared to say it. She sat silently shaping and reshaping the words in her head. Finally she looked at him. 'Alistair, I don't want to come between you and your family . . . I realize you love them too and, it . . . well, darling, it just wouldn't work if you were torn in two . . . Maybe your mother's right . . . perhaps it would be better if we split up now . . .?' Her whole speech came in quick breathless bursts, the words competing with sobs, which finally won.

Quickly, Alistair came round the table, knelt beside her, took the hands she was so ashamed of and kissed them. 'Oh, sweet Jane, you've got it all the wrong way about. I'm not going to have my family damage us, or come between us. It's made me more determined than ever to marry you and the sooner the better now. Come on, Jane, no more tears. You never warned me that life with you would be so damp,' he teased her as gently he dried her eyes.

'Alistair, I thought I was going to lose you,' and she shuddered at the thought.

'What rubbish! You'll find I'm much more difficult to get rid of than that.' He grinned. 'At least you can be proud of the way you stood up for yourself last night.' He got to his feet, chucking her under the chin, trying to coax her to laugh. 'Now, I've been very busy this morning. I've had a long talk with my father on the phone – he's in complete agreement with my plans, and he sends his love to you. I've phoned my lawyer and he's arranging a special licence for us to get married. This week, I hope. We have to go to your parents and get their consent since you're under twenty-one. My lawyer is bringing round a consent form today. Once we're married, then I think we should go away for a few weeks to let the dust settle a bit. There is one problem, though.' He leaned forward and looked at her intently. 'I have to return to Respryn, Jane. It's what I've spent all these years training for and I can't let my father down.'

'What about your mother?'

'My mother will pretend that all this hasn't happened; I know her. In fact, we need see very little of her: she tends to spend most of the week in London. We can have our own set of friends. So life there will be possible for you, if not altogether ideal. You do understand the position I'm in?'

'Yes, darling,' she said uncertainly.

'So, we settle at Trinick. We make love morning, noon and night. We'll have hundreds of children and live happily ever after. Agreed?'

'Agreed.' She smiled for the first time that morning.

The front-door bell rang. 'That'll be the lawyer.' Alistair jumped up to answer but returned with Lady Honor, who immediately took Jane into her arms.

'My poor, sweet, little thing! What a ghastly night, what a drama! Are you all right? I thought you were absolutely marvellous, Jane. What an exit! I do hope you didn't mean your threat – some of us are quite nice, you know.'

'That was temper, Lady Honor. I didn't mean it. I want to marry Alistair more than anything else in the world.'

'Thank God for that! And cut the Lady nonsense – call me Honor. You're family, or almost. Now, I'm off to Italy today and New York on Thursday but I simply had to see you two before I left. When are you getting married?'

'This week,' Alistair answered.

'Good, I'm glad to hear it. Very sensible. I should make it as soon as possible. I'd like you to have my villa for your honeymoon, if you have nothing else planned.'

'Thank you, Honor, fantastic. I can't think of anywhere I'd rather take Jane, it'll be perfect.' The front-door bell rang again. 'That must be the lawyer this time. Cheer Jane up, will you, Honor?' Alistair rushed off to attend to the lawyer.

'I've a pressie for you, Jane. Look.' Honor held out a red velvet box to the young girl. Gingerly Jane opened it. Nestling inside was a beautiful four-stranded pearl choker with a diamond clasp.

'Oh, Honor, it's lovely! I don't know what to say,' Jane exclaimed, stunned.

'It was my mother's. I know that she would have liked Alistair's wife to have it.'

'Honor, it's the most beautiful thing I have ever seen. I'll treasure it. Thank you.' Honor patted her hand. 'I can't help how I was born, Honor,' Jane suddenly burst out. 'I can't understand how one's background can be so important, how if it happens to be the wrong one you're treated as if you're an untouchable.'

'I know, my dear.'

'You don't think it matters, my being me, do you?'

'Loving each other and being good to each other, that's all that matters.'

'But, Honor, I just know Lady Upnor won't give up. She will still try to break us up. I sensed it right from the start. At least, I knew there would be trouble. I tried to warn Alistair, but he was so convinced that everything was going to be all right. I really feel sorrier for him – after all, it's his family.'

'Alistair's strong enough – don't you worry about him. He won't give in, it's Blanche who'll end up the loser. No, you must never let anyone come between you and the man you love. I did, you know. Years and years ago, I fell in love with someone my mother didn't approve of and she forced me to give him up. I've often wondered how my life would have been if they had let me marry Bob. Maybe I wouldn't have had so many husbands. And, you know, Jane, the silly thing is, he's a cabinet minister now and frightfully respectable. Stupid, isn't it?' She laughed, but Jane noticed a look of sadness cross her lovely face.

'But you're not against me, nor is Alistair's father. It's Lady Upnor. Why?'

'She's showing her middle-class origins, darling. They're the worst snobs of all.'

'What do you mean? You mean she wasn't born an aristocrat?'

'Good God, no! There was an awful shemozzle when Rupert fell for her. Her father was a manufacturer of something or other, filthy rich of course, but anyone in trade was beyond the pale to my mother. Blanche still has an enormous chip on her shoulder.'

'But she plays the part so well.'

'Of course. Expensive education, right clothes and the right training work miracles, but when the chips are down all her nasty, sordid middle-class pretensions come out.'

'But you'd think that she'd be even more understanding, then.'

'Heavens, no! She buried her origins: no one remembers any more. Now you'll stir them all up again. I can just hear the old ducks in the county trotting out, "Of course it's history repeating itself. The Redland boys always marry beneath 'em . . ." What a hoot it will all be!'

'But, Honor, I don't think any of it matters.'

'Of course it doesn't, darling, that's the great joke. You know it and I know it, only fools don't know it.' She lit a cigarette. 'What are your plans now?'

'We have to go and get my parents' consent. I'm under twenty-one.' Jane pulled a face.

'Problems?'

'Probably. My father's slightly left of Lenin. He'd abolish hanging and bring in the guillotine for aristocrats if he had his way.'

'Well, make sure he chops Blanche first!' Honor chuckled with joy at the prospect.

'What's the joke?' Alistair had appeared in the doorway.

'We're having a profound sociological discussion,' Honor announced airily.

'So early?' Alistair laughed.

'Anyway, darlings, I must fly – literally. I'll tell my staff to expect you any day next week.'

'You're an angel, Honor. I wish you could come to the wedding,' said Alistair. 'Any chance?'

'No, darling, impossible. In any case, with my track record, I find weddings deeply depressing affairs. I feel I put a curse on them if I attend, like the wicked fairy. Now, be happy, the pair of you. Don't let anyone interfere.' And she was gone.

'I like your aunt so much. She seems to understand,' Jane said as they heard the car drive away.

'She's probably enjoying all this secretly. She loathes my mother and I know it's mutual. Come on, sweet,' Alistair said cheerfully, pulling her to her feet. 'Now it's your lot's turn.'

There was little traffic on the road and they drove quickly out of London and through Kent. She guided him through the warren of narrow streets in her home town.

Alistair sighed. 'My God, this is depressing. You told me your childhood was bleak but I wasn't prepared for it to be as gloomy as this.'

'But all towns have rows of streets like this – you must have seen similar ones.'

'Yes, but I never really noticed them before. I never knew anyone who had to live in them. It makes one see them in a different light.'

She debated with herself whether or not to knock. Usually the sound of an unexpected knock on the door would throw her mother into a fit of anxiety. Certain knocks were expected and came at regular intervals – the rent collector, the club man, an insurance agent – but in these streets an unexpected visitor usually meant trouble. On the other hand, if she just walked in with Alistair her mother was likely to be angry since she hated to be taken unawares. At least a knock would give her warning and time to hide the papers under a cushion, or to stuff the washing in a cupboard.

Her father answered the door, in shirtsleeves and slippers.

'Oh, it's you,' he said without enthusiasm, turning his back to return to the living room, where he sat back in his armchair and resumed reading the newspaper. They followed him.

'Dad, this is Alistair Redland.'

Alistair stepped forward, his hand outstretched. 'Good morning, sir.' Her father looked at the proffered hand and the young man suspiciously. He shook hands and grunted something.

'Where's Mum?'

'Out the back, yakking as usual.'

She left Alistair standing in the middle of the tiny room, looking lost and embarrassed, and quickly went to find her mother, who was in the garden gossiping across the rickety fence with their next-door neighbour.

'Hullo, Mum, Mrs Green.' The two women looked up in surprise at her sudden appearance. 'Excuse me, Mrs Green, but, Mum, I've brought a friend home to meet you.'

Mother and daughter walked up the narrow garden path.

'Who is it?'

'Alistair. The one I told you about.'

'You could have warned us. You can't stay to dinner, the joint's not big enough.'

'That's all right, we didn't plan to, it's only a flying visit.'

'You look terrible. What have you been up to?'

'Nothing. Too many late nights probably,' she lied and her mother sniffed, knowing she lied.

They found Alistair very relieved to see them. He had stood there in silence and her father had not said a word to him. At least her mother was polite and offered him coffee.

'I think Alistair would prefer beer, Mum.'

'No, Jane, coffee will do fine,' Alistair interrupted.

'I really think you would prefer a beer, Alistair,' Jane said pointedly, imagining his puzzlement if faced with her mother's idea of coffee, which was boiled milk, a teaspoon of Camp coffee and far too much sugar.

'Well, if you have beer that would be very nice,' Alistair complied.

'Charlie, get the gentleman a beer,' her mother ordered.

'That's my dinner beer,' Jane's father complained.

'Get the beer, Charlie,' her mother said with barely controlled anger.

'I'll get you some more, Dad,' Jane promised. Still muttering under his breath, her father reappeared with his jug of beer. They settled themselves around the dining table while her father sorted out the glasses. She had never thought about the smallness of the room, but now, after her visit to Respryn, the contrast was ridiculous. This one room would have fitted into the drawing room at Respryn a dozen times. It was not that they were untidy; it was that the room was so small that one person made it look crowded. With the four of them it was chaotic. Her father took out his tobacco tin and laboriously began to roll a cigarette.

'And to what do we owe the honour of this visit?' he enquired, unpleasantly.

'I wanted you to meet Alistair, Dad.'

'You this Cambridge chap she's been knocking about with?' her father asked.

'Yes.'

Her father concentrated further on the rolling of his tobacco. An awful silence hung in the air.

'Actually, sir,' Alistair began, 'I've come to ask your consent to marry Jane.'

Both parents looked at her simultaneously.

'Your nursing, Jane. You won't be allowed to finish. Oh, what a pity!' her mother exclaimed.

'I realize that, Mum.'

'But after all the sacrifices I made! You should have a qualification, Jane. You never know what's going to happen, and with nursing you can always get a job anywhere.'

'She will be well provided for, Mrs Reed, I can promise you that.'

'Quite honestly, young man, I'd rather you waited until Jane has finished her course and is qualified. It all seems such a waste of time otherwise.'

'We don't want to wait, Mum. Having decided, well, we want to get married now. I've never been really happy nursing, I'll be glad to see the back of it.'

'First I've heard of it,' her father interjected. 'If my memory serves me right, you made enough fuss to start nursing, against my wishes. Now suddenly we're to believe that you don't like it.'

'We won't go into that now, Charlie.' His wife stopped him. 'Where would you live? Finding a house isn't too easy these days, you know.'

'Alistair is going to help his father and we'll have a lovely house of our own. It's so pretty, Mum, right in the country, with two bathrooms, imagine that, Mum. And it's got a huge garden and no traffic.'

'You could come and stay any time, Mrs Reed, any time you wanted. All you'd have to do is phone and we would come and get you.' Alistair smiled. Jane could see that her mother was beginning to succumb to his charm.

'It all sounds lovely.' Her mother sighed wistfully.

'And this job with your father, what does that entail?' her father enquired.

'At first I'll be watching and learning.'

'Oh yes, what?'

'Farming.'

'And what sort of wage can you expect?' her father persisted.

'Well, I won't actually get paid.'

'Not paid? Then you're a bloody fool. If you're worthy of hire then you're worthy of pay commensurate with the work you do.'

'It wouldn't actually be necessary, sir.'

'Money not necessary? What a strange world you must live in, young man, where there's no need for money. How will you eat, may I ask?'

'Oh, I'm sorry, sir. I misunderstood. I already have enough money to support us from my investments.' Alistair smiled broadly.

'Investments?' Jane's father's eyes glinted dangerously. 'You mean you make money sitting on your arse while the poor bloody workers tear their guts out for bloody peanuts?'

'Charlie . . .!' Her mother tried to stop him.

'I don't think that's quite fair, sir. If no one invested then there would be no work for anybody.'

'If the parasites didn't invest, then the government would be forced to step in and then maybe the profits would go to the right people, the workers who created the profits in the first place, and the fucking drones in the City would get nothing!' Her father sat back with a satisfied expression on his face.

'But it doesn't work that way, sir,' Alistair said almost desperately.

'I know it bloody doesn't, more's the pity. But it will one day, oh yes, one day it will!'

Alistair nervously tightened the knot of his tie. Jane sat helpless, knowing too well that when her father got into his stride, there was no stopping him. He would continue to pursue, needle and goad Alistair.

'But you said something about farming. That's a proper job, Charlie. Farmers work really hard,' her mother interrupted helpfully.

'Real farmers do,' her father sneered. 'He isn't going to work that hard if he isn't going to get paid for it, is he? Stands to reason.'

'It's like an apprenticeship, really. A way of learning to manage the estate – '

'Estate?' Her father pounced eagerly on the word.

'Yes, sir. So that when I inherit – '

'Inherit?' Her father's eyes shone with anger as he spat the word out venomously. 'Estate? Inherit? Inherit what?' he said as if the words left an unpleasant taste in his mouth.

'Well, everything, sir. The land. The house. The title.'

'Title?' Her father's voice was too controlled now. It frightened Jane.

'Oh, of course, sir, I'm sorry, you probably don't know,' Alistair continued blithely. Jane desperately pulled a face at him across the table but his eyes were intent upon her father's face. 'Silly of me, sir. I'm Viscount Redland and my father is the Earl of Upnor.' Jane noticed her mother surreptitiously straightening her skirt.

'Jesus Christ!' The oath exploded from her father's angry and distorted face.

'Oh, that's nice,' her mother simpered.

'The answer's no,' her father announced loudly.

'Dad!'

'No, and that's that.'

'But I'll be twenty-one next year and then you can't stop me.'

'Right, do what you bloody well like next year but until then the answer's no, understand, N-O.'

'Might I ask why, sir?' Alistair asked.

'You can, young man, and I'll tell you. I've no truck with the likes of you and never have had and never will have, and I won't rest until your sort's dead and gone for good.'

Alistair reeled back in his chair at the vehemence in her father's voice and the hatred which showed in his eyes.

'But, Dad, Alistair can't help who he is – it's an accident of birth.'

'He can't help it, Jane, I agree. But I can stop you joining them and stop you I will. Christ, I'd be a laughing stock on the shop floor.'

'Typical of you, that is, Charlie. As usual, it's not Jane you're thinking of but your stinking bloody pride and what your bloody workmates will say. When have you ever thought of her, I ask?'

'I am thinking of her, you stupid cow – it won't work, it never does. She'd be miserable. Stick with your own class, that's what I say. His lot won't ever accept her: she'd always be an outcast.'

'On the contrary, sir, my father likes Jane very much and is very fond of her already.'

'Your father, you say, what about your mother? I notice you don't mention your mother,' her father said sharply.

'It goes without saying, sir.'

'Nothing goes without saying, sir.' Her father sarcastically emphasized the 'sir'. He stood up. 'Well, if that's all you came for, I'm off to the pub.'

'Charlie, you can't leave like this. If Jane's made up her mind and he seems a nice young man – '

'You women are all the same. A good-looking boy, smarmy manners, a title, and you're wetting your knickers with excitement. Women, you're all pathetic!' He slammed out without saying goodbye.

'Whew!' Alistair whistled.

'I did warn you,' Jane said miserably.

'My husband is an animal, um . . . Viscount . . . an animal!' Jane's mother twisted her hands in anguish. 'He's done nothing for Jane, it's been all me. He's never taken an interest, then suddenly he decides to play the father.'

'Can Mum sign?' Jane perked up at the thought. Alistair dug out the form and studied it.

'It doesn't make it clear, it says "parent or guardian".'

'Then it doesn't matter which parent signs it. You sign it then, Mum.'

'Jane, I daren't. It's hell living with him as it is.'

'Please, Mum,' Jane pleaded.

'No, I'd better not.'

The three of them sat looking at the form on the table. Jane was the first to speak.

'Mum, I think you'd better sign. I'm pregnant!' Her mother stared at her, a look of disgusted horror twisting her face.

'Jane, how could you? You dirty little bitch, you slut, letting a man do that to you!' She shuddered. 'My God, the shame, the whole street's been waiting for something like this to happen, they'll laugh their heads off over this.'

'Jane?' Alistair looked at her quizzically.

'It's true, Mum, you'd better sign it. So the street laughs, but it'll be better than having a bastard grandchild, won't it?' She pushed the form across to her mother.

'That's me finished with you, Jane, I don't ever want to see you again. How could you, after all I taught you? And after all I've done for you – the sacrifices, all those hours in that bloody factory, and this is how you repay me! You can count your lucky stars that this young man here has some sense of decency and wants to do the right thing by you. It's more than you deserve,

my girl. You give me no bloody choice then, do you, you mucky little cow!'
Jane watched her mother signing the paper, writing her name with an angry
flourish. The set of her mouth was even more bitter than before. Jane felt a
flicker of anger at her mother's predictable reaction.

'Thanks, Mum, you won't regret it.' Jane hurriedly snatched up the form
and stuffed it quickly into her handbag. 'Come on, Alistair, let's go.' Alistair
said a hurried goodbye and her mother replied automatically. Alistair drove
the car down the street, round the corner, and stopped.

'Jane, what the hell was all that? You're not pregnant, are you?'

'No. But I knew it was the only way to get one of them to sign.'

'But that was cruel.' He sounded shocked, but there was a small glimmer
of amusement in his eyes.

'I know, I didn't want to lie to her but it seemed the only way. I'm afraid
that if we don't get married right away, we never will. And I'm her child – I
can be as bitchy as they are.'

He put his arms about her. 'Of course we'll get married. Do you think that
we should go back and explain to your mother, though?'

'No, Alistair.' Jane laughed a hard little laugh. 'You heard her, she's not
worried about me, only what the street will say. And I can assure you that the
fact that I'm not pregnant is irrelevant to the street. They will presume that I
am, anyway.' She thought a while. 'I'll tell her when we're safely married.'

They drove out into the country and stopped for lunch at an old coaching
inn. As he was eating his roast beef, Alistair began to laugh.

'What's the joke? I thought that was a bloody awful scene back there,' Jane
complained.

'Jay, it's the funniest thing that ever happened,' he spluttered over his food.
'Imagine, neither of us is socially acceptable to the other side. God, it's so
incredibly funny!' She began to laugh with him. He pushed his plate away,
unable to eat more for laughing. 'I just wish that my mother could have heard
all that.'

15

On the Monday they applied for and were granted their special licence to be
married on the following Thursday.

Alistair was immersed in a whirlwind of preparations, making arrangements with lawyers and the bank, as well as travel plans.

With only £14 to her name, Jane had to face the problem of what she was
to wear at her wedding. She would have liked to buy a new suit but that was
out of the question. It was then she remembered Mrs Baum's suit. A year ago
a grateful patient had given her a grey silk outfit by Hartnell, hardly worn.
Jane was used to receiving chocolates, nylons, the odd scarf, but nothing like
this. Mrs Baum had insisted she accept it, saying the silk matched her eyes,

but Jane had never worn it, thinking it too dressy for her. She did not even know why she had bothered to pack it for this holiday. While Alistair was out, she tried it on. Twirling in front of the mirror, with full skirt billowing round her, she admired the pinched-in waistline, the tight-fitting bodice. It really was perfect; she wished she'd been nice to the patient now. She studied her reflection thoughtfully – perhaps a little too long. She'd ask Mrs Evans to help her alter it.

Jane took the bus to Battersea, the suit in a box beside her. She was excited at the prospect of telling her second family the news.

'My, Jane! What excitement, taken me really by surprise,' said Mrs Evans over tea. 'I do hope you're not rushing things.'

'I love him so much I could burst.'

'And how are you so certain it's love?'

'Oh, I know it is. I mean, I wouldn't mind peeling potatoes for him or washing his socks!'

Mrs Evans laughed. 'That sounds like true love. Mind you, I don't think you'll be doing much washing or peeling of spuds, from what you say.'

'It's like a fairy story, isn't it?'

'It's that all right. With the mother as the wicked fairy.'

'She's dreadful, Mrs Evans, really terrifying. Ten thousand times worse than Matron.'

'From what you say, she may be called "Lady", but it doesn't sound as if she behaves like one to me. I've never heard of such rudeness!'

'It was so unexpected. I knew she didn't approve, but she'd hidden it well until that last night, and then . . . wow.'

'Mind you, Jane, what that woman says is right in some ways. You're taking on a lot and even more will be expected of you. Marriage is hard enough without the problems and added responsibilities you'll be facing.'

'I'll learn, Mrs Evans, I know I can.'

'Let's hope you're right, Jane. It's a shame you'll have to resign. Have you seen Matron?'

'No, I'm too frightened to. I'll write.'

'Matrons have that effect.' Mrs Evans laughed. 'Now, what about this skirt that needs shortening?'

Jane slipped on the skirt and stood on the kitchen table while Mrs Evans began to pin up the hem. 'You were wrong to lie to your mother, though. I'd never have expected it of you, Jane,' she said through a mouthful of pins.

'I know.' Jane blushed. 'But, you see, if I don't marry him now, I know his mother will work on him and stop it. I couldn't risk that.'

'If he really loves you, nobody can change his mind, not now or in six months. And, Jane, I want you to write to your mother straight away and tell her what you've done – it's wicked, Jane, the poor woman will be sick with worry.'

'Yes, Mrs Evans, I will, you're right. You will come to the wedding, won't you? Thursday at noon.'

'Come? You try and keep us away – we'll all be there, I promise. Do stand still, Jane, or this will take hours.'

'I want Sandra as my witness. I hope she can get off duty. If she can't make it, will you stand in for her?'

'Don't you worry, my love, Sandra will be there, if she has to abscond to do it.' She stood back. 'Is that the right length? Right, you put the kettle on, Jane. This'll take me just a minute to hem up.'

It really had been the most satisfactory day, Jane thought, as she returned to Fulham. As she let herself into the house she heard raised voices coming from the sitting room. She peeped around the door in time to hear Roderick Plane saying, 'But the poor woman is prostrate with grief.'

'She brought it on herself,' Alistair answered stiffly.

'Hullo,' Jane said shyly.

'Dear Miss Reed.' Roderick bore down on her and took her hand. 'Such exciting news!' From his reaction Jane could only presume that overnight she had become a person of importance to him. 'Miss Reed, I am here from Lady Upnor. She is in such distress. She wants to see you.'

Jane looked across at Alistair. 'It's up to you, darling, you must do what you want,' he said.

'Will you come?' she asked hopefully.

'No, I'm afraid I can't. I've arranged to meet my father at his club in half an hour – it's important. After that I want to take you out for a very special dinner. Do you realize, we haven't celebrated yet? You go if you want – Roderick will take you – but if you don't want to, I'll quite understand.'

'I'll go,' she quickly decided. It was the last thing she wanted to do but she knew she must. She had to grasp at any chance to patch things up: perhaps that was what Lady Upnor was hoping, too.

'That's a good girl,' Roderick lisped and bustled her out of the house to his waiting car. He talked incessantly as they travelled through the rush-hour traffic but she barely listened to what he had to say. The car halted in front of an imposing double-fronted house which dominated the square in which it stood.

When Banks opened the door to them, Jane greeted him as if he were a long-lost friend. He bowed solemnly and led them across the black and white marble hall and up the wide imposing staircase; the brass handrail glinted in the evening sun pouring into the stairwell from a glass dome above. Generations of Upnors gazed down stiffly at them from the gilded frames which marched up the walls of the staircase. The house was intimidating in its opulent elegance. The butler opened shiny mahogany double doors and led them through the large drawing room and into a smaller sitting room, where the curtains were half drawn and a single lamp glowed in the corner.

'Miss Reed and Mr Plane, Your Ladyship,' the butler announced in a loud voice. In the dim light Jane could just make out Lady Upnor lying on a chaise longue, a book unopened on her lap. She raised her arm feebly and Jane was not sure if this was to dismiss Banks or to welcome her.

'Miss Reed.' Lady Upnor indicated a seat beside her. 'I thought we should talk.'

'Yes, Lady Upnor, I agree.'

'Please sit down. No, Roderick, I want you to stay,' she said as the little man sidled towards the door. Jane saw him lick his lips as though in anticipation at the interview ahead.

'Miss Reed, the other night was so unnecessary.'

'Oh yes, Lady Upnor, I do agree,' Jane said warmly and smiled with relief.

'Had you not been so tactless, none of this unpleasantness need have happened.' Jane felt her face stiffen, her smile disappear. 'However,' Lady Upnor continued, 'one thing is certain: you do appear to care for my son and so you won't marry him, will you?'

'I don't understand,' Jane said shakily.

'Miss Reed, you're an intelligent young woman, you must comprehend how unsuitable you are for the position my son will eventually hold. It is imperative that he marries someone of his own class. You could only harm him, and, if you really care for him, you will not want to be an encumbrance to him.'

'I don't see that I would be an encumbrance, as you put it. I want to marry him because I love him. I think our love for each other is all that matters.'

'I am fully aware of what you think, Miss Reed, but I must disagree with you. This love that you speak of . . .' Lady Upnor shuddered as she used the word 'love'; she spoke it reluctantly, almost as if she were uttering an obscenity. She coughed discreetly. 'Love is not enough. For one thing, it never lasts, and when it is no more, what are you left with? Two completely unsuitable people, with nothing in common, inflicting unhappiness upon each other.'

'I think that love can last.'

'That is because you are young and naive, Miss Reed. You will become a burden to my son, a very embarrassing burden.'

'I thought I'd come here to be friends with you.'

'I assure you, Miss Reed, I choose my friends with far greater care than my son does.'

'My God, Lady Upnor, you're so bloody rude!'

'How dare you speak to me like that?' The older woman sat bolt upright, her book clattering to the floor. 'Such impertinence!'

'Then watch what you say to me!' Jane retorted quickly, with anger.

'Ladies, ladies,' Roderick intervened. 'Please, this will get us nowhere.' He turned to Jane. 'What Lady Upnor says is true, my dear. You have no idea what will be required of you in the future.'

'I can learn.'

'My dear girl, we are talking about breeding, you can't learn that,' Roderick continued in a patient voice as though speaking to a small child.

'I gather Lady Upnor has learned,' Jane said sharply.

'Well, really!' Lady Upnor exclaimed.

'Behaviour is ingrained,' Roderick persisted. 'It cannot be acquired. Small things, I agree, like not calling Banks mister, those can be learned, but not the important attributes like grace and style.'

'I call Banks mister, because he is a mister and he's older than I am and it would be rude to call an older man by his surname.'

'But Banks is a social inferior and is used to being called Banks. It embarrasses him to be called anything else.'

'Have you ever asked him? And, in any case, this whole argument is because I am socially inferior, too. In that case, how can I be superior to Mr Banks?'

There was no answer to Jane's logic and Roderick slumped back into his chair, giving the floor once again to Lady Upnor.

'Is there anything you have not told us about that perhaps we could help you with?' Lady Upnor continued, forcing herself to speak calmly.

'I don't understand,' said Jane.

'Miss Reed, what do you want from me?'

'I've told you, I want to marry Alistair and I wish we could all be friends.'

'Might I, Lady Upnor?' Roderick insinuated himself again. Lady Upnor waved her hand at him in a gesture of exasperation. 'Miss Reed, what Lady Upnor is trying to say, I think, though of course being a lady she is finding it very difficult, is, well, are you pregnant and do you want help with an abortion? These things can be easily arranged. No one need know.'

'Pardon?' Jane exclaimed in horror.

'Oh, my God,' Lady Upnor sighed. 'She says "pardon"!'

'Are you pregnant?' Roderick repeated.

'I heard you the first time! No, I bloody well am not and if I was, what business would it be of yours?' she shouted.

'Well then,' the unctuous little man continued, 'how much do you want? Lady Upnor is quite prepared to be generous, say £2000? That's a good sum of money, my dear Miss Reed.'

'I don't believe this is happening!' Jane exclaimed, jumping to her feet. She was shaking with rage. She wanted to smash the face of this horrible man, see his blubbery lips split wide open. 'You can stop calling me "dear", I'm not your dear,' she yelled angrily at him. 'I'm getting out of here. You tricked me into coming ... I don't want to hear any more from either of you!' She stumbled across the room and, as she left, her unbelieving ears heard Lady Upnor wail, 'But Roderick, he can't marry her – she says "pardon"!'

She sped down the sweeping staircase. Banks, standing in the hall, watched her descend with genuine concern on his face as he saw the expression on hers.

'Mr Banks?' He looked at her enquiringly. 'Mr Banks, do you mind me calling you mister?'

'It's unusual, Miss Reed.' He thought for a moment. 'But I must confess I find it rather charming.' He smiled.

'Thank you, Mr Banks,' she said with a sense of triumph.

He opened the door for her, she stood on the steps and, taking a long, deep breath, put two fingers in her mouth and summoned a taxi with an ear-splitting whistle. As she got in the cab, she turned to see the discreet Banks standing on the steps, a broad grin on his face.

In the taxi she began to calm down a little. She felt as if she had been in a bad play and someone had forgotten to give her her lines. The whole situation was turning into a farce. She began to laugh.

'What's the joke, miss, can anyone join in?' the taxi driver asked her.

'People, that's the joke.'

'People! That says it all, miss. They are the biggest comedy around. Learn that and you'll be all right, I can tell you.'

She was relieved, as she paid the taxi off, to see that the lights were on and that Alistair had returned. She found him in the sitting room, mixing himself a drink.

'How did it go?' he asked. She started to laugh.

'You can't marry me, I say "pardon".' She laughed and could not stop laughing, and the laughter began to hurt. She leaned against the wall weakly but still the laughter came, rising to a crescendo. Alistair stepped across the room and slapped her face sharply. Immediately she stopped, surprise registering on her face.

'I'm sorry, darling, but you were hysterical. I think you need a stiff drink,' he suggested.

She sat with her drink while Alistair coaxed out of her a confused account of what had happened at his mother's.

'Shit!' he exclaimed. 'The old bitch, and I thought I knew her. In front of the greasy toad Roderick, too.'

'But why can't I say "pardon"?' It was the only thing she could think of, it was becoming a fixation.

'You're supposed to say "What?" or "I beg your pardon". It's one of those words that are supposed to label people, like saying "toilet" instead of "loo" or "serviette" instead of "napkin".'

'You mean, on top of everything else, I've got to start relearning my own language?' she asked in disbelief.

'No, my love. You can say what you damn well like. I love you when you say "pardon".' He smiled broadly at her and playfully smacked her rear end. 'You see, there's another one, you'd say "bottom" and I'd say "arse"!' He laughed.

'No, I wouldn't, I'd say "bum".' She laughed too as she took a swipe at his.

But she remained perplexed. Everything about this family puzzled her. They spoke too loudly, almost shouting at each other. They roared with laughter, displaying filled teeth and tonsils. They made noises when they ate, they burped – why, she had even heard Lord Upnor fart, and instead of ignoring it, everyone had joked about it. And now there was a vocabulary which was different from everything she had learned. A code by which people graded each other. And what was oddest of all was that if she had said

'What?', her mother would have hit her. Of one thing she was certain: she was not going to bother; people would have to take her as she came or not at all. She was not going to change for anyone.

That night Alistair took her to the Connaught. Family treats, all his life, had been held here, he explained. She gazed around the opulent, plush room which, although full, seemed to have more waiters than clients. All round her were faces she recognized, faces from the cinema, the newsreels. Alistair was amused at the simple pleasure she took in spotting the famous. She, in turn, was amused by the attentive service as her napkin was unfurled, her wine glass refilled, her peach peeled, her cigarette lit.

'Makes me feel just like a baby,' she said, as she sipped her liqueur contentedly.

On the way back to the house, Alistair stopped the car on the Embankment. They leaned on the parapet where they had stood the night they had first met.

'Jane, I want to give you this.' She looked down: in his hand he held a beautiful, antique sapphire and diamond ring.

'Will you marry me, Jane?'

'Yes, please, Alistair, oh yes.'

He slipped the ring on her finger. 'It had to be here,' he said 'where we first kissed.' And he kissed her again. It amazed Jane that after a year, the minute Alistair touched her, her body reacted, needing to be caressed and closer to him.

Remembering the scene at his mother's, Jane began to laugh.

'What's so funny?' he asked, bewildered. 'This is a serious moment.'

She told him about her defiant whistling for the taxi and Banks's amused smile. He started to laugh too, clutching her shoulder.

'At last I know the real reason why I'm marrying you,' he said.

'Why?'

'Think how useful you'll be when I'm old and riddled with gout and it's pissing with rain in Bond Street.'

16

Jane walked jauntily towards the house in Fulham. She swung her carrier bags almost triumphantly. In one was a perfect wisp of a hat; in another, dove-grey, peep-toed shoes. And lastly there was a dreamy white nightdress. She would have liked to buy the gloves she had seen in Harrods – Italian, with the new gauntlet effect – but her money had run out. She would have to make do with an old pair. However, in her present mood, the lack of new gloves was a minor disappointment. Everything was working out perfectly. Her passport was ready at Petty France in her future name. They could collect it after the wedding in time to catch the flight to Italy. Everyone seemed bent on helping them. Everyone, that is, except Lady Upnor. Jane shook her head, hair flying loose, in a gesture of defiance. She had decided not to worry about her. There was nothing she could do about Lady Upnor's attitude. Nothing and no one, she was determined, would mar the day after tomorrow. She was in love, she was loved, that was all that mattered.

She continued along the leafy road, the early evening sunshine dappling the pavement. She was smiling, she could not seem to stop smiling. People passing her, seeing her smile, continued on their way, made happier by the young woman's evident joy.

As she put the key in the door, the telephone began to ring.

'Miss Jane Reed?' A man she had noticed standing by the gate had followed her up the path.

'Yes?' she replied, smiling, struggling to turn the key and get to the phone.

'Francis Greenstone,' he announced, digging in the pockets of the rather grubby raincoat he wore, despite the heat, and produced a card. Juggling with the bags and the key, Jane popped the card between her teeth.

'Excuse me. Minute. Phone,' she muttered. And, despite the card, she still managed to smile. She slipped into the narrow hall and picked up the receiver. 'Hullo?' The door slammed shut. She swung around, her smile disappearing immediately. The man had not only followed her into the hall, but had shut the door and was leaning against it, his arms folded, watching her. Jane felt afraid. 'What the hell?' She started. 'No, not you,' she explained into the phone. She looked at the man and then at the telephone, unsure which to attend to. 'Yes, hullo?' She finally decided.

'Miss Reed?' a voice asked. 'This is the *Daily Bugle*. Is it true that you are to marry Lord Alistair Redland on Thursday?'

'Yes.'

'And is it true that Earl Upnor's objecting?' She slammed the phone down, her stomach lurching, making her feel suddenly sick.

'Press?' the man asked. She nodded, white-faced, her mind racing. 'I'd take the phone off the hook, if I were you,' he said, almost kindly. As he spoke, the phone rang again. She jumped and looked at it, wide-eyed with alarm. 'Shall I answer it?' he asked helpfully, and picked up the receiver without waiting for her reply. 'Hullo,' he barked into the instrument. 'It's for you,' he said, handing her the phone.

'Who the hell was that?' she heard Alistair demand.

Remembering the card, now crumpled in her hand, she glanced at it. 'Oh, darling, he's a reporter, please come quickly, I don't know what to do or say.' Her voice expressed the mixture of relief and alarm she was feeling. Relief that he was not a burglar, and alarm that he was from the press, an unknown quantity, but one that made her feel vulnerable.

'Don't say anything,' Alistair ordered and, before she could say more, the phone went dead. She replaced the receiver on the cradle and immediately it rang again. Without a word Francis Greenstone swooped on it.

'Too late, mate, *Echo* here, piss off!' He disconnected the call. 'As I suggested, Miss Reed, you'd better leave it off the hook. Do you know what, I could do with a cup of tea, and you look as if you need one, too.'

Wordlessly she led him down the stairs into the basement kitchen and put the kettle on. As she did so, she noticed the man peering into her carrier bags.

'Do you mind, that's mine.' She grabbed the bags and stuffed them under the table.

'For the wedding outfit? Any chance of a preview photograph?'

'No! Certainly not!' She glared angrily at him, and then added, 'Do you take sugar?' The mundane question struck her as ludicrous in the circumstances.

'Three, please,' he answered. As she spooned the sugar into his tea she noticed her ring. 'Nice ring you've got there. Part of the Upnor collection – or wouldn't his lordship cough up?'

'There's no point in you staying, I'm not going to say anything to you.'

'I can't go, I'd get the sack. I'm only doing my job. Shall we wait for your fiancé? It's all the same to me. You make a good cup of tea, by the way.' He smiled amiably at her. As they sat in silence, drinking their tea, he seemed totally oblivious to Jane's anger and discomfort. After what seemed an age she heard Alistair's key in the lock. She rushed to meet him on the stairs.

'Alistair, thank goodness you're here! Get him to go, darling, please, he gives me the creeps.'

'Good evening, Lord Redland. I've just been trying to have a chat with the young lady here.'

'Get out,' Alistair ordered. 'We don't want anything to do with damn reporters.'

'What you want and what you get are two different things, M'Lord. I suggest you cooperate with me. It'll be better in the long run.' The pleasant tone of his voice made his words sound even more ominous. Jane shuddered.

'I don't want to give any interviews,' Alistair said.

'I think you will, M'Lord. You see, at this moment one of our reporters is with Miss Reed's parents and if you don't cooperate with me, then we'll just use that interview instead.' He smiled. 'Got a match?'

'Oh, Alistair, Mum and Dad can't cope with this.'

'What we want, Lord Redland, is complete exclusivity and in return we'll keep the other papers away from the old couple, and that's a promise. All we want is an interview with you two and a nice photo with the parents, OK?'

Despondently, Alistair shrugged his shoulders. He picked up his car keys.

'We'll take my car, Lord Redland, more satisfactory in the long run.' Again he smiled, but each time he did so, it made Jane even more alarmed. It was an automatic, unfeeling smile. A professional smile, she realized.

Outside, the man whistled and a car drew up, driven by a young woman with bright blonde hair. 'Lottie Carter,' he said, introducing them. The young woman barely acknowledged Alistair and Jane as they climbed into the back seat and grimly held hands. Francis Greenstone swung around in his seat and leaned over towards them.

'Now, just a few questions, like where you met, that sort of thing.' Alistair coldly told him that they had met through mutual friends, and added no details.

'And has Miss Reed met your parents?'

'Of course.'

'Sticky, was it?'

'I don't know what the hell you mean.'

'I mean, Lord Redland, the difference in your backgrounds. She's not exactly what your parents expected, I'm sure.'

'Mr Greenstone, I don't like your attitude. Of course my parents have no objections. Why should they? They have met Jane, like her and are very happy that we're getting married. I don't know where you got these peculiar ideas.'

The reporter did not look convinced. 'Bit sudden, though, isn't it? Any particular reason?' he asked, looking pointedly at Jane's stomach. Alistair shifted his arm and put it protectively around Jane's shoulder.

'I don't like the implication of your question.'

'I'm sorry about that, Lord Redland, but I'm only doing my job.' There was a detachment about him and Jane knew he was telling the truth. It was just a job to him, it didn't matter one way or the other what they did or said; he would write a story, print it and move on to the next one. The feeling it gave her, of not being of any real interest to him, was a chilling one.

Halfway to her home, they stopped at a mock-Tudor road house for a snack. The two journalists were obviously on expenses and determined to make the most of it. Jane ordered orange squash, she wanted to keep a clear head. Alistair ordered beer, but Francis and Lottie ordered double whiskies and steak sandwiches. 'Best steak sandwiches in the Home Counties,' Greenstone announced, but the last thing Jane or Alistair wanted was food. Jane stood up to go to the lavatory. 'Where are you going?' asked Francis Greenstone. Jane swept past him without answering.

Lottie joined her in the ladies'. The young girl stood at the mirror playing with her hair. Jane locked the cubicle door, glad to be alone for a moment. She supposed it was funny, really, that the only place she could find peace was in a lavatory. Funny or sad? One or the other. When she came out the girl was still looking in the mirror. Jane washed her hands.

'You've been sent to spy on me, haven't you?' she said accusingly.

The girl laughed. 'Well, I'm supposed to keep an eye on you, if that's what you mean.'

Jane angrily piled her make-up into her bag and swept out to battle her way through the crowded bar back to Alistair.

'Alistair, we've been kidnapped!' she announced dramatically, her eyes flashing with indignation. 'That girl's been spying on me.'

'Yes, darling, I'm afraid so. They're protecting their story.'

'But what possible interest could we be to anyone?'

'Plenty, Miss Reed,' the reporter interrupted. 'You're a big story. It's not every day of the week a working-class girl like you marries a lord, now is it?'

'But how the bloody hell did you find out where we were?' Alistair asked.

'Impending marriages are always pinned up on the notice board in the Register Office – they're inspected every day. It was clever of you to put your father's address and not your own, though. It took the others a time to find out where you were.'

'You didn't answer my question,' Alistair persisted.

'I was luckier, I had a tip-off. Not only where you lived but also that there were – how shall we put it – a few difficulties?'

'But who told you? Nobody knows.'

'Sorry, Lord Redland, I can't give secrets away like that – just an impeccable source, close to the family, as we say,' he said, tapping the side of his nose with a grubby finger.

Alistair and Jane looked at each other. 'Roderick Plane!' they said in unison. The reporter grinned but said nothing.

'The bastard!' exclaimed Alistair angrily. 'The slimy little bastard.'

'It's a very lucrative business, informing on friends in high places,' Greenstone told them.

'That's the end of that little creep's weekend house-partying,' Alistair said bitterly.

'I didn't say it was him, Lord Redland.'

'You didn't have to. He's the only person who knew anything, outside our families.'

Francis Greenstone abruptly stood up. 'Now, if you two lovebirds are ready, I think we'd better be on our way.'

They drove in silence and an hour later pulled up at Jane's house. The lights were on in the front room, a sure sign of momentous events. The front door was wide open and from inside the noise of a monumental row could be clearly heard. They rushed in, in time to see one young man hitting another and splitting his lip open, then grabbing his camera and removing the film.

'Hullo, Jimmy, what seems to be the problem?' asked Francis Greenstone.

'Local press, Francis, he won't leave.'

'Oh no? I think you'd better, sonny,' and so saying he manhandled the astonished young reporter out of the door, throwing his camera after him and slamming the front door firmly shut. They found Jane's mother in the front room.

'Thank God you're here! It's been like a zoo and with your father on nights, I've been at my wits' end,' Jane's mother complained.

'Mrs Reed, I'm so sorry, I'd no idea,' Alistair apologized.

'That's all right, dear, it's not your fault, it's these wolves. Disgusting behaviour! That poor local reporter – that was Maggie Baker's eldest, Jane – he was only trying to do his job.' She glared at the London reporters. Jane thought that if she heard just one more person claiming that they were only doing their job, she would scream.

'And what do you think of your future son-in-law, Mrs Reed?' asked

Francis Greenstone, ignoring her thunderous looks with nonchalant detachment.

'He's a very nice young man.'

'And what about him being a lord?'

'He can't help that, can he?' she snapped back.

'Splendid.' The reporter laughed. 'What a quote! And what about your daughter becoming a lady?'

'She's one already, thank you very much, young man.' Her mother sniffed audibly. Alistair and Jane looked at each other astonished at the assured way her mother was handling the reporter.

'Mrs Reed, have you got a nice photograph of Jane we could use?'

'Sorry, no. I gave it to that nice young reporter from the local paper.'

'You did what?' Francis Greenstone groaned. 'How the hell did you let that happen, Jimmy?'

'Sorry, Francis, I was in the loo when he arrived, she must have slipped it to him then.'

'That's our bloody photo exclusivity gone for a burton.'

'It was my photograph, I can give it to anyone I want. I didn't "slip it", as you put it, young man. He asked for it and I gave it to him. I really don't know who you people think you are,' Jane's mother said angrily.

'Of course, Mrs Reed. Never mind, what's done is done. At least he didn't get a photo of you three together. How about our taking one now? Would you mind?'

Lottie stopped filing her nails long enough to pose them and to take the photos of three very stiff and unsmiling people.

'Are you going to the wedding, Mrs Reed?'

'I doubt it, if people like you are going to be there.'

For the first time in the whole evening Jane and Alistair laughed. Try as he might, the experienced reporter could get nowhere with Jane's mother. Resigned that no more information was forthcoming, Francis bundled them back into the car, leaving the young reporter, Jimmy, guarding Mrs Reed from the attentions of the other papers.

The car sped back to London. It was a silent journey. Francis appeared to be asleep, but both Jane and Alistair were afraid to talk to each other in case he was not. So they sat lost in their own thoughts, tightly holding each other's hands.

Finally, the car ground to a halt in front of the loading bay of a tall building. They were ushered out of the car and through a door, and only when the door was firmly shut were the lights put on. Francis led them to a lift, and they travelled several floors up to emerge in the newsroom of the newspaper. The place was a hive of chaotic activity, reporters frantically typing, shouting across the vast room at each other. Several telephones were ringing; some were answered, others ignored. No one took any notice of them. Francis opened his desk and took out a bottle of whisky which he offered them and this time they did not refuse. For the first time in the whole evening Francis left them alone, but no doubt one of the many staff in the room had been instructed to keep an eye on them. The frantic activity began to decline, desks were opened and bottles appeared. Finally Francis returned.

'Our compliments,' he said and handed them a sheet of still-wet photographs. They were terrible: in all of them they looked stiff, rigid and far from happy.

'Can we go now?'

'Not just yet, Lord Redland, if you don't mind. We'll run you home, of course. I must say you've been very helpful. If I might suggest, I'll pop round first thing in the morning, keep the rest off you, though it's a bit late for them now.' He laughed.

A sudden gigantic shuddering reverberated through the building.

'What on earth's that?' Jane asked alarmed.

'It's the presses, Miss Reed. The paper's been put to bed, we can all go home.'

'You mean it's safe for you to let us go. I presume that all the presses of your rivals will be rolling too by now?' said Alistair.

'Well, give or take a few minutes, yes. Nothing will stop them now except the Queen dying or World War Three starting.' He laughed again.

Wearily Jane stood up. It had been the most extraordinary evening in her life. No one had been unpleasant to them, but what had happened was far from pleasant. For a whole evening they had lost control of their own lives and wishes.

By now Lottie had gone home and it was Francis who drove them, at breakneck speed, back to Alistair's house. 'See you in the morning,' he called cheerily as he drove away.

'We want to have a lie-in,' Alistair shouted to the departing car. As they turned on the pavement they were blinded by the popping flashbulbs of a dozen cameras.

'Lord Redland, could you comment on the rumour that your father has disinherited you?' shouted a voice from the darkness.

'Oh, go to hell, the lot of you!' Alistair stormed into the house, slamming the door with a resounding crash.

17

The phone rang at six in the morning. No sooner had Alistair angrily replaced the receiver than it rang again.

'Don't these bastards ever sleep?' Alistair muttered bitterly.

'Francis Greenstone suggested I took it off the hook, yesterday. It'll never stop. I'll make us some tea.' She slipped a shirt of Alistair's over her naked body and quietly padded down to the kitchen. It was going to be a lovely day.

She wound up the venetian blind to let the sun in and opened the window. The figure of a man popped up from nowhere, framed by the window.

'Miss Reed? Do you have any comment to make . . .?' A camera shutter clicked.

'Leave us alone!' she screamed, slamming the window shut and racing out of the room and back up the stairs. 'Alistair! Alistair! Come quick, they're everywhere! They're even outside the kitchen window.'

'Bloody bastards! It's unbelievable,' he muttered as he pulled on his slacks and a pullover. 'You'd think there were enough people who actually wanted publicity.' She heard him run down the stairs, and then the sound of raised voices, Alistair shouting, the door slamming. Jane huddled under the sheet, beginning to fear that at any moment a camera would poke out at her from somewhere else. Nowhere seemed safe. Alistair returned with their tea.

'Can't we complain to their editors?' Jane asked.

'It's the bloody editors who sent them in the first place. Thank God, we'll be away from all this tomorrow.' He peered out through the curtains. 'The street looks full of them. They're like locusts.' He looked at her sitting white-faced and dishevelled, the sheet still clutched about her. 'My poor darling Jane, I'm sorry about all this. I expect you always planned a lovely white wedding in a rustic church with bridesmaids – the full works – and look at the carnival this is likely to turn out to be.'

'I'm OK, darling. They startled me, that's all. I mean, you don't expect it, and me in your shirt too.' She managed a wan grin.

'I feel so useless. I don't know what to do to protect you. I should have guessed this was going to happen.' Alistair banged one hand into the palm of the other with frustration. 'The press have sniffed around me all my life, but nothing like this.'

They spent the rest of the day in a half-light with all the curtains drawn because as soon as a crack appeared they saw the sinister, black snout of a camera. Francis Greenstone arrived at nine, as he had promised, and, to her surprise, Jane was glad to see him, hoping that he might provide some measure of defence against the men outside.

'Can't you get rid of them?' she implored him.

'Too many, I'm afraid, they wouldn't listen to me. Any chance of some tea?' Jane poured him a cup.

'I'll try reasoning with them,' Alistair said, going to the front door. Francis Greenstone gave a short laugh over the rim of his cup. The clicking of cameras heralded Alistair's appearance on the doorstep. It was as if a swarm of crickets had descended on the street. She could hear their raised voices as they fired questions at Alistair. 'Where's the bride?' she heard several shout, but she could not catch what he said in reply.

Alistair reappeared. 'Jane, I think if we agree to let them take our photograph, they might just go away.'

'But I look such a mess.'

'You look lovely.' Jane hurriedly dragged a comb through her hair and went to the front door, holding Alistair's hand tightly. The reporters had agreed to photographs only but, as soon as she appeared, they began shouting questions at her. They asked about Alistair's parents; they asked her when the baby was due. Alarmed, she ran back into the house. They had had their photographs, but they did not go away.

She tried to concentrate on doing her ironing and packing their cases. She had even become resigned to Francis, who sat reading the huge pile of newspapers he had brought with him. His only requirement was countless cups of tea.

'Seen your press?' he asked, handing her a copy of the *Echo*. The headlines in bold print announced: 'HE CAN'T HELP BEING A LORD' SAYS EX-STOKER'S WIFE – 'HE'S REALLY VERY NICE!'

Below was the terrible photograph of the three of them. 'Turn to centre page for full story – ' but she could not bear to see any more. She thrust the paper back to Francis. She did not know why but she felt overwhelmed with shame at what she had seen.

'It's ghastly, I don't want to see any more.'

'Pity. I thought it came off rather well.'

A loud banging on the door began. Alistair bellowed up the stairs to them to go away, but the banging and bell-ringing continued. It even disturbed Francis, who, with a sigh, heaved himself up from the table and, muttering, 'I'll see to the buggers,' disappeared up the stairs. He reappeared with John and David, who were grinning from ear to ear.

'Crikey, what a song and dance! We had to rugby tackle our way in,' John declared.

'Your phone's broken,' David informed them.

'We took it off the hook. But am I glad to see you two! Beer?' Alistair asked them.

'Anything we can do?' they asked, gratefully gulping at the tankards of beer.

'Keep us sane!' suggested Alistair.

'I'm about to write a couple of letters that you could post for me,' Jane replied. 'I'd begun to think I wouldn't be able to post them. I didn't know who to trust,' she said, looking pointedly at Francis. 'I've written to Sandra – I'm frightened she won't get it in time. You couldn't pop into the hospital and leave her a message? Tell her it's noon at Chelsea Register Office?'

'I'll go,' John volunteered. 'I don't think David had better show his face in there.' They all laughed at the memory. It was wonderful to be laughing again; Jane had feared she would never again see the funny side of anything.

She left the men heatedly debating with Francis Greenstone the right of the individual to privacy. Upstairs she struggled with her letters.

Jane wrote to Matron first, handing in her notice. The letter to her parents to explain her lie about being pregnant was more difficult. She made several attempts before she got it right. Alistair, bringing her a glass of wine, read them both.

'They're fine, darling. I'm sure everyone will forgive us eventually. Look, I'm sorry I hadn't told you, but I'm having dinner with my father tonight.'

'Alistair, do you have to? I don't think I can cope with that pack of jackals on my own.'

'Jay, I promised my father: it's a mini-stag-night he's laid on for me. Francis reckons that if I leave here, most of that lot will follow. Perhaps it's best if I'm not here tonight.' Jane's grey eyes widened in panic, and Alistair took her hand. 'Sweetheart, imagine the pictures in the papers, the snide remarks, if we leave for the wedding together. I've asked John and David to stay with you. No one will get in if those two oxes are here, will they? And they'll take you to the Register Office in the morning.'

'Well,' she said uncertainly, 'it is supposed to be bad luck to sleep under the same roof the night before you marry. But where will you sleep?'

'I can stay the night at my parents'.'

'Is your mother there?' she asked anxiously.

'If she is then I'll sleep at my club. I promise.' He laughed tenderly. 'She won't get me to change my mind, you know.'

'I worry . . .' She smiled lamely.

'Don't stand me up, will you?' he said, kissing her gently before he left.

She made the boys some supper and left them playing cards with Francis while she went to bed early. But it felt wrong to be in bed there without Alistair.

She woke far too early to a glorious, perfect June day. She spent as long as possible getting ready, taking immense care over each fingernail, each strand of hair. At last, finding nothing else she could do to her appearance, she nervously entered the sitting room.

'Jane, my love, you'll slay them,' David said appreciatively. 'Scared?'

'Absolutely terrified.'

The two boys shielded her with their massive rugby players' shoulders and cleared a path through the mob of newsmen to a waiting taxi. Outside the Register Office a crowd had gathered. Jane braced herself for their stares but relaxed visibly as they shouted good-luck wishes. Francis Greenstone bounded up to her with a bouquet of gardenias. 'Compliments of the *Echo*,' he said, kissing her on the cheek, and for the first time gave her a genuine smile. A bouquet was the one thing they had forgotten to arrange. She thanked him, and the reporters were finally rewarded with a photograph of a happy bride-to-be.

She was to remember little of the actual ceremony. She was vaguely conscious that the room was full, but she saw only Alistair. He told her later that she had stumbled over the words. At the time she had not even noticed, but she did remember the look of love in Alistair's eyes as he bent to kiss her.

'Good morning, Lady Redland,' he whispered in her ear.

Only then did she see their guests and was amazed that there were so many of them. Sandra was there with several other nurses from the hospital, tears streaming down their faces. She saw some friends of Alistair's and, right at the back, Mr and Mrs Evans with their children looking as if they had been polished for the occasion. Sitting in monumental isolation, smiling like a Cheshire cat, was her aunt, in a voluminous magenta dress and hat with the most dramatic feather Jane had ever seen.

'Auntie Vi!' Jane rushed into her aunt's expansive embrace. 'You wonderful person, you came!'

'What did you think? When I saw the paper yesterday I was straight over to your mother's, but she wouldn't budge. You're not pregnant, are you?'

'No. I lied.'

'I said you had. I said, "Our Jane isn't that stupid." Even if you were, they should have been here – silly behaviour, I think. Your mother thinks you're going to get hoity-toity with us.'

'Auntie Vi! I never would.'

'Course you won't. Your mother's a doomy old cow sometimes. Your husband looks very nice, Jane.'

'Heavens, yes, my husband!' Jane said with wonder. She introduced her aunt and the Evans family to Alistair. The atmosphere of the Register Office was rapidly becoming like that of a party.

'Excuse me, Lord Redland, but I do have another wedding in ten minutes,' the registrar said apologetically.

With difficulty Alistair shepherded the noisy group out to a line of waiting taxis, inviting everyone to join them for lunch at the Connaught. Alistair and Jane stayed to pose happily for photographs. Finally the press let them leave, and to cries of 'Good luck' they stepped into the Upnor Rolls-Royce.

'Who arranged all this – the taxis and the Rolls?'

'Pa did. He's organized the lunch too. He's at the Connaught now. He felt that if your parents weren't coming it was better if he stayed away from the Register Office as well. The press would only twist it.'

'You can't win with them, can you?'

'Never, Lady Redland'

'Oh, please, don't call me that. It makes me feel silly.' She tried to smile at him. That might be her name now, but she knew it was going to take her a long time to get used to it.

By the time they arrived at the hotel, everyone was into their second glass of champagne. Sandra was first to throw her arms about her friend.

'Sandra, thank God you're here! I was so afraid that you wouldn't get time off,' Jane exclaimed, hugging her.

'I'd have gone sick, I wouldn't have missed this for anything. You should have been at the hospital, though, Jane. What a laugh! Home Sister crashing around in her curlers like a demented hen, flapping the newspaper and yelling, "She can't do this, she's Senior Nights next week!" God, it was so funny!'

'Don't even talk about it – I couldn't face them, I wrote to Matron instead.'

Mrs Evans and her aunt hit it off immediately and, looking like two brightly coloured galleons come to rest, were soon deeply engrossed in conversation. As the champagne flowed, so the colour of the two women changed from pink to bright red. Aunt Vi eventually matched the magenta of her dress. Alistair's Cambridge friends began to flirt with the nurses. The Evans children, sampling champagne for the first time in their lives, were rapidly becoming overexcited. Lord Upnor beamed with pleasure on the whole proceedings. It was a wonderful, happy lunch. Much to his amusement, she thanked Lord Upnor at least a dozen times for his kindness. She was so afraid he wouldn't realize how much she appreciated the lunch, and especially how much she appreciated his being there.

The cool, oyster-grey interior of the Rolls-Royce epitomized the change in Jane's life. She leaned back against the soft leather upholstery and smiled a broad, satisfied smile. The bathroomless terraced house, the ugliness, the lack of privacy – that life had gone for ever and she could contemplate the fact with no regret. A new life now beckoned. She faced it eagerly, determined to succeed, determined to show them all that she could.

'What are you thinking?'

'That you're my husband and no one can separate us now, ever!' She kissed him gleefully. 'And bathrooms for the rest of my life!' She flung her arms excitedly into the air.

'Now I know why you married me,' he teased.

'That's right. For a bathroom and because I love you.'

He took her in his arms and they saw none of the suburbs of London as the car glided on towards the airport.

By nine that night they were driving up to Honor's villa. Her staff stood on the steps waiting for them, headed by her major-domo, Guido. He ushered them into the villa like a fussy nanny.

Whiteness. Everything was white, she had stepped into a marble, silken, luxurious, shimmering cube of white. Everywhere she looked, walls, floors, furniture, flowers, the billowing lawn curtains and the ornaments were white. Only the paintings on the wall were coloured – magnificent, blazing abstracts – and in their bedroom there were subtle pink tuberoses whose scent filled the air.

For fear of hurting the feelings of Guido and his staff, they had to eat the dinner prepared for them. They sat at a marble table on the wide, white marble terrace. Below them, far away, the lights of a little town reflected in the sea. The warm air clothed her like a light wool coat. The black sky seemed to hold a million new stars which shone brighter than she had ever seen stars shine before.

They bathed together in the sunken bath, water pouring from gold dolphins. They sat in the water, the air heavy with expensive perfume, and toasted each other in the chilled champagne they found at the side of the bath.

'Alistair, darling, it's unbelievable, like a Hollywood film set.'

'Great fun, isn't it? My mother thinks it's vulgar.'

'I think it's lovely. Lovely, extravagantly lovely!'

'Opulent decadence.' He laughed.

They climbed into the giant bed, their bodies slipping between the fine lawn sheets. The setting and the night air, sensuous with the heady smell of unfamiliar flowers, contributed to their passion. As Alistair slept in her arms she looked at him and knew that she would never love anyone as much. She had found him, and now she would use her life to love him.

It was an idyllic month. They had plans to go touring and sightseeing, but these came to nothing. Instead, they whiled the days away in their white villa making love, drinking Frascati, eating fresh figs, just as Alistair had promised they would. They grew brown and he more golden as the sun drenched his hair. They began to put on weight with the delectable food which arrived in astonishing variety each day. They purred like cats as the staff spoiled them, pandering to their every wish, treating them with that special understanding that Latins give to lovers.

She did not want to leave. For a month she had been able to forget the problems at home, to be herself, to be alone with him. But a letter from England settled their plans. Alistair had been mildly vexed that, because of his mother, he would not be able to go to Scotland to shoot as he always did in August.

'Fantastic!' he exclaimed over his letter. 'Listen, darling, it's from Mother: "I presume you will be arriving at Drumloch as usual in August? Shall you be bringing your wife? Will she be a gun? Let me know . . ." Isn't that great, Jane? She's obviously coming around.' His eyes were shining. 'I think we should leave here at the end of this week.'

'We'll get back to Trinick and start getting some order there. We can stay with Father.' Jane pulled a face. 'It'll be all right, darling, Mother will be in Scotland. She always goes up first to open the house. It will just be the three of us.' She listened to him happily making his plans.

'I wish we could stay here for ever,' she sighed.

'I know, Jay, but you'll love Scotland, too.'

Three
1957–69

1

Without Blanche Upnor's presence, Jane was happy at Respryn. Rupert, as he had now insisted she call him, gave them free run of the attics in the big house to choose whatever they wanted for Trinick House. It was like sorting through a large antique shop but with no bill to pay.

They spent several days in London choosing wallpapers and fabrics. The elegant designers' showrooms they haunted were as far removed as possible from the Co-op wallpaper department to which Jane was used. Jane wallowed happily in a sea of prints, chintzes, silks and fabrics of which she had never heard. Attentive, epicene young men plied her with emphatic ideas of what she should choose, of what was the rage this season. She blithely ignored their advice, confident, with the picture in her mind's eye, of how their house was to look. Having ordered carpets and curtains, they returned to Respryn, the car loaded with wallpaper and paint.

Nothing moved fast enough for Jane. If only the house could be finished overnight – instead she had to wait patiently for the workmen to finish one room at a time. But, as soon as one was finished, she was moving furniture, polishing, hanging paintings, unpacking the cases of porcelain and china they had chosen from the seemingly endless treasures of the attics of Respryn.

Jane's excitement knew no bounds, nor her burgeoning pride in her home. She would willingly have done without the trip to Scotland, so desperate was she to move in, but Alistair was adamant.

'When we return from Scotland will be time enough,' he insisted. 'Time for the smell of fresh paint to have disappeared. In any case, the curtains won't be ready until we get back.'

She found an old rocking horse called, incongruously for such a fine dapple-grey, Fred. He had been Alistair's. She rescued him from the dark attic, washed and polished him, patiently combed his mane and tail and placed him in the hallway.

'That's a strange place to put Fred.'

'I think he looks nice there,' she replied.

Alistair stood back and studied the horse. 'You know, you're right. I have to hand it to you, Jane, you really are putting this place together well.'

'You needn't sound so bloody surprised.'

'You needn't snap.'

'Well, you needn't be so patronizing! Just because I'm working-class doesn't mean I have no taste or that I'm colour-blind,' she said crossly.

'Jane, please, don't be so prickly.'

'What do you expect, for Christ's sake?'

'You know, darling, I shall call you Hedgehog if you continue to be so sensitive.' He smiled at her but she did not smile back.

'Of course I'm sensitive. You can blame your family for that!' She glowered in return.

'I'm sorry, darling. I didn't mean to sound patronizing. I'm so proud of what you're doing.' Gently he coaxed her back into a good humour; she was so happy that she could not remain angry for long.

In this fortnight, not only did she begin to build her home, but she began to consolidate her friendship with Alistair's father, whose acceptance of her, she confidently felt, was total and genuine.

Too soon the fortnight was over, and as the day of departure for Scotland drew near, her spirits began to sink.

Life with Alistair was turning into a long series of firsts. With him she had experienced her first champagne, foreign food, fine wines, gin and tonic. Her first trip abroad, with her first flight; and now Scotland, as they set out with Rupert on her first journey on the overnight sleeper. She loved the train, the comfort of their tiny sleeping compartment, the noise of the train thundering through the night, its whistle echoing across the sleeping countryside. At each stop she peered out, trying to make out where they were, as the train took on mail. She loved the hiss as the great steam engine was fed water and great clouds of steam billowed out across the station. As they progressed north, so the accents on each station changed, until finally she heard the lilt of the Scottish accent. When she awoke properly, it was to the beauty of the northern Highlands. She was to learn that the Highlands had their own special colours – with the improbable purple of the heather, the violent yellow of the broom and the scarlet of the rowan – as if God had mixed an especially bright palette for Scotland. At Inverness they left the train and she breathed air as crystal clear as gin.

The Rolls, with Tucker, the chauffeur, was waiting for them. Once off the main road, they seemed to travel for hours along single-track roads no better than cart tracks. They travelled up glens so narrow she had to peer to see the sky. Waterfalls cascaded down the mountainsides like liquid silver and yet the rivers frothed like brown beer.

'Why are the rivers so brown?'

'The peat,' they answered.

'What's peat?' she asked. They explained, astonished that she had never heard of it. Suddenly on the skyline they saw a magnificent stag silhouetted against the blue sky. Tucker stopped the car so that they could get a better look.

'Pa, look at that! If only I had a rifle on that beauty.'

'He must be a royal,' his father answered. 'Fine beast.'

'Alistair, you couldn't kill anything as beautiful as that, surely?' Jane asked, horrified.

'I damn well could, my girl,' he replied firmly.

After two hours of bumpy, curving roads, they arrived. The house had always been referred to as a 'lodge'. Jane had been expecting a small gatehouse. No one had explained a Scottish lodge to her and she was astonished when Drumloch Lodge appeared in all its grandeur. Turrets proliferated, windows were positioned in the most unexpected places and she saw a front door through which an elephant could have passed.

'What do you think?' Alistair enquired, smiling.

'It's very grand,' she answered unsurely.

'I always think it looks as if it was built by Ludwig of Bavaria on a bad day,' Rupert laughed.

She knew without going into the house that she did not like it. It was too big. It did not look as though it belonged here in the way that Respryn looked as if it had grown from the soil. It was so large and the place so inaccessible that she wondered how many men had toiled and for what pitiful wages, and how many had died, to build this giant, crenellated house in this remote place. Some Lord Upnor in the last century had ordered a castle, had chosen a design, said 'put it here' and then basked in the stone and mortar which were proof of his own importance.

Large deerhounds lolloped out to greet them exuberantly. Banks was at the door, and Jane smiled with delight. 'Mr Banks, how lovely to see you!'

'Lady Redland.' The butler bowed. She hated her new name, felt embarrassed by it, as if she had no real right to it.

The hall was like a banqueting hall. It seemed that every square inch of the walls was covered with the heads of dead animals; their staring glass eyes seemed to follow her everywhere. Animal skins were scattered over the floor, some with heads on, some without, so that crossing the floor was like an obstacle course.

Banks showed them to their room. He led them up a dark, creaking staircase and along a narrow corridor on both sides of which large portraits of dour-looking men in kilts glowered down on them. Like so many rooms in this strange house it was circular, and a large oak four-poster with tartan curtains dominated the room. The window was small and set in walls several feet thick; very little light filtered into the room and Jane searched for a light switch.

'There's no electricity here – oil lamps only,' Alistair informed her. 'We've a small generator for the fridges and the kitchen, but that's all. Fun, isn't it?'

'Yes,' she said, unconvinced. She would never like this house: she already loathed this dark cold bedroom and she hated the dead animals everywhere.

'I'm going for a walk. Coming?' he asked.

'No, thanks, I think I'll unpack.'

'Leave it to the maid, come on.'

'No, thanks, I'd rather sort things out myself.'

He shrugged and left her. As soon as he had gone she regretted her decision, the room seemed to press in on her. No sounds penetrated the thick walls and there was a chill in the room that an extra sweater did not eliminate. She started to unpack but the silence was unnerving. Leaving the cases for the maid, after all, she grabbed her coat and ran out of the room, down the long staircase, hoping to be able to catch up with Alistair.

She found her way out into the grounds – there was no garden that she could find. On either side, the dense forest seemed to come almost to the walls of the house itself, as if trying to engulf it. Only at the front of the building did a vista of meadows lead down to a steel-grey, glinting loch with the mountains rising majestically beyond. That view was breathtakingly beautiful and now out of the house with its oppressive atmosphere Jane felt distinctly happier. She sat on a wall admiring the view.

The sound of running water attracted her attention. She eased herself from the wall and made her way into the trees. She paused to enjoy the sweet, unfamiliar scent of the decaying leaves, and for the first time the comforting, warm smell of the soil. She bent down and inhaled deeply: it was a new idea to her that from death and decay should emerge something so consoling.

The sound of the water was louder. She walked further and found herself standing on a ridge above a river, the water flowing fast, as brown and frothy as stout, between the jagged rocks it had once carved and shaped but which seemed now to guard it. A short way up the river a waterfall tumbled urgently. She carefully clambered over the rocks to reach the bottom of the fall, amazed that here the frenetic water formed a dark, almost still pool. She sat mesmerized by the water.

From the corner of her eye she was aware of something moving. She looked up. There was nothing there. About to turn away, she stood rigid with astonishment as a large fish, the sun glinting on its scales, shot out of the peaty water of the pool like a silver blade and propelled itself into the air with such power that it cleared the fall. Another one appeared, missed the fall and crashed back into the river only to emerge again, seeming to balance on its tail fin and once again unleash its great force in another jump. The pool seemed to boil with swirling fish, all jumping, some clearing the fall, others falling back into the pool time and time again, only to try once more. She found herself cheering them, willing them to succeed. One poor fish mis-judged his leap and landed at her feet on the rock, half stunned. Gingerly she felt it, frightened that it would be slimy to her touch: instead, she enjoyed its cool smoothness. As she gently picked it up to replace it in the water, the fish jerked into life, and Jane was staggered at its strength as it broke her hold and knifed across the pool like a javelin.

For over two hours she sat, fascinated by the courage of these great, shining fish, before she reluctantly made her way back to the house to be on time for lunch. Several cars now stood in the forecourt, a crowd of young people spilling out of the latest arrival. Her sister-in-law was among them. Clarissa looked straight at Jane and pointedly turned her back. Jane steeled herself to walk past the group, her head held high, conscious of their stares as she let herself in the door.

Banks was in the hall, accompanied by some maids bearing huge silver trays of glasses and ice buckets. She asked Banks where she should go, and he ushered her into a large sitting room. The furniture was surprisingly shabby compared with Respryn. Large chintz-covered sofas, their seats sagging, their covers worn, were scattered about the room. It was a comfortable, lived-in room and was light compared with the rest of the house, with four large casement windows looking down across the meadows to the loch.

'There you are. Where have you been?' Alistair asked.

'I found a waterfall and a pond. Darling, it was magical – these great big fish, so brave, some of them, they jumped it, they actually jumped the waterfall.' Her eyes sparkled with excitement, the words tumbling out. 'What were they, Alistair? They were beautiful.'

Clarissa and her friends, who had followed Jane into the room, burst into laughter.

'Salmon, you ignoramus!' she heard Clarissa sneer. She swung round to her adversary. So, there was to be no respite from her sniping and bitching.

'I've never seen a salmon, so how the hell was I to know? We haven't all had your advantages, Clarissa,' she said with spirit.

'That is painfully obvious to us all,' Clarissa drawled.

'Clarissa, behave yourself or leave the room,' her father admonished her. Behind his back Clarissa pulled a face at him. 'They are beautiful, Jane, you're quite right.' Rupert spoke reassuringly. 'I must speak to Mac tomorrow, Alistair, there's obviously a grilse run on. We should get some good fishing in the next few days.'

Immediately Jane regretted mentioning the fish. By talking about them she seemed to have ensured that someone would go out and kill them.

In her excitement she had not noticed Lady Upnor sitting in a large wing chair. She greeted her and apologized for the lapse, but her mother-in-law ignored her and said to Alistair, 'Could you make sure that your wife keeps to our timetable while she is here?'

Alistair looked thunderous, but said nothing. Jane felt the usual wave of fear which this woman engendered in her. Like so many of her generation and class, Lady Upnor was an imperious being who would brook no dissension. Since her own mother-in-law had died, her word had been law at Respryn and no one could recollect her ever being contradicted, except by her husband. So she sailed on a sea of rudeness and bigotry, oblivious to the harm and hurt she caused: everyone accepted her behaviour as her right and perfectly normal in the scheme of things.

Jane survived lunch, but only because she was sitting at Rupert's right hand. She had already learned enough to know that she was placed there because of Alistair's title. What a strange woman Lady Upnor was, rude to the point of ignoring Jane herself yet strictly observing the codes of etiquette as far as Jane's position in society was concerned. As the only other married and titled woman present, Jane was given the seat of honour beside Rupert. It showed a depth of hypocrisy that only widened the gap between Jane and her mother-in-law.

More guests arrived in the afternoon and in the bustle of greetings, Jane was able to slip away. She decided that the oppressive room was more welcoming than Lady Upnor.

Alistair, in high spirits, joined her to change for dinner. She watched with fascination as he donned the paraphernalia of Highland dress. It made him look different, more masculine somehow: even the way he moved had altered, with a proud strut as the kilt pleats swung behind him.

'You look fantastic, Alistair.'

'I like wearing the kilt. I'm told I've the ideal arse for it. Don't you agree?'

She laughed at him preening in front of the mirror.

'What happens tonight, Alistair? Why the party clothes?' she asked.

'Pa's first night here is always a party. Lots of local friends come over. But you can slip off to bed when you want – the ladies usually do. We men tend to drink the night away and play billiards. It's great fun!'

The hall certainly looked different. Giant candles lit the room and a huge log fire burned in the grate; the long table was ablaze with more candles. Fortunately the walls were in shadow, so that Jane was spared the dead animal heads glaring accusingly at her.

Lord Upnor's friends began to arrive, the men all kilted and the women in soft, coloured, long cashmere skirts and jumpers. They all knew each other and the noise of their reunion was deafening. A piper appeared and piped them in to dinner, where the food was the best Jane had tasted in an Upnor house: a succulent saddle of venison with perfectly roasted potatoes and bright red rowan jelly. As a married couple, Jane and Alistair were separated at the dinner table and he was seated several places away. Jane found herself between a deaf old general, who tried to hear what she said but with whom conversation was impossible, and one of Clarissa's smooth male friends from London.

'Pity you missed the May ball,' he said without preamble.

'What May ball?' she asked.

'First week in June. It was good fun. Alistair was in cracking form. He's topping fun when he's drunk, isn't he?' The man chortled.

'I was working,' she said, her face stiff with the inner shock she was feeling.

'Yes, Alistair said you were. Ghastly job, nursing, I mean. What?'

As if from a long way away she heard the young man prattling on, but for Jane conversation was impossible. She sat isolated at the noisy, glittering table. It seemed to her that everything had gone dark. She could only sit and try to sieve through the turmoil of her thoughts. What she minded most was not that Alistair had gone to the ball, but that he had not told her about it. There had to be an explanation, she reasoned. She would not think about it now.

She must not let her thoughts spoil this evening. With great control she turned once again to the young man to ask him what he did.

After dinner they returned to the hall where the large refectory table had been manhandled to one side. The piper reappeared. People took up positions on the floor, talking idly while the man tuned his pipes, making an agonizing wailing noise as he did so. Everyone seemed to know exactly which reel he was going to play, for as soon as he started, the dancers hurled themselves into the patterns of the dance. In the afternoon Jane had noticed a gallery above the hall and, finding the staircase, she climbed up to get a better view. Beneath her the dancers moved from one reel to another, each of them knowing the steps perfectly. No one put a foot wrong. Jane was reminded of the ever changing patterns of a child's kaleidoscope as she watched the swirling tartans of the kilts, and the plaids worn by the women across their shoulders. There was much whooping and shouting from the men as they twirled the women around in intricate formations. While the dances were beautiful to look at, there was a barely controlled violence to them.

By one o'clock she felt tired enough to drop, and searched out Alistair.

'Can we go to bed now, darling?'

'Don't be daft, the night's young. You go if you want. I'm not.' With a loud whoop he put his arm round a pretty girl and led her off in another dance.

Jane slipped away and found their room with difficulty. Two oil lamps glowed, casting long, dark shadows on the walls. She slipped into the giant bed and peered into the shadows. She began to hear noises, a faint tapping and a strange sighing. She was shivering and put on a jumper and a pair of Alistair's socks. She longed for Alistair. She was hurt that he had not come when she asked – after all, they had only been married for seven weeks – but realized this was unreasonable. He was having such fun she should feel happy for him. But she did not. She knew she could not have fun without him beside her; yet he seemed capable of it without her. On the other hand it was not his fault that she could not dance the reel. She would learn: yes, she would ask a maid or someone to teach her, then she would not have to stand and watch. It must look odd, though, she thought, newly wed and he downstairs while she was alone in bed. She lay wide-eyed in the flickering light, trying not to think of Alistair dancing with other women, and of him at May balls without her. She shivered again. She knew she would never get to sleep in this ghostly room . . .

Despite her fears she slept, only to be woken by a heart-stopping shock as Alistair crashed drunkenly through the door.

'You missed a good party,' he slurred as he struggled out of his finery.

'God, you startled me, Alistair! This room is creepy.'

'Christ, Jane, don't be so bloody wet!' he snarled.

His tone of voice was so contemptuous that she felt as if she had been struck. The whisky fumes on his breath made her turn her head away in disgust. Violently he made love to her and she cried out because he hurt her, but he either did not hear or did not care. Finished with her, he slumped to his side of the bed and quickly fell into a deep sleep. For Jane sleep was a long time coming.

2

'Come on, darling, up you get! It's the Glorious Twelfth. It's the big shoot today.'

She opened her eyes. There was her Alistair, the man she loved, not the violent stranger of the night before. He kissed her tenderly as he did each morning.

'What's that?' he asked, pointing at a large bruise on her breast.

'It's a bruise. You made it last night.'

'Darling, I'm so sorry. Was I a brute?'

'Yes.' Her voice was cold.

'I was drunk.'

'I know.'

'It won't happen again, I promise.'

'I'm your wife, you know, not a whore,' she spat at him.

He looked so downcast that, despite herself, she felt a rush of love for her husband. Surely he meant it this time. Abruptly she changed the subject. 'Darling, I was scared stiff last night. Before you came up, I heard these terrible noises.' She attempted to imitate them, and he laughed.

'Poor darling, I should have warned you. It was the wind howling in the turret and the hot-water pipes tapping – and then I crash in like a monster . . .' He held her in his arms, kissing her hair, the bruise on her breast. 'This won't do, though. Come on, we'll be late. I want you to see the shoot.'

'What are you shooting?'

'Grouse, of course.'

'What's grouse?'

'Jane, you're so funny. You don't mean to say you don't know what grouse are? They're birds, delicious things.'

'I never heard of them.'

'You know, sometimes it amazes me how ignorant you are.'

'I'm sorry,' she said stiffly. 'I don't think you get grouse in Kent and, if you don't mind, I'd rather not go.'

'I do mind. I want you to come, it's great fun. You can stay in my butt with me, and I'll even let you have a go.'

'But I know I'd hate seeing animals shot, and I certainly have no desire to "have a go".'

'For heaven's sake, Jane, they're only birds, don't be so soft. Why on earth do you think we came here?' He tugged at the blanket. 'Come on.'

Reluctantly she did as he bid. She knew this constant carping was bringing out the worst in both of them. They ate a quick breakfast and then joined the rest of the party in the hall. The others were dressed in hairy tweeds and thick boots and sported the most extraordinary collection of headgear. The whole party looked shapeless and sexless.

'Jane coming? Good girl,' said Lord Upnor.

'Yes, Pa, I want her to see the shoot.'

'Well, she can't go dressed like that,' his mother snorted. Jane was conscious of everyone looking at her in her slacks and Wellington boots, trench coat tightly belted, and with a scarf on her head.

'I haven't got anything else to wear,' she retorted, glaring pointedly at Alistair, who rarely noticed what she was wearing.

'She'll get soaked,' Lady Upnor snapped.

'I've got another riding mac she can borrow,' one of the other women volunteered pleasantly.

'Thank you very much,' Jane mumbled in furious embarrassment.

'You should come properly attired,' Lady Upnor continued to complain.

'I would have, if someone had told me what to wear,' Jane defended herself. Rather, if you'd had the bloody courtesy to tell me, she thought.

Jane's clothing finally sorted out, they climbed into Land-Rovers and drove up on the moor. As the vehicles climbed, they left the good weather behind and a soft mist began to fall. Eventually they could drive no further and so the party trudged across the moorland, the dogs leaping and barking excitedly around them. Jane soon discovered that the heather, which looked so soft and inviting to walk on, was very difficult to cross. Her Wellington boots kept slipping and, as she stumbled, she tended to drop behind the main party; she began to feel wet and miserable. She could sense Alistair's irritation as he had to stop frequently to wait for her.

They finally reached the butts, a long line of heather-covered fences shaped into little boxes. They found the butt which Rupert had allocated them and settled in on the damp earth, with Alistair's loader standing behind them.

'You shooting, M'Lady?' he asked.

'No, thanks,' she replied firmly.

'Of course she'll shoot, Fergus. Load her a gun. Look, Jane . . .' He proceeded to explain the gun's mechanism to her. 'There'll be a hell of a bang, so stand firm or it'll knock you over. Keep the stock tight against your shoulder and slide your left hand well up the gun, at the top to the fore-end. Then hand the gun back to Fergus here and he'll give you another. Look,' he said excitedly, 'look, here come the beaters. I used to do that as a lad.'

She peered through the mist and saw across the hillside a long line of boys and men walking towards them, their arms moving rhythmically as they beat the heather with their sticks. A flock of birds began to rise in front of them, and, in their panic to get away, swooped low towards the line of guns. The firing started.

The noise was deafening. The little birds, desperately trying to gain height away from this new danger, fell to the ground in droves. Jane crouched, horrified. The shooting ceased and out went the labradors, returning with the pathetic, dripping little carcasses in their mouths, tails wagging at their own cleverness. Alistair turned to her, his eyes blazing with excitement.

'Isn't it fun?'

The tears rolled down her cheeks. 'I think it's horrifying,' she cried.

'Christ, Jane, you can be such a bore at times. If you feel like that, why don't you bugger off then?' he shouted at her.

'I didn't want to come here in the first place!'

'I wish I had bloody well listened to you now!' They glared at each other with angry resentment. She turned her back on him and stalked off towards the Land-Rovers in the valley below. She tried to walk with dignity but her feet kept slipping and she lost count of the times she fell as she stumbled through the undergrowth. A young man was leaning against the nearest Land-Rover, and she noticed him hurriedly put out a cigarette as she approached.

'Would you be wanting tae get back tae the house, M'Lady?'

'Yes, please, if it's no bother.'

'Nothing's never nae bother, M'Lady.' Skilfully he turned the vehicle around in the soft mud. She offered him a cigarette.

'I shouldnae, really,' he said.

'Why not? You smoke, don't you?'

'Aye, but we're nae supposed to smoke in front of the gentry.'

'Well, I'm not gentry, so you're not breaking any rules if you smoke with me.' He gratefully accepted the cigarette, smiling at her words.

'D'ye nae like the shooting, then?'

'I hated it,' she said vehemently.

'Trouble is the wee birds make fine eating and someone's got tae shoot them if we're tae eat them.'

'Sure, but that's a massacre up there, and they call it sport!'

'Aye, shooting for the pot is fine. I have tae agree with you, it can go too far. A friend of mine works further south. He says the pheasants are the worst. They hand-rear them and then shoot them, and them poor birds learned to trust man. At least the grouse is wild.'

Jane shuddered. Sensing her mood he changed the subject, telling her the names of the various hills, talking about the wildlife which abounded, the badgers, the pine martens, the wild cats, the deer which, in winter when forage was low, would become so tame that he could feed them from his hand.

'Do you shoot them?'

'It's my job, M'Lady. It's necessary tae cull them or the poor beasties would get diseased and starve.'

'Do you like doing it?'

'It depends. If I've a stupid beast in me sights, then, aye, it deserves tae die for the sake of the rest, you see, before the bad blood gets passed on. But if I get a good, intelligent beast that I've stalked all day, and he's led me a real dance, then like as not I'll let him go. He'll breed again and maybe his intelligence and courage will enter his bairns.'

'I suppose it's really just another extension of the survival of the fittest.'

'Aye, M'Lady, something like that,' he said.

'But I don't understand how everyone enjoys it so. I mean, you do it for the good of the animals, really, but then Lord Upnor, why does he do it?'

'Ye know, M'Lady, he does nae shoot like he used tae. You see that, time and time again, the old men, they seem tae tire of it, would rather watch the animals than kill them. A day like today, well, it's traditional and his guests would expect it, but I've been on the hill with himself, and we've stalked a stag and at the end, he's got it in his sights, and he's just said bang and let the beastie live. Aye, you see it often. It's as if, as their own time approaches, they have nae got the same love for the killing. He's content with the fish.'

Jane liked this man who had such understanding of men as well as animals. She looked at him: he was tall and heavy, his muscles indicating enormous strength, but there was a sensitivity about him which seemed sadly lacking in the men of the house party. He promised to take her out one evening to see what they could find. 'The evening's best, they all pop out then. I suppose they feel safer. Perhaps they know that's when the guns are having a wee dram.' He laughed.

Back at the lodge, as she thanked him for bringing her home, the front door swung open and the rest of the female party appeared, carrying large picnic baskets.

'Given up then, sister-in-law? Get too much for you?' Clarissa taunted her. 'Couldn't take it?'

'I get cold easily.'

'Ha! Really? Expect us to believe that?'

'Believe what you bloody well like.' Jane turned away and climbed the steps to the house.

'Do you always have to sound like a fishwife?'

'It takes one to know one,' Jane countered.

'Mac, take us to the butts,' Clarissa imperiously ordered. Jane noticed with a quiet satisfaction that the man did not smile at Clarissa and her party as he had smiled at her.

She wandered down to the waterfall and watched what she now regarded as her fish. She had been married only seven weeks and already she and Alistair were having their first row. She wanted to leave this place where people only seemed to think and talk of killing. It was as if something had happened to change Alistair, who was behaving like a demon, she decided. She did not belong here and she did not want to belong. But she was married to Alistair, and that gave her every right to be here. She did not wish to be here, that was the difference. But what the hell was she to do? She could learn to set a table, seat people at it correctly, a million and one things, but she could never learn to enjoy the slaughter she had just seen.

She was reading on the big four-poster in their room when Alistair returned.

'Sulk over?' he snapped.

'I'm not sulking.'

'You could have fooled me.' He stomped about the room, scattering his damp clothes on the floor. 'You were a bloody disgrace up there on the moor. Made me look a bloody fool, stalking off like that, leaving me alone in the butt.'

'If I remember rightly, you told me to "bugger off",' she shouted angrily back at him.

'A real bloody fool,' he muttered as he stormed off to the bathroom. She lay on the bed tense with anger at the injustice.

'Why did you bloody well come then?' he asked, returning from his bath towelling his hair roughly in his rage.

'I won't again.'

'Good,' he snapped. 'At least I can have some fun if you're not there.'

'Fun! You call it fun, slaughtering poor little birds that don't stand a chance?'

'Jesus! I'm married to a St Francis of Assisi! Of course the birds stand a chance. We don't shoot them all – hundreds get away. In any case, how the hell do you think your food gets on the table? If you feel that strongly about it, then become a vegetarian. At least you wouldn't be a bloody hypocrite.'

'Don't you dare call me a hypocrite! That's the last thing I am. Your mother's reserved all the hypocrisy for herself. She's a bloody professor of hypocrisy!' Jane stormed.

'Leave my mother out of this.'

'A bit difficult to do as she's intent on making me look a fool at every turn.'

'You're fucking paranoid, I always said you were,' he shouted. 'You made yourself look a fool this morning, and me into the bargain. Bad-tempered little bitch, you were –'

'Alistair, stop shouting at me. I can't stand being shouted at. I'm sorry, I've said I'm sorry,' she screamed. 'I didn't know it was going to be like that, I've never seen anything killed in my life, it made me feel ill. If I'd known how awful it was going to be, I'd never have gone in the first place. But, please, for heaven's sake, stop saying what fun it is!'

Silently he started to get dressed. 'It's time you changed for dinner.'

'I don't want to go down to dinner.'

'You've got to.'

'I haven't got to do anything,' she snapped angrily.

'You're bloody well coming down to dinner. What the hell will people think if you stay sulking up here? They'll start to say I can't control my own wife.'

She picked at the bedcover. 'Did you enjoy the May ball?' As she spoke, she knew this was not the time to ask, but she could not seem to stop herself.

He swung round, glancing quickly at her, but then averted his eyes, guiltily, Jane was certain. 'So, did you have a good time?' she persisted.

'Yes, as a matter of fact, I did,' he answered defiantly.

'Without me?'

'Yes, I'm quite capable of enjoying myself without you.'

'You probably enjoyed it more because I wasn't there.'

'I didn't say that.'

'You didn't have to.' They glared at each other across the white counterpane. Alistair began to brush his hair and then to splash aftershave on his cheeks, but in his agitation more landed on his shoulders than on his face. 'Why didn't you tell me?'

'I didn't think.'

'Why didn't you ask me to go?'

'I didn't think it was the sort of thing that you would be happy at.'

'Is that another way of saying – "out of place"?'

'If you like, yes.'

'Too posh for me?'

'Don't be silly.'

'I'm not being silly. I'm stating facts, aren't I? You didn't invite me because you were ashamed of me. Thought I'd be a duck out of water – '

'Christ, Jane, you've got one hell of a bloody chip on your shoulder!'

'Who did you take?' She had gone too far now, but she had to know all there was to know, no matter how much it hurt.

'I went with Clarissa and a whole gang. I didn't take anyone in particular.'

'I think you're a shit,' she hissed at him.

'God, woman, listen to you.' He looked at her with disgust. 'OK, I'll tell you the real reason. I didn't ask you because I knew you'd start bleating on about me drinking and having fun. There, that's the truth. You spoil things for me,' he added as a petulant afterthought.

Jane bent her head to hide the tears. His last remark was too near the bone. She had only herself to blame. She had engineered this row, just as her mother used to do. Alistair looked across the room at her, her dark hair falling loose across her breasts. Changing his tactics, he came over and put his arm about her.

'Jane, come on, love, I don't want to quarrel. You're right about everything. I should have warned you about the shoot. And it was unforgivable of me to go to the ball without telling you. It was the last, defiant gesture of a bachelor. I'm sorry, my darling. Forgive me. I didn't mean those horrible things I said.' He made her look at him. 'Come on, Jay, cheer up – let's be friends, Jane, please?' She put her arms up to him and he kissed her. 'That's better. Get changed, there's a good girl.'

Quickly she dressed and hand in hand they went down to dinner. The talk all through the long evening was of the 'bag': who had killed what and how many. The game book was produced and ceremoniously filled in with the details. Jane found she could hardly eat the food put in front of her.

That night, she again slipped off to bed before the others. In the middle of the night a drunken Alistair once more blundered into the room, into the bed. This time she recoiled in terror, desperately trying to escape his grasping hands. She rolled off the bed. He leaned across and grabbed her, pulling her back towards him. Her attempts to escape him seemed to amuse him for he laughed loudly as he tore the fabric of her nightie. Her nightdress in shreds, she covered her bare breasts with her hands.

'Alistair, please.' But her pleading only seemed to inflame his passion further, as violently he possessed her.

The two weeks dragged interminably for her. There was a wildness to them all here that was not present in England. Certainly everybody seemed to drink more, but Jane also wondered if some of the wildness was not induced by the excitement they found in the shooting. How else could she explain their pleasure in hurling billiard balls at each other, smashing the glass in the prints around the walls? Sometimes, in the night, one of them would climb the tower and hurl chamberpots from the battlements for the others to shoot at drunkenly. And what possessed them to 'mine' the carefully tended front lawn with thunder flashes which exploded with a terrifying crash when triggered by the front door being opened by an unsuspecting Banks? In the morning the lawn was completely wrecked, and the gardener was in despair, but it was still regarded as enormous 'fun' by everyone – except Jane. It was the violence of their humour that disturbed her most of all.

She was lonely. She spent most of her time reading, watched her fish for hours at a time and walked in the forest. Her mother-in-law continued to ignore her, which heightened her feeling of isolation. The talk seemed always to be of death: the dead animal's heads in the house haunted her. She wanted to be anywhere else. Each night the husband she loved, the gentle, considerate lover of her honeymoon, staggered late to bed and raped her.

She longed for her home, and for the Alistair she knew and loved, to return to her.

3

He did return, but not until they were safely back in their house at Respryn. He never mentioned his behaviour in Scotland, never apologized, as if he had no recollection of the incidents whatsoever. Jane reasoned that the courteous, kind person he normally was would certainly have said he was sorry. As in Cambridge, when he had crashed through the glass door, the only link was whisky. It seemed to act like a poison on him. Since he rarely drank spirits in England, there seemed no point in mentioning it. She would try to forget about it herself, but she knew that she never wanted to return to Scotland with him, never wanted to relive the nightmare of the past few weeks.

She settled happily into their house, Trinick. She took pride in the beautiful possessions which Alistair barely noticed. He was so used to being surrounded by lovely things, but they were a constant source of joy and wonder to Jane.

Upon their return, Alistair had arranged for her to interview several women for her staff. She was horrified at the prospect.

'But I don't want any staff,' she argued.

'Don't be silly, darling, of course you do. The house isn't that small. How could you possibly manage?'

'I'd go mad with not enough to do all day.'

'That's ridiculous, there would still be masses to do. I don't want you turning into a drudge, my sweet.'

'No, really, Alistair, I'd rather not. I want to do it myself.' She was afraid to have staff: she knew that she would not know how to handle them, or what to say to them.

'You're afraid to have staff,' he said accusingly.

'Don't be daft,' she lied. It was strange how often she told little lies to him these days, when in the past she had told only the truth, she thought.

'Well, at least have a char.'

'I might do that,' she acquiesced. She thought she could deal with a charwoman, it would be no different from asking one of the ward maids to do something. In fact, it would probably be far easier than dealing with the ward maids, a fiercely independent breed, united in their jealousy and hatred of the nurses. 'Yes, all right. I'll have a char.'

'Good. And a cook. Now we can't exist without a cook, can we?'

'Oh, Alistair, you are funny. Of course we can exist. I want to cook for you. That's most definitely my job. And, anyway, what about the expense?'

'The expense is no problem. When will you get it into your head that you don't have to worry about money any more? If that's all that's bothering you, we'll arrange a cook immediately.'

'No, no,' she said hastily. 'I want to do it myself.' She knew that she would be at a disadvantage with a cook, for the cook would know more than she, would sneer at her behind her back, at her ignorance of which sauce went with what. Not until she had taught herself some of the basics would she even consider such a prospect. But she did not explain any of this to Alistair.

'But you can't cook.'

'I'm learning.'

'That could take ages. Think of my poor stomach, meanwhile.'

'I'll learn quickly, I promise.'

She kept her promise. She bought a pile of cook books which she studied as seriously as any student preparing for exams. She talked endlessly with the butcher and fishmonger, asking their advice. Complimented by her interest they were happy to advise her, selling her only the very best and recommending methods and times of cooking.

Inadvertently the butcher helped her to put her marriage drama into some sort of perspective. Returning one day, she unwrapped the dog's bones from the newspaper they were in, only to see her own and Alistair's faces smiling at her from the newsprint, like strangers. Why had she felt so ashamed at the time? She spread the crumpled paper on the kitchen table and studied the blurred image. Alistair had been right when he told her it was a one-day wonder and that they would be used to wrap fish and chips the next day. All that drama, the reporters popping out at them from the darkness, the feelings of panic, of shame, of embarrassment – to end up as a dog's bone wrapper! At last, this made it all seem as ridiculous as it should have seemed at the time.

Alistair had found a gardener who began rapidly to transform the garden. Jane took a great interest in everything he did and why, poring over seed catalogues and gardening books, but always referring back to the wisdom of Bert, who confided to his wife that he had never been happier in a job. He felt appreciated for once.

Alistair had given way to her on the question of servants but had insisted that, while she could do what she liked, he was going to have a valet. All married men in his position had valets, he stated. Mark joined their small household a few days later. Unlike most valets, he was willing to turn his hand to any job and help Jane with the odd repairs about the house: he cleaned the silver and even peeled the potatoes. He had been all over the world in his job and Jane would sit with a cup of coffee at the kitchen table, listening entranced to his gossip of life in high places. He was a mine of information of how things should be done and how people should be addressed – Jane used him as her personal etiquette expert. Unknown to her, their odd domestic arrangements were the talk of the neighbourhood.

Alistair had been right: she saw little of his mother. Lady Upnor came to Respryn only at weekends, preferring the social life of London during the week. They were rarely invited to the big house and then only when there was a large party where their absence would have been noted, and where it was possible for Lady Upnor to ignore Jane in the crowd. Yet while she was apparently ignored, Jane was aware of the older woman watching her all the time, waiting for her to make a fool of herself. It made Jane uncomfortable and even more nervous. She hated these evenings and attended them only for the sake of Alistair and his father.

Rupert had taken to popping in several times a week for coffee. He would sit at the kitchen table while Jane cooked, enjoying her company and talking about everything under the sun. Had she had a cook, she pointed out to Alistair gleefully, Rupert would not have felt nearly as free to come and relax with her. As the weeks went by, she began to love Rupert deeply for his kind, wise personality and his instinctive understanding of her problems.

Honor was a regular visitor whenever she was staying at Respryn. She would often invite herself to dinner rather than eat at the big house. As she explained, the food and company were better. But Honor never stayed long enough for Jane, who would have been happy if she had stayed for months at a time. Instead she would alight at Respryn for a couple of days and then rush off to some distant spot.

Alistair enjoyed working for his father, learning much from him and Lockhart, the estate manager. He was away early each morning but he would return for breakfast and lunch, and with Rupert's visits as well, Jane never felt lonely. As the weeks went by, the hard physical work that Alistair insisted on doing, for it was the only way to learn, he said, made his body more muscular and even more attractive to Jane. The long hours in the open ensured that he was always brown. She marvelled at the fact that the man she had thought perfect became daily more handsome in her eyes.

As her cooking improved, she gained confidence and they began to have friends to dinner. They had begun to form friendships with Lockhart, the local doctor and the vet, who were young and, like themselves, recently married. With these people she was relaxed; she could entertain them confidently, make them laugh, be herself. She was amazed one evening to discover that none of them had ever been invited socially to the big house.

'Never, Richard? But you're their doctor, too.'

'I know, but it's a throwback to the Victorian and Edwardian eras when doctors were classed with farriers and expected to use the tradesmen's entrance.'

'But, Richard, you don't use the tradesmen's entrance, do you?' she asked, shocked.

'Not likely. On principle. But my father did during all the years he treated them.'

'God, that's awful, isn't it, Alistair? After all, who's more important than your doctor and your vet?'

Alistair was as surprised as she. He had to apologize: he had never given it a thought, he explained. Later, among themselves, the others discussed how things would change when the old boy and his wife died and what a breath of fresh air Jane would be. But they never told her how they regarded her.

It was Alistair who suggested that her parents should come to stay. Her mother had answered the letter she had written the day before her marriage. It had been the only letter she had ever received from her parents and it was a strange mixture of forgiveness and admonishment. This was followed by a large parcel containing a lurid pink, heavily embroidered eiderdown which she loathed on sight and knew she would never use. Yet she wept over it, for it was far too expensive for them to afford and its very garishness seemed to highlight the great gulf that lay between them. That had been months ago and now she had guiltily to admit to herself that she rarely thought of them these days. The life she had led with them and this new life seemed a million miles apart. She confessed that she did not want them to be part of her new life. But Alistair insisted.

'You can't just cut yourself off. They are your parents, after all.'

'I know, but I've got you now. I don't need anyone else. We've nothing in common. Hell, they never write or anything.'

'I still think you should invite them. Perhaps they're waiting for you to approach them.'

'Father won't like it here. He'll probably be rude to you.'

'Then we'll be quits over my mother.' He laughed, and she had to invite them, despite her misgivings.

Alistair was busy, and since she had not yet passed her driving test she sent Mark to pick them up. Inadvertently she insulted her parents, who felt slighted and were a little sulky when they arrived.

Jane purposely kept the food simple, knowing her father's taste. Even so, he toyed with his roast beef and left all his vegetables.

'Didn't you like the veg, Dad?'

'They weren't cooked,' he grunted.

'But that's the proper way to cook them, with a little bite still in them,' she explained.

'It might be the "proper" way to you, it isn't to me. I don't like raw vegetables – gives you worms.'

Despite Jane's efforts, neither parent made any attempt at conversation during the meal and she remembered the silent meals of her youth. Already she had changed, already she regarded good conversation as important a part of the meal as the food.

She noted much about her parents that she had not seen before or of which she had been unaware. How loudly her father ate, how careless he was at putting the food in his mouth. He virtually shovelled it in so that it was unpleasant to watch him. She became fascinated by the way her mother grimly held her knife and fork between mouthfuls, the handles firmly clutched in her fists, standing sentinel over her plate as if she were afraid that if she laid them down, her food would disappear. Had she always eaten like that? With horror Jane listened to her mother's strangulated accent: presumably she thought that it was an improvement on her normal speech, that she sounded genteel, but it was merely dreadful. At the dining table and later in the drawing room, her mother sat poised and uncomfortable on the edge of her chair as if she were about to spring up and leave. Jane longed to push her back on the cushions, tell her to relax, wishing she could help her mother, who was so obviously ill at ease, but unable to think what to say. She asked if they would like to meet some of her friends while they were staying. Her mother hurriedly, too hurriedly, said no, they did not want to bother with other people: it was Jane and Alistair they had come to see.

The next morning Alistair took them both for a ride around the estate in the Land-Rover. He returned, looking hot and bothered, without her parents.

'What happened?' she asked.

'He refused to ride with me, insisted on getting out halfway round, after lecturing me that my father's ownership of the estate was an obscenity and that I was a parasite, and what would I be fit for when the great day came and all the land was nationalized? He's gone off now to talk to the "workers", as he put it. Wants to talk to them without any "bosses in tow".'

'That sounds like Dad. Where's Mum?'

'She went with him, looking all flustered.' He managed to laugh.

'Mum will have gone to try and stop him getting into any fights. I did say I didn't think there was much point in them coming. He was certain to hate all this. Like a lot of working-class socialists he's against anybody having anything he hasn't got – that is, until he gets it.' She laughed ruefully.

Eventually her parents returned and her father went immediately into the study and settled down silently with the newspaper.

'What happened, Mum?'

'Right bloody fool he made of himself. Started asking all manner of questions of these farmworkers we met – rude questions, I thought – like how much did they earn and how many hours they worked, and what about overtime, that sort of thing. Then he began to run the system here down, and those men gave him a right mouthful. They told him they didn't need his nasty Commie talk here, that they were very happy and if all he'd come for was to be rude about Lord Upnor and his son, then he had better get off their land or they'd throw him off!'

'Oh, dear. Poor Dad.'

'Poor Dad, my aunt Fanny. He's a bloody stubborn old fool and he just seems to get worse.'

'Mum, would you like to see the big house this afternoon? She's not there this weekend, so you won't run into the old ogress.' Her mother was thrilled at the idea but her father refused to accompany them, saying he did not want to see any more trappings of decadent wealth. They left him with his newspaper while she and her mother toured the house together. When they returned, it was to find her father standing in the hall, with their bags packed beside him, demanding to be taken home.

'But, Dad, this is silly,' Jane pleaded. 'You have a couple more days yet. And Alistair's father will be here tomorrow. He so wants to meet you.'

'I'm not being silly. I don't like it here, I don't like the system, I don't want to be part of it, even for a weekend. I feel I'm betraying my class by being here. And if you think I'm waiting around here to meet a bloody earl or whatever he is, you've another think coming.'

'Dad, that's ludicrous.'

'It's not ludicrous, Jane. You've gone over, but not me. We have nothing in common any longer with you, Jane, or your husband. I'd rather not be involved, I'd rather go.'

She arranged for Mark to drive them back. She felt she should be sad, but she was not. They had never been her friends, so why should anything have altered now? While she found her father stupidly bigoted, she had to admire the fact that he stuck so steadfastly to his principles. Her father was right, they did not have anything in common any more, only the accident of birth. This was her home now, her friends were here, her security was here. She took the eiderdown which she had put on her and Alistair's bed for the duration of her parents' visit, wrapped it carefully, packed it with mothballs and put it at the back of the large airing cupboard.

4

As the months sped by, Jane's confidence in herself and her ability to manage grew daily. Their circle of friends was still small, partly because they met few people. The people in the other large local houses did not invite them, except for the Duchess of Wessex, who had them to dinner several times and who, in turn, had visited them. Jane felt as much at ease with her as she did when Honor or the vet and his wife came to dinner.

'Did you use to be invited to all the other houses?' she asked her husband one evening. That morning Rupert had been telling her of the dinner dance they had been to at the neighbouring estate.

'Yes.'

'Then why not now? Because of me, I suppose?'

'I think it's more that they've heard that my mother doesn't approve and they're frightened to offend her and perhaps not get invited to the parties at Respryn.'

'But the Duchess has us over.'

'She doesn't have to give a monkey's what Mother thinks. It's all about the old pecking order, isn't it? The Duchess can do what she likes about us, because Mother dare not be offended or she won't get invited to the castle! Remember, duchesses are the heavy artillery in the English social scene.'

'Heavens, it's like a game of musical chairs. I hope I never get like that – not having people around because I'm frightened of what those higher in the pecking order might think.'

'No, darling, I don't think you'll get like that for one moment,' he laughingly assured her. 'I don't mind either, you know that.'

'But Linda and Bertie Talbot have been very kind, and she's as thick as thieves with your mother.' It was true, the Talbots had gone out of their way to be friendly, often having them to supper, and Jane had an open invitation to pop in any time she wanted, which she often did.

'I've wondered about them,' Alistair said thoughtfully. 'It's very strange. As you say, she's very close to Mother. Have you ever thought that perhaps Mother's using Linda to report back on what we're up to? Or maybe she believes in keeping a foot in each camp so we'll still have her over when I inherit.'

'Alistair, how can you think such a thing? They've been so kind to me. I think, having no children of their own, they like young people about. I was scared of them at first but now I'm really happy to go there. Perhaps because they're so eccentric your mother overlooks their being nice to me as just another quirk?'

'They certainly work hard at being eccentric,' Alistair answered enigmatically.

Eccentric they surely were. Jane delighted in it and admired the total confidence in themselves which enabled them to look and act as they wanted, and to hell with everyone else. They lived in a large Palladian house which, through sheer neglect, was falling apart about their ears, the Talbots being of that breed of house-owner which feels that owning a property is enough. In consequence the house was literally crumbling: large cracks had appeared in its façade, masonry lay where it had fallen from the balustrade. The steps were cracked and weed-choked, the drive a nightmare of unfilled potholes. The inside of the house was no better; their furniture looked shrivelled from neglect and lack of polish. The dogs dirtied the beautiful old carpets, the smell of boiled cabbage filled the air. Linda was very like her house, her once fine face now wrinkled and dried from years of neglect and undernourishment, her clothes a total hotch-potch of old tweeds and strange shapeless jumpers which she knitted in random stripes. A meal there could be a fine dinner eaten from lovely porcelain with crested silver, or baked beans on toast eaten sitting on the floor, with the dogs and cats fighting round about.

Both Talbots were more right-wing than anyone Jane had ever met, but she was able to enjoy their political views because they were too extreme to take seriously. Linda's conviction that Communists lurked everywhere, not only under the prime minister's bed but probably in it as well, only added to Jane's amusement. She liked them and she trusted them, found it easy to talk to Linda and had begun slowly to confide in her. She would often ask her advice about a menu or how to answer a letter or address an envelope to some titled person.

The Talbots' vegetable garden was as weed-choked as their drive. Now that, thanks to Mark's patient help, Jane had passed her driving test, she had fallen into the habit of dropping in with baskets of vegetables from the abundant flow her own gardener supplied. One morning she rang the bell as usual, but there was no reply. This was not uncommon, so she let herself in, as she had been told to do. She could hear Linda's strident voice on the telephone in a room off the hall, and she waited.

'I know, it's a desperate problem, she's out of her mind with worry,' Linda barked into the phone. There was a pause as the other person spoke. 'I have them over quite a bit, really, so that I can let her know what's going on. I mean, she tries hard enough, I'll give her that. She's always dropping in and asking advice. My dear, if I told you the things that gel doesn't know, you'd be amazed!' She laughed stridently. 'It's no good, though. It's not going to work. It's the vowels, you see, the vowels always let them down.' Another pause. 'Oh, very pretty, but it won't last, she'll run to fat. All tits and arse, as Bertie says.' Linda laughed again, loudly. Heavens, thought Jane, what a bitch

Linda could be at times! Strange in such a kind woman. 'Yes, I know,' Linda's voice continued. 'Well, I've told her to pray for a divorce and hope it comes before a brat is born. Poor old Blanche, she doesn't deserve all this.'

Jane heard no more. She stood rooted to the spot. She wanted to run but her legs felt leaden and would not move. The blood was drumming in her ears and made her feel faint. Linda appeared in the doorway.

'Jane, what a lovely surprise! Let me get Bertie to see his favourite neighbour. How long have you been here?' she asked pleasantly.

'Long enough, you cow! You hypocritical cow!' Jane shouted. 'I trusted you,' she wailed, and with a heave she threw the bag of vegetables at the astonished Linda. Jane rushed out of the door and ran down the steps, stumbling in her haste on the moss-covered step. She drove at breakneck speed back to the haven of her house. She had no need to explain to Alistair, because, on his return home in the evening, he received a long phone call from his mother. When it was over, he came back into the drawing room.

'What happened?' he asked. When she told him he said, 'I see, I'm sorry. Perhaps it would have been better if you hadn't called her a cow and thrown the veg at her.'

'She is a cow.'

'I know, but you shouldn't have said it.'

'Why not?' Jane demanded angrily.

'It will only be used against you. You only prove to them their theories about you.'

'I don't care what they think about me. I'll say what I bloody well like.'

'I know, I know, Jay. But sometimes it's more dignified to walk away from a situation – silently.'

'Sod dignity. She hurt me, don't you understand?'

'I understand. I'm just trying to warn you, that's all. What's for dinner?' he asked, and the incident was never mentioned between them again.

But the damage to Jane was enormous. The confidence she had so painstakingly begun to build was shattered. She had lost her capacity to trust, and she had lost faith in her own ability to judge people. She met people now only with reluctance, and the happy little dinner parties ceased.

She had said she did not care what people thought, but that was not true: she cared very much. She had been so determined to succeed, to show them that she could learn, become what people wanted her to be. She bought the book on correct word usage that Alistair had mentioned once, as a joke, and studied it surreptitiously. She made lists of words to memorize. Some were easy – her 'handbag' became her 'bag', though she still winced when she bravely said 'loo' instead of 'toilet'. She now sat on her 'sofa' instead of her 'settee'. She had learned to say 'What?' to Alistair but maintained her 'pardon' for the char and the girl who helped with the ironing, for she still had a deep distrust of this rude word 'what'. But some words she could not remember: they sounded too awkward and clumsy on her tongue and refused to lodge in her brain so that she still had a 'mantelpiece' instead of a 'chimneypiece' and hers was a 'mirror' and not a 'looking glass'.

She approached vowels with wariness and fear. A, E and U seemed the kindest but even these, when combined with the dreaded O and I, lurked to trip her up. She learned cunning with her use of words and asked people if they wanted their tea black, for no matter how she tried she could not say 'milk' as she knew it should sound to 'them'. She invited people to her place instead of her house. In conversation she adopted a slight stutter in a pathetic attempt to disguise her panic as words full of the dreaded vowels loomed ahead in a sentence. Silliest of all, she could not say 'vowel' either.

Once a month they would go to London for a long weekend. She looked forward desperately to these trips. They would see Alistair's friends from Cambridge who now had jobs in the City, and Sandra would come to dinner. Sandra was now a staff nurse and engaged to an aspiring estate agent, Justin Clemance, who was quiet and a little pompous, not at all like the extrovert Sandra.

Only in London did the old Jane come out of her shell. Occasionally Alistair insisted they should give a dinner party at Trinick but she was never able to enjoy them. She felt sick with nerves for days beforehand. She was wary even with the few friends they had made. She would have only one friend here in the country, Alistair.

The following August she refused to go to Scotland with him. They had a blazing row, which frightened her with its intensity, and she nearly weakened in the face of Alistair's anger, but finally she was adamant. Alistair was furious and sulked for days but Jane was certain that by not going she was protecting their relationship, not harming it.

Their joy in each other when he returned was magical. She now knew she had been right not to go. On his return they made love with more depth and a new urgency. She was not surprised, a few weeks later, to find that she was pregnant. Alistair and his father were beside themselves with excitement. Even Alistair's mother relented sufficiently to buy some exquisite baby clothes, and Alistair reported that she was thrilled at the prospect of a grandchild, even if it was growing in the wrong body.

Jane had looked forward to being pregnant. She hated the reality. Not for her the joy of a placid pregnancy, or the compensation of floating through it with an ethereal beauty. She was sick. She felt clumsy. She became fat. She wanted her body back.

Alistair was a considerate expectant father. If Jane felt ugly, he was at pains to reassure her that to him she was beautiful. He put up with her fluctuating moods. The only disagreement between them was over the question of a nanny.

'But I don't want a nanny, I'm not letting some other woman look after my baby.'

'Jane, it's eccentric enough that you won't have a cook. We're having a nanny and that's that.'

'All right then, I'll get a cook and look after the baby myself.'

'No, my child has a nanny. You'll be tired when the baby is born. With a nanny here you'll have time to relax.'

The argument was still unresolved when Jane, on a beautiful June day, went into hospital and a boy was born. They called him James Rupert.

Jane held the unfamiliar bundle in her arms and scrutinized him for imperfections. But there were none; he was perfect. She wondered if he would love her and, as she wondered, became aware that, if he did, a day would come when he would love another woman more than her. In the acceptance and the mental preparation for it she had already shut a part of her heart away from him, though she did not realize it. Her feelings for him puzzled her, he must mean more than life itself to her – that was what being a mother was all about. But he did not. She still loved Alistair more than she loved her child.

Alistair described the party his father had given for the estate workers. The men had made a cradle for the baby and their wives had sewn a beautiful layette. Jane was touched beyond words when Alistair told her.

When she returned from the hospital with the baby, it was to find a sour-faced harridan in charge of the nursery and a cook in the kitchen.

'Alistair, she's horrible. She won't let me pick up James when I want, and I virtually have to make an appointment to go into the nursery.'

'It's your own fault. You should have agreed and then you could have chosen your own nanny, instead of my having to ask mother to find one.'

'Your mother! Oh no, they'll be in league together, she'll report back all the time. I can't live with her,' Jane wailed.

'All right then, make other arrangements. It's your department, not mine, but you'll have to sack her.'

Jane found a pleasant girl in the village who had trained as a nursery nurse and she plucked up courage to tell the terrifying nurse to go. It was the right decision. Both James and Jane liked Clare from the start and the baby thrived under her care.

Again August loomed, and Alistair asked her, 'Will you come to Drumloch this year, Jane?'

'I can't – the baby,' she excused herself.

'There's plenty of room for the baby and nanny and well you know it. Am I to take it you're refusing again?'

'I'd rather not go, Alistair.'

'Why not, for heaven's sake? I get bloody lonely up there without you – and horribly frustrated.'

'I'm sorry, I just can't come.'

'But why not? You needn't go on the shoots or anything, you know that – I agreed. Mother's easing up with you slowly, especially since James was born.

You can't spend the rest of your life pleading that you don't fit in. You've got to sooner or later.'

He kept questioning her, demanding to know the real reason why she would not go; Eventually she broke her pledge to herself.

'It's the change in you, Alistair. I can't bear it. You become a different person when you're there.'

'So, occasionally I get drunk up there. Heavens, it's the only time I do.'

'It's not just that, I don't mind you getting drunk. It's the way you behave when you are. I can't cope with it.'

'I don't know what the hell you're talking about.'

'I know, Alistair. And that's half the problem.'

'Come on, Jane, what do you mean?'

'You rape me, Alistair. Each night last time at Drumloch you raped me.'

'Don't talk such rubbish, Jane. You're exaggerating. Rape, that's too strong a word.'

'It's not too strong a word. It's best I stay here.'

'Well, don't be surprised if I'm unfaithful to you up there one of these years,' he shouted at her.

'She's welcome to you like that,' she shouted back, as he stormed from the room. His head reappeared around the door.

'Sometimes, Jane, I want to hit you!' He slammed the door shut. Always Scotland, that was the only time they rowed. What was it about that house?

So this year, as before, he went without her. To distract herself, Jane did what she often did now when she was upset – she embarked on a bout of vigorous housework, and decided to spring-clean the house.

Alistair had been gone a week, and she was beginning to enjoy the sheer physical effort the house demanded of her. Her figure was rapidly returning to normal and she was full of energy again. She and her cleaning woman were busy in the drawing room late one morning, when the telephone rang.

'Jay, darling.' It was Alistair, but his voice sounded strange, thick and muffled.

'Darling, can you speak up? The line is dreadful. You sound as if you're at the bottom of the sea.' She laughed.

'Jane, it's Pa – he's dead. Please, come quickly.'

Jane stood stunned. 'Oh, my poor darling! Yes, of course, I'll come immediately.'

'Get Lockhart. Get him to arrange an aeroplane for you. You can fly from Plymouth to Inverness.'

'Yes, darling, of course. Are you all right?'

'Bloody.'

'I love you,' she said, but the phone had already gone dead.

Lockhart, stunned as she herself was, arranged the hire of a light aeroplane. Jane hurriedly packed their bags, while Clare, the nanny, prepared James for the journey. Within a couple of hours they were in the air. They had to refuel on the way and she waited impatiently, desperate to be with Alistair to find out what had happened, hardly able to believe what she had heard. There must be some ghastly mistake. Not Rupert, not that darling man.

They landed at Inverness. Tucker was waiting for her with the Rolls-Royce. He touched his cap.

'A sad day, Lady Upnor.'

Jane swung round, looking for her mother-in-law – but there was no one there but Clare and the baby. In that moment she knew that Rupert was dead, but in his dying her life had taken another enormous lurch forward. She was the countess now.

5

Jane settled the baby and Clare in the back of the Rolls and climbed in the front with Tucker.

'What happened, Tucker?' she asked as the car sped through the gathering dusk.

'We are not sure, M'Lady. After breakfast his lordship went for a walk. When he didn't come back, and the guns were waiting, we went in search of him. We found him down a gully by the Maid's Pool. You know, M'Lady, the stretch where the river really narrows through the rocks?' She nodded. 'Lying half in the water, he was, and soaked to the skin. He was still alive, but only just. We got him back to the house and called the doctor, but it was too late.'

'So he died of his injuries?'

'We don't know, M'Lady. They've taken him to Inverness for the doctors to find out, M'Lady.'

They drove on in silence. If only someone had been with him on his walk. If only he had called. If only . . . if, if, if . . . Had he lain in the water unable to move but conscious that he was dying? The thought was too painful to contemplate, as was the idea of such a kind man as Rupert dying alone.

'How's my husband?' Jane asked, trying to blot out the images in her mind.

'He's bearing up, M'Lady. It's been a terrible shock.'

They finally drew up in front of Drumloch Lodge. Jane did not wait for the door to be opened for her, but ran into the house. The large hall was deserted, and there was a strange stillness about the house as if it knew that its master was dead. Jane looked up and for one lunatic moment it was as if the animals' heads were smiling. She shook her head at the trick the light was playing and went quickly into the drawing room, where she found Alistair sitting with his mother and some house guests whom Jane vaguely remembered from her one visit here. As she entered, Alistair jumped up and rushed across the room to her, his face grey and drawn, his arms outstretched. As she held him, he clung to her with a desperation that made her wince with pain as his hands dug into the flesh of her upper arms.

'Jay, thank God, you've come. I needed you,' he said with quiet intensity.

'I know, my love, I know. I'm here now,' she comforted him.

'There really was no need for you to come, you know. Quite unnecessary,' her mother-in-law said sharply.

'Lady Upnor, I can't begin to tell you how sad I am. I had to come and be with you all,' Jane said gently, her eyes filling with the tears that until now she had controlled.

'Really? I wonder. Are you?' There was a cold cynicism in Lady Upnor's questioning.

'I loved him, Lady Upnor,' she answered simply. 'He was kind to me. I shall never forget him.'

Banks had quietly entered the room. 'Excuse me, M'Lady,' he said to Jane, 'but Nanny wants to know, should she take Lord James upstairs now?'

'Yes, please, Mr Banks.'

'You brought the baby?' Lady Upnor asked, her voice dangerously raised.

'Yes, of course.'

'What on earth for? There's enough to worry about without a baby.'

'But I couldn't leave him – I mean, his feeds.'

'Oh yes, of course.' A look of distaste spread over Lady Upnor's face. 'I would appreciate it if you could keep your bovine activities to the upper floor.'

Jane felt as if she had been attacked physically. She felt herself redden, but bit back her angry words. This was not the moment. The house guests shuffled out of the room awkwardly, both obviously shocked by the older woman's assault on Jane.

'Mother, for God's sake, can't you drop it? At a time like this, especially,' Alistair pleaded.

'What, Alistair? Drop what? To what are you referring?'

'I'm referring to your stupid attitude to Jane. Can't you let it drop, just for now? I wish you'd get it into your head, Mother, she's my wife, I love her, and you sicken me with this endless carping, especially now, with Pa . . .' He couldn't finish his sentence.

'I don't know what you mean. Of course, I realize that Jane is your wife, I'm hardly likely to forget, am I? All I asked was that she not feed the baby in public.'

'As if she's likely to.'

'One never knows with people of – ' She stopped.

'Of my class? Was that what you were going to say?' Jane asked bitterly. 'We do know what modesty is, you know. I'm not exactly a peasant. Look, Lady Upnor, I came because I thought I could help. Please, I don't think any of us can cope with this sort of thing now.'

'Help? You? What could you possibly do to help me?' the older woman asked with a shrill laugh.

'She's a help to me, Mother, and I'd appreciate it if you didn't forget it. You're obviously overwrought, and there's no point in carrying on like this. Come on, Jane, let's go and see James. I've missed him.'

He put his arm about Jane and led her from the room.

'What on earth brought that on? I really had begun to hope that with James's birth things might get a little better,' Jane said sadly.

'Perhaps it's the jealousy of the old queen towards the new,' he answered wearily.

Jane took the baby from Nanny and carried him into their bedroom to feed him. She sat on the four-poster bed, cradling her son. Alistair paced up and down the room, stopping now and then to gaze at them, as James sucked contentedly at her breast. Satiated, the baby hiccoughed softly and went to sleep. Gently Jane laid him on the bedspread.

'James'll never know him now,' Alistair burst out. 'I wish he had. Pa still had so much to give us, so much to teach us.' As he spoke, the tears began to roll down his cheeks. Jane held up her arms to her husband and held him to her.

'Jay, I'm not going to cope. I'm not ready yet. It's too much for me, I don't know how to do it, not like he did.' His voice was muffled with tears.

'Darling, you will, you'll manage beautifully, I know you will. And I'll be with you, I'll help you.' She held him tightly as the sobs tore his body. Her heart ached for the pain he was suffering. Slowly he calmed down.

'I'm sorry, darling,' he spluttered. 'Blubbing like little James here.'

'No, it's better you should cry, darling. It'll make it easier for you in the long run.'

The crying subsided. Alistair wiped his eyes. 'He wanted me to go on that walk, he'd suggested it the night before, said he wanted to talk to me. And I bloody well overslept!'

'He'd have understood, Alistair. Anyone can oversleep.'

'Yes, but I feel so guilty. Oh, God, Jane, what have I done?'

'You've done nothing, darling. I expect the doctor's report will show he had a seizure or something. He wasn't young any more.'

'You don't understand, Jay.' He put his head in his hands. 'I overslept because I'd been awake all night making love to another woman.' He looked at her with anguished eyes.

Jane felt cold, ice cold. She let go of his hands. She stood up and walked like a mechanical doll to her case, and slowly and methodically searched for a sweater. Carefully she put the sweater on. She walked to the chest of drawers and poured a glass of water from the pitcher. She felt dizzy, the patterned rug seemed to leap from the floor towards her. She took a deep breath to quell the wave of nausea she felt. Her coldness persisted.

'For God's sake, stop fiddling about, say something,' Alistair begged. She turned to him, her eyes full of pain. He saw her expression and looked away. 'Don't look at me like that,' he shouted. 'I can't bear you looking at me like that.'

'I wish you hadn't told me,' was all she said. 'I'd rather not have known.'

'Jane, I'm sorry, so bloody sorry. I had to tell you. All day I felt so guilty. If I hadn't done it, Pa might still be alive.'

'And will telling me bring him back?'

'I had to confess.'

'So that you can feel better? Destroy me, so long as the guilt's removed?' She did not cry, she felt no tears. She wanted to be warm, feared she would never be warm again.

'I did warn you it might happen, if you persisted in not coming here,' Alistair said defiantly.

'Yes, you did, I remember.' She heard her voice, a long way away.

'So you're partly to blame too.'

'Yes, I probably am,' she said wearily.

'Is that all you've got to say?' he asked.

'I don't know what else there is to say, not now. I can't think of anything to say, I don't know what you want me to say.'

'I want you to understand and forgive me.'

Jane looked at him, silently, for a long time. She looked at his handsome face, the dear mouth, the mouth that kissed her and whispered sweet words to her. The mouth that had kissed another woman, given pleasure to another woman. Had it whispered sweet words to her too?

'I understand, you're different when you're here. I can understand that, but I can't forgive you yet. Don't even ask me to,' she said in a strange, controlled voice.

'She's nothing, Jane, she means nothing to me.'

'She meant something last night. And the night before?'

'She's gone. She's a friend of Clarissa's, she – '

'I don't want to know. I don't want ever to be told,' she suddenly screamed at him, making him jump back with surprise registering on his face. The baby jolted awake, his little fists windmilling in the air, and he began to cry.

'My darling, I'm sorry, did Mummy make you cry?' She scooped the baby into her arms, caressing the child, lulling him. All her attention was focused on the baby; Alistair stood helplessly by. He answered a gentle knock on the door, and she heard him talking.

'Jane, the doctor's back from Inverness. You coming? He's waiting for me.'

'No, Alistair, I want to sleep. I'll see you in the morning. I want to be alone.'

'Jane!' He stepped towards her.

'Don't touch me,' she hissed at him.

She gave the baby to the nanny to settle for the night and prepared for bed, moving like an automaton. She washed, brushed her teeth, got into bed and then, uncertain, got out and cleaned her teeth again. She lay in the dark and began to shiver. She could not stop. She wanted to think and she could not. She shivered, her teeth chattered, and all she could think of was Alistair's mouth on another woman's body.

She awoke at dawn exhausted. She lifted herself on one elbow. Across the room, slumped in a chair, Alistair slept, his head on his chest, his hair falling forward into his eyes as it so often did. Beside the chair was a half empty bottle of whisky. She watched him as he must have sat in the night and watched her. What thoughts, what fears had threatened him then?

Now, at last, she was able to think and with a clarity that surprised her. She loved him, nothing he ever did could alter that. She wanted him to hold her, to heal her pain with his kisses and his words of love. He had made one mistake. Was that enough to destroy all the happiness which they had and would have together in the future? She had always thought it would be, that if he touched another woman everything would be over, her love for him would die. But it had not. Her love was strong enough to weather this. She slipped from the bed, crossed the room and knelt beside him.

'Alistair,' she whispered, 'Alistair.' He stirred. 'Darling, I love you.' He was awake.

'Jane, my love, say that again.'

'I love you.'

'Thank God. Oh, my darling.' He lifted her and carried her to the bed. 'Jane, I love you. I've been a bloody fool. I'll love you always, Jane, I want you, only you.' He began to shower her with kisses, his fear heightening his passion and his need for her.

Later as they lay together, entwined about each other, tears finally came and, as his tears mingled with hers, he vowed that he would never hurt her again.

The next few days were a bustle, with guests arriving for the funeral and local people calling to pay their respects to the family. Jane was fully occupied, arranging food and drink and bedrooms for overnight guests.

The report from Inverness confirmed that Rupert had had a severe stroke which had rendered him unconscious immediately and that, had he survived, he would no doubt have been paralysed and speechless. They all felt secret relief at the doctors' report.

Lady Upnor was marvellous, Jane had to admit. She never broke down; she received sympathy from friends and neighbours with quiet dignity and her outburst of the first night was not repeated. Jane decided that her mother-in-law's attack must have been a distorted form of grief. With her own sadness for Rupert she found for once that she could forgive her. Finally Lady Upnor even went so far as to thank Jane for all she was doing.

Honor arrived. Her grief for her brother was terrible to see. It seemed she grieved more for her brother than Lady Upnor for her husband. Jane spent many hours with Honor, patiently listening as she went over and over stories of their childhood together. The two women walked miles over the estate and, without the guns banging in the distance, Jane could appreciate fully the beauty and the glory of the place.

'You know, Honor, if I was ever really rich, I'd buy a place up here and never let anything be killed on it, unless it was hurt or there wasn't enough food for them all. Wouldn't it be paradise?'

'What a lovely idea! I hate the killing, too. It's why I rarely come here. Let's hope you're rich one day and can do it.'

One morning they sat by Jane's salmon pool watching the fish, content in each other's company.

'You've changed, Jane, what's happened?'

'What do you mean, Honor?' Jane asked, startled.

'You've been hurt, Jane, it's in your eyes. There's a look that wasn't there before, a wariness. What happened?'

Slowly Jane began to tell Honor. She explained how she wanted to forgive Alistair and forget the whole incident, but that it would not go away, kept her awake at nights. When she looked at him she could not stop herself imagining his mouth on another woman's flesh.

'Poor Jane. Bloody fool Alistair. Why on earth did he tell you?'

'To remove his guilt, I think.'

'Men always think that, the fools . . . "If I tell, if I say I'm sorry, it will all be better again . . ." I sometimes despair of men: they are so infantile.'

'Yes, I think he thinks it's all over and forgotten, that he merely had a narrow escape.'

Honor nodded her head sadly. 'You don't have to tell me. They're all the same. The truth is the other women really are unimportant to them, mean nothing, and yet they never understand the pain they cause. Pain like that can alter a relationship for ever. Why they do it is beyond me, especially when they have a good marriage. I mean, there's nothing wrong in yours, is there?'

Jane looked at her hands. She knew it was not right that she had always to pretend an orgasm when they made love, but could Honor help, could she explain? No, she could not confide in her: it was wrong, disloyal to Alistair. Reluctantly she let the chance slip away.

'Honor, apart from his mother, and her awful friends, I thought everything was perfect.'

'What happens when he does it again?'

'No, Honor, I couldn't forgive a second time.'

'He'll be unfaithful again, you know. They always are, once they've taken the plunge. It's like a dog that's worried sheep and tasted blood. It becomes a compulsion with them.'

'Oh no, Honor, I don't think he will. He promised me. I think he thought he had lost me.'

'I sincerely hope you're right and I'm wrong then, Jane dear. You know,' she suddenly said, lightening the conversation, 'I sometimes wish I were a lesbian. I'm sure they're so much nicer to each other.'

'But what guarantee would you have, even then?' Jane asked, laughing at last.

'None, I suppose. God, life can be such a bitch at times, can't it?'

Linking arms, they strolled back to the house for tea.

Rupert was buried the following day in the Highlands he had loved so much. Led by a piper playing a lament, the mourners followed the coffin up a steep hill. The strong, kilted estate workers carrying the coffin strained under its weight and the steepness of the path. The cortège wound through the woods, past the river, and up – up to the top of the hill that looked down on Drumloch and, spread out as far as the eye could see, the old Laird's land. They laid him to rest, the plaintive skirl of the pipes echoing in the valley below and tearing at the pain of all those who heard.

The lawyers had come from London and, after the funeral, the will was read to the family. As expected, he had left all his estates and his house in London to Alistair. He had made provision for his wife to receive a sizeable income for the rest of her life and left a lump sum to Clarissa. There were small bequests to members of his staff who had served him for many years and then, right at the end of the will, was a bequest of a flat in Chelsea and £20,000 to a Miss Jean Robins.

Alistair spent long hours with the lawyers and when he finally came to bed, he looked ill with fatigue.

'It's bad, Jane,' he announced. 'The bloody death duties are enormous.'

'Tomorrow, darling, we'll worry about it then,' she said comfortingly. He smiled gratefully.

'Jane, my love, make love to me.'

Later as they were staring into the darkness Jane asked, 'Darling, who's Jean Robins?'

Alistair laughed. 'My mother wanted to know that, too. Miss Robins was Pa's mistress, and had been for the last twenty-odd years. She's a nice woman, I met her several times – she made lovely chocolate cake and was very funny.'

'What on earth did you tell your mother?'

'I lied. I said I didn't know who she was. I decided to let someone else tell her. I couldn't face it.'

'Weren't you shocked by your father when you found out?'

'Good God, no. Why? It didn't harm anyone, did it? And a fellow needs some fun,' he replied unthinkingly as he settled down in his pillows. But Jane could not get to sleep and lay worrying, Honor's words endlessly turning in her head – 'He'll do it again, they always do.'

When sleep finally came, her dreams were of savaged sheep and blood dripping from the fangs of large, grinning dogs.

6

Despite the loss of Rupert, the next couple of years were to prove two of the happiest of their married life. The financial problems facing Alistair were so enormous that they had to work as a team to solve them. And they worked well together.

They continued to live in the dower house at Trinick. Each morning, after they had breakfasted with James, Alistair would leave for the big house. Jane would stay and play with James for an hour. She would then drive to Respryn in her red Mini. At Respryn she had her own office. Her main job was to catalogue the contents of the house for the official valuation. She had happily started the job, ignorant of what was actually involved. It was a complicated and lengthy task. It was soon obvious that she was going to need help, so a secretary was employed; and in the university holidays, a student from Cambridge acted as her researcher. No inventory had ever been done before: there had been no need. But with death duties and the spectre of the Inland Revenue at their shoulders, it finally had to be tackled. Lady Upnor took great exception to her activities. To anyone who would listen she complained that Jane was checking up on what she owned. But Jane was learning to ignore her mother-in-law.

Together they worked and planned. Deciding on economies here, investment there, always planning for the long-term future – ensuring the continuation of Respryn for their son. Jane was in her element and happy that Alistair really needed her.

The talk was continually of the dreaded death duties. Properties were going to have to be sold, but which ones?

Two of the farms at Respryn were sold. Alistair had been told that by selling his father's collection of rare maps a very considerable sum would be raised, but he could not bring himself to sell these – his father had loved them so much. But he could not save the Book of Hours nor two paintings – a Constable and a particularly beautiful Stubbs – which were taken to the sale rooms, leaving unsightly patches on the walls where they had hung, no doubt, since the day they were painted.

Alistair insisted on going to the sale and Jane went with him. At the end of the sale of Rupert's paintings, Jane glared angrily at the man who had successfully bid for them both. A week later she and Alistair were intrigued when a large wooden crate was delivered. Inside were the paintings and a scrawled note: 'Hang these for me, darling. Love, Honor.' As they joyfully supervised their rehanging, it was like having old friends back again.

Still more money had to be raised. Jane secretly hoped that Alistair would decide to sell Drumloch. She would be content never to see it again. But Alistair, after endless meetings with accountants and lawyers, was advised to sell the London house. It was an unproductive but valuable piece of real estate, whereas Drumloch produced revenue. Alistair was happy with the decision: since his father was buried at Drumloch he had dreaded having to sell the Scottish estate. Lady Upnor was in hysterics. At least her anger at losing her London mansion sidetracked her from her suspicion of Jane's activities. Now it was her son she complained of, telling her friends that he was throwing her out of her town house. As his mother became more difficult, so Alistair's irritation with her grew. Jane would not have been human if she had not felt pleasure at the rift she saw growing daily wider between mother and son.

Lady Upnor continued to live in the large house. She was observing a year's mourning which, she had announced at the funeral, she would be spending at Respryn. The year had almost passed but still she showed no signs of moving, had kept all her staff and, despite her mourning, continued to entertain as she had done when her husband was alive. Alistair found himself paying her expenses, since his mother was adamant that the allowance her husband had left her was for her personal needs only, and not for wages and food.

'Look at these bills,' Alistair said angrily one morning in Jane's office, flinging a pile of statements on her desk. 'Just look at them! We can't afford this kind of expenditure.'

'You're going to have to tell your mother she must cut back.'

'She'll never cut back while she's here. We'll have to get her to move to Trinick.'

'Alistair, no!' Jane said, horrified. 'Please, don't even think of it. I love Trinick. She's welcome to stay in Respryn. I don't want to live here, the idea is too daunting. And think of the effect on your mother. We're happy as we are.'

'We have to move here, darling, you know we have to. It's expected of us. She knows the score better than you do, Jane. She knows she should have moved to Trinick months ago, that the widow always does. She's just being pigheaded –'

'Who's being pigheaded?' his mother asked, sweeping into the room. She smiled icily at her son. 'See to these, Jane.' She handed Jane a list.

'What do you want me to do with it, Lady Upnor?'

'Type it, of course, on that machine of yours.' Lady Upnor waved her hand vaguely at the typewriter and Jane's secretary who was cowering nervously behind it. 'It's my instructions for the staff for my house party at Drumloch.'

'Mother! You can't be thinking of a shooting party so soon.'

'Of course I am. Your father would have wanted it.'

'Firstly, Mother, I think we should give it a miss this year. After all, it's the first anniversary of Father's death. But also it's the expense.'

'I beg your pardon, Alistair,' Lady Upnor thundered at her son. The young secretary, fumbling for her notepad, quickly excused herself and scuttled from the room. 'How dare you speak to me like that in front of the staff?'

'I'm sorry, Mother. I forgot the girl was here. But I'm angry. This can't go on. Look.' He showed her the bills. 'The only solution I can think of is to shut up most of Respryn, to cut back on staff and, with some economies, I think you'd be more comfortable at Trinick.'

'I hate discussing money, Alistair, it's too vulgar.'

'I'm sorry you think so, Mother. But I'm afraid you're going to have to steel yourself to do so.' There was no humour in his voice.

'I could live in one wing.' She was bargaining now.

'Don't you listen to anything, Mother? We can't afford to keep a whole wing open. What's more, all the time you're here, Jane can't be mistress of her own house.'

'Fine mistress she is likely to make.' Jane looked coldly at her mother-in-law who continued as if she were not present. 'It will be the end of Respryn, if it's left in her hands.'

'Mother, don't start that. I'm not interested in your stupid vendetta. Be fair, I've leaned over backwards to help you. I can't afford it any longer. If you're off to Scotland next week, I suggest that, while you're away, we move your possessions over to Trinick for you.'

'I shall hate that poky little house.'

'And, while I'm on the subject of economies,' Alistair continued, ignoring her protest, 'we can't afford a large house party at Drumloch this year.'

'But I've invited everybody.'

'Well, you're just going to have to uninvite them. They're all friends, they'll understand.' His mother complained volubly and bitterly but Alistair was unyielding.

'Will you be coming to Drumloch with me, then?' She knew she was defeated.

'No, Mother, I've too much to do here.'

His mother swept out of the room as imperiously as she had entered. Jane relaxed in her seat. The woman was impossible, but still, Jane was beginning to feel sorry for her. The adjustments in the older woman's life were going to be enormous. But she was overjoyed at the news that Alistair would not be going to Scotland. She had been dreading it, knowing that this year, had he gone, she would have had to accompany him.

While his mother was away, Jane supervised the change of houses. For themselves, within the large house, they had a set of rooms which amounted to a house. In the west wing, which had a door to the courtyard, they had a large drawing room, a dining room and study. Upstairs was their own bedroom, dressing rooms and bathrooms and two guest rooms. On the next floor were James's nurseries and his nanny's room. The rest of the staff slept in the old servants' wing, just as they had always done. Alistair would occasionally sigh at the way they lived but Jane thought they were magnificently housed.

Laying off some of the house staff was painful for Alistair, who had known most of them all his life. Some were pensioned off in cottages on the estate; for others he found new jobs. There was endless talk of economy and discomfort. Jane's childhood was still too close for her to be anything but amused by this family's idea of hardship. Banks was kept on, with one footman. Lady Upnor's cook and kitchen maid decamped to Trinick. Jane had a new cook at Respryn, and a scullery maid. Alistair kept his valet, Mark, and insisted that because of her new position, Jane must have a lady's maid. With no hesitation she asked for May, and welcomed the girl like a long-lost friend. The chauffeur, Tucker, remained secure in his flat over the garage where the gleaming Rolls still stood; the baby had his nanny. The gardeners were cut from twelve to three and an army of cleaning women came in each day from the village. They still lived in one of the most beautiful houses in England; they still had their house in Fulham and the estate in Scotland. Economy, she learned, was a relative word.

Suddenly the press re-emerged in Jane's life, taking an inordinate interest in her reactions to her new position. Once again the telephone became a threatening instrument which she avoided answering, in case it was an aggressive, nosy reporter. She was left with a fear of the machine which she was never able to conquer.

Despite the fact that she was now the countess, she did not feel that she was, just as she had never really felt she was Lady Redland. The use of her title continued to embarrass her: she always felt a fraud when using it. In London, where she could be anonymous, she took to calling herself Mrs Upnor, and felt much more comfortable with that. But Alistair found out and was furious. Angrily he told her to pull herself together and to stop being so neurotic; she was his wife and as such would be treated with the respect that his title deserved. This argument only made Jane more confused. How could a title, which after all was merely a word, confer respect? Only a person should be worthy of respect. 'Think of the advantages,' she was told, but she found it difficult to find any. Honor claimed that it ensured better cabins on liners, hotel rooms with the best views, and VIP treatment at airports, but since they never travelled, those advantages escaped her. There were distinct disadvantages, for Jane was convinced that prices went up when her title was mentioned. She soon realized that everyone reacted in some way to it when they were introduced to her. Some people became obsequious, others belligerent, and some tended to stand back as if fearing to be friendly, in case this should be misinterpreted. Sadly, these were the people whom Jane would most have liked to know. Even old friends' attitudes seemed to have changed: they were almost deferential, which only embarrassed Jane further. No one, it seemed, in this society, remained neutral to a title, except those who already possessed one, and Jane still felt ill at ease with them.

To Jane, her mother-in-law was still the countess. Jane was relieved that old Lady Upnor kept on various charitable positions which would otherwise have fallen to Jane, who did not feel ready to be the president or the chairman of anything yet, if ever.

Society, which had cut her dead, now courted her. The invitations poured in and the telephone rang continuously. Jane was amazed at the way these people chattered to her as if their silence and rejection of her had never happened. She was fêted, and she despised them for it. She was wise enough now to realize that should anything happen to Alistair, the procedure would go smartly into reverse. Had it been her choice, she would have had nothing to do with these people, but Alistair insisted that she entertain and be entertained by them. He was certain they were now aware of their error. 'You see, my darling,' he would say, 'they're acknowledging how wonderful you are. People aren't that bad, are they?' She wondered at his naivety, but did as he asked. She was amazed at how easy it was to be hypocritical, as she smiled at them, talked to them, ate with them, and still, inside, hated them. But about one thing she was adamant – Linda and Bertie Talbot entered Respryn over her dead body – and Alistair conceded.

Their trips to London were few – there was still too much work to do at Respryn – but occasionally Alistair had to go to see his lawyers, accountants and brokers, and Jane usually went with him. It gave her a chance to forget who she was.

Sandra was married and living in Cambridge. When Jane was in London she would try to get to town so that they could have lunch together and do some shopping.

Jane had visited her parents once since Rupert had died. But it had not been a success. It was not just the stares of the neighbours that bothered her, but the knowledge that her parents' way of life was so different now from her own. She wished she had money of her own to rehouse them. She did not like to ask Alistair, who had problems enough – if on a different scale. So she took to inviting them to London, where they would have tea, always in a Lyons Corner House, which was her mother's favourite. Then they would go to a show, usually a musical, and after a steak supper her parents would take the train back. She had given up trying to persuade them to stay the night. They seemed happy with these outings and it was a neat compromise as far as Jane was concerned.

Jane worried about Alistair. There were days when his new responsibilities seemed to weigh far too heavily upon him, and he seemed to age before her eyes. Then, just as she decided she must say something to him, he seemed to shake the problems away and the light-hearted, slightly wild Alistair of old would return. Usually, he would insist on a party, always at Fulham and always with the old friends from Cambridge. These parties seemed to be a safety valve for him. And if he got drunk on the wine, never whisky, she said nothing: it was as if he needed to.

They did not make love as often as they had. But Jane was not worried. She had read in a new women's magazine that sexual activity tailed off after the first couple of years and she guessed that she and Alistair were average in their lovemaking. In a way, she was relieved since, when she faked her orgasm, she always felt as if she were lying to Alistair. This way she did not have to lie so often.

As the problems at Respryn eased, Alistair finally took his seat in the House of Lords. Jane sat with Lady Upnor in the peeresses' gallery and watched the age-old ceremony unfold below her. The drama and solemnity of the occasion, in the dignified surroundings, brought home to Jane a fuller understanding of what her husband's position entailed.

7

London was beginning to swing, but Jane was happy for it to do so without her. She was happiest at Respryn. The city girl she had once been had completely disappeared. It was the country life she lived for. She began to take a great interest in the farm. With Lockhart's guidance she and Alistair began the long task of building a prize herd of cattle. They began to buy rare breeds, and imported a couple of Highland cattle from which to breed. Jane collected chickens and became a passionate admirer of goats. She lived in jeans and Wellington boots. She even went to the local point-to-points. So much for Lady Upnor's fears that Jane would miss the bright lights.

She had already discovered an interest in gardening while making the garden at Trinick, but now, with the large walled garden and the yards of greenhouses at her disposal, she was in her element. She planned and planted one garden, based on the scent of flowers, which even her mother-in-law admired.

Lady Upnor was less of a problem. Alistair had bought her a flat in London. At first she had complained that people of her status did not live in flats. This one was large, however, and, in Regent's Park: she soon discovered its advantages and returned to her previous life-style of weekdays in London and weekends in the country.

It was three years before Alistair could bring himself to go back to Drumloch, but the estate needed to make more money if he were to keep it. Jane and Alistair returned together. It was June and in the Highlands yellow gorse bloomed profusely, reflecting the bright sunshine that shone every day. The rhododendrons were a chaotic riot of colour. May blossom scented the air. There was none of the drizzle of August and there were no midges to drive them mad. Scotland was at its best and Alistair, relieved of the pressures of the south, was once again the carefree husband Jane remembered. In this peace, and her contentment, she began to love the place as Rupert must have done.

After long consultations with the factor and ghillies, it was decided to let the estate to the many rich Americans, Brazilians and Germans who were eager to rent stalking and fishing in Scotland. For the grouseshooting in August and September it was decided that Jane and Alistair would host large parties which would be lavishly entertained in the old style.

That first August Jane discovered that the very rich were demanding and never ceased to complain. She found it almost impossible to pretend excitement over a large 'bag' which she was expected to admire. But she had to be there for only a month each year, and then she could return to Respryn. It was the price she had to pay so that Alistair could maintain his beloved Highland estate. Without her saying anything to him, Alistair had stopped drinking whisky while they were there.

James was a quiet little boy, thin and rather shy, but with his father's fair hair and brown eyes. By three he was already studious and would rather sit with a book than play with his soldiers. Of one thing there was no doubt, he adored his father, and would follow him everywhere about the estate, even copying the way Alistair walked. Jane was relieved that he felt so strongly for his father, for to her surprise, tinged with a certain amount of guilt, she found that though she loved the child, she did not have Alistair's patience with him. And she knew that, despite all the talk of the power of maternal love, she still loved Alistair more.

With memories of his own isolated childhood, Alistair agreed wholeheartedly with Jane's idea that they should set up a nursery school at Respryn for the child, and invite the very young children of the estate workers and village to join. Clare was in charge, and they were relieved to see that with his own age group James was not shy at all.

By the time he was five they decided to go one step further and enrolled him in the village school, the first Upnor child not to have a governess. Alistair's mother was up in arms and blamed Jane entirely for the decision.

Now that Alistair had taken his seat in the House, he was invited to join various boards of directors and he took over the charitable patronages of his father. A large part of his week had to be spent in London, but there were also the estates to oversee. Despite his initial fears, he was managing well. There was a new assurance and maturity to him.

For a couple of years Jane dutifully went to London as often as she could manage. It was hard for her: she found that she could not share his enthusiasm for his new life in London.

His business life she found dull. Many of the dinners he had to attend and give were boring affairs with people much older than themselves. Jane could now hold her own in country society talking of country matters but, having no interest in the world of business, she found herself once again reduced to monosyllabic conversation.

Alistair had also taken a fancy to the social life, which left Jane feeling that all the confidence she had managed to build was stripped away from her. She liked the tennis at Wimbledon, but Henley and Ascot were a different matter: there she had to talk to people, there she had to look elegant and self-possessed. She was aware that, compared with the other women in their set, she looked wrong. She could buy whatever she wanted – the problem was that to look 'right' entailed going into the sort of shops where Jane still felt intimidated by the assistants. She knew full well that she could now spend on a dress four times what these supercilious *vendeuses* earned in a week, but the knowledge did not help her. She was angry with herself but she was trapped, as always, in the mesh of insecurities which so often, she knew, were of her own making. In consequence, her outfits were often remarked upon unkindly. But if they sniped at her dress sense, no one could find anything unkind to say about her face, which with its haunting grey eyes was increasingly beautiful.

Alistair accepted every invitation that came his way. Tentatively she suggested that she would prefer to stay most of the time at Respryn, that she did not really like London and his friends. She was too relieved by his agreement to be hurt by it. This did not prevent her, though, from wishing that their old life could have continued as it used to be. And she spent her time longing for his return or a phone call from him.

Rupert had been dead for over five years when the most momentous changes began to take place. Respryn was losing money: something had to be done. It was Jane who first suggested that they should open the house to the public. It seemed wicked that all its beautiful contents should lie unseen, covered in dust sheets. Properly managed, the house should be able to pay for itself.

'Do you think you could organize it?' Alistair asked her one evening soon after she had suggested the idea.

'Me? You're joking!' She laughed.

'No, I'm not. I can't do it. I just don't have the time. I've too many commitments as it is.'

'I'm not sure I could.'

'Nonsense, of course you can. Look how well you run this place with me away so much. I sometimes feel I'm redundant at Respryn. It's always amused me how much you've proved my mother wrong.' He laughed. 'Think about it, Jay.'

Certainly, she had proved Lady Upnor wrong. Her training at St Cuthbert's, much as she had hated it, had taught her discipline and organization. She was surprised to find she enjoyed running the large, unwieldy household. She did not mind the cut-backs in staff and was quite capable of getting a bucket and mop and giving a hand when necessary.

But what Alistair said was not strictly true, for she had learned that most valuable of lessons, to delegate. Much of the running of the household was done by the true professionals, Banks, the cook, the head gardener and Lockhart. They were all far more capable than she of knowing what to do, what to serve, whom to place with whom, and what to plant and when to sell. Far from despising her, they appreciated her confidence in their abilities.

She decided to try to organize the opening of Respryn. She spent a busy few months touring other stately homes, sometimes as a guest of the owner, more often as a plain tourist – she found she learned more that way. The other owners were most helpful. Her head was dizzy from the advice they gave. Some advocated animals in the park; others told her to keep clear of them at all costs, that they would only ruin the trees. Some thought funfairs were the best money-spinners; others warned her that these only encouraged riff-raff. All were in agreement that the most important factors were good loos, and a restaurant serving nonstop tea. One duchess was adamant that half the trippers came just to say they had peed at her castle.

She naively hoped to open the following year, but she had not reckoned with the local planning authorities, who were obsessed with lavatories, fire regulations and crowd control.

It was not only the local authorities with whom she had to deal. Once their plans became known, representatives of protection and conservation societies appeared from nowhere leaping to the defence of Respryn. She wasted precious hours placating, reassuring and explaining to them. She was becoming expert at handling people.

She had the estate carpenter build her a mock-up of the house and she spent hours with it planning various routes for the guided tours.

She enjoyed compiling the guide book. Her work on the inventory had given her a good knowledge of the house's contents and of which things to illustrate in the book. She wrote a potted history of the house and family. She organized the printing. Alistair watched her activities with pride.

She turned the old servants' hall into the necessary cafeteria, with gingham tablecloths. She ordered robust china with the Upnor crest, arguing with Alistair that everyone liked eating off crested china. She arranged for a group of village women to make the jam and cakes they would sell. Since this would be the first money the women had ever earned in their own right, there was no shortage of volunteers.

She bought boats for the lake, had the swimming pool relined. Parts of the park were designated picnic zones and furnished with rustic tables and benches and giant wastepaper baskets. The old racquet court was converted into a gift shop. The mounting costs worried Jane but Alistair, bravely signing the cheques, pointed out that one never made money without spending it first.

The loos, though, were her pride and joy. Their white tiles gleaming, the brass taps burnished, the wooden seats shining, they were tucked away unobtrusively behind the stables.

She rejected the idea of wild animals in the park, or a funfair. Respryn would stand or fall on its beauty alone.

A year later than she had planned, they eventually opened. It was a success and the funniest thing of all was that Jane found she was one of the chief attractions. Everyone wanted to say they had met the 'working-class countess'.

Alistair's mother treated the whole operation with disdain, regarding it as nothing better than a vulgar circus for which she blamed Jane, and from which she distanced herself totally. Honor, on the other hand, was far more philosophical. Times had to change, she acknowledged. On her visits she became an enthusiastic and popular guide.

Outwardly the changes in Jane were many. She had a far more confident air: everyone was agreed on that. Her ability in organizing Respryn had given her a veneer of authority to which others responded. She did not even realize that she now said 'What?', 'loo' and even 'bog' and 'arse' as a matter of course. But inside her there was no change, she was still afraid, still self-conscious, still desperate for Alistair's love. What the years had given her was the ability to hide her inadequacies and to fool the world into believing that she was now a competent, self-assured woman.

She loved Alistair more with each passing year, but then she had always known that there could only ever be one man for her. It seemed unbelievable that they had been married for ten years, for the years had slipped by so quickly.

She was tired. It had been a busy day. She was glad of her bath and now, with her well-earned gin and tonic, she sat contentedly by the fire at Respryn waiting for Alistair to return from London. The phone rang.

'Darling?'

'Alistair, where are you?'

'London. Sorry, darling, but I've got tied up here in a business meeting and I can't get away.'

'Poor you. Never mind. We were going to have salmon – I'll get cook to put it back for tomorrow.' She started to chatter about her day, but he seemed distracted so, reluctantly, she rang off, disappointed. Recently Alistair had become so busy in London that he was often delayed.

The next day, Saturday, was a full day for Jane. She had acted as guide, sold souvenirs and helped out with the teas, and it was not until the last car drove away that she had time to realize that Alistair was not back and had not phoned. She tried the number of the Fulham house several times and listened bleakly as she heard the phone ring in the empty house. At ten he phoned.

'Darling, where are you? I was worried, I've been trying the Fulham number all evening.'

'Sorry, sweetheart, I got delayed. Look, it seems silly to come back now. I'll stay in town until next week.'

'Oh, Alistair, do you have to? I'm missing you.'

'I've got a board meeting on Monday anyway. It's daft to travel all the way down just for Sunday. I'll see you Monday evening.'

'Alistair, please come.'

'No, darling, I've just told you I'm bloody tired. It makes more sense this way.'

She heard a burst of laughter in the background.

'Alistair, where are you?'

'I'm at Clarissa's. Look, darling, I must fly,' and she heard the phone go dead.

She felt little tendrils of fear in her stomach. She thought he had not seen Clarissa for years, not since she married a merchant banker called Hector, who, like Clarissa, could hardly speak a civil word to Jane. Why go and see her now? He loathed her, he was always saying how much he disliked her. Had he, over the years, been seeing her, and thought it better not to tell Jane?

If he could deceive her over seeing Clarissa, what other things had he not told her? When he had first confessed his infidelity to her, she had watched him like a hawk, convinced that she would know if he were unfaithful again. There had been nothing, she was certain. But what did she expect? Was he to appear with a sign around his neck 'I am an adulterer', like some creature in the medieval stocks? How could she be so certain? How much about his life away from Respryn did she really know?

She cancelled dinner, she did not want to eat. She tried to watch TV but could not concentrate. She sat staring into the fire, a large gin and tonic in her hand, knowing instinctively that her greatest fear had materialized.

8

She spent a restless night, anger, mistrust and jealousy devouring her.

When morning broke Jane tried to rationalize her fears. Maybe she had overreacted. It was true, Alistair was very busy in London these days and he did get very tired. If he had bumped into Clarissa, what would be more natural than that she should ask him back for a drink, to see her new house perhaps?

All day Sunday she filled the hours with hard work, anything to stop herself thinking. That evening she sorted through all the cupboards and wardrobes in her dressing room. 'Busy, I must keep myself busy,' she kept telling herself.

On Monday evening she sat waiting nervously in the little study which, in the interests of economy, they used as a sitting room. She heard the dogs barking and knew that he had arrived. She felt certain that, when he entered the room, she would be able to read the truth in his face. But as he approached her he looked the same, the same sweet smile, the tender kiss. Perhaps she had imagined everything.

'My, you look pretty, M'Lady.' He grinned at her, poured himself a drink and freshened hers.

'Did you have a nice time?' she asked.

'Nice time? Oh, you mean at Clarissa's? Yes, fine. She doesn't send love, by the way!' He laughed at the thought.

'What's the house like?'

'Fine.'

'Is it big?'

'Average. Is dinner ready? I'm starving.'

'Nicely furnished?'

'Yes.' He studied his drink.

'Has she had designers in?'

'I wouldn't know. God, Jane, why all this sudden interest in Clarissa's house?' He poured himself another drink. 'When is dinner ready?' She sat opposite him and knew that he lied. He had not been to Clarissa's, his answers were too evasive. The thought lurched through her. She knew she was relying on instinct which could be a dangerous thing to do, but she could not stop herself.

'Who else was there?' she continued, relentlessly.

'At Clarissa's? No one, just Hector.'

'I thought I heard a lot of people laughing.'

'No. Just us. Ah, Banks! Dinner, at last.' He smiled at the butler. They settled themselves at the table in the little dining room. 'Tell me about your week,' he said.

'It's been a good one. We had over 600 on Saturday.'

'Splendid.'

'But I'm tired. I've been thinking, Lockhart could manage without me for a few days. How about you and me getting away for the weekend, together? How about next weekend?'

'Darling, I'm sorry. I accepted an invitation to go to Wallace Hawkins's and you know you never enjoy it there with all that horse talk.'

'Without me!'

'As I said, you hate the hunting and shooting fraternity. What's the point in your going?'

'I like the weekends with you, Alistair.'

'I know, my pet, but I really ought to cultivate Wallace a bit more. Just this once. We'll arrange something for another weekend, I promise.' He smiled at her.

After dinner they sat and watched television and she was almost grateful for the flickering screen which made conversation unnecessary. She wanted to probe further but at the same time she was afraid to.

'Will you be long?' she asked, deciding to go to bed.

'No, I'll just watch the end of this.'

She lay waiting for him. The light on the telephone console flickered on, indicating that the phone was being used. She longed for the courage to pick it up but was afraid of what she might hear. The call was a long one: it was a good half-hour before the little light went out and the receiver pinged. He came to bed.

'Not asleep?' he asked unnecessarily. 'God, I'm tired.' He yawned. He climbed in beside her but did not turn to take her in his arms as he always did when he had been away for a few days. Then she knew for certain. It had not been her imagination: the dream was over.

He was home for two more nights and, although he behaved to her in the same way, he never touched her or made love to her. Her body longed for him; she would lie beside him wanting to touch him but frightened of his rejection.

On Thursday he left, saying he would phone and that he would be back on Monday. She watched his car disappear down the drive and then, knowing what she must do, she called May.

'May, I want to go to London for some time. Do you think you could manage to look after James and me? It'll just be the two of us for a couple of months until James starts at his new prep school.'

'Of course, M'Lady, no problem at all.'

'I want to have a nice long holiday, alone with James, before he goes to boarding school. Perhaps you would pack his bag and some of his toys, and a couple of cases for me?'

She called Lockhart, told him she would be away for a while and instructed him to take charge for her. She got out her BMW, her thirtieth birthday present from Alistair last month. With May and James in the back she drove across the park which looked magnificent in the June sunshine. She did not once look back.

She knew that it would be safe to go to Fulham, it was unlikely he would take another woman there. May was thrilled with the little house and did not mind sharing a room with James.

'How long will we be here, M'Lady?'

'I don't know. May, would you do me a great favour? Please stop calling me "M'Lady", I hate it. Call me Jane.'

'M'Lady!' said May in a shocked voice. 'I don't think I could do that.'

'Please, May, I want you to. Everything's different now.'

'I'll try, but I think it will be difficult . . . Jane.'

There was no telephone call that evening. Not until late the following evening did it ring. She sat with her drink in her hand and watched it, willing it to stop. Over the weekend, the telephone sounded intermittently and each time she sat and looked at it, longing for the noise to cease in case she weakened and answered it.

It rang again when they were sitting at the kitchen table, while May and James ate their supper.

'Why don't you answer it?' May asked eventually.

'I don't want to,' Jane replied.

'Jane, I'm sorry to say this, it's not my place, but I've got to. M'Lady, you look terrible. You should eat. Just drinking is not good for you at all, and won't solve anything.'

'I can't eat, May, I just can't.'

'Oh, M'Lady, please, M'Lady, what's happening?' May began to cry.

'Don't cry, for God's sake, I can't stand it. I'll be all right, really I will. Just give me time to handle this in my own way. And I asked you to call me "Jane".' She heard the irritation in her voice and felt ashamed that she should snap at May.

On the Sunday he came. She was sitting in bed, too desolate to get up and face another day burdened with the knowledge which lay like a cancer within her. She heard May talking to him, heard her take James out for his walk, heard Alistair bounding up the stairs.

'Jane, for Christ's sake, what are you playing at? I've been worried. What the hell are you doing here? Why don't you answer the phone?'

'I've left you, Alistair.'

'You've what?' he said, astonished. 'Why, for God's sake?'

'You're being unfaithful to me again.'

'Don't be so bloody ridiculous, Jane – just because I go to Wallace's for the weekend without you.'

'Yes, but who did you take with you? Don't pretend, Alistair, there's no point. I know.'

'Who told you?' he asked urgently.

'No one.'

'Someone must have. That cow Clarissa!'

'No one had to tell me anything. I know, that's all.'

'How the hell could you possibly know?'

'Because I love you, Alistair. I didn't need anyone to tell me.'

He sat heavily on the bed. 'I am so sorry, so terribly sorry.'

'You said that last time.'

'But I mean it, it's nothing. She means nothing to me.'

'You said that last time, too. No doubt you would say it the next time.'

'But I love you, Jane.'

'I know, that's what makes it so bloody tragic.'

'Jane, come on, pack your bag. We'll all go home. I promise it will never happen again. We love each other, you've just said so, we can't throw that away. We'll work it out, I'm certain we can.'

'No, Alistair, you don't understand. I can't bear the thought of you touching someone else. I can't share you. It's all or nothing for me, it always has been, I told you that the day we got engaged. I warned you. How the hell do you think I felt lying next to you these last nights with you not touching me, not wanting me? I've thought a lot these last few days. I think I'll be better alone. The pain of being with you, like this, is too much to cope with.'

'Jane.' The anguish in his voice hurt her. She longed to hold him close to her. But she knew that if she touched him she would be lost and her pain would only intensify.

'I think you're being overdramatic,' he suddenly announced in a completely different tone of voice. 'It's only a little affair. I repeat, it means nothing to me.'

'It means everything to me.'

'Jane, be reasonable. How often do I go off the rails?'

'Once too often, I'm afraid, Alistair. Don't you remember we made vows to each other?'

'Oh, Jane, don't be so bloody working-class.'

'I am working-class, don't you remember? That's what all the fuss has been about all these years.'

'But everybody does it.'

'Everybody doesn't do it. I'd rather stick with my working-class morality, thank you, than be an aristocrat with the morals of an alley cat,' she spat at him. His hand flashed through the air and hit her hard across the face. She could feel her skin begin to swell, she felt her eyes smarting, but she did not flinch, did not touch her face. Instead, she looked at him, steadily.

'Jane, I'm sorry, I didn't mean to do that but I can't understand what's happening. If you love me, why leave me?'

'Because I want to continue to love you. If I stayed with you and this kept happening, then I might hate you.' He sat back on the bed, his head in his hands. 'But why, Alistair, tell me? I have to know. What did I do wrong?'

'Nothing, Jane, you've done nothing wrong. You've been marvellous, putting up with my mother and sister, all you've done at Respryn, your hard work at Drumloch, and loving me the way you have. It's I who am in the wrong. I admit it. I don't know why I do it.' He paused. 'I guess I get bored every so often and want some excitement, you know.'

'No, Alistair, I'm afraid I don't know.'

'Jane, all marriages end up like this. Surely you realize that? Hell, I wouldn't mind if you had the odd fling, provided you were discreet about it. It wouldn't alter our love for each other. My little adventures haven't, have they?'

'Oh, Alistair,' she said, a deep sadness in her voice. 'I've been such a stupid, blind fool. I thought it had just been that once in Scotland, but it hasn't, has it? There have been others, haven't there?' He did not answer. He did not need to: the guilt on his face spoke for him. 'Then there really is no hope. No hope for us. I'd rather you went now.'

'But James, what about James? Have you thought of him?'

'Of course I've thought. You can have him each weekend – it's the only time you're at home anyway. I'll look after him in the week. In any case he goes to boarding school in September, poor little boy.'

'Poor little boy? It's a good job he's going if you're planning to be as stupid and selfish as this. What sort of life will that be for him? He needs us both.'

'We'll sort something out about the holidays. Share him, or take it in turns.'

'My God, you're a cold fish. I'd never dreamed it of you – parcelling out your son like that. I thought . . .' His voice was drilling into her skull. He was so clever, she knew that it was only a matter of time before he managed to make her feel guilty, as if it were all her fault. She had to stop him.

'Will you go now, please, Alistair? I'm very tired.'

'"I'm very tired." Christ, what are you made of? Break up my marriage, deprive our child of his home life and you sit there calm as can be and say you're bloody tired.' He stood over her, shouting.

She flinched from his anger. 'I didn't break up our marriage,' she said, fighting her tears. 'You did.'

'Oh, didn't you? Didn't you? The perfect Jane, the perfect bloody wife. Are you? Tell me, are you?'

'I tried to be.'

'Tried is the right word, and failed. Dear God, how you failed!'

'I don't understand. I loved you the only way I knew how.'

'Loved? Loved?' His voice rose to a screaming crescendo. 'You smothered me with your fucking love.'

'Don't say that,' she cried, putting her hands over her ears to shut out the hateful words.

'And do you think for one moment you fooled me with your moaning and writhing in bed, pretending to me, your husband? You and your famous honesty – the most important thing in our lives and you deceived me. You're no bloody use in bed. You're frigid, hear me? *Frigid!*'

'I'm not, I'm not,' she sobbed.

'And you're smug too. Bloody smug, thinking you're always right and criticizing my friends, my way of life and my family, ad nauseam. God, why did I ever marry you?'

She looked at him with horror. 'Christ, why were you ever born?' echoed in her memory from all those years ago.

'Why, then, tell me why you bothered, if you were going to give me all this pain?' she screamed.

'Because, fool that I am, I felt sorry for you.'

'Get out . . .'

'Yes, I'll go. I'll go where I can get some bloody warmth and understanding,' he shouted. The front door slammed and the sound made her wince with pain. She stared into space. She did not cry but sat silent as another part of her soul died within her.

She found the calm practicality of the lawyers helpful. They dissected her marriage and drew up the separation contract, in a clinical way, like legal pathologists. Alistair gave her the Fulham house, a sum was agreed for the support of James, and he insisted that May's wages were his responsibility. Then the lawyers began to negotiate her allowance.

'I don't want an allowance from you, Alistair, I'll get a job.'

'Doing what, for heaven's sake? What could you do?' Alistair sneered at her across the lawyer's desk.

'Perhaps if you'd pay for me to do a shorthand and typing course . . . I think I'd like that. Having organized the opening of a stately home to the public shows I have some ability,' she said with pride, fighting the tears she felt were not far away. How sad, she thought, that they did not seem able to speak to each other normally.

She enrolled at a secretarial school. It was strange to be back at school, sitting at a desk. The other girls were school-leavers and at first she felt shy of them as they talked nonstop of their boy friends and music groups of which she had never heard. She felt dowdy beside these exotic young women with their bright miniskirts and bleached beehive hair. But they were kind to her, took an interest in her. She decided that they were a much more caring generation than her own had been.

Life settled into an orderly routine which helped her. She attended school each morning and each afternoon, with May, she took James to a park, a museum or the zoo. Her evenings were devoted to studying the squiggles and swirls of shorthand. They lived simply. She found sleep difficult. And she felt completely dead inside.

Three months went by. Sandra called whenever she was in town. She had many worried conversations with May, without whom Jane would never have been able to manage. May cared for the house, looked after James when Jane was at school, cooked for them, and tried as best she could to help Jane through her depression. It was a difficult task which May had set herself, for Jane would sit for hours, a drink in her hand, listening to music, not wishing to talk.

'Jane, love, you've got to pull yourself together.'

'I'll be all right, May.'

'But you've been saying that for months now.'

'It takes time, I feel I'm mourning a death. It's the only way I can describe it. Please, May, be patient with me, give me time,' she pleaded.

Alistair phoned one day to suggest that he take James with him on a short trip to Italy, before the start of the school term. Jane agreed; it would be a holiday for the boy and it would give May a chance to go home and see her family. Since they had been in London the girl had not had a day off. Even so, May was worried about leaving her but Jane insisted; she felt that if she were completely alone for a time, perhaps she would be able to heal herself.

Alistair's car arrived. James had been watching for it from the window for the past hour.

'Come on, Mummy, Daddy's here.' The child rushed out to greet his father, who was standing on the doorstep. Behind him Jane could see the car and, sitting in it, a pretty blonde-haired girl. James rushed up to the girl and gave her a smacking kiss on the cheek; the girl greeted him with the ease of an old friend.

'Who's that?' Jane asked her husband, a dreadful coldness filling her.

'My girlfriend, Samantha.'

'You're not taking her to Italy?'

'Why shouldn't I?'

'But with our son? That villa, it's our place, our time.'

'Don't talk such romantic crap, Jane. That's all over now. I do need some comforts, you know. Of course she's coming. Really, Jane, it's none of your business whom I take with me,' he snapped. He looked at her closely. 'You look bloody awful, Jane, it's about time you pulled yourself together. You won't even get a job, let alone a lover, looking like that.' She slammed the door angrily in his face and turned to look nervously in the mirror. It was as if she looked at a stranger. A stranger with a puffy face from too much drink and too little food. Dull hair hung unkempt and limply about her face. The eyes that gazed back at her from this stranger's face were devoid of expression: they looked like the eyes of a dead person. She could not bear to look at this face – she picked up an ornament and smashed the mirror.

'I love you, you bastard!' she screamed, her voice echoing around the empty house, bouncing off the wall and beating into her brain. Sobbing, she poured herself a drink. With shaking hands she lifted the glass to her lips and downed the contents in one gulp, then quickly poured herself another one. With exaggerated care she placed her favourite recording of Sibelius's Fifth Symphony on the record player. From the cupboard under the stairs she dragged the large paisley cushion, now worn with age, and sat cross-legged on it in the middle of the floor, staring out of the window at the snippet of sky above the house opposite.

She remembered the very first time she had sat on this cushion, on this floor, in this room. Where had she gone? Where was he? What had happened to them? Where did dead love go? All that energy, created by their love, did it just dissipate into the air, did it wander about looking for other lovers? He hated her. She had heard it in his voice when he spoke to her. She had begun to cope with knowing that he no longer loved her, but how was she to live with the dreadful knowledge that he hated her? And now there was someone else, someone who knew how to love him and not smother him as he accused her of doing. Someone who screamed with real passion in his bed. He had gone for ever now; she had no place in his heart. Her love, her precious love, the only thing of any value she had to give him, was no longer needed. He was the only reason for living – and now he did not care if she lived or died.

She stretched her hands into the air and clutched at the space with desperation and folded her arms, cradling her unwanted love to her breast. She began to rock. Back and forth she rocked, and she began to make a strange whimpering, mewing noise. She watched her patch of sky as she rocked. She saw the night come and then the day, then night, then day again. The darkness and the daylight sped across her window as she rocked and mewed to herself.

Sandra found her three days later. Jane did not recognize her friend. She could not stop rocking, could not take her eyes from her little piece of sky.

Kind hands came and gingerly straightened her legs. She was not conscious of the pain in her cramped limbs. Gently they lifted her onto a stretcher and covered her with blankets.

She missed her sky, she could not rock but still she whimpered – her song for her dead love.

The days and nights filtered past her in uncounted progression. She felt she was a bird, a little green and yellow bird, and she watched patiently for hands to come and hold her, caress her gently, with tenderness. Hands that would love her.

Faces came and peered at her, talked about her as if she did not exist. She did not understand where they got the idea that she was unaware of them. It was funny because, of course, she knew them. She watched her friend Sandra, May, Mrs Evans; she learned to recognize the different doctors. She just did not want to speak to them, could not raise the energy, but, oh yes, she knew they were there. She waited for one face, but it never appeared. She longed for his face, then she would talk, she would make herself talk, she wanted to speak to him, explain everything, and once he understood then he would love her again. But she never saw his beloved face. They tried to frighten her into talking, for one man they sent had no face. Each day the faceless man looked at her and each day she screamed and screamed until they led him away. And then they stopped sending him and she felt happier.

She watched her sky, the sun shone brighter for her, the clouds scudded faster, the stars shone more clearly. She allowed the needles to be pushed into her. She liked the feeling that the drugs gave her: they allowed her to float above herself, as the bird that she had become.

She had been sleeping, drifting in and out of her own dream world, and when she awoke it was to see a new face looking at her with concern.

'Honor,' she cried, and she held her arms up. The woman took her and rocked her like a baby, crooning to her, and Jane began to cry. As the tears flowed from her eyes, as the pent-up emotions flooded out, she explained to this woman whom she loved the sadness that rotted her soul. Then and only then did her sanity begin slowly to return.

Her doctors were pleased with her: the change in her was miraculous, they declared. She had had a nervous breakdown, a severe emotional shock. Nothing to worry about, she would be fine now, she was well on the way to recovery, they told her. She knew that they were wrong; she knew that a part of her had died, that she could never be the same again. A new doctor came, a young man called Nigel, who talked to her, wanted to know about her. She found it easy to talk to him, to tell him of her need to be loved, the loneliness inside her, the emptiness she felt. In the talking came a measure of healing.

Honor came each day. They would walk in the grounds of the hospital and talk of everything – but never of Alistair. After that first outburst, Jane could not speak of him again, except to the nice, young doctor who, she felt, did not mind being told.

They sat in the sunshine in the garden and she felt peaceful and almost happy.

'I want to go home, Honor.'

'Yes, darling, you shall.'

'But today, Honor. Will you come with me? I want to be in my little house. I want to see James and hold him again.'

'Not today, darling, but soon,' Honor promised.

She talked often of James now, she could not imagine how she had forgotten him. They explained that she was not quite ready yet – a few more weeks and then she could return home. So she concentrated hard and willed herself better, incomplete as she was, so that she could see her son again.

Despite the racking pain of rejection which tore her apart inside, she had learned to smile calmly at them, to sit quietly, her hands folded in her lap. She knew this impressed the doctors, who would then keep telling her how well she was doing. There seemed no point in speaking of the pain within her: she doubted they would understand.

'We feel you are nearly ready to go, Jane,' the doctor told her. 'However, I don't think it's a good idea for you to go home yet. Lady Honor has suggested you go to Italy with her, but quite honestly I would prefer that you stayed in this country for, let's say, another three months. Then you could go to Italy for a good, long rest.'

'But I want to go home to James,' she complained. She noticed Honor and the doctor glance quickly at each other. 'What aren't you telling me? Is there something wrong with James? Tell me, please.' Her voice was raised with fear.

'James is fine, darling. He's with Alistair.' Again they glanced at each other and she saw the doctor nod his head almost imperceptibly. 'You see, darling,' Honor said gently, 'Alistair had to take the boy when you were so ill, and no one knew how long it would take for you to recover.'

Jane nodded, smiling. 'That was kind of him. But I want James back now.'

'The trouble is, Jane,' Honor continued, taking hold of her hand, 'when you were ill, well, Alistair applied to the courts and they gave James to him to care for.'

She sat in silence allowing Honor's words to sink in. 'You mean he had me declared unfit to care for him?'

'Yes.'

'Had me committed?' she asked calmly.

'Yes. He didn't know what else to do, Jane. Someone had to decide about James.'

She sat quietly, apparently examining this information. But within, she screamed in her anguish. She did not understand. 'Honor, he didn't have to go that far. I could only have James to myself while he was small. Alistair knew I understood that. I've always known that in the end he would be happier with Alistair, and he belongs at Respryn. A boy needs his father, doesn't he?' She knew she would begin to shake. She sat rigid, fighting the tremors which began to ripple through her body, fought with all her strength, for if they saw, they would never let her go.

'Jane, are you all right? Can I get you something?' the anxious doctor enquired, quickly opening the bag at his side.

'Don't worry, Nigel,' she said hurriedly. 'I don't need your drugs any more. I'll manage. I'll be all right in a moment. It's the shock, you see.' She turned her face to them and both Honor and the doctor averted their eyes from the pain in hers. 'I'm having to adjust to the fact that to all intents and purposes I've lost my son. I have, haven't I?' Honor was distressed at her words. 'But he need not have gone as far as to have me committed. I wouldn't have gone anywhere. I like it here.' The doctor and Honor looked intently at their hands. 'Why did he never come to see me, Honor? I waited every day for him to come. Had he come, I'm sure I'd have recovered faster.'

'But he did come, darling. Every day for weeks he came, but you screamed so much that in the end the doctors wouldn't let him see you. He's been beside himself with worry,' Honor explained.

'I didn't know that he had come. I couldn't see him.'

'No, of course not, darling, you weren't aware of anyone when you were so ill.'

She decided not to explain to them about the faceless man: it was too complicated and, as with everything else, she doubted if they would understand.

'Now, where are you to go? That's our immediate problem,' the doctor asked kindly. 'What about your parents?'

'God, no! They would be ashamed of me. Mental illness frightens people like them. It wouldn't go down well in the street.' She laughed a tiny laugh. 'In any case, I don't belong there any more, I wouldn't fit in. I do have one friend who might look after me before I go to Italy – Sandra, we nursed together.'

'That would be ideal. Especially since she's a trained nurse. Then she can keep an eye on you for us,' Nigel said, pleased with the arrangement. 'Do you want to see your husband?'

'No, thank you, not yet.' She could say it without thinking. She knew she had to have time before she could face him.

Everything was arranged for her. Sandra agreed immediately to take her friend and care for her until the doctors agreed that she was ready to fly to Italy for a long holiday with Honor.

A year after her collapse, outwardly well but precariously stitched together inside, Jane set out with Sandra, with whom she had shared her London adventure, to Cambridge, which had other memories for her.

Four
1969–70

1

Sandra drove Jane's car carefully. The traffic was heavy. Jane sat stiffly, flinching, as the large lorries hurtled towards them.

'It's all right, Jane. I know this road like the back of my hand.' She patted Jane's hand comfortingly.

'A year without traffic is a long time,' Jane explained. 'I'd forgotten how busy the roads can be.'

She made a conscious effort to relax, to let her hands lie flaccid on her lap. Breathe deeply, she told herself, as they had instructed her to do in the hospital, when, as now, anxiety crawled over her body insidiously, like invading slime. She felt transparent, as if her nerve endings were on the outside. Breathe deeply, she repeated to herself with more urgency. She had to control herself; it was important. She must not let anyone see how she was feeling, or she would be returned to the hospital she had just escaped from.

This must be how prisoners feel, newly released from jail, she thought, as she watched with strangely reawakened eyes the never ending flatness which stretched as far as the eye could see. Where the land met the sky, there appeared to be no division between earth and heaven. She remembered, fondly, the gentle hills of Respryn and the noble mountains of Drumloch, and she felt a wave of homesickness engulf her.

As if reading her thoughts, Sandra turned to her. 'You get used to the flatness. I didn't think I ever would, but I love it now. It has a beauty all of its own and, with no hills in the way, one is more aware of the fantastic skies.' Jane smiled at her friend. They had both changed. Jane was razor thin. Her cheekbones had deep hollows below them. Her clothes hung loosely on her. That was the first thing she must do: get something that fitted. How could one begin to feel normal in clothes like these? But Sandra had changed too. Her plumpness had gone – in its place an angular slimness, which did not suit her as well as her previous rounded curves – but the beautiful eyes and dimpled smile were still the same.

Sandra spoke of old friends from their hospital days. An inveterate letter-writer, she seemed to have news of everybody. They spoke of her family, her children, Lance and Michelle, of the new house they had just bought, and said nothing of Jane's illness or her marriage. Jane felt herself finally relaxing. The wave of anxiety had passed.

They left the main road and entered a village. Jane clapped her hands with pleasure as they sped past the village green where, in the shade of an oak, stood the quaint thatched pub; on the village pond ducks pottered busily; and the village shop had bottle-glass windows. It was a chocolate-box village, and brought a smile to Jane's face at last. The car snaked over a packhorse bridge, swung up a lane and they entered a modern housing estate. The houses stood in staggered formation, to give a measure of privacy to the occupants, but to Jane this element of privacy looked to be an illusion. Each house stood on an immaculate, unfenced lawn, giving the impression of wide open spaciousness, unless, like Jane, you were used to rolling parkland which made these lawns look like pocket handkerchiefs. Some attempt had been made to vary the minor details of each house. There were three types of front door and two types of door knocker, and some houses had porches while others did not. The houses were made individual only by the choice of curtains, or the make of car in the driveway. Since the houses had all been built at the same time, the gardens were at the same stage of development, and looking around it was as if only two trees, the weeping willow and the flowering cherry, were indigenous to these islands.

They came to a halt. 'There. What do you think?' Sandra asked.

'It's very nice,' answered Jane, unsure of what to say about a house that looked so uniformly ordinary.

'Of course, for you, after Respryn, it must seem like a hovel.'

'It's lovely, Sandra, really,' Jane said hurriedly. 'If I sounded a bit vague it was because I thought you still lived in Cambridge.'

Sandra's husband, Justin, was waiting for them in the sitting room. The first thing that struck Jane, as she looked about her, was how small the house was, and how bare it seemed, despite plenty of furniture. Everything gleamed in its newness, from the shiny Dralon-covered three-piece to the large wall unit which housed the stereo, TV and books. Apart from a Utrillo print and one vase, there were no ornaments and it was their absence that made the room seem naked. She felt as if she were standing in a showroom in a furniture store. The large picture windows were draped in net curtains so that it was impossible to see out. Dominating the room was a rough stone fireplace which rose from floor to ceiling; beneath a shiny copper hood was an electric fire, the artificial coals glowing too red.

'What do you think?' asked Justin, expansively waving his arm.

'It's a bit big, isn't it?' said Jane unthinkingly, fascinated by the monstrous fireplace.

'Yes, we're lucky. This style of house is the "Executive Elite", so we have a separate dining room, and four bedrooms. Our garden is the largest on the estate, always a good selling point, that,' he said proudly, misunderstanding Jane completely, much to her relief.

'Justin! You sound like an estate agent. I shouldn't think for one moment that Jane cares about the virtues of our house.'

'It's very interesting,' Jane said, quickly.

'Go on, I bet you'd be more interested in a drink. I know I would. I'll show Jane her room, Justin, while you organize the glasses.' Jane followed her friend up the open-plan staircase and into a back bedroom, whose walls were covered in a nursery wallpaper.

'Sandra, I didn't think. You haven't got room for me. The children . . .'

'Of course we've got room for you. The kids are bunking in together. They don't mind one bit.'

'But I thought that Justin said you had four bedrooms?'

'We have, but that's the agent in him talking. The fourth is so small you couldn't swing a cat in it. It's got my sewing machine in it – that's all there's room for.' Sandra laughed.

'Look, Sandra, I'll just stay the weekend. I'll be fine in Fulham.'

'You bloody well won't. We'll manage. I promised everybody I'd look after you. Hell, I virtually had to swear on the family Bible.' As she spoke, Sandra moved about the room, straightening the already straight curtains, smoothing down the smooth bedspread, checking the empty cupboards. 'The bathroom's across the landing. See you downstairs in the lounge.'

'Sitting room. Only hotels and airports have lounges,' Jane thought automatically, so well had she studied her book on accepted word usage. In the pretty, wallpapered bathroom, the tiles on the walls gleamed, the taps shone. Every corner of this house was a triumph of cleanliness and tidiness. Frilly net curtains hung unnecessarily at the small frosted window. She studied her face in the mirror of the medicine cabinet. Lounge, sitting room, drawing room, it did not matter a damn any more, and she could say what she wanted, but it was odd that she had flinched at that word 'lounge'.

Back in the sitting room, they waited for her. Small bowls of nuts and crisps now stood on the ceramic-tiled coffee table beside an ornately scrolled, silver-plated tray on which glinted carefully polished cut glass.

'What's your poison, Jane?'

'What?'

'To drink? Sherry?'

'Oh, gin and tonic, please, ice, no lemon.'

'Sorry, Jane, we're out of gin.'

'Don't fib, Justin. We don't run to spirits, Jane,' Sandra announced and her husband glared angrily at her. She stared back almost defiantly.

'Anything then, anything you're having,' Jane answered, flustered. 'Sherry will be lovely.'

As Justin poured the drinks, Jane saw that Sandra seemed incapable of relaxing. Even when she was sitting down her hands were endlessly fiddling, straightening the folds of her skirt, patting her hair, picking unseen threads from the arm of the chair.

Justin presented her with a small glass of sherry, which he carefully placed on an embossed leather coaster on the tiled table.

'Well,' they both said in unison, and then both laughed, awkwardly. 'After you, Justin.'

'I was going to say that my parents have invited us all to dinner the day after tomorrow. If you would like to come?'

'I'd like that very much, thanks.'

'I was going to suggest,' Sandra said in turn, 'that if we could get a baby-sitter, we should go out for a curry.'

'If you don't mind, I'd rather have an early night. But if you two want to go out, I'll baby-sit for you.'

'I don't think that's – ' Justin stopped in midsentence.

'Thank you, Jane. We'll take you up on that, won't we, Justin?' Sandra said, looking pointedly at her husband.

'You needn't worry, Justin. I'm not dangerous. I didn't hurt anyone, only myself. The kids will be safe with me, I promise,' Jane said to a very red-faced Justin.

'Jane, I didn't mean . . .'

'Yes, you did, Justin.' Jane laughed good-naturedly at him and the embarrassing moment passed.

The children returned from their tea party and Sandra refused Jane's offer to help bath them. She was left alone with Justin. He stood with his back to the fire, legs straddled, the glass of sherry in his hand. He had a paunch now and the good looks of youth had given way to a smooth, self-satisfied face. Jane noticed the fingers around the stem of the glass were podgy and looked as if they'd be sweaty, too. He did not talk to her, rather he lectured in a hectoring tone. She listened but made no reply. Instinctively she felt he was not interested in anything she had to say. Jane thought that she did not like Justin very much any more.

At last, Sandra was ready and they left. Jane sat in the sitting room, the two children standing in front of her, solemnly inspecting her. She talked to them, but neither said a word, merely stared with round eyes in their angelic faces. Finally, she suggested that she read them a story.

'No!' five-year-old Lance said.

'No, thank you,' corrected Jane.

'Piss off,' the child replied.

'Pith off,' Michelle, his little sister, echoed.

'That's not a very nice thing to say to me, is it?' Jane asked, feeling more surprised than shocked.

'Don't want you here. Don't like you,' the boy announced.

'Don't like you . . .' his sister aped.

'I can't say I'm very impressed with either of you,' Jane said angrily. 'If you're going to be that rude, then you can both go to bed, now.'

'Shan't!'

'Shan't!'

'Yes, you damn well will, or I shall smack you.'

'You hit me, I'll tell my granny.'

'Tell her what you like. I'm sure she would agree with me that you deserve a good smack for such bad manners.'

'My mummy never hits us,' the boy stated proudly.

'Then perhaps she should.' Jane did not know how to handle this situation. She had never been very good with children, in fact, apart from James, she did not like them very much. Lance stuck his tongue out at her, and her hand itched to slap him. 'Go to bed,' she said as calmly as she could.

'Shan't!'

'Shan't!'

'Bed!' she yelled. Startled, the little girl ran screaming from the room, but the boy stood his ground, staring insolently at Jane. Suddenly he raised two fingers at her, stuck out his tongue again, and then dashed hurriedly from the room before she could reach him.

Jane poured herself another of Justin's far from good sherries and wished they had some gin. She leafed through the records but gave up on finding that they were mostly light music. She was surprised, Sandra had always loved classical music. She sat on the slippery, Dralon-covered armchair and remembered the wonderful softness of the velvets and cretonnes she had become used to.

That scene with the children had been extraordinary. They were awful, even someone who liked children would have to agree with her on that. They looked angelic and were monsters. She had presumed that Sandra's children, with her idyllic childhood behind her, would be perfect.

And why was Sandra so thin? There was a jumpiness about her which was alien to the carefree girl she had once been. There was something very wrong. Jane was certain she was not imagining it: her time in hospital had given her what she liked to think of as antennae which were able to pick up moods and atmospheres quickly and incisively. She had not yet worked out if this facility within herself had come as a result of her illness or whether, surrounded as she had been by people in a precarious mental state, she had developed it as a means of protection. There was an atmosphere of edginess bordering on aggression in this house which was a tangible thing to her.

She looked about her. This was a dreary room, it was totally lacking in character. She began to feel claustrophobic, especially with that vast fireplace looming over her. If one had pitons one could climb it.

She sat bolt upright in the chair. What had got into her? She should not be thinking this way. She was so used now to Alistair's standards that they were normal to her. Separated from them, she missed them, and realized she wanted to live no other way. Yet, when she had been a schoolgirl, this house would have been the height of her ambitions. Fifteen years later she sat here, sneering at it.

What right had she to sneer? It was bare, but from the odd remark that Sandra had dropped, it was obvious that they were short of money. She was turning into a possessions snob. It was not a pleasant thought.

Tired of all this self-criticism, she began to think of her future. After her holiday with Honor, what then? It had been one thing in the lawyer's office to state proudly that she wanted nothing from Alistair. Now, if she did get a job, she would certainly not earn as much as Justin. If they were hard up, how could she afford to pay the electricity bills, the rates, buy drinks? While she had had James, she could with a clear conscience accept an allowance for all those things, but now, what on earth was she to do? Maybe she had acted too rashly. She could not have known that she was going to be ill, and for so long, or that she would lose custody of James. The repercussions of that wretched illness were going to be with her for a long time. But one thing she had learned: never again would she be so involved with one person. In the future, in the unlikely event that she should meet someone she could care for, she would reserve a part of herself to fall back on if things went wrong. She would never allow herself to become so vulnerable again. She was certain that if she had not wallowed in her grief for Alistair, she would never have become ill. She had allowed her mental resistance to get too low and so she had succumbed. Just like catching flu, really, only more inconvenient.

It was strange that she should begin to think of all these things now. It was almost as if a curtain had lifted in her mind and she was faced with stark reality for the first time. It was a frightening prospect, but at the same time she realized with relief that she was facing it rationally and reasonably calmly, despite her fears.

She looked at the telephone on the table beside her and wished she felt free enough to phone Alistair, talk to him. Would she ever ask him for help? She did not know, she doubted it. Maybe one day she would have to swallow the stupid pride which had landed her in this muddle in the first place. Now all she wanted was to hear his voice, to tell him she was all right, that she missed him, that she was sorry, that she loved him. 'That she loved him' . . . it was always going to be like that. She might let herself think of being involved with someone else, but it was a futile exercise. She would never love anyone else: it was as simple as that, she thought. Hadn't she always said to Sandra, all those years ago, that there would only ever be one man for her? They were just romantic words then; now they were reality. Perhaps she should have shut her mind to his affairs. He would never have left her, she knew that; he would always have come back to her and their marriage. That pain would have been preferable to what she had just been through, preferable to this fear for the future. Would she ever have the courage to tell him all this? What if he gave her an ice-cold look? What if he spoke to her in that controlled way he now had, with barely concealed irritation? There were too many imponderables. By now, one whole year later, he was probably living happily with someone else. How was she to know – hadn't she refused to discuss him with anybody?

She patted the telephone affectionately, drained her glass, switched off the light and went to bed in the room with aeroplane wallpaper, in the narrow child's bed, and lay a long time wondering what was to become of her.

2

Jane had overslept. She apologized to Sandra, whom she found, a can of Pledge in one hand, briskly polishing the kitchen cabinets.

'Tea or coffee?' asked Jane. 'I'll do it, just tell me where everything is.' Jane opened the cupboards Sandra indicated. 'Crikey, you've changed. They're so tidy!' She laughed. 'Remember your cupboards at the Nurses' Home? Always in a mess.'

'I wasn't that bad.'

'You were, you were dreadfully untidy, far worse than me,' Jane teased.

'I don't remember.'

Jane settled herself at the table and, digging in her dressing-gown pocket, took out her cigarette case and lit up. 'Got an ashtray?'

'I'd prefer it if you didn't smoke, Jane.'

'What?'

'It's a filthy habit.'

'I know, sorry.' Quickly she put the cigarette out. 'You given up, then?'

'Heavens, yes, ages ago. Justin doesn't like it.'

'I see. Does that mean I can't smoke here?'

'Good gracious, no. It's just I'd prefer you didn't in your bedroom and here in the kitchen.'

'Perhaps you've got a handy garden shed?' Jane grinned, but Sandra ignored the remark and continued with her polishing. 'Do you always polish the units? Isn't washing them enough?'

'I don't like to see finger marks,' she said, standing back and looking critically at the shining doors. Then she got a bucket, filled it with water, and proceeded to wash the floor.

'Don't you want your tea?'

'When I've finished this,' she replied.

'Why are you so unrelaxed?'

'Me? Unrelaxed? What a strange thing to say, Jane. I have work to do, I'm just getting on with it. We can't all afford servants to do it for us,' she said tartly.

'Sorry,' Jane said in a singsong voice and, clutching her mug of tea, tiptoed over the washed floor and into the sitting room. She lit a cigarette and took a few puffs but, conscious of the smoke curling into the air of the tidy room, she hurriedly put it out. Wandering back upstairs, she paused in the bathroom to run herself a bath. In her bedroom Sandra was making the bed.

'Heavens, Sandra! What the hell are you doing?' she exclaimed, shocked.

'Making your bed. What's it look like? I feel uncomfortable if I know there's an unmade bed in the house.' She busily straightened the counterpane.

'Sandra, love, I'd have done that. Honestly, you're making me feel embarrassed.'

'Sorry, I can't help that, I have to get finished. Is that the bath water running?'

'Yes.'

'I wish you'd asked, Jane. We only have so much hot water and I wanted to do a wash today.'

Jane felt herself blushing with confusion. 'Hell, I'm sorry, I didn't know. I'll stop it.'

'You might as well have it now, rather than waste it. We'll fix a time for you in future. It's the immersion heater, you see – for economy it's only on at certain times of day.' Satisfied with her bedmaking, she turned to the door. 'It's my morning for coffee, if you'd care to join us?' She smiled and left Jane alone.

Sandra was very confusing to be with, Jane thought, as she lay soaking in her bath. One minute she was so prickly, the next moment she was smiling that beautiful smile. The last person she had expected to become a house-proud woman was Sandra. She smiled as she remembered the arguments they had had when, for three months, they had shared a room in the Nurses' Home. Both were equally untidy, and the chaos they had created should have led to disaster, but somehow they had weathered it, and later used to laugh about it. Yet now Sandra denied that she had ever been untidy. She was hyperactive. Nobody changed that much without a reason. In her present sensitive state, Jane was finding Sandra and her house unnerving.

When she arrived in the sitting room, to her delight it was full of young women with their children. She stood in the doorway overcome by sudden shyness, watching them chattering happily with each other, as they drank coffee and ate cakes. The children divided into two groups, those who tumbled about together and those who clung to their mothers' skirts, sucking their thumbs, and solemnly watching the others as if wanting to join them but lacking the necessary courage – Jane knew exactly how they felt.

'Ah, Jane, here you are. Everybody, this is my best friend, Lady Upnor,' Sandra said in a proprietorial tone. The women stopped talking and, as one, turned and stared at Jane. 'Don't just stand there, Jane, come and have some coffee.'

One of the women made room for her on the sofa. Since some of the others were smoking, Jane took out her cigarette case and lighter and offered a cigarette to the plump, fluffy-haired girl who sat beside her. The girl was already balancing a baby, her coffee cup and cake plate with admirable dexterity, and still she managed to take a cigarette.

'Thanks.' She smiled. 'My name's Liz Turner-Green.' She looked longingly at the cigarette case. 'That's a beautiful thing. May I look at it?' Jane, not sure which to relieve her of, took her coffee cup in preference to the baby, and handed her the heavy gold case which carried her initials picked out in sapphires – a birthday present from Alistair. 'Gosh, it's heavy,' Liz exclaimed. 'Look, Dodo, isn't that the most beautiful thing you ever saw?'

'Is it real?' the woman called Dodo asked. She was red-haired, not in a soft, green-eyed way, but with sharp features and a spiteful expression.

'Of course it's real.' Liz laughed.

'I think it's vulgar,' Dodo said matter-of-factly. Jane felt acutely uncomfortable as the pale-blue eyes surveyed her coolly. She put out her hand to take the case back, but already it was being passed from one girl to another, making Jane wish she had left it upstairs.

'Does it offend your socialist principles then, Dodo?' asked another girl with rosy cheeks and large muscular legs which must have served her well on a hockey field. 'Lady Upnor, don't let Dodo upset you. She'd love to own it, really. She's just jealous.'

'Hilary, you needn't think for one moment that you can upset me. I only take note of people of intelligence,' Dodo said in a cool voice, but Jane saw that her eyes were blazing with anger. Jane braced herself for the ensuing row, but instead the large-legged girl merely laughed louder than ever, and Sandra took the heat out of the moment by offering more coffee.

'You staying here long, Lady Upnor?' Liz asked her.

'Jane, please call me Jane. Well, I was, but I didn't realize the house was so small. I don't think it's fair for me to stay too long.'

'Too small!' the young woman shrieked. 'Did you hear that, everyone – Jane here thinks this house is too small. Heavens, it's the biggest one of the whole estate.'

'I didn't mean it like that. Please. I mean with the children . . .' She blushed with confusion, and felt angry with herself. She had looked forward to meeting a group of women of her own age who lived normal lives. She wanted to talk to them, learn from them, and here she was inadvertently putting her foot in it at every turn.

Their astonishment at her remark subsided and conversation became general again. They discussed their electricity bills and there was a long debate about whether or not it was more economic to turn the immersion heaters off at night. They complained of how little their husbands helped them in the house. They all agreed that it was not immoral to economize on their housekeeping and to keep the excess for themselves to buy make-up and tights. Jane learned that the local shop had a sixpence discount on Nescafé – the middle-size jars, not the large. Hilary announced that she thought she might be on to a window cleaner, at last. This information caused great excitement. Jane listened intently and felt isolated. If she was to build a new life, she thought, how could she succeed if she felt she had nothing in common with women of her own age? She supposed she could learn, but, on the other hand, she was not sure if she wanted to: nothing they talked of interested her. Yet they seemed contented, and was not that what she herself longed for?

'Sandra's always talking about you,' Liz suddenly said, and Jane jumped, jolted out of her sense of isolation.

'We've known each other a long time.'

'She's wonderful, isn't she? I mean, she's so efficient, everything is always perfect. And her kids' socks are always immaculately white. Me? If I can find my lot one pair between them it's a miracle.' The girl laughed, and Jane warmed to her.

'You live here too?'

'Yes, opposite. We were first here. It was lonely to begin with, but now it's lovely with most of the houses sold – there's always someone to talk to.'

Jane wondered what they found to talk about, day after day. Sandra and she used to debate everything under the sun and yet there was her friend, across the room, deep in discussion on the best way to remove ring marks from furniture . . . Jane leashed in her thoughts and felt ashamed – she was getting arrogant, in the true Lady Upnor mould. She turned to talk to Liz. 'Tell me about your house,' she said.

'Oh, I'd much rather talk about yours,' Liz gushed. 'I visited it last year when we were on holiday. I shouldn't have been so rude, laughing like that when you said this one was small. I saw that I'd embarrassed you. Sorry. I mean, it really would be minute after Respryn, wouldn't it?'

Jane smiled gratefully at the plump young woman. 'It isn't really – you see, we only live in a small part. We can't afford to live in the whole house.' She realized she had used the present tense. How long would it take, she wondered, before she would be able to talk of having lived there?

'Do you mind the trippers crashing about?' Liz continued.

'No. Most people are very appreciative of what we do. It's good for the house, too, to be full of people and noise. And it helps with the expenses,' Jane replied, uncomfortably aware that the conversation had died down and that everyone was listening.

'Bet the heating bills are dreadful?' another voice enquired.

'Horrendous. But you learn to run a lot in winter to keep warm.' She managed a laugh but wished inwardly that they would return to their normal conversation. She found herself getting flustered as she was unable to answer some of their questions. The financial, day-to-day running had never been her concern.

'How many staff?' 'Do you have a butler?' 'Does a lady's maid wash your knickers?' 'Bet you've a Rolls-Royce?' 'A chauffeur?' 'What do you do all day?' The questions continued thick and fast. Jane wished her answers did not sound so apologetic. While some of the women had a genuine interest in Respryn, there were others from whom she sensed a distinct feeling of animosity. She had a strange feeling of *déjà vu*: she might just as well be back in Respryn, all those years ago, with Clarissa and her cohorts taunting her –

except that now everything was reversed. Then she had been attacked for being working-class; now the ill-feeling was because she was a countess.

The door burst open and a harassed young woman, with a young child on each hip, stood anxiously in the doorway.

'Who owns that blue BMW out there?'

'I do,' Jane said, blushing inexplicably.

'Oh, Christ, I'm sorry – I've just reversed into it. My bloody foot slipped and I just shot backwards.'

'What's the damage?' asked Sandra anxiously.

'I've dented the bumper. I'm so sorry. I'll pay for it, of course. Christ, Chris will kill me,' the young woman wailed and both children, sensing her distress, began to cry loudly.

'That will cost a bomb, BMWs don't mend cheaply,' Dodo said unhelpfully.

'Oh, please, don't worry,' Jane said, relieved. 'If it's only a bumper, that's no problem – after all, what are bumpers for except to be bumped into?' She smiled brightly. No one smiled back.

'Shit! How grand can you get?' Dodo sneered.

'I don't understand,' Jane said worriedly, alarmed by the antagonism. 'What have I said?'

'Well, really, if you don't have to worry about a bent bumper, if you've got so much money it's of no importance, quite honestly I think it's disgustingly ostentatious of you.'

'What the hell do you mean? What the hell do you know about my finances?' Jane flared back, her vulnerability making her defensive.

'You've been boasting enough all morning.'

'Boasting? I have not, people asked me questions; I didn't bring up the subject of my home. Would you have preferred it if I'd ignored your friends' questions? In any case, it isn't – Sod it, I don't have to explain anything to you.' Jane felt herself begin to shake. Abruptly she stood up and walked across the room, conscious of the stares of the women upon her. As she got to the door, she turned and, forcing herself to smile, said in a dangerously sweet voice, 'But if it makes you feel happier, Dodo, I'll send your friend the bill.'

She swept from the room and into the kitchen. She started, vigorously, to do the washing-up. Suddenly her shoulders slumped and she clung to the edge of the sink. She took deep breaths, counting between each intake, just as they had taught her ... but the control she needed eluded her. From deep within, anxiety wormed its insidious way to the surface, snaking along each nerve fibre, escaping from each follicle, bathing her in a fine film of sweat. She was conscious of the subdued voices of the women in the hall, and the unconcerned shouts of their children as the party broke up. Sandra must not find her like this, not even Sandra – they would shut her up again. Grabbing her handbag, she searched helplessly for her cigarettes. Turning the contents of the handbag out on the kitchen table, she hurriedly clicked open the case, put a cigarette in her mouth and, with trembling fingers, lit the lighter. The cigarette was soaked, her hands still damp from the washing-up. Cursing, she threw it away, quickly lighting another. Calm down, you stupid bitch, she told herself with exasperation, inhaling deeply. The hospital had given her pills. She wondered if for once she should take one. Until now she had resisted them because she had an ex-nurse's fear of drugs, and also because, if she were to regard herself as recovered, it had to be without the crutch of tranquillizers.

Sandra came into the room, went straight to Jane and put her arm about her.

'Jane, love, I'm so sorry about that.' Through the silk of her blouse, Sandra felt Jane shaking. 'Love, don't get this upset. It's only Dodo, she's a painful cow.' She looked intently at Jane, seeing fear in her grey eyes which was out of all proportion to the incident. 'I don't know why we put up with her. I suppose primarily because we feel sorry for her. Her husband's a bastard – thinks he's God's gift to women and is always having affairs with young students.' She spoke quickly in an attempt to distract Jane.

'Is he a teacher?' Jane asked, not because she was interested, but needing something to occupy her mind.

'He's a lecturer at the tech. He's got the most enormous chip on his shoulder – feels second-rate compared with the university lecturers.'

'She reminded me of my sister-in-law, the dreadful Lady Clarissa.'

'God, how funny. I must tell the others. I mean, she's so left-wing she's almost a Commie. But then that's the tech again: it's almost mandatory there, it seems to me.' An uneasy silence settled over them, as Sandra could not think of anything else to say. She looked anxiously at Jane as she sat at the kitchen table, a blank look on her face.

Jane took another cigarette, forgetting Sandra's rule about smoking in her kitchen. 'You see, Sandra, I begin to think I don't belong anywhere any more. I don't know where I'll ever fit in,' she suddenly said, sadly.

'Oh, darling, of course you will. You and I get on just as before.'

'Yes, with you. But you don't understand. I can't go home to my parents – there's nothing there for me now. I never really fitted into Alistair's world. My hope was yours . . . but look what happened. So where do I belong?' She looked anxiously at her friend, who had no answer for her. 'Funny thing is, your friend Dodo's probably got more money than me, anyway. I'm skint.'

'Jane!' Sandra exclaimed. 'You're not serious? Oh, God, you are. Have you got a cigarette?'

'But you said – '

'I was being crabby. I hate these bloody coffee mornings – they bore me to tears – and whenever it's my turn I'm bad-tempered. I don't smoke officially: Justin would hit the roof. I'm a closet smoker.' She chuckled.

'Thank Christ for that,' said Jane as she opened the case which had started her downfall at the coffee party.

'Right, now tell me. What's all this nonsense? No money?'

Jane explained her problem and how she had no one to blame but herself.

'You're a bloody fool, Jane. You must go back to your lawyers,' Sandra advised.

'I can't do that. My pride won't let me.'

'Pride is a principle you can't afford, my girl.'

'I said I would manage and manage I will.'

'That's being pig-headed. It's as much his fault that you're not an SRN. He married you and prevented you from finishing your training. Had you done so, you wouldn't have had any job worries. Let's be practical then. What have you got? What can you do?'

'I'm very good at opening stately homes to the public.' At last Jane grinned.

'I don't think there's much call for that.' Sandra grinned back.

'I've done three months of a secretarial course – Alistair was paying for that. I don't mind asking him to pay for me to finish it. But how do I live until I get a job? Coming here has been a good lesson for me, Sandra. It's making me think of practical problems that I've never had to give a thought to – like how to pay electricity bills and the rates on the house. I haven't had to handle money since the day I married. I never see a bill. I have accounts everywhere. The most I ever carried with me was enough to pay a taxi. I used to joke about it and say I was like the Queen, never carrying money, but now – '

'House, you said, what house?' Sandra jumped eagerly on the word.

'Alistair gave me the house in Fulham, but I can't see how I can afford to live in it.'

'Jane, you're a clot. It's simple. You rent out the house, furnished – you'll get a small fortune for it. Then you rent something cheaper and live off the excess until you can get a job. Then you'll be laughing.'

'Do you really think it would be easy to rent? I hadn't thought of it.' At last Jane felt the vestiges of her panic recede. 'I thought I was going to have to sell it and I hated the idea.'

The back door burst open and Michelle rushed in, home from nursery school. Having kissed her mother, she turned and gave Jane a kiss, too.

'I thought you didn't like me?' Jane asked, surprised by the child's attention.

'I do,' the child answered indignantly. 'You're pretty,' she said as an aside, as she banged out of the room and rushed up the stairs.

'What was all that?' Sandra asked.

'Nothing, just a joke.'

'No, it wasn't. Lance was horrible to you last night, wasn't he?'

'Well . . . he's at a difficult age.'

'No, Jane, he's becoming a monster! I'm at my wits' end with him. What did he say?' Jane related what had happened and Sandra sighed. 'What upsets me is that he's beginning to affect Michelle and she's such a sweet child. It's his bloody grandfather – he spoils him rotten. He spends virtually every weekend there and comes back impossible.'

'Stop him going,' said Jane reasonably.

'Ha! Easier said than done. I can't. The old man would hit the roof, and Justin would be angry. His old man owns the agency Justin works for, you see. He's a real bastard, I hate him. He doesn't pay Justin nearly enough and always hanging over us is the threat that unless we toe the line he'll kick Justin out.'

'Sounds a really attractive character! But Justin, surely he'd rather be disinherited and be his own man?'

'I wish he would, but he's shit-scared all the time. The old bastard's a martinet. He's short, that's the problem.'

'Short! What on earth has that got to do with it?' Despite her friend's obvious distress, amusement sounded in Jane's voice.

'Don't you know the theory about short men? They have to bully to compensate for their lack of inches, to prove how masculine they are. Like Hitler and Mussolini. And I have to land up with one as a father-in-law.' As she talked, Sandra was picking away at the label on a sauce bottle.

'Sandra, stop fiddling. Do you realize, when you're not working, you're always fiddling with something?' To Jane's consternation Sandra began to cry.

'Oh, Jane, you don't know. I'm so bloody unhappy.' It was Jane's turn to put a comforting arm about her friend, but it was some time before Sandra's tears subsided.

'You're always listening to my problems. Now let me listen to yours for a change,' she said. Sandra blew her nose on a large piece of kitchen paper. 'Is this why you've turned into such a frenetic housewife?'

'I suppose it is. You see' – she helped herself to another of Jane's cigarettes – 'his father was so angry with Justin for marrying me in the first place. It's the only time he's crossed his old man, but then he didn't have much choice – I was pregnant.' She laughed, bitterly. 'I'm not good enough for his son, he thinks I'm a liability. I suppose that's why I have to have everything so perfect all the time, trying to prove what a good wife I am.' She began to pick at the sauce bottle label again and Jane waited patiently for her to continue, knowing there was more to come. 'And it's Justin, too. I mean, the kids come back from their grandparents like wild animals. They wreck the place and then if everything isn't all spick and span when he comes in, he hits the roof. He's so edgy these days, and so conscious, all the time, of what people will think and say. Sometimes I'm afraid he's going to end up just like his father. I seem to irritate him constantly. He's becoming a bully. He even hit me the other day.'

'Bloody hell!'

'It's this awful house: God, I hate it. We had a lovely house before, off Mill Road. It was smashing, but, no, Big Daddy decides the area isn't good enough for his son. That it's time we were incarcerated in this miserable executive box, on this bloody executive estate, with all the other boring young couples crawling painfully up the bloody ladder to success. And what happens? We're lumbered with an enormous mortgage we can't afford, for a house I never wanted in the first place.'

'But you seemed so happy just now?'

'Oh, don't get taken in by that. That's part of the "wife-of-successful-businessman" act that I'm very good at. Most of the women bore me to tears. They moan all the time – about their lives, their husbands, their bloody periods. And either they're getting too much sex or not enough. Sometimes, Jane, I feel that all my personality, what strength I had, has all been sucked out of me. But I love him. I just don't know what to do.' She began to sob. Jane took her hand, attempting to comfort her friend. 'Oh, hell, Jane. I'm sorry. I shouldn't be burdening you like this. I'm supposed to be cheering you up.'

'But you are helping me. You're putting my problems into perspective . . . and I thought I was alone . . . But you've got to put your foot down, Sandra, before it's too late. Get a job, that'll help with the mortgage and get you out to meet people,' she advised. 'You're going to crack up at this rate.'

'I know. It sounds awful, but when I used to visit you in hospital, I almost envied you your breakdown – you'd got right away from everything.'

'What's your mum say?' Jane asked.

'She doesn't know. She's so proud of me and my lovely home, I can't bear to disillusion her.'

Jane looked thoughtful. 'Come on, Sandra, we need cheering up. I'll go into town and get us some booze – we'll get pissed together.'

'Would you? Tonight's ideal. Justin's at some Rotary do. Get loads of fags, too!'

Jane drove into Cambridge. At least that had not changed, except that the students looked younger. She went first to the top floor of Heffers and browsed through the paintings. There were some good abstracts, but she decided on a conventional oil painting of the Fens, certain that Justin would prefer it. She went to Millers and bought recordings of the Brandenburg Concertos and Mahler's Third Symphony. She bought a bottle of gin and a couple of bottles of wine, then went to Adams and loaded up with exotic cheeses.

They put the children to bed early, saw Justin off to his dinner and, like conspirators, settled down to the serious business of getting drunk. For one blissful evening they were back together again – just as in the old days.

'There is just one thing, Sandra.'

'Wha's that?' Sandra slurred into her glass.

'Do me a favour, don't introduce me to people as Lady Upnor. I hate it, I get all embarrassed.'

Sandra sat bolt upright and looked earnestly at Jane, her eyes filling with tears. 'Oh, Jane. Don't ask me to do that. I love it, I'm so proud of you. I get such a kick saying it. Don't you realize – you're the excitement in my boring life.'

3

They drew up in front of Justin's parents' house, a pseudo-Georgian mansion, looking, with its columned portico, like a miniature Parthenon. They entered a large, imposing hall full of reproduction antiques, including a fake suit of armour.

Justin's mother, a thin, nervous woman, whose greying, mousy hair exactly matched the long dress she was wearing, showed them out to the swimming pool, where drinks were to be served. A shaggy green carpet stretched to the edge of the pool which was surrounded by gleaming plastic plants. Mrs Clemance could not settle, fluttered about them like a rather dull moth, serving drinks, plumping up cushions, emptying ashtrays. She seemed fond of Sandra, fussing over her almost protectively. Her genteel voice, a product of hours of elocution lessons, was hard to listen to, as each word issued forth half-strangled.

After an hour Mr Clemance finally joined them. Since Sandra always referred to him as 'the old man', Jane was unprepared for his apparently youthful appearance. With jet-black hair and dressed in fashionable, tight-fitting, flared trousers of green velvet, topped by a boldly striped shirt, he looked more like Justin's brother. But as he shook Jane's hand she saw that the hair was dyed, and the face was not, as she had thought, unlined – instead, the wrinkles were disguised by a heavy tan, which looked suspiciously even. The Clemances made an odd couple, so contrasted that Jane was reminded of a cock bird with his hen.

They began dinner, a meal of overcooked lamb and soggy vegetables, washed down by a 'Choice of the Month' wine from Mr Clemance's wine club, of which he was inordinately proud.

Mr Clemance dominated the conversation. He leaned back in a large, intricately carved chair, his stubby hands splayed out on the table in front of him. A miasma of smugness enveloped him. He did not speak to anyone in particular; rather he spoke as if the sound of his own voice was satisfaction enough.

Throughout the meal Sandra was silent. When not eating, she stared fixedly at the pattern on her plate. The only time she smiled was in response to her mother-in-law who fussed around them, communicating in a silent semaphore of arched eyebrow, questioning smiles and tentative gestures.

Justin seemed to enjoy his father's company. Sitting in a smaller chair, he leaned back, too, a carbon copy of his father, not in looks but in attitude.

Back at their house, Justin went to bed. The two friends settled for a nightcap.

'Your father-in-law is a male Lady Upnor. Perhaps they're related. What an ego! I don't think I've ever met anyone quite so pleased with himself before.' Jane laughed.

'I wish I could find him funny,' Sandra said. 'Do you see what I mean now? If it wasn't for Mrs Clemance, I'd begin to wonder if I existed.'

'Justin puzzled me, though. He was ignoring you too.'

'I know. So, am I to presume that he agrees with his father's opinion of me? That's the question that haunts me. And what makes me really sad is, I'm not a bad wife. But that old bastard won't rest until we're finished and he can marry him off to someone he thinks more suitable.'

'And I thought it was only me having problems about being accepted by gruesome in-laws. You'd think that now, in the so-called liberated sixties, things would have changed, wouldn't you?'

'Perhaps it's because we've done nothing. I mean, you read of working-class film and pop stars, even hairdressers, who're courted by everybody. Maybe if we'd done something with our lives we might have been more acceptable . . .'

'You have done something, you're an SRN. But those others, you can take my word for it, they're only taken up temporarily – like fashionable cabaret acts.'

They finished their drinks and made their way to bed. Jane lay in the dark, worrying about Sandra. All the fun and sparkle seemed to have gone out of her. She was in a vicious circle of being so terrified of Mr Clemance that she could not assert herself, and the more she cringed, the more he despised her. There was no doubt in Jane's mind: Sandra was on the verge of a breakdown. She would talk to Justin about it. One of the good things she had learned in the hospital was the value of talking things out; it solved so many problems before they took serious root in the mind. Self-awareness they called it, but Jane always felt that it was more like cleaning out a cupboard – taking the muddle out of one's mind.

The next morning while Sandra was doing the school run, Jane sat opposite Justin at the breakfast table.

'Justin, I'm worried about Sandra. I think she's on the verge of a nervous breakdown, unless we do something quickly,' she announced baldly.

'Really? I can't say I've noticed anything odd about her,' he said, sounding uninterested, peering over the top of his newspaper.

'Surely you have, Justin. She's so nervy. She never stops cleaning. Look how jumpy she is.'

'She takes pride in our home. I don't see anything wrong in that.'

'Of course not, not normally, but this cleaning of hers is obsessive, bordering on paranoid.'

'My, haven't you learned a lot in that hospital of yours?' he said, unpleasantly. 'Are you now trained in such matters?'

'Of course not, but I can't help noticing things. I think she needs to get right away. I think you should sit down with her and talk this through. It'll help both of you.'

'I don't think any of this is your business, Jane. I'd prefer it if you dropped the subject,' he said coldly.

'I can't. Hell, she's my oldest friend. I can't just sit back and see her cracking up because your father doesn't approve and is turning her into a nervous wreck. It has to be faced, discussed,' she said, a shade too excitedly.

'My father has nothing to do with this.' Justin methodically refolded his paper.

'But, Justin, your father has everything to do with it. Gracious, he's even turning her children against her.'

'That is arrant rubbish. How dare you. And who the hell are you to lecture me about my wife and my home? You haven't made such a great success yourself, have you? Just out of the loony bin, your marriage in tatters. What right have you to criticize me and mine?'

'It's because I've just got out of the "loony bin" that I'm in a position to say it. I can see signs in her that perhaps you're not aware of yourself. In the hospital – '

'I think, Jane, that you're a very arrogant woman. Just because you queen around with some stupid title doesn't give you the right to interfere like this.'

'I do not queen about. I am the last person who can be accused of that.'

'Oh no? You don't think I haven't noticed you sneering at our life style, because I have. And last night at my parents' you hardly opened your mouth and I know why, too – because you were uninterested and felt superior.'

'It's quite easy to feel superior to your father. Not your mother. I felt sorry for her – who wouldn't? But OK, yes, I didn't like your father: I thought he was pompous and rude, and horrible to my friend.' Horrified, she realized she was shouting. How much of that, she wondered, was to cover her discomfort at Justin's precise reading of her thoughts? The very thoughts she had been so ashamed of.

'Right, Jane,' he said, collecting his newspaper and coat, 'I thought it was a bad idea your coming here in the first place. I was certain that you would upset my wife. I would appreciate it if you weren't here when I return from work this evening. I really have no room for your interference and rudeness in my house.'

She should not have lost her temper, Jane thought, as she despondently packed her case. They had drummed that into her at the hospital. Calmness and logic, those were the keys, not flying off the handle and insulting a man's parents. She really had been trying to help. She had become so used to sitting in a circle, analysing others' problems, that she had quite forgotten that the outside, sane world did not behave that way.

'Oh, Christ!' Sandra exclaimed when Jane told her what had happened. 'But thank you for trying.'

'I did it all wrong. I was inexcusably rude about his father. And losing my temper, antagonizing him like that, isn't going to help you – and that's all I wanted to do. Oh, Sandra, I'm sorry.'

'I'm sorry you're going, but I'm proud you stuck up for me like that.' The two friends hugged each other.

'I suppose we'd better find somewhere for me to live.'

They phoned a couple of agencies and were given details of several flats. They telephoned one and made an appointment for Jane to view it later in the morning. Until it was time for her to go, they sat miserably smoking cigarettes and drinking cups of coffee.

'At least if you rent somewhere in Cambridge, you'll be near and I can pop in and see you to have a good old moan,' Sandra said bravely. But as Jane loaded her cases into the car, her friend began to cry.

The address she had been given was of a large house in Newnham. She drove up a shrub-infested drive and stopped outside a large house which looked in desperate need of a coat of paint. The garden was a riot of weeds, and the bell she rang was half hanging off the door. It was answered by a woman in her forties, her ample form covered in a multicoloured, flowing, none too clean kaftan. Her long hair was blonde, the roots showing black on her scalp; in her hand she wafted a long cigarette holder.

'Mrs Upnor? Welcome . . .' She waved Jane through the door, squeezing her bulk against the jamb so that Jane could manoeuvre past. 'Bloody hell, I just seem to get fatter and fatter.' She laughed loudly, as she showed Jane across the hall. Every inch of wall space was covered in paintings, the unpolished wood-block floor was strewn with random piles of books. They entered a bright kitchen which was a jumble of more paintings, books, plants, unwashed dishes and unironed clothes. 'Hope you don't mind clutter?' She grinned and pushed a fat, sleeping, white cat from the chair. 'Magnificat, move! Coffee?' She busied herself at the Aga, grinding beans, and moving, despite her obesity, with agile grace. Soon the kitchen was filled with the smell of freshly made coffee.

'They forgot to give me your name at the agency,' Jane said, savouring the delicious taste.

'Silly sods. Zoe Potterton, the old boiler, that's me.' She laughed loudly at her own joke. 'Have you lived in Cambridge before?' Jane was fascinated by her voice, which was low and husky: even when she was not smiling, laughter seemed to bubble through. It reminded Jane of Honor's voice with its hints of all manner of secret enjoyments.

'No, London mainly. But I have friends here, and when I found myself having to decide where to go, I thought of Cambridge.'

'Divorced?'

'Separated.'

'I hope you're not hoping to find a new husband here? Everyone's peculiar, you know. It's an odd place to live. Nothing's real here, it always seems to me. And the people take a bit of getting used to.'

'Marriage isn't a priority of mine at the moment,' Jane said lightly. 'I want to sort myself out, I've been ill, you see. I've just got to learn to pick up the pieces and build a new life.'

'You've chosen an odd place to try, then. Everyone seems to be off their rockers here. And most people are so self-centred, intent only on what they are doing, no real interest in anyone else. I always think that going to a dinner party in this city is like going to listen to half a dozen monologues.' She produced a large tin of cakes and offered them to Jane, who refused. As she bit hungrily into one, she suddenly said, 'I suppose you think I shouldn't be eating this, too fat already?'

'No, I wasn't.' Jane laughed at the question.

'Being fat is my own personal statement. This town is impossibly full of glorious, gorgeous, gilded youth. I can't compete, so I decided not to try and to be what I am, uncomplicatedly fat. No, I'd resolved not to say that any more. I'm not fat, really, I'm just under-tall. If you stretched me out a bit, I'd be lovely and thin, wouldn't I?' Again the full-blooded laugh rang out. 'Do you drink?' Jane nodded. 'Smoke?'

'Devotedly, I'm afraid.'

'Drugs?'

'Gracious, no.'

'Good. I like you, you'll fit in. I like people who drink and smoke. Drugs can be a bit wearying and trouble with the police and what have you. But I'd never have nondrinking, nonsmoking types as lodgers. They wouldn't fit in, and I'd be endlessly worrying myself about what vices they did have. Still, I expect you want to see the flat.' She led the way, talking nonstop so that Jane found herself watching carefully to see when she managed to take a breath. Jane could not understand how she could possibly have decided to like her since Jane had had little chance to say anything.

'See, you've got your own entrance,' Zoe said, unlocking the door and showing Jane into the flat. Built onto the back of the house, it had a large sitting room, with sliding glass doors opening onto the garden. A large, black, Swedish wood-burning stove stood on a central hearth; a spiral staircase led up on to a balcony which was arranged as a small study, and off it were two bedrooms. A beautiful kitchen, fitted in pine, and a bathroom completed the flat. 'You're welcome to use the garden, any time, and there's a lake at the bottom where we all swim and frolic in summer. What do you think?'

'It's perfect, Mrs Potterton. How much is the rent?'

'Call me Zoe, please. How much can you afford?'

'I'm not sure. I'm going to rent my house in London, I'm not sure what I'll get for it, but no doubt you want to rent straight away?'

Zoe thought for a moment. 'Tell you what we do. You rent your house in London and give me a third of what you get. How about that?'

'Are you sure?'

'Oh, I'm sure. The money doesn't matter. It's having congenial neighbours that's important. I've already said no to half a dozen the agency sent.'

'Heavens, what a compliment!'

'Do you want to move in now?'

'Well . . . I'm a bit short until I rent my own house.'

'Just owe it to me,' Zoe said airily.

Gratefully Jane accepted her offer, unloaded her cases, packed her things in the drawers, and then telephoned Sandra with her new number and address. After going to the shops to buy food and some drink, and fortified with a large gin and tonic, she telephoned Alistair.

It was a long time since they had last spoken – and then they had been screaming at each other in anger – but, when she heard his voice, all the old longing returned. Her mind raced with dreams and plans while her voice prosaically made arrangements to meet him at Fulham, to sort out what things he wanted to remove. She sat for a long time afterwards, her hand on the receiver, as if by touching the instrument she was, in some way, still in contact with him. He had sounded warm and kind and had offered to make the letting arrangements for her. It had been a big step for her to take, to speak to him, but now she wished they could have talked longer.

Jane was highly agitated as she approached the house in Fulham. It was the first time she had been there since her illness. She was almost afraid to enter in case she would catch it again, like a contagious disease, and never recover. She was afraid to see Alistair, too. It was one thing to talk on the telephone but an entirely different proposition to be face to face with him. But still, she argued with herself, speaking to him had been one hurdle, seeing him was only another. He was already there and opened the door as she put her key in the lock.

'You look well, Jane,' he said, kissing her quickly on the cheek.

'So do you,' she replied, unsure of what else to say.

'I think your Cambridge idea is a good one. Better to get right away.'

'Yes.'

'Are you sure you wouldn't prefer to sell the house altogether?'

'No. I'd rather rent it. I don't want to lose it, it's so much of the past . . . isn't it?'

'Quite.' He walked past her into the sitting room. She paused at the doorway, afraid to enter, afraid to look at the point on the carpet where her mind had left her that dreadful day. He stood in front of the Picasso. 'You can take this, if you like. You didn't believe me when I told you that you'd grow to love it, did you?'

'No.'

'So, do you want to take it?' he asked, unaware that she had not yet followed him into the room. He studied the painting. 'It needs reframing. I'll get that done for you as well, shall I? And I think you should replace the china and glass: it's far too good for lodgers. I spoke to the agent and they'll see to all of that for you. Odd bits of silver should go. I don't want anything. You're welcome to the lot.' He was speaking quickly and, as he spoke, he roamed about the room collecting ornaments and pictures which he felt she should take with her. She watched the familiar figure, the beautiful hands which had caressed her, and she longed to shout, 'I want to come back to you. Take me back. I love you.' But fear would not let her speak; wordlessly she nodded at his suggestions and silently she packed the objects he gave her

221

into the boxes he had thoughtfully provided. He did not look at her once; she wanted him to look at her – perhaps then he would see the naked longing in her eyes. 'Right, I think that's all. Didn't take long, did it? You'd better give me your phone number. I'll bring James over one of these weekends, shall I?'

'Yes, please,' she said huskily, the happy thought making her breathless.

'Right.' Satisfied, he looked about the room. 'That's it, isn't it?'

'Yes, I suppose so.'

'Funny, really, when you think of all the time we spent here, our life together. Now it's just a room, waiting for lodgers, isn't it?'

'No, it'll never be that to me,' she said, turning away, tears brimming in her eyes. He helped her carry the boxes out to her car, laid the paintings carefully on the back seat.

'Anything else?'

Hesitantly she explained her need for some money until the rent from the house started to arrive. Equally hesitantly she asked if he would pay her fees at a secretarial college. She wished he had simply offered and she had not had to ask.

'Of course. I think even with the rent coming in you'll have a struggle, you know. Better let me help you out on a regular basis.'

'That won't be necessary,' she said with dignity, as she accepted the wad of pound notes he gave her and climbed into her car.

As she cleared the London traffic, she felt overwhelmingly sad. What had she expected – that on seeing her he would run into her arms and beg her forgiveness, plead with her to return? Yes, she supposed that was exactly what she had hoped for, but things like that only happened in fairy tales. This was life, real life, where it seemed there were to be no happy endings.

4

She settled into her new life in Zoe's flat. She had wondered if it would be difficult for her to meet people, but as an endless procession of people visited Zoe, so she would be summoned by Zoe yelling out of a window for her to come and be introduced. Her life became a succession of new faces and celebrations, since Zoe needed only the weakest of excuses to open yet another bottle of wine.

They would sit for hours around the large pine kitchen table, Bach or Mozart filling the room from the giant-reeled tape recorder. They were a motley crew – university lecturers, worried by their work or disillusioned by it; homesick students; lovesick nurses; menopausal women whose children had left home and who could no longer find ways of filling their days; men whose wives had just left them; homosexuals set on another destructive affair – all of them in some way wounded by life.

People would arrive at any time, day or night. Coffee would be put on or wine opened. Zoe would settle her expansive bottom on her special cushion, in the biggest chair. With her giant breakfast cup or the equally large rummer in front of her, she looked just like one of Goldilocks's bears. She could coax, wheedle and persuade them to tell her everything – and they did, at length. Zoe always seemed to have time. In fact there was not even a clock in the kitchen to remind anyone of time passing by.

In this company Jane felt at ease. She listened to their tales, and just as Sandra's problems had helped her put her own life into perspective, these new friends consolidated that perception. Her sudden bouts of anxiety passed, the pills were flushed down the lavatory. Jane felt calm. Luckily, she was aware that it might be a false calm, for she could not say she lived in a normal world. She was surrounded by the walking wounded of life; apart from trips to the corner shop she never went out; and she had the security of Zoe's strength to protect her like a huge, warm blanket. But it was giving Jane respite, a plateau on which her mind could heal and renew itself.

The reason for Zoe's size soon became apparent. She was a cook of passionate genius. She never minded how many she cooked for; her only proviso was that she was never to be left alone in the kitchen.

'I can't stand being alone. I start thinking, and too much thought is a dangerous exercise,' she laughingly explained to Jane one day, as she avidly and expertly chopped the ingredients for another gargantuan casserole. The rest of the house seemed to hold no interest for her. Jane only ever saw her in the kitchen. She supposed that Zoe must have a bedroom somewhere, and that there were other rooms, but Jane never saw them, and could only presume that they were slowly falling into decline from neglect, as the front of the house was doing.

From far away in the large house, Jane would hear Benjamin tapping away on his typewriter. He was a successful novelist. He worked hard and was rarely seen in daylight hours. Telephone messages would be taken for him; anyone who wanted to see him would have to wait patiently until his tall, lolloping figure wandered into the kitchen, his big nose over his wild, bushy beard sniffing the air like a huge shaggy dog's at the tempting smells coming from Zoe's Aga. They adored each other, and Jane loved to watch them as they greeted each other every evening as if they had been separated for weeks, not just for one working day.

'Benjamin works so hard,' Jane commented one afternoon: the tapping of the typewriter had been a constant background noise all day.

'Yes, it sounds as if it's going well. I dread it when a book's finished: he gets very depressed that all the characters he's created have gone away. Then he stays depressed until he starts another one.'

'It must be wonderful to be that successful.'

'It is. On the other hand, because he's successful, the intellectual snobs here sneer at him. He was a Fellow, you see, once, then he committed the unforgivable crime of writing a bestseller. Now some of his old colleagues ignore him. He says it doesn't matter, but I know it hurts him.' Zoe looked angry at the thought.

'They're probably jealous of all the money he earns.'

'Yes, that's probably it.' Zoe laughed, her expression lightening.

Jane spent more and more time with Zoe as the weeks went by. Zoe cooked and Jane would help clear up, do the washing and ironing; and she took on the weeding of Zoe's precious herb beds and vegetable garden. If the front garden was a jungle, the back was a model of order, with row upon row of vegetables flourishing. The arrangement worked well, for Zoe had all the tasks she hated to do done for her, and Jane was never alone.

Jane had always enjoyed writing letters, and now she had the time. Honor was high on her list, Alistair and May, too, and Nigel, her doctor, and her parents. It was as if by writing long chatty letters to them she was proving how much better she was. Each week she wrote to James, hating the thought of him now at boarding school, and though it was often difficult to know what to write, she was certain he must look forward to the post. Each week he replied, short stilted little notes, thanking her for hers, rarely any news.

Sometimes three or four letters would be posted before Alistair would reply, always news of the estate, nothing personal. His phone calls were infrequent, and she began to feel more isolated from him.

Honor never wrote but instead phoned often in reply, enquiring how she was and never failing to ask if there was anything she wanted. Each time the invitation to go to Italy was repeated and each time Jane declined. For the moment, Jane felt safer with Zoe and Benjamin; her days were full of chores and people. At Honor's Jane knew that she would have too much time with nothing to do but to think, and she was not ready for thinking, yet.

The letters done, Jane began to write for the pleasure of it. She tried to put into words what had happened to her and to her surprise found that the exercise helped her further. As the days sped past, Jane kept putting off her plan to enrol at the secretarial college, there just didn't seem any need somehow.

Sandra called whenever she was in Cambridge. On each visit, Jane was aware that she was witnessing the gradual disintegration of her friend. Each time she looked gaunter, each time she was thinner. She chain-smoked now, and her hand as she reached for her cup had an almost imperceptible tremor. One day she was more agitated than usual. Not only had Mr Clemance announced that he was taking the children on a month-long cruise, but he had suggested that on his return they move into the big house with him. Justin seemed to think all this a good idea: it would solve his money worries. But Sandra was in despair.

'That friend of yours is going to have a breakdown any day now,' Zoe declared after Sandra's latest visit.

'I know. I don't know what to do. I tried talking to her husband but he threw me out. She's frightened to do anything in case Justin sues for divorce and gets the children.'

'That's unlikely.'

'His father's very rich. He'd finance Justin to fight her through every court in the land for those brats. She loves him, you see, though I don't understand why. I think he's a creep.'

'Does her mother know?'

'No, she's too ashamed to tell her.'

'Phone her up, you tell her.'

'I can't do that . . . it's none of my business.'

'I've never heard anything so wet in my life, Jane. I thought you were her friend. I'll phone, what's the number?'

Zoe went straight to the phone and in graphic detail told Mrs Evans what was happening to her daughter. The next day, a shocked Mrs Evans arrived and, within an hour, had assessed the situation, had packed Sandra's and the children's cases and was speeding back to Battersea with the three of them. That evening the telephone lines to Cambridge bristled as Mrs Evans vented her spleen on Justin and his father. She was adamant: Sandra and the children were to stay with her until Justin decided what he wanted – his father or his wife. Zoe and Jane waited impatiently for the outcome.

Six weeks later a radiant Sandra appeared. She seemed beside herself with happiness. She and Justin had been on holiday together while Mrs Evans looked after the children. She was coming back, but on her own terms. Now the children were only to see their grandparents once a month. According to Sandra, the time spent with her mother had worked wonders on the children, especially Lance. The house outside Cambridge was up for sale and they were searching in the city for something cheaper. Once she had left him, Justin had realized how much he loved her, and had plucked up the courage to demand a raise from his father. With the mortgage pressures off him, and more money in his pocket, Sandra was certain that the bullying, hectoring Justin would disappear – everything had been getting him down too. Sandra herself was applying for a part-time job at the hospital. Jane watched this speedy revolution with envy and wished that she had been able to solve her own problems as neatly as Sandra had done, but then, as Zoe pointed out, Jane did not have the formidable Mrs Evans behind her.

The weekend she had longed for arrived, and on a crisp autumn day, Alistair was due with James. She was nervous as she awaited their arrival, and unsure if this stemmed from the prospect of seeing Alistair or excitement at seeing her son again. When she saw Alistair getting out of his car, the old longing flared up in her body. The little boy who climbed out of the car in his smart school uniform looked like a stranger to her. The boy stood in the driveway, his cap clenched in his hand, staring intently at the ground and aimlessly kicking a pebble with his shoe, as his father kissed Jane on the cheek. James turned his head away, abruptly, as she tried to kiss him.

'Kiss your mother, James,' Alistair demanded. Anxiously Jane saw the small hands clench his cap more firmly, his jaw set in a determined line as he went on kicking the pebbles. 'James!'

'It doesn't matter, Alistair. He'll kiss me when he wants to, won't you, James?'

The boy did not answer. His eyes darted everywhere, looking at everything but Jane. She was distressed that his lovely blonde hair had been cut with short back and sides, accentuating the slimness of his young boy's neck. She saw the fine blonde down on the nape of his neck and she longed to nuzzle him there, suddenly remembering the warm, earthy smell of little boys. She asked him about school. He replied shortly, called her 'sir', and kept a mental as well as a physical distance from her. Over a year was a long time in the life of a child of nine. She would have to learn to be patient with him; but, even as she thought this, she realized that she did not mind his distance; shockingly, it did not seem to matter.

They spent a stiff afternoon in the botanical gardens. Jane and Alistair walked ahead of James who lagged a good ten yards behind, as if proclaiming to the passers-by that he was not with them, or rather, she thought, with her. Alistair, irritated, would call him, they would pause and wait for him, but as soon as they set off, the boy would lag behind again. They had tea in the Copper Kettle, then wandered back to Newnham. She gave Alistair a drink. James sat on the edge of the sofa, giving the impression that he was ready for instant flight. She turned the television on for him, but he did not watch; instead his eyes never left his father, waiting for the first sign that they were about to leave. When it was time for them to go, it was Alistair to whom she hated to say goodbye.

After this initial visit, they came twice a month during the school holidays. James's air of detachment persisted. Alistair was distressed by the boy's behaviour. He cajoled, nagged, reasoned with and yelled at James, but to no effect. Jane suggested that, perhaps, if she were alone with him for a few days, it would be easier for them to reforge a relationship. Alistair refused her request: he was regretful but he quite openly admitted to her that he was afraid she was not fully recovered yet. She could have argued with him, she supposed, but she did not want any bad feeling between them, so she dropped the idea. In a way, she was relieved at Alistair's refusal. She felt she had suggested it because she should, not because she wanted to. In reality, what would she have talked to the boy about? What could she give the boy when he so obviously did not want any part of her?

On each visit, her main hope was that Alistair would say something of how he felt about her, about them. But he never did. Instead, she felt he treated her with a distant but tender concern.

'Will you ever go back to him?' Zoe asked her one night as they sat alone, drinking chilled white wine and eating dolmades.

'I shouldn't think so. He's never shown that he wants me back.'

'I wouldn't say that – he looks at you at times as if he could eat you.'

'I've never noticed. He never makes any advances and he's never said he misses me.'

'Has he found anyone else?'

'I should think there's an army of them.' Jane laughed.

'Perhaps he's waiting for you to make the first move. He strikes me as a somewhat inhibited individual where emotions are involved.'

'He's not particularly inhibited where leaping into beds is concerned,' she said ironically. 'I couldn't make the first move, though. What if he rejected me? I just don't know how I could cope with that.'

'You'll never know unless you try. You can't hide behind your breakdown for ever, miss.'

There were times, Jane thought, when Zoe's bluntness was hard to take. But she was right. Jane knew she used her illness as a barrier to life, something behind which to cower. She never went anywhere, clung always to the security of Zoe and her kitchen. She was going to have to do something about it – well, some time, she would.

'There's something else, Jane.' Zoe interrupted her thoughts. 'You'll probably hit me for saying it, but you don't seem to be involved with that little boy of yours. You seem – '

Jane stood up abruptly. 'You're right, Zoe. I would like to hit you. If you'll excuse me, I'm off to bed,' she said coolly, picking up her cardigan and leaving Zoe to the rest of the wine.

She lay on her bed, frowning at the ceiling. She felt threatened by Zoe's assessment. But she was not ready to talk about it to anyone. Alone, she often worried about her attitude to James but, even so, she felt she did not worry enough. When she was with James, it was as if she were watching someone else with the boy. She was certain that the boy regarded her as a boring duty, a visit that had to be got through, politely, before he could get back to the life she now knew nothing about. It should make her sad; it was odd that it did not. Part of the trouble was that, try as she might, she could not remember what it was like to be a mother. She just could not seem to remember what their relationship had been like before her illness. When she thought of the past it was always of her life with Alistair, almost as if the child were an adjunct to that life, not a true part of it.

She fumbled on the bedside table for her packet of cigarettes, lit one and watched the smoke curl up to the ceiling. Perhaps her attitude was a defence mechanism. Having lost Alistair, was her mind refusing to cope with the possibility of losing her son? Or was it that they were reaping the whirlwind of her childhood? How could you love as a parent if you had not been loved as a child? Maybe Alistair was right: maybe, as a result, she could not love, only possess. Agitatedly she puffed at the cigarette. That could not be true. She knew she loved Alistair, whatever he chose to say. And knowing how she felt about Alistair, there was Zoe, always nagging her to find a boyfriend, telling her she would get crabby without sex. Jane laughed softly. If only Zoe knew – sex, and the lack of it, did not bother Jane one jot. It was the lack of love that made her sad.

She stubbed out her cigarette, and searched for the light switch. Beside the lamp, Alistair's face smiled at her from a photograph. She gently traced the outline of his lips. She had placed it there so that it was the first and last thing she saw in her day. Alistair, not James.

'Oh, dear, I am weird,' she said to the darkness.

5

Autumn slid into the marrow-freezing cold of a Cambridge winter. The winds whistled in from the North Sea, crossing the Fens but apparently losing none of their bitterness and ferocity on the way. They even acquired the ability to go around corners, so that wherever one huddled in the city, the wind would find one out. This would, Jane thought, have been a logical time to go to Honor's, but Zoe had invited her for Christmas, which coincided with Benjamin's birthday and the big party they always held. In the New Year she would go to Italy for a month, and when she returned she would start her secretarial course again.

The food for the party would have fed an army. Hearty, robust stuff to line the gut and mop up the wine, in total contrast to the delicate canapés and wafer-thin sandwiches she had ordered for parties at Respryn.

Armed with a big brush, Zoe marched across the kitchen. 'Care to help get the party room ready?'

Jane willingly followed her across the hall and into two intercommunicating, darkened rooms. Zoe wrestled with the shutters and, as the thin winter light filtered into the room, Jane burst out laughing. Before her was a room totally bare of furniture, except for large cushions scattered about the floor, a stereo unit with massive speakers, and everywhere dirty ashtrays, upturned bottles and empty glasses.

'Oh, dear, I should have cleared it up after the last party. I always forget. Still, it hardly matters now, does it? We'll just empty the ashtrays and wash the glasses, it'll be in just as much of a mess again in the morning.'

'Zoe, I love your logical mind!'

Jane was excited at the prospect of the evening. It was such a long time since she had been to a party. She dressed with care in a new black suit she had bought from Wallis especially for the occasion. She studied herself in the mirror. She had never worn so short a miniskirt before: the style had never seemed right at Respryn. She liked the way it seemed to make her legs look longer, and the fact that the chunky patent-leather shoes accentuated their slimness. She buckled a chain belt around her waist and decided to wear her hair loose. The black suit with her dark hair made her look interesting and intellectual, she decided, laughing at this new image. Now that, thanks to Zoe's cooking, she had filled out a little, the new clothes suited her.

Zoe looked magnificent in a turquoise kaftan, shimmering with gold thread which competed with her freshly bleached hair. As Zoe glittered about the room putting the finishing touches to the food, Jane was aware that she was nervous. It was an extraordinary discovery: she had thought that nothing could frighten Zoe. But here she was, fretting and worrying in the same way that Jane had done at Respryn.

Jane circulated dutifully about the room, but could find no one to talk to – plenty to listen to but none to talk with. She wondered what it was about male academics that made them smell, a strange musty sort of odour, akin to unwashed socks or a damp day on the London tube.

She finally gave up circulating and stood quietly watching the crowd form and reform like live cells under a microscope. She smiled at the sight of Zoe, deep in conversation, her arms whirling like a turquoise windmill as she argued animatedly with another middle-aged woman.

'Hullo, who are you?' A dark-haired young man with a distinct cockney accent was standing beside her.

'I'm Jane Upnor, Zoe's lodger, in the flat.'

'One of her lame ducks, are you?'

'Yes.' She laughed. 'I suppose that's a fair description of me.'

They stood side by side, surveying the crowd. She glanced at him out of the corner of her eye. He looked interesting, different, she thought. She searched for something to say to prevent him moving off.

'What do you do?' He spoke for her.

'Nothing, just trying to survive at the moment.'

'Hope you haven't told the other geezers here that you do nothing. It wouldn't go down at all well.'

'I've learned that already. It's the glazed look that comes over them and the speed with which they shuffle off.'

'That's 'cause you're no use to them, you see, if you do nothing. Everyone is on the lookout for contacts, people who'll give 'em a leg up, see?'

'You mean no one wants to know me for myself?' Jane said in mock horror.

'Christ, no. What an antiquated idea! Only use you'd be to this lot is to listen to 'em.'

'I've done a lot of that tonight, actually.'

'"Actually", have you?' he said, mocking her voice, but this only amused her. 'What you've got to do, my girl, is to emote. E-bleeding-*mote*, as our American mates would say.'

'Sounds messy, like having an emetic.'

'I like that. You're funny. Yes, emetic, much the same really, give out, spew your personality out. 'S good, that.' He laughed, showing a fine set of white teeth, so white they made his full lips look redder than they really were. There was a film of moisture on his lips which, to her astonishment, Jane found she would like to touch.

He stood in front of her now, as if shielding her from the other guests. She was pressed back against the wall. Used to peering up at tall men she found, for a change, that she was looking at his face with ease: he could only be a few inches taller than she. Dark, piercing brown eyes looked at her with an amused glint. His hair was long and black and one hank kept falling across his forehead, which he would impatiently flick back with his hand – just like Alistair did. He leaned forward, and the black shirt he wore, unbuttoned, revealed a hairy and muscular chest. She felt totally encompassed by his short but powerful body. There was an animal quality about him which, with mounting surprise, she realized was exciting her. 'So, what do you do?' she asked, the huskiness in her voice betraying what her body was feeling.

'Tom Hutchins. Painter by profession.'

'A painter? Of houses?'

'Good God, no. Pictures.'

'You mean, you're an artist.'

'No, I mean I'm a painter. I can't call myself an artist. Picasso, he's an artist, or Bosch, or Turner. Me, I'm learning, I'm still a painter.'

'So one day you'll be an artist.'

'Oh yes.' He smiled a strange sardonic smile, removing, momentarily, the deep furrows on either side of his mouth which gave a look of bitterness to his face. She listened fascinated as he talked with intensity of painting, of pictures he loved, of how important his work was to him; a day without putting brush to canvas made him feel incomplete, he said.

'Would you like to see my work?'

She hesitated only for a moment. 'Yes.'

'Come on, then.'

'But . . .'

'You either do or you don't.'

There was such a crush that they would certainly not be missed. It would not matter, she thought, if she popped out for an hour.

They heaved their way out of the crowded house. He walked so rapidly that she almost had to run to keep up with his hurried strides. They finally turned into the warren of streets behind Mill Road and stopped in front of a small terraced house. By the street lamp she could see that the windows were covered in dust and that the curtains were old blankets. The door was painted a bright emerald green and in the very centre a large, painted, purple eye looked at them. He pushed the door open. A plump, rather dirty-looking young woman was in the hallway. Her long, dark hair reached her waistline; she wore flowing, brightly coloured clothes which swirled about her, and around the hem of her dress were little bells which tinkled as she moved.

'This is Beth, she's our group mum.'

'How do you do, Beth?' Jane said politely.

'Peace,' the young girl said, raising her hand. Smiling a dreamy, unseeing smile, she glided into the front room, tinkling as she went. The smell of joss sticks pervaded the air. Tom led her up the steep, uncarpeted staircase. The walls of the small room into which he showed her were covered from floor to ceiling in paintings. Canvases were stacked one on top of each other against the walls, and the smell of turps was overpowering. There was a small table covered in paints and a mattress on the floor, but nowhere to sit, as far as Jane could see.

'That's where you sit,' he said, indicating the far from clean mattress. Jane lowered herself onto it and he handed her wine in a cracked cup. Gingerly she sipped it: the sharp, acrid taste made her throat constrict and she coughed.

'Used to better, I suppose?' he asked, holding up the bottle.

'It went down the wrong way,' she lied.

He took a painting from the stack against the wall.

'What do you think?' The large canvas, painted in primary colours, was full of enormous, laughing people. The group was at the seaside, fat bottoms straining the brightly striped deckchairs, plump children eating ice creams covered in sand. It was like the postcards which her aunt used to send from the seaside, with one difference. There was one monstrous figure in the painting, with an ugly, distorted face – and it was not laughing.

'They're so funny. But why the devil, who's that?' she asked. He ignored the question. 'Tom, they're so true. It reminds me of my childhood.'

'Your childhood.' He snorted.

'Oh yes, caravan trips to the seaside with my aunt. She had a big bottom like that. I was always scared that the canvas would rip whenever she sat on a deckchair. Is it for sale? I'd love to buy it.'

'No.'

'Which ones are?'

'None of them.'

'Don't you sell your work?'

'I'll have to one day, just to make room for more. I don't want to. I don't want to become some fat pig's investment. I've warned 'em, mind you, that some of 'em are going to have to go. They didn't like it much, I can tell you, bleeding well sulked for days.' He continued to talk as if the people in his picture were real. He produced more and more of the funny paintings, each with its devil leering in the corner. He seemed too serious and intense a person to paint such happy paintings.

'Good, aren't they.' It was a statement rather than a question. She watched fascinated as he produced a tobacco pouch and began to make a roll-up cigarette. She had forgotten about them; she had not seen it done since she had watched her father. From another pouch he took a strange-looking lump, which looked like a nutmeg, and with a sharp knife began to shave some of it into the tobacco. Carefully he rolled it up.

'What's that?' she asked curiously.

'Oh, come off it, you're not telling me you don't know hash when you see it?' She looked shocked and he laughed at her expression. 'It's good for you, gets rid of all those bleeding inhibitions,' he said, lighting it and inhaling deeply. Then he handed it to her.

'No, thank you,' she said primly.

'Oh, come on, don't be unfriendly. Try it.' Cautiously she sucked at the cigarette, inhaling the strange-tasting smoke. Nothing happened, so she inhaled some more.

'Here, don't hog it.' He snatched the joint back. 'Why do you live here in Cambridge?'

'I've friends here, and I like the atmosphere. I like all the young people about the place.'

'You're not that young though, are you?'

'Put so bluntly, no.'

'How old are you?' he asked, and passed her the joint.

'Thirty-two in May.'

'Over the top, aren't you?'

'How charming you are, Mr Hutchins. How old are you, then?'

'Twenty-nine.'

'There isn't that much difference between us, then.' She laughed.

'Oh yes, there is, lady. I'm still young, you see, and you're middle-aged. It's all in one's attitude, you were probably born middle-aged.' He began to giggle inanely. 'You getting high, my poor old middle-aged bird?'

'I don't think so.'

'It'll work next time.' He lay contentedly on the pillow looking at the ceiling, apparently oblivious to her presence. She began to wonder if she should leave, when suddenly he sat up again. 'I should like to see your tits,' he announced. Instinctively she crossed her arms across her chest, which only made him giggle again. 'God, Jane, you're so funny, so bleeding funny. Like an old maid.'

'You surprised me. I'm not used to people speaking to me like that.'

'Jane, you can't be true. You must know you've got great boobs. What's more natural than that I should want to have a dekko at them? Come on.'

'No, I think I'd better go.' His only response was to laugh even more loudly. He began to roll another cigarette.

He handed it to her. 'It's lonely being high on your own. Come on, love, try again.'

She knew she should get out, knew that it was madness to be here smoking joints with this strange, wild young man, but she did not want to go. There was a fascination about him and the whole situation that kept her. Again she took a deep breath of the pungent smoke, felt it burning as it swirled down her throat, decided that she did not like the taste one little bit and that this was a pointless activity when . . . she felt suddenly as if her blood was made of honey. She felt her brain expand: suddenly she was totally free, she had no problems. She laughed and the characters in the paintings laughed back at her.

'Good girl,' whispered Tom. 'Now let's see those lovely tits.' She enjoyed being undressed by him, enjoyed the wonderful feeling as his large, sensuous mouth closed over her nipple. How slowly he did everything! She felt she was floating, certain that she was the little green and yellow bird again, but this time the little bird was safely held in loving hands, oh, such loving hands . . .

'Tweet, tweet.' She laughed uncontrollably. 'Tweet, tweet.'

'To-wit-to-woo,' Tom replied. It was all so funny, so deliciously, sensuously funny. Why on earth had she ever thought she could never be happy again, never enjoy what this wonderful man was doing to her? She heard a strange moaning, which grew louder and louder, and she realized that it was herself; she heard herself moaning and sighing until with a body-shattering explosion, and for the first time in her life, she reached a shuddering climax.

6

'Aha, and where did you get to last night?' Zoe teased Jane when she finally arrived back at the house.

'Well I . . . I . . .' Jane did not know what to reply and, to her annoyance, felt herself blushing. She wondered if there would ever come a time when she would no longer blush – it seemed so undignified in a grown woman.

'There's no need to answer, Jane – you look marvellous.'

'I feel marvellous. I feel so relaxed, so . . .' She hugged herself.

'Splendid. May I ask who the lucky fellow is?'

'He's a painter, Tom Hutchins.'

Immediately, the benevolent smile disappeared from Zoe's face. 'Oh, Jane. Not Tom, he's not right for you. You could find somebody much better than that creep.'

Jane felt a surge of anger. 'What do you mean? What makes you say that?' she demanded. Zoe ignored her questions and continued, energetically, to whisk the cake she was making. 'I like him.' Still there was no response from Zoe. 'I said, I like him, he's fun. I had a lovely evening. I'm not going to fall in love, Zoe. Neither of us wants any great involvement, just to enjoy each other. That's what's so marvellous about it.'

'You've changed your tune in a hurry, haven't you?' The two women glared angrily at each other across the kitchen table. 'I'll remind you, you said it was all or nothing for you – '

'I didn't know I was going to meet anyone like Tom, then, did I? I've changed.'

'You haven't changed. Not enough for a sexual fling with a bastard like Tom. That isn't you. You'll be disgusted with yourself if you go on with this. Hell, Jane, I'm so angry.'

'I can see that.' Jane laughed bitterly. 'So what is it about Tom that makes you so angry?'

'I could write a book on what I've got against that young man.' She shook her balloon whisk at Jane before returning to the cake with renewed fury. 'You bloody fool, don't you see, I'm angry with you because I love you, and you're in danger and you don't have the sense to judge and to see. You've led such a sheltered life that you don't know danger when it's staring you in the face.'

'I don't think being ditched by my husband and having a nervous breakdown is leading a sheltered life.'

'Of course it bloody well is. If you had lived a bit more you wouldn't have crumbled so dramatically, would you?'

'You're not answering the question. Leave that flaming cake alone and tell me,' Jane shouted.

'He's dishonest. He steals things, usually from his friends – that sort of charming dishonesty.'

'That's slander.'

'No, it's not, it's true. Ask anyone.' An oppressive silence hung over the kitchen. Jane was too shocked to speak and Zoe still too angry to do anything but beat the poor innocent cake. 'He takes drugs, too,' she added, finally.

'Everyone takes drugs these days.'

'Everyone doesn't, my girl.'

'It's only pot and that doesn't hurt you. I'm sure he's not taking anything else, and pot's not serious.'

'That remark shows just how little you know, then, young woman. One thing leads to another. I've seen it time and again.'

'For goodness' sake, Zoe, stop mothering me. Let me lead my own life.'

'Normally I would, I'm only interfering because of that creep. I bet you smoked pot last night?'

'Yes, but only a little, and I won't do it again, I promise.' She saw Zoe's massive bulk relax. 'Please, Zoe, let's be friends. I'm so excited, I wanted to tell you about it. You see, I had an orgasm last night for the first time in my entire life. Isn't that amazing?' The wonder of the experience still lingered in her voice.

'Oh, child, if you were high on pot ... that was an illusion. Don't you see? There's no difference between that and if he had fucked you while you were pissed out of your mind.'

'You don't understand, Zoe. It was real. I know, I've tried before – making love drunk – but it never happened ... and then last night ... And he didn't "fuck" me – he made love to me.'

'Tom! He's incapable of anything but fucking. All he does is copulate.'

'Shut up, Zoe!' Jane screamed putting her hands over her ears. 'Don't use such horrible language to me. Don't spoil my happiness.'

'I'm not, I'm trying to preserve what little happiness you've managed to make for yourself. I warn you, Jane, he will use you, just as he uses everyone.'

'Maybe I'm using him too,' Jane replied defiantly. Zoe sat down heavily on her chair. She looked defeated and weary.

'Zoe, please don't make me fight you. I need you.'

Zoe sat silent for a moment, deep in thought. 'You're right, Jane, it's your life.' She smiled at Jane. 'I'll say no more. But I warn you, when he's hurt you and you come in here crying, I shall say "I told you so" – I promise you that.'

On the few occasions that Jane saw Zoe in the following weeks, she kept her promise. Tom was not mentioned by the two women again.

Jane's happiness was total. She felt like a sixteen-year-old again. They seemed able to extract enjoyment from the silliest things. They would go to the park and swing on the swings, shriek as they slid down the slide, and when the park-keeper appeared to tell them angrily to clear off, they would run away, giggling, like the naughty children they felt they were. They played 'knock door ginger' and Jane could not remember when she had had such fun or laughed so much. They ate fish and chips from the paper, washed down with cheap red wine. And they made love – long sensuous hours of exploring each other's bodies. She did not try very hard to keep her promise not to smoke more hash. The liberated feeling it gave her was too seductive. She spent little time in her flat; most nights she slept in Tom's room in the dusty, dirty little house in the back streets of Cambridge.

Tom shared the small house with Beth and four other men. The lack of privacy made Jane feel uneasy: casually she suggested after a few weeks that she get a new flat where they could move in together.

Tom thought for a moment. 'All right,' he finally said. 'But there is one thing. If I move in with you, don't you get all "married" with me, will you? No set meal times, no "Where have you been?", no washing my socks.'

'I promise, darling.' She laughed with relief. She knew she would have promised him anything.

'And don't call me "darling", it's bourgeois. I can't stand it.'

'All right – Tom.' She smiled, too happy to feel hurt.

She returned to the house in Newnham to pack her possessions. Zoe appeared in the doorway.

'What are you doing?'

'I was just about to pop over and see you, Zoe. I think I should look for another flat.'

'Jane, why? Don't do that. We enjoy having you here so much.'

'It's difficult. You see, Tom and I have decided to move in together and I know how you feel – you wouldn't want him in your flat.'

Zoe stood silent for a moment. 'No, you're wrong. It's your home and you have every right to have whoever you want with you. I've not mentioned again how I feel, have I? I've kept my promise: I shall continue to keep it.'

'Really? You wouldn't mind?' She flung her arms round Zoe. 'That would be so marvellous. I don't want to go. And really, Zoe, I think he's changed. You might even begin to like him again,' she said hopefully.

'Yes, Jane, maybe I will, for you.'

She rushed back to Tom with the news, and cheerfully helped him pack his few possessions into the back of her car. Almost triumphantly, she drove him to her flat.

7

Tom took one of the bedrooms for a studio and moved in his paints and pictures, which was all he seemed to own. That first evening they hung his paintings throughout the flat, light-heartedly arguing about where best to put each one. She enjoyed the novelty of having a man to cook for, and with their first meal there they drank a bottle of good wine.

'That's one proviso I make,' she said, laughing at him over the rim of her glass of wine. 'No more vinegar plonk. My liver can't stand much more.'

'So long as you don't expect me to pay for it, who am I to complain?'

She watched eagerly as he got out his tin of tobacco and began the ritual of rolling the reefer for them. She shut her mind to the thought of Zoe across the patio in her kitchen, and the promise she was about to break again. All she could think of was the effect the drug had on her, longing already for the physical release it gave.

They settled into a routine. She would get up in the morning, leaving him asleep, and would clean the flat as quietly as possible, so as not to wake him. Then she would go to the shops and buy their food, feeling like a million other housewives for the first time in her life. But there the similarity ended, for when she came home, he was either locked in his studio, which he would never let her enter, or he was out. She never knew where he went and did not dare to ask because he was increasingly irritable. Each evening she would cook their supper, hoping that he would come back in time to eat it. More often than not he did not. So, although he lived with her, she saw less of him than she had in that first rapturous month. And a different sort of loneliness began to seep into her life.

Most evenings she sat alone in the flat. She had stopped writing her letters to her friends – she was afraid she might reveal too much of herself in them. Instead she began again to write, playing with words. Nearly all of her efforts ended up in the wastepaper basket. But Jane found she enjoyed seeing her thoughts emerge in black and white.

Late one night when he returned home, Jane was already in bed but got up to tell him his supper was in the oven.

'I told you,' he shouted, 'no bloody hot dinners. I don't want to be looked after. Don't you understand plain English, you stupid bloody cow?'

'Don't speak to me like that, Tom, I can't bear it.'

'You'd better get used to it. You're living with me now, not some bloody lord.' He leaned menacingly over her and, frightened by his anger, she went back to bed as he slammed into his studio.

So she gave up cooking for him, and since she could not be bothered to cook for herself, she began to lose weight at an alarming rate. She lost interest in her looks. She would have been welcome in Zoe's kitchen at any time, but she avoided going there. She was far too proud to confess her increasing unhappiness. In a strange way she felt that Tom was testing her, setting the parameters of their relationship. Surely, she thought, things would improve once he was convinced that she would make no demands.

Now, it was only in bed at night that she thought she was happy – when the ritual smoking took place, and her body relaxed, her pent-up and complicated emotions evaporated. In the mornings she tried not to face reality. But her fear of being alone again made her cling to Tom.

He had been picking on her all morning. Whatever she did was wrong. He objected to the record she put on and tore it from the turntable, scratching its surface. Perversely, he grumbled that she did not feed him, then threw the fried egg she had cooked across the kitchen, complaining that she could not even cook an egg. He criticized her choice of books, her clothes, her hair. She stood listening to the familiar tirade and wondered why she did not cry. Instead, she wanted to scream at him. Longed to tell him what a cruel, thoughtless bastard he was, twisted, abnormal, a deviant – the angry words tumbled about in her brain. But, she remained silent. Silently she wiped the egg from the wall, and picked up the shards of broken plate.

'What the bloody hell is this?' He was standing in the doorway, holding a pair of jeans in front of him. 'Why have you been going through my things?'

'There was a tear in them – I mended them.'

'Leave my clothes alone!' he stormed.

'I was only trying to help.'

'Then don't. I like them torn.'

'Tom, that's ridiculous, you can't wear them torn.'

'I can, and I do. I don't want you doing things for me, all right? I don't want a domestic scene, I don't want to have to say "thank you" to you for anything,' he shouted.

Neatly she washed the egg out of the cloth. Rinsed out the plastic bowl. Wiped the draining board. Then she collected her coat and bag and, while Tom was in midsentence, slipped out of the flat.

She walked along the Backs, not seeing the beauty of the colleges, the skeletal fingers of the winter trees. She sank down on the bank, oblivious of the damp grass, and intently watched the river slide by. Something had happened, she decided – she had not cried, had not even wanted to. Was she becoming impervious to his intolerable moods?

Distractedly she tugged at the grass. Why did she stay with him? She did not even like him any more; he did not make her laugh as he used to do. She did not seem to care whether he stayed or not. She knew she did not hate him: hate was a violent, passionate emotion but she felt empty.

How could she have ended up with someone like him after Alistair? Perhaps because they were complete opposites – the only similarity was the way their hair fell down over their foreheads. Was she punishing herself? she wondered. But for what? For failing, perhaps. Failing in that previous, precious relationship. Wouldn't Nigel and the other psychiatrists have a field day with that theory? she thought, smiling to herself.

A swan approached the bank, looking for titbits, and stared solemnly at her. She remembered that other river, that other swan, and her whole being ached for the past, the lost happiness.

But what was she to do? She dreaded the thought of being alone again: she knew she could not face it. And there was the sex. She smiled. Zoe had been right: that was all it was – copulation, not lovemaking. But she enjoyed it still, would go so far as to say she was hooked on it. Without doubt Tom was good in bed. How could she adjust to living without the physical excitement he gave her? Perhaps he was the only man in the world who ever would. Again she tugged at the grass: a small pile now lay beneath her hand. She would get rid of him soon, she promised herself. But not yet. It was as if her body were demanding the orgasms it had been cheated of in the past.

Purpose in her life – that was what she needed. She stood up, aware at last of the damp patch on her trousers. She shivered, pulled her coat secure about her and walked purposefully into town.

She found the office of a secretarial college she had seen advertised. She enrolled herself as a full-time student and, to the principal's surprise, asked if she could start there and then. When she returned to the flat that evening, Tom was out.

As before, Jane enjoyed the course. Once again, the shorthand needed such concentration that she was able to shut out the part of her mind where her worries and discontent lurked. Tom, too, seemed much happier with this arrangement and nagged her less, even became quite pleasant again.

'Nothing personal,' he explained. 'It made me feel uncomfortable with you being around all the time, I felt I had to talk to you.' He even surprised her by giving her £50 one day. 'I like to pay my way,' he muttered, giving her one of his rare, sardonic grins.

'But you needn't,' she exclaimed. Even as he insisted that she took the money, she wondered where he had got it from. At regular intervals after that he would appear with odd sums of money for her.

During the day, while Jane was at college, he filled the flat with his friends. She did not like them: she thought they despised her, and they made her feel uncomfortable. She did not confide her feelings to Tom for she was too afraid to hear him accuse her of paranoia: it was not a word that she could contemplate with ease. If she did not like his friends, he had no time for hers, either. She had foolishly invited Sandra and Justin to dinner one night. The evening was a disaster, as she should have predicted. How on earth had she expected Justin and Tom to get on?

It was as if she led two lives. In the daytime she had college and visited her friends on her own; at night she became another woman, moaning, writhing.

It was as if they only met on the mattress these days. She knew it could not go on; she knew that this self-deception was likely to damage her, but still the fear of loneliness persisted. And always the thought of their sexual passion kept her in a trap of her own making.

She had not seen Alistair for nearly three months. Blizzards, a flu epidemic, everything seemed to have conspired to prevent him coming with James. Not until late February was it possible for him to come. She was relieved when Tom announced he would be out during Alistair's visit.

When Alistair arrived on his own, she was surprised.

'Where's James?'

'He's got a filthy cold, I thought it better to leave him at home.'

'You shouldn't have bothered to come, then,' she said, but was pleased that he had.

'I like to see you,' he said simply. 'In any case I had to deliver the Picasso: it's been reframed,' he said, putting the parcel on the floor. 'You hardly need it, though, do you?' He nodded at the paintings on the wall. 'Who did them?'

'A friend of mine. Thanks for the Picasso. I love that picture. It's a sort of bond with the past, if you know what I mean.' She smiled shyly.

'I ought to give it to you outright.'

'Good gracious, no. You've been generous enough to me. No, just allowing me to borrow it is enough.'

He took her to Panos's restaurant for a long lunch and afterwards they walked along the backs, their breath curling in white tendrils in the cold air. They paused and watched the birds on the water.

'Do you remember our swans on the Thames?'

'Yes, and Mr Rat, do you remember Mr Rat and how he looked at us with those intelligent black eyes? And that breakfast – I still think of that as the best breakfast I ever had,' he replied. For the first time she found that they were able to talk about the past, reminisce about places and people.

'Do you have to get back to London early?'

'Not particularly.'

'Shall we go to Fitzbillies and get some crumpets and chocolate cake? Remember how we used to spoil ourselves when you were an undergrad?'

He took her hand as if it were the most natural thing to do. They collected their cakes and walked back to her flat; she could almost pretend that nothing had ever changed between them. She made the tea, and they toasted the crumpets on the fire. She sat on the floor as Alistair relaxed in the big armchair, his long legs stretched out in front of him. They sat in the half-light watching the flames.

'Jane, come back,' he said suddenly.

'Alistair . . .'

'I need you, Jane, I love you.' She could not believe the words she was hearing. She had dreamed of this scene, known exactly what she would say, and now she sat in stunned silence.

'Look, Jay, I've been a fool, a bloody fool. I miss you and I need you – that hasn't altered. There's never a day goes by that I don't regret what I said to you, what I did. I can't pretend there haven't been other women since you left, but it's you I want.'

'Alistair, I – ' she started to say.

'Anyone home?' With sinking heart she heard the front door slam and the sound of Tom's voice before he burst into the room. Alistair stood up, rigidly. He looked from Jane to Tom and back again. 'Darling, crumpets, how lovely,' she was astonished to hear Tom say.

'I see, Jane. I really must apologize. It was very presumptuous of me,' Alistair said with a hard look on his face. 'I'm obviously not up on the developments in your life. I'll be in touch.' Before Jane could speak he had left the room, slamming the door shut.

'Did I butt in?' asked Tom.

'What?'

'Did I interrupt a pretty little reunion scene just then?'

'No, of course not. He was just leaving,' she lied. She had no intention of giving him the satisfaction of knowing what he had done.

'What's that?' He indicated the parcel.

'It was meant to be a surprise,' she answered, but with little enthusiasm in her voice. Tom tore the wrappings off the painting.

'Bleeding hell, I don't believe it!' Reverently he touched the painting with his fingertips. 'I can't believe I'm touching this, that it's here. You never told me about this.' He sat cross-legged on the floor gazing at the painting. 'I wouldn't want to live on this planet without Picasso on it, too.'

'You're going to have to one day, he's an old man after all,' she said in an automatic voice, wondering what the hell she was doing discussing Picasso's death when her own heart was breaking.

'No, when he dies, I go too. I wouldn't see the point of living when he's no longer around. I don't want to talk any more. I just want to be left alone to look at this.'

She was only too relieved that he did not want to talk, for she wanted to think. She lay on her bed in the dark. Life played such cruel tricks. She had been so close to having the man she loved back again, and now he was gone and, from the look on his face, no doubt for ever. How unfair it was: he had had God knows how many affairs, and she had had only this inadequate relationship. He had obviously, over these months, imagined her alone and waiting for him. She had waited for him but she had been lonely. Tom had none of her love: he did not want any and would run away from such involvement. The only thing he would ever love was an old man far away in a château below a French mountain; second-best for him would be to sit and gaze at the old man's paintings. How could she explain that she lived with Tom out of loneliness? How could she ever explain that the only way she could make love to Tom was to smoke his dope so that the drug took her out of herself and she became another person?

She buried her head in her pillow and cried softly.

Much later Tom came to the room. He began the ritual of rolling his cigarette; she watched him uninterestedly.

'Tom, don't bother for me, I'm not in the mood.'

'You what?' He looked hard at her. 'Been crying?'

'No.'

'Yes, you have. You don't mean you've been crying over that wet drip of a husband, for heaven's sake?' He laughed unpleasantly.

'I have not been crying, and he is not a wet drip,' she said angrily.

'I hate twits like him, never had to graft and scrounge to survive. Smug self-satisfied bastard.'

'Tom, please . . .'

'I'm so sorry, do I offend M'Lady?'

'Tom, I don't want to row.'

'Neither do I. You're not worth rowing with. You're a nothing and a nobody. What have you ever done in your life except lie on your back, open your legs and let a man screw you? That's how you've got where you are – you're a bleeding parasite! Christ, you bore me.' He slammed out of the flat. She could only feel relief that tonight he had gone, for now she could lie in the dark and think of Alistair. She could dream of a different future, and plan the letter she must write to him explaining everything.

The next day she posted her letter. Each day she waited in vain for a reply or for the phone to ring. She was puzzled. If he had really wanted her back, would he let Tom stand in his way? Had he perhaps been seduced by the happy day, the firelight, the memories of his youth here? Had it all been one of those illusions that seemed to pepper her life at the moment?

There was no word from Tom. She was relieved that he had gone, that she had not had to make the decision. Occasionally she felt sexually frustrated but soon learned that if she did something active, something as mundane as scrubbing the kitchen floor, the feeling went away. And why had she mooned around thinking she was alone? She had a good friend in Zoe – how could anyone be alone with a Zoe in her life?

Two weeks later, Tom returned.

8

She took him back, she never knew why.

They slept together but in the mornings, although her body might feel relaxed, her mind was in increasing turmoil. With her emphatic views on love, she was cheating on herself, and the knowledge was becoming increasingly difficult to live with. She had lost patience with him weeks ago; now she was losing patience with herself.

The winter finally faded and Easter came. A stilted letter arrived from

James but still no word from Alistair. Sandra had invited her to lunch at her new house across the city in Chesterton. A German friend who was staying with her had spent hours painting eggs in beautiful intricate patterns for a treasure hunt. Before, Jane would have hoped to interest Tom in the eggs, now she did not even bother to tell him she was going.

'No Tom?' said Sandra.

'No, he's doing one of his walkabouts. I don't know where he is.'

'I can honestly say that I don't think we'll miss him,' Sandra said with a grin. 'Rotten for you, though.'

'Oh, I don't mind.'

'Yes, you do. It's Sandra here, Jane, your old mate. You don't have to pretend to me.'

'Okay, so I mind. I mind not having a relationship I mind about. If you can work out such a convoluted sentence.' She laughed wryly.

'Jane, for heaven's sake kick him out. Can't you see what he's doing to you? You're as thin as a rake and you've a dreadful, haunted look about you. You can't cope with this sort of setup. You need to be loved, Jane, and he's on such an ego trip that he can only love himself.'

'I know you're right, Sandra. It's easy to say. But falling in love doesn't happen that easily. Maybe it'll never happen to me again. Remember, I always said it would be once for me.' She sighed. 'I suppose I've got into a sort of rut. If I throw him out, what then? Try again? Have the same thing happen again?'

'I should never have let you go. You weren't ready, I knew that. I should have stopped you, sorted something out with Justin ... You were ripe for landing in a messy relationship like this.'

'No, Sandra. I've got to learn. It would have happened whenever I set up on my own. I know I would still have gone through something like this.'

'Not if you'd met someone decent, someone who really cared about you. That's the trouble with Zoe's, she only ever seems to have misfits or crackpots there – never anybody normal.'

Jane had to laugh. This was the old Sandra. 'Well, I certainly fit that description!'

'I didn't mean you, you clot. Do you keep him?' she suddenly asked.

'No, he gives me money from time to time for his keep. He's intermittently quite generous.'

'Where does he get it from?'

'I don't know, I presume he must sell the odd painting,' she said hurriedly, wishing that Sandra had not, as usual, gone straight to the crux of the matter and asked the very question that worried Jane.

'I doubt it. Zoe says he never sells any of his paintings. Zoe says she reckons he's dealing in drugs.'

'Oh, Zoe's got a thing about drugs. I'm certain he's not on anything. I'd know if he was.'

'Would you? I don't think I would. Wherever he gets it from, I doubt if it's honestly.'

'Sandra! I know he's a bit odd, artists usually are, aren't they? But I don't think he's a criminal. He can be fun sometimes, Sandra, honestly, and it's someone to look after,' she finished lamely.

'Pity he doesn't appreciate you more. Trouble is, all the time you're with him, how are you going to meet anyone else?'

The children clattered into the room, and the question remained unanswered. Jane enjoyed the lunch, which stretched into tea and then supper. It was past eleven before she left. She refused a lift. She wanted to walk back and enjoy the smell of spring in the air. It would not be long till summer now: in the sunshine everything would look better. It was probably this long, endless Cambridge winter which was making her see everything so bleakly. As she let herself into the flat, she was pleased to see that the lights were on: she hated coming back alone to a darkened house.

The sitting room was full. Apart from Beth, the faces were all new to her. Jane felt conspicuous and overdressed in her pretty Laura Ashley dress. The men were in jeans and T-shirts, with dirty sneakers on their feet, and most of the women were in long, flowing Indian dresses, with dirty, bare feet protruding beneath the hems. The smell was overpowering: mixed with the heavy, musty smell of marijuana was the acrid smell of unwashed bodies. The room was a shambles. There were bodies everywhere, and upturned wine glasses on the carpet. She swooped on a cigarette end as it burned the edge of the coffee table.

'Tom,' she said, trying to keep the irritation out of her voice, 'are you going to introduce me, then?'

'My apologies.' Tom jumped up. 'Everybody, I'm so sorry, I forgot my manners. Let me introduce your hostess, Countess of Somewhere, Lady of Nowhere. Now everyone up and curtsy to your betters.' The group stumbled to its feet and, laughing and falling about, curtsied to her in a grotesque parody.

'Tom, please,' she pleaded.

'No, M'Lady, we all know our place. We must touch the proverbial forelock to you now, mustn't we?'

'Or foreskin!' someone shouted, 'We must touch our foreskins to her ladyship!' Unzipping his trousers he took out his penis and waved it in the air, tugging at his foreskin. The other men began to remove their trousers. With mounting horror Jane watched the ugly scene, her face twisted in disgust as the men began to dance about her, writhing obscenely. Repulsion filled her as the women's cackling rang in her ears.

'Tom, stop them!' she screamed.

'I think it's great.'

'I want them out, now.'

'No, I'll say when they're to go. They're my friends. If you don't like it, then piss off, you boring cow,' he spat at her. 'Get out, Jane!' he shouted. Frightened by the violence she saw in his eyes, she ran up the stairs and, pulling a chest of drawers across the doorway, barricaded herself into her room. Sleep was impossible, not just because of the noise they made but because of her feelings of self-disgust. She had become a nobody in her own home. He was mad. If she were not careful, he would make her mad again. Suddenly she saw the dreadful risk she was running. She had been so busy bothering herself with her introverted self-analysis that she had not seen the real danger she was in. She had had enough. He had to go.

At daybreak she went downstairs. Bodies lay everywhere in jumbled heaps. Ornaments were smashed on the floor; the carpet was covered in wine stains and would have to be cleaned if not renewed. With dismay she saw that the curtains had been pulled down, the curtain rod wrenched from the wall. Cold anger gripped her, and she kicked Tom, who stirred lazily.

'Tom,' she said clearly, 'I am going out. I shall be back early this afternoon. When I return I expect to find you and your friends out of here and this mess cleared up.'

'Sod off,' he grunted in reply.

She walked for miles about the city, then had lunch in a pub and drank two large brandies.

The flat was quiet as she entered it. She opened the sitting-room door: the room looked devastated but at least it was empty. With manic energy she began to clear the chaos; she scrubbed the carpet, washed the walls, tenderly picked up the pieces of broken porcelain. She threw the windows wide open and the foetid smell began to disappear.

When order was restored she went up to her bedroom. Nausea filled her as she saw Tom and Beth sprawled naked across the bed. She shook Tom.

'Wake up, you bastard!' she screamed. Tom turned over and stretched contentedly. 'Get up and get that woman out!' she continued to shout. Beth woke and smiled dreamily at Jane.

'Do you have to shout so loud?' Tom asked in a reasonable tone of voice.

'Yes, I do, I'm angry.'

'I don't like anger. I don't like aggressive vibrations,' announced Beth, sliding off the bed and walking, naked and unconcerned, across the room.

'You get that ugly, dirty cow out of my house!' Jane yelled.

'She isn't that dirty,' Tom said, laughing. 'Or you'd have caught something yourself by now.'

'What the hell do you mean?'

'I mean what I'm saying. I've been screwing Beth every day since I met you. She's better than you are. Laugh is, you were too bloody dumb to realize it.' Jane stood speechless with anger. 'I've been thinking,' he continued in his reasonable voice. 'I've decided to move her in here with us – a nice cosy *ménage à trois*. It'll cut down on my travelling and you might manage to learn a thing or two about screwing from her.' He smiled at Jane.

The smile was the last straw. Jane leaped across the room and hit Tom hard across the cheek. Very calmly and precisely he hit her back.

'Look, Jane, I'm not angry yet, but I'm likely to be. I do as I want, you understand. No one orders me around. Get that into your stupid, thick skull and I'll stay, otherwise I'm off.'

'Get out, you bum, you sickening filthy bum!'

'Language, M'Lady. You can't insult me – there's no point in trying. And don't look all hurt and offended. I've only given you what you wanted, kept you from going barmy, fucked you. You've been taking from me just as I've been taking from you.'

'I want you *out*. I mean it, I never want to see you – ever again. Get out!' Her voice rose, as she used every filthy word she could think of. But as she shouted, she knew that her anger was more at herself than at him.

'OK, don't yell. Keep your hair on. We'll go.'

Jane did not wait to hear more but raced to the bathroom and locked the door. She stripped, jumped under the shower and began methodically to scrub every inch of her body with her nailbrush, oblivious to the pain.

'Dirty bastard. Dirty bastard,' she repeated to herself over and over again, like a mantra.

When she emerged, the flat was empty. All his paintings had gone, his studio was bare. The silence hung oppressively about her. She slumped on the sofa, wanting to curl away in some dark corner – ashamed. She sat there as if frozen. Then slowly and gradually she felt the web of anxiety begin to build within her. She began to rock, back and forth, rhythmically.

'Not bloody likely. He's not worth that,' she said aloud, grabbing the phone and asking for International. She waited impatiently for the connection to be made.

'Honor, please, can I come?'

'Darling, immediately, I insist,' she heard the loved voice say. Five minutes later her plane ticket was reserved: Jane was amazed at how simple it had all been.

Through that night, she packed. It was only then that she realized what Tom had meant when he had said 'taken from you'. He had been clever, he had not stolen anything big that would be noticed straight away, so she had not registered that the odd piece of silver was missing. It was the same with her jewellery: he must have noted what she wore, and then taken only small pieces that he had seen she rarely used. How he must have laughed at the joke of paying her with money raised from the sale of her own possessions. She cursed her stupidity, but at least her anger with him and with herself doused any hysteria.

'Zoe?' she said, entering the kitchen the next morning and seeing the familiar figure at the kitchen table. 'Zoe, I'm sorry . . .' She stood with her shoulders slumped. 'You can say it, Zoe, – "I told you so."' She managed a weak smile.

'I've nothing to say,' Zoe replied. 'But you look as if you could do with a good breakfast.'

'Zoe, the flat is in a dreadful mess. I've cleaned up as best I could. Can I leave you a blank cheque to replace the carpet and get the place redecorated?'

'Are you going away?'

'Yes, to my friend, Honor, in Italy. I know I ought to stay and sort out the flat but I feel I've just got to get right away, now.'

'Don't worry, I'll see to it. Are you coming back to us?'

'If you'll have me. I was happy in the flat until . . .'

'Of course we want you back. How long will you be gone?'

'Three weeks, a month at the most.'

Zoe insisted on driving Jane to the station; it was the first time that Jane had ever seen her outside her house. She hardly noticed the journey. Not until she was on the plane and looked down to see the coastline of England receding did her mind jolt into focus. Things were not as bad as they seemed. So, she was still vulnerable. Perhaps she was not as stable as she had fondly thought. But, on the other hand, in the months with Tom, she had never let go, had not had any crises of anxiety; her mind had weathered Tom.

Finally she decided what she was going to do. She knew that she could not return, not until she was so strong that no one could hurt her or use her – so strong that she would never again involve herself in a second-class relationship in the hope of solving her problems and, in so doing, make them worse. She had to take care, for some time to come, but she knew it: that was the beauty of it.

Five
1969–76

1

Everything was the same and yet everything was different. She stood on the terrace of Honor's villa, knowing, as she looked at the timeless view, that she was a different woman from the young girl who had stood here on her honeymoon – not so long ago in time but a long time in living.

She felt, on her arrival, almost like an invalid, and from the concerned way in which Honor looked at her she had to presume that she looked like one, too. She allowed herself to be looked after, sitting on the terrace wrapped in a blanket, by Guido, Honor's manservant. Guido was horrified that she wished to swim – April was far too early in the year, she might catch cold, it could only harm her, Guido fretted. She ate well because Guido seemed to take it as a personal insult if each dish was not finished. She drank too much Frascati, but consoled herself that it did less damage than the gin, of which she had begun to drink far too much in Cambridge.

As the spring sun gathered strength her skin became golden. The mouth-watering Italian food brought the gentle curves back to her body. Zoe would have been proud of her. Her long hair began to shine once more and the grey eyes regained their sparkle, appearing even larger in her tanned face. Jane was becoming a beautiful woman again.

The peace of the place was everything she needed. She was not yet ready to talk or to explain and Honor, sensing this, did not pry. As her physical state improved, so did her mental wellbeing, until she was able to begin to sort through the turmoil of her mind. Like a filing clerk, she extracted each problem, each puzzle. Whether it was to do with Alistair, James, Tom, herself, or a combination of all of them, she would examine and study it, then file it back into her mind. Each time she went through this process, she began to create new order within herself.

Over a month had passed in this way. One evening the two women sat after dinner in a companionable silence, when suddenly, without preamble, Jane began to talk. She began at the very beginning. She told of her childhood, right through to the shame of the last four months. She told of her fears. Of her worry about her son. Of her craving to be loved. She opened compartments of her mind which, until now, she had kept closed. She felt no embarrassment as she spoke of love – her needs, her failures – for Honor knew so much about love and being loved. It was as if she were talking of another woman in another time. Honor sat, moving only to pour more wine into a glass or to light another cigarette, and she listened with an intensity that made talking easier. When the monologue finally ceased, she kissed Jane tenderly, 'It will be better now, I promise.' She led the now exhausted Jane to her bed, and tucked her in as if she were a small child.

Jane slept a long, deep sleep. When she awoke, she found that Honor had been right – she did feel better – and she found that her hope for happiness, which had for so long deserted her, had returned.

They never sat and discussed all the things that Jane had told Honor. But as the days slipped by, an odd word here or a sentence there would remind one or other of them of that long conversation and then, minutely, they would discuss some issue of Jane's life.

'You are wise,' proclaimed Jane one morning after Honor had for the umpteenth time put into perspective the jigsaw puzzle of her mind.

'God, darling, don't even think it. Me, wise? It's too funny to contemplate. I've just lived longer, that's all. It's always so much easier to see other people's problems. You never recognize your own. If I were wise, I should hardly have made the balls-up of my life that I have, would I, darling?' She chuckled in her deep-throated manner.

'Do you wish you'd had children?'

'Good God, no! I'd have been the world's worst mother.'

'I think you would have made a super mother.'

'No, you're wrong. I could never have stayed still long enough, and I can't stand babies. I might have enjoyed my children when they were adults, as I enjoy you and Alistair, but think of all the damage I could have done in the intervening years.' She laughed at the very idea.

'I don't think I'm a good mother.'

'What if you're not? James has a good father, hasn't he? We may not agree with what he's done to you, but he seems to be a caring father, much to my surprise. Why should you automatically be expected to be a good mother? That's the problem with having babies. You don't really know until you've had one if you're going to be any good at it, do you? So dreadfully random of nature, don't you think?'

Jane smiled. 'It must be lovely being you – so confident about everything.'

'Rubbish, no one's that confident about anything. If they are, they've usually led dreadfully boring lives. The trouble with you, Jane dear, is that you think too much. It's a dangerous occupation.'

'Zoe says that, too.'

'She's right. You spend hours worrying about love and being loved. All the time that you're thinking about it, you're never going to find it, are you? You must try to forget about it. It's more likely to happen then.'

'But, Honor, you've misunderstood. I don't want anyone else's love but Alistair's.'

'Piffle! You can't spend the rest of your life clinging to the past.'

'I'm not clinging to the past. It's in my present that I still love him. I know I couldn't love anyone else and I can't have a relationship without love. Look what happened with me and Tom.'

'Bah, Tom was an unpleasant interlude, a little bitty mistake. We've all made them,' she said with a shrug. 'You'll see, he'll be of no importance in a few weeks' time.'

Once again Jane returned to the problem of James.

'Jane, darling, all the time he's at Respryn there's nothing you can do. It's that old bitch, I'm sure of it, poisoning his little mind against you.'

'She wouldn't go that far, surely?'

'That old cow is capable of anything.' Honor was launched on her favourite subject – Blanche Upnor. Honor seemed to have an inexhaustible supply of stories about her and every wrong that the woman had ever done.

'What irritated me most about her was that she was always ready to criticize me. Always watching for me to make a cock-up, but she never once told me what to do or how to do it,' Jane complained.

'But darling, she wanted you to fail, to prove her right. She's so stupid, so bigoted. If Alistair lets her back into the house, he's madder than I thought he was.'

'Is he thinking of it?'

'He hasn't so far, but men are funny about their mothers, aren't they? I've often wondered if it's guilt – giving them all that pain to come into the world. And mothers of sons always seem to win in the end, haven't you noticed?'

Jane loved it best when Honor reminisced about her youth and how Respryn had been in the old days; her life as a debutante in London, the crazy things she and her friends had done. It was like listening to someone who had lived in another century rather than someone who was describing a way of life recent in years but irretrievably destroyed by the war.

The advantage of being here with Honor was that it bore no relationship to her other life. The opulent luxury, the release from the worries of day-to-day living, the upside-down life style – where they might sit the night away talking and then sleep all morning – all helped Jane to divorce herself from her past and to see herself as a different person.

Occasionally, half-heartedly, Jane would say she really should go back to England. She felt guilty about Zoe and the empty flat. But Honor would hear none of it and was adamant that Jane should stay for as long as she liked, for ever, if she wanted. Jane needed little persuading.

'Jane, darling, next month masses of friends will be coming. Will you mind?'

'Why should I mind? Who's coming? How exciting!'

'The whole of the world.' Honor laughed. 'The season begins now. You see, as it gets hotter the cities empty and the villas are all opened up until by midsummer there's no one left in the cities except the tourists and the poor souls who have to work for a living. We shall be very busy. Will you like that?'

'Yes, I think I will.' Jane was genuinely surprised at her reaction. 'In any case you must be bored stiff with just me.'

'What a silly thing to say! I've loved having you here all to myself. I've enjoyed watching you get better and feeling that I might have helped. Normally I should have been off on my travels, round and round like a goldfish in a bowl. Instead, I feel relaxed and at ease, wondering why on earth I spend all that time rushing about when I have this lovely home. No, it's been such fun having you here, watching you – what is that divine new expression? – "get your head on"!' She laughed. 'Oh, I do wish I was young enough to be a hippy, such fun!'

That week they shopped. Honor approached shopping like a general planning a campaign. Magazines were consulted for the latest trends, phone calls were made to friends in the fashion industry in London and Paris. Lists were drawn up. Wardrobes were inspected and ruthlessly culled of garments of the wrong length, line, colour or fabric. Shoes of the wrong height went the same way and only hats that could be retrimmed were reprieved. It was a long process, for so many of the clothes that had to be discarded reminded Honor of a happy day, or some lover until now forgotten, and she would sit on her heels in the chaotic muddle and tell Jane of this and that in her life. Eventually, enough space had been cleared and ideas gleaned for the serious shopping to begin.

They did not so much enter a shop as descend upon it, for at the sight of Honor owners and managers would drop everything, as if she were the only customer. In each shop she was welcomed like a long-lost friend, chairs were arranged for her, drinks appeared, and hours passed in the choice of fabrics and the exchange of gossip. If a shade were not quite right, new bolts would be ordered from Rome. Nothing was too much trouble to make M'Lady Honor happy. Jane seemed to live in a sea of silks, crêpes and chiffons. Once the fabrics had been chosen, each seamstress had to be visited. Honor had a different woman for each garment for, as she explained, you could not expect one who could make a jacket to be an expert on trousers, skirts and blouses as well. So Maria made their shirts for them, Pepe the trousers, Franca the day dresses, Lela the evening dresses and, of course, only Sofia could be trusted with the chiffons. Shoemakers measured their feet, patterns for handbags were selected and the glovemaker brought out his best skins.

The biggest surprise of all was how swiftly the clothes appeared. They were cut and fitted one day, given a second fitting the next, and finished the following, each one beautifully sewn, each a perfect fit.

'They're lovely,' exclaimed Jane.

'Yes. I'm satisfied.'

'But, Honor, I can't afford all these. One or two, yes, but not this avalanche.'

'Don't be ridiculous, darling, I'm paying.'

'Honor, I can't possibly accept.'

'Why not? Don't be so stuffy. Of course you can accept, it's giving me pleasure, and in any case I can't have my niece appearing in front of my friends dressed exclusively by Marks & Spencer. What would they say?'

'But the expense!'

'Don't be vulgar, darling, what would Blanche say – talking money?' She laughed loudly at her joke. 'I can afford it, I like to do it. Please don't spoil my fun.'

Jane relented. It was not difficult, for the clothes were more beautiful than any she had ever worn and, as each box was delivered, she would unpack excitedly and try on the contents, gazing with satisfaction at the image that the mirror reflected. She wore colours that she would never have dared choose herself: rich, jewel-like colours which, in this bright sunlight, enhanced her dark looks to perfection.

Honor prowled around her protégée, scrutinizing the fall of the skirt, smoothing a wrinkle which only her eyes, seeking perfection, saw.

Jane was an apt pupil, taking Honor's advice without question. Each day she became sleeker, better groomed and more confident.

'You're spoiling me rotten.'

'Fun, isn't it?' Honor smiled gleefully at her. 'I do so enjoy being rich. What's the point of money, if you don't spend it? I think it's wicked just to stick it in a bank, amassing away. But the bloody stuff just keeps coming, so I have to spend as much as I can, spread it around a bit. See what a good socialist I am.' The husky laugh rang out happily.

'But where does it keep coming from?'

'Did I never tell you?' Jane shook her head. 'I told you about my Bob, didn't I? The one who's now a cabinet minister? Divine man.' She sighed. 'Well, when my parents wouldn't allow me to marry him I was so angry – dear God, how angry I was – I wanted revenge. I bided my time, looked around and eventually found the ideal candidate in an American called Wilbur Calem. Imagine, a self-made American, my father nearly had apoplexy. He was thirty years older than me, and even his name sent shivers down their spines – there's something ridiculous about Wilbur; sounds like a hamster, doesn't it? Worst of all, he was in "trade" – dirty word in my family. He'd been everything in his life: lumberjack, waiter, crook, probably, you name it, Wilbur had done it. Then somehow he got into making sausages. It was too perfect: imagine the only daughter of the Earl of Upnor married to a man who made sausages. You can imagine the shock and horror at Respryn. So, I eloped with him.

'When I met him I'd realized that he was rich. I mean, there would have been no point in eloping with someone penniless just to get my own back, because father would be sure to cut me off without a penny, and the satisfaction in a cold garret would have been less than in a suite at Claridge's. But it wasn't until we were married that I realized how rich. The dear man was absolutely loaded with money. By then the sausages had enabled him to go into real estate, oil, everything under the sun. It was lovely, the way he spent money on me, like living in an avalanche of gorgeous presents. But then it all went wrong. I'd intended to marry him to teach them a lesson. Then I was going to ditch him and they were going to welcome me back with open arms – really dreadful bitch I must have been. But I fell in love with him, crazily, totally besotted. I couldn't help myself: he was the kindest, most considerate man I have ever met. Of course I had to tell him what I'd done and he roared with laughter and said he'd known all along and he hadn't minded because he loved me and was convinced I would grow to love him, given time. He'd even guessed why I had married him, and the dear soul just thought it was dreadfully funny. God, how I adored him – that's why I still use his name after all my other marriages.'

Honor paused a long time. Jane sat on the edge of her seat, eager to hear more.

Honor sighed. 'He died. The silly man died after only five wonderful years. Just got up one morning, turned to me, told me he loved me, and then simply keeled over, stone-cold dead. I wanted to die, too: there seemed no point in living without him.' Tears formed in her eyes at the memory but she quickly brushed them away. 'He had no family, you see, no one but me, and so I inherited everything. There's so much income that I couldn't possibly spend it all each year – silly isn't it, all that money just for me? I don't have anything to do with administering it, of course: lawyers and accountants beaver away looking after it and they just send me cheques which I busily try to spend.' She laughed.

'Then what happened?'

'Disaster, that's what happened, unmitigated disasters – three, to be precise. First an alcoholic racing driver, failed, of course. But luckily his liver hated him as much as I did, in the end. Then I married Marcus Telling, poor man, such a dreadful actor. The trouble was he didn't think to tell me he was queer.'

'And then?'

'Wayne Higgins – I do seem to have a thing about odd names, don't I? I met him soon after he'd come out of jail. But he just couldn't stop being a crook, you see, even when he had all my money to spend. He seemed to need the excitement. We were in America – off he trots and robs a filling station, bopping this poor man on the head. That was the end.' Honor got up to pour more drinks.

'But what happened to him?'

'Oh, he got life. And I got a divorce.'

'Honor, you're so funny. Do you think you'll ever marry again?'

'Good God, no! I suppose, in a way, I'm like you: I'll always love my darling Wilbur. But, unlike you, I enjoy my little adventures. And the way I live now, I'm in control. They go when I tell them, no nonsense, no alimony.'

'I'm so sorry about Wilbur,' Jane said gently.

'Bloody inconsiderate of him, if you ask me,' replied Honor, but she was not laughing.

As Honor had promised, it did seem as if, suddenly, the whole world had arrived in this tranquil spot. The quiet roads began to fill with the roar of expensive motor cars, Maseratis and Ferraris in droves. New boutiques appeared like a rash in the small town at the foot of the hill. Smart hairdressers from Rome opened their summer salons. The beaches filled with the beautiful bodies of young men and women, staking out their positions for the duration of the season, greeting each other excitedly after the winter. At night their hillside, which until now had been dark, glistened with lights like giant glow-worms as villa after villa was opened up. Jane hadn't even been aware that the villas were there.

Now the phone rang constantly, people dropped in, and a quiet evening at home on the terrace was only a memory, for each evening they went out to dinners or parties. She would watch Honor's friends, admiring their elegance, their perfect grooming, their confidence, wanting to be like them. They were kind and charming to her, and she blossomed but could not help being amused at the way they all called her the *contessa inglese*.

Dutifully she flirted with the men, for it seemed to be *de rigueur*. But, as she flirted, she felt nothing. It was just a social game to be played; it was expected of her and she did not wish to offend.

She regretted that she only had O-level French while this glittering group would switch from English to French, German and Italian, almost without taking breath, and she determined that this winter she would learn a language.

Usually she left long before Honor, and always alone. Honor seemed to have an insatiable appetite for socializing. Jane found she did not have the same stamina. In any case Jane loved the mornings. She would sit on the terrace and watch the mist roll up the hillside from the town, until everything was bathed in the glorious sunshine; and she liked to swim at this time of day, before her breakfast, while it was still cool enough to be exhilarating.

She never saw Honor in the mornings, and only occasionally at lunchtime. Honor would appear in the afternoon, showing no signs of fatigue and eager to start the social whirl again.

One morning, Jane found the lunch table on the terrace set for four. Two handsome young Italians suddenly appeared and bowed graciously over her hand.

'Umberto,' announced one.

'Federico,' said the other.

She could only smile for she had no Italian and they appeared devoid of English. So they sat smiling inanely at each other until Honor arrived.

'Darlings, you've met.' She swished to her seat. 'What do you think of my find, Jane? Aren't they divine? So handsome and virile. Umberto is superb.'

'But . . .' Jane glanced embarrassed at the young men.

'Don't worry, darling, they can't understand a word we say.'

'Are they staying here?'

'For the time being. I met them at Constanza's last night after you'd scuttled off, and I just couldn't let them escape. They're just too marvellous, like book ends.' She laughed and the young men grinned happily. Honor talked rapidly to them in Italian, at which they bowed again to Jane and she laughed too; then everyone was laughing but no one except Honor knew at what.

'But two of them, Honor?'

'I know, terrible, isn't it? But such fun. When one flags you've always got the other one,' and she burst out laughing again.

'But Honor . . .' The sound of shock was apparent in Jane's voice.

'Now, darling, don't be so stuffy. You're a big girl. I told you ages ago I liked living here because it was easier to be naughty, didn't I?'

Jane looked around the happy, smiling group. There was a strange innocence about them all and Jane felt ashamed of her initial reaction. It was none of her business; Honor was a grown woman, free to do as she wanted, and she was hurting no one.

Now, when they went shopping, there were four of them clattering about the streets, exploding into the shops, sipping Campari and soda under the huge umbrellas of the pavement cafés, watching the world go by. Each morning the young men joined Jane for her swim and began to teach her Italian. She supposed that when people saw them all together, they presumed that one of the boys was Jane's lover: as she did not want to be involved with anyone, the arrangement was really quite convenient.

2

'What a busy little scribbler you are, Jane.'

'Honor! You're up early, it's not even lunchtime,' Jane teased.

'Couldn't sleep. Who are you writing to, anyone I know? Can I put a message in?'

'That one's to James. Shall I add your love? Now I'm writing to my friend, Sandra, and I was just thinking – it's strange: if you asked me, I'd say I prefer men to women, but all my best friends are women and they're all very similar, too. You, Sandra and Zoe are all warm, practical and logical. I was wondering if one chooses one's friends because they have the qualities lacking in oneself.'

'I'd hardly say you lack those qualities, my sweet.'

Jane lay back on the lounger. 'I've been trying to describe my life here to Sandra, but it's impossible. This life is like a dream: it's all so exotic and glamorous and I think I'm beginning to forget what ordinary life is like.'

'Would you like to lead an ordinary life?'

'Like Sandra? I envy her security, but I don't know if I want to live like that, or even if I could.'

'You couldn't. Once you get taken out of your environment, there's no going back. Alistair spoiled you for any other sort of life. You can go up in style, but you can't go backwards.'

'Hell, Honor. Don't depress me. I'm going to have to learn to settle for less.'

'Nonsense, not if you play your cards right.'

'You mean if Alistair wants me back.'

'Certainly not. The world is full of miserable people giving marriages a second try. It never works. I mean here – you could find someone if you wanted to.'

'Oh, Honor, you never give up, do you?' Jane smiled fondly at the older woman.

'Have you any emeralds?' Honor abruptly changed the subject.

'No, I'm clean out of emeralds,' Jane replied with a giggle.

'I've noticed you never wear jewellery. You didn't leave it all behind, did you?' Honor asked anxiously.

'Of course I did, except for my engagement ring, a cigarette case and some small pieces. And the choker you gave me.'

'That was silly, Jane. You should always hang on to your jewels and furs. You never know when you'll get replacements and buying them for yourself is never the same as being given them by a lover.'

'Honor, you're so funny. I could hardly have walked off with the Upnor collection, could I? Alistair never had enough money to buy me expensive stuff anyway. Why do I need emeralds?'

'Tonight we go to a ball at the Palazzo Villizano, and everyone will be there, in best bib and tucker. I thought you should wear the green silk that Lela made for you. You'd better borrow my emeralds, they'll be a perfect match. I don't need them – I'm wearing my sapphires tonight.'

'Whatever you say, Honor. You're the boss.'

'It'll be enormous fun. There'll be masses of divine men for you and by the end of this evening I expect to find you in love. Otherwise, I shall have lent you my emeralds for nothing.' Honor laughed at her.

That evening Guido drove them up into the mountains. The boys had been sent into town earlier by Honor. Umberto and Federico seemed to accept their occasional dismissals with good humour.

Across a steep valley, Jane saw the castle. It stood, floodlit, on top of a steep hill, a small town clustering around the lower slopes like the folds of a skirt. It was so improbably beautiful, with its turrets, its hundreds of glinting windows, that it was like an illustration in a book of fairy tales. The car stopped in the town square at the bottom of a steep hill, and they joined the long line of people walking up to the castle. Several horse-drawn carriages clattered past, taking the elderly and those who could not manage the climb. On either side of the road, the townspeople stood, applauding dresses that pleased them, and shouting encouragement to the party-goers. As Honor and Jane appeared, there were cries of '*bellissima!*'

Through massive, heavy, wooden gates they entered an immense stone courtyard lit by flickering tapers. Here they joined the queue of people climbing a long flight of worn stone steps to the entrance which led into a large medieval hall. Jane stood awestruck at the sight. The hall was already crowded and the women in their bright silks and satins whirled in a never ending kaleidoscope of colour. From the ceiling brilliantly coloured pennants hung, swaying in the heat from the throng below. An orchestra was playing and, at every turn, servants in scarlet silk knee breeches with white slashed doublets were serving drinks. Jane felt she was stepping into a Renaissance painting.

She had never seen so many exquisitely dressed women. But in her classically draped emerald-green silk dress, Jane, though she was unaware of the impression she made, could hold her own with any woman in the room. Her dark hair gleamed and her golden skin looked flawless. Honor's emeralds shone at her neck and wrist but were no match for the excited sparkle in her wide grey eyes.

Honor swooped like an exotic bird from one group of friends to another. People had travelled from all over the world to this ball, and Jane found herself searching hopelessly for a face she knew.

'Honor!' They both swung round at the voice. A dark-haired man approached them, his hands spread wide in expansive greeting to Honor, who fell immediately into his arms, shrieking with pleasure. Perhaps this man was the reason why Umberto and Federico had been left behind, thought Jane, and she looked at him with renewed interest. She guessed that he was in his forties but could not be certain. She had learned that it was difficult to assess the age of the rich, for it seemed that, lacking financial worries, their faces did not wrinkle in the same way as those of ordinary people, and their permanent tans made the middle-aged look years younger than they really were. At least this man made no attempt to hide the silver speckling his dark hair. He was far from handsome, with a large aquiline nose which gave his face an arrogant look that disappeared the moment he smiled. His shoulders were wide and muscular, his hips trim, and his physique so well proportioned that Jane was at first unaware of his lack of height. Yes, thought Jane, he would be admirably suited for Honor: though younger, he was nearer to her in age than the two boys. He had that indefinable aura which, she was now aware, invisibly cloaked only the very wealthy.

'Roberto, darling!' Honor cried. 'Where have you been? Why were you so long in coming this year? We have missed you dreadfully.'

'Problems, Honor. Always problems.' For the first time he smiled and looked enquiringly at Jane.

'Jane, allow me to introduce your host, Il Principe Roberto Michele de' Verantil di Villizano.' The names rolled expertly off her tongue. 'Roberto, this is my niece, Lady Upnor.'

Jane's confusion at the long list showed on her face. 'Roberto is sufficient,' he said, in an attractive, deep voice with only the merest hint of an accent, as he bowed elegantly over her hand.

'Roberto.' To her annoyance Jane realized that her voice emerged as almost a whisper. The dark eyes watched her intently, making her uncomfortable, and she lowered her eyes from his stare.

'Charming, charming. It is my greatest pleasure at last to meet the beautiful *contessa inglese*. Everybody speaks of your beauty, Contessa.' He smiled warmly at her. 'But, I forget myself, have you two ladies dined? No? Allow me.' He guided them to a table set in a bower of flowers away from the main throng. Several of the exotic servants appeared immediately at his side and he issued instructions. Their dinner arrived, a bewildering assortment of beautifully prepared dishes, and wine in huge crystal goblets. She did not need to talk for, throughout the meal, Honor kept up a stream of chatter, animatedly telling their host of all the parties and the people he had missed. As they talked of people she did not know, Jane allowed her attention to wander around the vast room, enjoying the parade of elegantly dressed people, the display of jewellery which must be worth a king's ransom. Once or twice she glanced at the Prince, and each time her glance seemed to coincide with a look from his fine, dark eyes, smiling at her. Hurriedly she looked at her hands in confusion, and could not understand why. It was as if, at one glance from this man, all the gloss and sophistication she fondly thought she had acquired in the past weeks deserted her completely.

'Darlings, there's Josh Phelps, I haven't seen him all summer, do be angels and excuse me a moment.' Before Jane had a chance to stand and join her, Honor swept away. She was at a loss for what to say to the Prince.

'Please don't bother with me,' she finally said. 'You have so many guests to attend to.'

'They seem quite happy.' He gestured to the throng. 'Would you care to dance, then you won't have to try to think of what to say to me?' He was laughing at her, but she stood up with relief. 'Which do you prefer, Contessa? Dancing to this orchestra, or I have one of those 'groups' the young seem so fond of. You are so young, perhaps you would prefer the latter?'

'I really don't mind. I like old-fashioned dancing.'

'Old-fashioned – how charming!' He laughed.

'I'm old enough and young enough to enjoy both.'

'How fortunate you are. Me? I don't pass this test, I prefer the old style. I like to hold a woman when I dance with her. And some of the gyrations I see I prefer in the bedroom and not in public. I suppose it means I grow old.' He sighed, laughingly, as he took his arm and led her into a quickstep. He did not talk as they danced and Jane could concentrate on the music and the pure pleasure of dancing with someone so adept and easy to follow. The music changed to a cha-cha. His hips moved only slightly, but provocatively. Jane liked to dance but she had never before danced with a man who could make her feel as sensuous as this. She was disappointed when the music stopped and the musicians, taking a break, put their instruments away. He led her back to their seat, where there was no sign of Honor. She expected him to excuse himself but instead he sat down beside her, ordered more wine, and offered her a cigarette.

'You're a good dancer,' he said as he leaned forward to light her cigarette.

'Not as good as you.'

'Not yet, but you will be. You have the feel for it. It's rare in an Englishwoman.'

'Aren't generalizations dangerous?'

'I'm not generalizing, it's a fact. They're too self-conscious, always aware of people looking at them, wondering what effect they're creating. You can't dance like that. Only the music, the rhythm and your partner should matter, you see, just like making love – the sound, the rhythm, your partner.' He smiled mischievously at her.

'Really?' She hoped she sounded more confident than she felt.

'Ah, yes. You'll be good at that too – one day.'

'One day? And what makes you think that I'm not good now?' Her rising anger made her speak boldly.

'I know these things.' He laughed at her. 'I make you angry, I like that. I like the sparkle in your eyes that your anger gives.'

'I'm not angry. Why should I be? You can think what you like. You're unlikely to find out one way or the other.'

'Yes, Contessa.'

'I'm not angry,' she almost shouted.

'Yes, Contessa.' He continued to smile his infuriating smile. He was insufferably rude, she thought. The dignified thing would be to move away – but she did not.

'I wish you would stop calling me Contessa, too. My name is Jane.'

'Then I accept the honour you give me and I'll call you – Jane.' It was ridiculous, how could the sound of her name make her feel as if she had been caressed?

'Are you enjoying Italy?' he asked, switching back to the role of considerate host, so that she could almost believe she had imagined the suggestive conversation.

'It's wonderful.' With relief she began to tell him what she loved about Italy.

'Is this your first visit to my country?'

'No. I was here several years ago. I regret that I didn't return sooner.'

'I too.'

'I'm sorry?'

'I regret that you didn't return sooner also. It would have been a joy to me to know you better.' Once again the tone of his voice had changed. She felt herself blushing and cursed inwardly as the familiar warmth suffused her face. She lowered her head, hoping that he had not seen, but he put his hand under her chin and made her look up at him.

'Charming,' he whispered. She did not want to look at him. He was not just flirting with her, he was seducing her with his beautiful voice and the suggestion in his eyes. It frightened and, at the same time, excited her. But it was not what she wanted. She did not want to be involved with anyone – except Alistair. She closed her eyes to shut out his expression.

'Are you tired?' he asked, concerned.

'A little hot.'

'Would you like to walk outside? It's very warm in here.' He led her through the crowds, not stopping to speak to anyone despite the dozens striving to catch his attention. They walked out onto a wide terrace where the heady scent of jasmine filled the warm evening air. They leaned on the wall and together they looked down at the village twinkling far below.

'It was a clever place to build a castle,' she said.

'Yes, no one has ever managed to conquer it. If my ancestors didn't like someone they could just drop them over the wall.' He laughed. The music seemed a long way away now. She was conscious of his closeness, would have liked him to touch her, yet perversely dreaded his doing so.

'You are a sad lady,' he stated.

'I'm not sad. I'm having a lovely time.'

'Ah, the famous British stiff upper lip. You cannot deceive me: it is in your eyes, such sadness.' He touched her hand. 'I would love to be the man to remove that sadness.' She turned her face away from him. 'I'm sorry. I startle you. Look at me, please. My dear Contessa, I can tell you one thing: we shall be important to each other, I promise.'

'Please,' she said, suddenly shivering, 'I want to go in now. I should try to find Honor.'

'Of course, forgive me.'

Back in the castle they could not find Honor in the crowded halls.

'Honor will not want to go yet, I'm sure,' he said, taking her arm. 'Perhaps you would like to see my gallery? I promise, I will behave like the perfect gentleman.' He smiled good-naturedly at her. 'Come, we shall be respectable art lovers together, instead of the other sort.'

At the top of a long flight of shallow stone steps was his gallery, which housed a fine collection of paintings. At each picture they stopped to admire, and Roberto told her its provenance, about its artist, the mediums used.

'You know so much about the paintings. Are you an expert?'

'Good heavens, no, but you cannot live all your life with these beautiful paintings and not know them, not explore every inch of them as one would a woman one loved.' That voice again, Jane thought, flustered. 'Come and meet my family,' he said, leading her into a side gallery. 'Ancestors, may I introduce to you all Lady Upnor, the charming English countess?' Laughingly he waved at the ranks of portraits on the walls. Jane sank low in an elegant curtsy to the paintings. Roberto, enjoying her gesture, with equal elegance gave her his hand as he helped her rise. 'You see, Jane, what dreadful rascals some of them look, but others I think I would have liked to know.'

'There's a definite family likeness, I think it must be the nose,' she said, scrutinizing his face.

'Yes, the famous Villizano nose, as bad as the Habsburg lip, isn't it?'

'Oh no, I think it's a very regal nose,' she protested.

'Regal?' He postured, turning his profile to her. 'Yes, I like that concept of my nose,' and he laughed. She decided then that she liked him: he could laugh at himself. So many men and most of the Italians she had met took themselves far too seriously.

'What a lovely portrait!' Jane exclaimed as they halted in front of the last picture. 'The artist has caught your expression and your fine eyes exactly.'

'Have I fine eyes?'

'Beautiful eyes.'

'If they are so, I think, it is only because I look at beauty and it reflects in my dull eyes.' He turned to her and smiled. His extravagant compliments made her feel awkward, like a gauche young girl again. A little too quickly, to cover her confusion, she said, 'Why is there this big gap here?'

'That is for the portrait of my wife.' At his words she felt a momentary and ridiculous sense of disappointment.

'Has she not had her portrait painted yet?'

'No, not yet. She can't, you see, I haven't found her yet.'

'Oh, I see,' she said and was shocked at the sudden happiness his words gave her. They were interrupted by the swishing of silk as Honor fluttered towards them.

'Darlings, I hate to interrupt, but I've got this dreadful headache. Would you mind terribly, Jane, if I left you? I can send Guido straight back to wait for you.'

'That's not necessary, Honor. I'll come with you,' Jane said, concerned.

'No, darling, I wouldn't hear of it. And Roberto here would never forgive me for dragging you away.'

'No, I insist. If you're not well, I'll come with you.'

'Dear Honor, of course Jane must travel with you. I am only sad to lose two such lovely women from my party, but . . .' he said, shrugging his shoulders.

He insisted on escorting them to the courtyard and waited while their car was summoned. As Jane settled herself in the back, Roberto spoke softly with Honor. He came around to her side of the car.

'Jane, I hope we meet again very soon.' He bowed and kissed her hand.

'That would be lovely,' she heard herself say. Guido skilfully edged the car out of the courtyard. Jane would have liked to look back to see if he were still there, but she knew it would look unsophisticated.

'Sorry, Jane, darling, to drag you away like that.'

'I was ready to go, Honor. I really am tired,' she lied. 'Are you all right? I've never seen you ill before.'

'Heavens, I'm not ill. Just a stupid, silly headache. Too much booze recently, I should think. An early night and I'll be as right as rain.' She grabbed Jane's hand. 'I think our prince is rather taken with you. He asked me if he could call on you, as if I were a chaperone – too divinely quaint.'

'He's very nice.'

'"Nice" isn't exactly the word I would choose to describe Roberto.' Honor laughed. 'He's an impossible fish to land, that one.'

'Oh, Honor, I don't want to "land him". It was a lovely evening and he was the perfect host, nothing more. In fact, I thought it was you he was interested in.'

'Me?' Honor hooted with laughter, wincing with pain as she did so.

'Oh, this stupid head. Darling, I'm far too old for Roberto. In fact, I'm even surprised at his interest in you. Don't get me wrong, I only meant that he's normally trailing some empty-headed creature of twenty around with him.'

'To be honest, he frightens me.'

'Darling, I know what you mean. It's that world-weary air of dissipation about him. Dreadfully exciting, though, isn't it?' She chuckled quietly.

3

The haze that shimmered above the sea began to lift as if an invisible hand were gently unpeeling the mist to reveal the little town. It was Jane's favourite time of the day, and she watched entranced, as she did each morning after her early swim. Guido appeared across the terrace, the phone in his hand.

'Il Principe di Villizano,' he announced, indicating the phone.

'I don't think we should wake Lady Honor this early, Guido, not even for the Prince.'

'No, Contessa, he wishes to talk with you.'

Nervously she took the telephone. 'Hullo?'

'Jane, good morning. I just knew that if I called this early I would find you awake. It's a beautiful morning, isn't it?'

'Fantastic. Thank you for the lovely party, Roberto.'

'It was my pleasure. Honor is better, I hope?'

'I don't think we shall know that until this afternoon,' Jane said, laughing.

'So, your aunt will sleep all day? You'll be alone?'

'Well, yes,' she said uncertainly.

'Perhaps, then, you would take luncheon with me? It would give me great pleasure.'

Jane did not hesitate. 'Thank you, Roberto, I should like that.'

'I shall call for you at eleven.'

Replacing the receiver, she looked at the telephone and wondered why on earth she had accepted with such alacrity. It was hardly the sophisticated thing to do, and it was not as if she were really interested in him. He was not her type, and he was too old. Gracious, he was not even handsome. Still, there was no harm in lunch – dinner might have been a different proposition. She jumped up and, grabbing her large beach bag, hurried to her room – Honor would never forgive her if she went out with the Prince, of all people, not looking her best.

Everything went wrong. Her hair refused to do what she wanted and she had to wash it again. The same with her nails: twice she had to start from scratch and repaint them. Choosing something to wear took for ever. Honor's generosity meant she now had so many clothes that it was always difficult to choose, but today she was even more indecisive. She tried on half a dozen outfits, pirouetting in front of the mirror, before deciding on an aquamarine silk pyjama suit, which she dressed up with the junk jewellery that Honor adored and had taught her how to wear with style. She never failed to be surprised by the difference wrought by her new clothes and accessories. None of her friends in England would have recognized this sleek, bronzed woman.

Having scribbled a note to Honor, she was waiting on the steps when, on the dot of eleven, Roberto's black Maserati drove up in a cloud of dust. This morning he was dressed in the casual clothes that Italian men wear so well. He settled her in the car as if she were a precious package, and within a minute they were roaring off down the drive.

'I do like punctuality, thank you,' he said, and smiled at her. She had not noticed last night what a generous mouth he had, nor that his teeth were so white and even. She hoped they were his own, it would be awful to be kissed by someone with false teeth. What a silly thing to think – she was not going to kiss him, anyway, so what did it matter? She smiled back at him, not knowing what to say. She hated being punctual; all her life she had wanted to be one of those scatter-brained women who are late for everything, and with whom no one ever seems to be cross. Her inner clock always made certain that she arrived on time, and frequently early. But this was the first time anyone had ever complimented her on this.

He drove at a fast and furious pace, sounding his horn loudly and making other cars scuttle out of the path of this gleaming, black monster. She closed her eyes with terror as the car seemed to skim the very edge of the coast road: the drop to the sea looked far too steep for survival if anything went wrong.

'Are you afraid?'

'The road is very narrow.' She managed to control her voice.

'Don't you find speed sexually exciting? I do.'

'No.' She laughed nervously. 'That's the last thing I find it. All I feel is sheer terror.'

'Then I shall slow down,' he announced, and reduced his speed to 70 miles an hour, still far too fast for comfort on these winding roads. Jane gritted her teeth and, for the next hour, closed her eyes every time they hurtled round a bend. Her sigh of relief when the car finally screeched to a halt turned to a cry of pleasure as she opened her eyes to see the small white hotel nestling in a cove, the blue sea lapping a pale sandy beach, pine woods protecting it on the landward side.

'Roberto, what a heavenly hideaway!' she exclaimed.

'Worth the journey, wasn't it?' He grinned at her, and then gently took her hand and brushed his lips against it. She felt a surge of excitement as he touched her, which was not at all what she wanted. He let go of her hand. 'I have told no one of this little place, none of my friends. That way it stays like this. It's very simple food but excellent.'

The innkeeper appeared, bowing low to Roberto, speaking excitedly, far too quickly for Jane to catch a word. Roberto's reply was equally unintelligible to her, but the man nodded his head in vigorous agreement before turning to scuttle away up the road down which they had just come.

'What on earth did you say to the poor man to make him run away like that?' she asked.

'I have asked him to go and put up his "Full" sign. I don't want anyone else here to spoil our peace.'

'Roberto, you're joking. And he agreed?' she said, astonished.

'Of course.' He shrugged his shoulders. 'At a price, naturally.'

'Roberto, you're extraordinary!'

'No, not extraordinary. What is more natural than that I should want to be alone with you, here?' She laughed, delighted at his extravagant compliment but disconcerted by the pounding of her disobedient heart.

'Did you bring a swimming costume?' he asked suddenly.

'Yes, I've learned never to go anywhere in Italy without this,' and from the car she pulled the large beach bag that went everywhere with her these days.

'Come.' He took her hand and led her into the hotel. The shadows of the interior and the coolness of the tiled floor were a welcome contrast to the heat outside. Still holding her hand, he led her up the plain pine stairs and opened a door to a bedroom. The immaculately clean room was dominated by a wide pine bed with startlingly white sheets. Jane looked nervously at the bed.

'You change here, Jane, I will await you on the beach,' Roberto said, quietly closing the door behind him and leaving her in the room. Jane sighed audibly: for one dreadful moment she had thought that the whole day was about to be spoiled by a clumsy attempt at seduction. Even as she changed she realized that this had been a stupid thought – that would not be Roberto's style.

On the beach she found Roberto supervising the *padrone*, who was folding up the sunbeds and replacing them with large beach blankets. An umbrella shaded a wine cooler in which a bottle was already chilling.

'So much better for one's tan, don't you agree?' he said, indicating the blankets. 'And so much more intimate,' he added, smiling mischievously. Instead of replying, and to cover her confusion, she plunged into the sea and swam through the crystal-clear water to a large rock. From its top she could see the tiny fish darting in and out of the rocks. She watched, amused, Roberto on the beach still issuing instructions to their host, who rushed about anxiously fulfilling them. Then, with firm strokes, Roberto swam out to the rock and climbed up beside her.

'Wonderful, isn't it?' he said. 'The water is always so clean here, because of that line of rocks, I presume. Did you enjoy your swim?' She nodded, and sat, knees drawn up, arms folded about them, her body safely cocooned from eyes that constantly looked at her. Gently he brushed the sea water from her upper lip, his finger softly outlining her mouth. She shivered at his touch, quickly stood up, dived into the sea, and swam back to the beach. She flopped onto the rug, put on her dark glasses and lay down, facing the sea. Behind the dark lenses she watched him secretly as he dived time and again from the rock, his muscular body arcing gracefully. She was amused at the knowledge that this display was for her. He joined her, sinking down on the rug beside her. Gently he removed her sunglasses.

'Don't hide those wonderful eyes. I think you're a witch. Only a witch would have such grey eyes with black hair. A man could die just looking at those eyes.' Jane was sure there must be a sophisticated response to such compliments, but she could only laugh, shaking her wet hair which splashed him with water. Blushing at her clumsiness, she lay on her back, and pretended to soak up the sun. Even with her eyes closed she knew he was looking at her, felt certain that now he was studying the swell of her breasts. She half opened her eyes. She was right: Roberto was leaning on one elbow, gazing down at her. She sat up and, groping for her towel, hurriedly wrapped it round her shoulders.

'May I not look? Just look? You're so English. Why be ashamed of such beauty?'

'You make me feel uncomfortable and you make me blush just like an adolescent.'

'I know, I find it adorable. I love that delicate blush. It shows you're still pure.'

'I can hardly be that,' she replied wryly.

'It's possible, rare but certainly possible, to lose one's virginity and still remain a virgin in the mind,' he said seriously. Jane smiled vaguely: she did not understand his riddles.

'Come, lie back. I will not touch you, I promise.' She lay back; though he was not touching her, it felt as if he was. He lay so close to her that she could feel his breath on her skin, feel the warmth of his body, conscious always of his dark-brown eyes upon her.

'You're laughing at me,' she protested.

'Am I?'

'Yes. It makes me feel awkward.'

'I apologize. I don't wish to disconcert you – never. Instead of my gazing at you with adoration – not laughing at you, as you claim – we shall talk. OK?' He grinned at her and for a moment she felt safe.

'You speak wonderful English. You've hardly any accent at all.'

'You shame me that I have any accent. I get lazy these days.'

'Where did you learn?'

'I was at school in your country and I was at Oxford.'

'That explains it, then. Did you enjoy it?'

'Yes and no. England is such a civilized country to live in, such delights to be found there – the tea, the armchairs, crumpets, Ascot, the shopping, the Russian-roulette weather, Guinness. But on the other hand, I hate the weather, the rude shop assistants, warm beer, dog hairs on the armchairs – endless lists. Worst of all is that the English are never comfortable with foreigners. I found it difficult to make close friends. I had friends but I was always conscious that I didn't really belong, that behind my back I was "that greasy wop". My breeding and my background meant nothing to the arrogant English.'

'How did you stand it?'

'At first I felt enormous anger, but then it amused me. Such incredible arrogance has to be admired, such total conviction that God is English, C of E and a Tory.' He laughed loudly.

'You know I'm married?' she asked suddenly.

'Yes, I was told. Your husband must be a madman to allow you to be alone, here.'

'I don't think my husband gives a damn where I am.' She gave a sad, bitter little laugh.

'Then he's not simply mad, but certifiably so.' A shadow flickered across her face and, sensitive to her mood, he changed the subject. 'How long will you stay?'

'I don't know. Honor keeps persuading me to stay longer. It's easy to give in, it's so lovely here, it makes my problems seem a million miles away. I'll probably stay to the end of the summer, then return to Cambridge and look for a job.'

'A job? What for?' He sounded surprised.

'To earn money, of course.' She knew her answer would surprise him even more. Suddenly she wanted to challenge his assumptions about her.

'But it's your husband's duty to look after you.'

'He would. I don't want him to. I don't want his help or his money.'

'You're a woman of spirit, too. You must hate him a lot not to be willing to accept his money.'

'Oh, I don't hate him, I love him,' she said simply. 'No, I want to be independent. I want to do something for myself, I don't want just to be the wife of someone. You see them all the time, everywhere, in the shops, at the hairdresser's, women full of self-importance, which they've done nothing to earn. They spend the rest of their lives feeling important, being noisy about it, because of their husband's position or wealth. I don't want to be like that, I want to be myself. And if I achieve anything, it will be because of what I've done – not because I happened to have slept with someone. Even if it's only a typing job. Otherwise, it's a form of whoredom, really, isn't it?'

'You've set yourself a difficult goal. Young as you are, it's a little late to start again, isn't it? I think it might be easy to think this way, now. But what about when you're older? How will you feel then?'

265

'I shall have a career behind me and a pension.' She could not help laughing at his pained expression. 'And you, what will you do when the summer is over?' she asked.

'I have to go to Rome for a while. And then to Paris in the autumn: it's always more amusing there. In winter, I go to my estate in the north for the shooting of the wild boar. You pull a face? It's a great sport, but not for women. I don't like these women who shoot, pretending to be men, it's unfeminine. I might go skiing, see old friends, and if the winter gets too depressing I'll go to the sun. It's a busy life.' He laughed at himself.

'So you're what they call a jet-setter, then?'

'Good God, no. Nothing as glamorous, or vulgar.' He looked appalled at the idea.

'Do you work?'

'Yes, very much so. I have estates to administer, and I have other business interests. Even my socializing is a form of work: I know a lot of people, they tell me things. I hear of a deal here, another there. I weigh them up, investigate, contact other people about them, and because I met so-and-so at Gstaad, for example, I can fix something up. It all depends on whom you know, really, the way I do business.'

'Doesn't it always?' she asked with a touch of bitterness. 'What matters is who you were at school with, Oxbridge, who your cousin married and who you're related to. I hate that system,' she said with vehemence.

'I'm sure you do, my love, many do. But you'll never alter it. Occasionally people think they have broken in, been accepted, but if their credentials are not quite right they never are, and when the chips are down, no one will go to their rescue. It's always been that way, no doubt it will continue so. But don't let's quarrel. This conversation is much too serious for such a beautiful day.' He filled her glass.

They sipped their wine. She did not know if it was because of the heat, the wine or the proximity of his body, but she felt dizzy. He was telling her about the wine, but she did not hear the words. As she listened to his voice, she felt a physical need which had been dormant in her for some time. She felt that if he touched her again she would be lost ... but he kept his promise and did not do so. Only his voice caressed her, as he spoke of impersonal things.

Their host arrived to tell them that lunch was ready.

'Do you wish to change?' Roberto asked.

'No, if you and the *padrone* don't mind me like this,' she replied as she slipped a short towelling robe over her bikini.

'I'm sure he's as happy with the way you look as I am.'

It was cool in the deserted dining room. They selected a table by the window. The food was delicious, as he had promised. All the time the *padrone* hovered near their table, his keen eyes watching for any signal from Roberto. Roberto ordered several bottles of wine, insisting that she sample each. She noticed that, though he drank with pleasure, he never finished a glass.

'This one is lovely,' she said, sipping the golden, chilled wine. 'Where is this one from?'

'I want to touch your breasts.' His hand snaked across the table and took hold of hers before she had time to remove it. 'I want to see them, I want to take them in my mouth, I want to feel your softness. Dear God, I ache with wanting you.'

Jane sat transfixed with astonishment, his words, echoing Tom's so closely, sent shivers through her body and made her shake. Still he held her hand. 'I want to bruise you, I want to make you moan with desire for me.' She looked at him, her eyes wide with horror, and she saw naked desire in his eyes, saw that his mouth was slightly parted, imagined that mouth on her. She felt a shiver of excitement flood through her, and snatched her hand away.

'Roberto, please. The man!' Beside them the *padrone* still stood, smiling and nodding his head. Jane hastily wrapped her robe tighter about her.

'Ignore him. He speaks no English.'

'He doesn't have to. Just one look at you, and he must know what you're saying,' she said spiritedly.

'Darling Jane. Forgive me, I couldn't stay silent any longer. Last night, the moment I saw you, I wanted you. I wanted to take you away from the ball. On the beach just now I wanted to tear your costume from you and mount you and possess you . . .'

'I'm not a bloody horse.' She tried to laugh but the laugh died and emerged as a half-strangled sigh.

'I don't joke, Jane. I want to give you the pleasure that I know you have never known. Let me be the one to teach you.'

'For Christ's sake, Roberto, send that man away, I can't bear him grinning at me like that.'

He spoke quickly to the man who virtually ran from the room. Roberto turned back to Jane, and took her hand again. 'Now, my darling, now, let me make love to you for the rest of the day and all night.'

'Roberto!' Her eyes pleaded with him.

'You're not going to let me, are you?'

'No, Roberto, I can't.'

'Why not? Who is here to see? There's that wonderful bed upstairs waiting for us. Can you not imagine what beauty of feeling awaits us, in that room, on that bed?'

'Please stop, I'm sorry you feel this way. But I don't think I've done anything to make you think that I would or could.'

'You may think that but your body feels differently. All morning I've sensed your need for me. I know you've been fighting this feeling all the time. Jane, imagine my weight on you, the power of me within you.' He spoke quietly, urgently.

'Roberto, it wouldn't be right. I don't want to, you're wrong, I don't want ever to make love to another man.'

She wished he would stop. With every word he spoke she could feel herself weakening.

'No, my sweet one, you must not talk like that. Of course you must make love to me. Your beautiful body was made for it. You have nothing to fear, my darling. This fellow is very discreet.'

'Is he?' Jane sat upright, anger flashing in her eyes. 'You know that for a fact, do you? Come here often, then, do you? It must cost you a small fortune hiring the place so often to be on your own with your latest pick-up.'

'Contessa, don't be angry with me. As a matter of fact, I don't make a habit of coming here. I thought it would appeal to you,' he said gently. 'I did not plan this. I beg your forgiveness, Contessa. I apologize, blame the wine, the sun, your intolerable beauty.'

Jane ran from the room and blindly up the stairs. Her legs were shaking. What the hell was wrong with her? Her body was completely aroused. She looked at the bed: he had been right, she did want to make love to him. She wanted to see his body naked looming above her, to smell him, to . . . 'No!' she shouted out loud. 'No!' That was lust. She did not love him; she loved only Alistair. If she went to bed with him, she would despise herself. She could live without sex. She was not going to repeat the mistakes of the last six months in Cambridge with anyone.

He was waiting for her in the hallway. He helped her into the car, and she thanked the *padrone* in her faltering Italian. As they drove back, quite slowly, he talked casually and did not attempt to touch her, and it was as if the incident had never happened.

Back at the villa, Honor was on the terrace with Umberto and Federico. The two boys eyed Roberto with unconcealed resentment. He merely glanced at them once and then ignored them.

'And what have you two darlings been up to?' Honor asked archly, raising her eyebrows.

'Nothing, my dear Honor. I took your lovely niece for a swim, a delicious lunch, perhaps a little too much wine, and I return her safely to you.'

'*Quel dommage.*' Honor looked unconvinced. 'I was anticipating news of a delightful little affair. How sad!'

Roberto accepted tea – Honor's was the only house where proper tea was served, he said – but declined her invitation to dinner. Jane, becoming used to the complexities of her new feelings, found that she wished he had accepted. After tea, she walked with him to his car.

'It would have been nice if you could have stayed to dinner,' she said shyly.

'Not for me, my entrancing Jane. It would have been unbearable. To sit in a room with you, for hours, to look at you, and to want to touch you without being allowed to – that's too much for me. I can only permit myself to see you for a few short hours.' He bent forward and kissed her full on her mouth and the shock of his lips on hers made her quiver. He stood back and looked at her with a strange, knowing smile, and almost imperceptibly nodded.

'All in good time, my little one. All in good time.' He waved his hand and was gone.

4

That evening, pleading tiredness, Jane did not go to a party with Honor and the boys. She wanted to be on her own. She had forgotten that for months she had been terrified of being on her own; now at last she had chosen it.

She had intended to write some letters. Instead she sat on the terrace, attempting to analyse her fluctuating emotions and attitudes. One moment she wanted never to see Roberto again, the next she was miserable at the thought of not seeing him. Later, when he phoned to invite her to lunch the following day, she accepted, feeling elated and excited at the prospect.

This time they drove into the mountains. He laughed at her expression, as she surveyed the crowded restaurant into which he led her.

'You see, my darling Jane, you will be safe from me here.'

'Roberto, I don't think one is ever safe with you anywhere,' she countered.

'Perhaps you've been thinking; perhaps you don't really want to be safe?'

'Oh yes, I do. But I'm sure you're a gentleman, and I enjoy your company, so I thought it was worth taking the risk,' she parried.

The head waiter made much of them. With a flourish which entailed much flexing of his elbows, he removed Jane's chair and seated her. He flicked open a large damask napkin with a sharp movement of his wrist, making the linen crack like the sail of a boat. With hands darting like quicksilver he rearranged the flowers, altered the position of the ashtray, and straightened the already perfectly aligned silver. He clicked his fingers at his acolytes and with a bow presented Jane with the menu. Jane was aware that she had just witnessed a virtuoso performance.

Roberto surveyed the other diners. There was much waving and bowing. Jane noticed that some he rewarded with more enthusiastic waves than others. For some he bowed from the waist, to others he inclined his head. Having done so, he then proceeded to ignore them all.

'Please, if you want to go and speak to your friends...' Jane smiled, indicating the room with a wave of her hand.

'No, my darling, I am with you. They're of no importance,' he replied with an ingenuous arrogance that made Jane smile even more.

'You seem to know everyone here. It's extraordinary, I think I've met more people since I've been staying with Honor than I ever did while I was with Alistair. We lived in the country, you see. We didn't mix much socially.'

'This husband of yours is a strange man. He allows you to be here on your own, but when you're at home he does not introduce you to society. He should want all the world to know and admire you.'

'But I didn't want to be part of society. It had rejected me and I was frightened by it. It was a very difficult situation for Alistair, too,' she said lamely. She wanted Roberto to understand, but here in this restaurant it all sounded so unlikely, even to her.

'And why did this society reject you?'

'As you would say, my credentials were wrong.' She smiled wryly.

'Poor little one. Your husband failed you. He married you, so he should have made society accept you.'

'It's more difficult in England.'

'No, it's worse here – the society, the caste system. Having married you, he should have made a stand. He knew before he married you how it would be; he knew the system better than you. He sounds a very stupid man; what was he trying to do, change the order of things?'

'Oh no, I don't think he ever thought about it. He said he married me because he felt sorry for me after his family had been horrible to me.'

'Then I was right, he is very stupid. He only made matters worse for you, didn't he?'

'I suppose so but, honestly, I don't think he knew it was going to be as difficult as it turned out to be. He meant well, and he loved me.'

Roberto frowned. 'I find this conversation makes me angry. I don't want to talk about your husband, Jane.' His voice was suddenly cold.

'Then you shouldn't have brought the subject up, should you?' she replied, heatedly.

'I don't like to think of you in the arms of another man.'

'But that's silly, Roberto. I'm not a twenty-year-old virgin.'

'I wish you were, and had known only me,' he said wistfully.

'This food is delicious.'

'Dear Jane, always so English when the conversation goes the way she does not wish it to go.'

Their coffee was served and they lingered over a brandy. 'Why does your aunt live with those dreadful gigolos?' he asked abruptly.

'They're not dreadful and I'm sure they're not gigolos.' She felt indignant on Honor's behalf.

'Of course they are. It's such a sad waste.'

'What's a gigolo, then?'

'Jane, you know full well.'

'I want to know what you think a gigolo is,' she persisted.

'A gigolo is a young man who makes love to an older woman for money.'

'How do you know she pays them? I'm sure she doesn't.'

'Well, perhaps not in money, but she feeds them, takes them about with her, probably buys them clothes and jewellery.'

'And had I gone to bed with you yesterday, what would have been the difference between them and me? Would you have despised me, too, thought me dreadful?' She stared angrily at him, exasperated with his pompous hypocrisy.

'Of course not, that's entirely different.'

'What's different? You're older than I am, you buy me meals, no doubt if I had an affair with you you would buy me presents, too, and clothes. I've no money, I can't repay your hospitality.'

'Darling, I adore you when you're angry. Those eyes of yours are even more beautiful then. That wonderful grey takes on an entirely new depth, a depth with great fire . . . wonderful.'

'You don't take me seriously,' she said, growing more irritated.

'Of course not, I think you might be winning the argument.' He smiled, took her hand, raised it to his mouth and she felt his breath on it. It was a sensuous act, more so than if he had kissed her hand.

'What you should have said was, "Why does your aunt have such young lovers?" Then I would not have taken umbrage, but gigolo – it's not a pretty word, is it?' She took her hand from his grasp but she smiled at him.

'True. So why does she?'

'I think she's fed up with husbands. She says they're too expensive a hobby.' Roberto laughed loudly. 'This way she's in control, they go when she wants, no alimony. If you're a very rich woman, I suppose it's a good system. Don't think I disapprove, because I don't. They're very kind to her, and they're really very sweet. They make her happy, so I'm grateful to them because I love her.'

'I was wrong to criticize. I apologize. You're right, if she's happy, then . . . She must be very lonely sometimes.'

'Honor, lonely? I've never thought of that. She's always surrounded by so many people that it doesn't seem possible.'

'That's a sure sign of loneliness. She drives some of my friends mad, you know. There are many who would love to please her,' he said with such a soulful expression that Jane had to smile.

Their lunch finished, he drove her home. Again he had tea with them, and again refused an invitation to dinner. For a week the routine was varied only by the restaurants to which he took her for lunch. Each day he flirted gently with her, but he made no further attempt to force himself upon her.

She did not go out in the evenings any more. He always phoned in the evening, and always at a different time. Until his phone call, she was restless and would wander about the villa aimlessly.

One evening, Honor was having a rare quiet night at home.

'For heaven's sake, Jane, do settle. Read or something.'

'I'm sorry, Honor. I can't settle. I'm like this every evening until Roberto phones. I'm always afraid that this evening is the one that he won't. But I'm still restless even once he has phoned, I don't know why.'

'Jane, you're impossible. Of course you're restless. You go out with a sensuous man like Roberto, he brings you home by early evening and then leaves. I'm not surprised you're like this. Why, you should be in bed with him by now, not wandering around here driving me mad. I presume he has tried to seduce you?'

'Yes,' Jane said, half embarrassed and half proud that he had.

'And you turned him down?'

'Of course.'

'Why "of course"? I should think he's everything a young woman wants. He's not handsome in a conventional sense but he's bloody attractive in an off-beat way, such fun to be with, and very kind. Mind you, I doubt if he's ever been treated like this before. He must be intrigued by you – women are queueing up to get into his bed. It's very clever of you, darling.'

'I'm not trying to be clever. I could never sleep with him, Honor, I don't love him.'

'Piffle, of course you could.'

'It would be all wrong. How could I sleep with him, pretending it was Alistair?'

Honor shrieked with laughter. 'Jane, darling, if you slept with Roberto, I can guarantee there's not the slightest chance you'd want to pretend that it was Alistair – or anyone else. The very idea,' she snorted, obviously well pleased with the joke. 'But Jane, seriously, you can't spend the rest of your life with no interest in men. Be sensible.'

'I admit I'm very attracted to him: it would be difficult not to be. And if I'm honest I'll admit I love his attention. But if I slept with him it would just be for sex and I never want to do that again.'

'Jane, you're so divinely old-fashioned.' Honor chuckled, but then added seriously, 'You're not still hoping to go back to Alistair?'

'Well . . .'

'Jane,' Honor exclaimed, 'I don't understand you. After the dreadful way he treated you.'

'Sometimes I think I was too rash. If I'd kept my eyes and mouth shut, I'd be happy now.'

'Bullshit! I've never heard anything so stupid in my life. You'd be perfectly miserable by now. I love him dearly but he'll never change: he's too much like my brother – he always had to have a little woman on the side, too. You'd become a martyr – the shires are full of them. You see them at point-to-points, too hippy, too loud, too fond of the sherry, with set mouths, sad eyes, and besotted with their dogs.' Jane had seen so many women who fitted Honor's description that she could not laugh. 'You're too young to live in the past,' Honor went on. 'Remember, Jane, you're living your memories now: make sure they're not dull, sterile ones for the sake of the old woman you'll be one day.' Jane shivered at Honor's chilling remark. 'Roberto would be an ideal start for you. He's charming, rich, sophisticated, experienced in bed and he would make you happy.' Honor efficiently enumerated Roberto's virtues.

'But I don't want to marry again.'

'Darling, I'm not talking about marriage. Oh, dear, you're so innocent. I'm talking about a delightful affair, a light summer soufflé of a relationship. You take everything so seriously, too seriously.'

'That's true.' Jane smiled.

'You must forget about marriage where Roberto is concerned. Firstly, you'd be a divorced woman, which would kill his stuffy old mother and he'd have a guilt complex for the rest of his life. And, you know, despite appearances, Roberto and people like him stick to the strict order of things. When he's fifty, he'll marry a suitable young girl from a suitable family, who, no doubt, has already been picked out for him. She will produce his babies and he will continue to have mistresses, several of them.'

Jane shivered, as if with cold. 'Several, really?' She tried to sound nonchalant, but she felt sick inside, and that night she found it difficult to get to sleep.

It seemed that finally he was bored with her. Now that she knew he had many mistresses, this was not surprising. For five days he did not telephone, despite her making all manner of bargains with God. On the sixth day, when the phone rang she ignored it. When Guido handed her the phone, she knew she sounded overeager as she accepted his invitation to dinner the following night.

'Honor, he's invited me to dinner, not to lunch.' A flushed and happy Jane exploded into the room.

'Thank goodness for that. For Christ's sake, sleep with the delicious man this time, then perhaps we can all have some peace.' Honor laughed at her.

The following night she asked Honor's advice about what to wear at least half a dozen times before settling on a plain, full-skirted, black taffeta dress which made a delightful swish as she moved. Honor insisted on lending her a diamond necklace and earrings. It was a very sophisticated-looking woman who rushed out of the door like an excited schoolgirl as she heard his car arriving promptly at eight.

The road seemed familiar to her this time. 'Where are we going to dine?'

'At my home. I'm tired of crowded restaurants and noise. We shall dine peacefully à deux.' Jane found herself both relieved and apprehensive at the words.

Tonight there were no lights in the castle as they drew up. As he led her through a side door, along stone-flagged corridors and up and down innumerable stone staircases, her high-heeled shoes clattered and echoed in the silence. He ushered her into a room which, but for the view, could have been one in any large English house. Comfortable chintz-covered chairs and sofas, a log fire and, to complete the picture, two large dogs which merely raised their heads as they entered, then returned to their contented slumber in front of the fire.

'Gracious, it's so English. Even an open fire, in Italy, in summer!'

'It can get very chilly in the evenings in these mountains. I'm glad you think it's so English. I went to great trouble to create the illusion.'

'Except for the view, it could be England,' she said, crossing to the large full-length window which framed a view of mountains tinged with the rose colour of the setting sun.

'Crikey!' She jumped back in fright: beneath her was a sheer drop to the valley far below. Roberto caught her as she stepped back, twisting on her heels in her haste. As he touched her she leaned her body slightly towards him, but he steadied her and then, to her disappointment, let go, crossing the room to pour the drinks.

'I'm sorry, I should have warned you. It's quite safe, though, the glass is very thick. It looks dangerous, that's all.'

'I forgot for a moment that the glass was there, it made me jump,' she said in confusion, caused, she knew, more by his touch than by her fright. He settled her in a chair beside the fire with her drink and, selecting a record, put it on the turntable. As the beginning of Sibelius's Fifth Symphony filled the room, Jane jerked nervously and spilled half her drink.

'Jane, darling, what is the matter? You're a bundle of nerves tonight – and you're as white as a ghost. Darling, what has frightened you?'

'It's the music, Roberto, please, anything but that . . . I can't stand it.'

'But it's so beautiful to listen to, especially when the sun is setting on the mountains.'

'Please, Roberto, please change it.' The urgency in her voice made him cross to the record player at once. Instead, he put on some Mahler.

'Does Mahler frighten you, too?' He smiled gently as she began, frantically, to dab at her dress. 'Would you like me to get a robe for you? The servants can see to your dress.'

'No, it's nothing. Look, it's all mopped up – so clumsy of me. The Mahler is lovely,' she said quickly.

'What was it?'

'Oh, I was being silly. It reminded me of something that happened a long time ago and that I prefer not to remember, that's all. I'm fine now.' She smiled brightly at him.

'Was it reminding you of some sad love affair?' he persisted.

'No, nothing like that.'

'Pain in a woman's life is always caused by a man, even at second hand.'

'I suppose that's right.'

'Will you tell me about it?'

'I can't, Roberto, I'm sorry.'

'I want to know everything about you, even the bad things.'

'But I can't think about it, let alone talk about it.'

'I would like to kill anyone who has ever hurt you,' he said vehemently, and kissed her gently on the forehead. 'You will tell me one day, you promise?'

'I'll try. But not yet, Roberto, please?' and the almost begging tone of her voice made him change the subject.

A servant appeared and stood silently to one side. He said nothing to Roberto, who continued to talk and sip his drink. Ten minutes must have passed while the mute servant stood there, before Roberto stood up and told her that dinner was ready. The servant moved silently and opened a door concealed in the bookcase to reveal a dining room, also furnished entirely in

English style. Two more servants stood there, dressed in black livery with gold trimmings and immaculate white gloves. While they ate, the men stood at attention behind their chairs. As courses were finished, they moved in unison to remove the dishes and replace them with new ones; in tandem they poured the wine. Jane watched but she could see no signals pass between them.

'I thought you said we were dining *à deux*?' she said pointedly.

'We are.' He sounded surprised.

'How can it be *à deux* with so many in the room?'

'They're servants: they don't count.'

'That's a dreadful attitude, Roberto. I hope they don't understand English.'

'Of course they don't. But if they did, it wouldn't alter the fact. They know their place and I know mine.'

'I could never adjust at Respryn to having servants. It always embarrassed me, being waited on – I always seemed to be apologizing.' She laughed at the memory.

'How strange. You must have confused them terribly.'

'Did I?'

'There's no shame in being a servant, you know, provided you're a good one. Your embarrassment could have insulted them.'

He turned and spoke quietly to the men, who silently left the room. 'Better?' he enquired, smiling at her. 'I don't want you to feel uncomfortable, do I?'

'I hope they don't feel insulted.'

'On the contrary, they will assume that I have dismissed them because I want to be alone with you. But obviously you were not brought up with servants. Tell me about your life.'

She told him her story, everything but the illness. She was ashamed of that.

'Of course, now I remember you. I remember your face – I saw it in the newspapers. I thought then what a beautiful face it was, but you look very different.'

'Thanks to Honor. I was pretty dowdy before. She's done what she calls "glossing me up".' Jane laughed good-naturedly.

'She has done a wonderful job, but she had the best material to work on. You have no vanity: that's rare in a beautiful woman.'

'But I don't think I'm beautiful; in fact, for years I thought I was ugly. My mother was always at pains to tell me so.'

'How very strange of her. Your parents, do you see them often?'

'No. My father thinks I'm a traitor to my class, poor old thing. And my mother, well, I just don't seem to have anything in common with her. We're both uncomfortable with each other. I write and let them know how I am, and send presents, but I haven't seen them for ages.'

'It wasn't just your husband who put that sadness in your eyes.'

'I wasn't sad,' she said. 'Not really. Just angry, and determined that things would get better. But there are advantages to an unhappy childhood: nothing ever hurts you as much again, after being rejected as a child.'

'Doesn't it?' he said, unconvinced.

'Well, it's different, shall we say? And you have a better chance of surviving what gets thrown at you.'

'And what has been thrown at you?'

'Rejection. My parents first, then society, my husband . . .'

'How did he reject you?'

'He had an affair.'

'So, you left this husband, whom you claim to love, because he had an affair?'

'Well, several, it turned out. But one or several, it's all the same.'

'Poor man. To lose you . . . He should have been more discreet.'

'It wouldn't have made it any better and I would have found out anyway. There were people who would have made certain I did.'

'Don't you think you were too hard on him? We men are weak creatures, you know.' He smiled, spreading his hands expansively as if in apology for all men.

'No, I don't. I expected fidelity. I was faithful to him. If I were to be unfaithful it would be because I no longer loved. It has to be the same with a man.'

'Does it? You sound so sure.' All the time he spoke he smiled gently, but Jane had the feeling that he was laughing at her, that her views were amusing him. She found it disconcerting.

'I *am* sure,' she said emphatically.

'I have always found it difficult to be certain of anything in this life.' He sipped his wine and gazed at her over the rim of his glass for what seemed a long time. 'And me, when you have your affair with me, what if I am unfaithful?'

'It would be the same.'

'I see. And what about now, what if I told you I had a mistress?'

'I know you have. Several in fact.'

'How interesting. Who told you?'

'A little bird. But we are not having an affair, so it's none of my business what you do, is it?'

'True. But how do you feel at the thought that, when I take you home tonight, I shall kiss you chastely, go to the arms of another woman, and spend the night making love to her, when it should be you?'

'Should it?'

'Of course, as you well know.'

'But it won't be, so again it is none of my business where you sleep tonight,' she answered lightly, but inside her was a tumult of distaste and distress at the very idea of him with another woman.

He smiled enigmatically. 'Shall we take our *digestif* in the sitting room?'

No servants appeared. She curled up on the comfortable sofa. He put on more music and sat down opposite her.

'You don't flirt with me any more,' she said almost petulantly.

'I never stop,' he replied, laughing.

'I haven't noticed.' She pouted.

'What was I doing just now?'

'I don't think talking about your mistresses amounts to flirting with me.'

'Doesn't it?' He smiled. 'Are you getting just a little jealous, Contessa?'

'Of course not, I don't mind what you do. We're good friends – that's all.'

'And do good friends normally flirt?'

'Some do.'

'Jane, Jane, you're so contrary. What you mean is that I have stopped trying to seduce you. I haven't stopped flirting with you. But I thought we had a pact?'

'Oh.'

'You tell me not to seduce you, so I don't. Then you don't like it when I stop.' She smiled shyly at him. 'Do you want me to start seducing you again? I will with pleasure.' She saw the merriment in his eyes.

'I really did mean flirting,' she parried.

'You did not answer my question.'

'I don't know what to say,' she replied, becoming flustered.

'Then you're a little more uncertain than before, which is good. It's a pity you're not yet totally convinced that I'm right for you. Never mind, you will be.'

'You're always so certain.'

'It's easy. It's in your eyes when you look at me so shyly, so slyly. It's in the way you move your body when you're close to me. You want me. You're deciding – even at this moment you argue with yourself. You waste time with your games, your little teases, but no matter. We have time, and it adds to my pleasure in savouring the prospect of you.'

'You make me sound like a dish of food.' She laughed, but he looked seriously at her from across the room and said, 'When you have decided, you will let me know immediately, won't you?'

'Yes,' she said breathlessly, willing him to come to her and touch her, knowing that if he did, she would not resist, not tonight.

'Good. And now it's late, and as we both know, I have business to attend to. I think we had better go,' he said, to her acute disappointment and annoyance.

5

'Jane, you've let me down. What on earth are you doing here?' Honor asked, as she swept into the room with Umberto and Federico.

'What's the time?' Jane asked blearily.

'It's gone four. What happened?' Honor asked, and then told the two young men to go to bed.

'Nothing happened,' Jane said when they had gone. 'Nothing at all. We talked about his mistresses – that was the high spot of the evening. I think he's bored with me. He didn't ask me to go to bed with him, anyhow.'

'Darling Jane. He's not bored with you, he's playing games with you. I bet he knew exactly how you were feeling tonight and decided to pay you back for all the indecisions of the past weeks. In any case, men like Roberto don't ask you to go to bed with them – the very idea! – they lead you to it with a word here, a glance, an innuendo. Nothing as vulgar as asking.' Honor snorted with laughter at the thought. 'You're so divinely unsophisticated, Jane, it must be driving Roberto mad with desire.'

'I couldn't sleep so I came in here to listen to music and at least I've made my decision. I'm not going to have an affair with him. He's conceited and I think there's something decadent about him. Imagine having a whole army of mistresses – it's revolting.' But Honor's only reply was to laugh even louder. 'I don't think it's funny. Anyhow, I've decided that I don't want to be a member of his private sex army.'

'Perhaps, if he had you, he wouldn't want the others.'

'I doubt it. You yourself said the other day that men never change, they just begin to lie better. I'm not taking the risk.'

'Well, it's your decision. I still think it's a pity. He would have been such a good education for you. So, can we go to bed now, if that's decided? I've a splitting headache.'

'Honor, don't you think you should go and see a doctor? You often have these headaches now,' Jane asked anxiously.

'No. It's too many late nights at my advanced age, and I drink too much. I ought to wear my specs for reading, too, but I can't bear to. I look so ugly in them!' She chuckled.

In bed, Jane tossed and turned. It was hard to contemplate not seeing him again, but it was stupid to continue like this: it was not fair to either of them. When he next phoned, she would thank him politely for the good times they had had and explain that since she could not be what he wanted, it was better that they stop seeing each other.

But she did not get the chance, for he did not phone.

'Don't mope, Jane,' Honor said briskly. 'You've only yourself to blame, and it's boring me, this long miserable face about the villa. I like happy people. Pull yourself together and come to the Pattersons' with me tonight?'

But the evening did not distract her. She was even more despondent when they returned to the villa to find a note from Guido saying that the Prince had telephoned four times.

'Four times?' shrieked Honor excitedly. 'Now we know he's been playing games. When he finally phones – how long has it been, a week? – instead of your being in, which he's now used to, you're out all evening and Guido is far too discreet to tell him where. Oh, what fun, four phone calls! I think he must be feeling that he's overplayed his hand just a teeny-weeny bit.'

'You make it all sound so complicated. There must be a reasonable explanation.'

'Affairs are complicated things. I've had years of practice and I know what's going on in our divine prince's head.' She clapped her hands with glee. 'What's the time? One o'clock? Right, I guarantee he will call by two. If you've any sense, you won't answer it – really give him something to worry about.'

'How can you be so certain?'

'Oh, I am. I'll switch the phone through to your room – that's how certain I am.'

At two minutes past two, Jane wearily put her light out. At five past she quickly switched it on again. She sat mesmerized watching the phone as it rang. She let it ring half a dozen times before she picked it up.

'Hullo?' She tried to sound sleepy.

'Jane? Is that you? Jane, I am in Rome. I was called away.' He paused. 'Jane, are you there?'

'Yes, Roberto, I'm here.' Her ploy to sound sleepy was not working: she could hear the eagerness in her voice.

'Where have you been? I was calling all evening.'

'Out,' she said casually.

There was a pause before he asked, 'Darling, how are you?'

'Oh, I'm fine. I've been busy.'

'Did you miss me?'

'Yes.'

'Good. Perhaps you weaken, a little?'

'Maybe.'

'Nothing more definite?'

'No.'

'Look, Jane, I may be delayed in Rome a few days yet. Should you need me, Honor has my number. I would love to talk to you but, darling, I'm busy, I must go now. Ciao.' The phone went dead. To hell with him, she thought angrily, what could be keeping him busy at two in the morning but another woman? He had probably crept from her bed to call Jane. Damn him, he could go and boil his head as far as she was concerned. It was ridiculous that grown men and women should be playing games like this.

Honor, though satisfied to have been proved right, was not happy about the outcome of the call, especially when Jane began to suggest that she should return to England to start looking for a job.

'Darling, you can stay with me for ever. I love having you here.'

'You're sweet, but I can't live off you like this for ever, can I?'

'I don't see why not. If it doesn't bother me, why should it bother you? Too silly.'

Jane finally promised to stay for another month. Honor went out to lunch and then with Guido to the shops. Jane was left alone in the villa. When the phone rang, her instinct was to ignore it, but the caller was persistent and finally Jane went to answer it.

'Honor?' The voice made Jane start. 'Honor, is that you?' it asked. The sound of the familiar, warm voice excited Jane.

'No, Alistair, it's Jane.'

'Oh.' there was silence as she waited for him to continue.

'How's James?' she eventually asked.

'He's fine. He's really happy at his prep school.' Perhaps it was her imagination, or did his voice sound colder?

'And how are you?' she asked almost shyly.

'Rattling around, much the same as usual.' There was a pause. 'Jane, I'm glad I got you. I want to talk to you, it's important.'

'Yes?' she said breathlessly, happy that, at last, he wanted to talk to her.

'You are OK now, aren't you? I mean, fully recovered?'

'Oh yes, Alistair. I'm right as rain now.' The words bubbled out of her: she was sure his questions could mean only one thing.

'Anyone else?'

'No, no one,' she answered, perhaps a shade too quickly.

'I see,' he said shortly. She had expected him to sound more pleased.

'So?' She laughed.

'I think it's time we got a divorce.'

Momentarily, she took the receiver away from her ear and stared at it with a puzzled expression. She could not have heard him correctly.

'It really would make everything simpler and a lot tidier if we got divorced,' she heard him continue.

Jane felt as if she were boxed into total silence. This was not how the conversation should go. And what had happened to the clock – why wasn't the clock ticking? What the hell had gone wrong? He should be asking her to catch the next flight out.

'Look, you needn't bother yourself with a thing. I'll get the lawyers onto it straight away. Of course, it goes without saying that you can divorce me for adultery – it's customary,' his voice went on relentlessly.

'You'll what?' Her voice suddenly exploded into life. 'Oh, thank you, Alistair,' she said with heavy irony. 'How really kind of you. What an honour, letting me sue you.'

'Jane? What's got into you?'

'What's got into me? I'm angry at your bloody nerve.'

'I don't know what you're going on about. It's always the gentleman who is sued: that's how things are done. But don't forget I could, in law, sue you with that weirdo in Cambridge.'

'You might have the legal right, Alistair, but what about the moral right? I never wanted any of this to happen. If you hadn't played around, we wouldn't be in this position now. Do you remember, or have you conveniently forgotten?'

'It takes two to break a marriage, or have you forgotten that?' he countered.

'Bastard!' she snapped.

'Look, Jane, I don't want to argue with you.'

'Don't you? I don't hear from you for months and then you blithely phone up and ask for a divorce. What do you expect?'

'At least we can try to be civilized about it.'

'Civilized? You?' she sneered, while her mind was screaming, I don't want a divorce. I love you. Instead she yelled, 'Oh, do what you bloody well like!'

'I will!' he shouted back, and the phone was abruptly disconnected.

The clock was working. That was strange – she had been certain it had stopped, but now its relentless ticking was deafening. She picked it up and stuffed it under a cushion to prevent herself hurling it out of the window. The bastard had hurt her again. He knew how she felt: she had poured it all out in that letter which he had not seen fit to answer. And this, at last, was his reply. She kicked the sofa. What about her pride, her wonderful pride which was in shreds now? How could she ever face him? The sod, the rotten sod! She sat with her head in her hands. If only she had not answered the bloody phone, then none of this would have happened . . . She felt the prick of tears, and shook her head. She was not going to cry: she had cried enough over him. 'I'll show the rotten bastard,' she muttered to herself as, feverishly, she rifled Honor's desk, searching for her address book. Half an hour later, tears were running down her cheeks but they were tears of frustration at her inability to make the operator understand what she wanted. She heard Guido's car and rushed to meet him.

'Guido, thank God you're here. Please get me this number, quick.'

Guido calmly obtained the number and smilingly handed the phone back to her.

'Roberto?'

'Contessa?'

'I miss you. I'm so miserable.'

'I'm sorry you're so sad.'

'Roberto, may I come to Rome?'

'Of course.'

'Tonight?'

'You've decided?'

'Yes.'

'Then come, my love, come quickly.'

It was Guido who found out the times of trains for her, and it was Guido who lent her the money for the fare to Rome. A single ticket would do, she told him, and he smiled knowingly. She raced up the stairs two at a time and frenetically began to pack her bags, hurling an assortment of clothes into them, instinctively picking her best clothes. She swept the contents of her dressing table into her make-up valise. Never, since she had been at Honor's, had she ever showered, changed and made up in such record time. Guido drove her to the station and promised a hundred times that he would phone the Prince the minute he got back to tell him her time of arrival.

The train was travelling too fast for her and yet not fast enough – such was the turmoil inside her. She wanted to see Roberto before she changed her mind again. She wanted this train to speed up and to race her away from the past. And yet it thundered towards him too swiftly. This time she knew that she could not resist: the time for playing games was over. But after so many doubts, what sort of happiness could she expect with him? What number mistress was she to become? How could she learn to bury the principles of a lifetime and accept the inevitable infidelities? How could she learn to hide a love for another man which had burned in her for so many years? She was going for all the wrong reasons – what if he detected this and left her in anger? What the hell was she to do with her life? Mercifully, the emotions of the last few hours, the endless questioning of her mind, forced sleep upon her and she awoke with a start when, at nine, the train pulled into the station.

Anxiously she searched the faces on the platform as she stood alone, isolated in the seething crowd of Italians noisily and emotionally greeting each other. Perhaps he had changed his mind, perhaps he would not come . . .

'Jane.' He was beside her, his arm protectively about her. He was smothering her face with hungry kisses and suddenly she was part of the milling Italian throng.

'I missed you, Roberto, darling,' she said honestly.

'That is the first time you have called me "darling" or anything but Roberto,' he said happily, as he took her arm and held her tightly, as if fearful that she might slip away from him. Gently he ushered her through the hordes of pushing, shouting people. Having stowed her cases in the boot, he got into the car beside her and took her hand.

'Do you want me to book you a room in a hotel, Jane?'

'No.'

'You're certain. No more games?'

'No, darling, no more games. I want to sleep with you tonight, if you want me.'

'Want you? Oh, sweet Jane.' He laughed at her. 'Yes, I want you, I want you.'

With skill he threaded the car through the crowded streets, in the fast city traffic. She had never been to Rome but this night she saw only him. In the train she had feared that she had come only because of Alistair's rejection of her – she had been certain of it. But now, beside him, able to touch him, to smell him, it seemed equally certain that she had come because Alistair's news had jolted her into a decision that she needed to make, that it was natural for her to make. She lifted her hand and stroked his cheek.

'What happened?' he asked, taking his attention off the road for a second as he looked at her searchingly.

'What do you mean?'

'What made you decide to come?'

'I missed you too much. I realized what I wanted and how stupid I had been.'

'Nothing more? Nothing happened to make you change your mind?'

'No, nothing,' she lied.

6

Everything in Roberto's life seemed to move on oiled wheels. The wrought-iron gates of his Roman house opened silently as they approached. The front door was opened, like the gates, by unseen hands. In the huge, white marble hall stood a row of silent servants in dramatic black and gold livery. When they moved, it was with silence and smoothness across the marble floor. The sound of Jane's heels seemed unnaturally loud.

To her surprise, Jane was immediately dispatched to her room with instructions to change quickly for dinner. She was in such a hurry that she had no time to take in the splendour of her room, did not see the Manet hanging on the wall or the fine Venetian looking-glass. Not till later did she notice the exquisitely inlaid French bureau, the Persian rugs scattered on the highly polished floor. She cursed herself for having packed so fast – everything was badly creased, and only the black taffeta she had worn the other night was wearable. She felt even more dishevelled when she skidded back to the hall to find Roberto immaculate in his dinner jacket.

'Are we going out to dinner?'

'Yes. You'll like the place we are going, it's a beautiful old monastery which Mussolini turned into a restaurant.'

'There's no need: a sandwich will do me.'

'What you're really saying is that you're surprised I did not rush you into bed immediately?' He smiled teasingly at her.

'Well . . .' She felt a traitorous blush flit over her face.

'No, my darling, that's not my way. These things have to be done properly, with grace and with – anticipation.'

The restaurant was everything he had promised. Old as time, and yet with all the comfort of the twentieth century. The view across the Tiber to the floodlit Castel Sant' Angelo could not have been more romantic. He had ordered their meal while she was on the train and seemed genuinely delighted at her pleasure in his choice. As the meal progressed he talked easily and entertainingly, leaning across the table to her, speaking with intensity on many subjects but not once about themselves. Occasionally he would stroke her arm, touch her hair; and always there was his warm, seductive smile. But she began to feel edgy. She supposed she had expected a repeat of the frenetic seduction scene at the beach hotel – but there was nothing.

As the time passed and he continued to talk animatedly to her as if she were a good friend, she began to wonder if she had imagined everything. And yet he had asked her if she wanted to stay in a hotel. Surely that could mean only one thing? Maybe she was not beautiful enough for him this evening in her crumpled dress. Maybe he had met someone else and this dinner was to let her down lightly. Maybe she had delayed too long and he had tired of the idea of her. She had been determined never to have an affair with him; now, contrarily, she felt acute disappointment at the thought that nothing would happen. He did not hurry his food, as one might have expected an eager lover to do, but lingered over each mouthful. Even when the meal was finished, he did not ask for a bill, but ordered cognac and slowly, oh so slowly, he drank it. It was past two before they left the restaurant and made their way back to the house.

Even at that time in the morning the ritual of the swinging gates was repeated. This time, Jane spied a very old man, bent almost double as he bowed low to them. In the hall the servants waited, taking their coats, opening doors for them. She found these silent figures everywhere disconcerting.

'When on earth do they go to bed?' she asked in a whisper.

'Why, when I do, of course.'

'But that poor old man outside, he should be retired, or at least in bed hours ago.'

'If I did not use Giovanni he would die: if I suggested he had an early night he would think that I did not like the way he worked. I am his life, my darling, don't you understand?'

'No, I don't – it's feudal.'

'Yes, it is. So feudal that it makes my responsibilities, my expenses, enormous. But why do we always end up discussing servants?' He looked pained.

'It's a subject that fascinates me.'

'Reserve some of the fascination for me, will you?' He smiled as he crossed the room and poured them each a brandy. She did not want a drink: her nervous anticipation had reached a peak where she felt she would scream at him if he did not touch her soon, kiss her, anything . . .

'Oh no!' she wailed.

'What is the matter, my darling?'

'My handbag, I left it in the restaurant.'

'It will be perfectly safe, don't upset yourself. I'll send one of the men first thing in the morning to collect it for you.' She gulped nervously at her drink. 'Darling, what is the matter? It will be returned.' He smiled at her, amused by her agitation. She was in despair: inside the bag was the last of the marijuana she had had from Tom. If she had not fooled Alistair with her faked ecstasy, she was hardly likely to fool someone like Roberto. Why couldn't she just be honest with him?

Having put on the same Mahler record he had played at dinner the other evening, Roberto came and sat opposite her, not beside her as she would have liked. He sat in his chair, his glass in his hand and stared at her with that deep, dark, penetrating stare which, although it frightened her, excited her too. She sat transfixed as she felt his gaze wander over her body, resting for a moment on her breasts, then moving on down her body. She wished he would speak, for she could think of nothing to say.

'Darling Jane, you're so tense, what is the matter?'

'It's the way you stare at me, I don't like it.'

'I'm sorry. I am enjoying so much looking at you. I've waited: it would be wrong to rush things now. I told you, I enjoy anticipation. Take your shoes off, lie back and relax, darling.' His beautiful voice did not soothe her as she lay back on the couch, feeling as stiff as a board.

'It's no good.' She swung her feet to the floor and looked at him with desperation in her eyes. 'Roberto, I . . .' She stopped, blushing, and hating as always that telltale colouring of her face. He looked at her enquiringly. 'Roberto, have you by any chance . . . have you got any dope?' she said in a rush, in a tight, little voice, her blush deepening.

'Did I hear correctly, Contessa? Dope?'

'Yes.' The redness deepened.

'What for?'

'It's nice, of course.'

'I'm aware it's nice. No, it was something in your voice, the way you asked, it was strange.' He crossed the room and sat, at last, beside her. He took her hand, but she could not look at him. 'Yes, I've some grass, but I would like to know first why you want it so desperately.'

'I just like it.'

'That's not the only reason.'

'It helps me.'

'Helps you what?' Stubbornly she sat silent. Putting his hand under her chin, Roberto forced her to look at him. 'Helps you what?'

'I don't want to tell you. Can't you just give it to me?'

'No, darling, I want to know. I don't like this air of desperation about you. Tell me. I insist.'

'Well, if you must know. It helps me make love.'

'But darling, we need nothing, especially tonight.'

'You don't understand. I can't make love unless I'm high.'

'Jane, darling?' he said, concerned as he saw tears begin to gather in her eyes. 'My darling, don't upset yourself.'

'It's true,' she sniffed. 'I just can't, not without dope in some shape or form. And I don't want to deceive you by pretending.'

'Dearest, you could not deceive me. Don't you realize I already understand every mood you have? How could you deceive me in our bed?'

'It's the only other way. I don't want to spoil your pleasure so I would have to pretend. You see, I like the beginning and the end, it's the important bit in the middle that leaves me cold.' She smiled a lopsided smile.

'Darling, it's all important, every moment. I will show you what it is like to be really made love to: you won't need anything with me.' As he spoke he began gently to kiss her face, her neck, nibbled her ear. She lay back against the cushions as his hands moved over her. He bent and through the silk of her stockings she felt his soft mouth as he began to kiss her feet, her ankles. She felt his hands search for the softness of the inside of her thigh, involuntarily she arched her back. 'Come, my love,' he said and, sweeping her into his arms as if she were a child, carried her from the room and up the stairs.

They entered a different bedroom. In the centre of the room stood a large, gilded four-poster bed; enormous candles lit the room but their light did not penetrate to the corners. He laid her, gently, on the bed. Looking up, she saw that the canopy of the bed was a huge mirror and she lay watching fascinated as with grace and expertise he began to undress her. With an exquisite slowness he peeled her stockings from her. With care he removed her dress. He paused, admiring her in her black silk lingerie, all the time telling her how beautiful she was to him. He uncovered her full breasts: she would have loved him to touch them, caress them, but instead he feasted his eyes on them. The slowness of his movements, the deliberation, his sensual expression, the low, sexual tone of his voice, heightened all her emotions. She felt no shame, only total abandonment to him. Never taking his eyes from her he began to undress himself, pausing frequently to gaze at her with naked longing in his eyes, talking gently to her. Naked he knelt beside her; languidly she raised her hand to caress his fine muscular body. Still he knelt, quietly talking to her, telling her of his joy in her, of the pleasures of the night ahead, of what he was going to do to her, and what she would do for him. At the sound of his relentless voice, the husky sexuality of it, her desire for him became a desperate need. She began to rock her head from side to side, her body began to writhe rhythmically. 'Please, darling. Please,' she heard herself plead. His answer was to touch her gently. The relentless whispering continued, gently his lips brushed her breast, first his fingers sought her, then his mouth and her body shook uncontrollably as he brought her to a climax. She sank back on the pillows. He knelt above her and laughed.

'Don't!' she yelled, hiding her head in the pillows.

'Such a sensuous little English girl. Does she still need her dope to enjoy me?' He continued to laugh with delight.

'Roberto, don't look at me. I feel so ashamed!'

'Ashamed? What on earth for?'

'You hardly touched me and look what happened. How is that possible?'

'Many things are possible, my darling, many things.' He bore down upon her and kissed her with a hard passion, his lips bruising her mouth in their intensity. As his hands, his lips, his tongue ranged over her body, searching out the secrets of her flesh, she was begging him to enter her and take her. She screamed with her longing, and then he was driving himself into her.

She was to learn so much that night. Not only that such lovemaking existed, but also that she could come again and again, as if her body was an instrument he could control at will. She found that as she climaxed so she wanted more of him, that overnight she had become insatiable in her need of this man and his body. She learned so many variations, each appearing more enjoyable than the one before. He taught her that there was no shame in love, if both enjoyed what they did to each other, then there was no sin, no disgust, only pleasure. She learned to let him do whatever he wanted to her for what he wanted she wanted, and she experienced total possession. She had not known that her body could feel like this, and had never known what wantonness was within her. And for the first time she met the unselfishness of a man who desired only her pleasure and delayed his own until she felt sure she was almost dead from the passion of the night.

She awoke to his voice and his gentle kiss. He stood beside the rumpled bed, freshly bathed and shaved, in an elegant silk robe. Beside him was a tray of coffee and croissants.

'Breakfast, my love?'

'I don't need food.' She smiled at him, contented as a cat, as she lazily stretched against the fine lawn pillows trimmed with lace.

He laughed. 'So, do you think I cured you?'

'Oh, Roberto, you were . . . I had no idea what love could be like.'

'I told you you were pure. You see, I knew that body had never known real love. Had never been truly awoken. We make good love together. Now you will never want to leave me, will you?'

'Never. I couldn't anyway, it would never be like that with anyone else, never, never. You may live to regret last night – I shall always be creeping into your bed now.' She laughed with delight at how bold she felt.

They drank their coffee and suddenly she found she was ravenous. They ate the plateful of croissants and then rang for more. She bathed, a long, luxurious bath, the water full of sweet-smelling oils, and he sat beside the bath and talked and talked; and he insisted on washing her, and drying her, and powdering her. He brushed her hair, he dressed her in a negligee of cream silk, handmade lace cascading around its neck and hem.

'There, my first present to you.'

'It's so lovely, Roberto, when did you buy it?'

'Yesterday.'

They returned to the bedroom. The bed had been made with fresh sheets.

'Oh, my God, look! Someone's made the bed. Crikey, those sheets, what will people think? How embarrassing!'

'Not at all. My laundress will be very happy for me. There is no shame in lovemaking in this country, my darling, only joy. You must get used to that.'

They lingered all day in the room, making love, talking, laughing.

'Don't you have work to do?' she asked guiltily.

'No.' He smiled.

'But I thought you had been called away on important business.'

'No.' He burst out laughing. 'That was a little lie. I thought if I went away suddenly, it might help you make your mind up faster.'

'Roberto, that's deceitful!'

'Of course, but then about the only sensible platitude in your language is that "all is fair in love and war".'

They bathed and dressed; Jane found her clothes neatly pressed and hanging in his dressing room. Roberto took her out to dinner. He took her to Frascati to drink the wine, and then they returned to the giant, mirror-canopied bed which seemed to be becoming the centre of her world.

For five days the routine was the same. She was satiated with love and she had never looked more beautiful or felt more relaxed and content.

On the sixth day he asked her to live with him. And on the sixth day they had their first row.

7

'So, will you come and live with me?'

Jane looked up, startled, from her coffee cup, at Roberto lying languidly at the foot of the bed, casually lighting his cigarette. His tone of voice seemed to her the same as if he had asked her where she would care to dine.

'The way you ask me makes me think that my reply is about as important to you as if you had asked me if I prefer tea or coffee,' she replied sharply. It was Roberto's turn to look in surprise at Jane, reclining against the pillows, her long, dark hair spread over their silky smoothness, apparently enjoying her morning coffee, her skin glowing with that special sheen of a woman well loved.

'I beg your pardon?'

'You heard!' she snapped.

'I heard, I mean I don't understand the sharpness in your tone.'

'It's a very big question you are asking me, one that could alter my life, and you lie there as if you were totally unconcerned what my answer might be. Or are you so conceited that you have taken my saying yes as a foregone conclusion?'

'Jane, what has got into you? You're very grumpy this morning.' He was laughing as he leaned across the bed to take her hand. Angrily she brushed his hand away. 'Darling, please.' He looked perplexed. 'Of course it is a big question, for both of us. And it is one that I do not ask lightly.'

'Then why sound so offhand? It's my life we're talking about.'

'My life, too.'

'It's a bigger step for me than for you. I can say goodbye to my reputation.'

'My love, I am aware of that, but you will have my protection. My friends will understand. What is more natural than that two people in love should want to be together all the time?'

'What about your family?'

'They would think it perfectly normal that I should take . . . that I should live with the woman I love.'

'Mistress. You wanted to say "mistress".'

'Yes, my mistress. It is an old-fashioned word, but yes, that is what you would be. I see no shame in it for you.'

'What we lack is a word for you, really, isn't it? Pity I'm not filthy rich – then you could be my gigolo, and we'd be quits.'

'Darling, don't sound so bitter. I would offer you more if I could.'

'Offer me what? Marriage? Hardly.' She laughed but it was a short and hard sound.

'Don't you think that if I could marry you, I would?'

'I can get a divorce,' Jane said quickly.

Roberto was silent.

Jane did not know what devil was working in her. Part of her was ecstatic that he had asked her and the other part of her was a tumult of anger that he should dare. She knew full well that had he asked her to marry him, she would have refused. She knew she could not face again the social problems such a marriage would cause. So why was she making such a fuss, why was she needling him like this? 'It's not just that I would be a divorced woman in a Catholic country, is it?' Still Roberto did not reply. 'Is it?' she persisted.

'No.'

'What is it then?' He did not answer. 'It's because I'm a peasant, isn't it, not good enough for your snooty family, is that it? I wish you would speak to me,' she said, her voice sharp with anger.

'Jane, that is a silly thing to say. You of all people should know that it is not possible. Good God, girl, there are families in my society who will not entertain people in their houses who are not in the Almanach de Gotha. Can you imagine what those people would do to you? It wouldn't stop with us: they wouldn't accept our children either. Could you live with that? Compared to my society, your English one is liberated.'

'And of course you are in the Almanach de Gotha,' she sneered.

'Jane, don't be perverse. Please try and understand my position. If I could change things for you, I would, but I can't. I have my family to consider, too, my mother – it would kill her.'

'Isn't her son's happiness important to her?'

'She belongs to a different generation. Duty is of more importance to her than happiness.'

'Christ, it's archaic! It makes me so angry. What is so wrong with me? I'm not a bad person, a thief, a bitch. I just want to love you, and to do that I have to accept that I'm second-class. Well, I'm not and I won't accept it.'

'Darling, everything you say is true. But we cannot change things. This society would destroy us.'

'It's such dreadful hypocrisy – they will accept me if you're screwing me, but not if you marry me.'

'Jane, Jane, this language does not become you.' They sat on the bed, glaring angrily at each other. 'I'm sorry to hurt you, Jane. I thought you understood, after your experiences. I would never have asked you if I had thought to hurt you so. I cannot marry you, I am sorry, there is no argument to pursue. But as my mistress you will be accepted in the circles I move in. I can offer you my protection, which is immense, and my love for you, which goes without saying.'

'And what about me when you get married?'

'I have no thoughts of marriage.'

'No, but in the future when they wheel out that little schoolgirl for you. What about me then?'

'What schoolgirl, what are you talking about?'

'That kid that your family has already decided you will marry, when you're fifty.'

'Darling, where do you get these ideas from? There is no one chosen for me, I promise you.' He almost laughed at her notions.

'It's not funny. You could desert me.'

'Of course. And you could desert me, it goes both ways. Look, darling, I'm not offering you an affair that will be over by Christmas. I'm offering you a life with me as my companion until the day we no longer make each other happy. And when that day comes, I promise to look after you until you meet someone else, or all your life if necessary. I cannot be fairer than that, can I?'

'Marvellous. A pension plan. Is it index-linked?'

'Jane, you are making me angry.'

'You've already made me angry!' An oppressive silence descended on them. 'Mistresses? What about all your mistresses?'

'I wouldn't have any.'

'Oh no?' she said, the disbelief evident in her voice.

'No, I would not do that to you. I am an honourable man. If I say I will not, you will believe that I won't,' he shouted at her.

'It's going to cost you dear, moving that lot out of your various houses, pensioning them off.'

'Jane, you must believe me, I have slept with hundreds of women. I have always had women available to me, but I have never lived with one of them. Not as I'm inviting you. If you don't want to come and live with me, share my life, then just say so, but don't create all this unpleasantness about us. Jane, I love you.'

'It's easy to say.'

'At least I say it. You haven't once told me you love me,' he shouted back. 'Do you love me?' She sat silently. 'Jane, I asked you a question. Do you love me? Answer me! I demand to know.' He was shouting again.

'No, I don't love you, so there,' she said in a singsong voice like a petulant child.

'I don't believe you. We could never have what we do without love.'

'You use the word so easily – probably a lot of practice with it. But for me, it's a bloody big word in my vocabulary.'

'I am amazed it is even included in your somewhat limited vocabulary.'

'I haven't had your advantages in life, so you needn't start sneering at me.' She wanted to cry. She had awoken so happy and now she felt wretched. But like someone on a helter-skelter, she felt she could not stop, now they had started.

'I apologize, that was low and unforgivable of me. Please, Jane, forgive me? Please?' He put out his hand and lifted hers to his mouth and kissed it. She looked at him, tears overflowing her eyes. 'Oh, my darling, this is so wicked of us, we have such happiness and we begin to destroy it.' He kissed her full on the mouth and she responded to his touch. 'Do you really not love me?'

'Roberto, we have just made friends, don't start again.'

'But if you don't, why can't you lie? Why do you have to hurt me?'

'We have gone too deep for lies.'

'I can't believe you don't love me, I just can't. If it's true, what do I have to do to make you love me? I will, you know, I will make you love me.'

'You can't make someone love you. It happens or it doesn't.'

'We have everything. What is stopping you acknowledging it? I want to know,' he persisted.

'I would rather not say.'

'I insist. Jane, tell me, now.'

'I love my husband. I told you right at the beginning, nothing is going to change that. I always knew I could only ever love one man. What I have for you is nearly that, but not quite.'

'You talk rubbish, utter rubbish.' He looked as if he wanted to shake her with exasperation.

'I didn't want to tell you: you made me.'

'You are cruel, Jane. You have your little fantasy and you inflict it on me. And you risk destroying what we have with your stupid lie.'

'It's not a lie. I love him,' she shouted defiantly. Roberto swung round and hit her hard across the face, then he twisted her long hair around his hand and shook her.

'You little bitch! How dare you talk of loving him in front of me when I give you so much and he has given you so little. The bastard couldn't even make you happy in bed.'

'That wasn't his fault, it was mine,' she shrieked back at him. 'And don't you hit me, don't you ever dare hit me again!'

'Listen, you stupid little fool. You're in love with a memory, don't you understand? A memory, that's all it is, memory of your first love – we all have those sorts of memories but we don't mistake them for love.' He was screaming and she was crying now, and still he continued. 'You cling to it from fear. You're afraid of life! That's why you took so long to come to me. But don't for one minute think that what you feel is love, it isn't. It's me you love, me, you understand.' He threw her back across the bed.

He paced agitatedly about the room as she lay on the bed sobbing. His anger was a fierce force in the room. Why had he asked her? she thought. Everything was spoiled now, it would never be the same again. She felt the bed give as he came and sat beside her.

'Jane, I'm sorry. I should not have hit you. I lost my temper because I am so afraid of losing you. You think I'm a playboy, that I'm toying with you, that I'm not serious about you. If only you could understand, my darling, how much I need you, how desperate I have been for a love like this. And now I've probably lost you.'

Blindly, through her tears, she held up her arms to him. 'Roberto, I don't want to fight. Of course I want to live with you, I certainly can't live without you now. I was being oversensitive. You're right, marriage would be impossible: I know I couldn't go through the sort of rejection Alistair's mother and friends inflicted on me, ever again. I know you're trying to protect me, I really do. Forgive me.'

They made tender love and when they later lay on the bed, watching their reflections in the mirror, Roberto turned to her.

'I will make you love me,' he whispered. 'That's a promise.'

'Yes, darling.' She smiled.

'We shall live as if we were married but, with us, when there's no love left, we shall separate with respect, dignity, no recriminations and friendship.'

'Maybe we shall never separate?'

'True. In that case, my love, I shall marry you when I'm seventy and to hell with all of them.' He laughed.

They lingered on in Rome. The city was empty of people he knew, all his friends had gone to the mountains or the sea to get away from the heat of the city and so Rome was left to them and the tourists. They joined the throngs of sightseers and he showed her the city he loved. He knew of little, out-of-the-way churches which the tourists never found. And tiny squares with bubbling fountains where the tourists never wished. He showered gifts upon her and took her to small restaurants where they would sit for hours, talking. She began to think that life with him would be a joy. Only that loveless child of years ago who still dwelled within her stubbornly prevented her acknowledging that she loved him. But those who saw them together – holding hands, devouring each other with their eyes, unashamed of their blatant, physical need for each other – knew that she did.

Finally and reluctantly they returned to the coast. A party had been arranged at the castle, and it would have been unthinkable to cancel it. Late one afternoon they drove up to Honor's villa.

'So here you are! What on earth was there in Rome to keep you two in that dreadful heat?' she teased them fondly. Jane clung to Roberto's arm.

'We fell in love, Honor,' he said simply, and grinned as sheepishly as any callow youth.

'Darlings, how marvellous.' Honor clapped her hands excitedly. 'It's a champagne occasion, isn't it?' She called to Guido to bring champagne. 'Now, tell me all.'

'I've come back to pack, that's if you don't mind, Honor. I'm moving in with Roberto.'

'Why on earth should I mind? At last you've taken my advice.'

'I want her to move immediately before she has a chance to change her mind,' Roberto explained.

'Is she likely to?'

'If you knew the job I had persuading her.'

'She's always had a streak of obstinacy,' Honor said with a husky laugh.

'So I learned. And pride.'

'Oh, dreadful pride, I thought it would be the ruination of her,' Honor merrily retorted.

'Would you two mind not talking about me as if I wasn't in the room?' Jane grinned. 'Any mail for me, Honor?'

'On my bureau.'

While the two friends chatted, Jane collected her mail. Apart from a letter from the bank there were three letters for her. Recognizing James's childish writing she tore that one open first, and shrieked with joy as she read it. 'Oh, Roberto, Honor, it's from James, he wants to come and visit. I haven't seen him for months. He's always so shy and awkward with me, I never dreamed he'd actually ask to come and see me. All I ever get are his funny, stilted little letters. Roberto, can he come?'

'Of course, my darling, but he is the only male from your past I'll welcome.' The significance of his remark was not lost on Honor, who glanced sharply from one to the other.

'Oh, how sad!' said Jane, reading her second letter.

'What's sad?' Honor asked inquisitively.

'It's from May, do you remember her, Honor? My lovely maid from Respryn who came to London with me? She got married but it's broken up. She's back at Respryn and she's unhappy there – she says it's not the same without me and is there any chance of a job with me? I wish I could help her.'

'Write back and ask her if she minds working all round the world.'

'Roberto?'

'Darling, you'll need a personal maid, what better than to have an English one? Mind you, she'll have to be good.'

'Oh, she's the best. But Roberto, I can't afford her.'

'I'm not asking you to, I'll pay her, you silly girl.'

'Roberto!' She jumped across the room and flung her arms about him. 'She's so special to me, Roberto, thank you so much. Gracious, how much happier can I get?'

Honor and Roberto smiled indulgently as she ripped open her last letter. As she read it, the smile disappeared from her face to be replaced by a heavy frown.

'I don't believe it,' she said, horrified, sitting down heavily, her face white. 'The bastard!'

'Jane, what is it?' Honor rushed to her side.

'It's from my lawyer. Alistair is suing me for divorce and he's named Roberto as co-respondent. But the date – ' She scanned the letter for the date. 'This is impossible, it's dated a couple of days after I left for Rome. How did he know, how did he find out? He lied, he said I could sue him. I told him there was no one in my life: how could he have known? How could he do this to me?'

'You told him when?' Roberto asked sharply.

'The day I left for Rome,' Jane said, unthinkingly.

'So you spoke to your husband that day?'

'Yes, Roberto.'

'I see,' Roberto said, his face closing with anger.

'No, Roberto, you don't see. It wasn't like that. I promise you it made no difference.'

'What are you two talking about? So many people are here, he probably found out from someone who had seen you two together.'

'It's unimportant how he found out. That does not concern me. I talk of lies and deceptions, Honor, that's what concerns me.' He looked coldly at Jane.

'Roberto?' Jane looked at him with anguish.

'If you are coming, Jane, I suggest you pack quickly. I have much to do at home,' he said suddenly, and Jane with relief excused herself and went to pack some more clothes, leaving Honor apologizing for her nephew. When Jane returned, she crossed the room to Roberto and kissed him on the cheek.

'I'm sorry, darling, to cause you these problems.'

'I do not mind being named as co-respondent. No, Jane, that's not the problem we have to resolve,' he said ominously.

They left Honor still admonishing them not to let anything spoil their happiness and warning Jane to contact her lawyer immediately. She was still calling to them as the car began to spin down the drive. It was a silent drive back to the castle. Roberto was hunched over the steering wheel, a cold and angry expression on his face. As usual he drove far too fast but Jane was too afraid of his anger to say anything. She should have told him about Alistair's call before. It was so easy to be wise now, but at the time, silence had seemed the best policy.

Roberto must have warned the servants that she was coming, for a set of rooms had been prepared for her. Of all the bedrooms she had occupied in her life, this was by far the most beautiful. She sat at her dressing table gazing through the large windows to the valley and watched the sun setting behind the mountains. It was a breathtaking view. She wandered about the room admiring the pictures, amounting to a fortune, which hung on the walls. How strange her life was! Sitting in this beautiful room she could hardly remember the tiny bedroom of her childhood. To have come from that life to all of this was like some fairy story. In England the memories of her previous life had never left her: always she had remembered her past, it had been a strong part of her present. But here in this foreign land, in this castle, with Roberto by her side, it was no longer part of her. The past was the dream world, not the present, and when she looked back at the girl she had been, she saw someone else.

8

'Do you like your rooms?'

Jane swung around from her dressing table, startled by his voice, to see Roberto standing in a doorway which was so cleverly concealed in the massive wall tapestry that she had not noticed it. The maid who had been tidying her clothes bobbed to Roberto and silently left the room.

'I didn't hear you come in, you made me jump.' She laughed nervously. After the silent drive, she had not seen him until now, a full four hours later. His absence had made her nervous, for he usually came, drink in hand, and talked to her while she had her evening bath. It had become a ritual with them, until tonight, when she had waited in vain for him. 'I missed you,' she said simply.

'I had much to attend to.' His words reassured her: perhaps it was not anger, after all, which had kept him away from her.

'So do you like your rooms?'

'Darling, they are superb. I spent ages just gazing at that wonderful view and watching the sun set. They're perfect, I've never lived in such style.' Again the nervous laugh. 'I mean, my dressing room and bathroom, they're so luxurious, and this room, just look at it, it's big enough to have a ball in . . .' She heard herself prattling on. 'Is that really a Gauguin over there?'

'Yes, of course.'

'It's lovely,' she said lamely, her nervousness making conversation difficult. He crossed to her dressing table and opened her small jewel box.

'Who gave you these?'

'Honor gave me the pearls, the rest were presents from my husband.'

'I would prefer it if you did not refer to that man as your husband. He does not deserve the title.' He scattered the jewellery on the dressing-table top. 'Apart from Honor's gift, I would prefer it if you did not wear any of this, do you understand?' He gestured, dismissively, at her small collection of jewellery. She nodded, though she did not understand. 'I will buy you whatever jewellery you need. I don't want you to wear another man's gifts in my sight.' The coldness in his voice was mirrored in his expression. 'And while I'm on the subject, I do not want you to have any contact with this man, except through your lawyer. Should he telephone, or write, I wish to be informed. I have left instructions with my staff and I expect you to obey my wishes also. It is an order, Jane.'

'But – '

'There are no buts. You accept these conditions, or you pack and return to your aunt.'

'Darling, please don't be so angry with me. I know I was wrong, that I should have told you about Alistair phoning. I was going to, really. I would have, honestly, I just forgot . . . you see how unimportant it was to me, I forgot.' Even as she spoke, she had a chilling feeling that he knew she lied.

'Sadly, dear Jane, we shall never know if you would have told me. At least one thing we do know for sure, you lied to me at the station. I shall take time to forget that lie.' She could not meet his eyes but instead intently studied her hands. She had apologized but she refused to beg. The silence between them was oppressive.

'Is your maid adequate for you until your own arrives from England?' She was relieved not only by the change of subject but also by the change in his tone.

'She's fine, thank you. Mind you, we had a bit of a job understanding each other – we managed finally with mime and drawings.' Her laugh sounded more natural this time.

'You must learn my language.'

'Yes, I must. I know a few words already but I would like to speak it properly.'

'I shall find you a tutor.'

'Books or Linguaphone will do fine. I don't think I would like a tutor, someone actually hearing my ghastly mistakes.'

'Jane, you're a funny creature. So sophisticated in some ways and still a child in others.' Lovingly he caressed her hair. It was going to be all right, she told herself. He crossed the room into the dressing room, threw open the large mahogany wardrobes, lined with white silk, and began to study her clothes, which looked so few in the cavernous interior. 'We shall have such fun filling these cupboards,' he announced. His cold mood seemed to have disappeared completely. Taking her by the hand, he led her to the small sitting room where they had sat the first night she had dined here. It was becoming apparent to her that their quarters were in one wing of the castle, a house within a house, like Respryn except that everything was larger and grander. Over dinner they began to talk of the party to be held the following day.

'What should I do about the party?'

'Do? Darling, what do you mean?'

'I'd like to help, and I'm good at organizing things – food, flowers, that sort of thing.'

'Good heavens, that won't be necessary. The staff know exactly what has to be done. You needn't worry about such matters.'

'But the household, I must be able to help manage the household?'

'I wouldn't hear of such a thing. My darling – worrying about such mundane matters. My staff run all my homes expertly, they would be horrified if you wanted to help.' He looked equally shocked at the notion.

'But what on earth shall I do all day?'

'Be beautiful, for me.'

'You say the loveliest things, Roberto, but I can't spend my life titivating – I'd go bonkers again.'

'Again?' he enquired sharply. Jane felt herself blushing, and began to study her hands. 'You know, darling Jane, it's a good job you have hands to stare at so intently each time you are confused.' She looked up to see him smiling fondly at her. 'So what is this? Something else you haven't told me?'

'Only because I feel ashamed – no other reason.'

'Why be ashamed? I presume you were ill? What is there in illness to be ashamed of?'

'I suppose it's a hangover from my childhood – mental illness must never be discussed, must be hushed up, a slur on the family, that sort of thing.'

'Poor Jane, was it dreadful?'

'Yes, it was . . .' Almost with relief she began to tell him of the horror that had engulfed her, swept her away with it as if on a rip tide.

'And yet you still say you love this man?'

Again the long studying of her hands. 'Yes.'

'Such strange creatures, women,' was all he said.

'Anyhow' – she shook her head, as if shaking the conversation away – 'what am I to do all day?'

'As I have said, you'll devote yourself to beauty.'

'All day? It can't take all day!'

'That is all my mother ever did, that and a little charity work.'

'I don't think mistresses would be welcome as charity workers in Italy,' she said lightly. 'I shall have to find a hobby. Painting, I liked painting at school: that would be fun.'

'And your Italian. You will be so busy at this rate you won't have time for me,' he teased.

After dinner, they lingered over their cognacs, and took a last walk on the terrace. When Roberto suggested it was time for bed, she agreed eagerly. In her room he kissed her cheek, and then passed through the concealed door in the tapestry. Quickly she prepared for bed. She sat in the vast four-poster and waited. She read for a while, but he did not come. Her body began to ache for him. As she remembered their nights in Rome, she became restless. The book did not interest her; she kept rereading the same page. She fell asleep, propped up against the pillows, the book open in her hand, the light making an oasis of the bed in the large darkened room.

She awoke with a start. Daylight was streaming into the room and he stood by her bed, an old woman beside him with a breakfast tray.

'Good morning, Jane. Your breakfast is here.'

'But I hate breakfast in bed.'

'You liked it in Rome.'

'That was different, you were with me.'

'I have work to do, I have been up since six and now it is nine. Rome was a holiday for me.'

'Then I shall get up at six, too.'

'For heaven's sake, you will not! A lady should breakfast in her room.'

'I don't want to. I hate eating in bed.'

'Then you must get used to it, it's not seemly that you should breakfast with me.'

'You are being stuffy, Roberto,' she cajoled him.

'No. I am teaching you how you will behave in my household,' he replied carefully and yet Jane heard a sternness in his voice which worried her.

'You did not sleep with me, last night,' she complained.

'No. Now we lead a new life. You have your suite of rooms, I mine. When I want you, I will come to you. Last night I did not want you,' he said coldly and Jane felt her smile freeze on her face. 'So,' he continued as if he did not notice her expression, 'so, the party is tonight. As I told you there is nothing for you to worry yourself with. I shall be unable to see you until tonight, I have business to attend to. I apologize, but it is unavoidable.' Now his tone of voice was pleasant again and he kissed her gently and left.

As she drank her tea, she was perplexed. He seemed to switch from mood to mood in the space of a sentence: one minute gentle with her, the next with that dreadful coldness in his voice which confused and frightened her.

Jane spent the day wandering aimlessly about the castle. The staff scurried busily about, each knowing exactly what they were to do. Even her offer to help with the flowers was curtly refused by an abrupt and efficient young woman. She was aware that wherever she walked, busy as they were, the servants stole sly glances at her and once or twice she was certain she heard a muffled giggle. Irritated by their staring and by her own uselessness, she strolled out of the castle and down the hill to the village. From behind windows and half-open doors she was again aware of the sly glances, the whispering, certain now that she heard giggling as she walked past. She must curb her irritation and the feeling of anger that was welling up in her. This was not England in the early seventies, this was Italy, and an Italy which time seemed to have passed by. She could not expect understanding from these people: to them she was a kept woman. If she were to win any respect from them, then she would have to behave with circumspection and dignity, not anger.

The heat was intolerable and she had not thought to wear a hat. As the midday sun beat down on her she felt dizzy and exhausted. Listlessly she reclimbed the steep slope to the castle and with some difficulty found her way to her room. She supposed it was lunchtime but where a meal would be served she did not know, and had not the energy to find out. Instead she lay on her bed trying to cool herself and realized that, if she were to survive here, she would have to find something to do with herself. Otherwise this inactivity would drive her mad. She would have to campaign to be allowed to do something about the running of the house, or else she feared she would always feel like a guest in it. She had never been able to understand women who took hours to have a bath: she could not imagine what took them so long.

Her walk and her worries had tired her and she slept fitfully, to be woken by the smiling maid waiting to help her to dress for the party.

As the party progressed, she forgot her daytime fears. Roberto was as charming and attentive as he had been on that first night when they had met.

He never left her side, held her hand, caressed her hair, her cheek, proudly introduced her to his friends. At about one in the morning he insisted she was tired and must go to bed; she longed to stay but he was adamant and escorted her to her room and kissed her cheek as he said goodnight. She lay in the dark listening to the distant music, longing to be part of it, perplexed that he had made her leave when she was obviously enjoying herself. She strained her ears, hoping to hear his footsteps returning to her. The dawn was breaking, music still filtering into her room when she finally fell into an exhausted and restless sleep.

The days began to fall into a lonely pattern. She found it surprisingly easy to take hours over her bath. She wrote endless letters – to James, to Zoe and Sandra, to Honor. She devoured books but without enjoyment, and she would stare for hours out of her window at the view without really seeing it. She felt the dreadful lurching sensation of misery returning.

They went to parties and to dinners, or would dine at home, and wherever they were he was charming and affectionate to her. Each night she was certain that his mood had passed and each night she waited in vain, peering through the darkness at the little door in the tapestry, praying for it to open, cursing it for always being closed. One night she tried to open the door but found that there was no handle, it was a secret door with a secret mechanism. She ran her fingers over the tapestry, trying to find the hidden lock. In a frenzy of frustration she beat on the door, hoping he would hear her, not knowing if he was on the other side, or even where it led, or even where his rooms were. Her sobs rang around the empty room and she cried herself to sleep, huddled by the little door. He found her there in the morning and gently picked her up and carried her to her bed, but said nothing about it, merely talking of the weather and his plans for the day.

Inside she was screaming with the pain of his rejection but she was beginning to feel a terrible rage, too. She had thrown herself on his protection, the protection he had promised her. She began to withdraw into herself and, as one week passed into another, began to fear that she was in danger of another mental breakdown. All the signs were there. She had to force herself to eat, force herself to concentrate, force herself to smile, to talk to people, wanting only to be alone, to hide away. She was certain that she was dying inside. And then he would smile at her across the room, that secret smile of lovers, and hope would surge within her that the nightmare was over. She began to hate her hope, wished it would evaporate, and finally let despair take over completely, for perhaps desperation would force her to decide what to do.

One evening, two weeks after she had moved in with him, after a quiet and pleasant dinner with him, he had, as usual, left her, and she sat in front of her dressing table absent-mindedly brushing her hair. She began to remember how peaceful it had been in the hospital – one whole year of peace and quiet, no worries, no responsibilities – everyone had been so kind to her then. Why couldn't she now shut out of her mind anything that upset her, as she had previously made Alistair's face disappear? If she was honest, it had been quite a happy time, really . . . The hairbrush clattered onto the dressing table. With horror she stared at her reflection. Christ! She was beginning to think of the oblivion of her breakdown with affection. She must leave, she must get right away from him. It was dangerous for her here. She did not understand this game he played. Whatever his motives, it was a cruel game. She had had enough, more than any soul should be expected to endure. With rising panic she began to suspect that he was attempting to destroy her. This was no innocent play, this was retribution. Fighting the hysteria welling within her, she wrenched one of her cases from the wardrobe and began to throw her clothes into it. She would go to Honor, first thing in the morning . . . thank God for Honor. Sobbing, she cleared the bottles from her dressing table.

'And what is my little one doing?' The bottle of perfume clattered from her hands onto the floor; the stopper rolled under the table and the liquid began to make a rivulet across the marble floor, the large room filling with its scent. 'I shall have to buy you another one,' he said, smiling gently at her.

'Roberto,' she sobbed. 'I don't want to leave you.'

'Then don't, my darling.' He swept her into his arms and carried her to the bed, where she clung to him with all the desperation of her near madness. He began to make love to her and time and again he brought her to a screaming climax. The relief of her body and mind reduced her to a frenzy of tears.

They lay exhausted in each other's arms. 'Why, Roberto?'

'I wanted to make you hate me.'

'Oh, Roberto! I could never hate you. You frightened and saddened me, but to hate you . . . never!'

'But I thought if you hated me you would leave.'

'But why? Do you want me to go?' Icicles of fear tingled through her.

'God help me, no.'

'Then why did you do this to me, to us?'

'Each morning I would stand by this bed determined to tell you to go, to get out of my life. And you would open your beautiful eyes and smile at me and I was lost . . . And then, each night I would pace the floor fighting with myself not to come to you, to take and possess you, and each night I resolved again to tell you to go and then each morning . . . the same helpless ritual. I told you weeks ago you were a witch.' He smiled and, lifting a strand of her hair, kissed it. Jane sat up and looked intently at him.

'Roberto, darling. Please, I don't understand why, when we mean so much to each other, you put me through these two terrible weeks.'

'You lied to me about your reasons for coming to me in Rome.'

'What if I had been honest with you that night? What would have happened? Would you still have wanted me? What else could I have done?'

'But I thought you had come to me. And then to find out that you were running away from your so-called husband . . .' His mouth twisted with bitterness. 'To have to know that I was being used as a means to forget your own unhappiness.'

'But darling, that night I didn't really know what I was thinking. How could I be totally honest with you when I wasn't sure if I was being honest with myself? Like you, at first, I thought that was the reason I had come, but then I began to think differently, I began to realize that in fact he had jolted me into a decision I had wanted to make all along.'

'How can I ever be certain?'

'You have my word.'

'Will you ever know what you did when you lied? But I don't seem to be capable of deciding to stop loving you.' He laughed at her. 'It has been a great shock to me. From the very start I couldn't believe it, I, Roberto Villizano – rake, sophisticate, womanizer, in love! I didn't even recognize it at first. How could I, it had never happened to me before? I thought you were just another conquest, but each time I saw you, I wanted you so desperately that other women ceased to exist. You have made me so vulnerable: that's what fills me with fear, that is why I wanted you to go. I feel as if I am in uncharted seas in my relationship with you.' He sat staring moodily into space. 'And you had the coolness to tell me that you loved him. I wanted to die when you said that, but I wanted to kill him first.' 'But, Roberto, listen to me.' She took his hand in hers. 'Listen, I begin to think it's a different kind of love.'

'You just say these things to make me feel better.'

'No, darling, I don't. I'm being honest with you as best I can. Heavens, Alistair and I were children when we married, mere kids, we grew up together, went through a lot together. I can't just stop loving him, but I begin to see that it isn't the love of a lover. You can't just throw away the past.'

'If only I could be certain. If only . . .' He looked longingly at her. She bent towards him, her bare breasts brushing against his skin. Aroused, he took her in his arms and kissed her with a forceful intensity. As he drove himself into her his great need filled her with such happiness but this time, as she reached her climax and cried with joy as he always made her do, she also cried, 'I love you!'

He wept. This strong, confident man sobbed in her arms and at last, as she held him and consoled him, she believed that she loved him.

'Roberto, I've been such a bloody fool. We nearly lost so much,' she said.

9

Her long lonely days were a thing of the past for she and Roberto were now almost inseparable. If he had business on his vast estate she would go with him, sitting patiently for hours while he talked with his tenants in a patois she could not understand. Just to be near him was happiness enough. She was welcomed by these simple people with a dignified deference. If this woman made their prince happy then she was welcome. Nobody stared at her, or sniggered, when he was with her. Now he lunched with her, took English tea with her. Only breakfast he ate alone. The morning ritual remained unchanged. Each day she was woken by him, the old maid beside him with her breakfast tray, grinning her toothless smile.

Roberto had changed her. She was always conscious of her body now. She cared how she looked, for him. No matter what she was doing, she was aware of herself, aware of her femininity. The more he made love to her, the more she craved from him. She was always ready for him at any time of the day or night.

Sunday was the only day she disliked. She hated the tolling bell that never seemed to cease, the sound dolefully soaring up the valley from the village below. It was not a joyous noise, not like the church bells at home. Its mournful note matched her mood on Sundays, for Roberto would visit his mother that day, and though nothing had ever been said, she knew better than to ask if she could go too. The old princess, well into her eighties, lived across the valley in yet another castle owned by this astonishing family. 'How many castles does one family need?' she had asked him, laughing, one day.

'Too many,' he replied. 'They ruin me, these dreadful stone mistresses.'

If she was lucky, Honor might visit, but that was rare, for Honor disliked travelling so far into the hills, away from her villa and friends. Roberto would not hear of her going to Honor's without him. So Sundays were a hateful day, but the memory of his treatment of her when she first arrived was too fresh in her mind for her to object strongly. She waited, from ten in the morning until ten at night when he returned, trying to hide her growing resentment. Once or twice he brought some cousins back with him, but always male cousins: her correct assumption was that she was deemed too wicked to meet his female ones. Sometimes she raged inwardly at the injustice but otherwise she was happy and, she reminded herself, it was only one day out of the seven.

When alone she would spend hours exploring the castle, realizing that she had seen only a small part of it. There was none of the cheerful clutter of possessions she was used to at Respryn or Drumloch, where different styles and periods of furniture stood happily side by side, where unimportant and inexpensive objects could be found scattered among the priceless pieces. Here each piece of furniture, each ornament, each sculpture was placed so that its beauty could be seen to perfection. At Respryn, she had felt free to rearrange things, but here there was no question of it, for everything had its place; it would have seemed a sacrilege, she felt, to move anything. Roberto's two houses, despite their differences of style, period and size, were similar. There was a silence about them both which was almost tangible. The servants here moved in the same silent way, like noiseless acolytes, so that sometimes she would jump, thinking that they were ghosts as they flitted past her. Both houses were places of dark shadows, which varied from the deepest black through all the shades of grey and green, so that sometimes she felt she lived in a magic castle under water. It was the shutters and blinds that created this illusion: their gentle movement as they swayed in the breeze or the sun sneaking through the latticework, made rippling patterns of the shadows. In every room the sun was fought as a fierce enemy of the treasures inside. Both houses echoed. As she explored, her footsteps would make a deafening clatter on the stone or marble. Feeling guilty at breaking the silence of centuries, she would tiptoe or often, to the staff's amusement, could be seen, shoes in hand, as silent as they, wandering through the rooms and galleries. Respryn was like a doll's house compared with this magnificent, castellated, arrogant building.

He had been right: her help was not needed and would probably have been resented by the servants, who went smoothly about their allotted tasks.

She found Roberto's attitude to his staff strange. He never seemed to speak to them, and yet they always knew exactly what he wanted. It would not have been unfair to say that he virtually ignored them, as though they were pieces of furniture. But instead of the smouldering resentment that she expected, she began to notice, with astonishment, that they looked at him with undisguised adoration.

A letter arrived from Alistair.

'Do you want to read it first?' She waved it at him. 'It's probably about James's visit. Nothing more ominous.' She grinned, confident now in their love for each other.

'Read it to me,' he replied with a smile. Within seconds of opening it, she was in tears.

'He won't let James come and stay with us,' she said in disbelief. 'Listen: "I have spoken to my lawyers, who agree with me that the household in which you are now living is not a suitable one for a child of James's tender years to visit",' she read.

'What?' Roberto stood up, an expression of anger spreading across his face.

'There's more, "Until you get rid of the gigolo with whom you choose to live, I'm afraid, Jane, you can't see James. Sorry about this, but I have to think about the boy, and my lawyers assure me I'm within my rights ..." Roberto!' She looked at him with an expression of horror, only to see that he was beginning to laugh. 'What's so bloody funny? How dare you laugh when I'm so unhappy?' she stormed at him.

'My darling, forgive me, it's the idea of me as a gigolo – I find it so amusing. But you're right, I should not laugh. This Alistair of yours is a very arrogant young man.' Pulling himself together, he crossed the room and put his arms about her. 'He is wicked, this man, I shall never forgive him the repeated pain he causes you. Come, my little one. We shall consult lawyers, too.'

'It won't do any good. They will probably all say the same thing.'

'It's a dreadful price you are being asked to pay. I would understand if you felt you had to leave me for your son – that I could forgive.'

'I couldn't leave you, Roberto.' Her voice was firm now. 'It would make little difference, he'd find some other excuse to stop me, or rather his bloody old mother would. This is her work, I can smell her in this.'

'He must be a very weak man then, if he allows his mother to rule him so.'

'He's not weak, it's just his mother's so bloody strong. Even the devil would run and hide from that terrifying old hag.' She managed a bitter little laugh, thinking as she did so, that there did not seem much to choose between Alistair's mother and Roberto's.

'Then he's trying to get you back.'

'Alistair, wanting me back? No, there's no risk of that,' she snorted derisively.

But that day she did not go with Roberto; instead she went to her room, pleading tiredness. It was cruel and unfair, she thought. Was she supposed to believe that Alistair lived like a monk at Respryn, never had girlfriends to stay? Unlikely, unless he had changed out of all recognition. But to have her declared an unfit mother on moral grounds, that was despicable. She knew there was not a court in the land that would allow her to have her son now. Only a year ago he had asked her to return to him, yet now he could do this to her. He wasn't a vindictive sort of person, nor was he a prude; it had to be that old bitch, still warring away in the background against Jane. Still terrified that if her grandson saw too much of his mother, she might contaminate him with what Blanche saw as the obscenity of her background. It might be wicked to hate but, by God, she could not help herself. She thought of the consequence of leaving Roberto, but what for? She knew the answer – a life of loneliness, devoid of love, and, if she were lucky, the chance to see her son once a month. She could not live like that, not again. Perhaps later, when Roberto was more secure in his relationship with her, trusted her again, perhaps then he would let her go alone to spend a few days with her son. It was the only thing she could hope for.

She was depressed for several days and only cheered up with the arrival of May. Roberto shrugged resignedly when she insisted they meet her off the plane rather than send a car. He watched with disbelief as the two women excitedly hugged each other in greeting, tears streaming down both their faces.

'But May's not just a servant, Roberto, she's my friend,' Jane explained to him later, but the concept was beyond his comprehension.

Happy as she was here, she was hungry for news of Respryn. Who had had babies, who had died, who was feuding with whom?

'And you got married, May?'

'Yes, daft thing to do. I'd always said I'd never marry and I should have stuck to the idea. Daft I was. Drove me mad, he did, nasty smelly thing, and he snored too.'

'Who was he?'

'A new footman, Felix. Oh, he's good-looking enough, and he was pleasant, but his socks smelled something dreadful . . .'

'Hardly grounds for divorce, May.' Jane laughed.

'No, it was wrong of me to marry him in the first place. I don't know what got into me, I suppose I was lonely. Respryn isn't the same without you and of course I'd had to go back to being a parlour maid. I didn't like that, I can tell you – the other cows laughing at me behind my back 'cause I'd come down in the world. In the middle of me being fed up, Felix popped the question and I said yes, and after I'd said it, he seemed so pleased I didn't like to say, "Sorry, I've changed my mind."'

'Oh, May!'

'His Lordship was real kind to us, he really was, gave us a lovely cottage, up by the home farm. I enjoyed doing it up, getting it nice, then I got bored and Felix wouldn't let me go back to work . . . and he drank . . . and . . .' She looked at Jane as if making up her mind about something. 'It was the sex,' she stated. Jane sat silently, waiting for her to continue. 'Well, I couldn't be doing with it, it was disgusting, he was like a bloody animal . . .'

'May, I am sorry.'

'Nothing to be sorry about. It's my own fault – always listen to your inner voice, my mum says, and I didn't. Anyhow, it's one of them new quick divorces for us, two years apart and it'll be over.'

'I meant I was sorry you didn't enjoy the sex,' Jane said gently.

May shrugged dismissively. 'Landed right on your feet here, haven't you, him a prince and this lovely castle. No day trippers here, I'll be bound!'

'No, May, more's the pity. There should be.'

'I never did understand you and the trippers – you actually seemed to enjoy them. Untidy lot, leaving their litter about. These houses should be for the families and nobody else.'

'May, you sound just like old Lady Upnor,' Jane protested.

'When you getting married then? When your divorce comes through?'

'I'm not getting married, May.'

'Why ever not?'

'It would be too difficult and complicated, me with my background and being a divorced woman. One's bad enough, but the two together – ' She flicked her fingers, as if cooling them, in an unselfconscious Italian gesture.

'Who says?'

'We both do, May.'

'Does he love you?'

'Oh yes, he does.' Jane smiled.

'Then I don't see the problem. Lord Upnor didn't let society stand in his way with you, so who's this prince think he is to treat you like this?' May said angrily.

'May, don't be cross with him. It's my choice, too, I couldn't go through all that social thing again, I couldn't. We're happy as we are, very happy.'

'Well, I don't like it and that's flat. You someone's mistress: it doesn't seem right.'

'It's the seventies now, May. Times have changed.'

'Not that much, they haven't. Where's your security, I'd like to know? And if times have changed so much as you say, then why can't he do the proper thing and marry you?'

Her logic was unassailable. Jane gave up the argument. 'May, let's leave it alone, eh? I love him, he loves me; I'd rather be with him like this than live without him, don't you see?'

'He seems very nice and a real gentleman, for a foreigner. And he has got lovely eyes, and that voice . . . it makes me go all wobbly.' May giggled. They never discussed the situation again.

Jane's Italian lessons had started in earnest. Each day a young woman appeared and for two hours they toiled away together. Jane had not found languages easy at school, but now, wanting to please Roberto, she learned quickly.

Roberto was away for the day and Jane had taken the opportunity to do some extra work in the comfortable study he had given her to use. Her pen ran out, and she opened the desk drawers to search for another. A large box full of reels of films caught her eye. Home movies! How lovely. She pressed the button that swung the bookcase open to reveal a screen, another button and the projector appeared from the wall. Expertly she wound the reel of film on to the machine: she had watched Roberto do it often for he refused to go to the local cinema, which was a dingy, smelly fleapit, and had new films sent from Rome. Jane settled down in the large, leather chair as the film flickered into focus.

A young girl appeared on the screen, lying on a large bed. Unselfconsciously she began to undress. Jane's eyes opened as wide as saucers: it was a blue movie. She had never seen one in her life and she sat forward in the chair with excited curiosity. A man loomed out of the shadows and began to caress the girl, his face turned to the camera. It was Roberto. Transfixed Jane watched as his hands slid over the girl's breasts . . . with a horrified gasp, and with nausea rising within her, she leaped for the projector and with shaking fingers switched the machine off. She could not believe what she had just seen. It was disgusting and there was something else about it – that bed, it was somehow familiar. Dear God in heaven, she exlaimed, it was the bed in the house in Rome. The bed they had made love in, the bed with the mirrored canopy . . .

It was evening before Roberto returned. All afternoon Jane had been in a turmoil of indecision about whether to mention the film or to ignore it, pretend it had not happened. As their dinner wore on she found it increasingly difficult to forget what she had seen. They took their cognac through to the adjacent sitting room.

'You're very quiet, Jane. Is anything the matter?'

'Nothing.'

'It doesn't seem like nothing to me. Tell me, what is the problem?'

She looked at him, as he smiled his gentle smile, remembering the sight of his hands creeping sensuously over the naked girl's body.

'I found some films,' she stated baldly.

'I see.'

'Well, I don't!'

'Perhaps you shouldn't pry in people's drawers.'

'I wasn't prying. I was looking for a pen. And you said I could use that room as if it were my own.'

'Yes, I did, that's true. I was stupid – I should have moved the box.'

'You certainly should have moved the box. It was disgusting . . .' Roberto said nothing. 'I mean, how could you? It's sick, degrading.'

'Why did you watch it, then?'

'I only watched the beginning. When I realized you were in it I switched it off immediately.'

'Ah! I see. It's not the fact that it's a pornographic movie, it's the fact that I'm in it that disturbs you so?'

She ignored the implication of his argument. 'And the others, are they dirty pictures too?'

'Yes.'

'You're perverted!' she shouted at him.

'They were made before I met you, I can't see what concern they are of yours.'

'Can't you? I think it's very much my concern that you are decadent.'

'Yes, you are right, I was decadent, but no more, don't you understand, my darling? It's the old romantic story, the dissolute hero reformed by the love of a good woman,' he said calmly.

'You're bloody well laughing at me! How dare you? How can you be so cool about it when I'm feeling sick inside with disgust and anger?' she shouted.

'Jane, calm down, let me try and explain to you, please. I don't apologize for those films being made. I'm sorry you found them and that your curiosity got the better of you – '

'You don't apologize?' she snapped with disbelief.

'Shut up a minute and listen to me,' he commanded. Jane subsided in her chair, still smouldering with anger. 'Yes, I was a different man then. I had been spoiled in life, so much money makes conquests easy, you know. By the time I was twenty I was well tutored in love. By my midthirties, I was bored and jaded. Nothing excited me anymore. These films, they were a little conceit and, eventually, they were an aid to me. It excited me to know what the camera was recording, it made it easier for me to copulate with those young women. That's what it was . . . a physical copulation, nothing to do with the mind.' He poured himself another drink. Jane, despite her anger, sat listening intently to every word. He continued. 'There is much in my life that I hope you will not discover. I have done many dark things, mainly from despair,

307

but, oh yes, I was decadent. And then the miracle happened and I met you. I could not believe what was happening to me: to make love to you was a joyous experience, you reawoke my body, you gave me a physical and mental satisfaction I had not known since I was a young man. You gave me back dignified love ... If only you could understand. That was another man, it's not the person I am now.'

'I suppose I can understand, a little,' she said doubtfully. 'But it was such a shock. And seeing you with another woman, I wanted to kill her.'

'My poor love.'

'I didn't trust that bed when I saw it.'

'It's very vulgar,' he said sheepishly. 'Am I forgiven?'

'If you destroy the films.'

'Immediately.' He hurried from the room and was gone for some time. When he returned he smiled apologetically at her. 'They are all burned.'

'All of them?' He nodded. 'Roberto, I've been thinking. That bed, where was the camera?'

'Above the mirror.'

'And ...'

'Yes, my darling, I'm sorry, you too – but only once.'

Jane put her head in her hands, 'Roberto how could you?'

'I can only say I'm sorry.'

'Get rid of that bloody bed, promise me?'

'Yes, I promise.'

She had been afraid that the thought of the films would destroy her need for him, but when they went to bed, to her relief, she found she was as eager for him as before. But first, much to his amusement, she insisted on clambering on a chair to inspect the canopy of this bed for hidden cameras. Later, as they lay in each other's arms, she turned to him.

'Roberto? Have you ever slept with another woman in this bed?'

He kissed her gently. 'No, my sweet. Only you.' Satisfied with his answer, she drifted into sleep.

10

The summer ended. They were in Rome for three weeks. Roberto kept his promise and the bed with the mirrored canopy was gone. But still Jane could not feel relaxed, not until they had moved to another room. Even then she began to doubt if she would ever be happy in this house: it had an air of foreboding about it, which she had not noticed before but which haunted her now. In a strange way, she felt the house did not like her and wanted her to go, and she began to feel homesick for the castle.

She could not have been happier when Roberto announced that they were going to Paris. May was beside herself with excitement. Until her trip to Italy, the furthest she had travelled had been from Respryn to London, and now the whole world was beginning to open up for her.

Roberto had a large, elegant flat in Passy, staffed by French servants. All Jane's hard work at learning Italian was of no use to her here, and she knew that her attempts to communicate with the staff in her bad schoolgirl French only made them laugh.

'They're sneering at me behind my back,' she complained to Roberto.

'Darling, you're too sensitive. What does it matter? They're only employees. In any case the French sneer at anyone who doesn't speak their language perfectly.'

'How can you talk about your employees like that? Your arrogance is incredible sometimes,' Jane said with a brief laugh. 'But maybe you're right about the French. That housekeeper's certainly a stuck-up old bitch.'

'Then she shall go.'

'Roberto, I didn't mean . . . Heavens, I don't want to be responsible for someone losing their job,' she said lamely.

'Then she should do it better.'

The next morning Jane realized with guilty relief that the housekeeper was not to be seen, and she felt it was not her imagination that the staff were treating her with much more respect. May hated the place. She had liked Italy, had enjoyed the Italian food, had made friends with the servants, had even picked up enough Italian to talk with them. But in France she had nothing but complaints. She moaned about the plumbing, the water, the house, the smell of garlic. She hated the food – convinced that the sauces were only to cover up the taste of bad meat – and existed on a diet of poached eggs which entailed a daily row with the arrogant young chef, who resented her presence in his kitchen. To add insult to injury, May refused to allow him to cook her eggs.

'He'll only put some filthy sauce all over them,' she complained to Jane. Because of Jane's bad French it was left to Roberto to create calm in the kitchen, a role he did not relish.

'That is the first and the last time I have been in one of my kitchens. It is no good, Jane, you will have to learn French. I am not going to spend my time sorting out the domestic arguments created by your maid.'

'But I haven't learned Italian yet,' she wailed.

A compromise was reached by employing a new housekeeper who spoke English, was courtesy itself and who made friends with May. It was just as well for, as the days sped past, Jane doubted if she would have had time to learn another language. Her days were full.

With great seriousness Roberto supervised the restocking of Jane's wardrobe. She was fascinated that a man should take as much interest and care in how she looked as Honor had done.

'It takes a man to dress a woman,' he informed her. 'Left to their own devices they look a mess.'

'Thank you very much.' She grinned. 'I'll tell Honor that.'

'Ah, Honor is unique in women – she has real style.'

'I really don't need any more clothes, Roberto. Honor bought me so many.'

'But winter comes. You need a different wardrobe. And in any case you need better clothes. I shall be judged by how you look.'

His boyish arrogance amused her and she allowed herself to be led from one great couture house to another. He would sit critically eyeing the clothes paraded before them, choosing first one garment, then another, never allowing her any say no matter how much she protested.

'But, Roberto, I love that dress so much.' Wistfully Jane eyed a dreamy concoction of frilled broderie anglaise.

'It is not your style, darling. That is for an ingénue. You would look wrong in it totally.' The *vendeuse* nodded her agreement.

The *vendeuse* in each house terrified Jane. It was not that they were unkind or rude, only that they were so perfectly groomed that no matter how good she thought she looked when she arrived, the moment she saw these impeccable women in their neat black dresses, with their smooth make-up and pristine hair, she felt a mess. Their skirts never seemed to wrinkle, their make-up never needed touching up, their shoes were never dusty.

'Why can't I look like them?' she would complain to Roberto.

'You will. It is just a matter of time. Your deportment needs attention. Watch how they move, how they sit. Always they are conscious of their bodies. Note how unobtrusively they arrange their clothes as they sit. They wear the clothes, not vice versa: they do not allow themselves to be intimidated by what they wear. Watch the mannequins, they are saying, "Look at me, I am beautiful", but they say it with their bodies, their subtle movement.'

'I can't strut around like them, don't be daft! Everyone would laugh at me. I don't want to look like that.'

'Of course not, but you must learn to be proud of your beauty. Then you will walk correctly, then the clothes will look right on you.'

'But I don't think I'm beautiful.'

'Don't be silly, Jane, and stop fishing for compliments.'

But it was true. She was not confident in her own looks. She wanted to be blonde and have curls, to be tall and willowy, not dark and small. She could not see that in Roberto's eyes her petiteness was one of her great charms. Her total lack of conceit was another.

Her efforts always to look her best were an exhausting regime to maintain. May was kept hard at work pressing and sponging, dressing her hair, manicuring her nails. Visits from beauticians and masseuses took up much of her time. It was unthinkable to Roberto that she should go to a salon – the salon came to her. If they were invited to an important dinner or reception, he would enjoy watching as her *maquillage* was applied – she could no longer think of it as mere make-up, because the preparation of her face now was a very skilled and long process, almost an art form. Roberto would sit looking at her with loving pride, offering suggestions. Sometimes, she told him, she felt like a giant Barbie doll he had bought to play with. He found the idea amusing and would enrage her by calling her Barbie at the most inopportune times.

She had thought, after the practical life she had led, that she would hate it all; in fact she found she loved it. She loved the beautiful clothes and what they did for her, she loved the attention and the fuss. She loved the pride Roberto had in her, and she worked hard to please him. She even learned to walk differently for him, when a dreadful, bossy woman was employed to improve her posture. She had changed, she knew it: she was no longer the frightened girl who shopped in Marks and Spencer because the assistants in the dress shops terrified her. She was growing in confidence, which lay thick upon her, not from the knowledge that she looked wonderful but from the certainty of this man's love.

They returned to Italy for the shooting, staying at another of Roberto's houses. In this shooting lodge deep in the forest she immediately felt at home. The scenery reminded her of Drumloch, but the house was far more beautiful and comfortable than Drumloch had ever been. Since Roberto did not want her to go shooting with him, she could pretend it was not happening and would while away the days reading, walking and making herself beautiful for his return. The house party was large and she began fully to appreciate that Roberto's households ran themselves. Despite thirty house guests, and sometimes as many as fifty for dinner, none of the problems were hers. The major-domo arranged everything: where people were to sleep, where they were to sit at dinner, what they were to eat. She had all the time in the world to look after herself, and each evening, as the company assembled, she found it easier and easier to move among them as the gracious hostess Roberto expected her to be.

They skied. They went to the West Indies. They joined an American on his yacht. They sailed the Java sea. She fell in love with Bali. Everywhere there were new people, new experiences, and the amusing realization that she need never be without a tan.

His friends were charming to her. With them she felt welcome and never tongue-tied or gauche. Here the criteria were that, as a man, you should be rich, successful and amusing, and, as a woman, beautiful, intelligent and amusing. She did not know why but she had presumed that these people would be empty and frivolous, and that she would be bored. Nothing was further from the truth. The women shamed her with how well read they were. Their knowledge of art and music was frequently encyclopaedic. In England she had been used to a society that regarded an intelligent woman as unfeminine and a threat, whereas here she was regarded as a jewel. Beside them she felt ignorant. As she had learned how to dress and how to present herself, now she began with a ferocious intensity to learn.

She had expected the press would be everywhere, but their peace was never disturbed. But they did not go to nightclubs or first nights, they dined in one another's homes or on each other's boats. She learned that publicity could be avoided if one were rich enough and chose to be invisible to the press.

Most of Roberto's friends, like him, owned land and dabbled in business; it was as if they moved around the world in a large club. They were a sophisticated group and Jane's role in his life was accepted without question. There were many other women who were mistresses, too, but Jane soon learned that she was luckier than they, for Roberto loved her, and she was a rarity in that she was permanent in his life, whereas most of the others came and went. It was not unusual to be friends with a man's mistress one week, the next to be chatting to his wife. And when it was the turn of the wives, she was always the only mistress present and knew that therefore she had a special place in his life.

The world was suddenly a very small and different place. These people caught planes as other people caught buses; to fly across a continent for a party was not uncommon; excellence in everything was the unspoken norm. She noticed that, in her new world, colours of clothes had a greater subtlety, silkworms seemed to make softer silk, sheep grew finer wool, brocades and velvets were more lush. Doors seemed thicker and they shut with a satisfying dunk, as did the doors on her cars now. Windows shone more cleanly, the glass was thicker. Gold was heavier and glowed more richly. Dirt did not exist and ugliness was removed. Poverty was something glimpsed distantly from a limousine window or read about in the newspapers.

When she thought of Alistair these days, she found that her life with him seemed as far removed from the present as her childhood had been from her life with him. This elegant woman could happily hold her own wherever she was.

A whole year had passed and they were back in Italy. There had been nothing further from Alistair about their divorce and she had almost forgotten about it, thought it was of no importance to her. It was Roberto, his face black with rage, who heard first of Alistair's plans.

'He is suing me in the Italian courts for enticing you away from him, and thus denying him his conjugal rights. Such a charming gentleman, your beloved husband!' He stormed about the room, waving his lawyer's letter angrily in his hand.

'I don't believe it. But you didn't entice me away, I didn't know you.'

'Exactly.'

'What are you going to do?'

'Kill him, probably.'

Instead, many phone calls and an aeroplane flight later, Jane found herself in Alistair's lawyer's office. The room seemed full. Her own lawyer and aide were present, and Alistair with his, but it was Roberto and his anger that seemed to fill the room. It saddened her to see Alistair in these circumstances – still the fine, boyish face, the elegance, the way he had of flicking his hair from his eyes. He had not altered: he was still beautiful to her eyes. But how had it all come to this? What had happened that they could not be friends?

'I had presumed, Prince Villizano, that you would have brought your advisers with you from Rome,' Alistair's lawyer, Mr Strong, said.

'That won't be necessary,' Roberto replied shortly.

Alistair stepped forward, his hand outstretched. 'We've never met,' he said. Roberto looked at the hand offered him and slowly turned his back. Alistair coughed. 'You look wonderful, Jane.' He sounded surprised.

'Thank you, so do you.'

Roberto swung round and glared angrily at Jane, who hurriedly took her seat. Without preamble, the two sets of lawyers began to argue terms. As she listened, Jane felt humiliated. They talked as if she were some sort of package, up for barter to the highest bidder.

'Am I to gather that this meeting is for us to come to a financial arrangement so that it will not be necessary for this distasteful matter to be brought to the Italian courts?' Roberto enquired so calmly that Jane felt a flicker of irritation that he was not upset for her.

'Exactly, Prince Villizano,' said Mr Strong, with obvious relief that he was speaking to a man of the world who understood these matters.

'And that you are bringing this action in the Italian courts because of the liberal divorce laws you now have in this country, since 1971, I believe?'

'Quite.'

'If the law says I have to pay for the privilege of Lady Upnor's love, so be it.'

Alistair and his lawyer sat back appearing relaxed and satisfied, content in the knowledge that only the amount remained to be decided.

'However,' continued Roberto, 'it does seem somewhat unfair to me, since it was Lord Upnor who was the first to commit adultery, thus precipitating Lady Upnor into a serious nervous breakdown which culminated in this gentleman here having her committed as a lunatic to an asylum. Am I correct?'

'Well, a private mental hospital, a very luxurious hospital, may I add?' Alistair's lawyer interrupted hastily.

'He then acquired custody of their child since he had her declared an unfit person to care for him?'

'Er, well, yes,' Alistair's lawyers agreed, somewhat uncomfortably.

'I'm not surprised you don't want all this brought out in the English courts. We have all heard of British justice: I can imagine what the famous British justice would think of this claim. But we have justice in my country, too. I doubt if the courts there would consider my having to pay for a cast-off, lunatic, childless wife as being exactly fair justice, would you?'

'Well, couched like that, no. But you have to admit that because of you, Lord Upnor has been deprived of the love and comfort of his wife.'

'But they weren't living together.'

'They might have been reconciled had it not been for you, Prince Villizano.'

'But he doesn't seem to have made much effort to effect a reconciliation.'

'We do not know what attempts he has made,' Mr Strong argued.

'He does and I do.'

'Prince Villizano, I do not understand what you are getting at.' Mr Strong was agitated now.

'Then I shall explain. Lady Upnor and I have discussed this at great length. We have decided that she has paid enough already in pain, humiliation and anguish. We are quite happy for the whole sad story to come out in court in whatever country you choose. Then the judges can decide if I am to pay or not.'

Pandemonium broke out. Roberto stood up. 'No doubt you will wish to discuss this matter. Come, my darling.' He offered his hand to Jane. 'We are at Claridge's, gentlemen – once you have decided.'

Alistair jumped to his feet. 'Jane?' He looked at her and she felt there was almost a look of pleading in his face, which puzzled her.

'Goodbye, Alistair,' she said with dignity, and hand in hand with Roberto she left the room. Outside, she turned to him. 'You fox, we never discussed anything! How I kept quiet I shall never know.'

'They annoyed me, talking about you as if you were a commodity, something in the marketplace. It was distasteful. They won't press the claim, we shall hear no more. Now, my darling, where would you like to have lunch?'

He was right, they heard no more. The months slipped by and the whole sordid incident passed from her mind. Their life settled into its exotic routine. She was in the West Indies when she was informed that her divorce was going ahead and several months later, in Singapore, she heard that a decree nisi had been granted. Three months later she was in New York when the news reached her that it had been made absolute. She looked at the paper in her hand and she felt an overwhelming sense of loss and failure. She had embarked on that marriage with such shining hope and confidence, all her youth had been invested in that union. Now this paper said it was no more. It really was the end of that era in her life. Strangely, although so much time had gone by, and despite her happiness with Roberto, as she looked at the paper, she suddenly felt an emptiness within her.

11

Another year with Roberto slipped by with clockwork smoothness. She had lived with him for three years. And for three years she had not seen her son.

At first she had written every week but as the time went by it became more difficult for her to write to a child who was rapidly becoming a stranger, one whom she no longer knew. Soon she was writing once a month, then only intermittently and at birthdays and Christmas.

In an ornately carved sandalwood box, tied with blue satin ribbon like the letters from a lover, she hoarded the few letters the child had written her, dog-eared now from endless rereading.

She had photographs of him, too, which she would study by the hour, sometimes with a large magnifying glass, poring over them, searching his features for a sign of herself. The shape of his eyes, she felt, was like hers, otherwise he was a replica of how Alistair must have looked at thirteen. She knew so little about him, what his interests were, who his friends were, for his letters were dutiful and unemotional. She wished now that she had been more positive when he had come to visit her in Cambridge, had made more effort to get to know the child. For now she wanted to know him and it seemed it was too late.

To all intents and purposes she was Roberto's wife. Each year the rules of their relationship relaxed a little more, so that now she had met most of his family, women as well as men. The moves to meet his family had started tentatively with the arrival at the castle of a cousin and his new wife. His report back to the family on Jane must have been favourable for it was followed by an invitation from his father, Roberto's uncle, and from this visit others grew.

Jane was amazed by this family and the scale of their living. She had often heard, in England, snide remarks made about European aristocracy, as if their claims were spurious, and they were regarded as poverty-stricken, living in crumbling ruins, taking jobs as guides to rich Americans to make ends meet. Certainly not in the class of their secure and smug English counterparts. Nothing was further from the truth with the Villizano family. Each branch of the family had its own castle, a palazzo in Rome, and at least one shooting lodge.

The wives were always Italian, always of noble birth – not one corpuscle of unacceptable blood flowed in their veins. They were appalled by the English aristocracy's habit of, as they put it, 'marrying out', a dangerous foible which would only dilute the precious blood. Jane had tried to explain that it did not weaken, but strengthened. And in this century the American heiresses, whom many families had sought, had saved a number of country estates. 'Tut, tut,' the Italian women exclaimed, flicking their elegantly manicured hands through the air, the light shining on rings at least 200 years old, and again they explained to Jane the necessity of pure blood lines. They did not speak of social unsuitability, of liability – such mundane thoughts did not enter their heads. No, they talked as racehorse owners talk. Looking at them, Jane saw that these women had been bred and refined to a fine-boned elegance, just like the horses whose blood was regarded with equal importance. So Jane was never offended, it was a theory they discussed: she never felt here that the conversation was directed at her.

Closest to them in distance as well as age were Emilio and his wife Francesca. Both were cousins of Roberto, from different sides of the family. Emilio was the same age as Roberto and his wife a year younger than Jane, a sophisticated couple whom Jane particularly liked and felt as if she had known for years.

She sometimes began to hope that Roberto would relent and marry her. From being adamant that she would never marry him, it was now the thing she wanted most in the world – that, and to see her son. Only Roberto's mother, she was certain, stood in their way. Perhaps when she died? But as the old lady entered her nineties, hale and hearty, Jane learned how young men must feel waiting for dead men's shoes. She had never discussed the subject with Roberto – but she had a sense of permanence with him, an inability to imagine life without him.

May had at long last come out of what Jane referred to as her 'bangers and mash' period and had become a true cosmopolitan. She loved her work, took great pride in Jane's appearance, had even forgiven Roberto for not marrying her. Wherever they went, there was May, an iron in one hand and the heated rollers in the other, no mean feat on safari in Africa.

At thirty-five, Jane showed she was one of those lucky women who improve with age, as if her inner contentment and confidence had worked outwards to her skin, her hair, her figure. As the beauty of youth faded, another, more striking beauty took its place.

They were back from their annual travels to spend the summer in the castle in Italy. It was the usual mix of summer people including, as always, Honor, whose friendship Jane valued increasingly. Roberto, trusting her more, had relaxed, and on Sundays as his car turned one way to visit his mother, hers would turn the other and she would visit Honor.

Honor never failed to astound Jane. She had known her now for over fifteen years and in all that time she had barely changed in looks, outlook or manner. Jane had no idea how old she was: Honor was not the kind of woman who discussed her age. Jane was sure this was not out of conceit but because, to Honor, age was irrelevant and she would have been surprised by anyone finding it necessary to ask such a question. Jane presumed she must be in her late fifties, could be sixty even, but she still had the looks and vitality of a thirty-year-old.

It was a hot Sunday in August, and the two women were relaxing by the pool after a light lunch, gently gossiping, Jane's foot stirring the water of the pool. They would have a siesta soon, then friends would arrive for cocktails and dinner, before Jane went home to Roberto. That was her unchanging routine every Sunday.

'What on earth's the matter with Guido? He never runs,' Honor commented as they watched the now decidedly portly Guido puffing towards them along the terrace, the long extension cable of the telephone trailing behind him like a writhing snake.

'He looks dreadful. Something's happened, Honor,' Jane said, alarmed, her first thoughts of Roberto, who, despite her protestations, still drove like a maniac.

Too breathless for speech, Guido handed Jane the phone.

'Hullo? Jane Upnor speaking,' she said cautiously.

'Jane, love. Sorry to disturb you. It's James. Little blighter fell out of a tree . . .' she heard Alistair say.

'Is he all right?' she asked, knowing as she spoke what a futile question it was. Alistair would hardly be calling her if it was not serious.

'No, he's not too good, Jane. He's been calling for you . . . and the quacks think . . .'

'Where is he?'

'St Cuthbert's.'

'I'll be there this evening.' She quickly replaced the receiver and, for the first time ever, dialled the number of Roberto's mother. As the phone rang she turned to Honor, with terror on her face. 'It's James, he fell out of a tree, he's in hospital!'

'Don't panic, Jane. If he's got the Upnor head, he'll be OK.' She smiled supportively. 'I'll get some things packed for you.'

Roberto came to the phone, his voice full of concern, knowing that for her to call him there, something very wrong had happened. She explained.

'Get Guido to drive you to the airport, I'll get the pilot organized. Be brave, little one, I'll see you there.'

'Will you come with me, darling? I'm so afraid.'

'I have that meeting with those German financiers tomorrow and the Americans on Tuesday. I can hardly – '

'Please, Roberto.'

'Darling, I can't get hold of Herr Schramm at such short notice, but I can cancel the Americans. Send the plane back and I'll fly to London tomorrow afternoon. OK?'

'Bless you, Roberto.'

In the car, Honor held her hand as Guido raced like a demon down the mountain roads. Roberto was waiting for her by his new aeroplane, which was ready to taxi off.

'My passport, I haven't got my passport . . .'

Smiling, he handed her the familiar blue book. 'I called May,' he explained. He took her into his arms and kissed her forehead. 'Now, my love, stop worrying so. Boys are always falling out of trees and landing on their heads.'

'But he could be paralysed, or dying of a brain haemorrhage . . .'

'Then the sooner you get there and find out, the better, my sweet.' He helped her into the plane. She looked down at the two people she loved so dearly, and as the plane took off and circled the dusty little airport she waved and waved until their figures were two tiny dots she could scarcely see.

It was early evening, and raining, as the taxi drew up in front of the familiar doors of St Cuthbert's, but the worried woman who got out seemed unaware of where she was, appeared to have forgotten the years she had spent here herself as a nurse. She entered the private wing and was shown immediately to the third floor. It needed every ounce of her reserves to push open the door of the room the nurse indicated. It was three years since she had seen her son, and now it might be too late.

She burst into an anguished cry of relief as she saw the young boy with a sticking plaster on his forehead and a wide grin on his face, shovelling large spoonfuls of ice cream into his mouth.

'Thank God!' she said, unaware that in that exclamation lay all the maternal love she had feared she was incapable of. Alistair stepped quickly across the room and took her arm.

'Sorry, Jane. Right scare I must have given you. But he suddenly sat up as bright as a button. It was too late to call you back.'

'Hullo, Ma.' James smiled shyly at her.

'James.' Jane rushed across the room, forgetting in her relief that the boy did not like to be kissed, and flung her arms about him and hugged him to her, smothering his face with kisses. It was some time before she realized that the child was cuddling her back with equal intensity. 'Crikey, you frightened me. What happened?'

'I was climbing a tree, and a branch broke. I landed on my head. Did I see stars! Everything went black . . .' James laughed, evidently enjoying the drama he had created.

'Is he all right?'

'The doctors say yes, he's been X-rayed, no concussion. They want to keep him in overnight, that's all. Sorry, big drama over nothing.'

'Don't be sorry. I'm just so relieved he's going to be fine.' She smiled fondly at them both. She had often wondered how she would feel on seeing Alistair again. This was the first time she had seen him and their son since the divorce. Would she be bitter, would she be cold with him, would she tell him how much anger and pain he had caused? None of these – she could never remain angry with him. Whenever she saw him, that smile, the unruly hank of hair flopping forward on his forehead, and his guilty, boyish expression enabled her to forgive him anything. She knew that it would always be like this.

At eight they were asked to leave. Outside it was still pouring with rain.

'Haven't you got a coat?'

'No. It doesn't often rain in Italy in August, remember?'

'Put this round you then.' He took his jacket off and slipped it around her shoulders. 'I'll get a taxi.' She stood in the doorway, aware suddenly of the familiar smell of his coat round her. Strange how one never forgot smells, and how quickly and sharply they brought back memories. Alistair's smiling face appeared at the taxi door. 'Have you eaten? Fancy a bite?' he asked.

'I should get to a phone and call Roberto.'

'Phone from the restaurant,' Alistair suggested.

It was a pleasant little French restaurant in Kensington. The proprietors were none too happy at her request to call Italy, since there was no pay phone. Persuaded by a ten pound note from Alistair, they agreed. Roberto had not yet returned from his mother's. She left a message.

'That must be about the most expensive two-minute phone call to Italy ever,' she said, laughing, as they settled at their table.

'Anything, for M'Lady.' He bowed.

She was surprised how easy it was to talk to him. This is how it should be between two people who once loved each other, she thought contentedly, as she sipped the wine he had ordered.

'You know, Jane, I've been a real bastard over James. When that poor little bugger was calling for you, I realized the dreadful thing I'd done to him and to you. I'd no right to stop you seeing him.'

'It was cruel, Alistair. But I must admit, there was a time when I didn't seem to mind. I don't know why. But in the last couple of years I've ached to see him.'

'I'll make up for it now, I promise. Would you like to have him come to stay with you when he's over the bang on his head? Before he goes back to school?'

'Alistair, would you? I'd love that.' Her eyes shone with excitement. 'With Roberto there too?'

'Yes, of course. I hear he's a nice enough bloke for a wop.'

'Alistair, you fool! James will love Italy. We're there until the end of September. Perhaps you would let him come skiing with us after Christmas?' she asked hopefully.

'We could see how it fits in with his school terms.'

'How wonderful, how bloody wonderful!'

'It's quite a life you lead now, isn't it?'

'It's different.' She grinned at him.

'When are you going back?'

'I had planned to stay until James was better so that I could see as much of him as possible – while you allowed it.' She smiled slyly at him. 'But if the doctors are satisfied with him and if you promise that he can come in the next few days . . . well, tomorrow, I guess.'

'Can I book him on a flight to that local airport that's opened up?'

'Don't bother. I'll get the plane sent to pick him up. He'd probably love that.'

'Christ, Jane, how grand!'

'Sorry, does sound a bit flash, doesn't it? It's Roberto's latest toy – he's in love with it, I think. It makes sense, though. You see, we spend so much time travelling and he's always having to rush back from somewhere or other. But what about you? What are you up to these days?'

'Oh, I flit about, bit like a bee really, little bit of nectar here, then on to the next flower. I keep busy, nothing serious. Just hasn't turned up.' He shrugged.

'You'll probably meet someone when you least expect it. That's what happened to me.' She smiled fondly at him and patted his hand. 'How's your mother?'

'Still bossing.' He groaned. 'Still hating you,' he added with a grin.

'After all this time. Extraordinary. And Clarissa?'

'She's got two kids now. Poor little sods, she ignores them completely. Mind you, she ignores poor old Hector too.' He laughed. 'She's very bitter, of course.'

'Bitter, why?'

'Didn't you hear? Hector lost a packet in some mad investment scheme, nearly wiped him out. Clarissa's standing by him, though if I were Hector, I'd wish she'd piss off.'

'Poor Clarissa.'

'Do you mean, poor as in "what a shame" or poor as in "got no money"?'

'I meant I was sorry for her. I should think Clarissa would find it more difficult than most to adjust to less money.'

'You're something else, Jane! Why should you feel sorry for her when she's been such a bitch to you?'

'That was all a long time ago. It's very easy to be forgiving when one is happy, isn't it?' She smiled.

'I shouldn't feel too sorry. She's not that poor. It's all relative. To most people she's still rich: it's only Clarissa who thinks she's on the breadline.'

'Poor Hector, then.'

'That's much more to the point. Of course I have a great time telling Clarissa of your various adventures. You see, I keep tabs on what you're doing.'

'What on earth for?'

'I like to see her go green.' He roared with laughter.

'I meant, why the interest in what I'm up to?'

'I do care about you, you know.' He smiled his devastating smile at her and she warmed to him, but then she remembered the trouble his interest had caused, and she frowned. 'Honest,' he said, taking her hand and squeezing it. 'Let's have another bottle of this Sancerre, shall we?'

They lingered over the wine.

'Where are you booked in?'

'Gracious, what's the time? Damn, it's gone eleven. I didn't bother. I went straight to the hospital. I'd best get a taxi to Claridges and hope they're not full.'

'Why not stay at the house in Fulham?'

'It must be all damp and musty.'

'No, I often stay there, since you don't rent it out any more. I didn't think you'd mind. In fact, that's where James and I were staying – it was the tree in the garden.'

'I don't want to put you out.'

'Hell, you wouldn't be putting me out. It's your house, anyway. It's damn cheeky of me to squat in it, I suppose. No, I'll go to my club, no problem, and I can assure you the house is as dry as a bone.'

'It would be nicer than a hotel . . .'

'Of course it is. I'll come and settle you in, make sure there are no mice. Do you remember how scared of mice you used to be?' he reminded her as he paid the bill and hailed a taxi. They drove to the familiar street. It seemed strange to be standing once more beside Alistair as he put the key in the lock. The house even had the same smell about it, she thought as she walked into the hall.

She went straight to the study to telephone Roberto. He laughed at the excitement in her voice as she told him that James was to come and stay. 'I'll get a commercial flight back. I want to stop off in Paris.'

'Why?'

'It's a surprise. You must wait until tomorrow night to find out,' she teased him. 'I love you.'

'Hurry home, my little one.'

In the drawing room Alistair was uncorking a bottle of champagne. 'Remember the first time we had champagne together?' He grinned.

'Am I ever likely to forget?'

'That was a special night, and so is this one,' he said, pouring the wine into the flutes.

'Why?'

'Because we're friends again. Because we can begin to forget all the bad things we've done to each other.' He lifted his glass to her in a silent toast.

She looked at him sharply. She could not recollect anything that she had ever done to him, but he was in such a good mood and the evening had been so perfect that she let the remark pass. She wandered about the room, admiring the new pieces that Alistair had added, exclaiming with pleasure as she recognized an ornament, a painting. Their old sofa was still here, and the ornately carved Indian table.

'Remember how proud of that sofa we were?' He noticed her looking at it.

'Yes. And how your mother hated it.'

'The day it came, wasn't that when I took you to your first Italian meal?'

'You know, I think it was.' She looked about the room. 'It's still the same, isn't it?'

'Nothing ever really changes.'

She had been happily exploring the room until she reached the spot on the carpet where, on that dreadful day, she had sat and had slowly and deliberately, she now believed, let her mind drift away from her. She shivered. She felt his arm about her shoulders. He turned her towards him.

'Don't think about it, Jane.' He took a strand of her hair and twisted it between his finger and thumb, playing with it as, long ago, he had loved to do. 'Forget the sadness,' he whispered.

'You're right. It's fatal to remember the past. I learned that.'

'But how do you forget, how do you erase all the magic and beauty that's there in the past too?' he asked her huskily. 'Jane! Jane!' he said urgently. 'I've been such a bloody fool. I love you, I need you. Come back to me, I beg you.'

'Alistair . . .' she began to say in astonishment, but before she could finish the sentence his lips were on hers and she was held securely in his arms, his hands feverishly running over her body. 'Alistair . . . it's all too late . . .' but her body and her memories betrayed her. She was too tired and too vulnerable to protest further, and she leaned against him. It seemed to her the most natural thing to do. As she felt she belonged in this room, was relaxed in it, so she belonged in his arms. He took her hand and quickly led her up the stairs. She followed like someone in a dream. In their old bedroom, he held her, gazing at her face, and kissed her again.

'You're so beautiful,' he sighed as he gently laid her on the bed and crossed the room to pull the curtains. 'Jay . . .' He knelt down on the bed beside her. 'At last . . .'

From far away in time the physical excitement that his touch had always given her was reawoken. As his hands once more explored her body so she was lost. She had no past, no future, only this exhilarating moment.

His passion intensified and she felt that timeless power that all women feel as a man loses all consciousness except for her, her body and the pleasure she can give.

Wiser now in the ways of his body and her own, as she had not been in the past, she responded expertly. Their bodies entwined, broke loose, re-entwined. Their passion mounted in unison. He rode into her with an intensity that neither had experienced together before. Deeper and deeper he plunged into her. Her body arched to receive him, inviting him, exciting him, sucking him into that minideath of shared oblivion. Her voice screamed, 'I love you!' and together they climaxed. She held his sweat-soaked body to her as he lay slumped with exhaustion upon her. At last, at long last, she had given him what he had always wanted from her. This time she had not failed him.

He rolled away, lit two cigarettes, and handed her one. His arm about her, they lay in silence, the smoke from their cigarettes entwining above them just as their bodies had done. To Jane, it was as if the years in between had never happened.

'Jane, darling,' he said at last. 'My God, that was wonderful. You were sensational.'

'I didn't have to pretend this time.'

'No, that was obvious. Heavens, it was shattering, wasn't it? Marvellous!' Pleased with his words she snuggled closer against him, feeling secure as she lay beside the beautiful body she had never forgotten. 'Crikey, Jane, I've had plenty of sex in my life but I tell you one thing, you've learned one hell of a lot since the last time,' he said sleepily.

At his words, the blood in Jane's veins seemed to turn to ice. She shivered, and did not know what to say. But there was no need for words: with disbelief she heard Alistair's breathing settle into the regular rhythm of someone deeply asleep.

She lay in the dark, frozen with despair. Nauseated with reality. A yawning void opened where her heart should have been.

Relentlessly her mind came back to life, and she wished it had not, as myriad emotions assailed her. She had to be the stupidest woman that walked this earth. She had fooled herself. She always seemed to do that. He didn't love her, he hadn't said any words of love to her, only congratulated her on her sexual ability. Nothing had changed. No doubt at this very moment he was being unfaithful to some other woman, with her. She dreamed of love and to him she was only another conquest.

How could she be so stupid? Why did she always have to wrap everything up in romance?

And here she was blaming Alistair, but really wasn't she the same? So for a split second then she had dreamed of a future with him but wasn't that because of the pleasure they had enjoyed with each other? She had allowed her vagina to rule her head and her heart, so who was she to criticize him? She was Roberto's and she had betrayed him. There was nothing to choose between the two of them.

Roberto! All the love he gave her, all the passion. Roberto never had 'sex'. Roberto made love. And he made love with an unselfish generosity which perhaps she had begun to take for granted. How could she possibly muddle the two like this time and again? She had had a narrow escape – she should have been content with the deep affection, love, call it what you will, that she and Alistair had for each other. With Roberto she was loved as other women could only dream of being loved.

She slipped from Alistair's arms and hurriedly dressed. For the rest of the night she sat in the drawing room watching the slowness of the clock, wishing she was safely back in Italy. She thought to wake Alistair to explain that she had been a fool and had made a dreadful mistake, but decided against it. She did not want Alistair to think she put too much emphasis on what had happened. It was best just to slip from the house – no note, no explanation. That way, with luck, he would think she, in turn, regarded him as just an amorous adventure.

At five she silently let herself out of the house and by seven was on the plane to Paris.

Her appointment there took longer than she had anticipated and she missed her flight for Italy. She caught the later one, and it was late evening before her car swung into the courtyard of the castle.

The castle had a strange, deserted air about it. She had expected to find the German industrialists there. It was odd that Roberto had not invited them to stay – he usually did. Their private sitting room and his study were both empty. She raced up the stairs but he was not in her bedroom. She ran along the corridor and swung open the door of his room. 'Roberto! Such exciting news!'

'What news, Jane?'

'Roberto!' Her mouth formed the word but no sound came out. Across the room, in the large bed, lay Roberto; beside him was a young fair-haired man. She lifted her hand and swept it before her eyes as if to remove the image she saw. She wanted to move, to run away, but her legs felt as if they were filled with lead. With enormous effort, she turned and walked slowly from the room, stumbling as she did so. She fumbled her way along the corridor, groping against the walls for support, bumping into furniture as she went, bruising herself yet not noticing the knocks. She moved like a zombie into the safety of her own room. She leaned against the bed, fighting for breath. A strange noise was issuing from her throat: she was trying to say 'Roberto', but instead she sounded like an animal in pain.

The door in the tapestry opened, silently. 'Tell me, Jane. What is this exciting news you have for me?' He smiled coldly at her.

'I don't understand,' she managed to say.

'What don't you understand, my dear Jane?'

'Roberto, what is happening?'

'Aren't you in a better position to tell me that?'

'I don't understand!'

'So you keep saying,' he replied in an ice cold voice.

'How could you do this to me?'she cried.

'Do what?'

'You know bloody well what! That bastard in your bed.'

'That young man. Very good-looking, don't you think?' Jane could feel her mouth hanging open with astonishment. 'Don't look so startled, Jane. Didn't you know I liked young men, too? How remiss of me not to tell you. How impolite.' He laughed. He was actually laughing. Jane clasped her hand over her mouth as a great engulfing wave of nausea hit her. She raced for the bathroom and, shoulders heaving, she hung over the lavatory bowl. Loud retching noises filled the room, but she had not eaten, she could not be sick, could not relieve this nausea within her. She slumped on the floor, sweat running down her face, dry, racking sobs shaking her body.

'Calm down, Jane, for goodness sake. You sound like an animal.' Roberto stood in the doorway.

'Calm down! After what I've just seen. How could you, Roberto? How could you be so cruel? And when we have so much . . .'

'What have we got, Jane? Lies and deception? I'm not the only person in this room capable of cruelty.' From his pocket he took a piece of paper, a telex message. He thrust it at her. 'Read that,' he ordered. It said little and it said everything; as she read it she thought she was going to faint.

'26, BATHURST ROAD, FULHAM. 11.30 P.M.—5 A.M.' The words of the telex seemed to dance before her. Blood was drumming in her head. She shook herself: she was angry now, very angry.

'You had me watched! You had me followed! How dare you? What right had you to do that?'

'The right of every man who doubts the integrity of his woman, as I doubted you.'

'So,' she snapped. 'Five a.m. So what? Yes, I went to Fulham, I didn't want to stay in a hotel. It is my house, after all. What's wrong in my going there? What your telex doesn't tell you was that Alistair was with me, I freely admit it. He came with me because I was afraid to be on my own. And I left at the crack of dawn to fly back to you. To you!' she shouted. 'It doesn't mean anything.'

'The subsequent telephone call did. You were seen in the bedroom, silhouetted artistically against the window, before you pulled the curtains. You in the arms of that unspeakable bastard!'

She sank against the side of the bath, despair filling her. 'Nothing happened,' she lied desperately.

'I don't believe you, Contessa.'

'Is this to be my punishment then? That creep in your bed?'

'It amused me. After all, you had been amusing yourself, so why should I not have a little fun, too?' He smiled at her, but it was the smile of a death mask, the muscles rigid, no warmth in the eyes.

'You cruel bastard!' she spat at him. 'Not even a woman to punish me with, but a boy to humiliate me. You rotten sod!'

Swiftly he crossed the room and hit her hard, her head banging against the marble wall. 'Don't you ever call me names.' He hit her again. His heavy, muscular body loomed above her.

She scrambled to her feet. 'Don't you hit me! What right do you think you have? You don't own me. I'm not your bloody wife.' She spat the words, angrily, at him.

'Just as well you're not my wife, in the circumstances,' he shouted back.

Their anger filled the room, each one fuelling the fury of the other. Suddenly he slumped against the wall, staring at Jane, an expression of disbelief on his face. 'Oh, Jane, how could you?' She averted her eyes with shame. 'You took my love and you squandered it,' he said in a quiet voice which was more menacing than if he had continued to shout at her.

'No, Roberto. You're wrong. I was coming back. I was so excited. Roberto, listen to me. Please.' She grabbed his arm as he turned as if to leave the room. 'I'm sorry, Roberto. I know "sorry" sounds inadequate for what I've done. Believe me, I don't know how it happened, or what got into me. I was drunk. You must believe I was drunk, I didn't know what I was doing. It just happened, forgive me, for God's sake.' He did not look at her as she tugged desperately at his clothes. 'Darling, I know I did wrong. But, truly, I think it will help us. I'm sure I've buried the ghost of the past once and for all. I've been fooling myself. I pretended to myself that Alistair didn't matter but he's always been there like a ghost between us. Now, he really has gone. I know for certain, totally and utterly, that it's you I love. And I realize now how much you love me.'

'I fear you may have reached these conclusions too late, Jane. I despise you. You have no dignity. That you could let that man even touch you is beyond belief.'

'But it meant nothing – nothing at all. I thought for a minute . . . but it's gone, it's over . . .'

'You whore!' he shouted, his words echoing off the marble walls. 'You stinking, filthy whore!'

'I love you,' she pleaded.

'Love! You love? You cannot begin to comprehend what love is. You took my love, you used me, declared your love for me and all the time creeping about in your sordid mind were thoughts of him. When I fucked you, did you pretend it was him? Did you want it to be him?' He was screaming at her, his face almost black with rage.

'No, I didn't. It wasn't like that. It was all so complicated. It just happened, I don't know how or why. And, Christ, I wish it hadn't, don't you see?'

'All I see is a hypocritical whore who pontificated about fidelity, how faithful she was, and she was lying. You are deceitful. I shouldn't even call you a whore – at least a whore is honest. You're lower than that.' He looked at her with such loathing in his eyes that Jane had to look away. 'You cheap bitch! Get back to the gutter where you belong. Get out of my house and out of my life. Now!'

'But Roberto, I went to the doctor in Paris. Roberto, I'm pregnant.'

He looked at her coldly as he opened the door. 'Then, Madame Contessa, I suggest you have an abortion.'

12

'Oh dear!' said Honor, sitting Jane down and pouring her a very stiff drink. 'You're going to have a splendid black eye, too. What on earth have you and Roberto been up to?'

Through her tears, Jane told Honor the whole story. 'Honor, I'm so unhappy. What am I to do?' She looked up and saw a stony-faced Honor staring at her. 'Honor, don't be cross with me, not you as well.'

'I'm more than cross. I'm furious. You stupid, silly little bitch! What on earth got into you? I thought you were so happy with Roberto. Good gracious, just recently I had begun to think he might even end up marrying you.'

'Me too. But he won't now.'

'Of course he won't and can you blame him?'

'What about him? In bed with a man! He's not so innocent, either,' Jane defended herself indignantly.

'I would bet everything I own that it was just an act. He wasn't doing anything with that fellow, had no intention of doing so. It was meant to humiliate you.'

'He succeeded. The shock! I'd no idea he was queer, no idea at all.'

'He isn't. Even when he was really wild, in the days before he met you, I heard all sorts of tales of orgies and drugs and so on, but never men. Not our Roberto.' Honor gave a short laugh. 'You have hurt him dreadfully, young woman. And with Alistair of all men! I thought that was dead and buried ages ago. If you had doubts, why on earth didn't you come and talk to me about it? I would have put you straight. God, you've been so stupid!'

'Please, Honor. Don't keep telling me I'm stupid. Don't you think I know?'

'But what on earth made you do it?'

'I don't know. I really don't know. It just seemed . . . shit! I was emotional about seeing James again, and so relieved he was all right, there was nothing to worry about. Alistair took me out to dinner, we drank too much, it was fun, and then, back at the little house which had been our home . . . I can't explain it, Honor, but it just seemed so natural.'

'It's a pretty lame excuse. We've all had nice evenings out with too much to drink but they don't end in going to bed with the one person who can ruin one's life. I just don't understand you – I thought you were so sensible.'

'I don't understand myself. He just kept saying, "Do you remember . . .?", and it just all sort of happened.' She shrugged her shoulders despairingly.

'Ah! "Do you remember . . .?" Dreadfully dangerous words they are! Yes, I begin to see. What a mess.'

'You see, Honor, I'm so confused, but I think I love them both. To be honest, I didn't just jump into bed with Alistair without a thought. I wanted to. And yet I know I love Roberto. His hating me is the worst thing to bear. I'll never forget that look of hate I saw in his eyes.'

'Poor Jane. It's quite common to love two men – but one has to make a choice and live with it. You're not the first woman to wish we lived in a polyandrous society. At least you have a solution – forget Roberto and go and live with Alistair,' Honor suggested, practically.

'But he doesn't love me. I'm just a sexual conquest to him. And in any case I'm pregnant with Roberto's child.'

'Good God, girl, how careless of you! Do you have any more shocks for me, or is that it?'

'Nothing more. In any case it couldn't get worse, could it?' She smiled weakly.

'Maybe, with the baby on the way, Roberto's crazy enough about you to forgive you, eventually,' Honor said, but Jane heard the lack of conviction in her voice and it made her start to cry again. 'For Christ's sake, Jane, do pull yourself together. All this crying is just going to give you wrinkles. It's not getting us anywhere. We must be practical and think what you're to do. You know you're very welcome to stay here, both you and May, there's plenty of room. It would be such fun to have a baby about the place. Guido would be beside himself with happiness. Yes, do stay . . .' Honor held her hand out to Jane.

'Honor, it's sweet of you. I can't. It's too near him, too near all the happiness we shared. No, I had best get right away. I'll go back to Cambridge. I've friends there.'

'As you wish, darling,' Honor said lightly. 'But what about money? Will you let me help with that?'

'Hell, Honor, you're too good. No, I managed before, I'll manage his time.'

'But with a baby on the way, darling? You won't have two halfpennies to rub together. Let me help you, I'd like to.'

'I got myself into this mess, I'll get myself out of it. I can always finish my secretarial course.' She managed to laugh. 'That bloody course. I seem to have been doing it for years, and whenever I do, something catastrophic happens.'

'It's going to be a fearful adjustment for you to make after your life with Roberto. It really will be riches to rags, won't it?'

But it was not the loss of riches that was worrying Jane. It was the thought of a life with no love in it that frightened her.

Early the following morning cases came from the castle containing all Jane's possessions. She sat on the floor sifting through them, repacking all the clothes Roberto had given her, and his presents of jewellery.

'God, girl, you're not sending that all back, are you?'

'Yes, and a note to tell him to dispose of my clothes in his other houses.'

'Is that all it says? Isn't that a bit cold?'

'I did all the begging I'm going to do last night. He's made his mind up. There's nothing else to say.'

'You're too proud, Jane. It's been your downfall once before. And you're making a dreadful mistake – at least keep some of the jewellery. It will keep you for years. Heavens, Roberto can afford it, and it's his baby after all.'

'I can't, Honor. You know I can't.'

'Such a pity! Goodness knows when you'll get another wardrobe like this. He's got such good taste for a man.'

'They're not exactly the sort of clothes that would look right trundling a baby round the supermarket, are they?' Jane managed a weak laugh. Even so, she thought that Honor would cry as the trunks full of her lovely wardrobe were loaded back on the vans to be returned to the castle.

It was a wrench saying goodbye to Honor. But by late afternoon she and May were on the plane to England and by late evening they were sitting in Zoe's kitchen with Zoe and Sandra. Jane had telephoned them both from Heathrow. It was like coming home. She had forgotten what a haven Zoe's kitchen was.

'You must stay here, Jane. I never re-rented the flat when you wrote to say you wouldn't be back. Too lazy, I suppose. Your stuff's still there. It's plenty big enough for you and May.'

'Could I really? Just for a while. Zoe, you're an angel. There's another problem, you see. I'm pregnant.'

'Oh no!' Sandra exclaimed.

'That complicates things,' Zoe stated.

'Does he know?' Sandra asked.

'Yes. He suggested I had an abortion,' Jane replied, fighting back the tears.

'The bastard!' said Sandra.

'Men!' exploded Zoe.

'No, I don't blame him. I treated him atrociously.' To the astonished ears of her two friends she confessed, fearful as she did so of their condemnation, but feeling a compulsion to tell it in all its sordid detail.

'What a sorry tale, Jane. You've been such a clot. But you must think of the future now, and the baby. And, speaking of babies, the most sensible thing is that you get some sleep,' Zoe bossed.

Zoe, May and Sandra sat for hours drinking wine and discussing Jane's situation, once she was in bed.

'That bloody Alistair! He's always popping into her life and wanting her back and then pissing off again. I could kill him,' Zoe said angrily. 'If he'd just kept out of her life she would probably have got over him years ago.'

'I think he meant it, this time,' May said. 'After she left Respryn he had a procession of girls but none of them lasted long. You could see he knew he'd made a mistake.'

'I think he was serious, too. After Jane telephoned today, I phoned St Cuthbert's. I know the sister on that ward, she trained with us. James was never in danger, he was just in for routine observation. He was never delirious nor was he calling for her.'

'My, my. I take it all back then. But how could she go back to him if she's pregnant with Roberto's baby?' Zoe asked logically.

'She can't, can she?' Sandra looked depressed.

'She might have an abortion, as Roberto suggested.'

'Jane? Never. I can't see her doing that.' They solemnly sipped their wine. 'What's Roberto like, May?' Sandra asked.

'He's lovely. He's not handsome or anything – he always reminded me of a monkey, he's got one of those funny, ugly, attractive sort of faces. And so kind, I think he's the kindest man I ever met. And he adored her.'

'Then maybe he'll forgive her, take her back?' Zoe said hopefully.

'No, Mrs Potterton, I doubt that. If he'd loved her a little bit less he might have done, but she was on such a pedestal to him. And he's a Latin, of course, they don't easily forget, do they?'

In the morning, a much calmer Jane began to sort out the muddle of her life. The first priority was money. She telephoned Alistair, who did not sound in the least surprised to hear from her so soon and was eager to see her.

'No, Alistair. I don't want to see you, not for some time. The other night was a stupid mistake. I'm phoning to say that I want to sell the house in Fulham and perhaps get something smaller here, in Cambridge. I hoped you would make the arrangements for me – you know how useless I am.'

'You've left him, then?'

'You could say that, yes.'

'I'm glad. That wasn't the life for you.'

'About the house . . .' Jane continued, ignoring Alistair's remark. She had no intention of arguing with him about Roberto, not now, especially.

She was not alone in making decisions. Zoe and May had made them too. Over lunch they told Jane the conclusions they had reached. Zoe wanted no rent for the flat, and when the baby came May would move into the main house to sleep. May would help Zoe in the house so that Jane need not worry about her wages.

'I can't let you do that.'

'Why not? I like May, provided I can get her to call me Zoe, I couldn't stand that "Mrs Potterton" bit day and night.' Zoe smiled at May. 'No, it makes sense, I need help, you know better than most what a pigsty this place is. And you needn't bother spending your money on a house. It's simple.'

'Yes, it's beautifully simple. But don't you see, Zoe, it's too generous of you. I've got to learn to stand on my own two feet.'

'Why? It's silly saying that. You needn't worry about money anyway: Benjamin's making so much, now his books are being made into films, money is the least of our worries. Those Hollywood nymphets, that's what my nightmares are about.' Zoe laughed her loud, good-natured laugh.

'Until the baby's born, then. But once he's here, I have to think again.'

'I have every confidence you'll bounce back some way or other, Jane. You seem to be destined to be one of those people who drive around in Rolls-Royces or Minis but nothing in between. You'll soon get out of this year's Mini,' Zoe said.

'I like your faith in me. For the moment I can't see a way out. No, it's modest living from now on for yours truly.'

It was comforting being back in these familiar surroundings, with Zoe just across the patio whenever she needed her, with May coming in and out; and there were the large, rowdy meals in Zoe's kitchen with a new batch of lame ducks. She missed Roberto desperately, far more than she let the others know. She would sit for hours looking at the phone, trying to muster the courage to telephone him, but she never succeeded.

Jane was baby-sitting for Sandra. When Sandra and Justin returned and Justin had gone to bed, the two women sat up talking, just as they used to do.

'Jane, I never told you before but, you know, Alistair set you up. James was never at risk.'

'I know, Sandra, "set up" just about sums it up.'

'You know? Oh. But that was the wrong phrase to use. I really think he wanted you back.'

'Sandra, I was just another body to him. It was probably his way of getting back at Roberto.'

'Alistair? He never struck me as a vindictive type. You sure?'

'Positive.'

They sat for a while in silence. 'Jane, can I ask you something?' Jane looked quizzically at her friend. 'It'll probably sound daft, but ... I've only slept with Justin ... what's it like with a different man? I mean is *it* different?'

Jane laughed. 'Wondering if you're missing out, Sandra? Yes, it was different ... but then it wasn't ... maybe I was different – I just don't know.' Sandra looked puzzled at Jane's riddle of an answer. 'Oh, God, I miss him!' she suddenly burst out. 'I ache for him. I want him so badly. No one will ever be able to make love to me like that again.'

'Jane, I'm so sorry, I thought you'd got over him, you never say a thing. But you'll find someone else, I'm certain.'

'No, Sandra, you don't know what it was like. He made my body come alive and he kept it that way. When he took me it wasn't just my body he took, it was a part of my soul, too. Each time he made love to me, I thought I would die from the sheer ecstasy of it.'

'It doesn't sound at all what Justin and I get up to,' Sandra said with irony. 'I mean, it's all very nice and enjoyable but I can't imagine our little gropings could ever reach those exalted heights.' She laughed, making Jane smile at last. 'You know, you and I were born at the wrong time. We missed out on the sixties. All that fun and freedom, the pill. Hell, I'd got varicose veins by the time it was being prescribed, and how can you be promiscuous lugging a Dutch cap around in your handbag? There we were beavering away looking after husbands, house, brats, all the things we had been told it was our duty to do, and everybody else was having such fun! Now it's all too late – 35-year-old hippies just look sad.'

'I wonder if it is such fun. I wonder if they really enjoy all that casual freedom. I think we felt safer.'

'God, Jane, you're a right one to talk – at least you've lived in sin.'

'"Living in sin" sounds so wicked, as if you're having an orgy every night. But Roberto and I weren't like that. We lived a very staid life, really, a very married life: all that was missing was that little bit of paper.'

'But think of all the opportunities that are open to young women these days, don't you envy them that? I do.'

'Not really. I haven't changed much, Sandra. I still would love to have a man to look after, to be waiting for the sound of his key in the lock every evening. Someone to grow old with.'

'I'll swap for your past any day,' Sandra said wistfully.

'I think you'd want to swap back pretty fast. I'd have given anything for the sort of security you have with Justin. You might think it dull, but I envy you it.'

'Then don't ever get involved in an argument with the Cambridge women's libbers. They'll tear you apart with fury.'

What she had said was true, she thought, as she drove herself home. Her desires were simple and seemed destined to be unfulfilled. She did not want freedom, sexual or otherwise. She did not want a career. She wanted a husband and the emotional security such a relationship would give her. But, feeling as she did about Roberto and Alistair, how could she ever hope to find another man?

Honor came on one of her whirlwind visits. As Jane had expected, her three friends took an immediate liking to each other. Honor even persuaded Zoe to leave her kitchen and took them all out to lunch at Panos's. It was a noisy lunch. Jane thought that May would die from laughing as Honor, Zoe and Sandra capped each other's funny stories, one after the other, like machine-gun fire. They then trooped through the city, like a gaggle of giggling schoolgirls, marching into one department store after another, where Honor insisted on buying not only a complete layette, but all the furniture for the nursery, too. Before she left at the same breakneck speed, Honor took Jane on one side.

'Have you written to Roberto?'

'No, Honor, I can't.'

'I think you should. He's desperately unhappy. He's virtually a recluse, darling. No one sees him, poor old thing.'

'No parties or anything like that?'

'Nothing. The castle appears closed up, but I know he's there, lurking in the shadows, like a sad ghost. Too morbid, darling.' She shuddered.

But she did not write. What was there to say? She had told him she was sorry, had begged his forgiveness, said that she loved him, and he had not wanted to know. What else was there to write to say?

A month after Honor's visit, she was in Zoe's kitchen when a breathless May rushed in.

'He's here,' she blurted out, interrupting Zoe in midsentence.

'Who's here?' Jane and Zoe asked in unison.

'The Prince!'

She looked a mess, she thought, as with pounding heart she raced across the patio. All this time and all she could think of was how she looked! She was convinced she had not heard May correctly. But there he stood, in the middle of her sitting room, looking out of place in his elegant clothes in the ordinary surroundings of her flat. He looked tired, desperately so, and she felt anguish for him and wanted to rush across the room and hold him to her.

'Hullo,' she said shyly, instead. She was conscious of his eyes looking at her swollen belly and she instinctively put her hands in front of her. 'It's getting big. Not very glamorous, I'm afraid.' She tried to laugh, but her nerves would not let her. Instead a strangled, stupid giggle emerged.

'Honor told me about the baby,' he said without preamble.

'She was here last month. Where did you see her?'

'Paris.'

'You went to Paris as usual, then?'

'Yes.'

'How's the apartment?'

'Why didn't you let me know about the baby?'

'I did. I told you that . . .' She could not finish the sentence.

'I didn't believe you. I thought it was a trick. Why didn't you get rid of it?'

'It isn't the baby's fault. It didn't ask to be conceived. And . . .' She stopped.

'And?'

'It's part of you.' Her eyes filled with tears and she hurriedly turned away.

'Jane, I think we should get married.'

Her head jerked up. She could not believe what she was hearing, she knew that her mouth hung open inanely in astonishment. She could not speak from excitement.

'It would be better for the baby, if he were legitimate. It would not be fair to deprive him of his heritage because of our errors. As you say, he did not ask to be conceived.'

'It might be a girl,' was all she could think to say.

'If we marry, he is secure,' Roberto continued as if she had not interrupted. 'I wouldn't try to take him from you, not like Alistair, I'm not cruel like that. No, but I would expect to share him with you. I would like to see him each summer, and I would like to have him for the skiing and, when he is older, for the boar-shooting. I would like that all decisions to do with his education are mine. I would prefer him to be educated in Italy, I should like him to be an Italian, not an Englishman. I would wish to pay for his upkeep and his servants and, of course, for you.'

'It would be fairer to him,' she said softly, amazed that she could sound so reasonable as she stood, her hopes smashed in little pieces about her. 'I wouldn't want you to pay anything for me, I don't deserve anything, but I can see you would want to support your child. It wouldn't be a question of servants – there's only May.'

'This is not suitable accommodation for you,' he said, looking about the sitting room. 'You must look for a house and I will buy it for you. Perhaps an estate in the country, it would be healthier for the boy, and he should learn to ride . . .'

'I like it here, Roberto. I don't want to move. My friends are very kind to me, we don't need a big place.'

'I don't wish to be difficult. Stay here by all means for a while, until he is older. Should you change your mind meanwhile, then let me know.'

It was all so coldly businesslike. She looked at him with longing. Nervously she stretched out her hand and gently touched his. 'I love you.'

'I love you too, Jane.'

'Then why?'

'I cannot forgive what you did to me. I could never trust you again.'

'Will you stay with me here, now?' Her voice implored him.

'No. I've rooms at the Garden House, I shall see you each day.'

He kept his word in the days before their wedding. He took her to dinner each day, and there were moments of such ordinary intimacy between them that she would allow herself to hope. But then she would say something, or touch him, and he would look at her coldly and all hope for reconciliation was dashed. The very closeness of him was a perpetual agony to her as she remembered the joy his lovemaking had given her. At night she would plan not to see him, but each morning she relented – just in case.

He had planned their marriage with great care. He had chosen a day when a world-famous film star was to marry in London, and his ploy worked: not one reporter appeared at their wedding. Sandra and Benjamin were their witnesses and Zoe and May their only guests. They stood in the biting December wind on the steps of the Shire Hall while May insisted on taking their photograph with her Instamatic camera. Jane thought wryly how different it was from the last time, as she smiled into the lens. Zoe cooked a magnificent dinner, and Benjamin served champagne, but it was a restrained party.

Then it was time for Roberto to leave. They crossed to the flat for a moment alone together.

'You really are going then?' she asked.

'Yes, I fly home tomorrow.'

'We could make it work, Roberto,' she said, urgency giving her the courage to say what she thought – what had she to lose?

'I would make your life hell, Jane, never trusting you, never letting you out of my sight. You would be a prisoner.'

'I'd learn to cope.'

'No, in time you would hate me. This way is better. The baby has his father's name, his inheritance is secure and you'll be free to lead your own life.'

'But I want to be with you, on any terms.'

'Then you don't know yourself at all, my dear Jane. You have too much spirit for the restrictions that I would put upon you. I don't wish to argue any more, Jane. I have decided.'

'Very well.' She tossed her head with a gesture of defiance. 'You will regret it, though.'

'We shall see,' he said as he made for the door.

In the months that followed she would often wonder if she should have pleaded with him more, if she should have begged, implored. Could she have handled him better? But it was all too late, she told herself frequently. She had only herself to blame this time.

She wrote to James to tell him about the baby, fearful of his reaction. But now she concentrated all her energies on the baby growing within her. She fought any sign of depression, fearful that her moods might infect the child. She wrote long rambling letters to Roberto, which she never posted, knowing that he would not have answered them. But the letter-writing was a form of contact with him that was necessary to her.

In March, on a crisp, golden day, when the crocuses ran riot on the Backs, a lusty, black-haired boy was born, just as Roberto had predicted.

Sandra had arranged to inform Roberto of the arrival of his son, and the following day a large basket of flowers arrived at the nursing home, followed by a telegram which said simply, 'Welcome, Giovanni Roberto Michele Umberto.' Jane laughed: such a long list of names for such a little soul.

She had him christened in the Roman Catholic church. It seemed the right thing to do. She had written to Roberto to tell him which day it was to be. But he did not come.

She was left with his son, his name, and an unquenchable fire in her body for him.

13

Jane had wondered what she was to do with herself once the baby was born. She had not realized that, to this child, she was to give willingly her total time and attention. She would begin her secretarial course at the technical college next term, she said. Next term became the term after. And finally next year seemed early enough to start. Roberto's allowance was generous, so that, having no need to look for a job, she concentrated happily on the child. She knew that even had she lacked money, she would have moved heaven and earth not to have to work, so that she could spend her time with him.

She was the first to admit that she enjoyed this baby in a way that she had not enjoyed her first-born. Perhaps it was because she was older and had more patience and was more aware of how transient babyhood was; or because, she thought, when she had had Alistair to love as well, her affections had been more divided. Or maybe, having been deprived of so much of James's life, she now overcompensated with this little one. Whatever the reason, it made her single-minded and surprisingly content in her life with her son.

She had forced herself not to think about Roberto. At first she had spent hours longing for him, remembering the past, planning a future: then, one day, she realized with a jolt that once again she was allowing the past to rule and threaten her present. She had to stop this, take a grip on herself. It was finished with Roberto: her son needed her full attention, not the depressed, discontented woman she risked becoming if she allowed herself to dream. It had been difficult. The intensity of Roberto's passion had followed her, it seemed. But slowly she succeeded until, a year later, she could live a whole day without thinking of him. But at night it was different – then she would lie in bed and her mind, relaxing its guard, allowed her body to announce its hungry need for him.

She had expected that she would have difficulty adjusting to a more mundane existence, that she would long for the excitement of life with Roberto, the travelling, the clothes, the parties, the endless parade of people. But she did not miss this life at all. Now she began to realize that the life which she had thought so full had, in fact, been empty. It was the perpetual motion more than anything else that had generated the idea of excitement. Roberto and his friends, she realized, lived a life with as much rigid routine as the office worker catching the 8.35 each morning. It was the exotic locations that had confused her.

With a sense of relief she found she could delay washing her hair until the next day – it did not matter. She enjoyed putting on old jeans and sneakers and staying in them all day. It was wonderful that a broken nail was no longer a major tragedy. It was odd, though, she would think: she was certain that, when she was living the exotic life, she had enjoyed it. Maybe she was far more adaptable than she had thought.

One thing upset her. She never heard from Roberto's friends. She sent Christmas cards but received none in return. She had felt that they had liked her for herself but clearly she had been mistaken. Only Roberto's cousins, Emilio and Francesca, kept in touch, though she would have expected them automatically to side with Roberto. Francesca wrote regularly with news and sent photos of her son, born two weeks after Giovanni; and they even invited her to stay.

But none of these conclusions was reached overnight. And now she knew herself well enough to wonder whether she could have reacted and adapted so well without Giovanni's welcome demands on her.

She did not lack friends, however. Living with Zoe, it was impossible to be lonely, and it was a rare day that she did not see Sandra. But she made no attempt to find a lover. She did not look at men as possible lovers. It was as if Roberto had destroyed that potential in other men for her. And what if he still had her watched? It was not worth the risk.

Alistair telephoned frequently. He would ask her out to dinner, and several times he invited her to join him at a house party. She always refused; she was afraid to accept. Alistair, she feared, was the one man who could still excite her physically. She could not face the old romantic need for him, either. She knew that such reactions would make her despise herself. She wanted to long only for Roberto.

James came. Of his own initiative he phoned one day to ask if he could come for half term. Jane was torn between terror at the prospect of spending days alone with the boy, and longing to see him again. He was fifteen now: a solemn and serious young man arrived on her doorstep with none of his father's charm and lightness. His first visit was strained but it was as if the child wanted to build a relationship with her, for he persisted and called regularly.

Her greatest joy was to see her two sons together. Despite the great age difference, James was entranced by his small brother and would play with him for hours. She learned that he was not as humourless and serious as she had thought: he had a delightful, off-beat sense of humour. He was still not demonstrative but the dreadful distance she had felt in the past had gone. It should have been worse since Lady Upnor now lived at Respryn with her son. Jane wondered if, perhaps, the old lady had overplayed her hand, had gone too far in her condemnation of Jane, and had turned the boy towards her. She did not know for certain, she never asked and, since the boy did not talk of his life at home, the subject was never raised between them.

One year passed without her having to relinquish Giovanni to his father, but in the second year, Roberto insisted and May and the toddler travelled to Italy for the summer, leaving Jane alone. She missed both the child and May, and one evening, sitting alone in the flat, feeling too depressed to join the others, she was surprised when Alistair appeared at her door, unannounced, resplendent in his dinner jacket.

'I'm up for a college dinner,' he explained. 'I've got a couple of hours to spare. Thought it was silly that we see so little of each other these days. We should see each other more.'

'Should we?' she asked, pouring them drinks, already uncomfortably aware that she was pleased to see him.

'Yes. Jane, I've known you longer than most of my friends. Makes me shudder to think just how long. It's terrifying the way the years are slithering by, isn't it?'

'I'm not sure what you mean.'

Alistair took a gulp of his drink, stared intently at the glass, and then said quickly, 'I've been a real bastard to you in the past, haven't I?'

Jane smiled. Alistair seemed nervous. She wondered why and what he was leading up to.

'Jane, there's something I've wanted to say for ages. It was bloody of me to try and sue Roberto like that, wasn't it?'

'It was a long time ago.'

'Well, it was, wasn't it?' He leaned towards her, frowning, as he waited for her answer.

'Yes, Alistair, if it makes you feel better, it was bloody of you.' She laughed at him.

He seemed to relax a little and sat back in the armchair. 'I was angry, you know, and jealous. That's why I did it. That day in Cambridge when I asked you to come back to me, I had taken months to pluck up the courage to ask you, and when I did eventually ask, that bastard Tom walked in. I could have killed him!'

'But Tom was nothing to me, I explained all that in my letter to you.'

'What letter?' He looked up sharply from his glass.

'I wrote to you that same night, telling you that I loved you and trying to explain about Tom and me.'

'Jane, I never got any letter! Where did you send it?' he asked incredulously.

'To Respryn, of course.'

'But I went to London. I went on a monumental binge. I can't remember much of what happened but I do know there was no letter.'

'It must have got lost in the post, then. How strange! I wonder what would have happened to our lives if you had got it?'

'Letters don't get lost in the post, Jane. It's the sort of thing one says to one's bank manager.' Anger flickered across his face. 'I know what happened to it.'

'Your mother?'

'I'd stake my life on it. Interfering old bitch. God, what else has she done to ruin my life?'

'She is a bitch. But she interferes only because she loves you, Alistair.'

'Jane, sometimes you can be too reasonable. You ought to hate her for what she has done.'

'I used to, but I can't now. I just don't have it in me to hate anyone. In any case, I believe in fate: we weren't meant to get back together, so your mother was just an instrument of fate. You've got to admire her tenacity, though, she never gives up on me, does she?' Jane gave a rueful smile.

'But we could have been so happy,' he said seriously.

'On the other hand, we might have been as miserable as sin together. And I wouldn't have Giovanni. Perhaps, inadvertently, I have your mother to thank for him.' She smiled to herself at the thought of the strange tricks life played.

'And now?' His voice insistently interrupted her thoughts.

Jane looked at her hands. She remembered that night, in Fulham, remembered so clearly her moment of joy; but she also remembered his words, 'You've learned a lot since the last time'. Those words she could never forget. She shuddered almost imperceptibly.

'So?' she heard him say, softly.

Jane looked at him. Apart from the grey in his hair he looked the same, still handsome, still charming. It would be so easy, she thought. One word and there was the chance that he could be hers again. But could Alistair ever be anyone's totally? How long before the affairs started again? How long before the rot of rejection would eat into her soul?

'We're friends now, aren't we? Let's keep it that way. I value our friendship,' she said, her calm voice belying the control she was exerting.

He seemed about to say something else, but stood up suddenly, his drink unfinished. 'Well, the Master and Fellows await me, I'd better be going. But I meant it, Jane – let's have the odd dinner together. You can't spend the rest of your life mooning about in this little flat, worrying about babies.'

'That would be nice, dinner occasionally,' she said, letting him out of the door.

After he'd gone she sat for a long time in the twilight. It was as she had feared. It had taken all her willpower not to slip into his arms, feel his lips on hers, want to feel his naked body and his hardness within her. What was it about her? Other women were content with one man in their lives, but not she – always the same, always wanting the two and now unable to have either. She smiled at herself. It wasn't strictly true that she just thought of babies; she had not told him, but she had a job now.

It had happened completely by accident. She had always enjoyed writing letters, long newsy ones. As she scribbled away in Zoe's kitchen one day it was that practical woman who suggested she should try writing for money. She had sent off an article to the local paper on a subject close to her heart, the difficulties of marrying out of one's class. To her excited astonishment they printed it and sent her a cheque. It was a one-off, she decided, and was surprised when they asked for a series of articles. In the evenings and while

Giovanni rested in the afternoons, she had sat at her desk tapping away at her new portable typewriter. She was thankful that at least her haphazard attendance at secretarial courses had taught her to type. She found the articles surprisingly easy to write and she loved the thrill of rushing round to the newspaper office to meet the copy deadline. She was amazed one day to get a phone call from a national women's magazine, commissioning some articles. Staggered by how much they were prepared to pay, she took particular care over them, and sent them off nervously. Three weeks later the assistant editor rang to ask if she would be interested in writing an advice column. The prospect unnerved Jane, but Zoe brushed aside her objections and insisted she accept.

It was a success. She enjoyed the work, which she could do at home, was happy if she could help people, and was appalled by the sadness and fear in so many women's lives. She discovered it was not just women like herself who had married into difficulties: there were those working-class women who had married a working-class sweetheart only to find that, as the man's career advanced, the pressures on them were enormous – how to do things correctly became an ever present nightmare. It seemed silly to think that not knowing how to lay a table when the boss was coming to dinner might lead to divorce, but Jane got letter after letter that said just that.

What saddened her most was that nothing had changed. She might be happy in liberal, easy-going Cambridge but out there the social jungle was in good heart. Society was still as spiteful and those on top were still as busy kicking at the fingers of those just below them on the ladder of success.

Being able to say she was a professional journalist made life in Cambridge a lot easier for her. She no longer had to suffer the blank, bored stares that saying she did nothing had elicited.

Her life seemed to have settled into a pleasant, comfortable routine, one which, if she was lucky, would go on for ever.

It was late as she sat at her desk writing her column. The flat was lonely without Giovanni, but she had peace to work. The phone rang shrilly. Irritated, she looked at her watch as she crossed the room to answer it.

'Jane, darling. It's Alistair. I don't know quite how to tell you this. It's bad news, it's Honor. I'm afraid she's dead.'

Jane leaned against the wall as she felt her legs buckling under her. She felt enveloped in ice.

'Honor? What on earth are you talking about?'

'It's a shock, I know, Jay, but I'm afraid it's true.'

'This is crazy. I was going to phone her tomorrow, ask her if I could go and stay with her for a couple of weeks,' she said, as if the fact of her intended phone call proved the falseness of his news. 'She can't be dead, I won't believe it.'

'Guido just phoned – '

'A car crash, that was it, wasn't it? Maybe she's just hurt.'

'Jane, love, I'm sorry. It wasn't a crash. Guido found her in bed a couple of hours ago.'

'Of course he'd find her in bed, it's late, isn't it?' she snapped, her rising hysteria reaching her voice.

'Jane, love, you standing up? If so then sit down, take some deep breaths. I know it's hard but you've got to take a grip on yourself.' Obediently she did as he said. The deep breathing made her regain control but did not remove the ice-cold blackness that surrounded her. 'Her light was on, apparently she hadn't been too well recently. He went to see if there was anything she needed, and he found her, dead.'

'Alistair!' She began to sob. 'I wish you were here.'

'I wish I was, too, Jay. It's a devastating blow. I know how fond of her you were. I thought I should tell you immediately, I didn't want you reading about it in the newspapers.'

'But what did she die of? She always seemed so fit.'

'I don't know, love. I expect there'll be a post mortem.'

'God, how ghastly! Poor Honor.'

'I thought you'd want to be at the funeral. It's next Wednesday at Respryn. You must stay the night, it's too long a drive. James will want to have you here, he's upset. He was very fond of her.'

'Of course, Alistair. Thank you for letting me know.' She was calmer now but it was the calm of disbelief. She replaced the receiver and sat there well into the night, her mind refusing to accept that a world without Honor was possible.

14

The following Wednesday as she drove through the lodge gates of Respryn and crossed the familiar park she felt a mixture of emotions. Above all she felt an overwhelming sadness that bright, shining Honor was no more, that a glittering piece of magic had gone from the world. She felt a loneliness tinged with fear that Honor would never be there to turn to again. She felt guilt that she had not been to see her sooner – if only she had been there, Honor need not have died alone. She stopped the car and looked round at the beautiful parkland and took comfort that some things never changed. She felt strangely happy to be back here again on the land that for so long had been her home. As she sat and watched the deer, she laughed at herself, for lurking under all these varying emotions was an old familiar feeling of apprehension at the prospect of seeing Alistair's mother again. It wasn't just the parkland that never changed.

Alistair and James were waiting for her and Banks gave her a kindly, warm welcome. She was shown to her room. It was the same room she had occupied the very first time she had come here. She sat on the bed and, looking around the room, saw that nothing had changed here either, except herself. She wondered if the gauche, badly dressed young girl who had sat here, too afraid even to leave the room on her own, would recognize herself in this groomed, sophisticated woman? She had been too long with Roberto and he had been too good a teacher for the veneer that he had given her to disappear. She might not wear couturier clothes any more, but with her acquired sense of style it was easy for her to make her cheaper clothes appear far more expensive than they were. She knew instinctively now the best way to dress her long hair. Her make-up was discreet and perfectly enhanced the large, grey eyes, still unlined, the high cheekbones. Her figure had a svelteness that made it hard to believe she was the mother of two children, one of whom was almost an adult.

Yet, Jane knew that the changes were outward; inside, the differences between the girl she had been and the woman she had become were minimal. She was still longing for love, still not really belonging anywhere, and always, it seemed, in awe of Alistair's mother. But there was one difference: her feelings for Lady Upnor could amuse her now.

Lady Upnor had hardly changed. A few more lines on her face, perhaps, but the same upright carriage which belied her years. Clarissa would not age as well as her mother. There was too much hardness and bitterness in her face, and already she had the set lines of a sour middle age.

Jane was greeted by both in the same manner: an almost royal inclination of the head, a limp handshake. Sufficient courtesy for her not to be offended, but not enough to make her feel welcome. At least the years seemed to have taught Clarissa to disguise her contempt.

August. It seemed to be a significant month in her life. In that month she had met Alistair, Rupert had died, she had finally given herself to Roberto, had betrayed him in that month and had left him too. And now Honor . . . she wondered if Honor's death had interfered with the shooting party at Drumloch. She hoped it had; perhaps it had had to be cancelled. How annoyed Blanche Upnor must have been!

The funeral was beautiful in its simplicity. Estate workers carried the coffin from the house through the knot garden, the rose garden, as if Honor were saying goodbye to them, through the little garden gate and into the tiny church so close to the house that it appeared part of it. The church was packed. As the men lowered the coffin onto the bier in front of the altar, Jane began to weep, it looked so small. Honor had been tall in life, and it was strange that death should make her seem tiny. They buried her in the family vault alongside her ancestors, beneath the oaks, looking down on the home of her childhood.

The congregation made its way silently back to the house. Drinks were served and people stood in embarrassed little clusters whispering to each other. 'You all right?' Alistair asked her, handing her another drink. 'I got you a gin and tonic. I know you loathe sherry.' He smiled at her.

'I hate to think of her alone out there.'

'She's not alone. Calem, her first husband, is with her.'

'How come?'

'She had his ashes in an urn. She's carted them around the world with her for years. She told me yonks ago, "When I snuff it, put Calem in my coffin with me. He was so divine in bed, I'd like to share my coffin with him." So I did. They're both tucked up together.'

'Dear Honor, how lovely! Outrageous to the end.' Jane laughed with delight at the thought of Honor reunited with her Wilbur Calem. As her laugh rang out, several groups turned and stared at her with disbelief and she saw Lady Upnor's mouth twist with distaste. 'Alistair, tell me a funny story, quick, make me laugh again. Honor would have hated us like this, all sad and miserable.'

'You're right. Let me see.' He embarked on a long shaggy-dog story, and when he got to the punch line, Jane laughed loudly, joined this time by Alistair. A deathly silence fell upon the room, and there were more disapproving looks. Alistair clapped his hands. 'Everyone, listen, don't be shocked. Jane had just pointed out to me that Honor would have wanted us to have a happy time. You remember, all of you, how she loved a good party. Well, I suggest that we cheer up in respect and honour of her memory.'

There were murmurs of assent, the whispering ceased and conversations were in normal voices. A laugh rang out, then another, and the volume of noise increased until soon the level was that of a good cocktail party in full swing, one in which Honor would have been very much at home. Instead of the customary two sherries for the ladies and whiskies for the men, Banks and the footmen were dispatched for more liquor and the party went on into the early evening. It was such a success that, as he left, one young scion of a noble house thanked Lady Upnor for 'an absolutely super party' . . .

Finally only Jane, the family and their lawyer, Mr Strong, were left. Jane noticed the lawyer begin to remove a sheaf of papers from his briefcase. She moved silently towards the door; if the will was about to be read, she would slip away.

'Excuse me, Princess, I would be grateful if you would stay.' Jane turned in the doorway.

'I really don't see any reason for this woman to stay, Mr Strong. This is family business,' Lady Upnor said imperiously.

'With Your Ladyship's permission, I would prefer it if she stayed,' Mr Strong said smoothly as he settled his papers on the desk in front of him, ignoring the glare that Lady Upnor gave him. Jane, looking around for somewhere to sit, chose as always a window seat.

The lawyer began to read the will. It was long, for Honor had had many friends and everyone seemed to be remembered. As each bequest was read out, there was a message from Honor for the recipient, whether they were present or not, all read in Strong's passionless, legal voice. It was a touching will and a funny one too – she had left a large sum of money to Guido with the instructions that he buy himself some land, but Honor suggested he stick to olive-growing since, with his liver, vines might be too big a temptation. Jane heard Alistair's name mentioned: Honor had left him the land she owned here, saying that she wanted it to revert to the Respryn estate. For the first time Jane realized that Honor must have bought much of the land which had had to be sold when Rupert died.

The lawyer took a sip of his drink and looked anxiously around the room. Clarissa and her mother sat on the edge of their chairs, probably unaware of how eager they both looked as they strained to catch every word. The nub of the will, announcing the disposal of Honor's considerable fortune, had been reached.

Mr Strong cleared his throat and went on. '"My paintings, my furniture, my motor cars, my jewellery, my flats in New York and London, my villa in Italy, I leave outright to my dear niece and true friend, Jane Upnor née Reed."'

The gasps in the room were audible. 'Really!' Jane heard Lady Upnor exclaim, but, undeterred, the lawyer, having taken another sip of his drink, continued. '"The rest of my estate, my portfolio of stocks and shares, my various businesses and business interests, and any monies I have at the time of my death, I leave to my great-nephew Viscount Redland, possession of which he is to enjoy only upon the death of his mother Jane. Total control of my estate and its income is to be hers to enjoy outright with, as Jane would say, 'no strings attached' until her death.

'"Now I expect at this very moment there's a lot of muttering going on, so let me explain. I have done this, Jane, because I learned to love you and you became a good friend to me. I admire your integrity, and I know James's money will be safe with you.

'"I have done this, Clarissa, because you have always been a mean-minded, spiteful little bitch and you were cruel to Jane when she needed friends and understanding. But in any case I never liked you and, Jane apart, would never have bothered to leave you anything.

'"As for you, Alistair, I could never forgive the way you treated Jane, the dreadful cruelty of taking away her child at a time when she needed love. No doubt you were influenced by your dreadful mother, but that is no excuse. I tried to forgive you but I couldn't. I could never understand Jane's faithfulness to you and the love she bore you for so long. Since I spent long hours trying to persuade her to ditch you, it would be hypocritical of me to leave you anything other than what belongs to Respryn and the future. So I chose to benefit your son.

'"I would prefer, though I doubt if it is likely in the circumstances, that you do not vent your spite in your collective disappointment upon Jane. It is not her fault I have chosen to act in this way."'

The lawyer paused a long time and took another long sip of his drink.

Finally, as if screwing up all his courage, he continued, ' "My only regret is that I won't be with you all just to see the expression that is, undoubtedly, on Blanche's face right now." '

Everyone turned to look at Lady Upnor, whose face was mottled grey and maroon and twisted with anger. The lawyer laid the papers down, took off his spectacles and polished them carefully. He looked like a man who knows that all the furies of hell are about to break upon him. The silence hung oppressively. Jane waited for the onslaught to begin.

'I don't believe it!' Lady Upnor finally said, her voice strangely thick with emotion.

'The bitch, the filthy degenerate old bitch!' Clarissa screeched.

'Does that mean I'm rich?' James asked.

'Not for a very long time, it seems, James, unless you're lucky,' his grandmother interjected, glaring at Jane venomously.

'Can you two shut up a minute and let me say something?' Alistair demanded but Clarissa ignored him and continued unabated, though in a quieter voice, which, after her initial hysterics, was more frightening.

'You're a cunning bitch, aren't you, Jane? Wheedling your way into the lonely old bat's life, always looking as if butter wouldn't melt in your mouth, and bloody scheming all the time.' To Jane's astonishment she saw that Clarissa was crying; somehow she had never thought her capable of tears. Hector, her husband, put his arm about her shoulder to comfort her but angrily she shrugged him away. 'It's not fair, we needed that money so badly,' she wailed. 'She's not even family.' Angrily wiping the tears from her eyes, she jumped to her feet. 'We'll fight it, that's what we'll do. We'll get the will overturned.'

'Lady Clarissa, I do not advise that,' the lawyer interrupted. 'You would spend a lot of money and get nowhere. A will made by a person sound in mind is almost impossible to upset and only then by a close relative. Your relationship with Lady Honor would not be regarded as close enough.'

'But she wasn't of sound mind. She was mad, always had been, everyone knew that. You knew her, Mr Strong.'

'Eccentric, yes, Lady Clarissa, but mad in medical and legal terms – no.'

'I think it is appalling, Mr Strong, that my children should be deprived of their rightful inheritance in this way. That's the will of a spiteful, vindictive woman,' Lady Upnor said angrily, the mottling on her face even more marked. 'It doesn't sound like a proper will to me. I'm sure no court would accept it.'

'I know what you mean, Lady Upnor. It is a most unusual will, but then Lady Honor was a most unusual person.' The lawyer tried a placatory smile but, getting no response, he continued. 'However, it has been duly witnessed and I can assure you Lady Honor was of sound mind when she made it. I remember her exact words to me. "I want a will that everyone can understand, no legal jargon," she said. It is a proper will, albeit not couched in legal terms.

Of course you may take other opinions, Lady Upnor, but you will find they agree with me.'

'When was that will made?' Lady Upnor angrily enquired.

'It is dated December 1970. Nearly three years ago by my reckoning. She came to my office when she was here on a Christmas visit.'

'You were in Italy then,' Lady Upnor said accusingly, stabbing the air with a long bony finger.

'Yes, I was,' Jane said quietly.

'There you are, then, Mr Strong, undue influence from certain quarters, no doubt.' Lady Upnor continued to emphasize her words by pointing her finger menacingly at Jane.

'I was no longer living with Lady Honor, I had left. I take exception to your accusations, Lady Upnor. And I would appreciate it if you would stop wagging your finger at me in that aggressive manner,' Jane said in such an even tone that only Alistair was aware of the hint of humour in her voice.

'How dare you? You impudent hussy!' Lady Upnor spluttered, but Jane noted with satisfaction that she folded her hands on her lap.

'Shacked up with your gigolo, were you?' Clarissa snapped.

'Clarissa, what is the point in insulting me like this? Don't you ever give up?' Jane felt exasperated.

'What do you expect? That I just sit back and let you steal our money?'

'I'm not stealing anything. I repeat, I knew nothing about Honor's intentions. I knew she didn't like you and I admit that I agreed with her assessment of you. What the hell did you expect after all the years of sniping I had to put up with? But I'd no idea she'd go this far.'

'You see, Mr Strong, she admits it. She worked on the old cow, it's obvious,' Clarissa shrieked.

'If I can get a word in edgeways in the midst of all this backbiting, I for one would like to say I'm very pleased for Jane. You keep going on about rightful inheritance, Mother. This money has nothing to do with us. It was Wilbur Calem's originally: Honor was free to leave it to a cats' home if she wanted.'

'She's done that,' Clarissa said childishly.

'I would prefer it if you didn't mention that loathsome Calem's name.' Lady Upnor said haughtily.

'You might have found him loathsome, Mother, but your loathing appears to stop short of his money.' Alistair grinned triumphantly.

His mother shook her head angrily but ignored his jibe. 'I think Clarissa is right. I think Jane wormed her way into my sister-in-law's affection, Mr Strong. Something she had no right to do.'

'That's not fair, Lady Upnor. I loved Honor, she was a good friend to me. I always presumed that Alistair would get everything.'

'Liar!' shouted Clarissa. 'Your whole life has been one long scheme. Look how you conned Alistair into marrying you. He denies it, but I bet you told him you were pregnant. He'd never have married a common little tart like you for any other reason.'

'Aunt Clarissa!' James had leaped to his feet. 'How dare you speak to my mother like that?' He crossed the room to stand protectively beside Jane, who smiled gratefully up at him.

'You don't know her, James. Christ, I always had my doubts about Honor, I wouldn't be surprised if the two of them were a couple of lesbians and we didn't know.'

'Clarissa! You've gone too far,' Alistair shouted at his sister.

'A little family loyalty from you wouldn't go amiss, Alistair. Hoping to screw your way back in to some money, little brother?'

'Clarissa, so help me, I'll hit you.' Alistair lunged forward as if to strike her but Jane grabbed at him.

'Alistair, please don't bother. It doesn't matter. Honestly.'

'I'd no idea this family could be so bloody,' young James said with disbelief.

'You haven't heard the half of it, James. Why do you think your father wouldn't let her have you? Ever thought of that? I'll tell you, because he knew her for what she is, and he didn't want any of her nasty working-class mentality rubbing off on you.'

'Grandmother, this is terrible. Please stop, Aunt Clarissa.' The youth looked, wide-eyed with horror, from one relation to another. Jane took hold of her son's hand and squeezed it, hoping to convey that she was no longer upset by this family and its attitude to her. She looked at the angry faces, Lady Upnor's still dangerously mottled – absent-mindedly, Jane wondered if she had had her blood pressure checked recently. Clarissa's carefully larded make-up was beginning to melt with the perspiration her anger was creating – she'd be furious when she saw her face in the mirror. She watched and listened and realized that they were no different from any family haggling over an unfortunate will: money really brought out the best and worst in people. Money. How much? she wondered. It must be a considerable amount. Look at the way Honor had lived; look at the hysterics she was witnessing. Inwardly she smiled. What fun, what power! No, that wasn't a pleasant thought – Honor had never used it as a weapon and she wouldn't, either. Imagine, though, after all these years, here she sat, no longer the least bit in awe or hurt, and rich, too. A smile broke on her face – what a sense of humour Honor had! She became aware that Lady Upnor was talking to James. She shelved her thoughts for the moment, and concentrated on what the old bitch was saying.

'I'm sorry, James, but you're a man now, it's better that you know the truth. This family has never been the same since that woman, your mother, came into it.'

'I'll tell you the truth, James.' Alistair spoke up. 'My mother thinks I got custody of you because I loathed your mother and she thinks she persuaded me. It wasn't that. I thought, wrongly, as it turned out, that if I got you she would come back to me, but she didn't. You were all I had left from our marriage, and when she didn't want me, I knew that if you got to know her too well you would love her more than me. That's the truth. And I suggest that, if you two can't shut up and behave with a modicum of civility, you both leave the room,' he added forcefully to his mother and sister.

'I'll leave the room, willingly. Oh yes, I'll leave the room but I'll see that bitch in court. Come on, Hector, Mother.' The two women swept from the room with a sheepish Hector tagging along behind.

'Another Scotch, Strong? You look as though you've earned it,' Alistair said, the tension visibly draining out of him.

'Thank you, Lord Upnor, another drink would go down well. I do so hate these occasions when people are disappointed. The trouble is, they get so carried away that I think they forget I'm here,' he said, almost sadly.

'Mr Strong, what does this will mean?' Jane asked.

'It means, Princess, that you are an extremely wealthy woman. Not only do you have complete control over Lady Honor's assets, but you will enjoy her very large income from them for life. You are also free to dispose of those properties left to you outright. She did mention that she thought you might like to keep the Italian villa: she felt it was a special place to you.'

'Yes, that's true. But I would like to help Alistair in some way. James's school fees are so high and in a few years there'll be the cost of university. His expenses will be heavy. I'd like to pay them if there's enough.'

'Very proper in the circumstances, might I say? It's your privilege entirely whom you assist.'

'After death duties, there would be enough, then?'

'My dear Princess, I don't think you have any idea of the vastness of Lady Honor's estate, even after death duties are taken into consideration.'

'Dear old Calem.' Jane smiled.

'Jane, I don't want you helping me out. James, yes, but not me, I don't deserve it.'

'Yes, you do, they were magic years.' She held out her hand to Alistair.

Mr Strong packed his papers away.

'I almost forgot. There's one thing here for you, Princess, a letter. The instructions are on the envelope.'

Jane took the thick white envelope with Honor's distinctive, bold hand-writing on the front: 'Jane, read this when on your own, your feet up and a large G & T in your hand.' She slipped it into her handbag.

The lawyer left and Alistair poured his son and Jane another drink.

'Here you are, James. I think today is a day we won't count your drinks.' He laughed affectionately at his son.

'Can I get this straight, Pa? Ma has control of Aunt Honor's money but it's all mine one day?'

'That's right. I don't think you have any cause to worry. I can't imagine your mother ever letting you run short.'

'So we're rich?'

'You could say that – filthy rich would be more accurate.'

'Wow!' exclaimed his son.

'Do you have any idea how much, Alistair?' Jane asked.

'None whatsoever. I do know that the Calem empire is enormous and very diversified. She explained it to me once but I wasn't really listening – it all seemed to be companies within companies. I don't think darling old Honor really understood, she just spent it.'

'What about death duties?' Jane asked, remembering Alistair's problems at Respryn.

'It won't be like when my father died. She had an army of accountants and lawyers looking after her affairs, and she was no longer resident in this country. Don't look so worried, Jane. You'll inherit her advisers along with the money. I should just listen to them.'

'Granny and Aunt Clarissa were bloody,' the young boy announced suddenly, looking anxiously at his mother. 'Poor Ma.'

'James, don't worry yourself, it's been going on for so long now that I'd have felt there was something terribly wrong if they had been nice to me,' Jane said with a shrug.

'I have listened to them sometimes in the past. Ma, I'm sorry . . .' The boy's face twisted as he fought to control tears that were not far beneath the surface.

'Darling, I understand.' She put her arm around her son and looked closely at him. 'Darling, listen to me. It's not important. We're friends. We love each other, that's all that matters.'

Mother and son stood holding each other. Alistair crossed the room and in turn put his arms around them both. The three of them stood silently holding each other, taking comfort from each other.

She could not stay the night now. Alistair accepted that the atmosphere would be intolerable for her. In the small hours she finally arrived home. She was tired from the long drive, but still she poured herself the drink Honor insisted on, and sat down, her feet up, as instructed, and opened the letter.

Darling, darling Jane,

Isn't this too divinely ghoulish? Just like in the films!

Did Blanche's face go all slack with shock and horror? Such fun, I do wish I could have been there. I did toy with the idea of making one of those video tapes from the grave, like they have in America, but I decided that was a wee bit too vulgar!

I expect you were called all manner of names, scheming bitch etc. But you know and I know and that's all that matters. With no children, it is sad and chilling to know that one is dying with no one to leave favourite knickknacks to. But I loved you, so you were the logical choice.

Yes, I knew I was dying. Remember those silly headaches? They'd started just before you came to stay. I saw the doctors and they gave me a year to live. Be buggered, I thought, I'll fight this, and I did. Nothing for three years and then, whoosh, the bastard peeped up again. It was when you left Roberto. I so wanted you to stay, I was so low then and afraid. I should have told you, begged you to stay, I suppose, but you were so afraid of seeing Roberto, remember? Anyhow, with my luck the tumour went dormant again. I was a bit weak and wobbly but by cutting down on the late nights and the booze I could manage reasonably. Then this year it came back with a vengeance, there was no mistaking its intentions this time. It's here to stay and the pain is sometimes intolerable. It's obvious which of us will win the battle this time.

They can't operate, you see. The only thing they could offer me was radiation treatment and chemotherapy, but with a very slim chance of recovery. They were quite honest with me, I'd lose my hair (imagine, after all the money I've spent on the bloody stuff, having it all fall out!), I'd slip slowly into being a paralysed, incontinent vegetable. Well, I can't let it happen, Jane, I just can't.

I found an obliging doc who's given me some pills that will just carry me off, no fuss, and everyone will think my heart gave out.

I shall take them one day when the pain is like a circular saw in my head. I'll lie down with a nice gin and tonic and beat the bastard at its own game.

Forgive me, darling, but there's no other way. I wanted you to know, but don't tell a living soul. You see, I want to be buried at Respryn with the rooks and wood pigeons cawing and cooing away above me, and the scent from the rose garden wafting up to the cemetery. I don't know what the law is about suicides in consecrated ground, and all that guff – or is that just Roman Catholics? Anyhow, I'd rather not take the risk of some busybody finding out and insisting on digging me up. Too macabre for words, darling!

Remember when we were at Drumloch, when poor old Rupert died, you said if you had a place like that you'd never kill anything. Buy one, darling, you can afford it, and it's a nice idea. Do get in touch with Roberto, I beg you.

Honor

Jane sat clutching the letter for a long time, her large gin and tonic forgotten. Her mind led her back unbidden over all those years to the many times when her wise friend had comforted, counselled and loved her. Gradually the awful void Honor's death had left in her heart began to fill up with the memories, both happy and sad, that their friendship had left. Honor had been too full of the joy of living to endure a living death. She had taken the only way.

Curiously at peace with herself now, alone, Jane said goodbye to her beautiful, glittering friend.

15

A piece of paper had so changed her circumstances that there was no way she could ever lead a normal life again. Overnight she had become a very wealthy woman and from now on, her accountants advised her, a tax exile. Long hours were spent with lawyers and the ever present accountants, rationalizing her fortune and her future.

Her days seemed full of decisions and the nights full of wondering if she had made the right ones. Decisions about Honor's investments were easy to make – she just left everything as it was, and would rely on the same team of experts that Honor had depended upon. Deciding to sell the New York flat was easy, too. She did not want to live that far away, so everything was sold. She dithered about the flat in London. It might be useful, and James could use it when in London, and Alistair too, if he wanted. But then she saw it. Elegant and enormous, the flat was for parties and soirées; she would merely rattle about in it on her own. She put it on the market immediately.

A few weeks into her wealth, the realization that it was not all going to disappear overnight finally fixed itself in her mind. She travelled to her home town, and within a couple of hours had found a house on a leafy avenue, with gardens at the front and back, bay windows, a fitted kitchen and a tiled bathroom. Not until the contracts had been exchanged did she return.

It was strange entering her childhood home. It was even smaller than she remembered and shabbier, too.

'This is a surprise. We thought you'd given us up,' her mother welcomed her. Jane chose to ignore the gibe. What was the point in arguing that they hadn't gone out of their way to keep in touch with her? Instead she jangled the keys of the new house and put them on the table.

'That's for you two.'

Her father picked the keys up, suspiciously. 'What are they?'

'They're keys to a house on Sunny Avenue. I remember Mum always dreamed of a house there. And it's close to the football ground for you, Dad.'

'What's this, then, conscience money?' her mother asked, her customary bitter expression distorting her face.

'No Mum, it isn't. I would have done this years ago, but I was never in the position to. Now I can. I want to see you both more comfortably settled.'

'This money hasn't come from that greasy wop you've been living with, has it? 'Cause I'll tell you now, if it has, you can tell him where he can stuff his bleeding keys.'

'No, Mum, it hasn't come from him. I was left some money by Alistair's aunt. It's my money.'

'Why did she leave it to you? What about Alistair? And James?' she asked sharply.

'She left it to me and James.'

'Oh, that poor dear boy Alistair, what he's suffered because of you. You were a stupid cow to ever leave him, a nice gentleman like that.'

'Who left who is academic. He broke the marriage up, not me.'

'Not without reason, I'm sure. You always were impossible to live with, and that's a fact. And then to choose a greasy wop!'

'Mum, I'm beginning to get irritated by you. He's not a greasy wop, and I'd prefer it if you didn't talk about him like that. Now, do you want this bloody house or don't you?'

She had planned this surprise so meticulously; she had presumed her mother would be beside herself with happiness, but it wasn't going at all as she had anticipated.

'Thank you, Jane, it's very generous of you. We'll enjoy living there.' To Jane's astonishment, it was her father, accepting graciously.

'I thought you always said you'd never accept charity,' her mother snapped at him.

'I don't regard a gift like this from our only child as charity. Can we go and see it?'

On seeing the back garden, he immediately and enthusiastically began to plan what he was going to plant. Her mother stalked about the house, inspecting it, sniffing audibly as she opened cupboards and tried the windows.

'It's filthy!'

'Empty houses always look dirtier than they are. They were very nice people, I'm sure you'll find it's just the bareness makes it look dirty.'

'It's a nice kitchen,' her mother said grudgingly. 'But the heating – it'll cost a small fortune. Your father's retired now, we're not rolling in money, you know.'

'I've thought of that. I'll make you an allowance for things like rates and heating.'

'It's a long way from the shops.'

'Mum, stop carping. If you look in the garage, you'll see a Mini. Why don't you just give in and accept it as a nice house, and one you'll be happy in? I sometimes think you prefer being miserable.' Jane was rapidly becoming disenchanted with the whole exercise. She wandered into the garden and joined her father.

'What d'you think, Dad?'

'It's a little palace, Jane. It's very good of you. We weren't exactly the best parents, me especially. And then you do this. You're a good girl, Jane.'

Unused to kind words from him, she was puzzled by the change in him and did not know what to say. So she leaned forward and kissed him on the cheek. It felt odd to be doing so, the flesh unfamiliar, the flesh of a stranger. Her father began to cry.

'Oh, Dad, please don't cry, it's supposed to be a happy day. That's if Mum will allow it to be.' She was embarrassed, she hated to see him cry, but was not sure what to do or say to him. She did not know him well enough to be able to comfort him.

'Sorry, I'm getting to be a sentimental fool in my old age. And ashamed, too. It should have been me buying this house for your mum, but somehow, I never seemed to make it.'

'You've got it now. Does it matter who bought it? Perhaps she wouldn't have moaned so much if it had been you.'

She managed a weak laugh. Perhaps that was the reason for the change in her father: old age, as he said, making him look differently at things, at her.

'Yes, she would. But she'll come round. Your mum's only really happy when she can have a good moan, bless her. It's more a ritual, really.' He smiled at her. 'Heavens, even God can't get it right for her! It's either too hot or too cold, too wet or too dry.'

'Maybe she should have been a farmer.' The sad moment had passed. She had always presumed that they hated each other, but now her father had just shown that he was fond of his wife. As love could turn into hate, was it possible that hate could turn to love?

She stayed a week in the old house with them. Her Vuitton luggage looked incongruous in the bedroom of her childhood. She washed at the kitchen sink, she trotted out to the outside lavatory. Stoically she ate her mother's cooking. Having had her token moan, her mother settled happily into planning for the new house. Each day they set out shopping for furniture, carpets and curtains, a washing machine, a gleaming new cooker. What had started as a duty became a pleasure and Jane was as excited as her mother when they found exactly the right wallpaper for the sitting room. It was an odd experience, being in her home town again. Had it always been so drab? Had the people always looked so downtrodden and dejected? It fascinated her to think that as she walked along the High Street, she was probably brushing shoulders with women she had been at school with. She scanned the faces of those who she thought were her own age. It was days before she realized that she was searching for the wrong faces. She had been looking at women with young faces, like hers; now she realized that had she stayed here, she would have been one of those with faces marked with premature middle age. It was a sobering experience. Once or twice her mother stopped someone and said, 'Jane, you remember so and so here,' and Jane would lie and say, 'Yes,' and a stilted conversation would begin; then the old acquaintance would start to look embarrassed and, since there seemed nothing to say, they would move on.

She was glad to get back to Cambridge and to May and Giovanni returning from Italy. A momentous amount had happened since they left. Tanned by the sun, Giovanni looked far more Italian: he could even say one or two words in the language. She purposely did not ask May about Roberto, and May, presuming she did not want to know, said nothing. Giovanni was too young to say more than a few garbled phrases about 'Papa'.

That Christmas Jane went wild. She was so happy to be able to give.

She showered all her friends with presents. When invited out, she took only the best wine, a pot of caviar, fruit out of season, exotic plants. Just like

Honor, she found it 'such fun'. If rich people were unhappy, it was because they had not learned the sheer exhilarating joy of giving, she decided.

And then the unpleasantness started. Snide remarks were made about her wealth, and sly comments on the cost of her clothes. Her jewellery was inspected a mite too closely. She began to feel intensely guilty that she had so much. Some blatantly asked for help and she was only too happy to give it, but she was puzzled when she saw them later: often these same people would cross the street to avoid her. Others came to her with schemes that needed investment, all of them impossible, but she was not prepared for the abuse she received when she refused to invest. Only Zoe and Sandra never changed, but then Zoe was wealthy, too, and understood, and Sandra had been a friend too long to be anything but happy for her and was, in any case, incapable of malice.

The last straw came when Jane found herself in the ladies' in Eaden Lilley, stuffing the dress she had just bought in Vogue – the exclusive shop she loved – into a Marks and Spencer bag, just in case she met someone she knew on the way back home; anything to prevent the catty remarks that would be made about her choice of shop. 'This is crazy,' she thought. 'I can't live the rest of my life being ashamed, and doing potty things like this.' Sadly, the conclusion she reached was that she could not stay in Cambridge. Being rich had its penalties and other people's envy was the hardest. Since her lawyers had advised her that after a year she would have to become a tax exile, she decided to go now. To Italy. If she bumped into Roberto it was too bad, but at least in financial terms she could face him as an equal. And if she found she could not live so close to him, then she would sell Honor's villa and find somewhere else in the world to make her home.

She gave May the option of staying with Zoe, but May insisted on going with her and Giovanni.

'You need me more, now you're rich. At least I might stop you doing anything daft.'

To her surprise, Guido was still at the villa. He looked sheepish as he opened the door for them.

'But what about the smallholding that Lady Honor gave you the money to buy?' Jane asked him.

'Principessa, I couldn't leave this beautiful villa, it has been my home for too long,' he burst out desperately. 'Principessa, you will allow me to stay here with you, please?' His pleading decided her that there could be no sale of Honor's villa. If Roberto were to be awkward, she would just have to learn to live with the problem. In any case, Honor had been right: this was a special place to her. Already she felt relaxed and happier.

She meant to telephone Roberto as soon as she arrived but she delayed, admitting to herself that she was frightened, fearful of the effect the sound of his voice would have on her hard-won equilibrium. The summer slipped by in a haze of happy days with Giovanni by the pool. The villa was a quieter place without Honor's friends racketing in and out and with the phones rarely ringing.

Autumn came and still she had not phoned. But now, Christmas was only a few weeks away, and in fairness to their son, she must speak to him – they should, for the child's sake, celebrate it together. She telephoned the castle. The Prince, his major-domo told her, was still in Rome, too ill to come this year.

'Too ill? What's wrong with him? Is he in hospital?'

'No, Principessa, he is in his house in Rome.' A strange moaning noise issued from the telephone. 'Principessa! He is dying!'

Never had she packed so fast and never had Guido driven so rapidly. He drove direct to Rome, she did not have patience to wait for a train. She needed to be moving. When they arrived at the *palazzo*, Jane leaped from the car before it had even halted. The same old man opened the gate for her, his body still bent, but now with the added burden of grief. On seeing her, he looked as if he would cry, speaking in Italian too garbled and fast for her to understand. She raced up the sweeping marble staircase. The house oppressed her immediately. She opened the door of Roberto's suite of rooms and found her way barred by two nurses.

'No visitors allowed,' they said stiffly, in unison. The male nurse grabbed her arm and pushed her back through the doorway.

'Get out of my way. I am the Principessa Villizano, I demand to see my husband.' It was the first time she had ever called herself that and she must have said it with authority, for the nurses stood respectfully aside to let her pass. She crossed the anteroom and gently opened the door into his bedroom. Tiptoeing towards the ornately canopied bed, she stopped, transfixed with horror at what she saw. A frail old man slept there, his thinness accentuated by the large, opulent bed. His body was not fine and muscular like Roberto's but wasted, the skin stretched taut across the bones. Roberto was always tanned but this man's skin was putty-coloured, with a sickly, yellow tinge. Roberto was dark-haired, not grey like this man. There must have been a hideous mistake, someone was playing cruel tricks on her. Then the figure on the bed opened his eyes, the fine, dark-brown eyes focused on her, and she put her hand to her mouth to stifle the gasp. Only the eyes were those of the Roberto she knew.

'Ah, my Contessa.' He took her hand and with difficulty lifted it to his mouth. 'You came.' The words were a sigh on his lips.

'Roberto, my darling, what has happened to you? What is wrong with you? How long have you been like this?' The urgent questions tumbled out of her.

'Forgive me, my dear, I know, I look terrible, not the Roberto you remember. It is difficult to realize that it is me, isn't it?' He tried to smile.

'Why on earth didn't you send for me?'

'How could I? What right had I?'

'You should have sent for the woman you knew loved you.'

'Do you still love me, Contessa?'

'I never stopped loving you, my darling.'

'You never took another lover?'

'No, my darling.'

'Then it is an even greater tragedy.' He sighed.

'But what on earth is wrong with you?'

'I have a form of leukaemia. It has been mercifully quick. I feel no pain, but I am very tired.'

'America! We must go to America, immediately. They are so much more advanced there,' she said in desperation.

'No, my sweet. It's no use. It is my time to die.'

'You mustn't talk like that. I won't hear it! You will live, I will make you live.'

'As I made you love me? Remember how you said it was impossible?' He laughed, but the effort was too much for him. He closed his eyes and she held him to her, terrified that the shock of seeing her had weakened him and that he would die now, just as she had found him again.

'We've been such fools, Roberto, such bloody stupid proud fools,' she said as he opened his eyes and smiled. She took his hand and covered it with frantic kisses.

'It's so easy to be proud and foolish when you think you have years of life ahead of you. But you're here now. You'll stay? You will stay with me to the end?'

'Darling, of course I'm staying. For all the years we have left, I'll be with you. You're not getting rid of me this time.' She tried to joke. He sighed contentedly and she sat and held his hand and watched him as he slid back into a deep sleep.

While he slept she summoned his doctors. They assured her that there was nothing further to be done. There was no point in taking him to America; they themselves had arranged for the world's experts, including the Americans, to see the Prince. They felt that her coming was the best thing for him, for he had spoken often of her.

'But this house. I hate this place. It's so gloomy. Could we not take him to the castle? He loves that best of all: I'm sure he'd get better there.'

'I very much doubt if he would survive the journey, Principessa.'

'We could fly him.'

'Not even a short flight.'

'How long then?' The dreaded question hung in the air between her and the sober-suited doctors.

'A month, Principessa, at the most.'

She turned away from them. It was impossible, a month. She could not, and she would not, believe it.

There was already the gloom of death about the house. The servants shuffled silently about, their faces long and mournful. The windows were shuttered, and the large rambling palazzo was a place of shadows and despair.

Before Roberto awoke, she had ordered the shutters to be opened. Roberto had loved the sun, had followed it all his life; if he were to die, it was intolerable that he should die in this half-gloom. Even the weak December sun which filtered through was better for him than that. She ordered boxes of flowers to be delivered immediately. And she told the servants that, on pain of dismissal, they were to smile and be cheerful in front of the Prince – they could keep their mournful looks to themselves. Once he was awake, she had all the medical paraphernalia removed to the anteroom; his bedside table was cleared of medicines and bottles, and flowers took their place. She had the large stereo set up in his room, so that throughout the day and at night when he could not sleep he could have beautiful music filling his room. The first record she placed on the turntable was the Mahler he had played her years ago.

'Already, it is better.' He smiled at her. 'It becomes a home and not a charnel house.'

In her room she found nothing altered. The wardrobes were still full of her clothes, the dressing table contained her make-up and perfumes. Each day she would change her clothes several times, even though they were now very out of date. She would groom herself with the special care that he had once demanded. He remembered each outfit, where they had bought it, where they had had lunch that day, whom they had met, and where they had gone that evening.

Each night she would prepare herself for bed with elaborate care as if going to a lover and each night she would lie beside him and hold him, talk to him when he could not sleep, snatching sleep herself whenever he drifted off, but waking the minute he stirred. Only his eyes could express the longing that he still felt for her.

His spirits improved as she fought for him, like a tigress. The dreaded month passed and he was still with her. The doctors had been wrong.

Christmas came and, against the doctors' advice, she sent for Giovanni and May. The doctors feared that the child would weaken and tire him. Instead, the presence of his son and the child's happiness strengthened him. They decorated the tree; Roberto was carried downstairs and sat in his favourite chair, issuing instructions on where the coloured lights should be, teasing her, bantering with her, and smiling now, always smiling.

This house had become her world, his room the centre of that world. She never went out, was never far from his side. She began to plan; they would talk of Giovanni and what they both wanted for him. In the New Year they started him in kindergarten, and in the evenings, the child would sit on his father's bed and together they would look at his books and what he had done that day. She began to plan for them, where they would go this summer, whom they would see. He would smile at her and agree and she would try not to see the sad resignation in his eyes.

Now it was spring. There were days when the sun was warm enough for them to wheel Roberto into the garden, and he would sit, his face turned to the sun he loved so much. But there were days he could not be moved. Her indomitable spirit and her devotion impressed everyone. She would not speak of death, she would not accept it. As spring turned into summer she began to believe that she had won. A month, they had said, and that had been seven months ago.

He was sleeping peacefully. She sat beside the bed, holding his hand, gazing with love at the face which, even with this terrible illness, still had a nobility to it. He awoke and his dark eyes smiled at her.

'Promise not to live in the past, little one,' he whispered. 'Don't waste any more of your life. We've wasted too much already. You promise? You must live. You promise, my Contessa?' he asked with a strange urgency. They were the last words he was to speak to her. He fell asleep but this time did not wake up. He slipped silently and imperceptibly away from her into a deep coma. He lay suspended in that sleep before death for three long days. Days when Jane could not accept what was happening, a time when she never slept but talked to him, softly, willing him back to her. She knew he heard, for sometimes he smiled. Jane was certain that, since he could hear her pleading, he would fight, he would return to her. But, on the fourth day, he died in her arms. She held him a long time after he was dead, loath to let him go, loath to give his body to the waiting nurses. Eventually, ignoring her cries of anger, they forced her to give him to them.

It was a sad return to the castle. As the train bearing Roberto home drove into the station, it appeared that the whole village of Villizano was waiting. First they went to the church for a solemn requiem mass. Then the coffin was placed in the gleaming, black and silver hearse, pulled by six fine, black horses, black plumes dancing on their heads, their feet muffled as they pulled the precious load up to the castle, along the road lined with silent, weeping people. Roberto was laid to rest in the white marble mausoleum of his ancestors. Through it all, Jane, with Giovanni at her side, felt as if she too were dead: she seemed to feel nothing. She wondered why she did not cry, loving him as she did. All around her people wept, but Jane stood stoically, her face a rigid mask.

His family closed ranks around her, shielding her from the curious. For the first time she felt part of his Italian family. Francesca took Giovanni and drove off with him to play with her son. Supported by Emilio, Jane steeled herself to enter the castle. In the large, formal salon, the windows, the mirrors, the paintings were all draped in the same fine, black material which billowed in the gentle breeze like the sails of ships in mourning. Only large arum lilies, their sickly-sweet smell filling the air, decorated the room. Groups of people stood in whispering, huddled groups, dressed from head to toe in black. There was no question of this gathering becoming the light-hearted party that Honor's wake had been. Here the ceremony was so awesome that it shrivelled the soul.

Emilio led her by the arm to the centre of the room. In a large chair sat an old woman, wizened with age and the only person seated.

'You must meet my aunt, Jane, Princess Renata Villizano, Roberto's mother.' Nervously Jane approached the black-clad figure whose face was entirely covered in a heavy veil. Emilio spoke quickly to his aunt. With a surprisingly agile flick of her wrist she swept the veil back. Beautiful dark eyes shone brilliantly in a face wrinkled and yellowed by age. They were so like the eyes of her son that Jane suppressed the cry that welled up within her. The eyes studied her closely.

'This is a sad day, daughter,' the old woman said in a strong voice and in impeccable English.

'Sadder than I have words for, Principessa,' Jane replied softly.

'I am more fortunate than you, I shall see him sooner,' the old woman announced with no embarrassment, and Jane envied her such faith. 'But we have his son, and for him I thank you, Jane.' Jane bowed her head. 'I gather my son had told you of his wish that Giovanni be brought up as an Italian?'

'Yes, Principessa, please do not fear. I shall fulfil Roberto's wishes.'

The old woman fell back against the cushions of the chair. Her eyes suddenly dulled as if a light in them had been extinguished. 'Thank God,' she sighed in a quiet, tired voice. She waved wearily to a manservant who came and with ease lifted the old woman into his arms and carried her away. She had achieved what she had come to do.

Somehow, Jane saw the other guests away and was finally left with Emilio, James, who had flown out to be with her, and yet another army of lawyers. There was no need to worry that Giovanni's estates would not be well managed: it was clear that they would go on just as before. But she decided to shut up the houses until he was old enough to take charge of them. She loved this castle but, without Roberto here, it was too painful for her to remain.

Now, with everyone gone and the lawyers dispatched, James suggested they explore the castle, which he had never seen before.

'Darling, I don't think I could. It's too painful for me yet. I'll wait here for you. Maybe Emilio would be kind enough to show you?' The two men left her, and she opened the door to what had been their private sitting room. She wanted to be alone. Perhaps here, where they had spent so many happy hours, the tears that were inside her like a painful tumour would be set free. She had known him seven years, but she had only lived with him for three years and seven months. Encapsulated in that short time were all the memories she had of him. She heard a scratching noise. When she opened the door, a golden retriever entered. It crossed the room and sat gazing at Roberto's chair, and whined. She knelt down and stroked the dog.

'Hullo, old boy, who are you? Did you love him too?' She comforted the whining dog, but still she could not cry.

'Ma! Ma! Come quick,' James called. Nervously she ran to him. He was standing on the steps to the picture gallery. 'You never told us about this. It's sensational,' he said, walking quickly ahead of her to the wing where the portraits hung. 'Look!'

Jane cried out with disbelief. Beside Roberto's portrait was a full-length one of herself. She was dressed in the emerald-green silk dress she had worn when she had first met him, Honor's emeralds about her throat. It was an astonishing likeness.

'You never told me you'd had such a beautiful picture done?'

'I couldn't tell you, I didn't know.'

'But . . .?'

'Roberto arranged it,' Emilio explained. 'He called in several artists. The place was full of giant photographs of you, Jane. Honor lent him the jewels and I gather the dress was already here. He must have had a dozen paintings done before he was satisfied with this one.'

'It was what I was wearing the night we first met.' Jane's voice faltered.

'He loved you very much, Jane.'

'I know, Emilio, as I loved him. We were fools, I most of all. But Emilio, why didn't you tell me he was so ill? Why didn't you send for me sooner?' It was a question that had haunted her ever since she had seen Roberto. Why had no one, not even May, told her?

'He forbade us, Jane. All of us. He said he didn't want you to come back out of pity . . .'

'Oh God,' she sighed, turning away from her portrait, not daring to glance at the one of Roberto hanging by its side. 'I must get out of here,' she said hurriedly.

As they were getting into the car, the major-domo gave her a heavy wooden box which the Prince had instructed him to give to her after his death. The dog still twined itself around her legs.

'Was this the Prince's dog?'

'Yes, Principessa. He has not seen the Prince for a year and he pined dreadfully. And today, it is quite extraordinary, but today, I know he knew he had come home and he has been inconsolable.'

'What's he called?'

'Harry, Principessa.'

'Harry! What a weird name for a dog,' James exclaimed.

'I think it's a fine name. Prince Hal. Shall we take Roberto's dog with us?'

They loaded the box and the dog into the car.

'Jane, do you think it would be better if Francesca and I kept Giovanni for a few days more?'

'Would you, Emilio? It would be kind of you. I don't think I could be a good mother at the moment.' Emilio kissed her hand. Jane eased the car out of the courtyard and down the mountain to the villa.

Late that night, alone in her room, the dog already settled for the night on her bed, she gingerly opened the box. Inside lay all the jewellery he had given her. And beneath, wrapped in tissue paper, was a cine film, with a note attached. She had hoped that there would be a letter, like the one Honor had written her; instead there were only a few words: 'Forgive me, Contessa, I lied, I could never destroy your beauty!'

'Roberto!' Her longing and agony for him sounded in the cry. The dog raised its head and nuzzled her. She sank her head into his soft fur and she began to cry.

Six
1977

1

Jane seemed to live in a world full of the swirling fogs of grief. Daily she grieved for Honor and Roberto. At first she could not go out, nor did she want to see anybody. She knew that this was wrong, that she should be attempting to build a new life. But as she began to fight back from her despair, it was as if she were suffocating in a giant sponge of cloying loss that would not let go of her.

James stayed in the villa with her for a few weeks after the funeral, but when he announced he must return to England she felt only relief that she was to be left alone. Giovanni returned from his cousins'. She looked forward to the child's return, certain that with him to consider she would soon recover. Instead, she found his demands irritating, and the child increased her irritation by making her feel guilty that she should feel this way. When Giovanni, fractious with boredom, demanded to return to the happy home of his cousins, she quickly, too quickly, she knew, made the necessary arrangements.

'You can't go on like this, Jane. It's ridiculous,' May admonished her as the car, taking her young son away, disappeared round the curve of the drive.

'May, don't nag me. He's better off at Emilio's. There are kids to play with, there's more for him to do.'

'He needs his mother now that his father's gone, poor little mite.'

'I know what I'm doing. I need this time alone.'

'Self-indulgent, that's what it is.'

'May! You can be so hard. I have to grieve, and in my way.'

'It's Giovanni I worry about. When he was here you hardly noticed him. Poor kid, he must wonder what's going on, when you virtually smothered him with love before.'

'Christ, May, I've just lost my husband! Don't you see it'll take me time?'

'It's not as if he was a proper husband. You hadn't lived with him for years.' May stood, arms akimbo, looking sternly at Jane.

'Don't you ever say that to me again, May!' Jane swung round angrily to face her friend. 'I never stopped loving him, as you bloody well know. He was my husband here . . .' Dramatically she thumped her breast.

'I shouldn't have said that, Jane, I'm sorry. Of course you never stopped loving him, but life must go on. I don't want you getting ill like you did over his lordship.'

'I won't do that, I promise. I just need time. I know I'll never be the same again, but eventually I might find a different way of living.'

She knew May was telling her the truth in her usual down-to-earth manner. She knew she was doing wrong. She just did not seem to have the will or energy to do anything about it.

Christmas came and Giovanni returned. They bought a tree and decorated it. They shopped for presents and Jane carefully wrapped them. Guido dressed up as Father Christmas. They had turkey, wore funny hats from the crackers and Guido and May played blind man's buff and hide-and-seek with the child, while Jane sat curled up in a chair, a gin and tonic in her hand, and watched them, unsmiling.

Giovanni went back to his cousins. Jane was left wandering aimlessly about the beautiful white villa, fully aware that the ghost of Honor would be appalled by her.

'You'll end up losing him just like you lost James if you're not careful. You're a fool, Jane. You need that boy. Don't push him away like this,' May pleaded.

'I know what I'm doing. Give me a year.'

'What then? I bet you'll be whining, "Give me another year"! You're drinking too much, too.' May frowned at the glass in Jane's hand. 'Oh, and by the way, Guido and I have decided to get married.'

'You've what?' Jane's glass clattered onto the marble table. 'That's wonderful news. I had no idea.'

'Of course you hadn't, you've been so wrapped up in yourself you wouldn't have noticed if we'd developed bubonic plague.'

'May, I'm sorry. Am I that dreadful?'

'Yes. Not enough to do, that's your trouble. If you'd been left with kids to support instead of all this money, you'd have had to pull yourself together.'

As always, May was right. Having money should have made deciding what to do easier, instead it made it harder.

The wedding of May and Guido in February seemed the only happy occasion for a long time. It was also the event that finally forced Jane into action. She decided to take a holiday and leave the couple alone for a few months.

But where to go? With no set plans she motored slowly up through Europe, stopping where the mood took her, sometimes for a day, sometimes for a week, visiting the cathedrals, castles and museums without the summer crowds about her. She seemed to have been unhappy for so long that it was several weeks before she realized that she was enjoying herself.

Finding herself on the coast of France, on a whim, she took the ferry for England. As the boat churned across the channel she sat in the bar and wondered where to go next. It was then she decided to go to Scotland and find the house that Honor had urged her to buy. It was an obligation, and one that must be fulfilled.

She took the motor rail to Edinburgh, visited estate agents and then drove, zigzagging across the country, searching for perfection. She saw many estates; they were all beautiful but none of them seemed just right. The exasperated estate agents began to despair of her. She tried to explain that she would know the minute she saw it, that an inner voice would tell her she had found it, and they, behind her back, decided she was demented.

She went further and further north in her search. As she drove over Drumochter Pass, despite the bright sunshine, there was still a scattering of snow on the tops of the mountains which made them look like giant Dalmatian puppies huddled in sleep. A strange elation filled her and she was certain she was near the end of her search.

Jane had not realized that buying a house could be like falling in love, but she learned. As she drove around the corner of a sadly neglected drive, the house loomed in front of her in the bright Highland light, and she fell in love. It could have been riddled with dry rot and deathwatch beetle, but she did not care – she had to have it.

The house was white, tall and proud; two large towers with fine pepperpot roofs stood at either end, like sentinels. The windows were large, the door wide and welcoming. The house stood protected against the winds by old beech trees and the views to the moorland were breathtaking. It looked as if it had been transported by magic from some valley in the Dordogne: it was far more like a small French château than her idea of a Scottish castle. As she drove towards it, she knew the search was over.

She waited impatiently for the lawyers to complete the sale. While they worked, she stayed in the local hotel. There was an elation in her now, long missing, a new excitement. In a strange way she felt she had come home. If this was to be a new start, she must slough off the past. She decided to revert to her maiden name, and determined that no one here should know her as anything else.

She ferried herself about searching for furniture and pictures, arranging for builders and workmen to be ready to start the day the house was hers. She had the furniture from Honor's London flat, which had been in store, sent up. She wrote excited letters home to May in Italy, to tell her of her find, and was unaware that the letters relieved May of a lot of worry. Jane, she felt, was going to be all right.

At last she had possession. And the work began. Eager for it to be finished she donned dungarees, wrapped her hair in a scarf and made herself the decorators' mate, much to the workmen's surprise. It was not at all how they expected rich Sassenachs to behave, but they respected her for it. And each night she went to bed exhausted and happy. She found a gamekeeper willing to work her land with the strange instructions that nothing should be killed, unless it was necessary, or for his pot. He would laugh about her to his mates, but the more he thought about it, the more he liked the idea. She found a couple willing to move in and look after her while she was there, who would care for the house when she had to return to Italy. She loved their soft Highland accent, and recognized in Margaret, with her kind face and deceptively gentle manner, the same steely personality as May, which would put up with no nonsense and would tell her what was what in no uncertain terms. Only the accent was different.

Her birthday came. Alone, she faced the fact that she was forty. The years had slipped by with an unfair rapidity, she thought, and laughed at herself, knowing full well that this was what everyone reaching that ominous milestone must think. She looked at herself critically in the mirror. She looked good, she told her reflection. A few lines now, but as she turned her face from one side to the other, she decided they added to rather than detracted from her face. She had no grey hair yet, and her figure looked as firm as ever. The gloss that Roberto had given her still remained. Even in jeans and headscarf there was an elegance to her.

Scotland healed her. As she walked across her gun-free land, she could enjoy the peace and tranquillity of the place, the lack of urgency that pervaded it. The vastness of the scenery helped her to put a sense of perspective into her life. She would stand on the top of a hill and admire a view unchanged for a million years and it made her, Jane Reed, seem very unimportant.

One day a large trunk arrived. Hearing of her new home, Alistair had forwarded the things she had left at Respryn when she had left in such a hurry. It was an odd feeling to open this casket from the past. It held little things she had collected over the years – photographs, letters. She spent a happily morbid afternoon rereading Alistair's love letters to her, their attempts at poetry. She found the book she had bought with the list of words that it was OK to use, and she laughed at the memory of the poor, insecure creature she must once have been. With due ceremony she put it on the fire and let the flames destroy her old self once and for all.

Her accountants pestered her daily to return to Italy before the Inland Revenue ruined her. Reluctantly she began to pack. She did not want to leave this new home, which had assumed so great an importance in her life in such a short time. Was it because it was the only house that had really been hers? All her life she had lived in other people's houses, never one that she had created. And because she had never lived here with a man, it was devoid of painful memories. She hated to leave but she wanted to see Giovanni, needed to see him. She had been right and May wrong, she had needed time away from him to resolve their future together.

She knew now without a doubt what she had to do. She realized that she had distanced herself from him almost as if in some strange way she had been preparing herself for the decisions she was finally to make. As, in the end, it had been better for James, with his heritage, to stay with his father, so she resolved it was best for Giovanni to spend a large part of the year with his Italian family. She could not teach him to be Italian, she could not help him learn how to be a great landowner. If he stayed with her, in a few years he would go to prep school: she could not let him go through that, not years of being despised by the English for his noble Italian blood. She would ask Emilio and Francesca to keep him with their ever increasing family, to grow up as an Italian. She would have him for the holidays and would visit him much more than she had visited James. There would be people who would say she did not love her child, had cast him aside, but they would be wrong. This was the right decision for Roberto's son.

As she sat in the dining car of the train taking her to England, she was suddenly aware of a woman behind her reading a story to her children. How strange, she thought, she knew the words, knew what was coming next. With a start she remembered – it was the book about Jane Squirrel which her father had given her so long ago and which she still cherished, for he had inscribed it 'with love'. It pleased her to think that the book was still read and loved.

She took the long car ferry from Southampton to Le Havre. With Roberto she had never really enjoyed hurtling from one country and one culture to another. She enjoyed the hours on the ferry which gave her time to adjust from Britain to the Continent. She sat in the bar, by the window, watching the grey waters of the Channel slip by.

'May I have the pleasure of buying you a drink?' a heavily accented voice asked her. She looked up to see a young man smiling at her. Dark-haired and dark-eyed, his face had the intelligent intensity peculiar to Frenchmen. His clothes were expensively well cut, his body lithe and slim. She paused imperceptibly before accepting, with an equally warm smile. His English was bad, and she was surprised to find how much French she managed to dredge up from her memory. As drink followed drink, her French became more fluent. He told her he was from Paris, his name was Jacques, he was thirty-two and worked in banking. He asked her where she was travelling to and when she said Italy, he smiled broadly.

'How wonderful! I am going to Rome.'

'Are you driving?'

'No.' He patted his pocket. 'Train.'

'Do you drive?'

'But of course.'

'If you wouldn't mind sharing the driving, I can give you a lift to Florence, if you like.'

'That would be marvellous.'

'Are you in a hurry?'

'No, no, I have all the time in the world.'

The boat docked at Le Havre and together they made their way to the car deck. She was amused by the startled expression on his face as she unlocked the door of the Rolls-Royce.

'I had no idea,' he said, almost as if in apology.

'It's very easy to drive.'

Since speed was unimportant, they decided to avoid the motorways and to meander down through France on the secondary roads, doing some sightseeing, stopping when the fancy took them.

'Do you know the Relais Château hotels?' she asked him. 'They're wonderful.'

'Of course,' he replied, but for the first time she heard uncertainty in his voice.

'I would like to stay in them. I shall insist on paying.'

'But, Madame, I could not hear of such a thing.'

'In return for your helping with the driving, of course.'

'Ah, well, in return for the driving, *d'accord.*'

It was pleasant driving through the beautiful French countryside with a companion. He was knowledgeable about his country's history and architecture. He was funny, too, and made her laugh. Using the joke that he was her chauffeur, she was able to pay for their meals and hotels with no embarrassment to either of them.

On the third night, as she settled down to sleep, he crept stealthily into her room and climbed wordlessly into her bed. For a second she thought she must ask him to leave, but as his arms went around her and she felt the comforting sensation of his bare flesh against hers, she wondered whom it could hurt now. No one. It would be nice to know a man again, to feel him in her, and so she turned to him and the pleasure of his soft mouth on her body.

He was not going to Rome. There was no job in banking, and with disarming honesty he told her he had not even the money for a train ticket. She liked his honesty, enjoyed his company. She was happy with his lovemaking, which was skilled and expert, and unselfish. It did not drive her to the heights of ecstasy that she had experienced with Roberto, but she knew that physical perfection like theirs happened only once in a lifetime, if that. So in some strange way she felt she was not being unfaithful to Roberto's memory. She decided to take him back to the villa with her.

On their arrival, May could hardly wait to get Jane alone. She was beside herself with anger.

'He's young enough to be your son!'

'Hardly,' Jane insisted. 'He's over thirty.'

'Is that what he told you? Twenty-five, more like.' She sniffed audibly.

'May, don't sniff like that, you remind me of my mother.' Jane laughed but May did not join in.

'What happened to all that famous grief, then? Barely a year since the Prince died. It's disgusting, Jane, that's what it is.'

'I thought you were the one who told me to pull myself together,' Jane replied smartly.

'So I did, but not this way. You're making a fool of yourself.'

'May, it's my life and I would appreciate your not speaking to me like that. I do employ you, after all, or have you forgotten?' Jane flashed angrily.

'No, I haven't forgotten and you'd better give me the sack now if you expect me to do anything for him, 'cause I won't serve someone like that.'

'May, dear God, what are we doing? I don't want to fall out with you.'

'I've always spoken my mind, you can't expect me to stop now,' May replied, tears glinting in her proud eyes.

'I know it must be a shock to you, but May, he makes me forget, he gives me a sort of happiness. I still grieve for Roberto, I will for the rest of my life. This is something different, Roberto would understand.'

'He wouldn't, he'd have had a fit. You with a gigolo!'

'If it was good enough for Honor then it's good enough for me.'

'You don't think that woman was happy, do you, the way she carried on?'

'No, not really happy. I shall be surprised if that ever comes again, but this is a good second-best. He's a nice enough young man.'

'You've got into a panic, haven't you, just 'cause you're forty?'

'May, don't talk so daft. Being forty has nothing to do with it.'

'Well, the only solution I can see if he stays is that you get someone else to look after him, 'cause I'm not and that's flat.'

'May!' Jane exclaimed.

'You can "May!" me all you like. I'm not waiting on the likes of him.'

'You are being stuffy, May. Who can it possibly hurt?'

'*You*, you fool!' and May slammed out of the room.

Exasperated, Jane phoned the agency for a new servant. When the woman arrived, May calmed down, but she kept her promise and would do nothing for Jacques. But for once May was wrong, it did not seem to hurt Jane. The lovemaking was pleasant enough but it was his company she enjoyed most. It was good to have someone with whom to go shopping and sightseeing, someone to talk to as she ate her dinner, instead of those interminable, lonely meals.

The summer slipped by. She did not know what made her change her mind. Perhaps the blue-rinsed American matron they had seen last week, with a young man fawning over her. Or was it the way she had noticed Jacques look at young girls in bikinis? Or was it, finally, her honesty which had made her see the way she was going, realize that perhaps May had been half right about Jane's reaction to that fortieth birthday? Whatever the reason, she decided suddenly that he had to go.

As she watched Jacques pack his bags, she felt no remorse, no pleasure. If she felt anything at all, it was a mild irritation that he was taking so long.

'I don't understand, Jane. Why do I have to go?' He kicked the door of the wardrobe shut as he removed the last of his clothes. She heard the question but she did not reply for she did not know the answer.

'What has made you change so suddenly?' he asked as he bundled his clothes into the last open case. That was very unlike him, she thought; he was usually such a tidy person, almost obsessively neat with his clothes.

'You shouldn't pack your things like that, they'll get all creased,' she commented helpfully.

'What do I care about that?' He turned to face her, holding out his hands. 'Jane, please, for God's sake, tell me, what have I done wrong?' She heard the note of pleading in his voice and she shut her ears to the tone, not wishing to hear it, not wanting to start feeling sorry for him. She regretted now that she had not left him to his packing. She did not even feel guilty for her lack of feeling. She just wanted to get the whole scene over and to be on her own.

She could understand his bewilderment, it had been a very sudden decision on her part. Her lack of explanation must be perplexing for him, but, in truth, she felt as confused as he. His normally handsome face was now set in sad lines. He usually looked so happy. She hated to see him look like this, and for what? Was it worth it? Would she miss him? How would she manage being alone again?

His heavy gold bracelet caught on the webbing of his case, and he swore softly. She hated that bracelet, and the gold medallion he always wore around his neck. She hated them, not because he had been given them by her American predecessor, but because, like badges of office, they proclaimed what he was and so what she had become. She shuddered. Vigorously she shook her head to dispel the indecisions worming into her brain. He had to go.

She smiled at him, fondly, she hoped.

'You've done nothing wrong, Jacques. It's me, I want to be by myself, that's all.' She searched in her handbag and took out an envelope stuffed with dollar bills. 'Here, take this.' She handed him the money. He made no attempt to refuse.

At last he had loaded the car. She had forgotten about the car. She had given it to him on his birthday and maybe, in view of it, she had been too generous with the money in the envelope. Did it matter? It was too late now, she could hardly ask him to give her some of it back.

'You're a strange woman, Jane,' he said as he climbed into his car. 'Look, here's an address where you can find me when you change your mind.' He gave her a card and attempted a smile.

'I won't change my mind, Jacques. I'll just remember what a wonderful summer we had.'

She did not know what had made her say that. It had been pleasant enough, but not wonderful, not like some of the summers she had known. In contrast this had been a sad substitute.

She gave a small wave as he drove off, its brevity calculated. He might have misinterpreted a more energetic goodbye, especially after her remark about the summer.

She stood and listened until she could no longer hear his car and then walked back into the empty villa. In the white marble hallway, she paused – it felt odd. The house was not used to silence either. It stood in its white, luxuriant splendour as if listening for the noises to return. She lingered for a moment, accustoming herself to this unusual quiet, allowing it to wrap around her. She crossed into the long, white drawing room, poured herself a large gin and tonic and went out on the terrace. The sun was beginning to set in the hurried way it always does in the Mediterranean, the sky ablaze with improbable colour. Only in Britain did the sun seem to set gently and with dignity. She felt an overwhelming longing to be home again, to be sitting in the soft, balmy cool of a Scottish evening, not here in this searing, baked heat. What on earth was she doing here, anyway? She should never have allowed herself to be persuaded to live abroad, always to be a stranger. She had already found her place to live, the place where she was most at peace with herself. She was homesick. Not just for the house but for the contentment she had begun to feel there. She had listened to accountants and lawyers, people concerned only with her balance sheets, and she had let them persuade her to leave the security of her home and to come to this foreign land in order to save, in taxes, money that she did not need.

She sipped her drink and watched as the lights came on in the bay far below her. Across the terrace Harry, Roberto's dog, padded towards her. He sat at her feet and regarded her with an expression of devotion. Idly she patted his head. How lovely to be a dog, she thought, everyone accepted that a dog just wanted to be loved. God, she was getting so full of self-pity these days . . .

She had to find something to do, May was right, she was too rich, too idle. She did not know what that something would turn out to be, but she was sure that some day she would know.

Seven
1977–85

1

For nearly three years she had lived in Scotland. Her business affairs meant that she had to make trips to London and New York, but she made them as short as possible and then quickly returned to her haven in the northern Highlands, so quickly that she would sometimes liken herself to a furry animal scuttling back to its lair.

She had not returned to Italy but allowed friends to use her villa whenever they wanted, for she was happier and felt safer where she was. The villa had too many memories that still haunted her. But she had not been short of company. Giovanni came four or five times a year, often with his cousins. Various combinations of Sandra's large family visited, all married now, with children of their own. And Sandra herself, sometimes with her family, often on her own. In summer there was an endless tide of James's university friends and when the other lodges opened, the young from them visited in droves, so that it seemed her son was embroiled in one endless party. And there was the memorable and drunken week when Zoe had finally abandoned her kitchen and caught the shuttle, complaining bitterly at the size of the seats. Her parents came once, but moaned constantly about the weather and the isolation, and cut short their visit to return to their suburban comfort.

But something had happened to Jane. While she would look forward, eagerly, to these visitors, within a couple of days she resented their presence, with the exception of her sons, found the duties of being a hostess irksome and longed to be alone again. She never once saw anyone off on the plane or train with regret.

She saw little of Alistair. When she was in London, she rarely saw him, for he had given up most of the directorships and committees that had kept them apart when they were married, and preferred these days to spend most of his time at Respryn. He had invited her to Drumloch several times but she had refused. The Highlands had become an oasis of calm and peace for her, and she knew the guns at Drumloch would distress her more than ever. He was always too busy to come and stay with her and in a way she was relieved, for she did not want to find that she would want him, like the others, gone in a couple of days. But still, it seemed a shame that they had drifted apart, especially now when she was certain that she could see him and not want him, for since Jacques she had not felt the need to bother with another man.

She would have been hard pressed to explain how she filled her days, but she did. She spent hours walking her dogs, now six in number, and just watching the light on the hills, enjoying the colours, the changing seasons and the birds and animals.

But the longer she stayed, the more she realized that living in Scotland was full of paradoxes. She learned that she could love and hate this strange, wild country at the same time. Always, Scotland had two faces, like a beautiful and deceitful woman. A lush and lovely day with the air gin-clear could turn within the hour to a nightmare of mist or blizzard. A stretch of green that invited her to walk on it would become a slimy, stinking bog. The placid sea, with the rocks sitting in the sparkling water as if scattered by God in a playful mood, could, the next day, turn into a writhing maelstrom and, whipping up a shrieking wind to cover their screams, dash a boatload of strong men onto the jagged rocks.

This duplicity seemed reflected in the people: honest as the day is long and yet capable of cunning trickery; kind and thoughtful or mean and cruel in their thoughtlessness; funny to the point of hysteria or dour to a soul-numbing dullness; proud with the pride of centuries and tribal laws and loyalties, or craven with a shame of their heritage. Men who could one day risk their lives to save a man and yet the next damn him to isolation with their malicious, meaningless gossip.

Jane learned that even as the sun beat down on them, the long preparations for their cruel winter began. Winter here was an old enemy to be faced and beaten by careful planning. And so, while the holidaymakers enjoyed the quaint, idyllic scene, the Highlander cut his peats and stacked and dried them in neat piles beside each door. The fish and meat were hung and smoked, the eggs were pickled, the potatoes stored, the wood cut. The cracks in the house were mended, the shutters secured. Winter here stormed in, a heartless enemy.

She sensed a wariness towards her in the locals which only time would allay. She realized that because she was English she would never be fully accepted but she wanted to live here and was willing to settle for second-best. She could understand the hatred for her race engendered by years of oppression and abuse. She could see that in each generation it was blue-printed in their very cells, so that even if they knew no history, even if they could not read, the hate was second nature. So she would hear such comments as 'He's nae so bad for an Englishman!' and know that this was the nearest to a compliment their heritage would allow.

She distrusted the 'gentry'. Such an antiquated term to describe them; one long dead in England, but used daily here. Listening to the tone of the Highlanders' voices as they said it, she was aware it was not a term of respect. The 'gentry' were divided into two groups, those who stayed the year long, most of whom strutted around like feudal kings, and those who came for the shooting and scuttled back to the delights of the south as winter came. Of the two, it was the latter the locals most disliked. The absentee landlords were an emotive and a political issue. But when they came up for the fishing and shooting they seemed blithely unaware of the resentment they caused with their big, fast cars on the narrow roads, destroying the peace for the weeks they were here. It was a shock to Jane when she became aware that Rupert, greatly respected though he was, had been one of these. And Alistair – he was still one of the absentee landlords, she thought wryly. Most of all, she saw, the Highlander's loathing was reserved for the young of the house parties who descended on the local bars and, with their loud, braying voices and their arrogant manners, fertilized annually the hatred for the English lurking in the Highlander's soul. But the Highlander needed them and the money they brought and, canny to the last, would touch his forelock, oblige, perform and, in the safety of his croft, would laugh at and hate them.

On her arrival, there had been a flurry of invitations for Jane; her coming had sent a wave of titillating curiosity through the local 'gentry'. But once they had met her and, like dogs sniffing out each other's pedigrees, had found she was not one of them, the invitations ceased. She did not mind. She had not come here to try, after all this time, to be accepted. And, in any case, as she saw endless replicas of Lady Upnor, she was relieved to be left alone. Nothing was ever going to change. But she had changed, for it no longer mattered to her: she could watch them and not want to be part of their society. It puzzled her now why she had ever wanted it.

Since throughout her adult life she had not felt she belonged anywhere, there was a comfort in knowing that here in the north of Scotland the rejection was historical, not personal.

2

Jane sat at the dinner table of the Impingtons, the only local couple she visited regularly. She liked Liz Impington who, being American, sailed unbothered through the sea of class divisions, inviting to her table anyone she liked and who amused her. But tonight, surrounded as she was by owners of great estates, Jane should have known better . . .

'But what about the ordinary people?' Her question hung in the air of one of those pools of silence that occur at a dinner party, waiting for the ill-timed remark to drop noisily into its waters.

'There's more at stake here than people,' thundered the red-faced and heavily chinned man opposite her.

'What can be more important than people?'

'Our heritage, Mrs Reed. Our heritage, our land. We're only custodians of all of this, you know.' His chubby, lily-white hands swept vaguely through the air. 'We don't own it, we care for it for future generations.' Noisily he took a sip of his wine and sat back, pleased with his sentiments. Jane looked around the assembled company at the well-fed, well-wined faces as they, sanctimoniously and in unison, nodded agreement – like a row of well-controlled puppets, Jane thought. 'The land is sacred,' the noisy, hectoring voice persisted. 'The beasts, the fowl, the flora must be protected. Allow this development to take place here and what have you got? Before you know it, Mrs Reed, another part of our heritage ruined for all times.'

'I agree with you that our heritage should be guarded wherever possible, but people's needs must still come first. I mean, the level of unemployment here is dreadful.'

'You don't for one moment think this development will create jobs locally, Mrs Reed? They will utilize the local work force to do the labouring, and when that's done, they'll be laid off, as poor as ever, but discontented that the big wage packets are over, and with another part of their heritage lost for ever.'

'Then, this time, extract guarantees for permanent employment for the community,' Jane answered reasonably.

'You are singularly naive, Mrs Reed, if you think that there is a remote possibility that such guarantees would be forthcoming. And, if they were, employ them as what? Navvying is all they're fit for –'

'Really, Lord Ludlow, I hardly think that's a fair statement to make. I've been struck by just how intelligent people are here. I reckon they could be retrained to do anything.'

'As an incomer, Mrs Reed, I don't really think you're qualified to have an opinion and I don't think any of this is your business. Like so many, you arrive, think you know it all in six months, and, probably, in another six months you'll be gone.'

'And how can you be so sure?'

'Seen it all before. I've seen your type before.'

'And what's my type, Lord Ludlow?' Jane asked, her eyes glinting dangerously.

'Too much money, too little sense. You're not born to the land, you don't understand it and the passions it rouses. I hear you don't even allow any shooting on your land.' The man snorted derisively.

'Oh yes, Percy, and how long have your family owned your estate? Fifteen years or thereabouts, isn't it? Just after you got your life peerage, wasn't it? Where were you before, Birmingham, was it, or Manchester? I doubt passions about land run very high there.' Jane looked up to see a pair of clear, intelligent, blue eyes smiling mischievously at her. As Jane smiled gratefully, one of them winked at her. 'I think Mrs Reed is right, people are more important than a stretch of scrubland running down to a beach that no one ever goes to anyway.'

'But the birds,' Percy Ludlow persisted.

'Bah the birds. They're not daft, you know. They'll soon find somewhere else to go.'

'You're a philistine, Fran, and we all know about your politics,' he said darkly, appealing to the others, and a rumbling murmur went round the table.

'I'm not a philistine, Percy, I'm a realist. And my politics are irrelevant when we're discussing something as fundamental as the future of a whole community. Jobs, Percy, that's what this area needs, jobs, not more birds. Jobs for men to go to, earn a decent wage packet, regain their dignity. There's thousands of acres left for the birds.' The blue-eyed woman thundered as loudly as Lord Ludlow.

'Dignity,' boomed his lordship. 'What dignity? They're all layabouts anyway, you won't get them interested in work. All they're interested in is their government hand-out, paid for by you and me . . .' The row swirled on, and Jane sighed inwardly: it was as if she were back on that first night at Respryn.

'Fran, Percy, you're getting overexcited down that end, and ruining my dinner party. I'm sure you're both right.' Mrs Impington smiled with a patient expression which showed she was used to Fran and Percy's battles. She rose to her feet. 'Ladies, shall we . . .?' Gracefully she gathered the ladies about her, like a careful hen with her chicks, leaving the men to the port. The old order, thought Jane; just as things were getting interesting, off they had to troop to powder noses, drink filthy coffee and talk about servants and education.

In the drawing room the blue-eyed woman made straight for Jane.

'Fran Nettlebed. I was longing to meet you before dinner. You're the glamorous mystery woman who bought the Murchon estate a couple of years back, aren't you?'

'I'm not so sure about glamorous.' Jane laughed. 'But yes, I'm Jane Reed.' They shook hands. The blue eyes sparkled in a face that glowed with health and was as square as her body which, enveloped in a royal-blue kaftan, looked twice the size it probably was. She reminded Jane of Zoe.

'It's odd we haven't met before.'

'I don't go out much. I enjoy the solitude. But I like Liz Impington, she's interesting. So I usually come here when they're up.'

'Implying you don't think much of the others?' The bright-blue eyes twinkled at her.

'Let's just say we don't have an awesome amount in common,' Jane said. 'I was so enjoying that argument in there.'

'I'd promised myself I wouldn't get involved tonight. Now I'll have to apologize to Liz. But that bloody man gets right in my craw, he really does. He's so pompous – silly old fart.'

'Wasn't he the man who made a fortune out of property and gave the socialists a pile of money?' Jane said, laughing at Fran's colourful language.

'That's him.'

'He doesn't sound very much like a socialist.'

'He isn't any more.' Fran laughed loudly. 'Human leopards are quite capable of changing their spots.' She slung the end of a long feather boa over her shoulder, the feathers floating agitatedly through the air as she did so.

Unconcerned, she spat out those feathers which had found her mouth. 'Load of crap this lot spout, I can tell you.'

'Do they all think like that?'

'Mostly. And none of them has a right to an opinion anyway, they're never here – come up for the shooting, casting the fly, and then sod off back to London when the weather gets tough. No time for them at all.'

'You live here all year, then?' Jane asked.

'Yes, in fact I prefer the winters when this lot go. Mind you, I don't count Liz in that number.'

'Why have anything to do with the others, then?'

'I have to be seen to be one of them, you see. You have to in local politics – keep up, I mean.'

'Why?'

'They own everything. Even from London they bloody control what's going on. So you've got to keep in to know what's what, what plans are afoot, who to contact, who to try and coerce.' Fran threw back her head and guffawed, just the way Zoe did.

'This planned development – where is it, and what is it? I'm afraid I just dived in without knowing anything about it.'

'You interested? Great!' The stubby hands clapped together with glee. 'Come to lunch tomorrow, I'll take you over. About twelve do you? Then you can tell me all about yourself, I'm dying to know. No one seems to know a thing about you.' She gave Jane her card.

'There's nothing interesting about me,' Jane assured her.

'Ha! Don't give me that. I can sniff out interesting people at a hundred yards.'

Noisily, the men rejoined the party and, as in a game of musical chairs, everyone changed places. Jane walked towards Liz and Percy Ludlow, whose fat paunch made his sporran stick out at an angle as if he were blessed with a permanent erection. Seeing her coming, he pointedly turned his back. Ah, well, thought Jane, what does it really matter? Instead she talked to a young New Zealand playwright whom Liz had picked up as a hitchhiker. One dram later, Jane found herself yawning. She thanked Liz Impington and left the party.

3

Next day, at noon, Jane drove up Fran's driveway. She had not known what to expect – not a croft, certainly, but neither did she expect the beautiful Georgian house she found. A pack of dogs tumbled down the steps in friendly greeting. Fran came out to welcome her and in cords and sweater she looked not only thinner but far more comfortable than she had the night before.

Jane had imagined that Fran would live in chaos and was unprepared for the muted, beige-and-white, ordered elegance into which she was shown.

'It is lovely, isn't it?' Fran said, noticing Jane's admiring gaze. 'But difficult to keep with the brats about. I ban them from here. You have to have one safe haven, don't you?'

'How old are they?'

'Fourteen and twelve, vaguely civilized at last, thank God. Gin?'

'Is your husband here?'

'No. He's got itchy feet; he's a geologist, spends more time abroad than at home, unfortunately.' She handed Jane her drink and pushed an enormous ashtray towards her.

'He doesn't want to settle and farm, then? I mean, is that your land out there?'

'Yes, but we rent it out. Jack doesn't like the countryside, you see. He distrusts it. He'd much rather live in the middle of some filthy city, but, since he's away so much, it seemed only fair that I should choose where we live. Good old London boy, my Jack: the country is for looking at, nothing more. You farming?'

'No.'

'What do you do, then?'

'Not much, really. I walk the dogs and think about what I ought to do,' Jane said lamely. 'What about you?'

'Meddle in politics – I'm on the local council, small stuff. I'd like a real job now the kids are older but I don't know what I want to do, and fitting in with Jack's schedule makes any nine-to-five job impossible.'

'How did you get involved?'

'Accident, really, and conscience. Jack earns a fortune and I've got some money of my own, so I have the time. I think you have to put back into the community if you're one of the fortunates, don't you?'

'I'm ashamed to say I've never given it much thought. Too self-centred, I suppose,' Jane said apologetically.

'Perhaps you've never regarded yourself as one of the fortunates?' There was no note of sarcasm in Fran's voice but Jane looked sharply at her and was rewarded with Fran's expansive smile. 'So, Jane. Put me out of my misery. Explain all the mystery. Who are you? What are you doing here?'

'Got a few hours?' Jane smiled. She found it easy to talk to Fran.

'All day.'

She had lived so long as Jane Reed now that as she told her tale, it felt almost as if she were talking about someone else.

'I thought I knew you. Your face, it was plastered all over the papers for years, wasn't it? Of course, and the Prince. What a gas! And no one here has twigged?'

'Well, no, I just say I'm called Reed, you see. And it was all so long ago.'

'I suppose you want to keep it deadly secret. Hell, I'd love to tell some of the old crows around here. The last story I heard about you was that you had won the football pools.'

'How typical!' Jane said lightly.

'So tell me, in this extraordinary life of yours, what affected you the most?'

'Bathrooms,' Jane said without hesitation. 'I have never got over the luxury of having a bathroom and running hot water.' She laughed at the surprise on Fran's face. 'Did you think I was going to say something a lot more socially significant?'

'Well, yes, I thought you'd rattle on about becoming obsessed with class or something, not bathrooms,' she protested.

'But I did become obsessed with class. I still am.'

'And how do you regard yourself now, as a princess?'

'Good God, no. Working-class, of course.'

'You certainly don't look it in clothes like that.' Fran eyed the understated Yves St Laurent suit, the Hermès bag and shoes.

Jane laughed, smoothing her skirt. 'That's the influence of my second husband. He made me into a clothes snob, I'm afraid. But seriously, if I had said I thought of myself as an aristocrat when I was married to Alistair, I bet you'd have thought, "Who the hell does she think she is?" If you're a working-class child, that's what you stay, especially when the chips are down. Haven't you noticed, when people are angry, they always revert to the accents of their origins? You can't have a decent row in an assumed accent.'

Fran laughed in agreement. 'You're like my husband – he's working-class and makes no secret of it – but what about those who manage to cover their tracks?'

'They never do, they're only fooling themselves. The upper classes will always sniff them out. It's a closed shop with its own rules, codes and network absorbed with their mother's milk. They might let me in to the club but only as an honorary member and only for as long as it suits them.'

'True. Right old expert on the subject, aren't you? Are you rich?'

'Yes.'

'Hasn't that made a difference?'

'I don't really know. I don't think anyone here knows how rich I am.'

'It would make one hell of a difference, I can assure you. You should see them with the sheik who bought that estate last year.'

'Bet they're foul about him behind his back.'

'True.'

'So it wouldn't make any difference, would it? No, thanks. I don't give a fig any more.'

'Good for you. How about some lunch?'

Fran led her into a farmhouse-style kitchen. The red Aga, the long pine table, the Portmeirion pottery, the herbs hanging drying from the ceiling, all reminded her of Zoe's kitchen. She felt at home. Fran was one of those rare people, warm and giving, whom she felt she had known for years. Jane was not in the least put out when Fran suddenly asked, 'Do you think you'll get married again?'

'I shouldn't think so. I was lucky twice, I can't expect such luck a third time.'

'You don't sound as if you've had much luck – one divorce, then being widowed.'

'I meant I can't complain about my marriages. You make mistakes, and the tragedy is you only realize when you're older and it's all too late. But still I'm lucky. I've got two marvellous sons, and I'm very fond of Alistair.'

'Most people seem to hate their exes' guts, not talk of being fond of them.'

'Well, that's their loss,' Jane said.

Fran was an excellent cook and the wine was superb, and it was a contented and well-insulated Jane who set off with Fran to look at the land that was causing all the problems.

Strathleith was a small estate of 15,000 acres. Unusual for this area, it was mainly flat, and swept from the foothills of the mountains to the sea. The land was rough, not agricultural, and there were no trees. It was rather dull except for the beach, which was a beautiful sweep of golden sands. The two women stood on a headland, the wind from the sea whipping at their clothes.

'The beach is lovely but I've seen more beautiful places up here. Surely no one could object to this being used?' Jane said helpfully.

'Everywhere you go up here is beautiful. It's our blessing and our curse. No matter what you want to do, the environmentalists do have a case, it's all so sodding lovely.' Fran angrily tugged at a piece of couch grass.

'I'd have to look on the map, but I'm certain my land must join onto this.'

'It does,' said Fran. 'I checked last night.'

'And what exactly is it you want to do here?'

'There's a small group of us on the council would give our eye teeth for this land. We want to start an industrial complex here, small work units. We don't want big business here. Have you heard of the smelter they built over on the east? Marvellous, it was, until it went bust and all the men were laid off. We can't afford all our eggs in one basket – we must diversify.'

'That makes sense.'

'Fantastic! You understand,' Fran shouted excitedly, beaming from ear to ear as if Jane had understood the secret of the universe. 'You've no idea how many don't understand that concept. They drive me bonkers.'

'But surely everyone wants to bring employment into the area?'

'Those fat cats sit on their estates pontificating away about the benefits of bringing employment to Scotland, but only if the industry stays in Glasgow and Motherwell – it mustn't come and upset their grouse and their stalking. A hint of that and they're on the ecology bandwagon straight away.'

'And what about the government? Can't the government buy it?'

'Christ, Jane, haven't you been listening? Those bastards *are* the government. If not in power, my love, they know or are related to those who are. Went to school with them, served in the army with them, shoot with them, fornicate with them.'

'Times are changing.'

'Balderdash! What were you saying back at the house? The system never changes and the people up here are the victims of it just as you were, but in their case we're talking of survival, not just the odd insult at a dinner party.' Fran's face was red with anger.

'But I've seen in the paper . . . large grants from the government . . .'

'Fish farms and craft shops, Jane. I tell you, if I see a planning application for another craft shop I'll run naked through the streets of Inverness, and that'll frighten them.' She laughed loudly, the wind scooping up the laugh, accentuating its hollowness.

'What do you think will happen?'

'I expect old Rimbish will buy it, it marches with his land.'

'It's all so depressing.'

'That it is, my girl. It's perfect for what we want. The main road is only three miles away, no distance for up here. The bay is deep enough for ships. Hell, the railway cuts across it, that is, if the line isn't axed . . .'

'Poor Fran.'

'Poor Fran, my arse. Poor Highlanders.' She kicked angrily at the sand. 'I don't know why I get so worked up, no one gives a damn.' The blue eyes looked angrily out across the water. 'My particular bandwagon.' She suddenly grinned again. 'Come on, Jane, fancy some tea?'

That evening, at home, Jane sat in her small library, surrounded by her dogs, and thought for a long time. She wanted the woman to like her. She feared that Fran despised her for the rich, spoilt, self-centred person she must seem. She had wasted too much of her life worrying and caring what people thought, seeing injustice at every turn. She knew she had lied when she said she did not care what people said any more. Obviously, if she were honest, one of the reasons she had hidden away up here was to escape, not to have to face reality, to avoid being hurt. She had been wrong. She had allowed herself to become obsessed with slights and insults instead of getting on with living.

She spent the next morning with paper, pencil and a calculator, making telephone calls. She made copious notes. She surprised her accountants, whom she had meekly obeyed until now, signing whatever was put in front of her, by asking for a complete set of her business accounts and a total breakdown of all her assets. She had a long telephone conversation with James. And she returned to Strathleith and walked the land.

She waited anxiously for the parcels of accounts, balance sheets and bank statements to arrive. Once they had, the large drawing-room carpet disappeared under a sea of paper. Never seriously involved in business, Jane worked late into the night and all the next day trying to untangle the web of how much she was worth.

'Donald, it's Jane.' She finally phoned her chief accountant. 'There's an estate up here I want to buy.'

'Another one, Jane? Of course, if you want, just give me the name of the agents.'

'I don't want to live on this one, Donald. I want to do something with it.'

'Like what?'

'I want to build an industrial estate on it.'

'There's a lot of money to be made that way these days, Jane. A good investment.'

'No, Donald, you don't understand. I don't want it, I want to give it away.'

There was a long silence on the phone. 'Give it away?' Jane smiled at the pain in her accountant's voice.

'Yes. I've worked it all out. I'll set up a trust and the people who work it will own it. It will need houses and schools, even an airport eventually . . .'

'Jane! Jane! What on earth are you talking about?'

'I'm talking about putting back into the community, Donald.'

'But, Jane, you're talking about millions if not billions.'

'I know, isn't it exciting? I realize it can't all happen at once, but I intend to raise money from everywhere – industry, banks, government.'

'And what sort of industry have you in mind, Jane?'

'Computers to start with, a Highland Silicon Valley, the air's so clean up here – '

'But you don't know anything about computers, Jane.'

'Of course I don't, as I know nothing about creating industrial estates. I shall employ those who do,' she heard herself snap in reply to his patronizing tone of voice. 'I shall buy the land out of income, Donald, and when it gets going I want to use my money, none of James's. I've worked it out – I can well afford it.'

'What about James in all this? I mean, even if you use what's yours, he has every right to expect it to be his one day.'

'He's excited. He's coming up next week to see it and he's got masses of ideas, too.'

'And does this land you want have planning permission?'

'No.'

'Then I must ask you to be cautious. Without planning permission the land will be almost worthless.'

'I'll get planning permission.'

'Jane, it isn't that easy. It might prove impossible to get the necessary permits.'

'Oh no, Donald, it won't. I know exactly what I'm going to do.'

4

Two months later the *Scotsman* had barely hit the breakfast tables before the phone began to ring. It was not surprising – 'Italian Princess saves Strathleith Estate.' Two cats out of the bag, she thought.

Lord Ludlow was one of the first to congratulate her. Jane explained nothing; she did not want to and, in any case, Ludlow did not give her time to, so fulsome was his praise of her. The phone never stopped ringing: the local nobility were welcoming her with open arms – for the time being.

As the phone rang for the umpteenth time, Jane heard the noise she had been expecting all morning, the roar of Fran's Ferrari as it screeched to a halt outside. Fran burst angrily into the room.

'You bitch! What the hell are you playing at?'

'Fran, I – '

'You're just like the rest of them and I, bloody fool, thought you were something different,' Fran shouted, tears welling in the beautiful blue eyes.

'Fran. Shut up! Sit down and listen for once,' Jane ordered. Fran sank sulkily into a chair, still blazing with anger.

'Want a job?' Jane asked.

'Job? What job?'

'Chairman of the trust I'm setting up.'

'Chairman? Trust? What the hell . . .?' The intelligent eyes watched Jane sharply.

'Strathleith. I'm forming a trust. I'm giving it to the people who'll work it.'

'Sodding hell!'

'Very expressive, Fran.' Jane laughed at the open-mouthed astonishment on her friend's face. 'You see, your industrial estate will be built. But I want to go one further, I want a whole town built. It's to be done well, the best architects. I want it beautifully landscaped so that no one can say, "Look at that God-awful hole."'

'Jane, I don't know what to say . . .' There were tears again in Fran's eyes.

'We'll need training facilities. We shall insist that as many locals as possible are used, not just as labourers to build the place but trained to do skilled work. It'll take time but that must be the end result. This is to help this community, not to make money for people down south. The women, too. And the children – I must go round all the schools and see what computer courses are being taught.' The words bubbled out of Jane in a breathless torrent.

'Computers?'

'We won't just stop at computer-related industries. There's so much unused talent here. We can have our own weaving factories, textiles. Laura Ashley did it, why not us? Bottled water – hell, it's wonderful stuff here, why buy Perrier? I've so many ideas. Fran, it's so exciting! I've been dying to tell you but I was frightened something would go wrong and I didn't want to disappoint you.'

'Exciting! Jane, it's mind-blowing. But hang on a minute, how?'

'I'll kick it off. Hopefully it'll all be self-sufficient in ten years or so.'

'But it will cost – '

'Millions. I know.'

'But, Jane, where's the money coming from?'

'I'll start, and others will help us – industrialists, big businesses, banks and then the government will have to chip in. This is the big one, Fran. Everyone will want to help . . .'

'And you mean you can even contemplate this sort of money? Christ, are you that rich? Like Hughes, like Getty?'

'Not personally, but I have access to almost as much.'

'Bloody hell,' Fran said, open-mouthed with astonishment. 'But Jane, what about the planning permission? They'll still stop it.'

'No, they can't. We won't be applying for planning permission for individuals, we'll be applying for a whole community, a whole new way of life. With the general election eighteen months away, who the hell will dare to refuse us with the unemployment at the level it is here?'

'They will. They'll shut it up somehow. You don't know those bastards like I do. It'll be done in such a way that no one will ever get to hear of your plans.'

'But people will know. I'm that weird thing in our society, a personality. For years I've hidden from the press; now, if necessary, I'll court them, newspapers, radio and TV. No, I don't think we'll have any problems with our applications.'

Fran looked unconvinced. 'They'll throw everything at you – conservation of endangered species, destruction of the environment. They'll stop you,' she declared knowledgeably.

'Look at all those horrible conifer plantations, they've destroyed more of the Highlands than any light industry has ever done. And who planted them? Why, the people you think will stop us.'

'That's different, nice little tax breaks in forestry. They'll find some rare bug, last on the planet.'

'Then I shall employ experts to check every inch of land to make sure that we aren't about to destroy anything.'

'You'll make enemies, Jane.'

'I'll make friends, too.'

'But who will really join us?'

Jane reeled off a list of internationally known names.

'Wow! You know all those people?'

'Yes. Roberto knew everyone and he was in business with lots of them. I've talked to them, they're interested. There's loads of reasons why they should be – old obligations to Roberto, tax breaks, honours, you'll see.'

'Why, Jane? Why are you doing all this?'

'So many reasons, Fran. Something you said that first day we had lunch together, it made me sit up and take stock. I'd been feeling sorry for myself for too long, wallowing in self-pity, thinking too much. I love it here, I want to give in return. And, to be honest, I want something to do. I guess I've always wanted something. I never found out until now what it was.'

'Hell, I started all this. So let me just say two things, love. First, I think you should keep some financial involvement in this project, say 25 per cent.'

'But I don't want any financial benefit from it.'

'Maybe not, but people won't trust you if you don't. If they see that you've invested in it for yourself, put your money where your mouth is, then they're much more likely to regard it favourably, and help. Otherwise it all sounds a little too good to be true.'

'Do you think so? Yes, I see what you mean. All right, I'll keep a portion for myself. At least it'll please my accountant.'

'The other thing is, I don't want the job as chairman.'

'Oh, Fran, I can't do it without you.'

'You don't have to. I'd love a job, but as your assistant or something. You have to be the chairman. You're the one who's worked it all out, you're the one with the clout.'

'OK, assistant chairman or chairperson, or whatever you like.' She danced a little step of glee. 'Oh, Fran, darling, isn't it all so wonderfully exciting?'

'Jane, I didn't know you had it in you.'

'Neither did I, Fran, neither did I!'

5

Fran advised that they should work secretly in the planning stages. She feared that, if news of Jane's intentions got out, objections would snow down thick and fast, and the less warning the opposition had, the better. Fran's husband was the only local whom they told. He wished them well as he left for his job in the East again, but he sounded as if he doubted there could ever be a happy outcome.

Together they travelled the length and breadth of the country and to Europe, to America, anywhere they could study the concept of a new town. They visited factories by the dozen, workshop units by the hundred. And after each trip the files containing their plans and ideas grew larger.

Within the first month an American company, in which Roberto had invested heavily, showed interest in the possibility of setting up a European factory. At a party in London, Jane met the head of a large cosmetics firm, who began to think seriously of setting up in her town. Designers who had until now seen Jane as just a good customer began to regard her, excitedly, in a new light, when she asked them to investigate the weaving of fine silks in the Highlands, thus saving them the need to stalk the suppliers of Europe. Taking a necklace whose clasp had broken into the jeweller's in London that Roberto had always patronized, Jane moved quickly on hearing the owner say he was toying with the idea of going into clockmaking. A furniture manufacturer, a toymaker, the ideas flowed thick and fast: getting tenants was not going to be a problem, and they had not even started to investigate how many small, subsidized units would be needed by people who could not afford to start big. Everyone was sworn to secrecy at this stage.

She was listened to sympathetically by businessmen who had been part of Roberto's vast network of contacts. As they had respected the man, so they respected his memory, and to his widow they pledged the level of donations she would need.

With this backup, they decided the time was ripe to begin to have unofficial, exploratory talks with the local planning officer. Since the council had wanted the land in the first place, Jane was not surprised by the enthusiasm and advice they received from him; and, knowing the problems they were likely to face, he was equally keen that, for the time being, their talks should be confidential.

The botanists, zoologists, ornithologists and all the other experts Jane had marshalled searched and scoured the land. It took weeks, but finally their reports arrived. Nothing of any rarity or of an endangered species had been found on the estate.

James, newly graduated from university, was excited by his mother's plans. He tried, unsuccessfully, to persuade her to use some of the Wilbur Calem millions that would one day be his, and then, the greatest surprise of all, he gave up his new job in a City bank to join her and Fran. It was like a shot in the arm to Jane that he should have such faith in the outcome and that he wanted to live and work with her.

'It's incredible,' Fran said as they relaxed over dinner in London after a long afternoon spent in the deep leather armchairs and gentlemen's-club atmosphere of the senior partner of Ormerod Brothers, the merchant bankers. 'Money really does make money, doesn't it?'

'True, and so unfair.'

'Not this time, my old mate, not this time. There are moments, though, Jane, when I think it's all too easy, that something's got to go wrong.'

'You're a dreadful pessimist, Fran.'

'No, Jane, I'm not. You're just an incorrigible optimist!'

Over six months later their outline planning application was rejected on its first presentation. Jane and James waited with frustrated anger for Fran to arrive.

'The sods!' exclaimed Fran as she bounced angrily into the room. 'I shouldn't have resigned from the flaming council. At least we'd have known something was going wrong.'

'You would have had to declare an interest, Fran, so it probably wouldn't have made any difference,' James pointed out.

'But we would have had some warning that things weren't going completely our way.'

'The Neanderthals must have known right from the outset. So much for all the promises of confidentiality.'

'Neanderthals?' asked Fran.

'James's word for the opposition.'

'But it was inevitable. After all, our application had to be published weeks ago,' Fran said as reasonably as she could manage.

'But not time enough, Fran, to set up all these new environmental groups. No, they've known right from the beginning, I reckon.'

'What groups?' Fran demanded. James began to read a long list of societies dedicated to the protection of every aspect of flora and fauna, from the birds to the buttercups, from the sea to the slugs. 'I've never heard of half of them.'

'Exactly, Fran, that's what James means: they've been set up in the past twelve months – probably the same people belong to all of them.'

'It was pretty naive of us, really, if you think about it, Jane. Once we began putting feelers out in the City, then the word must have been out in the bloody clubs, gossip shops more like.'

'But they promised, all of them, even Ormerods.'

'Yes, Ma, but to them, promising to you was one thing; their loyalty has to be with their own sort, so they could welsh on you with a clear conscience. It's the old-boy network.'

'I can't see your father doing something like that.'

'But he's not really one of them, Ma, is he? Never has been.'

'That's true.' She laughed. 'Or you wouldn't be here, would you?'

The old Jane would have been cast down with dejection but this new Jane resolved to fight back. And she needed every ounce of that resolve, for the tentacles of vested interest seemed to be everywhere. There were days when she felt she was in a web of intrigue and plotting so dense that there was no way out. Time and again the people she tried to contact, to talk to, to persuade them to see things her way, were out to her calls and never returned them. Many letters to important people mysteriously went astray.

Since so many avenues seemed suddenly closed to her, she approached the one group who welcomed her with open arms – the press. She courted them, but it was hard: she had hidden from them for so many years. Everything about her past was dragged into the light. For each complimentary article there was always an equally derogatory one. Once again her steps were dogged by eager young reporters with notepads, while photographers ran backwards in front of her. She had to steel herself to see her face on television. She had to adjust to losing her anonymity.

The first letter came as a shock. Her hands shook violently as she saw the word DEATH crudely made from newspaper headlines. But this one was mild compared with those which followed: from them she learned a new vocabulary of invective. When the abusive phone calls started, she retreated behind a screen of secretaries who sifted and sorted through the mail, answered the phone for her, and protected her from hate.

When her car was pushed off the road and into the river she emerged unhurt but soaked, her rage delaying the inevitable shock, as she screamed angrily at the retreating black car which sped back up the glen.

The police, though they assured her it was probably a chance case of reckless driving, thought it would do no harm if she had a bodyguard with her at all times. She was not fooled by their bland-faced reassurance.

Now, not only could she not open her mail, pick up her phone, answer her own front door, but she had lost the freedom to drive wherever she wanted and, worst of all, to wander alone on her beloved moor.

It was not surprising that there were days when she wondered if she should not give up. But then the spirit which had saved Respryn from financial chaos, given her the courage to raise Giovanni, and the strength to will Roberto to live for those precious extra months, re-emerged and she and Fran carried stoically on.

When the second planning application was thrown out, Jane decided she had to see someone at the top. Since so many doors were now closed to her, she used her new allies, the press, to announce her intention to put her case to the minister for industrial planning. In the face of so many questions in the tabloids about why he did not see her, he had to relent.

As Jane was shown into his office, her heart sank. In front of her stood a replica of so many of her adversaries – the neat pinstriped suit, almost a uniform; the Guards' tie; the smiling mouth beneath the unsmiling eyes. His cheeks, pouched like a well-fed hamster's, were an ominously high colour – the bright red of years of best claret and hours spent stalking on the hills. His colour said it all: she did not need to look at the photograph in the crested silver frame to know what his wife would look like, and she did not need to ask if the painting on the wall was of his own ancestral pile. He was charming, almost unctuously so. How grateful they were for her generous intentions but he was powerless to help, he smoothly informed her. 'A local matter,' he said, one eyebrow arched expressively.

'But I can't see it as just a local matter, like something of no importance. I've promises from manufacturers that, for a start, will ensure 2,000 jobs. That's just the beginning. And you know that number of jobs in the Highlands is like 10,000 jobs anywhere else.'

'Princess . . .' he started.

'Reed, Jane Reed.'

'Miss Reed, of course, how remiss, I had quite forgotten you prefer . . . But have you thought perhaps, if you wish to give so generously, that the National Trust for Scotland or the RSPB would be only too pleased . . .'

'I didn't buy it for them. I want to create jobs in a community that desperately needs them, permanent jobs that last years, not just when the tourists come, with the long winter lay-off when they've gone. I want to build decent houses, with room for people to move in, not rabbit hutches. I want to give people hope.'

'Most commendable, Miss Reed, but I'm afraid my hands are tied.'

'And you won't untie them?'

'It's not that easy, my dear. As I've explained, this is not a government issue.'

'Then it bloody well ought to be and if you were half a minister you would get off your arse and make it one.' Angrily she picked up her handbag and gloves. 'And, minister, I'm not your "dear" anything. I should be obliged if you would remember that in the future dealings we shall be having with each other.'

She had the satisfaction of seeing him speechless, gulping like a stranded fish, though she realized she could now expect no help from him. Still, she knew no help would have been forthcoming anyway.

The solution, like most solutions, came in the middle of the night. And like the best solutions it was so blindingly simple that she wondered why on earth she had not thought of it before.

She would play the game their way, with their ploys and using their rules.

Anonymously, she joined all the societies for environmental concern that had suddenly proliferated like mushrooms. She compiled a list of the principal officers and telexed the list to the New York offices of the Wilbur Calem conglomerate. The powerful computers sifted, searched and analysed and less than twenty-four hours later the answer lay in her hands.

Jane telephoned Alistair and two nights later she sat opposite him in the Caprice.

'Like old times, Jane.'

'I don't remember ever coming here with you. Roberto, yes, but us?'

'I meant being together. We should see more of each other, Jane.'

'It's my fault, but I'm so busy, there's so much to do. And you're rarely in London these days.'

'I'm getting like my father, I suppose. I'm happiest at Respryn, I can't be bothered with the rat race of London.'

'But you used to love the London scene so much.'

'That was just a youthful phase,' he said, looking sheepish. 'Perhaps I've grown up.'

'Oh, Alistair, don't do that, it would be awful if you grew up. James is grown-up enough for the two of us.' She laughed.

'But a fifty-year-old Peter Pan is somewhat undignified, don't you think?'

'No, and in any case I can't believe that you're fifty – it only seems like yesterday, doesn't it?'

'Yesterday and a million years ago. Jay . . .' He put his hand across the table and covered hers. The movement was so unexpected that for a long moment Jane left her hand where it was. At his touch her mind raced back to that last time they had made love. The nerves of her body tensed as she remembered the feel of his lean, strong body. She looked at the generous line of his mouth . . .

'Penny for them?' He was smiling easily at her.

'I wanted to talk to you about my trust,' she said quickly, fearful that her eyes must reflect the intimacy of her thoughts.

He removed his hand from hers. 'Don't you think that perhaps you have taken on a bit more than you can chew, Jay?'

'It's funny to hear you call me Jay. No one else does,' she said, finding it increasingly difficult to concentrate on the reason they were here.

'Our word. That's nice.'

She looked across at him, now, in his middle years, even more attractive than in his youth, something she would not have thought possible. The blonde hair was now totally white, the same silver white that his father's had been. The lines on his face added to its distinction, and his body was as slim and spare as when she had married him. And strange, too, being with him and remembering the past, how quickly her pulse seemed to race . . .

She shook her head, trying to erase the thoughts that were plaguing her. This was ridiculous – Honor would have told her to go out and find some nice, uncomplicated young man. 'Alistair, do you approve of what I'm doing?' she said, suddenly unsure of herself.

'The idea, yes, of course. It's a wonderful concept and typical of you – you always had a guilt thing about wealth and privilege, didn't you?'

'With my background, what would you expect?'

'Remember how you used to sit on the floor of the Rolls when we went through towns because you were embarrassed to let anyone see you in it?'

'It wasn't just that. I always thought how disappointed people would be, expecting to see a film star or a pop star and instead getting us.' She laughed at the memory.

'The idea's all right,' he said, suddenly serious. 'But I worry what it might be doing to you. James told me about those pleasant fellows in the car and how you now have a personal ape to mind you.'

'Oh, that's nothing, people will soon forget, once I've really got it going. But you do approve?' she asked anxiously, realizing that she needed his approval more than anyone else's.

'I approve. Of course Mother doesn't. She's convinced you're frittering James's inheritance away.'

'I'm not, Alistair, I'd never do that.' She leaned across the table, studying his face for any hint of suspicion.

'I know, darling. She's old and she can't grasp it. I've tried explaining and James has, too, but at eighty-five it's all too much for her.'

'I shouldn't think her age has anything to do with it. She would have to object on principle, if I was involved.' The mention of Lady Upnor brought her back to the purpose of their meeting. 'Anyhow. Would you do me a favour?'

'I'll try.'

'Do you know Lord Ludlow and George Fraser-Brown?'

'I know George. I was at Cambridge with his son, John – you know, the minister for industrial planning.'

'We met,' she snorted derisively. 'What about Ludlow?'

'I don't know him socially, only in the Lords. Can't say I like him much. I mean, if you get your life peerage from one party I think it's pretty cheap to cross the floor the minute you're safely ensconced. Bombastic old toad I've always thought him. What's your interest in them?'

'Those two are stopping my plans.'

'You sure?'

'Oh yes. There are others but they're the main ones. If I can make them crumble, the rest will soon follow.'

'I can't see either of them giving way, especially to a woman. God, they both live in the Middle Ages where women are concerned. You do realize that George is old Rimbish's brother-in-law, and his estate is bang next door to your little venture – you could hardly expect him to agree.'

'But, Alistair, he's got thousands of acres and he's so rarely there.'

'I take your point. Of course Ludlow would object on principle, just to ingratiate himself with the real nobs he aspires to be like. So what's your plan?'

'I've discovered that an American bank, a subsidiary of the banking section of the Calem conglomerate, has large loans out to Ludlow and Fraser-Brown. Put simply, either they get off my back or I arrange to have the loans called in.'

'Ha! I like it! How much?'

'Ludlow nearly 5 million, Fraser-Brown just two.'

'Shit! It would finish Ludlow. I know for certain he's in a bit of a mess at the moment, had one or two catastrophes. He'd never get anyone else to back a loan of that size. But Fraser-Brown's a different matter, lot of money there, you know. It would just be a temporary setback for him; he'd raise it again, no problem. My, my. Little Jane, you have changed! Quite the ruthless career woman, aren't you?'

'I don't like doing it – I think it stinks – but then what they're doing to me stinks, too. Do you know, Alistair, that land had been on the market for five years before I came along? No one wanted it then, hardly anyone knew of its existence. I know it's a rotten thing I'm planning, but they chose the rules, not me. I'm only playing the sort of hand they're expert at.'

'So where do I fit in?'

'I hoped you'd know something about them, have some idea what I could do.'

'We're going to have to find something else on the Fraser-Brown lot. Obviously it would be most helpful if we could find something on Fraser-Brown junior, wouldn't it?' He smiled at Jane, his eyes sparkling. 'Most definitely. I think I'm going to enjoy all this.'

'If we could get something on the pompous minister, it would be marvellous. You see, it's all getting to be so big that we'll need the government in on this eventually.'

'I'll do it.' He laughed. 'I know how to handle John Fraser-Brown. Not very pleasant but then he was a pompous fart at Magdalene, and Ludlow's the sort of lord that gets us all a bad name. Don't worry, we'll sort them out, together.' He looked at her, momentarily serious. 'It's amazing, Jane, but you seem to get more beautiful the older you get.'

'It's all an illusion, Alistair. It's wonderful what money can do.' She tried to sound casual. Alistair was not given to compliments.

'I want to make love to you, Jane.'

To Jane it was as if the sound in the restaurant was suddenly shut off. She felt she was in a child's game of statues, as if the other diners and waiters were frozen in that moment. She looked at Alistair, saw the naked longing in his eyes, felt the fatal longing of her body for him. And then remembered, 'You've learned a lot since the last time . . .' his voice echoing back and forth in her brain. The noises of the restaurant returned, the waiters and diners were moving. She turned her face away.

'Don't spoil the evening, Alistair,' she heard herself say, almost primly.

'Sorry, Jane. But I had to say it.'

The spell was broken. They finished their coffee, and Alistair handed her into a taxi, kissing her lightly on the brow. From the taxi she watched his familiar, long-legged walk as he disappeared down the street, and she wished that things, that she, could be different.

A week later the phone rang in her Scottish home. 'Jane? Alistair here. Mission accomplished, collapse of stout parties. Have you ever seen a puce-faced peer turn green before your eyes? I have. Not a pretty sight. Anyhow, the word's out to all their little minions. I should reapply forthwith if I were you.'

'What did you turn up on John Fraser-Brown?'

'Oh, that was rather naughty of me,' he said with a chuckle. 'I just conveniently remembered that one day at Cambridge, he hadn't sported his oak, and I walked in. It seemed odd that he should have his trousers down round his ankles and the beefy fencing blue with him likewise. I just reminded him, that's all, and out of friendship thought I'd better mention that I'd probably told you at some point along the way.'

'Alistair, fantastic!'

'It is, isn't it? He can't afford any scandal, especially not of that nature, if he's to fulfil his ambition and become prime minister.'

'Alistair, you're wonderful. I love you, I really do,' she said with glee. There was an awkward pause. What on earth had possessed her to say that? she thought.

'I'm glad to hear it, Jay. Perhaps you could whisper it in my shell-like ear one day soon, instead of down this infernal machine,' he quipped with practised, social ease. She relaxed: that was the kind of bantering flirtation in which her bank manager indulged.

This time everything progressed with the smoothness of the best-oiled machinery. Jane's trust application was passed and, over a year since the day she had bought the estate, Jane watched Fran turn the first sod of earth. The minister for industrial planning made a smiling and well-received speech of gratitude as he declared the Wilbur Calem Trust a reality.

Jane, in turn, smiled charmingly at him. To give him and his father their due, they had lost graciously, unlike Ludlow, who continued to bore anyone who would listen about the ruthlessness of Jane Reed. But in the way of the world, no one listened to him any more: as always, money and success triumphed.

6

Everything began to move with satisfying speed. It would have moved faster but for Jane, who rejected one set of plans after another from an ever increasing army of architects. She knew what she wanted: they were just not producing it. She had explained, she thought, quite clearly. She wanted buildings that would blend as far as possible into the environment in which they stood, and that would offer functional yet pleasant working conditions. In her endless travels, time and again she found factories where the offices, the planners and the designers worked in large-windowed, carpeted luxury, while the work force toiled in noisy, windowless, featureless blocks. It seemed illogical to Jane that those with the more interesting jobs enjoyed the most comfort, while those with the dull, repetitive tasks had the least.

She had hoped for a Scottish firm, but her search finally ended in a pretty, wooded valley in Devon at a small textile factory. The architects were two young men whose largest contract this factory had been. As they listened to her plans, their dark, intense eyes glittered and their floppy bow ties seemed to quiver with excitement. Their views mirrored hers, her enthusiasm matched theirs.

Around her now she had an army of advisers. Her solicitors and accountants had been joined by financial experts, marketing and publicity men. All were up in arms at her rejection of yet another set of plans and at her choice of new architects. She had been foolish, they would have liked to say; instead they contented themselves with telling her she needed a large, experienced firm, not two young lads fresh out of college, and the publicity and marketing people, who were Scottish, deplored her choice of Englishmen. But Jane was learning fast and getting tougher with the learning – she knew what she wanted and no one was going to stop her, certainly not local nationalist feeling.

'I'm the one who's been doing the searching, and I know just how difficult it's been to find a firm who understand what we want. I couldn't care less what nationality they are. If they were Eskimos I'd still have asked them.' Such views, now expressed firmly and with confidence, silenced her advisers. They might moan behind her back, but it suited Jane to use her power and their burgeoning fear of her to achieve her own ends.

The plans for the factories and work units that they already knew they would require began to arrive. Jane was thrilled; the two young men had planned exactly what, until now, had been her dream.

Their plans for the housing, therefore, came as a disappointing shock.

Jane stood in the small, cluttered, but brightly lit office of Colin and Renton and silently studied the exquisitely drawn plans for the housing development. She frowned. Colin nervously straightened his red polka-dot tie; Renton's hands restlessly played with the large cowboy buckle on his belt. The silence seemed endless; they were not used to Jane frowning.

'This isn't what Fran and I asked for,' she said quietly.

'There are 200 units, Jane, the number you stipulated,' Renton's high-pitched voice explained.

'In boring, uniform rows! It looks like a plan more suited to the Industrial Revolution.'

'It's the most cost-effective use of land.'

'We're not exactly short of land, Renton.'

'I realize, Jane, but with the factories costing so much, we thought we should economize somewhere.'

'Who asked you to?'

'Well, no one . . .'

'These are rabbit hutches. You can't expect people to live in conditions like that.'

'They conform to the minimum square footage for living space laid down in the building regulations.'

'Then the building regulations are inhuman. Sod regulations. This whole concept is built on defying rules and regulations. I want larger houses, landscaped for privacy, big gardens – we're dealing with country people, they're going to want gardens they can plant vegetables in, not just sit in.'

'How about a large allotment plot, Jane, each house to have its own, if they want? Then the gardens needn't be so big,' Fran suggested helpfully.

'Oh yes, Fran, I like the allotment idea. That's good – we'll do that. It doesn't alter the fact that I want them to have good-sized gardens.' She continued her careful study. 'But they're all the same – why are they all the same?'

'Well, cost-effectively – '

'Renton, Colin, I don't think you can have listened to a word that Fran and I said to you.' Her irritation made her voice hard. 'Maybe we need a different firm for the housing.'

'You tell us what you want, we'll do it,' Colin said hurriedly.

'But we did tell you what we wanted, excellent housing. How can you design such beautiful factories and then do this?' Angrily she stabbed at the offending plan.

'We're rather good at factories.' Renton laughed nervously, only to be silenced by Jane's angry glare.

'For your benefit I'll outline it just once more. We want houses of different sizes – not all people have 2.2 children. I don't want our children sleeping four to a room. We need small units for the unmarried only. Family houses must have at least two rooms downstairs.'

'But we've done them with two rooms just as you said; both Colin and I would much rather have had a large open-plan room, but you were so insistent on two rooms.'

'You couldn't swing a cat in either of those rooms. We want a large family room, and a smaller, quieter room, for being alone, a study . . .'

'Study? Jane, you're kidding! These houses are for artisans.'

'And don't workers also need peace and quiet? Doing homework in a crowded family room is an impossibility.'

'There are the bedrooms.'

'Bedrooms are always colder. Children like to be near what's going on, not isolated in their bedrooms.'

'As you like, Jane, but it'll be few families who'll use them that way.'

'You don't know that,' Jane snapped sharply. 'And why are the walls so thin?'

'That's how houses are built these days, Jane.'

'Then I don't like it. We must have solid, soundproof houses.'

'But the cost?'

'That's my worry, not yours.'

'Honestly, Jane, I think you would just be throwing money away. This is normal building-reg housing.'

'Have either of you ever lived in a house where you can hear your neighbours rowing, gobbing, farting, copulating?' she asked angrily.

'Well, no, but –'

'I have. It's hell. It creates family tension and arguments, let alone ruining your sex life.' She was almost shouting at the two startled young men. From Fran a large snort of laughter exploded.

'She's right, boys. Hell, we can't be responsible for ruining the Highlanders' libido, can we?'

Suddenly they were all laughing and Jane calmed down, her point made and taken. She surprised herself these days by just how forceful and arrogant she could be to ensure the realization of her dream.

A month later she was in possession of the housing plans, and at last they met with her approval. The building began in earnest.

7

For three years Jane worked, planned and schemed. She found reserves of energy she did not know she possessed; her attention to detail, her insistence on perfection became legendary. As her town grew, as more factories opened and new families moved in, she had thought that she would not need to work so hard, but nothing was further from the truth. As her fame spread, so the demands on her time were increased and she spent weeks and months away, travelling the world, lecturing, advising, consulting – her diary full for months to come.

She was proud of her success but as the years sped by, seeds of discontent began to grow within her. To achieve what she had, her personal life had been sacrificed. She saw far too little of Giovanni, who was becoming more Italian than English, instead of the mixture she had hoped he would be. She had not had a holiday in years. She rarely saw her old friends now. She still wrote to Sandra and Zoe, but their replies only emphasized the growing gulf between her life style and theirs in Cambridge. Though she met people by the thousand, she was never in one place long enough to establish any friendships. She was forty-seven, beautiful, elegant and assured, but she had become resigned, not without regret, to the idea that she would end her days alone.

When she saw Alistair it was only ever for a quick meal, before jetting off somewhere. She made sure they were never alone together. She was still afraid of the effect he had on her. It would have been so easy to phone him, arrange a meeting, get into bed with him. But Jane was determined not to repeat her mistakes. Other men left her cold; she kept them firmly at arm's length. Despite her wealth and success, her fear of rejection was a powerful force. Jane was unaware that her frenetic work schedule was in fact a defence mechanism – it did not allow her time to think of her own life.

Into her organized, tabulated world, the news that her father was ill came as a shock. In her new life there was no time for illness. But for his she made time.

She flew down to England and took the car to the neat house which was now her mother's pride and joy. His decline had been rapid and she was not prepared for the emaciated figure she found, huddled in front of a large fire that did not seem to warm him, the *Daily Mirror* folded on his lap. His radio had been replaced by a large television set which flickered in the corner, the sound off.

'What's this then, Dad? Malingering, are we?' She tried to joke to cover the pain she felt at his appearance.

'Something I ate, I reckon, don't know what all the fuss is about,' he said lightly, but looked at her with frightened grey eyes, flecked now with the yellow of age, which seemed to plead at her for an explanation. 'I can't seem to keep anything down. It's like a bloody hangover that won't go away.'

'Should put more water in it.' She laughed nervously and averted her eyes from his agonizing gaze. 'Who's your doctor?'

'Useless bugger!' her mother exclaimed. 'Fresh out of medical school, he doesn't know his arse from his elbow, if you ask me. He isn't even English,' she added darkly.

'I'll arrange for you to see a specialist in London, Dad.'

'See, I said she would –'

'No, you bloody well won't!' Her father managed to raise himself in his chair, indignation giving him strength. 'I've never approved of private medicine, jumping the queue, you can't expect me to change my ways now.'

'Oh, come on, Dad. It would put Mum's mind at rest –'

'No. National Health's good enough for me.'

'But Dad . . .'

'I know you mean well, girl, but I've got my principles.'

'Fat lot of good they ever done you.' He chose to ignore the flash of her old bitterness in his wife's voice.

'I understand, Dad. Forget it.' And she squeezed the thin, blue-veined hand. It looked transparent and frail.

He picked at the rug that covered his knees and, without looking at her, said in a barely audible voice, 'I'm very proud of you and what you're doing in Scotland. Seems there must be some of me in you after all.' She heard an unfamiliar, almost embarrassed pride in his voice.

'It looks like it, Dad.'

'Bloody waste of money, if you ask me. I bet Lady Upnor thinks the same way, wasting James's money like that.'

'I'm not wasting James's money, Mum.' She tried to sound patient instead of irritated. 'I used my own money and we raised the rest. In any case, Lady Upnor's dead, so her views don't come into it any more.'

'Dead? Why didn't you tell me? When? What she die of?' Her mother leaned forward with her customary interest in the news of death, illness and catastrophe.

'You'd never met so I didn't think to tell you. She died in her sleep, at Respryn, last year. She was in her eighties, after all.'

'She'd had a good innings, then.' There was a hint of disappointment in the woman's voice as she trotted out the platitude. Jane's mother preferred gory deaths. 'Did you go to the funeral?'

'No. I didn't see the point.'

'See the point! You have to go to funerals, Jane, even if you don't want to. That wasn't nice of you at all.'

'She'd hated me for so long and I never liked the woman. It would have been hypocritical to go. Alistair understood.'

'Quite right, Jane. I'm glad to see you've got principles. Now, if you two would stop your clacking, I want to check my pools.' The clawlike hand manipulated the remote-control button and the television set burst into noisy life.

Jane followed her mother into the kitchen where the older woman, filling the kettle, suddenly slumped against the draining board looking weary and beaten.

'You shouldn't have given up so easily, Jane. You should have insisted on another doctor.'

'You know what he's like, Mum. I'll phone his doctor and check what's going on, see if there's any more we can do. But in the end it's up to him, we can't make him see a specialist. It's his life, after all.'

'His death, more like.'

'Oh, Mum, don't say that.'

'It's the truth. And it's not just him. What about me, doesn't anyone ever think of me? I've a right to insist on him seeing another doctor.'

'I'm sorry, Mum.'

'You seem to have spent your life saying "sorry" to me. About time it stopped.'

'What, saying sorry?'

'No, doing things that make it necessary for you to say it.' She lit the gas, angrily, it seemed to Jane, who sighed inwardly at the prospect that things were likely to degenerate into a row, even at a time like this.

'I'll lay the tray,' she said hurriedly.

'What am I to do, Jane, how the hell am I to manage?' the older woman suddenly burst out. She stood awkwardly, knotting and unknotting the teatowel in her hands, appearing embarrassed by her own sudden outburst. Jane looked up, taken by surprise at the change in her mother's voice. 'I don't understand anything any more. All those years when I wished the old bugger would fall under a bus, the quarrels, the rows, why, I've never stopped nagging him, I still do. And yet, I'm filled with such dread at him leaving me, the emptiness there'll be . . .' She began to cry noisily, using the teatowel as a handkerchief.

'It's because you do love him, Mum.'

'Don't talk so bloody daft.' She sniffed derisively and with shaking fingers attempted to light a cigarette. Jane steadied the match for her. 'You always were sloppy, Jane.'

'There's nothing sloppy in acknowledging you love somebody.'

'I've never been one for words.'

'I know, Mum. He loves you too, I'm sure of it.'

'Well, he's never said so, and he's a funny way of showing it.' She sat down heavily on the kitchen chair.

'You stayed together, didn't you, despite everything? And you're not the easiest person to tell, you know. I love you, but I've never been able to say it.'

Her mother sniffed again loudly. 'We don't see much of you – if you love us so much you'd think you could find the time to see more of us.'

'We don't get on, Mum, we never have, it's safer if I don't see you, but that doesn't stop me loving and caring for you.'

Her mother twisted in the chair as if she were uncomfortable with the way the conversation was going. She appeared relieved when the kettle began to whistle, and she got up to make the tea. 'He's going to get worse, Jane.'

'When he does I'll pay for a nurse to help you.'

'He won't have that.'

'Then lie to him, tell him it's on the NHS.'

'Yes, I might do that,' she said, picking up the tray.

Later that afternoon Jane visited her father's doctor. He confirmed her fears, the prognosis was bad. All the tests that could be done had been done, all the treatment available had been tried. Her father's tumour was inoperable. Another opinion, the doctor felt, would only confirm what they already knew and would exhaust her father further. To her mother's anger, she accepted the decision.

Jane would have stayed longer but an urgent call from Scotland arrived and her father insisted she left to attend to it. She planned to be away for only a short time.

The nurse was not needed. A week later, her father died, neatly and quietly, watching a football match on the giant television set she had bought him.

Jane stood by the open grave, her body shuddering with sobs. Back at the house, she helped serve the ritual ham-salad tea, with South African sherry. The tears kept streaming down her face.

'I don't see why you're so upset. He was never much of a father to you,' her mother said, when the few guests had gone, and they sat sipping tea that neither of them really wanted.

'We had the odd moment of closeness,' Jane said, a strange mixture of defence and pride in her voice.

'Few and far between, if you ask me. I don't think he ever liked you, if you want to know the truth.'

'I'm not asking you and I don't want to know. That's cruel, Mum.'

'It's the truth, but then you never liked the truth, Jane, all that airy-fairy romantic guff in your head. For goodness' sake, pull yourself together,' she snapped as Jane began to cry again.

'If you must know, I'm crying because it's all too late, he'll never love me now,' she cried out.

'There you go, sloppy talk again.'

'Christ, Mum, don't you ever give up?' Jane shouted angrily at her mother who sat rigidly in the chair opposite.

'There's no need to shout at me like that. You are getting bad-tempered, Jane.' Huffily she sipped her tea. 'I was surprised Alistair didn't come.'

'He offered, I said no.'

'And what right had you to do that?'

'It was the same as me with Alistair's mother: Dad never approved, so it wouldn't have been right for him to be there. Alistair understood.'

'Your father liked Alistair, it was what he was he didn't like.'

'Oh, I see, he liked Alistair but not me?' She sounded bitter.

'Alistair's a fine man. You were a fool ever to leave him. Look at you now, all this money, rushing about the world, showing off. It's all right now, but what about the future? Look at you – you'll be fifty before you know where you are. Still on your own, a fine, lonely old age you're going to have.' Jane admired the way her mother could sniff her critical snort and sip her tea at the same time.

'Age isn't that important. Fifty isn't old these days, and the attitude that every woman needs a man is gone – that's old hat,' she said with spirit.

'Old hat it might be, but it's still the truth, people need people. And mark my words, seventy will come galloping along in no time.'

'Thanks for cheering me up, Mum.'

'I think I might move in with your aunt.' Her mother abruptly changed the subject. 'She's on her own now and it's silly, the two of us rattling around in two houses. She's always good for a laugh, too – not that I can see much to laugh about at the moment.'

'That's a good idea. I would have been happy for you to come to live with me.'

'No, you wouldn't. As you said the other day, we've never got on. In any case I don't like Scotland and I couldn't live in your grand way.'

'I don't live in a grand way. My life style is quite simple, really.'

'Bah, don't give me that! Do you see much of Alistair these days?' Again she changed the subject as if suddenly tiring of one and needing to distract herself with another topic.

'Not as much. But I'm seeing him next week. It's his birthday – he's having a big party at Respryn. I promised I'd go.'

'That's nice. I must remember to send him a card.'

At last her mother stopped talking and Jane was relieved when she announced that she thought she would have an early night. It had been an emotional day for Jane and she was finding it a strain to deal with the sudden shifts in her mother's moods. As always she did not really know what to talk to her about.

As she lay in the dark, thinking of the day, she puzzled over her mother's attitude. Less than two weeks ago she had been dreading this day, and had been in tears at the prospect, and yet today she had shown no emotion and had even been irritated by Jane's grief. So Jane was both surprised and relieved when through the wall she heard the unfamiliar sound of her mother weeping. She did care, after all. Jane lay listening, wishing she could go and comfort her mother but knowing she would not appreciate the intrusion on her grief. It was sad, thought Jane, that one could know someone all one's life and still not be close enough to help them.

8

It was a strange feeling for Jane to be motoring through the park at Respryn and to know that there was no Lady Upnor waiting at the end to sneer at and torment her. She had felt guiltily elated when the old woman died but now, as she approached the house, she felt a sense of emptiness. How strange. Just like her parents – hating in life and grieving in death.

She swung the car into the courtyard. She must be the first guest to arrive: there were no other cars parked.

Banks was no longer there to greet her. He had retired to a cottage on the estate several years ago, and she hoped she would have time to visit him. The door was opened by an impeccably dressed young butler with a superior air and more than a hint of a sneer on his face. His manner was correct but Jane felt he was too perfect – more like a stage butler than the warm and welcoming Banks.

She was shown to her habitual room and given Alistair's apologies for his absence: a drama with his prize bull had called him away to the farm.

She was glad to have time to rest: she seemed to have been travelling for weeks. She bathed, and selected a dress of kaleidoscopically coloured silk she had bought at Saks in New York. She stood in front of the cheval glass and studied her image. She smiled at the thought that this mirror had seen Jane in all her different phases, from the gauche, badly dressed young nurse through her dowdy period to the present day and the sleek, perfectly groomed woman she was. Jane could now look at herself and acknowledge that she was beautiful. Lucky, too, for age had been kind to her and her face with its fine bones was still lovely, the eyes were still clear, the long hair still shone luxuriantly.

At the summons of the first gong she made her way to the drawing room and found Alistair alone, waiting for her.

'Happy birthday!'

'Jay, you look ravishing. What a dress – Honor would have approved.'

She spun round, demonstrating the fullness of the brightly coloured silk. 'Yes, it's very Honorish, isn't it, more suited to Italy – but I felt like cheering myself up.'

'Of course, your father – how did it go?'

She shrugged. 'All right, I suppose, as funerals go, but difficult. You know. Mother and I still not communicating, Mother still carping. Nothing's changed – I guess it never will. Here . . .' She handed him the carefully wrapped parcel she had brought. Like the little boy she so often thought he was, he unwrapped it eagerly.

'Hey, look at this, it's sensational,' he said, placing the large glass bowl gently on a table. 'Look at the workmanship!' He studied the engravings of Respryn, Drumloch and Trinick which she had commissioned.

'Look at the bottom.' She was smiling, pleased with the success of her idea.

He peered into the bowl. 'Why, it's the little house in Fulham.'

'All the houses you've lived in, you see.'

'All the houses we've lived in, you mean. It's the most thoughtful present I've ever had.' He kissed her cheek, his hand lingering a second longer on her arm. 'G and T?'

'Where's everybody?' she asked, as she took the drink.

'Everybody who?'

'The party guests.'

'Oh, I cancelled it,' he replied airily. 'Couldn't be bothered.'

'What am I doing here, then?'

'I can always be bothered with you.' He grinned the still boyish grin. 'I'll be honest – there never was going to be a party. I pretended.'

'What on earth for?'

'You're always so busy and surrounded with acres of people these days, I thought it was about time we had dinner on our own, without half a dozen of your minions around. I sometimes feel you do it on purpose – the people I mean – as if you're avoiding me.'

'Alistair, don't be silly.' She laughed.

'Am I? Anyhow, I hope you don't mind.'

'How could I? It's a very sweet compliment. So it's just the two of us, no other house guests?'

'Totally à deux, as the Frogs would say.' The silly, weak joke made him seem almost shy with her.

The butler appeared and announced unctuously that their dinner was served. Ceremoniously taking her arm, Alistair led her into the small family dining room.

Jane looked around the familiar room where they had eaten so many times together in the past. The blessing of Respryn was its continuity. It gave her, as it always had, a sense of security.

'So how's James? Still beavering away for you up north?' Alistair asked when the butler finally withdrew.

'He's wonderful!' Jane's eyes gleamed with pride. 'He works so hard, I really don't know how I would cope without him. He does more and more off his own bat now. He's so smart: he's more aware of what's going on than I am. I think I'm becoming redundant.'

'Good, then maybe the rest of us will see more of you.' He grinned.

'Actually, I've some exciting news. He asked me to tell you . . . he's getting engaged.'

'Really? To whom? Do I know her?'

'I doubt it. As soon as he arrived, the local matrons trotted out their daughters but it didn't work. He's fallen in love with my gamekeeper's daughter – she's one of my secretaries.'

'Ha!' Alistair roared with laughter. 'I like it. Full circle. A chip off the old block, after all, and I thought he was too serious ever to be like me.'

'Perhaps it's as well that your mother didn't live to see it. I'd have got the blame for influencing him.' She laughed too.

'Let's hope he doesn't make a mess of it, as I did.'

'Oh, come on, Alistair. We were both at fault. It took me a long time to realize it but I must have been a pain, with my insecurities and those massive chips I carried around on my shoulders. Katriona's different, though: she's far stronger and knows exactly who she is – God help anyone who tries to put her down.'

'Nice name. Is she pretty?'

'She's stunning – black-haired and grey-eyed, you know, with that lovely pale complexion some Scots have.'

'It's not just the Scots who look like that.' He lifted his glass to her and, stupidly, she thought, after all these years, she was blushing. 'When do I get to meet her?'

'I have to fly to New York again this week. He's planning to announce it when we get back. Perhaps you could come up that weekend?'

'I'd love to.'

'I was thinking of offering them the villa for their honeymoon, but I wondered if that was too schmaltzy.'

'I don't think it's schmaltzy at all. As I remember, we had a rather spectacular time there. Let's hope they do too. I often think – '

The oily butler reappeared, and Alistair stopped in midsentence. With exaggerated ceremony, the butler served them the next course, bowing as he withdrew.

'He's creepy.'

'Who, Uriah?'

'That can't possibly be his name. Uriah!' she protested.

'Uriah Heep – it's my secret name for him. I think he's called Justin de Beaune or something. I usually avoid calling him anything.'

'He's not like a butler at all. Banks would have a fit.'

'I don't think he is, I'm sure his references were fake, but you know me, I meant to check and never got around to it – you used to do all that sort of thing. I reckon he's an out-of-work actor playing the part.'

'That's what I thought the minute I set eyes on him. It's funny how we think the same things after all this time.'

'Are you lonely?' he suddenly asked.

'I don't get the time.' She did not know why she lied: remnants of her stupid pride, she presumed. 'And you?'

'Very. I doubt if there's a day when I don't kick myself for losing you.'

'Alistair, don't fall into that trap,' she said quickly. 'For years I rued the day I walked out. But I learned there's no point in ruining the present because of past mistakes. Honestly, love.'

'Don't look so alarmed.' He was laughing. 'Candlelight always has this effect on me,' he said, grinning, lightening the mood. Jane looked across the table at him: the light shining on the white hair played tricks with her eyes so that it looked as blond as it was when she had first met him. With his boyish charm it was always difficult to know when he was serious and when he was joking, she thought.

'What would happen, Jane, if I crept into your room tonight?'

Jane just caught the glass that she knocked sideways. 'I'd scream for Uriah Heep.' She giggled, desperately covering her confusion.

'It was a serious question, Jane.'

She stopped laughing. 'I don't know, Alistair, I don't even know if I'd have the courage to say come in.'

He smiled. 'I know how you feel. I wonder if I would have the courage even to knock.' He laughed again. 'Ah, well, if we're such cowards I guess we'll never know.' He shrugged his shoulders and poured more wine. As if the previous conversation had not taken place, he asked politely about the town's new airport. The moment had passed. Jane felt a strange mixture of relief and regret.

He took her arm to lead her into the small drawing room, and sat opposite her. It was a pleasant evening and passed quickly as they talked of old days and friends, of incidents that one remembered and the other had forgotten and some memories still fresh to both of them. They discussed James's wedding and what they should give him. Then Alistair escorted her to her room.

'Night, Jane,' he said, kissing her gently on the mouth. 'Thanks for a super birthday – best for a long time.'

She watched him as he disappeared along the red corridor that led to what had once been their suite of rooms.

Jane was restless as she lay in the dark, waiting for sleep. She wished she had not come: she knew the effect he could have on her. It was unfair of him to tease her. Look at her now, tossing and turning, half longing to hear his knock on the door and half terrified that she would. She wished that when he had kissed her, she had responded; she should have flung her arms about him, kissed him back. So, if she really wanted to sleep with him, why hadn't she? Even as she thought the question, she knew the answer – her fear of rejection, the hurt pride of that young woman she had once been. She knew that his mild flirting was part of a game, his suggestion that he visit her, simply an exaggerated form of politeness. She could hardly think him shy – after all, he'd shown no shyness in the past with his numerous sexual adventures – so why should he suddenly be timid now, especially with her? It was just a diversion to him.

But all the same, if he did come, she wondered what she would do. She could acknowledge she was beautiful still: people were always telling her that. Her hands ran up and down her body. She was slim, and still had a good figure, but it was not the body or the skin of the young woman he had known. Even if he really did want her, his desire was probably for the woman she had once been and not the one she was now. Eventually sleep rescued her, and when she awoke in the morning, he had not come.

They had breakfast together. Neither referred to the conversation of the night before. Alistair came with her to visit Banks in his cottage by the home farm. She inspected his horses, and felt almost relieved when it was time to go.

'Keep in touch, Jay.' He smiled at her through the window of the car and, kissing his fingers, gently placed them on her lips. 'See you next week.' He waved gaily as her car slid out of the courtyard.

Her appointments kept her in London for three days before she was able to travel north to pack and to collect her papers and her thoughts for the trip to New York. Hating flying, she dreaded these trips, but it was necessary for her to attend regular meetings at the Calem conglomerate.

And there was increasing interest in her trust in America and more of her time these days was spent lecturing and explaining the concept.

Among the pile of mail that awaited her, she was surprised to find one in Alistair's familiar handwriting, with 'Very personal' underlined twice. It was years since she had had a letter from him – he always phoned. She opened it. It was short but to the point.

Jane,

I always make a mess of things with you. I had laid my plans so carefully. I was going to seduce you, somehow wheedle my way back into your life. I haven't got the technique, that's my problem – need lessons, I suppose. I admit it's never been a problem before! But I'm so afraid of hearing you reject me.

Please come back to me, please love me again, please marry me again. There, no flowery language, just plain English, but said with as much if not more feeling than if it was all wrapped up in pretty phrases.

I keep telling you what a bloody fool I've been over the years. Last time I managed to get you into my bed I knew, even as I spoke, that I had blown it. I lay there pretending to be asleep, sensing you awake, hurt and thinking what to do. I just didn't know what to say to make it right. And I think that sometimes when I'm trying to tell you you just think I'm flirting with you. Odd, I've never been a letter writer but it seems easier to write than to say it to you. Maybe I should have taken up letter-writing sooner . . .

I've done so much to hurt you in the past, I know, but now please let me love you. I need you, Jane.

A.

Jane sat stunned. She reread the letter three times. How extraordinary: all that time he was afraid of rejection, too. Her hand went out to pick up the telephone –

'There you are, Ma. I heard you were back. I hope you don't mind but I've arranged for us to go a day early. We're flying out tonight.'

'Perhaps that would be better,' she said in a faraway voice.

'What do you mean, better? I thought you'd be annoyed.'

She smiled. 'Have I time for a bath at least?'

'If you're quick.'

She bathed hurriedly; her cases were already packed. Her mind was in turmoil, but she would have time to think on the plane. Her hand shook as she slipped the letter into her handbag.

Epilogue

The jet skimmed eastward across the Atlantic. Jane was returning home to Scotland.

'Jane,' Fran's voice whispered. She opened her eyes. 'Fancy a drink before we eat?'

'Lovely.' Jane stretched her body.

'Nice sleep?'

'I was thinking.'

'Long think. Anything interesting?' Fran asked, alert, her hand darting towards the ever present pen and pad.

'No, Fran, you can relax. I was just thinking about myself and my life.'

'How boring,' Fran teased.

'Totally self-indulgent. Bloody hell, I'm tired, Fran. Dynamic, go-getting Jane Reed is tired.'

'I'm not surprised. The number of meetings you managed to squeeze into four days was ridiculous. Why, you even exhausted the Americans. You need a holiday, my old mate. Why don't you go to that lovely villa of yours? You never use it.'

'Do you know, Fran, since Honor died, I guess I've only been there half a dozen times. It would be nice, a holiday – any chance of your coming?'

'Jane, love, I'm the last person you need. We practically live together as it is. What you need is a feller with you, my girl. Why not ask Alistair, I bet he'd jump at it?'

Jane leaned back on the cushions. There Fran went again. She's psychic, thought Jane; how the hell could Fran know that Jane had been thinking about Alistair since they left Scotland? Maybe she had talked about him without realizing it, maybe she had let something drop.

The villa. Honor's magic world. It would be nice to be there and relax for a couple of weeks, to forget all the business problems, the worry, shed the responsibilities. Could she do that at the villa? Wouldn't the memories she'd been so intent on running away from haunt her?

Across the aisle, James sat quietly working through a mountain of paper-work. He worked so hard, was so conscientious, she knew he would be only too happy to take more of the load off her. If she were honest with herself, she had to admit that he was quite capable of running everything himself. She was a figurehead, really: she could and should do less.

He sensed her looking at him and smiled. How like his father he looked, she thought – the same blond hair, the fine-boned face. He was too serious, though, and lacked his father's sense of fun. That was their fault: he had had a lonely childhood which could not have been made easier by his grandmother's continual interference. Jane could still remember the illogical sense of freedom she had felt the day Alistair had phoned to say his mother was dead, freedom from that malevolent spirit.

Giovanni had been lucky not to have a Lady Upnor in his young life. Her two sons were so different; it amazed her that they should be such good friends. She thought fondly of her Italian son, so handsome with his flashing brown eyes, improbably white teeth and Roberto's wonderfully sensuous smile. He did not seem to have a serious thought in his head. Already at twelve he showed signs of turning into an out-and-out playboy, interested only in fast cars. Before long, no doubt, it would be girls. Maybe one day he would settle down, just as his father had done.

Absent-mindedly she picked at the food the stewardess had given her. Perhaps Italy would be a good idea. But she would have to take somebody with her, someone to shield her from the past.

Could it work? She took the letter from her handbag and read it for the umpteenth time. She smiled as she remembered the years when she would have gone flying to him. What stopped her now? The romantic girl who still lurked within her, dreaming of the perfect love? No, that wasn't true. About one thing, Jane had been right all her life. She had said she would love Alistair and through everything she had. No, it was fear and pride. Stupid wasteful emotions. What if he were unfaithful to her? Hadn't she for years now admitted her mistake, admitted that infidelity need not mean the end of love? Yes, it would hurt but not as it had before. He did seem to have changed. And with the sexuality that Roberto had unlocked in her, she too had changed. Could she make love to Alistair again, though? She knew now that sexual attraction was still an important ingredient in her feelings towards him. Platonic love lay many years away for her yet. But she felt strangely shy at the thought of his seeing her naked again. In an odd way it would be easier to go to bed with that Brazilian diplomat she had met last night than with Alistair.

'Oh, Lor'.' She sighed. It would be lovely to be back at Respryn, with someone else to fill her thoughts, someone to care for her and to love her. She sighed again. It would be wonderful to wake up in the night and sense him beside her. She moved restlessly in her seat. God, that last time had been wonderful: she remembered the way she had screamed as he brought her to her climax. What was so wrong in having learned to use her body, how to excite his? Stupid Calvinistic shame which the sophisticated Jane Reed could never quite shake off. She smiled at herself, and at the memory of that night.

'What's that strange smile for, Mother?' she heard James ask.

'I was just thinking how nice it would be to sleep with a man again,' she replied, startled out of her reverie.

'Mother!' James laughed in surprise.

'Did I shock you? Maybe I'm not as old as you think. The old hormones are still scudding about.' She laughed.

'There's always Father.'

'Darling James, you never give up, do you?'

'Neither does Father. He still loves you, Mother.'

'I love him, too.'

'Then what's stopping you? I think you're both bloody mad, rattling around in your huge, great houses. You'd save a fortune in housekeeping.'

'My darling son, where did you inherit such an accountant's mind from? I don't think housekeeping economies are quite the best basis upon which to rebuild relationships.'

'You know what I mean, Ma. And I still think you're both daft.' He returned to his papers.

Maybe Alistair would like to come to Italy with her ... after all, if the memories were what frightened her, what was more logical than to invite one of the memories to come with her? Perhaps in Italy she could come to a decision – just the two of them alone – and maybe the villa would work its old magic.

It was obvious what she wanted. Then why didn't she grasp it? What held her back? Fear, stupid fears that had plagued her all her life.

Roberto had understood. That first argument, he had told her the truth about herself. That she was afraid of life, of loving. Roberto would have thought she was wasting her life now. He would have accepted her business success with pride; but he would never have comprehended her denying herself physical pleasure.

Thinking, thinking, that's all she seemed good for. And where did it get her?

The seatbelt light came on. She slipped the letter back into her bag. She checked her make-up. The plane banked and swept in a circle over the town below. This was the only moment in the flight that Jane loved. She could see the whole town beneath her, ablaze with light.

The plane swirled down and landed on the newly built runway. At the terminal building, cars waited. The door of the plane swung open and she stepped out. Dame Jane Reed was home in Strathleith.

She stood beside the plane. Across the tarmac a crowd was rushing towards her. She could see the architects, her accountant, at the front one of her secretaries clutching a sheaf of messages for her. Beyond them the hospital committee waited. Beyond them who else?

Jane opened her handbag. From inside she took a pad and pen. The pen poised indecisively for a moment. She wrote hurriedly. 'Darling,' she said, turning to her son. 'Could you telex this to your father? I haven't time. I promised to go to a meeting of the new hospital committee before I go home.'

James glanced at the paper. 'You haven't put your name on it. It doesn't make sense.'

'He'll understand.' She smiled.

James glanced again at his mother's familiar handwriting and shrugged his shoulders. He turned into the administrative building and soon the telex chattered.

'Why not? But get rid of Uriah Heep!'

Advances

For Suzanne Baboneau,
with love, and thanks for having
such wonderful ideas

I should like to thank my friends in the worlds of writing and publishing who helped me with this book, even if sometimes they were not aware of it.

In particular: Alison Samuel, Gail Lynch, Billy Adair, Suzanne Baboneau, Tom Burns, Philippa McEwan, Martin Neild, Jane Wood, Vivienne Worldly, Mic Cheetham, Marina Oliver and the many others too numerous to mention. And especially Billy Jackson for his constant support and patient Carol Slater who typed it all.

Part One

1

The white fog clung damply to the window. Julius Westall moved the heavy brocade curtain to one side and peered out, remembering other fogs, other days. Fogs which had billowed without warning across the square, blanking out man and buildings with their great swirling yellow clouds. Fogs sulphurous in their density. Fogs in which anything could happen, untold adventures could begin . . .

He turned from the window abruptly. An old man losing touch with reality in daydreams, that was what he was becoming. Senility lay that way and life was already complex enough without giving in to advancing age.

On his desk lay last year's audited accounts. He stood, a tall, patrician figure, looking down at the glossy black spiralled folder. His thick hair, once blond, was silver now, the once-piercing blue eyes were faded and with the aureole of age around the iris. But the figure was upright, that of a man who looked fit even though he knew he was not.

He was tired, that was his problem, nothing more ominous he was sure. Tired of fighting against the odds, of hoping to balance books which never would, of losing money, of responsibility, of family relationships which he could not heal, of every damned thing. He had to cling to the idea of normal fatigue: if he didn't he was afraid what lack he might find in his mental resilience.

From a cabinet at the side of his desk – a fine marble-topped desk with outspread golden eagles at either end for legs – he took a glass and a bottle of Glenfiddich and carefully poured a large measure.

'Give up the whisky and cigars for a start, Julius,' Sir Archibald McKinna, his socially smart and elegant Harley Street physician, had said that morning. But Sir Archibald had been known as 'Baldie' in his schooldays, and it was difficult for Julius, remembering the snotty-nosed fag Archibald had once been, to take anything he said seriously. Or was he using those memories as an excuse? Had he known, even as his old friend lectured him, that he would take no notice – could not face the consequences of doing so?

Did he want to live what was left of his life without the drink, the cigars, the rich food he loved? For what? An extra year, maybe two. Extra time to worry about the business, to war with his children and be ignored by his wife.

Certainly he should slow down. He might even learn to enjoy it. There were his roses, after all, he would like to spend more time pottering among them. Odd how he had come to gardening so late in life. He had never before felt any inclination to garden, could never understand those of his friends whose passion it was. Gardens had been places for others to tend and for him to sit in occasionally. And then, quite suddenly, just after his sixtieth birthday, he had the notion to plant his rose garden and for the past five years he had lavished his love, spare time and money on it. He realised now that the roses had taken over when Gemma, last of a long line of mistresses, had left him for someone younger and richer. In the past he would have sallied forth and quickly found a replacement except, after Gemma, he found he really could not be bothered – hence the roses.

It was ironic after sixty-five years of life, years packed with amorous adventures, to find himself thinking of his love for the flowers. But then, what else, who else was there to love?

Certainly not his family. Jane, his wife, six years and two children into their marriage had coldly announced that there would be no more sex as if, by producing the children, she had done her duty and would now rest on her laurels. Not that Jane had referred baldly to 'sex', she was far too genteel even to acknowledge the word existed let alone the practice. No, she had met him one evening on his return from work to inform him that his things had been moved from *her* room, that he now had a room of his own. The implication of such a move did not even need to be discussed between them. He understood. He was not surprised. A considerate lover, whatever he had tried had failed to awaken any passion in his otherwise perfect wife. He had felt sorry for her – then. How bleak never to know the fulfilment and relief of a good physical relationship. If he was honest he was relieved, as if her frigidity was no longer his responsibility. Julius had not liked the sense of failure her lack of response gave him – it made him feel that he had let her down – but then, in his defence, he doubted if there was a man alive who could rouse Jane.

After the night of his dismissal from her bedroom, he'd been unfaithful for the first time. He felt he had every right to; she did not. And as mistress followed mistress he had watched Jane's pretty face turn thin-lipped, bitter and shrewish. She had loved him once but Julius had seen that love turn to hatred, ice cold, polite, but hatred none the less. Jane had the final revenge – she refused to divorce him.

Divorce. In this day and age divorce would have been automatic, and no one would have thought the less of him – a modern Julius would have had no qualms about it – but he had been brought up in the old ways and divorce was out of the question. Appearances had to be maintained and now it was too late to bother. He had accepted the ground rules of their relationship –

the façade that all was well – but when he contemplated the lost and empty years, he wondered why and for whom he had done so.

Inevitably his liaisons became known and he had acquired the reputation of a roué. Unfair, when all he had ever wanted was a happy, loving marriage. Jane, on the other hand, while not much liked – she was not an easy woman for anyone to like – received sympathy as the wronged wife. Julius had never explained the true situation to a living soul, not even his army of mistresses. It was not his way.

And his two children? He did not even know them, did not even want to now. John, his son and heir, had rejected publishing for banking and was now nearly forty, suitably pompous with a large enough gut to proclaim to the world how successful he was. Caroline was a bigot who lived in the country with her minor 'landed gentry' husband who tried to lord it over a community, which these days refused to cower satisfactorily.

He had once overheard someone say that it was possible to dislike your children but nothing could ever stop you loving them. Well, he could put the lie to *that* theory, he thought, as he poured another whisky, raised his glass and silently toasted Sir Archibald.

All he cared for was this room, the company and his roses. Julius leaned back in the high-backed wing chair and looked with satisfaction at his office, as he often had over the thirty years since he had inherited it from his father. He had always worked long hours – invariably the first in and the last to leave – and from the very beginning he had resolved that if he was to spend more time here than in his home, then he would make this room as beautiful and comfortable as it could be. Hence the valuable desk, and the two enormous George III breakfront bookcases, containing every book he'd ever published, bound in best Morocco leather, the Chippendale library steps, the fine Amritsar carpet and the pictures. Ah, the pictures, his pride and joy. Sutherland, Hitchens, Bacon, Spencer, each purchased with love, each now worth a small fortune.

The company Westall and Trim had been founded by his great-great-grandfather in 1859. Each generation that followed had taken up, with pride, the running of their 'house'. Trim's descendants had long ago faded from the scene, bought out one by one by Julius's predecessors. By the time he had joined the firm, the name was merely part of the logo. Westall was a name to be proud of in the literary world, a name anyone would care to follow – all, that is, except his son who, with his ruthless accountant's eye, had scanned the balance sheets and opted for what he saw as the safer world of banking.

On that score Julius had to admit John was right: there could be no arguing with such a conclusion. Working at Westall's would not have bought him the fine house in Ebury Street, the small farm in Sussex, the bolt-hole in the Dordogne. But banking could never provide John with the excitement that publishing had given Julius all his working life. He was convinced there was nothing in the world to compare with finding a new writer, taking that first gamble on an unknown. Nothing could match the satisfaction of nurturing him or her, supporting, persuading, cajoling, sympathising, dealing with the tantrums and the self-doubt, having the patience of Job, all for that end product – *The Book*. A book that might sink without trace, but at the same time a book that might, just might, be lauded, awarded and sell. The authors thought it was they themselves who were important but for Julius they were a means to an end – the production of that precious volume. Where in banking could he find the pleasure of having an idea and matching it to the right author – the next best thing to being a writer himself? It never palled. Each time a new book arrived from the printers, encased in the dust jacket over which the designers had argued and laboured, Julius always felt the same sense of excitement and pride.

He had taken many gambles – books that, in the end, he realised only he and the author loved, and others that he had known would never return the outlay but which he had still gone ahead with because he was a publisher and he felt they *should* be published. Publishing to Julius was about books, not profit, and that, in the 1990s, was where the problem lay.

All his predecessors had had other means – share portfolios, property with which they had been able to cushion their lives against the ups and downs which had always been the way of publishing – but Julius had none of these. After death duties, what had been left had gradually been eaten away by the necessary injections of cash that this insatiable monster – his 'house' – required to stay afloat.

In the old days, once an author joined you, they stayed until they wrote no more or died – Julius had found the two usually came together. But that had all changed. He still had that precious asset which made him a good and highly respected publisher, the ability to spot talent – often when others had passed it by. He would do his part of the job to perfection but invariably the great conglomerate sharks lurking out there in today's murky waters would strike, offering enormous advances which his firm could never match. Author loyalty was long dead. He did not blame them and always sent them on their way with his congratulations and wishes for their good fortune ringing in their ears. For who but the richest could turn their backs on such seducers?

Those advances! He hated the word, loathed the lengthy negotiations they invariably involved with rapacious authors hiding behind equally rapacious agents who did the dealing for them. Time was when an author accepted a couple of hundred pounds as a loan against future royalties – a modest sum to tide him over. Once that couple of hundred had been earned he was paid his royalties. Now there were authors whose advances were so high they never earned a penny in royalties. Advances so huge – half a million pounds, a million, anything was possible – that the publisher could never hope to earn the money back. It was madness, all of it.

Of his own authors he could rely on only two: Gerald Walters, knighted now for services to literature, Nobel Prize winner and doyen of English writers whom Julius had first met at Cambridge and whose first book Westall's had been proud to produce. Every three to four years a chaotic manuscript would arrive on Julius's desk. Gerald, he often thought, must be the only author alive who was allowed to present his work like that rather than neatly typed.

Then there was Sally Britain – crime writer *extraordinaire*, winner of the Golden Dagger award, who each September, for fifteen years, had presented him with yet another beautifully crafted thriller. A sweet woman and one with whom he had enjoyed a happy summer affair soon after she had joined them. Sally did not strike one as a romantic but as the years went by and she still stayed with him, he often wondered if it was for old times' sake.

Each year Julius was anxious, knowing that both these writers would be approached by the larger publishers with promises of untold sales and promotion but, luckily for him, they had always refused. But then, both were in that small band of successful writers who were content with the money they made and could afford the luxury of loyalty.

The others, one by one, had left what, he supposed, they saw as a sinking ship. And new blood, initially sycophantically grateful, was, once Westall's had done the groundwork on their careers, seduced away by offers which, to Julius, resembled telephone numbers.

It wasn't as it used to be ... There he went again, that's how old men thought and talked ...

The solution was easy. He had only to hint he wanted out and the bargaining from the conglomerates would be deafening, the cheque books would flash, the piranhas would strike, and Westall and Trim would never be the same again.

His family was as aware of this as he and there had been many discussions, usually slipping into arguments, as they pointed out what a selfish fool he was. Maybe so, but he could not sell out. He'd rather die in harness. But he needed new blood in the company, sympathetic blood, someone who could look at the dear old lady and drag her, screaming if necessary, into the new decade.

Not Crispin, though. Never! He still rued the day he'd listened to his sister, Marge, and agreed to take on his nephew, cocky and fresh from Oxford, as a junior editor. Now he was financial director – from ability certainly, Julius wasn't a total fool and certainly not where staff were concerned. But Crispin, with his thrusting arrogance, his streak of ruthlessness, his greed, was not a person Julius could ever like and certainly not the person to entrust with this love of his life. If he did, Crispin would sell out within twenty-four hours he was certain.

He supposed he had to listen to old Archibald, though – if not for himself at least for the firm. He was not ready to give up yet, he still had things to do. He needed help, he realised that now. Someone younger, but someone who thought as he did. He had a number of ideas stored away in the back of his mind. Perhaps it was time to bring them out, dust them down and mull them over seriously.

The clock on the mantelshelf chimed the hour. Julius checked it against his watch. Ten. Hardly worth going home. He closed the ledger he should have been studying and locked his safe. Carrying his bottle of Glenfiddich and with a typescript under his arm, he mounted the stairs to the attic where, years ago, he had created a small flat for himself, the scene of many of his conquests.

Stupid old goat! He laughed at himself. All that was over and thank God it was. As a young man he could never have imagined a day would dawn when he would be grateful that the hormones had quietened down. Now he felt it was one of the greatest advantages of age, even the memories did not bother him any more.

He opened the small refrigerator to see what Roz had bought for him just in case he slept over. The perfect secretary, Roz. Pity she had blotted her copybook, in his eyes, by having an affair with Crispin – not that he was supposed to know.

2

Like many housebound women, Kate Howard had a moment in the day that was more special than any other. Before it could be reached, however, the chaos of the early morning had to be surmounted. First, she had to sort out her family ready for work and school. She had winkled them reluctantly out of their beds. She had searched for and found a vast range of things they could not find – items of clothing, satchels, briefcases, last night's homework, dinner money – all of which were invariably in the place she had suggested. She had mediated in an argument that had erupted from nowhere and over nothing. She had fed and watered them, arguing with her dieting daughter about the need to eat and reprimanding her son whose bolting of his food was putting his future digestion at risk. Long ago she had resigned herself to her husband hiding behind his paper, loftily impervious to the noise. As usual she had waylaid the morning post, secreting away the electricity or telephone bill knowing, from experience, that such matters were better received at the end of the day rather than at the beginning. She had kissed them goodbye and waved them on their way. Then the front door slammed on the last of them and a silence descended upon the house, a silence like no other, a moment like no other.

Kate now sat at the table in the kitchen and looked with distaste at the dirty breakfast crockery which littered it. She leaned back in her chair and let the quiet wash over her, calm her and set her up for the rest of the day. She felt the peace of the house seep through her as if it was flowing in her veins.

Kate was not a morning person and never had been. When the alarm clock rang it was a rebirth for her, and an agonising one too. She always rose first and had a quick shower, cleaned her teeth, brushed her hair and, these days, avoided looking in the mirror over the pampas-green basin with its gold-plated taps. Then she padded quietly down to the kitchen to put the kettle on.

She was always first down, too, not out of any sense of duty but rather because it gave her half an hour before she had to speak to anyone. If it was necessary for her to speak before then it invariably emerged as a snap which put the whole household out for the rest of the day.

For years she had thought guiltily that it was only *her* family who faced such chaotic mornings, that in some way they were all her fault, for she had made the mistake of comparing them with the calm of her mother's house where everything worked like clockwork and no one ever had a cross word with anyone. She knew better now. From friends she had learned she was not alone, that the behaviour in this household was the same as in a million others. Her mother's house was the odd one out.

When the family had gone Kate ate, or not, depending on whether she was dieting, or whether she had given up on the latest one, the latter being the more common. But first she cleared the offending dishes from the table, loaded the dishwasher, wiped the cooker down and then made her tea and toast. When she thought of the amounts of food her son and husband consumed without putting on an ounce, she resented bitterly the guilt she felt as she ate her toast and put a spoonful of sugar into her tea. Then she lit her first cigarette of the day, the one she enjoyed most, and finally was at comparative peace with the world.

She could not enjoy a total peace for Kate had reached the point in her life where she had begun to feel as confused as she had as an adolescent. As her hormones thrashed about in their dying phase, she found her moods swinging alarmingly. If she felt happy and elated she could not rely on it to last for she knew full well that a dark feeling was always lurking ready to take hold. When it came she tried to fight it, to make it go away, for she knew that if she allowed it to linger long, it would sneak into the centre of her soul, and the consequences could be disastrous. It had crept stealthily over her, so slow and subtle its onset that neither she nor those around her were aware of the change in her.

Kate called it a feeling because, in fairness to herself, it wasn't a true depression, not a medically diagnosable condition. Rather, she felt as if the joy had departed from her life and much of her spontaneity disappeared with it. She felt herself becoming, by insidious degrees, empty and colourless and the more she felt this the more rapidly she began to look as she felt – so much so that a passer-by in the street would no longer notice her, would pass the insignificant woman she had allowed herself to become without a second glance. Even her walk had changed. These days she walked with eyes downcast, not wanting to glance up to meet the blank stare of a stranger, knowing that in the uninterested glance was the proof that her youth had gone once and for all, that she was middle-aged.

She was surprised by her reaction to the loss of more youthful looks. She had not expected it. She had assumed that only beautiful women cared. Kate had never been beautiful and had imagined that she would be able to shrug off advancing years when her skin lost its elasticity, the wrinkles appeared, her waist thickened, when she would meet men and see that they were not attracted.

She found she thought constantly about that lack of interest. She had never played around, had not wanted to – but now that it was all too late, she found a reservoir of regret within her that now she never would. A sadness that she would never know what it was like for another man to make love to her.

Discontent, unknown to her before, had begun to infiltrate her life. Yet the life she lived had not changed, only herself. Her routine was the same as it had been for nearly twenty-four years – a routine she had not questioned, had been too busy even to think about. But now she found she was beginning to resent it, and sometimes felt as if her home was becoming a prison from which there was no escape.

That was when the guilt began to surface, for what had she to be so discontented about? She had everything that a woman could want – or, rather, what her upbringing had taught her a woman should want. Tony, her husband, worked hard for them all – too hard, in fact, for she would have preferred him to spend more time with them than he did. He did not drink excessively, he was not a womaniser, all his free time was spent at home and many of her friends, with husbands who strayed, envied her. Lucy and Steve, their children, were healthy and good-looking. They had never been a problem, there had been no unsuitable friends, no drugs and she and Tony had even been spared political views alien to their own, which, she knew, in other homes had led to rows of volcanic proportions. They were ideal children. Lucy, bright as a button and about to finish her A levels, had opted for a career in law just like her father, which had pleased him immensely. Steve, a bit slower than his sister but with far more charm and about to take his GCSEs, wanted to be a landscape gardener. Tony could not understand this ambition and, Kate felt, found it somewhat *infra dig*. Of the two she was most at ease with her son.

Kate's life had been predictable. She had lived with her parents – solicitor father, housewife mother – in their large semi-detached Victorian villa in a good part of Bristol. She had done moderately well at school and if, in her teens, she might have dreamed of travel and adventure, she had known these were only dreams. She had been brought up to marry a suitable man and have children, the best role for women – she should know, her mother had told her often enough.

Her only time away from home had been at teacher-training college where her speciality had been domestic science. Most weekends she returned home and took little part in the college's social life for by then she had met Tony, articled to her father's firm. She had never taught for as soon as she had her diploma she married him. Her life was pre-ordained. It was to be the same as her mother's, and rightly and gratefully so, Kate knew that.

The young couple had lived for a happy year in a small flat in Bristol until one day when Tony returned in a high state of excitement with the particulars of this house, then in need of repair and restoration. It would be an expensive and long-term project and the only way they could afford it was by delaying the family they planned. There was no question of Kate working to help, Tony would never have countenanced such an idea.

It was hard for Kate not having a baby when she so wanted one and as much as she loved the house she felt she would rather they had bought something cheaper and she be allowed the children she wanted. But Tony had set his heart on it and Tony always had his own way. He expected it and she accepted it, for had not her own father always decided everything?

They had worked on the house for nearly five years – Tony regarded her decorating skills more as a hobby than as work. When the second bathroom had been fitted the news she longed for came – Tony said they could start a family. First Lucy, followed a couple of years later by Steve. They were a perfect family in their perfect home.

It was a gem of a house, old and built in beautiful Cotswold stone and standing in a village which nestled in the folds of the Mendip Hills. Nothing here had changed in centuries if one discounted tarmacadam, electricity, telephone, TV aerials and running water. Kate had an *en-suite* bathroom, an Aga in the kitchen, a lovely garden and her own car, even if it was secondhand, in the garage. She had the best of the old world and the new. She had everything.

So why had she begun to question it, to feel that she had missed out in life and that, in some way, everything was over?

At night in bed, when she felt so hot she couldn't sleep, she knew the answer. She wanted to do something, to be someone, not just a wife and mother but important to others, too. The thought would give her hope, make her feel that all was not lost. But in the morning it became no more than a dream and the 'feeling' would take hold of her for the rest of the day.

Breakfast over, her second cigarette alight, Kate read the *Daily Mail* from cover to cover – the only time she felt was hers alone to be so self-indulgent.

There were times when she dallied with the idea that if they were richer she might not be feeling the way she did. Her husband must be earning a good salary as the middle partner in a firm of solicitors in the nearby town of Graintry. She did not know since Tony had never told her what he was paid, only that there was never enough and she must be careful.

For years 'being careful' had been a challenge that she had taken pride in meeting. She worked hard at domesticity, wrote 'Homemaker' with pride on forms. And the reputation she had acquired among their circle for being a good manager had filled her with a sense of purpose.

Lucy, cleverer than Kate at manipulating Tony, had recently acquired a dress allowance from her father, which Kate, tired of asking for money for her own clothes and often having to make them, had to admit she envied. But when she had *wondered* if she should not have one too, the request was met with a look – there was no need for words. *Wondering* was Kate's way of asking. Early in her marriage she had discovered that she got nowhere with Tony by asking outright for something. It appeared to irritate him and his 'no' was virtually automatic.

Kate would wander round Debenhams and look at the make-up, the moisturisers, the anti-wrinkle creams. She could have bought them, the housekeeping allowance would stretch to the occasional treat, but she did not. She could never quite bring herself to spend that sort of money on herself, feeling it would not be right and certainly unfair to Tony. The supermarket was her main beautician. She had her hair permed twice a year and managed it herself in between times. Her only extravagance was shoes, in that she only ever bought good quality, expensive ones, but that had been drilled into her by her mother, so it was not really her decision.

She made all the curtains, lining them, stiffening the pelmets, making a job of them that a professional would be proud of. She had never opened a can of soup in the whole of her married life and her pantry was a joy to enter with its rows of home-made jams, chutneys and bottled fruits lined up neatly on the shelves.

Kate was a paragon of a housewife. But recently in her quiet moments, she had looked about her immaculate kitchen with loathing and would sit and dream of hair appointments and manicures in expensive London salons, of throwing out all her carefully hand-made clothes and shopping for new in the expensive boutiques in Graintry, of buying face creams that cost a whole week's housekeeping, of going to a health farm and being cosseted for a week. She would imagine herself in some exotic island location, the warm tropical wind riffling through her newly streaked hair. In this dream there was always a shadowy figure in the background – male, of course. And, although she had not put a face to him, she knew it was not Tony.

Kate was at a dangerous age. An age made more dangerous because she could see no way out of the domestic trap in which, at forty-five, she found herself, and where she dreaded remaining for the rest of her life.

3

Crispin Anderson had not meant to enter the restaurant quite so surreptitiously, thereby attracting far more attention than he had intended, but, in the circumstances, it was difficult not to look shifty. Fearful of being overheard he had made the appointment from a call box; he had lied to his secretary, telling her he was going shopping; he had ordered a taxi for Harrods and there had changed cabs, knowing that his destination would appear on the taxi firm's account. By the time he arrived at the restaurant, situated far away from any prying eyes in Bloomsbury, he felt quite elated and sure he knew how a spy must feel. The venue he had chosen was in the nether regions of

Battersea. He had felt like an intrepid traveller crossing the river – rather like crossing the Rubicon, he thought, and chuckled quietly at his own joke. He rarely joked and even more rarely understood the witticisms of others – hence his inordinate pleasure in this one.

He rejected the first table he was shown to, in the window, and asked for one at the back conveniently hidden by a large potted palm. He looked about the less than half-full room to make certain he knew no one there, and relaxed. But then, who would travel this far for lunch? And, as far as he was aware, he knew no one who lived in this district.

Crispin resided in a tall white-painted house in Chelsea, generously bequeathed him by his paternal grandmother. Even with what he and his wife earned they would never have been able to afford such a prestigious address from their own resources. They claimed the house was Regency, which it certainly looked. He kept secret, even from his wife, the fact, gleaned from the deeds, that it was Victorian. Everything about the house was perfect and nothing in his and Charlotte's lives could mar it. They had no children and no intention of having any, and Charlotte's wish not to procreate had been the deciding factor in his marrying her. They had no dog, cat or even gerbil to shed hair, puke, pee or fart.

They had searched painstakingly to find the right fabrics, wallpaper, furniture, objects and paintings. All were in period – if one ignored those irritating few years that placed the house in the wrong era. They ate off bone china and drank from glass made before the mid-nineteenth century. Both would have died rather than have plastic in the house – even their tooth-brushes were tortoiseshell, the bristles of which were restored at regular intervals.

Such electrical equipment that, given their busy lifestyles, they needed – washing machine, drier and the vacuum cleaner their cleaning lady adamantly demanded – was relegated to the basement so that their sensitive eyes need not be offended and they could pretend the intrusive gadgets did not exist.

Among their small group of closest friends, all of whom lived in identical houses, they were famous for the exquisite dinners they gave, the whole house lit by candle-light, coal fires glowing – they had refused to install central heating. Crispin had a fine line in embroidered waistcoats and cravats while Charlotte nursed a collection of antique dresses. It pleased him to watch her prettily fussing about their guests in her sprigged muslin, which allowed him to fantasise that he was about to screw Jane Austen.

In reality the house was their own private dream world. Neither of them took their fascination with the past into the outside world of business: Crispin was always impeccably suited by Savile Row, Charlotte by Catherine Walker. It fascinated him that, in effect, Charlotte was two people, the soft, daintily adorned woman inside the house and the other suitably dressed outside for her powerful position at Phipps and Secton, one of the largest advertising agencies in the Western world.

Peter was late, for which he was glad. It gave him the chance to study again the figures in his briefcase. He had no need to do so, he already knew them by heart, but Crispin was meticulous where business and figures were concerned.

He ordered a Perrier with a slice of lime. Crispin never mixed alcohol with business, he had seen too many fail that way. His Uncle Julius was a prime example, taking pleasure and pride in his long, heavy, alcoholic luncheons. Probably a contributory cause to the mess he was in right now. Crispin had no patience with such people or such behaviour.

He looked with satisfaction at the neatness of the rows of figures. Roz had done him proud this time. One of his most sensible decisions in the ten years he had been at Westall and Trim was the one made, nearly a year ago when he first started seriously to plan his future, to seduce Julius's personal secretary.

It was his uncle's fault that he was having to act like this: Julius had a romantic, stupid attitude to publishing that for some time had been driving Crispin mad with frustration. There was money to be made, big money – he saw it happening in the go-ahead firms unencumbered with a dreaming old fool at their head – but not with the independents. They'd had their day. Crispin had every intention of joining the ranks of the rich conglomerates as soon as possible.

That day was moving nearer now that he had all the information he needed. At first he had had all manner of wild plans to oust his uncle from control but thanks to Roz's help he had not made such clumsy errors. He had learned he would have to wait but, it transpired, not for too long. Now was the time to begin to put out serious feelers within the industry so that the minute the old man died he would know which course to take.

There had been times in the past year when the expense of a mistress, coupled with an expensive wife, had made him wonder if the outlay was ever going to be worthwhile. In the beginning, his main stumbling block had been the inconvenient discovery that Roz was infuriatingly loyal to Julius. It had required enormous patience and self-control on Crispin's part to bide his time with her.

Not that it had been difficult to recruit her in the first place. Crispin was handsome, smart, and could turn on that easy charm which, all his life, those women he had selected fell for. It was one of the reasons he despised women as much as he did, for Crispin was fully aware how superficial it was. He regarded it as just another useful tool, like his intelligence and his good looks.

Using charm, it had taken him just six months to get Roz to dig out the share register of Westall and Trim – since it was a private unlimited company it had been impossible to find out any other way. His mother held shares but, typical of her, she had refused to tell him how many.

He should not have been surprised at her attitude: all his life his mother had been irritatingly secretive, almost pathologically so, he thought. The result was that after thirty-three years he did not know her at all. She had been a widow for six years and although he had tried to find out her financial standing and whether she had any followers she might marry, he had failed – as he always did where she was concerned. Sometimes he had the feeling that it was only with him she was secretive, that she did not like him. He did not mind in the least since he felt nothing for her. If he thought about his father these days it was to feel sorry for him for having shared his life with someone like Crispin's mother. He did not know what her attitude was towards her brother Julius, which made planning more difficult than it need have been. He had once thought of soliciting her help, confiding his long-term plans to her, but when she had told him to mind his own business over the shares he had resolved not to rely on any maternal feelings.

Knowing who held which shares, however, had not helped him one iota. Julius owned 49 per cent, his brother Simon – a painter of little distinction, in Crispin's view, and less success – held 20 per cent, as did Crispin's mother, Marge. Julius's wife Jane held 9 per cent and the Lepanto Trust held the remaining 2 per cent.

In the unlikely event of Crispin being able to persuade his mother, Uncle Simon and Aunt Jane to go along with him they would still only equal Julius's 49 per cent. The key, therefore, to a majority holding would be the trust. What or who this trust was had beaten both his own and Roz's investigative abilities. The last dividends had been paid into an account at Hoare's Bank, no address available. At this rate he'd have to acquire another mistress, at Hoare's, to find out.

He had been despondent until last week, unable to see any way of gaining control of Westall and Trim. What had changed the whole scenario was discovering from Roz that the old boy had been to see his doctor in Harley Street. Crispin had been unable to do any work that day, he was so excited about the possible implications of his uncle's appointment. At first Roz had refused to tell him anything, pretending she knew nothing. But Crispin knew that if the old boy had told anyone anything it would have been Roz – he was ridiculously fond of the girl in Crispin's eyes. He had not pushed the issue but had invited her out to dinner and cleverly manipulated the conversation so that she thought she had brought up the subject herself. At first she had wittered on about promising not to tell a soul, that she could not break a confidence. He had pretended to respect her wishes, changing the subject, talking about a mythical happy childhood in which his uncle had played such a loving part. It did the trick, she burst into tears and spilled the works. It appeared that Julius's heart was in bad shape and that the doctor had told him that unless he gave up drinking and smoking and went on a strict low-fat diet, he could die at any time. Crispin was suitably distressed, an act difficult to maintain when Roz, crying even more, told him how worried she was since Julius seemed to be drinking even more in a crazy act of defiance. To get her to commit the final treachery he had had to promise her the ultimate – that he would leave his wife for her if only she would open Julius's private safe and photocopy his will.

It never failed to amaze him, in this day of sexual equality, the power men could exert just by promising marriage. Not that he had meant it. He would never leave Charlotte for anyone, least of all Roz. She was a nice enough girl and far more enthusiastic in bed than Charlotte had ever been, but she was not right for him. Once or twice he had been horrified to notice she wore clothes blended with man-made fibres, and she had the most vulgar collection of earrings. But she had believed him and last night, in bed in her small flat, she had presented him with the longed-for copy of the will.

The will was the other key. It had always worried him what Julius would do with his shares. Julius had never made any secret that he loathed his children so Crispin had feared he might leave his shares divided among old, loyal employees or to Battersea Dogs' Home or whatever.

His relief when he read the document was total. Julius was just like all the others of his generation: he had left the lot to his children – all except his flaming paintings which he'd bequeathed to the Fitzwilliam Museum, Cambridge. Crispin did not mind that. They were a load of rubbish, as far as he was concerned, even if they were worth a small fortune. Crispin much preferred a nice understandable still-life or landscape. All the same, it might be useful to dig in the accounts and find out how they had been paid for – they might belong to the firm, one never knew.

With this information he could really begin to plan. He knew his cousins John and Caroline. Neither had any interest in publishing and both needed money, John because he collected the stuff like other people collected stamps or butterflies, and Caroline because her small estate in the country was always needing money – the place devoured every penny she and her husband could raise. Both would be only too happy to sell to the highest bidder – and bidders, he knew, there would be aplenty. Westall and Trim was a distinguished name and half a dozen firms, both English and American, would be only too happy to acquire such a house.

'Sorry I'm late.' Peter Holt slipped into the seat opposite. 'I know you said discretion was essential but isn't this going a bit far?' He grimaced.

'I'm told the food is surprisingly good.'

'I hope you're right,' Peter said with feeling. 'Double gin and tonic,' he instructed the hovering waiter. Crispin's lip curled ever so slightly with disdain. 'I presume, with all this skulduggery, you've something secret to tell me?' he went on, as he flicked his napkin across his knee and opened the menu.

'Wine?' Crispin asked, delaying any business since he knew he was going to enjoy this interview.

'But of course – red, if it's all right with you.'

Crispin studied the wine list. He would like to have chosen a cheap house wine since he wasn't drinking but, realising he must have Peter on his side, steeled himself to order a particularly expensive Burgundy and a bottle of Perrier for himself.

'What's the news, then?' Peter asked as he ripped his roll to pieces, crumbs flying all over the place.

Crispin had to force himself to ignore such brutishness. 'I phoned you, Peter, for as you know I've always had the greatest respect for you and value our friendship greatly.' Peter said nothing to this since it was all news to him. He smiled instead, he hoped graciously. 'I've approached you – and only you, I hasten to add – since fairly shortly I shall be looking for interest from a larger firm.'

'You're leaving Westall's?'

'No.' Crispin hoped he did not sound too irritated. 'I mean I shall be in control of Westall's. Let's face it, Peter, the day of the independent is over. I've always respected what you and Phillip have done with Shotters. You're *the* success story *par excellence* in postwar publishing. We, the family, shall be selling up and all of us would prefer you to be the buyer. I shall, of course, have one or two expectations – a seat on the board, Westall's to remain as an imprint with me in control . . .'

'And a sack of money,' Peter laughed.

'Of course.' He tried not to lean over, tried not to appear too desperate.

'The old boy retiring, giving you the whole bang shoot, then?'

Crispin shrugged, thereby saying nothing.

'When?'

'I'd rather not say at the moment. And I'd prefer it if you didn't mention this meeting to a living soul. I just wanted you to know, for when it happens there will undoubtedly be a rush. I wanted you to be in a position of strength.' He dug into his briefcase and slid a black folder across the table. 'Those are the firm's figures for the past ten years, plus projections, plus details of business in hand.'

'You're taking one hell of a risk giving me all this.'

'I trust you implicitly, Peter.' Crispin smiled his most charming smile.

'Well, thanks.' Peter stuffed the folder into his own briefcase. 'Right, where's that wine? I've one rule, Crispin, I never mix food and business.'

Crispin had to agree, he had no choice, but he was disappointed. Peter could have been his Uncle Julius speaking.

After lunch, Crispin took a taxi to Harrods. He purchased two Sea Island cotton shirts, some silk socks and a box of Irish linen handkerchiefs. Then he went to a phone booth and made three calls. The first was to the managing director of Tudor Holdings UK, the English arm of a large American publishing conglomerate, the second to the chairman of Pewter, the largest of the English publishing empires. Then he called his cousin, John Westall.

4

Peter manoeuvred his Mercedes into the space reserved for him in front of the large office block of Shotters. He collected his papers together, strode rapidly across the pavement and into reception, nodded pleasantly at the girl behind the desk, and stepped into the lift which shot to the top of the building and the wide, white-painted lobby of the executive floor. At sight of him there was a flurry of activity as his secretary collected memos and Ben, his personal assistant, walked quickly to open the large double mahogany doors at the end of the hallway. The green suit Ben was wearing today was more lurid than usual, and Peter disliked his hairstyle – extravagantly quiffed in the front, and flat as a board on top, as if he spent the night standing on his head. He supposed he should speak to him about his appearance but, even as he thought it, he knew he would not. He would have resented such criticism at Ben's age and he liked the young fellow – besides, he was the brightest assistant he had ever had.

Several people had been sitting in large comfortable dark blue leather armchairs, which matched exactly the blue of the carpet woven specially with the Shotters logo of a small pistol in gold. Peter had had doubts about the carpet at the drawing-board stage and had voiced them, but the combined sulks and cajoling of his wife and the epicene designer had finally persuaded him. Anything for a quiet life. Too often he gave in for that reason and then despised himself. It didn't help that he had the satisfaction every day, as he walked on the thick carpet, of knowing he had been right: it was unbelievably vulgar. He smiled, as if in apology, to those waiting as he hurried past. He looked at his watch, he was running late again.

He walked through the door, still held open by Ben, and into the vast room which was his office.

'You know, Ben, I'm quite capable of opening a door,' Peter said, with an unusual flash of irritation.

'Sorry?' Ben said, puzzled.

'Oh, never mind. Who's out there?' He nodded curtly towards the hallway, annoyed at himself. That was twice this week he had snapped at Ben, plus shouting at Em and reducing her to tears. It was not like him. Maybe he needed a check-up, a holiday, or something.

'Your two-thirty and your three-fifteen appointments. The three-fifteen is bloody early.'

'Must be keen,' Peter said with a grin, hoping the grin would excuse his earlier bad manners. He threw his document case on to the desk, which was so large that although the black leather case skimmed across its surface it did not slip off. He shrugged out of his jacket and took from his secretary, Em, the sheaf of telephone messages. He glanced quickly through them. 'Anything important?'

'Your wife telephoned to remind you about the opera tonight. She says she'll meet you here at seven. Joyce Armitage insists on speaking to you personally. She refuses to discuss whatever it is with Gloria, who thinks it's probably something to do with the new artwork,' Em said apologetically. Peter rolled his eyes with exasperation at authors who thought they knew better than the art department. 'And a producer from BBC Bristol called. They want to know if you'd be interested in appearing in a programme they're planning on publishing. I said you wouldn't be free to return his call until late afternoon, he said he'd be there until seven. The rest can wait.' Em closed her notepad.

'I hate doing TV,' Peter complained.

'Think of the free publicity. Perhaps they'll want to do it here – you could have all the latest books lined up behind you,' Ben said, excitedly, already arranging the books and posters in his mind's eye.

'I think you're wonderful on television, Peter.' Em smiled her shy smile.

'Thanks, Em – you and my mother.' He laughed. 'Would you be an angel and rustle up some coffee? I've just had one of the foulest lunches of my life. So, Ben, who's waiting?'

'Stone, from Stone and Solomon, with the layouts.'

'Who?'

'They're doing the hoardings for Bella Ford's new one.'

'Oh, yes, I remember. She's becoming a sticky bitch – too demanding.'

'Her sales on the last one are up.'

'I could almost wish she'd fail, and then the pleasure I'd have rejecting the next book. I loathe the woman. You'd best get the art director up. Bella will hit the roof if we get it wrong this time. Who else?'

'Your three-fifteen is Marsh – they're a public-relations firm, specialising in book promotions, poor bloke's probably touting for business. And there's a young fellow, Chris Gordon, he's looking for a job.'

'Then send him to personnel.'

'He says his mother met your wife at a charity lunch and she suggested he drop by. Apparently she said you wouldn't mind.' Ben smiled to himself.

Peter loosened his tie with exasperation. He wished Hilary wouldn't do that sort of thing, but it just wasn't worth the ensuing row not to see the fellow – there he went again, giving in. 'Very well, but he'll have to wait until after I've seen the others and made my calls. And get some info on him – look at his CV. Phone Lorna, ask her what jobs are going, if any. Right, tell Em I'll have the coffee in five minutes.'

As Ben let himself silently out of the room, Peter threw himself lengthwise on to the six-seater sofa. He levered off his fine black leather loafers, closed his eyes and, concentrating on his toes, made himself relax. He lay so for four minutes then stood, refreshed. It was a trick he had learnt from a hypnotist who had lectured the Parapsychology Society when he was a student and it always worked, even though he knew it had led to a host of jokes in the outer office. He crossed the wide room, opened a concealed door in the mahogany panelling and entered the small shower room. He splashed his face with cold water, brushed his hair, noting a few more silver hairs in the faded blond, now bordering on mouse. He inspected his nails, put on his jacket again, pressed the button on his desk and was half-way across the room, hand held out in greeting, as his two-thirty nervously entered the room. An assistant followed him, weighed down by the large leather portfolios that were the stock-in-trade of advertising men, designers and the like.

'Stone – a million apologies – the traffic . . . Now, let's see what you've got – I've been waiting all day to see . . . Bella Ford is so excited . . .'

It was gone six before he had completed all his appointments and calls – early for once. From the document case he removed the folder Crispin had given him, laid it out on the desk and began to study the figures.

'So, what was the mystery lunch about?' Phillip Stern, his partner, had popped his head round the communicating door of his office.

'Come in, Phillip. Crispin, up to no good . . .' He pointed to the open folder.

Phillip loped across the room on his long, thin legs and glanced down.

'Is this for real?' He slumped down on a chair, looking quizzically at Peter.

'It would seem so. He claims he's tipping us off first – that it'll be up for grabs shortly. Wants a seat on the board, etc, etc . . .'

'That creep comes in the door, I walk out. I'm serious.'

'Don't worry. I have to admit he's bloody good at his job, for all his old-fogey ways, but who could work with a shit like that? You'd be spending all your time watching your back.'

'I can't believe old Julius is retiring.' Phillip shook his head in disbelief.

'Neither can I. Undoubtedly he knows nothing about this.'

'Is he ill?'

'It's the only explanation I can think of.'

'And the figures?'

'Grim.'

'What's he asking?'

'We didn't get that far but from the odd hint dropped I should say he's thinking in the region of twenty million.'

'You have to be joking. He's mad!'

'Crispin's a greedy little fart. He's putting too big a value on the name – maybe it had it in the eighties but not any more. The money's not around.'

'And what is it worth?'

'I've only glanced at these.' Peter pointed to the folder. 'Of course they've got the freehold and they've Gerald Walters and Sally Britain. The rest?' Peter rested his chin on his hands. 'What else is there? Honourable literary losses. I'd say in the region of five million. It needs revamping, more staff, more authors, more money – lots of money. It's a creaking dinosaur. It's a miracle it's survived this long.'

'Julius must have been funding it with his own money. Fatal. But it won't be the same without him around, will it?'

'No, it won't. Poor Julius. I'd put money on it that Crispin's already lined up three or four of us. Offering it to us first, my eye!'

'Bet he's been on to Tudor Holdings then. Who else? Sovereign?'

'No, my guess is Pewter's. I'm seeing Mike Pewter tonight, I'll see what I can fish out. Drink?'

'No, thanks, I've got tickets for the Stones. Milly's waiting for me downstairs.'

'Philistine.'

'That's right, mate, that's me and proud of it. Enjoy your Verdi or whatever . . .'

As Peter showered he was thinking. He never stopped thinking and planning: he'd long ago resigned himself to the fact that he couldn't even take a holiday without his mind still whirring away. Even when he slept he was likely to dream about business.

Wrapped in his bathrobe, he padded across to the drinks cupboard and poured himself a large whisky. He took it to the sofa, selected a small cigar and lit up. He sat staring into space.

Poor Julius indeed, he thought. One of the last. It was a dreadful indictment of the business he was in that there was no longer room for the gentlemanly, creaking approach to publishing which was Julius's style. If the old boy went it would be everyone's loss, that was the tragedy. But then, was he not himself one of those to blame?

It was Julius who had given him his first job when, against parental advice, he had insisted on going into publishing. He smiled to himself as he looked about his palatial surroundings with the plate-glass sliding doors which opened out on to the huge terrace. He'd certainly come a long way from the small chaotic office at Westall's – more a cupboard, really. He knew which one he preferred. He still felt uncomfortable in this place, almost as if he were trespassing. It was like a set for a Hollywood film on big business and he sometimes felt like an actor and at any moment a director would shout, 'Cut.'

He looked gloomily into his glass. Great days they had been. Julius listened: that was his great strength. It did not matter how junior you were, he always had time to listen to your schemes and ideas. He had listened when Peter had pounded into his office, breathless with excitement, with a typescript he had taken off the slush pile, the large heap of unsolicited manuscripts that plagued every publisher. At Westall's, when they had time on their hands they had been duty bound to take from the slush pile. At weekends, evenings, Julius expected them to read from it. 'Who knows what gems lie in there?' he would repeat time and again to his frequently bored and exasperated staff, the cynics among them snorting behind his back with derision. But at least when Westall's returned a manuscript with a rejection it had been honestly read, not like some publishers – or his present operation if he was honest.

Once, though, he knew he had found the gem that Julius was convinced lurked there and Julius had agreed. That had been Tain Ross's first novel. It had gone on to win the David Higham Prize for Fiction. His second novel had been shortlisted for the Booker. Then Tain had gone, left poor old Julius, ungrateful sod, but for ever more, Peter was famous in literary circles for discovering him. Give Julius his due, he always gave credit to those who had earned it. Peter took a sip of his whisky.

But that was exactly what he had done too – left Julius. He had been seduced just as the authors had, bribed away to Freehold's with a salary Julius could not match, let alone top, and with promises of more responsibility. A disaster, that move had been. He should have realised that a megalomaniac like Bartholomew Freehold with his huge business conglomerate would know nothing about publishing and would, consequently, interfere unmercifully. That's what being a megalomaniac was all about, he supposed. Julius had warned him and he had chosen to ignore the warning. As the books they published became seamier and seamier, Peter became ashamed of the list and resolved to quit. Luckily for him that was the precise moment his father had died leaving him a tidy sum, so with Phillip, his friend from Cambridge, equally suddenly endowed by a departing grandfather, they had started Shotters. 'Let's have a shot at it,' one of them had said, they could no longer remember which. Hence Shotters.

Now those really had been the happy days. Toiling away all the hours God gave in those cramped offices off the wrong side of Tottenham Court Road, as close to the magic of Bloomsbury as they could afford.

Even Hilary had cared then and had worked long hours as an unpaid secretary. Come to think of it, with the pittances they paid themselves, they were all virtually working unpaid. Now she did not care a jot about the business so long as the money kept rolling in.

He had poached too. He had taken writers from Julius just like everyone else. Julius never appeared to mind, but he must have. He would shrug his huge shoulders, smile, wish everyone luck and plunge back looking for fresh writers to nurture. What the hell would they all do without Julius and his unnerving ability to spot talent? Find their own, and about time too.

Peter had known right at the beginning that his father had been wrong, he only wished he had lived long enough to see the success his son had become. Peter and Phillip were the whizz-kids of publishing. Their rise had coincided with the City's discovery that publishing was 'sexy'. They had grabbed at the opportunity long before anyone else had woken up to what was happening. From taking on board small houses which were in difficulties they had moved up the scale, gobbling up the middle ones, absorbing them like an insatiable amoeba. Now they were there up at the top with Sovereign, Tudor's, Pewter's. Up there with the big boys.

From two cramped uncomfortable rooms to this fine purpose-built office block, purveyors of dreams. Bah! He drank deeply.

He sighed. He knew why he sighed. He had been sappy then and now he was not. He was no longer a publisher, he was an accountant and administrator. Too often recently, he would dream of jacking it all in, of selling. He would come out with a fortune, his family would be safe. He wanted to go back to the heady days of a two-roomed office, the excitement and the despair, the fear of the bank breathing down his neck. How Julius must feel, he supposed, every working day . . .

He could get out if he wanted. He had only to hint that Shotters was up for grabs: two American firms and one German had already indicated interest. He knew Phillip, the dreamer of the two, would not mind. He would be the first to admit that the power was Peter's, and the ability too. Provided Phillip had his state-of-the-art sound system, his cannabis, his tumbledown house in Shropshire and Milly, his flower-power wife, whose petals had never wilted, Phillip would be happy. What would they get? Clear of outstanding debts? He stroked his chin as he calculated figures. He could set up a trust for the kids, pay off the mortgages and start again with the rest – far more than he had started with last time. He stretched his legs and wiggled his toes at the joy of the dream . . . but a dream none the less.

'Good God, man, aren't you even dressed? I told Em seven.'

The door had opened and there stood Hilary, his beautiful, expensive wife. He got slowly to his feet.

'I needed to think.'

'We'll be late,' she snapped.

'No, we won't. We'll leave the car here, Em will have called a cab.' He crossed the room to the small dressing room. As he slipped into his dinner jacket he sighed again. Out there in the main room was the biggest obstacle to his dream of turning back the clock. Hilary would never countenance his risking everything he had made for the sake of a dream. She enjoyed being the wife of one of the most powerful publishers in the country. He was no longer sure how much he enjoyed having her as his wife.

5

Michael Pewter's father had been knighted for services to publishing. Mike wanted a life peerage. 'One up on the old bastard,' he was fond of saying to anyone who would listen. That his father was dead and would never know if his son succeeded in getting one was neither here nor there: the hatred of the son for the father was so deep-rooted that ambition had become obsession.

It puzzled Mike that he was not elevated already. He had done, and did, all the right things. He had married well – Lady Lily, insatiable worker for charity, and daughter of a Duke – he gave more than his tithe to charity each year, he knew everyone of importance and entertained right royally, quite literally. He should have been ennobled years ago but as he read in each honours list the names of lesser mortals, he would slump in his chair, his large brown eyes filled with tears, his hurt awesome to witness.

Mike Pewter did not have an enemy in the world. He did not need one for he was his own worst. Mike was big and loud and lovable, like a giant brown bear. No one took him seriously. He had become a joke, the court jester and, sadly, he was unaware of it.

Six feet four and a good twenty stone with a large, ruddy face, he boomed and chuckled his way through life. His appetites were as gargantuan as his size. Many a society hostess's heart quailed, fretting that her cook might have miscalculated on quantities, as she watched the food pile on to his plate. He drank with equal enthusiasm and a night with Mike always ensured everyone else under the table as he called for yet another bottle of port. He adored women and they him, despite his size. Lady Lily turned a blind eye to his many infidelities, for he was always discreet and she had long ago tired of his stupendous weight crushing her into the mattress. Not that he did that any more – that was too athletic by far – but women without number were willing to sit astride him and make them both happy.

He should have been dead, of course, and it was a constant puzzle to his doctors that he was not. But each annual medical showed his blood pressure low, his organs in tip-top shape, and even his lungs, assaulted daily by the smoke from forty cigarettes and a minimum of three fat cigars, still functioning without a wheeze or an obstruction. Carouse as he did, he had never had a hangover in his life. His appetites had never cost him a day's work. He could drink all night, grab three hours' sleep, and still be in the office on time, bright-eyed and bushy-tailed. And everyone adored him – everyone, that is, except the Honours Selection Committee.

Pewter's was, with Westall's and a few minor firms, one of the last entirely family-run publishing houses left in the country. But Pewter's did not have Julius's problems. Founded a hundred years ago, backed by a fortune amassed from steel-making, Pewter's had never had a liquidity problem. They were so wealthy and successful that failures were easily absorbed, cushioned by an enormous technical and educational list. It was a rare child who did not have one of Pewter's language dictionaries in their school satchel. Few motor mechanics, engineers and plumbers would have qualified without Pewter's handbooks. And Pewter's had been first to lead the field into the computer-manual boom. In addition, there was Pewter's Book Club, the largest, and moving rapidly into Europe.

Mike was rich, but in the way of the really rich he had not the least idea how rich he was. He was happy, for he was of that lucky band who love their work, so that it had never been irksome toil but always pleasure.

At Covent Garden, Peter and Hilary were shown up immediately to the Pewter box. Peter was relieved. Hilary had strong views on the state of dress of the majority of the audience and was quite capable of saying so, loudly.

Peter greeted Lily with enthusiasm. He liked her and found her an honest woman. If pushed to explain what he meant by this description he would have said it was her naturalness. He liked the way, at fifty, she was growing old gracefully – not like Hilary who waged a bitter, expensive and, he was sure, painful war against flab, cellulite and wrinkles. Lily never whined, nagged or cajoled. If she wanted something, or something upset her, she said so outright and expected a discussion and a solution to the problem immediately. She was kind and thoughtful and there was a calmness about her that made one aware that here was a natural confidante. She did not give a fig for fashion and wore what was comfortable. Invariably she was the most feminine woman in the room.

Peter did not like *Cosi Fan Tutte*. He would have been quite happy to explain he preferred something with a good tune, but rarely did so – it would have given Hilary apoplexy. He sat in the darkened box and from the lights of the stage could see Hilary sitting just in front with Lily. He looked at her with sadness and wondered what had happened to them.

When they had married – she at twenty and he at twenty-four – she had been so different, sweet and fun. God, he had loved her then, could not get enough of her, wanted her every day, several times. Looking back he supposed they'd been happy for ten, maybe twelve years. She had supported him in his plans, had faith in him, worked with him. And then success had come and the money with it and everything had changed.

Suddenly the comfortable but slightly shabby place in Battersea was not good enough and they had crossed the river to Chelsea to a fine Georgian house and a mortgage which had given him nightmares. He had become used to the house and the mortgage eventually, he even enjoyed living there, until five years ago when it no longer suited Hilary and she had demanded they buy a manor house in the country. He had sold the Chelsea house, bought a flat in the Barbican, gritted his teeth and negotiated an even larger mortgage which even now, rich as he was, made him sometimes wake up in a cold sweat. The country house was a source of embarrassment to him still. It had become a cliché these days: it seemed that everyone they knew who had made some money scuttled off to play at being country folk. Hilary had thrown herself into the country life, nurturing suitable friends, hunting, doing good works. It bored Peter stiff: he loathed riding and he found their neighbours bigoted and unattractive. And the rows he had endured with Hilary because the one thing he would not do 'for a quiet life' was to take up shooting. She was in a sulk at the moment because she wanted a swimming pool. When Hilary wanted something she wanted it immediately. The beautiful Elizabethan stone manor house and a swimming pool just did not seem to go together in his eyes.

He would not mind so much if everything he did for her, and bought for her, made her happy. But it did not. He was watching her becoming more bitter with each year that passed as if she was angry with him. Yet he did not know what it was he had done to make her so.

'Fancy a smoke?' Mike hissed in his ear. He thought it was a whisper, but Mike's whispers never worked and he was rewarded by a spate of shushing from those close by.

Peter followed as quietly as possible as Mike knocked his chair over and inadvertently slammed the door.

'I hate bloody Mozart,' Mike said with feeling, stripping the band off his cigar and searching in a cavernous pocket for his cigar cutter.

'I must admit I'm not too keen on his operas,' Peter took out his more modest cigar. He rationed himself to two small cigars and three cigarillos a day. He had once smoked cigarettes with the best of them and had given up ten years ago. At least he told himself he had given up, but he often wondered how true this was when he watched others smoke and found himself wanting to tear the cigarette out of their mouths. He supposed the longing might go eventually.

'If you don't like Mozart what are you doing here?' Peter asked.

'Something to do with one of Lily's charity dos. Didn't you realise? She'll be worming a cheque out of you before the night is out.'

'No, I didn't. Hilary sees to all that sort of thing.'

'Quite right too. So, what do you think about Crispin?'

Peter coughed on the smoke of his cigar. 'Sorry?' he said, playing for time. He had meant to decide on what strategy to use with Mike and instead had been mooning about his relationship with Hilary.

'You mean he hasn't been in touch? He's carting Julius's figures around, touting them for anyone to see. Fellow should be shot.' For someone as good-natured as Mike this was serious talk.

'Yes, I have seen him. I was going to talk to you about it but, of course, I didn't know if you'd want to say anything.'

'Bloody right I do. This isn't the normal cut and thrust, this is treachery.'

'What did you make of the figures?'

'Right mess – in fact, with interest rates as they are, more like a bloody disaster. Julius can't be having fun any more with that lot slung round his neck. You've got to be able to make mistakes in this game or you might just as well give up.'

'What are we going to do about it?' Peter asked, since a solution entirely escaped him. He was disappointed to hear Mike's reply.

'I don't see what we can do. Crispin's obviously got some shares. I'd always been led to believe he had none. That's a complication. And Crispin's no fool. If Julius is giving up, then Crispin will sell to the highest bidder. I presume he's been in touch with Tudor's – they're acquiring like crazy at the moment.' Mike puffed thoughtfully on his cigar and then smiled slyly. 'We could make it so that no one would want it.'

'How?'

'I'll take old Walters on – he'd slot in nicely. You can have Britain – more your imprint than mine.' Mike waved his cigar airily. Peter smiled at the implication. He had never made any claim to being a literary house: commercial fiction, DIY, cookery, hobbies generally were his strength. The others might make the odd snide remark but everyone these days had to do more popular books. If he let his guard slip for a moment, he would have to defend his properties with an axe in the stampede to sign up Bella, Heather

Gardens, Shiel de Tempera or Grace Bliss, any of Shotters' stable of incredibly successful female writers.

'Walters and Sally Britain wouldn't leave Julius.'

'They might if they knew what was afoot.'

'I don't think I could do that to Julius, it would break his heart.' Peter paused. 'Anyone else but not him.'

'I'm glad you added that rider, thought you were getting soft, that would make things boring.' Mike guffawed and the laugh rumbled around his huge chest, escaped and bounced off the flock-covered walls of the corridor.

'I think we've got to talk to Julius,' Peter said.

'I hoped you'd say that.'

'I'll arrange a weekend. Do you think we'll be missed?' Peter nodded towards the door of Mike's private box.

Mike shook his large head vigorously. 'No. They're both in seventh heaven – mystery to me. Let's go to the bar, they'll know where to find us.'

Across London Crispin was just being let into his cousin John's house in Ebury Street. He was agog with curiosity. He had never been here, they were not a close family, and he had never had anything in common with John – until now.

The servant showed him into the study where John waved at him and mouthed apologies that he was on the telephone. It was a long call and obviously to someone in the States; figures were being rattled around as if he was discussing his shopping list. Crispin was certain the call was being made on purpose to impress him. He carefully set his features into a bored expression.

John finally and, Crispin was sure, reluctantly put down the receiver.

'This is a surprise, Crisp. What couldn't wait? Whisky?'

'I'd prefer white wine. I never touch spirits.'

'Fine, Crisp. I'll have to ring for my man.'

Crispin managed not to shudder or show by the twitch of a muscle just how annoyed he was at the use of his childhood nickname. No wonder he had never bothered with John.

'So?' John asked once the drinks had been dispensed, the servant had withdrawn and polite but uninterested enquiries had been made as to the health of respective wives.

'Do you like your father?' Crispin asked, deciding not to employ his usual subtlety.

'An odd question,' John answered, and looked thoughtfully at Crispin as if deciding how to reply. 'As a matter of fact, we've little in common.'

'I didn't ask you that. I asked if you liked him. It's important.'

'Well, I wouldn't want it repeated, but, no, if you must know. We've never been close.'

'He's dying.'

'My mother hasn't said anything,' John replied in the tone of voice used for discussing the weather.

'She probably doesn't know.'

'Then how do you know?'

'I found out.'

'I see.' John smiled in a particularly unpleasant way. At that point Crispin would have liked to tell him to get stuffed, but he needed him. So he smiled back.

'By accident. His secretary was less than discreet – the poor girl was devastated, you realise.'

'Ah, ha . . .'

'The point is, John, the company is going down the chute and fast. We had the audited accounts last month. He lost £400,000 last year.'

Crispin had the satisfaction of seeing John's discomfort at this information.

'I hate to tell you this, John, but your father is behaving most oddly. I'm concerned about his will and to whom he might leave the business.' Crispin spoke in a soft, caring voice, as if his cousin's future was of the utmost importance to him.

'He's left it to me and my sister. I know. He consulted me about it.'

'Really?' Crispin failed to keep the cynicism out of his voice. In view of the relationship between John and Julius, well known within the family, it was more likely that John had been doing a bit of judicious snooping himself. 'He could change it, though. I told you he's very odd at the moment – people can go funny when they get old. I want to ensure the future of the company. I want a proper stake in it.'

'When it's losing as much as it is?'

'I love the company, John. It's my family too, remember. I've worked nowhere else, it's my life. Without a Westall and Trim, publishing would never be the same again.' Crispin was proud of the feeling that he had put into that little speech. Quite moving, he thought.

'My sister and I had decided to sell when he goes. I'm reliably informed I can get quite a tidy sum for the name and, I think they called it, "the backlist". And, of course, there's the freehold.'

'Would you mind telling me how much?'

'My friend said confidently five million.'

Crispin could have sighed with relief. He'd thought a banker would have been better informed.

'A little on the high side, I'd have said, more like three million,' he lied effortlessly, with all the assurance of a financier who bandied these sums around daily. 'But there's no need to sell. With the right management, a more go-ahead approach, a fortune could be made. And I'm the man to do it. But I need the security of a holding in the company.' Crispin was amazed at how easily lying came to him once he had started.

'But whose shares?'

'That's the point. As you know, I'm sure, your father has forty-nine per cent. If I can buy in, then, with the backing of everyone else, I can get him to move with the times. You need someone who knows the ropes there and who's loyal to the family. If he dies and, God forbid but I think we should look at the worst eventuality, if he left it outside the family, then we would have control of the company over the beneficiary.'

'Whose shares? My mother has her nine per cent. Julius needed some money some time back and sold them to her. I advised against it, but she wouldn't listen.'

Crispin tutted sympathetically. So that's how she'd got her hands on the shares, he'd presumed as much.

'I'd want more than the nine.'

'What about your mother?'

'My mother?' Crispin snorted. 'She'd never help me, you can bet on that.'

'That leaves Uncle Simon.'

'Exactly.'

'What would you offer him?'

'Three hundred thousand.' Crispin spoke quickly, as if by doing so the sum would diminish.

'And you have that sort of money?'

'Yes,' Crispin said, staring steadily at his cousin. He had, almost. The bank he had approached was impressed with his figures. They were deciding right now; he should hear next week. They would have preferred Julius to die, of course, but it seemed they were willing to gamble with Crispin. He was going to have to put his house up as security, that was painful, but it would be worth it in the end.

'I'd recommend him to sell to you for that. He's old and, as you know, not too successful with his painting. It will help all the family if he's cared for now rather than later.'

'That's settled, then?'

'He's away at the moment – painting trip to Italy, odd time of year, isn't it? I presume you would like me to give him a buzz in a couple of weeks when he's back, tell him you want to see him. You do realise that a special meeting would have to be called, all the shareholders given twenty-one days' notice, and they would have to agree by a majority for any shares to change hands other than to another member of the board – which, of course, you are not, Crisp, even if you're called financial director.'

'I can't see any problems, can you?' Crispin smiled his most charming smile, ignoring his cousin's gibe.

'Well, there is your mother.' John laughed. He actually laughed. Crispin was amazed.

'Oh, I don't think she'll mind so long as it doesn't cost her anything. If you could speak to Uncle Simon, I could then visit him with your blessing?'

'Of course, Crisp, old chap.'

Crispin stood up to leave, amazed that it had all gone so smoothly. It wouldn't matter now if Julius lived or died, he had a stake. And his £300,000 could grow rapidly to four million when he persuaded the others to sell up. It made his mind reel.

John showed him to the door, his arm about his cousin's shoulders, which Crispin did not enjoy. He did not care for physical contact with virtual strangers, but for the sake of his plans he accepted the comradely gesture. The door was just about closing and Crispin was having to fight himself not to leap down the steps, when John called out.

'Tell me, Crisp, what about the Lepanto Trust? That could be a sticking point. Julius has always had its proxy vote. We've never managed to get out of Julius who, or what, it is.'

'The Lepanto? Oh, no problem there,' Crispin said brightly – he hoped not too brightly.

6

Kate looked up from the sink where she was peeling the potatoes for the evening meal. In the window she could see her reflection – lank dull hair, spectacles slipping down her nose, overweight, dowdy, done for . . . She had got to pull herself together, she told herself for the umpteenth time that week.

The door of the kitchen burst open.

'Mum, have you seen my grey blouse anywhere, the one with the high neck?' her daughter Lucy asked.

Kate continued to gaze at the window. But forty-five was no age, she thought. How had she let herself get like this? Look at Joan Collins, how attractive, how desirable she still was but, then, she had had the courage to grab at life by the throat, live it to the full, not like Kate, cruising aimlessly along, getting nowhere, endlessly feeling sorry for herself.

'Mum, coo-ee!' her daughter shouted, standing close to her.

Kate jumped. 'Lucy, you did give me a start. I'm sorry, were you speaking to me? I was miles away.'

'I'm looking for my grey blouse.'

'Is it in the laundry room?'

'Oh, Mum, no! Does that mean you haven't done it for me? I did ask.' Lucy ran out, slamming the door behind her, and Kate could hear her noisily opening and shutting the doors of the washing machine and drier in the laundry room. She returned to the kitchen, the damp blouse hanging limp in her hand looking like a drowned cat.

'You did promise,' Lucy said accusingly.

'Well, I forgot. Wear something else.'

'But I wanted that blouse.'

'But you can't have that one, can you, not if it's wet. Be sensible.'

'I asked you ages ago. I told you I wanted this blouse for tonight. You don't seem to remember anything these days! Nothing gets done around here any more,' Lucy whined in an aggrieved tone.

Kate looked at the anger in her daughter's face, the discontented expression, and would have liked to slap her hard. She found herself wondering, quite dispassionately, if it was possible to love someone even when one thought one was beginning to dislike them.

'Maybe it's about time you did your own washing for a change. At seventeen I'd have said you were old enough,' she said.

'That's right, make me sound in the wrong.'

'I didn't mean to. It was just a suggestion so that at least one reason for the unpleasant scenes we keep having would be removed.' Kate spoke calmly and with exaggerated patience.

'And when am I supposed to have the time to do this Widow Twanky act? Tell me that.'

Kate leant against the sink feeling an intense wave of anger surge over her. 'Make time!' she shouted, throwing the vegetable knife into the water, splattering the front of her own blouse as she did so. 'I'm sick to death of this family and its endless demands on me. I'm fed up with being regarded as the hired help around here. I'm a person too, you know, or have you not realised?'

Lucy stepped back, an expression of shocked surprise on her face. She looked as if she was about to argue but, apparently thinking better of it, turned on her heel. At the door she swung round. 'You're really getting menopausal, you know.' And before Kate could answer had slammed out again.

Kate searched in the muddy water for her knife, aware that she was shaking. She forced herself to peel the potatoes again. She wondered how many she had peeled in twenty-four years. Laid end to end would they girdle the earth? Fiercely she concentrated her thoughts on the potatoes, knowing that if she did not she would want to cry. This crying was a new thing come to join the feeling of despair she so loathed. She resented the tears. She played a game: if she could peel this one in a complete piece, everything would get better. Slowly and carefully she peeled, the skin curling below her like a snake. She cheated, digging hard into the potato flesh, but despite her care and her cheating the peel broke off. She watched it sink into the water in the bowl and, as she watched, knew that, despite herself and the games she played, she was going to cry, and that she would despise herself for doing so.

She was not crying over Lucy, they argued too often for that. In fact this evening she was feeling rather pleased with herself for shouting back. Usually she tried to understand her daughter's frustrations. Not any more, she had enough of her own.

Lucy's 'menopausal' taunt puzzled rather than hurt. She felt it bordered on treachery coming from one of her own sex, and from one so much younger. She wondered if it was the female equivalent of a young stag taunting an old one. But, then, over the years any mood she had, any irritation she had shown, Tony had invariably blamed on her hormones. Just recently he, too, had taken up the menopause cry instead of pre-menstrual tension as explanation for her behaviour. It was as if women could not be like the young, or men, but were expected to live on a saintly plateau of calm, emotionless equanimity. It seemed never to have struck Tony that there could be any other cause for her changes of mood.

Now the menopause, which had taken the blame when it did not exist, had finally come, and Kate wasn't enjoying it. Secretly she'd always looked forward to the 'change' as her mother coyly referred to it, doing away with all that monthly mess, getting her moods on the level everyone expected of her. Her mother had made such a drama out of her own menopause, making the whole family's life hell, but Kate had resolved she wasn't going to be like that – it was a blessing to look forward to, not misery. The reality was different: her hot flushes were mild, but the aching joints were more of a problem, especially first thing in the morning when she was certain she would never move easily again. She wished someone had warned her about the unsightly bristle which suddenly appeared on her chin and which, with each plucking, grew longer, stiffer, blacker – like a walrus's tusk, she told her friend Pam. She would also like to have been warned that it was wiser to cross her legs when she sneezed. Nor had she realised that her waist would thicken quite as quickly as it did. Still, her skin had not dried out yet: she had few wrinkles. And she didn't have hysterics – but sometimes she wondered if she wasn't going mad.

She hated shopping now. She found – in the street, in the car, in the middle of Sainsbury's, anywhere – that she would, without warning, suddenly panic, certain the car was about to crash, whole buildings were about to collapse and kill only her. She thought about her death a lot, she would even admit to becoming obsessed by it. Yet it was a subject she had preferred not to think about. She had trotted out the old clichés – 'we've all got to go some time', or 'when your number's up', that sort of thing – but now 'some time' seemed uncomfortably close. Then there was this fight not to cry. She cried not because she was unhappy, but simply because her tear glands produced fluid that squeezed out of her eyes and trickled down her cheeks of its own accord – it was rather like having a runny nose from a bad cold – she had no control over it at all.

Tony appeared, kissed her cheek, asked what was for supper and disappeared into his study to work until his food was ready. Lucy banged out of the house without a goodbye, and Steve would not be home from the camera club until ten. It was just Tony and herself, an evening alone. Once they would have been excited by that prospect, now it meant nothing, she thought, as she laid the table.

When they sat down to eat, she automatically asked about his day, though she rarely listened to the answer since he did not often have anything of much interest to say. Graintry did not go in for juicy divorces or murders.

'Lucy tells me you were horrible to her this evening,' he said instead.

'Did she? She shouted at me, I shouted back, that's all.'

'A trifle undignified, wouldn't you say?' he asked in his measured tone.

'She asked for it. She treats me like a servant and I've had enough of it.'

'She works hard at school, she can't be expected to work at home too.'

'Well, that's where we differ. I think it's about time she did help more. In fact, I think it would be nice if everyone did a bit more to help me.'

He did not respond but continued to eat. The rhythmic click of his knife and fork made her want to scream.

'This is a good bit of meat. Did you get it at Flitch's? Damn good butcher, Flitch.'

'Do you realise, Tony, that of every piece of meat you have ever eaten in this house, you've made that self-same remark?' She spoke brightly enough as if she believed she was camouflaging her annoyance.

'Have I? Well, it's true.' He looked up at her, slightly puzzled.

'It's also bloody boring,' she said defiantly.

'I beg your pardon? And what do you mean by that?'

No sooner had she said it than she began to regret it. It was such a pointless conversation and one that could lead to an argument if she was not careful. Or was that what she wanted? she suddenly thought. A row? Just to relieve the tedium?

'I'm sorry, that was unpleasant of me.' She looked down at her plate.

'I should think so.'

'I said I was sorry.'

'If you hadn't said it there would have been no need to apologise, would there?'

She did not reply, thinking she had better not, afraid of what else she might say, feeling she was teetering on the edge of something and not knowing what it was. She put down her knife and fork.

'Tony, I don't want you to take this as any form of criticism of you. I don't know what's wrong, but I feel so discontented these days.'

'Do you?' He looked up from his plate with as much animation as if she was talking about the electricity bill. Come to think of it, she thought, he would have been a lot more animated if she had been.

'I feel so restless. Unhappy inside . . .

'Perhaps you need a check-up.'

'I've had a check-up. There's nothing wrong with me. The doctor was his usual helpful self,' she said with an irony which was completely lost on her husband. She certainly was not going to go into the useless interview she had had with old Dr Plaistow, whose reaction, when she had plucked up the courage to ask about hormone replacement therapy, was a shocked lecture on unnecessary chemical interference. He had not said that when he'd put her on the pill, she had thought. It was tempting to think there was a male conspiracy against women, just to keep them down because of their biological differences.

'I sometimes feel, Tony, that apart from producing two children which, let's face it, any healthy woman could do, I've done nothing with my life – '

'Oh, God, Kate, not this again.'

She looked down at her plate. 'I'm sorry. It's just that I feel everything is passing me by. I . . .' She jumped at the clatter of his knife and fork on the plate, and looked up to see him staring angrily at her.

'What's so special about you? Don't you think we all feel like that sometimes? Do you think I'm happy with the routine of my life? It's life, that's all. Grow up, Kate, for goodness sake.'

'I was just wondering if we couldn't do something – go away for a weekend without the children, just take off . . .' Her voice trailed off lamely at the irritated expression on his face.

'Don't be stupid.'

'But we seem to spend so little time together. You're always working.'

'That, Kate, is how the bills get paid, or didn't you realise?' he said sarcastically.

Kate stood up and collected the empty dishes.

'It's apple crumble. Do you want cream with it?' she asked equably, as if the previous conversation hadn't taken place.

'Please.' He picked up his book, he always read between courses. She frequently thought he would prefer to read throughout the meal rather than have to talk to her. She wished she had the courage to pick it up and hit him over the head with it.

As soon as they had finished Tony took his coffee and disappeared once more into his study. She often wondered what he did in there. He said he worked but they only had his word for it. He could have a woman or the biggest collection of pornography in the world secreted away, or he might just sit and twiddle his thumbs, she wouldn't know. She began to load the dishwasher. Well, that was a pointless exercise, she thought to herself. Where had it got her? Nowhere. The telephone rang.

'Kate, have you ever heard of a Felicity Marchmont?' She heard the confident voice of her friend Pam Homerton who never announced herself but blithely presumed that whoever answered the telephone would recognise her immediately.

'No, I can't say I have. Should I?'

'I haven't either. She's a writer. She runs a writers' circle, they meet every Wednesday morning over at Little Moreton. Let's join.'

'I don't write.'

'Neither do I, but we can learn.'

'Oh, I'm not sure . . .'

'Come on, Kate. It could be fun. I don't know any authors and I'd like to see inside her house – there are some lovely houses in Little Moreton, and I bet she lives in one of them. It would be something different to do, something to relieve the bloody boredom of our lives,' Pam said in a dramatic tone and then laughed. Pam was never bored, she was one of those lucky ones who always found something to amuse her even in the most mundane of circumstances – but then, Kate thought, she wasn't menopausal yet. It would be interesting to see what Pam would be like when she was.

'All right. I don't promise to stick at it but we could give it a whirl.'

They chatted on for a while about the happenings in their locality. They were just like schoolgirls who rush to the telephone on returning home to talk to the friend they have just left. They had seen each other only yesterday, but they still found plenty to talk about.

As she finished her conversation, Steve clattered in from his club. She smiled at the noise he made: when he was trying to be quiet he invariably made even more noise than usual. She looked up with affection at the tall and gangly youth who, at nearly sixteen, had reached the point of accelerated growth where no part of his body seemed to match any other.

They spent a few minutes together while she admired the latest batch of photographs he had developed. It was not hard to do, for they were good and she found herself wondering whether Tony would regard photography as a more acceptable career than landscape gardening. She told him of her and Pam's plans.

'That's a wonderful idea, Mum. Take you out of the house, and doing something interesting instead of looking after us lot.'

She smiled at him and not for the first time thought how much easier it was to love her son than her daughter.

Ten. She poured the two whiskies that she and Tony always had as a nightcap, knocked on his study door and waited for his reply. Tony hated anyone to enter without knocking, hence her fantasies as to what he got up to in there.

'Was that Pam?'

'Yes.' She handed him the glass.

'Anything interesting?'

'They've definitely decided to go to Provence this year to look for a holiday home.' This she said rather wistfully, for she knew Tony's views on how unproductive was the use of capital invested in a second home. 'She thinks Carol might have a new boyfriend.' Tony was yawning. 'And we're both enrolling in a writers' circle. A local novelist has set one up.'

'You've what?' Tony looked at her with incredulity. 'You don't write.' He laughed.

'I've always wanted to,' she lied.

'News to me.' He snorted. 'Maybe it will cheer you up, make you less neurotic.'

The look she gave him was a mixture of hurt and loathing but it was a waste of time, he had returned to his papers. She turned to leave the room.

'Oh, by the way,' Tony said. 'I forgot to tell you at dinner. We've been invited to a party the Saturday after next. You'd best splash out on a new dress and get something done to your hair.'

Involuntarily she patted her hair. 'Whose party?' She knew she sounded surprised, but for Tony to tell her to buy a frock was rare indeed.

'Sir Barty Silver's,' he announced, grinning at her, waiting to see her reaction.

'Barty Silver?' she repeated. 'I didn't know you knew him.'

'I don't. He's thinking of buying some property in the Bristol area. He wants someone in the vicinity involved, not his London solicitors, and he wants to meet one of us. Tom's away visiting his daughter in Australia, Freddie's tied up, so that leaves me. Apparently he likes to do business at his parties.'

'Barty Silver,' she said again in a dreamy voice. He was one of the people she read about in Nigel Dempster over her toast and marmalade when everyone else had left the house. He was not someone she had ever dreamed of meeting. 'I wish I'd known earlier, I could have told Pam.'

'No doubt you will tomorrow, pushing up the telephone bill . . .'

That night in bed Tony made love to her. At least, that was what he called it. She wondered if he had done so to try to make her feel better about herself, for he did not often deviate from his Saturday and Wednesday routine. No doubt he would be shocked and hurt if he knew it made her feel even more depressed. She sometimes thought that Tony, when taking her, had a chart in his head – like painting with numbers. She certainly could have reeled off the order of his caresses for it never varied. A kiss on the mouth, then a nuzzle of her ear. First he rubbed one nipple between thumb and finger, then the other, just as if he was fine tuning a radio. A quick grope between her legs, a little heavy breathing and then he was on top of her and in her and it was over in minutes.

Not that she wanted him to prolong the act, it had become so irksome to her. She wondered if the same had happened to him. Now the closest she got to an orgasm was reading about it in *Cosmopolitan*. She'd heard that sex improved the longer one knew a person, which certainly had not happened to them. She supposed she had enjoyed it once, she could not be sure for she could no longer remember. And then she wondered if she did not remember because she no longer wanted to. But as she lay in the dark looking at the ceiling she could not help wondering what it could be like.

7

From her kitchen Kate heard the faint throaty roar of Pam's car as she approached the village. She looked quickly about her, making a last-minute check. She unlocked the cat-flap, moved the tea-towels from the bar in front of the Aga for safety, picked up her handbag and the spiral-bound notepad she had bought, and was standing by the gate as Pam screeched to a halt.

'You must be psychic, you always know when I'm arriving.' Pam was smiling as she leant over and opened the passenger door for Kate.

'No, just good hearing – and this car's roar would be difficult to miss.' Kate kissed her best friend in welcome.

'Roar? My darling purrs, positively purrs, don't you my sweet?' Pam patted the fascia of the E-type Jaguar, her current pride and joy. 'Are you excited? I am,' she said as she put the car into gear.

'I'm a bit nervous. I mean, I've never written a thing in my life apart from school essays and letters. I don't really know why I'm going and I certainly shan't know where to begin.'

'Oh, go on, don't be such a wimp. It'll be a laugh if nothing else,' Pam said with her easy confidence as the sleek red car with its long snout sped quickly through the lanes towards Little Moreton.

Pam loved to drive and did so with far more panache and expertise than most men. Kate enjoyed being driven by her for she herself was one of those women who saw motoring as merely a means to get from A to B. She could not have cared less what she drove provided it was reliable and not too big to park easily. Pam, on the other hand, always had high-performance cars which she changed with extraordinary rapidity. This red Jaguar was the only one that Kate had known her to keep more than six months. She had nearly died of shock when Tony had told her how much these old cars cost. It had been a birthday present from Pam's husband and Kate did have a frisson, not exactly of jealousy – she would not have wanted such a car in the first place – no, it was more of longing and curiosity to know what it must feel like to have a husband so rich that such a present was a normal thing.

The Homertons lived, for the moment, in a large imposing mansion, near Graintry, about ten miles from Kate's village. They had two hundred acres. The heated swimming pool was in its own custom-built house which looked like a giant Victorian Gothic gazebo. There was a tennis court, horses in the stable – not that Kate had ever seen any of them ridden – and a four-car garage. Their son was at Marlborough and their daughter at Benenden. Pam did not have a wardrobe for her clothes, she had a whole room. Their *en-suite* bathroom was so huge and plush that Kate always felt she was slumming when she returned to her own more than adequate one.

They had lived in this house for three years which for them was a long time. In the eighteen years she had known Pam and Doug they had moved at least seven times, always to a place bigger and grander than the one before. 'Trading up', Doug called it but Kate thought it must be a dreadful way to live, like nomads forever packing up, never settled. Pam joked that it was the only way that she kept her cupboards tidy but Kate often wondered if she was really as happy with the arrangement as she made out.

The talk among their group was that this time the Homertons were finally settled, for where could they 'trade up' this time? They had the most imposing house in the area, to get anything bigger or grander they would have to move further away from Graintry and everyone was certain that was something Doug would never do.

Doug was the true 'local lad made good' of people's dreams. He had left school in Graintry at sixteen with two O levels, in metalwork and technical drawing. He had started working for a local builder when a lucky, but modest, win on the football pools had enabled him to set up on his own. Six years later he had bought out his previous employer who was retiring and then bravely borrowed a fortune and built houses, in the process making himself a fortune. He had stayed in building but had also diversified into so many other ventures that Kate was never sure how many there were. She knew of a bingo hall, a carpet warehouse, several pubs and a string of video-hire shops but was aware there were others. So, when recession came and the building trade was inevitably sorely hit, Doug was safe and could ride out the storm while others collapsed. More often than not it was Doug who bought up the bankrupt businesses at rock-bottom prices. He was unpretentious, funny, kind, generous and Kate admired him.

Tony had been in the vanguard of those who had prophesied that he would fail. Even now, eighteen years later, when Doug appeared fire-proof, Tony could not bring himself to admit he might have been wrong and still tutted and frowned and said, 'Wait and see.' Kate had the horrible idea that Tony would be pleased to see Doug fail. Further, she had reached the conclusion that her husband was riddled with envy, which did not, however, stop him accepting Doug's hospitality, frequently.

'Doug's going to buy me a word processor,' Pam said as the car climbed the hill out of Kate's valley.

'What on earth for?'

'To write on, of course. All writers have them these days.'

'Do you know how to work one?'

'No, but everyone says it's easy.'

'Rather you than me. Tony has horror tales about the one in the office.'

'I looked at it this way. If that thick cow in Doug's office can get the hang of it, so can I. You can come and use it any time.' Pam smiled across at her.

'Thanks, but I think it's unlikely I shall be needing one.' Kate laughed and looked at her friend with affection. That was the endearing thing about Pam, she always wanted to share everything. 'Doug's pleased you're going to this writers' circle, then?'

'Ecstatic. He thinks it'll keep me out of his hair for a while.'

'Tony just laughed. He thinks the idea of my writing anything is a joke.'

'Then prove him wrong,' said Pam, not pausing in the conversation as she overtook a surprised septuagenarian on a particularly difficult stretch of road.

That was an approach Kate had not thought of but, as they sped along, and the more she considered it, the more she thought, why not? Why did she automatically think she could not do it, could not write, would fail? Because Tony had implied it, that was why.

'Thanks, Pam,' she said. 'I might just try to do that. It would be nice to prove him wrong for once.'

'I never understand why you snipe about Tony like that. He's such a nice man, a wonderful husband. You don't know how lucky you are, that's your problem,' Pam said quite sharply. 'And at least he still makes love to you,' she added for good measure.

If you can call it making love, thought Kate, but said nothing, for loyalty would never allow her to discuss Tony's sexual inadequacy, not even with Pam. Pam herself suffered no such inhibitions.

'I sometimes think if I was a balance sheet then Doug might screw me again,' Pam said, as if reading Kate's mind. She was laughing but Kate knew her well enough to know that it was a laugh to mask the hurt and frustration that was her sexless marriage. 'We had a row last night. I told him straight that, at forty-two, I was not ready to give up on the nooky.'

'You're not forty-two.'

'I am next April. I said if he didn't get his act together then I was going to look for a lover.'

'What did he say?'

'Not much. He shrugged and asked me if I'd like a word processor. I ask you! Am I supposed to shag that? It's guilt of course, that's all. I know how his mind works. Give the nagging bitch another pressie and she'll shut up.'

'Poor Doug. Maybe he can't any more – look at the pressure he works under. Have you thought of that?' Kate said, and thought how strange it was how she was always defending Doug while Pam was Tony's best advocate.

'Poor Doug, my arse! He never has been one for it. It's a bloody miracle to me that I managed it twice and got two kids.'

Pam's rather lurid turn of phrase was totally at odds with her appearance for she was lovely and had the fragile beauty of a Dresden figurine. Kate was always aware of what an odd couple they made. She spent her time fluctuating from eleven to twelve stone while Pam was always striving to stay at seven. Kate was always dressed sensibly and, although she tried to be neat and tidy, after half an hour she always looked a mess. Pam dressed immaculately, designers' initials proclaiming the cost. And she looked as good at the end of the day as she had at the beginning. Her nose never shone, she did not eat her lipstick and her thick red hair, once combed, obliged by staying in place.

Pam's eyes were dark brown, soft like a puppy's and Kate envied her for she loathed her own grey ones. She had once had blue contact lenses made for her short-sighted eyes in the hopes of jazzing them up a bit. She quite liked the effect even if it meant her world was permanently tinted slightly blue. But one day, while gardening, she had sneezed and one lens had flown out never to be found. When Tony discovered that, in the interests of economy, she had not insured them, he had refused point blank to give her the money to replace it. She regretted its loss, she felt she had looked better without her spectacles. Not that Tony had said so, but she was almost sure she did.

The two women had lapsed into the companionable silence that is allowed in a long friendship. Kate looked out at the passing scenery. It was one of those crisply cold autumn mornings which Kate sometimes thought she preferred to spring or summer, until, that is, those seasons came in their turn. As they broached hill after hill, down in the valleys small hamlets nestled. They were all alike, a collection of old houses clustered around the church, as if for solace, built in the same bleached Cotswold stone. Only the names were different. Smoke was rising from several of the chimneys in straight white columns and the air was full of the distinctive sweet smell of burning wood. The pale golden stone houses seemed to be hiding in the gauze-like shroud of the morning mist which still lingered. An early frost was painted on to plants and grass making them stiffly sculptural. The hedgerows glistened with the frozen dew on a thousand webs. Rooks called noisily to each other and the barking of a distant dog was so clear it could have been alongside the car.

Such a village was Little Moreton, its claim to fame being that it had rather more than its fair share of small but architecturally important Elizabethan houses.

'God, just look at those wonderful houses. I've always wanted one of those ones with flagstones and a panelled cross-passage hallway. Lovely.' Pam sighed.

'You on the move again?' Kate asked with a smile, recognising the emergent signs of another Homerton decampment.

'They must be so convenient, not like our mausoleum,' Pam replied.

They were disappointed as they followed the instructions Pam had been given to find that Felicity Marchmont did not appear to live in one of them as they had expected. The car finally slid to a halt outside a cottage that evidently had once been two. It was old and pretty but not in the league of the houses they had so admired.

Kate hauled herself out of the almost prone position required to sit in the E-type, and was glad that there were no men around to see the expanse of fat thigh she exposed as she did so. Pam slid effortlessly and elegantly from behind the steering wheel.

They rang the bell, and pulled their coats around them against the chill as no one answered.

'You sure you took the address down correctly?' asked Kate. She knew it was an unnecessary question: Pam might appear vague but in fact was highly organised.

'The Grange, that's what I was told.'

'It doesn't look much like a Grange to me, more like two artisans' cottages knocked into one.'

'Try the bell again. I'll go round the back and see what I can find.'

Kate was stamping her feet with cold when Pam reappeared.

'There's a tray of cups and saucers laid out in the kitchen so someone's expected. It's probably us.'

They both spun round as the gate creaked and a small, dowdily but neatly dressed woman with the under-nourished look of a vicar's wife, scuttled almost apologetically towards them.

'Are you Felicity Marchmont?' asked Pam in the tone of voice which implied she could not believe she was Felicity and, if she was, that Pam was sorely disappointed.

'Me? Good gracious no. I'm not nearly clever enough to be Felicity. I'm Mavis Crabtree. I live over there.' And she pointed to by far the largest and grandest of the houses they had so admired. 'Silly question, but have you rung?' She tittered nervously.

'Twice.' Pam and Kate answered in unison.

'Oh dear, I do hope Clarissa hasn't forgotten us again. She leads such a wonderfully busy life, the house always teeming with people and children and dogs – it's all so jolly. And she's so clever with her hands, restoring and painting and making things. I don't know how she manages with it all, clever young thing.'

At which a bedroom window opened and the 'clever young thing's' head appeared.

'Hello? If that's the baker just leave me a bloomer will you?' A voice of brittle accent called down.

'It's us, Clarissa. It's your turn for the circle . . .' Mavis twittered again but almost admiringly at such vagueness.

'Golly, gosh! I'd completely forgotten. Crikey, you've caught me completely on the hop. Everything's in the most unholy mess. Hang on . . .' The window slammed shut and Mavis, Kate and Pam smiled inanely at each other. As they were wondering how long they would have to wait outside in the freezing cold, an MG sports car screeched up out of which stepped a tall, slim, smartly dressed young woman whom Mavis introduced as June Fleming. She lived, she told them, close by on an executive housing estate which Doug had built – not that Pam mentioned it.

'Clarissa isn't claiming to have forgotten again?' June said with a sigh of exasperation.

'The poor dear has so much on her plate,' Mavis fluttered.

'My eye. Filthy manners more like,' June muttered.

'You said, June dear?'

'Nothing.' June angrily rang the bell again.

'Oh Christ, she's not up to her stupid tricks again is she? It's too bloody cold to stand about, freeze the brass knobs . . .' an even younger woman in a lurid cerise and lime-green shell suit said as she joined them and was introduced as Tracey Green. At last they heard a bolt being drawn and the door being unlocked. 'About bloody time,' Tracey said for them all making Mavis wince.

'Come in, my dears . . .' A dark, long-haired, perfectly made-up though barefoot Clarissa ushered them in with no apology for making them stand and wait.

The sitting room covered most of the ground floor of the house. It was tidy, a log fire crackled in the inglenook fireplace. The room was a brave attempt to disguise that they were hard up: the shawls artfully flung over the sofas were undoubtedly to hide holes. And Kate dreaded to think of the state of one chair which was completely covered in a white sheet. The coffee table was an old door, painted gloss green, balanced on a pile of books.

There was the fusty smell of furniture from secondhand shops. Most of the ornaments were Victorian bric-à-brac and the paintings were nondescript watercolours of the sort that Kate always imagined were done by impoverished relations of grand families who took them in out of duty not love.

'You see the fearful mess. Golly . . .' Clarissa trilled as she busied herself taking coats. 'I'm Clarissa Steele-Greene – with oodles of 'e's.' She giggled. 'And you two must be Kate and Pam and which is which or who is who?' She laughed, a forced little-girl laugh as if a bolder, louder one might be being kept in check. Who was who having been sorted out, they were told to take their seats while Clarissa just had '. . . to fly into the kitchen, just for a second, and get the coffee ready. Such mundane things . . .' And she whisked away.

Kate and Pam looked significantly at each other and while both were fully aware of the social games some people played they were both flummoxed at what conclusion to draw from Clarissa's alleged absentmindedness.

Clarissa swept back, talking non-stop, saying nothing really but leaving sentences hanging with no end to them like smoke trails disappearing in the air.

'Money . . . I really think . . . don't you?'

'Yes, of course. How much?' Kate asked.

'It's Felicity . . . money . . . she finds it all so vulgar . . .'

'My arse!' Pam whispered but not softly enough.

'She's artistic,' Clarissa said sharply.

'Of course,' the friends replied.

'Well, now . . .' Clarissa explained about the joining fee and each week's subscription. 'And a little extra for the coffee and things . . . that's for me, coffee, you understand . . . so expensive.' The false laugh tinkled. 'If you're paying by cheque make it out to Doris Miller – that's her real name, not that she ever uses it . . . well, one doesn't, does one?'

'Of course.'

Kate was opening her handbag and wishing it was the last week in the month rather than the middle and was already juggling menus in her mind.

'I'll get this.' Pam was already delving into her handbag which, as always, was overflowing with money and had settled the bill before Kate had even found her pen.

Kate had never met a writer before and was not sure what to expect. In the event she was somewhat disappointed by the stout grey-haired woman, in a tweed skirt with a voluminous navy jumper over her ample breasts and a voice of deepest profundo. She reminded Kate uncomfortably of her old headmistress and she felt frightened of the bright brown eyes which stared intently at her as if reading her thoughts.

'So pleased to see our little circle growing,' Felicity boomed. 'You're not the Mrs Homerton who lives at Felix Park?'

'Yes, that's me.'

'Such a lovely house. I used it for the setting in my Regency *Feud of the Soul*.'

'Really, how exciting,' said Pam, politely if a bit vaguely. 'Regency? I'm afraid I don't understand.'

'It's a *genre* term, my dear, for a period novel.' Felicity rolled the word genre around her mouth as if enjoying the sound of it immensely.

'But the house is mainly Victorian,' Pam said, sweetly.

'Artistic licence, my dear. Tell me, you must know dear Peter and Hilary Holt, they live your way.'

'I've met her, at a gymkhana, that's all.' Pam forebore to say that she had found Hilary stuck up, and that upon discovering Pam's husband was a builder Hilary had lost interest in Pam immediately.

'You must look her up. Contacts, my dear, so important in publishing.'

'Hilary's a publisher?'

'No, but dear Peter is, why he *is* Shotters. Let's to work, ladies,' Felicity called, making them all jump and obediently begin to sort out their notepads and pencils with a flurry of clicking handbags and briefcases – all except Tracey who carried everything in a Tesco carrier bag. Felicity waited until everyone was settled. 'Now, with newcomers we must all explain ourselves and our plans and strategies. Shall I go first?' which she did since she was not the sort of woman anyone present was likely to argue with.

'I started writing nearly twenty years ago. I have written over a hundred short stories, I've lost count of my articles and eleven of my books have been published. I am presently at work on my twelfth book, a saga set in medieval England at the court of Mathilda. So you see, both of you, I think I can honestly say that I am well qualified to lead our little group, don't you?' She beamed, for the first time displaying a fine set of dentures with bright pink gums.

'Such a lot of books. You must be very proud,' Kate said with admiration. Felicity bowed her head graciously.

'I don't know how to say this, Felicity – I read the most massive amount, but I've never read any of your books. Have you, Kate?'

Kate, greatly discomfited and wishing Pam was not always so forthright, agreed she had not.

'You'll find them in libraries.'

'Not in shops?'

'My publishers – Drummond and Lock – specialise in library books not for sale to the general public.' This was said as if there was something not quite nice about selling to the public.

'That explains it, then,' Pam said brightly. 'I never go to libraries. I never want to return the books.'

'We shall have to rectify that, won't we, Pam?' The pink gums were flashed again but Kate was concerned to see it was not a happy smile.

'Do you make as much money selling to libraries?' Pam asked, apparently all innocence, and Kate wished she would drop it.

'You must not believe everything you read in the papers about money paid to authors, it's mainly all lies,' Felicity announced airily. 'Now, Clarissa . . .'

One by one they listed their successes – not many – and their ambitions – numerous.

Clarissa was writing a novel of the destructive love of a man for a woman as his soul descends to hell. But, importantly, she wanted there to be another main character in the book, the moorland where the two lived. Kate sensed that Pam was about to blurt out that it had already been done but managed to press her thigh against Pam's with sufficient pressure to warn her off.

Mavis admitted she attended more for the company and found it a help in compiling her nature notes for the parish magazine and then, almost as an afterthought, told them that the magazine *Hearthside* had, just yesterday, confirmed they were buying a short story.

'That's wonderful,' Felicity said rather stiffly, and the others went wild with excitement and congratulations for Mavis who became quite pink.

June said she wanted to learn to write, something she had always wanted to do, and in any case she was bored with housework. Tracey said she had had two stories taken by *Teen Life* and wanted to be published by The Paradise Club, make a fortune and retire to the Isle of Man.

'And you, Pam?'

'I want to write a bestseller – you know, the ones you see at airports – and appear on chat shows,' Pam answered, much to Kate's surprise. It was the first she had ever heard of it.

'Quite.' Felicity smiled in a very superior way. 'Wouldn't we all? And Kate?'

'I'm not sure,' Kate said, feeling flustered and unprepared. 'I've never written anything. I don't know what I could or couldn't do. Perhaps I'd be best starting off with a short story or two.'

'Short-story writing is a particularly difficult genre, you know.'

'Is it?' Kate asked, wondering why Felicity seemed so intent on putting people down.

'Remarkably so. Now, first things first. I repeat this every week and shall continue to do so. Market trends,' she spoke these two words as if they were in capital letters, 'market trends are the key to everything. Once you've identified your market then you'll know what to write.'

'Can't one just write whatever is inside one?' Kate asked.

'Not unless you're a second Iris Murdoch. Not if you want to sell you can't,' Felicity told her sharply.

There then followed a bewildering list of books to buy on how to write, magazines that must be read – not the magazines in newsagents but the trade press – *Publishing News* and *The Bookseller* – and two for aspiring authors. 'And there's no harm at this stage in getting Macmillan's *The Writer's Handbook*. Our bible, isn't it, girls?' She beamed at her little flock, who not only hung on every word but wrote it down as well.

What followed next Kate found awful and she doubted if she would ever have the courage to participate. One by one they read out passages they had written on the subject Felicity had set them the previous week. They then proceeded to criticise each other's work. What was most surprising was that the sad-eyed, depressed-looking Mavis was the most vicious critic of them all. And soon, sleek, confident June was sobbing until Felicity told her sharply to 'Pull yourself together, June,' and proceeded to lecture them that this was good for them, that professional writers must be used to criticism for how else would they cope with unfavourable reviews?

Tracey held her own magnificently and shrugged off her critics as of no importance.

'But you kept repeating the same words,' Clarissa pointed out gleefully, for she had just, thin-lipped with exasperation, absorbed an attack from Tracey on her use of pretentious words.

'I did it on purpose.'

'Why?'

'For emphasis, and it works.'

Clarissa's lips went thin again, and Kate found herself agreeing with Tracey, it had worked, and of them all she thought it was Tracey who could write.

By the time they broke for coffee, Kate felt as exhausted as if she had been writing herself. The sharpness and envy had all disappeared and everyone appeared to be friends again.

'There's a writers' weekend just before Christmas, which, if you're quick, you might just get on,' Felicity told Pam and Kate. 'It's essential to meet other writers. Cross-pollination, I like to call it.'

Kate found it was a nice feeling to be referred to as a writer even if she had not written anything. And another even stranger thing was happening. As Felicity set their project for next week – three hundred words on 'A Winter's Romance' – Kate found that ideas were flying about in her mind, like small black birds beating at the inside of her skull in desperation to be let out.

'What did you think?' Pam asked when they were eventually driving away in the direction of Graintry.

'To be honest I feel oddly elated.'

'Me too. It's exciting, isn't it?'

'I'm not too sure of Felicity, though,' Kate said. 'She strikes me as a bit of a bossyboots if you let her get away with it. Mavis is intriguing, isn't she? Such a quiet, unassuming little thing and yet she was quite bitchy. Maybe she's led a hard life.'

'Mavis? Don't see how. She's married to Crabtree's Cough Lozenges – they've loads of money. Doug built their gazebo, cost an arm and a leg. Why don't we go to Smiths, get all these books?'

They had driven back to Kate's after buying the books and magazines – or rather Pam had bought them for there was no way Kate could have afforded all of them. It was not until they got to the house and were sitting over coffee and sandwiches at the kitchen table that she discovered Pam had bought everything in duplicate.

'Pam, I can't take them.'

'Of course you can. Don't spoil my fun. We've got all this bloody money. I don't know what to do with it half the time.'

'You're always so kind to me, but I'm paying for my subs,' Kate said getting out her cheque book.

'What about this writing weekend?'

'Oh, I don't know. I don't think Tony would like me away all the weekend.'

'Sod the men. Let's do it. I'll pay.'

'No, you won't. I'll talk to Tony about it. Here's my cheque. Now bank this one, not like the last.'

'Maybe I will, or maybe I'll keep it as a souvenir when you're a famous author.'

'You've a long wait, then.' Kate laughed.

Once Pam had left Kate sat with her pile of women's magazines, flicking through them reading a story here and there.

She learnt one thing. She did not think that writing romantic short stories was what she wanted to do. And then she realised she had learnt something else. This morning, she thought, she had listened to the others and she knew she could do better. It was not conceit, it was something inside her that told her so.

8

It had been a pig of a day, Gloria thought, as she pushed open the small gate with her hip. Such an awful day that she felt it inevitable that the hinge of the gate should choose this evening to grind painfully and the gate, in slow motion, swing back at a drunken and broken angle. It had been wobbly for months and she should have had it mended. She could just hear what her mother would have said: 'A stitch in time . . .' At that thought she turned round and kicked the gate with irritation. The pile of books and papers she was carrying slipped in the crook of her arm and slid to the ground. She lunged to save them and dropped her keys. The strap of her large, cumbersome handbag slewed across her chest and the bag banged against her knees, tripping her, so that finally, as a *coup de grâce*, she knocked the bottle of milk flying from the doorstep. Elephant, still clutched safely under her other arm for he was the last thing she would ever drop, yapped excitedly as if laughing at her.

'It's all right for you, you can smirk.' She chucked the little Yorkshire terrier under his chin and began searching in the dark for the keys. She cursed mildly as she did so. She was not cursing the keys but her own clumsiness, for this clattering of her possessions down the small garden path was an all-too-common occurrence these days.

Once she had located the keys, she undid the mortice lock and then the Yale and as the burglar alarm whined she sprinted for the box in the fifteen seconds allowed before the neighbours and police complained yet again. This frantic daily race was her own fault. It was she who had insisted on the ugly box of the burglar alarm being hidden away, so that instead of being conveniently situated in the hall, it lurked under the stairs in a cupboard containing all the things she didn't know what else to do with.

Elephant jumped from her arms and raced for the kitchen. She returned to the steps and retrieved the scattered papers and books, dusting them down – at least it had not been raining, she thought, as she added them to a precarious pile already sitting on her desk. Then she did what she always did, ran around the small house, switching on all the lights. It always made her feel better, safer somehow.

An imperious bark from the kitchen informed her that Elephant was not prepared to wait much longer for his food. Dog food! 'Oh, Lord,' she mumbled, burrowing in the cupboard, Elephant looking accusingly at her as if about to say, Not again! Right at the back she found a small tin.

'See, you're wrong. There was one,' she said to the dog, who was excitedly leading the way to the drawer where the tin-opener lived. The cat-flap rattled and Mog appeared, sliding sinuously through. Elephant looked at the cat and then at the tin-opener and decided to stay with the food.

By the time she had fed both cat and dog, emptied the rubbish bin she should have dealt with that morning, taken supper, enough for two, out of the freezer and made herself a cup of tea, she felt exhausted as she settled on the sofa, kicking off her shoes and wriggling her toes in liberation. On days like this she thanked God she did not have kids or a husband. There were other times when she came home from work and the house depressed her with its emptiness. Then, she would dream of what it must be like to have a family waiting for her. But today she marvelled at how some of her friends managed, those who, after a disastrous day in the office, had to return to demanding children, their chatter and noise, help with homework, fulfil demands for fish fingers and baked beans, wash their clothes, see them to bed. They would be followed by husbands who wanted sympathy for the day *they* had had and who were quickly sniffing around wondering what was for dinner. Letitia did it, and Jenny – how? She shook her head in wonderment at the organisational abilities and strength of character of others, so lacking in herself, and pressed the playback button on the telephone answering machine.

There were several messages. First was her mother complaining that Gloria never phoned, not that she actually complained, she was far too subtle in her dealings with her daughter for that. The long message was punctuated with the odd strategically placed sigh, and the wistful tone of her voice was a complaint in itself. Gloria was left feeling riddled with guilt, which was what her mother, no doubt, had set out to achieve. Next was the service engineer about the washing machine – she had missed him again. That would mean another week at least that she would have to lug her washing to the launderette. She had recently edited a book about all manner of happenings in a London launderette, including the heroine falling in love. No such adventures had happened to her; she found the place depressing in the extreme. Then there was a call from a woman desperate to sell her a new kitchen followed by another equally keen on double-glazing, and two calls from people who had chickened out and left no message – the most infuriating of all. But the call she wanted, and all the way back in the car had almost prayed for, was not there. Were everyone's messages as relentlessly boring as hers? Surely other people returned to urgent, exciting messages, not tele-sales people and their mother!

Elephant, having finished his supper, barked to go out into the garden. Patiently she unlocked, unbolted and unchained the back door. These security precautions irked her daily, making her a self-imposed prisoner in her own home. Some days she hated London and longed to be in the country again, where front doors could be left unbolted. The feeling never lasted though. She loved the city and now wondered why she had not gone mad with the tedium during all those years of her youth in her parents' house in Cornwall where the routine was always monotonously the same.

'Why can't you use the cat-flap? You're small enough,' she complained, opening the back door. With great dignity Elephant ignored her question and sallied forth into the night.

She prodded the packages she had taken from the freezer – of course they were still solid. She peered at the backs of the outer wrappers, wondering why the makers of frozen food always wrote the instructions in the smallest print possible and often in green or red ink, always the hardest to read in artificial light. 'Not suitable for home freezing', she read on one of them. 'Oh sod it,' she said aloud. Probably won't hurt, Gloria thought hopefully. She could just imagine her mother's hysterics if she saw that lot, followed by a lecture on price and nutrition. Replacing the packets on the worktop she picked up a glass, opened the fridge door, took out the ice tray, did futile battle with it for a minute or two, then threw it into the sink. She picked up a bottle of vodka, returned to the sitting room, and poured herself a stiff measure. She wondered whether to rerun the tape in case she had missed his message, and then told herself not to be so stupid.

Still, she thought, he might just turn up, he did not always telephone. From the pile of papers on her desk she took a typescript off the top, rearranged its pages in order, settled down under the reading light and tried to concentrate on what she should have finished days ago. She quickly scanned the reader's report and found when she got to the end that she could not remember what it had said at the beginning. With exasperation she threw the typescript onto the sofa, and took a sip of her vodka. She never used to be like this. In the past the most reliable member of staff at Shotters had been Gloria Catchpole: give it to Gloria – it got done. Ask Gloria – she'd have an answer. 'I can't find it' – Gloria could.

But in the past six months things had changed. Her once tidy square of office, in which she had known exactly where everything was, had become, to say the least, untidy. The floor was littered with Elephant's toys. Unread manuscripts stood in piles, the curling of their paper an indication as to which had lain there the longest. Her in tray was full and the out was empty. The rubber plant on the windowsill had died of neglect. Compared with the other offices, glimpsed over partitions, and through the potted plants of the open-plan office, hers was a disgrace.

Without doubt one of the reasons for this state of affairs was the environment she worked in. She hated the vast room, close carpeted, and the large windows that never opened. It was always too chill in summer from the air conditioning and too hot in winter, as if a mad engineer controlled their working temperature. A no-smoking policy was in force and although she had never smoked herself she would think with longing now of the fug in past offices. There was little clutter, camaraderie was sorely lacking. It was as if the building made everyone, crouched over their VDUs, anonymous within it.

Gloria had worked in publishing since leaving university fourteen years ago. She had begun as a junior secretary at Westall and Trim and had been there only a month when Julius had called her into his office and suggested that she might like to try her hand as assistant to the publicity manager. In the years she had spent with Julius he had nurtured her career with as much care as he took over his authors. She had worked in every department, even having a short stint on the road as a rep. Consequently there was little about the business she did not know. For the last two years with Julius she had been what she had always wanted to be – an editor.

Then she had left. She always frowned when she thought of that, her act of betrayal. But she had been invited by Peter Holt to join Shotters which he had recently started up and which he had been running on a shoestring ever since. She had gone for the challenge and excitement and she had received both in spades. Life at Westall's had been satisfying, at Shotters it was knife-edged excitement tinged with terror most of the time.

The general women's fiction list had been her responsibility. She was proud that, without doubt, her efforts had helped Peter reach the position he was in now. It was she who had discovered Bella Ford and Shiel de Tempera. It was she who, working subtly and patiently, had poached Heather Gardens and Grace Bliss from other publishers. These four were in the vanguard of women's literature, their sales enormous. The writers she had garnered had helped in the upsurge in Shotters' fortunes. And when Peter had bought Blades, about to expire but once famous for its mainstream fiction, Gloria and her writers had become part of it, and she had been instrumental in nursing it back to health and viability.

Sometimes, though, she wondered if she had done Peter a favour. There were days she had serious doubts. As Shotters became more successful, as it bought in other ailing publishing houses and grew larger and larger, she had watched Peter change from brilliant publisher into astute businessman. But was he happy?

In the old days, in the cramped offices off Tottenham Court Road, he had been different. Then he seemed charged with electricity as he bounced ideas about, excited at the challenge ahead of him. Then he was approachable on any problem. Now she sensed a dullness about him, he even seemed to walk differently. These days, although she kept an eye open for him, she rarely saw him, stuck away as he was on the top floor in that ludicrous suite of offices.

She had been in love with him then. Sometimes she thought he was the only man she had loved. Not that he ever knew how she felt for he was married, and if there was one rule Gloria had it was that she did not mess with married men. In any case, at the time she had liked Hilary. But Hilary had changed too. Once she had been one of them, but now, with Peter's success and money, she had become grand and detached. Gloria could not remember the last time she had seen her, and now, if she did, she would not be in the least surprised if Hilary cut her dead.

As the firm leapt up the ladder of success one set of offices was exchanged for another. Each move was into premises more convenient and spacious than the last but they had all been offices where the intimacy remained, where the feel of books was in the air. All that had gone with this last move. Now, when at work, Gloria could imagine herself anywhere – an insurance company, a broker's.

There were days when Gloria had begun to think the unthinkable – that she was in the wrong job. But what else could she do? This was all she knew. She had toyed with the idea of setting up as an agent, which was what most discontented editors did. Certainly she had the contacts and the push needed to succeed. But then she would not be doing what she was best at. How could she bear to find an author and then hand him or her on to somebody else to tend and prune and polish?

It was not just the office though, she had to be honest. The problems of the past six months had begun when she had been passed over for promotion to editorial director, a post which she was not alone in regarding as hers for the asking. Instead it had gone to that wimp Norman Wilton whom she could have wiped the floor with: he lacked her intelligence, experience, and certainly her instincts. Once she would have rushed to Peter with her anger and disappointment but not any more. He was too remote, and since the senior management structure had mushroomed to include a small army of people with grand-sounding titles, she doubted if the decision would have been his alone.

She had become despondent and the 'couldn't care' attitude towards work was spilling over into her home, once her pride and joy. She just could not seem to be bothered about anything. The restlessness inside her was as physical as any itch on the outside.

And then there was Clive. He was the latest in a long line of romantic catastrophes. The men Gloria knew she should have gone for – sensible, hard-working, reliable types – just did not interest her. Time and again it was the drifters, often artists, writers, actors, all handsome, virile and usually younger than herself, who excited her.

Clive Renshaw was typical of them. At twenty-five he was ten years younger than her. He was handsome, intelligent and without doubt the best-endowed man she had come across – and he knew how to please her. She did not love him nor he her. He was a good lay. There had been a time when she would have congratulated herself on her luck but, just recently, she found herself longing for something more than sex.

She never knew when he would turn up. They had a relationship of sorts but it was strictly on his terms. Such behaviour was normal with the men in her life, and it was an attitude she had encouraged. 'No commitment' could have been her motto. But she had changed, she would have liked to know where she stood with him, she wanted a normal life.

What was different with Clive from the other affairs was that until him she had not felt hurt; each had used the other. But with Clive she felt used and almost angry that she did not love him, as if it was his fault.

Even Jenny, her friend, did not understand. At least, she had been her friend until last week, and then they had rowed – over Clive, what else?

Gloria had been having a moan about Clive, trying to express how empty she felt when Jenny had gone too far. 'It's your own fault, Gloria,' she'd said, standing by Gloria's desk and smiling as she spoke. 'You enjoy the drama, you enjoy being badly treated. You search these men out on purpose just so that you can be hurt. You're a mental masochist. The good sex that comes from it just isn't worth the pain . . .'

The ensuing row must have been heard all over the editorial floor – certainly people seemed to have been looking at her in an odd way ever since. She and Jenny passed each other without speaking and Gloria now regretted ever confiding one word to her. What a thing to say. Gloria shook her head as if to blot out the memory. She looked at her watch. Eight-thirty. If she had a long bath, maybe he would arrive in the middle of it – then they could bathe together. That is what she would do.

During the following hour she shaved her legs, removed her nail varnish, plucked her eyebrows, washed her hair. Still he had not come. She dried herself, perfumed herself, changed into her new Marks and Spencer pyjamas that looked and felt like silk and took ages over painting her nails. Still he had not come. She stood studying herself in the mirror as if the image could give her the reason for his absence. It did not. She liked what she saw. She might have problems but not about her looks, she had always been confident of them. She was a tall woman with a face more striking than beautiful; her hair was her best feature, dark, almost black, thick and naturally curly. Her brown eyes were sharp and intelligent. With her strong bones she had a forceful face which she was aware frightened some men away – but that was all right, she supposed, she would not have been interested in such wimps, anyway.

Maybe she was not meant to find a man, maybe this was how her life was to be led. Jenny was wrong, she hated being hurt like this, loathed the humiliation. This time she had not heard from Clive for ten days – that was too long, even for him. He would not change, she realised that: if she had learnt anything from the past it was that no man ever changed his ways. Maybe she should try to forget him, maybe she would have more luck with someone nearer her own age. She sighed at that thought. 'Fat chance,' she said to the mirror. She knew from the experience of her other friends that men her own age were, if unmarried, either weird or gay. And the tales she had heard of divorced men riddled with guilt, pining for their children and with never enough money, were enough to put off a woman for life. She let herself out of the bathroom. Elephant was sitting on the landing.

'I'm better off with you, aren't I, Heffalump?' She bent down and patted the small dog who licked her hand excitedly. 'Shall we go to bed or go and have some supper?' The dog looked up at her, head on one side, and turned to the top of the stairs. 'Yes, you're right, I should have something to eat.'

Back in the kitchen her meal was still partly frozen. She rinsed the carton of *moules* under the hot tap, then knocked the contents sharply on the bottom of the box into a non-metal dish. She placed this in the microwave and gave it an extra few minutes for the icy bits. She looked with disgust at the resultant over-cooked mess and scraped it into the bin, then she threw the other packages after it. She wondered how many dinners she had got out, just in case he came, that had ended up ditched like this.

'Bed, then.'

She settled Elephant in his basket covering him with his blanket and kissing him. Even as she did so she knew it was no way to treat a dog, knew that she was making the little dog a substitute for the emptiness of her life. She knew she should not, but she could not stop now.

Gloria climbed into the large and very empty bed. She did not even bother to wind the clock. Saturday tomorrow, she could have a lie in. Tomorrow was Barty Silver's party. She had meant to surprise Clive with that – it would have been an important party for him to attend. Goodness only knew which important actors and producers he would have met there, any one of whom might have offered him work, let alone Barty himself. Serves him right, she thought, as she turned off the light. She would not answer the telephone tomorrow, she would go by herself, let him suffer for a change.

On Saturday evening Gloria dressed with extra care. She might, last night, have thought she was destined never to find a man, but she wasn't willing to give up trying yet. Tall and with good legs, the short Hempel dress in dark blue taffeta suited her. It had cost her several months' salary – she didn't care, no matter what her mother would think. She liked good clothes and, thanks to a grandmother and two great aunts all dying at nearly the same time and leaving her money, she had no mortgage to pay, so she could afford the odd splurge.

She checked her make-up one more time and kissed Elephant, locked the kitchen door, had a moment of panic about her car keys and finally set out into the night.

'Aren't you going too fast?' Kate craned her neck to see the speedometer but, in the cluster of spinning dials, she was not sure which one it was. He ignored her question. She fumbled with the cigarette lighter, unfamiliar with its position in this new Rover speeding up the M4 to London.

'You smoke too much,' Tony replied, waving his hand in the exasperated way of a non-smoker. In the darkness Kate rolled her eyes with aggravation and inhaled deeply in defiance.

'You didn't answer my question,' she said.

'We'll be late. And don't smoke there, Sir Barty abhors smoking.'

It had all the makings of a strange evening, she thought. First, this unexpected invitation to such exotic circles. Then he had told her she didn't have enough make-up on. And then, biggest surprise of all, he had shyly given her a small box containing a pretty pair of gold earrings. Now he was driving too fast. Tony never speeded, never got tickets, in fact he frequently embarrassed her with his sedate pootling along, annoying other motorists and, no doubt, causing all manner of accidents in his wake.

She hoped the dress was all right. She had bought it in a small shop in the local town, feeling unable to cope with the crowds in Bristol. She was not used to attending smart London parties and it had been difficult to know what to buy, having no idea what women wore outside her own small circle. She had opted for a safe black crêpe one, loose to cover up the bulges she knew she had but never seemed to have the will to do anything about – like most things these days.

'You're quiet . . .'

'I was just thinking.'

'You think too much, that's half your problem. Look in the *A to Z*. It must be close to here . . . Clarendon House, Silver Street. Found it?'

9

Joy Trenchard sat in the white, gold and beige drawing room of her elegant house in Holland Park.

With her sleek head of short-cut straight blonde hair, her pale skin, the expensive beige silk dress she wore with a large gold Butler and Wilson lizard snaking across it, it was difficult to tell if the room had been decorated to suit her or she to go with the room.

She was reading a book. At least, it looked as if she was reading but for the past half-hour she had been looking fixedly at the same page. She did not read, she could not, for the words were blurred from staring at them for too long and the book was of no interest to her. It was a prop in case someone should come into the room and find her still sitting and waiting.

She looked up at the sound of whispering outside the door.

'Come in, Hannah,' she called, her sad expression disappearing immediately, her face transformed by a beautiful smile.

Hannah, her four-year-old daughter, entered, closely followed by her nanny, Sheila. The child's hair, as fine and blonde as her own, freshly washed, hung loose and long, spread on the pink of her pyjamas. She clutched a small and almost bald teddy bear.

'Do you like the new pyjamas?'

'I like the Snoopy dogs on them, Mummy.'

'I wish I had such lovely ones. None of mine have dogs on them.'

'Why don't they make grown-ups' pyjamas with Snoopy on them?'

'I really don't know, my darling. Kiss?' Joy held up her face to be kissed, Hannah scrambled onto the sofa beside her to be able to reach her. 'Ready for bed?'

'You will read to me, please.'

'Not tonight, darling, Mummy's going out in a minute.' She did have time to read, it was just that she could not, she knew she would not be able to concentrate. 'I'll read you two stories tomorrow and that's a promise,' she said, at sight of her daughter's look of disappointment. 'Off you go.' She gently patted her daughter's small rump. Joy stood up and faced the nanny, a woman she loathed but who was super efficient. Sheila was so reliable that Joy could never find any reason to sack her, especially when Hannah adored her. 'Sheila, Mr Trenchard has been delayed in chambers. I'll wait a few minutes more but then I'll go on to Sir Barty's on my own. I've written the number on the pad in the hall should you need me.'

'Yes, Mrs Trenchard,' Sheila said as she began to usher her charge towards the door. 'Shall I tell Mr Trenchard that's where you are when he comes home?'

'That won't be necessary, he'll probably go straight on to the party.'

'Of course, Mrs Trenchard,' Sheila said with such an expression of disdain that Joy had to look away quickly, as though it could scald her. Once the door was closed she crossed to the drinks tray and poured herself another gin and tonic. This was her third so far in the last hour. She knew she should not drink so quickly, not with Barty's party to go to, but she could not help herself. It was Charles's fault if she got drunk – at least, that's what she told herself. Where was the bastard?

From a table beside the sofa she picked up the telephone and dialled his chambers. She listened to the monotonous sound of a telephone ringing in a deserted room. She did not think it was her imagination that telephone rings sounded different when there was no one there to answer – like the way one could always tell when a house was empty. Five more rings she would give it, she told herself. Three, four, five. Reluctantly she replaced the receiver. She did not know why she had bothered, she had been phoning at regular intervals since six to remind him of the party. There had been no reply before, so why should there be one now?

No sooner had she replaced the instrument on its cradle than it rang. She virtually dived for it, spilling her drink in the process, but mercifully on the sofa and not her dress.

'Yes?' she said breathlessly.

'Joy, it's me, Betty. I'm in a fix, I don't know which way to turn.'

'Tell me about it,' Joy replied patiently, managing to disguise her deep disappointment that it wasn't Charles.

'It's gone – totally. I can't write,' Betty said dramatically in her husky, smoker's voice.

'What do you mean, you can't write? Of course you can, you write beautifully.' Joy was using her most professional and soothing tones.

'I can't, Joy. The stuff that's coming out isn't me at all. I've lost my style, I've lost my voice.' Betty Farmer sounded virtually hysterical.

'Betty, try to calm down. Tell me what it's like.'

'Short sentences, staccato almost.'

'What are you reading?'

'Reading, what do you mean?'

'What book are you into for relaxation.'

There was a long pause. Joy smiled to herself. When she had been an editor she had had this conversation on more than one occasion with an hysterical author. Whatever it was she was reading, Betty didn't want her to know.

'Well, there's my research . . .'

'No, Betty, I need to know what novel you're reading.'

'The latest Jackie Collins, actually.' Betty's deep voice was ripe with embarrassment.

Joy laughed. 'That's it, then. Collins has a particularly strong style and you're catching it, it's easily done. Good read, isn't it?' Joy was laughing again, but silently, for Betty Farmer liked to think of herself as something of an intellectual. Her books were far from being so, but Betty did not see it that way and took her writing far more seriously than the content warranted.

'I think one should keep abreast of trends,' Betty said defensively.

'Essential,' Joy replied soothingly.

'And that's all you think it is?'

'I'm sure, Betty. While you're writing stick to encyclopaedias or *Whitaker's Almanack*, anything but Jackie Collins or other writers with such distinctive prose.'

'You're such a pet, Joy. Always so good-natured and understanding.'

'It's what I'm here for, Betty.' Odd, she thought as she spoke, how normal she could make herself sound when she was cracking up inside – she did it all the time.

The call eventually over, she raced out to the small cloakroom and dampened a hand towel. With it she worked quickly, mopping up from the sofa the spreading damp from her drink. She was in a panic. She had had such a fight with Charles when she had chosen this expensive white slubbed silk covering, she could imagine his fury if his worst fears had materialised and the sofa was ruined. She stood back and looked carefully at it from all angles. She had been lucky, it had not stained.

Poor Betty, she thought, as she replaced the dirty towel with a clean one and checked her face in the mirror over the basin. It must be hell to be a writer, always so insecure – far better to be an agent. She wished she was an agent with an office, though, then she would not have to field that sort of call when at home, often when it was the last thing she wanted to do.

She did not have the capital to set up an office, that was her problem. She had asked Charles to help but he did not take what she did seriously enough to invest any money in her. He had suggested she try the bank. She had no luck there either; it transpired that her manager had known more than one client like herself, bored, married to a rich man, who had set themselves up as a literary agent, thinking all that was needed was a telephone and a typewriter. They all gave up within the year when the money did not come in as they anticipated, and the outgoings became far more than they had ever dreamed possible.

Despite these setbacks she had carried on, using her dress allowance to finance herself so that Charles could never complain about the telephone bill. She had asked for an electric typewriter for her birthday and was now about to ask for a fax machine for Christmas. She was determined to succeed, to show him that she could do it. She needed one writer who would earn her a substantial commission, a deal which would make people sit up and take notice. It would come, she was sure, for she loved the work, loved the excitement that each new writer could be the one.

She had not had much luck in the six months she had been in business. There were plenty of writers out there, she had advertised only twice in writers' journals and after that it was a rare day that new work did not arrive. But out of the piles of manuscripts she had waded through – some almost indecipherable – she had found only two she thought might have the spark, if she could persuade them to revise certain parts. There was Betty. If she reworked a couple of sections, Joy was convinced she could sell her book to Wallers who specialised in women's lightweight romantic fiction. But she knew the sum they would get was unlikely to be as much as Betty dreamed of, nor would they be the publishers she hoped for. And, unfortunately, Betty took the trade press and knew exactly what sums some authors were getting.

She had had one success with Brian Hoskins – he was thirty, a journalist –

who with his first novel showed great promise. He had been accepted last week but the sum which she would eventually get as her commission would not even cover the amount she had spent on lunching likely editors, on telephone calls, and photocopying the manuscript. She had been so elated, almost as if she had written the book herself, but Charles had been unimpressed. She had, with aggrieved irritation, pointed out to him that she had to start somewhere. His reaction only fuelled her determination to prove him wrong.

Back in the drawing room she looked at the carriage clock on the mantelshelf – eight-thirty. She would give him another fifteen minutes. She poured herself another drink. She had spilt the last so that did not really count, she told herself. She sat again on the sofa, stroked the telephone and debated whether to call again or not. Her hand fell to her lap – what was the point?

She would often say, always with a laugh, that in the fourteen years of her marriage to Charles she had lost count of the times he had been unfaithful. This, of course, was a complete lie. It was the sophisticated, throwaway remark she made to her friends to cover up her hurt. In fact Joy remembered every one of them, their names, ages, what they looked like. She remembered every ounce of pain, every lonely evening she had spent. The humiliation of keeping appointments without him or, worse, not keeping them and lying to her hostess, saying she was unwell, had become a sickening repetitive routine. Especially as she knew that none of them was taken in for one moment. The whole of London knew about Charles.

She loved him, that was her curse.

She had loved him the moment she had set eyes on him at a May Ball in Cambridge when she had been with someone else – his friend, in fact. She had seen him, tall, blond, blue-eyed with his long-legged elegance, and had known she did not want to marry anyone else. It had taken her six months to get him and a further six before he proposed, and only six months into their marriage he was unfaithful for the first time. That time, since she was pregnant, she had told herself was understandable. Poor Charles must have been put off by her lumbering body. She had lost that baby. They never spoke of it, but she sometimes wondered if, like her, he blamed that particular affair, with the stress it had caused her, for her miscarriage. He was wonderful to her for some time after that. He was contrite. He loved her, he told her a dozen times a day. But then the signs came again that another affair had started – the lateness from work, the truncated telephone calls when she walked into a room.

Over the years, she had tried to rationalise the problem. He was like an alcoholic really, except it wasn't booze with him, it was the constant renewal of fresh pussy he was addicted to. Her pain at his rejection of her had often goaded her into confronting him. They had had scenes without number when she had angered him by threatening to leave. Then he would hit her. But it was almost worth it for then he always said he was sorry, he would promise her, swear to her that he would never do it again, that she was the one he loved, and she the one he would stay with until his dying day. That said, he would sally forth for another fling as if his promises to her exonerated him – until the next scene.

The one thought she would not allow herself to dwell on was the one that told her he should never have married in the first place. She supposed she should have become used to it, but she had not. What she had become adept at was hiding her feelings, burying the pain so that all their friends, while amazed at her relentless cheerfulness, her apparent understanding of her husband, could only assume that she condoned what he did.

But this time was different and this time, on top of all the usual emotions of rejection and unhappiness, she felt fear.

In the past she had been able to convince herself that the women were transient. There was a form of comfort in the sheer volume of turnover. She had also met most of them – it appeared to give Charles pleasure for her to meet his mistresses. Doing so had, in a way, removed fear. They were all young, vacuous, women he was certain to tire of quickly and come back to her as he always did.

Penelope Hawkins was a different proposition, however. Charles's affairs usually lasted, at most, three months. But this one had been going on for over six. Penelope was older than they usually were, more beautiful and, most worrying of all, she was highly intelligent. Like Charles, she was a barrister and so they had much in common. Had he been a criminal barrister, Joy herself could perhaps have been interested in his work. But a tax expert? It was not a subject she could get excited about nor could she cobble together a great deal of small talk on the subject for use over the dinner table – but Penelope could.

She realised now that she had always been waiting for someone like Penelope to enter his life. Now it had happened and she did not know what to do. She had nothing to offer him that Penelope had not more of. While beautiful herself she could acknowledge, in that cold calculating way in which women assess each other, that Penelope was more so. Undoubtedly she was better company for him and, at thirty, was five years younger than Joy. In her mind, each day since the start of this particular affair, Joy had made herself feel more and more inadequate so that in the end she felt there was nothing of value about herself at all.

Previously she had always comforted herself that her position was inviolate, for Charles loved their daughter as much as she did – he would never risk losing the child. But this year, for the first time ever, he had missed Hannah's birthday party. His love for the little girl was no longer an assured comfort to her.

Her marriage was over. That's what she thought, in those long sleepless hours, in the depth of night when everything is blackest. Usually one can laugh at such night-time notions when daylight dawns. Except Joy couldn't this time, the idea persisted night and day.

She knew she should fight back and despised herself for not doing so. If she could only find a lover for herself, maybe Charles would be beside himself with jealousy, begging her to return to him, vowing never to stray again. It was something she was never likely to put to the test. The problem was, if you loved someone as Joy loved Charles then no one else held any attraction for you, the very thought was anathema. She could not bear the thought of anyone else kissing her, stroking her, inside her, no, she knew for certain there was no other man for her. Who else could give her the pleasure in bed that Charles could? Those times when she knew he was with another woman caused her physical pain. She wanted him, needed him, was fixated with him.

She looked at her watch. Ten to nine. She tried the phone one more time. No answer. She really had thought he would turn up for Barty Silver, an important client. This time she would not telephone with an excuse, this time she would go alone. She needed a big book to establish herself, to make the publishers, as well as Charles, take her seriously. She planned to try to have a word with Barty Silver tonight. She wanted to suggest he write his memoirs and she act as his agent. She knew a dozen publishers who would fight to publish them. She also knew that many before her had badgered Barty and failed. Difficult though it might be, she was going to have to find the courage to speak to him.

She got up and collected her handbag. She stood up straight as if steeling herself to go alone. In the hall she slipped into her coat and let herself out into the night, hoping she would pick up a taxi quickly.

10

Sir Barty Silver was a master in the art of party-giving. He should be, he had had enough practice. He gave more parties than anyone else in London; it appeared to be his favourite hobby. In fact it was not, it was how Barty liked to do business. Just as well, for Barty's hours did not fit in with most people's idea of a working day. He never woke before noon, having rarely got to bed until dawn. He then had a leisurely breakfast, served by his Mexican manservant, followed by an equally leisurely bath; by the time he had changed into freshly laundered silk pyjamas – his chosen mode of dress for this part of the day – one and a half hours had passed. His secretary would come to take down letters and to deal with any business in hand, for which he allotted a further hour, not a minute more. He would then deal with his tailor or his shirtmaker, his masseur, herbalist, hypnotist or take a swim in his sumptuous indoor pool. This he called his maintenance hour. He then spent the next two on the telephone, calling business contacts in all corners of the earth, with scant regard to which time zone they were in. At five-thirty he would nap until six, when he would change again.

On the dot of six-thirty his aides arrived, all young men, all noticeable for their extraordinary good looks, charm and elegance. They were male for, if the truth were told, Barty was uncomfortable in the presence of all but a few women friends. The aides were handsome for Barty liked to surround himself with beauty. At this point, his day could go in two directions.

On those he called *drudgery* days he would have a stiff martini, check the figures and the weekly ticket sales sent over from the various theatres where his shows were on. He would then sally forth to one of those theatres selected at random and inspect his show. The knowledge that he was 'out front' put fear into the heart of even the most famous actor, for after the performance there would be a lengthy backstage post-mortem, which had been known to go on for hours. Such discussions could, and frequently did, result in Barty cold-shouldering those who had not reached his demanding standards – Barty expected perfection. He dined late, at a supper club he had founded simply so that he would always have somewhere to eat at any hour of the night. There, he did business into the small hours over several bottles of claret while those about him tried to stay awake. These nights he would go home early, for him. In bed by three o'clock, he would then speed-read scripts that were sent to him by the sackload. Those who had written plays or musicals chosen by him for further consideration were, if the work was finally selected, assured of a golden future. Barty's touch was infallible. It was a mystery to all the other impresarios in town, who worked far harder than he and at more conventional hours, how Barty could be the runaway success he was.

The other days he called his *relaxation* days – not that anyone else in his entourage would agree with the description. Such evenings would begin with his usual stiff martini followed by a light supper. Then he would go to a party – he never went to a party without setting up some deal or other. His interests were vast, not just the theatre, but a stage school, real estate, several night clubs, the supper club, three pop groups, two public houses, an Italian restaurant. These were his visible assets, but they alone could not explain his extreme wealth. In addition, he dealt astutely in all the markets of the world – his portfolio was a treasure chest.

The hostesses at these events knew that when they invited Barty they would have to invite one of his aides as well, which, when it was a dinner party, vexed them dreadfully. But Barty was so socially powerful that no one ever dared to refuse him. It did not matter if he had been to a dinner party, a party or a reception, he would always end up at his supper club and, to everyone's amazement, would have another meal.

But the relaxation days he liked the best were when he gave his own parties, two or three times a month. These he preferred for the simple reason that his parties were always the best. And they were the only nights when he did not go to the supper club – he had no need, for at about two in the morning his chef always served a late supper.

One of the secrets of the excellence of his parties was that there was never that awkward hiatus period when the party was not yet under way, when few people had arrived and those who had just stood about unsure what to do or say, waiting for something to happen. If the invitations said eight, it was certain that a number of people, chosen for their extrovert characters, would arrive extra early so that a small party was already under way before the main one had even begun.

And Barty set great store by champagne cocktails.

'Get the buggers tiddly-poo the minute they arrive, then it'll go with a swing – sober 'em up later.' He said this so often that people said it should be carved on his tombstone. The first two cocktails he offered were extra strong on the brandy. There was then a subtle lessening of the potency of the drinks so that the euphoria was judiciously kept topped up, but it was rare for anyone to get legless at his dos. How his staff knew who was at which drinks stage was one of the wonders of London society.

Barty was also adept at juggling his guest list so that the widest cross-section of people was invited. It was possible at any of his parties to meet someone you might need in your passage through life. There was always a sprinkling of the beautiful and young so that the possibility of romance hung heavy and excitingly in the air. A bishop, monsignor or rabbi was invariably present should the possibility of marriage arise. Estate agents from the larger establishments were usually there, brains packed with information on desirable residences. Barty took an inordinate interest in his health so a smattering of Harley Street specialists would be on hand, and if an obstetrician was not among them they would be only too happy to recommend one. The world of finance was represented by bankers, stockbrokers, financial advisors in droves. Lawyers abounded for pre-nuptial agreements, divorce and wills. Actors, writers, painters, musicians – classical and popular – were on hand to amuse. One person who was a more frequent guest than most was Sir Hugh Morangie – the most famous gerontologist in the land – for Barty was taking as much care of his future as he did of his present. And, of course, the bishop, monsignor or rabbi were also there to arrange a nice burial or memorial service and so complete the circle.

Barty's house was a dream. Many had offered to buy and all had been refused. Large, white and imposing, built by a courtier at the time of Charles II, it stood in a small street in Chelsea shielded from the noise of the city by ten-foot walls and a huge wooden gate that thumped shut after each arrival so that the casual passer-by only ever caught the tiniest glimpse of the huge gardens with their immaculate lawns and fountains, the graceful sweep of the driveway.

Only royalty and the lame were allowed to drive through the gates to the front of the house. Everyone else, without exception, was made to park elsewhere and walk, for Barty hated his front drive cluttered with cars. This had led to frequent altercations with the gate-keeper by those who did not know better. Many were the threats to his occupation, many were the tossed heads, the fury, and the declaration that they'd never been treated like this before nor so insulted. It made no difference, either they accepted the rule or they did not come. The majority did. Those who had fallen by the wayside were an American female singer of stunning vulgarity and wealth, a particularly pompous, and newly created life peer, a High Court judge who everyone knew had a propensity for child pornography and the exclusion of these three was generally welcomed.

The house contents were worthy of a museum. Looking about it people shuddered at what the insurance premiums must be.

Barty's study was the room where his parties took place, spilling out if necessary into the adjoining drawing and dining rooms, when the double doors were opened and the three huge rooms interlinked. But the core, and where the cognoscenti gathered, was the study. Told to go there, new guests were not prepared for what was in store. It was a vast room, which had once been a ballroom. Long sash-windows opened on to a balcony that wound round the ground floor of the house. At one end, on a dais, was Barty's desk, threateningly wide and heavy, behind which were french windows and steps leading down into the beautiful garden. It was decorated in lush Pompeian red, the mouldings and cornices picked out in white, gold and black. Rich, wild silk curtains, which matched the walls exactly, hung heavily pelmeted and swagged at the windows. On the highly polished oak plank floor were scattered priceless Persian rugs. Against the walls were ebony bookcases, the books all re-covered in black, red and white bindings of finest kid. Upon black plinths, set at intervals around the room, were marble busts of Roman emperors. On the many tables were Barty's collections – lapis lazuli, jade, gold, silver, crystal. And everywhere were photographs of Barty with royal persons – only the more important ones – and presidents – from only the major powers.

Very few people had ever ventured as far as Barty's private apartments. There, they would have been even more impressed, for stepping into these was like moving into an Arabian Nights of colour. His bedroom was decorated as if it was a Bedouin tent, the opulent wall hangings spread across the ceiling in a graceful arch, caught in the centre by a solid gold sculpture of two cupids. His low bed was covered with a counterpane made from the fur of thousands of mink throats, the antique tapestry cushions scattered about it seeming to glow with the richness of their colours. Here there were no paintings as in the other rooms, except opposite the bed where hung a discreetly lit Russian ikon for which the Russian government would happily have paid millions. At the touch of a switch the rich hangings on one wall parted to expose his computers, faxes, telephones, all the hardware that kept him in touch with the rest of the world.

Everything about the house, and the man, was rich, exclusive and amazing. Not bad for an ex-Dr Barnardo's boy, deserted at birth by his Cockney mother who would not divulge the name of his father. Amazing for one who had started his working life selling, from an attaché case, doubtful items of jewellery outside Selfridges in Oxford Street.

He was ready for his party and excited. He always was – another reason why he was such a successful host. The day he did not feel this excitement would be the day he gave his last party. He was dressed in a dark green suit of the softest French velvet, his cream silk shirt was finished at the neck with an equally fine silk cravat. On his feet were matching green slippers, his initials finely embroidered in gold. It was a vulgar outfit which, on Barty, lost its vulgarity. It would have been fashionable in the sixties but without doubt, by tomorrow, copies would be being made for sale in the shops by the end of the week.

He was short, and surprisingly muscular. His hair was white, thick and luxuriant. There was much debate as to whether his hair was his own or a wig, and the question of whether he had a face-lift was of great interest to many. He had a smooth, round face with deep-set grey eyes and an unblinking stare with which he observed everything.

How old he was nobody knew, and he never said. Forms of any description requiring his birthdate were left blank, so that consulting *Who's Who* was of no use. His passport, when travelling, he kept strictly on his person, while at home it was locked safely away in his personal safe. He looked to be in his mid-forties but had been famous for too long to be anything but in his sixties.

The majority assumed he was a homosexual – his exotic house, his obsession with the minutiae of entertaining, his style of dressing, his coterie of beautiful young men, his unmarried state, were all given as proof of his sexual proclivities. The truth was a long way from this. Barty wasn't homosexual, bisexual or heterosexual: he had no interest in men or women, never had. He had not experienced love as a child, and never in his whole life had he been hugged or kissed. He had survived, and could see no benefit to be gained from physical contact with another human being. Or from any emotional entanglement. Perhaps a psychiatrist would have said he was an incomplete person, a damaged individual, but Barty would have scoffed at such a notion. He genuinely could not understand all the fuss about sex and felt quite strongly, from observing his friends, that it invariably led to grief.

His excitement was gained from making money. He loved the stuff, or rather the buzz it gave him, with a deep passion. Money to him was life, without it he would not have wished to continue living.

Now he stood at the door to his study, a glass of champagne on the table beside him, and waited to welcome his guests with that inner feeling of delicious anticipation at wondering what deals, what ideas he would be given tonight.

11

Kate had not even reached the large wooden gate and already she was feeling sick with apprehension. They were in Silver Street, part of a long queue of people edging along. She wondered if Sir Barty had bought his house because of the name of the street or whether the street had been named after him.

The crowd was noisy with excitement and there were frequent shrill cries of recognition from the women. They reminded her of the parakeets in the zoo calling to each other. She was amazed at the number of fur coats she saw, and even more amazed that people were still brave enough to wear them. But, then, the women wearing them looked so groomed and sleek that, apart from this party, it was unlikely they walked anywhere at all. Certainly she could not imagine them shopping at Tesco or doing the school run – such an idea was ludicrous. These women would be protected, by chauffeur-driven cars and exclusive, guarded shops, from the more extreme of the animal-rights people. They had such an air of superiority that she found them frightening. But then, she told herself, they were women just like her, they must have the same worries and fears. Undressed, they had two boobs and no doubt worried about the passage of time, as she did. They might all be smiling and appearing happy, but were they? Did they find their husbands irksome? The routine of life restricting? And she found herself wondering what they did with their lives, how their days were filled. Was it fun being rich, never having to worry about the bills? Or could luxury become boring? Was it possible they were as discontented with the lives they led as she was with hers?

Those women who weren't in furs wore evening coats or swirling capes in silks and satins. Kate pulled her serviceable tweed closer to her and knew with a sinking certainty that her dress was not going to do at all.

This was confirmed in the ladies' cloakroom. It was more like the cloakroom of a hotel or a smart restaurant than a loo in a private house. There were four lavatories for a start, each behind doors painted with wonderful *trompe l'oeil*. Four basins with gold-plated taps were set in a vast vanity unit; over each hung a fine Chippendale mirror. On the marble surface, and at each basin, was a full set of make-up by Charles of the Ritz and a selection of perfumes in the largest size bottles that money could buy. Beside them lay silver-backed brushes and combs. On a table was a stack of gleaming white hand towels. Comfortable armchairs were scattered about the white marble floor, marble which appeared to be veined with gold, and on a low coffee table were copies of all the latest magazines. In attendance was a maid, in uniform black dress and crisp, starched apron, who was taking the coats and wraps through to an adjoining room.

Her coat taken, Kate felt even worse as she saw herself in the long mirrors that covered one wall. She looked like a fat black crow in the midst of a flock of exotic birds. If Pam were with her she could have told her which designers had created the dresses about her. Everyone was expensively clothed, made-up and coiffed – everyone, that is, except Kate. She glanced quickly into one of the mirrors, peering at herself over the head of a particularly sophisticated woman in crimson silk, whose body did not appear to have an ounce of fat on it and whose face, though rigid from a face-lift, looked as if it had been painted by an artist. Kate would like to have picked up one of the bottles of perfume – she'd spied Joy, a smell she adored and could never hope to afford

– and have a quick dab, but no one else was doing so, and she did not like to. Her Estée Lauder would have to do.

In the hallway the men waited for their women, milling about confidently, greeting each other far more quietly than their female counterparts. It was all right for them, thought Kate, in their dinner jackets. They did not have to suffer the humiliation of not being smart enough. And their middle-aged spread was counted a sign of success, not a sign of neglect. It was an unjust world, she thought, as she looked about for Tony and tried not to gawp at some of the famous faces around her.

Sir Barty Silver looked exactly as he had in the copy of *Hello* magazine she had picked up in the hairdresser's – what a fuss they had made of her when she had shyly said she was going to his party. Never one to boast, she had quite taken herself by surprise at even mentioning it. But she was so excited and so proud that it had just slipped out.

They edged slowly towards him in the receiving line, slowly, since Sir Barty seemed to have a word for everyone. She noticed that as each guest approached a young man surreptitiously whispered in his ear – so surreptitiously that it was barely noticeable.

'Mrs Howard, thank you so much for coming to my party.' She found her hand being firmly shaken, and noticed with surprise that he spoke with a pronounced Cockney accent.

'Thank you for asking us,' she said. She knew it sounded inane but she felt almost weak-kneed as if in the presence of royalty.

'And the children, are they well? Steve and Lucy, isn't it?' He looked straight at her and Kate found the unblinking stare disconcerting.

'Very well, thank you.' She was aware that she looked half-witted in her astonishment that he even knew she had children.

'And Mr Howard. I'm so looking forward to our chat, say in ...' He turned towards the young man hovering behind him, who without even glancing at the paper in his hands, whispered again. 'Fine, nine-thirty, in the small library. We'll talk then, Gervase here will show you the way.' And they found themselves standing the other side of Barty, ushered there by the gentle pressure of his hand, as he turned to the next guest. A waiter was hovering with a tray of glasses. Kate took one, smiling her thanks.

'Don't drink too much,' Tony hissed in her ear.

'How did he know about Steve and Lucy?' she asked, curtly.

'He obviously does his homework.'

'Then what else does he know about us?'

'There's not a lot to know, is there? We've hardly got any dark secrets.' He laughed.

'You can say that again,' Kate muttered into her glass. This really was a lovely drink, cool, bubbly and yet giving one an instant lift.

'What did you say?'

'Nothing,' she replied, and wondered how often women said that little word to their men. She used it all the time. Saying the word gave her a measure of satisfaction when irritated by him, as well as avoiding a full-scale row.

'We ought to circulate,' he said, looking about the room with a smug, self-satisfied expression on his face.

At sight of the half-filled room, Kate knew she would never have the courage to do that and she took a huge gulp of the comforting drink. 'I can't,' she hissed back at him. 'I just couldn't. I feel shy.'

Tony looked at her with undisguised irritation. 'Don't be so feeble. Well, I'm going to,' he said, and plunged into the nearest group.

Kate stood on the sidelines and watched. She had to admit to a degree of smugness herself as she noticed the blank looks on the group's faces as Tony, a shade gushingly she thought, introduced himself.

For a while she was occupied in studying, with genuine interest, the tables holding Barty's collections of *objets d'art*. She accepted another drink gratefully and longed for a cigarette. She looked about her but, Tony had been right, no one was smoking. She wished it was not winter, then the french windows would be open and she could have escaped on to the balcony and had a quick puff out there. Everyone knew everyone else, except Kate who knew no one, and, it appeared, was of no interest to anybody else. It looked as if she was in for a boring evening.

And then she recognised, in a corner of the room, sitting regally in a chair, wearing a dress of cobalt blue which made her eyes look even bluer, a mass of white hair framing her fine face and observing the scene with an almost cynical smile, Joyce Armitage.

Kate clutched at her throat with excitement. Joyce Armitage! Kate had read every book she had written. Read was the wrong word for the pleasure they had given her, devoured would have been a better description. Everyone knew about Joyce – she was the sort of woman who gave other middle-aged women hope. At the age of fifty-eight she had had her first book published, never having written a single word before, not a short story, a poem, nothing. Her husband had left her for a younger woman, her children, grown-up, had left home, and Joyce, instead of crumbling into a self-pitying heap, had put pen to paper and written the whole sorry tale – beautifully. Fame had not come immediately, that was another lovely part of the story about her, she had become successful by word of mouth. Out in the country, women told other women of this new writer, keen to share their discovery with others. Her publishers had had to reprint six times – it was all part of the legend. Now her novels, one every other year, five in number, leapt straight into the bestseller list.

Here was someone Kate wanted to talk to, someone she knew she would get on with, she knew that from the books, for what Joyce wrote was what Kate so often thought. She grabbed at the sleeve of a passing waiter, and took another glass. Silly of her, she thought, she did not need courage to speak to this woman who, from the way she wrote, was already a friend, but she drank it all the same. She approached Joyce.

'Mrs Armitage?' she began.

Joyce Armitage swung slowly round to face her and Kate found two bright blue eyes looking at her unquestioningly.

'I was sure it was you. I do hope you don't mind me approaching you?' Kate found she was clutching her hands together tightly. There was no response from the writer. 'Only, it's just that I find your books such a joy – totally. I can't tell you the pleasure they give me and my friends . . .' Kate realised she was prattling but found, now she had started and with no response from Joyce, she did not know how to stop. 'I've all your books. I wish I'd known you would be here, I'd have brought them with me – got you to sign them . . .' She giggled stupidly.

The blue eyes stared at her with an expression which lacked any interest at all; Kate felt herself begin to panic. 'I'm sorry,' she said, miserably. Suddenly Joyce smiled, her face transformed. Kate sighed inwardly.

'Peter, I hoped you'd be here,' Joyce cooed in a soft and very attractive voice.

'Joyce, my dear, and how's my favourite author?'

Kate swung round to find two men standing behind her. She stepped to one side, flustered.

'I'm sorry to interrupt your conversation,' the younger of the two men said to Kate.

'You aren't interrupting anything. Peter, sit here with me, I insist.' Joyce patted the arm of her chair and Kate wished the ground would open up and swallow her.

'Hello, Joyce, I'm glad to see you looking so well.' The older man spoke.

Joyce looked at him, and through him, and turned her attention towards the man she had called Peter. The older man shrugged his shoulders expressively and turned to Kate.

'Your glass is empty, let me get you another.' He attracted the attention of a waiter, took two glasses from the tray, handed one to Kate and took a step away from Joyce. Kate followed. 'My name's Julius Westall.' He held his hand out to her.

'Kate Howard.'

'Are you a writer?'

'Me? Good gracious, no.' Kate laughed at the very idea.

'You should be with a name like that – it's perfect.'

'Is it?'

'I can just see it on the spine of a book – short, neat, memorable.' He was laughing now.

'Are you one? A writer, I mean?' she asked.

'No, a publisher.'

'Of course, how stupid of me . . . Westall and Trim.' Kate felt confused again at not making the connection. 'It's funny, though, you asking me that, I've just joined a local writers' circle. Just for fun,' she added hurriedly, for she did not want this nice man to think she was being pushy. He might go and then she would be alone again.

'I've known many writers who have started that way. I wish you luck. You know Joyce?'

'No. I think I might have just committed a dreadful gaffe. I'm a fan of hers, but she didn't want to know me. I expect she gets fed up with all the adulation.'

'It's not that, she's just a very unpleasant woman and, to compound it, a crashing snob.'

'You know her well?' She was shocked by his assessment but at the same time the gossip in her wanted to know more.

'I know her, she'd rather not know me,' he said, smiling. 'I was her first publisher, you see.'

Kate did not see, but was saved from having to comment by the arrival of the younger man whom Julius introduced as Peter Holt.

'Are you a writer?' he asked. 'With a name like that . . .'

Both Julius and Kate began to laugh.

'We've been through that, Peter,' Julius explained.

This was the point where, if she took Felicity Marchmont's advice, she should make herself known to Peter as someone living in the same area, interested in writing. Only she could not do it. She was amazed at the prospect of anyone being able to advertise themselves, it was against everything she had been taught.

'Kate's a writer,' Julius said, smiling kindly at her.

'Oh, hardly, Mr Westall.' She laughed nervously. 'I've only just begun.'

'Really?' said Peter in such an uninterested voice that she was glad she had not mentioned where she lived, or anything about the circle.

'Peter, have you noticed how many publishers are here? You, me, I saw Mike Pewter, Anthony's over there.'

'I know. I've just been talking to Martin and he said that there's four or five from Tudor's. What's our friend Barty up to?'

'I trust he's not thinking of going into publishing. With his track record of success we'd all be bust by the end of the year.'

'There's something I want to talk to you about, Julius.'

'Here?'

'Excuse me, I think I should go and find my husband,' Kate said, feeling that she was suddenly in the way. Since neither man made a move to ask her to stay she turned away, just as the younger man invited the older one to his home for a weekend. But in turning, Kate knocked the arm of a man standing closer than she realised. The drink in his glass slopped dangerously close to the rim as he held it away from him with both hands, balancing it carefully.

'I'm so sorry,' Kate blurted out.

'Nothing to be sorry about. See, not a drop lost.' He laughed. He was grey-haired and with the kind of deeply lined face – more crevasses than wrinkles – that implied a life led to the full. He was tall and large and well padded and he shambled, reminding her of a bear. His laugh was deep and rumbling, which for some reason made her think of molasses – if molasses could laugh, she told herself.

'Stewart Dorchester,' he said in introduction holding out his hand to her.

'Kate Howard and clumsy.'

'Not at all. I like Barty's party but he will invite too many for my taste. You can't really talk to people.'

'I know what you mean,' she said with feeling.

'Do you know Barty well?'

'No, not at all. And you?'

'I've known him for years but I don't *know* him but, then; I don't think anybody does. A man of mystery.' He smiled this time and Kate noticed deep crow's feet around his eyes, sign of one who smiles often.

'Are you a publisher too?'

'No, a mere journalist.'

'Really?' Kate's voice perked up with interest. 'That must be such a fascinating career.'

'Not as glamorous as it seems. Everything becomes routine in the end.'

'But there's routine and routine. There's mine which I wouldn't wish on anyone but then a brain surgeon has a routine but he's . . .' She didn't finish the sentence. A young woman in a skimpy skirt, thick make-up and long heavy earrings, which threatened to distort her ear lobes for life, had sidled up and put her arm through his.

'Stewart, the very man. You simply must meet Sylvan, she's *the* face of the future,' she said confidently, completely ignoring Kate, and tugging at Stewart to follow her.

'Excuse me, Kate. These pushy PR people!' He pulled a face of apology. 'See you later?'

'Yes, I'll be around.' She found herself giggling and wondered why on earth she was.

She watched him go with regret. She liked him, he seemed warm and sincere. There were so many things she would have liked to ask him about his work. Tony often told her she should not get people to talk shop, that it was boring and insensitive of her. Yet she always found that people talking about what they knew best were always fascinating. 'Stewart Dorchester,' she said to herself. Of course, she had only been talking to one of the leading journalists in the land famous for his in-depth interviews. What an ignorant fool he must think her, not even realising. God, what she would do for a cigarette. Perhaps there were ashtrays in the ladies.

Gloria had been round the room twice and her feet were killing her. Professionally it had been a good evening. She had met two highly successful authors, more than discontented with their present publishers, and had invited both to lunches to talk about the possibilities of their moving. She had chatted up Marina Smallwood, the international model. Over the hill now, perhaps, but with the life and lovers she had had, from politicians to pop stars, not to mention a stretch in Holloway on a drugs rap, she was ripe for a ghosted autobiography which could be a smash hit. And, Marina had confided to Gloria, she could do with the money. She was so keen that Gloria had been able to arrange an office meeting. That would please the accounts department for a change, they were always querying her expenses. She gossiped with several publishers and agents. Much could be gleaned from a party such as this. Secrets, which it would have been impossible to find out in working hours, were freely whispered when alcohol had loosened tongues. Serious secrets, such as who had paid what for whom, projects hoped for, where discontents lay, some of no interest, others to be stored for future use. She had managed to avoid Joyce Armitage, whose editor she was and wished she was not. The woman was impossible, arguing over every changed comma let alone phrases. To get her to cut anything needed all the skills of a diplomat – skills Gloria felt she was sadly lacking these days. Yet they were crucial to her job. On a personal level it had been a success too. She had given her card to one young man who had taken her fancy – so much for her lecture to herself last night to find someone more suitable. But, she thought, if she did not get out of these shoes, she would hit someone. Gloria was used to the cocktail circuit and always brought a second wellworn pair with her to change into once she had made her entrance and that all-important first impact.

Joy was late arriving, she had walked miles before picking up a taxi. She had looked a mess when she arrived and had spent ages repairing her make-up and thawing out in the cloakroom. She knew the maid, Sylv, from past parties and the woman had kindly got her a large brandy.

Barty was no longer receiving when she finally joined the party. He was moving slowly about the crowded room, his aides picking out the chosen with whom Barty wished to have a further word. Butterflies were careering about in her stomach as she joined the crowd hopefully trying to catch the attention of Barty or one of the aides. Barty moving about his guests always reminded Joy of the Queen at a Buckingham Palace garden party.

She didn't have to jostle long for Barty himself saw her and moved towards her.

'Joy, my love.' He approached her with hands held out in expansive greeting, took hers and squeezed them tight. He did not kiss her, everyone knew that Barty never kissed anyone. 'Where's the old man?' He looked around.

'He was delayed at the office, an important case,' Joy lied loyally.

'Oh, yeah?' Barty smiled kindly at her. She looked away, knowing he probably knew more about Charles's affairs than she did. She took a deep breath, it was now or never.

'Barty, might I ask you a favour?'

With a nod of his head, Barty indicated that they should move away from the circle about them to the relative privacy of the dais on which stood his desk. 'What's that, ducks?'

'I'm a literary agent now – it means I can work from home. I'd love to represent you, Barty.'

'Me? I don't write. I don't even write me own letters.' Barty laughed.

'You wouldn't have to. We could find a ghost, who'd do the writing. I'm talking about your memoirs, Barty. They'd sell like a bomb.'

'I'm sure they would, girl. But I'm not about to tell nobody nothing. I think me memoirs will have to wait till I'm in me box – I know a little bit too much about too many people.' He tapped the side of his nose with a forefinger.

'I suppose you're always being asked to do them.' Joy tried to keep the disappointment out of her voice.

'You could say that,' he answered kindly, and then as he saw her begin to sway, 'You all right, love?' he asked, concerned, but looking about him wildly for someone to support her should she fall.

'Yes, I'm fine,' Joy laughed, holding on to the side of the desk. 'Probably drank your bloody champagne cocktail too quickly.' Her laugh was brittle and false. Barty looked about him. At the end of the long room he saw what Joy had seen – Charles with Penelope beside him standing in the doorway, relaxed and smiling.

'Joy . . .'

'Excuse me, Barty. I need some water . . .' And she slipped away from him, her lovely face white and wraith-like.

Kate was sitting behind the locked door on the lid of the lavatory seat, deeply inhaling the smoke from a cigarette – at last. The maid was no longer here, having a break, Kate assumed. She had looked about the luxuriously appointed room but saw nothing that she could be sure was an ashtray. There were several pretty bowls but they looked too valuable for stub ends. She was sitting in a cloud of her Estée Lauder, she had sprayed the air just in case someone else walked in and smelt what she was up to. She stiffened as she heard the clatter of high heels on the marble steps leading into the room.

'Sylv, you there?' A voice called out. 'Sylv, it's me Gloria Catchpole, I need my other shoes. Sylv? Sod it, where's the woman got . . .' The door of the cubicle beside Kate slammed shut. Kate lifted her feet so that they stuck out in front of her and tried to hold her breath. The cistern flushed. The cubicle door banged. Gingerly Kate lowered her legs, and began to breathe normally again as she heard the woman washing her hands across the room. A further clatter of heels announced the arrival of another. Oh, Lor', thought Kate, how long was she going to be stuck here? She lit another cigarette from the end of the first one, raised the seat, threw the stub in the pan and winced at the hiss it made. Might as well be hung for a sheep . . . she decided, settling back on her perch with difficulty as she curled her legs under her, the less likely to be seen under the gap at the foot of the door. There she crouched on the lavatory lid for all the world like a black, bespectacled gnome on a toadstool.

'Joy, darling. You look bloody awful. What's happened? Sit down . . . come on, come over here. There . . . Now what's the matter, tell me,' the voice called Gloria said, brimming with bossy concern.

'I can't, I'm too mortified.' Joy was obviously crying.

'You stay here, darling. I'll be back. You look as if you need a drink.'

Kate sat, wondering whether to slip out quietly, but when she heard the remaining woman begin to sob noisily, she felt she could not. Something very bad must have happened to upset her so much, and Kate's presence might make matters worse.

'Here you are. I met Sylv. She got me a bottle of champagne. I told her to try and head other people off – there's another loo along the corridor. Now, you drink that.'

'I want a smoke.'

'I don't have any, I don't.'

'In my bag . . . there . . .' Joy spoke through her tears. Kate, in her cramped prison, rolled her eyes with exasperation. So she could have smoked after all and need not have got into this stupid situation.

'Was it Charles?'

'Yes. The bastard's out there with that whore Penelope.'

'No!'

'He's done it to humiliate me. Nearly everyone I know is here.'

'But why?'

Kate sat trapped and could not help but listen to the sad tale Joy was blurting out between sobs and large gulps of champagne. Normally she would have found it riveting. As it was, she was acutely embarrassed to be eavesdropping in this undignified manner. The right thing to do would be to make a noise, flush the loo, brazen it out – but she could not. She had been too quiet for that.

Gloria made sympathetic noises at intervals until Joy stopped, obviously talked out.

'You should leave him, Joy. He's only going to get worse. Women are like a drug to him, you must have learnt that by now.'

'I love him.' Joy sniffed loudly.

'How can you? He's a bastard, he obviously doesn't love you or he wouldn't do this to you.'

'Don't say that!' Joy wailed.

'Well, someone's got to, darling. He's going to make you ill. Get out, take Hannah, make a new life for yourself.'

'How can I? I've no money. I can't even make any.'

'Go to a lawyer, get a settlement. He'll have to pay you, support the two of you.'

'Bah!' Joy managed to laugh. 'Have you ever heard of a barrister whose wife came out on top in a divorce? They close ranks, it happened to a friend of mine. She couldn't find a lawyer for love or money who'd give her the right advice. The legal profession is famous for sticking together.'

'Shop him then, I would. Write to the Lord Chancellor. He can say goodbye to silk then, the law doesn't like divorce in its midst.'

'He is a silk already.'

'Then perhaps they'll take it away,' Gloria said hopefully. 'You know what, Joy? I bloody loathe men, they're nothing but grief.'

The two women were silent for a while and to Kate's horror she realised she had got cramp in her leg. In the constricted space she tried to twist her leg round, to ease the pain. She was hot now and her spectacles had slipped down her shiny nose. As she grabbed at them before they fell her handbag slid to the floor with a clump.

'What was that?' Gloria said. 'Is there anyone in there?' There was a pause and then she was banging on the door. 'Are you all right?' she shouted.

Kate stood up, straightened her skirt, took a deep breath, opened the door and emerged blushing furiously.

'What must you both think of me? I can't apologise enough. I didn't mean to listen. I was desperate for a smoke and locked myself in there. Then I heard you two and I was so scared at being found out, I got stuck in there. Oh, Lor' . . .' She felt the blush deepening and longed to leg it quickly out of the room.

Gloria looked at Joy, and Joy at Gloria, and both burst out laughing.

'Are you a journalist?' Gloria asked, suddenly straight-faced.

'Me, no. I'm a housewife.'

'That's all right, then. Have a drink.' Joy was waving the bottle at her with one hand. 'And a smoke.' She held out a packet of cigarettes with the other. 'Could happen to anyone. Sit down, join the party.' Her speech was markedly slurred.

Kate, not sure what to do, decided that perhaps it would be best to join them, perhaps she could explain better. They did not seem too cross with her. 'Thanks,' she said, taking a glass and a cigarette. She looked about her guiltily before bending her head over Joy's wavering lighter.

'Barty doesn't mind you smoking here, it's banned in the study with all those lovely rugs and only at the big parties. He once saw someone stub one out on a particularly precious rug,' Gloria explained.

'How dreadful,' Kate said with genuine shock. 'You can't blame him, then, can you?'

'There's a lot of creeps around,' Gloria said sagely, pouring herself another glass and topping up Joy's as she did so.

'And my husband's the chief creep out there,' Joy announced. 'Is your husband a bastard?' She looked closely at Kate as if trying to focus.

'No, he's not a bastard, but . . .' and to her utter astonishment she heard herself say, 'but he's a dreadful bore.' Having said it aloud, Kate felt a wonderful and strange feeling of liberation as if saying that had peeled the scales from her eyes. She saw it all now, understood everything, knew why she was so fed up. She had been blaming herself when all the time it was his fault. This ladies' loo was her road to Damascus. 'Boring as hell,' she said loudly and gleefully, as if testing that it wasn't all a dream.

It appeared that holding such sentiments about her husband made her an immediate member of this circle. The other two held their glasses aloft.

'Down with boring men,' Gloria toasted.

'Let all the bastards rot in hell,' Joy added.

And Gloria thrust another glass of champagne at Kate. To her equal astonishment she found she was telling them about her discontent, her menopause and how she loathed being overweight and middle-aged – all things she had not even discussed with Pam. In return she learnt that Joy was a literary agent and she was filled in with more of Charles's misdemeanours and an insight into the life of the rich which, it seemed, wasn't nearly as good as Kate had presumed. And Gloria had a good moan about her young men and her own dissatisfaction with her love life, her career as an editor, with everything.

'We should all meet up again, this is fun. It must be the ambience.' Joy was giggling. And Kate agreed, she'd never normally have chosen a lavatory for such confidences, she said. Joy was reduced almost to hysteria and in attempting to give Kate another drink managed to pour it straight down her dress. This upset Joy out of all proportion to the act and she burst into tears again.

'Poor bitch,' Gloria said over her head to Kate. 'I think I'd best get her home.'

'You're not thinking of driving?' Kate asked, concerned.

'God, no, I'm way over the top. I'll get a cab.'

They stood up and Kate helped Gloria get the very unsteady Joy on to her feet, a now very maudlin Joy who was slurring her way through, of all songs, 'Stand By Your Man'.

'I'll pay for the dry cleaning,' Joy stuttered.

'It doesn't matter, honestly.' Kate was not lying, she had felt so ugly all night that she had vowed never to wear this dress again.

'It's the least I can do. Gloria, in my bag ... my card ... give darling Kate one ... Such a lovely woman. She understands, Gloria, she understands everything ... Now, you send me the bill, you promise.'

'All right, then,' Kate said as she took the card.

'Nice meeting you, let's hope we meet up again some time.' Gloria shook her hand. 'Come on, Joy, old girl. Let's find Sylv, get our coats, I'm taking you home.'

Kate felt strangely lonely after they had gone. As she walked up the steps to go back to the party and find Tony her legs felt dramatically unsteady.

'Where the hell have you been?' Tony snapped on seeing her.

'I've been in the ladies' loo,' she said with total honesty and dignity.

'You sound drunk.'

'You know something, Tony? I think I am.'

'That's disgusting, I loathe drunk women.'

'Do me a favour, Tony. Sod off,' she said, before she passed out on Barty's favourite rug.

12

The consequences of Barty's party reverberated like the rumblings of a distant summer storm.

Tony virtually frog-marched Kate down the steps of Barty's house and along the street to their parked Rover. He slammed shut the door of the car, crashed the gears noisily, then mounted the kerb, knocking a dustbin flying, and did not even bother to get out to see if his precious vehicle was damaged. Kate leant back in the seat and closed her eyes, thinking that silence might be best in the circumstances. However, she found that closing her eyes was an unpleasant experience: something had happened – everything was whirling out of control.

'You do realise you've probably cost the firm a very valuable contract?' he eventually said in a tight-lipped way.

'Um . . .' replied Kate, finding that if she turned her head slightly to the left the whirling was a little better. In fact, if one allowed it to take one over it was quite a pleasant sensation, like being on a fairground carousel.

'If this gets out we could lose other clients.' He then began a monologue of her faults until well past Reading. Not only was she a disastrous wife and mother but she was a social catastrophe. Her behaviour would undoubtedly lead to Tony's partner's children being removed from their fee-paying schools, and their lives ruined by contact with the hoi-polloi in the state system. The senior partner's wife would no doubt have to give up her horses and God alone knew when anyone would have a holiday again. When she did not react to that threat he finally looked at her. Kate was snoring contentedly, a tiny whiffling sort of snore. So enraged was Tony that he pressed his foot down hard on the accelerator. The Rover, feeling itself liberated at last, kicked itself into action and leapt down the M4.

They had almost reached their junction turn-off when he heard the chilling wail of a police siren. Dutifully he pulled over on to the hard shoulder. He smilingly apologised for his speed, quickly explaining he was a solicitor and that it was the first and last time he had ever exceeded the speed limit. It would never happen again, he promised. Tony's attempts at charm had little effect on the constabulary who insisted on breathalysing him. He failed.

Kate eventually woke up as the car, driven by a strange policeman, pulled into the police station car park.

'What happened?' she asked, fear clutching at her. Was Tony ill? Had she been kidnapped?

'Your husband's up ahead, in custody.'

'In custody? Tony? I don't believe it . . .' And she began to laugh drunkenly at the ridiculous prospect.

They eventually took a taxi home in sullen silence. It cost nearly thirty-five pounds, an amount that neither could raise between them and the driver was none too happy at the prospect of accepting a cheque. Guiltily Kate slipped into the house leaving Tony to deal with him. In the kitchen she put some coffee on.

'I'm sorry,' she said, shamefaced, when Tony eventually appeared.

'Sorry? You think you can stand there and say "sorry" and I'm going to forgive you?'

'I didn't make you get drunk,' she said defensively.

'Drunk? You were the one who got drunk.'

'I wasn't the only one, according to the police.' In the circumstances she felt quite pleased with such a sharp retort.

'I was only just over the limit, if you must know.'

'*Just* is quite sufficient.' She knew she smirked, knew she was being unpleasant when she had set out to be sympathetic. She knew she was rousing his anger.

'Look at you, you look dreadful. I'm ashamed of you. You of all people. Well, Madam, you are going to have to live with the consequences of your gross behaviour, I can promise you that.' He was shouting at her. She found herself stepping backward until the Aga prevented her going further. He's going to hit me, she thought with alarm.

'Coffee?' she asked, in as normal a voice as she could muster.

'I want nothing from you. I'm finished. I'm sick to death of you and your bloody moods, your whining, and now this.'

'And have you ever wondered why I get moods? Has it ever crossed your mind that I might be bored to tears with you, this house, my life, with everything?' She spoke firmly now, anger sobering her long enough to enable her to argue.

'You ungrateful bitch. After all I've done for you – the hours I work, the money I lavish on you.'

Kate laughed, a short, sharp and mirthless laugh. 'Why, Tony, you sound just like my mother. You never did, or gave me, anything that you didn't want to. Everything here, everything you've ever done has been for your own ego, for your self-satisfaction. I'm just a possession to you, not a person in my own right.'

'In your own right? You're nothing without me. And just look at you – you've no style, you look a permanent mess. Do you want to know the truth? I was ashamed to be seen with you tonight.' His head was thrust forward, his eyes bulging.

Kate stood silent as if absorbing his words. She threw her head back and laughed. 'And who are you? Adonis? Have you looked in the mirror recently? Seen your gut? Counted your chins? Noticed your hairline? If you don't fancy me any more, that's fine by me. You know what you can do about it.' She was shouting now, saying things she did not mean, things she did not want to say, but did not seem able to stop.

'And what's that?'

'Try and find someone else who'll put up with you and your nasty little habits as I have done.'

'What habits?'

'You pick your nose when you think I'm not watching. Your feet smell and you slurp your soup.'

'This is childish. I'm going to bed. I'll speak to you when you are in a more dignified condition.'

'Good, I can hardly wait.' She was close to tears now, and turned back to the Aga. 'And you scratch your balls!' she managed to shout before the kitchen door slammed shut. The coffee was heated, Kate poured herself a cup, black, with plenty of sugar. Angrily she wiped a tear away with the back of her hand. No, she was not going to let bloody tears get in the way this time, she'd show him. 'Pompous twit,' she muttered to herself as, with exaggerated care, she carried her cup to the table. She slumped down on a chair and gazed morosely into space. She wondered why it was that people, when arguing, always ended it by announcing they were going to bed. She sat at the table and thought about this for some time and then realised that the amount of effort she was having to put into its contemplation could only mean one thing – she was still drunk.

'I'm going to bed,' she said to the cat, not to be outdone.

Upstairs she wavered outside her room. That was another thing about rows with one's spouse, it always seemed bizarre to end up lying together in the same bed. Ah, well, she thought, maybe he'll have calmed down in the morning. But even as she thought it she doubted it would be so.

The bed was empty, Tony's pillows missing. He must be in the guest room. She took off her dress, crossed to the bathroom, cleaned her teeth, looked at her reflection and laughed – she certainly looked decidedly blotto. She never got drunk, rarely drank to excess, only at Christmas. It must have been such a shock for him to see her in that state. That was what had made him fly off the handle at her, shock, she reassured herself, preferring to draw a discreet veil over her finale at Barty's. She turned the light off – her face would have to wait, she had not the energy. Similarly she couldn't be bothered with her bra and tights, so she crashed into bed half-dressed.

When Kate awoke it was eleven and pouring with rain.

'Oh dear,' she said in the time-honoured way of the morning after the night before. She turned and looked at the empty space beside her. She put out her hand and touched where he would normally lie. They had never slept apart because of anger before. She stretched – she enjoyed the freedom of the large bed to herself, always had in the past if he was away overnight on business. She wondered if he would return to it and found this morning she did not mind if he did not. Certainly she would not miss what passed for sex between them. She did wonder if her disinterest in him sexually was because she no longer loved him, whether it was what to expect at her age – a slowing down of desire. Desire? She laughed. Had she *ever* desired him? No, she did not think so. Maybe when she was very young, but that was where her memory let her down again. But then, *if* it had all been wonderful once, surely she would have remembered?

She turned restlessly in the bed. Had she lost all interest in sex? The truth was, no. She fantasised, and when she did she was ashamed, feeling it was almost a betrayal of Tony even to think of herself with another man. She consoled herself with the thought that perhaps Tony did also which made it a bit better.

It would be easy to allow herself to dream of that man Stewart she had met last night. He was not conventionally handsome, nor was he young, but all the same there had been something about him, and a quickening of her pulse when he spoke to her, and the way she had felt quite skittish. But she had not seen him later and probably wouldn't again. And what conceit made her even dream that he had felt awakened by her?

She sat up, thumped her pillow, and shook her head as if to rid herself of such thoughts. She looked at the window and watched the rain lashing the glass, the greyness of the sky mirroring her mood. She should not have said what she had, though, about his paunch and his hair, it had been spiteful. But, then, she thought, he had been the first to make personal remarks – he'd asked for it.

She raised herself with effort on to the pillows. He had certainly told her straight last night. 'I'm finished,' he had said. What did he mean by that? She had to admit she had been so obsessed with her own problems and feelings it had never crossed her mind that he might be thinking the same. It was a shattering prospect. She would never have regarded herself as arrogant, but certainly she had been over this.

Was he thinking of leaving her? She felt a frisson of panic at the prospect. She hugged her arms about her for comfort. What on earth would she do? She had no career to fall back on, all she knew how to do was homemaking. He managed all their affairs, decided how to invest their money, paid the big bills. She knew nothing about organising her own life. Could she learn? Could she cope? Loads of other women did, she told herself, she knew of three within their own circle. After the initial shock they seemed to have settled, to have come to terms with the new situation. In fact two were positively jolly in their new freedom. Freedom. What an odd word to spring to mind for such circumstances. She sat up straight, she was feeling less panicky now.

She looked about the room on which she had lavished much love and thought over the years. A room furnished bit by bit as they could afford it, everything in it chosen with care. If he went, what would she be left with? She could not afford to run this house on her own. Would he buy her another, smaller, cheaper to manage? She would have more time for herself with a smaller house to run, that was for sure. Had he met someone else already? Well, last night she had given him permission to go to her . . .

She shook her head, puzzled. She should be feeling terrified, but the panic had subsided and she was beginning to feel a strange sense of excitement and anticipation. What did that mean?

All the same, she was going to have to face him. Goodness knows what she was going to say. She owed it to him to apologise – sober this time. It had all seemed funny last night, but he had been right, she had behaved badly. If he hadn't been so angry with her he would have driven home at his normal sedate pace and the police would not have stopped him. In his position – a solicitor, governor of the local school, respected freemason – a court case would be a disaster. It was unfair on him, he was normally so careful, so law-abiding. It was mainly her fault, there was no question about it.

Gingerly she slipped her legs over the side of the bed and stood up. She deserved to feel dreadful but in fact she felt fine. She showered quickly, scrubbing off the remains of last night's make-up, disgusted with herself for being such a slut. She dressed quickly in skirt and jumper, brushed her hair, put on a little make-up – she felt she should try to look as attractive as possible. But she had to hurry, they would all be starving by now.

The kitchen was deserted. Dirty breakfast plates stood on the table. Kate pushed back her hair and tried to smother the feeling of irritation that they had not bothered to put them in the dishwasher for her. Propped against the milk jug was a note.

Who's been a naughty mummy, then? Tut, tut. Dad's gone to see Freddy to discuss a 'limitation exercise' he said. He is FURIOUS. I'm spending the day at Mandy's. Steve's gone to Tom's. There's a note from Pam in the hall. How's your head?
Lucy.

He need not have told the children, she thought with annoyance. That was a mean thing to do, she would have covered up for him. In the hall she found Pam's note telling her that she had enrolled them both in the writers' weekend, that it was all paid for and it was to be Kate's birthday present. Kate smiled to herself. Her birthday was not until next June and, no doubt, by then dear Pam would be giving her something else.

She went back to the kitchen. She stacked the dishes in the dishwasher, wiped the kitchen table down. She put on an egg to boil and found she was going back over everything again, the thoughts whirring around trapped in her skull. Abruptly she turned, crossed to the dresser and collected pen and paper which she put on the table. She stood a moment, looking down at the pristine white paper, deep in thought, until the pinger sounded and she collected her egg.

Breakfast over she pushed the dishes to one side and sat, pen in mouth, gazing out of the window at the pouring rain. She began to write. She began slowly. When she had covered a quarter of the page she stopped, read what she had written, screwed it into a ball and started again. Four false starts she had, but on the fifth she began to write with speed. She was thinking so quickly now that her writing could barely keep up with the flow of words tumbling about in her mind.

Once the dishwasher had finished she was unaware of any noise in the kitchen apart from the scratch of her pen on paper. She was so absorbed that she did not hear the clock ticking, the low hum of the refrigerator, the sibilant hissing of the Aga, the occasional swish of a car's tyres on the damp road outside. When she finally laid down her pen it was past three and beginning to get dark. She had covered sheets of paper. She collected them together and laboriously began to count the words – she had written three thousand five hundred and forty-two!

She put the kettle on, made herself a mug of tea, switched on the light, lit a cigarette, realigned the papers in front of her and, taking a deep breath, began to read.

She sat back in the chair and smiled. She was surprised, she liked what she had written. What was more she had enjoyed doing it, it had been such fun. She realised she was not depressed, she had not wanted to cry once, and she wanted to go on, and on . . .

She took a clean sheet, thought for a moment and then printed, A WINTER'S INTERLUDE by KATE HOWARD. She held the page up and studied it. She preferred this title to 'A Winter's Romance' and that nice man Julius had been right, her name looked beautiful.

Sylv, the maid who had supplied Kate, Joy and Gloria with the champagne, was summarily dismissed by Barty. No pleading on her part would make him change his mind – she knew the rules about the supply of drink to guests and she had broken them. Dismissal was to be expected, the housekeeper had informed her. She was given two hours to pack her bags and leave.

Gloria was woken by the telephone ringing. Immediately she looked at the pillow beside her – he had gone. She had to cough several times before she could get her voice to work properly.

'Gloria Catchpole,' she rasped.

'Gloria, my dear, did I waken you?'

'No, no,' she lied, frantically trying to put a name to the familiar voice.

'I wondered if we could have lunch one day soon?'

'I'd love to,' she replied, and immediately realised she had left it too late to ask who was speaking.

'I don't want anyone to know I'm talking to you. Sorry to be so cloak and daggerish about it, but you'll understand when I explain everything. But say the Gay Hussar, next Thursday?'

'That would be lovely,' she said, still racking her brain for a clue to her caller.

'See you, then.' And the phone went dead.

Gloria replaced the receiver, turned and stroked the pillow beside her. She lay down burrowing her head into it, searching for his smell. She had done it again. Fool, she told herself.

Clive had been here waiting for her when she had returned from the party. She had found him lying on her sofa fast asleep. She had stood for a while looking at him, fuddled with drink, not sure which emotion to grasp hold of. She was angry with him for his neglect and for his assumption that she would be pleased to find him here. She could not continue to drift like this, she must finish with him to maintain her own self-respect. She should waken him, tell him to go, instead she watched him, trying to memorise exactly how his long black lashes appeared to lie on his cheek. She put her hand out wanting to touch the hollow of his cheek, outline the fullness of his lips. Her hand hovered. She did not touch him. Not this time. This time she was going to finish with him for good. And then he had opened his eyes and he smiled his lazy smile. 'Sorry,' he had said. And she was in his arms, lost once more, instead of reading the riot act to him.

He had said he could only stay an hour. She had argued with him for where was there to go at this time? He would not tell. Still, she had thought, once in bed he would forget, he would stay.

She knelt beside the sofa and with agonising slowness unzipped his jeans, all the time watching him, her eyes sparkling with anticipation, the tip of her tongue moistening her lips. He was already hardening as she held him in her hands, stroking gently, enjoying as she did the almost miraculous velvety texture. But she was enjoying even more the feeling as it became rigid in her grasp. And she could see the expression of lust in his eyes.

'Like it?' she asked.

He did not answer but took her head in both hands and guided her to where he wanted her to be. Her mouth felt full of him as she sucked at him like a greedy child. His hands found her breasts and he began to play with her erect nipples. She was writhing with pleasure. He groaned. She let go of his penis and pulled him down towards her on the floor and quickly, almost desperately, she pulled down his jeans and as quickly pulled off her own pants. She searched in the pocket of his trousers and found what she knew would be there. Gently and so slowly that he began to groan, she slipped a condom over his huge throbbing member. Then she was astride him and he jerked upwards and easily into her and she was riding him. As he thrust deeper into her she cried out. She lifted her hands above her head, breasts thrust forward, dark curly hair falling about her face. She lifted her head, looked down at him. She was happy, so very happy. And then she climaxed and her body jerked as her orgasm seemed to explode within her. Then he came and it was over and she slumped on to his body; that fleeting moment of happiness had slipped away, again.

'Hand me my fags,' he said, flexing his body under her to make her get off him, ridding himself of the condom.

'You bastard,' she said.

'After that?'

'You don't understand, do you?' She rolled off him and leant across the floor for his cigarettes and lighter.

'What more do you want?' he asked, putting a cigarette in his mouth.

'Oh, nothing,' she replied. She would have liked him to say he loved her, even if it was not true. But he never did. But it would be nice to hear, she thought, hunching her knees up, putting her arms round them and hugging them.

'Women!'

'Men!' She smiled.

He did not go immediately, instead they had a glass of wine and then he led her to bed and there they made love again.

She must have fallen into a deep sleep, and he had quietly left her bed, avoiding her pleas to remain the whole night.

She sat up and thumped the pillow feeling wretched. She could not blame him this time, it was she who had instigated it. She pushed her hair back. Why did she do it? Why did she so often allow her pussy to rule her head?

'That, my girl, was the last time,' she said aloud, pleased with the conviction in her voice. She climbed out of bed and walked out of the room naked. An annoyed Elephant was sitting on the landing waiting for her. 'Sorry, my darling. That's the last time. That particular one won't be back to banish you.' She entered the bathroom, the little dog with her, who, once her bath was run, took up station on the bathmat as if guarding her.

In her bath Gloria made herself puzzle over the voice to stop her thinking of Clive. It was familiar, obviously someone who knew her well enough to be confident of being recognised, and someone she liked enough to have given her home telephone number to. It was also the voice of an older man, so it could not have been the young man she had met at the party. It was an annoying habit, not announcing yourself like that, arrogant really. Still, she would go. For a start she was intrigued and, secondly, just to eat at that restaurant once more would be nice. She would not eat the day before and then she would have the wild cherry soup and the chicken-stuffed pancakes with paprika. She used to eat there often, now rarely. Hopefully she'd remember the name to go with the voice before then.

Joy Trenchard woke with a fearful hangover and felt very sorry for herself. She lay in the bed in her large white and pink bedroom, looked about the room, which contained everything a beautiful woman could possibly want, and felt she had nothing.

She covered her face with her hands at the memory of last night. Her thin shoulders shook under the silk of her nightdress as she began to cry. Was she doomed to spend the rest of her life weeping? Looking up she caught sight of herself in the mirror opposite. She saw a thin, bedraggled woman, her face blotched from her tears, slumped pathetically in the huge bed. She loathed the sight.

Angrily she felt for a tissue in the box on her bedside table and wiped at the tears and blew her nose noisily. God, what a mess she looked. What if he came back and found her looking like this?

'So what?'

She looked up abruptly. That was the sort of thing Gloria would have said, not her. But Gloria was not here, so had she said that? Or was she hearing things?

'So what?' she said aloud. Yes, she *had* said it, and yes, she meant it. 'So what?' She tried it again and she smiled, admittedly a rather wan smile, but a smile none the less. Two little words that made her feel better, two words out of all proportion to their size.

She slipped from the bed, crossed to her bathroom and ran herself a bath. She lay a long time soaking and thinking. She forced herself to return to last night and to go over in detail what had happened. She made herself remember who was there. This time Charles had gone too far. How could he have humiliated her by arriving at Barty's with his mistress, to a party where he knew there would be many of their friends? Not only did he not love her any more, he did not respect her. She had done nothing to lose it except to acquiesce too easily to his previous indiscretions. She had been a fool, a weak despicable fool. Now she was in danger of losing her self-respect. The loss of that would be far greater than the loss of Charles's for her, she decided. She was going to have to change. She did not know how, but change she would.

An hour later she emerged from the bathroom and she was angry, very angry.

She took a long time dressing and doing her face but as she worked on her make-up she suddenly realised she was taking care for herself and not for him. The thought made her calmer, gave her confidence and she saw herself smiling in the mirror.

In the kitchen she found Hannah and her nanny having a mid-morning mug of hot chocolate.

'You look pretty, Mummy.'

'Why, thank you, my darling, and so do you.' She bent and kissed her daughter's cheek.

'I assume you'd like some black coffee, Mrs Trenchard?' Sheila asked. It was the tone of the question that made Joy's hackles begin to rise.

'No, thank you, this chocolate looks delicious.' She took a mug from the cupboard and helped herself to some – the last drink she wanted, but she forced herself to sip it.

'Mr Trenchard didn't come home before I went to bed, last night, so I couldn't give him your message.' Sheila persisted in the cold, clipped voice which had always irritated Joy.

'No. We met at the party.'

Sheila's disbelieving smile made her wish she could slap the supercilious bitch. She sipped at the chocolate, looking hard at the nanny, enjoying the thought.

'Daddy said we could go to the zoo this afternoon.'

'He's had to go out on business.'

Joy knew it wasn't her imagination that Sheila smiled again with the expression of one who knew that Charles hadn't come home at all last night. It was an almost triumphant look. Sheila didn't respect her either, that was patently obvious now. She wondered what it was about last night that had suddenly made her see everything so much clearer.

'It is my afternoon off,' Sheila said petulantly.

'Of course, Sheila. Am I likely to forget? If Mr Trenchard is held up, I shall take Hannah myself.' She plonked the mug, barely touched back on the table. 'I've got to go out. I'll be back by one, Sheila, don't worry.'

'I've an appointment –'

'I said I'd be back.'

'There are a lot of promises made in this house –' Sheila began, and then as if thinking she might have gone too far, shut her mouth tight like a clam shell shutting.

'And what does that comment mean, Sheila?'

'Nothing.'

'It had better not,' Joy said sharply. She kissed her daughter again, let herself out of the kitchen. In the hall she slipped into her white cashmere coat, checked herself in the mirror over the console table, picked up her car keys and let herself out of the front door and raced through the rain to her car.

She found a florist open and spent so much on flowers that she had to use a credit card to pay for them. As she watched the girl slide her American Express card into the machine the thought crossed her mind that perhaps she should use her cards with enthusiasm during the next few weeks – hit him where it hurt. On a small card she scrawled two words. *Sorry, Joy.*

'We can deliver if you want, we've a Sunday service.'

'No, thanks. There'll be someone there.'

She drove towards Chelsea and wondered why she was doing so. She could have written, could have telephoned even. She could have had the flowers sent. But she felt she had to do this in person. Even if she did not see him, taking the flowers herself, hopefully, would make the apology appear truly sincere, all the other ways were too easy. She felt certain he would understand the gesture.

Barty was in and although he did not normally receive people without an appointment he made an exception for Joy. He was impressed, she had courage, there were not many who would face his anger the next day.

'Barty, I can't apologise enough,' Joy stepped forward her face half concealed by the huge bouquet. 'You can see how embarrassed I am, I wouldn't normally buy such a vulgar profusion of flowers.'

'They're lovely, Joy. My favourites, all of them.' He grinned as he relieved her of the huge bunches of flowers and laid them carefully on a table. 'I'll arrange them myself.' He nodded.

'Apart from letting you know how ashamed I am at my behaviour last night, I felt I had to come, I didn't want the maid, Sylv, to get into trouble. I know your strict rules.'

'I've dismissed her.'

'Oh, Barty, no. Oh, how awful. That makes everything worse. She's worked for you for years. We made her get the drink, you know.'

'She needn't have.'

'But you know Gloria when she wants something, no one can resist Gloria's powers of persuasion.' She laughed a tiny, useless laugh. 'And we were only a little tiddly.' She rushed on recklessly. 'I mean no harm was done, was it?' There was an anxious tone to the last question since her own memory of the end of the night before, and her part in it, was vague to say the least.

'You know why I control the drink the way I do? Let you all get a bit sozzled so as you enjoy the party and then sober you all up before you go?'

Joy shook her head to show she had no idea.

''Cause one of my best mates killed himself drunk driving.'

'I'm sorry.'

'He had every right to kill himself but not the poor little bird with him. He got drunk in my house, and I vowed I'd never have anything like that on my conscience again.'

'Oh Lord. I'm sorry. It was my fault entirely. I was fed up.' An awkward silence descended. Joy could not think what else to say.

'You got off a bit better than your friend Kate,' he said suddenly.

'Kate?'

'Kate Howard – dull little mouse of a woman. She passed out after telling her duller husband to "sod off".' Barty laughed loudly at the memory and Joy, sensing his anger was long over, managed to join in.

'What you going to do about that bastard of a husband of yours, then?' Barty had stopped laughing as abruptly as he had started and his expression was serious now.

'I'm going to divorce him,' Joy heard herself say, to her complete astonishment. 'Yes, divorce would seem the only sensible action,' she added trying to inject a confidence into her voice she was far from feeling.

'That's my girl, and about time too. Stay to lunch, talk about it with me if you like.'

'Barty, I'd love to but I promised my little girl I'd take her to the zoo. Charles had promised to take her but I can't rely on him turning up.'

'I like that.' Barty nodded his head sagely. 'Never let the nipper down, that's how it should be. Tell you what . . .' he paused and looked at her with a strange expression, almost as if he was shy. 'I wouldn't mind joining you both.' He grinned, sheepishly.

'Barty, we'd love you to come. Two-thirty, at my place?'

'Right on.' He nodded his head with satisfaction.

'Then I'll know I'm really forgiven.' She smiled at him.

'I wasn't angry with *you* in the first place.' He laughed, putting his arm under her elbow and guiding her to the door. Even as he did so Joy realised it was the first time she had ever known Barty touch anyone, other than a handshake. At the door he paused.

'You like Gloria, don't you?' he asked.

'Why, yes.' She looked at him curiously, wondering why he asked. 'She's a good friend to me.'

'And what makes a good friend?'

'She's loyal and loving, she gives you her time. And I admire her enormously.'

'Why?'

'Mainly, I think, because she doesn't give a damn about what anyone thinks of her. I don't think Gloria knows what fear is.'

'And you do?'

'Don't we all?' Joy laughed nervously, surprised by the intensity of Barty's expression.

'You trust her?'

'I'd trust Gloria with my soul.'

'You're lucky. I think I could do with a mate like that.' He was smiling as he opened the door for her.

As soon as Joy had gone Barty went to his study. He rang for his butler and told him to send Sylv to him. Within five minutes Sylv was reinstated. He took a call from Gloria who was sufficiently apologetic also to be forgiven. Then he faxed Charles's law firm announcing he would be dispensing with their services in future. He made a note for his personal assistant to inform all his contacts of what action he had taken – where Barty went everyone else would follow.

Wandering about the zoo, a place he had not been to in years, Barty could not remember when he had enjoyed an afternoon so much. To Joy's embarrassment he insisted on thanking her time and again for permitting him to come. It was raining and cold and they only had a short time before it was dusk and the zoo closed. They returned reluctantly to Barty's Rolls-Royce, all excitedly planning another visit when the weather was better and they could stay longer.

Joy never knew why she asked him back for nursery tea, but she did, and he accepted with surprising alacrity. As she watched him playing snap with Hannah, after sausages and chips followed by jelly which he had eaten with gusto, Joy wondered if she was not watching a lonely man who, although he might declare he disliked children, deep down wanted a family just like this but knew it was something he could never have. He was like a hungry child in a Dickens novel who, having been found looking through the window at a happy family, had been allowed in.

He had kept saying he must go and did not, but finally he was putting on his coat. He turned to her.

'My autobiography – you're on, girl.'

'I beg your pardon?' She knew she looked astonished.

'You heard.' He was grinning.

'Wonderful, but why?'

'I don't like bastards who walk out on their kids,' he said simply, and quickly slipped out of the door as if he was saying too much, allowing too much of himself to be known.

13

It was as well it was Sunday. Crispin rarely drove and consequently his ideas of road management did not necessarily coincide with those of other road users. Crispin's policy was to set off in the direction he wished to go – and just go. He did stop at red lights and junctions; he was fully aware of the danger if he did not. But roundabouts were a different matter: he went into them without pausing, oblivious to the mayhem he invariably left behind him. Neither he nor Charlotte possessed a motor since neither of them fully approved of them – they took taxis and relied on other people. He had borrowed this 2CV from an artist friend. He felt less revulsion for this particular brand mainly, he thought, because it was so unlike a normal car.

He wished it wasn't raining, driving was hazardous enough because of road hogs without the addition of rain, he thought, as he drove the little car off the slip road on to the motorway, totally ignoring the large articulated lorry which was already in the lane he chose.

Perhaps when he was a millionaire he might have to have a car – he shuddered at the thought. Perhaps a vintage Bristol would not be so vulgar, he would have to discuss it with Charlotte when he returned.

He was in a very good mood. Last night at one of their dinners, not only had Charlotte excelled herself with the food, but an old friend had asked permission to bring a friend who turned out to be the banker of Crispin's dreams. Everything was set up over the port and cheese, no having to wait for decisions. He knew Charlotte would have liked to have accompanied him but he had resisted her requests. He wanted to do all this alone – she was too clever by half and might hijack the proceedings. He could only rely on Charlotte being sweet and submissive inside their house. Outside it she was, he knew, far more hard-headed than he would ever be.

He glanced at his watch. Ten-thirty. With luck he would be at his uncle's within the hour – reluctantly he had to admit that motorways had made travelling so much quicker. He had planned on an hour to persuade the old codger and then he would be out of the house by lunchtime. He wished his uncle lived in Oxford rather than Cambridge, there were better restaurants there, but he'd try the Blue Boar. He had many a good lunch there as an undergraduate when he visited on union business.

In fact he was later than he had planned: as always when in Cambridge, he found himself seduced by the beauty of the Backs and the chapel of King's

College rising mysterious and ethereal from the hazy mist of the drizzle. He saw a car moving out from a parking space and, neatly, he thought, swung the 2CV over the road and slipped in. A burly man driving a Mercedes, who had been waiting patiently for the place, banged his fist on the steering wheel and stuck two fingers in the air at Crispin. Crispin acknowledged the gesture with a gracious inclination of his head, slipped on his coat, locked the car and walked quickly over the bridge towards the college.

He stood for a moment, oblivious to the rain, and breathed in deeply, as if inhaling the sheer beauty and magnificence of the place. Two Fellows emerged from the chapel and, with gowns billowing, stalked self-importantly across the lawn in the centre of the court. Crispin watched them with admiration as they walked across the grass from which all others were banned. What a life they must lead, rooms in these stunning buildings, High Table, civilised people to talk to, time to think. That is what he should have done, instead of rushing into trade. He should have stayed on at Oxford as an academic, become a Fellow and undoubtedly have ended his days as the Master of a College, a life far more suitable to someone as sensitive as himself. And then the thought came to him, hit him, made him suck in his breath with the sheer beautiful simplicity of it. Of course he could now! Once he had all those millions, he could return to academe. He wondered how Charlotte would react to the prospect. Even if she did not like the idea of living in Cambridge, it would not matter. They would have so much money they would be able to have a home in London and one here – he would have the best of both worlds.

Crispin had never visited his uncle at home but he knew Cambridge well enough to find the house off the Madingley Road with ease. He had anticipated that his relative would live in one of the solid, large Edwardian houses that were common in this part of the city, a period of architecture that he could appreciate even if he never wanted to live in one. When he pulled up in front of the address he shuddered visibly. He had never contemplated the thought that anyone he knew, let alone was related to him, might choose to live in such a monstrosity.

'What an abortion,' he said with horror as he looked at the offending house. In fact, the house was famous as a prime example of thirties' architecture with a preservation order on it, something Crispin would never have believed. It was built of concrete, painted white. There were no sharp edges to its profile, all was a symphony of curves. Even the windows, large and steel-framed, swept gracefully around the sides of the house. To appreciative eyes the house looked like a liner, docked in a wild garden where shrubs had been allowed to grow in unchecked profusion. To Crispin, it should have a large stash of Semtex placed under it.

'My dear Crispin. It is Crispin, isn't it?' Simon Westall stood in the doorway, towering over his nephew – Crispin had forgotten how large his uncle was, how the sheer bulk of the man had frightened him rigid as a child. He remembered how in the night when he could not sleep and his sadistic nanny would not let him have a night light, he had convinced himself that this particular uncle was the giant who ate Englishmen. He had not expected him, as an old man, still to be larger than himself.

'Yes, it's me, Uncle. Did Cousin John tell you I'd be calling?' He spoke briskly, endeavouring to quell such childhood fears.

'Yes. Such a surprise hearing from two of my nephews in such a short space of time. Dulcett, come here, it's my nephew. Such excitement . . .'

Crispin had the grace to feel guilty at the genuine warmth of his uncle's welcome.

'Come in, dear boy, come in.'

Crispin found himself in a surprisingly spacious hall, whitepainted like the outside, an uncarpeted, well-constructed oak staircase leading off from the end, and with good, sturdy, oak doors.

Crispin approved of the excellent carpentry – he might like the interior if only he could forget the exterior. The paintings on the walls he could never like however, far too abstract and modern for his choice. He preferred not to look at them, feeling they assailed his fine senses.

A dark-haired woman with large breasts on a slim frame, fine bone structure, huge luminous eyes and, despite her fifty-odd years, considerable beauty, smiled shyly at him.

'Whatever you do, don't call me Aunt Dulcett,' she laughed with a delightful low chuckle as she held out her hand to be shaken. Surprisingly Crispin found himself stirred by her – unusual, for he did not normally find himself attracted to older women. But he could just imagine the comfort and security he would feel with his head cradled on those fine breasts, white they would be and finely marbled . . .

'Dulcett . . .' His voice was husky as he spoke. She laughed at him and he realised in one appallingly embarrassing instant that she knew what he had been thinking. 'How do you do,' he said, and the danger passed. For Crispin was appalled at the rough, calloused hand he found himself offered and he let go of it as quickly as possible. There was no way he would allow such hands to touch his tender body. No woman should have skin like that, like a navvy, he thought, as he smiled his most winning of smiles.

He was ushered into a large room which, in a normal house, would have been a drawing room but in this house was a mixture of sitting room, studio and dining room judging by the table already set for a meal. Crispin could not stop his lip curling with disapproval at the heavy, chunky, gaudy china on the table. The whole room was a mélange of objects of the cottage-industry type, rough rush matting on the floor, books cluttering every surface and the unmistakable smell of turpentine in the air. Crispin, who worshipped order and neatness, was doomed to feel an alien in it.

'You'll lunch with us?' Simon was smiling broadly at him.

'I wouldn't dream of imposing, Uncle. I just meant to stay for five minutes, have a chat.'

'We wouldn't hear of such a thing, would we, Dulcett? We shall have so much to catch up on after all these years.'

'I've cooked for three,' Dulcett said moving away, presumably to the kitchen. Despite her hands, Crispin once again found himself admiring her: he liked the way she walked, head held high, an almost regal walk.

'Beautiful, isn't she?' Simon was grinning proudly. 'When I met her I thought she was the most beautiful creature I had ever set eyes upon, I never dreamt that she would get more beautiful as the years passed – and did you note her knockers? Lovely, aren't they?'

Crispin found himself blushing for his uncle. What a disgusting way to talk! In Crispin's view old men did not notice women's breasts, let alone comment upon them. 'I didn't even know you were married, Uncle,' Crispin said stiffly, his mind racing, wondering if she might make things more difficult for him, trying to gauge how intelligent she might be. He knew he need not worry about Simon's level of intelligence, it was well known in the family that he was not very good at anything – particularly painting, Crispin thought as he avoided looking at the lurid pictures, in various stages of completion, scattered about the room.

'I'm not. Never have been.' Simon laughed loudly at the shocked look on Crispin's face. 'Dulcett and I have lived together for twenty years now. You wouldn't want me to be unconventional, would you?' He threw his head back and Crispin averted his face from the display of ugly fillings as his uncle roared with amusement.

'Unconventional? I'm afraid I don't understand,' Crispin said limply.

'I believe in conventions, as an artist I toe the line, you see. It would be too unconventional of me to be married.' And he was laughing again, at what Crispin hadn't the least idea – as always jokes were a mystery to him.

'Is this your work?' Crispin tried to inject enthusiasm into his voice, knowing he was going to have to talk about the pictures sooner or later.

'Yes, but the sculptures are Dulcett's.'

'They're wonderful,' Crispin said insincerely, forcing himself to look at the strident colours of his uncle's paintings and the large, lumpen, ugliness of Dulcett's sculptures, which at least explained the state of her hands. He was puzzled by the paintings. Julius had several examples of his brother's work, but they were not like these. Crispin had always thought them rather poor imitations of Augustus John. 'You've changed your style quite dramatically,' he said.

'I still do the old potboilers, but this is the real work.' Simon waved his hands at the large canvases, all of which, as far as Crispin could make out, were of the same subject, a tree of life or some such allied theme, he assumed.

'Potboilers?' Crispin asked, innocently, he hoped. This was a good indication, serious artists who stooped to such work were seriously hard up, he thought.

'Still lifes, odd portraits, that sort of stuff. I've got to keep the shekels coming in somehow, now your publishing house rarely pays a dividend.'

'Not my publishing house, Uncle.' Crispin smiled but in his haste it wasn't one of his more charming ones but emerged rather unctuously.

'What's gone wrong, Crispin? Whenever I ask Julius I don't seem to get anywhere.'

'Ah well, it's rather a long story,' Crispin said apologetically, hardly able to believe his luck. He had expected an uphill struggle to get Simon to listen and here was the old boy asking to be told.

'Sherry?'

'Thank you.'

Crispin, once started, was soon in fine form explaining Westall and Trim's problems, in depth, to his more than receptive audience. They were soon joined by Dulcett with their meal. All through lunch Crispin continued, patiently answering the many questions showered upon him. He really had to congratulate himself on how well he was doing. He never once blamed Julius – blood was a funny thing he knew from experience. No, instead he gave a masterly dissertation on the state of publishing in Britain in the nineties, and the hopelessness of Westall's position. It was just as well he was so engrossed in his own cleverness, for otherwise he would have had problems consuming the nettle soup, the vegetable cutlets, and the execrable parsnip wine.

'What's the solution, then, Crispin?'

'Please don't think me ungrateful, Uncle, for what I'm about to say. I love Uncle Julius, I owe him so much, but – ' He paused dramatically. 'We need younger blood, we need a big injection of capital.'

'Well, don't look to me for it.' Simon gave one of those laughs which Crispin was finding increasingly unpleasant on his ears. 'Dulcett and I haven't two halfpennies to rub together, have we, my darling?'

'But we're happy.' Dulcett put out her hand, took hold of her lover's and squeezed it. 'And we've this beautiful house.'

'And a bloody great mortgage . . .' Simon said gloomily, helping himself to another glass of parsnip wine which Crispin hurriedly refused, using the need to drive as an excuse.

'But I thought . . .' Crispin began delicately, and coughed, thus indicating that he was treading on ground far too personal.

'The potboilers don't pay the bills, old boy. I had to raise money on the house about ten years ago. The point is, Crispin, we're getting on, Dulcett and me. It's always been my dream to settle in Tuscany, better for the old bones.' Crispin flinched, prepared for the raucous laugh, but for once it wasn't coming. 'Your cousin John hinted that you might be interested in buying me out?'

'Well, yes.'

'How much?'

Crispin's mind was scudding about. The old boy had said that John had hinted, did that mean John hadn't mentioned any exact sums? What if he said £200,000 instead of the three he'd planned, or knocked the odd fifty thousand off? He stroked his chin, he always felt the gesture added a certain gravitas to his persona when he did so. Best not risk it, not when everything was going so well.

'Three hundred thousand,' he said quickly, before he could change his mind.

'Yes, that's what John said.' It was Uncle Simon's turn to stroke his chin as he studied his nephew carefully from under his bushy eyebrows. 'I think I might consider it for another fifty thousand.'

'That's more than your share is worth.' Crispin spoke quite sharply. How dare the old codger ruin it when everything was going so smoothly?

'Now, but not if you get bought out by some American multiple with more money than you and I can ever imagine.'

'But none of us would ever let that happen to Westall and Trim.' Crispin injected a fine degree of emotion into the sentence, only to be rewarded by a cynical snort from Simon. Perhaps the family was wrong, perhaps they had misjudged Simon's ability all these years.

'What I don't understand, Crispin, is, if things are as bad as you say, why are you risking such a lot of money? A young chap like you could lose everything.'

'I'll be straight with you, Uncle. It's the young blood and expertise that's needed. With me as a shareholder I can get capital, I know I can. I've banking friends, you see . . .'

'I don't, but I suppose I have to take your word for it. It wouldn't be nice to lie to your old uncle now, would it?' Simon leant across the table at him, menacingly, Crispin felt like he was a little boy again and Uncle was frightening him . . .

'Could you imagine me doing anything so dastardly?' Crispin's perfect white teeth flashed. 'There's just one thing, I'd prefer you not to mention anything to Uncle Julius, not just yet, not until we're sure. He's not been too well recently, I don't want the dear man unduly worried.'

'Ill? Nothing serious?' Simon leant forward anxiously.

'No, no. Just a nasty bout of flu he's had difficulty shaking off. You know Julius, fit as a flea.'

'I'll think about the offer. I won't worry Julius.'

'But I need a decision,' Crispin said.

'Then you're going to have to wait, young man. It's not every day I have to contemplate selling my heritage.'

'When would you let me know?'

'I'd like a few days to think about it. Now, tell us all about your wife. Any children?'

Crispin had to endure another hour of their company before he thought courtesy could allow him to take his leave. The initial guilt he had felt upon meeting his uncle had completely disappeared, destroyed by boredom and irritation that he was not going home with a decision.

Crispin's 2CV had not cleared the outskirts of Cambridge before Simon was on the telephone. Dulcett could have told Crispin that Simon had never felt it necessary to honour a promise.

'Julius? It's me. Odd thing's just happened . . .' And he told Julius of Crispin's visit and his offer.

'I'm not surprised,' Julius said calmly. 'Don't take it. When I croak they'll sell the whole bang shoot and your share will be worth millions.'

'Crispin said they would never sell.'

'Don't you believe it, Simon. My dear son and daughter will be in the marketplace before I'm cold.'

'But your own son advised me to accept, said they would never sell.'

'Did he, now? When?'

'A couple of days ago. It was he who telephoned to say Crispin was coming and to advise me to accept. But I've asked for more.'

'Very commendable, Simon.' The irony in Julius's voice was completely lost on his brother.

'But if you're right, I could be an old old man before I saw anything. You're as fit as a fiddle, fitter than me, aren't you, Julius? Crispin said you'd been unwell, nasty attack of flu or something? You are all right, aren't you?'

At the other end of the line, Julius frowned. He should be straight with his brother, should tell him what the doctors said. But he couldn't. If he said it, it might happen even sooner. And Simon's concern, what was it for? Concern for him, or concern that he might be making the wrong decision? He didn't blame him. Why shouldn't he look after his best interests?

'I'm fine,' he said shortly, suddenly feeling very weary.

'So you don't think I should sell then?'

'No. You'll regret it.'

'Thanks, Julius, then I won't, that's a promise. Fancy buying any pictures?'

Julius laughed, he already possessed going on for fifty of his brother's works, all purchased for double their value, all purchased with love and, if he was honest, a sense of guilt that the company didn't pay Simon more. 'I'm a bit strapped myself these days, Simon,' he said apologetically.

'These are hard times, Julius, old boy, hard bloody times.'

Julius slept soundly that night, Simon didn't. He and Dulcett sat up long into the night with several bottles of parsnip wine, and one of elderflower, as they went over the best course of action.

'But Julius could live for ever,' Simon kept repeating.

14

Gloria had long ago decided that if she had been God she would never have created Monday. No matter how she planned, how organised she thought she was on Sunday evening, by Monday morning everything had gone to pot. And this morning was to turn out to be a cracker.

The traffic was heavy as she slowly edged her way across Albert Bridge towards her office. It would have been faster by tube but Elephant did not like public transport. People assumed it was because he was small and was easily frightened, but Gloria knew better. Her dog was a snob. So, each morning she braved the worsening traffic chaos of London while Elephant sat grandly beside her barking instructions at other road users.

Gloria drove her Golf down the ramp to the cavernous underground car park beneath Shotters, and into her allotted bay. She might not be happy working in this huge publishing house but this car park and her parking privilege, she knew, saved her a small fortune each year in parking tickets and fines.

In reception she stood waiting for the lift, clutching Elephant close – he did not like lifts either – and pushed her way into the next one that stopped. There was no need to say which floor she wanted: at this time of the morning it stopped at every floor. No one spoke, everyone stood in that dazed manner of office workers returning after a weekend, like battle-fatigued soldiers in the frightening lull before the next assault.

On the fourth floor she got out. Immediately outside the lift, on the deep red wall, was the gold shape of a scimitar, Blades's – this particular branch of Shotters – logo. As she walked into her office, the telephone was ringing.

'This will not do, Gloria,' a voice screeched at her without preamble.

'Belle! My, you're up bright and early.' Gloria tried to sound pleased but Bella Ford was nobody's favourite author, certainly not first thing on Monday morning.

'You have to be up early to stay ahead of the rats in this game,' Bella said unpleasantly, and Gloria's heart sank. Trouble!

'What can I do for you, Bella?'

'Have you seen the latest *Publishing News*?' Bella demanded. Gloria sighed. Monday was the day when this type of call was common, when those authors who bothered to take the trade press had read something over the weekend that displeased them.

'Yes,' said Gloria, already on the defensive and racking her brains for anything in the last edition about Shotters and Bella that might have offended her.

'Did you see what Pewter's are laying out in publicity for Philomel Greensward's next book?'

'No, I didn't.' Gloria did not ask how much. She knew she need not bother, that Bella would quickly tell her – which she did.

'Philomel's useless, written out. I sell more than her but I don't get a budget like that.'

'You mustn't believe all you read, Bella. There's a lot of lies told and exaggeration in this business. Why, only the other day I saw an author, who shall be nameless, claiming she had sold over a million worldwide and I know for a fact her book is about to be remaindered.'

'Don't try and be smart with me, Gloria.'

'Bella, your own publicity budget hasn't been decided yet. As soon as it is I'll let you know,' Gloria said, lying through her teeth. If there was one rule in publishing it was never to let the author know what the publicity spend was to be – it was never enough for them. Not unless, as Pewter's had done, the sum was so vast that it was worth banging the drum to awaken interest early from the booksellers. 'Peter Holt is taking a personal interest in all the artwork for your publicity,' she said in a soothing voice. 'And we're all so looking forward to you coming to the sales conference. You know you're everyone's favourite author.' Gloria pulled a face at this bare-faced lie. Bella was to be at the sales conference because with her fruity vocabulary and her ability to consume copious amounts of alcohol and still stand up, she was a favourite with the reps – the only people she was ever nice to.

'I'm looking forward to the conference too. At least with the sales force one is meeting fellow professionals,' Bella snapped. Gloria chose to ignore that thrust. 'And I'm glad Peter is condescending to take an interest. But I can't be soft-soaped or distracted from my original point. I'll expect an equivalent sum, Gloria, I'm warning you.'

'It's not up to me, Bella.'

'Then make certain those people who decide know my strong feelings.'

'I will, Bella . . . I will – '

But the line had gone dead without even a thank-you. 'Grasping, ill-mannered, cow . . .' Gloria muttered to herself.

As if she had been waiting for the call to end, her secretary Rachel popped her head over the top of the partition.

'Now or later?' Rachel grinned apologetically.

'Now – why not? After Bella, what could possibly be worse?' Gloria laughed.

'Production are screeching for dates for Heather Gardens' – '

'Sod . . . I haven't finished the line edit. I thought we had a good two months to play with,' she said, turning to the shelf behind her desk and manhandling a large typescript off it. 'I've still a third to do, then Heather has got to have it back. She works fast but . . . we need one month at least. Why the sudden panic?' she asked as she riffled through the pages of typescript as if hoping to find she had done more than she thought.

'They've had to bring the publication date forward a month. Apparently Grace Bliss is having trouble getting the end of her book right, so the whole list is being shuffled.'

'Again? That bloody woman is incapable of delivering on time. Production should realise that, make allowances. Why wasn't I told?'

'You were, Gloria. Last week.' Rachel pulled her funny face again, the one she always used when apologising or when she thought the going might be getting rough. It was an expression which was unnecessary, working for Gloria. Rachel was envied by the other junior staff for having Gloria as her boss. She was not one of those women, abundant at Shotters, who found it necessary to prove their seniority by behaving like Attila the Hun. Responsibility sat lightly on Gloria's shoulders. If she shouted it was only to equals and those senior to herself, never the juniors.

'Was I?' Gloria's voice was resigned.

'I put the memo on your desk myself.'

They both looked at the paper-strewn desk, a desk which looked as if no order could ever be achieved from it. Gloria grimaced and shrugged her shoulders at the muddle. 'I'm sure you did, Rachel, my fault entirely.' She smiled up at Rachel. 'Be a love, make me some coffee?'

'Sure? Dieting or not?'

'Not.'

She hung up her coat, checked Elephant's water bowl, sharpened four pencils and was straightening the typescript when Rachel returned with her coffee.

'Bless you. Hold all my calls, say I'm in a meeting. All that is except – '

'Clive?' Rachel asked, laughing.

'Yes. I know what you're thinking but don't say it and ruin a perfectly good relationship, will you?' Gloria said good-naturedly.

'Don't forget you've got to see the art manager this morning over Bella's stuff and Adam in production would like a word and – '

'For God's sake, what else?'

'Top floor want you. Logan has summoned you.' Rachel rolled her eyes heavenward.

'Give me an hour of peace with this. I might go home with it this afternoon and work on it there.'

She chewed the end of her pencil looking abstractedly out of the window at the blank side wall of the building opposite. What could Logan want? He was the chief accountant in charge of overall finance and a person one rarely saw unless it was bad news. But her sales figures were up this year, not like most. She had no idea what the summons was for.

Gloria turned her attention to Heather Gardens' *Dawn Chorus*. Six hundred and fifty pages of double-spaced A4, four hundred and fifty edited, another two to go. As she read Gloria's attention was total. This was what she loved to do best. Her only regret was that she was being harassed and this type of editing needed to be done slowly, patiently. Other editors eagerly farmed this work out to juniors, not Gloria. She did not do it for all her authors – there was not time. But someone like Heather, whom she had discovered, whose hand she had held through various writing crises, numerous writer's blocks, whose book she was nursing through every stage of the process – Heather's she insisted on doing. Some authors resented this process, argued over each comma altered, but Heather wasn't one of those. She saw the edit as Gloria did, a polishing process. Taking the book line by line, ferreting out the disorderly syntax here, the repetition there, improving, honing the whole way, making it perfect without removing Heather's voice. It was a challenge, and ideally one over which author and editor worked in unison. For an hour Gloria worked steadily.

The art manager, Bart Friars, was dealt with quickly. He had wanted her to see the proofs of the jacket for Bella's new book. As usual there was a rush on – there always was. Publishing dates, ideally, should be fixed a good year ahead – the publisher's catalogues had to be produced, the sales team needed time to whip up interest with the booksellers. But it was not an ideal world. Too often dates had to be altered: frequently it was the writers themselves not finishing on time, occasionally the legal department stepped in, unhappy with a possibly libellous passage in one book which sent the whole list of books into a reshuffle. In this case, Bella's new book, due out next June and one which they were promoting heavily, would, they had discovered, coincide with a mega-seller from Tudor's by the American writer Tympany Fox. This news had sent publicity into a spiral of hysterical despair. With Tympany, all slink, sex and seductiveness, in town to promote it, Bella's fluffy faded prettiness would not get a look-in with the profile writers and chat shows. Hence this rearranged schedule to get her out in May. It would not have been so bad if Bella and her agent had not rejected the first two jacket roughs. There had once been a time when an author was presented with a jacket design and if they did not like it they had to lump it. Now, any self-respecting agent inserted a clause in their contracts demanding the right of consultation in all aspects of the production process.

'If the old bitch doesn't like this one, I'll murder her personally for you, Bart,' she promised as she slipped from the art department and next door into production.

Adam Preston presided over his domain in a permanent state of dyspeptic confusion. It was he who selected and bought the paper, sometimes buying tons in advance, like a futures broker on the market. He chose the typeface, decided on the design of the book. He haggled with the printers to get the best deal. He checked the artwork and liaised with the sales force. He pulled together all the various strands that went into producing a book. Nothing ever went smoothly no matter how hard everyone tried. As she had suspected he, too, was in a Bella panic.

She listened to his anguish over the number of changes Bella had insisted upon making to the proofs. Gloria apologised for her inability to control this author, and commiserated with him over the row that was now brewing with the printers about who was to pay for the changes. She tutted patiently. Bella was one of the worst at having second thoughts, she explained. Now he was worrying what they would do if she did not like the latest jacket design.

'Don't worry, Adam, I'll take the artwork over personally and I'll make her like it.'

'Sales are screaming for jackets. What else are they to sell on?'

'Her charm perhaps?' Gloria smiled sweetly. 'Maybe not,' she snorted.

She grabbed a quick coffee before taking the lift to the top floor and the senior executives' offices. Compared with the bustle downstairs it was a bit like entering a church up here where silence reigned and the most beautiful of the receptionists smiled charmingly but blankly at her.

'Gloria Catchpole for Logan Perriman.'

'Oh, yes, Gloria. Logan is expecting you,' the girl said in a soft sing-song voice as she picked up the telephone. 'Pandora? India here, Gloria Catchpole for Logan.' She smiled up at Gloria as she spoke, as if including her in some sort of conspiracy. It was an odd thing in publishing these days, Gloria thought, everyone had such daft names. She could only presume that these were the latest crop of débutantes' names. Publishing paid such lousy salaries that only girls with a daddy who would help out could afford to work here in the junior positions. Pandora, tall and willowy with an abundant mane of hair and dressed from head to toe in St Laurent, sashayed towards her.

'Gloria Catchpole?' she queried, smiling an empty model's smile. Gloria longed to snap, 'Yes, I am, Senior Commissioning Editor for Blades, with Shotters from the beginning and important.' She did not, of course, merely followed dutifully like a little dog along the wide swathe of blue carpet to the large mahogany door of Logan's office.

'Gloria, great to see you. How's things?' Logan, all six feet and ten and a half stone of tightly coiled energy, sprang across the huge expanse of office and was taking her by the hand and pulling her into the room as she shook it. 'Coffee? Perrier?'

'Gin and tonic, please, ice no lemon,' Gloria said with malicious satisfaction. Logan, she knew, never drank and disapproved strongly of those who did, especially during office hours. But a summons here could only mean bad news so Gloria reckoned she needed something strong.

'Well, if that's what you want,' said Logan, looking pointedly at his watch.

'Make that a large one,' said Gloria to Pandora as she swayed towards a bookcase, pressed a concealed button and a drinks cupboard appeared. How naff, thought Gloria.

Logan waited until Gloria had her drink and Pandora had silently let herself out of the room. Bet she listens on the intercom, thought Gloria.

'As I was saying, Gloria, how are things?'

'Apart from the normal Bella panic, fine,' she lied.

'I wish I could say the same. Times are bad, Gloria, couldn't be worse.'

'Don't worry, Logan. You know publishing as well as I do. There are always these ups and downs. What specifically? Christmas orders not looking so good?'

'Disastrous.'

'It'll pick up, it always does. All those last-minute shoppers panic-buying and before you know where you are the twenty-four-hour ordering lines will be glowing.'

'I hope you're right.'

'And it always gets better come spring and summer. Remember what old Gladys Hellman used to say? "Get the bums on the beaches, only time the buggers read."' Gloria hooted with laughter at the fond memory of Gladys who had worked as Peter's assistant and general factotum for years until she had been run over by a number 39 bus which, given the scarcity of buses on that route, was an achievement in itself.

'It's more complicated these days, Gloria, as well you know. Too many books, that's what I keep telling Peter.'

Gloria clutched her glass tightly. No editor liked to hear those words. It was true, of course. The number of new titles every year was reaching monumental proportions yet the size of the reading public remained static. But it was always others' lists that should be cut, never one's own.

'I've been looking at your sales figures, they're good.'

'They are, aren't they? Better than most, well over target,' she said pointedly. The target system had been brought in a few years back and everyone hated it. Now they all had goals to reach. Each editor had a set amount of money they were expected to earn the company each year and woe betide them if they slipped below this mark. Their projected sales figures, on what they anticipated each book to make, were critical rather than the hit-and-miss affair they once had been. Gloria would frequently be over-optimistic on some but had never once slipped below her target, using the expedient of always downgrading projected figures of the Bellas of this world just to be on the safe side.

'Yes, they are good, but rather by manipulation than judgement, wouldn't you say, Gloria?' Logan smiled his icy smile, sitting bolt upright and rigid opposite her. Gloria found herself wondering what he would be like in bed. She could not imagine one part of his anatomy, even the most important part, being warm to the touch.

'I don't know what you mean,' Gloria said, smiling, because she was still distracted by the thought of the doubtful body heat of his penis.

'Look at these figures on Bella. You know damn well she'll sell almost double that. Come off it, Gloria. You write her down to puff the others up. It doesn't make sense and you know it.'

Gloria sat silent, she was not smiling now. It did make sense, if not accountancy sense. She knew that if she did not inflate the figures on some of her books they would never get published in the first place. No new author, unless well known to the public in some other field, ever sold thousands. It was her way of keeping her stable supplied with fresh talent, writers she would coax along so that by the third or fourth book the figures were becoming respectable and she could leave them to survive on their own.

'There's dead wood here, Gloria.'

'There's what?' Gloria slammed down her glass, splattering its contents on the desk's leather surface. She hastily began to mop it up with a Kleenex. 'I'm sorry about that, but I can assure you there's no dead wood in my list,' she said angrily.

'For a start I can see a couple, if not more, we have got to drop. Concentrate on the earners.'

Gloria sat aghast as Logan in his dry, lifeless voice quoted figures of her authors who were in the various stages of beginning on the treacherous road of writing. If Shotters dropped them, their chance of being picked up by the others, especially now with publishing in one of its periodic doldrums, was remote. Logan was not exaggerating, times were harder but hardest for those writers who did not sell in mega-figures.

'Look at it this way, Logan,' Gloria began, fighting to keep her sense of outrage from her voice. 'What if Bella fell off the twig – now there's a pleasant thought . . .' She laughed, he did not. 'Seriously. If Bella and Shiel and all the big earners suddenly stopped writing, or were all killed in a bus on a writers' day out, say, where would we be? We need to be bringing on others to take their place.'

'Actuarially it's unlikely they'd all die or get writers' block together,' he said stiffly.

'They could move, go elsewhere to be published,' she said, with a sense of glee at the scenario that shot fear through the heart of all financial directors. 'I was over at Tudor's the other day. I could swear I recognised one of Shiel's typescripts on the senior fiction editor's desk.' Gloria had seen no such thing but it was worth a try, she reasoned with herself.

'And how could you possibly know it was hers?'

'Because I do, that's how. The first thing you learn as an editorial assistant is to read a manuscript upside down on somebody else's desk.' She was grinning, he was not.

'We look after all our top earners and they know it. They're loyal to us,' Logan said staunchly.

'If you think that, Logan, then you're naive and know bugger all about publishing. They're an egotistical bunch who'll leave at the drop of a hat if they think the pickings and the ego-massage will be better elsewhere.'

'I'm sorry, Gloria. This is getting us nowhere. Your list must be shortened. I know it's hard. It's always hard telling a writer their next book isn't good enough.'

'I won't say that to them, not one of them. It wouldn't be true and imagine the damage it could do to their confidence. You want to know what I think, Logan? I think a few less ludicrous advances to some of our writers would sort out a lot of our problems. First novels are notoriously difficult to sell, as well you know. But those you picked out are getting there. Next time their figures will double and so on.' Logan moved uncomfortably in his chair. 'Look at that bloody awful book last year by Gail Storm. OK, the publicity generated good sales but remember the obscene advance we paid her? That will never be earned back. We need the good, reliable workhorses of writers to bring the money in for mad flights of fancy like Gail, who is unlikely to write another thing – if she wrote the last one,' Gloria said darkly. She had not liked Gail's book, in fact had refused to edit it. She had not come into the business to work with pornography, she'd said, and, give him his due, Peter had accepted her objection. She was not sure but she believed the damn book was taken on simply because the ex-model Gail was Hilary Holt's best friend – she knew Peter, anything for a quiet life.

'You don't seem to understand, Gloria. This is not a matter open to discussion. I asked you here to tell you, not to argue the toss with you.'

'We'll see about that.' Gloria was standing now and very angry. There were two things Gloria was passionate about: Elephant and her authors. 'You'll be hearing from me.' She turned, stormed from the room and into the reception hall. India stood up to greet her but Gloria swept past in the direction of Peter's office.

'You can't go in there,' India wailed, tripping down the hallway on her Manolo Blahnik shoes. 'Peter's in conference, he's not to be disturbed.'

With a defiant flourish Gloria opened the double doors to Peter's office.

'Gloria, what a nice surprise,' Peter said, looking up from the *Beano* he was reading.

At sight of her chief executive's reading matter, Gloria burst out laughing. 'Some conference,' she spluttered.

'What can I do for you?' Peter grinned back, threw down his comic and leant back in his chair. He was always pleased to see Gloria. She was so straight in her dealings and never played games. She was lovely too, she always had been, but was one of those women who, he thought, was improving with age – confidence suited her. 'What's the problem?'

'Either my list stays my way or I'm resigning.'

'Who have you been talking to? Logan? Ah well, I might have guessed. How about lunch? I'm free if you are. We'll thrash it out over a good bottle of claret. Always makes everything clearer, a good claret.' He grinned at her.

'Yes, I'm free.' She found herself calming down. 'I'll just go and tell Elephant.'

He took her to the Caprice. They ordered and he asked for the claret to be served as they waited for their food. Gloria did not waste time but went straight into the attack. Peter sat silent listening to her tirade, watching the emotions flit across her honest, expressive face. How he envied her, he thought, as he sipped the wine he had promised them both. This was how he had once been. There had been books he had felt so passionate about he sometimes used to wonder if he would kill for them.

For a good fifteen minutes Gloria spoke non-stop and then stopped suddenly, embarrassed as she became aware that their starter had arrived and she had not noticed and that Peter had not said a word.

'That's it.' She slumped back into her chair.

Peter looked at her for what seemed an age.

'God, Gloria, you're so lucky. You're still in love with it all, aren't you?'

'Yes, I am. But I'll be honest with you, I hate Shotters as it is now. I wish we could put the clock back, have it as it used to be.'

'You're not the only one. But this is progress.'

'How can it be if it stops new writers coming forward?'

He laughed. 'Tell you what. Just for twelve months don't take on anyone new, keep the Logans of the world happy.'

'We can't do that. If the agents twigged that, we wouldn't see anything worthwhile when we were ready.'

'We could prevaricate. Anything you find keep them dangling.'

'No, I won't do that. Who suffers when we hold back on typescripts for months at a time? The poor bloody authors. I've always prided myself on making quick decisions. Well, I used to, I've got a bit sloppy with my reading these past few months. No, I can't do that.'

'Enough publishers do.' He rubbed his chin with his hand. 'You win.'

'You mean my list stays?'

'Yes.'

'And I can still take on new talent?'

'Let's ration it for twelve months – say, two new writers, if you can find them.'

'Peter, thank you, thank you.' She grabbed at his hand and squeezed it but she noticed he did not smile. Still holding his hand she looked closely at him. 'You're not happy, Peter, are you?'

'Not very.'

'Do you want to talk?'

'There's not much to say, Gloria. I'm probably being stupid, I just feel discontented and what have I to be discontented about?'

'Quite a lot,' she said. And it was true. She knew he felt as she did about publishing, this conversation had proved that, and there was Hilary. How could he still be in love with her as she was now?

'Oh, it's nothing.' He shook his head and looked away embarrassed.

'Well, if you ever want to talk, I'm always around, you know that, don't you?'

'Yes, Gloria, I know. Thanks. We haven't been fair to you recently, have we?'

'Promoting that prat Norman Wilton over me annoyed me, yes,' she said, shaking her head defiantly.

'It wasn't my choice,' he said apologetically.

'Quite honestly, I don't see the point in owning a company if you are not in total control,' she answered sharply.

'Point taken. It's just that everything has become so large . . .' He leant forward. 'Look, Gloria, I understand why you're unhappy but don't do anything rash, not at the moment, will you?'

She looked at him with a puzzled expression, taken back by the intensity of his stare. 'No, all right, I won't.'

'Promise?'

'What is this?' She laughed. 'OK, I promise – Brownie's honour.' She joked. It was not necessary – even after all this time she knew she would promise him anything.

'How about some more claret?' He managed a smile.

'That would be lovely. Why not? Blow the office.' She grinned and removed her hand from his and he found he was disappointed that she had.

15

Each day of the following week involved a mish-mash of drama for all concerned.

Crispin, not having heard from his Uncle Simon if the deal was on or not, had worked himself into a lather of fear and apprehension. Meeting Roz on the stairs he had snapped at her most unpleasantly. It was unnecessary but then, he felt, it was equally unnecessary of her to burst into tears. The sight of her mascara rolling unbecomingly in black rivulets down her cheeks was so unappealing that he marvelled that he could ever have gone to bed with her in the first place – he certainly did not want to again. He had begun to apologise for his behaviour when it struck him that he already had most of the information he required from her and, since she was as much in the dark about the Lepanto Trust as everyone else, now might be the best time to divest himself of her – and he told her so.

He returned to his own office feeling quite satisfied with his morning's work. He felt good for the first time since the weekend when he had seen Simon. But the feeling did not last and within the hour he was back to tearing out his hair with frustration.

His hand hovered frequently over the telephone receiver but he fought a battle of wills with himself and refrained from calling his uncle. He must not appear too keen or concerned or the old fool would smell a rat.

For the past two days he had resisted telephoning his cousin also. He did so on two counts: he so loathed the man that he couldn't bear to talk to him even at a distance, and he did not want John to know that anything was awry with his plans. He could just imagine the toad smirking at him if he sensed that Crispin's grand plan was about to fail.

Frustration finally won, however, and he called John at his bank. He was told that his cousin was in a meeting and could not possibly be interrupted. He had to wait two miserable hours until his call was returned.

'Meeting go well?' Crispin said airily.

'Meeting?' John answered, and Crispin smiled to himself, he had caught him out. Or had he? Was John making sure he knew there had been no such appointment? 'Fine, yes of course. Money rolling in,' John chuckled. 'So Crisp, what can I do for you?'

The knuckles of Crispin's hands whitened as he clasped the receiver with pent-up anger at the use of that name.

'I suddenly realised the other day that we had never had you and dear Poppy to our place. I thought perhaps a light dinner, say tomorrow?'

There was a self-important rustling of a diary's pages.

'Sorry, Crisp, no can do. New York beckons, I'm afraid.'

'Perhaps when you return?' Crispin tried to sound as pleasant as possible, hard in the circumstances.

'Hang on. I've just remembered. I have a cancellation – a client flying in from Japan has got himself held up in Bombay with engine trouble. I could manage tonight.'

'Tonight?' Crispin's mind was racing. If he said yes it implied he and Charlotte had no social life. If he did not, he might have days of this agony. Charlotte would not be happy, normally she liked several days to prepare for a dinner party. 'Why not? Wonderful.'

Five minutes later he was not so self-satisfied. Not once he had spoken to Charlotte.

'What the bloody hell do you mean? A dinner party tonight! It's out of the question, can't be done.'

'But, Charlotte, my sweet one, it's important to me. I must find out what Simon's about. This is the only way.'

'No.'

'Charlotte, please.'

He winced at the language as Charlotte harangued him. It was strange how forceful and coarse her language could become when away from their delightful home and ambience, he thought, as he held the telephone away from his ear.

'Very well, my darling. You're right, I should not have been so inconsiderate. I do understand. I'll get one of those catering Sloane types to come in and do it – save you the bother.'

'You'll do no such bloody thing!' Charlotte shrieked, just as he had known she would. If there was one thing his wife would never countenance it was someone else in her perfect kitchen, messing about with her precious *batterie de cuisine*.

Crispin had only met his cousin's wife once, at their wedding. The creature who stood on his doorstep at seven-forty bore no relation whatsoever to the sweet, fresh-faced bride he had remembered. This Poppy was hard-faced, Knightsbridge-chic and bored before she had even crossed the threshold. What was even worse, she smoked. Since none of their friends indulged in the disgusting habit this was a state of affairs that had never happened before. He saw the strained face of his wife as Poppy lit up without even the courtesy of a 'Do you mind?' He prayed she was not a chain-smoker. She was.

At such short notice, Charlotte had surpassed herself. The lightly seasoned consommé was masterly; the turbot in a gentle coating of subtly coloured sauce nantua was sublime; the crisp sorbet of peach was delicious; the rack of lamb, so moistly pink with its vegetables moulded into pretty castle shapes, was accompanied by a rowan sauce of such delicacy that Crispin could have wept at its excellence. Charlotte had arranged the salad that followed with such an eye for colour and design that he could have fallen in love with her all over again. Her cheese board was famous. And the flim-flam that followed was a delightful surprise.

It was a feast of taste, smell, colour – and Poppy left practically everything, being that abomination at a dinner party, a woman on a diet. John ate with such disgusting and noisy relish that it quite spoilt his compliments.

By the end of the meal, when Charlotte rose prettily and suggested that she and Poppy should withdraw, she was ashen-faced with despair.

Crispin placed several knobs of coal on the fire while the maid they always employed for dinner parties cleared the dishes. He collected the port decanter and walnuts and leant back in his chair. He was suddenly aware that John was looking anxiously about him.

'Something wrong, old chap?' Crispin asked.

'No, nothing,' said John, and slipped his hand into his jacket pocket and brought out a cigar case.

'No, thank you, I don't.' Crispin waved his hand at the offensive object John was offering him.

'Mind if I do?'

'No, no, carry on,' Crispin said almost hysterically. But then, he told himself, fighting to calm down, Poppy had done so much damage with her weed what was a bit more?

'I spoke to Uncle Simon. I told him we were coming here tonight.'

Crispin choked on his port with surprise and a dribble landed on his waistcoat, a particular favourite. He dabbed miserably at the stain.

'Sorry, didn't mean to startle you, Crisp.' John smirked at him.

'I wasn't startled. The damn port went down the wrong way. How is the dear old chap? I had a wonderful lunch with him and Dulcett. Quaint couple, aren't they? I've been meaning to get hold of him but, with one thing and another, I've been too busy.'

'Really?' John smirked again and Crispin marvelled at the paucity of facial expressions the man possessed. He noisily slurped from his port glass so that Crispin was made aware it was empty. 'You wouldn't have got hold of him,' he said once he had refilled his glass. 'He's in Tuscany.'

'Tuscany?' Crispin asked lightly, unsure of the significance of this news. 'He said nothing on Sunday.'

'Went as soon as he'd seen you. He's gone away to think what he should do, he says. I've got his number, of course. I think he's looking at property. Working out how much more he should screw out of you.'

'I couldn't go higher. I agreed top price with him.'

'Think you might have to, old boy. The old cove isn't nearly as stupid as he appears.'

'What do you think he'll do?' Crispin loathed himself for asking the question but, on the other hand, nothing could have contained his anxiety.

'Take it and hop off to Italy with his fat and horny-handed whore, no doubt.'

'Let's hope you're right. Some Stilton, John?'

At least Crispin bored John as much as vice versa so it was only half an hour later, after a tisane in the drawing room where they had found Poppy sitting with a tumbler of lemon barley water in her hand and a surprised expression on her face that she had not been offered a brandy, that they left.

Their car had barely started before Charlotte was rushing about the rooms opening windows and lighting a month's supply of scented candles.

'How could you, Crispin? How could you have invited such crass and vulgar people to our little nest?' Her pretty eyes brimmed with tears. Her pert white breast swelled becomingly over the top of the forget-me-not-sprigged Empire line dress she wore. Crispin could feel himself hardening at the sight and at the thought of the night ahead. She looked so distressed and agitated that he thought they should definitely play the virgin-bride-on-her-wedding-night ravished by her dastardly-brute-of-a-husband game. They both enjoyed that one immensely.

'I'm sorry, my sweet one. But it was business.' He leant forward and gently touched the white, marbled flesh so temptingly displayed.

'But we promised each other, Crispin. We promised never to let the horrible twentieth century into our home. You've let me down so badly.'

'Dearest heart. It's over. The bad man's gone away. You've only this bad man now. One who's going to bruise those pretty little breasts of yours.'

'Oh, Crispin, fuck you – and your stupid bloody games!' she shouted raucously, hit him hard across the face and rushed from the room slamming the door with such force that two particularly sensitively executed watercolours smashed to the floor.

Crispin fumbled towards the nearest chair and slumped into it, his face white with shock. What had gone wrong? What was happening? Why had she spoken to him like that? It was not allowed, not here. He could cope with most things but not that, not the loss of his wonderful, delicate, sweet world. And he put his face into his hands, as if to shut out the confusion.

16

To say that Charles Trenchard was surprised to find his bags packed and in the hall when he eventually returned home was something of an understatement.

He prodded a case with his foot and it fell on its side heavily. It was full. Joy was not playing games. It looked as if she meant business. Surely not?

'Oh, Lord,' he sighed, and scratched his head. If she was serious, why? She knew him, knew he always came back to her. She had forgiven him enough times in the past; it was reasonable for him to think that she would continue to forgive him. Of course, he thought, peering at his face in the hall mirror, it had been stupid of him to turn up at Silver's party with Penelope. But he had been drinking champagne, and Penelope had begged him to take her. He had never been able to resist a pretty woman's pleas.

What the hell had changed? He did not understand women. Joy had everything she could wish for – just look at this house and the lifestyle he gave her. She had known what he was like when they had married: he had never made a secret of his predilection for women. His mother had never complained about his father, so why should Joy? Indeed, she was more fortunate than his mother for he had hinted, broadly enough, that he did not mind in the least if she took a lover – provided she was discreet.

He looked again at his cases and wondered what she had forgotten to pack. In a strange way he felt a sense of relief. He had to admit this fling with Penelope was different from all the rest for she *was* different – intelligent, on his wavelength and beautiful, too. He had even begun to think he might be in love with her. But then, even taking into account Penelope's virtues over the usual bimbos he chose, he doubted if it would last, they never did.

It was not his day, he thought ruefully. The accountancy firm for whom he acted as consultant were none too pleased with him in view of the amount of suddenly cancelled business. This morning he had endured a painful interview with the senior partner. Charles had offended Barty Silver and, he was told, only a bloody fool did that. He could only assume the self-righteous poofter objected to him with Penelope. He aimed a kick at another case. Interfering bastard! No doubt he was behind this too. Joy would never have done it without someone goading her into it. How was he to handle her? He liked his women, but he loved Joy, this house, Hannah and, no, he had no intention of losing any of them – not even for Penelope. He would talk to Joy, calm her down, buy her a new piece of jewellery – that usually worked. Maybe they could go away for Christmas. He had always won her over in the past but, then, she had never packed his bags before. Best face her, he thought, get it over with, and he bounded up the stairs two at a time.

Joy was on the telephone and barely looked up as he entered the room, intent on listening to whoever was on the other end.

'Why are my bags in the hall?' he asked, in such a reasonable voice that this might have been an everyday occurrence. 'Am I going somewhere I don't know about?' He smiled, knowing it always made him look more handsome.

'Do you mind? I'm busy,' his wife said, looking at him coldly and placing her hand over the mouthpiece. She deliberately turned her back on him and continued with her conversation.

It was that action that made Charles lose his temper. He was not used to being ignored, and never by women. 'I'm talking to you.' He raised his voice.

'Excuse me a moment, Barty. Something's turned up . . .'

Charles wrenched the receiver from her hand. 'The "something" is me, her husband, you jumped-up oik!' he shouted into the telephone before slamming it back on to its cradle.

'How dare you! That's my most important client.' She stepped back from him, rubbing her wrist which he had hurt.

'I want to talk to you –' The telephone rang, Charles bent down and wrenched the socket from the wall. 'What are you playing at?' he demanded angrily.

Joy laughed, a shrill, ugly laugh. 'You have the audacity to ask me that? I'm not playing at anything, Charles. I've woken up at last. Woken up to the true bastard you are and the realisation that you're sick. You can't keep your prick in your pants, it's like an obsession with you.'

'My, my. The perfect, cool Joy talking dirty. I like that.' He threw back his head and laughed. 'There's hope for you yet!'

'Yes, there's certainly that. I've seen a solicitor and I want a divorce.' Joy faced him squarely and although she was speaking calmly it was a forced calm, for she was shaking with emotion. 'I've talked it over with her, and she says –'

'Her, did you say?'

'Yes, I thought I'd get a fairer hearing from a fellow female. I know you lot and the way you stick together.'

'Don't be paranoid, Joy, it doesn't suit you.'

'I don't want to make any trouble for you so I won't be suing you for unreasonable behaviour. I'm happy to wait the two years and we'll go for irretrievable breakdown of marriage.'

'I don't want a divorce.'

'Well, I do. Have it whichever way you want. But I want this house.'

'Don't be naive, Joy. How the hell do you think you can continue to live here? I can assure you that I would so arrange my affairs that your alimony wouldn't cover the cost of running this place, let alone the shopping and the clothes you so love.'

'I don't want any money from you, just this house.'

'Good God, woman, what do you think this house is worth? You needn't think I'm going to give you a fortune in property without a fight.'

'I've a right to a roof over my head.'

'Yes, but not this one.'

'All right, then. I agree, we sell this and you buy me something smaller.'

'That was not an invitation to an agreement.' Suddenly he smiled. 'And how are you going to eat if you're so proud that you won't take an allowance from me?'

'I can work.'

'You? It would interfere too much with your social life, the trips to the hairdresser's, lunching with your vacuous friends.'

'My friends are *not* vacuous! They filled the long hours.' She ignored him as he played an imaginary violin. 'With my work I shall be satisfied, it will fill my days.'

'You'll starve before you become a success. Why, what have you done? You've just been playing at being an agent, the reality is far harder.'

'I'll succeed. I've Barty Silver as a client now. The interest in his memoirs is already monumental and they aren't even written.'

'Oh, yes, dear Barty. You realise he is trying to ruin me? Since that bloody party the firm's lost a stack of business.'

'You don't know it's him,' she said, but her voice wavered – it was just the sort of thing Barty would do. He was a wonderful friend but a fearsome enemy. 'Why should he bother with someone like you?' she asked, for if it was true, then she was in serious trouble with her husband.

'I don't know, I haven't worked it out, but I'll get to the bottom of it, one way or another. Maybe he fancies you.'

'Don't be so stupid.'

They had been standing facing each other like combatants. Suddenly Charles turned and walked to the drinks tray. 'G and T?' he asked, his voice once again normal and pleasant after the shouting and sneering.

'Why, yes, thanks . . .' she said, caught off guard. He often did this when they were arguing, switching moods so that she did not know where she was, making her feel like one of Pavlov's dogs.

'I can't believe we're having this conversation. I just don't believe it's happening to us,' he said with feeling as he handed her her drink. She sat down on the sofa.

'It has to be done, Charles, if we are ever to find any peace,' she said, getting the strength from somewhere to stand her ground. 'You're obviously not happy with me. If you were you wouldn't need these mistresses. It makes me unhappier than I can describe. And then there's Hannah to think of. Our relationship will eventually begin to affect her. I know you love her, and we must handle this so that she is not damaged in any way. I shall make no difficulty over access.'

'No – ' he started to say. The word burst forth, then he was silent, looking into his drink. She watched him anxiously, trying to fathom what he was thinking. His mind was whirling; the one thing he could not argue about, at this point, was his daughter – his one vulnerable spot. He would have to move cautiously, he could not put his possession of Hannah at risk. If Joy went ahead with this divorce one thing was certain, he swore to himself, she would not get his daughter. He had not been handling this right, he told himself, best not to shout at her, best to watch it. He looked up at her, the expression on his face changed to one of pleading.

'Tell me why, Joy? You've always understood my little peccadilloes in the past.'

'I didn't understand, Charles. I put up with you. But no more.'

'Please, Joy, I don't want us to end.'

'It has to.'

'No. You don't understand, I love you.'

'I'm sorry.' She looked away from the pain she saw in his eyes, she dare not look at him lest he made her change her mind.

'Please, darling . . .' He put out his hand to take hers but she moved away from him, to the corner of the sofa, knowing only too well the effect his touch might have on her.

'I won't let you do this to us,' he said softly.

Joy looked at him, her expression a mixture of pity and disbelief. 'Oh, Charles,' she said. 'Just listen to you. I'm not doing anything to us – it's you, don't you see that? You're unfaithful not just to me but to those other women also. You screw around and never think of the consequences, the pain you're inflicting. You never stop to think why you are as you are. What's wrong with *you*? If you did, maybe you'd finally grow up.'

'Joy forgive me. I do think, honestly. I know I've hurt you. But I promise, my darling, I won't stray again, I promise. Tell you what, let's get away for Christmas – somewhere warm, just you, me and Hannah.'

'I want my freedom. You have no choice. My solicitor says – '

'Shut up about your bloody solicitor!' He was yelling, his temper, which he had always had difficulty in controlling, slipping away from him again. 'So you think I have no choice. Well, you're wrong. I've got a choice.' And he stood up, moved quickly towards her and before she could escape he had grabbed her by the arm, was pulling her up from the sofa and marching her, she protesting, towards the door and up the stairs.

He kicked open the door to their bedroom, pushed her in front of him into the room and slammed the door shut. He took hold of the bodice of her dress and deliberately and slowly ripped it to the hem. She stood rigid, making a strange mewing noise of fear, desperately scrabbling at the torn cloth, trying to clothe herself with it.

'See. This is my choice,' he said his eyes glinting dangerously.

'Please, Charles, I don't want to,' she pleaded, pulling away from him. 'I beg you – please . . .'

He scooped her into his arms, virtually threw her on the bed and, pinning her down with one hand, began to unzip his trousers with the other.

'This is my choice and you love it, always have, haven't you, ice-cool Joy? The best times have always been when I've just come from another woman's bed. Admit it.'

She lay still, imprisoned by his legs, as he straddled her. She remained silent.

'Admit it!' he shouted and slapped her hard across her face.

'Yes,' she whispered.

'Louder.'

'Yes.'

'Tell me you like it,' he ordered, his hand raised ready to strike her again.

'I like it,' she sobbed.

His mouth was crashing down on her. She tasted the salt of her own blood, and felt she would suffocate as his full weight was upon her and, with no concern for her or the pain he was inflicting, he was ripping what little remained of her clothing from her.

As he entered her, involuntarily she groaned. Rhythmically he began to thrust, back and forth, his large penis seeming to grow inside her. She felt her body betraying her as it rose in time with him.

'No!' she shouted, attempting to push him from her. 'No!' Her mind tried to resist him but her senses won. She arched her back allowing him to penetrate deeper, and she screamed as she climaxed, her whole body shaking with the intensity of it.

When he had finished with her he rolled away, raised himself on his elbows and looked down at her.

'Better now?' He smiled, raising one eyebrow quizzically. 'You never could resist a good fuck, could you?'

Her blue eyes were dark, almost black with emotion. She pulled herself up in the bed. 'I hate you. Hate you!' she screamed, but who did she hate, him or herself for enjoying it? And as if her hand had a life of its own it lashed out, hitting him across the face. He did not pause for a second but hit her back, far harder.

'Want some more? Want it rougher?' He was laughing.

Sobbing, Joy made to get off the bed, but he grabbed her. She fought against his hold and abruptly he flung her from him. She fell against the side of a chest, banging her head. She was past feeling pain and it was almost with surprise that she felt the warmth of blood trickling down her forehead. She picked herself up and stumbled towards the bathroom, locking the door behind her.

She slumped against the basin, shivering, retching with shock. She looked in the mirror. The cut was deep, her face ashen and where he had hit her the skin was already discoloured.

'Joy, Joy, I'm sorry.' He was banging on the door. She clutched at her throat with fear. 'Darling, I'm sorry. I shouldn't have done that. I was angry. When you spoke of Hannah and taking her this red mist came. I don't know what came over me.'

Like all the other times, she thought sadly to herself. She splashed water on to her throbbing face. 'Not any more. He's never going to treat me like that again,' she told the reflection in the mirror. In her dressing room, she put on a loose dress, grabbed a raincoat and, throwing some night things into a bag, unlocked a door on to the landing that was never normally used. She looked nervously over her shoulder, afraid he would remember there was another way out, but she could still hear him banging impotently on the bathroom door. She raced down the stairs. As she reached the hall the front doorbell rang. She opened the door wide and with a little cry pitched headlong into Barty Silver's arms.

'Well, now,' Barty said holding her awkwardly, nodding frantically at his assistant Gervase to come to his rescue. 'What's all this, then?' he said, pushing her gently away from him. He saw her bruised and bleeding face. 'A fine kettle of fish and no mistake, you'd best come home with Barty, ducks.'

Barty, who never liked to become involved with the lives of others, was inadvertently becoming heavily involved with Joy's.

Even as the Rolls carried them from Charles's house to his mansion Barty realised he had made a tactical error. For a start, what was he to do with a bleeding, near hysterical, woman? And secondly, even a bachelor such as he knew that she should never have left the matrimonial home. He, by stepping in, had undoubtedly made matters worse.

'Who'd ever've thought it?' he kept saying as the large car purred along, 'a smart, sophisticated, cool-as-a-cucumber geezer like Charles behaving like a raving monster. Who'd ever have thought it?'

Back at his house his personal physician was summoned and photographs were taken of Joy's face, despite her protests.

'Evidence, my girl. You never know when you might need it.'

'I couldn't admit to this, I'd be too ashamed.'

'Why should you be ashamed? It was him did it.'

'I can just hear everyone talking. "Why did she stay with him? She must have liked it," you know the sort of things people say.' She accepted the glass of brandy which the doctor had said she should not have but which Barty thought was essential.

'You mean this isn't the first time?'

'No.' She shook her head and then winced because it hurt. 'And if I stayed it wouldn't be the last time.'

'Bloody animal,' Barty growled. 'Who'd ever have thought it?' he repeated. 'And him appearing so nice and respectable – amazing. Why?'

'I used to think he couldn't help it – he's always had a short temper. I thought it must be my fault, that I annoyed him so much I made him do it. I know better now. I know he enjoys it.'

'Joy. I'm sorry.' He shook his head in disbelief, for if there was one thing Barty could not stand or understand it was physical violence.

'I'm sorry too, Barty, landing you in it like this.' She was curled up in the corner of the large sofa in his study.

'You look like a little girl, sitting there like that,' he said softly.

She tried to smile but it would not come.

'Look, love, I don't think you can stay here.'

'I know, Barty, I'll go to a hotel.'

'Looking like that? What if some mucky reporter sees you?'

'I'll risk it.'

'No, you can't do that. Tell you what. You stay here tonight – I was going out anyway. I'll just stay out all night – we've got your reputation to think of,' he said seriously.

At that Joy did smile, for the very idea of anyone thinking that she might misbehave with Barty was just too silly to contemplate.

'I've got a little service flat you can move into tomorrow, till you get yourself sorted out, see your brief, that sort of thing.'

'Barty, you are so kind.'

'I've got to look after my agent, now, haven't I? Who wants me book, then?' he asked, more to distract her than to hear the outcome.

'I've only floated the idea so far and it's had a wonderful reception.' Barty had the satisfaction of seeing Joy brighten up considerably as she talked about their project and the reactions provoked during the past two days by her talks with various editors. 'When I've found a ghost-writer you feel you can get on with – I've several in mind – I think we should auction it.'

'Me? Being auctioned? Now there's a funny idea. How's that done, then? Haul me along to Christie's?'

'No. We offer it around to a selected group of publishers and invite them to bid within a set deadline. They can do so by telephone or by sealed bids. It's up to you which way. Then you choose which one you want. In a case like this it's a way of seeing, right away, what the highest bid will be.'

'Sealed bids, I like that idea. But I don't want Shotters to have it.'

'But they're likely to be one of the highest bidders. Such a book is just right for them, they would market it beautifully,' she said feeling disappointed.

'Let them bid, we don't have to accept them.'

'But why, Barty?'

'Secrets, Joy,' he replied, winking at her and tapping the side of his nose with his finger. 'Know what I mean?' he said with a jerk of his head. 'An auction, I'm tickled pink. I'd like to know me price.' He laughed, and Joy was laughing too even though it hurt. But she realised she suddenly felt safe.

17

Tony had not spoken to Kate since the night of the party three days ago. He was still sleeping in the guest room and had moved more of his stuff into it. She found that his silence did not make a great deal of difference to her. He had always been taciturn at breakfast, and spent so much time in his study, that it was only at supper and when she was undressing to go to bed that she missed conversation.

But it was far from an ideal situation. The atmosphere in the house was unpleasant, the rancour between her and Tony almost a physical thing. While she could enjoy the lack of nagging on his part it was ludicrous and childish to be relaying messages through the children, and goodness knows what it was doing to their authority with them.

She had made use of this to her advantage, however.

'Lucy, would you tell your father that I am going away for the weekend with Pam?' she said, as they were eating yet another meal in uncomfortable silence.

Lucy grinned broadly as if enjoying the situation immeasurably. 'Mum says – '

'I heard. I'm not deaf,' Tony growled.

'So?' Lucy spoke with her mouth full, a habit Kate had never been able to break and doubted if she ever would now. Though she sometimes wondered if Lucy only did it to annoy and ate perfectly normally when with other people.

'Do you have to eat with your mouth open?' her irate father asked her.

'Yes,' Lucy said, masticating even more noisily. 'You didn't answer.'

'Answer what?'

'Answer Mum.'

'Your mother can do what she flaming well likes,' Tony said, standing up and flinging his napkin down on the table with a dramatic gesture.

'Good,' Kate said with equanimity, and began to clear the dishes. Tony slammed from the room and Kate sighed at the damage all this bad temper must be causing to the house. Much to her surprise Lucy followed her into the kitchen with a tray of dirty dishes and began to help her clear up without being asked.

'Why are you two behaving like spoilt brats?' Lucy asked, picking up a tea-towel.

'Your father blames me for his getting breathalysed.'

'That's not fair. You didn't pour the drink down his gullet, did you?'

'No. But I'm afraid I laughed. Unforgivable where men are concerned, Lucy.'

'Where are you going this weekend or is it a deadly secret? I won't tell if you don't want.' Her daughter grinned at her.

'It's no secret.' Kate was smiling. So, it was nosiness that was making her daughter help, not a reformation in her character. 'Pam has booked us in to a writers' weekend. We go on Friday to Weston and I'll be back on Sunday evening. I'll leave food organised and notes to tell you what to do with it and – '

'A what?' Lucy stopped drying the saucepan lid in her hand and stood stock still like a statue.

'It's a weekend arranged for people who want to write. There are lectures by well-known writers – Bella Ford is coming to this one.'

'Bella Ford? Wow!' Kate was pleased to register that Lucy was impressed.

'Then there are workshops, seminars, we get tips on being published, that sort of thing. And we discuss each other's work . . .'

'You're having me on, aren't you?'

'No. Of course, it might be dreadfully boring. But Pam and I thought we ought to find out. Well, the truth is more that Pam decided, I had nothing to do with it.' Kate smiled.

'I don't believe it.' Lucy was laughing. 'It's just too silly. You, a writer!'

'Why?' The smile disappeared from Kate's face and she felt herself becoming defensive.

'I suppose there's no reason why not, except you're not, are you? A writer, I mean. You can't be taught how to write, Mum. You're born one. I mean, you haven't done any. Or have you?'

'As a matter of fact I have. I've written the start of a novel. Pam and I joined a writers' circle in Little Moreton, I'm sure I told you.'

'Can I see what you've done? Go on, let me.'

'Well . . .' Kate paused and, seeing the blatant amusement in Lucy's face, turned away and rapidly wiped down the draining board.

'Come on, Mum. Get it out, let's see it.'

'No, I'm sorry, Lucy. I couldn't. I know it's silly but, well . . . I feel shy about it.'

'But you just said you'll be discussing your work with these other so-called writers.'

'Yes, but they'll be different. They'll know what it's like, they'll understand. At least, I think I'll show it to them. I'm still not sure. It's mine, you see, precious to me.' She swung round, her face alight with excitement. 'Oh, Lucy, it's such a wonderful feeling to know I'm creating something which is all mine. I'm so thrilled about it and what's happening to me. Do you understand what I'm trying to say?'

'Nope. You haven't got any spare tights, have you?'

'Top drawer of my dressing table,' Kate replied automatically and began vigorously to wipe down the work surfaces, trying to ignore the disappointment she felt. She had wanted to share her feelings with Lucy, to try to explain the importance of it, but there was no point. Lucy would not understand. Why should she?

She finished tidying the kitchen quickly and laid the breakfast table. She had been doing everything fast since Sunday because, once started on this book, she did not know how to stop. She certainly knew she did not want to. She squeezed her writing into any available moment. When not doing it, she was thinking of what she would be writing next. Tony's sulk had helped her enormously. She had taken to getting up in the morning and preparing everyone's breakfast, putting it in the warming oven of the Aga and then going back to bed. She did not go there to sleep, instead she sat up, all the pillows puffed up behind her, and wrote. She had discovered that this was the best time of day, when the ideas came pouring out, so that her pen had difficulty in keeping up with them. It was as if she had her own private cinema in her head. She would sit on the bed, start the film and write down the images, the scenes, the conversation that was taking place on this personal screen. At night, without Tony to consider, she worked into the small hours. When she eventually put out the light she lay in the dark, thinking about what she had just created, working out ways to improve it in the morning. She found now that she was even dreaming her plot.

The three hundred words that Felicity had told them to write on 'A Winter's Romance', had, in Kate's hands, become nearly ten thousand words on 'A Winter's Interlude'. Her excitement at what she was doing was so overwhelming, such a surprise, that Lucy was the only person she had told – even Pam did not know.

A novel. The very thought made her sigh. It was all so impossible – and yet was it? And to her! The book, her book, had, in this short space of time, taken over her life completely. She, who had always been such a good housewife, in the past few days had become slipshod. She hoovered and dusted quickly, skimming over the surfaces, only bothering with the bits that were seen. She was behind with the washing and ironing. She cooked only meals she could knock together as rapidly as possible and the store cupboard was emptying fast as she had delayed her weekly trip to the supermarket. She found that she resented anything that interfered with her book. And as she got out her paper and pens, she paused and smiled. She had not realised until now, but that stupid crying had stopped.

Kate read what she had done this morning in bed and the little she had managed this afternoon, and the pages she had ripped through while watching the vegetables cook for supper. They all joined together neatly. Her fear had been that working in this haphazard way the writing might be disjointed. She wanted to know what progress she was making. How long should a novel be? Was there an easier way to count the words than one by one? She should study *The Writer's Handbook*, that might clarify things. It would have to wait though, she could not do it now, she had words desperate to be put down.

Kate's euphoria vanished smartly at the next meeting of the circle. When it was her turn to read her work she explained that she had got somewhat carried away and had written thousands instead of hundreds of words. She smiled, expecting an avalanche of congratulations.

'The whole object of the exercise is discipline, Kate,' Felicity said, standing four square on the carpet, reminding Kate even more forcefully of her late headmistress. 'We could all write on and on, there's nothing special in that. I asked you for three hundred words for a reason – to teach you to write to a specified number. The Paradise Club is not interested in writers who write on and on. They want fifty thousand words and they expect fifty thousand words.' Kate felt herself redden as she saw Clarissa begin to smirk. 'What if you wrote a short story for *Hearthside* and instead of one thousand submitted two? What would happen? I'll tell you, rejection.' The last word boomed out.

'But I know now I don't want to write short stories.'

'Maybe, Kate, it would be a good idea for you to learn to walk before you can run. Now let us hear the first three hundred words of this opus, shall we?'

Kate began to read, diffidently at first, and then as the pleasure in what she had written took over, with growing confidence. She stopped after two pages.

'Well, yes,' Felicity started, after what seemed an age. 'As I said, you must be prepared to learn – there's plenty of room for it.'

Kate clutched her exercise book to her, horrified to find that she wanted to hit Felicity over the head with it.

'Bit purple in places, wasn't it?' Clarissa asked as she smoothed a piece of ancient material on the arm of a chair which she had just acquired. She was inordinately proud of it, but Kate had noticed it stank of cats.

'I can't put a name to it right away but I'm almost sure I've read that piece somewhere before,' Mavis said, smiling innocently at Kate.

As the criticisms mounted Kate felt hurt – not for herself, she realised, but for the book. She wanted to run out of the room, shut these horrible words out of her ears. She had believed she could take criticism but she could not. This was different, this was painful.

Later, as she and Pam drove away, she asked her friend if it had been that bad.

'Well,' said Pam, serious-faced. 'I think it was a bit wordy, if you know what I mean. It could have been condensed.'

'I don't see how,' Kate said despondently.

'That's why we joined. As Felicity said, we've a lot to learn – if we're willing to listen,' she added pointedly.

'At least they liked your piece,' Kate said. She had been surprised by that, she had not liked it herself but she had not said so, for she would not have put Pam through this agony.

'Yes, they did, didn't they? Mind you, I was as nervous as hell. I shan't be next time. It's so constructive, all of it, isn't it? I tell you, Kate, I really like this writing lark.'

Pam pulled up outside the house. Normally Kate would have invited her in for a snack lunch and a gossip. She did not, she had no time for gossip now. She excused herself, pleading too much housework. A rather stiff-faced Pam drew away from the kerb.

Once in the house Kate decided the ironing could wait; she would get something out of the freezer for supper. She would reread her work and see where she had gone wrong, where she could alter and improve it. It was childish and counter-productive to react to criticism as she had done. Pam was right, she must listen to others. She did not even bother to take off her coat. She sat down at the kitchen table, pushed aside the breakfast dishes that she had not had time to clear away this morning, and concentrated.

An hour later she looked up from her task. They were wrong, she was sure. All her misery was dispelled. This was good. It was not perfect yet, it could be improved – anything could be. But it had pace and interest. She could write!

The kitchen clock showed two. She had planned to go to Sainsbury's. Never mind, she would go tomorrow. This was more important. If she worked on until four she would still have plenty of time to clear up before Tony returned.

When she heard the front door slam she expected one of the children to come in. With a shock she saw it was dark outside. She looked up at the clock – it was five-thirty and the voice that called out from the hall was Tony's. She looked wildly about the chaotic kitchen. Hurriedly she began to load the dirty breakfast plates into the dishwasher, which was full of unloaded clean plates.

'Drat it,' she muttered as she squeezed the dirty ones in among them.

'What on earth have you got your coat on for? Is there something wrong with the central heating? Has the Aga gone out?' Tony was standing in the kitchen doorway.

'No, no, I've been out, just got back,' she half lied. 'I didn't realise it was so late. Where are the children?' she fretted.

'It's Wednesday or have you forgotten? Lucy's got drama and Steve's got football practice.' He stepped into the kitchen and glanced about him. 'Good God, what an unholy mess.'

'I know, I'm sorry, I stayed out too long . . .' she said, riddled with guilt. She flung a tea-towel on the table in a vain attempt to cover up her exercise books.

'You're not still doing that scribbling? I hope that doesn't mean we're all destined to starve?'

Kate began to relax. Something had happened, he was speaking to her and laughing as well.

'You're in a good mood,' she said and immediately regretted saying it, the implication was obviously that he normally was not.

'Yes, I am. And so will you be. Get changed, I'm taking you out, let the kids fend for themselves. We're celebrating.'

'Celebrating what?'

'My drink-driving charge. I had a phone call from the police today. They're dropping the charges. It would seem their equipment was faulty. They're confirming by letter tomorrow.'

'Tony, that's wonderful.'

'It is, isn't it? Leave all this, take a bath and we'll try that new Italian in Graintry. Fred says it's very good.'

'Shall we take a taxi?' she smiled up at him slyly.

'Perhaps we should,' he said, patting her on the rump. 'Cheeky!' But all Kate could think about was the worrying idea that he would want to return to her bed. How would she keep up her work?

18

Gloria was early for her appointment at the Gay Hussar. She had thought it the best tactic. This way, whoever had invited her would have to approach her, and it would be less embarrassing all round. She ordered a Perrier water while she waited, feeling it would be presumptuous to order a drink since she did not know who her host was. One only did that sort of thing with a good friend.

Several heads were raised in appreciation of the smart attractive woman seated by herself. She had gone to a lot of trouble to look right for this mysterious assignation. In fact she had even shopped especially for it – or that was what she told herself. She had on a short black dress by Jean Muir she had had some time, and her pride and joy, her new classic Armani jacket in pale yellow which she had been promising herself for years, and which she resolved to hide should her mother come to stay, as she often threatened. The truth was that she had not bought the Armani jacket just for this meeting, it had been a consolation too, something to cheer her up because Clive had not rung – but she preferred not to dwell on that sign of weakness.

She opened the menu and, to avoid the curious eyes of the others lunching, studied the choice intently. Maybe she would not have the soup, maybe she would have the boar's head brawn in aspic instead . . .

'Perrier, Gloria? Whatever next? Don't tell me you're on the wagon, that will never do.'

'Julius!' Her voice rang with pleasure and surprise. 'It was you!'

'Yes, it's me.' He shook his head, puzzled, as he took the chair opposite.

'I didn't recognise your voice, I should have, I know it well enough. But I was still groggy with sleep when you telephoned. I've been agog all this week wondering who it would be.' She laughed.

'Then I hope I'm not a disappointment?'

'Good gracious, no. I can't think of anyone I'd rather be with.' It was true, it was a rare woman who could resist Julius's particular charm. Charm that could make even the plainest woman think herself, for a moment, a raving beauty and the most important woman in the world. But even as she spoke her sharp mind was wondering why he had invited her. They were old friends but not lunching friends – that was business. Supper she would have understood.

Julius ordered them both dry martinis. He took a long time discussing the menu with her, consulting the waiter, before deciding what to order. He then took an even longer time pondering upon which wine to drink. He finally handed the menus to the hovering waiter, leant back in his chair, sipped his martini with appreciation, and smiled at her.

'You are so beautiful, Gloria. The colour of that jacket becomes you.' He was that rare creature, a man who could compliment a woman without it sounding sickening, false, or a come-on.

'Thank you. It's a consolation present to myself.' She laughed with pleasure.

'And why on earth have you need of consolation?'

'Men.' She shrugged her shoulders.

'Then they are fools. If I were only a few years younger . . .' He smiled and made a Gallic gesture of despair with his hands.

'I wish you were too,' Gloria said with more heartfelt expression than she had intended.

'You're unhappy?' he asked with concern.

'Not really. Nothing changes with me, Julius, still making silly mistakes where my heart is concerned. I'm feeling rather stupid, that would be a better description.'

'Still choosing the bad ones, then?'

'All the time.' She laughed.

'It's strange that some women always go for the wrong ones, time and time again, as if they never learn. Oddly too, I've noticed, it's invariably the more intelligent ones who do. It makes me think that maybe what we are led to believe is the ideal relationship is in fact too boring for words, and only bright women like yourself have gathered this.'

'Somewhere in there is a compliment – I think. And what were you, Julius?' She smiled at him.

'Me? I tried to be good but you know, Gloria, it's a very hard thing to do. I never meant to hurt anyone, but, unintentionally I always seemed to land up doing just that.'

'We'd have been made for each other.' Her laugh was a delight to hear. 'I get masses of advice – go for someone older, more settled. I try. But they never excite me, Julius. There'd be no challenge.'

'I understand totally, my dear. But I would not be your friend if I did not warn you that our way leads to much loneliness when you get to my age. But such philosophical talk is for after midnight and too much wine. Not lunchtime. It has earned us another martini, though, wouldn't you say?'

Julius ordered and they talked of little until the waiter had served them their drinks.

'Are you lonely, Julius?'

'I think I am, but I do begin to wonder if I say I am because the adventures are over, or whether, in truth, I might have been lonely all my life.'

'I can't believe that,' she said, but at the same time she shivered at how close to her own truth he was.

'You're not like most women. You haven't yet asked me why I invited you.' He changed the subject, sensing her discomfort.

'I presumed you would get around to telling me.'

'I asked you to find out if you would be interested in coming back to Westall's.'

'Me? But you don't publish what I'm good at. Westall's is too literary for my sort of list.'

'I'm planning a new imprint – popular women's fiction. You would have total editorial and budgetary control. Whatever Shotters is paying you and the rest. Car. No interference.' He leant back in his chair, smiled across the table and watched her absorbing this information that he had rattled at her like grapeshot.

'Popular women's fiction? Westall's? I can hardly believe it.'

'We should have gone along that path a long time ago. I've been too pigheaded to see it. Crispin has warned me time and time again. My ostrich attitude, my hoping always that we could go along as before, is why we are in the doldrums now.'

'They'll crucify you, Julius. Westall's publishing schlock? The heavens will fall in. It would be like a bishop becoming a pimp.' She shook her head at the very idea.

'I've never regarded what you do as producing schlock, Gloria. Women's fiction has always had an honourable place in English publishing. You're being over-sensitive to the literati and their sniping. Who's to say what is schlock and what isn't? And, in any case, I don't think a generation can judge what will and will not last. I've always said it takes the hindsight of at least fifty years to sort out the sheep from the goats. Look at Emily Brontë, none of her contemporary critics, who lambasted *Wuthering Heights*, would have dreamt it would now be regarded as a masterpiece, would they?'

'I know what you mean but I can't see anything written by Bella Ford being a set book in schools in fifty years' time.' She chuckled at the very idea.

'Maybe not her but who's to say that out there somewhere, scribbling away, there is not another Brontë?'

'Darling Julius. Always the dreamer. I remember you and your slush pile, each day certain you were going to find a priceless piece of literature in there.'

'I still do.'

'My genre is not so easy. The manuscripts come in droves but to find anything . . .' She shrugged at the endless frustrations of her work, the many disappointments when something that looked as if it might be good on page one had petered out by page fifty.

'You must keep faith, Gloria. Look at du Maurier, never out of print since thirty-eight. If you had been around then you would have stood as good a chance as any of discovering her.'

'You're preaching to the converted, Julius. It won't be me you'll have to persuade. It'll be the rest of the board, the booksellers wondering if Westall's is being serious and can really produce the bestsellers the public will want to buy, the reviewers who will tear them to shreds – simply because it is you doing it. Why, even your reps are going to hate it. They've always regarded themselves as a cut above everyone else for selling your books, or didn't you know?' She looked at him slyly: it was well known that the Westall's sales team behaved very much like the members of an exclusive gentlemen's club – for of course they had no women on the road, all the reps would have resigned *en masse* at the very suggestion. They did not use the hard sell with the booksellers like everyone else these days. Rather, they graciously dropped in for a chat about books, preferably over a glass of claret or a good sherry. The talk was that they were part of the reason Westall's was in the mess it was now.

'Revamping the sales team is the first of my priorities,' Julius said a shade defensively. He knew full well what they were like, but how could he complain when he felt very much the same? Bookselling should be a leisurely occupation, not the rat-race of pushiness it was becoming. He mentally shook himself at such an idea: thinking like that was why he was here, his resistance to change had caused all his problems.

'I could never work with Crispin. I'm sorry, I realise he's your nephew –'

'You wouldn't have to. I said this would be totally autonomous, an imprint within an imprint. You can choose the name for it, if you like.' He leant forward eagerly.

He was deadly serious, she realised. She began to feel excited. Back with Julius. No more committees, no more interference from jumped-up accountants. Lovely offices, total control . . .

'Julius, I can't.'

'I don't expect you to make your mind up here and now. It is obviously something that needs a lot of thought. I can assure you I'm not speaking about this to anyone else.'

'Julius, I think you should. It's a marvellous offer and one I would love to jump at. But, you see, I promised Peter Holt something the other day. I don't think I could go back on it, not to Peter.'

'Look, Gloria. Let's leave the offer on the table. Odd things happen in publishing. Well, that's over. Business out of the way. Did you order the wild cherry soup?'

'Yes. I starved all yesterday so I could have it.'

'Thank God I'm not a woman.' He laughed fondly at her.

19

If there was one thing Hilary Holt could not be faulted on, it was her style of entertaining. An invitation to a weekend at the Holts' country retreat was always welcome.

On this particular cold and wet early December evening, the house, standing in its own parkland, glowed with welcoming light from every window so that from a distance it looked like a giant doll's house lit up. Two cars, carrying the Pewters and the Westalls, had barely halted on the neatly raked gravel drive before the large imposing oak door opened and more light poured out onto the arriving guests.

A housekeeper ushered them into a large hall with a flagstoned floor on which were scattered antique rugs whose colour was intensified by the warm grey of the floor. The fine collection of highly polished oak furniture reflected the logs blazing in the ten-foot-wide fireplace. Large vases were full of out-of-season blooms and the air was scented with the sweet smell of burning wood and the lingering scent of lavender polish.

Hilary raced into the hall, hands held out in greeting, slightly breathless as if she had been running. She was dressed for riding, her slim figure made sexier than usual in the tight-fitting riding breeches and beautifully cut hacking jacket. There was much social kissing of the air in the vicinity of the guests' cheeks and cries of pleasure at their arrival. She showed them to their respective bedrooms where their luggage had already been stowed away.

The bedrooms were elegantly furnished. Fires glowed, flowers bloomed, fruit waited, polished, to be eaten. This month's magazines lay in serried, unsullied ranks. The drinks trays were complete down to ice, lemon, olives and the latest fashionable bottled water. The newest books from Shotters were on the bedside tables.

'Good God, this bang shoot must cost Holt a fortune,' Mike Pewter said, as he eased his bulk into an easy chair and began with one foot to ease the shoe off the other.

'Lovely curtains,' Lady Lily said.

'Bloody fortune,' he repeated. 'I don't see how he does it,' he added, with the puzzled air of one whose fortune is based on old money and, unable to comprehend the new, feels an illogical resentment towards it.

'You're not the only successful publisher, Mike my dear,' said his wife. 'Don't be so catty. Fortunes have to start somewhere.' Lily had an unnerving way of reading his mind

She opened one of the doors to find a bathroom containing an imposing Edwardian bath encased in shiny mahogany with brass taps burnished to reflect the bather. 'Just look at this bath, and we had all ours torn out. Now they're back in fashion again, how confusing. And so much Floris...' she exclaimed happily.

'It's her, I reckon. Not Peter. I can't see him wanting all this high-falutin' living,' Mike announced. 'It's a bit like one of those damned chintzy and oh-so-genteel country-house hotels, where you can't fart and it costs an arm and a leg to pretend you're a nob for a day.' Mike hauled himself out of the chair and in stockinged feet lumbered across the room to inspect what drinks were available. 'Laphroaig. My favourite.' And he poured himself a tumblerful, ignoring the ice and the water.

Lily was still exploring her quarters. 'It's so exciting, sleeping somewhere different, isn't it? Reminds me of when we were children and went on holiday, and finding everything new and strange.' She opened a second door to find that she and Mike had been allotted adjoining bedrooms. 'How very thoughtful,' she said. When staying with friends it always worried her that she might be expected to share an uncomfortable night with her overlarge husband. 'Are we here for any specific reason or is it purely social?'

'Julius is in a mess.'

'Again? Oh, the poor dear man. He deserves to succeed. You can always rely on one of his books to be all right – nothing nasty, if you know what I mean.'

'No fucking in them, you mean,' Mike bellowed. 'Soft porn makes money, though, that's the dilemma, or not, whichever way you look at it.'

'And you and Peter want to help. That's nice.'

'His greedy nephew is up to all manner of tricks. We thought he should be told.'

'Do you think that's wise, Mike? It's not a good idea to get involved with family problems. It only leads to trouble. You could get hurt.' Others who thought they knew him would have been surprised by this conversation, but few were aware that the loud rumbustious Mike was as sensitive as a shy maiden at times. Lily knew.

'I know there are risks, Lily. But we can't just stand by and see the poor old boy shafted. Especially by that slimy bastard Crispin.'

'It's not only the nephew you should be concerned about. His wife is greedy too, and more dangerous . . .'

Across the upstairs hallway Jane Westall was also exploring her room. But she did so in a far more ruthless manner than Lily Pewter. The curtains were inspected, the quality of their fabric, their linings, whether they had been correctly weighted with lead shot. She lifted the bowl of fruit to see its maker's mark. She pinged the glasses to check if they were crystal. She fingered the flowers to make sure they were not silk. She seemed almost disappointed that she could find nothing false.

'It's nice to see some publishers know how to make money,' she said icily.

Julius, inured to years of his wife's carping, poured himself a large Glenfiddich and thought how kind it was of Peter to remember his particular favourite.

'If you had had the courtesy to ask, I would have said I'd like a dry sherry.'

'I'm sorry. I didn't think you would want one – a bit too early for you,' Julius said pointedly, measuring out the sherry.

'It's not too early for you so why should it be for me?' she said sharply. 'It's all desperately *nouveau*, don't you think? A little too perfect.' She waved her hand to encompass the beautiful room.

'I think it's all very nice. They have gone to a lot of trouble.' His voice had the resigned quality of one who had had this conversation many times before.

'He can afford to.'

'Then good luck to him.' Julius downed his drink, poured another and, noting the disapproving expression on his wife's face, topped it up making it even larger. Such little victories gave him inordinate pleasure, he had discovered.

'Did you notice Hilary didn't smell of horse at all? She hadn't been near a horse, that's what I reckon. She was just dressed up like that to impress.'

'Really?' Julius did not even bother to argue with her. What was the point?

'Why are we here?' she asked, taking the sherry.

'Does there have to be a reason?'

'Hilary would not be wasting her time on us if there was not a reason. We're not rich or important enough for her.'

'I'm sure it's just social,' he said. He went into the bathroom and turned on the taps. 'Mind if I bathe first?' he called. He did not really want or need a bath, having showered in his flat before they had left London. But in here he could get away from the sound of her voice and the bitterness that dripped on him like a Chinese water torture.

He began to lay out the silver-backed brushes given him by his godfather at his coming-of-age and rebristled so many times he had lost count. Of course it was not purely social. Pewter and Holt had something up their sleeves. They had been approached by Crispin, after he had had access to the share register, after he had heard of Julius's visit to the doctor, before he had approached Simon. He knew all that – a tearful and repentant Roz had confessed to him. He had reassured the girl, for what could Crispin do for the moment . . . He shuddered at 'for the moment' and then put the thought of his own death to the back of his mind. Crispin had no shares and his brother was unlikely to ignore Julius's advice and sell to him. Simon had always listened to Julius even when they were young. He lowered himself into the warm water, his glass of Glenfiddich close at hand. After all, there was always the Lepanto Trust, his own personal defence.

In the master bedroom Hilary was sitting at her dressing table staring vacantly into her looking-glass, displeasure writ large on her face.

'If you have to invite your publishing cronies you could at least have invited someone interesting.'

'I thought you liked the Pewters – you accept their hospitality often enough,' Peter said, twisting to right and left, trying to see around her and into the same mirror, to check his bow tie was straight.

'Mike is a buffoon with the manners of a pig and Lily talks only about her charities, her flaming garden or her smelly dogs. You should keep anything to do with publishing in London. I don't mind helping you out there – it's my duty – but not here.'

'But why, Hilary? I can't switch off just because it's the weekend.'

'It bores me rigid.'

'It didn't bore you once . . .' Peter began, and then thought better of it. 'It pays for everything,' he said, equably enough.

'But why couldn't I have had a big dinner tomorrow? Invite an interesting mix?' She was wheedling now. 'We still could. I could phone up, say there had been a change in your plans – the Websters wouldn't mind, nor the Flynns – they're always good for a laugh. What do you say?' She had brightened up at this idea and was already reaching for her fat Filofax. Peter laid his hand over it to prevent her from picking it up.

'No. I want a quiet weekend with my two friends discussing business. I don't want the Websters here, let alone the Flynns. To tell you the truth, Hilary, your friends bore me as much as mine obviously do you.'

'Well, we know where we stand then, don't we?' she said, turning round abruptly and looking at herself in the mirror again.

'What does that mean?'

'I'll hostess for you this time but it's the last. So don't repeat it, not unless I can have my friends too.' And she concentrated on her make-up. 'And one other thing,' she said, as Peter moved to leave the room. 'No business tonight, I'm sure the other wives don't want it. I'll take the women to Graintry tomorrow, look at the shops or something. You can talk then.'

'Thanks, Hilary. And about tomorrow evening, if that's what you really want, invite who you like.'

'There. I knew you would see sense in the end. Gracious, the others might be bored to tears too. What a silly you are.' Already she was picking up the telephone.

*

On the Saturday morning with the women away on their shopping trip to Graintry, Peter would normally have suggested they take a walk. But, knowing Mike's aversion to exercise of any description, he suggested they meet in his study for a mid-morning coffee. He had grinned at them as he suggested this, knowing full well the coffee would only be drunk by himself. How the other two could drink mid-morning and still function was a mystery to him.

His guests were now settled in comfortable wing chairs, glasses in hand with whisky bottles close by. Peter stood with his back to the fire. He had worried about what to say to Julius, but decided that the truth and no prevarication was the best approach.

'Julius, I invited you here under false pretences. Mike and I want to talk business with you – your business.'

'Oh, yes? Can't say I'm that surprised.'

'Business is bad at the moment for everyone, but Mike and I know that you've been harder hit than most.'

'You could say that.' Julius smiled good-naturedly.

'The truth is, Julius, we have both been approached by Crispin with an offer to sell Westall and Trim.'

'I know. Bloody little fool . . .'

'You know?'

'Yes.' Julius did not explain further.

'And you've spoken to him?' Mike asked, leaning his considerable bulk forward in his chair.

'No.'

'Don't you think it would be wise to?' Peter was sitting now.

'Why? There's nothing he can do.'

'Well, he must think he can, or he wouldn't be bothering, would he?' Mike asked logically.

'He approached my brother Simon, offered to buy his twenty per cent shareholding. I advised him not to sell – Simon will listen to me. I told him that when I pop my clogs those shares will be worth a fortune to him, but not now.'

'You're not thinking of retiring, then? It was the only reason we could think of for him moving now,' Peter said tactfully.

'You're not ill, are you? Been given the proverbial life sentence?' Mike, lacking Peter's finesse, jumped in.

'I'll die in harness.' Julius side-stepped the question. 'I'm resigned to the business being sold when I'm dead – I can only protect it so far. But while I'm alive it continues. I've got the odd plan.'

'Look, Julius, we both want to see Westall and Trim last, even when you're no more. I know I'm a fine one to talk, the way Shotters gobbles up other publishers. But your firm is different. It's always been there, one of the last of the old-time independents. It's a part of everyone's heritage really, like the Crown Jewels.'

'It's a nice sentiment, Peter. But I don't see how.'

'Peter and I were wondering if you would sell us your shares,' Mike began. 'We could have it all tied up, no funny business, so that we, in turn, could not sell – maybe set up some sort of trust just so that it remains independent.'

'And who would run it?'

'Now? Why, you, of course, just carry on as you are.'

Julius looked long and hard into the fire. He closed his eyes so that the others could not see how close to tears their offer had brought him.

'It's a wonderful offer and a tempting one. But, gentlemen, I can't. Westall's is my responsibility and I could not let anyone else own it – even if it was token. And in any case how could I let such good friends risk their money?' Julius laughed.

'The offer's there, Julius.'

'Thanks, Mike. I've got my plans though. Maybe they'll work, maybe they won't. But I've got to give them a try. And as I explained, there's no panic at the moment. Crispin can't do anything – my family knows which side its bread is buttered on.'

'There is one thing you don't seem to have thought of, Julius,' Peter said kindly. 'He's trotting around all over London. We know for certain now that Tudor's have seen the figures. Who else has he shown them to? If it got out how bad things were you could begin to lose your best authors and then what would you do?'

'Tudor's too? I didn't know that. I thought it was just you two and I knew neither of you would do anything without consulting me. You're right, though, I shall have to talk to them – especially Sally Britain and Walters. If they went then the game would well and truly be up.'

For the next couple of hours they talked of publishing, the love of all their lives and a subject which never palled. Before lunch Julius went for a solitary walk.

He might be being stupid but he couldn't help himself. It had been a generous offer, but would it have worked? Fine while those two were alive but what then, what would their heirs get up to? He had been in business long enough to know there was not an agreement made that a clever lawyer could not find a way round. He could not, after all this time, run Westall's, worry about it, and it not be his. No, that was not the way.

Hilary's Saturday evening party was a success, as far as she was concerned. The others were not so sure. Her friends were a noisy crowd, especially Pinkers Flynn. Peter had disliked Pinkers the moment he had met him. There was that stupid name for a start, given because pink gin was his favourite tipple. But there was an oily charm about the Irish bloodstock dealer that irritated him. He did not know if he was successful or if he was a con-man – he was not sure why but he sensed the latter. But the party hat put Hilary into a good mood and she appeared to be almost sad when they said goodbye to their guests after Sunday lunch.

*

Jane was mostly silent on the drive home but Julius felt elated at the good friends he had in Mike and Peter: discovering something like that gave one a lift never to be forgotten. But once in the house he was tired with a tiredness that was new to him. Last night had been noisy and late and his days of loud parties were long since gone. There were two urgent messages for him, left on the pad beside the telephone by the cleaning lady. His life had been full of such calls and it was one reason he refused to have an answering machine in his home: experience had taught him they were never as urgent as the caller implied, and certainly not on a Sunday. He needed to sleep, if only for half an hour – he felt he could barely stand.

'I think I'll take a short nap,' he said.

'As you please. It will be cold cuts for supper.'

'I don't think I want anything – too bloody tired.'

'You must eat,' Jane said sharply.

An hour later, refreshed from his sleep and before his supper, he called the first of the numbers, his brother Simon, back from Tuscany.

'Julius. I'm glad you called. I've done it.'

'Done what, Simon?'

'Decided to sell my shares to Crispin.'

Julius had been standing holding the telephone. He felt blindly behind him for a chair. The room, momentarily, had become foggy and seemed to be listing to one side. He took a deep breath.

'Why, Simon?'

'Dulcett and I are getting on. We've found this wonderful house in Tuscany. And, well . . . we fell in love with it.'

'You haven't told him?'

'Yes, I have. I couldn't get hold of you. No answer when I rang – and I did, Julius, all Friday evening and yesterday. Yesterday a cleaning woman answered, said she had popped in to feed the cat and she didn't know where you were. You see, the problem was urgent, the owners of the house had other people interested – they had to know I was definitely on by this weekend. I promised, you see.'

'Didn't it strike you, Simon, that people selling houses often say things like that?'

'I know. But it could have been genuine. So I got hold of Crispin. John told me to. When I couldn't get hold of you I rang him. John said I would be a fool not to accept. He is your son, after all. I could not imagine him advising me in any way that would damage you.'

'I could,' Julius said, but so softly Simon would not have heard. 'You do realise there has to be a special meeting to confirm that the other shareholders agree – there has to be a majority in agreement?'

'Yes, I knew all that. And it's all right. I called Marge and I spoke to Jane an hour ago – she said you were tired and having a sleep. You should watch yourself at your age, Julius. They've all agreed. What's more they think it would be a good idea for Crispin to be on the board. That only leaves you, Julius. You won't let me down, I'm certain of that.'

'I wish, Simon, that for your own sake you had listened to me. The company would be worth a fortune if sold outright.'

'I know that, Julius. I'm not totally stupid – could go for millions of pounds. But would I ever see a penny of it? That's what I had to ask myself. Don't forget I'm older than you. You could live for ever.' Simon laughed.

Julius was too fond of his brother to tell him the truth. He listened while Simon babbled on about his farmhouse, the plans he and Dulcett had for it. He even heard himself accepting an invitation to go and stay. When the call was finally over he did not stop to collect his thoughts. All he felt was betrayal and anger and a growing fear for the firm he loved.

'You stupid, arrogant woman,' he shouted at his wife when he eventually found her in the conservatory tending her plants. Julius, who never normally shouted and so rarely lost his temper, was shaking with the violence he felt growing inside him.

'What do you mean, raising your voice at me in such a way?' Jane said with indignation.

'Why didn't you wake me? Why didn't you discuss this with me?' He was pacing the conservatory, hitting one hand into the palm of the other with impotent rage when it was his wife's face he longed to strike.

'Because I already knew what your answer would be,' Jane said, stepping behind a table, putting it between her and this uncharacteristically furious husband. 'Your brother is fast becoming a liability,' she added quickly. 'You don't think that dreadful gypsy creature he lives with would have stayed with him much longer in view of the financial mess he's in? She would have been out searching for another mate before it was too late . . . before what's left of her looks – '

'Shut up, shut up!' he yelled. 'Why do you have to denigrate everything? Dulcett's a good woman, she truly loves him . . .' He sat down on a bench and put his head in his hands, feeling the energy draining from him, feeling defeated.

Jane squared her shoulders, taking control again.

'You and I would have ended up supporting Simon, something we can ill afford to do. He might even have hoped to move in here with us. Well, no thank you, Julius. Not if there's an alternative, as there is. This way he is set up for the rest of his life, and no doubt Dulcett will stay with him in the hope of getting something out of it when he eventually dies. I think we owe Crispin a large thank-you. What's more, I did it for your own good. You might not see that now, but you will eventually.'

'God, how you must hate me.' He looked at her with horror. 'I knew you did, but not this much. I'm going to London.'

'When should I expect you back?' The question was asked with no interest, it was a mere formality, and she turned back to the flower she had been tending when he had first walked in.

'Never!' And he turned on his heel and walked from the conservatory, walked out of the house he had juggled his finances so hard to keep for Jane. Tired as he was, he took the car out of the garage and drove round to the front of the house. He put the headlights full on and let them play on the carefully pruned and nurtured roses in his garden. He said goodbye to them and then, berating himself for being sentimental, swung the car round and drove at a furious pace down the long sweeping drive.

He had driven ten miles or so, his anger slipping away from him at every passing mile, when he pulled the car over on to the side of the road and switched off the engine. He sat, hunched over the steering wheel, staring into the darkness beyond. What on earth was he doing, hurtling off into the night, having a maudlin conversation with his roses? At his age, with so little time left, what was the point in running away? Nothing was different, Jane was behaving as she always did, jumping at any opportunity which might present itself to annoy him. He had lived with her long enough to be able to weather it until the end.

He switched on the engine again. In any case, why should he leave his roses? He turned the car round and headed home.

He met Jane in the hall. She ignored him, made no comment that he had changed his mind. That was the only moment he wavered, thinking how nice it would be to shock her out of her smug complacency. But no, it was not worth it, time was too short for stupid games.

He entered his study. And he called the second number.

'You left an urgent message for me, Roz?'

'Mr Westall, thank you for calling.' Roz, he was sure, was crying.

'What's the matter Roz?'

'Mr Westall, I've done a dreadful thing. I can't sleep worrying about it. I should have told you everything. You see, it wasn't just the share certificates I showed Crispin. Oh, Mr Westall, you'll never forgive me, I showed him the copy of your will.'

For the second time that night Julius sat down hard on a chair. He was conscious of his heart pounding painfully in his chest, and once again watched the familiar room become unstable.

'Mr Westall, are you there?'

'Yes, I'm here, Roz,' he managed to say, but fighting for breath.

'I'll resign, of course.'

Still he said nothing.

'He promised to marry me . . .' He heard Roz wail.

'Poor Roz. Your resignation won't be necessary,' he said and wearily replaced the receiver. Maybe he should have accepted her resignation, punished her for her treachery. But it would mean training another secretary in his ways and with so little time left he could not be bothered.

Once the call was over, Julius found he was no longer tired. He took pen and paper and sat a long time making notes and calculations. He then dialled a west country number, apologised for the lateness of the call and spoke on the telephone for some time.

20

It was Tony coming back from work at lunchtime on Friday that made Kate realise he was not happy with her weekend plans. Since her announcement that she was going he had said nothing about it, not even when they had made up their quarrel. Nor had he commented when, after breakfast, she had kissed him goodbye. He never came home for lunch.

'How do I get in touch with you if there's an emergency?' he asked, as he watched her put her case in the hall, ready for when Pam came to pick her up.

'What emergency could there possibly be?' She laughed, she hoped encouragingly, as she moved briskly into the kitchen.

'Something might happen to the children.'

'Oh, Tony, don't even say such things!' This was emotional blackmail, she thought, touching wood all the same. 'I've left the number of the hotel. You'll call me just as I would if you were away on business. After all, you go away yourself often enough and the house hasn't fallen down, has it?'

'I go away for business. I don't go away for pleasure,' he parried.

She turned to face him. 'Please, Tony, don't spoil this for me.'

'I'm not spoiling anything. I'm just saying the truth. When have you known me do something like this?'

She could have reminded him of the time he had gone to Spain with Freddy to watch some golf, or the time he had gone to Liverpool with friends to see the Grand National. She did not say anything, she knew better, he would only claim that both outings had been strictly 'business'.

'If you're beginning to feel guilty about going away that's your problem, not mine.' He stood leaning against the Aga, arms folded, his bottom lip thrust slightly forward giving him a petulant look, something he did when he was not getting his own way.

'I don't feel guilty, why should I?' she said staunchly. She had not, but he was beginning to make her feel just that. 'Look, I've left instructions for everything, you can't go wrong between you.' She showed him the lists she had written out for when various dishes should be taken from the deep freeze, how long they would take to defrost, their cooking times. 'And I've put a beef casserole in the lower oven which will be ready by seven. Here's the hotel's number. Now, have I got everything?'

'What I don't understand is why you want to spend time with a load of catty women.'

'At least they're women, you've no cause to complain on that score,' she said, checking the contents of her handbag for the umpteenth time.

'Don't go, Kate,' he said softly yet urgently.

'Oh, come on, Tony. Why ever not? You're behaving as if I was going away for weeks. You'll enjoy yourself without me around. You can spend the whole weekend locked in the study.' She smiled brightly, aware it was probably too bright. She was rescued by the loud tooting of a car horn outside. 'There's Pam, best not keep her waiting.' She stood on tiptoe to kiss him but he averted his face. 'Have it as you want,' she said sharply. If guilt had begun to take root, such a childish action on his part had wiped it all away. 'I'll phone this evening.'

'If you can find the time.'

'Goodbye, then.'

'Goodbye,' he mumbled grudgingly.

Kate had never shut the door of her house with such a sense of relief before. She ran down the path almost as if she was afraid he would follow and persuade her back. Pam was waiting in their large Mercedes. Tracey, to Kate's surprise, was in the back, complete with her Tesco carrier bag.

'Poor Tracey was going to go by coach so I offered her a lift,' Pam explained, once all the hellos were over.

'You should have seen my kids' faces when Pam arrived in this. I tell you, my standing on the estate rose.'

'Have you been to one of these weekends before?' Kate asked her as Pam manoeuvred the large car round in a three-point tum.

'Only once, two years ago – I can't afford more often. It's fun, everyone talking books. I wanted to come this time especially because one of the speakers is an editor from The Paradise Club. I want to try and nab her, show her my stuff.'

'You and most of the others, I shouldn't wonder,' Pam said.

'Yeah, I know, that's the problem. I raided the electricity meter so I can buy her a couple of drinks in the bar.'

'Who's looking after the children?' Kate asked.

'My Sean. He's on the dole so it isn't as if he's got anything better to do.'

'How long have you been going to Felicity's circle?' Kate enquired.

'Couple of years. I used to go to the one at Ferrington, then a year ago she started the one at Little Moreton, so I joined that – it's nearer, saves on the bus fares.'

'How many circles does she run?' Kate asked with surprise, she had presumed that theirs was the only one.

'Five. One for each day of the week.'

'Good Lord. How does she find the time to write, then?' Pam asked, concentrating on the road and them at the same time.

'Evenings, I suppose, like the rest of us.'

Both Kate and Pam looked embarrassed at this. It was women like Tracey with no money and little hope who, more than anything else, made Kate despise herself for being discontented.

'But she's successful, look at the number of books she's had published,' Pam pointed out.

'Her? She's as poor as a church mouse. That publisher she's with, Perry Lock, is a bastard. Don't get into his hands whatever you do,' Tracey said knowledgeably.

'What's wrong with him?' The other two asked in unison.

'He pays peanuts for a book. Sure, he promises you royalties on top of the couple of hundred he gives as an advance. Trouble is, he never prints enough for you ever to earn any royalties and never reprints – smart, isn't it?'

'Then how does he make his money?' Kate asked, puzzled.

'Volume, sheer volume – hundreds of women like Felicity, desperate to see their name in print. It costs him bugger all to produce the book. He uses lousy paper and the covers are a laugh. So deduct the pathetic cost of producing the book, Felicity's pathetic advance and the rest is sheer profit. Multiply that by the number he's churning out every year and he's making a nice little bundle.'

'How do you know so much about it?'

'I try to find out. I've learnt one thing, if you want to make money you've got somehow to go mainstream publishing or The Paradise Club – there's bugger all else.'

'Are Felicity's books any good?' Pam asked.

'Crap.'

'And what's so good about The Paradise Club?' Kate asked. Like everyone else she had seen the books everywhere, not just in bookshops but filling stations, at the supermarket check-outs, even in chemists.

'They're a different kettle of fish altogether. For a start, they pay ten times what Lock does as an advance for a book the same length. They sell in thousands so you stand a chance of royalties once your name is known by the readers. And then they sell abroad, and you really can get rich. *Then* it's Isle of Man time.' Tracey laughed.

'I must buy some, read them, see how it's done.' Pam chuckled.

'It's hard to get accepted – everyone's trying. But once you're in, they look after you real proper and advise you how to look after your money. I've given myself five years to crack it. Then it's growing mushrooms or raising angora rabbits for me.'

'I think you'll make it. I think you're good, certainly the best in our circle,' Kate said, askew in her seat so that she could see Tracey better.

'Thanks, Kate, but I don't agree. I'd say you were the best by far.'

'Me?' Kate was astonished.

'Yes, didn't you know? Don't you feel it inside you? You should.'

'But the others, they said – '

'You don't want to take any notice of them. They're jealous. The worse they are about your work the better you know it is. If they like it, forget it. Mind if I smoke, Pam?'

'I'm surprised you can afford it if your husband's on the dole,' Pam said sharply, her pretty face marred by a shrewish expression.

'Ta,' said Tracey, blithely ignoring the tone of Pam's voice as she got out a tin of tobacco and began to roll a cigarette. Oh dear, thought Kate, poor Tracey had forgotten the praise heaped on Pam. And then she saw Tracey wink at her and she was not so sure.

'What about Clarissa?' Kate asked, hurriedly changing the subject.

'What a pseud!' Tracey rolled her eyes heavenward. 'She thinks she's a literary writer. That absentminded crap is all part of her image. Mind you, I think she could do it, but it's more likely to be along Felicity's path than a contract with Westall and Trim.'

'I met Julius Westall at a party the other week.'

'You did *what?*' Tracey shrieked.

'You never said,' Pam said accusingly.

'I didn't think. I mean, it's not as if any of us are going to be published by him, are we?'

'But he's a publisher. I'd sell my soul to meet a publisher.' Tracey sighed. 'Crikey. I know someone who's met Julius Westall!' Kate noticed Pam's hands tighten on the steering wheel.

'What did you think of Bella's book?' she asked in a somewhat irritated tone.

'Were we supposed to read it?' Kate swung round to look at Pam.

'I told you. I said she would be there, and we were to read *Troubled Nights* for group discussion.'

'No, I haven't. Oh, God, what's it about?' Kate felt herself beginning to panic – she remembered that feeling from years back when she had not done her homework.

For the rest of the journey in her precise and analytical way Tracey gave a complete rundown on *Troubled Nights* for Kate.

The seaside hotel had the sad and seedy air peculiar to such places out of season. Not even the rather garishly decorated Christmas tree helped to lift the mood of the place. It smelt of stale tobacco trapped in unaired rooms with an overlay of beer and cabbage. The carpet in the entrance hall was so brightly coloured and heavily patterned it gave warning of worse décor to come. The wall lights, with tasselled parchment shades, had hunting scenes embossed upon them which shed as little light as possible. A harassed receptionist was at a small desk built into an alcove decorated with plastic Doric columns. She was trying, single-handed, to sort out the requirements of twenty women who had all managed to arrive at the same time. She was not helped by the reappearance of half the thirty she had already dispatched to their bedrooms coming back to complain they were not satisfied.

Kate and Pam sat on their cases and decided to wait for the rush to subside. Again, Kate had that strange feeling of being back at school, but a new school for most of the others were shrieking at each other with tribal cries of recognition.

There was only a sprinkling of young women. Several of them had welcomed Tracey with open arms and she had long since disappeared. They glimpsed Felicity in the corner, standing beneath a niche with polystyrene Regency architrave, which held a rigid arrangement of plastic flowers. She was regally holding court. Mavis was standing beside her like an attendant unsure of her role in life and nervous that, not knowing, she might get everything wrong. Her face lit up when she saw Kate and Pam and she sidled over, apologising to everyone and even the furniture as she made her way. Clarissa had not come, she told them, a large house party was descending on her.

'I bet. Couldn't afford it, more like,' Pam muttered.

Everybody was in pairs as if they lacked the courage to come alone. But what impressed Kate and Pam most was how intelligent the women looked. And Kate pointed out how well dressed everyone was but Pam, more expert in these matters, could not agree.

'New girls?'

They both looked up to find a confident-looking woman with black hair pulled back dramatically into a severe bun and dressed in scarlet chiffon, which matched exactly the red of her lipstick. Red, that's the colour, Kate made a mental note. 'I'm Siobhan Appsley, course organiser. Welcome,' she said in the measured tones of an actress and held out her hand. Both Kate and Pam leapt to their feet. 'Any problems, any queries, you come to me. You promise?' she said smiling, and they both felt themselves engulfed in a great wave of charm.

'Promise,' they obediently said in unison.

'You'll find your folders in your rooms giving the times when you should be where. Please try not to be late, we've a tight schedule to get through.'

'Of course,' they muttered, before Siobhan whisked herself away to welcome the stragglers.

'It's all very professional, isn't it?' said Kate. It was dawning on both of them that everyone here was very serious about the business in hand.

As soon as they were in their room and had sorted out who was to sleep in which bed – decided finally by a toss of a coin since both were too polite to opt for the bed by the window – Pam had her case open and a bar set up on the dressing table.

'Doug doesn't mind what I spend but woe betide me if I use the mini-bar – they're a right rip-off,' she said, as she poured them both large gins and tonic in the plastic tooth mugs from the bathroom.

'There isn't one.'

'Good job I brought the booze, then, isn't it?'

They sat on the beds with shoes off and went through their folders. The party was to be divided into four groups and they had been separated: Pam was in the 'Catherine Cookson' section, Kate in 'Danielle Steele', Tracey was in 'Shiel de Tempera' and Felicity in 'Jilly Cooper'.

'You wait. One day they'll have a Kate Howard group.'

'Or a Pam Homerton.'

'Never. I shall use a *nom de plume*. I thought about Emma Peel.'

'You can't use that, she was in *The Avengers*.'

'You know, I thought it sounded familiar when I chose it. What about you?'

'I think I'll stick to my own name. After all, it's got a right royal ring about it.'

Kate fretted over what to wear – the others were so smart. Pam had brought two cases of clothes with her and it really did not matter what she chose, for everything in them was delectable. Kate finally, on Pam's advice, selected a dark green velvet A-line skirt, which helped make her hips look less bulky, and a black jumper. Pam lent her a large Paisley throw in bright reds, blues and greens which quite transformed the outfit.

'You should wear brighter colours, Kate. You always go for the mousy dull shades and with your good skin you can get away with the more vibrant stuff.'

'You think so?' Kate said, so pleased with the compliment that the implied criticism of her wardrobe went unnoticed.

Pam herself chose a stunning black silk tuxedo with a huge spider diamanté brooch on the lapel.

'You look a star!' Kate exclaimed admiringly.

'So do you, my sweet. Ready?'

In the bar their fears that no one would speak to them proved unfounded. Everyone was welcoming, and all the talk was of books, agents and publishers and how to get into mainstream publishing and see your books at airports and WH Smith. As novices they listened attentively, absorbing all this new information. They could both have been excused for believing that there was a conspiracy out there in the big book world to stop anyone ever getting published. They heard, wide-eyed, tales of manuscripts going missing and publishers denying they had ever been received, of manuscripts having to be chased up after months, if not years, of no news, of manuscripts that everyone else had said were marvellous being rejected twenty, thirty, forty times by stupid publishers. They even heard one poor soul tell how, having had her book accepted, the publishers went bust and she had not seen a penny. They listened to complaints that only famous people were ever asked to submit novels, taking the bread out of the mouths of honest hard-working writers like themselves. There were assurances that someone who knew someone who knew another who really knew had told them that the slush piles were never touched, the manuscripts in them were merely held for a decent time and then sent back unread. And, they were told, a publisher would not consider you unless you had an agent but, then, no agent was interested unless you had been published. Therefore, those still unaccepted appeared to be trapped in a hopeless circle of frustrated ambition.

If publishers were not popular, agents were given even shorter shrift. 'Cowboys', 'sharks', 'bloodsuckers' were the most common descriptions they heard. Even those who had acquired one of these selective and elusive creatures did not seem to have anything good to say about them.

Kate found it difficult to believe everything she heard. If it were so, she would not read in her newspaper of new writers and first novels – which she did, quite often. She was left with the distinct impression that should one of these 'parasite' agents appear, there was not a woman in the room who would not lie down and die for the privilege of being represented by him or her.

They had wrongly presumed that everyone was a professional writer: they were not alone in being unpublished, and several like themselves had never submitted a thing in their lives and were just beginning.

It was at this point that the secretary of the Red Rose Society invited them to become probationary members, apologising that only published writers were entitled to full membership. Kate had never belonged to any society in her life, apart from the PTA and that did not count since it was duty. She glowed with pride as she signed her application form. She was being taken seriously.

In the dining room a hush fell when Siobhan entered shepherding her party of guest speakers to a central table where the flowers, unlike all the others, were real.

Kate recognised Bella Ford from the times she had seen her on television and in magazine interviews. Though rather hippy she was smaller than Kate had expected and the red curly hair was less ginger than on TV. The prettiness was of the faded type – too doll-like to be compatible with wrinkles. To compensate she had used a touch too much make-up which accentuated the lines rather than minimised them. But she smiled all the time, such a warm smile that Kate felt herself respond to it immediately as if the smile was just for her. She was dressed entirely in lilac, scattered with sequins, and had several long toning chiffon scarves around her neck which floated behind her as she walked to her table.

'Bet she's got one of those crinoline ladies over her bog paper,' Pam whispered. 'And a fluffy toilet-seat cover. And hasn't she put on weight?'

'I wouldn't know. She looks very sweet,' Kate said, feeling quite defensive towards a woman she did not know.

'Sweet? That one?' Pam snorted. 'Those fluffy, oh-so-feminine types are usually as hard as nails.'

'Who are the others?' she asked Tracey, sitting the other side of her.

'The one in black is Faith Cooper, she's Bella's agent. Old dyke, if you ask me,' Tracey said, a shade too loudly for comfort.

Faith was also in a black tuxedo suit but, better endowed than razor-slim Pam, the effect was not nearly as successful. She was tall with hair cut strikingly short but more magenta than the deep chestnut one presumed she had aimed for. She strutted in and smiled at no one. Following her was a quiet-looking, neatly dressed woman in a plain pale blue wool dress, with a small stock-pin at the neckline and a pleasant intelligent face, who reminded Kate of a Sunday-School teacher.

'That's Ann Cuthbert, she's the senior editor at The Paradise Club. She looks approachable, doesn't she?' Tracey whispered.

'Very,' Kate assured her.

After dinner, a welcoming talk from Siobhan, a lecture by Faith on public lending and foreign rights, delivered at such speed it was doubtful if anyone understood one word, Kate was tired.

'If you don't mind, Pam. I've got to telephone Tony. I think I'll stay in the room and go to bed,' she said, as everyone headed for the bar.

'Party pooper.' Pam laughed as she followed the others.

She let the telephone ring and ring but nobody was at home. That's odd, she thought as she turned off the light but was too tired to think further about it.

By the middle of the following morning Kate was in the swing of things and thoroughly enjoying herself. The weekend had been divided into lectures followed by workshops when, in their groups, they worked on various exercises set them by Siobhan. The guest speakers moved about these groups in turn, sitting listening, offering advice and help when necessary. Kate was impressed by how helpful everyone was, those with most experience advising beginners like herself. So much for Tony and his 'catty women' remark. She would have pleasure in letting him know how wrong he was. Criticism here was constructive, not hurtful as it was at Felicity's and soon her notebook was half full of hints and suggestions. In the breaks groups gathered around the guest speakers, hanging on their every word.

They had just finished one seminar in which Kate had read a chunk of her work. Reading aloud at the writers' circle had been bad enough, but this was far worse. Professional writers had been listening to her, and the presence of Faith, the agent, sitting at the back of the room, apparently intent on every word, had not helped. She had been so frightened by the whole ordeal that when the session ended she headed straight for the bar and had a quick whisky, which she downed in one, before going to the lecture hall for one of the high spots of the whole weekend – the lecture to be given by Bella Ford.

Everyone sat tense and excited, notebooks open, pens poised, and Bella, as if sensing this, smiled at them, making them relax.

'It was only a few years ago and I was one of you, hoping, praying to succeed. If I can, you can. Believe in yourself . . .' Her lecture began.

The room was silent except for the scribbling of fifty pens and pencils as copious notes were taken, as if any word might, just might, be the one containing the secret of the Holy Grail: how to be accepted. And how to be as successful and rich as Bella, for those who had been published but were, as yet, earning only a pittance.

She spoke of plot, and 'hooks', and pace and 'page turnability', which

made Kate feel more amateur than ever. She repeated constantly the importance of the first sentence, the first paragraph, the first page. She said how
essential was research, she likened it to the hidden part of an iceberg in
relation to a good book. She told of planning, of making in-depth character
profiles before a word was written. 'Know everything about your heroine. Did
she have measles as a child? Does she like champagne or does it make her
burp? Does she like horses, dogs? What colours does she prefer? Build her up.
Create her. Play God.' Bella lectured on with enthusiasm, eyes sparkling,
scarves whirling, hands waving dramatically. She explained her own filing
system as if imparting the secret of the runes. At length she made them privy
to her working methods, the discipline, the necessary routine. And the whole
lot made Kate slump with despondency. How on earth had she had the
presumption to think that she could write a novel, given her slap-dash
approach, her total lack of routine? How could her method of simply writing
whatever came into her head, of not knowing what the next sentence would
be, let alone the next chapter or the end, ever work?

Kate was the odd one out, the others poured out from the lecture
rejuvenated, fired with hope and optimism, buzzing with excitement. The
noise level, as they took their lunch, was deafening. Siobhan smiled at her
flock knowingly. She had seen this so many times – an author's enthusiasm
for her trade transferring itself to her listeners by mental osmosis.

Kate was helping herself to coffee in the bilious yellow residents' lounge,
overcrowded with tasselled gold Dralon chairs that did not quite tone with
the walls, when she was joined by Faith Cooper, dressed today in grey pin-
stripes.

'I liked that piece you read out this morning,' she said to Kate as she
poured her coffee from the Cona machine.

'Thanks.' Kate could feel herself blushing to her roots.

'Have you any work finished?'

'Nothing. I'm trying to do a novel but after listening to Bella, I don't think
there's much point.'

'Don't believe everything Bella says she does.'

'No?'

'In any case, every writer has her own methods. There's a lot of crap
talked, you know.' Faith spoke in the deep and gravelly voice of a heavy
smoker.

'I see.'

'So, how much of this novel have you written?'

'About twenty thousand words.'

'Typed?'

'Longhand.'

'Get it typed up – A4 double spaced – and send the first chapter to me.'

'Just one chapter?'

'I pride myself on being able to tell from the first page.'

'Thank you,' said Kate, fully aware of the importance of the offer but at the same time thinking she did not like Faith much and in any case, after Bella's lecture, she was worried about her own first page.

After lunch they all filed in for the second high spot, a talk from Ann Cuthbert for all those aspiring to be published by The Paradise Club. If Bella's lecture had seemed pointless to Kate, this one was even more so for the books published by this particular publisher were written to a prescribed formula, from length, to settings, to type of hero and heroine, their ages, hair-colouring, occupations, even the sort of ending – happy. Kate knew she could not write to such a strict set of rules, she was far too undisciplined for that and it would be like wearing a mental corset. She spent most of the lecture dreaming of her book and wondering if she would find the courage to send it to Faith. And then she remembered the woman she had met at Barty Silver's party. June, Joan somebody. The one who could not stop crying. Had she not said she was an agent? Surreptitiously Kate opened her handbag to see if she still had her card. She found it. Joy Trenchard. But would she even remember her?

If Bella had inspired everyone, Ann had made many of them burn with renewed ambition. There had been excitement before, now it was a real presence as, at the end, the women pressed round a rather harassed-looking Ann.

Kate, not wanting to write for The Paradise Club, went to the ladies' to wash her hands. Ann Cuthbert entered, looking agitatedly over her shoulder. She smiled nervously at Kate, who mumbled her thanks for the interesting lecture, and Ann quickly entered one of the cubicles and locked the door.

There was a commotion of raised voices outside and then the door flew open and Felicity marched in, followed by several other women. Her hair was askew, and there was a wild look in her eyes.

'Did Ann Cuthbert come in here?' She did not ask but demanded of Kate.

'Yes, she's in there.' She nodded at the cubicle door.

'Ann. Ann. It's me, Felicity!' Felicity bellowed, and bent down and peered under the door as if not believing Kate.

'I won't be a minute,' Ann called back.

'It doesn't matter. I'll give it to you now.' Felicity opened her voluminous handbag, took out a manuscript held together with an elastic band and, belly flopping on to the tiled floor, her large breasts squelching out on either side like squashed melons, she pushed the papers through the gap under the door.

Her action seemed to release her followers from normal restraint. One stood on the still recumbent Felicity and hurled her manuscript over the top of the door. One slipped into the booth next door and, standing on the lavatory, peered over the top.

'Ann, Ann, catch,' the woman called, dropping over her offering. Another two made for the booth the other side at exactly the same time and momentarily became stuck in the doorway. But then, like a champagne cork, they burst through, both clambering on the lavatory lid which creaked ominously. They jettisoned their manuscripts just as the lid gave way and two legs were wedged firmly into the bowl.

Kate stood open mouthed, and blinked. It had all happened so quickly she wondered if it had been real. Ann was screaming, accompanied, like a descant, by cries of genuine pain from the two women blocking the lavatory.

'What the hell is going on here?' Siobhan appeared, incandescent with rage.

'Siobhan. For Christ's sake, get me out of here,' Ann wailed.

'Ladies, ladies, this is so unseemly,' Siobhan was clapping her hands. 'Out, all of you,' she screamed. Felicity picked herself up, dusted herself down, collected her fellow conspirators around her like a fussy mother hen and, with great dignity in the circumstances, stalked out followed by those who could walk.

'I told you to get out,' Siobhan shouted at Kate.

'I haven't done anything,' Kate protested, wrongly accused. 'I only came in to wash my hands.'

'Siobhan, is it safe?' There was an anguished call from Ann who sounded as if she feared she had been forgotten.

'Ann, my dear. I'm so sorry. What can I say? What can I do?'

Ann stumbled out leaving behind a cubicle covered with scattered papers and fell sobbing into Siobhan's arms. 'They were like wild animals . . . I was terrified . . . What the hell got into them?' she gasped, between sobs.

'Was she one of them?' Siobhan pointed imperiously at Kate.

'No; no. You were washing your hands, weren't you?'

'Yes. I don't even want to write for The Paradise Club.'

'I'm not sure if I want to stay working there.' Ann moved gingerly towards the basin and began to splash water on to her face.

'Help us, please.' A pathetic voice issued from the booth with the broken lavatory.

'Kate, get the management. Get those stupid women out.'

As she passed the door she saw the two women, one leg stuck in the lavatory, clinging desperately to each other. In the hall she found a distressed-looking Tracey.

'What's the matter?'

'Ann won't talk to me now. She won't want to speak to anyone. She'll want to get the hell out of it.'

'You give me your manuscript when we get home. I'll get it seen for you.'

'You? How?'

'Trust me.' Kate smiled, thinking of Joy again.

The management were summoned, plumbers arrived and Siobhan called a meeting. A collection was taken for a bouquet for Ann as an apology from everyone. It was a subdued gathering. Of Felicity and her collaborators there was no sign, nor was Ann in evidence. The rest of the weekend passed quietly.

21

It would soon be Christmas and moving about London had become a nightmare with the crowds in town for shopping and to see the lights. Joy was fuming as her taxi was stuck in a monumental jam at Marble Arch, the traffic solid behind them and ahead down the length of Park Lane. She looked out of the window at the shoppers hurrying by in the drizzle and saw how, despite the weather, despite the crowds, they all looked happy. She, however, was dreading this Christmas.

She was fretting because she had an appointment with Barty in half an hour and at this rate there was no way she was going to get there on time. She knew Barty: if you were late you missed the appointment, he never allowed for excuses. Then when *would* she see him? He was flying out to Australia tonight for his own Christmas.

Barty, and his autobiography, were hot news; she had to be able to act now while he still was. Next week it could be someone else the publishers were all fighting over. What if Sean Connery finally agreed to write his autobiography, or a royal, or any of half a dozen gold-plated possibilities? It was very easy to become yesterday's news in this voracious profession. She opened her handbag and nervously lit a cigarette.

The sliding window between her and the driver opened. 'Look, love. It's miles round, but what say we nip up the back here, round to Holborn, sneak down to Trafalgar Square and through that way? Don't want you to think I'm cheating you.'

'Driver, to the moon and back if you can get me to Silver Street by three.'

For the umpteenth time she checked in her briefcase to make sure she had everything she needed. Her head was throbbing – it often did since the fall. To hide the scar on her forehead, she had had a fringe cut, which she knew did not suit her.

It had been a bad time. She had tried to see her daughter but had found the house with shutters closed and locks changed. Where Hannah was she did not know. When she called Charles invariably his secretary said he was out of the office. Her mother-in-law had slammed the receiver down on her when she telephoned, desperate to find her child.

What was the cruellest was that Charles, somehow, by employing detectives, she presumed, had found her hideaway in Barty's service flat. He did not call, but every day flowers were delivered from him, with no message, no news, only his name on the florist's card. It was as if he was taunting her, punishing her, when she had done no wrong.

Finally she had refused to accept the flowers and the deliveries had stopped. Then her action made her wonder if she should have continued to take them, that he would eventually have contacted her, but that now she had angered him.

She made an appointment to see a solicitor; the games had to end. But last week, out of the blue, the telephone had rung and it was Charles, refusing to tell her how he had acquired the ex-directory number. The call had upset her dreadfully, especially when he told her Hannah cried for her each night. Then, she was almost sure, he began to weep himself, certainly his voice sounded strange. But that did not stop him refusing to tell her where Hannah was. The following morning she had cancelled her appointment with the solicitor. Far better, she thought, that they try to work things out between them, better for Hannah as well as for them.

He did not call again. The telephone rang constantly but it was always Barty or a publishing contact to do with his book. She had had to learn, immediately, at the sound of the wrong voice to make her own appear bright and efficient, as if she hadn't a care in the world.

Now she found she was longing, praying for him to call. Anything to have contact with him, and through him her daughter. That's what she told herself . . . or was she deceiving herself? Was she not also longing for the calls just to hear his voice?

At such thoughts she made herself concentrate on something else. She could not allow herself to think this way. She hated him, she told herself a dozen times a day. But then at night, the telephone silent, alone in the little flat, the thought she could resist in the daytime wormed back into her mind. She still loved him, still wanted him, missed his body so that at night she could not sleep for longing for him. Then she would permit herself to dream of them back together, a happy family, Charles changed for good. But dreams fade in the morning.

It had been a busy week too. Word was out that Barty's autobiography was to be sold. All those editors to whom she had floated the idea, and had sworn to total secrecy, had let the cat out of the bag. But the fault was hers – she knew well enough that nothing stayed secret long in the writing world, that publishing was a giant galleon on an ocean of gossip.

When the various editors, agents and even writers in person discovered she was not at her usual number they had contacted Barty.

'Suss them out good and proper. Only give Joy's number to those you're sure are *bona fide* – certainly not her husband. Get it?' Barty had instructed his staff. Hence her telephone never seemed to stop; at the moment all she could do was stonewall everyone while keeping the interest whipped up.

'We're going to have to set you up in a proper office, my girl,' Barty told her over dinner one night. 'This is ridiculous. Ten lines I've got, and half the time they're blocked with calls for you. You're costing me a small fortune in lost business.'

'Barty, I'm sorry. I promise, I'll fix something up soon, after Christmas,' she said, with no idea how she was to manage it.

'No, you won't. I will. When I get back from down under. We'll find you a nice little office, with a nice rubber plant and a girl to help and all the gizmos.'

'Barty, I couldn't afford an office, not yet. When I find somewhere of my own to live I'll work from there.'

'What on earth do you mean? Barty Silver's agent working from a bed-sit? Never! I'd lose all me street-cred if you did it that way. Enough said. Barty will see to it.'

She had kissed him when he had said that, right in the middle of his forehead. Immediately she was horrified at her temerity and he was amazed to find he had not minded.

Barty was to be her partner. She had not suggested it, had not mentioned it. He had insisted. At this moment lawyers were working on their contract.

If her personal life was in tatters her career life was working out wonderfully. Barty, as she had known he would be, was her big break. Now she was being approached with projects from other authors asking her to represent them. If she worked hard and was cautious in her choice of writers to handle she could be the success she longed to be.

To gain that success, Joy was aware, would be an uphill struggle. Hannah and the never-ending ache she felt to hold the child in her arms again; Charles and her longing for him; her future, or not, with her husband had somehow to be compartmentalised, separated from her working day. How this was to be achieved she was not sure. She had known men whose wives had left them, taking children with them, and they had not crumbled but had continued with their careers. They could not afford to throw in the towel and say they were too sad to work this week. If men could do it, so could she, she told herself several times a day.

Some days it was easier than others. Today seeing Barty would buoy her up – he always did – even if this morning she was going to have to be stern with him. Publishers were hungry for this book, banging on her door for it, and not one word was written. Barty could not agree on who was to ghost-write it for him. There had been no shortage of volunteers, several were famous in their field as biographers and a couple were household names. Barty had turned them all down though he had agreed to meet two; both, in Joy's opinion, would have been ideal.

'Nothing personal, mate. Just wouldn't work,' he had said to them, one by one.

When Joy had tried to find out what the problem was, in the hope she could find someone who would suit, all he would say was that the chemistry had not been right. Today she was sure she had the solution for him, the ideal person. If he refused Brian Hoskins, she was not sure what to do next.

She looked at her watch as the taxi raced along the Embankment. Her hopes lifted, they were going to make it.

Now there was also the problem of Christmas to face. She did not know what to do. She had thought of going to a hotel but each one she had called was fully booked. She could not go to her mother's, she had already been deluged with censorious telephone calls telling her what a fool she was to leave such a wonderful husband, and what was she thinking of? She had not told her mother the full story, she could not. Pride, she supposed, the same pride that had made her rush out of the house and not call the police to report her husband had raped her, and make Charles the one to leave. Pride and that stupid middle-class fear of making a scene, of the neighbours knowing. And look where that had got her – no home and no Hannah.

The taxi screeched to a halt. 'There. Three minutes to spare.' The driver grinned at her.

'You're a wonder,' she said, tipping him a fiver.

Anxious-faced Brian Hoskins, her most talented client so far, stood against the wall of Barty's garden.

'Joy, I can't do this. It's madness,' he said in greeting. 'I don't know anything about writing autobiographies.'

'Of course you can, Brian. Would I have suggested it if I wasn't confident of your ability?' she asked, concentrating all her energies on gearing up Brian's confidence. 'You did research at Cambridge for a year. Then there's your journalism – it makes you ideal.'

'But I'm not a ghost-writer. I write books about serious matters.' His face screwed up into a feeble attempt at a smile which failed. Joy grabbed him and hugged him.

'You can, you can. You'll like Barty. This really is a worthwhile project, and you need the money right now.'

'Yes. But Barty Silver? He's not my kind of subject.'

'You're the right person for him, the only one. I know it.'

Barty was waiting for them in his study. It was one of the things she liked most about him: as he expected you to be on time for an appointment, so was he. There was no waiting around in anterooms with Barty; if he said three, then at that time he would be ready and waiting for you. A rare thing in a man of such success and power.

'So you're Brian Hoskins?'

'Yes, sir.' Brian shuffled miserably and looked everywhere but at Barty.

'You written anything before?'

'A novel and lots of newspaper articles.' Joy answered for him.

'A journalist?' Barty said suspiciously.

'Not the sort you're thinking of, Barty. Brian's more an investigative journalist – he did a wonderful piece on one-parent families and the DSS in the *Independent*, didn't you, Brian?'

'Yes,' Brian mumbled.

'And why should I choose you to ghost-write this book of mine when I haven't even heard of you?' Barty peered at Brian.

'He's coming new to this, as you are, Barty. A fresh approach, not the usual pedestrian biography at all. And he writes like a dream. You may not have heard of him now but you will,' Joy said staunchly.

'Can't he speak? All I've heard are two yesses.'

'I can speak and if you want the truth, Sir Barty, I'm not sure I want to be your ghost-writer.' Brian appeared to have suddenly woken up.

'And why's that?'

'I'm a novelist for a start, a bloody good one and . . .' Brian looked about the opulent room. 'Quite honestly, I don't think we've anything in common and what is more I don't really think your life would be of the slightest interest to me.'

'Well, there's a thing!' Barty laughed loudly. 'Got spirit then, have you? So have I. Let's have a coffee, let's talk.'

'You've got a lot more in common than you realise,' Joy said, quickly picking up her handbag, lowering her head so that neither of them could see her smile.

'Like what?'

'I'll let him tell you that. I've got some shopping to do. When shall I come back to see how you've both got on?' Joy said.

'Give us an hour,' said Barty. 'See if I can persuade this young man differently.'

Joy had no shopping to do, instead she walked up to the Fulham Road and found a café where she sat smoking and drinking coffee. Now she was alone her mind switched gear and she sat thinking of Hannah, and the more she thought the angrier she became. Not just with Charles but with herself for allowing this situation to rumble on. She would go and see him, camp in the chambers if necessary, embarrass him – that's what she would do.

She looked at her watch. The hour was nearly up.

The butler let her into the house and, anxiously, she approached the study. As she opened the door she heard laughter.

'And that's not all, Brian me lad. You should have seen him the next morning . . . Joy!' Barty leapt to his feet. 'You're a genius. We got along famously.'

'I knew it. I just knew you would.' Joy laughed. 'At last!' she added with feeling.

'We're like bruvvers, aren't we, Brian? It's not just Eton has an old boys' network you know, we Dr Barnardo's boys work the same way. Sly minx. Why didn't you say?'

'I wanted you to meet each other. I didn't want either of you to feel you were being pressurised.'

'I wouldn't have thought that of you, girl. But, you just think of it, Joy, what this boy's done – Cambridge, with his background. I'm proud as punch.' Barty was grinning from ear to ear as if he was talking about his own son.

'You haven't done so badly yourself, Barty,' she was surprised to hear Brian say. Few were the people allowed to call him by just his Christian name.

'Yes, but you're educated. That counts, Brian. That counts.'

'Now, to business. We must agree a fee . . .' Joy began trying to sound businesslike among all the euphoria.

'It's all done. I know, I know, it's your job.' He held up his hand as if to ward her complaints off. 'I'm sorry but we've agreed and it won't alter your firm's percentage, now will it?'

'Might I ask how much?'

'Brian's to get twenty per cent of whatever I get.'

'Oh,' said Joy, the wind taken out of her sails. With the sums Barty was likely to earn, and Brian's relative lack of experience, she would have asked for only five per cent. Brian would earn a small fortune this way.

'It's more than fair, Barty. But I think Brian is going to need some sort of subbing now.'

'All arranged. He's moving in, aren't you, Brian? Then we can work any old time. And he's coming to Australia with me for Christmas. We leave tonight, we can talk on the way out and back. Why don't you come, girl? Have a break.'

'Barty, I'd love to. But I can't. I'm determined to find a way to see Hannah.'

'Of course, wouldn't be right would it, you the other side of the world at Christmas, of all times? But you promise me one thing while I'm away and can't keep a beady eye on you. Don't go back to him. Understand?'

'Yes, Barty. I promise.'

Joy had intended taking Brian out for a drink either to celebrate or commiserate, but now, with packing to do, he did not have the time. There was no point in going to find Charles either – he would not be in chambers now. She returned to the flat and was running herself a bath when the doorbell rang.

Her heart lurched when she saw Charles standing in the hallway with a huge bouquet.

'Since you refuse to accept my flowers from the delivery man, I thought I'd best bring them myself,' he said, smiling at her. She stood rigid, holding the door as if in support. 'And I think we should talk, Joy, don't you?' he said quietly.

'Yes. Yes, we should.'

'Can I come in, then?'

'Sorry . . .' She stepped back, opening the door for him.

'Nice flat,' he said, looking around him and then pushing the flowers towards her.

'Thank you, they're lovely.' She put the flowers to her face, covering it so that he could not see her expression. 'Coffee or a drink?'

'Nothing. I need to talk to you, Joy. I won't say sorry again – there's no point is there? You can't forgive me my unforgivable behaviour, can you?' He said it in the beautiful voice which she had always loved to hear.

She did not answer.

'I've been thinking, Joy. You remember you said to me I never questioned my actions, the hurt I caused? Well, I have. I've faced myself and it wasn't easy. You were right.'

Joy laid the flowers on the table. 'Do you want to take your coat off? It's warm in here,' she said for something to say, afraid of the feeling of hope his words were giving her.

'I've been so selfish, my darling. I just thought I could cruise through life doing my own thing because you loved me and would never stop loving me. What a fool I've been. Now I've destroyed your love.' He looked at her sadly and her instinct was to rush into his arms and tell him she loved him still. She held on to the back of the chair to stop herself.

'Look, Joy. I know you can't forgive and all that but, well, it is Christmas and Hannah needs both of us. Come back just for that. I promise you I won't try anything – I'll sleep in the dressing room. Anything you want. But just for Christmas. What do you say?'

'Yes,' she answered simply. There was no other answer to give, not with him here in the room with her . . . so close . . . and Hannah.

So it was that before Barty's flight had taken off, Charles was carrying her cases from the taxi into their own home.

22

The huge jet aeroplane lifted its nose and rose quickly above Paris. Crispin settled himself into his club-class seat, opened his briefcase, took out a stack of papers and sat reading none of them. What to do or where to go was occupying his mind.

He realised he could not permanently delay seeing Julius but he hoped that being away now would give the old boy time to calm down and come to terms with what had happened. Crispin had been taken by surprise to find that he felt quite a measure of guilt – he had not expected that. It was not unusual for him to travel about Europe in December – he usually did, it was a good time to visit foreign publishers. Few others bothered to go because Christmas was so close. This way he need not see Julius until the New Year.

But what to do with himself in the meantime? Things were not good with Charlotte. They had barely spoken since that dreadful dinner party. At first he had felt sorry for himself but then decided he was glad they were not speaking. His initial shock and pain had turned to anger towards her. He would never be able to forgive her lapse in their nest. She had let him down, betrayed him. He found now that whenever he thought of her, it was her face that night, ugly with anger, her mouth shrieking those appalling expletives at him, that came to mind.

Most certainly he was not willing to spend Christmas with her. In one of their rare exchanges she had announced that she was going to her parents and he had announced that he was not. Shortly after their marriage he had visited them once, and once was enough. Upon meeting them, and seeing where they lived, he had understood her reluctance to invite them to the wedding. A bungalow in Budleigh Salterton did not fit his idea of a suitable background for his parents-in-law. Budleigh Salterton he could manage – a delightful place with some good architecture remaining. No, it was the bungalow and the tasteless interior that he abhorred.

That visit, he had thought what a miracle it was that she had overcome such beginnings to become the sensitive soul-mate she was. And he had nothing but admiration for her – then. Of course he had loved her – then. He did not love her now. And that scene had shown her in her true colours, proving that blood would always out.

He ordered a drink from the stewardess and watched her as she sashayed back up the aisle of the aeroplane – nice figure, pretty face, almost Pre-Raphaelite, perhaps a little too much make-up but that was expected of stewardesses, he supposed.

He had to decide, and quickly, what he was to do about Charlotte and his marriage. It was over, there was no doubt about it, he could never play games with her ever again – she had spoilt everything. The point was how to get rid of her without having to pay out too much. If he dithered, Julius might die and he could end up paying out a fortune to her in divorce settlements. Better to do it now, before she realised he had his shares. That had been a lucky break – her not speaking to him had made it possible to keep secret that Uncle Simon had agreed. The house would have to go – that was a pity, but then, he brightened up, he could always find something better when he had sold Westall's. Yes, that's what he would do. Once he was back he'd get on to his solicitors.

What about Christmas? Where could he go? He did not fancy being on his own, but staying with friends might be difficult, for it was early days, and until the dust settled he would not know which camp, his or hers, they might fall into. He did not fancy a hotel with all the false bonhomie. Maybe he should go right away – the Bahamas, or maybe Switzerland.

The stewardess returned with his drink. He smiled up at her and contentedly watched her reaction. Almost electric, he congratulated himself. Gently, very gently, he let his hand brush against hers.

'Any chance that you're free over Christmas?' he asked with no preamble, totally sure of himself.

'As a matter of fact . . .'

'Good. Where shall we go?'

Julius had not been looking forward to Christmas. This was nothing new, he never had enjoyed the enforced jollity that was his family's idea of fun. This year he was to be lucky. Jane's sister was suddenly taken ill. The woman was one of the few people his wife genuinely cared for.

'I must go to her, you do understand, Julius?' she had asked upon receipt of the news.

'But, of course,' he answered solemnly, while his heart lifted.

'I shall have to cancel the family coming here, but you must go to John's or Caroline's for the festivities. They will welcome you.'

'I don't think so, Jane. I don't want to put anyone out. I'll give Angus Fairley a ring. I'd quite like a break of a week or two up there.'

He called Angus. He had difficulty in extricating himself from Angus's immediate invitation to spend Christmas with them.

'You're very kind, Angus. And normally I can think of nothing I would rather do. But the point is, I need some time alone – I've one or two things to work out. I wondered if you had a cottage spare?'

It was not in Angus's nature to pry, so they decided on which of his numerous cottages was the most suitable and all mention of Christmas was dropped.

Julius, who in the whole of his life had never spent Christmas alone, was rather looking forward to the experience. He went to his wine merchant's and bought a selection of assorted malt whiskies. He went to Harrods and bought a Cumberland ham. He dug out his thermal underwear, his tweed plus-fours, packed his bags and caught the train for Scotland.

Kate had returned from her weekend to a frigid atmosphere. The reason she had not been able to get Tony on the telephone was simply because he was not there. She had returned to an empty house and a burnt beef casserole. He had taken the children to London. This had annoyed Kate. A few weeks back when she had suggested that she and Tony go away on their own for a weekend break, he had told her she was being ridiculous. It seemed a petty revenge on his part to punish her by giving the children the treat instead. However, she had tried to disguise her annoyance and felt she had succeeded. She had told him of her weekend, and the writing, and Faith's interest in her. He, by a blank look, a finger pointedly marking the place he had reached in the article he was reading, had told her he was not interested. If he thought this attitude was going to make her stop it had the opposite effect. It galvanised her into writing more and sowed a deeper ambition to succeed, if only to show him.

Kate was in a total whirl. She had set herself the task of typing her first chapter, double spaced, with two fingers, determined to send it off before the holiday period. If it had not been Christmas with its added expense she would have taken it to an agency to have it typed professionally – as it was she felt she could not afford to. The whole thing was taking so long to do that she was behind with all the other preparations.

On top of all this she had inadvertently upset Pam. She had declined a shopping trip to London and another one to Graintry; since they always did their Christmas shopping together, it was not surprising that Pam was upset. But then Kate had compounded it by saying she had decided to stop going to the meetings of the writers' circle.

'Why?'

'I thought sending only one chapter was silly so I'm doing two. I want to get it finished and off to an agent, and it's taking so long.'

'One morning won't make that amount of difference.'

'It will. To be quite honest, Pam, I can't see the point in going. Felicity isn't what she cracks herself up to be, and in any case I don't think I can face her after that fiasco in the loos. I think I'd probably be wasting my time, none of it's what I want to do.'

'And I'm not wasting my time?' The question was asked in a voice so frosty that Kate found herself looking at the receiver with surprise.

'I didn't mean that – you know I didn't. It's just that I'm not interested in writing sloppy short stories for *Hearthside* and I know I could never do anything that The Paradise Club would even want to look at.'

'Good gracious me. How long have you been writing? A month, six weeks? And already you're an expert.'

'Pam!'

'It was all such fun and now you're taking it so seriously and spoiling everything.'

'I admit I'm taking it seriously but I so want to succeed and Faith was so nice about – '

'One woman says she likes what you do and now you're imagining yourself in the bestseller list.'

'I think that's uncalled-for.'

'Do you? Well, I don't. When was the last time I saw you?'

'I've been so busy.'

'But not so busy that you could not find the time to drive over to Tracey's.'

'I only went to pick up her manuscript as I had promised – you know she doesn't have a car. This is silly.'

'It might be to you, it certainly isn't to me!' And the telephone went dead.

Kate sat for some time wondering what to do. She and Pam had never had a cross word before. She could not remember ever seeing her friend in a mood, let alone a temper. So what had she done wrong? If it had been Pam who had suddenly discovered what she wanted to do she would be happy for her, want to help her. 'Ah well,' she said aloud to the room. 'I've work to do.' And she set up the typewriter hoping to get another few pages done before the children came home from school.

The next day she had finished. She reread carefully several times, looking for errors. Then she could delay no longer. She crossed to the telephone. Despite Faith's encouragement, she'd definitely decided to approach Joy first.

'May I speak to Mrs Trenchard, please?'

'Speaking.'

'You probably won't remember me, but we met at Barty Silver's party – Kate Howard?' she said, unaware that had she called a few days earlier she would not have found Joy back in her home.

'Yes, of course I remember. Oh, what a disgrace that party was!' She laughed.

'Yes, I'm only just out of the dog-house with my husband, actually.'

'Your dress, I owe you for the cleaning bill.'

'Well, that isn't what I'm calling about, actually,' she said, and wished she could stop saying 'actually'. It sounded so gauche. She took a deep breath. 'You said you were a literary agent?'

'That's right.'

'It's probably rubbish, but . . . I started writing a book when my husband wasn't speaking to me . . .' She giggled and then regretted that as well. 'The point is, another agent overheard me reading a part of it and said she would like to see it.'

'Yes?' Joy's voice sounded interested. Kate felt bolder.

'But I wondered if I could send it to you first. I'm not sure I'd get on with her – bit bossy, if you know what I mean.'

'How nice. I'd love to see it!' Joy replied and would have liked to ask who the other agent was but stopped herself. She checked that Kate had her address and Kate explained that she had only typed the first two chapters and was that all right? Joy assured her it would be fine, at least it was a start.

'There's one other thing. I hate to be a nuisance, but do you know anyone at The Paradise Club? Only a friend of mine is desperate to be published by them. She works so hard and needs the money so badly.'

'It's an extremely difficult market to break into.'

'She knows that. They have rejected her twice already. But we learnt at this writers' weekend that it helps if you have an agent, and I was wondering . . .'

'Of course, pop it in with yours. And the dress, how much do I owe you?'

'Nothing.' Kate laughed. 'I threw the flaming thing away. I decided I looked like a pregnant crow in it anyway.'

Kate flew out of the house, clutching the large manila envelope to her. It was already sealed and addressed before she made the call. She drove into Graintry to the main post office – with the Christmas rush on she was not going to risk the local one. To make doubly sure she sent it by special delivery. Once she was home she poured herself a large brandy to celebrate having had the courage to call. She was astonished that she had done it – pushed herself. Amazing! A couple of months ago she would have shied away from doing any such thing. Now, she told herself, she had to pull herself together, forget all about the book until she heard from Joy, and start concentrating on Christmas and her family.

Undoubtedly it was finding his wife back in the familiar mould and the house spotless once more that must have convinced Tony he had won, for suddenly he was nice again. He even went as far as to apologise for his lack of interest and, as if to make amends, on Christmas Day the large box under the tree with Kate's name on it revealed a word processor.

Kate thought she was going to burst into tears. At last he understood.

'That should put a stop to all this nonsense,' he laughed. 'You'll never get the hang of the thing. I'd bet a month's income.' In truth, he'd bought the machine for himself and the children. He felt sure there'd be a return on his investment.

But his remark was to seal all their fates.

Gloria waited until Christmas Eve just in case Clive telephoned or turned up. Then, that morning, she put his present by the telephone, the cat in the basket, loaded all Elephant's toys and, with him beside her on the front seat, the cat complaining bitterly in the back, she set off for what she knew would be a dismal Christmas with her parents.

'Bet it rains,' she said to Elephant.

Peter Holt was in New York. Normally he liked its buzz and excitement and usually did well there. He liked Americans and their enthusiastic way of doing business and they in turn liked him. But this time nothing was working out as he wanted. He did not know what was wrong with him, for this trip he felt totally uninterested in everything. Physically he felt lethargic, and, oddly for one with so many friends here, he felt lonely. The city he loved and had always found welcoming suddenly felt cold and threatening. After one particularly unproductive and rather acrimonious meeting with a publisher – his fault entirely, he knew – he decided to cut his losses. He wanted to leave and quickly. He cancelled, with insincere apologies, the next two days' appointments and, thinking hang the extra expense, caught the evening Concorde home.

From the airport he stopped off at his office which, apart from the security men, was empty. He was not even sure why he had gone there. So close to Christmas it was unlikely anyone would still be working, but he wondered if he had come in the hope that someone would be here – Phillip, or Gloria preferably. But that was a forlorn hope: of all of them Phillip was always the first to scuttle away, and there was no sign of Gloria. Instead, on his desk, Em had left an urgent memo that he was to call Phillip the moment he arrived.

'We had a summons while you were away. Costas Carras wants to see us, like yesterday.' Phillip's lazy voice answered his call.

'I've just got in from New York. I left early, suddenly got fed up.'

'I know, I tried to get hold of you there. Are you all right?'

'I think I must need a holiday, or a check-up, or something. Nothing seems to matter any more,' Peter replied, laughing slightly, feeling he should really be apologising to his partner.

'You're getting there, my old friend. Nothing does matter, that's the great gas! There's nothing wrong with you, mate, just that you're beginning to see sense. Join the club.'

'Did Costas say what he wanted that was so urgent?' Peter asked, trying to get back to business, not wanting to be like Phillip.

'No, but I've a shrewd guess, haven't you?'

'And?'

'Up to you entirely, mate. You're the one who does all the work, makes all the money. I'm the drone who spends it.' Phillip laughed.

'We could talk, it won't hurt. It would be interesting to see what he's got to say.'

'*You* can talk. I'm flying out to the Seychelles first thing. I made an appointment for you tomorrow at ten, Claridges, hope that's all right. I leave it all in your capable hands.'

'When do you get back?'

'A month.'

'Carras won't wait that long.'

'I meant it, Peter. Whatever you decide, you've got my power of attorney, you always have.'

'You'll be contactable?'

'Maybe. I've left a couple of numbers with Em. I don't promise to be at them, mind you.' Phillip laughed.

'Fine.'

'Keep on trucking . . .'

Peter collected together a pile of papers, half a dozen files and a ledger. He called the security man to help him carry them down to the garage and flung them in the back of the car. After all, he thought, there was no harm in being prepared. The powerful car slid up the ramp of the underground car park.

There was no point in going to the country with such an early appointment. In any case, Hilary would not be expecting him for another two days. He drove to the flat, let himself into the darkened hallway and once again felt that loneliness which had been bothering him in New York. He crossed to the sitting room and switched on the CD player. He turned the volume down slightly as the music of Mozart filled the room. He kicked off his shoes, poured himself a brandy and soda and sat in his favourite chair. What the hell was wrong with him? Peter was not one for thinking about himself, there had never been time, let alone inclination. He had always felt that too much introspection could be a dangerous thing. And yet here he was, several possibly lucrative appointments cancelled, mooning in a darkened room with Mozart for company and feeling sorry for himself.

He had meant to study his papers, be prepared for Costas in the morning, but even that he could not be bothered to do. Yet there had been a time when looking at the company's figures was his favourite occupation, one that gave him indescribable pleasure. There was no fun any more. No fun anywhere at work or home – that was half the problem. This would not do, he told himself firmly as he downed the brandy in one. A good night's sleep, that's what he needed. Everything would look better in the morning.

He switched off the light, left the CD to play itself out, crossed the wide hallway and down the corridor to his bedroom. Halfway along he stopped and listened. He was sure he had heard something. Silence. He began to walk and then stopped again. There *was* someone, he had distinctly heard a muffled cry. Gingerly he opened his bedroom door.

Peter was just in time to see Pinkers Flynn ramming himself into his wife, pink arse heaving up and down between Hilary's white splayed legs. He saw Hilary's body rise in the bed in orgasm and heard her cry out in the throes of her passion. 'Pinkers, I love you.'

He stood in the doorway, momentarily frozen. Then he turned and quietly shut the door.

In the sitting room he retrieved his shoes and found that he was shaking. He closed his eyes as if trying to blot out the scene he had just witnessed. He picked up his keys, left the flat, collected his car and left.

He did not know how long he drove or where, he just felt he wanted to keep moving. He was angry, so angry that he drove too fast, quite unaware of other road-users, until an articulated lorry, blaring its horn at him, brought him to his senses. He pulled into a lay-by.

The engine switched off, he lit a cigar – one over his allowance he reminded himself, and he smiled. Then he wondered how he could smile after what he had seen. And why had he just walked away? Why had he not made a scene? Why had he not tried to kill Flynn? That's what a normal man would do. And then he remembered Pinkers's pink arse pumping up and down and he began to laugh – my God, he thought, what a grim sight that was. So if he was laughing where was his anger? Then he realised that these days, in all matters, what Hilary did with her time was of supreme indifference to him. Why should this not be the same? When had they last made love? He found he had to think long and hard to remember. Months ago, and then it had been quick, something to be got over fast.

How strange, to be sitting in this lay-by, accepting the end of a marriage and not caring. Once, this would have been unthinkable. Once, he would have been suicidal with despair. Once, he had loved her like no other. But she had changed and no doubt he had too. Sad.

He restarted the car, turned it round, and headed back to London and his club. On the drive he felt strange. He was not aware at first what it was he was feeling and then he realised it was elation. He felt free and he found he was singing. Perhaps the answer was to free himself of everything.

Peter was shown into Carras's suite at ten the following morning. He had met the man maybe half a dozen times and always socially but he knew he was about to sit down and do business with one of the most astute brains in the Western world.

Costas Carras was short, fat and bald, with an oily complexion. One expected him to be as gross in his attitudes and speech as he was in appearance but, meeting him for the first time, people were always surprised at his old-world charm and his impeccable Boston accent.

'How kind of you to come at such short notice, Peter.'

'Not at all, Costas. It's always a pleasure to see you.'

They shook hands politely and Peter towered over the smaller man who, as if feeling at a disadvantage, sat down quickly on a sofa and indicated Peter should do the same.

'And your charming wife? She's well, I trust?'

'Very. She couldn't be happier.' Peter smiled faintly as he spoke.

For the next few minutes they exchanged social pleasantries, Costas all the time watching Peter with a shrewd expression as if assessing him.

'So Costas. Why am I here?' Peter asked.

'I've heard a rumour,' Costas said as he flicked his fingers at an aide who hovered at the side of the room. 'Coffee?'

'What rumour would that be?'

'That you wish to sell Shotters.'

'Sell? Me? I'm sorry, Costas, I think you've been misinformed. Why should I want to sell?'

'For a lot of money.' Costas grinned slyly.

'Well, they do say everything has a price but I doubt if what I regard as a *possible* price for Shotters would be the same that you had in mind – that is, *if* I wanted to sell, which, I'm sorry Costas, I don't.'

So, with such games, two days of negotiations began.

Peter summoned Logan, Em, his personal accountant and solicitor, who came with their assistants.

The arguments washed back and forth. The negotiations became heated, then calm, only to hot up again. They would take breaks, both men gathering about them their advisors, in select and secret huddles.

On Christmas Eve the deal was finalised. Shotters had a new owner.

As he shook hands on the deal Peter realised he felt almost light-headed with excitement. He had not known he wished to sell. But now it was done he felt a surge of relief, of happiness.

He was free. Free of a wife he no longer loved and free from a business that, without him realising, had become irksome to him.

Part Two

1

The cottage stood high on a cliff. The Atlantic ocean far below pounded relentlessly and noisily at the shore. The house appeared to huddle in a slight fold in the land as if cowering from the ferocity of the wind which tore at the thatch on its roof, screaming through any available chink or gap in window or door. The rain, itself a victim of the wind, was not falling but being hurled in horizontal sheets against the granite walls. With sea and sky a dull gunmetal grey, it was impossible to see where the horizon began or ended. The tough grass, the bracken, were flattened by the onslaught and the one tree in the garden was bent low to the ground like a giant bow.

Gloria looked gloomily out of the window. She thought this holiday would never end and, not for the first time since her arrival, wished she had never come, and wondered how soon she could decently escape.

The weather was not responsible for her mood, the cause as always was her mother. They had never got on, never would. Gloria was a straightforward person but her mother chose to mask her criticism of Gloria – of which there had been a lot – in a fog of innuendo accompanied by much loud sighing.

'It's my own fault, Elephant. We shouldn't have come,' Gloria said to her dog. She often debated with herself why she had when she knew all her visits ended this way. She realised there was an element of duty involved, for her parents had been good to her and the least she could do was to visit them occasionally.

'I suppose we had better go and offer to help, Elephant. Or that will be wrong.' She crossed to the door leading to the kitchen, the dog at her heels.

'Anything I can do?' she asked brightly.

'I suppose you could do the Brussels sprouts for me,' Mrs Catchpole said grudgingly. Gloria smiled to herself, aware that her mother was annoyed that she had volunteered, thus depriving her of a source of martyrdom.

Gloria had barely begun to prepare the sprouts when the back door flew open and her father appeared from his trip to the village, accompanied by part of the storm, his mackintosh dripping onto the spotless kitchen tiles.

'Graham, really! Just look at the mess you're making,' his wife fretted, leaping up to collect her mop.

'I think you should see this, Gloria,' her father said, completely ignoring his wife – but, then, he might by now be oblivious to her ways, Gloria thought, as she took the copy of the *Daily Telegraph* he handed her. She glanced idly at it, and then, in the way of words hidden in a thousand others, those relevant to her appeared to jump off the page, blacker, larger than all the others. 'SHOTTERS SOLD.'

'Good God . . .' Gloria smoothed the paper out on the table and bent over it reading the copy, her heart beginning to pound. 'The bastard!' she exclaimed.

'Gloria! Really, your language – ' her mother began but her husband took hold of her arm and shook his head at her in warning. 'What's happened? Tell me.' Mrs Catchpole grabbed at her throat with anxiety and craned forward, trying to see what Gloria was reading.

'I just don't believe it!' Gloria slumped back on the kitchen chair. 'The creep! I had lunch with Peter Holt only the other day and he didn't say a thing.' She looked up anxiously at her father. 'Or did he? I said I was fed up at Shotters and he said to me, "Don't do anything yet." He must have known then. He needed me there, didn't he, to sell on? It wouldn't have looked too good, one of his senior editors leaving. He had to make it appear a happy ship.'

'These takeovers often come completely out of the blue, Gloria. I shouldn't judge him too harshly. It's quite likely he didn't know himself,' her father counselled.

'He's just upped and sold us like a load of cattle and you say don't judge him, Dad? Oh, come on . . .'

'And to an American company! Why could he not have chosen a nice English company.' Mrs Catchpole sighed.

'Because no English company would have paid him what that greedy bugger wanted.' Gloria stood up. Her chair scraping painfully on the tiled floor. She picked up her Filofax from the dresser and began to look for Peter's home number.

'What will you do?' her father asked.

'Resign.'

'Gloria, you can't do that, not with the position you have. Why, you said only last night that you hoped to be made a director soon.'

'That's what I thought he meant when he told me not to leave.'

'Maybe he'll recommend you for a directorship to the new owners. I'd be so proud of you.'

'Mum, it's no great deal, you know. Some publishing companies make staff directors at the drop of a hat. It doesn't mean you've a seat on the board. It's a sop in lieu of decent wages.'

'You've become so cynical, Gloria.'

'No, Mum. I've become a realist.'

She picked up the telephone. 'Oh, no, I don't believe it. It's dead.' She shook the instrument with exasperation.

'It's the storm.'

'I've got to go. I've got to get home.'

'Not in this weather, Gloria, please,' her mother begged, but Gloria was already half-way up the stairs.

An hour later she was driving to London, through the scudding rain. Because of the weather conditions the drive took nearly twice the normal six hours. By the time she opened her front door Gloria was exhausted. Quickly she fed the animals and then took a bath and went straight to bed. But she barely slept; instead she tossed and turned with anger. In the morning she left early for the office, leaving Elephant, still sleeping, behind.

It was 28 December and the building should have been empty. Instead, in every office, in the corridors, even in the lavatories, clusters of anxious people were gathered, each with a different worry, a different snippet of gossip.

'Gloria, I'm so glad you made it here.'

Gloria swung round at mention of her name to find Peter's secretary, Em, standing behind her, clutching a sheaf of papers. She noticed Em's eyes were rather pink and puffy.

'Hi, Em. What a cock-up! Can you tell us what the hell is going on? Where's Peter? Is anyone getting the push?'

'I tried calling you in Cornwall yesterday but the lines were down – a storm, they said.' Em avoided Gloria's questions. 'Peter was very anxious to speak to you personally and was upset when we could not get through. He's called a meeting in the canteen in half an hour's time. He asked specifically that you should hang on for a few minutes after the meeting is over.'

'What for?'

'I'm afraid I've no idea. But if you wouldn't mind?' Em smiled questioningly before excusing herself to speak to Blades's design team who had just walked into the office.

The atmosphere in the canteen was charged with equal measures of anger and fear. Peter finally arrived with Logan Perriman and they both climbed on to the small stage that only a short time ago had been the scene of the annual pantomime. Somebody switched on the spotlights. Gloria was shocked at how exhausted Peter looked. He fiddled with his papers; a nervous man, too, she thought. She would have liked to rush up to the stage and fling her arms around him. And then she scolded herself for being a fool. It was his own fault if he looked like that, he need not have sold. He was not worthy of sympathy. She must remember that.

'Ladies, gentlemen, thank you so much for coming to this meeting. I apologise to you for breaking into your holidays . . .' Peter looked up from the papers in his hand and smiled but no one smiled back. 'I thought it was best that I should see you all as soon as possible and explain a thing or two, and try to pre-empt any gossip.' Gloria wished he would stop smiling at them. He coughed and people began to shuffle, becoming restless. As if sensing this, he squared his shoulders and appeared to discard his notes. 'I realise this has come as a shock to you all – ' Someone at the back snorted with derision.

Peter looked about the jampacked room, not a seat free nor any standing space.

'You didn't have to bloody well sell,' a male voice shouted out.

'No, but it's better for everyone that we have.'

There was loud laughter at this but it was not caused by humour. It was derisory, bitter.

'Great, so you pocket millions while the rest of us can go to hell.' It was a member of the Blades art department on his feet, and shouting.

'Of course I've made millions. What do you want me to do, stand here and lie to you and say I haven't? But don't you be all pious and think you wouldn't have done the selfsame thing if you had been in my shoes. Be realistic, for Christ's sake.'

At last, thought Gloria, he's getting into his stride. His audience had sat up, were taking more notice. She even heard a few genuine laughs, and the odd murmur of agreement.

'It's a change of ownership, that's all, we carry on as before. Well, almost. Phillip is leaving, he wants to devote more time to his gardening.' At this there was a loud roar of approval: it was no secret in Shotters that Phillip's interest in gardening extended only to the fine crop of cannabis plants that he tended lovingly in deepest Berkshire. 'All those who worked for Phillip will be absorbed into other departments. There will be no redundancies, I assure you. Each imprint will continue with its own autonomy. We'll get what we need – a large injection of capital at a difficult time in publishing. I shall be staying on as chief executive. There will be one major difference. As some of you know, for some time I had been thinking of us starting up our own paperback house instead of selling paperback rights outside. Vertical publishing is the way forward, you don't need me to tell you that. This is exactly how Costas sees it, so we shall be looking to take on extra staff – not losing people. As from later this year we shall be starting Sabre, a completely new imprint that in three years, I predict, will be in the top four. I, for one, am very confident this is all for the best. Now does that make you all feel more secure? Any questions?'

Murmurs of approval greeted this, but, thought Gloria, if everything was so wonderful, why did Peter look so awful?

A junior editor stood up. 'This Carras person, what does he know about publishing?'

'Not a lot,' Peter said, joining in the laughter. 'He owns one of the largest private companies in America. He began in real estate, I think. He's recently acquired a publishing house in the States and one in Australia although nothing on this scale. But this is why I think he is a good person to sell to. He's interested in publishing but since he knows little about it he's going to leave it to us. Provided we are profitable, we'll be left alone.'

For a further hour Peter parried questions which, as time progressed, began to get more stupid, Gloria thought. Finally the meeting was over. Not that anyone said it was but it just fizzled out, having lost its momentum.

Peter left the stage and once he was out of the room the noise in the canteen was deafening, as everyone went over again what they had just heard. Like Gloria, several were unconvinced and said they were resigning. Or was it just bravado on their part? Gloria wondered. And did she herself mean to? She was no longer sure.

Em appeared and reminded Gloria that Peter wanted to see her. She took the lift to the top floor.

His office was crowded with men, the majority of them strangers to her. Upon seeing her, Peter excused himself and came over.

'You've been with me the longest, Gloria. There's a couple of things I should explain to you.'

'I'd appreciate that,' she said seriously.

'Let's go next door, it's a madhouse in here.'

They went through the communicating door into the calm of Phillip's office. They sat opposite each other. She looked with concern at his haggard face, he avoided her stare.

'Look, Gloria, I'm sorry. You must be feeling very let down,' he said studying his hands.

'You could say that, Peter. Thanks to you, I turned down another job just before Christmas.'

'Might I ask who with?' He looked up.

'Julius. He wants to start publishing commercial fiction. I was to – '

'That would have been no good,' Peter interrupted. 'Poor old Julius is finished. He's clutching at straws. If you had gone your job wouldn't have lasted long.'

'And who are you to say that? Have you got a hotline into the future or something? Julius and I would have made it work,' she said with spirit.

'I'm sorry, Gloria. I put that badly. You're safer here, is what I was trying to say.'

'You reckon?'

'Yes, I do. Costas is all right. And just think, with our own paperback house every book you buy is guaranteed publication in soft covers.'

'You reckon?'

'Yes. From day one we'll have combined decisions. No book is bought unless both hard and paperback editors agree.'

'Come on, Peter. That's a Utopia you're imagining. It will be worse than it is already. All it will mean is more committees to persuade on your choice of book. And who's going to run Sabre?'

'That's why I wanted to see you. How about Gloria Catchpole?'

'Me?' She shook her head. 'I don't think so, Peter. I'm an editor, not an administrator.' Gloria did not even have to mull over this suggestion.

'You'd have been an administrator at Westall's.'

'Yes, but look at the scale of Julius's operation compared with here. I would still have been able to edit.'

'It would mean a doubled salary and all the fringe benefits.'

'I still don't think so. What's more, my appointment would be a disaster for you personally. I'd let you down. I couldn't organise a teddy bears' picnic let alone a new imprint.'

'Nonsense! You were once highly organised.'

'*Once* is the operative word there. Perhaps I'm getting old. Perhaps we both are.' She looked sad.

'I'm sure Julius's offer seems even more appealing at the moment. But you're wrong. I also think you're wrong to turn down Sabre. I need you, Gloria. Please don't resign.'

'Why should you need me?' she asked, a shade suspiciously.

'Because I respect you and trust you. Because you're good. Because – ' He stopped abruptly, stood up and crossed to the window.

'Because what?' She waited.

'Nothing.'

They were silent, looking at each other.

'You could tell me one thing,' she said. 'If everything in the garden is so wonderful why do you look almost ill?'

'I'm tired, that's all.' He pushed his hand through his hair. 'It was a hard round of negotiations.'

'It's not just that. Come on, Peter, I've known you a long time.'

He turned and looked out of the window. 'I've left Hilary,' he said with his back still to her.

'Oh, Peter, I'm sorry.' She blurted out the words automatically – she wasn't at all, but then what else could she say?

'Don't be. I'm not. I should have done it ages ago.' He turned and faced her.

'Which came first – Hilary or selling the company?'

He laughed. 'Clever Gloria . . . But, no, it's not what you're thinking. I found out about the two almost at the same time. They seemed to slot in together. No Hilary, I don't need Shotters. No Shotters, then I doubt if Hilary would have stayed.'

'But then . . .'

'Let's just say I've spent the last few days coming to terms with quite a few things. It's not much fun facing the fact that you've wasted so many years with the wrong person.' He looked at Gloria long and hard and stepped towards her as if he was going to say more but he didn't. Instead he took a cigarette from his pocket and lit one.

'You're smoking again. Peter, that's silly.'

'I know. I'll stop once everything is sorted out.' He smiled at her, pleased by her concern for him.

'If there's anything I can do . . . You know, if you want to talk or anything,' she said feeling awkward and looking at her shoes intently.

'Does that mean you'll stay?'

'Yes, for a bit to see how things go. I've blown it with Julius anyway.'

'I'm pleased, Gloria. I promise you everything will be fine.'

'I do hope so, Peter,' she said, and wished she had the nerve to cross the room and hold him.

2

Christmas at the Trenchards' had gone surprisingly well. This was due, Joy was sure, to her having invited her parents to stay. She knew she was safe with them in the house for there was no danger that Charles would annoy her father – he was too rich and too important. She had changed, she had to acknowledge. Only a few short weeks ago she would never have admitted, even to herself, that this was so. Charles only bullied the weak, had been her unpleasant conclusion.

She explained nothing to her parents, allowing them to think she had merely had a row with Charles and had gone away for a few days' break and that everything was now fine. She could be a good actress when she wanted, she decided.

Over the holiday period Joy could not fault Charles. He had never been sweeter nor more considerate to her every need. She had lost count of the number of times, when alone, he had apologised for his unforgivable behaviour. He had swamped her with the most wonderful presents. He had vowed never to stray again.

Upon her return she had insisted he sleep in his dressing room – her parents need never know. But on Christmas Eve, although she blamed the alcohol she had drunk, she supposed it was inevitable that she would relent and take him back into her bed.

Charles was a consummate lover when he wanted to be. That night he had undressed her with an agonising slowness, all the time loving her with kisses and caresses which, by the time she was naked, had made her nearly desperate for him.

'I want you now,' she looked at him, her hunger blazing in her eyes.

'Don't be in such a hurry, little one. We've the whole night ahead of us.'

It was a night of exquisite, gentle torture as his mouth, his hands led her almost to climax and then he would turn from her, offer her a sip of champagne, all the time teasing her. So that when he finally took her she was screaming her passion and her need for him.

'Oh, why can't it always be like this?' she had said, as she lay cradled in his arms, totally relaxed after such intense love-making she thought that now would be a perfect time to die.

'It will be. This time, I promise you, my darling, nothing will alter.'

Now the holiday was over. Charles had returned to work and her parents had left that morning. After breakfast and a quick game of snakes and ladders with Hannah before she went for her morning walk with her nanny, Joy raced up the stairs and into her bedroom. There she picked up the Jiffy bag which had arrived by special delivery before Christmas. She had been longing to delve into it during the holiday but had forced herself to leave it until now. From inside she took two bundles – Tracey Green's complete novel and Kate Howard's two chapters.

She looked first at Tracey's. She was not a fan of The Paradise Club style of book, but from the first page she realised that this was very much what they were always wanting. In truth, it was better than most she had glanced at over the years. She skim-read, dipping here and there into the book to check that it stayed consistent with the first page. Half an hour later she telephoned Ann Cuthbert, senior editor of The Paradise Club.

Joy had known Ann for years, ever since they were junior editors in their first jobs. She liked it when she knew an editor quite well for she found it easier to talk to them, easier to convey her enthusiasm. It worked with Ann for she agreed to read the manuscript which Joy said she would send over by messenger. She hung up, anxious to get on with Kate's book.

She was only half-way down the first page when it happened. The hair on the nape of her neck stood up, her breathing was faster, her pulse raced, she felt butterflies in her stomach. She was almost too afraid to continue in case the magic of Kate's opening paragraphs did not continue.

She need not have worried. She read on with mounting excitement only to be deeply disappointed when she got to the end of the section and there was no more. She longed to find out what happened next. She leant back in the chair feeling elated. This was it, the book she had dreamt of finding. First Barty and now Kate. And a Kate she had met at Barty's, as if Barty held the key to her success. She did not hesitate but picked up the telephone.

'Gloria? It's Joy.'

'Are you all right?' Gloria asked anxiously.

Joy laughed. 'Couldn't be better.'

'You haven't gone back to him?'

'I have. I know what you're thinking, but – oh, Gloria, I'm so happy. I had the most wonderful Christmas. It's as if I've fallen in love with Charles all over again.'

At the other end of the telephone Gloria rolled her eyes with exasperation. There were times when she found her own sex frustratingly illogical but, then, who was she to criticise another woman? Wasn't she just as daft where men were concerned?

'And how's your love life, Gloria? Happy?'

'Don't even talk about it – non-existent. I've resolved to give them up.'

'That'll be the day.' Joy laughed, and Gloria thought how wonderful it was to hear her laughing again. 'You must come to dinner one day. How about next Wednesday?' Gloria accepted with pleasure: she had never been to Joy's house, or met her husband – she was curious to see what the big attraction was.

'I never expected to read that Peter had sold Shotters. I mean, it's his baby, isn't it? Will this new company work?'

'Of course, it's better all round. New capital, vertical publishing. New dynamism. The bigger the better in today's publishing world.' Gloria repeated the little pep talk she had been handing out to the authors and agents ever since business had started after the holiday. She had serious doubts, but it would be a disaster if they got wind of discontent in the office.

'I always thought Peter had got too big already. He's a publisher not an administrator. Now the firm will be even larger.'

'Oh, he loves it. He says he was born with the soul of an accountant.' Gloria forced herself to laugh. 'He's left Hilary,' she said, and wished she hadn't – she should not be gossiping but she was so pleased she wanted everyone to know.

'So I heard. And . . .?' Joy was laughing now, a small arch laugh.

'And what . . .?'

'I always thought you had a thing about Peter. Now's your chance.'

'Me? Don't be silly, Joy. He's just a very old friend. That's all.'

'Is that so?' Joy smiled to herself.

'What can I do for you?' Gloria asked, abruptly, wanting Joy's teasing to stop. It made her feel very uncomfortable.

'I've got the most marvellous piece of work for you to see. Two chapters and a rather vague synopsis. Honestly, I couldn't put the damn thing down. It's going to be wonderful. Mega.'

'Yeah?' said Gloria, unexcited, used as she was to the hyperbole of literary agents. Whatever they were selling was always the best, always unputdownable. One had to admire their tenacity.

'I know agents are always saying that about their books, but this time it's true. You remember that woman who was skulking in Barty's loo, having a quick fag? Well, it's her, Kate Howard. Marvellous name, isn't it? No need to alter that.'

'She was nice,' Gloria said, with more interest.

'It will be just up Blades's street. You'll love it. Bet you get as excited as I am. When I read it I knew you were the only editor for it and for Kate.'

'She didn't say anything about being a writer.' Gloria ignored the compliment. That was par for the course from agents as well.

'She wasn't then. That's the amazing thing. She tells me she has only just started and it's just pouring out of her.'

'I don't like buying first novels on so little. I prefer them to be finished. You know how it is, Joy. They start all fired up with ideas and enthusiasm and then it all peters out before they've got half-way and they run out of ideas or suddenly realise what hard work it is. I should think this nation is littered with wonderful beginnings of books stuffed away in drawers. Sorry, but I've had my fingers burnt once too often.'

'This is different, *she*'s different. I reckon she'll have finished it completely in six weeks if not less,' Joy said, mentally crossing fingers and toes. 'I'll bike it over to you,' she added emphatically. She had quickly learnt not to say 'Shall I?' to an editor.

'Do that, but I'm not buying, not until it's finished. I don't care how good it is. Anyone else seen it?' she asked, even though she knew it was a futile question. Half a dozen publishers might have thumbed it but the agent would always deny it. There had been a time when you could tell a typescript had been the rounds by its general tattiness, with thumb marks and coffee stains on the pages. These days, with word processors and fast, efficient photocopiers, scripts by the score could be churned out so that each publisher received a pristine one and there was no way to call the agent's bluff.

'No. I told you, I thought of you immediately. I've only just this minute finished it.'

'How are you doing on the Barty project? That was one hell of a coup, Joy. How did you manage it?'

'God knows. I'm waiting for him to return from Australia. I should have something to sell on pretty soon.'

'Well, let Shotters have a stab,' she said, loyal as always.

'I'll be auctioning this one. There's just one thing, Gloria. Don't tell Barty I'm back with Charles, will you?'

When she had put the telephone down she wondered what had made her say that; all she knew was that she did not want Barty to know – not yet.

She picked up the telephone again, not wishing to think too long about her motives for wanting him kept in the dark. As she dialled she thought this was the best part of her job, letting a writer know you liked their work. When she decided she didn't like a book enough to handle it, she never used the telephone but, like everyone else, hid behind the anonymity of a letter.

'. . . I just can't wait to read on. You do have more, don't you?' There was silence from the other end. 'Kate? Kate, are you there?'

'Yes, I'm here.' Kate's voice sounded faint and far away. 'I'm just overwhelmed.' And to Joy's horror she heard her burst into tears. 'I'm sorry.' Kate fought for breath.

'I loved it, absolutely. When can I see the rest?'

'I'm still struggling with my word processor but my son is helping me, it's not so puzzling any more. I'll get it to you as quickly as possible.' Kate gulped.

'Now, I'll tell you what I've done. Remember the other woman in the witches' coven at Barty's? Gloria. I've sent it to her. She's senior fiction editor at Blades who are part of Shotters.'

'I didn't know that.'

'It's always confusing. Publishers seem to buy and sell themselves faster than any other business. Even we get confused. And to confuse you even further Shotters has just been bought by Carras of New York. But don't worry, it doesn't affect the authors and Gloria is staying on. Anyhow, I've sent it to her.'

'Joy, I can't thank you enough.'

'Look, Kate, don't get too excited, it's early days yet. Blades won't buy an unfinished work – it's unusual unless you are a writer with a track record.

But the important thing is we'll get feedback from her. She'll love it and her enthusiasm will make you want to finish it.'

'I don't need anyone to make me finish it, I can't wait to find out what happens myself.'

'Gracious, you are an unorthodox writer.' She laughed. 'So you'll send me the rest? We must have lunch one day soon. Oh, by the way, Ann Cuthbert's agreed to look at your friend's book personally.'

When Joy replaced the receiver she hugged herself with sheer happiness. What a wonderful career she had chosen, she told herself. When things were going well what better was there?

Joy dressed quickly in newly cleaned jeans, a sweater, flat leather pumps and a navy blazer and took a taxi to the flat Barty had loaned her. She made a point of going every few days to collect any mail that might be there for her. So it was that she happened to be in the flat when Barty rang. She accepted his invitation to go straight over to his house for a light lunch, but warned him she was casually dressed. What one wore mattered to Barty.

'You're back early, I didn't expect you until next week,' she said, as she entered his study.

'Too damned hot for my liking. Felt homesick for some nice drizzle.' Barty fussed over her, taking her jacket, ordering her a drink.

'Then you must be sadly disappointed.' She nodded to the window where the sun was shining brightly and unseasonally.

'It'll come. I missed you, girl,' he said, grinning broadly.

'I missed you, too. How did it go?'

'Like clockwork. Brian and me, we get on like a house on fire. He understands me, Joy. I don't have to explain things to him, you see. He doesn't bore me.'

'I'm so glad. Getting on with your ghost-writer is so important. Do you know if he has written anything yet?'

'Love you, yes. We've mapped out a sort of synopsis, well, chapter headings really. And I know he's done the first chapter. That was hard that, things I didn't really ever want to think about again. But, there you go. I said I'd do it, and do it I will. And at least the first bit's over, the worst is done.'

Joy put out her hand and touched his gently. 'I'm sure it was hard. But you know, Barty, you've so much to offer people. When they read your story it will be an inspiration to so many.'

Barty produced a large white linen handkerchief and blew noisily into it.

'Did you know that Shotters has been sold?' Joy said, hurriedly changing the subject, embarrassed by Barty's obvious emotion.

'I told you, didn't I?'

'No.'

'Yes, I did, when I said I wouldn't sell my book to Shotters. Remember? You'd be no good in business, my girl, if you couldn't pick up on a hint like that, especially one from Barty.'

'How did you know? I don't think even Peter Holt knew until it happened.'
She laughed.

'Costas and I go back a long way. He's wanted to get into English publishing for some time. I kept an ear open for him, advised him. I felt Peter was restless, ready for something to happen. Told Costas to act now. I was right, you see.'

'A wonder!' she teased him.

'So's Costas. You think I've got a story to tell, why his would make your hair stand on end. Orphaned at five . . . now one of the richest men in the world.'

'Obviously the rest of us were at a disadvantage not losing our parents.'
She laughed gaily.

'Never say that, Joy. Never.' He had swung round and was facing her, his expression sad and serious.

'No, I'm sorry, it was tasteless of me,' Joy said quickly.

'I've got your new office for you,' Barty announced brightening up. 'All signed and sealed. Bloomsbury, that's the proper place for you. And there's a nice little flat above it, so your business and housing problems are solved in one, There's a garden for Hannah to play in and . . .'

'Barty . . .' She paused.

'Yes, girl?'

'Oh, nothing. You're too kind to me.'

'For a moment there I thought you were going to say you'd gone back to that bastard. I wouldn't like that.'

'No. I know you wouldn't,' she said, wondering what on earth she was doing by not telling him the truth.

After lunch, with Gervase in tow, they went to inspect the new office. It was in a house in the maze of streets behind Tottenham Court Road, that elegant and relatively peaceful part of London with its Georgian terraces, lovely squares and its literary past.

Barty had acquired the whole house, though whether bought, leased or rented he was not saying. The basement he had promised to a friend, he explained to her as he let them in to the main part of the house. Reception and the secretary's office were on the ground floor. Joy chose the largest room on the next floor for herself. Once the drawing room, it had fine mouldings and two large windows that stretched from the ceiling almost to the floor and the room was filled with the January sun. The other room on this floor they earmarked for another agent, when they expanded. They giggled happily at the idea. The flat above was on two floors. A huge sitting room, a small study, three bedrooms and a compact beautifully fitted kitchen which opened on to a small balcony at the back.

'Barty, it's wonderful.'

Barty was grinning at her, Gervase appeared with a bottle of champagne and two glasses.

'New beginnings, always exciting,' said Barty, raising his glass. Joy wished she had not lied to him but could not see any way out of it now, and she raised her glass to him in return.

3

Kate looked at the kitchen clock. It was half past twelve. They were giving a dinner party tonight. The senior partner of Tony's firm and a new client, both with their wives, were the guests. Kate did not mind giving dinners but she loathed not having met two of her guests, it always put her on edge. She sat at the kitchen table and looked at her tattered manuscript and stroked it gently. She still could not believe the conversation she had just had with Joy. She leafed through it. Nearly a hundred thousand words written, she guessed, and of that only the first two chapters were typed. But she had printed out the last two she had written, now that she was managing to cope with the word processor, though she was far too slow to do it all herself. When could she get it into town to be typed professionally? What about now? No, she told herself, she had too much to do. But still, she had made the puddings . . . how long would the starter take? She looked at the recipe she had cut from one of the colour supplements. She had wanted something different from the usual hot chicken liver salads or quails' eggs that everyone was serving at the moment. That was why she was about to break the rule of a lifetime and serve guests a dish she had not tried on the family first. She read it through: a timbale of puréed vegetable and smoked fish. No, it would take ages. If she made something else, if she got the ingredients in Graintry, then she would have time to get the typing into the agency. She would think what to cook in the car.

She hurriedly slipped on her coat. It was putting the manuscript in a Tesco's bag that must have reminded her that she had not telephoned Tracey to tell her her good news too. She went back to the kitchen. Tracey's reaction was the same as Kate's had been – she burst into floods of tears. Kate had to calm her down, and try to make sure she was not too excited, so she reiterated that it had only been sent to be read. And then Tracey insisted she tell her all over again what Joy had said.

It was not until she was in the car and heading, at last, for Graintry that she realised she had not cleaned one piece of silver and she still had the tablecloth and its matching napkins to iron – a pure linen one with drawn thread work, which was a work of art and a horror to iron. She felt herself beginning to panic, so much so that she misjudged a corner and narrowly missed an oncoming car by inches. The driver blared his horn and made obscene signs at her and she forced herself to slow down.

She parked on double yellow lines and raced to the typing agency, only to find it closed and due to open at two. She returned to the car in time to accept a parking ticket from the traffic warden which she stuffed into her handbag. That would make Tony happy, she thought with a grimace. She had to queue to get into the multi-storey car park and by the time she arrived at Sainsbury's she could not remember what it was she had gone there for. Pudding, that was it. She had to change the pudding, she finally decided. She wandered the aisles with her trolley, her mind on Joy not on shopping. Unsure what she would prepare she selected some kiwi fruit, a punnet of strawberries, flown from God knew where, and bought a lot more cheese from the delicatessen counter just to be on the safe side.

At the typing agency the fact that she had a novel to type caused a great deal of excitement. 'A4 paper, double spaced,' she repeated like a mantra. The cost came as a shock. Even more of a shock was the news that it would be ready the week after next. Her pleas that she needed it sooner than that met with the smooth suggestion that if she was prepared to pay extra then that, too, could be arranged. She steeled herself to write the cheque. At least, she reasoned with herself on the way back to the car, they were putting it on disc for her so that it would work in her own word processor. It was a one-off cost. You had sometimes to lay out money to make money, she remembered Pam's husband saying often enough. That would be the tack she would take with Tony when she had to explain the severe depletion of her allowance.

Her car refused to start. The AA were quick, but even then it was past five when she finally returned home. Steve was sitting at the kitchen table reading a comic and eating a peanut butter sandwich of such proportions that she feared for the safety of his jaw.

'You look in a bit of a tizzy, Mum.' He grinned up at her from behind the wedge of bread.

'I am, I am.' She flopped down on the seat opposite him. 'You'll never guess what's happened. An agent loves – not likes but loves, she said – my book and, I can hardly dare to believe this, she's sent it to a publisher.' She sat back, her turn to be grinning from ear to ear.

'Mum, that's absolutely brill. Just think of it, my mother a famous author.' His grin was even wider.

'There's a long way to go yet,' she said, trying to suppress her excitement, which refused to be suppressed. 'I'm so lucky. It can take years to get this far. Getting an agent is one of the hardest parts.'

'Hardly, Mum. Writing it is, more like.'

'Yes, well, after writing it ... Gracious, I must telephone Pam, I haven't told her yet. Oh, Lord.' She stood up. 'Look at the time. Why, oh, why, do we have to have guests tonight of all nights?'

'I'll help.'

'Would you? Would you really? If you could buff up the silver that would be wonderful. Now starter, starter,' she muttered to herself as, without bothering to take her coat off, she began to unpack the bag of groceries. 'Oh, my God, I've bought for puddings not starters. I'm going mad.'

'Not surprising, Mum, it's been a big day. Who gives a damn about starters on a day like this?'

The back door opened.

'Hi,' said Lucy as she breezed in. 'Mum, Christine and I are going to a disco, is my pink skirt clean?'

'Guess what, Lucy? Mum's book is being looked at by a London publisher,' Steve said excitedly.

'That's great, Mum. You know the pink one I mean, don't you?'

Kate had been burrowing in the depths of the refrigerator looking for inspiration for the wretched start to the meal. 'No, I don't. I doubt it, though, I haven't done any washing for days,' she said, straightening up.

'Oh, Mum, really.'

'I thought we had agreed that you do your own washing now. I don't have the time.'

'All you think about is that flaming book. Dad was right – ' Lucy stopped mid-sentence.

'Oh, yes, and what was your father right about?' Kate stood, hands on hips, between the door and her daughter.

'Nothing.'

'I want to know, and you, madam, are not going out until you tell me.'

Lucy flounced, flicking her long hair over her shoulders as she did so. 'Very well, if you must know. Actually, Dad said you were being selfish, but that it was only a passing fancy and that you'd get back to normal sooner or later.'

'Well, *actually*, what your father thinks of my writing is of no interest to me whatsoever – and you have my permission to tell him that.' It was not strictly true but she congratulated herself on how well it sounded. 'And what is more, Lucy, do you think that you and I are destined to spend our lives having conversations about the state of your laundry? If so, I can think of nothing more pointless or more tedious. Sort yourself out, Lucy, I'm not doing it, not any more,' Kate said icily, and returned to her fruitless search of the fridge.

'Well . . .!' pouted Lucy. 'God, why can't things be like they used to be?' she cried dramatically and stomped across the kitchen but at the door turned and poked her tongue out at Kate's rear.

'Childish brat,' sneered her brother.

'It'll have to be soup. Your father won't like it but he's going to have to lump it,' Kate said emphatically, collecting onions and potatoes from the vegetable rack. 'Bread!' she suddenly exclaimed, making Steve laugh as she raced across the kitchen.

'You're like a demented hen, Mum.'

'I've no rolls and the village shop will be shut by now. I can't give them soup without bread.' She ran her fingers through her hair.

'Croûtons,' said Steve, simply.

'Steve, you're a genius.' Kate dived into the large earthenware bread pot. 'Steve, you've eaten all the fresh, this bit's got mould on it.'

'Cut it off,' Steve said, 'it won't hurt them. Sorry about the bread, I was peckish.'

For the next hour Kate was running round in circles. The soup was bubbling. Luckily, looking at the bottom of her near-empty freezer, she had found an unlabelled bag of stock. She offered up a prayer that it was chicken, as she slid it, hissing, on to the gently sautéing onions and potatoes. She trimmed the pork fillet, cut it open and bashed it flat with the rolling pin. Into her Magimix she threw some prunes, apples, cooked rice and offered up another prayer of gratitude for progress. Deftly she stuffed the fillet, rolled it, tied it and browned it quickly in butter and garlic. She assembled the ingredients for the lemon and white wine sauce she would make at the last minute, using the pan juices. She parboiled the potatoes, sliced the leeks – they were too big to cook whole – and puréed the spinach, which she put into buttered ramekins to cook in her *bain-marie*. Was there enough? She would do parsnips in orange juice and brown sugar cooked in the oven – everyone always loved that. And then she fretted that perhaps the whole meal was going to be too sweet. She checked her tangerines stuffed with ice cream in the freezer and realised they were uncomfortably close to the parsnips with their orange juice. But then, she told herself, there was nothing she could do now. And what was more, she suddenly realised, she did not care. She had poured herself a large gin and tonic and was just starting to iron the tablecloth when Tony walked in.

'What on earth have you got your coat on for? This is always happening these days.'

'I've been in a rush.'

'You look like a peasant.'

'Good,' she said defiantly, and took a deep swig of her drink.

'Is it wise to start so soon?' he said, placing two large clinking carrier bags on the table.

'Mum's got the most amazing news,' Steve said from his station at the sink where he was carefully washing and drying the silver.

'What's that?' Tony asked absent-mindedly as he unpacked his wine bottles. 'I got one white and two red and a Sauternes for the pudding, that should be enough,' he said, without waiting to hear the answer and stood back to admire his purchases.

'It's pork. I told you it was.'

'You didn't.'

'I did. I asked you, shall I do the prune-stuffed pork and you said yes, you liked it.'

'If you had, why should I buy red?'

'I haven't the foggiest idea. But it doesn't matter, lots of people drink red with pork.'

'Well, I don't. Christ, Kate, you're useless, now I'll have to go back into Graintry.'

'There's an off-licence in Malt Lane,' Steve said helpfully.

'At Malt Lane prices, young man. No, I'll go to Peter Dominic's. What's the starter, we haven't messed that up have we?'

'It's soup.'

'Soup! Can't you do better than that with such important guests? What will they think?'

'Mum's soups are wonderful,' Steve chipped in.

'I ran out of time, Tony, I'm sorry. I had the most wonderful news, you see . . .' And excitedly, her eyes shining, she told him what Joy had said.

'You mean to say you've messed up this important dinner party because of that damn book of yours?'

'I had to get to Graintry to the typing agency.'

'Christ, how much will that cost?'

She told him in little more than a whisper.

'You're mad, bloody mad, do you realise?'

'Joy wanted it next week. I'm still quite slow on the word processor,' she added quickly to pre-empt him.

'I don't understand you, Kate. You used to take such a pride in everything – this house, yourself, dinners. Now everything's going to pot. You're being selfish, Kate, I hope you're aware of that.' And he slammed out of the back door.

Kate felt her face stiffen. It was one thing to hear Lucy repeat what he had said about her, but actually hearing him say it, that hurt.

'Here you are, Mum.' Steve handed her the glass of gin and tonic she had poured. 'Sit down and drink this. He didn't mean it.'

'Yes, he did.'

'Well, I'm proud of you. Even if the publisher turns it down, how many people get this far? Don't take any notice, Mum. The dinner will be lovely, they always are. Don't let him stop you, Mum. You do it. You show him. Tell you what, I'll give you another lesson on the word processor this weekend, show you all the short-cuts, shall I?'

'Thanks, Steve,' she said, giving him a hug, but all the pleasure of this morning had gone.

Although Tony was barely speaking to her – a state of affairs that was completely lost on their guests since he still appeared to be – the dinner was good, even if the company wasn't. Fred, the senior partner, was not one of her favourite people though she quite liked his wife, Philly, who made Kate laugh – Silly Philly they all called her behind her back. But the stumbling block was John Premier, the important client. He was pompous, loud and constantly putting down his wife.

The food, although good, was, as she had feared, unbalanced with too much fruit and too many sweet tastes. It was a mistake she would never have made in pre-writing days. But all the guests ate with gusto and much appreciation, especially, she was amused to register, for the soup.

Pre-writing days, everything had changed since then, she thought as she sat through the long dinner and watched her husband at the other end of the table. She would show him. She would succeed without his support, she did not need it.

'And what else do you do, Kate, other than produce food fit for the gods?' John Premier, sitting at her right, asked her.

'I write,' she said loudly and confidently.

'Kate, I didn't know you were a writer, how exciting,' Philly said, face alight with interest.

'Kate can hardly call herself a writer. You can only do that when you're published by someone,' Tony added from his end of the table.

'I didn't say I was a writer, I said I write.' She looked at Tony steadily.

'I'd love to be able to do that. You are lucky,' Margaret Premier said, totally unaware of the tensions building up around her.

'And have you a publisher?' John asked.

'My book is with one now. Blades, a part of Shotters.'

'My, the big-time. I thought you were going to say The Paradise Club.' John threw back his head and laughed. 'Right load of rubbish they are. Margaret spends all her time reading the drivel.' His wife looked embarrassed.

'In fact those books are very hard to write, it's a very special technique. I know I couldn't do it, I lack the talent,' Kate said.

'Oh, come on, Kate, any fool could do them,' John persisted.

'No, I mean it.'

'Well, their success is beyond me. Sell millions, don't they?' John asked.

'Yes. No doubt their success is due to the fact that they fill a void in many women's lives.' Kate said quietly, smiling at Margaret and ignoring the looks of fury being semaphored down the table from Tony. She stood up. 'Cheese everyone?' she asked with a smile.

4

Julius, alone in Scotland, could not remember when he had enjoyed himself so much. To find a time he would have had to return to the days of his youth, when, as an undergraduate, working for exams, he had rented an isolated cottage in Wales for a few days. In the intervening years he had always been surrounded by other people, bothered by their noise and problems. He had forgotten how pleasurable solitude could be. So great had been his pleasure in his own company, and with Jane still away at her sister's, he had prolonged his stay in the cottage in the wilds of the Northern Highlands for several weeks.

With no telephone there was no one to bother him. With no newspapers to read, no doubt the world was carrying on in its usual cruel, hysterical way, but without him having to worry about it. With no company and no television he had reread *Bleak House*, *War and Peace* and *Vanity Fair* plus a handful of easily consumed thrillers. His supply of malt whisky had been diligently depleted. If he had a complaint it was that he was a little tired of eating Cumberland ham or salmon and he had resolved it would be some time before he bothered with them again once he was back in what fools called civilisation.

Every couple of days or so he wrapped up warm and trudged across the snow-covered fields and through a wood of magical winter icicles to his friend Angus Fairley's improbably turreted castle. There he picked up mail forwarded by Roz. He had told her not to telephone unless anything crucial cropped up. To his delight, nothing had, apart from the notification of a directors' meeting of Westall's to be held at the end of January, to vote on the proposal that Crispin be appointed to the board and be allowed to acquire Simon's shares. The resolution was proposed by his brother and seconded, he noted with wry humour, by his dear wife.

He liked Angus, and Flora, his wife, friends of such trust and long-standing that explanations for his behaviour were not asked for, nor expected. They all delighted in each other's company and they all respected each other's need for privacy. Shortly after his arrival he had confided in Angus his death sentence and then wished he had not as he saw the pain and distress the news had caused this dear friend of a youth long gone. He had begged him not to tell Flora and resolved never to tell another living soul.

Sometimes he stayed with them and their guests for lunch – the invitation was always forthcoming. At other times he thanked them and scurried back to the small crofter's cottage beside a burn which flowed so swiftly it rarely froze even in the extreme temperatures here. At night it was to the sound of this water that he drifted off to sleep. When he first arrived he had thought what a wonderful sound it would be to die to. And then there were nights when he found he wished he would not wake up. But, to his sadness, the mornings came.

Such morbid thoughts were at the beginning, now he had changed. Whether it was the peace, the beauty of the place or the sheer magnitude of the scenery, he did not know, but now when he woke up it was with joy at the prospect of another day. He no longer wanted to die. He was so happy he had even tinkered with the idea of letting everyone have their way and selling up Westall's, giving Jane the house and retiring up here. But if he did that the years of work and worry would be for nothing. There had to be another way.

The day of the meeting approached and it was time to leave this idyllic spot. He felt immeasurably sad as he packed his few belongings and waited for Angus to come in his Range-Rover to drive him to Inverness to catch the night sleeper. He gave his friend the last full bottle of whisky, a Laphroaig. On the station platform he had to look away as he saw Angus's eyes fill with tears. He listened to the invitations to come back soon, to regard Burn Cottage as his whenever he wanted, or to stay with them, whichever he preferred. He accepted with gratitude but even as he did so he knew he would never return, and realised that Angus, too, knew he would not.

He climbed on to the train, waved goodbye, and settled himself in his sleeping compartment, unpacking the half-full bottle of whisky he had saved for the journey. He changed into his pyjamas and lay back on the narrow

British Rail bed. He wondered how he would readjust to living with Jane after his enjoyable solitude. Once or twice he had wondered if they should not part. Jane might find someone else, someone capable of making her happy – but, then, with his prognosis, what was the point? She would be a widow soon enough. It would be an expensive and pointless exercise.

There was also the company to think about, Crispin and Simon, and what to do. Could he let his brother down? His thoughts zigzagged around. Whichever way he turned them he did not like the conclusions he reached. This was one decision that refused to be resolved.

Crispin had had a strange time recently. Parts had been good and others bad. Confident that his deal with his uncle was finalised he was somewhat put out when the greedy old codger had asked for more – not a little but a lot. And Crispin had the devil's own job raising the extra. It was not in his nature to go cap in hand to anyone, least of all the banks, and to be turned down like a nobody was painful. He had finally raised the money, by the skin of his teeth, but to do so had been forced to sacrifice six paintings, some silver and a rug to the various dealers from whom he had originally purchased them. He knew he had been cheated; when money was needed quickly it was unseemly how rapidly the value of possessions fell. But there was no time to wait for an auction or to find that rarity, an honest dealer. He had accepted their money and vowed never to do business with them again. But nothing could assuage the loss of these objects, their absence would always leave a void in his heart.

Charlotte was being rapacious in a way he would not have thought possible. She was behaving like a shopkeeper with her interminable lists of what she regarded as hers – rapidly becoming the majority of the house's furnishings it seemed to him. The house was on the market – something he had not told the bank yet. Of course they would have to know eventually, since it was their security against his loan, but it was one of those irritating details he preferred not to think about for the moment, just as he preferred to ignore what was to happen when Charlotte discovered this fact. It had probably been unwise of him to forge her signature on the bank documents but, there, it was done now. It was not his fault, he had not known he was going to fall out with Charlotte, it had seemed safe at the time. And what was to happen if the bank insisted on their money the minute it was sold? And who had first priority, banks or greedy, divorcing wives? Unpleasant thoughts best not dwelt upon. The happy thought was that if everything was taken from him then there would not be enough money for the bijou mews residence Charlotte had set her heart on and had found with what he regarded as indecent haste.

His holiday in the Bahamas with the air hostess, Carol, had started off badly when she had insisted they go to a disco, of all places. He had enjoyed three nights of her body, though. She was at first delightfully insatiable, and was one of those rare women who did not mind what was done to her. But three nights was enough. He felt exhausted and was quite relieved that she had to leave to return to her job. He said he would look her up when he was back in London – something he had no intention of doing. She was disappointed that he was not travelling with her but by a piece of good fortune, he had bumped into an old Etonian chum, in real estate in Miami, with a holiday home on the island, who had most hospitably invited Crispin to stay. And then, at a party given by this friend, he had met a gem.

Brenda Benton. He had almost been put off by the name – Brenda was not a name conducive to a great passion, he thought. But, luckily for him, he had registered her surname just in time to give her the benefit of his full charm. Benton: the mass-market jewellers, hoteliers and fast-food chain. He had accidentally found himself a pretty, gentle, well-educated and docile heiress to millions.

He had returned to England with Bee-Bee, as he now called her, madly in love with him, desperate for him to meet her parents and sweetly hinting that marriage to him would make her happy. What to do? While divorce would cost him dear, marriage to Bee-Bee would quickly refill the coffers. Sex was likely to be a problem, however. From their nights in bed, he had learnt that Bee-Bee was a traditional girl – him on top and strictly no fellatio. She might change, of course, and he could have a mistress, but it was annoying.

Before he took such a step as matrimony, however, there were one or two things he would have to sort out with her father. There was still the extraordinary meeting at Westall's to go through. He had not had time to find out more about the Lepanto Trust – his foolish trip to the Bahamas had seen to that, and had he not found Bee-Bee, he would now be kicking himself for an indolent fool. But meeting her had, possibly, changed everything.

He had formulated a second plan. If Julius should dig in his heels over the shares, and Lepanto remain a mystery, he must not miss the opportunity that meeting Bee-Bee had given him. He had ingratiated himself with her father and had interested him so much in the world of publishing that he was pretty confident he could get old man Benton to finance him to buy all the shares he wanted, maybe even the company itself – once Julius was dead. But Crispin would want definite assurances before he went ahead with any nuptials. And if this was to be the outcome he was going to have to teach himself patience. Difficult, but important.

Today was the meeting. Crispin was in his office trying to appear as though he were working at the same time as his future was about to be decided two floors above. Even with the money arranged for the initial plan, even with his secondary plan incubating in his mind, he had an uncomfortably churning stomach. For who knew better than he did how quickly things in one's life could change? What if Bee decided not to marry him? What if her father were not as amenable as he had thought?

So he had plan three – a shot in the dark but all that was left to him. He could not imagine Julius voting for him so he had asked his mother, should Julius vote against his inclusion and use the Lepanto vote to scupper his plans, to insist upon seeing the authorisation papers for Julius's proxy. She would have the right and there was a faint chance the mystery might be solved – if the beneficiary of the trust was named on the proxy. Then he would be able to approach whoever it was, work on them to vote for him, and try again later. The problem with this scheme was that he did not know if his mother would act for him – he never knew with his mother. He bent his head over the papers in front of him, he had done all he could. Now he was going to have to wait.

The large boardroom at Westall's had been set ready. There were four ordinary chairs with blotter, pen and paper, water carafe and glass before them on the table. A larger chair stood at the head for the chairman – Julius.

Julius entered the empty room and crossed to the window. No matter which window he stood at in this building the sight of the square, unchanged since these houses were built, always pleased him, whichever the season. The room was called a boardroom but, with so few directors or shareholders, it was rarely used. The art department had long ago purloined it, using the large mahogany table to great effect for layouts of jacket and poster designs. Today their paraphernalia had been stacked on side tables and propped up against the walls.

He watched his sister Marge and his wife greet each other across the square. Even from this distance it was possible to see, from the stiff way they stood, the perfunctory handshake they gave each other, the careful distance between them as they began to cross the road, that here were two people who had no time for each other. He wondered if Jane was complaining about him. If so, she would get scant sympathy from Marge, who had loathed Jane from the minute Julius had brought her home to introduce to his family. Marge had liked him then, loved him even, and so close had they been that it was inevitable that no one would be good enough for her brother. Caring for him as she did then, it had always been one of life's greatest puzzles to Julius why, when he had gone ahead with his marriage to Jane, his sister had turned her enmity on him too. Enmity that had lasted to this day. It was extraordinary, he thought, just how long the female of the species could maintain a feud.

He turned as the door opened and Simon entered the room, crossing it immediately towards Julius, arms held out, in expansive greeting, which he wrapped around his brother in a huge hug. If pressed, Julius would admit to loving Simon alone in the family. But it would be hard not to, for the large bear-like man exuded such affection and was basically honest. And Julius was aware that, in all probability, Simon was the only one who truly loved him and would be scarred and saddened by his death.

The two women clattered into the room on immaculate high-heeled shoes, both equally expensively suited and scented. Both were unnaturally thin with the twig-like slenderness of the late middle-aged woman who has dieted too harshly and too long. Marge greeted him pleasantly enough and he was glad she did not find it necessary to kiss everyone welcome. Jane nodded curtly.

'So you're back? How kind of you to let me know,' she said coldly.

'I'm sorry, Jane. I travelled down on last night's sleeper. I called but you had already left. How's your sister?'

'Fully recovered, thank you.'

Julius mumbled how pleased he was and then thought how little it would matter to Jane if he had left her. If the cook handed in her notice it would upset her far more.

At two he called the meeting to order by taking his seat. The others slid into theirs where Roz had placed their names. There was much straightening of blotters and realigning of glasses, which Julius presumed indicated that none of them was as relaxed as they appeared. Quietly Roz took her place at the side of the room at a small table as secretary. Julius glanced down at the agenda.

'As always I have Lepanto's proxy on all matters, should any point arising necessitate holding a shareholders' meeting after this one.'

'So yet another year goes by and are we still not to be privileged to know who Lepanto is?' Marge smiled.

'Should anyone query my proxy they are at liberty to inspect the necessary documents.' He smiled. He had often wondered if this would ever be raised. He could smile, for he knew that only the solicitor who dealt with the administration of the trust had signed the document, on behalf of the trustee. Anyone studying it would get nowhere in discovering his secret. The Lepanto secret had always been a game with him but it was now turning into far more than that.

'I might,' Marge said, tightly.

They raced through the business but then, he was fully aware, none of them wanted to hear his financial report which was nothing but failure and gloom. In the past he had witnessed animated interest on their faces in the good years when the profits were high. He reported on his acquisitions, mentioned his plans for the future, none of which was of the slightest interest to them.

Finally they reached the all-important minute. The proposal that Simon be allowed to sell his shares to Crispin and that Crispin be elected to the board.

'Is anyone opposed to Crispin's becoming a shareholder?' Julius asked. There was silence. 'I would like it put on record that I, as chairman, am none too happy with Simon selling his shares and that I have indicated to him on several occasions that this is a course of action he might come to regret.'

Roz's pencil skimmed with speed across her shorthand notebook.

'Why?' asked Jane.

'Because my brother would do better to wait. When I'm dead this firm will realise a lot of money, that's why.'

'Why, are you thinking of dying, Julius?' Marge asked, her husky, heavy-smoker's voice full of humour.

Julius ignored his sister.

'They are Simon's shares to do with as he wishes. I don't think any of us has the right to stop him selling at this point if he wishes,' Jane said in her oh-so-reasonable voice. 'It will give him much-needed security,' she added, looking pointedly at her husband.

'I do need the money now, Julius, old chap. Not some vague date in the future.' Simon laughed nervously.

Julius rested his head on his hands and looked at the face of his brother. He could not let him do it, it would not be fair. Think how Simon would feel when he died and he realised how much he had lost. 'It's like this . . .' he began.

'Hold on, Julius.' Simon held up his hand. 'No need to do the protective brother act with me.' He laughed, nodding at the others around the table. 'When we were young he was always like this, never letting me get a word in edgeways, interrupting me when I had something important to say,' he explained, smiling fondly at Julius. 'It's my turn to speak up today, Julius. What I wanted to say . . . It's like this . . . I'm fully aware that if Julius dies I'd receive a lot of money from the sale of the firm – far more than Crispin is willing to pay me. But for a start I don't like all this talk about when Julius dies – he's my brother and I love him.' He coughed, his voice thick with emotion. 'Apart from that, if, and God forbid it does – if anything happened to Julius and everyone wanted to sell up, well, to be honest I wouldn't want a penny of the damn stuff. Selling would be a betrayal of Julius and everything he's worked for all his life. This way – selling to young Crispin – I can buy my house in Tuscany, have money enough to see me out, something to leave Dulcett and, most important of all, a clear conscience.'

It was Julius's turn to cough and to find his voice was husky too. 'Thank you, Simon, I appreciate that.'

'Of course, there is another matter.' Everyone looked at Marge who appeared totally unmoved by her elder brother's speech. 'Crispin is loathsome, driven by pure self-interest. Do we really want him on the board?'

'Really, Marge, what a dreadful thing to say about your own son,' Jane admonished.

'It's the truth. Tell me, Julius, do you like him?'

'No,' Julius answered.

'See,' Marge said pointedly to Jane.

'Who *does* Julius like in this family?' Jane snapped back.

'Certainly not you, if he's got any sense left,' Marge countered quickly.

Jane sat even more stiffly in her chair, turning her back slightly in haughty dismissal of her sister-in-law. 'He's good at his job, Julius has said that enough times. He knows the financial side of publishing inside out.'

'I'd like to cut the cackle and put it to the vote, if you don't mind.' Simon was getting restless, dreading the thought of his farmhouse in Tuscany disappearing, dreading the legal implications if he did not buy, since he had already signed the initial documents.

'Should I strike those last comments of Mrs Anderson's from the minutes?' Roz asked politely.

'No, keep it on the record,' Marge ordered. 'He knows what I think of him, I don't care if he reads it.'

'This whole voting is a waste of time, this meeting is a waste of time. We all know how Julius, with his proxy giving him fifty-one per cent, will vote, don't we?' Jane gestured with a thumb pointing downwards.

'Right. Those in favour of resolution five, please raise your hands,' Julius said smoothly.

Every hand around the table shot into the air – including Julius's.

5

Although she had known Joy professionally for years, Gloria had never met Charles. She had several married friends in the business whose husbands she did not know. When two people involved in any aspect of publishing met socially, it was rare that anything other than books was discussed. Consequently it was not unusual for people to keep their family and work lives separate. Gloria was curious to be meeting a man who from many talks with Joy she felt she knew personally but whom she had not yet seen.

She parked the car outside the large, imposing white house in Holland Park. A wrought-iron and glass canopied porch stretched from the door, down the steps, along the path to the gate. Gloria was most impressed: these places cost a fortune. Maybe that was why Joy had returned to him – money. Then, as she locked the car, she chided herself for such an uncharitable thought. Money did not matter to Joy, but then it need not, she had never in her life been without it.

The inside of the house was even more impressive. Gloria was shown into the hall by an incredibly handsome blond butler. He was far too young to be a proper butler, and Gloria presumed he was an out-of-work actor hired for the evening. The hallway was laid with black and white marble. Over a gilt Regency console table, with legs so slender it seemed a miracle they could support the heavy marble top, hung a large and very fine Chippendale mirror with candles lit in the sconces at its side. Gloria made a point of checking herself in the mirror for experience had taught her that the more expensive the mirror the more becoming the reflection in it.

The butler led the way to the wide sweeping staircase. He walked in such a stately manner that she was convinced she had been right in her original assessment of him. As he mounted the steps ahead of her she had an almost uncontrollable urge to pat his delectable buttocks. Gloria adored men's bottoms, the perter and tighter the better. She always claimed that it was going to school in Plymouth and, at a young and impressionable age, seeing *matelots*' buttocks in their tight bell-bottom trousers that had left her with this particular fixation.

Joy was waiting for her at the head of the stairs. Without waiting to welcome Gloria she grabbed hold of her arm.

'Barty's here. Please don't breathe a word about my being back with Charles,' she whispered urgently.

'But if Barty's here and Charles is here, won't he guess?' she whispered back, gesticulating questioningly with her hands, palms held upwards.

'Charles is in New York. Barty thinks I'm here to look after my daughter while he's away and that I'm borrowing the house for this dinner,' she said, speaking normally now that the butler had reached the foot of the stairs and was crossing the hall to answer the door again.

'If you don't mind my saying, Joy, aren't you in the process of creating the most awful muddle in your life?'

'I know, I know. But what else can I do?'

'Tell the truth for a start. It's hardly Barty's business if you go back to your husband, is it?'

'But it is, you see. Barty loathes Charles – he's even trying to ruin him. And if he finds out, he could do anything – cancel the book, break up our new agency.'

'But . . .' Gloria was about to point out that if Joy loved her husband, being in business with someone intent on his ruination seemed an odd way to show affection, but she thought better of it. 'Don't you think if Barty finds out from other people he's likely to be far more furious?' she asked reasonably.

'He won't, though, will he? Unless people tell,' she said, staring pointedly at Gloria.

'Rather you than me.'

'Ian, Peggy, hello.' Joy beamed at the new guests ascending the stairs. 'Be a darling, Gloria, go and talk to Barty while I welcome my guests.'

The drawing room into which Gloria stepped was a wonderful, light and airy room with the kind of flower arrangements that took hours of supreme patience to achieve – that or horrendous florists' bills. Elephant could efficiently have wrecked the white silk upholstery in five minutes. She was glad she had not asked Joy if she might bring him. But, for all its perfection, the room was cold and soulless, a bit like a too-perfect woman, Gloria thought. For her, rooms had to have a bit of human clutter to make them real.

Barty was in deep conversation with a young man over by the window. Rather than interrupt, Gloria studied a painting over the mantelshelf. It was of a man, so handsome and perfect of feature that he was beautiful. He had a pleasant smile, which told of immense charm, but the eyes that looked at her from the painting – blue and icy – told Gloria it would be of a smooth and superficial variety. Like the room, he was too perfect and what size ego did a man have who had a portrait of himself hanging in his drawing room?

'Cold-looking cove, wouldn't you say?' Barty was standing at her elbow.

'A bit surprising. I had imagined him dark, not blond. And with far more passion about him. It is Charles, I presume?'

'Yes, it's him all right. He's got the passion, too. Problem is he can't keep it in his trousers.'

'Poor Joy.'

'Not any more. She's made the right decision at last. She'll be OK now. She thinks a lot of you, by the way. I was very pleased about that.'

'How nice,' said Gloria, but was unable to find out why Barty should be so pleased, for Joy had come in with her other guests.

Ian, sleek and rather pleased with himself, was a banker of decided opinions. Judging by Barty's reaction to him he must have been quite important too for one could always gauge Barty's assessment of someone by the way he greeted them. Ian's wife, Peggy, was beautifully dressed with immaculate hair and fine jewellery. Every time she spoke she looked nervously at her husband before starting and then even more nervously when she had finished. A wife-beater, Gloria decided, and liked him even less.

She was then introduced to Ferdie, something in the City, early forties and affluent-looking but with a pleasant smile and an infectious laugh. And lastly there was Brian, Barty's ghost-writer, who was unkempt, somewhat ill-at-ease but with a rather wild expression in his eyes which intrigued Gloria. She wondered which of them had been invited specifically for her. She knew Joy of old and like so many friends when happily married, or, as in this case, enjoying a happy interlude in an otherwise turbulent marriage, liked to matchmake. Was she supposed to make a play for Ferdie or Brian? Of them all she fancied the butler most.

'How do you enjoy working for my friend Costas?' Barty had rejoined her, drink in hand.

'It's all right. It's really too soon to tell,' she answered, bestowing a dazzling smile on the butler as he handed her the vodka and tonic she had asked for in preference to a champagne cocktail which always made her legless.

The butler moved on to the next guest.

'He's not your sort, love. Eton and Christ's and his father's a viscount,' Barty whispered conspiratorially, his sharp eyes never missing a trick.

'Then why's he a butler?' she whispered back, glad that it took a lot to make her blush these days.

'For laughs, I should think. So why don't you like working for Costas?'

'Did I say that?' She spoke defensively.

'I would hardly think that "all right" means you're happy in your job.'

'The job's OK, it's the building. He's turned it into Fort Knox – passes, security guards.'

'Costas doesn't like industrial espionage. He's been caught before.'

'But this is publishing.' Gloria laughed at the very idea.

'So?' said Barty. 'In my experience if something's worth paying good money for then there's always someone who would like to nick it off you.'

Gloria sipped at her drink and to her horror found she had already finished it. 'By the way, I heard about the book. I hope Joy stitches up a good deal for you with it.'

'No worries there. With my Joy in charge it'll be the sale of the century. Clever little thing, isn't she?' He lifted his glass to Joy across the room and smiled a soft, gentle smile. Joy waved back. A thought so bizarre entered Gloria's head that she had to shake her head to rid herself of it, but she could not stop staring at Barty who, aware of her gaze, raised his eyebrows quizzically, so that she had to say 'sorry' and quickly turn away.

The dinner was wonderful but, then, that was what one would have expected from a perfectionist like Joy. Gloria was placed between Ian and Ferdie and had a difficult time deciding who was the most boring. Ferdie spoke only of shooting and money, while Ian's interests extended only to fishing and money. It was evenings like this that confirmed her belief that the ideal marriage her mother envisaged for her, with a successful monied husband, would be mental suicide.

At the pudding stage Joy made everyone change places. With relief Gloria now found herself between Joy and Brian while Barty had taken on the money men with relish. They were free to talk about what they liked best – books.

Looking across the table Gloria saw that the shamefully ignored Peggy, who throughout the meal had successfully semaphored the state of her empty glass to the butler, was sitting bolt upright on her chair fast asleep without making a hint of a whiffle.

'What a talent, I wish I could do that,' Gloria whispered to Joy nodding to the sleeping woman.

'Oh dear,' said Joy with a little laugh. 'I'd best say it's time we withdrew.' In the ensuing hubbub as chairs were pushed back and the men stood and the women looked for their handbags, Joy was able to wake Peggy without her husband noticing.

In the drawing room, large iced vodkas in their hands, Peggy already asleep again in the corner of the sofa, Gloria and Joy could get down to what they had been longing to discuss all evening.

'Well? What did you think of it?' Joy opened the proceedings.

'What?' Gloria replied with, she hoped, a good air of vagueness, because one of the first things she had been taught about her job was never to show too much enthusiasm – it could be costly.

'You know what I meant.' Joy pushed her playfully.

'Do I?' Gloria grinned.

'Yes. Have you read it or not?'

Gloria paused before answering and studied her shoes intently. 'I did.'

'And?' Joy leant forward.

'There's not enough to go on.'

'There's enough, you know there is.'

'A lot of work needs to be done on it.'

'Come on, it doesn't, editors always say that about every book.'

'I'd need to see a lot more.'

'She's lunching with me next week, would you like to meet her again? She'd love to see you.'

Joy crossed to the desk and took her bulky Filofax. 'Here we are. Tuesday, one, Panakies.'

'My, my, you're pushing the boat out for her, aren't you? One you say?' Gloria opened her Filofax.

'I expect great things from Kate, I believe in spoiling a good author.'

'What did you think of the other guests?' Joy changed the subject, her face alight with curiosity.

'Not a lot. I was surprised about them more than anything else, I'd have thought they were more up Charles's street than yours.'

'They weren't my friends. Barty asked me to invite them, I was hosting for him, you see.'

'Ah,' said Gloria, understanding a soupçon more.

At eleven-thirty she made her farewells even though there was talk of moving on to Barty's supper club. In the hall she managed to slip a note to the butler suggesting he meet her in an hour at the Groucho Club.

Barty had been right. He was not her sort at all. Polite and gentle in the extreme, he spoke of the metaphysical poets and Zen Buddhism until, to her shame, she had nodded off.

Now she was looking at herself in the bathroom mirror, wishing it had the kind reflection of Joy's Chippendale, and wondering what on earth had made her do that. And then she looked at herself sadly and wondered how many times she had asked herself that question and how many times in the future it was likely to be repeated. And what the hell to give him for breakfast with the fridge empty and the corner shop shut?

6

Kate had been so absorbed with her writing and the battle to master the word processor that it was some time before she realised she had not spoken to Pam on the telephone for days, let alone seen her.

She dialled Pam's number.

'Pam? I need your help desperately. Joy Trenchard, my agent...' She paused, she had not meant to, but those two words were like a dash of cymbals in her head. 'Joy has invited me to lunch at Panakies. That's a very posh place, isn't it? What kind of thing do you think I should wear?'

'I don't know, I've never been there in my life.' Pam's voice was distant and chill.

'But you're always going out to lunch in super London restaurants, please help.'

'Wear a suit, the blue one. Is that all you wanted? I really must be going...'

'Pam, what is it? You sound so cool with me.'

'Well, what do you expect?'

'I'm sorry?'

'If you must know, I was rather hurt to hear, from Tracey Green of all people, that you had found yourself an agent. In my book, that's big news. Something I could reasonably have expected you to share with me. After all, I am supposed to be your best friend, at least that's what you were always telling people.'

'Pam, I'm sorry. I just don't seem to have the time any more to do half the things I should. When I first heard from Joy, we had a dinner party that night, and I got into such a flap that telephoning you went quite out of my head. I do apologise.'

'You didn't manage to remember after that either, did you?'

'It's the book, I just can't seem to think of anything else. The next day I went back to the writing and well, you know what it's like, everything else goes by the board.'

'Felicity says you're probably being taken for a ride.'

'Really? Does she? Why?'

'She says London is full of so-called agents – cowboys, actually. Women setting up with a telephone, typewriter and fax, knowing bugger-all about publishing. She says that you're only really safe in the hands of the proper large agencies.'

'I don't think that's necessarily so. Joy's a lovely person and obviously knows the publishing world. I don't think that's a fair comment when Felicity hasn't even met her.'

'I'm only telling you what Felicity advises, but then you don't like Felicity, do you?' Pam's normally sweet voice sounded quite hard.

'It's not that. I'd rather be handled by a person who's working in a small way and can spend time with me, rather than a huge organisation which must be more impersonal.'

'You're the one who would know, of course, with all your experience.' There was no mistaking the venom behind the remark.

'Pam, please. Don't be like this. How can I make amends?'

'Perhaps, in future, it would help if you told me first hand what was going on.'

'I promise faithfully I'll call you next Tuesday – soon as I get back from London – and tell you everything. What I want, though, is for you to come shopping with me tomorrow. You know how hopeless I am at putting clothes together.'

'Sorry, no can do. Out of the question. I have to stick to *my* writing routine, you should understand that. There's just one thing, Kate, it's not very attractive only calling on friends when you want something.' The line went dead and Kate was left looking at the receiver with a surprised expression. It was her fault, she had been thoughtless and totally self-absorbed. In the past she had always been available, at the drop of a hat, for Pam. No wonder she was hurt and upset. Once she had finished the book she would try to make it up to her. Not yet, though, she was not going to allow anything to impede the book's progress.

'Tony, might I have a word?' she asked. There was an irritated rushing of the newspapers, Tony hated to have his Sunday-morning read interrupted. 'My agent wants to take me out to lunch on Tuesday.'

'How very nice for you,' Tony answered, and she was almost sure he was not being sarcastic.

'Yes, isn't it? The thing is, would you mind taking my typescript into the office tomorrow and getting your secretary to photocopy it for me? I need two copies.'

'But I seem to remember you spent a fortune last week having it typed.'

'They only made one copy and I need two.'

'Run it off on your word processor,' he said reasonably.

'I haven't got enough paper and I won't have time tomorrow to get more.' She did not look at him as she said this for it was an out-and-out lie, she had a large box of paper and another unopened in the cupboard, but she had already worked out that if she shopped in the morning, she could work in the afternoon and add another couple of chapters to what she already had ready for Joy.

'I suppose so. I don't promise anything, it depends on how much work the girl has to do. Leave it by my briefcase.'

'Thanks.' She let herself out of the drawing room and went straight to the kitchen where she quickly knocked up a chocolate mousse, Tony's favourite, rather than the shop-bought treacle tart she had planned to serve. That made and chilling in the refrigerator, she raced back upstairs to the spare bedroom. This room was rapidly metamorphosing into her study with paper and books littering the bed, and the word processor on the dressing table by the window for the light. She was soon tapping away. But she had learnt a thing or two and now she typed with an alarm clock beside her, set to ring when the potatoes needed to go into the oven.

Tony was somnolent after his roast-beef lunch and two large helpings of mousse. He was sprawled in his favourite chair, legs stretched out in front of the fire, looking as if he was about to fall asleep.

'You look very content.' She smiled at him.

'I feel it.' He patted his stomach.

'You have a nice sleep. I think I'll do some more writing,' she said, standing up. She paused in the doorway. 'Oh, by the way, I thought I'd go to Graintry tomorrow and get a new outfit for Tuesday – give me confidence.'

'You do that, Kate,' he said, yawning mightily.

Kate did not like using such ruses to get what she wanted. When she had first married she had despised any woman who stooped to such feminine wiles. But that was a long time ago, and experience and disappointments had taught her that it was often the only way with her husband. What if her book was accepted, what if she made some money, what would it be like to be able to buy what she wanted when she wanted and never to ask again?

'No!' she said firmly and aloud, back in her study, and purposefully switched on the machine. This was a silly way to be thinking. It was sure to lead to disappointment. She turned back to her work.

Kate felt almost sick with apprehension as she approached the restaurant.

'Madame?' A waiter welcomed her. Joy had not arrived. For a moment she managed to work up quite a good panic, convinced Joy had forgotten, but then, glancing at her watch, she saw that she was early. Joy had asked her to be there for twelve forty-five. It was only twenty to. She declined to be shown to the table immediately and asked for the ladies'. She had already spent ten minutes in the toilets at Paddington station, fiddling with her hair, her make-up, her clothes. She stood once again staring at herself in the mirror and for the umpteenth time wondered if she had not made a ghastly and expensive mistake. If only Pam had been willing to come shopping with her, to advise her, she would not be so worried and flummoxed now. At the same time she loathed herself for being such a wimp.

The black patent shoes with gold buckles were all right, so was the handbag, but that was about it. The rest of her, she felt, looked a disaster. The three-quarter length, fine wool, red coat was all wrong. It was too bright. And what on earth had made her listen to the shop assistant who told her she looked wonderful in the red and pink, swirling-patterned silk two-piece that matched the coat. She never wore such bright colours, and certainly not ones that clashed as much as these did. Looking at herself now, she looked like a child's kaleidoscope. She peered at her chin line and round her ears, checking there was no tidal rim of make-up – she never normally wore so much. And should she have worn her hair quite so loose at her age? God, she looked a mess, she thought mournfully. Would she ever wear any of it again? She doubted it.

The door swung open and Joy Trenchard, elegant in taupe and white silk, drifted in, short blonde hair straight and gleaming, make-up so discreet as to be almost invisible.

'Kate!' she cried out with genuine pleasure. 'Are we destined always to meet in the loos?' She chuckled.

'Hello,' said Kate, feeling huge and awkward.

'Yum, I love the outfit. Where did you get it? I'd die for that silk suit,' she said, as she glanced at her face in the mirror and then looked enquiringly at Kate.

'Graintry, a small shop,' she said, realising that Joy meant it, she really liked what Kate was wearing.

'Did you bring the rest of the book?' Joy asked eagerly.

'Yes, it's here, two copies as you asked.' Kate pointed to the rather shabby old briefcase of Tony's which was the only thing she could find big enough to hold two copies of her typescript.

'Wonderful. Let's go and order drinks.'

They were settled at one of the central tables and Kate, feeling happier now that Joy had said she liked her outfit, was looking around surreptitiously just in case there was anyone famous to tell Pam about. But they were the only customers, it was still too early for most people. Kate ordered a spritzer, primarily because that was what Joy ordered.

'I asked you early because I wanted time alone with you before Gloria comes.'

'Gloria? She's coming here?' Kate asked feeling all the anxieties rushing back.

'Don't look so frightened.' Joy patted her hand. 'She absolutely adores your work.'

Kate felt the room reeling and her skin burning and had to hold on to the edge of the table for support.

'There is a slight problem.'

'Of course,' said Kate, sinking back into her chair. Of course there would have to be, wouldn't there? she thought.

'As I warned you, Blades don't give advances on first novels until they're completed. Nothing to do with your work, it's company policy. It's in case the rest does not come up to standard and they will have thrown money away.'

'I could always give it back if they did not like it,' Kate said helpfully.

'Oh no! No one ever does that. Most authors I know spend their advances immediately. They're nearly always in debt, you see. Goodness, don't even suggest it, you'll start a revolution.' Joy laughed at her. 'But that was why I was so keen for you to bring more, keep Gloria on the boil until you can finish it. How far along are you, do you think?'

'I had some typed professionally, and now I'm much quicker on my word processor, so I was able to print out another chunk. I must be about three-quarters of the way through.' Kate plucked this figure out of the air because she had no way of knowing where she was in her tale. Since she had planned and plotted nothing it was difficult for her to say how far away the end was.

'Three-quarters!' Joy shrieked, and then covered her mouth with her hand to stop herself. 'You're amazing. You've only just started, how do you do it?'

'I don't know. The words just come out so quickly and I have to write them down in case they all escape.'

'How many words do you write a day, for goodness sake?'

'It varies, depending on what else I have to do. I have to squeeze it in. I managed seven thousand one day, but my husband was away, and the kids were out. Most days I hope to get three or four thousand words down.'

'Unbelievable.' Joy looked at her with admiration.

'The house has suffered and the garden is a shambles.'

'What do they matter? Someone else can always do them,' Joy said grandly, in the manner of someone who has such things done for her. 'It's the book that counts.'

'Yes, it is, isn't it?' Kate beamed, basking in this conversation with someone who obviously understood her compulsion.

'The thing is, Kate, don't be down-hearted if Gloria says little about it, will you? And if she does, and if – it's unlikely to happen, of course – but if she starts talking money, don't say a word. Understand? Oh, and by the way, if she does, you need the money.'

'Well, of course I do. Doesn't everyone in this day and age?'

'Good. I'm glad. If they think the money is unimportant to you and that they can get something for nothing they will. Gloria, over here . . .' she called.

'Kate, lovely to meet you again.' Gloria shook her hand and smiled at her. She sat down, slipped off her jacket, plonked her handbag on the floor, ordered a vodka and tonic and sat back and smiled again at Kate. 'I have to tell you, I liked the little bit of your book Joy allowed me to see. It promises to be good.'

'Thanks.'

'Guess what, Gloria.' Joy was leaning forward eagerly. 'Kate's already over three-quarters through the book. She writes at the most amazing speed. She'll have finished in a matter of days, won't you, Kate?'

'Hopefully, domestic crises permitting.' She grinned and felt herself blushing though she did not know why. Since they were talking about the book, was this the time to give it to Gloria? Or should she wait for someone else to make the move?

'She's brought you a copy, haven't you, Kate? Go on, dig one out for Gloria,' Joy encouraged her.

'Yes,' said Kate, covered with confusion, and she burrowed into the briefcase to remove one copy. It was an odd feeling handing it over to Gloria. She had posted the first section with excited glee. This was different. There was far more of it. Last time she had not expected much to happen, but now that so much hung on Gloria's opinion Kate felt almost loath to let it go. As Gloria took the large wodge of paper she felt suddenly bereft, painfully so.

'I'll look after it, I promise,' Gloria said. 'It must be an awful wrench giving it to me, like giving your baby to someone else to criticise.'

'Yes, it is.' Kate smiled at her, happy that she should be so understanding.

'I'll be straight with you both. I know we don't normally buy . . . The thing is, I'm in two minds on this one.' She paused, looking at the typescript, flicking through as if to see the number of pages. 'Tell you what. I'll read this and if it's as good as the rest then I'll talk to Joy straight away. I can't promise you more than that, can I?'

It would have been difficult to judge whose grin was the wider, Kate's or Joy's. Gloria put the typescript into her own case. She did not know what had made her say that. She did not normally let herself fall into any of the traps invariably set up by agents, nor even half promise things. But there was something about Kate she liked, a shy enthusiasm, a bewilderment at what was happening, almost. And she realised she felt keenly that she did not want to let her down. She always hoped a book was right, this one she longed to be so. She could wish Kate was a bit younger and wore contact lenses – publicity always wanted them glamorous today and only literary writers got away uncriticised for looking frumps. Still Kate looked better than the last time she had seen her, much smarter and prettier.

'I love that suit,' Gloria said. 'I love clashing colours, don't you?'

Kate mumbled, not sure if this was a compliment or not, as the waiter took their order.

On the train back to Graintry, Kate was certain it was not just the afterglow of the wine she had drunk that was making her feel so euphoric. A tiny bit of her was beginning to believe that the impossible was possible: she was going to be published. But then the other, more sensible, part of her squashed flat such a notion. Best not to think about it. Logically, what were her chances? Nil. She knew already the heartbreak suffered by other writers far more experienced than she. What right had she to think that she could possibly be that much luckier than everyone else? Ah well, she thought, if nothing happened, if she heard no more, she had lost nothing. She had had a lovely lunch, it was all a little adventure, really. And she had a super new outfit – she liked it now, she told herself, seeing her reflection in the train window as they entered a tunnel. One thing was certain, though: if no one wanted this book, it would not stop her, she would carry on with the next one. In the last few days new ideas had begun to float into her mind, like small motes which, each day, grew bigger.

Joy returned home to be met by the nanny who, with the greatest pleasure, told Joy that her husband had telephoned and would be late home.

Joy did what she always did when upset: she poured herself too large a gin and tonic and took a long bath.

Gloria had not bothered to return to the office. The three of them had shared two bottles of wine and work was out of the question. She returned home to a furious Elephant, not best pleased at not being taken to work, and she called Rachel to say she would be at home reading. She did not intend to do any such thing. She meant to have a bath and then to sleep until she woke up. She looked in her briefcase for some Nurofen – lunch-time drinking always gave her a headache. To find it she removed Kate's typescript. She glanced at it idly. Three hours later she was still reading it.

7

Gloria showed her security card to the uniformed guard, the barrier was raised and she drove down the ramp into the car park. She took the lift to reception, and joined the queue of employees waiting to sign the large book on the desk and to enter their time of arrival – they would be putting in a time clock soon, was the current joke among them. Here, again, she had to show her pass to the security officer on duty. These new procedures, introduced by the Carras organisation, were ridiculous, she thought, as she had thought every day since they had been instigated. She knew each officer by name and they her, but every time she entered the building the same ritual had to be gone through.

Getting into Shotters was like getting into a prison, she had decided, though friends who had odder friends assured her prisons were easier. She supposed Peter Holt and Costas Carras were the only people allowed in without this rigmarole. Even then, maybe Peter was in the same boat. She must ask him what he thought of all these ludicrous new regulations when she next saw him. She was sure he had not instigated them, he was far too casual a person for that. It would probably be a long wait: she saw him even less these days. She often wondered what the authors thought about it all when they visited but, then, they were no longer particularly welcome here. A memo had been sent to all departments pointing out that authors should not be encouraged to call at the office. It was only a matter of time before the authors were banned altogether as an unnecessary nuisance. A day would come when her authors would be voices at the end of a telephone, or senders of fax messages, or images on a video screen; people who would only be trotted out to appear at a launch party and to face the press on publication day, like performing puppets. This high security added to the atmosphere of paranoia which was now rampant here.

She stuck out her tongue at the TV camera which swept back and forth filming the crowd in the reception area. Pointless really since it certainly would not be Costas at the other end – he was in New York, only his aides remained. But she liked to imagine Peter might be there. She would like him to know just what she thought of him and what he had done, what he was allowing to happen.

He had lied to everyone. The promises of no redundancies had been empty. A massacre had taken place here and that was no exaggeration.

In mid-January a team of men from across the Atlantic had entered Shotters. Who was who was difficult to tell since they all wore identical grey suits, button-down shirts, and understated ties. Even their haircuts were the same. For a week some had pored over the bookkeeping while others prowled around the building with clipboards in their hands and, although they did not have stop-watches, they looked as if they should. Round and round they went, observing. It had been an unnerving experience for everyone.

The feelings of relief when they closed their notepads, packed away their clipboards, shut their briefcases and boarded their Boeings back to New York were enormous. Everyone had relaxed, blissfully thinking that they had passed some test, that now they would be left alone to get on with what they were good at doing.

There was peace for a couple of weeks and then the telephone on one editor's desk had rung with a summons to Peter Holt's office. Ten minutes later she emerged looking ashen and, with everyone in the office watching in horror, she silently began to pack her things – the first to be made redundant.

The others huddled together, reassuring each other, confiding one to the other that this editor had not been much good anyway. Dead wood should be cut out, they rationalised. But word filtered through from the other sections of Shotters that editors were falling like ninepins.

For the next week there was a strange stillness about the building. Where before there had been jokes and laughter and the constant buzz of conversation and discussion, now there was nothing. Sombreness permeated everywhere even down to the boiler room where the maintenance staff had been decimated. Telephones frequently rang for a long time: people were becoming afraid to answer them for fear of the summons.

Then attention was turned to the other departments. First publicity, then production, followed by the art departments. Teams were pruned. Then the announcement that everyone half expected, and although they might think it a logical step, it still frightened them – individual departments working on separate imprints were to be amalgamated into one, servicing all the various imprints within the group. What had been pruning became ruthless and radical surgery.

It was not over. Marketing and sales were finally confronted. Whereas each house within Shotters had its own sales team, now they, too, were to be joined into one large one. Large it might be, but not large enough, and reps who had been with Shotters from the beginning were shed as unfeelingly as the newcomers.

The whole huge building was now a frightened hive of rumour, the occupants like bees whose nest had been disturbed after the winter slumber. Heads of department walked about with the look of hunted animals, badgered as they were by staff for information that they themselves did not have but which everyone else believed they did. People slipped quietly about the building as if trying to make themselves invisible in case they reminded the powers that be of their presence.

Gloria had lost count of the tearful farewells, the attempts to cheer up with warm white wine those who had been sacked, the piles of Kleenex they were getting through. Redundant they were called but, at the end of the day, they had been sacked. It did not matter a jot what cosmetic words the bosses used. Sacked with a pay-off. What was there to say to them? Assurances that they would get other work were misplaced, for this could not have happened at a worse time. Business was slow in the book world and other publishing houses were also shedding workers – if not on the massive scale at Shotters. The bleak truth was there were no jobs to go to.

The survivors felt exhausted. Living with this amount of tension began to take its toll. Tempers became short, ailments that doctors could find no cause for affected many, marriages were under strain and colleagues had become rivals.

Blades's office space had been rearranged. Where she once had three editors Gloria now had one – Letitia. Editorial assistants, those who tradition-ally were being trained to become editors in time, were all gone. Secretarial staff had been cut ruthlessly. Rachel now worked for both Gloria and Letitia. The only good thing to happen was that Gloria had been given a private office, quite grand and large, and glassed off from the main floor. There had not been space before, but that was one thing Shotters had plenty of now.

The 'list' was now on everyone's mind. How long before cuts were to be made there? With this depleted staff there was no way they could continue to produce the number of books they had been, and which made Blades viable. As word went out and journalists picked up the story, so anxious authors began to telephone, worrying about their contracts, their options, the chances of their next book being picked up.

During this period, although she kept a sharp look-out for him, she rarely saw Peter. Then one day they had shared an uncomfortable journey in the lift. Neither had known what to say to the other. He seemed unable to look at her and spoke only of the weather. She knew she should have told him exactly what she thought. She could not, for she felt she was looking at a man who, from the loss of weight she noticed, the puffy eyes from drinking too much and the harassed expression, was facing the fact that he had made the worst decision of his life. But nor could she bring herself to put out a hand and touch him and tell him she understood and did he want that shoulder to cry on? She wanted to but something – shyness, perhaps – stopped her. After that encounter he seemed to be avoiding her.

If Gloria had started to become disillusioned with Shotters before, it was nothing to how she felt now. She had begun to dread entering the building, afraid of what the day might bring. She was trapped. How she rued the day she had honoured her pledge to Peter and turned Julius down.

On this day, as she made her way through the huge open-plan office, she had promised to write a reference for a wan creature who asked her even before she had reached her own door. Once inside she shut the door quickly as if she could shut out the misery outside it.

The telephone trilled. It was Lorna Willington's secretary from personnel asking for her immediate presence. In the past a summons from personnel usually meant some silly problem with tax or national insurance. Not any more. Her heart seemed to plummet.

'Lorna will have to wait,' she said, with a courage she was far from feeling.

'I'm sorry, Gloria, but she said it was important.'

'Half an hour,' she said, more out of bravado than anything else.

She sat and forced herself to think logically. She was too senior to be given the boot by personnel, only the junior staff had been told that way. People like her had been summoned to the top floor and given a stiff drink before hearing the news. So why was she being called? After her job her next greatest worry was for Blades itself: she had a nasty idea its days were numbered. How long before all the middle-market books produced under the various imprints were put under the editorial directorship of Tatiana Spence of Shotters, and the Blades logo was no more? When that happened Gloria was leaving, she had promised herself, with or without a job to go to. She loathed Tatiana. There was nothing wrong with the woman as an editor – she was one of the best, Gloria was the first to admit. No, she disliked her superciliousness, her perfection, her neatness, her organisation. In her presence Gloria always felt she was back in the Lower Fourth and being interviewed by the head girl.

She berated herself for getting worked up. Such a major decision would be told her by Peter, not by washed-out Lorna in personnel. She looked at her watch, the half-hour was up.

'Now, Elephant, you be a good boy. Mummy won't be a minute,' she said, and picked up her commodious handbag. That was another unpleasant change about this place, one couldn't leave anything of value lying around: someone was sure to nick it if you did. But she could leave the dog with confidence. Provided she told him she would be back he would stay patiently waiting for her; he never roamed and would bite anyone who tried to steal him.

'Morning, Lorna, what can I do for you?' Gloria said with breeziness to the head of personnel whose office was on the second floor. Lorna, a thin-lipped and dyspeptic-looking woman, was head of personnel for the whole group: at least here was one department that had not altered much.

She might manage to sound breezy but, for all her logical thinking, Gloria's heart was pounding.

'Gloria, thank you for coming so promptly.' Lorna smiled her wintry smile. From anyone else such a remark would be sarcasm, something beyond Lorna.

'I've an editorial meeting at eleven.' Gloria looked pointedly at her watch which showed a quarter to.

'I'll get straight to the point, then,' Lorna said, but instead of doing so began to shuffle papers about her immaculately tidy desk. Gloria was not surprised, Lorna was incapable of getting straight to the point of anything. She had always felt sorry for the woman, sensing she had strayed into a job that was way above her capabilities and was now doomed to a life of constant worry.

'So?'

'This is very difficult . . .'

Gloria waited, attempting a bored expression.

'I've had a complaint, well, several in fact.'

'What about?' Gloria's forced boredom continued in her voice.

'Your dog.'

'Elephant?' She did not pretend to be bored now, she was alert and on the defensive. 'What and who?'

'There are some who think it's unhygienic for you to bring that animal to work as you do. Not healthy at all.'

'What the hell do you mean?'

'I've received instructions to ask you to desist from bringing it.'

'*It*, as you call it, is a dog, *my* dog. Peter Holt gave me permission to bring him with me. I only work here on the understanding he comes too. No dog, no me.' She spoke clearly and coldly, not feeling at all sorry for Lorna now.

'It's the health risk. Certain matter has been discovered. It's not nice, Gloria, not nice at all.' Lorna was twisting her hands as if washing them in unseen water and soap.

'What "matter"?'

Lorna put her head on one side like a weary bird and lowered her voice. 'A motion,' she whispered.

'A motion? What the hell's a motion? Do you mean a crap, or a turd? If so, why can't you say so?' Gloria's voice was beginning to rise.

'You know exactly what I mean, Gloria, and it's not my habit to use the language of the gutter.'

'Elephant's been set up. He'd never crap indoors, he'd burst rather than do that. Whoever said that is a bloody liar. Who was it?'

'Gloria, calm down do, you're sounding paranoid.' Lorna was beginning to flutter.

'Paranoid? Me? Don't be so bloody patronising.' Gloria's voice was raised, and heads began to lift and peer towards the glass partition behind which the two women were now standing, glaring at each other. 'You know what you can do with your instructions, Lorna? You can stuff them. I've a meeting to go to.' Gloria picked up her bag and swept from the office.

'Well!' Lorna sat down heavily on her chair, not for the first time wondering if she was in the right profession.

Gloria returned to her office. She looked about the outer office with a hurt expression: she had thought these were her friends. She had been certain that everyone loved Elephant as much as she did. It was unbelievable that any of them would lie about the little dog. She reassured the dog loudly, for everyone to hear, that no one was going to besmirch his name like that again. People looked upset; it crossed her mind that it might not be anyone here. It might have been the blank-faced men from New York who had objected.

Her mood was not improved by being unable to find the reports she had prepared last night on two novels she had to present this morning. Now she was going to have to do it off the cuff. These presentations were new to Shotters, something the editors were learning to approach with nervous apprehension. Having found a book they liked and believed in, it was then their job to persuade the rest of the staff that it was good enough for the house to publish, and the book passed or failed on a vote.

In the past when Shotters had belonged to Peter, Gloria had had her own budget to work within. Any book she liked, up to a certain sum, she could purchase without consultation with anyone. What had usually happened, however, was that she solicited other people's opinions anyway, but from choice, it had not been a rule. Above that sum she would consult with Peter and Logan and they had always sanctioned what she felt strongly about. Then, editorial meetings had been held to report on books that had already been accepted for publication, reports on work in progress, discussion of ideas each editor might have had. But now everything, it seemed, was to be decided by a committee.

When she arrived it was to find Tatiana sitting in on Blades's editorial meeting.

'Tatiana,' Gloria said coldly.

'Do hope you don't mind me sitting in on this meeting.'

'Why?' Gloria asked the question everyone else in the room had been longing to ask but had lacked the courage to do so.

'Just interested in what Blades's spring list for next year might hold.' Tatiana never smiled as other people did. Her face was a rigid, perfect mask. One theory going the rounds was that, like some models and actresses, terrified of facial lines forming, she never smiled for fear of inflicting them upon herself. The other theory was that she was so devoid of humour she never found anything to smile about. As it was, for politeness' sake her lips, with bright red lipstick that never smudged, never seemed to be eaten, were stretched a millimetre or two, showing just the tips of her perfect teeth.

'Sure it's not to see what we've got that might fit an amalgamated general list?'

'Oh, Gloria, what on earth gave you that idea?' Tatiana laughed, but, with mouth almost closed, it emerged somewhat false and tinny.

Gloria found the meeting tedious and endless. She nearly nodded off as Peregrine Phelps, ex-Wykhamist with a personality problem, droned on about the biography list. She fantasised about the joy of strangling Jill Case as she twittered on about some new cooking star she had found and *longed* to sign. Jill always 'longed', never asked, demanded or wanted, and Gloria loathed her silly little-girl voice, so at odds with the body of a fat middle-aged woman.

'Gloria?'

Gloria looked up. Norman Wilton, her editorial director, was smiling encouragingly at her. She had forgiven him for being promoted over her and quite liked him now.

'Sorry, dozed off, I can't cook.' She grinned in apology thus upsetting Jill who was frequently hurt at the best of times. 'I had a rush, I'll have to send my reports round.' There was a shuffling at this – it was quite common for Gloria not to have her reports ready.

'Right. I've two completed works. *Revenge* title self-explanatory, by a new writer, Primrose Cooper, she lives in East Anglia. And *The End is Nigh* a modern romance, saga length, by Serena von Hohenzohe.'

'I hope it's not a medical with a title like that,' someone joked.

'That can't possibly be her name?' It was Jim Field from marketing. Gloria did not know him well but resented him, unfairly she realised, for he had replaced Chris Bootle. Chris, in her eyes, had been the best marketing manager she had ever worked with.

'It is. She's a lovely woman and as glamorous as her name, and lives in London. She used to freelance for several of the women's magazines, this is her first novel. The advantage with both of them is they are new and hungry writers, we'll get them cheap. Only Serena has an agent, so we'd get world rights, America, TV, the lot with Primrose. I've received from Joy Trenchard an historical saga by a Betty Farmer – I've not had time to do a report on it for you but I like it and if you would trust to my judgement? Joy is keen to hear since she's thinking of sending it to Wallers. She's certain they'll buy but at least we would get away with Wallers' rock-bottom advances.'

'Joy Trenchard – another rich woman playing at being an agent,' Tatiana drawled.

'She's not playing, she's highly professional. She signed up Barty Silver, after all,' Gloria said sharply. She then began her synopsis of the works in question, trying to convey in the too few minutes allotted to her the excitement and the pleasure she had felt upon beginning to read the typescripts, imparting to others the enthusiasm that never left her when she found a book she believed in and wanted.

The Betty Farmer went through on the nod – at that price they could take the risk on Gloria's word alone. Everyone was excited about Serena, especially when Tatiana announced that she knew her and confirmed what a glamorous, vibrant person Serena was. Copies were to be sent around; if the majority liked it they would offer on the lowish side but be prepared to double if necessary.

But on the first book she had talked about, and Gloria's favourite – *Revenge* – they stuck. It wasn't the plot, a searing tale of jealousy and revenge between twin sisters, well plotted, good characterisation, wonderful use of words. No, the sticking point was Primrose Cooper herself: she was fifty-four and a grandmother. She was too young to be published under the 'isn't she marvellous for her age, writing about sex in her seventies' school of thought. And she was too old to be a sex symbol herself.

'But it's a wonderful book.'

'Fifty-year-old grannies are hell to publicise. The chat show hosts want glamour,' Coco from publicity wailed.

'Not everyone watches chat shows,' Gloria snapped.

'Has she led an interesting life?' Jim asked hopefully.

'Her husband's a civil servant.'

A collective groan went up around the large boardroom table.

'You know the problem, Gloria,' Norman said kindly. 'Look at the number of these novels published each year. You've got to have a publicity hook. I'm sure it's a wonderful book – your instincts are always right, Gloria. But we need a personality, your Primrose sounds about as exciting as a ham roll.'

'And, after all, Gloria, we are stuck with the Kate Howard you bought before this new system was introduced. She's problem enough without another middle-aged frump to add to my troubles. I mean they're always so lacking in confidence. They dry up on radio, are worse than useless on TV.' Coco did not so much speak as whine. Gloria gave her an irritated look, which was completely lost on her, as she concentrated on the complicated doodle she had been doing.

'If I could be of help,' Tatiana said smoothly. 'Our list over at Shotters is already full for next spring. I know that Ann Cassell is keen to do a novel, I could get her agent to call Gloria.'

'I'm quite capable of calling her agent myself.' Gloria glared. She felt sick, she wanted Primrose's book badly. She had met the woman, she had already told her how excited she was by the book, she had probably said too much, cruelly raising her hopes – but she'd been so sure on this one. Now she felt she had failed her.

Around the table everyone was talking excitedly about Ann Cassell. Ann was a journalist who wrote a regular column on one of the Sunday papers, cross between a social diary and social comment. She was often to be seen on television, was young, beautiful, slim and articulate. Her novel would be a bestseller just on her name alone.

'You'd have to move fast, she only approached me first because we were at college together. Of course, with her readership each week she'll be looking for a hefty advance,' Tatiana continued smoothly.

Suddenly Gloria saw very clearly the way things were going. Tatiana knew already they were to be shifted – she wasn't going to let a catch like Ann slip through her fingers. She was offering her to them purely and simply because, by the time the book was published, Blades would be no more. It would be part of Shotters' general list and run by Tatiana. Blades would do all the work and Shotters' imprint would publish it and get the acclaim. Worse, the woman would be her immediate boss! Gloria sat silently, listening to the others, hearing the words she loathed – media interest, hype – and suddenly spoke up.

'God, this sort of publishing makes me feel ill,' Gloria said, loudly interrupting the hum of general euphoria over Ann Cassell. 'We don't even know if Ann can write a novel. Primrose has – a wonderful unputdownable book. My instincts are screaming – buy, buy. Handled and marketed well this book could be a megaseller. It's nearly as good as Kate Howard's and, admit it, you all loved hers. And yet you'll let Primrose slip through our fingers. You're all getting your knickers in a twist about a self-opinionated journalist whose idea of a long piece is a thousand words when we are in the market for at least two hundred thousand. To cap it all, you are willing to give an unknown quantity a stupid advance. I just don't believe what I'm hearing.'

'But Ann would be so marketable.'

'If she pulls it off. Look at all the journalists getting on the bandwagon. I'm sick to death of having to put heart into their books for them, that's *when* they deliver them. Never on time, I'd like to point out. That's what it comes down to. Primrose has written with feeling and with love, not for money. Writing for money doesn't work, you land up with a sterile nothing,' Gloria said.

'But they sell.' It was Jim again.

'But can she write a second? Answer me that. Primrose is halfway through her second,' Gloria said triumphantly. 'And with an advance for Ann of that size, what sort of publicity budget are you into? Word of mouth still works out there, Jim, with the great reading public. You know it does, it happens time and again. And the public isn't so daft, it can recognise a book hype at a mile. What do you say, Norman?' Gloria appealed to the editorial director of Blades.

'I'm afraid I'm with the others, Gloria. There are just too many fifty-year-olds out there already. Now if she was seventy – ' He stopped, obviously thinking better of it upon seeing the expression on Gloria's face. He coughed. 'And you know how sticky first novels are to sell. The booksellers loathe them, the reviewers never bother with them. Let her go elsewhere, we can always offer for her next when someone else has had the mammoth task of building her up.'

Gloria sat silent for a moment and looked around at the faces of the others. One or two had the decency to look shamefaced, no one liked a book they felt strongly about to be turned down. Tatiana's lips moved. It was probably that version of a smile that did it.

'That's it, then.' Gloria suddenly felt oddly lonely and very tired. She stood up, picked up her handbag and faced them all. 'I quit. This isn't a publishing house any more, it's a sausage factory.'

'Gloria, you can't. Sit down, let's talk this through.'

'No thanks, Norman. We've talked it through. I'm through. I'll return the car in the morning.'

As she left the room, head held proudly high, she had the satisfaction of hearing a buzz of consternation behind her. She was a good editor, she knew she was. She loved her job, the real part of her job, getting her hands on a book, working with the author, coaxing out of her the book she had meant to write in the first place and hadn't. She knew she would be sorely missed, not just by the house but by her authors too.

Back in her office she picked up the two typescripts she had been working on, walked into the outer office and dumped them on to the surprised editor's desk.

'There you are, Letitia. It's all yours and there's a rush on – I've quit.'

She did not wait to hear Letitia's comments but went back to her desk, emptied two boxes of computer print-out paper onto the floor and began to load her dictionaries, reference books, and signed copies of novels into them. She picked up a black bin-bag and emptied the contents of her drawers direct into it. By now there was a ring of concerned faces peering around the door frame, watching her.

'Gloria, you can't – '

'Gloria, stop it – '

'Gloria, calm down – '

Gloria swung round and faced them. 'I can do it. I'm not stopping and I'm perfectly calm, thank you. If you'll take my advice you'll quit too – before you're all axed. Anyone willing to help me with these?'

Staggering under the weight of the bag and boxes, it was a subdued procession that accompanied Gloria and Elephant to the lift and down to the car park. By the time she kissed her goodbye, Rachel was crying. The others looked white-faced with shock.

Gloria gunned the car, and defiantly turned the stereo up so that Elvis blared out, echoing in the cavernous car park. She felt excited and elated. The tyres howled in protest as she shot up the ramp.

At the top she slammed on her brakes, her way blocked by a large Mercedes whose driver was reversing into a reserved parking bay. Gloria, leaving her engine running, jumped out and crossed to the other car and began, angrily to bang on its roof. The window purred down.

'Gloria . . .' Peter smiled pleasantly up at her.

'You big creep!' she yelled.

'What have I done?' He looked nonplussed as he climbed out.

'You don't know, do you? Still you don't understand. How long will it take for you to realise you've sold loyal colleagues down the river? That you have ruined a wonderful publishing house. And for what?'

'But, Gloria. Let me . . .'

'Money!' she shouted, unable to stop. 'You're just like everyone else. Greedy. And I – ' She gulped for breath. 'And I was the fool who thought you were different.' She wiped her eyes with the back of her hand, horrified to find she was beginning to cry. She turned abruptly. 'I've quit.'

'Gloria, please, let's talk . . .'

'Don't give me that rubbish. What did you say? "Stay Gloria, I need you . . ." Bah! What for? When do I see you? When have you consulted me? We've nothing to talk about. Nothing. You're a Judas, Peter Holt!'

'Gloria . . .'

But already Gloria was stalking to her car. She opened the door and swung round to face him.

'But I'll give you one piece of advice for old times' sake. Watch your back. Watch Tatiana – she wants your job, Peter. Maybe then you'll understand . . . I do hope so.'

She slammed the door shut and, with foot down, shot out of the car park, past a white-faced Peter. Far too fast, she drove down the street, tears of anger and disappointment rolling down her cheeks.

8

One of publishing's curses, though in this case one of its blessings, was that gossip spread through London at the speed of a forest fire. By lunchtime Julius knew that Gloria was out of work and, what was more, every detail of her departure from Blades. By two he was on the telephone offering her the job he had planned for her. By one minute past she had accepted.

Julius replaced the receiver on its cradle and was smiling. He was pleased to be proved right. He could have offered the job to many editors, but he had chosen to wait, certain it was only a matter of time before someone as individual as Gloria would walk out of Shotters and into Westall's.

'Come in,' he called in answer to the knock on the door and felt his smile disappear. The knock would be Crispin. Julius had an open-door policy in his office, people were encouraged to pop in and out with ideas and problems at all times. Only his nephew knocked. It irritated Julius out of all proportion, probably since there was nothing he could do about it, for Crispin was only appearing to be polite after all. 'Appearing', for Julius was sure that Crispin knew that his knocking annoyed him and continued to do it on purpose.

'I don't know how many times I have to tell you, Crispin, but there's no need to knock. If the door is open it's because I'm available.' Julius sounded querulous.

'I know, Uncle. I just couldn't do that, it would seem so wrong. I have to knock.' He smiled his oleaginous smile.

Julius looked down at the papers on his desk to get away from that smile. He loathed the bugger more with every passing day. And, what was more, he hated Crispin calling him 'uncle'. It only reminded him of a relationship he would have preferred did not exist. But, again, there was nothing he could do about that, either.

'What can I do for you?'

'It's the Barty Silver autobiography.' Crispin placed the folder he had been carrying on the desk.

'It's good, isn't it? I don't know the young journalist who's writing it but he's got the sound of Barty, the feel of the man, just right.'

'It will be the autobiography of the year, undoubtedly. But I don't understand, Uncle. These figures here, they're in your handwriting.'

'Yes?'

'But with these figures we won't stand a hope in hell of getting it.' Crispin tapped at the top page with his perfectly manicured fingernail. 'I mean, Uncle. Really! The advance you're suggesting is almost an insult to the man. And the publicity and marketing budget, that's more than the advance. Have you made a mistake? Have you got them the wrong way round? Even if you have, it's still too low, far too low.' He flashed his teeth but his eyes were cold. The old fool's going ga-ga, at least he could do the decent thing by everyone and die, he thought dispassionately. He placed another piece of paper on the table. 'Look, I've done my own costings, presuming a first print-run of ten thousand and a major paperback deal – I suggest Thistle's. With serial rights and subsidiary rights, we should be looking at – '

'There's no mistake, Crispin.' Julius looked calmly at his nephew. 'You're getting carried away. We can never hope to match what the big boys will be offering for this one. I've heard that Mike Pewter's determined to get it and he'll keep upping his offer until he does. We don't have that kind of money. But what do we have to offer Sir Barty?' Crispin looked blank. 'We have our name and our reputation, that's all, that and what we can honestly afford to offer. Barty's no fool. If we offer a ludicrous sum he'll know we've nothing left in the piggy-bank to market it properly.' Julius waited for a reply but none was forthcoming. 'I agree with you, we don't stand a cat in hell's chance of getting it.'

'Then why offer?'

'Courtesy, I suppose. Barty will be in on every stage of this book – he's like that. No doubt he gave his agent the list of publishers he wished it sent to. I've known him for years, I'd hate him to think we weren't interested.' It was Julius's turn to smile at the look of total frustration on Crispin's face.

'I despair, Uncle,' he said.

'I know, I know. But these things can't be helped.' He returned to the papers on his desk as Crispin turned to leave. 'Oh, Crispin. One piece of good news. I've just heard that Gloria Catchpole is to join us.'

Crispin stopped dead in his tracks and stood still as if caught in a child's game of statues. He turned slowly. 'Gloria? What on earth for?' His lips were curled with disdain: he had little time for the popular fiction that was Gloria's speciality.

'We're going into women's mainstream publishing. Of course we shall have to start in a small way and build. It might take time, but if we're lucky and find a couple of blockbusters it won't. Hence Gloria – she could be the saviour of us all.'

'I don't believe you.' Crispin sat down sharply without being asked, something he would never normally do. 'I've never heard of anything so stupid.' The shock he was feeling had, for once, stripped him of his impeccable manners.

'Thank you for your judgement.' Julius laughed. 'I'm sorry you've taken it this way, I thought you would be pleased. You're always saying there's money to be made and we're not making it.'

'Yes, but not with schlock. We've our reputation to consider. Why, you'll be a laughing stock.'

'No one will laugh if we're successful. It's not part of human nature to scoff when money's being made. Gloria's good. Don't fall into the trap of thinking just because a book is popular it's rubbish.'

'I'm sorry, Uncle, but I never expected to hear you talk in this way.' Crispin frowned. 'I really think you should have discussed this with me first. This is a major change in policy,' he said stiffly and, he thought, with dignity, but only managed to look pompous.

'The policy of this company is my responsibility, not yours, not yet. In any case, there was no time. I only heard at lunch from Mike Pewter. Gloria would have been snapped up by mid-afternoon – no doubt by Mike himself.'

'The market is awash with out-of-work editors at the moment.'

'Ah, yes, but they're not Gloria, are they?'

'Our other authors are not going to like this one little bit. For a start, we risk debasing our name and reputation. Secondly, the advances some of these so-called writers demand will anger the literary ones with their more modest ones.'

'Then they'll have to be told the facts of life, won't they? If we can't generate more sales, then there won't be money for them to be published at all.'

Crispin snorted disdainfully to cover the anger he was feeling. Everything his uncle was saying was correct and something he had long thought necessary. Success now might push the selling price of Westall's up marginally, and that would be fine. But what he feared most was, if the miracle happened, and Gloria succeeded, and dividends were paid out – and the rake-off could be substantial there was no denying it – then, he feared, his family might find themselves suddenly becoming sentimental about the old firm, suddenly finding they like the kudos of owning a publishing house once more, and refuse to sell. He had too much at stake for success to befall Westall's at this late hour. With a few judicious dinners here and the odd whisper or two there, he had already set in motion his plans to return to an academic life. What was more, Bee-Bee was thrilled with the notion of life as an academic's wife. The dear girl, insulated all her life by the abundant rewards of trade, had a healthy snobbish dislike of where her money came from. This could ruin everything.

'So, Crispin, here's your chance to ask one of our literary authors. Sir Gerald is, if I'm not mistaken, about to walk through that door. He's due here at two-thirty and I've never known him be a minute late.'

Crispin swung round just as Sir Gerald Walters walked in carrying his Tesco shopping bag containing his latest manuscript. Crispin swooped on it like a bird of prey. It was everyone's fear at Westall's that vague, partial-to-his-drink Sir Gerald might one day leave a masterpiece on a London bus.

Sir Gerald was only half-way across the room and Julius was already pouring him a glass of Madeira. Sir Gerald drank Pernod in the morning, Madeira after lunch and port in the evening. A habit which his resplendent nose, swollen, red and pockmarked, proclaimed, but a habit which had never interfered with his writing.

'My dear Gerald. Here we are again. And what is this one called?'

'Julius, my dear boy, looking fit as always. This one? *To Whom the Bird Has Sung* – good title, don't you think?' He was already drinking as he spoke.

'Can't be, my dear friend. Don't you remember, we once published a book with that title by Ulrika.'

'Shit!' said Sir Gerald, doyen of the English language. 'It's been bothering me where I got it from. How is the dear old girl?' He stuck his nose into his glass and sniffed appreciatively. 'How about *Last Song*?'

'Agreed. I like it,' said Julius topping up the glass of Madeira. 'Well, Crispin, should you ask Gerald what he thinks of my plan?'

'Yes, Uncle, I think we should.' Crispin looked very serious. 'Sir Gerald, my uncle has come up with a plan that I feel I cannot endorse. I fear for the reputation of the house. I fear giving offence to our prestigious authors such as yourself . . .'

Crispin stood with hands folded, a pious, smug expression on his face. Just like a church acolyte, Julius decided. He had had to pause while Sir Gerald had a coughing fit, brought on by smoking one of the shortest, blackest, most evil-smelling cheroots it had been Crispin's misfortune to get a whiff of. The attack over, Crispin took a deep breath and relaunched himself.

'I believe you would wish to find another publisher, sir – '

'Good God, Julius, what on earth are you planning?'

'I want to make some money by moving into general fiction with those large, saga-type books for women,' Julius said, smiling.

'What, those big things you see in airports and stations, all covered in glittering letters in gold and silver?'

'Exactly, sir . . .'

'Full of sex and ripping bodices?'

'Undoubtedly, sir . . .'

'Splendid. I like a bit of soft porn myself,' Sir Gerald said, holding his glass up to his smiling publisher. 'I'll drink to that.'

Peter Holt felt his day could not get worse. He was still reeling from his encounter with Gloria in the car park. She had looked as if she hated him and that had hurt – God, how it had hurt.

She was right, she had not seen him to talk to, he had not confided in her. How could he? He was too ashamed to face her, of all people. She had been with him the longest, she was an important contributor to his success. No wonder she was bitter.

She was wrong that he did not understand. He had fought to help her in the past few weeks, when his masters from America like grim reapers were cutting back his staff. The men from America had adjudged Gloria too individualist for the corporate image – nor had they gone too much on the dog. Her leaving was the worst, for it was almost as if a part of his past was chipped away from him.

He should have stopped her. He should have grabbed hold of her, made her listen to him. Apologised to her, begged her to stay. Anything, rather than this awful emptiness he was feeling now that he knew she was no longer in the building.

He remembered how, in her anger, she had managed to look even more beautiful. Her dark eyes flashing, her fine-boned face arrogant with hurt pride. And he had caused that anger.

As if all this was not enough, he had had a lousy session with his lawyers over his impending divorce. It took divorce, he had decided, really to get to know who you were married to. As his lawyer had pointed out to him, unnecessarily since he was no fool, he could not have chosen a worse time for a divorce: having sold the company he was vulnerable to a large settlement.

'Give her what she wants,' he had said wearily at the start of their session together. He had changed his mind sharply when he had heard what it was she wanted. Now he was determined to fight such unreasonable demands. Why should he shell out millions for that pimple-arsed Irish creep, Pinkers, to enjoy? He had always prided himself on his liberal outlook and he had always thought the divorce laws fair. Now involved in the whole sorry business, he had changed his opinion.

He had had a long and lousy transatlantic conversation with the American financial controller, who had informed Peter that the cuts made at Shotters were not enough, that further savings had to be made in overheads. When Peter had pointed out that he could see no way of saving another penny, the fool had queried whether soft bog paper was necessary and how about using lower wattage bulbs? Was this what publishing was about? He had slammed the telephone down in exasperation and refused to pick it up again when the man called back.

Catastrophes seemed to be multiplying when he was told that Shiel de Tempera was moving publishers. After years of building her into a top-ten writer, the ungrateful woman was taking her wares elsewhere – to Mike Pewter with whom Peter had had lunch only yesterday. And Mike had sat through the lunch, which Peter was paying for, without giving a whisper away.

He picked up his telephone and asked Em to get him Faith Cooper, de Tempera's agent.

The connection was made.

'Peter, nice of you to call,' Faith's deep voice said. 'But I'm sorry, don't even ask, Shiel won't change her mind.'

'I don't expect her to, and even if she did I wouldn't have her back. I just wanted to know why she left.'

'She felt in need of a change.'

'Oh, come on, Faith. There's more to it than that. We paid her handsomely, we looked after her well, she's been happy here.'

'OK, Peter. I've known you a long time, maybe I owe it to you to tell you. Shiel was happy at Shotters until the last couple of years. She felt it was getting too big, the attention paid to her less. This sell-out of yours was the last straw. She doesn't like the idea of swimming in the pool with a crowd of other big fish. You've become very author-unfriendly, Peter. She was beginning to feel insecure. Too many changes, too fast.'

'Thanks, Faith. I'll remember that.'

He replaced the telephone and ignored the flashing light that told him another call was on hold. That conversation with Faith put it all in a nutshell. He could not blame de Tempera, nor could he blame Gloria. What was happening here was the total destruction of everything he had worked for. His American masters were playing accountancy games with something that such games could not be played with. Every book and every author was different. Publishing was not like any other manufacturing process. Publishing was about people, their sentiments, their fears, their egos. The end product was, in a sense, manufactured, in that a book was produced. But there was an ephemeral quality to it all which his new master was incapable of understanding. Where creativity was concerned, such ruthless accountancy should really fly out of the window.

He hated his job now. He dreaded the faxes and telephone calls from across the Atlantic. This firm was his baby and he was committing infanticide. He could do nothing about it either: he was a puppet and Costas's minions were pulling the strings. All the negotiating he had done, the watertight contracts he thought he had pulled off, were not worth the paper they were written on. Except one, his own contract. He could see no way of breaking out of it, certainly not with an expensive divorce on his hands.

He stood up abruptly. He had to get away from this place.

'Em, cancel all my appointments,' he said into the intercom.

'You've got Bella Ford at four.'

'Sod her. Get someone else to see her. Tell Tatiana. Tell Bella I've got a sudden attack of myxomatosis or something.

He picked up his briefcase, looked at it, threw it back down on his desk and walked out of the door, ignoring the jangling of his telephone.

9

Gloria opened her front door to find the normally immaculately dressed Peter somewhat dishevelled, standing on the step. His hair flopped forward over his blue eyes, his generous mouth was grinning at her, but in a rather sheepish manner. He carried, awkwardly, a cheap bunch of flowers. She was surprised to see him there, but at the same time suspicious and a shade defensive.

'Peter, what on earth are you doing here?'

'Might I come in?'

'I'm not coming back if that's what you're here for.'

'I wanted to say goodbye to you properly and to set the record straight, that's all.' He spoke so matter-of-factly, she felt it might be the truth.

'I warn you, Peter, nothing will persuade me to come back.'

'I wouldn't even dream of asking you to.'

'Well, thanks.' She laughed. 'That's hardly complimentary.'

'I didn't mean it like that. I don't blame you for leaving as you did, Gloria. I just wish I could do the same.'

'Oh,' she said, nonplussed. 'Come in, then.' She held the door wide open for him, feeling ashamed she had been so discourteous.

'I shall miss you dreadfully,' he said, as they walked along the hall.

She turned and looked at him closely to see if he had been drinking, but he looked sober and steady enough. 'Come on, Peter, don't give me that rubbish.' She opened the door to her sitting room.

'But you were *there*, that was the point. Now I feel completely alone in the salt mines. Elephant, and how are you?' He bent down to stroke the little dog who, at sound of his voice, had come rushing in to welcome him for Peter was someone of whom he had always approved.

'Sorry about the mess, I wasn't expecting visitors,' she apologised, and began to tidy the piles of paper which were littering the floor and furniture. 'I've been sorting out what stuff is mine and what is Shotters'. This for a start.' She hauled a large typescript from the sofa. 'This is a marvellous novel. For God's sake, back it now I've gone, Peter. Those charlatans might let it sink without trace, might even not go ahead with it. I only wish she had not signed the contract otherwise I would have taken her with me. Add it to that pile there. Perhaps you could take them with you when you go.'

He took the heavy pile of papers from her and glanced idly at the title page. The name rang a bell. He frowned, trying to place it. Then he smiled. No wonder it sounded familiar, it was the name of a Queen of England, after all.

'You've got another job already? That was quick.' He sounded hurt. 'Where are you going?'

'Westall's. Julius said he'd been waiting for me and hadn't even advertised the post. Said he knew it was only a matter of time before I left Shotters.' She laughed. 'I said he must be a warlock to know.'

'What's he up to?'

'There's no harm in telling you. He's already organised an interview for me with *Publishing News* to coincide with the announcement of his plans. He's going to build a middle list – women mainly.'

'You'll have an uphill task there. I often wonder if that particular market hasn't reached saturation point.'

'Thanks for cheering me up,' she said.

'De Tempera's left,' he said, taking a seat on the sofa from which she had cleared the papers.

'She's what?' Gloria turned round sharply. 'Why?' she asked with amazement.

'Something I should have thought about, been aware of. It's certainly something the new owners won't even begin to understand. It was all too big and impersonal, even someone as successful as de Tempera was beginning to feel insecure. "Author-unfriendly", is how her agent put it.'

'Where's she gone?' Gloria asked with genuine concern. She liked Shiel, a rare creature who had not let her success go to her head. Hadn't turned from a pleasant, co-operative writer into a demanding ego with a pen as did so many of the others.

'Pewter's.'

'She'll be safe there. Liz Baker's a good editor, I'm sure they'll get along.' She was standing in the middle of the room, clutching a pile of papers. She looked at Peter and saw how tired and dejected he was. 'Is it too early for a drink?'

'Is it ever?' He laughed, and suddenly realised how little he had laughed recently. 'It's good to see you.' He smiled up at her.

'Mutual,' she said, finding she had to turn away from the intensity of his stare which, for some reason, embarrassed her. 'Whisky, gin, wine?' she said hurriedly to cover up.

'Wine would be lovely, but only if you have any open.'

'Open and not drunk? Don't be daft! In this house?' She went into the kitchen, took down two glasses from the cupboard and a bottle of Australian Chardonnay from the refrigerator. When she turned round it was to find Peter standing in the doorway. She did not know how long he had been watching her, he might just have appeared, but his being there made her feel ham-fisted. 'Would you do the honours?' She handed him the bottle and opener.

'This is a nice house,' he commented as he uncorked the wine.

'Thanks, I like it. I've got all sorts of plans for it but they never seem to materialise. Of course, you haven't been here before, only to that tiny flat I had in Clapham – God, that seems like a hundred years ago.' She smiled, accepting the glass of wine he gave her.

'This is an improvement on that flat. More than three people and you had a serious case of overcrowding.'

'Do you remember that night when you came with Milly and Phillip and the three of you sat on my put-you-up and it collapsed, just as I'd given you your plates of spaghetti? I was finding bits of dried spaghetti in my bed for weeks after.'

'And the time you decided to give a fondue party and the burner under the doo-da blew up.' He was laughing again.

'I'd forgotten that. And that time when Phillip and Milly came with their new baby and swanned off totally forgetting the brat?'

'Yes, and we were all rushing down the road screaming at them to come back?'

'Poor kid, it was a good half-hour before they realised they'd forgotten him. Something like that could have marked him for life. How's he turning out?'

'You wouldn't recognise him as Phillip's son. He's a very serious young boy, highly intelligent and he wants to read law when he leaves school and eventually go into politics.'

'Heavens! An MP with a father growing the biggest crop of cannabis in the UK – what a hoot!' She was nearly crying with laughter. 'I mean, he can't, can he? Either the son gives up his ambition or Phillip burns his crop.'

'I think Phillip would leave the country, plants and all.'

'Dear Phillip.' She sipped the wine feeling the contented happiness that talking about good memories can give one.

'You know this house reminds me so much of Hilary's and my first house, the one in Battersea.'

'It's very similar. Not surprising, London is full of these little Victorian terraces.' The feeling of contentment passed, she did not want to be reminded of his wife.

'Nice garden?'

'Lovely. Do you want to see?' She unlocked the back door and, preceded by Elephant, they went out to the small courtyard garden she had created, full of pots and creepers climbing the wall she had whitewashed. 'Actually, it's bigger than you think.' She led him out into the main garden. 'There's not much to see at the moment, but come spring this will be a blaze of colour right through until late autumn.'

She was surprised at the interest he showed and his knowledge of the different plants – not so easy to identify with only their early foliage on, but he did.

'I didn't know you were interested in gardening,' she said when they eventually made their way back into the house.

'I love it. Mind you, now . . . well, the gardens we've got are so huge and formal, they have to have gardeners who would not appreciate me grubbing around in the flowerbeds.'

'You can always come and grub in mine, another weeder would be greatly appreciated.' She laughed gaily, began to put the table lamps on in her sitting room and selected a Chris de Burgh compact disc to put on the machine.

'I might take you up on that. May I?' He indicated the bottle and his empty glass.

'Help yourself. Where are you living now, since . . .?' She stopped, wishing she had not said that. For all she knew they might be back together again.

'I'm at our flat – no garden unfortunately, just some indoor plants. But I'm going to start looking for a small house. Something like this, I think. Get back to basics, shed some of the paraphernalia.'

'So you didn't enjoy the life of a country squire?'

'Me? No. That was for Hilary, really. She loved it, the social life, the horses. It bored me to tears to be quite honest. I've always been a bit of a Philistine where the country is concerned. To me it's for visiting, not living in.'

'I know what you mean. When I go home to my parents', at first I love it, the wind, the wide skies, the sea, and I think, how the hell do I survive in the smoke? And then – it usually takes a week – I'm longing to get back, longing for the noise and the bustle. So, is Hilary going to stay on in your house in the country?'

'Not if I can help it,' he said shortly.

It was a chill March and, although the central heating was on, it did not seem to be enough. She leant forward and lit the gas under the coal-effect fire.

'Bit naff, I know,' she said, and even as she did wondered why she should be apologising for something she had chosen herself.

'I think they're marvellous, no mess, they look so realistic. Of course – ' he began then stopped.

'Hilary wouldn't contemplate one.' She finished the sentence for him and smiled at him.

'I'm sorry, I didn't mean to come here and talk about her.' It was his turn to sound apologetic.

'Why did you come?' she asked, suddenly serious.

'Maybe I shouldn't have.' He began to stand up.

'Don't go. I didn't mean to sound rude.' She, too, had jumped up.

'The truth is, Gloria, I don't know why I did come. I just suddenly felt so depressed and trapped. I had to get out of the offices. I felt . . .' He stopped again and looked at the flickering flames. He was going to say 'lonely', but something stopped him. It did not seem the right thing to say to her, somehow. 'I wanted you to know that I understood your going. I wanted to say sorry for the way things at Shotters have turned out.' He had sat down again.

'Why did you sell?' She, too, had taken her place in her chair again. She refilled her glass and, kicking off her shoes, curled her long, shapely legs up under her.

'Why?' He shook his head. 'It was no longer right. We had already got too big for comfort, the intimacy had gone, there were employees whose names I did not even know. And there were certainly books we were producing that I had not even read. You yourself had picked up that I was fed up with it, felt I wasn't a publisher any more.'

'But this is worse. You're even less of one. I could have understood you selling up and starting again in a small way. Gracious, I'd have jumped at the chance of going with you.'

'I had to stay. My continuing as chief executive was one of the conditions of the deal.'

'Can't you leave?'

'It might be difficult. Before I came here I went to see my lawyer to see if there's any way out of my contract.'

'There must be. I bet Costas had a loophole built in in case he wanted to get rid of you. You can rely on that.'

'That's what my lawyer said. He said that a clever lawyer can always find a way out of a contract. I just hope he's clever enough.'

'If he isn't, find another one. But why Costas? I don't understand that, either. I know you said it was because he didn't know much about publishing, but surely that's why everything is in the mess it is now?'

'Do you want to know the truth?' He looked at her, she nodded. 'I found my wife in bed with a creep the very evening I found that Costas wanted to buy. Suddenly, there really seemed no point in carrying on with Shotters. Phillip didn't care one way or the other, so I thought, "Sod the lot of them," and rushed straight into the arms of Costas when I wasn't really thinking straight. I can see that now.'

'Oh, Peter, that must have been awful for you. I'm so sorry.' She felt a surge of anger that Hilary had treated him in this way and wished she could help.

'I'm not. I regret selling to Costas, of course, it was the act of a fool in a slough of self-pity. I don't regret finding Hilary out. Our relationship had been dead for years. I was just too lazy to face up to it.'

'And the kids?'

'They appear to have taken it quite well. They're used to their parents arguing and not being particularly loving to each other. I suppose only time will tell how affected they are. Josh is happy at school and at eighteen was already starting to drift away from us. In any case he will be away at university later this year. Rose, I don't know. She doesn't get on that well with her mother – I gather it's quite common for girls to have stormy relationships with their mums.'

Gloria smiled at him. 'Yes, I'd agree with that,' she said with feeling.

'I know I shall miss her. You know, daddies and their daughters.' He tried to smile but only succeeded in looking sad.

'Couldn't she live with you?'

'It wouldn't be fair, would it? She likes the horses and all the country crap. You know what sixteen-year-old girls are like.'

'Yes, I can still remember that far back,' she joshed him. 'At sixteen I'd have given anything to live in London. The horses by then were most definitely becoming a secondary interest.'

'But do you know what hurts me most, Gloria? It's the idea of that Irish bastard taking my place in Rose's life.'

'She's too old for that. No one will replace her dad, not now. I promise you.'

'Really?' His face lit up. 'I do hope you're right.'

'Shall we have another bottle of wine? I don't know about you but I reckon there's a government plot that's making the bottles smaller, they never seem to last as long as they did once.' She was laughing, hoping to cheer him up.

'Good God! Look at the time. Gloria, I'm so sorry, I'd no idea . . . I do apologise for boring you with my problems . . . I must be going, I'm keeping you . . .'

'Sit down. You're doing nothing of the sort. I've nothing to do but feed the cat and Elephant. I've not much to eat, mind you – some cheese, or we could get a take-away?'

'Let me take you out to dinner.'

'I'd love to.'

'You feed your zoo, I'll book a table.'

They went to the local bistro Gloria had suggested, chosen since it was unlikely that anyone they knew would be there. She had felt in his present mood he would not enjoy a too-sociable evening. But also she suggested it because she knew she wanted him all to herself.

They talked and Gloria could not remember the last time she had opened up to someone quite as honestly as she did to Peter. It was almost a relief to be with someone she trusted well enough to confess her loneliness and how unsatisfied she was in her personal relationships. Gloria was cursed in that to the world she seemed a sophisticated, confident, slightly hard woman. But Peter knew her far better than she realised. He was aware of the kind, vulnerable, rather frightened person she was inside. Had he not known he would have been most unperceptive not to realise it that night. She told him everything from her past, things she would prefer to have forgotten but which, strangely, she felt impelled to tell him.

'Good heavens, Peter. I can't imagine why I'm unburdening myself to you like this. Sorry.'

'Don't even think of apologising. I'm honoured you should trust me.' He smiled and, even though the light in the restaurant was dim, she could see the kindness and understanding in his eyes. He put out his hand and covered hers. She felt a pleasurable jolt at his touch. 'We all need friends, Gloria.'

She smiled back, feeling different, as if her confession had cleansed her. She looked at him with longing, wishing he needed more than a friend, and then felt quite taken aback by the thought.

'Isn't it odd how with some people it's easy to pick up the thread of true friendship, and with others it's impossible? They belong in a time and a place in the past and can't come with you into your present or future.'

'Takes a very special sort of friend.' Peter smiled at her, slightly lopsidedly, over his glass of brandy.

Then it was his turn and, in depth, he told her of what he now regarded as his empty years. He spoke of love and the lack of it in his life and in turn he talked of his loneliness.

They only left the bistro when the waiters noisily began to stack the chairs on the tables.

Though cold, it was a lovely evening with a clear sky and, they both agreed, a definite smell of spring in the air. When he took her hand she felt ridiculously happy.

As they walked along she knew she wanted to invite him in, knew she wanted him to kiss her, knew without doubt that if he did she would want to go to bed with him. 'Not this time,' she told herself. This time she would not make the mistake she had so often made in the past. She would be courted. She wanted him to wine and dine her, shower her with flowers and little presents, with notes and telephone calls. This time it had to be perfect as it never had been before. She wanted to try to recapture her youth.

'That was a lovely evening, Gloria. Thanks,' he said, as they stood on the pavement outside her house.

'It was.'

'We must do it again sometime.'

'Yes,' she said fighting the longing to hold him.

'Shall I call you?'

'Yes,' she repeated, wondering what his kiss was like.

'Right. Yes, well, I'd best let you get to bed.' He turned away and began to walk down the street.

She watched him go and although she had won her fight with herself she still felt let down. She kicked her gate open and its hinge finally broke and crashed to the ground.

10

Having signed her contract, Kate had banked her first advance cheque from Shotters. To do so she had opened a new account. She had not done this to keep it from Tony but, rather, she had decided to use it for the things she needed for writing, any new clothes that her lack of confidence demanded, and – the most revolutionary idea of all – to buy ready-prepared meals from Marks and Spencer that she could put in the freezer. Then, when she was writing, the family would still eat well. She had heard good reports about the food from Pam who rarely cooked if she could help it. If she was careful in disposing of the packets, Tony need never find out. It was not a lot of money but she hoped it would tide her over until the next tranche came when Shotters had accepted the final manuscript. They would pay her the last instalment when the book was published by which time, hopefully, she would have finished the second book, with which she was already tinkering. She had not meant to start on it so soon, she wanted to have the first one completely finished before she did, but her brain had other ideas, and with a new plot, and characters in her mind, she had found it necessary to begin.

It was as well this was so for things were not going too smoothly in her life at the moment. Steve had found himself a job, miles away in Yorkshire, working in the garden of a stately home.

'I've got to take it, Mum. These jobs don't come up that often.'

'But it's so far away. Could you not find something nearer?'

'Mum, you don't understand, these gardens are world famous, I'll learn so much there. The head gardener is well known. I'll get a job anywhere with him having trained me. Will you tell Dad?'

She had agreed to, not that she had looked forward to it. Predictably Tony was furious.

'What about his GCSEs? He can't give up on those.'

'He says he doesn't need them.'

'That's ridiculous. Of course he needs them – everyone does these days. He should go to horticultural college if he wants to go ahead with this crazy plan.'

'He says, quite honestly, that he wouldn't stand a chance of getting into one, that he's too thick.'

'He's not thick, he's idle.'

'Tony, I know it's hard when it's your only son, but Steve isn't very bright academically. If only you could face that, not dream impossible dreams for him. Isn't his happiness more important? Anyway, I'm rather proud of him, taking the initiative like this. Taking control of his own life.'

'Kate, you talk such twaddle at times. I know there's nothing we can do. But at least we should try and stop him, the boy need not think he'd have my blessing. Thank God we have Lucy.'

'Yes, dear, thanks for Lucy.'

He looked up when she said that and glared suspiciously, as if he had caught the shadow of sarcasm in her voice. But he said nothing, for she was smiling sweetly at him.

The atmosphere in the house had been difficult since this bombshell from Steve. There had not been a row but everyone was aware that one was brewing just under the surface. As she bought clothes for him that she felt he would need, and washed and packed for him, Kate felt such a weight of sadness. It had all happened so quickly. One day Steve was a toddler and now she was packing his case ready for him to leave, probably for ever. She had known it would come one day, but she had every right not to expect it so suddenly.

She had tried to persuade Tony to drive up with them, but he stolidly refused. His only concession, that showed he might be upset, was the cheque he had given Steve the morning he was leaving. 'For emergencies,' he had said, somewhat gruffly.

Kate knew that Steve had really wanted to travel to Yorkshire alone. He was afraid people would think him a wimp arriving with his mother.

'Let me, Steve. If I know where you are, what it looks like, it will be easier for me to imagine you there,' she had pleaded. When it came to the day, she sensed that he was relieved the arrangements had been made this way. She was not the only one who was tearful when it was finally time to say goodbye.

'Think, Mum, you'll have a lot more time to write with one less of us.'

'You were never any trouble.'

'You will carry on, won't you? You won't let Dad stop you, will you?'

'What an odd thing to say. Why should he stop me?'

'Because I think he's jealous of it, he'll hate it when you're a success – I shan't, I shall boast to everyone.' He smiled and let her kiss him farewell.

They had stopped off overnight on the way up to Yorkshire, so that Kate could get away early. It was a long drive back and, with no one to share her misery, a lonely one. Hence, instead of going straight home when she arrived in Graintry, she decided to make good her promise to herself and to go to Marks' and stock up with food.

She enjoyed the next hour as she ambled around the aisles of the large foodhall. She often bought clothes here, but had never bothered even to look at the provisions section. It was wonderful. Dishes she had often thought of making but had felt were beyond her, and dishes that were old favourites of everyone. Slowly and surely her trolley filled up.

So engrossed had she been with reading the packaging that it was not until she had almost finished that she became aware of the funny looks she was getting from the other women. She could just imagine what they were thinking: 'Look at that lazy bitch ...' '... What a dreadful wife and mother ...' and worst, 'No wonder she's so fat ...' All the guilt that Kate was normally fighting rose up in her and engulfed her and she almost put everything back. Then she saw a man, about her own age, with a trolley even more full than hers and totally unselfconscious, laughing and joking with the woman at the till. If he can, why can't I? she thought, and proceeded to unload the trolley on to the conveyor belt before she changed her mind again, but resolved even more firmly to stick to her diet.

It was seeing the café she and Pam often had a snack in, and the old coaching inn where they sometimes treated themselves to a proper lunch, and passing Pam's favourite dress shop, that made Kate long to see her friend. She wanted to tell her how miserable she was about Steve, she wanted them to be like they once had been.

Instead of driving home, she took the turning that led to Pam's. It was weeks since she had seen her. She had telephoned upon her return from her lunch with Joy and Gloria as she had promised. She had begun to tell her all about it but Pam had sounded so bored that she had stopped. She had kept her in touch with every development – all through the nail-biting days of waiting for confirmation that Shotters wanted her book, through the days of Joy's financial negotiations. She had done all that but there were times she wondered why she bothered because Pam was always so cool about it. She needed Pam and she was going to get to the bottom of the trouble between them.

Pam was surprised to find Kate standing unannounced on her doorstep. By no stretch of the imagination could her welcome be called warm.

'We're going out to dinner,' she said somewhat sharply.

'I just want to see you for a moment.'

'I suppose you had better come in,' Pam said ungraciously.

They played conversational games as they asked each other about their families, Kate finding herself wanting to delay anything deeper. They were in Pam's drawing room, a room of great opulence. Portraits hung on the walls – nothing to do with their families and, to give them their due, they never claimed they were. But Kate often felt sorry for the faces in the pictures for they were like orphans having lost their real families and unlikely ever to be traced.

This was ridiculous, Kate told herself. This polite enquiring was not why she had come. 'Look, Pam, I think we're being silly. I thought we had sorted everything out. I've telephoned you often. There's something else that's annoying you and I want to know what it is. And right here and now I'll say sorry, whatever it is.'

'Oh, Kate, I've missed you so,' Pam said standing in the middle of the room like a small exquisite doll and looking as if she was about to burst into tears.

'And I you. What dumb clucks we are.' Kate was laughing. 'What happened?'

'I don't know.' Pam shook her head. 'You remember what it was like at school and suddenly your friends were doing something else and you weren't included? It's been like that. I've felt so left out as if you were going away from me.'

'It's not just you, it's everything – the whole of my routine has gone by the board. This writing is like a drug.'

'Don't laugh at me, will you, but, I feel silly even saying this – I felt jealous of the book. Does that make sense?'

'Pam, I'm so sorry.' She put her arm around her friend's thin shoulders and hugged her. How strange, she thought, that Steve should say the same thing about his father, but she decided not to mention that to Pam.

'And there's something else . . .' Pam said looking anxiously at her.

'What, Pam?' Kate suddenly felt uneasy.

'I . . . it's nothing. It can wait. Don't look so worried, it's not serious.' And Kate relaxed as Pam laughed. 'Gin?'

'Please. Have you heard from the Red Rose Society?'

'Yes, last week. Shall we go?'

'Let's. It'll be fun seeing everyone again. I've got to have lunch with my publishers that day. We could meet up and go to the meeting together.'

'There you are.' Pam's shoulders slumped with dejection again. 'You're in a different world already.'

'No, I'm not. We're both in the same one. I'm just a step ahead of you, it'll be your turn next.'

'I doubt it,' Pam said morosely. 'Did you know Tracey's been accepted by The Paradise Club? Felicity is furious.' She managed to smile as she imparted this piece of gossip.

'I'm not surprised. Poor Felicity, all those years of trying and then Tracey and I have such good luck. How's your book coming along?'

'Slowly. No one takes me seriously. If I say I'm a writer people just grin. You have to be accepted before anyone will respect you and leave you alone to get on with it.'

'You must be firm and insist no one interrupts you when you're working. Make the family understand it's important to you. Think about yourself for a change. You've got to, to get anywhere.'

'You will help me when I've finished it, won't you? Like you helped Tracey?'

'Of course I will. You're my best friend, aren't you?'

'You wouldn't read what I've done? Take it with you, let me know what you think next week?'

'Of course I will,' she said as Pam rushed off to get her manuscript for her.

Later, back home, she wondered if it had been a wise decision. Pam had not written much, only fifty pages, but as Kate read them her heart sank. She did not understand it or what Pam was trying to do. She could not see it selling, she certainly would not buy it. It was as if Pam could not decide what sort of book she wanted to write or for whom. It slipped from a fantasy world and then back to a more normal one even in the same paragraph.

Once she had finished it Kate sat for a long time wondering what to do about it. Should she be straight with Pam and tell her truthfully what she thought about it? No. She could not bring herself to destroy something someone else had toiled over, nor risk ruining Pam's confidence in herself. Should she advise her, tell her where she thought the writing could be improved? No. What if Pam resented her interference? Should she lie and say it was wonderful? No. It would be cruel to lie. She would not like this herself, so why should Pam be different?

What then? Maybe she could ask Joy, as a favour, to read it. Let her do the dirty work for her. Joy did not know Pam, it would be easier for her. Yes, that was what she would do, she thought, as she slid the papers carefully back into their envelope.

11

The following week an edgy Kate, in a new skirt, blouse, shoes and jacket, stood in the reception hall of Shotters to keep her appointment. She knew she would have felt better if she was waiting to meet Gloria. Her call to tell Kate that she had left had been a shock. Although, apart from buying manuscripts, she was unsure what the role of an editor was, she had felt convinced that she would be able to work with Gloria. Now she was going to have to get to know new people.

She wished she had worn her red silk, with its matching coat, instead of this much safer navy-blue outfit. She knew she looked better, having lost weight, but she wished she had worn something with a bit more panache. She did not want to look too middle-aged.

She looked up at the photographs of Shotters' star authors hanging on the walls and inwardly laughed at the silly idea that one day she could be there in their hall of fame. On another wall were posters of all their latest books – those by the most famous, she noticed, were awash with embossed gold and silver lettering. In a locked cabinet were the books themselves, laid out on black velvet like priceless exhibits in a museum.

'Kate. So wonderful that you could get here.'

Kate looked up to find a young girl dressed entirely in black: black mini-skirt, large baggy black sweater, thick black tights that reminded Kate of her grandmother, and smart, suede ankle boots.

'I'm Cressida, Tatiana Spence's personal assistant. She's upstairs waiting to meet you – everyone is. We can't wait to get to know you.'

Kate stood up, far too fast she realised – it made her appear over-eager and she dropped her handbag in doing so.

'Oh, what absolutely scrummy shoes, I'd die for them,' said Cressida as she dived at the same time as Kate to retrieve the handbag. Kate wished she hadn't noticed them – black patent pumps from Bally with gold bows on them – for she was sure to have spotted Kate's ankles, swollen from the heat of a surprisingly warm April. They squeezed into the already crowded lift.

'I just adored *Winter's Romance*. Couldn't put it down, page-turnability in spades,' Cressida gushed, and Kate knew she was blushing as everyone in the lift turned to look at her.

'It's *Winter Interlude*, actually.'

'Yes, of course, silly me. Well. Never mind. Ah, here we are.'

The lift doors hissed open on to another large reception hall, close-carpeted in deep red, with matching red walls. Right opposite them two men, on ladders, were unscrewing what looked like a large gilt scimitar from the wall. Of course, Blades's logo, she remembered.

They walked at speed through an open-plan office towards a glassed-off section at the end of the large room. Kate did not think it was her imagination but she was sure people were staring at her. It made her feel uncomfortable.

Waiting for them was a tall woman with impeccably groomed blonde hair, perfect make-up, and a smart yet fashionable suit in navy blue, the skirt barely skimming her knees on which were sheer black tights. She too had black patent leather shoes on, but she did not look middle-aged at all. Beside her stood a younger woman in the shortest mini-skirt that Kate had ever seen, more like a pelmet in her opinion. Under them she wore tights of a mind-numbing complexity of colour and abstract shapes, and on her feet were boots that would have looked well in the Lake District. Her jumper was thick and white, scattered with embossed knitted fruits and Kate could not help but notice that on one nipple was a cherry and on the other a raspberry and she wondered if they were there by accident or design. At the sight of both of them Kate felt she had aged a good twenty years.

'Kate. *Wonderful* to meet you at last.' The older of the two women had stepped forward, hand held out in greeting. 'I'm Tatiana, your editorial director. It means I'm the boss.' She laughed her constrained laugh. 'This is Coco, your publicity manager. And here is Bart, your designer. Come in, Bart, do, meet dear Kate.' Kate was shaking hands with a young man with dreadful acne, wearing a rather grubby T-shirt with something on it in French, but her French had never been up to much so she did not understand it.

'How do you do?' she said stiffly.

'We all just know you're going to be one of our favourite authors,' Tatiana gushed, and Kate wondered what she put on her lips to keep them so shiny and glossy. Lipstick on Kate lasted a matter of minutes. 'And here's Letitia, she will be your editor, the one you liaise with the most. Letitia, meet darling Kate.'

Letitia was tall and thin, too, everyone was, which only made Kate feel more gross. Her earrings did not match. Kate wondered if it was a mistake but then, upon noting she was dressed in black and white spotted trews with a black and white striped sweater, she presumed that the one black and one white earring was on purpose. But she had a gentler expression than the others and Kate hoped that here was someone she would get on with.

'Kate, I just loved *Winter Romance*. I couldn't put it down, read it in one sitting. Page-turnability in spades.' Letitia smiled and Kate felt a jolt of *déjà vu* and wondered why everyone seemed to speak in italics and why no one could get the title right.

'We decided on a working lunch, Kate, hope you don't mind but we've so much to talk about. Coco, be a pet, tell Cressida to ring the canteen and rustle up some sandwiches.'

Kate said it was fine even though she felt disappointed. Lunch with one's publisher sounded so grand when one said it, and she had read of the extravagant hospitality of some famous publishers.

Chairs were pulled up and they settled around Tatiana's desk.

'There's just one tiny little thing, Kate. It doesn't affect you at all – not in the slightest. But, you see, Blades is no more. You're to be published by Shotters – far more prestigious, of course, than small Blades ever was. It's just an internal little thing, a rationalisation. We didn't want you to be confused.'

'Thank you,' said Kate, unsure if it was significant or not. The door opened and Cressida appeared with a tray of sandwiches and several glasses of Perrier water. Tatiana signed a docket with a flourish, Cressida took it and left the room shutting the door behind her.

'Now, Kate. Tell us *all* about yourself.'

'There's not much to tell you, really,' Kate said, voice heavy with apology as she launched herself rather tremulously into telling them about her very ordinary life. There was silence when she finished and she found herself looking at four blank faces and four sandwiches poised, half eaten, in the air.

'That's it,' she added, to make sure they knew she had finished, and she took a large draught of the Perrier and, finding she was no longer hungry, refused a sandwich.

'And you've done nothing else? Travelled, any interesting or unusual hobbies?' Coco asked after a pause that seemed to have gone on for ages.

'None, I'm afraid. I mean, cooking and sewing, well everyone does those, don't they?' She laughed but no one else joined in. 'Sorry, I'm not a murderess, an embezzler, or adulteress – nothing. Just me.' She smiled wanly.

'How did you start writing?' Tatiana asked, dabbing her mouth where there were no crumbs and where, miraculously, the lipstick still shone.

'It just happened, like a dam breaking. I mean, one day I started and I can't stop, it seems.'

'How many times were you rejected?' Coco enquired, her frown deepening.

'There's only been you.'

'Submitted to one publisher, that's very unusual.' Tatiana studied her nails.

'I know. I realise I've been very lucky,' she mumbled, and cursed herself for sounding so humble.

'How long have you been writing?'

'Let me see, this is April.' She began to count the months up on her fingers. 'Six months,' she concluded.

'Six months?' they all said in astonished unison. 'Good God!' they all added for good measure.

'But you must have written something else, short stories, articles?' Coco put her head on one side and one earring fell off. She scrabbled for it on the floor.

'Nothing. This is the first thing.'

'That's got to be your angle, Coco,' Letitia said.

'There's nothing else is there? Well, if that's that, if you'll excuse me, Kate, I've got *masses* to do – Bella Ford's new one is out next week.' She stood up, checking she had both earrings on. 'It's been just *wonderful* getting to know you. I'll be in touch. I need you to fill in one of my *dreaded* author profiles – everyone hates them. And I think we should talk about you having an author piccy taken.'

Coco slid out of the room.

'We've pencilled your publication date in for February,' Tatiana said, ostentatiously leafing through a large desk diary. 'It's one of the best months without doubt. You pick up sales with the book tokens after Christmas – everyone is too weary to cash them in January. And there are no big names for you to clash with. You'll have the field to yourself.'

'I see,' said Kate, and would have liked to ask why, if it was such a good month, no big names were published in it. But she thought it politic to keep quiet at this stage and in any case was far too scared to query anything.

'Oh, yes, Feb's a fab month for you,' Bart spoke for the first time. 'I've done some rough sketches for our catalogue – it goes out to the bookshops and some members of the public are on our mailing list. It'll be a bit of a rush job to get it in but with luck we'll manage.'

He showed her a rough outline of a book jacket. It showed a simpering blonde of chocolate-box prettiness, in her early twenties, against the background of a seascape.

'What do you think?'

'It's very nice,' she said doubtfully. 'It's just that my heroine is forty and there's no sea in the book at all. And the title's wrong – it's *Winter Interlude* not *Winter Romance*. Apart from that it's very nice,' she repeated for something to say as the others shuffled in an irritated way. 'But you've got my name right,' she added with a little more spirit.

'That's OK then.' Bart stood up. 'Wonderful to meet you, Kate. I just know we're all going to work wonderfully together.'

'The thing is, Kate,' Tatiana began once Bart had left, 'we really want to angle this book seriously at the women's market. Now, our research shows us that if you put the word love or romance into a title we sell double the amount, at least.'

'Yes, but – '

'It really is a better title, you know.' Tatiana flashed a smile at her and Kate wondered why she reminded her of a head girl at her school whom she had particularly loathed. It was strange how all through this writing process the comparison with school kept coming up. 'We do know what we're doing,' Tatiana added and Kate thought there was an unmistakable sound of annoyance in her voice.

'But, Tatiana, if you don't mind me pointing out to you, I haven't written a romance. Why, the end is sad, you couldn't have a sad end to a romance now, could you?'

'Yes, well, that was something I wanted to talk to you about. Sadly . . .' she looked pointedly at her watch, 'I've an appointment and must rush. But Letitia here will explain everything. Use my office, darlings. Finish up the goodies.' She pointed to the tray of curling sandwiches and the by now flat Perrier and in a rush and a cloud of expensive-smelling perfume she was gone.

'Right, Kate. With that lot out of the way we can get down to the serious business.' Letitia had taken Tatiana's place behind the desk. She opened a file and took out a sheaf of papers. 'I've had these photocopied for you so that you can take them home to mull over. Now, Kate, you must understand they are only my little suggestions. You must do just what you want. I'm only the boring old editor who will drive you mad on the commas and semi-colons and the syntax.' She laughed gaily, turned, and from the shelf behind her manhandled on to the desk what Kate recognised as her typescript. It was no longer the pristine one she had submitted, there were pencil marks all over it. Letitia laughed again when she saw the horrified expression on Kate's face. 'I know just what you're thinking. What have they done to my lovely manu-script? It's only pencil, Kate, can be rubbed out in a trice. Now . . .' Letitia bent over her notes and when she looked up it was with a very serious expression. 'I take your points about the cover rough. I know there's no sea in your book and, at the moment, the jacket design is all wrong. But we've talked about this at the highest level and well, Kate, it would be a help if you could alter the setting. Regional novels are so strong, you see, and this one isn't really set anywhere, is it? We thought Cornwall would be nice. Cornish novels always sell well – especially in Cornwall.' She giggled. 'Do you know it there? If not, why not take a holiday, take some snaps of the coves and *delicious* cliffs, absorb it.'

'I could, I suppose,' Kate said doubtfully.

'Of course you could, Kate. Anything's possible. Now the age of the woman.' She studied her hands intently as if searching for inspiration and looked at Kate even more seriously. 'It's a difficult one this, Kate. She's so old. We'd much rather she was young.'

'But – ' Kate attempted to interrupt.

'I know *just* what you're about to say – that you wrote her that way because you, well, forgive me, but that's your age. Please, Kate. Have a try. Knock twenty years off, that would be wonderful.'

'I don't think I can remember how it was to be twenty. And if I did, none of the rest of the book would make sense.'

'You'd have to tinker about a bit here and there. But try, Kate, you'd be amazed at how easy it is. And then there's the horny problem of sex. Oops,' she clapped her hand over her mouth. 'Unfortunate choice of words there.' And she laughed but Kate felt it was at a joke she had used many times. 'What we would love to have, Kate, and what would help your sales enormously, is, well, if you could put in a lot more sexual *frisson* – there's a dear.'

'I can't write sex, it makes me embarrassed.'

'Really? How riveting! Do try, though, won't you? Now the end, Kate. I mean it's wonderful and tight and dramatic – delicious. But an unhappy ending? Oh, dear Kate, our readers will *hate* it. And I can tell you now America won't touch it – they hate unhappy endings more than we do.'

Kate could not stop herself from slumping back into the chair.

'Come, come, Kate, it's not as bad as all that, these are just our little suggestions. We want to make it perfect, don't we?' Letitia stood up. Obviously the meeting was over and there was to be no discussion.

'Have you far to go?'

'No, I'm going to a meeting of the Red Rose Society.'

'The RRS – wonderful women. Several of our authors are members. Bella Ford is – do you know her? A wonderful woman. Tell me,' Letitia said, not waiting for Kate's reply as they walked towards the lifts. 'Any ideas on number two?'

'I have, actually. I've been working on some ideas for two women, set in the last war.' Kate began to perk up at this.

'Oh, no, really?' Leeitia pursed her lips. 'Difficult, Kate, the market's awash with books on the last war. Historicals are getting so difficult to sell. Best stick to moderns, there's a dear.' The lift whined to a halt. 'Now, Kate, any worries, any problems, you just give me a ring.' She kissed her on both cheeks, which Kate felt was a bit much since they had only just met and she had torn her book to pieces. 'I just know you're going to become one of our *favourite* authors. Absolutely!'

Kate took a taxi feeling far too demoralised to take the tube. She quickly flicked through the pages of her precious typescript. She could not find one page which was not covered by pencilled crossings out, corrections and lengthy suggestions in the margins. And with it were the four foolscap pages of more detailed instructions. She felt she wanted to cry. She stuffed the pages back into the large Jiffy bag that Letitia had given her and felt like hurling it out of the window. What was the point in her going on? They obviously did not like what she had done so why should any reader? But as the taxi progressed towards her destination there was a change in Kate and by the time she arrived, she was fuming.

She was late and the meeting had already started. She was shown the hall by a porter and although she opened the large, heavy door as quietly as possible it still made a noise and an even louder one when it slipped from her hands and swished shut behind her. She tiptoed down the long hall towards the group of chairs but the plank floorboards squeaked at every foot fall. Faces turned at her and glared and there was much shushing.

'Sorry,' she mouthed exaggeratedly as she slipped into a vacant chair in the back row. A chair of canvas and steel which rasped as she sat on it. 'Sorry,' she mouthed again.

Bella Ford was on the platform, introducing the guest speaker, in place of the chairman who was in the midst of a writing crisis. She was in lilac silk again, without the sequins but still with two long chiffon scarves about her neck, and paused pointedly in her opening remarks, drummed her fingers on the lectern and waited for Kate to settle. Unfortunately the interruption had made Bella lose her momentum and the rest of her introduction tended to ramble so that soon the whole of the hall was full of the noise of other chairs creaking under restless bottoms.

'So, it's my pleasure to introduce James Truelove. Really, Mr Truelove, with a name such as yours you, too, should be a romantic novelist.' Bella smiled louchely at him and fiddled with the scarves, flicking one over her shoulder in what was evidently meant to be a carefree, girlish gesture but succeeded only in appearing arch.

James Truelove began to speak. Kate went over the morning's interview in her mind and the fuming became a rock-solid anger.

'Where did you get to?' Pam rushed up to her even as the audience was applauding Truelove's efforts.

'What on earth was he talking about?' Kate looked up, startled, realising she had not heard a word.

'Copyright or something, I wasn't really listening. It hardly affects me, does it? So what did you think? I've been desperate for your call.'

'Sorry?' Kate said vaguely. 'What do I think about what?'

'My book,' Pam said, standing dejectedly in front of her. 'You haven't bothered to read it.'

'Pam, I'm sorry. Of course I've read it. I had such a wretched morning, forgive me. I've sent it to Joy and I've asked her to look at it and comment. You should have professional advice,' Kate said breathlessly, fearful Pam might register that she had not given her reactions, and feeling totally wretched about the whole affair.

'Kate, you're an angel. I love you so.' And Pam kissed her enthusiastically which only made Kate feel worse. 'So, tell me, how did it go?' Pam asked taking the seat beside her.

'It was bloody awful...' And Kate launched into the tale of her first experience with her publishers.

'That's dreadful. They can't make you do that!' Pam exclaimed.

'Oh, yes, they can.' A grey-haired woman in front turned to face them. 'Excuse me, but I couldn't stop myself listening. When you've been in this business as long as I have you'll have heard this tale time and again.'

'It's not that I didn't expect criticism and that there would be things that would need changing. I'd prepared myself for that. But this . . . this is something else. If I do everything they want then it won't be my book any more.'

'If you don't, though, they'll say the manuscript is unacceptable and refuse you the next payment of your advance,' the woman said kindly and introduced herself as Emma Scott, someone Kate was relieved to find both she and Pam had read and enjoyed so there was no embarrassment between them all.

'The worse thing is it wasn't the person who bought my book. Now, I think I would have got on with her. I don't think she would have asked for such draconian alterations.'

'Who was that?'

'Gloria something . . .'

'You should talk to Bella. Bella's livid, she's got a thing or two to say about Shotters at the moment, I can tell you.'

'I couldn't bother an important author like her with my problems,' Kate said, flustered, and dreading to talk to the woman after making so much noise in entering the hall and putting her off her stride.

'Every member of this society is important to the others. It's why it was formed, to give each other support and help. I'll introduce you.' Emma took hold of Kate's hand in a no-nonsense grasp and led her through the knots of women who were now slowly making their way to the next room where tea was to be served. Quickly Emma explained Kate's plight to Bella.

'Of course, I've heard a lot about you from the people at Shotters. A wonderful success my dear, your first book – the society is proud of you.' Bella smiled sweetly. 'And weren't you at the weekend at . . .?'

'Yes. Oh dear, what a weekend!'

'Everyone's laughing about it all now, even dear Ann Cuthbert, thank goodness. But this Shotters business isn't funny, is it? Gloria was my editor and a good one too. But my dear, this is dreadful for you, such a worry.' Bella led Kate to a chair and sympathetically coaxed out of Kate how she was feeling.

'What shall I do?' Kate looked appealingly at Bella.

'Don't do anything if you don't want to. They can't make you. Don't let them bully you,' Bella advised. 'Do you know what promotional plans they have for you, author tours, that sort of thing?'

'No one has said.'

'Insist. They'll fob you off if they can. You can always tell where you stand with your publisher depending on what tour they give you. Someone from publicity to attend you, aeroplane, first-class everywhere, five-star hotels, TV – you're a star. On your own, but first-class British Rail, four-star hotels, national radio – they've got hopes and plans for you. An Inter-City supersaver and local radio – you're sunk,' Bella rattled off knowledgeably.

'Really? Oh, thank you, Bella, you've been so kind.'

'Not at all, we fellow writers have to stick together. Now I'm gasping for some tea, aren't you?'

Kate glowed at being referred to as a fellow writer by someone so successful, and looked about for Pam. They enjoyed the tea: several women from their weekend at Weston were there and all, somehow, had heard of Kate's luck. Everyone congratulated her and she did not feel a tinge of envy from anyone.

On the drive home Kate thought that Pam was very quiet, but she did not mind, she was tired and she had a lot to think about.

Bella, upon returning to her flat, was quickly on the telephone.

'Tatiana? Sorry bothering you so late but I thought I'd best let you know. You're likely to have trouble with a new writer you've just taken on. Problem these days is they buy themselves a word processor and they think that's all there is to it.'

'Really? A new writer, you say? How kind of you to bother, Bella.'

'Not at all. I must look after my publishers' best interests, after all – you've all been so good to me.' She laughed.

'Who is it?'

'A Kate Howard. Silly woman thinks she knows it all.'

12

'I haven't heard from Kate, Tatiana. I'm sure if she was bothered about anything she would have been in touch with me.'

'I do hope you don't mind me contacting you, Joy, but as her agent I thought you should know,' Tatiana cooed into the telephone.

'It's kind of you, I'll have a word with her.'

'I mean, it's best to nip this sort of thing in the bud, isn't it? We see the problem time and again here – I'm sure you do too. The poor dears think they know best and, of course, you and I know they know nothing.' Tatiana laughed but laughing on the telephone is a dangerous occupation for the instrument only accentuates falseness.

'But you all got on well with her?'

'Everybody absolutely adored her. She's just so sweet, made us all think of our mothers. Of course, it's a pity about the spectacles and she could lose some weight. You don't think she'd agree to trying contact lenses, do you? And what about a health farm?' The false laugh trilled forth.

'It's rather personal, isn't it?' Joy sounded as shocked as she felt.

'I agree, it's terribly difficult but, then, it is for her own good, isn't it? The competition in her particular genre is so fierce and to be quite honest with you, Joy, publicity are a little bit in the doldrums about her. Perhaps if you had a teeny weeny word?'

Joy heard herself agreeing and sighed deeply as she replaced the receiver.

'Problem?' asked Barty from the other side of her desk.

'Do you remember that nice woman Kate Howard at one of your parties, the one, to our shame, that Gloria and I got squiffy? I've sold her first novel to Shotters. Now it seems they want to change bits and Tatiana the new editorial director has just been on the line saying she's been tipped off that Kate is going to refuse to do it.'

'Can't say I blame her. That's one hell of an achievement, writing a novel. I couldn't, and could this here Tatiana?'

'No, but one must be able to listen to criticism, especially as a novice, and be prepared to act upon it.'

'Depends upon the criticism and what you think of the person giving it, surely?' Barty countered reasonably.

'Yes, I suppose so. But now they don't like the way she looks and expect me to talk to her about it.'

'And will you?'

'How can I? She's pretty unsure of herself as it is. Still, you're not here to discuss my problems with Kate.' Joy pulled a pile of large envelopes to her. 'They're all here, the last one was biked over with two minutes to spare to the deadline.' She patted the pile, smiling excitedly at Barty.

'Looks a fat heap.'

'I told you everyone would want you.'

'Tell you what, let's go up to the flat and have a nice cosy cup of tea while we sort through them.'

'As you wish,' Joy said, and buzzed her secretary to say where she would be and to field any calls until she returned.

Barty held the door open for her and bowed her through courteously. She led the way up the stairs to the flat. She could never be sure when Barty would drop in, and he always seemed to want to talk in the flat and not the office. Joy was finding that making the flat look occupied was harder than she had imagined. She always put the newspapers up there and first thing each day she dampened the soap in the bathroom, ran some water in the kitchen sink, left some washing up on the draining board and made sure the tea-towels were slightly damp, all to make it seem she was living there. But for all that, the flat, to her, had the air of unused space.

She went first to the kitchen and put the kettle on, then laid the tea on a small tray.

'It's still very sparse, isn't it?' said Barty, standing in the doorway and looking at the sitting room behind him. 'That husband of yours is being dead mean with you. You need more ornaments, paintings, that sort of thing.'

'I don't want anything of his,' Joy said, not looking at him.

'You're a brave woman. I can't tell you how much I admire you.' Barty coughed as if embarrassed by this statement. 'I'll have to get you a few things.'

'No, Barty, I couldn't allow that, you've done too much for me already. I'll never be able to repay you.'

'Who's asking?' Barty coughed again. 'So, to business,' he said as she completed making the tea. He walked back into the sitting room, sat down on the sofa and pulled the coffee table towards him.

Joy was ripping open the large padded envelopes, and piling them in order. Once finished, she handed him the top one. 'You see I didn't even peep at one. That took some doing, I can tell you. I asked them all to give us an idea of their marketing and publicity budgets and how they envisaged selling into the bookshops. That top one's Tudor's.'

'Well, I never. Haven't they done me proud?' Barty was grinning as he removed the glossy, spiral-bound brochure that Tudor's had produced to persuade them both that they were the best, the only ones, fit to handle Barty's book.

Soon the coffee table was full and they moved on to the floor and the rug was quickly covered with similar brochures. Some had included artwork for proposed covers and posters. Every major London publisher was represented.

'We should have had Brian here, it's so exciting,' Joy said, looking up, eyes glowing with satisfaction at this, her first major publishing coup.

'I didn't think it was a good idea. He might have been seduced by money and that's not everything is it, gal?'

'No. But it's a big factor. If a publisher pays dearly he's got to spend on marketing to recoup his advance. Still, I'd never let you go to Merrytown – they're hopeless, all talk and no action.'

They began to weed the unsuitable ones out. Joy was about to put Westall's on the rejected pile.

'No, leave them in,' Barty held up a restraining hand.

'But their offer is derisory.'

'Do you think so? Maybe it's all they can afford.'

They debated and argued until the brochures were whittled down to four. Pewter's with the largest bid, followed closely by Tudor's, then Shotters and lastly Westall's.

'Westall's it's got to be,' Barty finally said.

'But I don't understand. Their offer is the lowest on everything – advance, marketing and publicity budgets. They haven't even bothered to do any artwork – the others all have. Quite honestly, Barty, I think you would be making a serious mistake. They really don't have the marketing exper-tise –'

'I wouldn't say they had done badly over the years,' Barty said, sharply. 'I like it because it's honest. We all know they're in a mess. Julius could have offered millions and we would know that he was lying. Look at Dewridge here . . .' He pushed one of the booklets across to Joy. 'Ridiculous. Bloody liars. They're on the slide and everyone knows it and yet look what they're promising me. Mark my words, if they're not taken over in the next six months they'll be bankrupt and where would that leave us?'

'Agreed.' Joy was disappointed, she felt thwarted.

'I'll tell you another thing, Joy my girl. Westall's is the best, isn't it? Me? I likes the best.' He nodded.

'I think Brian might be disappointed with his advance.'

'Don't you worry about Brian. He's as happy as a pig in shit. I'm looking after him. Right, I'm off, then. Highly satisfactory.'

Joy followed him down the stairs to the front door where Gervase stood waiting.

'We should celebrate this.' He turned as he was about to leave. 'Have dinner with me tonight, with champers, of course.'

'Why . . .' she paused a second, her mind racing, trying to remember if she and Charles had anything planned. She could not remember. She would have to risk it. 'That would be lovely, Barty,' she said.

'I'll pick you up here.'

'No, not here if you don't mind. I've appointments until late. Say the Groucho, will that do?'

Back in her office she felt exhausted. It should have been easy enough pretending to Barty since she was here every working day and she had bought timers to switch the lights on and off of an evening, just in case he should drive by. One thing she had not thought of was that he often telephoned her in the evening. She had got round the problem neatly by having an answerphone and calling it several times each evening, replaying the messages with her bleeper. She had explained the answering machine always being on by saying that it was safer, for a woman living on her own, to be able to intercept calls. Barty had accepted this as being eminently sensible. But now that he had taken to popping in, it was only a matter of time before she was going to have to explain why she was always out.

But then, it was *her* life. Why shouldn't she return to her husband?

She looked at the telephone on her desk. Who should she call first, Kate or Julius? One a nasty call and one a lovely one. She decided to deal with the problem of Kate first. Kate's problem was not new; when Joy had been an editor one of the first things she had learned was how to tell a writer tactfully that what he or she considered perfection could be improved. But there was no answer from Kate's telephone.

Calling Julius to tell him he was the successful bidder for Barty's autobiography was one of the nicest things she had ever had to do. She laughed at the total disbelief in Julius's voice as he asked her to repeat what she had just said. She might think Barty was mad for selecting Westall's lowest bid, but on a personal level she could not be happier. Because for this, the first major deal of her new professional life, she would be dealing with the straightest, the most honest man in the business.

Kate was not in because she was on her way to London to see Joy. She had tried telephoning all morning, but no one seemed to arrive in the office before ten. Joy was not in, and on calling again later, Kate was told she was in a meeting and could not possibly be disturbed.

Kate had had a sleepless night, too, tossing and turning, wondering what she should do. She had finally got up before dawn. Not being able to speak to

Joy had been too much of a frustration so she had collected her handbag, the typescript, the suggestions, and set off for London. She could not have endured another hour of twiddling her thumbs and seething at not being able to do anything.

She called Joy from Paddington. Joy could not see her until six and suggested that they meet at the Groucho Club. Kate spent the afternoon window-shopping and in the National Gallery, but both activities failed to divert her mind from the problem of her book.

Kate sat in the vestibule of the club in Soho, waiting for Joy, and watching the people who were breezily clattering in through the revolving door, depositing their mobile telephones at the desk like cowboys handing in their guns in a Wild West movie. She waited and waited. An anxious look at her watch told her it was twenty past six. God, she thought, people have such filthy manners these days. A door swung open and there was Joy.

'Kate! I'm so sorry. I was waiting for you at the bar. How silly of me not to check if you were here.'

Kate would like to have agreed with her but instead followed Joy back into the bar.

'Look, there's a free sofa,' Joy said, pointing across the room. 'Grab it quick, I've got to go to the loo.'

Kate inadvertently beat two young men to it, unaware that a sofa here was a prize. She sat down, burrowed in her handbag for her cigarettes and with one lit, looked about her.

The room was large, crowded and noisy. People were talking loudly, waving and shouting across the room at each other. She was reminded of the members at a Hunt Ball she and Tony had mistakenly gone to once. They had bayed at each other, just like these people. The bar was long and people were crushed around it two deep, desperately trying to attract the barman's eye. A pretty girl made her way calmly about the room, taking orders from those sprawling on the sofas. Such confident-looking people, Kate thought.

Each time the door opened people looked up to see who was entering. Those with well-known faces received sly but lingering looks. Nonentities were immediately ignored. No one seemed able to concentrate on their companions, instead they were looking about them constantly, as if searching for better company.

While she waited for Joy to return, Kate amused herself picking out famous faces so that she could tell Pam. She would be riveted by this, she thought, seeing a celebrated and titled writer sitting among a fawning group and noting with uncharitable satisfaction that she looked older than on television.

'Sorry about that. Drink?' Joy asked, as she flopped down beside her in the evidently approved fashion. Kate asked for a gin and tonic and assured Joy she was having a wonderful time just rubber-necking.

'Now, I gather you've got a few problems with Shotters?'

'You know?' Kate said with surprise.

'Yes, Tatiana called me this morning – someone tipped them off.'

'But I haven't spoken to anyone ... apart from ... but ...' Kate looked thoughtful, remembering her conversation with Bella. But surely she, a fellow writer, would not have welshed on her? 'Who?'

'I haven't the foggiest but I wish you had called me. It's my job to sort out any difficulties for you.'

'I did. I couldn't get hold of you.'

'I'm sorry. It's just that ... I've been so busy recently. It won't happen again, I promise.' Joy smiled at Kate who was quick to notice it was with effort. Joy would like to have confided in Kate, told her of the strain of juggling her two lives so that she felt her nerves jangling with the effort. But she resisted. It would not be professional she told herself. 'Now, what's the problem?'

'They want me to change the book out of all recognition. I don't want to be difficult or anything but the problem is I can't do it and that's all there is to it.'

'Of course I understand you feeling a bit disgruntled, but everything can always be improved, that's all they want to do. Present your book to the public the best way possible,' Joy said patiently.

'But it's not an improvement. I think they are going to ruin my book.' And Kate launched into a lengthy description of her interview at Shotters.

'That's not on. I'll speak to them for you, sort it out. Perhaps you'd get on better with another editor?' Joy said soothingly.

'No, I've made up my mind. I don't want to go ahead with it, Joy. I'll give them their money back, cancel the contract. We can do that, can't we?'

'Oh, Kate, I know how frustrated you must be feeling but don't act too hastily. So many writers would give anything for your good fortune.'

'I know all that. I know what I'm risking. But you see, Joy, the book is more important to me than anything else. I'd like you to find another publisher for me.'

'I'll do everything I can, but I must warn you, Kate, once this gets out it is likely to prove harder than you think. You'll be labelled a difficult author, and no one wants a problem writer on their books.'

'They were being difficult publishers,' Kate countered.

Joy, who had been smoking, quickly lit another cigarette. She could understand Kate's annoyance but it didn't alter the fact that she was asking almost the impossible. Not only would she damage her own reputation, but by association Joy's also. It was hard enough to get first novels published and now this. Still ... she sat up straight.

'Well, the problem to surmount is your contract.'

'You don't think they'll hold me to it? They can't make me write,' said Kate, voice rising with panic.

'Don't worry. In law they could but it is unlikely they would insist.'

'What about Gloria? She loved it,' Kate said, brightening up at the sudden idea.

'Gloria's at Westall's now and, Kate, I know, I understand how wonderful you think your book is but a house like Westall wouldn't even read it. They publish only literary fiction. But . . .' Certainly it was an odd career move for Gloria, famous for her editing of popular fiction, Joy thought. She hadn't heard any gossip on the grapevine of a change in Westall's publishing profile, but it might be worth talking to Gloria. 'Leave it to me . . . I'll sort something out.' Joy slumped back on to the sofa, suddenly feeling exhausted.

'What sad-faced ladies.'

They both looked up to find Barty Silver with his entourage standing by their table. A hush had fallen on the room and everyone was looking at them with envious expressions.

'Kate Howard, isn't it?'

'Why, yes,' she said, amazed that he should remember her.

Barty sat down and Gervase ordered champagne. At first Kate said she must go but Barty insisted she have a glass.

'So why the despondency?' Barty wanted to know, so Joy explained. He invited Kate to join them for dinner. She would have loved to, but she had just remembered she had not left Tony a note explaining where she was. She must get to a telephone and then home as quickly as possible.

'Thanks, but I must go.'

'Pity,' said Barty. 'Remember one thing, Mrs Howard. Listen to your instincts and you can't go wrong.' And he winked broadly at her.

13

By the time Kate put her key into the lock of her front door, it was nearly ten and she was tired.

'I've been worried sick wondering where you were.' Tony was standing in the doorway of his study as if he had been waiting for her.

'I did telephone as soon as –' She stopped at that, uncertain how to continue, how to explain her lapse without hurting him more.

'As soon as you remembered me. Was that what you were going to say? Thanks a lot.'

'Tony, it wasn't like that – honestly. I can't tell you the state I was in. I wasn't thinking straight. I just knew I had to get to London, see my agent and ask her to sort out the problems with the publishers for me.'

In the kitchen, Kate heaved up the lid of the Aga and scraped the large kettle across to the hotplate. She decided that the best thing was to try to appease him. She crossed to the dresser, took down two mugs, and got the instant coffee out of the cupboard.

'Coffee?' she asked, in a reasonable tone.

'I just don't know what's got into you, what's changed you, Kate. We used to have such a wonderful, happy life together.'

This was too much. Kate slammed the mugs down on the table. 'Wonderful for who? Who was happy? Certainly not me. I did everything just as my mother and you expected me to. And what was the result? I suddenly realised I'd become a cipher, nothing more. You didn't even notice what I did until the day I stopped doing it and your quiet, orderly, life was remotely disrupted.' Angrily she spooned the coffee into the mugs. 'You don't care one iota about me as a person. You don't give a damn about my book. Any normal husband would be pleased with what I've achieved, be proud of me. But you? What's your reaction? To whine and complain because, for once, I'm not here.'

'I do care. Didn't I say the minute you walked through the door that I had been worried sick wondering where you were.'

'Ha!' Kate's laugh was short and cynical. 'Worried that there was no supper on the table, more like.'

'That's unfair, Kate. I wasn't to know you were in this state.'

She turned slowly and faced him. 'But that's the whole point, Tony. You didn't know because you never listen to me. Ever since I began to write I've tried to involve you – but you haven't wanted to know. I tried talking to you last night. I told you the editor at Shotters had upset me. I knew you weren't really listening.'

'Not interested? Who bought you a word processor? And that wasn't cheap, I can tell you.'

'Fine, but do you remember what you said? I'll remind you. You said that the word processor would put an end to all this nonsense.'

'It was a joke.'

'My eye. For years I've endured hearing about your work, even when I didn't want to, even when it bored me or I didn't understand. But can you do the same for me? No. I'm warning you, Tony. I've got this far and nothing is going to stop me getting to the top. Not you, not the children, not this house nor your flaming suppers!' She was shouting and shaking and as she poured the now boiling water on to the coffee she slopped some of it on the Aga. She watched it hissing and steaming and forming into little balls shining, looking almost like mercury, as they scurried about the hotplate as if trying to escape. She felt like one of those balls of water.

'It's not just me. I saw Pam the other day. She said much the same, that you didn't care any more, that she hardly ever saw you.'

'Pam is playing at writing. I'm not. I know I don't see her so much, I don't have the time. If she was serious about it she wouldn't have the time either.' She placed the mugs of coffee on the pine table.

'We used to have real coffee once,' Tony said mournfully.

Kate looked at him, eyes blazing with fury. She picked up the mugs and hurled both of them across the kitchen where they smashed on the furthest wall. The cat leapt with a yell and rushed for the cat-flap as the broken china flew to right and left while the coffee trickled down the tiled wall, forming puddles on the floor.

'Then make it yourself.' She walked to the door, choosing to ignore the mess. 'Oh, by the way. I'm going to London again on Monday, you'd best make arrangements to eat out.' And she slammed the kitchen door shut behind her, ran up the stairs and into her workroom, shut the door and switched on her word processor.

Joy had lied to Charles when she telephoned to say she was having dinner with a client he did not know but, she reasoned, he had lied to her so many times that this little untruth hardly counted.

It had been a pleasant evening. Usually when one dined with Barty there were up to a dozen other guests. But tonight he had dismissed his entourage and it had been just the two of them.

It did not seem to matter where they went, Barty was always known and the management made an inordinate fuss of him and thus her. It was rather enjoyable and something one could easily get used to, she thought, as they left the bar he had taken her to after the Groucho. Dinner was to be a surprise, he had said, as the Rolls-Royce hummed along, out of central London, across the river and into the East End into suburbs where she had never ventured before. They stopped at an eel and pie shop where, once again, Barty was treated like visiting royalty.

Joy had looked at the plate of mashed potatoes, swimming in a sea of green juice from the mushy peas, with suspicion. Tentatively she forked a little into her mouth, only to find to her surprise, and Barty's delight, that it was delicious.

They had then gone to a pub and watched a drag show. Unsure at first if this was what she wanted to sit through, Joy was in for another surprise. It was one of the funniest things she had ever seen, made funnier by the wit of the audience of locals hurling remarks at the performers, who lobbed back retorts at such speed it was difficult to believe it was spontaneous. She told Barty it was like listening to a verbal tennis match.

From there they had travelled back up West to a jazz club where she had discovered that Barty's knowledge of jazz music was formidable. Once she had confessed she did not know a trombone from a saxophone, Barty set himself the task of educating her.

It was nearly four when they finally drew up in front of the office and the flat where Barty fondly thought she was living. The chauffeur opened the door and she slid out. Barty followed her. She stood on the pavement feeling awkward, not knowing how to proceed, feeling a little like a teenager on a first date.

'Barty, I'm so tired. Forgive me if after such a wonderful evening I don't invite you in for a drink,' she apologised with a weary smile.

'I wouldn't dream of accepting. Why, at this time of night, with a lady on her own? Good Lord, Joy, what do you take me for?'

She would like to have kissed him for his thoughtfulness, but knowing how he felt about human contact, she did not like to. Perhaps the biggest surprise of the whole evening was when, to her astonishment, Barty leant across and kissed her gently on the cheek.

'Night, little lady,' he said and climbed back into his car. Joy stood waiting but the car did not move and then she realised he was waiting to see her safely into the building. She unlocked the door, stood in the doorway – but still the car stood motionless. Sighing, she closed it, and climbed the three floors up to her flat. She put the lights on, crossed to the window, and moved the curtains so that Barty could see her. The Rolls-Royce purred into action and moved along the darkened road.

Joy waited five minutes and then raced back down the stairs, ran along the street and round the corner to her parked car. She drove at speed to Holland Park, praying all the way that Charles would be sound asleep and that she would be able to slip into bed without him realising what the time was.

Once in the house, she took off her shoes, and, not bothering with any lights, tiptoed up the stairs. Gingerly she opened the bedroom door. She stood a moment, listening for the safe sound of his regular breathing. There was silence. She crossed to the bed and looked down. It was empty. With a feeling of mounting sickness she switched on the bedside light. The bed had not been slept in. Perfect, unrumpled sheets told her everything.

Gloria was elated. It did not matter how often she told herself she was being stupid, the feeling of excitement kept bubbling up and most of the time she knew she had a silly smile on her face that she could not control either.

She was elated because she knew she was in love. She was excited because she was strangely confident that Peter was falling in love too. She told herself it was stupid to think this way because she had nothing to base it upon. They had enjoyed a pleasant evening together, they had talked – nothing more.

Reason could tell her one thing but emotions told her another. There had been an undercurrent between them that evening. There had been more to their unburdening themselves to each other than reason could explain. She had analysed why she had confided her past to him. Now she understood. She had told him everything, even the worst, so that he knew all there was to know about her, so that there was nothing about her that someone could surprise him with in the future. Clearing the emotional deck for him was the best way she could describe it.

Oddly she was not afraid of her honesty. She felt he had accepted it, as if knowing himself her reasons for doing it. And if she needed further proof it was the way he had said goodnight. The way he had not presumed she would invite him into her bed. That's what nearly every man expected these days, but not Peter. He *was* different, he was a gentleman, he would court her, she knew! She knew!

And if she really delved back into her memory she could remember feeling exactly like this about him all those years ago, when she had had that hopeless crush on him, a married man. But now he was separated and it seemed all she had to do was to uncork the memories, those old feelings she had had for him. It was as if she had been waiting for him, that all the other lovers had meant nothing to her because she had put her love on hold for him.

In love she might be but she had work to do. Her new job at Westall's did not begin until Monday, but she already had plans. First she called Julius to check with him that, although she was not yet officially employed by him, she could start negotiations with an author. He laughed at her enthusiasm, and wished her luck. Her next call was to Primrose Cooper to tell her Shotters had turned her novel down but that she was in the happy position of being able to offer her a contract with Westall's, the details of which they would discuss next week.

That done, and after a light lunch, she began something which had once given her pleasure and which she had not done for months – she cleaned her house from top to bottom. She knew why she was doing it, she had a purpose now. There was someone who cared for her, someone to share it with.

She hoped he would telephone soon and then she would take the initiative, she would suggest he came to dinner. If her plan worked out he would stay the weekend. And then – she felt almost breathless at the idea – within a week or two she would suggest he need not bother to look for a house, he was welcome to move in with her.

Perhaps thinking this way was proof, if proof were needed, of her feelings for him. In all other previous relationships she had never countenanced the idea of anyone moving in with her. She had been happy to have them stay for the odd weekend, occasionally for a week. But always she had begun to feel restless, wanting them away, wanting her privacy back. Not this time.

As she worked she wondered what they would do this weekend. Perhaps if the weather held they could go to the country. Maybe he would like to go to the theatre, the opera. On the other hand perhaps she should go shopping and get food in just in case he preferred to stay at home. She could just imagine them, eating, drinking, listening to music, making love. Yes, come to think of it, a weekend at home would be best of all.

The house cleaned and shining, Gloria drove to Sainsbury's and trundled round with the trolley, light-headed with euphoria. No more prepacked meals. She would cook for him. Good gracious, she thought, stopping dead in the shopping aisle, she had never wanted to do that for any of her other lovers, either. She began to run through possible menus in her head, selecting the necessary items. At the drink shelves she bought his favourite whisky – strange she should remember, from all those years back, how much he had liked Highland Park. Carefully she selected a dozen bottles of wine – six red, six white. And happily she paid the huge bill, enlarged because of the cantaloupe melons, the out-of-season asparagus and the side of smoked salmon, none of which she had meant to buy but had, because she was certain he would enjoy them.

She drove home singing, the prospect of a full and wonderful weekend ahead of her. Of course, she should have returned the car, but now there was not such a rush to do so. They could return it together tomorrow, then she would have a lift back home instead of having to take a taxi.

She pulled up in front of her house at the same time as a florist's van. She signed for the huge bouquet of flowers, a grin on her face of such happiness that she made the delivery man laugh. She decided to unpack the car first and then open the flowers, knowing full well who they were from.

She forced herself to pack away the last item of groceries, delaying the pleasure of opening the bouquet, enjoying in a masochistic sort of way the wait to see what message he had sent her. At last she allowed herself to pick up the scissors and attack the gaudy ribbon and the Cellophane encasing her flowers.

'Look what a lucky girl I am, Elephant.'

She slid the card from its tiny envelope.

'Oh, no!' she said aloud. The message slipped from her fingers.

Sorry. I won't bother you again. Peter was written on it. Nothing else.

14

'Welcome to Westall's, Gloria,' Julius said, beaming at her as she stood in his office on her first day with the firm.

'Thanks, I got here at last,' she said, and smiled. But Julius was quick to note it was not her normal big and happy smile.

'Are you all right, my dear? You look tired,' Julius said with concern.

'I'm fine, Julius,' she lied. 'I cleaned my house over the weekend – I think I'm past such violent activity.' She attempted to laugh but it only made her head feel worse. She felt dreadful. Over the weekend, that awful lonely desert of a weekend, she had managed to drink too much of the wine and too much of the whisky she had bought for Peter. She was left feeling a complete fool and was only glad she had not told anyone of her stupid feelings and dreams.

'I'm glad you brought the little dog with you. What's he called?' Julius asked, bending down to stroke it.

'Elephant. He's why I'm here. They suddenly banned him at Shotters.'

'No risk of that here.' He laughed. 'But I don't think it was just the treatment of the dog – it was only a matter of time. You're not a corporate creature, Gloria, or I don't know you very well.'

'You're probably right, Julius. This suits me better, this is a *real* publisher's.'

'Grimly hanging on by the skin of our teeth, but surviving – just. Ah, Crispin, come in. I'm glad you could make it. Of course you know Gloria.'

'We've met a couple of times at book fairs and whatever, haven't we?' She held out her hand to Crispin.

'And this is another new member of staff, Crispin. He's called Elephant, aren't you, old boy?' Julius said, grinning broadly.

Crispin neatly sidestepped the little dog with as much speed as if it were a

Rottweiler. He smiled in a sickly way – another indication of his uncle's senility, thought Crispin, who regarded anyone who anthropomorphised a dog as mentally unstable. Elephant, upon sensing that here was someone who did not like him, immediately sat down as close to his feet as he could get.

'Is it too early to hear of your plans, Gloria? I've mapped out what I think will be a reasonable budget for you. As you will see, you have almost complete autonomy. Only if you should want to buy in some mega-seller I feel we should have a wider discussion. I trust your judgement entirely, otherwise.' Julius handed Gloria a folder with all the financial details she would need to run her department. 'I think it's only fair that we tell you from the start that Crispin is not too happy with this new plan.' Crispin looked up, a pained expression on his face. That might be so but he did not think it necessary for his uncle to trumpet it from the rooftops. He decided to say nothing at this juncture. 'So I suggest,' Julius continued, 'that being the case, it would be difficult for you both to liaise as you would normally. So I, for this imprint, shall take the role of financial director. Fairer all round, wouldn't you say, Crispin?'

Crispin wanted to say no it certainly was not fair all round, but then, he thought, if it was a total disaster – as it was likely to be – the less he had to do with it the better.

'That's fine by me, Uncle,' he said.

'So, Gloria, what plans do you have thus far?'

For the next hour, she was able to forget Peter as Gloria did what she liked best – talked books. She told them of Primrose Cooper. She reported on the gossip, straws in the wind which might lead to them picking up several authors. She said how she planned to get in touch with the secretary of the Red Rose Society.

'The what?' Crispin said with disdain.

'It's an organisation of women writers. Most of them write for Wallers and The Paradise Club.' At mention of these two publishing houses, Crispin snorted. 'But they do have quite a few members who write mainstream books and a lot, I know, would like to cross over. I thought, perhaps, we could arrange a competition with them, the winner to be published by us. It shouldn't cost much. I'd rather delay doing this until the present chairperson steps down – in May I think. She's one of Shotters' writers and might let them know a little too much of our business. Tatiana might like the idea and pinch it for themselves.'

'I like the idea of a competition, Gloria. We could pick up quite a bit of useful publicity that way.'

'And free, too.'

'Crispin?'

Crispin laughed a slightly maniacal laugh. 'Whatever you say, Uncle. Who am I to object?'

'Fine,' said Julius, completely ignoring the sarcasm.

'Didn't you edit Bella Ford?' Crispin asked. 'Wouldn't it make more sense if you tried to get her and others like her to move over with you?' He would like to have added that doing so would make a lot more sense of her appointment, but he refrained.

'I intend to, but not Bella. She's more trouble than she's worth. There's a lot of disaffection at Shotters as you know, but I think some will prefer to go to Tudor's or Pewter's – more established in their genre, you see.' She smiled sweetly at Crispin. 'But I'll do my best.' Just before she left she asked about a secretary.

'I presumed you would want to find your own. Until then you could borrow Crispin's?'

After the satisfactory meeting Gloria ran down the stairs from Julius's first-floor office to her own.

'Miss Catchpole,' the receptionist called out to her as she passed. 'You've a visitor.'

Standing at the desk was a woman in a mackintosh, with a scarf on her head for it was raining heavily outside. She was familiar but for the life of her Gloria could not put a name to her.

'Yes?' Gloria said hesitantly.

'Kate Howard,' the woman said, holding out her hand. 'We had lunch . . .'

'Kate, forgive me. It's the light in here,' she said quickly, though it was true. 'Plus I've got a filthy hangover. But, you know, you look different. What have you done to yourself?'

'I haven't got my specs on, it's raining so hard out there I couldn't see through them. And, well, actually, I've lost some weight.' Kate blushed at this.

'You're telling me you have. It suits you, how much?'

'Over a stone.'

'Wonderful! And, you know, you have such pretty eyes,: you should wear contact lenses, the specs hid them.'

'I've made an appointment to have some fitted next week.' Kate was not used to compliments and those from another woman meant more, in a way.

'Good. So, Kate, it's lovely to see you again. What can I do for you? Come through to my office.'

She led the way along the downstairs corridor to the back of the beautiful building. Gloria's new office was on the ground floor, with french windows opening on to a wrought-iron balcony and steps leading down into a pretty courtyard garden which would be a delight to sit in when the summer came. The room was furnished with a chesterfield sofa, two fine wing chairs and a large mahogany desk. Between the bookcases, as yet unfilled, which lined the walls, the paintwork was a pretty Adam green and Gloria shuddered to think how valuable was the carpet at her feet. Compared to Shotters this was paradise.

'Tea, coffee?'

'No, thanks, but do you mind if I smoke?'

'Not at all. There must be an ashtray here somewhere.' Gloria rooted among the papers on her desk which she had been in the process of sorting when she was called to see Julius. 'Forgive the muddle, it's my first day here,' she said, emerging triumphantly with a large glass ashtray which she was pretty sure was crystal.

'How are things with Shotters?' Gloria asked calmly, but her heart was lifting, for she knew something must be wrong for Kate to be here.

'I know I've been incredibly lucky and everything and I know this might sound dreadfully ungrateful and everybody is going to think I'm mad but – well, I can't let Shotters publish my book.' Haltingly at first and then picking up more confidence as the memory of last week's humiliation came rushing back into her mind, Kate told of her experience.

'Oh dear,' said Gloria, when she had eventually finished. She nearly said she was not surprised but her professionalism saved her in the nick of time.

'There's one thing I have to find out, Gloria – for my own peace of mind. Would you have insisted on those alterations?'

'No, I would not have done any of those things. Your book would stand as it is. It needed tightening up here and there, and you repeat yourself a little bit too often but they were all simple editing jobs. The trouble these days is that too many publishers don't give the readers credit for any intelligence. You get one book that hits the best-seller list, then they're all rushing about like lemmings to try to find one similar. Publishing to me is trying to find new talent with a new way of telling a tale and, with luck, a new tale to tell, not a constant repetition of the old. That's what attracted me to your book. It follows no rules, no clichés. Why, look at the ending – it's sad but it's the only logical ending to have. I agree with you, Kate, don't let them touch your book, they'll destroy it. Over-edited and they could lose your author's voice. Gracious, what a lecture.' She laughed at herself and the passion with which she had been speaking.

'I've told Joy. Did she speak to you about me?'

'No, not yet.' Gloria frowned, puzzled that Joy hadn't if Kate had asked her to. 'Maybe she's been too busy,' she added kindly.

'I've asked her to get me out of my contract, I'll pay them back. I did mention you to her but she said this firm wouldn't be interested in me.'

'She can't have heard of our plans when she spoke to you. But it's only a matter of time and she will.' Gloria laughed. 'Gossip travels fast in publishing. Look at these . . .' She pointed at a pile of manuscripts on her desk. 'I only left Shotters last week, yet the news had begun to filter out and these submissions were waiting for me this morning.' She smiled at Kate who looked worried. 'It's all right, Kate, we'd love to publish your book. You know how strongly I felt about it. But my hands are tied until you extricate yourself from Shotters. I couldn't make any moves – it would be unprofessional and would look as if I was poaching and that would never do. Do you see?'

'But all is not lost?'

'No. You might have difficulties with Shotters but it doesn't sound as if they were too keen on my choice, anyway.' She smiled.

'Thank you, Gloria, you've been a big help.'

'Any time, and keep up the diet.'

As soon as Kate had gone Gloria was on the telephone to Joy. She sounded slightly harassed and a little irritated that Kate had approached Westall's.

'I think she just came in for a shoulder to cry on,' Gloria reassured her. 'But, Joy, she means it, she won't let them touch it. Get her out of it and I promise you Westall's will pick her up.'

After her call to Joy, Gloria telephoned her secretary Rachel at Blades to invite her to come and join her at Westall's. Rachel needed no time to consider the offer and it was she who told Gloria that Blades was no more. So I was right, she thought, as she replaced the receiver. But being right did not make her happy. She had liked Blades, been proud of it. She had created it, if truth be told.

Throughout the day Gloria found that if she kept busy she could keep her feeling of depression at bay. It did not go away, but lurked, waiting for an empty moment when it would hit her. She'd allowed herself to hope and had ended up feeling a complete fool.

It was finally time for her to return home with an empty evening stretching before her. She just hoped to God there was something decent on television; if not she would read the submissions she had pointed out to Kate.

Elephant leapt ahead of her along the passage which was her hall, barking excitedly at the noise of Pink Floyd blaring out of the CD player. She walked into the sitting room to find Clive, whom she had not seen in weeks, lying on the sofa, idly reading a book. Gloria crossed the room and switched it off.

'What you do that for?'

'I don't feel like listening to it,' she said, putting on some Mozart instead. She crossed to the drinks tray, neatly stacked with bottles, and poured herself some tonic water.

'Don't I get a drink?' he demanded.

'Tonic water?'

'Hell, you ill or something? Don't be silly. Vodka straight, if you don't mind.'

'Actually, I do mind.'

She walked through to the kitchen, he followed.

'What's the matter, Gloria?'

'Nothing.'

'Oh, come on. When a woman says that it means all hell's about to break loose.'

'Nothing's the matter. I just wish you weren't here, that's all.'

'I beg your pardon?' he said, having the audacity to look surprised.

'I don't see you for weeks. I don't know where you are, what you're doing, who you're with even, and in this day and age that matters more than anything else. And then you swan in as if nothing has happened.'

'You never used to mind.'

'Is that what you thought? Oh, I minded, Clive. I minded very much. I was stupid. But everything has changed. Now I don't care a damn what you do so long as it's not with me. I've been down your road once too often.'

'You've met someone else?' he asked.

Gloria laughed. 'Christ, what conceit. You think the only possible reason I don't want to see you any more is because there's someone else. Well, for your information, there isn't. I've just had you up to here.' She tapped the underside of her chin with the flat of her hand as she spoke.

'No one, eh? So who's this from? And why are those far from dead flowers in the rubbish bin?' He was waving Peter's card at her. She steeled herself not to swoop on it thus alerting him to the fact that it was important to her, that he had caught her at a particularly vulnerable time.

'It's from my boss, Peter Holt, we had a misunderstanding at work. It's his way of apologising.'

'Oh.' Clive dropped the card on to the table, evidently disappointed he had not found her out. She wondered if she might have acted differently if for one moment she had thought he was feeling jealous. As it was she looked at his handsome but vacuous face, the over-greased hair, the trendy clothes and she despised herself for ever having found him attractive. So, she thought with satisfaction, maybe if he had been jealous it would not have made one iota of difference.

'Look, Clive, you'll have to go. I've got friends coming for dinner.'

'You? Entertaining? I don't believe it.'

She opened the refrigerator which was bulging with the food she had bought for her imagined weekend with Peter. 'See for yourself.' She shrugged her shoulders as if not caring whether he believed her or not.

'Oh, I see. Well, I'll be getting along. Shall I be seeing you again?'

'No, Clive. I don't think so. And, if you don't mind, I'd like my key back.'

He dropped the key on the table and it landed on top of the card from Peter.

'As you wish,' he said with a shrug. 'Bye, Gloria.'

'Bye,' she replied vaguely, for she was staring at the key and the card and fighting tears. In an ideal world she would have been giving Peter that key.

She heard the front door slam, heard Clive's footsteps echo on the pavement outside. She poured herself a large vodka ignoring the tonic water. She raised the glass, toasting herself for the first sensible action she had made in her personal life for a long time.

15

Kate had an appointment with Joy. When Joy had called, it was with the good news that she was out of her contract with Shotters and that Kate was to bring a cheque with her to pay her advance back. Then they were both going to see Gloria to discuss the book. That was the plan. Instead she stood in the outer office of the agency and was worried.

'You don't seem to understand,' she was saying to the young girl in the office. 'I have an appointment with Mrs Trenchard. Please let her know I'm here.'

'I'm afraid I can't.'

'Of course you can.' Kate realised she was beginning to sound irritated. She must stop, it was hardly the girl's fault. 'Look, I'm sorry, but I've come a long way for this appointment.'

'Please, Mrs Howard . . .' The girl looked close to tears.

'What on earth's the matter?'

'It's Mrs Trenchard. I haven't seen her yesterday or today. I don't know where she is.'

'Have you tried her home number?'

'I didn't bother her at first. It was slack here yesterday and she's been so tired I thought she was resting. But today when I tried no one answered the telephone at first and then a child answered, but I couldn't get any sense out of her. I've been so worried and didn't know what to do.'

'Didn't you think to go round?'

'I don't know where she lives and she's ex-directory.'

'Did you try Sir Barty?'

'Yes, but he's away.' And the young woman finally burst into tears. 'Mrs Howard, I'm frightened.'

Kate searched in her handbag for the card, now rather bent, which Joy had given her all those months ago at Barty's. She picked up the telephone and quickly dialled Joy's number. She was frowning – something must be really wrong: Joy would not leave the poor girl to manage on her own. She let the telephone ring for quite some time and was just about to replace it, when she heard it being answered.

'Joy?'

'Yes,' a weak voice answered.

'It's Kate.'

'Kate, how nice to hear from you.' Joy's voice had a strange rasping quality to it.

'Joy, are you all right? You sound strange.'

'Oh, Kate, what day is it? Oh God, our appointment – I'm so sorry . . . Can we make it another day? Can't talk, not now.' And before Kate could say any more the line went dead.

Kate did not like the sound of Joy's voice. She must be ill. She reassured Joy's secretary, collected her things and was lucky to find a cab cruising outside. She gave the address in Holland Park.

Once there she rang the bell several times but no one answered. Perhaps she had acted precipitously, maybe Joy was simply taking a few days off. But then, she thought, if she was, how dare she treat her as if she did not matter? She rang the bell again. Kate was about to turn away when she was sure she heard a child. She lifted the letterbox flap and peered in. A small girl was sitting on the black and white marbled floor crying.

'Hello,' Kate called through the gap. 'Hallo-ooo . . .' The child looked up towards the door. 'Come here, sweetheart.' Slowly the little girl stood up and approached the door. 'Don't cry, darling. Is your mummy there? I'm a friend of hers.'

'She's upstairs,' the child said, wiping her tears with the back of her hand.

'Will you go and tell her Kate's here and I'd love a cup of tea?'

'She won't come.'

'Please, be a pet, go and ask her.'

'She's asleep.'

'Is anyone else in the house with you?'

'No, my nanny's gone. My mummy shouted at her and now she's gone – ' And she burst into tears again and moved back into the hall, where she disappeared from Kate's narrow field of vision.

Kate tried to stay calm which, in the circumstances, was difficult. One thing the little girl had said kept echoing in her mind. 'She's asleep.' What if she had taken an overdose? She had sounded distraught enough. Something was desperately wrong: Joy was not the sort of woman to leave a young child unattended like that.

She ran up the road, and round the corner. These houses often had a mews and a large garden, she reasoned. She was right. Twenty yards along the road, she saw the entrance to a mews. She stopped outside the house she was certain was Joy's. The black gate set in the wall was locked. Kate looked about her and saw a large dustbin; she pushed it against the wall. She was not designed for shinning over walls and had to huff and puff to pull herself up. Then she hung from the top of the wall and carefully lowered herself down the other side. There was still a small drop and she landed on her backside in a rose bush. She picked herself up, dusted her coat down, saw the damage she had done to the plants and prayed she was in the right garden. She ran up the garden path. There were steps down to a basement kitchen. She pushed at the door praying it was not locked, and it gave. She stepped in and found herself in a downstairs passage. She called out immediately.

'Is there anybody there?' She wished she could remember the child's name, but in her panic she had forgotten it. She climbed the stairs out of the basement. 'Hello,' she kept saying. Suddenly the child appeared at the head of the stairs.

'Have you come to see my mummy?'

'Yes, lovey, can you take me to her?' She held out her hand and the little girl put her small one into Kate's and led her up the long flight of stairs to the second floor.

'She's in there.' They had stopped outside a white-painted door.

Kate's heart was thumping so loudly as she pushed open the door that she was sure it was audible. The curtains were pulled and only one bedside light was on but Kate could see Joy sprawled across the bed. She rushed across the room.

'Joy,' she said loudly and then again even louder. 'Joy, wake up, it's Kate.'

'Kate? What the hell are you doing here?' To her relief, Joy opened her eyes and tried to focus on her.

'Joy, listen to me.' Kate was patting her hands urgently. 'Joy, have you taken anything? Answer me, do.'

'Taken anything? Me? Don't be bloody silly,' she said, slurring her words and trying to laugh. Then, she drifted off to sleep again. As her head flopped back on the pillow for the first time Kate noticed a large bruise on the side of her face.

Either she was very drunk or she had taken an overdose, Kate concluded. She looked at the bedside table but there were no empty bottles. Perhaps she should telephone for a doctor to be on the safe side? She looked around but could find no address book. She listened to Joy's breathing, which sounded normal enough, then crossed the room and out on to the landing where the child stood, looking wide-eyed and wan.

'What's your name?'

'Hannah.'

'Of course it is. Tell me, Hannah, do you know the name of your doctor?'

'He's called Doctor.'

'Yes, of course.' Kate stood biting her lip, thinking. 'Is there another telephone I can use? I don't want to wake Mummy, she's tired.'

'This way.' Hannah led her to another room and pointed to the instrument. Quickly Kate dialled Westall's number.

'Why, hello, Kate,' said Gloria. 'Aren't we meeting later?'

'Gloria, I'm sorry to bother you but I didn't know who else to contact. I'm at Joy's, I'm afraid she might have done herself a mischief.'

'A mischief? What on earth are you talking about, Kate?' Gloria laughed at such an antiquated turn of phrase.

'Hannah's with me,' Kate said pointedly. 'I can't find her doctor's number.'

'Oh my God. I'll be right over. What happened?'

'I don't know what happened. Come quickly, please.'

She replaced the receiver and smiled encouragingly at the small child.

'My mummy and daddy had a row and my daddy hit her and she's been crying all night – I heard her. Then my nanny said it served her right and they were horrible to each other and my nanny went.'

'Well, what a busy time you've had. You know what would be a good idea, if we made your mummy some coffee. Shall we do that?'

She checked Joy again, forcing her to wake up before going to the kitchen and making a large pot of black coffee.

Sitting her up in a more comfortable position Kate managed to get nearly a cup of the hot liquid down a complaining Joy.

'Why you doing this to me?'

'I'm afraid you've taken some pills.'

'Pills? Don't be silly, Kate. I took two, to sleep, that's all promise,' Joy said slowly and emphatically. 'And I wish to Christ you'd let me. I'm so tired.'

'And booze, how much booze with the pills?'

'Dear Kate ... so worried. I've a hangover. OK?' And she pushed the second cup of coffee away and slumped back on the pillows.

Kate stationed herself, for what seemed an age, at the window waiting for Gloria's taxi. The doorbell rang and she ran downstairs to answer it.

'I'm sorry I took so long, it was the damn traffic, I should have taken a taxi instead of driving. How is she?'

'Gloria, I'm sorry dragging you here, I think I overreacted. I think she's drunk.' Kate led the way back up the stairs.

'Don't worry, I wasn't busy. You did the right thing, I would want to know.' They entered the gloomy bedroom.

'Hello, Gloria, just like old times.' Joy giggled from the bed.

'You pissed?'

'Yes. And how!'

'Oh, Joy, what about Hannah?' Gloria said shocked.

'Hannah, is she all right?' At mention of her daughter Joy sat bolt upright in bed.

'No thanks to you. She was all alone downstairs. Thank God Kate came over and had the sense to break in.'

'But the nanny . . .?'

'Gone,' said Kate.

'Oh God.' Joy ran her hands through her hair. 'The bitch, the out-and-out bitch.'

'What happened, Joy?' Gloria sat on the edge of the bed and took hold of her hand.

'The usual, he's up to his old tricks, he didn't like it when I complained.' She stroked the ugly bruise on her face.

'And now? Haven't you had enough? Are you going to leave him, finally?'

'I know I've got to, Gloria, this time, I really have.'

'You need a shower, my girl. Kate and I will throw some lunch together, then I'll run you over to the flat.'

'Thanks, both of you.' Joy's eyes brimmed with tears.

16

'Why does she stay with him?' Kate asked Gloria as they sat in the flat over the literary agency, sharing a bottle of wine; while Joy and Hannah were asleep in the bedrooms above.

'She loves him, I suppose, poor cow.' Gloria topped up their glasses. 'God, I'm tired, aren't you?'

'Exhausted. How many trips did we make between here and Holland Park?'

'It must have been half a dozen but it feels more like twenty.' Gloria rubbed her aching shoulders. 'She had so much stuff.'

'Still you could see why she wanted to get it out if he's violent.'

'At least she's got the kid with her. Last time Joy left without her, and Charles wouldn't let her see Hannah. That's how he managed to get her back, I reckon.'

'What a bastard.'

'Yes, and apparently he's charm itself. Everyone thinks he's a really super bloke, only he tortures his wife behind the bedroom door. She wouldn't drink in such a self-destructive way if it wasn't for him.'

'Talking of which I shouldn't be drinking this. What about my diet?' Kate grimaced at the glass in her hand.

'We've earned this, Kate. You can go back on the diet tomorrow.'

Kate looked at her watch. 'I think I'll have another go at calling my husband, he should be home by now. He's not going to be pleased that I'm late – again.'

'We can't leave her though, can we? I mean, what if he came over here? If only the kid wasn't asthmatic and allergic to dogs, I'd stay.'

'Is she?'

'It's why they have no pets, Joy told me. I can't leave Elephant, you see. I've never left him alone all night.' Gloria looked questioningly at Kate.

'I don't know. Tony will be livid if I stay . . .' Kate said doubtfully. 'Let's see what she says when she wakes up.'

There were times with Tony when Kate wondered why she bothered to call, his reaction was so predictable. She explained about the problem with Joy but he was in no mood to hear explanations.

'You're still there?'

'Yes. She's asleep. Look, Tony, she's a frightened woman. I think I should offer to stay the night.'

'Sod the lot of you,' he yelled and the line went dead.

'Trouble?' Gloria said, half grinning, half anxious.

'Husbands!'

'Some days I'm glad I haven't got one.'

'Days like today I envy you. Actually I think I will have some more wine.'

'Atta girl.' Gloria laughed.

'At least I've escaped from Shotters.'

'That was wonderful news. I've been going to discuss the book with you. I can let you into a secret now. I still had a copy of your typescript, and I sent it round to Panda – you know, the paperback company. Jill Ravenscroft, the senior editor there, is a good friend of mine and I was able to swear her to absolute secrecy. Anyhow, she read it over the weekend, she loves it and they're interested. We should be able to do a joint campaign with them.'

'What's that?'

'It's better for you, is what it means. We shall offer together and we share the expenses of promotion, publicity, all that sort of thing. Panda is one of the biggest paperback houses. If they decide to back you you should get a first print run of more than forty thousand. Honestly, Kate, it's wonderful news for you.'

Kate looked deeply into her glass, biting her lip, a great lump in her throat.

'What's the matter?' Gloria asked with concern.

'Everything's so wonderful and yet I've no one to share it with. My husband doesn't give a damn, in fact he's irritated by the whole business. My daughter is never at home and, in any case, thinks only of herself. My son, the one who has shown the most interest, is working in Yorkshire. And, to top it all, my best friend and I seem so distant with each other and I miss her.'

'How did that happen?'

'The book. I don't know if you understand this, but once I'd started I just couldn't stop. Paradise to me would be someone to run my home so that I could write all the time. My husband resents the inevitable domestic changes. And my friend? I keep thinking I've sorted it out with her, but she seems ... well, if I'm honest – jealous of my success. It sounds a horrible thing to say.'

'Poor Kate. You're not alone, you know. I've lost count of the number of times I've heard this story. You can't do it all. You can't be creative and a success and still be as you were – but some families, I gather, don't understand this. You can't do what you've done – and don't forget it's a massive achievement – without changing. And you will change more, success does that, you'll become more confident, make other friends. You're paying a price at the moment, but if they can't accept what is happening to you, they risk paying an even bigger price later when you don't want to know any more.'

'It's all so confusing, Gloria. I mean, I was happy, I'm sure I was, a bit bored with the routine, but then who isn't? Tony's a good husband, he provides well, he's faithful, not a drunkard, not a wife-beater ...' She thought of Joy. 'We've a beautiful home. And yet this one thing, my writing, and he's shut his mind to me, apart from resentment. When I see him now, all we seem to do is row. Oh, Gloria, I'm getting so fed up with it.'

'Of course you are, and it gets in the way of your writing. With your talent you mustn't let that happen, and that's your publisher speaking.'

'What's the alternative? Say I did give it up, wrote no more, how would I feel? I know – frustrated and bitter at what might have been.'

'Don't give up. Let him adjust, I bet *you*'ve had to enough times. Be yourself, he'll probably come round. And I hate to say it, but quite quickly when the money starts coming in. If I'm right about *Winter Interlude*, I rather think it will.'

'You are kind – ' she began to say when the telephone rang. 'Shall I answer it?'

'Yes, if it's her husband she's not here.'

'Hello?' Kate said uncertainly into the telephone.

'Joy?'

'No, it's Kate Howard.'

'Not little Kate of "Sod off, Tony," fame?' A deep voice chuckled.

'I beg your pardon?' Kate felt embarrassed even though she did not recognise the voice.

'It's Barty Silver here. I remember you well.'

'Oh, Sir Barty!' she laughed. Gloria was pulling frantic faces at her; she shrugged her shoulders, not understanding what she wanted.

'Is Joy there?'

'She's asleep, tired out, poor dear. We had to move her out of her house to this flat – it took it out of all of us.'

Gloria put her head in her hands.

'Is she all right?' Barty asked anxiously.

'Yes, she's fine, just tired,' Kate said.

'Right, ta.'

Gloria picked up the bottle of wine and topped up the glasses again. 'Oh, Lord, that's done it.'

'What do you mean?'

'It's a long story and too complicated to tell right now. Just that he thinks she was living here all the time.'

'I wish you'd told me.'

'So do I. Do you fancy something to eat? I'm starving.'

In the kitchen they inspected the few groceries that Joy had brought with her. They had to settle on bread, cheese and some pickled gherkins.

'Isn't it odd the things people pack in an emergency?' Gloria said, spearing one of the gherkins.

'Yes, and they usually leave the most important. Me, I'm sure I'd grab my pruning shears and forget the silver.'

'I don't know what I'd grab, the tin-opener probably, otherwise Elephant would never speak to me again.'

'You love that dog, don't you?'

'Best friend in the world,' she said, suddenly looking sad. 'He never lets me down.'

'And someone else has?' Kate asked gently.

'You could say that. I should be used to it by now, but I'm not. I thought this was different.'

'Do you want to talk?'

'Not particularly, I'd probably end up howling.'

'It might be the best thing for you.'

'I don't think so,' Gloria said, and then, despite herself, despite her vaunted independence, she found herself telling this woman she barely knew the sad little there was to tell of Peter, the pathetic amount to which she had pinned so many dreams. She did not cry as she feared – oddly, she felt better for finally letting it all out.

'You should give him a call.'

'I couldn't. What if he refused to speak to me?'

'Then write him a letter.'

'I'm too proud.'

'Don't be, Gloria. It can be such a destructive emotion, pride. What's the point of being alone with just your pride intact? Go and see him.'

Gloria smiled at her, a smile that completely transformed her attractive face to one of beauty. 'Do you think I should? All right I will, I'll call him.'

'Who on earth's that?' Kate clasped her throat with worry at the sound of the doorbell. Gloria dived for the window and peered out.

'Oh, crikey, it's Barty in person.'

It was a sombre-faced Barty who entered the room a minute later when Gloria had let him in.

'What happened?' he asked, dispensing with any niceties.

'We don't know, Barty. They had a row. Kate found her a bit the worse for wear.'

'She got the little girl with her?'

'Yes.'

'That's good. You got some of her gear out, then.' He looked around the cluttered room where cases and cardboard boxes stood waiting to be unpacked.

'Yes, as much as we could.'

'I feared this. Silly girl.'

'She loves him, Barty. Some women will put up with a lot,' Gloria explained.

'No, I can't believe that. She went back for the kid.'

'I'm sure you're right, Sir Barty,' Kate said gently.

'She can't stay here alone. She ought to come back with me, my house is big enough.'

'She's too distraught and tired to move again, Barty. Kate has said she'll stay overnight.'

'That's kind of you, Kate. I shan't forget that.'

'It's the least I can do.' She looked down at the floor with embarrassment.

'Can I see her?' he suddenly asked.

Gloria led the way to the door and the stairs.

Joy was awake, sitting up in bed, gazing sadly into the distance as if unaware that Barty and Gloria were in the doorway. She looked wan, the darkening bruise on her cheek vivid against the pallor of her skin. Barty stood silent. He was angry, though it would have been impossible to tell. An intimate friend might have recognised the signs, but then Barty had no such friends. His family might have seen the same sign, but he had no family. The slight pulse, throbbing high on his temple, was the small indication that Barty Silver was bleak with anger.

Joy looked up to see them.

'Barty, it's you.' She smiled bravely.

'My poor little love,' Barty said, as soft as a sigh, and he crossed the room to the bed. Gloria turned on to the landing and quietly shut the door.

'I've been so stupid, Barty,' Joy said, close to tears.

Barty sat on the side of the bed and he then did something he had never done in his whole life: he leant forward and took Joy into his arms and held her to him. He could smell the sweetness of her hair, felt the smoothness of her skin as her cheek lay against his, was aware of how fragile and thin her body was. And then a strange thing happened. He felt a glow spread through him as if his blood had turned to warm honey.

'There, there,' he said suddenly feeling awkward as he patted her and was not sure what to say. 'There, there. Don't upset yourself . . .'

She looked at him closely and sighed and then leant back from his embrace against the pillows, now glancing everywhere but at him and Barty sat, hands in his lap, feeling inept.

'I've something to tell you,' she said eventually.

'Not now.'

'No, I must.' She sat upright. 'I went back to him, Barty. I promised you and I broke the promise I made to you.'

'I know, my dear. You needed to see Hannah, didn't you?'

She stared at him, she should tell him everything, be honest with him and explain it wasn't just Hannah.

'Yes,' she said, no more.

'You couldn't help yourself, a good mum like you. But I know.'

She frowned. 'How did you know?' she said abruptly.

'Gloria and Kate just told me,' he said hurriedly, realising from her reaction that she would not like the fact that he had always known – the friend he had put in the basement flat had reported to him, as he had asked him to. Joy would not like the idea of being spied on, no one would. 'Kate's offered to stay the night.'

'How kind, but not necessary. I'm all right now. I got drunk but I was so sad and he hurt me . . .' She put her hand to the bruise on her face.

'I hate him,' Barty said his voice full of anger. 'I'll look after you.'

'Barty, you're so kind to me, why?'

'I think I . . . I want to ask you something, Joy . . .' And then he stopped speaking and looked into the corner of the room, an embarrassed expression on his face.

'What?'

Barty shook his head. 'No, not now. It's the wrong time . . . later.' And he scooped her into his arms again because he felt a great need to and he wondered if he would experience that pleasant sensation again. He did.

17

Having been reassured by Joy that she was fine and not afraid, but, rather, feeling ashamed for her drunkenness, Kate had caught a mid-evening train home. She was no longer too concerned about seeing an angry Tony.

Before she had left Joy's flat, Barty had taken her on one side. 'Kate, I can't thank you enough for your kindness to Joy. You're not to worry. I'll keep an eye on her for all of us.'

'It was nothing, Sir Barty.'

'Barty, please. No, you need not have bothered, I'm grateful. I'd appreciate it if you could tell your husband I've got some more business I can put his way.'

Kate hoped that the message from Barty would put Tony in a sufficiently good mood that he would want to hear all her interesting news – she had discussed ideas for the cover with Gloria and planned a launch party. She hoped he was happier because she was going to have to tell him that Gloria needed her in London next week for a whole day to discuss the editing of the book. This time she was not concerned, she was sure that any suggestions Gloria had would be constructive ones.

It was therefore something of a let-down to find that Tony was not at home. She waited until almost midnight for him to return but tiredness finally overtook her and she went to bed.

He was not beside her when she woke in the morning.

She found him in the kitchen. He was taciturn in the extreme. Kate made herself sound cheerful but it did not last and soon they were arguing – about her trips to London, about money, about anything, it seemed, that he could dredge up which had annoyed him in the past. And, most ludicrous of all, he seemed to be hinting that she had met someone else.

'Dear God, Tony, I'm getting so fed up with this. Can't we have a reasonable conversation these days?' she shouted in exasperation. 'I've been with my agent. I don't know anyone else. Please stop this endless carping.'

'The choice is yours,' he answered coldly.

'I'm not staying here for this,' she said crossing to the door. There she turned to face him.

'Oh, by the way, Tony, Barty says to tell you he might have some more business to put your way.' She noticed his eyes light up with interest. 'But since you are so uninterested in my work I'm not sure I want him to help you. Barty's very grateful to me for helping out with Joy. And you know what, Tony? I reckon one word from me and he'll forget all about it – so think on that, husband dear.' And she slammed the door shut behind her.

She went upstairs, dressed quickly and, with coat on, was about to return downstairs when she met Lucy on the landing, returning from sleeping at her best friend's house.

'So, you're back,' her daughter said.

'Same could be said of you,' Kate snapped back.

'Sorry I spoke,' Lucy said with equal spirit. 'Where are you going now?'

'Pam's. Your father will tell you why,' Kate said, running down the stairs.

As she drove along, she wondered why she was going there. What was the point? It was not as if she and Pam were close any more. But some of that friendship must remain or why did she instinctively run to her, to cry on her shoulder?

Pam was surprised to see her so early. It was the only explanation for her seeming reluctance to let her in.

'Do I have to stand here all day?' Kate forced a laugh.

'Sorry, come in.' Pam held the door open for her. 'I'm in the kitchen. I was just having some coffee.' She led the way through the green baize door from the main hall along a long corridor to the kitchen, which was so perfect it looked like an advertisement for a kitchen-unit supplier. 'Why such an early visit?'

'I was in the dumps. I need advice. I need to talk to you. Doug here?' she asked, hoping he wasn't about to interrupt them.

'No, he's away for a few days,' Pam replied as she took a mug from the long dresser. 'What's up?' She sat down opposite Kate.

As Kate related her problems with Tony she began to feel uncomfortable. The bickering, the hurt, the rows they had had when told like this sounded like one great moan on her part. She knew she was not explaining well – she didn't need the somewhat cynical expression on Pam's face to tell her that. She finally finished.

'Well, if you want the truth, Kate, I feel sorry for Tony.'

'You what?' Kate sat bolt upright. She might have been expressing herself badly but not *that* badly, she thought.

'You must see it from his point of view. One day he wakes up and his perfect wife has changed. You *have* changed and I don't think you're even aware of how much.'

'Don't be silly! How have I changed? All right, maybe the house has gone to pot and I'm not jam-making and whatever else I used to do. But for God's sake, Pam, there's more to life than all that.'

'I'd agree with you. I always thought you were too perfect for your own good. No, it's more than that. You're more confident, you've gone away from us all just as I said you would. Poor Tony feels lonely.'

'Well, I never thought to hear you of all people talk like this.'

'I'm sorry. But that's how I see it. You've found something in your life, Kate, something more important than anything else. And good luck to you. You can't go back but you've got to learn to compromise a bit.'

'You don't understand what I'm trying to tell you. He's trying to stop me, he's still sneering at the book even now when it's to be published. That's spite.'

'That's an SOS.'

'Oh, really, Pam! You don't know what I've put up with.'

'Then leave him,' Pam said bluntly.

'Pam!' Kate was shocked.

'No good looking at me like that. If it's so intolerable, you'd no doubt be doing both of you a favour.'

Kate drained her coffee and picked up her handbag.

'I'd better be going.'

Pam laughed. 'Sorry, but you wanted advice and I can't help it if you don't like what I give you.' She followed Kate into the hall and opened the front door. 'By the way, what about my book? What does Joy say? Or have you not given it to her?'

'Pam, I don't think she can possibly have looked at it yet, the poor woman is in a mess – she's left her husband. I promise I'll nag her as soon as she has sorted herself out.'

'Maybe she can advise you,' Pam said laconically.

'I'm sorry I bothered you, Pam. It's not fair of me when you and Doug are friends to both of us. I won't bring it up again. But there is one thing. I'm going to need some new clothes soon. Will you help me choose?'

'I'd love to.' Suddenly Pam stepped forward and kissed her on the cheek. 'I really am your friend, you know. I do care,' she said abruptly.

'I know you do,' Kate said as she slid behind the steering wheel of her car.

A long-faced Lucy was sitting in the kitchen when she returned home.

'Mum.' As Kate entered the room she immediately crossed to her and put her arms about her mother. 'Mum, I'm so sorry, I can't tell you how furious I am with Dad.'

'You spoke to your father?'

'We had a row, Mum, I'd no idea he could be such a male chauvinist pig. I couldn't believe what I was hearing.'

'Where is he now?' she asked warily.

'Gone out. Gone to see Fred, I think. Coffee?'

'No. Blow the coffee, Lucy. Let's have some wine.' Kate stood up and went out to the pantry to the small fridge emblazoned with stickers saying, 'Tony's, keep out'. They had been a joke once, it was she who had bought them for him. She did not see the funny side today as she opened the door and deliberately chose the most expensive bottle she could find. 'Pouilly Fuissé,' she announced to her daughter, waving the bottle on high.

'I've got to apologise to you, Mum. I haven't taken your writing seriously enough either.'

'Lucy, you've your own life to lead, I didn't expect you to. Lots of people write but who could have guessed I would have the luck to get this far?'

'That's no excuse. I should have been encouraging you, been pleased for you. I think, in a way, I was afraid of losing you as a mum, that you wouldn't have time for us any more. That was stupid of me. Mind you, I'm proud as punch now. Everyone at school is fed up with the subject of my mum and her book.'

'Bless you.' Kate poured the wine. 'It's bloody hard being a woman, Lucy.

Take all this as a warning. Equal opportunity, my eye. It doesn't work that way in our circle. I've given twenty-five years to running this family, his life. Is it wrong of me to want to do something else now? I don't think I've been a bad manager – '

'You've been the best.'

'But you see, Lucy, it's *my* time now. It's *my* turn to do something. It's no longer enough for me to be a homemaker – those things are no longer important to me. I was happy doing that once, I couldn't be happy just doing that again.' She sipped at the wine. 'You know you used to tease me about being menopausal? It's true, I am. But, you know, it's as if that was a sign to me to get off my arse, to stop mooning about feeling sorry for myself, to *do* something. And since I have, I've found so much more energy. I've felt better, I'm alive for the first time in years.'

'Can I read it?'

'I'd love you to.'

'You don't think Dad's jealous, do you?'

'That I'll find another man? Well, evidently.'

'No, I meant the book. I wonder if he's afraid you're going to succeed, that you're going to be famous. Maybe he doesn't think he can handle it.'

'Steve said something similar. Oh, no, Lucy, that's too silly. No, he thought I'd found a fellow. Me? Laughable, isn't it?'

Barty had had the telephone numbers both at the flat and Joy's office changed to ex-directory. This was fine except that he had not told her. Nor did Gloria know.

She had been trying to contact Joy for a couple of days and was concerned when she could not get through and could not prise the number out of the exchange. She hoped Joy was not going to pieces. She could sympathise with her problems: they were horrendous. But what woman in business did not at some time or other have personal problems? No professional woman worth her salt could afford the luxury of showing she was upset, let alone give in to her problems by not turning up for work at all. Gloria knew that shows of weakness played right into the hands of those men who were always waiting for such opportunities. Men who would then be able to say, 'See, women can't have positions of power, their emotions get in the way.' It would be unforgivable if Joy was to let her own sex down.

Luckily Gloria was busy. The best thing to keep her mind off Peter, and what might have been, was work. She had still not taken Kate's advice to contact him. A couple of times she had even picked up the telephone to dial his number, but when it came to it, she found she could not. She resisted being the one who made the advances.

Gloria's new list at Westall's was to have an autumn launch, a whole season earlier than Julius had anticipated. She had been lucky in buying in two American novels, and she wanted Kate's book as the lead title. She wanted to launch it in time for the Christmas market, which was a risky thing to do.

Christmas was not the best time to publish a first novel: with so many other books released with gift-buying in mind a first novel could so easily sink without trace. But it was a strong novel, different from many others and, if she was honest, Gloria had to admit that she found the risk involved exciting.

She had already spoken to the Red Rose Society. At the party for the opening of yet another shop in the Cavendish book chain, she had bumped into Olive West, chairperson-designate of the society. She had known Olive for years although never published her, but gave a hint or two that this was a situation which might be changing. Olive was a sweet woman, very intelligent, a highly professional writer. She was easy to swear to total secrecy, so that Shotters would not find out, since she loathed Tatiana Spence perhaps even more than Gloria did. Gloria had floated her idea of a competition to run concurrent with Kate's promotion. Writers would be invited to submit the first chapter and a synopsis of a novel suitable for the women's market. The Red Rose Society would administer it, doing the first readings and choosing a short list to be judged by Gloria and a personality, yet to be chosen. The winner, apart from getting a cash prize, would have their completed work seriously considered for publication by Westall's. The society always had a banquet just before Christmas, which would be the ideal time to announce the winner. Best of all for Westall's, the organisation had a huge mailing list and a good press officer. Media coverage was sure to follow, which, while helping Kate's sales, would give Westall's valuable free publicity.

It was all very neat and Gloria was pleased and excited by the plan. To get the ball rolling in time it would have to be announced in the next Red Rose newsletter which was going out in June – next month.

The speed with which Gloria was working was making Julius sceptical. He did not like things to be rushed, especially books. If a book was good enough to be published then it was good enough to have time spent on it to make it perfect.

'Look, Julius, this list has to be got going as soon as possible, you said yourself we need the money. The sooner the better. I've got these two books from America – they'll sell in well, I'm sure, they're both established authors I've managed to poach.'

'Who from?'

'Dawn-Rose is from Pewter's and Reena from Tudor's.'

'Well done,' he smiled. 'It makes such a change – everyone normally poaches from me.'

'Those two need no editing – we can offset from the American editions – artwork is no problem either, we can use the existing jackets. That means we only have Kate to worry about and if we bring her out in October that gives us six months to do it in. The main problem with a totally unknown writer like Kate is the publicity angle. I've been talking to Val. She's very excited at the news angle of Kate – having started writing and then been published in under a year. It's unheard of. It's like a fairy story. If Kate and I work like the clappers we'll do it. Your art department say they can foresee no problems – we'll go for a simple, dramatic cover that can be done in-house. What's more, Panda are very keen we do – they want Kate for their lead title the following October.' Gloria took a long sip of water, she was so keyed up she wished it was a vodka.

'That good?'

'That good, Julius.'

'Well, it's your decision and I promised you total control . . . Good luck with it, I hope you make it.'

Kate had not resolved anything with Tony when she went for her editorial meeting with Gloria. She could not believe how in tune they were. Parts of the book, she knew, were flat, or had not turned out as she had wanted. Without fail Gloria had picked them out. She made suggestions as to what should be done and Kate could not imagine why she had not seen the solutions herself.

'It's all so obvious. Why didn't I think of that?' She smiled across the desk at Gloria after scribbling down yet another answer to a plot problem.

'Because you're too close to it. Every book needs new eyes to look at it.'

'I'm really enjoying this. It's like a polishing process, getting it perfect.'

'Let's hope you always think like that.' Gloria laughed, thinking of the arguments she had with some of her authors. 'We've got a publication date pencilled in. Last Thursday in October – Westall's always publish on a Thursday.'

'October?' Kate said. 'Gracious, so soon?'

'We wanted to do it then so it's under a year from the novel's conception to being published. First books are notoriously difficult to place but let's keep our fingers crossed and hope that you prove everyone wrong. It could be a wonderful month for you.'

'Shotters told me February was.' Kate could not help but laugh.

'You'd be amazed at the lies we have to tell to assure authors that any month is perfect. You should hear some of my fibs,' Gloria replied, also laughing.

Gloria should not have worried about Joy. She called full of apologies that Gloria had not been informed of her change of number.

'I do hope you haven't been going mad trying to get hold of me?'

'Good heavens no.' Gloria laughed as she lied. 'Just yelled at British Telecom. How are you?'

'Fine. I'm having a bit of a problem getting a nanny for Hannah – they turn their nose up at this little flat. But otherwise I'm OK – work, that's the solution.' She laughed and at the other end Gloria frowned. It sounded a rather false and brittle laugh.

'Don't do too much, will you? You've been through a lot,' said Gloria completely forgetting her own emotional problems.

'Don't worry about me. I feel wonderful, especially now I've got both Kate and Barty's contracts almost finished and am rid of my husband.' The strange laugh rang out again.

Charles was not having a good time either. Finding Joy's telephone number changed and unable to contact her, his anger with her deepened. He had been burgled, his car broken into twice and vandalised. He shut up the house and moved in with Penelope. Once there he gave vent to his paranoia. There was nothing she could say to persuade him that the burglary and trouble with his car were nothing to do with Barty Silver.

During this period Barty worked on his autobiography, made a million pounds from various businesses, and bided his time.

18

Joy was tired, which she could not admit to anyone. Undoubtedly it was this tiredness which had led her to shout at her secretary – something she had never done before. The young woman, having struggled into work despite a very heavy cold, understandably took umbrage and walked out. This left Joy with a word processor she did not understand, a telephone system she could not work, and a filing system which took time for her to find anything.

After two days of frustration in the office she employed her first temp who only lasted one day. Something to do with the buses, she had explained, but Joy felt it was because she was bored, alone in the office. She was now on her third temporary member of staff. She was getting weary of having to explain everything anew and was determinedly sweet with this one in the hope she might stay, if only for a week. Her search for a new permanent secretary was taking up too much time and her over-flowing ashtray indicated the strain she was beginning to feel.

Hannah, as if sensing all was not well, began to play up. If Joy cooked her a boiled egg for breakfast she demanded it scrambled. Each morning there was a fight over which clothes the child would condescend to wear. Normally quiet and placid, she had now begun to play games which involved much stomping, shouting and throwing things.

The search for a suitable nanny continued but so far the accommodation was not good enough for any of them. They all expected an *en suite* bathroom, a private sitting room, a car and their own colour television and video recorder, none of which Joy could supply.

With no nanny Joy was relying on Universal Aunts to supply her with a child-minder so that she could get on with some work. The problem was that each day a different woman turned up to care for Hannah and such lack of continuity was exacerbating the problem. But when Joy telephoned the company to ask them to send only those willing to work on a semi-permanent basis, they prevaricated so much that Joy was forced to conclude that the 'aunts' were refusing to return for another day with the fractious and difficult child.

Temporary staff of any description did not come cheap and Joy was becoming worried about money but was loath to bother Barty with her problems. A long consultation with her lawyer had not helped her equilibrium. Having finally left Charles for good, Joy hoped for a quick divorce before she could change her mind again. She was horrified to hear that to achieve this before the period of two years' separation was up, she would have to sue him for his adultery or unreasonable behaviour.

'Luckily you have photographs of your injuries and Sir Barty's doctor's report,' her solicitor said encouragingly.

'But that would mean everything coming out in court,' Joy said, horrified at the prospect.

'Unfortunately, yes. But people soon forget . . .'

'No, no, I couldn't do that,' Joy said emphatically.

To all her other problems was added the knowledge that she would be trapped in this marriage for a further two years. To escape these worries Joy worked even harder but, with Hannah to care for and no decent help, she was having to fit it in as and when she could. Most of her reading and paperwork she did late into the night when Hannah was at last asleep. And so her tiredness intensified.

There were evenings when she had to go out. Knowing what was going on in the publishing world was essential and one sure way of finding out was to attend the numerous parties that were part and parcel of the industry.

To save money she had begun to use the *au pair* of one of her friends as a baby-sitter – she cost less than the professional ones.

This particular evening she was due at an awards dinner, when her friend called to say that her *au pair* was ill and could not come. She gave Joy the number of another Italian girl who would be willing to sit. Not knowing the girl or anything about her, Joy was worried. But this function was important and, even more important, Tatiana Spence would be there. Joy needed to build bridges with Tatiana who was annoyed at Kate moving to Westall's and was too important in publishing for Joy to have anything but a good working relationship with her.

Joy called the new girl and made the arrangements. She cooked Hannah's supper, then took nearly an hour to persuade her to eat it. Hannah's bath over and her story read, she was put to bed and finally fell asleep. Joy was left with less than half an hour to bath and change – everything she did these days seemed to be in a rush.

The Italian girl was pleasant and spoke reasonable English. Joy set off content that Hannah would be well looked after.

It was as well she went. She found herself at the same table as Tatiana who was charming to her and Joy wondered why on earth she had been so worried.

Best of all, she talked to a well-established writer who was looking for a new agent and they made an appointment to talk. When she returned to her flat she felt better than she had for weeks.

It was past midnight when she ran up the stairs.

'Sorry, I'm so late,' she called gaily as she entered her sitting room, 'I got held up; – ' She stopped in the doorway. In the centre of the room, a deep frown on his face, stood Charles.

'Who let you in?' she demanded.

'No one. I walked in. The front door was open.'

'Where's the *au-pair* girl?'

'I sent her packing *when* she came back.'

'Came back, what do you mean?'

'I arrived here hoping to see you, hoping to talk some sense into you, since you won't answer my letters and I did not have your telephone number. The front door was on the latch. I rang the bell, no one answered, so I came in. The baby-sitter you had thought good enough to care for my daughter was out – '

'Hannah, is she . . .?' She turned to leave the room.

'Hannah is fine, no thanks to you. The baby-sitter claimed she had only popped out for a minute to get some fags. How was I to know how long she had been out? She could have been out all evening. You're irresponsible, Joy, totally so.'

'I'm not. Hannah is never left alone.'

'She was tonight,' he said shortly.

'I'll speak to the girl. That was very wrong of her even if she was only out for a minute.'

'Did you know this person?'

'She was recommended by a friend.'

'You'd no right to leave her with someone you did not know.'

'I'm sorry, Charles. But no harm was done.'

'Wasn't it? I've removed Hannah. You are unfit to look after her and obviously too busy.'

'Removed her? What the hell do you mean? What are you saying?' She ran from the room, racing up the stairs with a thumping heart to her daughter's bedroom. The bed was bare, Hannah's clothes had been packed, her toys taken. 'Oh, no – ' She stumbled back down the staircase. 'How dare you, Charles? You've no right to take her. Where is she?'

'I'm going to court tomorrow, I'm applying for temporary custody.'

'How dare you?' she repeated. 'I've managed on my own for a month well enough. Where is she? You have to tell me. She can't stay with you and that whore, Penelope, I won't allow that.'

'I don't think the choice will be yours to make, Joy.'

'Is she with her?'

'No, she's at my mother's. Penelope took her there.'

'In the middle of the night? Are you mad? You must have scared her half to death.'

'Don't be silly, Joy. It was hardly the middle of the night – nine to be exact. Of course she was not scared. She was pleased to see me – she does love me, you know. And she knows Penelope well. She'll be happy at my mother's until I can make other arrangements.'

'You talk as if it had all been decided. It hasn't. I shall fight you.'

'Oh yes, and how? With what? Going to go running to Daddy to help you?'

'Barty will help me.'

'He won't want to get involved with any nasty publicity, and I'd make it nasty if he sticks his nose in, I can assure you.'

'He loathes you, Charles. He'll help me.'

'You should choose your friends with a lot more care, Joy,' Charles said coldly. 'It won't look good in court when the judge finds out that your protector is a raving homosexual.'

'He isn't, that's malicious gossip. It would be beyond the comprehension of someone as obsessed with sex as you to understand that not everyone is like you. Barty isn't homosexual, bisexual or heterosexual, he's not interested in sex at all. Nor is he my protector, he's a friend.'

'My dear Joy. I can assure you by the time I've finished the judge will have no doubt what role he plays in your life. You will be found to be a most unsuitable person to care for my daughter. That's a promise.' He smiled at her as he walked towards the door. She couldn't believe that she had once lived for him to smile at her just like that.

She heard the front door slam. She poured herself a large drink. She was about to drink it, then suddenly slammed it down. No, that was no solution. She dialled a number which would connect her with Gervase on his mobile telephone, and where Gervase was there would be Barty.

'Barty, I'm sorry, I know it's late but can I see you?'

Barty was waiting for her in the hall of his mansion. He stepped forward immediately, hands held out in greeting, smiling gently. On the way here she had been full of anger and indignation but now inside Barty's house with him holding her hands, with the feeling of safety he always gave her, Joy broke down.

Barty led her to his private sitting room, a room she had never been in before and one which now, with tears cascading, she could not see. Barty sat her on the sofa and fussed about pouring her a drink, finding her a cigarette.

'When you're ready, Joy, tell Barty,' he said settling himself beside her, waiting patiently while, between sobs, she told him what had happened.

'First thing tomorrow we'll get the lawyers to slap an injunction on him. Don't you worry, he can't take your little girl away from you, a good mum like you.'

'It's not right using her like this.'

'Of course it isn't. The law can be dumb but not that dumb. The judge'll see through his nasty games.'

'Do you really think so, Barty?'

'Would I say it if I didn't?'

'There is one thing – he's going to use my friendship with you as grounds for showing I'm unfit.'

'Consorting with undesirables?' Barty laughed almost as if he was delighted with the accusation.

'Yes, I mean ... it's too awful, Barty. I won't have you dragged into this mess, it's just not fair.'

'But I am involved and honoured to be so.'

'Oh, Barty.' Joy looked up at him, her blue eyes blurred with tears. 'Why are you so kind to me?'

''Cause I love you, girl. That's the truth.'

Joy stopped crying, stopped wiping her eyes with his handkerchief. She looked at him with amazement. She did not say anything, she was too stunned.

'Bit of a shock, isn't it?' Barty laughed a small, rather embarrassed laugh. 'Took me by surprise, I can tell you.' He looked at her anxiously, his large round face devoid of any smiles. 'It's not what I expected, I thought all that had passed me by.' He paused as if waiting for her to say something, but she did not. 'I didn't mean to say anything. I thought, best to let it lie, tell no one, including you. After all, why should a lovely lady like you want someone like me? That's what I thought, but then I saw you looking so sad and crying and all ... I couldn't bear to see you like that. I want to protect you from feeling as you do, for ever. And, well, the words just sort of popped out. I'm sorry.' Barty hung his head so as not to see the expression on her face.

'Barty, my dear, what can I say?' She put her hand out and touched his gently. She was surprised, but deeply moved. Nothing had prepared her for such a conversation.

'Don't say anything, I'd rather you didn't. I know what you're going to say.' He was still looking down.

'Do you really know what I'm going to say?'

Barty was staring intently at where her hand rested on his. Joy's mind was racing. She was safe with Barty. She always felt a great blanket of security when in his company. There was no violence here. 'What am I going to say, then?' she said, softly.

Barty mumbled.

'I'm deeply honoured, Barty. More than I think you'll ever realise,' she said quietly.

He looked at her then with an expression of disbelief.

'Could you say that again?' He spoke in barely a whisper.

She laughed but it was gentle. 'I think you heard, Barty.'

'Perhaps you don't understand, Joy. I mean I love you and I would like to marry you.'

'I didn't for one moment think that you of all people, Barty, would be thinking of anything else.'

'You mean you would be willing to marry me, once you are free?'

'Barty – I need time. I'll have to think about it.'

'Oh my God!' Barty floundered for words. 'Of course. You take all the time in the world. Oh, Joy. I do love you. Not just words . . . not that I've ever said them to a living soul before . . . but, well, you know.' He looked at her.

'Yes, I know, Barty. It's not something that's easy to explain.'

Then Barty hung his head again. 'You won't want to go through with it when you've heard me out. I say I want to marry you, but it wouldn't be a marriage like other people's I mean, I wouldn't want to bother you, if you know what I mean.'

'Sleeping together, you mean?'

'Well, yes . . .' Barty's voice emerged strangled with many different emotions.

'I know, Barty, and I understand. But you see that's one of the things I'd need time to think about.'

'You understand?' Barty repeated, fully aware that he sounded like an idiot.

'Maybe it is possible to love without sex, I don't know. Perhaps it might even be better. What has all that ever brought me? Much unhappiness.' She spoke with conviction, she spoke the truth. They liked each other, they respected each other, it seemed the most logical thing in the world to do, it might work, she thought. And unfortunately she found herself thinking also of how annoyed it would make Charles.

19

Tony was speaking to Kate, but it was in a formal and rigid manner, as if he hardly knew her; there was certainly no conversation between them. She would not have been human had she not felt a certain smugness when he came to tell her she was wanted on the telephone and that it was Barty. She picked up the receiver, puzzled as to why he should wish to speak to her.

'Kate, I see you've an appointment with Joy on Wednesday. I thought I ought to put you in the picture. Joy's had a bit more trouble from that husband of hers.'

'Oh, no. What?'

'He's nicked the kid. Don't worry, my lawyers are working on it. Thing is, Kate, she's tired, poor little thing's had a lot on her plate.'

'I know, Barty. The office, looking after Hannah, she would have managed –'

'Exactly, this bit of bother is the last straw. I've insisted she has a complete rest. I've popped her into a nursing home I've an interest in – she's not ill, you realise,' he said hurriedly.

'No, of course not. Just needs a good sleep.'

'Right on, Kate. Thing is, the business. Joy has recommended another agent, a Faith Cooper, to help her out. We have every intention of expanding and this matter has brought things to a head sooner – Faith'll be looking after you until Joy gets back.'

'Give her my love, tell her not to worry. She's lucky to have you as a friend, Barty.'

'Oh no, Kate, it's me what's lucky to have her. And while we're on the phone maybe it's a good time for me to have a natter with that husband of yours, shall I?'

'Yes, Barty, that would be very kind of you.'

Kate was peeling potatoes when Tony came back into the kitchen.

'Thanks, Kate.'

'Thanks for what?'

'You know, not letting on to Barty that I've been a bit of a berk.'

'Have you, Tony?' She glanced down at the potatoes in the bowl. Was this a good time to mention she was off to London again? She felt resentful that this situation had arisen, making a prisoner of her again. She was going, there was no doubt about that. So perhaps it was best to get it over with. She felt he was trying to apologise; it was as close to an apology as she was likely to get from Tony.

'Tony, there's just one thing. I have to go to London again. I'm sorry, but there it is.' She said this with a finality that would brook no argument. 'My agent has a lot of personal problems and she wants me to meet her new partner. And Gloria, my editor, wants to see me to talk about publication plans.' She stated it, she did not ask him, she was not apologising. It was the best, the only way, to handle him, she had decided.

During their period of hostility, Kate had rationalised many things. The situation with Tony was not something she enjoyed, nor one she wanted to continue. When they had rowed after Barty's party and Tony had said he had had enough, she had faced the prospect of his leaving her with a sense of freedom, almost excitement. It was a feeling that she could not recapture. Now, when she thought of separation, she found herself afraid of the loneliness it might entail.

She now felt that if only he would accept her new career with grace, she would be content. She realised that one of her main problems had been boredom, she had solved that. These days there were not enough hours in the day.

She knew she no longer loved her husband, not as she presumed she once had – it still puzzled her why she had such difficulty remembering their early days together – but she was fond of him, and still grateful for all he had given her. She did not want her marriage to end. But if it was not to finish, something had to be done to save it.

It was so easy to fall into the trap of thinking that only her own viewpoint was right. She could see now that when Tony had called her selfish he had also been right. They had both been selfish, and that must stop.

If one looked at it in the fairest light Pam had also spoken the truth. The change her new career had made to this family had been momentous. And what husband would accept his routine being upset? She could acknowledge that she had allowed her book to become so important as to exclude everything else. While unfair to the family it was not a good idea for her. She had not read a paper, watched anything on TV, taken an interest in anything else for months. If she was not careful she was heading towards a trap even more demanding and restrictive than the one she had found herself in before.

She made several resolutions, even to the extent of writing them down and pinning them to the side of her word processor so she would not forget. She was determined, while writing her second novel, to restrict herself to set hours of work – she must make time for family and friends. The money she earned could and should be used to help make the house run as it once had, so that her family did not suffer from her absences. While the writing had become a joy to her she did not want to see it become a burden to others. Compromises were going to be made, and not just on Tony's side.

This time before she went to London she cleaned the house, did a wash and iron that left nothing dirty, shopped for provisions and cooked Tony's favourite meal for Lucy to heat up for him.

Kate went to her first appointment with Joy's new associate, Faith Cooper. And as at their first meeting at the writers' weekend, she was unsure whether she liked her. There was nothing wrong in the warm welcome she received. And Faith remembering her was gratifying, as was the fulsome praise for Kate's book she generously gave. Of course, Kate admitted to herself, she did feel embarrassed. After all, it had been Faith who had seen the spark in her and had asked to see her work. But Faith made no mention of this which, if anything, made Kate feel even more uncomfortable.

The only things that Kate could pin down were the somewhat brusque manner and a super-professionalism and efficiency which bothered her. There was a steeliness to Faith, a harshness, a feeling that she probably lacked humour. Kate sat opposite her and realised she felt more than a little afraid of her.

Faith had her new contract with Westall's, and a list of details in relation to it, to discuss. Kate's head was soon reeling, assaulted by percentages and fractions of percentages which Faith rattled off at speed. Since she had been hopeless at maths at school, she had to confess she did not understand a word

Faith was saying and that she would rely on her good judgement. By the merest lift of an eyebrow, Kate was left in no doubt what Faith thought of women who could not understand the mathematics of business.

However, unrelaxed as she was, Kate could not fault the deal Faith had finally worked out for her. It was to be a two-book joint deal with Westall's and Panda Books, the paperback house. Kate was bowled over by this news, and said so, for Panda was a household name.

'Imagine them wanting to buy my book,' she said, amazed at the very idea.

'To make it into the big-time as an author you need to be bought by one of the big two paperback houses. If you think of any of the bookshops you go to, which paperbacks are most prominently displayed? Panda and Eagle. Had you stayed with Shotters they would have insisted that their new paperback imprint – Sabre – should publish you. But how long will it take them to build up to the sales levels and profile of the other two? Years. So many paperback books are produced each year that it's a continuous battle, requiring endless negotiations between the sales managers and the multiple bookshop chains, to get the optimum shelf positions and their co-operation to promote you in-store. And you can't get much better than the sales team at Panda. So, for you, this is all very satisfactory.' Faith paused only long enough to light a cigarette and to offer one to Kate. 'Westall's probably won't sell the number of hardbacks that Shotters, with its huge sales team and reputation in your genre, could have sold. But, on the other hand, this is a new venture for them – they have to make it work, so money and enormous effort will be put behind you. It's a rare book that becomes a bestseller without help, Kate. No, it's the publishers *deciding* who they are going to push into making a bestseller that is relevant – and, lucky old you, they've decided to put the loot behind you.' Faith dragged deeply on her cigarette and chuckled, a delightful deep, bubbling noise so infectious that it made Kate wonder if she had not been judging her harshly. 'And we've still got the American and foreign rights to sell.' Faith rubbed her hands with satisfaction.

'America? Gracious, I hadn't even given it a thought,' Kate said, finally getting a word in.

'You should do – it can be a very lucrative market. Even if you don't get a huge advance, the country is so vast that their print-runs are enormous compared with ours, so royalties from that source can be considerable. Foreign rights – the advances are small, but when you think of the number of countries you can sell to – it all adds up, Kate. But don't set your heart on America. It's an incredibly difficult market to break in to. For instance, Bella Ford still hasn't made it and I could name you a dozen others. But I'll put myself on the line. I've got a funny feeling about yours, it could have a universal appeal. I think we might just be lucky.'

'Really?' Kate had thought with the acceptance of her book the excitement was over. It seemed it was only just beginning.

'I've discussed it with Joy and I've sent the typescript to an agent in New

York we've decided to use. It means higher commission for you, unfortunately. I know that Joy was hoping to deal with America herself, but quite honestly, Kate, we've decided we need an agent on the spot, talking to the editors every week, knowing exactly what they're looking for. Unless you're on the spot with an ear to the gossip you can easily come a cropper. I know of one author who was taken on by a new publisher and they turned out to be fly-by-nights who had set up an office with a couple of editors. They offered the moon and six months later they were shutting up shop. The author was left with nothing, and the big New York publishers don't want to know her. Our agent will be aware who's financially secure or not. Barty agrees with us.'

'Have you been an agent long?'

'Too long.' She chuckled again. 'I was an editor, loads of us were, but I prefer the cut and thrust of the marketplace to editing – more exciting. I've been with Ambert's – one of the biggest agencies, I expect you've heard of them – but it was getting too big and boring.'

'You sound like Gloria talking about the publishing conglomerates.'

'Exactly, and I think the agencies are next. We'll see takeovers and amalgamations there as well, you mark my words. I was fed up with all the committees and discussions. I wanted the challenge of a small operation again. Barty and Joy appeared at just the right time.'

'And you could leave at such short notice?'

'Barty is a wonder, he can always get whatever he wants. He's connected to Ambert's in a way I haven't yet worked out, so he could get me out of my contract, wham bam.' She lit yet another cigarette. For every cigarette Kate smoked, Faith smoked three – it made her feel much better about her habit. 'My coming here is an advantage to this agency since most of my authors will follow me, you see. So everyone is happy – you included, I hope.' She flashed Kate a huge encompassing smile.

'Of course.' Kate smiled back. 'Do you know when Joy's coming back full time?' she asked in all innocence.

'No, I've no idea,' Faith said stiffly. 'If you've any worries about my ability perhaps you should discuss it with Barty.' She sat bolt upright behind her desk, no smile, the expression of her grey eyes suddenly hard. She was bristling with indignation, Kate realised.

'Good gracious no. I was only enquiring about Joy. I heard about the problems with her husband, and Hannah.'

'Ah, I see.' Faith relaxed in the chair, indignation mollified – for the time being, thought Kate. 'So, if you're satisfied about this contract, I suggest you sign it here and now and everyone at Westall's will sigh with relief.'

'Where?' Kate picked up a pen.

Faith watched her signing. 'I suppose your contract with Shotters was the exciting one?'

'Not really. My husband was away, the kids were out, my best friend didn't answer my calls, so the cat watched me sign.' She could laugh now; it was not so funny at the time. She picked up her handbag from the floor, ready to leave.

'By the way, Kate, before you go. This stuff from Pam Homerton, Joy asked me to read it. Is she anything to do with you? Only there's no address.'

'Yes, she's my friend, actually. I hoped Joy would write to her about her work.'

'Could you give me her address, better still her telephone number? I'd like to talk to her. It's wonderful writing.'

'You think so?' Kate tried to keep the surprise out of her voice.

'Oh, yes. You must have heard of Sappho, the women's imprint? They'll kill for it.'

'Wonderful, thanks, Faith,' said Kate, mentally making a note never to do any reviewing or criticism, assuming she was ever asked. Never, it was all too subjective.

'No, we should be thanking you for introducing her. Of course, she won't make the sort of money you will make but she'll get the prizes and plaudits. You can't have everything in life, can you?' She chuckled again, inhaled deeply on her cigarette, and had a coughing fit.

At Westall's Kate met more of the team. Val from publicity, Ben from design, John in marketing. The first thing that struck her was how normal everyone's clothes were, and the second was that there were no outlandish names. She could not help but wonder why. But the biggest contrast of all was the enthusiasm she met. They talked as if *Winter Interlude* was the only book that mattered. She knew this was not so, but it did not stop her basking in their compliments. They loved her writing, they did not want this, that and the other changed. Incredibly they appeared to care as much about it as she did. She apologised for her ordinariness, fearing it would prove a liability in publicising her.

'Gracious, no,' enthused Val. 'We shall use that very fact to our advantage. Every other writer these days is a celebrity of sorts – you're a refreshing change. You prove everyone wrong. It can be done – that first book accepted and successful. And to embark on a new career in your middle years, why, Kate, you'll be an inspiration to thousands.' Val was grinning at her, her keenness infectious, and Kate thought how much nicer 'middle years' sounded to 'middle-aged' – less leaden.

She was shown the artwork for the jacket and could have hugged Ben, could have cried. It was just as she had envisaged it, how she would have drawn it if she had the talent: simple, eye-catching yet still dignified. It was a very special moment.

'This is one of those days when I'm afraid that if I pinch myself I might wake up and find it all a dream,' she said, thanking them all for their hard work.

'It's no dream, Kate, you're on your way.' Gloria smiled at her. 'There's just one other thing. It's dreadfully short notice but we were wondering if perhaps you could get to our sales conference next month? It would help the teams so much if you could meet them. It's easier for them to sell a new author if they've met you. Then they can tell the bookshop people what a lovely person you are. It all helps. Of course, your husband's invited as well. The team from Panda will be there too.'

'I should love to, how kind of you to ask. I'm not sure about Tony, though, he's so busy these days,' she lied. 'And, anyway, I'm not at all sure he'd want to come,' she added, which was the truth.

20

'I want something in red, an outfit for the sales conference,' Kate told Pam as they entered the exclusive dress shop.

'Why red particularly?'

'I don't know, I suppose because when we went on the writers' weekend every other writer was in red, it seemed to me. My book jacket's primarily red too, with gold lettering.'

'Then I can't think of a better reason.'

Kate had forgotten there had been a time, less than a year ago, when she had found shopping in Bristol impossible, but those dreadful feelings of doom and panic had now disappeared completely from her mind.

They finally settled on a scarlet silk dress with a dramatic jacket of red, gold and black sequins. In truth, Pam decided, Kate would never have had the courage to choose it herself.

'You know, Kate,' said Pam, as they left the dress shop, 'I'd no idea you'd lost so much weight.'

'Great, that's just what every dieter wants to hear. What's the point if no one notices?'

'I never think of weight.'

'You don't need to,' said Kate with feeling.

'You need a new face. Let's go into Dingle's and play with the make-up.'

Two hours later, with the back seat of Pam's car covered in carrier bags, Kate with a stunning new make-up applied *gratis* by one of the beauty consultants in Dingle's, they were about to set off home.

'What a day!' Kate sighed, leaning back on the comfortable leather of the seat. 'God knows what I spent, and it's all been paid for by me. No guilt, no apologies, no lying. Bloody wonderful!'

'And I just love that blue suit on you, it looked stunning. And the green blouse with it, that's sheer genius.'

'I didn't need that suit.'

'Of course you didn't, that's the joy of it.' Pam laughed.

'Nor did I need three pairs of shoes – two of them identical.'

'Of course you did. Red suede can scuff – you've got to look your best.'

'You're sure I'm not going to look like mutton dressed as lamb?'

'Don't talk such rubbish. But you've got to get your hair cut and streaked, I insist. It'll take years off you. And when do you say your contact lenses will be ready?'

'I've got them, I'm wearing them for a bit longer every day. By the time of the conference I'll be up to full-time wearing.'

'Do they hurt?' Pam shuddered.

'Not much, the odd prick. I had them once before, don't you remember?'

'You'd never get me putting things in my eyes. Horrible thought!' Pam turned round and took something from the back seat. 'There's just one other thing.' Pam handed Kate a small gift-wrapped parcel.

'What's this?'

'It's for you, because I doubted you. It's me saying sorry for masses of things.'

Mystified, Kate opened it. Inside was a gold fountain pen.

'For signing all your books and contracts,' Pam said shyly.

'What a lovely idea. What a thoughtful gift.' Kate leant over and kissed her friend. 'But what did you mean, that you doubted me?'

Pam looked embarrassed and looked all ways but at Kate. 'Silly of me, I suppose, but I just thought you'd drop everyone when you started meeting new people.'

'Yes, it was silly of you. Why should I do a thing like that?'

'And I thought you were becoming so obsessed with it all that you wouldn't have time or inclination to help anyone else, and I was wrong on that too.'

'Oh, go on . . .' It was Kate's turn to feel embarrassed.

'It's true. You bothered even when you didn't really like what I had written.'

'What gives you that idea?' Kate said, probably a shade too quickly.

'It's true, though, isn't it?' Pam smiled at her.

'Not exactly. More like I didn't understand what you were doing – that's nearer the truth.'

'Ha! Don't fib to me. Honest, I don't mind. I thought it was a load of old cobblers myself.' And she laughed and Kate joined in, but she was not too sure that Pam was necessarily speaking the truth.

'Well, you're on your way, just like I said. It'll be me helping you choose an outfit next year, for your sales conference.'

'Felicity says that not many authors are invited to the conferences, she said you had been honoured.'

'Felicity said that? That was nice.'

'Is Tony going with you?'

'He still hasn't made up his mind. In a way, I hope he doesn't.'

The hotel, in its own park with a herd of deer grazing and a river flowing through the grounds, was large, crenellated, turreted and opulent.

'It looks like something out of a Hammer House of Horror film.' Kate giggled nervously. She was not nervous at the prospect of staying in something so grand but at the ordeal ahead.

'They obviously don't stint themselves,' said Tony. Rather grudgingly, she thought.

'Or us,' she answered pointedly.

They had not said what time they were arriving but Penny, Val's assistant at Westall's, was waiting for them at reception and insisted on accompanying them to their room. She explained the timetable, asked if there was anything they needed, and left them.

'Well, just look at all this,' Kate said, already busily inspecting the suite. 'I didn't expect all this, did you?' She fingered the flowers on the coffee table which had a welcome note attached. 'Look, champagne!' she exclaimed opening the small refrigerator, cased in mahogany and disguised as a cupboard.

'I'm glad I'm not a shareholder in either company,' Tony said, loosening his tie, throwing off his jacket and sitting down in a large, beautifully upholstered wing chair. He began to read the complimentary copies of the newspapers left for them beside a stack of glossy magazines.

'I think I'll take a bath and get myself organised. I'd love a gin and tonic with loads of ice to drink in the bath.' She smiled brightly.

'Not champagne?'

'Oh, hardly, I don't think we should open that, do you? No, gin will be fine.' She would have loved the champagne but felt it would be a bit cheeky, and what if they were supposed to pay for their own drinks? Tony would have a heart attack at the price a hotel like this was likely to charge.

'Bit early to start, isn't it?' he said.

'We've two hours before we go to the pre-dinner drinks reception. I need something to bolster me up and a drink in the bath is such a treat.'

She ran the bath, poured the complimentary bath oil into it, noting with satisfaction that it was expensive. She wondered if she dared pinch the remaining sachets of it, and the shampoo, soap and conditioner? Or would people laugh at her? She carefully bound her newly styled hair in a scarf, accepted her drink from Tony and sank with contentment into the warm water. Now this, she thought, was real luxury, no supper to worry about, the next two hours just to pamper herself. She could get used to a life like this.

Half an hour later she was wondering what to do next. She had painted her nails, her make-up was complete, her hair was combed out as the hairdresser had taught her, she was in her underclothes powdered and scented, her dress was on the hanger, covered with a muslin bag to protect it, ready to be slipped on. She sat on the bed and looked about her. Pam said it always took her a minimum of two hours to get ready to go out. What on earth did she do that took so long? Mind you, she thought, the end result was worth it with Pam. She picked up the remote control for the television and flicked through the channels. It was not like the one at home: not only were there the normal channels, plus Sky, but three film channels too. The first one was showing a children's film – must be pampered children whose parents brought them here, she thought, clicking over to the next which had a film she had already seen. She switched to the last one. On the screen, filling it, were two of the largest breasts she had ever seen and certainly with the biggest nipples. Two hands, hairy and male, suddenly appeared and began to fondle the nipples which stood to attention like organ stops. Kate sat forward transfixed. Five minutes later she was rolling on the bed laughing – if this was porn they could keep it! She'd never seen anything so limp or pathetic, in all senses of the words, as this. Tony put his head round the door.

'What's the joke?'

'Tony, you've simply got to come and watch this. It's so funny. I've never seen such a lifeless penis in my whole life!' She shrieked with laughter. 'He's going to have to beat it to get anywhere with it.'

Tony was across the room in a second and the screen went black.

'What did you do that for? I was enjoying myself – it was a good laugh.'

'Don't be stupid, you have to pay to watch the porn channel. That's not going to look good on the bill, is it?'

'Tony, no!' Kate looked aghast.

'Yes, look.' He handed her the card which had been on top of the set and which she had not noticed. 'You pay for all the movie channels.'

'Can we pay quietly at reception so that no one will know? You do it, I'm too embarrassed.'

'It registers automatically, it will have already. Honestly, Kate, I'm surprised at you even wanting to watch such smut.'

'I was curious, I'd never seen anything like that before. I don't think I'll bother again,' she said, subdued now. 'But . . . How do you know so much about it?' She sat up with interest. 'Is that what you get up to on your business trips? Is that it? Watching movies like that?'

'Don't be childish, Kate.' He was kicking off his shoes.

'I'm not being childish. I'm interested. I mean, if you like them then we could watch one together.'

'Kate, really!' He was removing his socks.

'No, I'm serious, Tony. If that's your bag . . . I mean I don't mind.' She was kneeling up on the bed now. 'It might help . . .'

'What's that supposed to mean?' he said, looking up sharply.

'It might make it more . . . Oh, Tony, it's difficult to explain.'

'More interesting? Is that what you meant? Quite honestly, Kate, I'm appalled. I had no idea that you were interested in perversions of any description.' He was struggling with the zip on his trousers. 'Isn't it wonderful? First you were dissatisfied with your home life and now it's your sex life. I begin to think nothing will ever be enough for you ever again, Kate.' He strode towards the bathroom and slammed the door.

Oh dear, thought Kate, she had only been trying to help. She could think of nothing worse than Tony making love to her with something as ludicrous as she had just watched going on in the background, but she had heard that pornography could be a stimulus. How sad if he really was satisfied with their sex life as it was. She sighed, and then she smiled at how impossible it was for a man to look dignified in his shirt tails.

She slipped into her new red dress and shoes and admired herself in the long mirror. It looked good, she looked good. She fluffed her hair. Pam had been right, the shorter style did make her look younger, and she loved the highlights. Why had she not had them done years ago instead of creeping around looking like a mouse?

She wandered through to the sitting room and poured herself another drink. She picked up the notes she had made for her speech and practised them in front of the mirror.

'What on earth have you got on?' Tony asked when he eventually joined her.

'It's my new dress, Pam helped me choose it.' She twirled around the better for him to see it.

'And how much did it cost?'

'You? Nothing. I bought it myself with my own money,' she said with marked satisfaction.

'You look like a Christmas tree with all those vulgar sequins. Have you seen my cuff-links?'

'I'll get them,' she said, going back into the bedroom with head held high. That was spiteful of him. She supposed he was getting back at her over her remarks about the film. Well, she was not going to fall for it, not this time. She knew better now. The dress was dramatic and suited her. She looked better than she had in years, probably better than she had ever looked.

'You are going to change, aren't you?' He had followed her into the room.

'No, I like this dress and sequins aren't vulgar – they're all the rage. Here are your links.' And she sailed out and did not bother to offer to help him put them in.

There was a knock at the door. She opened it to find Val with someone she had not met before.

'Kate, you look wonderful!' Val kissed her on both cheeks. 'What a stunning dress, you'll put us all to shame. This is Jill Ravenscroft, your editor at Panda. Jill, meet Kate, our favourite author.' Kate had hated that expression when those at Shotters had said it, but Val saying it was different. When she said it Kate felt it was true.

'Hello.' The two women shook hands. Jill looked as young as Lucy, Kate thought.

'I loved the book, Kate. We're going to do big things with it.' Jill smiled. Kate relaxed – it was a genuine smile.

'Come in. Drink?'

'Lovely,' the two young women said in unison. Kate crossed to the small refrigerator.

'What would you like?'

'Any champagne?' They both said instantly.

'Yes, there is. Anyone any good at opening bottles?'

'Me.' Jill stepped forward. 'You can't work at Panda and not learn how to open champagne bottles.' And with amazing dexterity she had the bottle uncorked in a flash.

'Tony, let me introduce you.' Kate smiled broadly at her husband as he entered the room, willing him not to show he was in a mood. The introductions were made, the drink poured.

'You must be so proud of your wife, Mr Howard,' Val said, taking her glass.

'Yes, of course,' Tony said, happily enough, Kate thought, and he handed a glass to Jill.

There was an awkward silence and the two women looked at their glasses as if waiting for something and then at Tony and then at each other.

'I think we should toast the book's success, don't you?' Val looked about her.

'*Winter Interlude*,' she and Jill said, raising their glasses. 'Good luck to it, with mega-sales.'

Kate thought the book was so much part of her that she should not drink the toast, it might be unlucky.

'The book,' said Tony raising his glass. Kate wished he had not taken so long to do so.

'Kate's managed such a great achievement, Mr Howard. So few books get selected. You should see the number of manuscripts we reject in a month, and Westall's is one of the smaller houses. Imagine what it's like at, say, somewhere like Shotters,' Val said politely.

'I always say you stand as much chance of winning the football pools.' Jill laughed a loud, gutsy laugh totally at odds with her heart-shaped face and slim prettiness.

'I didn't realise publishing was a lottery,' Tony said.

'I didn't mean that, Mr Howard. I just meant that statistically the odds must be about the same.' Jill had stopped laughing and spoke rapidly.

'Did you like the book, Mr Howard?' Val asked.

'I haven't read it,' Tony admitted.

'No?' both women said, wide-eyed with surprise.

'What if I hadn't liked it? What if I found myself in it, and in an unfavourable light? That could have led to the most appalling friction *chez* Howard. I'll wait for the hardback to be published.' Then he laughed and Kate realised she was not the only woman in the room who relaxed. They don't like him, she thought. Why won't he ask them to call him Tony? Why's he being so stiff?

'Of course, understandable,' said Val, looking about for somewhere to put her glass.

'I can recommend it thoroughly,' said Jill, putting hers on top of the TV set and Kate wondered whether to confess about the blue movie or not.

'Well, if you don't mind, Kate, Mr Howard?' Val looked at her watch. 'Perhaps we should be making a move. There's a whole army of people out there longing to meet you, Kate.'

'Kate! It must be Kate.' A large ginger-haired man wearing red spectacles which clashed dramatically with his colouring, a large cigar between clenched teeth, encompassed Kate in a bear hug of welcome. 'I'm Sherpa Tensing.' He laughed loudly, not just at his odd joke but at the look of total astonishment on Kate's face. 'Teddy Fletcher, sales director of all you survey.' He swung his arm and cigar expansively to include everyone in the crowded room. 'And you must be Tony?' He held out a large hand. 'You must be a proud man, Tony my lad. Right, Kate. Everyone wants to meet you. You come with Uncle Teddy now.' He grabbed hold of her hand and they lunged into the crowd, which parted briefly and then closed around them again like a satiated sea anemone.

For the next half-hour Kate found herself becoming more muddled and perplexed by every introduction. There were too many people, too many names, and too many grand-sounding titles to too many jobs.

'Confused?' Teddy grinned at her, and putting his arm about her waist he gave her a comforting squeeze.

'Very.'

'Don't worry, you'll get us all sorted out eventually. I'm the most important person here, so provided you remember me, you're home and dry, petal. Isn't that right?' he said to someone over Kate's shoulder.

'Don't you listen to a word he says, Kate, it's all blarney.'

She swung round. 'Mr Westall,' she said, with marked relief at seeing a face she knew.

'Julius, please. What did I say at Barty's party? Writers' circles are a good way to start, aren't they?'

'You remembered?' Kate said, and hoped he did not also remember her passing out on Barty's rug.

'Of course. And didn't I say how well the name will look? Have you seen the proofs? Teddy, have you got a spare copy?'

'I didn't know they had been done.' Kate was surprised at the speed of everything.

'It was an unholy rush and Gloria is frightened the mistakes in it will be horrendous, but we needed it for my chaps to read to sell on, you see, petal. Charlie,' he bellowed, making all those around him jump in the air. 'Proof over here for my favourite author Kate, chop, chop.'

When she held the copy in her hands she touched it gently. 'I think I want to cry.'

'Ah,' said Teddy, looking sentimental.

'Wait until you see the hardback, then you really will. I've yet to meet an author who doesn't want to cry their eyes out when that first copy is finally in their hands.' Julius smiled at her.

'There seem to be so many high spots in this business. I keep coming across them convinced that's the last and then something else lovely happens.' Kate blew into her handkerchief as dinner was announced. 'My husband?' she said, suddenly remembering Tony and looking about the room for him.

'He's fine, he's over there with the MD of Panda,' Julius assured her. He took her arm, and with Teddy on her other side she was escorted into dinner.

She barely ate a thing, she was far too nervous and she did not dare drink fearing that, with the gin, the champage and the wine at the reception, she had already had far too much. She wished the meal would go on for ever but inexorably it came to an end.

Others made speeches and Kate sat bright red with confusion at the fulsome compliments paid to her. And then it was her turn. Kate, who had once given a talk to the Women's Institute on jam-making, and one impassioned plea for better sex education to the other committee members of the Middle School PTA, got to her feet. She looked at the expectant faces turned her way and longed to make a dash for it, but took a deep breath and began.

When she sat down everyone in the large room was standing and clapping. She had made them laugh, she really had. They had enjoyed it! And the first thing she did was to pick up her glass and take the largest swig of wine she had ever swallowed in one gulp.

'Let's go into the bar, everyone wants to buy you a drink.' Teddy stood up, collecting the large bouquet of flowers that had been presented to Kate.

'I'd like to put them in water,' she said.

Immediately Teddy signalled to Penny who happened to be passing. She took the flowers and Kate's room key and went off to do it for her.

'Can't have you getting tired out, petal.' Teddy fussed over her and Kate, not used to such consideration, glowed with happiness at the novelty of it all.

'You coming, Tony?' She looked at her husband appealingly. He had said little through dinner and was the only one not to congratulate her on her speech.

'I suppose so,' he said, getting to his feet. 'But if one more person says how proud I should be feeling, I'll hit them.'

'You must be feeling so proud tonight, Tony me lad,' said Teddy, grinning from ear to ear. He turned and winked broadly at Kate, who had to stifle a grin herself. Tony at least had the grace to look disconcerted.

In the bar it was impossible to buy anyone a drink. Tony tried several times but each time was refused and another round came their way. At last Gloria fought her way through the mass to where Kate was sitting.

'You look fabulous. What a dress. And you were wonderful. My table were in stitches. Did that really happen to an editor? Locked in the loo with hordes of rampaging fans? It rings a bell . . .'

'I exaggerated a bit. There were only five but two dozen sounded better. Was I really all right?'

'You were a star! I couldn't believe that you weren't used to public speaking every day of your life. Wasn't she wonderful, Mr Howard?'

'Wonderful,' Tony replied in an expressionless voice.

'You must be so proud of her, I know I am.' Gloria patted Kate's arm. Kate looked anxiously at Tony but he gazed fixedly at the drink in his hand.

'Don't be so formal, Gloria. You don't mind if she calls you Tony, do you?'

A grunt was the only description for her husband's reply.

At this point Teddy appeared with a bevy of men – sales manager of this, of that, promotions director, promotions manager, special projects director . . .

'Here we go again.' Kate laughed. 'I can't imagine what it is you all do.'

'We shall explain,' Teddy said grandly, shooing away those he deemed had sat at Kate's table long enough and launching into a noisy explanation of how useless everyone but him really was.

More champagne arrived. Kate realised she was becoming squiffy but it was all so pleasant. All the compliments and enthusiasm were giving her such a lift that when another bottle arrived it seemed the most natural thing to allow her glass to be refilled. It was half-way through this bottle that she realised Tony was no longer at the crowded table.

'Anyone seen my husband?'

Teddy, in his role of court jester, made a great play of looking for Tony under the table and then, to her acute embarrassment, stood on the table, clapped his hands for silence and asked if anyone had seen a lost husband, '. . . five foot eleven, dark-haired, with a hump, and wearing spectacles . . .'

'He doesn't wear spectacles.' Kate pulled at his trouser leg, giggling.

'But he's got a hump?' Teddy leaned down to speak to her.

'I think I'll go to bed.' Everyone looked up to see Tony standing at the side of the table looking at Teddy with dislike. 'You coming?' he asked, clutching a bottle of Perrier water to him like a shield.

'No, I don't think so, Tony. I'm enjoying myself.'

'I'm glad somebody is,' he said, before turning smartly on his heel and marching away.

'Whoops, have we upset him?' Teddy clambered off the table.

'He's very tired, he works hard,' Kate said loyally.

'Yes, I'm sure he does,' Teddy said quietly, suddenly serious.

Kate was glad she had not gone to bed with Tony. There might be a lot of horseplay down here but there was serious talk too. She learnt a lot that night, and not just about the plans for her book; she learnt that she had acquired responsibilities. In the past it had just been her and her novel; now there was a whole army of people to whom the success or failure of her book was an important issue. She was no longer alone as she had thought. They asked after her second book and she knew she owed it to them to make a go of that one too. It was not a game any more, it was serious business.

Kate had always enjoyed a good gossip, never more so than now – especially the most interesting snippet about Bella Ford. Her latest book had been rejected by Shotters and Bella was busily searching out a new publisher.

'Know what she did?' Teddy asked, eyes shining with mischief. 'She was booked into this swishy hotel. You know, one of those with shops in the hall? She bought a ton of stuff – Waterford crystal, a watch, handbags, underwear, you name it, Bella bought it. She put the whole lot on the bill and left Shotters to pick up the tab.'

'She didn't?' Kate said, shocked.

'Yes, she did. That's why they turned her down. Then Peter Holt telephoned everyone and told them what she had done. No one will pick her up now.'

'Oh, the poor silly woman,' said Kate.

'I shouldn't waste your sympathy on her, Kate. It was Bella who shopped you to Tatiana. My secretary Rachel was still there when it happened,' Gloria explained.

'Did they call the police?' Kate asked, full of indignation now that her suspicions about Bella had been confirmed.

'No, but that's my girl.' Gloria laughed at the change in Kate.

'Pity,' she said, emboldened by the champagne. 'I inadvertently watched a blue movie tonight and I see you have to pay extra for that. I'll pay of course.' She managed to say all this without blushing once.

'Inadvertently, you say? I should bloody cocoa!' Teddy roared with laughter, and Kate realised this was something she was never going to live down.

The next morning she awoke to a very bad hangover and no sympathy from Tony.

'You were drinking like a pig, serves you right,' he said, too loudly for comfort.

'I needed to relax, I'm not used to making speeches.'

'Is that what it was?'

She looked at him, a weary expression on her face. 'Why do you have to put down everything I do? Why can't you be happy for me?'

'I'd be happy for you if you weren't so intent on making a spectacle of yourself. Letting those men fawn all over you, giggling at that idiot in the red glasses with his fatuous jokes. I can tell you one thing, Kate, I'm not coming to another of these dos and that's a promise.'

'Good, I wouldn't ask you. What did you contribute last night? Bugger all. You sulked, you couldn't even put yourself out to talk to people. God knows what they thought of you.'

'Quite honestly, Kate, I don't give a damn what they thought of me.'

'Oh, Tony, listen to us, here we go again. I thought we were going to get on better. What more do you want?'

'I want you to give up all this nonsense.'

She sat back on the pillows and looked at him with astonishment. 'You can say that after last night? Didn't you hear what my print run is to be? It's wonderful! I'm going to be read by hundreds of thousands of people. I want to give people pleasure – '

'You want to be famous, isn't that it?' He sneered.

'Fine, what if I do? Is there anything wrong in being acknowledged for what you achieve? They respect me. They've made me see I've a talent not everyone has. I can make us a fortune.'

'Come down to earth, Kate. If it wasn't your book there are a dozen others out there they could have published.'

'That's where you're wrong –' But she stopped, what was the point? It wasn't only that he did not understand, he didn't want to.

'One book doesn't make a writer,' he said.

'I know what the trouble was last night. You couldn't take me being the centre of attention, could you? All the dinners and dances we've been to, it's always been you who people wanted to talk to. I was just the wife in the background. Well, now, Tony, you're getting a taste of what it's like to be the little woman. And it seems you are sadly lacking in the maturity required to deal with the role.' They were arguing, she knew they were, but to anyone else it would have sounded like a conversation, so normal was the tone of their voices.

'Sometimes, Kate, you talk a load of crap.'

'To your ears probably, but then you never have enjoyed listening to what you don't want to know.'

'We can't go on like this,' he said, so matter-of-factly that at first she wondered if she had heard him correctly.

'No, we can't.'

'And you won't give up this nonsense?'

'No, I can't.'

'Then I suggest we put the house on the market, divide the proceeds down the middle. Mind you, if you're right about your earnings, then I shall be coming to you for a divorce settlement. I'm not going to hold my breath, though. I think I'll go for a walk. Shall I see you at breakfast?'

'No, I don't think so, I'm not hungry,' she said, as he walked to the door.

Kate got off the bed, opened the refrigerator door and found some orange juice. She could hardly believe what was happening to her. Marriages did not break up with polite questions like 'Shall I see you at breakfast?' Marriages broke up with grand fights and screaming matches. Didn't they?

She sat on the bed in the luxurious hotel and knew that he was right. Neither of them could go on like this. Funny old world, she thought. She had come to help promote a book and was leaving with her marriage over and divorce a serious possibility.

She wished she had not debased herself by offering to watch porn movies with him. That was annoying.

Part Three

1

Crispin's divorce was made final in August and two weeks later, in September, he married Bee-Bee. The unseemly haste was intentional for he felt, more than anything, that it showed the contempt with which he now regarded Charlotte. He had given her everything she had asked for, which he also felt indicated his disdain. But he could afford to enjoy such little triumphs now, such as not arguing about the Regency chest-on-chest, or the framed set of eighteenth-century flower engravings.

'Have whatever you want,' he had said with magnificent scorn as if he were above such haggling, and had walked out of the house leaving a surprised and even more huffy Charlotte behind him.

He had explained to the other shareholders and his cousin at every available opportunity the madness of Julius employing Gloria to launch his new list – doomed to failure and inevitably more debts – and ensuring that everyone was keener than before to sell – if and when. Ah, when? He had taken trouble to consult medical friends and had purchased several medical textbooks. Now he watched Julius with all the care of a diagnostician. He was certain that there was a slight blueness about Julius's mouth that had not been there before, and he was convinced of a marked breathlessness.

Even Crispin could not fault the wedding arrangements. The Benton family's country house was in deepest Berkshire – a better county socially there could not be. The old house, which was huge and rambling and stuffed with valuable antiques, was perfect. The gardens were a by-word in horticultural circles. The local vicar, while initially opposed to a divorcé marrying under his church's Saxon roof, had a remarkable change of heart when a cheque from Mr Benton covering all the repairs to that precious roof and then some over was wafted under his nose.

It had been a happy time. Not only were they to be given a London house but they had the use of the dower house on Benton's estate – not that Crispin could see himself spending much time there, the pleasures of the countryside were an ongoing mystery to him. A new house in Chelsea was chosen and with furniture, wallpapers, curtains and carpets to be selected for it, many joyous hours were filled.

He had a new mistress, Cleo. Crispin had solved the problem of his sexually less than enthusiastic wife-to-be, and the problem of young mistresses desperate for marriage, in one go. Cleo was forty, rapacious for the sex her millionaire banker husband was disinclined to supply her with and, best of all, she was so socially prominent and domestically comfortable that the last thing she wanted was to be found out, let alone divorced. He was well set up.

So it was that as Bee-Bee, looking like an aristocratic virginal shepherdess in a Watteau painting, dress low cut and prettily panniered, with a gorgeously luxuriant headdress of fresh flowers from her family garden, swayed down the aisle towards him, he was able at the same time to see Cleo, sophisticated and elegant, standing in the congregation. At sight of both women he thought of the two things he adored – sex with Cleo, and money in the shape of Bee-Bee – and had such an erection that he had to approach the altar with both hands clutched firmly in front of his crotch, looking like a small boy caught scrumping apples.

Near the front of the church Gloria, stunning in a lemon-yellow and black fine linen suit with a large matching hat trimmed with black satin, stood and feared she would cry. She loathed weddings for that reason. She never knew why she cried. Was it because the brides invariably looked so beautiful? Or because she knew, like most people there, that statistically the likelihood of most marriages lasting was abysmal – and the thought of all that lost hope made the tears flow? Or because, and this she feared was the most likely reason, she had never been a bride and longed to be one.

She had taken great pains to look right today for she was sure that Peter Holt would be a fellow guest. As she had paid the horrendous bill for her outfit, even as she dressed this morning, she had assured herself she wanted to look her best just to show him she did not care, that she could get on just fine without him. But a nasty niggling thought would keep popping up and asking her if she thought he would find her beautiful.

They should have met before now and it was a miracle they had not. Publishing was such a small world that it was unusual not to see everyone on a regular basis at parties, launches and the like. Gloria had attended many and Peter's absence could mean only one thing: he was avoiding her. He would not be able to do that today, though. Everyone who was anyone in publishing was present. He must be here even if she had not yet seen him.

She wished that avoiding him was simply a matter of not seeing him. But it was more than that. Every day she thought of him and longed for him. Every night before she went to sleep she ached for him. She had tried to fill this void in her life but no man she met interested her. She still thought often of telephoning him, but then she always decided, To hell with him, and slammed the receiver down. Perhaps worst were the nights when she dreamt of him, and it was always so perfect that upon awakening she felt desolate that it was only a dream.

What would happen today? She did not know. Did she want him to see her and rush up to claim her? She smiled at the juvenile notion. Did she fear him ignoring her? No, he would not do that, he was too kind and gentle a man for that. Gentle? After the way he had behaved that was an odd word to choose. No, she just wanted to be near him, in the same room as him, breathing the same air, able to watch him, that's what she wanted. But to do that, she had to look her best, she thought, as she picked up her hymn book.

Julius stood in the family pew with his wife and felt sorry for the poor little girl who was marrying his nephew. He looked across at her father who was smiling with such pride and contentment. Julius was amazed that someone so obviously successful and, presumably, astute should have been taken in for one moment by Crispin. He could not be as intelligent as he looked otherwise he would be paying the boy a large sum not to marry his daughter. As it was, he was apparently lashing out a fortune to bless the union.

He took a handkerchief out of his pocket and mopped his brow. It was hot in here, he thought, too many people. He held the hymnal up but found difficulty in seeing the words. Must get my eyes checked, he thought.

Mike Pewter, taking up enough room for two in his pew, could, from his massive height, see everyone. He was astonished to note Peter here with Hilary. To his surprise, he had been pleased when Peter had confided to him that he was getting divorced. Surprised because he had not until then realised the extent of his dislike for Hilary. Now they seemed to be together again and he wished he had not been so open with Peter, congratulating him on his decision and unwisely mentioning that he had never had time for the stuck-up cow. He should have known better, should have waited for the divorce before opening his big mouth. Shotters must be turning the fellow mad. He'd advised him time and again to get out, that such an organisation was not for him. Why, he would be happy to set up something himself with Peter if he wanted a partner. Odd that Peter did nothing about it. Not like he used to be at all.

He caught sight of Gloria standing in the next aisle. Now there was an attractive woman, spirited too – he liked them with plenty of originality and vivacity. He had often noticed her, not that he had ever done anything about it. For a start he had heard she preferred young men to mature studs such as himself. What's more, he always avoided affairs with anyone connected with the business – it made things too complicated if anything went wrong, which it invariably did. If he had been Peter she was the one he would have gone for. He knew that. Peter fancied her – he'd confessed as much once when in his cups. But there he was with Hilary. Rather him than me. He rubbed his chin with his large hand; of the two, he knew which one he'd prefer in his bed. He snorted with amusement, a little too loudly, so that Lady Lily found it necessary to give him a sharp dig with her elbow. Mike gave his concentration to the proceedings once more and bellowed out the hymn lustily.

Peter stood beside his wife and wished he had not come. He found weddings depressing affairs, reminding him of the day he had taken the vital step himself. It did not help to find himself placed beside his estranged wife by an officious usher who had refused to seat him elsewhere. He wondered if Gloria would be here. He wanted her to be so that he could talk to her, find out why, even when he had sent her flowers, there had been this silence from her. But then he also hoped she wasn't, unsure of what he would hear, what he would say.

The hymn soared about him but Peter's mind was on other things. He must stop thinking of Gloria. He switched to work. Once he had thought about work non-stop because it was the best thing in his life. Now he thought about it because it was the worst. The figures were bad. Important authors were leaving in a haemorrhage which did not seem capable of being staunched and new authors were proving elusive to find. Sales were down. The economies made were not sufficient. And, to cap it all, Costas was coming next week and Peter still did not know how he was going to explain everything to him. He wished he could get into a car, a boat, a plane, he did not mind which, and just take off into the blue and not let anyone know where he had gone. That would be bliss.

Barty Silver stood a proud man with Joy beside him. Not that they were engaged, Joy had still to make up her mind, but as each day passed he felt her moving closer to that decision as their friendship, always good, deepened. He was hopeful that by spring he and Joy would be enjoying just such a ceremony.

He had planned it all. He had a house in the Bahamas: they would marry there, in the gardens beside the sea. He would charter a couple of Boeings to bring all his friends. He would take over the local hotel – he made a mental note to get Gervase to find out from his solicitor when he could hope for everything to be finalised.

Thinking of his house in the Bahamas made him decide that it would be a good idea if he took Joy out there next week, he would like her to see his other homes. Perhaps a holiday away from England and the lawyers would help her decide. He felt for her hand and gave it a little squeeze. She looked up at him and smiled wanly. She was not happy, he knew that; it did not matter what he did or what he gave her. She could never be happy when that bastard had her little girl. Barty had failed her there. His lawyers were good but Charles was better: he had temporary custody. Barty hated to fail in anything. Somehow he had to succeed, to see to it that that evil bastard would never keep Hannah, not while Barty Silver lived. The small pulse in his temple pounded.

Joy wished she could have smiled more warmly at him. No man could have been kinder than Barty had been and in return what did she give him? She was being a dismal companion, it wasn't fair. She tried hard but the emptiness inside her, the longing she felt for Hannah, made happiness elusive.

She knew what he must be thinking, weddings did that to people, they thought of their own – past or future. He would be planning theirs now. She still had not given him her answer and she did not know why. She had decided she wanted to marry him, knew that she loved him – if not like a lover then more than a friend. So why didn't she? Fear, perhaps, that by marrying him she would never get Hannah back. Fear that if that happened she would never know happiness again.

Now she was concentrating on translating the Latin wording on the monuments about her, anything to take her mind off one particular wedding, all those years ago when she had been happy and so beautiful. She dared not think of it for if she did she thought of Charles, and when she did that she felt guilty, for in doing so she felt she was betraying Barty.

'Dearly beloved, we are gathered together...' the vicar began and the congregation rustled with anticipation.

The wedding reception was in the great hall of the Bentons' large Tudor house where florists had worked through the night so that now it was like standing in a summer garden. Crispin was pleased: not many people had a hall of such magnitude that it could take the three hundred wedding guests. There was a marquee in the garden, but that was for the five hundred expected for the dance in the evening. Crispin was particularly delighted with the marquee, which he had had a hand in designing so that it was reminiscent of Brighton Pavilion. He had just the waistcoat to wear to the dance tonight, Regency in style, white silk with scarlet and gold birds-of-paradise embroidered upon it. He stood on the receiving line very much at peace with his world.

Invariably at any such function it was only a matter of minutes before Julius, Peter and Mike deserted their wives and found each other. This occasion was no different, and soon they were deep into the gossip that was so much part of their work and which they would, all three, have insisted was 'business talk'.

Roz approached Gloria and asked if she could stick with her. 'I don't know many people here – they're all too top drawer for me. He only invited me because he didn't think I would come.'

'Who?' asked Gloria, shuffling slowly along the long receiving line.

'Crispin, the creep!'

'Am I to take it you don't much like our financial director either?' Gloria laughed.

'Of course, you wouldn't know. We had an affair for ages. I thought I was going to marry him, more fool me.'

'You'd have been more of a fool if you had married him.'

'That's true.' Roz laughed this time.

'Is that why you left Westall's?'

'Yes. I thought I'd be able to stick it out, but I couldn't, especially when he got engaged. He seemed to gloat then instead of showing any embarrassment.'

'Bet Julius misses you.'

'I think he must. He telephoned me last night to see if I was coming. He wants to talk to me about something urgent. I'm to meet him in the bar of the hotel.'

'Maybe he's going to offer you your job back.'

'No, thank you, I'm happy at Pewter's. You don't know why he wants to see me?'

'No, sorry. Here we are, best foot forward, Roz, I'm right behind you.'

Both women passed along the receiving line, shaking hands, smiling, muttering inanities.

'How pretty you look, Roz,' Crispin said, almost with regret, Gloria thought.

'I always do, Crispin. Always.' Roz tossed her head and swept on.

From the other side of the marquee Peter saw Gloria. He felt a surge of excitement. With heart thumping he weaved his way across to her.

'Gloria, hallo.'

She had her back to him but she recognised the voice immediately. She turned slowly, delaying the moment when she had to see the polite expression on his face.

'Peter.' She faced him, smiling brilliantly, all charm, all self-possession, and then she looked at him and there was no expression of polite friendliness, instead he was looking at her with longing . . .

'Peter . . .' she said, feeling confused.

'I've got to talk to you, Gloria. I must. But not here. Are you staying at the big hotel? Sod, I can't remember its name – ' He was speaking quickly, urgently.

'The Deer Park Hall?'

'Yes, that's it. Later, when we've got away from here. About six, I'll ring your room.'

'Yes . . . I'll look . . .'

'Gloria, long time no see.' Hilary had chosen that precise moment to join them. 'Peter, there's some people over there I want you to meet.' She put a proprietorial arm through his. 'Excuse us, Gloria.'

Peter turned round, pointing furiously at his watch. But Gloria did not see, her eyes were brimming with tears.

'I'm getting out of here,' she burst out.

'Gloria, what's happened?' Roz called out, trailing behind her.

'Bloody men, that's what.' And she was running to get to her car, and to get away, right away.

Elephant, never a dog for strange hotel rooms, was beside himself with joy to see her back so soon. She was packed in a trice. Within minutes, bill paid and suitcase in the boot, Gloria and Elephant were ready to go.

'Where to, Elephant? I've a week off. Where shall we go? My mother's?'

Elephant sneezed.

'All right, then, not my mother's – it's too far, anyway.' The dog had made her laugh. 'Let's go to Oxford, I haven't been there for ages.'

Expertly she manoeuvred her car out of the crowded car park and was soon on the main road, her foot down, putting as much space between her and Peter as quickly as possible. What a complete fool she was. She had this week's holiday and no plans made. And why not? She had pretended, even to herself, that she wanted to act on impulse. It was not true. She knew why she had made no arrangements. She had hoped to see him, prayed something would happen between them, longed to get away – just with him.

'Fool!' She pressed down hard on the accelerator, Elephant yapped, he liked speed. 'I've got to get him out of my mind, Elephant. This is hopeless.'

Julius was waiting for Roz in the bar before dinner. Later they would have to return for the infernal wedding dance. He knew he would hate it but Jane was insisting they attend. He ordered a double whisky and the Buck's Fizz which he knew was Roz's favourite.

'Roz, my dear. Thank you for giving me your time.'

'It's entirely my pleasure, Mr Westall.'

'Didn't enjoy the wedding?'

'Not a lot. I might have if Crispin hadn't been there.' She giggled.

Julius's smile turned to a frown as he saw Peter Holt enter the bar, looking about him. He did not want anyone to join them or even sit nearby – he did not want to be overheard. He frowned even more as Peter approached their table.

'Sorry to disturb you, but you haven't seen Gloria, have you? I arranged to meet her and reception says she's checked out.'

'She left in a hurry. She was upset,' Roz said, looking at Peter with a loathing that Julius noticed, though he did not know the reason for it.

'Oh, I see. You don't know where she's gone?'

'No. I don't.'

'Thanks. I'll try her home.' And with a distracted air he left them.

'Something I've missed?' Julius asked.

'Gloria was talking to him and then she began to cry and ran out of the marquee. It must have been something he said to her.'

'Ah, young people.' Julius nodded, even more perplexed. 'Roz, I've asked you here because I want you to do me a favour. I need someone I can trust and I think I can trust you again, can't I? I need someone who does not like Crispin.' He smiled kindly at her. She blushed at the thought that he was trusting her after all she had done to him.

'I want to explain some things to you.' And he began. Ten minutes later he had finished. 'Do you think you would mind doing that?'

'Of course not, not for you. It gives me the creeps, though, just thinking about it.' Roz shuddered.

'You know how it is with me, Roz. You're one of the few people I have told.'

'Yes, but I don't like to dwell on it. I can't bear to think of you dying.' Roz fought not to cry.

'I don't mind so much, you know.'

'Oh, please, Mr Westall...' Roz produced a handkerchief.

'Sorry. Here it is, then. You'll look after it?' He handed her a large white envelope.

'Yes. As soon as I hear anything has happened to you, I'm to give this to Gloria.'

'That's right.'

'Excuse me asking, but why could your lawyer not do it?'

'I've learnt about office staff and their indiscretions once before...' He laughed gently so as not to hurt her too much.

'Oh, Mr Westall. You can trust me this time. You don't know how much this means to me, after what I did. I promise you, Lepanto is safe with me.' And this time she did not bother to fight the tears but let them flow. Julius glanced about the bar uncomfortably, afraid people would think he had been unkind to her.

2

Oxford held little interest for Gloria, which was indicative of her state of mind. This city was normally one of her favourites. The following day she went to Stratford where Elephant enjoyed barking at the swans, but she felt she could not face sitting through a Shakespeare play on her own. Cheltenham failed to amuse her and so she pressed on to Bristol. The Unicorn had the universality of a modern, purpose-built hotel and was not the type she would normally have chosen, but it was ideal in her present mood, for anonymity was hers for the taking. In a smaller, more intimate establishment she might have been forced into talking to strangers.

From her bedroom window the following morning she could watch the crowds of people ambling about the dockside looking at the ships, the houseboats, the sleek, elegant four-masted schooner moored below. Were they, like her, dreaming of stepping aboard, upping anchor and away – it did not matter where?

She took Elephant for a walk along the Watershed, window shopping, and they stopped for coffee and a cake. She persuaded Elephant to stay in the car, something he was not normally keen on, but she wanted to go to the Arnolfini to see the latest art exhibition. After taking a drink on the dockside, and Elephant for another walk, she did not know what else to do. She returned to the hotel and leafing idly through her address book realised that Kate lived in the area. Perhaps Kate would like to join her in Bristol for lunch tomorrow? she asked on the telephone. Instead she found she had been invited to stay overnight with Kate.

She pulled up outside Kate's house and envied her. The house and the village were perfect, almost ridiculously so. This place was everyone's dream of what an English village should be. She felt she had stepped into a jigsaw puzzle picture.

'Why the for-sale sign? This must be anyone's ideal. You couldn't let this go, surely?' Gloria asked after the hellos were over and Kate had welcomed her. The inside of the house was exactly as one would imagine it to be from the outside – comfortable furniture, the odd antique, gleaming copper, pot-pourri and the tantalising smell of baking in the background.

'Sadly so,' Kate said, taking Gloria's coat and fussing over Elephant who, with snout in the air, had also got a whiff of something interesting in the kitchen. 'It will be a wrench,' she said in a tight-sounding voice as she led the way into the drawing room.

'Then why sell?' Gloria asked practically.

'It's too big now, my son's away in Yorkshire and my daughter goes to Cambridge this term. She's there now, sorting things out. I shall miss – Oh, hell!' She tossed her head. 'Why am I lying to you? I'm getting divorced. We have to sell if both of us are to have roofs over our heads. Neither of us wants to lose it, but there it is. Drink? Sherry? Gin?'

'Kate, I'm so sorry,' said Gloria. Kate picked up the bottle of Gordon's and waved it at her with a questioning look. 'Yes, please. This is dreadful news, Kate. I thought there was something wrong at the sales conference, it was as if your husband didn't really approve. Everybody felt it, they all said so after you had left. Teddy was beside himself, he felt he might have gone too far and offended him – he's very sensitive, you know, even if it isn't at first apparent.' She laughed at the thought of their ebullient and noisy sales director who was famous for putting his foot in it.

'Good gracious, no. Do reassure him. Tony didn't really want to come and, if I'm honest, I didn't want him to either. I suppose we both thought he *should* go – better to go by instinct, isn't it?'

'Then it did have something to do with it?' Gloria said aghast, as she took the glass of gin and tonic.

'All it did was bring things to a head which had been bubbling madly for months.'

'Is it the writing?' Gloria asked.

'I suppose that's symptomatic of things. I started because, to be honest, I was so bloody miserable. No, saying it was the writing that broke up our marriage would be the same as saying another woman did. It's never one thing, it's a vast pyramid of petty things. And then something happens, there's an alteration in the routine. For us it was my taking up writing – and the whole edifice collapses.'

'Are you all right?' Gloria asked anxiously.

'I'm fine. A bit scared, of course. I've never lived alone in my whole life. It's a challenge really to see if I can.'

'Move to London.'

'I don't think so.' Kate shuddered at the thought. 'I'm sorry, I don't have your love for the city. I'm a country soul. No, I thought I'd get a cottage, in a village but nearer London.'

'Won't you miss your friends?'

'Most of those we have are Tony's by inclination. My one and only friend is Pam – do you remember, I told you about her? She's gone odd on me again, I can't keep up with her. I think, Gloria, that I might be reaching that point in life when one begins to think that old friends are more trouble than they're worth. They always seem to think they know what is best for you and that time has given them the right to tell you.' She smiled ironically but she did not say how when she had told her she was getting divorced Pam had said, in no uncertain terms, that it was all her fault, and since she had done nothing but moan about Tony for years it was not surprising the poor man had had enough. 'Would you be insulted if I suggested we lunch in the kitchen?'

'I'd regard it as an honour.'

Half an hour later she was trying to persuade Kate to write a cookery book.

'I couldn't. I wouldn't know where to begin.'

'You probably said that about writing a novel before you wrote one.' Gloria smiled.

'That's true. I did. Cooking, though?' She paused as if thinking about the project. 'No, I'm too slapdash a cook for that, I can't be doing with weighing and measuring. I just throw things together and pray they work.'

'Well, that lot certainly did,' Gloria said, patting her stomach with satisfaction. 'Joy needs some of your cooking. I saw her at a wedding over the weekend. She looks thinner than ever. She's going to marry Barty when her divorce comes through – she told me that in strictest confidence, she hasn't even told him and I probably shouldn't have told you.'

'I won't breathe a word. It's a surprise, though. Barty doesn't seem the marrying kind; does he? Is she in love with him?'

'I don't know. It's not something you can ask. I mean, normally you automatically assume people are in love. But I felt she was anxious when she told me, as if expecting me to be censorious.'

'And were you?'

'Me? Good gracious, no. I can't think of a nicer bloke, can you? It's rubbish about him being gay, you know.'

'But is he interested in sex at all? If he isn't, then she's in for a difficult time. You can't be a normal woman and live with a man you love and not have sex, it would be so sad. Let's hope she's just enormously fond of him, then it won't matter so much. More apple pie?'

'Heavens, I couldn't manage another bite.'

'Did you get in touch with Peter Holt?' Kate asked, taking Gloria completely off guard.

'No. I thought about what you had said for ages, but in the end I just couldn't. I must have picked up the phone a hundred times and always chickened out. I told you what a proud old hen I am.' She laughed, but Kate noted how hollow it was. 'Just as well I didn't. He was at the same wedding with his wife, he's obviously gone back to her. I think he might at least have told me.'

'Are you sure?'

'Saw them with my own eyes. In fact, I cleared off when I did. I was a bit upset,' she said with masterly understatement.

'Maybe they were together just by accident. If they knew the same people . . .? Hold on – ' Kate leapt up from the table, opened the door of the pantry and began to rootle in a pile of old newspapers 'Here it is.' She returned to the table. 'Look this is only last Wednesday's.' She opened the page at the gossip diary. 'See,

Will beautiful Hilary Holt take even more interest in horses now she is so often in the company of Pinkers Flynn, 45, roistering bloodstock agent and filly fancier? Successful publisher, Peter Holt, 45, Hilary's little-seen husband, does not share her interests it would seem . . .

'Look, there's a photo.'

'Let me see that.' Gloria leant over for the page. She reread the piece Kate had just read out. And studied the faces of Hilary and a stranger in the photograph. 'This could be an old picture, you know what these columns are like – they need to fill a space, they dig in the archives.'

'It was taken last week at a charity ball in London. Look at the caption under the photo.'

'This Pinkers bloke wasn't at the wedding.'

'Well, hardly. You don't trot your fancy man along to weddings and things like that, do you? What's more, everyone around here says they're getting divorced. Peter lives near here, you know – or used to.' She added meaning-fully, 'His estate is up for sale,' and began to make the coffee.

'Oh, Kate, what if it's true?' Gloria looked at her with eyes shining with hope.

'It might be a good idea if you found out if it was true or not, don't you think? There's the telephone,' she said briskly, and pointed to it.

'Shall I?'

Kate doubted if Gloria really required an answer so she continued with the coffee preparations.

'Em? It's Gloria Catchpole. Might I have a word with Peter?'

'Gloria, lovely to hear from you. Are you well?'

'Fine, thanks.' Gloria rolled her eyes with exasperation as Em prattled on about how she missed her and what was she doing, and who at Shotters was pregnant and who was having it away with whom. Gloria felt that if Em did not put her through to Peter soon she would lose her nerve.

'Em, it's lovely to hear all the news but I am in a bit of a rush. If I might be put through . . .?'

'Sorry, Gloria. Peter's in New York. Mr Carras was coming here this week, supposedly, and then changed his plans and sent for him. It's not right the way they make poor Peter run around after them, is it, Gloria?'

'When did he go?' Gloria asked, ignoring Em's impassioned defence of her boss.

'Monday night. He was trying to get hold of you all day Monday. Should I take a message? He'll be calling later, I expect.'

'Yes, tell him I called, would you. Tell him I'll be back home tomorrow, Friday. Thanks, Em.' She replaced the receiver. 'He'd been trying to get hold of me,' she said to Kate, eyes shining.

'There then, isn't that nice?' Kate beamed, and poured out the coffee. When the telephone rang she answered it. From the rigid way she stood and the rather stiff responses she made, Gloria wondered if she was speaking to her husband. She was.

'That's that, then. We've sold the house,' she said bleakly when she had rung off. She looked close to tears. 'It's really silly to feel upset. I expected it. They're very nice people – he's something in computers. They've got three young children. It will be nice for the house to have youngsters running about it again – makes a house alive, don't you think?' All the time she was talking, Kate was rearranging the lumps of sugar in the bowl, piling them up, then knocking them down. Suddenly she stopped and looked at Gloria. 'Oh, Gloria, it's so awful. This place has been my whole life . . .' and she began to cry. Gloria held her close. 'I'm sorry,' Kate said, grabbing for some kitchen paper and blowing her nose.

'I'm so sorry, crying all over you like that.'

'Why not? What are friends for?'

'It's just, I don't know how I'll cope . . .' She sat at the kitchen table, looking small and vulnerable as she systematically tore the paper in her hands to pieces.

'You'll cope, you're a gutsy lady. Remember in Barty's loo? You were bored. You'll never be bored again, not now you've got your writing.'

'God, yes, Gloria, imagine this happening and nothing to fall back on.' She shook her head as if pulling herself together. 'I'm being bloody stupid. I know Tony and I can't go on together, that it's a relationship that lost its way a long time ago – it was simply that neither of us was aware of it. And everything has happened so fast. I wish he wasn't so bloody laid-back about it. It's somewhat insulting.' She managed a weak laugh.

'Is there anyone else?'

'I don't think so.'

'Would you mind if there was?'

'I don't know, I doubt it. I don't feel like that about him any longer. It's fear of the unknown that's hard at my age. And not living here. I don't want to lose my home. I really think I feel worse about losing the house than my marriage ending. And what does that make of all those years? Wasted time?'

'Tell you what, why don't we do the washing up, get in the car and go and look at possible places for your cottage? We could go to some agents, get a few details. Maybe we could even view a couple. I love doing that – snooping about in other people's lives.'

'I had thought of the Thames valley, I like it there.'

'Then that's where we'll go, have a look-see.' Gloria began to stack the dishes.

3

Julius's morning had been very satisfactory. The first quarter of Barty's autobiography was finished and had been sent to Julius to reassure him as to its progress. He had read it and found it moving and riveting. It was early days but that morning he had a verbal agreement with the editor of the *Sunday Times* to buy the first serial rights of the book for a very hefty sum – a sum that would make the accountants happy for a change. Julius even allowed himself the pleasure of contemplating a trading-account balance sheet in the black again, something he had not dared to dream of for some time.

He had walked through the offices, which he always liked to do, seeing the various departments beavering away. But today was special, for today he had made his tour with good news to impart instead of lying about bad.

Lunch had been with Mike Pewter at his club. This had become almost a weekly ritual ever since the weekend at Peter's when he had turned down their offer of assistance. It was as if Mike and Peter were keeping a friendly eye on him. It amused him while he was touched by their concern. This lunch had been without Peter – away in New York with his masters.

'I don't like it, Julius. I don't like to see a good publisher going to rack and ruin as he is. It's not Peter's style to be at the beck and call of others. He should get out. Start up again if necessary. I keep telling him.'

'Maybe Costas's contract with him is watertight.'

'No, it isn't. I know. He told me his lawyers had found a loophole, should he want to jack it in. So why doesn't he?'

'A broken marriage and the inevitable divorce are probably problems enough for him at the moment without all the drama of resigning and starting again.'

'He hasn't even got a woman. It's unhealthy, an attractive man like him. He rarely goes out socially, just moons about that flat in the Barbican – like an expensive mausoleum, Lily described it.'

'I'd have thought another woman was the last complication he needed for the time being.'

'I thought he'd go for Gloria, you know. She'd suit him down to the ground – intelligent, attractive, as much in love with the business as he is. There's a woman who can raise the pulses if ever I saw one. Why doesn't he?'

'Really, Mike, I don't know. And if I did, I wouldn't dream of interfering.' Julius smiled with affection at the huge man opposite him who, being happy, like a child, wanted everyone else to be happy with him. 'I think I'll have the steak and kidney pudding, Mike. There's a definite nip in the air today – time for puddings, don't you think?'

'Always trust a man who likes his fodder, Julius, it's always been a rule of mine. Never fails. How about the Château Petrus? A marriage made in heaven, wouldn't you say?' He guffawed heartily and ordered for them both.

After his long, heavy lunch Julius walked in Hyde Park for an hour, in sunshine that had already lost its summer power, watching the nannies with their charges, enjoying seeing lovers entwined in each other's arms on the grass.

He had an appointment for tea with Sally Britain and, after signing his letters at the office, took a taxi to the Basil Street Hotel where Sally always stayed when in London. Women never failed to amaze Julius. Sally looked exactly as she had years ago. She must have aged, for sixteen years had passed since they were lovers. But to his eyes she was still the same, still as pretty, still as feminine. He enjoyed seeing her for in doing so he was able to capture, for just a little while, a whisper of the happy past.

It was September, so she was about to deliver to him her next book. It was a ritual they always indulged in. Tea with tiny finger sandwiches, Earl Grey, and then a cake or two. At that point Sally always said she should not eat one for the sake of her figure. And he always said what nonsense and how perfect she was. Then, laughing, from her briefcase she would present him with the perfectly typed manuscript, always wrapped in pretty paper and ribbons, like a present. That was the moment he always ordered champagne.

Two hours later, he kissed her goodbye.

'I'll read this tonight, and look forward to it,' he said, as he stepped into his taxi.

He collected his car and, hoping to avoid the worst of the traffic, decided not to bother with the motorway but to take the long route home. He had already called Jane to say he would be an hour late. The drive home was pleasant. The golden early autumn sun always seemed more beautiful than the white of the summer one. And as he motored along he noted the leaves beginning to change. Odd how some people found the autumn a sad time of year, he looked forward to it, loved it best of all.

Dinner was a light meal after such a lunch. Jane knew better than to prepare a rich one when he had been with Mike. That was an indication of advancing age, he had joked. Once he could have eaten two huge meals in a day, but the consommé and the sole were just perfect. He thanked her. He had reached the high spot of his day when he could go to the peace of his study, pour himself a large whisky and settle down to read Sally's manuscript.

At midnight, half-way through, he set the papers down. Wonderful, he smiled. Clever Sally, she never let them down. He had read this far and he still did not know who the murderer was. It was amazing that someone so sweet and feminine could produce such horror. He poured a small nightcap and climbed the stairs to bed.

He opened his window, sniffed appreciatively at the air, liking the hint of autumnal decay.

He climbed into bed and read for another hour. He puffed up his pillows to his liking and turned out his light at about one. He was quickly asleep for Julius never had trouble sleeping. At about three he died.

4

Crispin was very annoyed. He slammed the telephone down.

'Isn't that just bloody typical?' he said to Bee-Bee who was reclining on the bed in their suite, still breakfasting off a tray. 'Typical! He never liked me and then he ruins my honeymoon by dying.'

'Who died?'

'My Uncle Julius.'

'Darling, what super news! Now you'll be so rich and Daddy will be so pleased for you.' Bee-Bee beamed at him.

He crossed to the wardrobe and pulled down a case. He opened a drawer and began to hurl underpants and socks into it.

Bee-Bee set her tray on the floor and sat up on the bed. 'Why are you packing? You're not going back to England?' she asked anxiously.

'Sweetheart, I'm sorry, I have to. I know it's rotten for you. But there's so much for me to see to back home, I dare not risk being here.'

'But no one will expect you to miss your honeymoon for a silly old funeral.'

'I'm not just going back for the funeral. I've got things to do, wheels to set in motion,' he said with a pompous air. He looked at his watch, eleven, local time. With luck he could be back by three. His stomach was churning with excitement. At long last, he thought.

Mike Pewter had been in the office for an hour when his secretary buzzed him to say his wife was on the telephone. She had heard the news on the radio.

'Oh, Lily, no!' he groaned.

'I'm afraid so, my darling. But it was in his sleep, he didn't suffer. Think. Perhaps this is for the best, Julius of all people would have hated to be an invalid.'

'I bought him a huge lunch yesterday. Maybe it was too much for him. He'd hinted once or twice that his quack had told him to ease up a little.'

'Mike, no one could stop Julius enjoying his food and drink, it would be the same as someone trying to stop you.'

'Even so, Lily, I feel bad about it. It could be my fault. We did have two bottles of the Château Petrus, it seemed such a good idea,' he said sadly.

'I doubt if it made any difference. I've thought for some time that there was an air of resignation about Julius, as if he knew his time was short.'

'Oh, Lily. I feel so sad, I loved that man.'

'And he knew you did, that's important to remember.'

When he replaced the telephone Mike laid his large head on his arms and cried like a baby.

Barty Silver was informed as he sat under a large beach umbrella conducting business on three telephones and two fax machines. Gervase had come to him the moment he had picked the news up from the wire service. It was seven in the morning, local time. Barty would never dream of being up at such an hour at home, but when in the Bahamas he often worked this early, it was one of the reasons he was beginning to think seriously of spending more time here. 'Now that is sad,' he said. Barty hated it when people he knew and respected died and the older he became the worse it was. At his age, there wasn't time to replace these people in his life, was how he thought, and such people were becoming less and less in evidence.

By eleven he wondered if Joy was up. She spent too much time in bed, lying in late, and retiring soon after dinner. It was unhealthy, he thought, but he had not said as much to her, not really understanding the ways of women. But he did wonder if all this insisting on solitude and taking long walks on the beaches was a good idea. He had hoped this break would help her stop fretting about Hannah. Barty still had not resolved the problem for her and was frustrated he hadn't but her sadness over her daughter only made him all the more determined to succeed.

He summoned her maid and asked her to ask Mrs Trenchard to join him by the pool at her earliest convenience. Barty asked, he never ordered.

An hour later Joy appeared.

'Sad news, Joy, my girl. I didn't want anyone else to tell you.'

'Hannah?' she said immediately, clutching at her throat and going even paler than she was already.

'Hannah's fine. No, it's poor old Julius, went to sleep and passed on. What a way to go! I've got to go back for the funeral. Do you want to come, or would you rather stay here and rest?'

'I didn't know you were such great friends.'

'Oh, yes, Julius and I go back a long way. And in any case he was my publisher.' He smiled affectionately at her. 'Got to go, girl, show willing. And I've a thing or two to sort, know what I mean?' And he tapped the side of his nose with his finger, a gesture that irritated her. Her own reaction worried her.

'If you don't mind I think I'd rather stay here. It's harder in London, knowing Hannah's in the same city. Faith can go to the funeral in my place. There's sure to be a memorial service later, I'll go to that.'

'Of course, you stay and rest. I'll be back as soon as I can.' He patted her hand and wished he had the courage to lean over and kiss her. He did not for he was not certain of her reaction. He sensed that Joy was struggling with herself, reaching conclusions that he might not like.

Upon arrival in London, Crispin hired a chauffeur-driven car and made straight for Julius's house where, rightly, he guessed the family would have gathered. His mother was crying. Now that was odd, thought Crispin. She had despised her brother, and certainly never had a good word to say about him. Everyone knew that, so why the tears? He was quite shocked by Uncle Simon who looked as if he had aged ten years overnight. He seemed not to know where he was. But it was only nine months since he had been capable of screwing extra money out of him; he had been bright enough then, thought Crispin maliciously. Crispin could only conclude he must be drunk as he blundered about with Dulcett in anxious pursuit. His aunt Jane was a picture of composure but that was what one would have expected from her. John was stridently in evidence with his wife Poppy, who was already seriously bored at having to be in the country. Cousin Caroline, dry-eyed and steely, had appeared with her chinless husband, who appeared only able to talk about the weather and farm subsidies, subjects of stunning boredom to Crispin. It was a truly awful family he belonged to; thank God it was only necessary to see them at times like this. It was another indication of how inconsiderate Julius was – it was only last Saturday that he had had to endure them at his wedding. He could not wait to get away from his family. Diffidently he suggested that perhaps they should have a meeting to discuss the business.

Even he was surprised at the alacrity with which they had agreed; he had quite expected to have to wait until after the funeral.

He painted the gloomiest picture yet of the fortunes of Westall and Trim, neatly avoiding the coup of Barty's first serial rights. As financial director it was his sad duty to report that he felt the only possible solution was the sale of the firm to the highest bidder, even though it broke his heart, pained him, saddened him, all this said in as mournful a voice as he could muster and one which, to his surprise, he almost believed himself.

There was no hesitation from anyone; all agreed that the sale should proceed as quickly as possible. Perhaps Crispin could put out some feelers for them within the trade, they asked. Only Simon objected, wittering on that it was not what Julius would have wanted, and dabbing his eyes with a paint-stained handkerchief. To Crispin there was something obscene in having to witness old men crying, as if their bodily fluids were leaking. The others began to shuffle in their seats and look guilty. Crispin quickly pointed out that Simon had sold his interest, and with an expressive shrug of his shoulders implied that therefore his opinion was not worth listening to, let alone relevant.

Crispin declined his aunt's invitation to stay overnight, mumbling something about problems in London with his new house. He summoned his chauffeur and was driven rapidly back to London to the ever-open arms and thighs of his mistress Cleo.

Gloria had enjoyed her stay with Kate. She had insisted on taking Kate out to dinner the previous night in Graintry. Apart from wanting to repay her hospitality, Gloria had suggested the meal out for she dreaded Tony returning home, imagining how stilted the evening would be. She need not have worried, she did not even see him. He returned after they were both in bed and had gone by the time she was up in the morning.

'He eats out most evenings. I've offered to cook for him but he refuses. It's rather childish really, as if he's sulking,' Kate explained over breakfast.

Or as if he's got a bit on the side, thought Gloria, as she agreed with Kate.

They had spent most of that day in house-hunting again. They had found three possibles and Gloria felt she had left Kate in better spirits than she had found her.

It was six before she arrived home in London. Even though Elephant was telling her patiently enough that he wanted his supper she listened to her answering machine first. There was no call from Peter. And she had allowed herself to hope. Stupid of her. She turned on the television for the six o'clock news but she was in the kitchen feeding her dog when the report of Julius's death was repeated.

She poured herself a drink and wondered what to do with herself. She had been so convinced he would call that she had turned down Kate's invitation to stay another night – that would have been more fun than the prospect of an interminable evening alone. She supposed she could have a bath; after all, that was what she usually did when at a loose end.

She was half-way up the stairs when the front-door bell rang. Peter was on the doorstep.

'Peter! I expected you to telephone from New York. Not to turn up. What a wonderful surprise. Come in . . .' She was full of exuberance but it began to wane as she saw the serious expression on his face. Wrong again, Gloria, she told herself. He had come to tell her why he had returned to his wife – it was patently obvious. She led the way into her sitting room, glad to be in front of him so he could not see the bleakness on her own face.

He stood awkwardly, it seemed to her, in the middle of the room. She dived for the television and turned it off.

'Drink?' she asked brightly, anything to delay him telling her he was back with Hilary.

'You haven't heard?' he said.

'Heard what? Got some good gossip?' She forced herself to laugh.

'It's Julius. Last night . . . Gloria, I'm sorry there's no easy way to tell you this. He died.'

She stood there unable to take in what he was saying. 'Julius?' she asked, registering only that Peter was not speaking about himself and Hilary.

'In his sleep, apparently. I didn't know until I got off the plane an hour or so ago and picked up an *Evening Standard*.'

'You didn't get the message I left at the office? You came straight here?' Her voice was rising with excitement at the implication.

'I wanted to see you and be with you. I knew how desperately upset you would be. I knew you loved Julius too.'

It was then it hit her. It was then she realised what he had been saying. She felt self-repugnance that she should have reacted the way she did, thinking only of herself. 'Oh, no. Not Julius.' She began to cry, and he took her in his arms to comfort her.

It was some time before Gloria calmed down. Even as she cried she was unsure if all the tears were for Julius or if she was crying for something else. Was she also weeping with relief that Peter had come to her?

'We need a drink,' Peter finally said, when he was sure the storm of emotion was over.

'In the fridge,' she said. While Peter collected the wine, Gloria inspected herself in the mirror over the fireplace, dabbing with a Kleenex at the streaks of mascara around her eyes.

'Better?' he asked.

'Much. I'm sorry.'

'Don't even say it.' He smiled at her as he handed her a glass of white wine.

They sat reminiscing about Julius and the old times and had soon opened a second bottle.

They had both already had far too much to drink so it was a mistake to open yet another and she couldn't remember whose suggestion it was.

Nor, the following morning, did she have a clear recollection of who had suggested that he stay. When she awoke to find him sleeping beside her she had no idea if they had made love or not. She hoped not and yet at the same time . . . ?

As she watched him in his sleep, the strain from yesterday having completely disappeared, he looked young again. She would have liked to touch him, feel the stubble of his morning beard, touch his eyelids, but she stopped herself and contented herself with looking at him. He stirred, and then, as if her stare had woken him, he opened his eyes, blinked and then smiled a long lazy smile.

'Sorry about last night,' he said.

'Don't be silly, there's nothing to apologise for.'

'I was pissed. That's why I was so useless.'

'So was I,' she said, relieved that she had not let stupid, unthinking sex get in the way of this particular friendship, but wishing she could remember what had happened more clearly.

'I'm not now,' he said quietly, and she felt his hand under the cover tentatively search for her body. She felt a jolt of pleasure as his hand found her breast, she felt her nipples stiffen, felt that melting charge slide down through her body as if there was a hot line from her breasts to her pussy. Involuntarily, she moaned with pleasure. She did not want this, this was wrong, she would regret it, she must stop him. But then his mouth was at her breast and he was sucking her and she was lost.

He made love to her and she found herself responding to him in a way that was strange to her. She wanted to hold him, she wanted to give him happiness. His happiness was all that mattered. She did not think of taking from him, she forgot, so absorbed had she become in his contentment.

He was gentle, he was sensuous, he was rough, he was unkind, he was gentle. She had no idea what he would be doing to her next, all she knew was that she wanted him inside her – deep within her, safe, for ever.

Eventually she slumped back on the pillows, satiated and exhausted.

'Stupid old Hilary,' she chuckled.

'Lucky old me,' he grinned, and he was making love to her again and to her horror Gloria found she was crying. Tears were falling from her eyes, down her cheeks, damp on her body. They would not stop. He wiped them away gently.

'My darling, what's the matter?'

'I don't know. I'm sorry. It's so stupid. I think it's because I'm just so happy.'

'I didn't realise I was so good.'

'Oh, Peter . . . ' she said, and started laughing.

'I'm rather chuffed – after all, you must know what you're talking about.' He laughed with pleasure at what he thought was a good joke. Gloria froze inside. She looked away from him. He put his arm around her, she stiffened at his touch. He knew he should apologise, realised that his words could be so easily misinterpreted, but as so often with unfortunate remarks, they had slipped out before he had time to think. He opened his mouth as if to say something, and then changed his mind, afraid he might make matters worse. Instead he nuzzled her neck, and she turned to him and held him to her almost with desperation.

Roz had taken a long weekend break. Seeing Crispin the previous Saturday had upset her more than she had realised at the time. It was easy to pretend she still hated him when others were around but it was impossible to deceive herself. She knew he was selfish, cruel and self-seeking but he still had a hold over her.

She had borrowed an isolated cottage, belonging to a friend, near Brancaster beach in Norfolk. There was no radio and no television but Roz did not mind. She had come here for peace and quiet and to think. Her thoughts were concentrated on the thick envelope Julius had given her, realising it bestowed a considerable amount of power – enough to get Crispin back into her bed.

Roz slept in a bedroom with sloping ceiling and gingham curtains and the sound of the sea swishing on the sand. She slept, unaware that Julius was dead. At the foot of the bed was her handbag and in it, for safe-keeping, the letter from Julius to Gloria.

5

On the following Monday, Crispin was, to say the least, rather hurt by the unfriendly way in which both Peter Holt and Mike Pewter spoke to him when he called to say that, acting for the rest of the family, he wanted to talk about the sale of Westall and Trim.

'Good God, man! Have you no respect? You haven't even buried Julius yet,' Peter had snarled at him.

'Ghoul!' Mike had bellowed before slamming down the telephone.

If that was how they wanted it they could lump it, he said to himself. Tudor's had been very willing to talk and, what was more, he had an intriguing invitation from Barty Silver. Barty had made an appointment to see him, once Julius was interred. All this old-fashioned insistence on burial first was a waste of time as far as Crispin was concerned. Still, if that was what Barty wanted, he would go along with it.

He set about compiling figures for Tudor's. He knew they expected a snap decision, but they were not going to get it. He would let them dangle, certainly until he had seen Silver. And since Mike and Peter had been so rude, he would cast his net further afield. He made a call to a company chairman in Germany and planned what to say to his contacts in America, later in the day, when they were awake.

Mike and Peter met for lunch.

'What are we going to do about Westall's, Peter?'

'The way I snapped at Crispin, I shouldn't think Shotters is in the running.'

'The decision is not entirely his, is it? I don't have much time for Julius's son, but he's a good businessman, I hear. He'll want the best price and in the end the rest of the family will defer to him, the banker, not the publisher.'

'I don't know. I doubt if Shotters will be interested. Costas is screaming for retrenchment, not expansion. I had a rather sticky interview with him last week.'

'And . . .?'

'Oh, come on, Mike. I work for the man, you don't expect me to tell you the ins and outs of Shotters.' He laughed at Mike's hopeful cheek.

'Worth a try.' He bowed his head in mock shame. 'Did you know Barty is snooping about?'

'No. But then I'm not surprised. Ever since that party last year when the place was alive with publishers I've wondered what he's up to – he gave me a rare old grilling. And then, shortly after that, he started up that agency with Joy Trenchard. He's been flirting on the edges for some time.' —

'Yes, and then allowing his memoirs to go to Westall's when sense will tell you that they must have been the underbidders by thousands. Now why do that? Unless he intended one day to own it and reap the benefit for himself. I tell you, Peter, Barty in the business is not something I look forward to. The man seems to attract success like a fly-paper. What about you?'

'Sorry, what about me?' Peter put his head on one side, wondering what Mike had up his sleeve now.

'Why don't you bid for it? Get out of Shotters, have your own company again. You could afford it, they'll never sell for the amount Crispin is hoping for.'

'Me? No, thanks. For a start I could never work with Crispin and if I did do something – and I'm not saying I will . . .' He waggled his finger at Mike, laughing at him as he did so. 'If I did, I think I'd like to start again from scratch.'

'Crispin is the last thing to worry about. He isn't staying in publishing. He wants an academic life in Oxford or Cambridge and he's been sniffing around there like a weasel for months, sounding people out – so I've been told.'

'God help either university, then,' Peter said with feeling.

'What's Gloria going to do, I wonder?'

'For the time being she says she's staying put – she has her new list, which is important to her. She wants to see who buys before deciding anything.'

'Does she now?' Mike was grinning from ear to ear. 'So you've seen her again? Good.' He sat back with a contented expression, amused to see the discomfort on Peter's face.

'I had to see her about Julius.'

'Of course.' Mike folded his arms over his expansive chest.

'I knew how upset she would be.'

'Of course.'

'It isn't like that, Mike.'

'Oh no?'

'If we weren't in such civilised surroundings, I'd fling a bread roll at you.'

'You do that, Peter. You can't lie to me, my boy. I'm delighted.'

The atmosphere at Westall's was grim. Most of the women had been crying. No one could believe that Julius was not coming back – he had been so happy on Thursday, everyone was at pains to tell each other.

Little work was being done; instead people were meeting in offices in whispered huddles, wondering what was to happen to them all. This concern for their future in no way detracted from their genuine grief for the man and Julius would undoubtedly have approved of their concern for the future of his 'house'. Rumours were flying around.

By ten a strong rumour, emanating from the publicity office, was circulating that Julius's son was giving up banking and would be running everything. This news did not meet with any approval. They all had a reasonable and logical pessimism about those who entered publishing knowing nothing about it.

By eleven someone in the postroom said that one of the telephonists had overheard a conversation revealing that Crispin had bought out the family. This was met with feelings bordering on despair, for Crispin was one of the least popular members of staff. At that there was much bravado and talk of resignations.

Some felt that the family would never sell, that their sense of loyalty would be too great. These opinions tended to be held by the older members of staff – Liz, who had been an editor here for twenty-eight years, Effie, who had started as an accounts clerk twenty-seven years ago, and in any other firm by now would have been retired. And old Stan who burrowed away in the basement postroom and would never say how long he had worked for Westall's in case someone managed to work out that he was getting on for eighty.

'I hate to interrupt this conference, but we do have books to get out,' Gloria said, standing in the door of the publicity office where Val, Penny and several of the editors had been drinking copious amounts of coffee and smoking themselves silly. 'We've a week to *Winter Interlude*'s launch, or have you forgotten? I don't see over much in the publicity schedule for Kate yet. So, Val, if you don't mind?'

'Hard cow,' Penny said when Gloria had gone. 'How can she even think about the bloody book on a day like this?'

'No, she's right,' Val said. 'This endless debate is getting us nowhere. Mr Westall would not want the books to suffer in any way. Come on, Penny, have you spoken to the *Express* yet?'

The door to Julius's office was open, just as it always had been. Crispin had toyed with the idea of using it himself now he had so much checking to do, and so many telephone calls to make. But even Crispin was sensitive enough to know that it would not be popular, so he restricted himself to collecting some papers he needed for his calculations and congratulated himself that, with his cousin inheriting Julius's shares, he need not worry ever again about the identity of the Lepanto Trust – for whoever they were, their measly two per cent of the shares could not stop the sale, for millions, of Westall and Trim.

Gloria was trying to work but finding it increasingly difficult. She would have liked time to herself to think about last night and Peter but instead she was continually interrupted by the telephone. Those authors who had heard the news at the weekend were first to call and somehow someone, she did not know who, had delegated Gloria to deal with them and their worried enquiries. Then it seemed that all the authors had been calling each other, for a second wave of calls came from those who never bothered with newspapers or television but had been told by those who did. And so the reassurances had to be repeated all over again. Some of the calls were hard to take and Gloria felt as though she had spent the whole day in tears. The one from Sally Britain had been the hardest – she was beside herself with grief, and she and Gloria wept copious tears together.

By mid-afternoon she could take no more. She picked up a strangely subdued Elephant – he had been like that all day as if he had sensed that something was very much amiss – and called Crispin.

'Crispin, I'm going home. I'm sorry, but the telephone calls are getting me down. I've asked the switchboard to put them through to you. I'll see you tomorrow.'

'Fine, Gloria. Thank you for all your wonderful support today. By the way, the funeral is fixed, Thursday at eleven at his local parish church. I know I speak for the rest of the family when I say I hope you will be there,' he said, unctuously. Gloria longed to hit him.

Back home she began to prepare dinner. Peter had said he would come. She wanted him to come and she didn't. Part of her was longing to be in his arms and have him make love to her. Another, more logical, part was telling her it would be better not to see him and so avoid making a fool of herself by jumping to too many conclusions too quickly.

He had explained the note on the flowers. They were meant as an apology for boring her with his problems, something he would not repeat. The florist must have misheard him on the telephone and written 'bother' instead. When Gloria had not telephoned he had taken it as an indication that he had presumed on her friendship and had bored her to tears. His words had been music to her ears, but perhaps it was the siren song. It might be the truth, she told herself, but she was not willing to accept it entirely. She had been badly hurt, far worse than any other man had managed to hurt her. And like a person wary of fire because once badly burnt, she was not going to let it happen again. She still felt cold inside when she thought of his joke. Did he think that all she wanted was to be in bed with him? She realised men could and did sometimes say crass things when they had just made love – a form of shyness, she supposed. But, still, such reasoning did not help her. Last time, he had come here because he was upset: Gloria had left the firm that day, and he was still adjusting to the shock of his wife's adultery. This time he had come because Julius had died. She would believe him when both their lives were on an even keel, not now.

All the same, when he arrived she was pleased – even if she managed to disguise just how pleased.

'You seem distant, Gloria,' he said, as they sat eating the meal she had prepared.

'Do I? I'm sorry, I don't think I am.'

'You were so warm before.'

'Aha, well, things happen, don't they, Peter?'

'I don't understand, Gloria. What things? I've explained as best I can.'

'When I didn't call I don't understand why you didn't telephone me.'

'How could I? I presumed that I had offended you – as I had feared.'

'I want to believe you, Peter, but I'm not what you think I am.'

'And what's that?' He smiled, puzzled.

'I'm not interested in a one-night stand.'

'Nor am I.'

'I'm afraid of being hurt again.'

'I'd never hurt you, not intentionally.'

'I need time, Peter. My trust went wobbly.' She attempted to smile.

'Then you don't want to see me again?'

'Yes, of course I do,' she said quickly, and then immediately kicked herself for sounding so eager. 'At the moment, with the shock of Julius's death, we are both so upset that our emotions may not be reliable. We have to get over this before we can honestly look at each other and know how we truly feel.'

'Then you don't want me to stay tonight?'

'No, Peter. I can't risk it.' She was lying, she longed for him to stay, but she could not let him know. 'In a little while perhaps,' she said smiling at him, hoping he could understand her muddled logic.

Roz should have returned to work on the Monday. Instead she had telephoned in to say she was unwell but the secretary had not mentioned Julius's death. She wasn't ill, but she was enjoying the isolation. She took long walks on the beach debating what to do. Finally she had made a decision. It would be pointless to use the letter to try to get Crispin back in her bed. Nor could she bring herself to betray Julius's trust again – how would she ever face him? It would be better if she waited until he died. Then, hopefully, she would feel no guilt. Before giving the letter to Gloria, she could steam it open, photocopy it and then decide whether to invite Crispin round for dinner.

It was not until Tuesday evening that Roz set out in her ancient Mini for the drive back to London. Despite the car's age and rather dilapidated state, she sped along making good time, for the traffic was light. It seemed to Roz almost as if she was the only person awake in the world – there were so few lights on in the cottages and villages she passed. Her decision made, she felt quite lighthearted.

On the straight approach to Newmarket, she leant forward to fiddle with the radio, just as a front tyre blew. The car slewed across the road as she fought to gain control. She went for the brake but in her panic hit the accelerator. The small car slammed into a tree and burst into flames with an explosion that could be heard for miles. It was two days before her body was identified.

6

Publishers, authors, booksellers, friends, they were all there, filling the small church to overflowing, some having to stand outside in the drizzle, which everyone agreed was fitting weather. Julius would have been proud at the turn-out, they also acknowledged to themselves.

Gloria had travelled down with Peter and was glad she had for she loathed funerals, not as most people disliked them, no, more than that. She dreaded them, for invariably she disgraced herself by getting a fit of the giggles.

'I am the Resurrection and the Life saith the Lord . . .' The vicar appeared at the head of the procession intoning the words in a voice so sepulchral that Gloria longed to laugh. As Peter took hold of her hand and held it tight, she smiled a thin-lipped, desperately controlled smile at him.

She also knew that no matter how hard she tried she couldn't think holy thoughts. She never did. Somehow her thought patterns always went off at a silly tangent despite her efforts to order them otherwise. Today she found herself thinking she never wanted a funeral like this for herself. And she found herself wondering about being buried at sea. Which was also fine. But then she remembered her mother telling her that that was not such a good idea unless one took great care of the winds and tides – bodies were forever washing up at Mount's Bay, Penzance, so distressing to all concerned. This made her want to giggle so she hung on to Peter harder, which luckily he took as evidence of her grief. Such irreverence had nothing to do with her true feelings about Julius, it was how she was. Churches had that effect upon her.

The family were feeling pleased with everything. The turnout, the flowers, all had gone well. Sheltering under large umbrellas, which caused rather than prevented drips down the collar, John conducted his mother away from the graveside, followed by the family. Uncle Simon had been too poorly to attend; Dulcett had come but none of them regarded her as family so they all studiously ignored her.

One of the first to reach the family group was their lawyer, who scurried up with a young woman, dressed fittingly from head to toe in black. None of them recognised her.

'Mrs Westall, John . . .' Tristan Kemp said breathlessly, mopping not rain but sweat from his brow, unusual since the day was chilly. 'Is there somewhere private we can talk? It's rather urgent.'

'Now, Tristan? Hardly,' Jane Westall said, irritated with the epicene man she had never really liked but with whom Julius had insisted on dealing. Kemp's firm had always dealt with the Westalls' affairs.

'Yes, now, I'm afraid. This is Miss MacPherson from London.'

'How do you do?' Jane said in her most dismissive manner, and offered a limp handshake.

'I'm sorry to interrupt you now, Mrs Westall, at such a time,' Miss

MacPherson said in the clear accents of the Home Counties and not the Highlands. 'It is necessary, I am afraid, for I am acting on the express instructions of your late husband. You see, Mr Westall made another will and – '

'He did what?' John interrupted.

'Christ!' Crispin added.

'He left strict instructions that it was not to be mentioned until his funeral was over – he said he did not want any prior unpleasantness.'

'Have you seen this so-called will, Tristan?'

'Yes, Mrs Westall.'

'And?'

'I can see nothing wrong with it. Julius made it back in December. He wasn't ill or anything,' Tristan said lamely, aware that he was about to be the centre of a God-awful family row and wishing he was somewhere else.

'We shall see about that. Back to the house, everyone, and hurry – some of these people are coming back. You . . .' Jane pointed imperiously at the young woman. 'Have you a car? Then follow us.'

At which the family streaked for their limousines, leaving the congregation somewhat nonplussed as they stood waiting to make their condolences. Unsure what to do, the majority returned to their study of the many wreaths that lay on the grass which, incongruously, was scattered with confetti.

When a decent enough interval had elapsed, those guests considered sufficiently important by Jane Westall returned to the house to find Dulcett the only family member present. The rest were in heated conference in the library observed by a lachrymose Simon, who had not waited for their return before starting on the whisky.

Miss MacPherson was made of sterner fibre than Tristan Kemp. She moved not an inch in her deliberations despite being shouted at by the grieving family.

'I realise this must be most distressing for you, Mrs Westall, but the fact is that your husband made this will while of sound mind. It was duly drawn up, correctly witnessed. It is a valid will, Mrs Westall,' she said with such patent patience that Jane was doubly offended.

'You need not speak to me as if I were a five-year-old. Tristan, don't just stand there looking pathetic, tell us what we should do.' In her anger, Jane turned on the family advisor, who spoke hesitantly.

'I'm afraid there is nothing I can say. This is a proper will. I must say, I'm a little hurt he did not come to us, but no doubt Julius had his reasons.'

'Stop whimpering, Tristan. Of course, my mother will contest this will,' John said, pouring himself half a tumbler of whisky.

'I'm sure Mr Kemp's advice would be the same as mine, Mr Westall. It would be an expensive and futile exercise. Your mother has been most generously provided for – this house, and a considerable insurance policy. You and your sister have both been left a large amount of money from the sale of his paintings. A court would regard these legacies as fair and honourable. But apart from that there is this clause that your father insisted upon. I'm afraid if any of you do contest this will, or block the transfer of shares, then his instructions are quite clear, he wishes that his shares and proceeds from his paintings should go to the Battersea Dogs' Home. No, thank you, Mr Westall, I won't have a drink, I must be getting back. I've left a copy of the will with Mr Kemp. Thank you all,' she said, with more than a hint of irony, packed up her briefcase and left them.

'Kemp, get us out of this.' Crispin's voice had risen an octave with emotion.

'There's nothing to be said. Miss MacPherson has said it all.'

'I don't believe this.' John had slumped in a chair, his head in his hands in despair.

'This trust my husband has set up for his employees, is that legal? Could he do that?' Jane asked Tristan.

'Perfectly legal, Mrs Westall. A man may do as he wishes with his estate.'

'Well, it's wrong. This is just typical of Julius, he always was a vindictive man.'

'He bloody wasn't! How dare you say that of him.' Simon had leapt to his feet, tears of grief replaced by a scowl of anger. 'A better man there never was. His tragedy was ending up with you lot as a family. I'm not surprised he did this. He loved the firm, he must have known what you all planned. You know what? I'm glad, good for Julius!' And he suddenly roared with laughter.

'Oh, shut up, you senile old fool,' Crispin shouted.

'I wish you lot would stop caterwauling, I've got to think,' John said with irritation. 'Look, Kemp, if my memory serves me right, the terms of the Westall's articles are that shares have to be offered to the existing shareholders first. If no one wants to buy, then the new shareholders have to be agreed by a majority?'

'That is certainly so.'

'Then there's no problem. My mother, aunt and Crispin refuse to have the employees as shareholders.'

'We would have to buy them out,' Crispin said, but cheering up immeasurably. 'You could arrange the finance for that, John. We'd recoup the moment we sold out.'

'Hang on, where would that leave Caroline?' It was her husband Bertie speaking, a rare occurrence. 'It doesn't help her or John. They would lose out. All that would mean is that you existing shareholders would reap everything.'

'You'd have to trust us, Bertie, old chap.' Crispin flashed one of his biggest smiles, but Bertie looked very doubtful.

'No, that's no good. Bertie's right, there's too much at stake,' John said, having second thoughts and no intention of trusting any of them.

'Miss MacPherson has told you what would happen should any of you block the transfer of the shares to a trust for the employees. Mrs Westall would still benefit from the insurance policy, but this house would be sold and Mrs Westall would live in a cottage to be retained for her on the estate. And John and Caroline would not benefit at all. Now we don't want that do we?' Tristan smiled, he was feeling less in awe of them now. In fact, he was rather enjoying watching them squirm.

'I'm not losing out on the paintings as well,' John said with feeling.

'Aren't you all panicking unnecessarily? Everyone has done very well – even you, Caroline. Jane will be left most comfortably. And if it's what my brother wanted . . . It would be typical of Julius that even if the company is sold – and I do believe he thought that inevitable himself – that his employees should benefit.' It was Marge speaking up for the first time.

'Mother! I don't believe you're saying this.' Crispin faced Marge. 'You always said you loathed him.'

'Did I? I don't remember,' she said dismissively to her son. 'I may not have agreed with everything he did,' Marge looked pointedly at her sister-in-law, 'but he was my brother and I loved him. And, if you must know, I find this haggling over poor Julius's wishes unseemly in the extreme. I should most certainly vote in favour of the employees' trust.'

'I'm sorry, Crispin, but this house means too much to me and I cannot risk ending my days in a poky cottage. I think it is all grossly unfair and spiteful. I shall never forgive Julius, but I would vote for the employees' trust with Marge. You'd be outvoted, Crispin,' said Jane with a finality that brooked no argument.

'Good show!' Simon clapped.

'There's one thing you all seem to have forgotten.' Crispin drawled, proud he was able to conceal his seething anger. 'There's the little matter of the Lepanto Trust and its decisive two per cent. We have to find out who this wretched trust is, approach them, buy them out. All right, we lose half, but at least the employees' trust could not stop us selling the whole lot, for then we should be in the majority. And I'm sure that, after this fiasco, the less we have to do with the company in the future, the better.' There was a murmur of agreement to this.

'That bloody Lepanto Trust,' said John. 'I've tried many times to find out who it is. Have you had any luck, Crispin?'

'No, but then I was looking with my hand tied behind my back. I had no access to his study here, his safe . . . I'm sure now that it will be easy enough.' He smiled. He could afford to: whatever happened, it did not alter his share in the pay-out when the business was sold.

'Who is this Gloria Catchpole?' Jane asked, pronouncing the name as if it was something indescribable.

'She's an editor, she worked for Julius years ago,' said Crispin.

'And he wishes her to be the new managing director. Would she be capable?'

'Very, I fear.'

'And why make Peter Holt and that mountain of a man Pewter this trust's trustees?'

'Mischief, I should think. He knows they would fight tooth and nail to keep it as it is and never sell,' Crispin explained.

'Then we have to find out who or what the Lepanto Trust is before this unholy trinity do, don't we? Then we shall sell and that will be an end to all this nonsense. Now, if everyone will excuse me, I have guests to attend to.' Jane stood up and regally left the room, the others trailing along behind her.

Gloria could not understand why Mrs Westall was so rude to her when she offered her condolences. She had met her once or twice, but only fleetingly, and nothing she had ever done could justify the way the woman had swept past her ignoring her completely.

'What did you do?' Peter grinned at her.

'A difficult woman, I shouldn't let her upset you,' Mike consoled her.

'Well, well. What a clever little group we have here.' Crispin had sidled up to them. 'I really think that in the circumstances it would be more tactful if you all left my aunt's house, don't you?'

'What the hell are you going on about, Crispin?'

'Oh, come, Mike. You and my uncle were as thick as thieves. You're not going to tell me that you don't know what the old bastard has done?'

'Not the foggiest,' Mike said puffing a large amount of cigar smoke in the direction of Crispin, who ignored the smoke and looked at him with cynical disbelief.

'What did you have to do, Gloria, to gain such an advantage? Screw the old roué? No, I suppose at his age that was probably out. Little bit of the old fellatio? Was that it?'

'Crispin, you'll apologise for that.' Peter squared up to him.

Gloria said nothing but her hand swished out and slapped him hard across the cheek. It failed to remove his smile however, he merely stood rubbing his cheek where the blow had fallen.

'What other conclusions are we to come to?' Crispin sneered.

'I wish you would get it into your fat head, Crispin, none of us has an inkling what the hell you are going on about,' Mike growled.

'Julius's will. He's left the whole of his shares to an employees' trust – me excluded, of course, but that's what I would expect from my loving uncle. He has decreed that sweet Gloria here is to be managing director and you and Peter are to be the trustees. And you tell me you knew none of that?' At the expressions of total shock on their faces he began to wonder if they had spoken the truth after all. 'It doesn't matter, though. I'll tell you now, in your new capacity. You only have forty-nine per cent of the shares and the family intend to sell – but, I hasten to add, not to Pewter's or Shotters. Sorry about that.' He bowed and left the three standing, glasses in hand, looking at each other with total amazement.

'Good God, I'd no idea. You, Peter?'

'Not a word.'

'Nor me,' added Gloria.

'Good old Julius. He was always a fighter. Well, we can't let them sell, can we? Nor stay here. Need a lift?'

And without saying the customary goodbyes, they left, unsure still that it was true, and even more unsure how they were to stop the family.

7

As the day for the launch of her book came nearer, Kate felt herself being swept along by events.

Never confident of how she looked, she had taken a severe knock when, in Graintry, she had sat in the studio of the one and only local photographer.

'I hate having my photograph taken,' she laughed, feeling awkward, as the man fiddled with the lights and equipment. 'Hope I don't break your camera,' she giggled but seeing the bored expression on his face realised she was probably repeating a cliché he had heard a million times before.

'You sure you want black and white?' he asked.

'Yes, that's what I was told.'

'Most people want colour these days, the lighting has to be different for black and white.'

'Sorry,' she said and wondered what it was about her that made her feel she had to apologise for everything.

'What did you say this was for?'

'It's an author photo, for promotions, posters and book jackets, that sort of thing,' she said, brightening up, presuming he would be complimented by her choosing him to take something so important.

'Well, there's not much point in trying to make you look glamorous then, is there?' he had replied.

That had been a couple of months ago, now she held her book in her hand, the photograph on the back cover. He had been right, she certainly did not look glamorous, far from it, she looked ordinary – mumsy, if she was honest. But the book, that was something else. Julius had been right, she did cry when she saw it. She could not leave it alone, but kept picking it up, admiring it, stroking it, unable to believe that it had really come about. She wished she could tell him of her reaction to the book and thank him. She had been saddened to hear of his death; she did not know enough about publishing to know that it might mean her own future was at stake.

She was waiting, hair freshly shampooed and blow-dried, made up and smartly dressed in a red skirt and black sweater, for her first interview. Never having done such a thing before she did not know what to expect, but at least it was for the local paper, she consoled herself, which might be an easier baptism than the national who had asked to interview her next week.

Dee Masters was young, with too much make-up, dressed in a black leather miniskirt and a bright green cotton sweater so tight her nipples protruded. She played constantly with the dangling earrings she wore and which kept getting tangled in her long hair. She was evidently proud of her peroxided mane, for she played with that constantly too, brushing it out of the way, flicking it back, tossing her head so it swished from side to side. Kate was not impressed, merely hoped that with all that flicking, tossing and swishing she did not have dandruff.

Since the interview was to be about her and the book she was somewhat nonplussed when Dee blithely announced she had not read it.

'Ah, I see,' said Kate, though she longed to say, Why not?

'So many books land on my desk it's just impossible to read them all,' Dee said cheerfully as if reading her mind. 'In any case, it might be a bad idea. What if I hated your book? It might colour how I react to you as a person and so make for a bad interview. That's what I've found in the past.'

Knowing nothing about journalism there was no way Kate felt she had the right to argue with Dee, even though she found her argument somewhat weak. She felt that the more probable explanation was that Dee was too lazy and could not be bothered.

'Far better if you tell me what your book's about.' Dee produced a small tape-recorder from the copious bag she carried. 'You don't mind, do you?'

In fact Kate did mind: if having her photograph taken was agony, listening to her own voice played back on a tape-recorder was her idea of hell. She only had to catch sight of one of the machines and her voice changed its key, she sounded stilted and could only speak with a ludicrously exaggerated accent. 'That's fine,' she said, despising herself for not objecting. Diffidently, she began to talk. Writing it had been easier, she concluded, than having to explain it. The plot, when described as now, seemed weak and rather pointless.

'Sounds riveting,' said Dee, but still did not say she would read it. 'Right, now I want to hear all about you.'

Kate began the monologue of her ordinary life and, as she always did, ended up apologising for it. 'Not a lot for you to write about, is there?'

'Amazing achievement, though, I envy you. I'd love to write a novel.'

'Really? Why don't you? I'm sure that with all your writing you could,' Kate said encouragingly.

'Oh, I could do it easily enough,' Dee said confidently. 'It's finding the time, that's the problem. If I had the time, I would.' Dee flicked her hair for the umpteenth time. Kate, remembering how she had fitted in her writing around home and family, made no comment. 'Why do you think you suddenly decided to write?'

'I don't think I could have done it at an earlier age. I'd always been a full-time mother, you see. Bringing up a family requires a lot of energy – mental I mean, not just physical. But there comes a time when the children don't need you quite so much and you're left with this great reservoir of mental energy and what do you do with it? That's a dangerous time for a woman –

she can go on tranquillisers or she can *do* something. I was lucky, I found writing.'

'So you would say you were impelled by the menopause into writing?' Dee leant forward with interest.

'That's not exactly what I said. No.'

'Do you think that women like you write these books because they are disappointed in their own lives? That you create a fantasy world as an escape, where the men are perfect, the sex divine?' Dee chortled.

'No, I don't,' Kate said, offended, but more, she felt uncomfortable that Dee might be a little too close to the truth for comfort.

'What is more to the point, do you think you are really being fair to your own sex, Kate?'

'I'm sorry, I don't understand.'

'You write of a fantasy world with fantasy men and women – let's face it, I've never met anyone remotely like these heroes and heroines. Have you? It's all impossibly unattainable to a woman trapped in a council flat with three kids under five, it could make her even more bitter with her lot in life. Wouldn't you agree?' Dee smiled expansively, exposing overlarge teeth and swishing her hair over her shoulder with a confident jerk of the head.

Kate felt herself bridling. 'I don't see why women can't have a degree of escapism. No one criticises thriller writers – do men become frustrated because they're not 007? But, in any case, if you had taken the trouble to read my book you would have found out it isn't like that.' Kate wished she had the courage to ask this patronising woman to leave. But if she did, what would she write about her? 'It's all a matter of opinion, isn't it?' she added and loathed herself for being so wimpish.

'And your husband – Tony, isn't it?' Dee continued to smile as if she had not even noticed that Kate had been sharp with her. 'How does Tony feel about it all? He must be very proud of you.'

Kate made a fatal mistake. She laughed a small bitter laugh which Dee swooped on with all the instincts of a vulture.

'He's not proud?'

'I didn't say that. Of course he is ... I don't know ... I mean, he never said, he's not like that. And I didn't ask ...' Her voice trailed off lamely.

Dee leant forward and pointedly switched off the tape-recorder. 'There that's better, there are some things best not taken down on tape.' She smiled, a small sympathetic one this time, and patted Kate's hand. 'There. Quite honestly, Kate, I sense you are not totally happy with your success. I've turned the machine off, you can talk to me if you like.'

'No, really. I'm more than pleased.'

'It's not always easy is it, being a career woman? I know. You can't imagine the trouble I've had with my husband. He wants it to be like it was with his father and mother – me at home, cooking his meals, always there waiting for him. He hates me working, can't understand my ambition.'

'Really?' Kate said with interest. She made some sandwiches and opened a bottle of wine, and for the next hour she had a wonderful time talking to this woman who understood her problems. They talked of the impossibility of men, and how hard it was to be a successful woman in a man's world.

By the time the newspaper photographer came Kate felt she had made a new friend, and she could not understand why she had been suspicious of her. Dee even understood how she hated to be photographed. She fussed about, checking Kate's make-up, rearranging her hair, advising her where to sit and stand for the best results. Pictures were taken of her in the kitchen, drawing room, at her desk, in the garden. When it was time for Dee to go it was with promises that they would meet up again and soon.

During this period Kate felt intensely lonely. She was approaching so many new and exciting experiences and yet there was no one to share them with, no one to reassure her she was doing all right. She hardly ever saw Tony, he left early and returned late. At weekends he had taken to going away. She had initially asked where but he was obviously loath to tell her so she stopped asking. Lucy had been walking in the Lake District and was now involved with her imminent departure to university. Pam, following Faith's interest in her work, had embarked on a schedule of writing so strict that she did not have time to see Kate, she said.

As the date for the completion of the house sale approached she viewed it with increasing alarm. She knew she should be beginning to pack yet could not bring herself to do anything about it. That would be too final. Until the contract was signed there was always the chance that they might sort something out between them – if only she could get Tony on his own to speak to. It was all made worse when Lucy finally went and Kate had to cope with the peculiar emptiness of a house when a child had grown up and left. She had herself driven Lucy to Cambridge.

'You are sure you're going to be all right, aren't you, Mum?' Lucy had asked as they drove along.

'Of course,' Kate replied brightly. She could not tell her daughter the truth and spoil these first important and exciting days in a new environment.

'Will you be lonely when you move?'

'Good gracious, no. I'm getting used to being alone. What do I see of your father now?'

'Yes, but you've had me pottering in and out during the past weeks and what about leaving Pam and all your friends? Don't you think you should have stayed in the area?'

'No, that's one thing I could not do. Being the odd one out at dinner parties when once I'd been part of a couple. Perhaps meeting Tony at a function, which would be so embarrassing for everyone else. It's best to make a clean break, I think.'

'But you've never had to live alone before.'

'I've my writing, you can't be lonely when you've got dozens of characters in your head all longing to be let out.'

'Are you *sure* you're doing the right thing?'

'The decision has been taken out of my hands, Lucy. Your father doesn't appear to want to talk to me about it.'

'What do you want to do?'

'I'd like to stay just the way I am but with your father understanding and accepting my writing. Since there seems to be fat chance of that, I don't have much alternative, do I?' She shrugged her shoulders.

'Do you love Dad?'

'You know, Lucy, I don't think I know what love is any more. I might write about it but as for myself and your father, who the hell knows? I'm fond of him. But is that enough?'

'You might meet someone else.'

'Me? You must be joking.' Kate laughed.

'I don't know. You're very attractive, you know, especially now you've lost weight, and Pam was so right about your hair.'

'Me? Attractive?' Kate showed she was amused by her daughter's assessment, but secretly she was more than pleased. And on the drive back oddly she found herself thinking of Stewart Dorchester, the reporter she had met at Barty's party, all that time ago and who, she often found, popped into her thoughts for no apparent reason. She wondered if they might bump into each other again.

The tabloid papers were due in the shape of Sybil Cavay from the *Daily News*. She had been nervous enough waiting for Dee from the *Graintry Echo*; this day she felt physically sick. Sybil Cavay was known as the Shrew of Shrews. She was proud of the title and she honed her sarcasm carefully to retain it. It was a rare interview where Sybil did not lash out with her pen. The problem she set for publicity departments was that she was read by millions. On the days when her interview appeared sales of the *News* were larger than any other day. But occasionally someone took her fancy and then no one could be kinder or heap more praise. So risks were taken but, to protect Kate, Val had volunteered to be present.

Kate made herself up and not liking the effect cleaned it all off and started again, trying hard to remember all the tips the woman on the make-up counter in Dingle's had given her. She dressed and then decided the blue dress she had on made her look dowdy. She changed into a red one, which she thought made her look flighty. Eventually she chose a pair of black silk trousers and a baggy white lawn shirt she had just bought. She put on two long chains that looked gold even though they weren't, tucked a red scarf in the collar and laughed at herself that she had to have something red about her. Would this do? She looked at her reflection in the mirror, twisting round to try to see how she looked from the back, and hoping the girl in the shop had not lied when she had reassured Kate that her bottom was not too big for trousers, for Sybil of all people would write about it if it was. She glanced at her watch. She would have to do, the reporter would be here in five minutes. She took one last look at herself. Once on her own she would no longer be able to buy garments like these. She supposed she would be back to watching the pennies – still, it had been fun while it lasted.

She fussed about in the drawing room wondering where on earth had Val got to. And then the doorbell rang.

Kate opened the door with a smile on her face which she was sure looked as false as it was. But the smile changed into one of genuine pleasure.

'Stewart!' she exclaimed.

'Hope you're not disappointed it's me rather than Sybil?' He grinned.

'Disappointed? Relieved, more like!' she said, holding the door open wide and welcoming him.

'Sybil sends her apologies, she was held up and I volunteered to take her place.' He laughed the rich laugh that so attracted her when they had met at Barty's. He was not about to tell her that as soon as he had heard who was to interview her he had pulled rank and insisted he do it himself. There was no way he was going to allow Sybil loose on someone like Kate.

'I thought you concentrated on politicians and world leaders?' She showed him into the drawing room.

'Not always. I need some treats.' He smiled at her and she felt suddenly shy.

'I have to tell you straight away, Kate, I liked your book enormously. I read it in one sitting. Is it really a first novel? I'm amazed.'

From such a beginning Kate feared it could only get worse. It did not; talking to Stewart about her writing and the book was like talking to an old friend, one who understood instinctively what she was trying to say. Unlike Dee he did not seem to be particularly interested in her private life.

His photographer arrived when they were only half through and the ritual was repeated all over again – photos in every room, with the last in the garden.

The photographer collected his gear and left.

'Fancy lunch?' Stewart asked her.

'You're hungry? I could rustle up something for us.'

'You don't want to do that. Let me take you out.'

'Oh, I could hardly . . .' she began, flustered.

'It's on expenses,' he said, as if in explanation.

'That would be lovely,' she answered feeling that that would be perfectly correct, a professional lunch, no more no less. And she drove them into Graintry.

She didn't know why but when they entered the restaurant she wanted someone she knew to be there, to see her with this man. She felt strangely proud to be with him.

He insisted she had a drink and she accepted even though she had resolved she wouldn't. And when she began to decide what to eat, choosing carefully the less fattening dishes, he insisted she had the lobster as he was going to.

'But my diet . . .' she protested.

'I think you're perfect,' he said and she felt herself blushing. And he ordered sauté potatoes as if to confirm his opinion.

He looked after her, that was what was so strange and pleasant about this lunch. He seemed to want to please her, to try to anticipate whatever she wanted. Several times his hand brushed against hers and she wondered if she dared think it was not an accident.

She could not remember ever talking so much to someone who, after all, was a virtual stranger. But then she began to discover they had far more in common than she had realised. Stewart had been divorced for two years and he understood totally her feelings of confusion and fear.

'It's the sense of failure, that's the worst thing to bear, I found,' he said.

'Isn't it?' she answered with feeling. 'Wondering if all the past years have been a waste.'

'They're not, you know, that's what you'll learn eventually. And the guilt will go, one person doesn't cause a break-up.'

'That's what I keep trying to tell myself,' she said a shade woefully. He put his hand across the table and laid it on hers. She was struck by the warmth of his touch.

'Poor Kate, I feel for you. But I promise you, the guilt will go and the fear. There are advantages, too. Being able to do what you want, meeting new people. It's been an exciting time for me, finding myself again, if you like.'

'Do you really think so?' she asked, willing him to keep his hand on hers and feeling ridiculously disappointed when he removed it and offered her a cigarette instead.

They lingered over coffee and were reluctant to go but finally even they could not ignore the exasperated expressions of the waiters.

Shyly she asked him if he would like to come back to tea. He said he would love to but he had an appointment in London he could not miss. She covered up her regret and drove him to the station.

On the way home she wished she hadn't invited him. How foolish of her, too forward. He had just been friendly, nothing more. It was probably her loneliness that made her imagine and long for something more.

Unexpectedly Tony was at the house when she arrived.

'Had guests?' He nodded at the coffee cups she had forgotten to clear up in the drawing room before going out.

'A reporter from the *Daily News* and his photographer.'

'My, my. The big time,' he said.

She looked up, but he was smiling, he had not meant it unpleasantly.

'Yes. Apparently I'm very lucky, not many first-time novelists get much media attention.'

'Why you, then?'

'I think they're interested that I've taken it up in middle age – you know, there's so much fuss these days about the forty- and fifty-year-olds, with families away and with oodles of money and no mortgages to pay.'

'Then we're hardly typical of them, are we?' He was laughing.

'Would you like me to cook you supper tonight?' she asked, emboldened by his good humour.

'That would be very nice, thanks. I need to sort out some papers in my study. And, Kate, we should get down to thinking about who's having what, shouldn't we?'

She agreed even though it was the last thing she wanted to do. As she began preparing the meal she wondered if tonight she should talk to him, grab at this opportunity of him being there especially as he was in a good mood. At some point, before it was too late, she had to try to explain that this was not really what she wanted – that somehow circumstances had just seemed to scoop them up and rush them into making idiotic decisions.

They sat in the dining room. Kate had laid the table with special care and had even lit candles. She had cooked his favourite meal – duck breasts in an orange and brandy sauce with mangetout peas, and had asked him to select one of the better wines to go with it.

'I've made a list of the things that I would really rather have – my mother's bureau, the bookcase in my study and that picture of boats we bought in St Ives ... those sort of things.' He handed her a list of items, neatly typed, across the table.

'I haven't even begun to think about what I want to take.'

'How big's the cottage you've decided on?'

'Minute, compared with this. It's got three bedrooms but most of the bedroom furniture will be too big for it. And the sitting room's half the size of the one here.'

'We'll have to sell what's left over and divide the proceeds,' he said with uncharacteristic reasonableness.

'Tony ...' she looked at him a wistful expression on her face. 'Look, I don't want any of this. I never meant it to happen.'

'I thought you were bored to tears with me.'

'No, not you. I was bored with myself – an entirely different thing altogether. I know we haven't been getting on, but that's happened in the past and we've weathered it. Why can't we weather it this time?'

'Too much has changed, you especially. I don't think even now you're aware of how much you have altered, Kate. You're not my Kate any more.'

'That's silly, Tony. Of course I am. All right, I've a career now, but that's the only difference. And I've been thinking, with both children off our hands, I shall have so much more time that my writing isn't going to affect you nearly as much as it has done.'

'It's more complicated than that, Kate. It isn't just what has happened to us. It's what has happened to me.' He looked down at the book beside his plate for what seemed an inordinate time. 'There's someone else, Kate. I want a divorce because I want to marry again.'

'Oh, I see,' she said politely, while she felt her skin tauten, her stomach lurch, her mind rejecting such an unlikely idea. 'Well, that's that, then, isn't it?' She smiled bravely.

'Yes, I suppose so,' he replied, picking up his book as he always did between courses.

'I made a lemon mousse, you like that, don't you?' She escaped to the kitchen to fetch the pudding so that he could not see how close to tears she was. But she did not cry: the tears stayed locked inside her. They were not so much for losing him to another woman, but that her marriage had ended. It was marriage she wanted, not necessarily him. It was his picking up his book at such a critical moment in both their lives that told her that.

8

Prior to the meeting of the shareholders of Westall and Trim, when the employees' trust's shareholding was to be voted upon, Gloria in her capacity of acting managing director called all the staff together. Her position as a director was also to be voted on at the same meeting.

They gathered in Julius's office. For some, it was the first time they had been in there since he had died. The room was exactly the same, except the walls were bare where his pictures had once hung. Otherwise it was as if he had just popped out of the room for a moment. It even smelt of him. Gloria had chosen this room on purpose: with such important decisions to be made she wanted to feel his presence, wanted to try to be close to him, and instinctively she felt it was what the others wanted also.

'I'm not sure, but I think the family are likely to announce that they wish to sell the company.' Consternation and cries of 'Shame' followed this information. She held up her hand to silence them. 'Obviously we ourselves are going to have to vote on this issue. Our trustees Peter Holt and Mike Pewter have asked me to discuss it with you. Apparently, the decision whether to vote our shares for selling or not is theirs to make. They feel that it would not be fair for them to act without prior consultation with you. I gather that they would act on a majority consensus.'

'It would be wicked to sell. Mr Westall left us the shares to preserve the company not to let it go to the highest bidder the moment he is dead,' Effie from accounts looked upset and flustered as she spoke.

'I know, Effie, but we have to accept that there is a lot of money at stake. If it is sold, everyone in this room stands to benefit.'

'You sound as if you want it to go,' Ben from design said a little belligerently.

'Gloria hasn't been with us long,' Liz said with an audible sniff. 'It's not the sacred trust to her that it is to some of us.'

Gloria loathed emotional talk such as that and felt it could only cloud the issue. 'We all care, Liz, probably as much as you do. For some of us how the voting goes can affect our future careers,' she said pointedly. Liz was not only on the brink of retirement, but Gloria knew she had been one of the first to complain about the advent of Gloria's new list. 'You've obviously forgotten that my first job was with Westall's. I love this firm. And, in any case, as one of the newer members of staff now, I don't stand to get much money in the event of a sale. As you well know, Mr Westall made sure in the terms he drew up that those with the longest service in the firm benefit the most. I want everyone to know the facts and to know what they might be voting for.'

'What sort of sums are they expecting to get?' Ben asked. 'After all, let's face it, the poor firm hasn't been doing too well recently.'

'Peter says that Crispin is hoping for a ludicrous sum, but that between five and six million pounds is probably more realistic and even that, given the present market and our trading figures, is a long way from being guaranteed. Like everything that's for sale, it would depend on how desperate someone is to buy the name of Westall. So you see why we have to consider the facts. There are thirty-five of us. Those ten of you who have worked here the longest stand to reap a small fortune. Even for the rest it would be a considerable windfall.'

There was a lot of shuffling and whispered conversations between the group.

'Perhaps you would all like a little more time to think? Say you all sleep on it and we'll vote tomorrow.'

'When's the meeting?'

'Tomorrow afternoon.'

'I don't think we need time, Gloria. I think most of us have made up our minds. Maybe we should first vote on whether we should vote,' said Ben, who seemed to have taken on the role of spokesman.

There was a show of hands: the vast majority wanted to vote now. 'Let's get it over with,' someone shouted from the back of the room.

'Fine, then the vote is – should we ask our trustees to vote for or against the sale of this company?' Gloria said with sinking heart. 'I suggest we do a paper vote and that way no one will feel intimidated one way or the other.' She asked Rachel to cut up pieces of paper. 'A simple "yes" or "no" will suffice.'

'Do you honestly think the trustees will act on our decision if they don't have to?' Ben asked in the sort of sceptical voice that implied a lifetime of being overriden by those in authority.

'I think they will. Why else would they request that we discuss it and vote on it ourselves?'

Gloria felt tired. She had spent most of last evening arguing with Peter and Mike about the fate of Westall's. She felt strongly that Julius had made them trustees to ensure that this very situation did not happen. It seemed to her that if they let it go ahead they were no better than Crispin and the others. It was obvious, she argued, which way the employees would vote. Salaries in publishing were not high – Peter and Mike should know better than most since they paid them, she had said rather acidly. The workforce at Westall's was no different from any other – they had mortgages, children to educate and how many could afford to turn their backs on ready money like this?

'Don't you see what you're doing?' she had asked them angrily. 'By letting the staff decide the firm's fate you're ignoring Julius's wishes.'

'Gloria, we hear what you're saying.' Mike had spoken patiently. 'But Julius has put us in an invidious position. He did not make his intentions clear and there is no way we wish to be accused of mishandling the employees' affairs.'

'Legally it could be dodgy, too, Gloria. We could end up by being sued if we're not careful. There's no other way,' Peter had said firmly. Gloria had fallen silent but had looked at Peter amazed. How could they be lovers and have such different views? If she had been a trustee she would have taken the risk for the sake of the firm, she knew she would.

Rachel handed out the papers. Some preferred to go away and vote in private. It was an hour before Rachel had collected all the papers and placed them on Gloria's desk. She began to unfold them and to place them in piles. There were two spoilt papers with 'don't know' written on them. But Julius would have been proud: on the other thirty-three was written 'No'. He obviously knew his employees better than Gloria did.

The following day the shareholders met in the boardroom. There was an atmosphere of animosity as if Gloria and the other two had somehow engineered the whole thing. She was glad that she had the moral support of both Peter and Mike. As they walked in Peter took her hand and squeezed it encouragingly. She smiled gratefully. Everyone took their places around the table at the appointed time. Marge, as largest shareholder and senior family member, took the chair. No one objected.

'Who is Lepanto?' Peter asked pointing to the empty chair beside him.

'Ah, who indeed?' Crispin smiled superciliously, unpleasantly. 'The important thing is, they own two per cent of the shares.'

'So, a decisive interest.' Peter looked thoughtful.

'Exactly,' Crispin smirked.

'In the past, Julius always had their proxy,' Marge explained.

'So who has it now?' Peter asked.

'No one.'

'Were they informed of this meeting?' Peter was being very serious.

'They were,' Crispin said smugly.

'So where are they?'

'They'll be here.' Crispin spoke with confidence. He had written at length to the trust, care of the bank, explaining the reason for this meeting and its importance. He had outlined the amount of money that would be at stake if the company was sold and, using his figures, what Lepanto's share would be. He was confident that no one would miss such a meeting in the circumstances.

'How long do we give them, Crispin?' Marge asked.

'The meeting was convened for three. It is already five past,' Mike said authoritatively.

Crispin looked put out by this even if he did quickly compose his features. 'Should we not wait?' he said.

'I don't think so,' said Mike, in the voice of someone who was used to not being argued with.

'You're not even shareholders yet. Strictly speaking you shouldn't even be here,' Crispin said, more to annoy than anything else. He was not unduly worried that Lepanto, yet again, was not present. It was obvious which way the voting would go. Julius had slipped up, he had not made it a condition of the trust that they should not sell.

'Crispin, don't be tiresome. This is a mere formality, we agreed they might just as well be here,' Jane snapped with irritation at her nephew.

The vote to include the trust was carried by Marge and Jane voting for, their twenty-nine per cent of the votes being larger than Crispin's twenty per cent vote against. Gloria's position as managing director was grudgingly ratified and she could not help but wonder how long she would be able to work with these people who so resented her and her position.

'There is only one piece of business to be discussed and that is the sale of Westall and Trim,' Marge said in a businesslike manner. 'Those for?'

Crispin, Jane and Marge held up their hands.

'Those against?'

Peter raised his hand for the trustees.

'Oh, come on, Peter, you can't do that,' Crispin objected.

'We just have,' Peter smiled pleasantly.

'You've no right to cheat those poor people out of a small fortune,' Jane said crossly.

'We're not cheating anyone out of anything – ' Peter began.

'Julius only asked you to act as trustees because he knew how pig-headed you would be,' Jane added for good measure.

'On the contrary, the workforce had a vote of their own yesterday to decide what they wanted to do. What were the figures, Gloria?'

'Two spoilt papers and thirty-three in favour of the firm continuing.'

'I don't believe this.' Crispin was on his feet, staring angrily at them.

'You better had,' Mike said, laconically.

'Of course, it doesn't depend on us,' Marge said smoothly. 'There is the Lepanto Trust to be considered. They must be contacted again and another meeting arranged.'

'Exactly!' Crispin said with a confidence he was far from feeling and he looked shiftily at his aunt and mother and then down at the papers in front of him.

Soon after the meeting ended, Mike, Peter and Gloria were huddled together in Gloria's office over a bottle of wine.

'We look like the three witches.' Gloria smiled at the other two. Peter put his arm round her; she leant forward to pour the wine, away from his touch.

'I always think best with a drink in my hand,' Mike explained. 'I'm glad you've got a fridge installed, Gloria. I once heard of an author turning down a large offer from a publisher trying to poach her, purely and simply because they did not have a fridge in the MD's office, and she thought they might not be her sort of people and that they might be mean in other ways too.' He bellowed with laughter. 'She came to us instead.'

'Has her liver survived?' Gloria grinned.

'Right, to business,' said Peter, concerned that discussions should begin before Mike suggested another bottle of wine. He was finding it difficult to concentrate on business with Gloria so close. The meeting had been bad enough and he had forced himself to take the initiative when all he wanted to do was to sit and enjoy looking at her. She, as if reading his thoughts, smiled a warm intimate smile, and then looked away. She was maddening, he thought. He coughed, and sat up straight as if telling himself to pull himself together.

'You've never heard of this Lepanto Trust, Gloria?'

'First time today, Peter. I've racked my brains but I'm sure Julius never said a word about it to me.'

Again she smiled at him; she knew she was perplexing him, one minute encouraging him with a look, and then shying away from him. She wished she could explain her confusion to him, but how could she when she barely knew herself?

'It's odd that he didn't. The two per cent the trust owns in shares is critical – he knew that. Why did he not tell you or at least make arrangements that you would be told in the event of his death? Through his lawyer or someone.'

'Or a friend he could trust,' Mike added.

'Oh my God, no!' Gloria exclaimed. 'I wonder. Do you remember his secretary Roz – a rather quiet, shy girl? She went to work for one of your editors, Mike. She was at Crispin's wedding. She told me Julius wanted to see her to discuss something urgently. She asked me if I knew what he wanted, but I didn't. But . . .' She looked aghast.

'No problem then, we'll give her a call,' Peter said moving to pick up the telephone.

Mike put out his hand to stop him. 'No point, Peter. The poor kid was killed in a car crash last week.'

'God, how awful,' Peter said, but then, not knowing Roz well, added, 'There might be something, a note or whatever, she might have left.'

'If she had it with her then we've lost it – the car was a burnt-out shell, Peter,' Gloria explained.

'Oh, Lord, poor girl.' He looked into his wine glass. 'Do you think Crispin and Co. know who Lepanto is?'

'They must do,' Gloria said mournfully. 'And that's it. They'll persuade whoever it is to vote with them. Poor Julius, why on earth did he not make it a condition of the trust not to sell?'

'Because he thought there was no need,' Mike said mournfully. 'He obviously believed the Lepanto people or person wouldn't vote with Crispin. I can't imagine Julius leaving himself uncovered, like this. He must have told

Roz, or given her something that would ensure Westall was safe. It's obvious – not in a million years would he have thought that a young woman like Roz would die at the same time as himself.'

'I don't think they do know,' Peter said. 'Didn't you see Crispin at the end of that meeting? He looked really shifty, as if he had promised them he knew when he didn't.'

'Then we have to find out before they do,' Mike announced. 'It's as simple and as hard as that.'

They sat silent, each trying to remember something from the past that might point them in the right direction.

'Who's using Julius's office?' Peter asked.

'No one, no one has liked to. His son and daughter came and took the pictures – or, rather, they supervised the Sotheby's people removing them. And the odd personal things from his desk have gone. Otherwise it's just as he left it.'

'Selling the bloody pictures he loved with him hardly cold in his grave,' Mike moaned lugubriously.

'Then you've got to move into it, Gloria, and quickly.'

'I don't think I could, Peter.' She shuddered. 'It would be disrespectful somehow. That's Julius's office.'

'Nonsense, Peter is right. Julius would expect you to move in there, and with office space at a premium you can't afford to waste it,' Mike said practically. 'And if you're there . . .?' He looked questioningly at Peter.

'Exactly. If you're there, Gloria, you can see how much snooping Crispin is up to. And, what's more, it gives you the opportunity to look yourself.'

'But what am I looking for?'

'Use your imagination, Gloria, for goodness sake,' Mike barked. 'Go through the bookcases, the ledgers, his safe. Look for anything that has anything to do with Lepanto. It must be in that room somewhere.'

'Let's do it now.' Peter stood up.

'Do what? Begin the search?' Gloria looked up at him, and thought how tall and how handsome he was, how enchanting his smile, and then stopped herself. She had vowed not to look at him in that way, not for the time being. For when she did her body reacted, her pulse raced, she wanted him – it could not be, not yet.

'We'll give you a hand.'

Together they began to pack her books and papers into boxes which Gloria found in the postroom. It was a strange sight, she thought, as she watched Peter and Mike laden with cardboard boxes staggering up the stairs. The two most important men in British publishing working as removal men.

Once everything had been moved Peter looked at the books in one of Julius's bookcases and Mike the other. They climbed the library steps – even though Gloria feared for them under Mike's weight – and carefully checked the spine of each book.

'Anything?' she called.

'No sign of the word Lepanto here,' Mike bellowed down from the top of the steps.

'I wonder what it means?' she asked.

'God knows, but we're going to find out,' said Peter emphatically, looking down at her and wishing Mike would go and leave them alone. It was agony being with her and not able to touch her, caress her, love her. But that was wishful thinking on his part, he thought, as he returned to checking the books. Last night had been wonderful, they had been so close. But when he began to kiss her, first she melted in his arms, then suddenly she drew away from him and her wonderful body felt rigid to the touch.

'But why, Gloria?' he had asked, desire frustrated again.

'I don't know . . . it's so difficult to explain.'

And he had done what he did too frequently these days he had slammed into the night, his body aching with longing for her.

'There's nothing here,' he said, descending the library steps.

9

It was Joy's idea that Kate's launch party should be held at Barty's and he was quite happy to oblige for several reasons, not least that he would agree to almost anything that Joy asked. Gloria was overjoyed to accept the invitation on behalf of Westall's. Launch parties were notoriously difficult to arrange and many a publicity manager had sleepless nights over them. So many were held in London that the journalists had become blasé about attending them. They had become so picky that unless an author was a celebrity, it was a notorious book, the publishers came up with an original idea for a party, or loaded them with freebies, they frequently did not bother to show up at all. What was left was a handful of people rattling about a large room, hired to take far more. Instead of a throng, there was the handful of staff from the publisher's, the author, her friends and relations, all gamely wading through the canapés ordered for dozens and pretending they were having a wonderful time and that no one was in the least bit disappointed by the poor press turn-out. Launch parties were held more to impress an author the house particularly wanted to keep than to reap publicity. But with Barty's as the venue, the magic of his name would create an altogether different problem, that of keeping the numbers of the press to within reasonable limits.

Barty and Joy had arrived from the Bahamas two days before the launch of *Winter Interlude*. Crispin's appointment with Barty had been scheduled for the day before the party. Barty had met Crispin only a couple of times and had not been overly impressed. He was cynically suspicious of people who thought themselves as charming as Crispin evidently did. And he was equally suspicious of those with a superiority complex, for life had taught him they rarely had anything to be superior about.

'No doubt you realise why I've asked to see you, Mr Anderson,' Barty said, once Crispin had been welcomed and seated in front of his awe-inspiring desk.

'Not really, Sir Barty.' Crispin smiled, presuming it would be appreciated. It was not.

'I wish to buy Westall and Trim,' Barty announced baldly.

'Really?' said Crispin, hoping he did not look too surprised. 'I had no idea you were interested in publishing, Sir Barty.' He put on his gently quizzical face but Barty did not answer. 'Of course, it might be for sale and it might not be.'

'Oh, come, Mr Anderson. Have you not already approached every major British publishing firm? Not to mention Schubert's of New York, Tiffel of Munich and my friend Costas?'

'I might have put out the odd feeler.'

'Quite so, and I assume you just happen to have the figures there with you.' Barty indicated the smart Hermès briefcase on the floor beside Crispin.

'Oddly enough, I have.' He smirked and dug deep into the case for the folder.

'I shall wish to be informed of the bids offered by Tudor's, Pewter's, Shotters and whoever else you have begun negotiations with. For such a co-operation on your part I shall, of course, show my appreciation to you personally.' Barty spoke so matter-of-factly that it was several moments before Crispin realised he was being bribed.

'How very kind of you, Sir Barty,' he said smoothly. 'I can assure you I shall not be dealing with either Shotters or Pewter's – I'm not too pleased with Peter's or Mike's attitude,' he said pompously.

'I see,' said Barty, thinking what a stupid man he had sitting in front of him. Did he seriously imagine he was superior in any way to those two? And how unprofessional to allow personal animosity to get in the way of a deal, something Barty would never do. 'Should you approach other firms I wish to be informed who they are.'

'Of course, Sir Barty.'

'You would be well advised to tell me for I shall know, you realise. You act straight with me, I'll do likewise.'

'Surely. I can foresee no difficulties whatsoever.'

'You've solved who Lepanto is then, have you?'

At this, had Crispin been drinking, he would have choked.

'A mere formality, Sir Barty,' he said with an airy wave of the hand, while wondering how the hell Barty knew so much.

'I have to be straight with you, Mr Anderson, and tell you I should not wish you to remain with the firm. It rarely works, a member of the family remaining.'

'I'm desirous of leaving in any case,' Crispin said, with, he congratulated himself, a marked degree of dignity, while deeply insulted that there should be someone who did not wish him to remain.

'And I do not wish Miss Catchpole's life, within the firm, to be made difficult during this period of negotiation. I don't want her leaving in a huff. Know what I mean?'

'You would want Miss Catchpole to stay?' Crispin said, surprised that anyone should want to retain someone as difficult as Gloria, while at the same time wishing to get rid of him. Barty must be the same as his uncle, he thought – silly where beautiful women were concerned.

'I would. Thank you for calling, Mr Anderson. Gervase will see you out.' And Barty returned to the study of his papers, an obvious and insulting form of dismissal. Crispin was furious. We'll see about you, smart-arse, he thought as he stalked, head held high, the long length of Barty's study. It would be hard to turn down Barty's back-hander but, then, with the amount of money he would be getting, what would such a small sum matter? And this interview proved one thing to him: Westall's was a desirable acquisition. There would be no shortage of buyers, so the sky was the limit in money terms. Who needed Silver? He took the opportunity of slamming the door of the study shut with a satisfying bang.

Barty's next appointment was with the barrister dealing with Joy's divorce.

'I want this resolved, and quickly, Burrows.'

'We are up against one of the finest minds in law with Charles Trenchard.'

'Then if you're not up to him find me someone who is,' Barty said sharply. 'I don't see the problem. The man is a known wifebeater – we've got the photos and the doctor's report for that. Who's to say that he won't beat his daughter too?'

'But Mrs Trenchard won't allow us to use that evidence against him. She's worried about the effect of adverse publicity on her daughter.'

'I know, understandable. But maybe it's in her best interests to pretend you wouldn't dream of using it and then do so. She's hardly likely to stand up in court and make a scene, is she? I keep telling her that today's news is forgotten tomorrow.'

'But it would be unethical to act in such an underhand manner.'

'Ethics? Ethics? What's that, all of a sudden? How do you spell it? Don't give me that old cobblers.'

'He is being most objectionable about you, of course,' Burrows said with a discreet cough, not wishing to mention the allegations of homosexuality in actual words, but wanting very much to change the subject.

'Nearly every bishop in the land has given me a glowing reference, what more do you want, the Queen? What about the private detectives, have they come up with anything?'

'Mrs Trenchard finds the use of them distasteful.'

'And I don't. I'm employing them, not her. Get them back on the job – and fast – and don't let her know.'

'Yes, Sir Barty.'

'And next time you come here I would appreciate some good news for the fees I'm paying you.'

'Yes, Sir Barty.' The barrister hastened from the room, relieved to be escaping.

Barty was a different person when dealing with Joy as they sat over their lunch. Gone was the ruthlessness. Instead, he coaxed and cajoled her, trying to persuade her that every weapon in their armoury should be used.

'Look, my darling. I know it's hard for you, but divorce always is unpleasant and you do want your little girl back, don't you?'

'Oh, I do. And I know you're doing your best for me. But, Barty, you don't know Charles as I do. If he thinks we'll use his beating me as evidence, or gets wind of our using private detectives, it will make matters worse. I'd much rather stick with suing him for his adultery.'

'And Hannah?'

'Surely the judge will let me have her? It's nearly always the mother who wins, isn't it?' She said this anxiously: she was worried and finding it difficult to sleep. She was having to face the unpleasant fact that Charles was capable of anything and would use her friendship with Barty against her. She could imagine the slanderous innuendo of which Charles was capable – Barty's lifestyle, the young male aides, the question mark over his sexuality which he had never bothered to respond to, seeming instead to bask in the conjecture.

What would a judge think? If Barty was deemed unsuitable, then what would she do? Which would she choose? Hannah, of course, but what of Barty? She was not *in* love with him, but she loved him.

Those nights when she could not sleep a traitorous thought often slipped into her mind, demanding attention. Was she refusing to co-operate with the barrister because she did not want to alienate Charles too much? Because if she was reasonable with him he might see the error of his ways and return to her? And what sort of fool did that make her even to think it? And if she was thinking it, what was she doing stringing Barty along? Joy felt she was in a vortex of conflicting emotions.

The launch was in full swing. Dozens of journalists had come: an opportunity to see inside Barty's house was not one to let pass by. And they were even more intrigued to find out why this unknown author had such an influential patron. Barty was always good copy. As each one took their turn to talk to Kate, Val stood protectively close, like a nanny, Kate thought. A television producer from the *Goodly Hour* was there and, having talked to Kate, arranged with Val that Kate should be on the show tomorrow evening. Kate felt light-headed with the excitement of it all and everyone's satisfaction with how things were going.

'Hallo, Kate.'

She swung round to find Stewart Dorchester standing behind her.

'Oh, Stewart, how wonderful to see you,' she said excitedly, and standing on tip-toe kissed him full on the lips. She stepped back hand over her mouth, aghast at her behaviour. 'I'm sorry. I shouldn't have done that. I'm tipsy.'

'Be my guest.' He smiled at her and touched his mouth. Kate felt a surge of excitement.

'I wonder . . .' she began.

'Sorry, Stewart, you've done your interview. I need Kate over here.' It was Val taking her by the arm and with smooth, smiling professionalism, sweeping her away to talk to another reporter. When she had finished with him it was to see Stewart in the corner in deep conversation with a very pretty young woman. Stupid me, she thought despondently and turned to the next person demanding her attention.

It did not take the journalists long to find out the connection between Barty and Joy and two and two were put together and fantastic sums reached. The morning papers would be full of her liaison with Barty. This was exactly what Barty had intended to happen. He knew Joy far better than she realised and felt that the more established they were as a couple in the eyes of the media, the harder it would be for her to back away.

Kate, having apparently spoken to everyone who wanted to speak to her, was desperately in need of a cigarette. At the first opportunity, she slipped out to the ladies' for a quick smoke. She thought she would never stop laughing when she found Gloria and Joy already ensconced in there, sitting at the coffee table, a bottle of wine between them.

'We should have a reunion in here every year,' Gloria said, laughing too. 'Drink, Kate?'

'It's the only place in this damn house to get any privacy,'said Joy. 'Cigarette, Kate?' She proffered her case.

'From that remark are we to conclude that all is not well *chez* Silver?' Gloria asked, archly.

'Gracious, I must sound so ungrateful, but I feel almost smothered with attention.'

'Sounds lovely, don't you think, Kate?'

'I felt smothered with it out there but I have to confess I rather liked it.' Kate grinned. 'On the home front I think I could do with some of it at the moment.'

'Kate's getting divorced too, Joy.'

'Kate, I didn't know, I'm sorry. What happened?'

'I don't know to be quite honest, everything has happened so quickly. I thought we might be able to sort something out but Tony's found someone else, so there doesn't seem much point in trying any more. Best bow out with dignity.'

'You really think that?' Joy leant across the low table, clutching her glass of wine and looking earnestly at Kate.

'Yes, I do. What's the point of hanging on in if someone doesn't want you any more? You've got to keep your self-respect, haven't you?'

'Yes, but sometimes it's so hard.' Joy smiled weakly.

'At least you've got Barty,' Gloria said softly.

'Oh, yes, poor Barty. Honestly I don't know what I'm up to. One thing I do know, I'm not being fair to him. I know if I can sort out the custody of Hannah I should stay with him, but I keep thinking of Charles,' Joy said with a sigh.

'Joy, you must be mad,' Gloria said with exasperation.

'I know, I know, but I can't help it.'

'I expect you keep remembering the good times and have forgotten the bad. Bit like having a baby, isn't it? You forget the pain. I'm doing the same. I know it's best for Tony and me to split and then I think, it wasn't that bad . . .'

'Do you honestly?'

'Yes, but I'm fighting it.' Kate laughed. Joy did not join in the laughter.

'God, I'm in such a mess again. I just don't think I can go through with it with Barty and yet I'm too fond of him to tell him.'

'Why did you agree to it in the first place?' asked Kate.

'At first I think I genuinely wanted to but I'm beginning to wonder if it was not to get back at Charles. I thought the idea of me as Lady Silver with all this wealth would infuriate him.'

'What, and he'd come running? Oh, Joy, really.' Gloria looked at her in horror.

'Well, not exactly,' Joy lied.

'Quite honestly, Joy, you appear to be on a hiding to nothing. At this rate, you'll lose everything, Barty included, then where will you be?' Kate said quite crisply. 'Barty's no fool, he'll work it out before long – if he hasn't already. I think you have to be straight with him, see what sort of solution you can work out.' Kate helped herself to another glass of wine. 'And what about you, Gloria? We always seem to land up using this loo as a confessional, what's been happening to you?'

'Not a lot.' Gloria pulled a face. 'Not strictly true. Peter Holt's back in my life, only I'm being ultra cautious this time.'

'Why? I thought you were crazy about him.'

'I am, but I'm so scared of getting hurt. All the other times men have been bastards to me I've bounced back but this time, I don't think I would, that's the problem.'

'You mean you're not seeing him?' Kate looked perplexed.

'No, we go out regularly – dinners, the theatre. It's rather nice, really, like old-fashioned dating. He brings me home, we'll have a drink, he kisses me and goes.'

'Sounds lovely.' Joy sighed.

'How long before he gets fed up?' Kate queried, wondering why it was so easy to see other people's problems while one battled through a morass of misunderstanding of one's own. 'What's the point in letting happiness pass you by because you might, just might, get hurt? That's about the silliest thing I've heard in years.'

'Joy, cast your mind back to about a year ago. Remember a quiet little mouse got herself locked in the loo because she was too scared to let us know she was there? Dominated by hubby, wouldn't say boo to a goose. Where's she gone? Who's this?' Gloria laughed at Kate.

'Oh dear, am I being terribly bossy?'

'No, actually you're talking a lot of sense, isn't she, Joy? Problem is, will we listen?' Gloria grinned. 'But what's all this with you and Stewart Dorchester, Kate?'

'I'm sorry?' Kate said almost spilling her wine with surprise.

'You remember Sybil Cavay was going to interview you?'

'Yes.' Kate felt uncomfortable, sure she was about to blush.

'Well, publicity were poleaxed when Stewart telephoned to say he was doing it – he doesn't normally interview popular fiction authors. And he hinted, like a sledge-hammer, that Val need not be there to protect you. Well, I ask you?' Gloria rolled her eyes archly. 'We've been agog ever since.'

'He was very pleasant. It was just an interview, that's all,' Kate said quickly. She would have loved to talk to them of how she was beginning to feel about Stewart, but she didn't. They would probably laugh. After all, wasn't Stewart out there now talking to an attractive young woman? A romantic dreamer, that's all she was.

'But are you enjoying your launch, Kate?' It was Joy asking as if she sensed Kate's discomfort at the question from Gloria.

'It's wonderful, I've had the most marvellous time. It does one a power of good in the sort of situation I'm in to be so spoilt. It's going to help me get through the whole catastrophe, I know it is. That's what you should do, Joy, really throw yourself into your work – don't be dependent on a man, ever again. Whoops, there I go again, bossing. Sorry. I'll change the subject. Can you two help me? I've been invited on the *Goodly Hour* show, tomorrow. I feel sick with terror already. Why can't books just sell themselves? Why do we have to do things like this?' she complained. 'And what do I wear?' she pleaded.

'Sheena Goodly is very nice, she's only bitchy to know-alls.' Gloria advised. 'And you'll love it once you get going. You forget the cameras are there, you know. You'll be a trouper before you know where you are.'

'You'll be fine, Kate. But the clothes are important. Don't wear anything too fussy and don't wear red – it can "bleed" on the screen and make you look fuzzy. And don't wear white, it's too bright, they'll only make you change. And don't be scared, just be yourself,' Joy added.

10

In the hotel she had been booked into by Westall's, Kate had ordered every newspaper she could think of. They had been delivered with her early-morning tea. She had not wanted breakfast for she knew she would be too nervous to eat a thing all day. She leafed quickly through them. There was plenty of coverage but it was mainly about Joy and Barty – all the photographs were of them – though two papers had mentioned the party was for the launch of her book. She read Stewart Dorchester's feature on her and when she had finished hugged the paper to her. The dear man, it was wonderful. She turned to the book pages. She had only one review.

From the prestigious publishers of Sir Gerald Walters – Nobel Prize winning author and the greatest living writer in the English language, we now have *Winter Interlude* by Kate Howard, a housewife by profession and a profession she would be wise to return to. The reader's stomach will churn at this tale of, less an interlude, but more an interminable nauseous saga . . .

She could read no more for tears prevented her seeing the writing on the page. She did not feel anger, instead real misery swamped her. Until now, all she had heard was praise and enthusiasm for her work and nothing had prepared her for such a cruel and unthinking review as this. She was about to bury her head under the pillow and try to pretend she had not read it when the telephone rang.

'Yes?' she said hoping her voice would not betray that she was crying.

'Kate? It's Gloria. Have you see the review by James Oaktree?'

'Yes,' was her muffled reply.

'Don't take any notice. He's a spiteful toad – he's got acne, too, which does not help his personality problems.' Gloria laughed and waited for Kate to do so also. When she did not she began again. 'Julius turned down his first novel last year and he's finally having his nasty revenge. It's Westall's he's getting at, not you.'

'It's kind of you to say that, Gloria, but at the moment I'm afraid it doesn't help much.'

'You must listen to me, Kate. He's unimportant, a failed writer venting his spleen.'

'I didn't expect anything quite like this. I mean, I don't pretend to be a literary writer, so why attack me?'

'Believe me, a bad review is better than no reviews. It'll help your sales, honestly. At least the book was reviewed, your genre so rarely is and when it is they usually attack. Invariably either the reviewer's own novel has been rejected or it has earned peanuts. They're jealous of the sales and the advances writers like you get. Come on, cheer up. Get your hair done, it's a big night tonight.'

'Can you come?'

'Kate, I'd love to, and I will if I can, but I'm snowed under here. Val will be with you. If I don't see you, good luck.'

Kate forced herself to reread the review. It did not make her feel better but she vowed one thing: she would never read another review ever again.

*

Gloria was surrounded by papers and ledgers. Elephant liked this game and was jumping from one pile of papers to another like stepping stones. She sat on the floor in Julius's office and scratched her head. Nowhere was there a reference to the Lepanto Trust. She also had a shrewd idea that Crispin had been snooping about in here last night when she had been at the party. She had made a point of locking the door but then common sense told her that someone like Crispin was sure to have had a key made, probably long ago. The papers felt as if they had been touched by someone. It was not evidence, it was a feeling she had that he had been in here, and that was not proof enough to accuse him. But, then, she supposed, he had as much right to be going through everything as she had – and, as a member of the family, more so. The safe was still locked but that would not have helped him either, there was nothing in there.

Where now? She picked up her notepad and began to make a list. *1. Books – check backlists of publications.* She sucked her pencil. Everyone had always presumed that Julius had a copy of every book he had ever published in here in the large mahogany bookcases, but maybe he did not. *2. List books in bookcase.* They had better be put in alphabetical order, too, for simplicity – she would get Rachel to do that and to check off against the lists of books published. But how far was she supposed to go back? The year when Julius took control would seem logical. She'd have to find that out from someone who had worked here the longest. *3. Ask Mrs Westall if she could check Julius's library at home?????* She stabbed at the paper as she added the row of question marks. That was a hope! Why should Mrs Westall help what she would see as the opposition? *4. Have the royalty ledgers sent up from accounts.* She had already spoken to Effie about payments to the trust.

'I've already told Crispin, dividends were paid to the bank. I know nothing else about Lepanto,' she had snapped. 'I've work to do, if you don't mind.'

Effie was normally testy, people in accounts often were. They were always being harassed by someone. It was they who fielded the endless queries from paranoid authors convinced they were being cheated on their royalty statements, and dealt with belligerent agents when advances were a day late. It was not a happy department, but Effie was edgy even by accounts department standards. Gloria felt that she was not telling her everything but, on the other hand, that could have been because, Gloria sensed, the woman did not like her. She would ask for the royalty statements when Effie had gone to lunch – her assistant was a lot more helpful. After that she really had no idea which way she was going to turn.

In his office at Shotters Peter sat doodling at his desk. He spent a lot of time doing that these days. As more and more key men were being shipped over from New York he was finding less and less to do. Nothing had been said, or even hinted, that Costas wanted him out but the signs were becoming unmistakable. He supposed they would prefer him to resign out of boredom or a fit of pique but he had no intention of doing any such thing. If he did so, under the terms of his contract, he could end up paying to leave the firm he had created. They would have to terminate his contract and pay him compensation. It was a giant cat-and-mouse game, really – and Peter was not sure if he was the cat or the mouse.

He was waiting for the arrival of Drew Wincanton III, the head of Costas's American publishing arm, whom he had met once on a trip to New York. He did not much like the man. It had been an odd meeting: at the time, Peter had felt he was not supposed to like him, as if Wincanton was going out of his way to be antagonistic. Perhaps, he wondered now, the animosity had been deliberately created because Wincanton was likely to be his replacement here, and part and parcel of the plan to get him to resign. Well, he smiled to himself, they were going to have to wait.

He had had his daily row with Hilary. She telephoned most mornings at about eleven. He expected the calls now and felt he would be quite lost without them. This morning's had been typical – a list of bills that had arrived, and which she considered were his responsibility and he did not. There was usually a tiff about the ownership of something: today's had been about a painting which she said had been given to her as a wedding present when he could distinctly remember writing the cheque for it. He would probably let her have it in the end, but he had no intention of making it easy for her – not that he cared, just the principle of the thing.

He looked at the list of thoughts he had written about Lepanto. Once he had finished with Wincanton he would pop over to Westall's and use the mystery of Lepanto as an excuse. Anything to see Gloria again.

He sighed. He did not know where he was with her. She seemed to enjoy being with him, certainly she never turned down an invitation, and they had fun together. But when he took her home, convinced each time that this was it, that she would ask him to stay, she seemed to shy away from him like a frightened animal. He felt as perplexed as an adolescent boy having to learn how to deal with girls and with no experience to fall back on. It was ridiculous. The odd thing was that he had not wanted to go out with anyone else. He had had no sex for weeks now, but he did not want to sleep with just anyone, only Gloria. As each day passed, frustrated as he was, he was more and more convinced that he was in love. He wondered if he should tell her, or was that what she was frightened of – total commitment? If he blurted it out, would she run a mile? And if he didn't, would she continue to keep him at arm's length? God, it was all so complicated, he thought.

Ten minutes later he was angry and his voice was raised.

'No, Drew, I won't do that and that's flat.'

'I'm afraid you're going to have to, buddy.'

'I wish you would not call me your buddy when I'm not. I will not con my authors in this way and that's an end to it. Go back and tell your master that.'

'Look, Peter, Costas is fully aware that you would not like this proposal and he has given me authorisation to go over your head. It's been decided. As our authors reach the end of their seven-year contracts with other paperback houses, the licences will not be renewed. They will revert to us and those books will be reissued by Sabre. I don't see what you're getting so het up about. They're our authors, it's just good business sense.'

'It's lousy publishing ethics. Those paperback houses invested heavily in those authors and renewal has always been automatic. Losing their biggest earners in this way could ruin them.'

'Exactly, and Sabre benefits. Good heavens, man, you set Sabre up, don't you want it to succeed?'

'Of course, but honourably. This stinks. Why, you're not even consulting with the authors. You're just going to face them with it, *fait accompli*. They're not going to like this.'

'They won't have any choice, if you read their contracts.'

'Christ! I just don't believe this is happening.'

'You'd better believe.'

'I won't do it.'

'Then there's no alternative.'

'I'm not resigning.'

'We're not asking you to. If you could be out of here within the hour? Thank you, Peter.' As Drew stood up to leave, he slapped an envelope on the desk. 'Severance of your contract, cheque inside. Oh, and by the way, Costas was not too happy that you had not opened negotiations for Westall and Trim when you were one of the first approached.'

'It's not even for sale yet.'

'It's only a matter of time but we gather you were most unpleasant to the firm's principal – we expect better from our executive management than that, Peter.'

'Crispin – the principal! That'll be the day.' Peter laughed.

'Anyhow, it's all on line now, I've seen to that. So, Peter, I don't think there's anything else. Have a nice day.'

The door slammed shut and Peter sat at his desk for a moment as if poleaxed. Then he was suddenly galvanised into action. He buzzed for Em.

'I've just had the chop, Em.'

'Peter, no!' Em's hand flew to her mouth, her eyes filled with tears. 'Not you, you *are* Shotters.'

'Don't worry, Em. Do you know it's odd but I'm quite pleased, really. I've not been happy since I sold up. I want to issue a press statement. I'll dictate that to you and then if you could get hold of the MDs of all these paperback houses, I need to speak to them.'

The press release, unlike the usual '. . . parting by mutual and amicable agreement . . .' lies, told the truth. The morning papers would be full of Costas's plan. Authors and their agents would be on the rampage. Hopefully one of the richer ones would take up the cudgels for the rest. The managing directors of the paperback houses he contacted were duly grateful and within five minutes of his calls meetings were set up and lawyers were being consulted.

He was being underhand. He did not care, he felt no loyalty to this Shotters. It had long ceased to be the firm he had started. It was a money factory now and the authors expendable workhorses. To Peter this was not publishing.

An hour later, with help from his staff most of whom were in tears, he had packed the contents of his desk, the bookcases were emptied, his paintings wrapped in brown paper, his ornaments in boxes and his shower room stripped. The security men were carrying everything down to the basement where a van, hurriedly summoned, was waiting for them. Peter had thought of calling a meeting of heads of department and then decided not to bother. Most of his old staff were long gone, none of those remaining had been with him initially. He felt sad for Shotters and what he had allowed to happen to it but he did not feel sorry for himself.

Once out on the street he hailed a cab and set off for Westall and Trim. He tapped on the door to Julius's office.

'Any jobs going?' He grinned as he poked his head round to see Gloria sitting on the floor, surrounded by papers. Gloria's heart lurched as it always did when she saw him.

'Peter, what a lovely surprise. What do you mean?'

'I've been sacked.'

'No! Oh, my poor darling.'

'Yes, and for a devious reason.' But he was smiling, she had called him darling. 'They're reverting the paperback licences of our bestselling authors and reprinting them with Sabre,' he said, thinking what wonderful eyes she had.

'They're not! Hell, what will that mean to publishing?' she asked, noting, as usual, how elegantly he moved across the room to her.

'There won't be a paperback house that will feel safe to invest in an author hardbacked by a publisher with its own paperback arm, that's for sure. Paperbacks are going to have to buy into hardback houses or be bought by one and offer an author the whole package.'

Certainly her mouth was one of the sexiest he had ever seen, he thought. God, how he'd love to kiss her now, this minute.

'But that way there would be fewer publishing houses acquiring books. And authors scrabbling around for those few left – it's hard enough for first-time writers now. Who will pick them up then?' she said, wishing he would kiss her instead of talking business. He couldn't care for her as she did him otherwise he would, surely?

'It'll take time to shake down. But on the way over here, I was thinking in the end it might be for the good – everyone should be safer in the long run, publishers and authors alike. It's just that I think the existing contracts should stand. Authors feel intense loyalty to their paperback houses, more so, often, than to the hardback publisher. But that's Costas for you.' He watched her as she stood up, admiring her figure and her long shapely legs. As always she was wearing the sheer black stockings which made them even more stunning.

'What will you do?'

'Take a holiday.' He grinned. 'Fancy coming?' he joked but longed for her to agree.

'I can't think of anything nicer. But I've got to sort out Lepanto first if I'm to keep my job,' she said regretfully. How wonderful, she thought, to go away, just the two of them. Then she wouldn't be able to resist – but perhaps that was a good reason not to go. In any case, he had probably asked her as a joke.

'Have you come up with anything?' he asked politely. What had he expected? Of course she would refuse.

'I think I have, as a matter of fact – not that it gets us any further on, just deepens the mystery.' Gloria stood up straight, she was being silly letting her mind wander in this way. She must concentrate. It was Lepanto he had come about, not her. 'Effie seemed a bit shifty to me when I asked her about payments to the trust. While she was out at lunch I got the royalty statements going back fifteen years. And look,' she hauled a ledger towards her. 'See, here, each year there's a payment to Lepanto and it goes up a little each time. Here, you see, when accounts went over to computers, it's still there. But it just says the name of the trust, there's no book title mentioned as there usually is. Well, what book earns royalties for that number of years, and further back still if we get the relevant ledgers? I mean, someone like Gerald Walters does, but then we would know which book it was, there would always be copies around, we'd have them in the warehouse. It's a mystery.'

'Have you looked in the bank paying-in books, in the record of payments ledgers? Is there anything in them?'

'What would they tell us?'

'I don't know, but perhaps there's a discrepancy or something. It would be worth checking them.'

Gloria crossed to her desk and buzzed Rachel to go to accounts and ask Effie for the relevant ledgers for the past fifteen years. 'I can't go myself.' She giggled. 'Effie frightens me – you know, one of those slightly shrewish ladies who lie about their age and always think you're up to something sexually exciting in the next room.'

'Would that we were,' said Peter with feeling. Gloria looked up. Rachel quickly arrived with the pile of ledgers.

'I don't know what she's got to hide but Effie didn't want me to have these and she's very huffy.'

Gloria and Peter looked at each other, eyebrows raised.

'I'll take these and you those. The dates are easy enough, March and September are normal time for royalty payments. Make us some tea, Rachel, there's an angel.' Gloria sat back on the floor where it was easier to spread out the ledgers. There was silence for five minutes while both went through them. Elephant sat quietly, watching.

'Peter?' She looked up at him.

'I think I might have found the same thing. Here, in the paying-out book, a payment to Lepanto, and then in the bank paying-in book, the same date always, a payment to Westall and Trim from Julius Westall.'

'For the same amount.'

'Every time.'

'So what was he playing at?'

'God and Effie apparently know. Get her up here, Gloria, scared of her or not.'

A few minutes later an anguished-looking Effie had joined them.

'Perhaps you know what this is all about, Effie?' Gloria smiled encouragingly at her.

'Mr Julius wasn't doing anything wrong,' Effie said defensively, folding her arms over her small breasts.

'Of course he wasn't, we know that, but we're trying to solve the puzzle. It is for everyone's good, Effie, honestly.'

'Each year, as you see, he had me send out a royalty statement and cheque to the Lepanto Trust, it went straight to the bank. Then Mr Julius gave me a cheque for the same amount written on his personal account, which I banked in the company's account.'

'Do you know why he was doing this, Effie?'

'No. He never said and I never asked. I didn't think it was my place.'

'Of course not, Effie. But perhaps you had a theory?' Peter smiled at her kindly.

'Well, it's just my idea, I've no proof of course, but Mr Julius was such a kind man I always presumed it was to an author who didn't have much money.'

'But if that was the case why pretend there were royalties due?' Gloria asked.

Effie looked at her as if she was half-witted. 'It was obviously someone who would not dream of accepting charity. This way Mr Julius could help and yet the person would think that they had earned the money.'

'And you've no idea who it could be?'

'No. The system was already in operation when I came twenty-seven years ago. Mind you . . .' she paused and took a small handkerchief from an inside pocket, and dabbed at her eyes as if she was stopping any tears that might have the temerity to fall. 'I've often thought it must be a lady friend of Mr Julius. He would look after someone he had cared for, don't you think?' And she trumpeted into the handkerchief and made rapid excuses that she had work to do.

Over their tea Peter and Gloria discussed how far they had got, which, they both agreed, was not very far. They had an author, probably female, probably an ex-mistress, who had written a book published by Westall's which had disappeared, for they had no title. And why should that book not be here when every other book was? Because Julius did not want anyone to know who the author was, because he or she had the controlling shares. They had gone full circle. But at least the detective work had given them a brief respite from their longing for each other.

'Will you have dinner with me tonight? I think we've done enough here for one day.'

Gloria looked at her watch. 'I'd love to but I really should go to the television studios. Poor Kate's doing her first show and she's terrified. I said I would if I could.'

'Can I come?'

'Please, I'd love you to.' Gloria's heart lifted with relief. Because of the stupid way she was behaving she would not be surprised if he stopped asking her out. She packed the ledgers into one neat pile, switched off the light and they left the office.

Gloria should really have locked the relevant documents in the safe for within an hour of her leaving Crispin had let himself into the room. He was a little slower than they had been but by the end of the evening he had reached much the same conclusion.

'Bet it was one of his bits of crumpet,' he said to himself as he restacked the ledgers in the same order in which Gloria had left them.

11

'I'm going to be sick.

'No, you're not, it's just your imagination.'

'You want to bet?' A frightened Kate looked up at Val. 'I can't do it, Val. I'm sorry if I'm letting everyone down but I can't go through with it and that's that.'

'Everyone feels like that first time, you'll be fine.'

'Have you been on television?'

'Well, no – '

'Then you don't know what the bloody hell you're talking about,' Kate said, fear making her irritable.

'Would you like a drink? Would that help?' Val asked, unperturbed – this was par for the course with most authors racked with nerves.

'Gin and tonic, a big one.'

There was a tap on the dressing-room door and Gloria appeared. She had left Peter outside, certain that too many people would only make Kate more nervous.

'Hello, how are you?'

'She's fine, aren't you, Kate?' Val said in the over-bright manner of a nurse in the presence of a terminally ill patient. 'Situation normal,' she whispered in an aside to Gloria.

'What are you two whispering about? What are you saying about me?' Kate asked in the rising tones of paranoia.

'I was just asking Gloria if she'd like a drink, that's all.'

The door closed behind Val.

'She's like a broody hen, she's making me nervous,' Kate complained.

'Shall I tell her to go away, then?'

'Oh no, we can't do that, I don't want to offend her. Oh, Gloria, I feel dreadful. What's my hair look like? It's a mess, isn't it? It cost me a small fortune and then they made it look dreadful.' Kate appeared to be unable to stop talking.

'It looks very pretty, honestly. Why would I lie to you?' Gloria said when Kate looked at her disbelievingly. She hated these stints in television studios holding the hands of nervous authors. She felt for them – it was a wretched ordeal which none of them ever seemed to get used to. It always reminded her of having to wait in hospitals with relatives whose loved ones were undergoing brain surgery – not that she ever had, but this is what she imagined it must be like. 'Have you been to Make-up yet?'

'Oh, my God! If you can't tell I have, then they must have made an awful job of it.' Kate twisted round and anxiously scrutinised her face in the mirror.

'On the contrary, it shows what an excellent job they've done.' Gloria tried to keep any hint of amusement out of her voice. 'Is that your dress?' She nodded at a particularly pretty peach-coloured two-piece hanging up. 'Lovely colour.'

'It was the nearest I could get to red – red's my lucky colour you see. But I've got a red petticoat instead.' Kate opened the towelling robe she was sitting in to show Gloria. 'Oh, Gloria, what the hell am I doing here?' Kate sighed audibly. 'I wish I could put the clock back. Last October I was married, a housewife, normal. Look at me now, a wreck. I don't want to be a success, I want to go back to my mundane life, I really do. You know what's happening? God's punishing me for being bored and discontented with my life, that's why I'm here. I wish I could go home!'

'You're here, my love, because inside you there is a great hunger to succeed. That's what you have and it's like gold dust. That's the difference between you and thousands of other women who want to write and don't make it. You've worked so hard to be here, now enjoy it. You've earned it.'

'Can I come in?' Joy's head appeared around the door. 'How're you feeling, Kate?'

'If anyone else asks me that I'll scream!' Kate said, sounding as if she was verging on hysterics.

'Sorry. Hallo, Val, what have you got there? I do hope that's not for Kate, it wouldn't be wise.'

'It won't hurt, Joy. It's just what Kate needs, isn't it?' Gloria said soothingly.

Yet another knock on the door and Sheena Goodly appeared.

'Hallo, Kate, just popped in to see how you are – feeling terrified no doubt. Don't worry, you'll forget the cameras once we start. Just one thing, don't look directly into them, will you? Is that what you're wearing? Perfect.'

Sheena had on twice the amount of make-up that Kate had, and looked half the size she normally appeared on Kate's television screen at home. Did this mean Kate was going to look insipid and as large as a house? Sheena smiled brightly at her, but it was the professional smile of a performer, an instant let's-be-best-friends smile that, try as she might, Kate could not respond to.

'Who else have you got on?' Gloria asked.

'Barry Filmour – he's divine. Do you know him, Kate? I'll talk to him for a few minutes and then I've got that boring old trout Dame Fiona Martingale rabbiting on about abortions – not that I should think any man ever got close enough to her to impregnate her in the first place. Then last of all it's Kate with Sebastian Trumpington, and that'll be a wow!' Sheena spoke with exaggerated enthusiasm, just like Kate's games mistress had when she was trying to convince the hockey team they could win, thought Kate. If it was supposed to fire her up, then Sheena was failing, just as the games teacher had.

'Sebastian who? Who's he?' Kate demanded.

'He's a literary editor with rather strong views about women's fiction.'

'I can't talk about women's fiction. I'm not an expert. I've only written one book. I don't even have any views on the subject.' Kate's voice was rising in panic.

'Don't worry, Kate, I have. I'll lead you and you'll be surprised what opinions you do have when it comes to it. There,' she looked up at the intercom as it crackled and her name was called, 'I must fly. See you in approximately twenty minutes, Kate. Good luck.'

The small dressing room was overcrowded and becoming uncomfortably hot. Kate began to fantasise about locking herself in the lavatory, pretending she was stuck, and by the time they got her out the programme would be over.

When a young man with earphones and a clipboard eventually came to collect her she could vaguely remember everyone kissing her and then she was racing along endless corridors with anonymous doors, trying to keep up with the floor manager, as he turned out to be, in his Nike trainers, who said nothing to her except to repeat that she was not to look directly at the cameras. The senior floor manager said the same as she arrived at the side of the set and repeated it as he gently pushed her forward. Her legs felt leaden as she began to walk.

The lighting on the set was blinding. The roar of welcome from the audience as she was announced was out of all proportion. Why should they be cheering her when none of them could possibly know who she was?

When Sheena spoke to her she was amazed that she answered and sound emerged. But how the hell was she supposed to ignore the cameras with their large black blank eyes which seemed to be nosing everywhere. She felt her answers were dull, sensed the audience becoming restless and was not surprised that Sheena was concentrating on her fellow guest, the tall and rather languid Sebastian Trumpington. And then luck was with her.

'One of the scandals of modern-day publishing is the effort spent, ludicrous advances paid and paper wasted on popular and commercial fiction – the publishers have very many expressions to describe it.' Sebastian was speaking, slowly, pontificatingly. 'I have a better word for it. Now what was it?' Sebastian paused looking up at the lights overhead in an exaggerated play of searching for the lost word. 'To publish schlock, that's it. Schlock pure and simple, there's no defence for it.'

'I beg your pardon?' Kate suddenly sat up straight.

'Rubbish pandering to the common denominator, that's what this kind of fiction is. Like the worst television, like the worst of the gutter press. From my experience one cannot even say there is good and bad schlock, there isn't, it's all rubbish.'

'And who are you to say that?' Kate demanded.

'Because I've read some of it. I don't read it on a regular basis. I have too great a respect for my brain to do that. But what I have read has made me positively nauseous.'

'Just because you don't like it doesn't necessarily make it rubbish. Thousands would disagree with you. Look at the number of people who buy popular fiction.'

'That's no excuse for it.'

'That's every excuse for it. If people want to read these books then good luck to them. They entertain, they allow people to relax and escape the harsh realities of life. Who are you to be saying that they shouldn't?' Kate leant forward, audience, lights, cameras, nerves all forgotten.

'They would be better off spending their time reading Jane Austen, Proust.'

'Proust!' The word exploded from Kate like a gun retort. 'Are you joking? It might be hard for you but try to imagine – you've got two kids under five, a husband who drinks and gambles, you're trapped in your house all day, the debt collector's due and you're lonely, scared and with no hope. Or you're a middle-class woman whose husband bores her and she him; their life will go on in the same rut as it has for years and she knows it. And you're telling me they'll be made happier reading Proust. Oh really, Mr Trumpington. You're probably one of those people who sneer at Tchaikovsky just because everyone can hum the *Nutcracker*. People like you make me sick. You're nothing but a pseud, Mr Trumpington.'

The audience went wild. Sheena glowed. Kate beamed with a sense of triumph and Mr Trumpington was silent. By sheer chance Kate had the last word. The closing music began, the titles rolled, Sheena made her ending remarks, they were off the air. Then perfect strangers bounded up to Kate, kissing her, telling her how good she had been. 'You're a star!' they all exclaimed.

'You were a star!' Gloria hugged her as she came off the set.

'I was very rude.'

'He deserved it. How do you feel?'

'Wonderful. I could climb Mount Everest right now, run a marathon, write a dozen books.'

'You're on an adrenalin high. Come on, we're all going out to dinner. You joining us, Joy?'

'If you don't mind, Kate, I wanted to have a long talk with Barty tonight and it's one of the few evenings he's free.'

'Of course I don't mind. Do you know what you're going to say to him?' Kate asked.

'No.' Joy laughed nervously. 'But I've been thinking about what you said, I've got to be straight with him.'

In the restaurant, Kate thought she had never felt so elated in her life. 'What did you say was happening to me – an adrenalin high? This must be how you feel on speed – I think I could learn to like it.' Kate laughed loudly, bubbling with excitement. Throughout the meal she could not sit still; she drank too much too quickly and stayed sober, and she felt she wanted to talk and talk and never stop. If only one other person was here. Every time there was a flurry of new arrivals in the restaurant she looked up hoping one would be Stewart.

Joy felt nervous as she waited for Barty to return from a reception he had been to at the Swedish Embassy. It was all very well saying she was going to be straight with him, but where and how to start were occupying her mind.

'You look very pretty.' He kissed her cheek when he joined her in the little sitting room they used when they were alone. 'How was Kate? I hope Gervase videoed it for me.'

'She was wonderful, a natural, everyone said so.' She lit a cigarette, aware her fingers were trembling. 'I wondered if I could have a word with you before dinner, Barty?'

''Course you can.' He sat down beside her on the sofa. 'Why are you looking so serious?'

'I want to be honest with you, Barty. I don't think I can go ahead with our plan to get married.' She sat stiffly, not looking at him, hating herself for saying it and knowing she loved him too much not to.

'And why not?' he asked calmly.

'Because although I love you as a friend, I don't think I'm in love with you, and so it would not be right.'

'I'm fully aware of that. It's good enough for me.'

'But it's more complex than that Barty. What if the courts object to you as stepfather to Hannah? How on earth can I choose between you?'

'You wouldn't have to. We'll win her back.'

'But you can't be sure of that.' Joy sighed and looked intently at her hands. There was nothing for it, she was going to have to tell him everything. 'It's like this, Barty. I should hate Charles – but I don't. And – I'm loath to admit this – there are times I find myself wondering if we can't get back together again.' There, she had said it. She did not look at him but continued the study of her hands, twisting the wonderful ring that Barty had given her and which, until she was free, was on her right hand.

'I think I can wear that.'

'I'm sorry?' Joy asked, not sure if she had heard correctly.

'I'm not totally stupid, Joy.' He took her hand in his. 'There's always been the risk that you think you're still in love with Charles. But note I said "think". What you are in love with is the few good times you had with him – memories can be a sod of a thing. You're beginning to forget the bad times – but I won't forget. Never.'

'That's strange. That's what Kate said.'

'Kate's a wise woman. I'll be straight with you, Joy. I think that perhaps you agreed to think about marrying me so quickly in the hope that it might bring him to heel?' He glanced quizzically at her, a gentle smile on his round, bland face. Joy felt herself begin to blush. 'But he didn't come to heel, did he, Joy? And that's the point. I'm willing to gamble he won't in the future either. And also that the feelings you have for him are because you are confused and that they will fade too. And I love you, nothing has altered that. I told you what I could and could not give you, the offer remains.'

'But, Barty, I'm being unfair to you. I've been so hypocritical.'

'How come? It can't have been easy to say what you just have to me. I respect your honesty. I might be wrong, you might go back to him. If so, don't worry about me – I'd be sad but I'd recover. I can't say fairer than that now, can I?'

'Barty, I don't deserve you.'

'Don't be silly,' Barty smiled bashfully but resolved to get on to the barrister. This problem had to be resolved quickly.

Gloria lay in bed unable to sleep. It had been a lovely evening. Kate had been such fun, bubbling with excitement and sheer joy. She had not taken her car to the studio so Peter drove her home. She had felt so relaxed with him tonight, had felt so happy and, for once, sure of him. She had decided that tonight she would ask him to stay.

When they had arrived back at her house he had leant across to her and kissed her on the cheek.

'You look tired, Gloria, it's been a long day. No need to feel you have to be polite and ask me in for a drink. I'm ready for bed myself.'

'Thank you, Peter,' she had said, feeling as if a bucket of cold water had been poured over her. 'Thanks for the lift,' she had added politely.

Now she lay alone when he should have been with her. Just her and Elephant snoring gently in his basket at the end of her bed. She feared she might have been too cautious. She felt he had become bored with her and her stupidity.

*

Kate lay wide-eyed in the dark in her hotel room and thought she had never felt more lonely. She had experienced two of the most wonderful days of her life. She had been fêted and fussed and now, suddenly, she felt lower than she could ever remember. She looked at the empty pair of pillows beside her and felt sad. She wanted the success, the acclaim, but she also wanted to be loved. She did not want to be alone. She was afraid. And when she closed her eyes it was the image of Stewart, large and shambling, with his kind smile, that filled her mind.

12

Kate opened the door of her house and the minute she entered it she knew that something was different. She stood for a moment in the hall and told herself not to be so stupid. She listened but all she heard was the rumble of the central-heating boiler, the tick of the clock in the hall, the swish of tyre wheels on the damp road outside. All normal sounds. Why, then, was she imagining this silence to be leaden with something else, with anger, disruption?

She looked in the drawing room but everything was as she had left it. She pushed open the kitchen door and the cat mewed to her in welcome while the Aga burbled sibilantly. She crossed the room, pulled the kettle on to the hob and leant against the bar of the cooker. She felt depressed and yet last night she had been flying. In the run-up to her launch the telephone had never stopped ringing but this morning, at her hotel, it had not rung once. She had telephoned Gloria, who was not in the office, and spoken to Val who was polite but sounded distracted. Reason told her that they had moved on to the next book to be published, but it was hard to accept. For so long it was as if only her book existed for them too. She felt as if she was yesterday's news. Nothing was happening and she felt bereft.

She had been away for nearly a week and a pile of mail awaited her, mostly dull bills but among them, excitingly, was a note from Stewart Dorchester with an invitation to the *Daily News* best book of the year award, at the Café Royal, no less. It was in a couple of days, no time to write – she would telephone him to let him know she would love to go. It was also an excuse to hear his voice again.

She made her mug of coffee and walked to the pine table. On its surface was a copy of the *Graintry Echo* opened at a page where her face loomed up at her. They had used a photograph of her in this very kitchen standing by her Aga. She smiled, at least the photograph was a good one. Kate sat down and looked for the article.

Writing Ruins Local Author's Marriage

The words did not jump out at her, they careered from the page. There it all was, her confidential talk with Dee. She had written of Tony's disinterest, was he jealous? And a long section on men's inability to cope with their women's success. She covered her face with her hands. Even the menopause was mentioned ... 'Oh, God...' she groaned. No wonder she had sensed anger in the air. What must Tony have thought? The telephone made her jump. She let it ring, not wishing to answer it, not wanting to talk to anyone, she felt so humiliated. It stopped. Five minutes later it rang again. This time she made herself get up to answer it.

'So you're back?' Tony greeted her.

'Tony, I've just seen the newspaper. I'm sorry, it wasn't like that ... the woman has written things wrongly. It's not fair – '

'It certainly isn't fair, making me a laughing stock in my own town. How dare you discuss our problems with a total stranger?'

'But I didn't realise that I was.'

'Don't give me that crap, Kate. I haven't the patience to discuss anything with you any more. I've moved my stuff out, I've rented a cottage for a month until the house sale is finalised. By the way, saw you on television, nice to see you ripping into some other poor sod for a change.'

The line went dead. She walked slowly back to the table and her now tepid coffee. Was that how he saw her, a raving termagant? Well, one thing had come out of the whole fiasco: she had learnt a salutary lesson that nothing was off the record with certain elements of the press.

Still, she thought, there were other members of the press. She telephoned Stewart and while she waited for the connection to be made realised she had butterflies in her stomach. If she had any doubts about anything, that call from Tony had changed her mind.

'Stewart? Thanks for your note. I'd love to come.'

'Oh, great. I missed you at Barty's the other night. I looked for you but I presumed you had left early.'

'No,' she said, not liking to tell him she had been in the loo with Gloria and Joy.

'Never mind, we can make up for it at the awards. I'll leave your invitation at the desk for you. I might be a bit late, I've an interview with the Home Secretary in the morning.'

'I see,' she said, impressed. When she finally rang off she felt ridiculously excited, like a young girl, and immediately began to plan what to wear. She was putting the kettle back on when the front-door bell rang. What now? she thought, as she went to answer it.

'Doug? Good gracious, what a surprise!' She forced herself to sound welcoming, though the thought of entertaining Pam's husband right now did not appeal. But she had not seen him for months and it would be churlish not to invite him in.

'Saw you on the telly last night, Kate. You were a smash.'

'Thanks. Coffee? I've just put the kettle on.' She led the way into the kitchen.

'I'm sorry to bother you, Kate, you must be a busy woman these days – what with the book and everything. But I had to talk to someone or I thought I'd go mad.'

'Of course, what on earth's the matter? Sit down, you don't look well,' she said, for in the better light of the kitchen she saw he looked grey with fatigue.

'You don't know, do you?'

'Know what?'

'Pam, she's done a bunk . . .'

'Pam? Dear God, Doug, I'm sorry. I'd no idea, I haven't seen her in weeks, why we hardly even talk on the telephone these days. When did she go, where's she gone?' She had sat down, forgetting the coffee in her concern for the man.

'With your Tony. She's done a bunk with your husband.'

The familiar walls of her kitchen appeared to move inward as if made of rubber. She was aware that Doug was still talking and forced herself to listen.

'She told me about it last week – give her her due, she was ashamed and all. And then I got home from work last night and she'd gone.'

'You're not joking, are you?' She knew she was staring at him with amazement.

'No, sorry, I'm not.'

'He told me the other day he had met someone else, but, not in a million years . . .' Her voice trailed off as her brain tried to assimilate this information.

'It's been going on for over a year.'

'Over a year? Surely not.'

'Oh yes, a year ago last August apparently. She didn't want to tell me but I made her.'

'But how?'

'Remember Pam went to visit her sister in Harrogate? She'd flown back from Australia for a holiday . . .'

'Yes, yes, and Tony was at a conference on . . .' she laughed, a mirthless sound. 'Rather apt actually, a conference on children in divorce, if I remember.'

'Right. Well, they met, had a drink and the rest is history, as they say.' He smiled wanly. 'I tried to give her everything she wanted but it wasn't enough. It's my fault, but one thing and another, I wasn't much cop at, well, you know, sex,' he said with discomfort.

This time when Kate laughed it was with genuine amusement. Doug, in his misery, looked at her perplexed.

'I'm sorry, Doug, I know it's not really funny. But you see, poor Pam – she won't get much joy there either. Tony's useless in bed.'

'That's not what she said, made him sound like the stud of the century,' he said mournfully.

'She didn't? Oh, that was cruel of her. And it can't be true, not unless he's had a dose of hormones or something. Bloody hell, Doug, this is lousy, isn't it? One's marriage breaking up is bad enough but the deception?' She shook her head, not able to take in fully all the implications of this news. 'What about her writing?'

'She's given that up, said Tony didn't want her to do it. She said his happiness was more important to her.'

'That rings true,' she said with feeling.

'I want her back, Kate. I can't live without her, I know I can't.' And to Kate's horror the large, burly man began to cry.

'There, there, she'll be back. If he bores her half as much as he bored me, she'll soon come running home.'

She sat patting his hand, murmuring words of comfort and thought she had come full circle. She had confessed to his being boring that night she had met Gloria and Joy. Then, just speaking the words had been like a liberation to her. For the past year she had swung as if on a see-saw, first wanting him gone, then trying to save her marriage. Now she had said it again – he was boring, and once again the simple word had made her feel free of him. Nothing had changed in those twelve months where he was concerned and nothing would. But Pam? How could Pam have deceived her? They had gone on the writers' weekend together, shopped, nattered on the telephone as if everything was the same when it wasn't. She had thought she knew Pam better than any other woman, and she hadn't. She had put her occasional strangeness down to jealousy over her writing but it probably wasn't that at all – that was when Pam had shown her true colours. She had not liked what was going on, she had been embarrassed in Kate's company. Such a defence of her old friend cheered her a little and Kate felt no anger towards her, only puzzlement. 'Oh, Pam, you fool,' she said aloud.

That lunchtime Barty received a visit from the private detective he had hired. The man had a selection of photographs with him. They had been taken the night before in a brothel, one with a special room for 'correction'. There, smiling straight at the camera, was the face of Charles Trenchard, dressed from head to toe in black leather, a whip in his hand, a large erection and about to beat a woman trussed up in shackles like a chicken.

'Love a duck,' said Barty. 'The things people do!'

'The rest are even better, sir.'

'How did you get them, for God's sake? Why, the man hasn't even had the sense to wear a mask.'

'There's a viewing gallery, sir, behind a two-way mirror ... Simple. He wouldn't have twigged. The flash can be a bit dodgy sometimes but, as you see, he had other things on his mind. Fair old dick he's got on him, hasn't he?' The detective grinned at him.

'I wonder if he goes there often?' Barty said more to himself than to the man.

'He's booked in for tomorrow, if that should be of any help to you, sir.'

'Immeasurable help. See Gervase on the way out. He'll see you right.'

As soon as the detective had left, Barty telephoned an old friend of many years' standing.

'Gloria? I've the most wonderful book for you, it's so readable, I couldn't put it down. I'm having it biked over straight away.' Joy's voice bubbled down the telephone.

'You're working again, that's wonderful news.'

'I had a long talk with myself. I've been behaving stupidly and selfishly. Kate was right, work is wonderful for sorting oneself out. I'm going to stick to it now, and with Barty. Even if I don't get Hannah back I've got to learn to carry on and Barty's the best person to teach me. He's so calm, so sensible and kind. I would have to look a long while ever to find someone who cares as much for me as he does.'

'I'm glad. Will Faith stay on?' Gloria asked.

'Yes. Most of her authors are coming with her and with Kate's success and getting Barty's book, the work is pouring in, and it's going to need the two of us. I've done it, Gloria. The agency is a success!' She was laughing. 'Just one other thing, it's dreadfully short notice, but it's my birthday tomorrow. You and Peter don't fancy coming to dinner? Barty wanted to give me a party but I said I'd prefer just a quiet dinner with friends.'

'I'll have to check with Peter but I'm sure it'll be fine.'

Gloria was smiling when she replaced the receiver. Life with Barty was unlikely to be a bed of roses or a sea of passion but, Joy was right, kindness went a long way in a relationship. Look at the mess she had been making of her own life with her preoccupation with sex or no sex.

The telephone rang again.

'Gloria, I've an Ulrika Talbot-Blaize, for you,' said Rachel.

'Who?'

'She says she's one of our authors. Wants to arrange to have a manuscript picked up.'

'Picked up?'

'I know, sounds a bit potty, doesn't she?'

'You'd better put her on.'

The line deadened, then clicked as Rached rerouted the call.

'Is this Miss Catchpole?' a deep, gin-soaked voice, so husky it would be difficult to tell if it was a man or woman speaking, asked. 'I was so pleased to hear of your appointment, not enough women in positions of power these days despite women's liberation or whatever it is they call it. Just look at the Cabinet – it really is too bad the lack of women there after those poor suffragettes went through so much, wouldn't you agree?'

'Mrs Talbot-Blaize?'

'Miss, actually. I was never one for the fetters of the marriage vows myself, too restraining.' A chuckle as deep and rich as the voice burbled along the telephone lines.

'Your manuscript?' Gloria tried to keep the amusement she was feeling out of her voice.

'Yes, so sad, I had hoped to finish it in time for Julius to read it, but silly man curled up his toes before I'd finished. Of course I'm disastrously late with it, about twenty years, in fact, but time does fly so, don't you find? And I did get so bored writing the thing. I find that too, don't you? Memories are so turgid, one wants to be up and fornicating not writing about it. But it's done now, so could someone come and fetch it, please?'

'Can you not post it?' Gloria had difficulty controlling her laughter.

'Post it? Well, there's a novel idea. No, I don't think so, my dear. I don't want to risk it in the post, it's the only copy I've got. Better you pop in and collect it. That's what Julius did.'

'Well, of course, if that's what Julius did. Your address?' She picked up her pen. Miss Talbot-Blaize was someone she very much wanted to meet.

'Just pop into the pub, the Old Success in Sennen, they'll direct you. So nice talking to you, Miss Catchpole. Come for lunch, we'll sink a gin or two.'

'Sennen, did you say? How extraordinary, my parents live near there. I could come when I next visit them.'

'Capital. Give me a buzz, I'm always here. If not, Jago is.'

'Miss Talbot-Blaize, your book, what's it called?'

'This one? I thought *Last and Lingering Troubadour* ties in rather well with the other one, don't you think?'

One of the delights of publishing, Gloria thought as she rang off, was the differing characters of the authors. Certainly, there were the difficult ones like the Bellas of this world, but there were some lovely eccentrics, too, like this one, and they made up for all the horrible carping ones.

'Rachel, could you look on the computer to find out the name of the novel or memoirs – I'm not sure which – of Ulrika Talbot-Blaize. What a character!'

Gloria returned to the work she had been doing. She was managing, contrary to her original fears, to do some editing and was working on a new book by Grace Bliss, fitting it in between the now inevitable administrative chores.

'Can't find her, Gloria. Sorry, there's no one of that name on the computer and no one's heard of her,' Rachel reported half an hour later.

'That's odd. She sounded potty enough to have got the wrong publishers. Never mind, it doesn't matter. I'm to see her next time I go home. I'll find out before then.'

The next morning Gloria was in the postroom attempting to retrieve a letter she had sent down last night. She had written rejecting a manuscript, but last night, when she could not sleep, she had had second thoughts and decided she would publish it after all.

The postroom was in the basement. Shelves lined the walls. On one side were those for incoming mail. There were pigeon holes with the names of all employees above the table where letters were sorted and then delivered about the building by Stan, the old postman who had been employed here longer than anyone else. Several parcels and Jiffy bags were waiting to be dealt with. Those addressed to a specific person were left unopened and would be delivered later but the date of their arrival and the addressee were logged in a large book that stood on a central table, and which the recipient signed when they accepted the package. Those parcels addressed merely to Westall and Trim were opened and their contents, name of sender and date of arrival were entered, plus a given number, into another book on which was written Unsolicited Manuscripts. These were placed on the shelves on the other wall, under a number pinned to the shelf. This neat orderly row of typescripts was what was known as the slush pile, even if there was no pile. Although, like every other publisher, they accepted no responsibility for the safety of a manuscript, it would be a dreadful thing to lose one. This system and Stan had ensured that nothing was ever lost from here, even if there were often panics in the offices upstairs.

Gloria stood anxiously while Stan checked the post on the shelves on the remaining wall where post to be sent out was held.

'Sorry, Gloria, it would have gone out last night if you put it out to be collected before four-thirty.'

'I did. Never mind, Stan. We've probably lost the best book since what? *Gone with the Wind*. My fault, I shouldn't be a ditherer.' She turned to go and then had an idea. 'By the way, Stan, does the name Ulrika Talbot-Blaize mean anything to you?'

'Ulrika? Most certainly does. There was a woman for you.' He sighed at what was evidently a happy memory. Gloria stood by the door waiting patiently. 'Wonderful creature. Beautiful? There was never anyone like her, nor has been since, in my opinion. Like a film star. She walked down the street and heads turned. Racy she was, very fast, but charming with it. Oh, yes.' He nodded. 'She had charm and no side to her. "Hello, Stan how are you?" she'd say, just like I was important. One of Mr Julius's ladies, if you know what I mean. Bishop's daughter she was, they often are the raciest, so I'm told.'

'She wrote a book?'

'That she did.' He laughed. 'That caused a stir and no mistake. The lawyers had to labour over that one, her memoirs they were, you see. The people she had known in a very special way . . .' He raised one eyebrow. 'Half the Cabinet, actors, royalty, they were all in it. Scandalous it was. But what a read!'

'She's written a sequel.'

'Never? Good God, I'd have thought she'd be dead by now what with the amount of booze she packed away. Mr Julius had given up on ever receiving that book, I can tell you. I often mentioned it to him, but he said he doubted if she would ever finish it.'

'What was the first book called, do you remember?'

'Like yesterday. Lovely title. *To Whom the Bird Has Sung.* Some bird, some song.' The old man laughed.

13

Kate walked rather tentatively into the crowded reception room of the Café Royal. The noise was so loud it was like walking into solid sound. She took a glass from a hovering waiter and looked about her among the groups intent on their conversations, hoping to see Stewart and, if not him, then someone she knew. She stood to one side and watched. Every other face was that of someone famous. Some writers she admired and others she did not. A sprinkling of actors. And a few of that strange breed of person who was merely famous for being famous.

'Hallo, should I know you?' She turned to find a woman about her own age, smartly dressed and clutching a glass as if it was a life-raft.

'I shouldn't think so, my name's Kate Howard.'

'Kate Howard? No, name doesn't ring a bell, I'm afraid.'

'I write fiction – for women mainly.'

'What are you doing here, then?'

'I'm not sure.' She smiled. 'I was just invited.'

'I won my ticket. Every year the paper runs a competition, you get a copy of the winning book as well.'

'That's nice.'

'Not that they're my sort of book, a bit too literary for me. I like a good read myself.'

'Me too,' Kate said with more feeling than the woman realised.

'It was once for the most popular book – now they're too highbrow for me. Still it's a day out, isn't it? Oh, excuse me, I must go. Look, do you see? It's Gerald Walters over there! Now his books I do like.' And Kate was left alone again.

'Kate. Lovely to see you, what on earth are you doing here?' It was Sheena Goodly. 'Gracious, that sounds awful!' She laughed. 'It's just after the other night – well, this is such a literary turnout, isn't it?'

'I was invited.' Kate forced herself to smile.

'You should see the postbag we got about you. I'll send them on. Whoops! Look who's here, your biggest fan, Sebastian Trumpington.'

'Good God, my favourite author,' Sebastian drawled sarcastically. 'But what on earth are you doing at a turn-out like this – thought you regarded us as pseuds?'

'Not all of you,' Kate corrected him. 'I was invited.' But this time she was not smiling.

Although the room was crowded, she did not feel like trying to speak to anyone. She felt certain that if another person asked her what she was doing here, she might just hit them with her handbag. She was relieved when the master of ceremonies announced that luncheon was served. She was first at her table. She peeked at the place names either side of her. The one on her left meant nothing. But on her right she saw Stewart's name.

'Glad you could make it.' She looked up to see a smiling Stewart taking his seat.

'Stewart. At last, a friendly face. Could you answer a question that's been bothering me? What *am* I doing here?' She laughed.

'You're here because I loved your book and your writing – you should be one of the finalists in my opinion. But there you go – I'm not in charge of the selection. And the other reason?' He put his hand out and took hold of hers. 'Because I think you're a lovely person and I found I wanted to see you again. Do you mind?' He was looking at her with a serious expression.

'No, I don't mind at all,' she said, but she could not look at him for fear he might see the excitement that he had sparked.

Late that afternoon there was a police raid on a brothel in central London. Certain people were arrested. The male customers, as is so often the case, were given a warning at the police station, and sent on their way. The madame of the brothel and the prostitutes, as is so often the case, were charged.

As he let himself into his mistress's house, Charles Trenchard was feeling enormously relieved at the understanding attitude of the police.

'Darling, you have a visitor.' Penelope met him in the hall. Charles entered the sitting room to find Sir Barty Silver with an impassive Gervase awaiting him.

'Charles, long time no see.' Barty rose and smiled warmly.

'What are you doing here, Silver? We've nothing to say to each other that can't wait for the courts.' Charles crossed to the drinks tray and poured himself a whisky, pointedly omitting to extend the courtesy to others.

'Ah, Charles, that's where you could be wrong. If you wouldn't mind,' he smiled quizzically at Penelope.

'No, darling, don't leave, I'd rather you stayed. In fact, with the divorce proceedings as far advanced as they are, and my wife domiciled at your address, I don't think you should even be here, Silver.'

'Oh, I don't know about that, Trenchard. And if you take my advice, I think it would be better if the young lady did leave us.'

There was something in the way he spoke that persuaded Penelope that she did not wish to remain in the room. 'I've some work to do,' she said as an excuse.

'Well?' Charles looked at Barty with loathing.

'It's Joy's birthday today. I fancy giving her a really nice present.'

'So?'

'Like her daughter – Hannah.'

'No way, Silver.'

'I'm not so sure about that. Gervase...' Barty flicked his fingers at the young man who clicked open a briefcase and removed an envelope. Before taking it from Gervase's outstretched hand, Barty with slow deliberation took a pair of chamois-leather gloves from his coat pocket and slipped them on.

'Now, what have we here? Holiday snaps? No, Trenchard, we've got very nasty dirty pictures.' He shook the envelope so that the photographs scattered out on to the table. 'Of you.' Barty waved the envelope at Charles.

Charles did not even have to look at the contents of the package, he had already turned white.

'Not a pretty picture, as they say, is it?' Barty smiled a small, private smile. 'Now, we have one or two things to consider here, Trenchard. You come with me now and collect Hannah to return her to her mother, or, I'm sorry to say, copies of these photographs will be delivered, within the hour, to the other members of your chambers, and, I regret, the Lord Chancellor himself.'

'This is blackmail.'

'Yes, you would be correct in that.'

'You can't get away with blackmail, not in this country.'

'Can't you? So now, since these rather mucky photos have found their way into my hands, you'll stop blackmailing me, won't you? I know what you're implying about Joy and me – we'll see that the little lady is well chaperoned and make no mistake. And you've been lying about me, slandering me, making out I'm some sort of queer, so Joy can't have her little one with her. I'm not the pervert around here, Mr Trenchard – you are. And I'll make sure all those who should know, do know – including that rather pretty lady out there.'

'I demand the negatives.'

'And why not, Mr Trenchard?'

Charles picked up his car keys. 'Very well, then, but you haven't heard the last of this, Silver.'

'Oh, I think I have.'

'I suppose you were responsible for the raid this afternoon?'

'What a thing to say, Mr Trenchard! Whatever next?' Barty wagged his finger at him as he laughed.

By the time Gloria and Peter arrived for dinner, Hannah was installed in the nursery Barty had had decorated and he and Joy had filled with expensive toys. Several copies of the photographs of Hannah's father were installed in Barty's safe.

Joy was almost incoherent with excitement. 'The best birthday present ever,' she said, looking at Barty with adoration, the look Gloria had waited to see her give him. 'We should be able to get married in three months.'

'That's marvellous. Will you stop working?'

'Oh, no, remember what dear agony aunt Kate had to say. We women need our independence.' She laughed, taking hold of Barty's hand and squeezing it, laughing with the confidence of a woman secure with her man.

The dinner was sublime but Gloria was not surprised. With both Barty and Joy being such perfectionists, it was inevitable. In truth, they were a lot better suited than one at first thought.

'So, Gloria, are you enjoying Westall and Trim?' Barty asked.

'Very much so.'

'Brian's almost finished my book. It's good, very good.'

'That will be a launch and a half.' Gloria grinned. 'We're hoping for a summer publication for that one.'

'I've seen Crispin Anderson. I've told him I would be interested in acquiring the firm.'

'But, Barty, it's not for sale,' Gloria said, not sure of her ground.

'That's a shame,' he said noncommittally. 'We could have worked well together, you and I, I think. You come highly recommended,' and he smiled across the table at Joy.

'If anyone buys it I think it should be Peter,' Joy stated firmly.

'Me? Why me?' Peter looked puzzled.

'Because it's a wonderful firm, and not one that the conglomerates should be allowed to get their hands on. You'd keep it as Julius wanted it. And you need something to do, you'll go mad doing nothing.' Joy shrugged her shoulders. 'And, I think you and Gloria together would take Westall's into the twenty-first century and make it a force to be reckoned with.'

'Why thank you, Joy, that's a lovely thing to say.' Gloria looked with gratitude across at Joy. What a wonderful dream that would be, she thought.

'But what hope would I have of acquiring it with Barty in the bidding?' Peter said.

'Are you interested, Peter, seriously?' Barty asked.

'I don't know. I could be.'

'Oh, Barty, then you've got to drop out, that would be awful if you were fighting each other – and Peter needs it more than you. Please.' Joy was pleading.

'I can see marriage is likely to ruin me if I allow myself to listen to my wife too often.' He smiled indulgently at her. He sat thinking a moment, looking around the table, all faces looking at him expectantly 'All right, against my better judgement, I'll pull out. But I warn you, Peter, I'm in the market. The next opportunity that presents itself, I buy. Then we'll be rivals.'

'That's a horrendous thought, something Mike Pewter and I dread,' Peter said laughing.

'Mind you, I think it would be better if I didn't tell Crispin Anderson. I could be of use to everyone if he thinks I'm still interested – get my drift?' He winked. 'So, Gloria, you've solved the mystery of Lepanto, then?'

'How on earth did you know about that? And what makes you ask?'

Barty tapped the side of his nose. 'I know lots of things.' Joy watched him and with relief found the action did not irritate her. 'The only way you could confidently say it was not for sale was if the employees' trust had control of the Lepanto shares, that's all. So it's a mystery no more?'

'I wouldn't say that.' Gloria shook her head. 'Up to yesterday I thought we were getting nowhere. Then an author contacted me out of the blue. And I've got this feeling she might be the key to it. I'm going to see her and try to find out though I don't know how to approach the subject when it's only a feeling.'

'Feelings usually have reasons,' Barty interrupted.

'She wrote a book years ago and we can't find a copy. That's odd, you see. We think Julius had copies of everything, so why not this one?'

'What was the book called?' Joy leant forward with interest.

'A lovely title, it sounds like poetry, but I've never heard it. *To Whom the Bird Has Sung.*'

From the end of the table, Barty coughed. 'Allow me,' he said. Everyone looked in his direction.

> *'The last and lingering troubadour,*
> *To whom the bird has sung,*
> *Who once went singing southward*
> *When all the world was young.'*

Barty sat back with a wide grin.

'Barty, that was lovely. What a wonderful poem.'

'We learnt a lot at Barnardo's, you know.' His grin had become mischievous.

'Who's it by?'

'G. K. Chesterton.'

'No one knows any Chesterton, these days.'

'More's the pity. But I do, Gloria, I do.' Barty was laughing now.

'What? Why are you laughing at me? What is it, Barty?'

'Do you want to know, really?'

'Barty, come on, don't be horrible to poor Gloria.'

'Want to know the title, Gloria?'

'Of course.'

'"Lepanto", Gloria, that's what it's called. What about that, then?'

14

During the afternoon of Barty's dinner party, Crispin had been busy. Since the identity of Lepanto was not at the office, he reasoned it must be at Julius's house in the country. He had telephoned his aunt and requested that he be allowed to do a thorough search of the library there. They had searched it once but not well enough for Crispin's satisfaction. He arrived mid-afternoon and after a pleasant chat and a cup of Earl Grey with his aunt, he settled into the library-cum-study that had been Julius's domain.

It was rather creepy being alone in the room for Julius's presence was very strong, and Crispin had the uncomfortable feeling that at any moment the door might open and his uncle walk in and demand to know what the hell Crispin was doing rummaging through his desk.

The desk held no clue, nor did a bureau which was stuffed with papers. Crispin had quite an amusing time with some letters he had found there. They were from various women, some so old the ink had faded. The sentimental old fool must have been keeping them for years. Odd he should keep them here where his wife might find them but, then, maybe the man did not care. Of course, if Jane found them she might burn them so he stuffed them in his briefcase. Archives should never be destroyed, he told himself. He would keep them, one never knew. Some person some day might wish to write a biography of Julius and he might be able to sell them.

He sat for some time at the desk, trying to get into the man's mind, wondering where he could have left a clue or made a slip. Only the books were left. He crossed to the large bookcase opposite: at least he had kept the books published by Westall's together. But he had been through these at the office. And then his eye saw one book. He frowned. A vague memory stirred. He took it down from the shelf, and, professional that he was, studied the cover, removed it, inspected the hard covers, the gold printing on the spine. Nice work. But it was the title that bothered him. He was sure he had not seen this book in the office, and that someone had mentioned it – recently. *To Whom the Bird Has Sung.* Sir Gerald Walters, that was it, he'd wanted to call a book by this title. He flipped the book open – dedicated to Julius himself. Now that was interesting. And then he saw the poem, saw who it was by, saw the title. He dived for the telephone, dialled directory enquiries and rang the number he had been given. Five minutes later he had an appointment for the following morning with Ulrika Talbot-Blaize, who, most satisfactorily, had said she had been expecting to hear from him. He telephoned British Rail and booked on the overnight sleeper to Penzance; it arrived just before eight in the morning. He went in search of his aunt to tell her all was solved.

Once everyone at the dinner party had realised the full potential of what Barty had said, pandemonium broke out. Barty, who had always claimed he did not like personal contact, was engulfed in hugs and kisses from both Joy and Gloria. Their excitement was infectious and Barty relinquished himself to the onslaught. Though he would never have dreamed of admitting it to anyone, he rather enjoyed it.

'I want to cry,' Gloria said, looking very much as if she was about to.

'Well, cry, my darling.' Peter put his arm about her.

'I just don't believe we've solved it. This nutty Ulrika woman – she simply has to be Lepanto, doesn't she?' Gloria looked at the faces around her as if pleading with them to agree with her.

'Telephone her, ask her,' Joy suggested practically.

Gloria looked at her watch. 'I can't, it's gone ten, she's old and probably in bed.'

'We could drive down through the night, and telephone her at a more civilised hour,' Peter said.

'Would you come?'

'You're not driving all that way on your own.'

Gloria, unused to being looked after by anyone, became quite fluttery with pleasure. 'If we leave about midnight we'd be at my parents between six and seven depending on the traffic.'

'What on earth will they say if we turn up at such a God-awful hour?'

'It isn't, to them. My father is always up by six. We could bath and change and call Ulrika about ten. What do you think?'

'We'll do that.'

'That settled, how about more coffee and a brandy?'

'No, whoever's doing the driving no more booze,' Barty ordered. And since they were sharing the driving they both had coffee.

'What a birthday!' Joy smiled contentedly.

Kate lay in the hotel bed and listened to the unfamiliar sounds of London outside the building. She lay on her back, looking at the ceiling, conscious of a wonderful feeling of lethargy as if she had been asleep for a hundred years and would need another hundred to wake up fully. There was no going back. Tony had said she had changed, now that change was complete. Writing her book had freed her mentally but now she was freed physically. She looked down at the man cradled in her arms and could have wept with happiness. The unimaginable had happened, someone she had found attractive had wanted her also. Where would it lead? Where did she want it to lead? She did not know. All her life she had wondered what the future held. Worried about it, if she was honest. Now she did not care. It was this moment that mattered, this contented minute of lying holding a man who had given her a pleasure she had not imagined existed. If it never happened again, so be it, she had experienced joy untold, she had memories now, real, worthy memories.

It had been wonderful. Being here with him had been the most natural thing in the world. After the awards, they had spent the afternoon together going to the zoo. They had talked and talked. She had told him things about herself, dreams and hopes, fears from the past that she had never told a living soul, never thought to put into words and certainly not to Tony. They had dined and as the meal progressed their physical need for each other became so strong that neither said anything, suggested it nor hinted at it – it was not necessary for both knew what the other wanted. They had left the restaurant and walked until they had found this hotel. He had looked down at her, a gentle smile on his face, and she had nodded, even then had not spoken.

He had undressed her, slowly, so slowly that her longing was intensified into a great ache inside her. She was embarrassed he should be looking at her – the second man in her life to do so. She wanted to cover herself, hide her body from his gaze. He had stroked her sensuously and had kissed her body with soft caressing kisses. He had knelt before her and she found she was no longer embarrassed but a woman hungry for her man.

He stirred and, as if aware that new arms were holding him, woke quickly. He sat up and looked down at her, smiling gently.

'Why so serious?' he asked.

'I'm angry, if you must know. Angry that all my adult life I've been cheated of the pleasure you gave me last night.'

He leant forward and kissed her. 'It was something wonderful and different for me, too, you know.'

She put up her hand and gently caressed his face. 'I just can't believe it happened. I mean, at my age you don't expect this.'

'Speak for yourself.' He laughed. 'I'm older than you!'

'Yes, but you're a man.'

'I gathered that. I'm glad you did, too!'

'No, you know what I mean.' She smiled shyly. 'It's different for a man. Your grey hair is distinguished, mine is an indication that I'm over the hill. I'm overweight, that's middle-age spread, a man's overweight and he's a fine figure of a man.'

'I think you're beautiful.'

'Please don't say things you don't mean. It's not fair.'

'I never would. I do think you're beautiful. I don't know what has happened to you in the past, Kate, that makes you feel you must knock yourself, but I intend to put a stop to it. No more putting yourself down, right?'

'I'll try.' She was laughing now, feeling a confidence so new to her she did not even recognise it.

'So where do we go from here?'

'I don't know, Stewart.'

'You don't regret last night?'

'Don't be silly.'

'I want to see you again and again, Kate.'

'Good. I do, too.'

'I never expected anything like this to happen to me again in my life.' He sighed. 'I have to go to Edinburgh today, a big book launch. How about the weekend?'

'That would be lovely.'

'Shall we meet here, in this hotel?'

'No. Come to my house. We'll be more comfortable, more private there.'

*

It was early still when Kate drove into her driveway. Pam's car was parked outside.

'Pam? You're an early visitor,' she said with no rancour.

'I was just about to drive off. I need to see you, Kate.' Pam's face, pink with embarrassment, looked up at her.

'Of course, come in.'

In the kitchen Kate did what she always did, put the kettle on even before she had taken off her coat.

'I had to talk to you, Kate, tell you how sorry I am. I've hardly slept worrying what you must think of me. I know it's unlikely but I still want to be your friend. I know what you must be thinking of me.'

'I doubt if you do, Pam.' Kate was smiling at her. 'I was a bit shaken at how long it has been going on, I thought that was a bit tacky.'

'I know.' Pam hung her head in shame.

'But I do understand why it happened. You were lonely.'

'But my best friend's husband? It's all so shitty. I can't believe I did it.'

'You've gone back to Doug, haven't you?'

'Yes. I was mad to leave. But when Tony said you and he had split up and were getting a divorce, I felt responsible in a way. And then when he phoned to say he had found us a house to rent, I thought I had to see it through. I realise now I was playing a game. It was the excitement when it was illicit, it was like a drug. Now it's in the open . . .' she shrugged, 'I found I wanted Doug.'

'He does love you, you know, desperately. Tony would have been so wrong for you. There are people who suck other people dry of their personality and he's one of them.'

'Can we still be friends?'

'I don't know if we will ever be the same again, with each other.'

'You'll feel you can't trust me? What a fool I've been.' Pam was close to tears.

'I'm trying to be honest, Pam. I don't know, but I don't blame you for taking away from me something that had already disappeared. It wouldn't be fair. I would just be blaming you for something that Tony and I had caused to happen.'

'I wanted to see you and patch it up, but you being so reasonable is making me feel worse,' Pam said contrarily.

'I don't feel like screeching at you, that's all. Coffee or tea?' She smiled at the ordinariness, the mundane question.

'Coffee, please. But are you going to be all right? Tony said you'd found a cottage, but you've never lived alone in all your life.'

'Now's my chance. I've found a place, near Henley, but I'm not sure about it any more. This morning I've been wondering whether to get a flat in London.' She paused and wondered if to continue, and thought, what did it matter? She was a free agent now. 'I've met someone, you see.' She heard herself saying the words and shook her head in amazement that she, of all people, could be saying them.

'No! How exciting.' Pam was leaning over the table, red hair falling round her pretty face, eyes sparkling with interest – just like old times. 'Tell me all.'

'Don't pinch this one.' Kate laughed, shocked by what she was saying – it was all right for Pam to take her husband, not her lover. If she needed anything to show her the futility of continuing with her marriage, then that comment did.

But as she spoke of Stewart she wondered, if she had not found him, would she have been quite so understanding with Pam?

On the long car journey west, driving through the night, for the first time Gloria felt totally relaxed with Peter. Whether it was the pleasant evening they had enjoyed, solving the Lepanto riddle or simply being so close in the confines of the car, she did not know. But as she sat beside him occasionally glancing at him as the lights from oncoming cars lit his face, she felt safe, just as she had that first night in the restaurant. She snuggled down into the seat of his large BMW and sighed.

'That sounds like a very contented sigh.' He took one hand off the steering wheel and touched her gently.

'Don't laugh at me, but I suddenly feel secure with you.'

'And you haven't before?'

'No.'

'What's changed?' he asked and glanced across at her, his hopes rising.

'I don't know. I haven't been playing games with you, you know.'

He did not answer but turned off the motorway and into the brightly lit parking area of a service station. He stopped the car and turned to her. It was now or never, he thought.

'Look, Gloria. I don't think we've been straight with each other,' he began.

'I know,' she said, her heart sinking.

'The point is. Well, I think I've been stupid but what with Hilary and then Julius . . .'

Gloria looked straight ahead, her mind screaming, don't say it. She had been right, then. He had turned to her for comfort, nothing else. Fool again, she thought bitterly.

'What I should have done, right at the beginning, was tell you.'

'Yes,' she said, in a small and miserable voice.

'Tell you how much I love you and can't live without you and . . . honestly, Gloria, I can't go on like this.'

She turned to face him.

'What did you say?'

'I love you.'

'Oh, Peter. I love you, too.'

'But then why?'

'Because I was afraid that you didn't. I couldn't bear it, loving you and you not loving me.'

'What idiots we've been,' he said, taking her in his arms.

'No. What an idiot I've been,' she managed to say before his mouth was covering hers. And a couple of long-distance lorry drivers cheered them as they ambled by.

Mrs Catchpole was none too happy with Gloria for bringing a guest unannounced. Her annoyance was somewhat mollified when she discovered who he was. She fussed about them, cooking bacon and eggs and making proper coffee rather than the instant she and her husband usually drank. But Mrs Catchpole was no fool. She sensed a closeness between her daughter and this man, and what an improvement he was on some Gloria had brought home to introduce to them. This one was worth making an effort for.

'Do you know this Ulrika woman?'

'Slightly. She's quite mad, of course, not someone one would invite for sherry. A somewhat racy past I've heard,' Mrs Catchpole added in a whisper which, since they were the only ones present, seemed extreme. 'What's more . . .' This time the whisper was accompanied by a quick glance over her shoulder to check she was not being overheard. 'It's rumoured that her gardener – an appallingly rude man – is rather more than a gardener, if you know what I mean. It's disgusting at her age! And she smokes.' This last was Mrs Catchpole's final statement of disapproval.

'Jago Arscott isn't that bad,' Gloria's father said. 'He's just not one for the small talk.'

'What did you say his name was?' Gloria spluttered behind a wedge of toast.

'Arscott – it's a common enough name in the West Country. He's more of a handyman.' Her father winked at her and Gloria and Peter collapsed with laughter leaving Mrs Catchpole quite nonplussed.

Crispin was feeling disgruntled. He had hardly slept a wink all night, what with the noise of the wretched train, the way it had kept stopping and inconsiderate railway people shouting at each other on stations. Now he had arrived at Penzance and it was cold and raining. If Crispin loathed the countryside there was something he loathed even more and that was the seaside. An out-of-season seaside was even worse – depressingly so.

The buffet was closed and, in any case, railway station buffets were not his idea of places to eat. He found a taxi and asked to be taken to the best hotel for breakfast.

'They'm all closed. Out of season you see,' the man muttered at him. 'There's a Little Chef up Hayle way, that that'll be open.'

So Crispin found himself eating the American breakfast in the sort of fast-food outlet he would never normally be seen dead in. That he enjoyed the meal was neither here nor there; he was just relieved that there was no chance of anyone he knew seeing him.

The taxi returned for him at nine-thirty and he ordered the man to drive him to Sennen. At least the driver was of the silent variety, which Crispin regarded as a blessing. The truth was that the man was not speaking to him for, in his velvet-collared cashmere coat, with his arrogance, he epitomised all the taxi-driver loathed most about 'they' who lived the other side of the Tamar.

They had had to ask directions of a fisherman, who was leaning on a railing studying the sea with an expression of terminal doom. Crispin could not understand one word of what he said, but luckily his driver could.

Crispin eventually found himself standing on the top of a cliff in the teeming rain. He entered a gate and started on a vertiginous descent of steep steps cut into the rock. Below him he could see a granite house, perched like the poop deck of a man-o'-war on a wide shelf half-way down the cliff. The sea was pounding ominously close on the rocks below. And the wind was howling around him as if spitefully trying to pluck him off the cliff. The creeper on the house was lashed by the wind, which screeched as if in a tantrum or as if complaining that it could not gain entrance to the house. By the time Crispin battled to the front door he was soaked and bitterly cursing his dead uncle for such self-indulgent mysteries.

The door was opened by what Crispin could only describe as a horny-handed churl, who looked at him with the same suspicion as the driver and the fisherman. So much for merry peasants and sons of the soil. Did no one with any charm live in these parts? He sighed inwardly.

'I've an appointment with Ulrika Talbot-Blaize. Crispin Anderson.' He smiled more out of habit than conviction. The man did not speak but held the door open, not wide, but a measly foot more which just allowed Crispin to slither in. 'Such a storm,' he said, mopping the rain from his face.

'Storm! This? Nonsense, a little light wind.' A deep voice, bubbling with laughter, called from the doorway into another room. The owner stepped forward. 'Crispin? I've been expecting you. I'm Ulrika Talbot-Blaize.' Crispin found himself shaking hands with a woman of gargantuan proportions in a loose-fitting dress of shimmering green silk. He did not like shaking the hand: Crispin did not like people who were over-large for to him it showed a lamentable lack of self-discipline. 'Jago my handsome, don't just stand there, take the man's coat, and get the port. This way, Crispin.' She held up her hand to guide him through a low doorway and smiled at him. Crispin, half-way through the door, stopped and looked at her with a puzzled expression. For the smile transformed the woman's face. It was like the moon shining on a romantic ruin, softening its lines, and for a short moment the ruin was again the beautiful building it once had been. And then she stopped smiling, the illusion was gone and she was a fat old lady again. But she laughed as if she was fully aware of the effect her smile had had upon him, as if it was something that was frequent in her life.

15

As Gloria and Peter drove up to the cliff-top, having followed her mother's directions, they saw a taxi standing waiting. They parked behind it and as they were getting out of the car the gate opened and Crispin appeared.

'What a pleasant surprise seeing you two here. Now, I wonder what on earth could bring you to this neck of the woods?' He smiled superciliously. Gloria felt her heart plummeting. They were too late, he had beaten them to it. No doubt, in that over-smart briefcase, he already had the signed power of attorney over that precious two per cent of votes.

'My parents live here,' she said, not wanting him to see how upset she was. Peter took hold of her hand.

'Of course, you're wasting your time. You do realise that, don't you?' Crispin said as he slid into the back of the car. 'Bloody awful weather and you say your people actually *live* here? Extraordinary! Any chance of a lift back to London?'

Gloria felt like exploding with rage at the audacity of the man.

'Sorry,' Peter said for her. 'We'll probably stay on a few days and meander back.'

'Oh, quite.' Crispin smirked. 'Not much point in rushing back is there, Peter, now you've no job. Right, driver. The station. See you two.' He slammed the taxi door shut and waved. Peter made the V-sign at him.

'Sorry, but I can't stand that creep,' he said.

'He's beaten us, hasn't he? What lousy luck. Is there any point our going in?'

'Of course there is. Don't you have her new manuscript to pick up?' He held the small gate open for her and gingerly, clinging to the handrail, they made their way down the cliff. Half-way down, Peter paused. 'What a position! I'd give anything for a house like this, wouldn't you? From the road no one would even know it was here.'

'Prefer it to a Cotswold manor house?'

'You bet. Shall we look for somewhere like this? A bolt-hole. The train only takes five hours.'

'That would be nice,' she said, her heart jolting at the implication.

This time the door was flung open wide and Ulrika stood waiting for them. 'At last, you've come. I've been waiting for you, nearly gave you up. Come in out of the rain, get by the fire, have a drink.' Ulrika busily ushered them into the small but beautifully furnished hallway. 'This way, my dears.' Despite her large size, Ulrika was fluttering about them as if excited to see them. They entered a long beamed room. It was far bigger than one would have expected, for from the outside the house looked quite small. The room was cluttered with furniture, wonderful oak, and the chairs covered with ancient tapestry. The walls were in need of paint, but it did not matter since they were covered with paintings of all shapes, sizes and periods. They were pictures that, because of their random age and content, one felt had been collected with love rather than an eye to investment. There were bowls of gold and bronze chrysanthemums, their distinctive scent filling the air. And in the fireplace a log fire crackled; in front of it lay a snoring bulldog who did not even open one eye in greeting, and beside her a large, tailless grey cat. From a big window all one could see was the sea and sky – nothing else was visible.

'My God, it's wonderful, like being on the bridge of a ship.'

'Fun, isn't it? My great-grandfather built it. There was a cottage here, and he added on and then my grandfather and father added, too. That's why it's called Bishop's Rock – nothing to do with the actual rock, no, they were all bishops, you see. You'd never get away with it, these days, what with planning officers and miserable little farts like that. Get by the fire, Gloria, my dear, you're soaked. Jago!' Ulrika yelled in her deep husky voice, making both of them jump. A small very dark man, looking more Spanish than English, appeared. 'Drinks, please, Jago. What would you like? I'm having port myself, warms the cockles.'

'Any wine? That would be lovely,' said Peter, thinking what a dreadful hour to be drinking but sensing she would be hurt if they refused.

'Jago, did you hear?' she said, so loudly that Gloria felt only the dead would not. 'There's a darling, get some for us, will you?' She smiled at the man and both Peter and Gloria were taken aback by the magical change in her face when she did. She was no longer old, no longer fat, her face was alive, animated and beautiful still. The man shuffled out. 'He's as thick as two short planks, but hung like a donkey.' She guffawed loudly and neither of the other two knew quite where to look.

'What happened to the cat's tail?' Gloria asked hurriedly to cover her confusion.

'Bloody mink got it. Poor Rupert was nearly a goner.' She bent down and stroked the animal who rolled lazily on its back. 'I'd given up fur coats, felt they were wrong. But after that verminous creature got hold of my cat I went straight out and bought one – Rupert's revenge, you see. I'm just waiting for one of those animal liberation people to nobble me. I'll tell them about mink, that I will.'

And Gloria thought, yes, she would, and God help them.

When the drinks had been poured and the fire was beginning to thaw them out Gloria asked after the manuscript.

'Oh, my dear, that was a ruse. I'm afraid it's still not finished but one of these days I'll get around to it, I will. No, I called you because you had not contacted me and Julius had told me you would as soon as he had curled his toes up. Well, you didn't so I thought I had better call you and drop a few hints. I couldn't tell you all, you see, because Julius had made me swear on the Bible that I never would let on about the trust to a living soul – except Jago, of course. He was so afraid of that frightful family finding out – oh, that's funny, did you notice the alliteration there?' She stopped to have a chuckle. The others waited patiently. 'Well, I was not sure if my vow still counted now he was dead. But I thought I had better not, just to be on the safe side. I hoped you would work things out yourself and come and find me. And you did, so clever of you.'

'But Julius's nephew worked it out too, and got here before us,' Gloria said with a sad expression.

'What, that little shit? Dreadful man. But doesn't he fancy himself? Last Christmas, or thereabouts, Julius telephoned me and warned me. He told me about his nephew and his plans to harm my darling's company. No, no. I told Crispin I hadn't the foggiest notion what he was talking about. I said I'd never heard of a trust. He didn't believe me, of course, but I said it must be a coincidence – the Lepanto poem in my book must have given Julius the idea of using that name. He seemed to swallow that.'

'So you didn't give him power of attorney?' The question tumbled out of Gloria and she was almost afraid to hear the answer.

'Good God, no. I've the papers here, all ready – been here for weeks, waiting for you. My lawyer in Penzance drew them up for me.'

'And it was Julius set the trust up for you?'

'No, that was my father, after the book came out. It did rather well you see, and he thought I was rather wayward – I can't imagine why. And when he died he added my inheritance to it as well. Mind you, that's worth bugger all these days. When Julius gave me the shares in Westall's we just added them to the existing trust for safety – he thought I was somewhat wayward, too.' She chuckled, a wonderful dark and happy sound.

'Julius gave you the shares?' Peter asked, entranced by this strange but very feminine woman.

'Bless him, yes. We had a wonderful summer once. I love summer affairs best of all, don't you, dear?' She smiled at Gloria. 'It's something about the sun, I think, makes one more lustful than in the winter. I've always said it was a good job I didn't live in the tropics, I'd have been flat on my back all my life.' She laughed and then stopped abruptly and gazed into the fire as if at ghosts from the past. They waited for her to speak for it was a silent moment, a very private one. 'I suppose I shouldn't have accepted them really, but then, I thought, why not? I'd made him happy and he me, and if he wanted to give me a little present, then why should I spoil his pleasure in giving? So I took them. He was such a wonderful man and the only one I ever really loved, and I like to think that I was something special to him too.'

'Oh, I'm sure you were,' Gloria said with a lump in her throat.

'And then each year he paid me royalties I knew I had not earned, and I took them, too. He thought he had hoodwinked me, but he hadn't. But, you see, it made him so happy to give them to me – a link with the past, I suppose. I could not have let him know I had guessed and take away his joy in giving. And, I'll be quite honest, these last few years it has helped enormously.' She suddenly sat upright in her chair. 'Still, to business or you'll be bored rigid with my rattling on. But it's so lovely to have people here who knew him too, you see, such a dear man.' She sighed. 'We'll get my cleaning lady to witness the signatures and everything – she'll be here soon.'

'Can't Jago witness?' Peter asked.

'Good Lord no, my dear. He's my trustee.' She laughed very loudly at their surprised expressions. 'I beat father and Julius, come the end. Jago's ideal, he can barely read but adores me and does just what I tell him. More wine, dear hearts?'

It was long past lunchtime when Gloria and Peter eventually left Ulrika. They were laden with presents – a small watercolour of the view that Gloria had admired and which Ulrika insisted she take. A bottle of the wine for Peter after he had said how good it was. Some of the pickle they had had with their ham at lunch after both had said how delicious it was, and a signed copy of *To Whom the Bird Has Sung*.

'What are we going to do about her royalties?' Gloria asked as Peter drove very carefully back to her parents' cottage. 'You heard what she said about them coming in handy.'

'We'll have to keep them on. But, if she wants to sell her shares, I'll happily buy them, then she'll be set up for life. I didn't mention it to her, I think she should have advice from someone not involved, don't you?'

'That's why I love you, you're such a kind, sensitive, man.' Gloria smiled at him.

They had reached her parents' cottage. But instead of going in Peter suggested they walk awhile in the rain. They walked to the Great Carn, an outcrop of rocks perched on the top of a cliff overlooking the Atlantic. Peter sat on one of the boulders and patted the space beside him for Gloria to join him.

'Bit more romantic than a service station, isn't it?' He smiled, gesturing to the great sweep of sky and sea, the Longships lighthouse wailing a warning of incoming fog.

'You could say that.' She snuggled close to him.

'I wanted somewhere special. I want to ask you to marry me, Gloria, once I'm free.'

'Peter . . .' It was all she could say, she was too happy for words to come.

'Is that yes?'

'A million of them.'

'I love you,' they both said in unison and they sealed their promises with a kiss.

He looked at her a long time as if to memorise this moment. 'Did you notice Ulrika called us dear hearts? That's what I'm going to call you from now on, my dear heart.'

'She was a magic lady. No wonder Julius loved her, what a character.'

'Like someone else I know.' He nuzzled the side of her neck.

If things were to be resolved, there had to be more meetings. Peter and Gloria talked long into the night about his buying the family's shares in

Westall. He had delayed making this decision for, unsure as he had been of Gloria's feelings for him, he did not want her to think he was rushing her, and also he had been worried that perhaps she would not want him involved in what was increasingly *her* publishing house. Now everything had changed, but still he wondered if maybe marriage to each other should be enough. He need not have had such fears and doubts for, as they talked and planned the future of the company, both were bubbling over with ideas and schemes. They could not wait to work together and they couldn't wait to be man and wife.

When they finally went to bed it was to separate rooms. Gloria felt too intimidated by the close proximity of her mother even to contemplate their sleeping together. She was relieved that Peter made no suggestion that he slip into her room when her parents were asleep.

They had planned to set off the following morning but Mrs Catchpole insisted they stay for lunch, and then for tea, so it was almost midnight before they drove up to Gloria's house. She felt oddly shy as she invited him in for a drink. But still he said nothing, made no move towards her. He stood to go as he was now used to doing. Gloria had not expected this, not now he had said he wanted to marry her.

'Peter ... this is difficult ... I hate making the advances, but please stay,' she said, feeling ridiculously gauche.

Laughing he bent forward and kissed her. 'I was only teasing,' he said, taking her by the hand and leading her towards the stairs. As they ascended he put his arm about her as if afraid she would escape. He pushed open the bedroom door and slammed it shut and they were in each other's arms.

There was a soft whimpering from the landing.

'Excuse me,' Peter said. He crossed the room and opened the door. 'Hallo, Elephant. Left all alone? We can't have that, can we?'

With great dignity Elephant stalked into the room, tail held high. He crossed to his basket, turned round five times and lay down, and immediately his eyes were closed.

'Oh, Peter, I love you more for that.' Gloria laughed at him.

In his basket Elephant was not asleep, just pretending. He settled further into his blanket. He had always liked this particular gentleman the most.

In the past few months, Gloria had dreamt often of Peter making love to her again, but nothing in her dreams was to match the reality. His hunger for her matched her own need for him. They tore their clothes in their haste to be rid of them and their desperate longing to feel the flesh of each other. He knelt in front of her admiring her naked body and then, with deliberate slowness, pulled off her black silk stockings, looking at her all the time, which was enough for her to be ready for him. His hands held her hips, and his mouth found her and his tongue was finding every secret place. Gloria felt her body jolt rigid, her legs buckle from the ecstasy he was giving her. She screamed with joy as she climaxed and fell back on the bed, but still he held her hips, still continued to pleasure her, and she lost count of the times her body arched in passion. Then he was upon her and thrusting into her, and she felt his flesh, his sweat and her love for him.

Mike was overjoyed on two counts – that Peter and Gloria were at last together and that his old friend had decided finally to bid for the family's shares in Westall. But if he was to do so, it was not proper that he remain a trustee and so another one had to be found. Barty Silver was approached and agreed to replace Peter. If he could not own the company, he reasoned, then the next best thing would be to be a trustee of the employees' trust.

Everyone reluctantly agreed that no matter how much they all loathed Crispin he had done a good job of whipping up interest in the sale. The offers began to come in and it soon transpired that Peter would be the under-bidder by quite a large sum. He would either have to borrow heavily – and how long would it be before, like Julius, he found himself in difficulties? – or he would have to take a partner, which he was most reluctant to do.

Then a very strange thing happened. One by one the other publishing houses who had shown interest began to withdraw their bids. A week later, only Peter's offer remained. Crispin was beside himself with anger and fury. He telephoned, he wrote, but suddenly people were not in for his calls and his letters went unanswered. Everyone had their suspicions, but nobody liked to ask – only Joy. Barty confessed to her that, yes, his tentacles were broad and far-reaching. He had done nothing wrong, he said, wide-eyed and innocent. All he had done was to ask a few people who owed him favours to repay them by withdrawing from a deal he had an interest in. He was only making sure that Julius's wishes were fulfilled.

Peter now owned the shares. Lepanto remained. Both Mike and Barty had decided that perhaps it was better if Lepanto shares were not owned by either Peter or the employees – the buffer of two per cent in the middle might be as good a thing in the future as it had been in the past. That was the plan until Gloria received a telephone call from Dulcett. She and Simon had married and as a wedding present he had given her a lump sum of money. They were both wondering if any shares were available that she might buy. Simon had agonised over selling his shares against Julius's wishes and late in the day he wanted to make amends. He felt he was too old but would like Dulcett to be involved with the firm. And her name was now Westall.

'How romantic,' Ulrika had said, with marked satisfaction, when she was asked if she would like to sell her shares to Dulcett.

The day that everything was finally signed they planned to celebrate. That afternoon, Kate, in London to see Stewart, called into the office with the first three chapters and a synopsis of her next book, *Autumn Fever*.

This was always a worrying time for author and publisher alike. Many people could write one book, but did they have it in them to write a second? Gloria would like to have read it there and then. Instead she controlled herself and placed it on one side.

'You look pleased with yourself.' She smiled at Kate, who looked particularly attractive in a cherry-red suit and black leather boots.

'I'm very excited. Joy's sold my American rights. I couldn't believe her when she said for how much. I had to sit down, I must have smoked a whole packet of cigarettes in five minutes.' She laughed.

'That's absolutely wonderful news. Joy hadn't told me, but I'm seeing her tonight for dinner. Why don't you join us? Are you free?' Gloria asked.

'I am, if I might bring someone?' she said, knowing she was blushing.

'Kate! No! How wonderful, who is it?'

'Stewart Dorchester,' Kate said feeling ridiculously embarrassed and proud at the same time.

'So there was something between you two! I knew it!' Gloria was beaming with pleasure. 'He's a sweetie. Oh, I do approve. No wonder you look so stunning. There's nothing like love, is there?'

As soon as Kate had left, Gloria settled down with the manuscript she had brought with her. Half an hour later she sat back with a satisfied smile. It was wonderful. Kate was a real writer, no question.

So it was that at the celebration dinner which followed the three women were together – a little over a year from the day they first met.

'How everything has changed,' Kate said. 'I still can't believe the new path my life has taken.' She looked proudly at Stewart.

'And we're all happy, aren't we?' said Joy, thinking of Hannah peacefully asleep, and smiled at Barty.

Gloria leant her head against Peter's shoulder. 'And for a change,' she laughed, 'we're not in Barty's loo!'

Breeders

This book is dedicated to
Gertie and Gussie with love.

And in fond memory of:
Paddy, Brutus, Fanny, Sammy, Sappho,
Rita, Emma Dane, Kefti and Shin.
But especially Buttercup.

Acknowledgements

It was my agent, Mic Cheetham, who suggested that I write about the world of dogs, whereupon my editor Jane Wood enthusiastically agreed and has never wavered in her belief in the project. I'm grateful to my publisher, Anthony Cheetham, for liking big books and to everyone at Orion involved in its production.

The members of the Special Operations Unit of the RSPCA have been incredibly helpful in sharing their experiences. Officials of the Kennel Club supplied me with information and explanations about the frequently confusing world of dog shows. Elizabeth and Helen McCreath were so hospitable and patient with what must, at the time, have appeared to be a lot of stupid questions about dog breeding. Pat Brigden, Jenny Ziman, Alex Briggs, Andy Foxcroft, Don Balfour and Pauline Lockyer helped me enormously, as did the many breeders I talked to at Crufts '95. I shall always be grateful to Steve Glanvill MA, Vet MB, DBR, OVS, MRCVS, who, despite his busy schedule, found time to check various aspects for me. Rebecca Leith drove many miles meeting and talking to people when I was too crocked to do so. My thanks to David Macmillan and the real Bandage who was the inspiration for the fictional one. Gertie, Gussie, Portia, Marble and Hero helped in their own way. And Billy was always there.

Although many of those mentioned above helped in checking what I have written, if mistakes have been made then the responsibility is entirely mine.

Il y a aura toujours un chien perdu quelquepart qui m'empêchera d'être heureux.
There will always be a lost dog somewhere that will prevent me from being happy.

Jean Anouilh

We are alone, absolutely alone on this chance planet; and amid all the forms of life that surround us, not one, excepting the dog, has made an alliance with us.

Maurice Maeterlinck

March

1

Fear was the dominant emotion in the speeding car. She sat, huddled, in the passenger seat, her breathing heavy with anxiety. He drove fast, far too fast for the atrocious conditions. He was angry. She had no way of knowing why, or what had caused this latest furious outburst. In the short time she had been with him she had learnt to be afraid of his temper, which could erupt at any time and over anything.

The heavy black Mercedes slowed. He did not stop, but with one hand still on the wheel he dragged her across him, opened his door and hurled her out on to the rain-sodden road. She fell heavily, grazing her chin. The car roared away into the night.

She tried to stand, but one leg collapsed beneath her. She attempted to drag herself to the verge, but the pain was too great. She sank on to the road, blood oozing from her damaged chin, her large dark eyes brimming with terror. Helpless and dejected, she lay awaiting whatever fate might bring.

Thomasine, driving slowly because of the foul conditions, decided that such weather was a fitting conclusion to an all-out awful day. She had overslept, laddered two pairs of tights in the mad scramble not to be late, had had her credit cards stolen, got divorced, endured dinner with a disapproving mother, and now this storm. Still, nothing much else could go wrong, she told herself.

The windscreen wipers clunked noisily, the black blades streaking in an hysterical rhythm back and forth, yet failing to clear the screen. Thomasine sat hunched over the steering wheel, clutching it firmly in her hands, as much for comfort as control, and wished she were anywhere but here, on this roadway, and on such a cold and stormy night – more like midwinter than the first month of spring.

She wished she were safely home in London – not in the present but three years ago, before her husband's betrayal, before all the anger and pain – not returning to an empty, strange house facing an uncertain and lonely future. It was hard to accept she was divorced when it was the last thing she wanted to be. Despite everything she still loved her husband with a painful longing.

Over dinner with her mother, Di, she had tried to hide these feelings. And although her mother had said she was well shot of the deceiving bastard and the sooner she found someone else and stopped mooching about the better, Thomasine was sure her mother had seen through her and despised her for being weak and indecisive.

Thomasine sighed. It was easy for her mother; she was one of those dogmatic individuals who never doubted they were right and who seemed immune to hurt, as if they had an extra layer of skin. Di was puzzled and irritated by her lack of ideas and plans for what she wanted to do with this new, unasked-for, freedom. If this had happened to her elder sister, Abigail, she wouldn't be afraid of an empty future. No doubt she would already have enrolled in a mind-improving course, be working for an Open University degree, while doing a full time job perfectly. Abigail would never waste a moment dreaming about what might have been. But then, it wouldn't ever happen to Abigail with her orderly, busy life, a paragon of a husband who would never stray, and three ideal children.

Divorced, dinner with mother, and her credit-card wallet nicked. 'It isn't bloody fair,' she said aloud as a large black car overtook her at speed. It swung sharply in front of her, far too close, its fat wheels kicking up a dense cloud of rain and mud which impeded her vision even more.

'Inconsiderate bastard!' she shouted at him impotently, and peered, trying to make out his number, but registering only an A. She reduced her speed even further. The sudsy water in her windscreen washer, caught in a slipstream, slid in foamy tendrils across the sheet of glass, compounding the mess. The wipers faltered, made an agonised screech and stopped.

'Oh, no, I don't believe this!' Thomasine, with all vision totally obliterated, slowly stopped the car, not wanting to aquaplane on the wet surface. She flicked on her hazard lights, tied a scarf over her head, grabbed the cloth she kept in the glove compartment and, cursing under her breath, did what all women travelling alone are told not to do – she opened the car door and got out. The rain-drenched wind whipped around her, hugging her tight, tugging at her dress. About fifty feet further along the road, she saw what she thought was the culprit car. It was moving, even though its huge rear brake lights were glowing red.

Within seconds she was soaked to the skin, her hair, despite the scarf, hanging lank and damp against her face. She wiped at her windscreen with her cloth – it only made matters worse. The wind lashed at the trees on the roadside, shadows darting amongst them as the branches arched and bowed in a wild dance. Any number of maniacs could be hiding in there, she thought, and the risk she was taking raced head on to meet her. She quickly climbed back into her car, hoped the rain would ease and prayed that she wouldn't be shunted in the rear, but even that seemed preferable to the alternative of standing amongst those trees. Nervously, she double-checked the car locks. She was cold, scared and wished she was home.

The rain gradually began to clear the windscreen. She switched on the engine; the wipers, now there was no mud, worked again. With the headlights on, she eased into gear and set off at a slow pace.

She was still in third gear when she slammed on the brakes, feeling the back of the car dance skittishly. In her headlights she saw the bedraggled figure of a small animal. 'Drive round it!' common sense whispered. 'What if it's hurt?' compassion replied.

'Call me St Francis,' she said aloud, and with a hefty sigh she climbed out of the car again. Cautiously she approached the creature, which was lying in the road, shivering from head to toe; two large dark soulful eyes stared at her and then looked submissively away. It was a dog.

Thomasine knew little about dogs, except that it would be foolish to touch a strange one, especially if it was hurt. She stood looking down at it wondering what to do next. If she left it in the road the next car to come along might not see it in time. She was aware that the creature was watching her with its expressive eyes, as if reading her mind. She shook herself at that, ridding herself of such stupid fancies – she was going to have to make a move or get run over herself.

She bent down, but it cowered away from her. If it was that scared, maybe it had no intention of biting her. On the other hand, perhaps a frightened animal was even more likely to attack. 'Here, have a good sniff.' She thrust her hand out, but the abrupt action made the animal lift its head, avoiding any contact with her. She waited patiently. The dog sniffed the air a good foot from her hand, paused as if registering what it smelt, and then wriggled slowly towards her on its front. Thomasine was unsure if she should talk to it or not, and decided to compromise by making a cooing, soothing noise, much as she had used to her daughter, Nadine, when she had been a baby.

The dog appeared to interpret these noises as encouraging, for it risked sniffing her hand intently. Thomasine gently patted its head. Round the massive neck of the dog was a black leather collar with large, wicked-looking metal studs on it. Feeling more confident, she looked for an identity tag, but there was none.

She looked at the dog; it studied her, head on one side. The beautiful eyes held hers for a moment but then were cast demurely down again, like a shy maiden. The animal was waiting, she was sure, for her to decide what to do. She returned to the car and opened the passenger door. 'Here, boy, girl, whatever you are.' She patted her leg encouragingly. The dog scrabbled desperately at the tarmac, its long black claws scraping on the surface, afraid it was about to be left. It heaved itself up using powerful shoulder muscles, but its back legs could not support it. The dog flopped back into the road. 'Hang on Buster. First things first, let's put this newspaper on the seat, you're a mite wet for the good of my upholstery.' She felt a bit self-conscious talking to a dumb animal, but she seemed to have got its confidence, so maybe the sound of her voice would continue to reassure it. 'Come on then.' She bent down and, putting her hands either side of the dog's stomach, with difficulty lifted it up into the car. 'Wow! You weigh a ton. You ought to be on a diet.'

Evidently used to car rides, the animal settled on the seat. A tip of pink tongue emerged between smooth, black lips, and the noise it was making sounded friendly.

Thomasine put the interior light on. 'What are you?' She registered the heavy muscles, the deep folds of skin, a pushed-back nose, and a massive jaw. 'I hope you're not a pit bull, I don't fancy a ride with one of them.' The dog made a snuffling, snorting sound and looked expectantly forward, as if waiting for them to move. A car overtook them at speed, blaring its horn, angrily flashing its lights.

'Roadhog!' she yelled, putting the car into gear.

As she drove along Thomasine, aware of the heavy breathing beside her, found the dog's presence rather comforting – it was not large, but heavy and obviously powerful; anyone would think twice before trying anything funny with you, she thought. It was nice, for once, to feel safe alone in a car at night.

Thomasine was on the Morristown by-pass. Despite the weather, she put her foot down, for joy riders from the Forest Glade Estate in the town were known to frequent this stretch of road. There was a large police station in Morristown and she supposed she should have taken the creature there, but she found the town frightening with its bleak tower blocks, badly-lit walkways and cavernous multi-storey car parks. There was too much violence in Morristown for anyone, especially a woman, to enter it at night with any degree of equilibrium. So she pressed on to the A road which would lead her to the pretty market town of Shillingham; it had a much smaller police station, but an atmosphere of security and well-being.

She parked outside the police station and, with difficulty, carried the heavy dog inside.

'What have we here then?' a constable asked her, opening a hatch in the wall and leaning over to peer out at them both.

Thomasine lowered the dog onto the floor where it stood, looking pathetic, on three legs. 'I found this dog on the dual carriageway ten miles the other side of Morristown. I think it might be a very large pug, they've got squashed in faces like this, haven't they?'

'That's a bulldog,' the constable said, peering down at the dog.

'Are you sure, aren't they usually bigger than this? There's one at The White Hart, that's huge – Butch, they call it.'

'This one's a female,' the constable said sagely, and pointed to the chart of dog breeds hanging on the wall. 'That's why it's that much smaller. I've never known a bulldog to be dumped before, they're too valuable.'

'Dumped? You mean, people abandon their dogs on motorways? But they could be killed.'

'Oh, that's the general idea, Miss.' He smiled knowingly. 'Poor things hardly stand a chance, do they, with all them articulated lorries?'

'But why?'

'Saves on the vet's bill – that way there's no need to pay to have it put down. Splat!' And he slapped one balled fist into the flat of his hand.

'That's awful! I'm not that mad about dogs, but how could anyone . . .?'

'Takes all types,' the constable said, with all the sagacity of his profession, sucking through his teeth at the same time. 'I've dealt with all sorts,' he continued, as if glad of an audience. 'When the dangerous dog legislation came in we had a lot of pit bulls and Rottweilers. But I've dealt with a wolfhound, a St Bernard – could cause a nasty accident, a dog that size.'

'But why, if someone has gone to all the trouble to buy an expensive dog, should they do that?' she questioned, puzzled.

'Dad loses his job or does a runner, dogs have to be fed. Or it's grown too big, or they're bored with it. It's easy, kick it out on the road, make a quick getaway and let a nice lorry do the dirty work for you.'

'I feel sick.' And she did, and had to sit down on the bench against the pale green wall.

'Great nation of animal lovers, aren't we?' he said sardonically, as he pulled his pad towards him. 'Best take your details.'

The paperwork finished, the constable came round to her side of the counter, a lead in his hand. The dog moved towards Thomasine and hid behind her.

'There, my lovely.' The constable put his hand out to grab at the collar, but the bulldog moved away as quickly as she was able to on three legs.

'Then you don't think this is a lost dog? His owner isn't going to come through that door saying "Fido, darling!"?'

'Unlikely. Possible, but unlikely. Did you have trouble with it? I mean, did it get nasty?'

'No, nothing like that. Here, give me the lead.' The dog allowed her to clip it on. She felt touched by its faith in her, but also guilty that she had tricked and betrayed it.

'Thanks,' said the constable, and began to drag the dog away.

'Its leg. It's hurt its leg,' she said, but he did not appear to hear. The dog pulled hard, looked back at her with those large brown eyes. Thomasine turned her back and hurried from the police station, away from their stare.

In the car, the newspaper the dog had sat on was crumpled and wet. She screwed it up and threw it on the floor. The car smelt of damp hair too. 'Horrible,' she muttered, switched on the ignition and swung out of the car park.

As she drove she kept thinking about the dog. She tried to put other thoughts in its way, to blank out the recurring memory, but the dog always won. Or, rather, the dog's eyes won. All too easily, as she remembered them pleading with her, begging her for help as it was dragged across the police station floor.

'For God's sake, woman, stop it,' she said aloud as she waited for a set of traffic lights to turn green. A lone male figure was walking towards her and she pushed down the central locking switch, felt the familiar tensing of her body at a possible danger, drumming her fingers on the steering wheel, urging the lights to change. She'd felt safe with the dog in the car, if it were here she wouldn't be reacting like this.

The green light shone. Still, she thought as she gathered speed, there was more to owning a dog than feelings of security. They were a pain, she'd heard friends who owned them moan often enough – even when they loved them. They messed up the house, chewed things, piddled, caught fleas, ruined the garden, you couldn't leave them, they smelt. No, she'd been wise never to have pets – one was freer without.

She was five miles the other side of Shillingham, two miles from her new house in the village of Middle Shilling, when she abruptly stopped the car, reversed into a field gateway, and shot off again at speed.

'What will happen to her?' she asked as she burst into the police station, bringing the wind and rain with her.

The constable looked up. 'We'll keep her in the kennels here for seven days and then, if no one has claimed her – ' He made a slicing action across his throat. She clutched at her own with her hand. 'No, that's what we used to do.' He laughed; she didn't join in. 'She might be lucky,' he said more soberly, aware she did not appreciate his attempts at humour. 'One of the lads might take a shine to her. And we get lots of people looking for their own dogs; someone might want her. Failing that, we give them to a refuge and they'll try to re-house her. If they're full, mind you . . .' He did not finish.

'Can I take her?' she said, interrupting him almost breathlessly, as if afraid of what she was saying, as if part of her did not want her to do so, and she might change her mind. 'I could look after her until someone wanted her. Just temporarily, you understand. Is that possible?'

'You'd be doing me a real favour, Mrs Lambert. The kennels are full to bursting, I blame those travelling people, you never see any of their dogs on leads. Should anyone want a bulldog, should I send them over to you?'

'Yes, fine.' She waited while he went to collect the dog. Alone, she doubted the wisdom of what she was doing. Should she just slip away? Her hand was on the door when the constable returned, dragging the dog along on its rear.

'Careful, it's hurt,' she said, feeling a surge of anger towards the policeman. She picked the dog up, and it licked her face. 'No!' she said, turning her cheek away. 'Just temporarily,' she said to the policeman as he held the door open for her.

Jim Varley was bone-numbingly exhausted. He felt like a deep-sea diver with his boots on as he walked across the cobbled yard at the back of the practice in Middle Shilling. He was cold as well; it was unusually cold for March which, according to the locals, meant a bad summer ahead. He swore to himself when, at the back door of his house, he had to go through the layers of his clothes searching in his various pockets for the keys. He could still remember a time, not so long ago either, when he had never bothered to lock a thing, certainly not his back door. But now it was like getting into Fort Knox – twice fools had raided the surgery for drugs, what were things coming to when they stole veterinary medicines? Last time it had happened he could only pray that they knew what they were doing, since they had stolen sufficient pentobarbitone to put an army to sleep, for good!

In the back porch he hung up his soaking Barbour to finish its dripping on the quarry-tiled floor, slung his cap on a peg and eased off his muddy boots. In thick-green-stockinged feet he padded into the warmth of the kitchen. His old mongrel, Castille, lifted her head from her basket and her tail beat a tattoo on the side. He bent and patted her head, telling her what a fine girl she was. She looked up at him with her rheumy eyes – time was running out for the old girl, he knew that, who better? Not yet, though, not yet. It was something he did not like thinking about, and very quickly put out of his mind. He turned his attention to the pine table. There was a note, there always was, propped against a pretty arrangement of dried flowers – Beth's hobby. From the beams hung huge bunches of flowers and grasses, which she had picked and dried herself. *Supper's in the slow oven. Pudding's in the fridge. EAT! Beth.* He smiled; poor patient Beth, how many suppers had she prepared and left in the Aga, only to find them still there in the morning? He'd do better tonight.

From the rail in front of the cooker he took the duck-shaped oven glove and retrieved his food, but seeing how dried up the chops were, he decided to eat only the pudding. He sat at the pine table and began to eat. Beth had left him a wine glass along with an unfinished bottle of red wine. He pushed it aside and instead collected a bottle of Glenfiddich from the work top, poured himself a lethal measure, and drank deeply before returning to his pie.

'You've got to eat, Jim,' a voice said from the doorway.

'I am eating,' he said, hurriedly spooning up a mouthful of pie.

Beth, a flower-sprigged dressing gown wrapped round her full breasts, her long, naturally curly, brunette hair swinging loose on her shoulders, joined him at the table.

'Whisky?' he asked, indicating the bottle.

'I am honoured,' she laughed, since he guarded his malt jealously. 'But no thanks. I'd prefer a small glass of wine.'

'You're pushing the boat out tonight,' he teased her, for Beth rarely drank. She said nothing, merely smiled her thanks.

Seeing the chops, she grimaced. 'No wonder you're not eating, they look grim. Let me make you an omelette? Bacon and eggs?'

'I'm fine with this. I think I'm past a proper meal.'

'You look tired, Jim. Was it a difficult foaling?'

He brushed his hands in front of his eyes as if pushing the fatigue away. 'You could say that. A breech. The trouble with Ben Luckett is he thinks he knows all there is to know about nags. He should have brought me in hours before he did. He may know how to ride the bloody things, but that's about all.'

'Maybe he didn't want to disturb you on a night like this,' she said reasonably.

He hated it when she was so tolerant, especially when she was right, for that was exactly what Ben had said to him tonight. He poured himself another measure and she frowned imperceptibly, but refrained from comment.

'What was it? The foal.'

'Oh, a filly. Pretty little thing. Were there any calls?'

'Nothing that appeared urgent. I've put them on your desk. Let them wait until morning.'

'I'd better look now – just in case.' He stood up. 'Thanks for supper,' he said like a polite little boy.

'You're going to have to get a partner, you know. Your workload's impossible. It would kill even a younger man.'

'Thanks, dear Beth, I'm not *that* old.' He laughed good-naturedly. 'Goodnight, sleep tight,' he said at the door and, carrying his glass and bottle of whisky, left the room. Beth stayed where she was, staring at the door. Then she sighed deeply, gathered up his dirty plate and loaded it into the dishwasher.

Jim sat in his study, though study was really too grand a word for the chaotic room where he did his accounts, kept up with the latest in the professional journals, and did a lot of thinking. He never let anyone in here to clean. He liked the muddle, knew where everything was and could lay his hands on it in a second; if anyone tidied it then the filing system of a lifetime would be lost. Give Beth her due, she was the only woman he had ever met who accepted the room as it was. Even Ann, his wife, had not understood, and had often suggested decorating the room and getting new office furniture in. It had been his father's study when he had been the vet here, and when the old man had retired, he had taken over the practice and the room.

He sat in his battered Captain's chair and lit a cigarette – he was down to five a day and proud of it. He riffled through the telephone messages Beth had stacked neatly on the desk; she was right, nothing that couldn't wait until after surgery in the morning.

Beth had been a godsend. For two years after Ann's death he'd muddled through, and then a year ago, his friend Fee Walters had taken things into her own hands.

'You look a bloody mess, my dear Jim, like a vagrant. I know just the person to help you out.' She had told him about Beth Morton and he had grudgingly agreed to meet her. What Fee had failed to tell him was that Beth came with Harry – five years old and with a permanently running nose. As soon as he knew this he had every intention of turning her down. But there was such a look of desperation in her eyes, like a cornered doe, that he had found himself saying 'yes' instead. He'd never regretted it, though he could have wished for fewer of her dratted dead-flower arrangements. Still, he'd never said, she seemed to get so much pleasure from them. He had even got to quite like Harry. Once the child was plugged into his Sega games he was no trouble to anyone, though Jim did have twinges of guilt that something else should be being done with him.

Beth had made life almost bearable again. She seemed to understand his pain, but without the need to say anything about it, nor to pry. He topped up his whisky. She was right of course, he did need help. The last three years had been hell. He was permanently tired, since there was no one to share the night calls with. And he was stressed too, he knew that – he might have cut down on the smoking, but he knew he drank too much, all to relieve the bloody stress. Times had changed, people had greater expectations for their pets these days than his father had ever known. New techniques, new medicines, made it possible for animals to live longer when, even ten years ago, they'd have been put to sleep. But such advances made for extra work, extra outlay on equipment, extra time to learn about developments, and all of this combined led to the extra stress which in turn led him to the whisky bottle.

He couldn't remember when he'd last had a holiday. With locums charging up to a hundred and fifty pounds a day – if you could find one – a holiday was out of the question. He couldn't just shut up shop, not when he was the only vet in the area. What would happen to the animals then? No wonder vets had the highest suicide rate of all the professions.

He was aware of all this, but he also knew why he hadn't looked for an assistant or partner. It was irrational, he could never explain it to anyone, the persistent feeling that if he got a new partner he would be betraying Ann's memory. They had met at college and worked side by side since they qualified, he treating the large animals, she taking care of the small-animal side of the practice. He was pretty sure that behind his back people were saying it was time he got over his wife's death, but he knew he had a long way to go yet. Too often, as now, the memory surfaced of that last morning as he'd watched her lithely swing herself into the saddle of her hunter and wave him goodbye. He didn't hunt, didn't like it. He'd never seen the point in spending his life patching animals up to go out on a Saturday and try to kill them. So he wasn't with her when the large horse had tripped as it jumped a fence, failing to see a wire. Ann had fallen and then the horse had crashed down upon her. She was dead by the time she reached the local hospital, and he'd not been able even to say goodbye. He'd sold the horse immediately, he'd had to, for part of him wanted to kill it there and then. But reason had prevailed and he'd known it was the last thing Ann would have wanted him to do.

He often wondered whether, if he'd been with her, he'd feel differently, if things might be easier. But now he'd never know.

*

It was past midnight before Thomasine carried the dog into her kitchen and put it down on the floor. It looked up at her expectantly, head on one side again, as it had in the road. She checked its leg. There was a nasty cut, and the underside of its large white chin was badly grazed. She filled a bowl with warm water, bathed the wounds and patted them dry with kitchen towels.

'You want something to eat? I haven't got any dog food, you realise that? You'll have to make do with last night's lasagne. Do dogs eat lasagne?' She put some in a soup bowl, and poured water into another. Dogs did eat lasagne, and with gusto. 'I should have asked you if you wanted more parmesan.' She laughed and poured herself a glass of wine, which she sipped as she watched the dog, still on three legs, eating with noisy enjoyment.

On the roadway she had thought the animal was black, but that had been the rain darkening her coat. She was drier now, and Thomasine could see she was fawn with a slightly darker saddle. Her ears were black, and when Thomasine had touched them in the car, she had found them softer than the softest velvet. Her nose was like a small black button beneath eyes of darkest brown. Thomasine was aware it was those beautiful eyes which had made her stop thinking straight.

'I don't want you, you know. I should have thought about this, not jumped in blind. What if no one claims you? You can't stay, you do realise?'

The dog put down her injured back leg as if testing it, and finding it felt better, then put her rear in the air, her forelegs parallel to the floor, and rested her head on her paws. Then she stretched her whole body and farted mightily.

'Well, that's a case in point. Phew!' she exclaimed, amused.

In answer the dog rolled on its back, kicked four legs in the air and spun round and round like a top, another trick that made her laugh. Was she doing it on purpose, she wondered? To amuse her? To get attention? When the dog finally finished this game she stood up and pointedly turned her back on the blanket which Thomasine had found for her in the laundry room and had placed in front of the wood burner.

'Well it's that or nothing. You'll just have to sleep on the floor then. I'll sort a box or something out in the morning. Now, I'm going up to bed. You're perfectly safe here, no one will hurt you.'

She bent down and began to undo the large, ugly collar. 'I don't think we need this, do you? Horrible aggressive thing.' She opened the cupboard housing the Hoover and threw the collar into the back. 'There, it's hidden well away.' This was madness, talking to a dog, she told herself, as she crossed the kitchen. Before she turned off the light, she blew the dog a kiss. 'Good-night,' she said, for all that.

As she undressed, she thought how much she had dreaded returning here today – divorced, official, rubber-stamped, new status. She had lived alone in the London house for over a year, so she should be used to it by now, but everything there had been familiar and comforting, now all was new – house, neighbours, even the shops. She had moved last week in time for the divorce; she had probably clung on to her old home too long and should have come here sooner.

She climbed into her brass bed, lay back on the lavender-scented pillows and began to think those thoughts which she knew were futile, and yet which, most nights, she thought anyway. Thoughts of when she and Robert had been happy together, when he was content with her and their marriage. For the umpteenth time she wondered why she had lost him, worried about how she might have played things differently.

The memory of the evening he'd told her he had met Chantal and wanted a divorce was bitterly clear, even now. She'd gone to pieces. She shuddered at the dreadful scene she'd made, crying out in disbelief. Then ranting at his duplicity. Then begging him to return to her, getting onto her knees, clinging at his trouser legs, pulling at him. Coldly he'd prised her hands away, retreating from her in horror and contempt. He had left that same night.

Thomasine had cried for three days non-stop, but then had begun to plan and scheme. With a superhuman effort she'd pulled herself together and forced herself to play it cool. She had turned herself into such a calm, patient and understanding wife that she'd marvelled at the performance she'd put on. Rational meetings took place, plans were calmly made, though all the time she was shrieking with pain inside.

As a strategy it had failed. The idea had been that he was to see her as such a wonderful wife that he would not be able to let her go, that he'd ditch Chantal and return to her. What an idiot she had been!

'But you must have known something was afoot?' her mother had said at dinner this evening.

'No, honestly. It was a bolt from the blue.'

'Then you must be either blind or stupid,' her mother had said with her characteristic lack of tact.

'Both, probably,' she'd replied, demoralised to the point of resignation.

She half sat up, aware of a snuffling noise from the kitchen below. At least finding the dog had kept her mind occupied for the last couple of hours. She wondered what it was called. She smiled into the darkness. This was something new, she'd begun to think of something other than Robert and all the sad and wasted past.

Half an hour later she could stand the barking and scratching from the kitchen no more. In her pyjamas she ran down the spiral stairs from her mezzanine bedroom. 'What on earth's all this racket?' she asked angrily, an anger which disappeared immediately when the dog's rump waggled back and forth in welcome. 'Come on, then. Just for tonight,' she said, not realising that those were the most fatal words a dog owner could say.

The dog settled happily on the floor beside her bed. What did it matter that it was in her room? She could get a basket for here too. 'A two-basket dog, there's luxury for you,' she said, forgetting she'd earlier promised it a box. But the dog was asleep, judging by the wiffling noise emerging from the small, black, button-like nose.

In his weekend hideaway two miles outside Middle Shilling, Oliver Hawksmoor tossed and turned. He had a bad cold, which he'd convinced himself was 'flu and which he'd been nursing carefully for several days. He felt as miserable as sin, and wondered if it was being ill or the new situation in his life which was making him so. Christ, this bed was bloody uncomfortable! He moved his rear only to discover the problem, a swathe of crumbs from the toast he had made himself this evening. He clambered out of the bed and stripped off the offending under-sheet. He bundled it into the dirty washing basket and opened the linen-cupboard door.

'This I do not believe! The bitch! How could she!' In front of him was a cupboard, empty, except for one bath towel, two hand towels and a pile of embroidered tray cloths. 'Oh sod it.' He slammed the door shut angrily. In the bedroom he dressed in jeans, a black silk polo neck and a pale blue cashmere jumper slipped over the top. He splashed some cologne on his face to wake himself up, stuck his tongue out at himself in the mirror and, not liking what he saw, popped it back into his mouth. Downstairs he scribbled a note, which he left propped up against the kettle, apologising to Grace White, his cleaning lady from the village, for the mess.

He drove at a sedate speed for him, only a maniac would drive fast in these stormy conditions. He shoved a CD into the player and Sutherland's voice filled the black leather cocoon of his BMW. Sophia should not have taken all the linen; the cottage and its contents were not part of their agreement. Everything in Bishop's End was as it had been the day he had inherited it from his great-aunt Phoebe. Dear old Phoebe, he wished she were alive now. He wondered what she would make of the state of his life. She had not liked Sophia – 'Why can't she call herself Sophie? That "a" makes her sound suspiciously foreign to me. Was she baptised thus, that's what I'd like to know.'

'English born and bred, Aunt Phoebe.'

'Trade, are they?' Phoebe had asked with a sharp incline of her aquiline nose, which always reminded him of a face he had once seen on a Plantagenet tomb in France.

'What on earth makes you say that, Aunt?'

'She studies the furniture a little too closely for my liking, as if she's a shopkeeper stock-taking. A well-brought-up girl would never do that. I think you might be making an unfortunate mistake, Oliver, my dear.' Phoebe had said it totally without malice, merely stating the facts as she saw them.

Aunt Phoebe, if not pleased to know how upset he was, would have been pleased to know she was right about the furniture. Sophia had insisted on Sotheby's being brought in for a valuation of the contents of his London home. Not nice, not nice at all. They had agreed on who was having what, but after the linen incident, could he be sure she had kept to it? It had seemed a simple enough division; she had agreed that if she could have the farmhouse in France and a property in London, then he could keep the Holland Park house and Bishop's End. This cold could prove more expensive than he had realised. She had planned to move her stuff out of their London base yesterday. Perhaps he should have been there keeping a beady eye on things, instead of feeling sorry for himself in his bed at Middle Shilling.

He drew up outside his smart house – another reason to thank Aunt Phoebe, whose legacy to him had bought it. Phoebe had had the ability to churn out romantic fiction by the yard, for which she was paid handsomely. She had amassed a large fortune, judiciously invested, all of which she had left to Oliver, her favourite great-nephew. Such good luck had not endeared him to the rest of the family, but it was something he had learnt to live with – not, after all, too hard a task.

It was three in the morning when he let himself into the house. The first thing he noticed was that the console table and mirror had gone. He entered the drawing room to find it bereft of virtually everything. She had left him a sofa, a coffee table, a side table and one armchair. The pictures that remained, he was gratified to see, were his most valuable; no doubt her nerve had failed her at taking those. Still, he knew he would mourn the loss of the less valuable just as much. He sat down on the armchair, looked about the denuded room with a doomy expression, and lit a cigarette.

What the hell had got into the woman? How could one be so wrong about someone? He had loved Sophia the moment he had set eyes on her at the varnishing dinner at the Royal Academy. Oliver collected paintings and she had been a student of art at the Courtauld – they had so much in common. She was pretty and delightful in the way of a young woman who had never wanted for anything in her life and to whom it had never been anything but sweet. When he learnt that her father had recently bought an estate near Middle Shilling, Oliver reasoned that fate had intended them to meet one way or the other, and he'd rushed out and bought the LP of Kismet. Her father was enormously wealthy from his property development company, which he'd manoeuvred skilfully through the various recessions and collapses of the past thirty years – not that Oliver had ever let on to Aunt Phoebe where the money came from. Sophia's divorced mother, Constance, was the daughter of an earl whom Ben Luckett had snapped up to give him a bit of social cachet. She now lived in the South of France off her alimony and had been perfectly adorable to Oliver. Mind you, come to think of it she had warned him not to marry her daughter which, at the time, he thought was a bit odd coming from a mother. Sophia loathed her mother only slightly less than she loathed her stepmother, Cora, whom she regarded as a vulgar gold digger. He liked Cora, which had annoyed Sophia no end.

He supposed he should go right through the house, check the lot, see his lawyers. Would he? He doubted it, come the morning he probably wouldn't bother. It was the hassle he hated, the letters that would fly back and forth. It was only money, after all. He might have no wife and no children, but he'd plenty of *that* to see him through, since Phoebe's books still sold in their thousands. Amazing how money helped one recover from most things.

He put out his cigarette and wearily climbed the stairs to bed. Wonder upon wonders, he thought, as he entered the bedroom, she had left it very much as it had always been – her dressing table had gone, but then if it hadn't he would probably have thrown it into a skip. He sat on the edge of his bed and began to remove his shoes.

What had gone wrong? Was it having no children? Was it that simple? But then it wasn't his fault they hadn't had any, the quacks had given him a clean bill of health on that little number. And he'd spent enough money trying to sort out why she could not reproduce, she'd been everywhere for treatment. He had felt genuinely sorry for her over that, she'd certainly seemed to long for children, though how they were going to fit into her busy social calendar would have remained to be seen. He would have liked a son, carry on the name and all that drivel, but when nothing happened he had merely regarded it as his bad luck, something that was not to be.

Basically he had wondered if she was just bored with him. He had suggested this to her, but she had screamed at him for making her sound shallow. He could not have blamed her; he supposed he was boring. He had his work – in which he was not a high flyer, since he lacked the necessary ambition. But Oliver nursed a strong work ethic, and so he worked in a firm of brokers in the City and made a reasonable living from that also. Since he did not feel passionately about the career he had chosen he rarely mentioned it to Sophia. In fact, come to think of it, he couldn't now remember what they spent their time talking about – certainly not his fishing. Even their shared interest in art had waned, now that Sophia was enraptured with the avant-garde, which Oliver cared nothing for. Nor did she share his love for Bandage, his bull terrier.

'Bandage,' he called. He stood up and crossed the room to his dressing room where Bandage's basket normally stood. It was not there. He checked his bathroom. Bandage had an endearing habit of standing in the corner of a room if he was depressed, worried about something, or sulking. All emotions Oliver knew for sure his dog felt. Bandage could often be found, his back to the room, his chin supported on the wall, and there he would be sometimes for five minutes, once for over an hour. But this time there was no sign of him. He ran down the stairs two at a time and into the kitchen, where Bandage often lurked and where he had a second basket. The basket was there, his toys piled neatly in it, but there was no dog. 'Bandage,' he shouted. He bounded back up the stairs calling his name as he went.

'Wimpole, where's Bandage?' he asked the sweet-faced, grey-haired woman who had appeared on the landing, still putting on a shabby, blue wool dressing gown. Wimpole was his nanny, who had lived with him since the first day of his life and would remain with him until the last day of hers.

'What the fuck's all that row?' she demanded angrily.

'Wimpole! Language!'

'Well, you gave me a fright. What's the matter?'

'It's Bandage, where is he?'

'Your dear wife took him,' she said sarcastically. 'Said she was taking him to her father's. She wouldn't listen to Wimpole.'

Oliver slumped against the wall of the staircase, half-registering that the Hockney had gone too; so much for his theory of her being afraid to remove the best. 'She took that painting of the swimming pool you liked so much, as well as some from the drawing-room. Rapacious moo, isn't she?'

'She can have the bloody paintings, I don't care about them; she can't have Bandage.'

'That's what I said. She said she had bought him so he was hers.'

Oliver sighed. 'That's true, she paid for him, but he was a present to me.'

'Some present. You can't go around giving presents and then taking them back when it suits you, can you? No class, that family, I always said, so did your Aunt Phoebe. Good job the old trout isn't here to see all this. Fancy a drink?'

'No thanks, Wimpole, but you go ahead. I've got to think.'

'You should never have gone to Bishop's End. You should have been here – then it would never have happened. Or taken the hound with you.'

'I usually do take Bandage. But, I remember now, she said her father wanted to show him to a friend and she'd take him to the Lucketts'. But he should have been back by now.'

'So what are you going to do?' They were back in the drawing room and Wimpole was busily pouring herself a very large Scotch on the rocks.

'If she's planning to keep Bandage she can forget it!' he said, with conviction.

But later, alone in his bed, Oliver did something he had not done in years; he covered his head with his pillow to keep the bogey man at bay. He could take anything but the loss of his dog.

At Oakleigh Kennels, far enough outside the village of Middle Shilling so that the barking of the dogs would not be a problem to anyone, Eveleigh Brenton was finally going to bed.

What a day it had been! She doubted if she would sleep, the excitement was almost too much for her. Crufts. She had returned that evening without winning a prize, she hadn't expected to this year. It did not matter. Just being there had been enough. Meeting the other owners and breeders, talking to the judges, being surrounded by people who knew what it was like to have dogs who were the most important creatures in your life. It was a joy not having to explain this love she felt. And she'd spied a fine St Bernard dog; already she was imagining the puppies that he and her Brünnhilde might produce. The dogs were excited too, and had taken a long time to settle in their kennels.

No doubt about it, she said to herself as she turned to switch off the light. There was nothing in the world like Crufts.

The lights were on in every room of the smart Georgian terraced house in Shillingham, and outside the carriage lamp shone above the bay tree in its white wooden tub. Viewed through the windows, its predominantly peach decoration made it warm and welcoming. The house was artfully perfect. The hall had a black and white marble tiled floor – shush, tell no one, Gill tended to say with a laugh, but it's Amtico's best. The carpet in the sitting room was palest cream, the sofas and chairs were covered in a rust-and-green-striped silk fabric – or rather it looked like silk but was, in fact, sixty per cent polyester, just another of those little secrets. The secretaire was Chippendale. The Canterbury music stand, filled with the latest glossy magazines rather than sheet music, was Georgian, as was the slender nest of occasional tables. Chippendale, Georgian and Hepplewhite, all the best reproduction furniture that Brights of Nettlebed sold.

The two bedrooms were white with the merest hint of peach. The bathroom suite, Edwardian with reproduction brass taps, and the Provençal pine kitchen, were wonders thanks to MFI.

It was a veritable palace and Justin and his friend Gill – pronounced with a hard 'g' as in fish, as he was fond of saying – had scrimped, saved and worked their little arses off for seven years to achieve the effect.

There was only one jarring note in the whole house, and that was in the sitting room. Tucked in one corner was a shabby, fawn, dralon-covered chair. Slung over it was a kelim which had also seen better days, but its orange, scarlet and brown design toned in reasonably enough.

This chair belonged to the third member of the household – Sadie. Sadie was her pet name but officially she was known as Saradema, Princess Light of Snippers, offspring of Champion Felix, Prince of Darkness of Barton. She was a white miniature poodle, with coal-black eyes set in a pretty and intelligent face. She was important and knew it, for she always sat in her chair with her snout in the air and the regal expression of one who expected to be waited upon.

Sadie was the love and joy of Justin and Gill's life. They doted upon her in the way that only the almost middle-aged and childless can. Both of them were certain it would be impossible to love a human child more than they loved their canine one. It was a theory never to be tested. Since they made no secret that they did not believe in God and regarded children as noisy and messy but, if mankind was to continue, necessary evils, they found it odd they'd both been invited, countless times, to be godfathers. Sadly, they reached the conclusion that their heterosexual friends were moved by matters fiscal; since they would never have children of their own, a godchild might cop the lot when they went to the great hairdressing salon in the sky. So they always refused.

They knew they were cynical. Life had made them so. It was harder being gay in the small market town of Shillingham than in cosmopolitan London. So they had grown carapaces against the whispers, the funny looks.

On the rare occasions clients asked them to parties, it was, they sensed, more for their entertainment value than for friendship. They camped it up, especially Gill, a bit like singing for their supper, for they knew that was what was expected of them – sad no one wanted to know them as they really were, but they could handle this.

But in the last six months something new had come to haunt them – a group of louts who congregated by the fountain in the market square. It was not what they said: as Gill recited often enough, 'Sticks and stones . . .' No, they were genuinely afraid of them, and with reason. Their salon was just off the square in a chic little cul-de-sac of shops, but the only way home was across or round the square. On Saturday evenings when the yobs were to be found lolling around the Cromwell fountain they had to run the gauntlet of the oafs, who screamed abuse, spat at them and accused them of being HIV positive. As if this were not enough, what upset both Justin and Gill further was the way the noble, honest and true citizens of Shillingham looked embarrassed, lowered their heads, and en masse appeared to be deaf.

Of the two Justin was the more sensitive, and thus the more upset. It was understandable, for as a child he had been cosseted in Upper Shillingham vicarage where his father was the incumbent, followed by the sheltered life of a chorister in Norwich. A choral scholarship had taken him to Kings College, Cambridge, like-minded friends, a lot of fun and a poor third class degree. He had spent a miserable year working as a trainee manager for a large company making chocolate until he had met Gill in a bar in London and had become a hairdresser instead and now only sang in his bath.

Gill's route to Shillingham had been rougher and harder. Born to a hard-drinking, wife-beating bricklayer and a valium-distanced mother, he had survived, just, on a council estate in Morristown. The place reeked of despair and neglect. The walkways were filthy, the graffiti beyond a joke. The lifts rarely worked and had become latrines instead. Burglaries were commonplace, though there was little to steal. Muggings were too frequent to be anything but the norm, and rape went unreported. It was called, ironically, the Forest Glade estate, but not one council-planted tree had survived the attentions of the bored unemployed youths who swept through the place like locusts.

Gill realised early in his life that he was different from his neighbours. He was brighter, cared about his appearance, and liked nice things. As a result he was bullied at school and beaten up out of school on a regular basis. He lived in a society which ruthlessly rejected the unfamiliar. He knew that the hatred was based primarily on jealousy, but knowing that was not much comfort when the boot was going in.

From his bedroom in the high-rise flat, he could look out and see in the distance green fields, and far beyond that was London, to which he longed to escape. In view of his father's attitude, he could forget any dreams of university and a degree. So Gill found a job as an apprentice hairdresser in the shopping precinct. He washed hair, swept up, stood and watched, all for a pittance which he squirreled away for three years until he could get to London and the life he knew was waiting for him.

Meeting Justin was the best thing that had ever happened to him. He had been in London for six years and done well, was already a stylist at Frederico's of Mayfair, building his own list of clients. He had had lovers galore and, at twenty-six, had reached that point in life when he longed to settle, to find someone with whom he could have a steady relationship. He found him in a smoky bar, and he got to him before anyone else could. It was love at first sight and they'd been together ever since – ten years in all.

It was Justin's father dying and leaving him a legacy that had enabled them to look around and find a permanent base. Seven years ago they had come to Shillingham. Neither could explain satisfactorily why they should choose a town close to where both had spent their childhoods, for neither would have thought their roots mattered to them. 'There's nowt so queer as folk . . .' Gill often said in his good imitation of a north country accent, which always made Justin laugh. Shillingham was pretty, relatively crime-free, but most importantly they were able to afford the Georgian house of their dreams and still have enough to buy the lease on a shop and open their salon, which they had called Snippers.

If the house was all peach and charm, then Snippers was slick and efficient. Black, white and chrome. It was state of the art and they loved it as they loved their house, as they were later to love Sadie. There was constant music, Vivaldi, golden oldies, that sort of thing – they would have preferred Mozart and Manilow, but they had to think of their mostly middle-aged customers. They both wore black, and Gill had taught Justin everything he knew.

Sadie had entered their lives three years ago, when they had decided how nice it would be to have a pet. Books on breeds were bought, dog magazines studied, but since they were both hairdressers a poodle was a foregone conclusion. Choosing Sadie from a litter of six had been difficult – they would have liked them all – but there was something about Sadie that made her stand out, an air of aloofness, as if she knew she was different, and it struck a chord with them, a memory was rekindled, and Sadie it had to be.

Sadie was different from your run of the mill poodles; she won prizes. For a bit of fun, they had entered her in the dog show at the local church fête one summer day. She won the prettiest dog category. Then just as they were leaving the woman judge had found them and told them they had a corker of a dog there, and they should show her. At that point they were not to know that everyone in the dog world listened to Eveleigh Brenton, champion breeder of St Bernards, show judge, and passionate advocate of dogs' rights.

Eveleigh had been right. Sadie did win. They had bought a glass-fronted cupboard to display the silver cups, glass bowls and rosettes which she had won while climbing the show ladder until she had won sufficient qualifications recognised by the Kennel Club to be eligible for showing at Crufts. That was a day of such excitement that neither of them would ever forget it; Sadie missed being Best Poodle Bitch by a whisker, though Gill to this day was convinced it was fixed. On Sundays they cleaned the trophies and Sadie had a major grooming. They took it in turns to trim her. She returned their devotion a thousandfold. On the days they did not take her to work with them she welcomed them back with a joy bordering on hysteria. Through her they experienced a love that demanded nothing; she accepted them as they were. No one had ever loved them like that except each other.

Tonight the men were in a state of dither. Sadie was whelping or, at least, she was due to whelp. But Sadie appeared to be taking no interest in the fact that it was long past three and she should have whelped yesterday.

'Do you think we should call the vet?' Justin asked anxiously, for at least the twentieth time. 'He said we could call him any time if there was an emergency.'

'I don't think being three hours late amounts quite to that, Justin.'

'Gill, you're always so calm and sane.'

'It's not that, remember what Jim Varley said, that sixty-three days is the average, that she could go to seventy-one. And she's shown no inclination to build a nest, and look how she turned her nose up at the one we made.'

'My God, I couldn't stand the strain of another eight days.'

'Open that Chardonnay in the fridge, it'll help us relax.'

As Justin rummaged in the kitchen, Sadie suddenly stood up, slid from her chair, walked behind the sofa, let out a soft whimper and collapsed into a heap on the carpet.

'Justin, come quick, I think she's started!' Gill shouted.

Justin appeared, bottle in hand, a tea-towel in the other. 'What should we do? Oh, where is she?' Gill pointed to behind the sofa. 'Oh, no, the carpet, the mess!' Justin waved the tea-towel impotently.

'Drat the carpet, we can get another. If that's where Sadie wants to have her babies then that's where she shall have them.'

The next few hours, instead of being a trial, were some of the most beautiful and exciting of their lives. At twenty-minute intervals, with the minimum of fuss, out popped another puppy. Sadie elegantly licked away the membrane that covered each of them, gave them a good rough washing, put them beside her teats and got on with having the next one. In the end they had five puppies, and both Justin and Gill were in tears at the sight of their Sadie, a new mother, knowing exactly what to do.

'Champagne, we should wet the puppies' heads,' suggested Justin, and when they had poured the wine into their flutes, they gave a saucer of it to Sadie, who much appreciated it after all her hard work.

In the countryside outside Shillingham the rain continued, and as the night progressed the wind rose and was soon battering senselessly at the corrugated iron roof of an outhouse on Tom White's smallholding, Primrose Acre. As the storm intensified, from within the shed an agitated rustling began. At first it was a few growls and then there was a bark and then another, and then one dog started to howl, followed by the rest.

The shed stank of faeces and urine and now, as the rain poured through in several places, to those smells was added the smell of wet pelt.

In the far corner of the shed lay an emaciated bitch. The elbow joints of her front legs were suppurating with sores from the endless rubbing on the concrete floor of her pen. There were no blankets, no straw, just a few urine-soaked rags which she had pushed into one corner, for she was a clean dog. It would be impossible to say what breed of dog she was, for she had lost much of her coat from a bad attack of mange; what little hair was left was crawling with fleas. Her teats sagged beneath her. She was a large dog, and her enclosure was too small for one of her size to lie down comfortably.

It was noisy in the shed, for the other dogs, some in boxes standing piled one on top of the other, were unable to sleep and moved restlessly. A large wave of muscle rippled down the bitch's side. She had a resigned expression as she lay on the floor, the pain ripping through her body. She struggled, panting, but there was no water to ease her thirst. It took longer for the first pup to appear than it had in the other eight whelpings she'd had in her five-and-a-half years. She was exhausted as she licked it, cleaning it. Her body shook as muscle after muscle contracted until one muscle in particular contorted deep within her and she sank back on the concrete as her heart fluttered and faded. With waning strength she scooped at the newborn puppy with her paw and guided him to her nipple and then sank back. Within her, six puppies kicked and fought in their effort to escape her dying body.

In the morning Tom White came and cursed the sight of the dead dog, and one dead puppy, as if it were her fault. He kicked the corpse of the Old English Sheepdog; they were a popular breed, he could not afford wastage like this, he thought, as he threw her corpse onto the rubbish tip.

2

When Oliver was a child, putting a pillow over his head to keep the bogey man at bay had always worked. It appeared that now, although he was an adult, and very tired at this late hour, it was not going to. He could not sleep, he felt insufferably hot, so he gave up the effort, sat up with the pillow propped behind him, lit a cigarette, and spent the small hours re-evaluating his life. He had heard of friends who did this at frequent intervals. Oliver had never felt the need; he had merely drifted amiably and contentedly through life. No doubt he would have continued to do so if Sophia had not put a stop to it. She had gone; she had taken most of his possessions with her; his marriage was irretrievably over, so now what? What did he want to do with the rest of his life – that really made him shudder, for if he said 'rest' then he had to think of it ending also. No, he didn't want to think about that, he'd stick to the immediate future.

He could easily afford her allowance, so was there any need for him to continue with his work? Perhaps he could find something else to do? This was a rather pleasant thought. Here he was, forty-five next birthday – happily a good six months away yet – maybe it really was time for a complete change. He looked at this thought from all angles because it was a new one to him. In Oliver's world, men went to work at nine in the morning, returning at six o'clock at night, if not later. Their aim was to make as much money as possible to give their families the luxuries of life and a secure future. But with no wife, only himself to consider, what were the luxuries he wanted?

Should he stop work entirely, or might that be a mistake? He knew that inside him was a great band of idleness which, if indulged, could swamp him. He could well imagine himself content to lie on his back in a water meadow, a piece of grass stuck between his teeth, watching the clouds scud by. A slight exaggeration possibly, but seductive all the same; he did find the prospect of idleness perhaps a little too attractive. Why not? said a voice inside him, one he had not heard before. 'Why not?' he said aloud. 'I can do what I bloody well want.'

He lit another cigarette. He could work at something else. Make a complete change. But what? He found himself thinking of Aunt Phoebe's house and how contented he was during the weekends he spent there. What if he should sell this London house and move lock, stock and barrel to the country? In the recesses of Oliver's mind was a secret which he had never told a living soul. Oliver had a sneaky idea that he had inherited slightly more from Aunt Phoebe than a house and money, that maybe he had some of her genes too. He thought he'd like to try to write – nothing serious, something that was fun and gave people pleasure, very much as the old girl had. Bandage would like it there, dogs were happier in the country with a big garden to roam; here in London one had to use the park with all its restrictions.

How would Wimpole react? She was a game old bird, but would she accept life in the country? She liked the city. He never really thought much about what Wimpole did when he wasn't around. He supposed she must have friends, and therefore maybe would not want to come with him. He would sound her out in the morning.

He felt enormously happy now. Happy for the first time in weeks, he realised. Not that he'd known that he'd been particularly *unhappy*. When Sophia had announced that she wanted a divorce he had admittedly been rather suprised. But on the other hand, once she'd said the words, 'Oliver, I've decided this isn't working, I want a divorce,' he had thought, yes, of course, how logical. So he hadn't really known that he'd been a bit miserable about the break-up of his life. It only registered now, when he had decided to reorganise himself. Now he knew that perhaps he'd been unhappy for a very long time but, with his nature, had decided not to acknowledge it.

At six he got up, padded downstairs to the kitchen, prepared not to look at Bandage's empty basket, and made himself a pot of tea.

'What's got into you?' asked Wimpole, as she bustled in in her blue woollen dressing gown. 'Not like you to be up this early, lazy bugger like you.'

'I couldn't sleep.'

'Told you last night you should have had a drink,' she said. She crossed to the long pine dresser and took down her mug, which said *Meg* on it, although Oliver was never quite sure why, and wondered if perhaps Meg was her name? She'd always been Wimpole to him. He didn't ask her if Meg was her name, it would have seemed too much of an impertinence somehow. Wimpole she was, and Wimpole she'd stay.

'Enough in that pot for me?' she asked. He replied by pouring tea into her mug for her.

'So, what *are* you doing up so early then?' she said, taking her tea from him.

'I've been re-evaluating my life.'

'Sounds like hard work in the middle of the night. Doesn't sound like you at all, Oliver.'

'It was a bit of a shock coming back and finding most of my things had gone, I couldn't sleep and I thought, well, maybe she's done me a favour. Maybe I should start looking at my own life.'

'Was it the picture or Bandage that upset you?'

'Why should I be upset about Bandage? I'll go and pick him up this morning. No, the picture doesn't matter either, saved me more moving costs.'

'Moving costs?' Wimpole pounced on the words.

To delay his answer, he busied himself topping up his own cup of tea. 'Have we got any biscuits?' he asked.

Wimpole shuffled across to the dresser, and came back with a biscuit tin. 'Moving? What's that mean?' she said.

He spent a few seconds rooting amongst the biscuits; looked up at her sitting opposite him, saw the anxiety on her face, saw how suddenly she looked old and afraid. Oliver realised in that moment something that had probably been so all his life and which he'd never thought about because it had never been necessary. Suddenly he realised that he loved her.

'It's just an idea, Wimpole. I wondered how you felt about our going to live at Bishop's End? I don't need this large house any more.'

'Why there?' she said, and stirred her tea. 'If anything it's bigger than here – rambling old thing. How many bedrooms has it got?'

'Six, I think. Maybe seven,' he said vaguely.

'And then there's that blooming draughty hall with all those rotting rafters exposed. What did your aunt call that?'

'The Great Hall. It was her work room, where she wrote all her books. I might hang the pictures in there. What do you think?'

He hoped that his voice did not sound as anxious as he felt. He watched as she sat concentrating on her tea, which she was still stirring rhythmically, irritatingly. She sipped the tea, and finding it not to her taste, added more sugar and began the stirring ritual again. 'So?' he asked, impatiently. 'What do you think?'

'Well, I've never been much of a one for the countryside. I've never actually trusted it, get what I mean? You know where you are in the city, don't you? You know what you got to look out for. Muggers, pickpockets, rapists, traffic. But the countryside, well, that's a creepy place, I tell you that.'

Oliver laughed gently. 'Wimpole, you are funny. If someone bangs you on the head in the city, who's going to come running? People just don't care.'

'You've never said a truer word, Oliver.' She sipped her tea with the same rhythmic action as, he realised, she always drank her tea, as if her arm were a metronome, taking two sips, down on the table, up, sip, sip, down . . .

'Mind you,' she said. 'Who's going to bloody *hear* you in the countryside if some bugger comes along and hits you on the head?'

'It's just that it's less likely to happen, Wimpole, that's the point.'

'Maybe I've been watching too much *Eastenders*. Maybe all that's gone, really, that friendliness in the street, that I knew when I was a kid.'

'I think it might have. I think you might just be able to recapture it in the country. I hope so, anyway. But, Wimpole . . .' He put his hand out and covered her small work-worn hand, worn from working for him, and squeezed it comfortingly. 'Wimpole, there's no question of me doing this unless you want to come with me. If you don't like the idea, I won't go.'

She grabbed her hand from under his, fumbled in her dressing-gown pocket, came out with a man-sized handkerchief and trumpeted into its folds. 'You see, Wimpole, I love you,' he said, and coughed because it wasn't a word he used an awful lot.

At that Wimpole cried, tears she did not dab at, as if unaware of them. She certainly wasn't ashamed of them.

'Oh, Oliver, you've never ever said that to me, ever.'

'Well, you know, didn't think I needed to,' he said, and wished he had.

'It means a lot to me that, Oliver. I mean, you get to my age, I'm sixty-three next birthday, and okay, I'm fit and able and I can find plenty to do and I help those useless Filipinos Sophia insists on employing – thank God they've gone with her. But I do sometimes wonder, what when I'm seventy and I can't get around so much, what happens then? What's to become of me?'

'Wimpole, I should have said, I mean, I just thought that you understood. I'd look after you, I will always look after you, I promise. And if you don't want to go to the country, we won't go. We can sell this and get a smaller house, one that won't be so difficult to run. I don't expect you to decide now, it's a big decision to make, I realise that. You think about it, and let me know what you want to do.'

'I did a good job on you, didn't I?'

'Sophia wouldn't agree,' he laughed.

'Bah, what would a stupid moo like her know? Nothing.'

An hour later, at just past seven-thirty, Oliver pulled the BMW into the car park of a Little Chef and went in and ordered the American breakfast, an orange juice and a cup of coffee. His 'flu was definitely on the wane. He had set out far too soon to see his father-in-law who, although an early riser, probably would not appreciate him clattering into the house at this time in the morning. He dawdled over his breakfast, smoked three more cigarettes, got back into his car, and arrived at Ben Luckett's half an hour later.

He paused in the driveway, as he invariably did, for the house always gave him immense pleasure. It was a beautiful, stone Elizabethan house, the outside of which Ben Luckett maintained to perfection.

Inside was a different matter. Ben and his wife Cora's taste did not marry happily with the age of the house. Dralon-covered sofas, green onyx coffee tables, huge paintings of wildlife charging across the veldt, and Cora's almost bordello-like fixation with ruffled curtains didn't quite suit the starkly beautiful Elizabethan interior. Oliver admired Ben's self-confidence, to have exactly what he wanted in his house. The enormous television set in the linenfold panelled drawing room might scream out that it was an anachronism, but to Oliver, it was a statement. *I, Ben Luckett, can afford the biggest, largest, most vulgar television set on the market, and I shall put it in my beautiful house, so there.*

Cora had, according to Ben's daughter, been a bit of a mid-life mistake. Oliver wondered if this was so, or was it just jealousy speaking? For if Ben felt Cora to be a mistake, then he managed to put a good face on it. Cora had once been a pretty, dim, peroxide blonde. Such looks had not travelled comfortably into her mid-years. She wore too much make-up, her hair was over teased, lacquered and coloured and she ate so little, in order to maintain her slim shape, that it was a miracle she survived. Her dimness had, of course, accompanied her. In her youth it had been girlishly attractive, but it did not suit a mature woman nearly as well – at least, according to Sophia it didn't. Oliver, however, found it rather endearing and certainly more relaxing than Sophia's rapid, sharp mind. Maybe Ben hadn't been so daft after all.

Ben Luckett, like many self-made men, had all the accoutrements of a successful country gentleman. On the immaculately raked forecourt, with its pristine flower beds in front of the large house, stood the four-wheel-drive Range Rover, dog guard in the back. Snuffling around on the forecourt were two fine black labradors and a Jack Russell, which charged at his car in hysterical welcome. Before Oliver even got out of the car, on the steps appeared Ben Luckett himself, his face glowing claret red, in his tweed plus-fours, and already sporting the sheepskin wrist-warmers that he wore for shooting.

'You're early, Oliver,' he said, holding out his hand in welcome. Oliver wished that people would stop making remarks about him being up early for once.

'I've come for Bandage,' he said. 'I gather Sophia's brought him here.'

'Sophia's not up, not yet.'

'Oh, I'll just pick up the dog and go.'

'Have some breakfast.'

'No thanks, I already have.'

'You'd better come in now you're here. You might have a long wait, Bandage is upstairs in Sophia's room – unhygienic, I say, but she won't listen.'

'Bandage sleeping with Sophia! In the same room! God Lor'.' This information made Oliver feel unsettled. Why should Sophia do that, when she'd made such fusses about Bandage sleeping in his dressing room?

Oliver allowed Ben to lead him back into the house. In the hall he paused. 'Where's the oak chest that stood over there, Ben?'

'Cora said it was a dust trap. She sold it. Sophia's a bit miffed. Said we should have let her know, she'd have liked it.'

Oliver did not wish to make any further comment on Sophia's current acquisitive nose for furniture, and smiled to himself instead. Cora and this house were a trial to Sophia, who had such exquisite taste that she worked as a consultant on a new magazine which was taking the British public by storm. It was the sort of magazine town dwellers loved, full of glossy photographs of tarted-up Tuscan farmhouses and tatty English cottages, with collections of old, junk-shop bottles arranged artistically to look like a display at the V & A. The loss of the intricately-carved chest would have pained Sophia; he was grateful to Cora for selling it.

Ben Luckett had been in the middle of breakfast, and Oliver accepted the cup of coffee he offered him.

'I haven't said anything, you know, about you and Sophia.'

Oh God, thought Oliver, here it comes – heart to heart time. 'I appreciate that, Ben,' he said, craftily he thought.

'Of course, I'm sad. And I don't understand. I like you, Oliver, I hope we keep in touch.'

'Well, thanks, Ben. Me too.'

'Don't get me wrong, Oliver. I love Sophia deeply. But I can see she's not the easiest of people to get along with – and to live with.' He added this with such feeling that Oliver realised that Sophia's visit had obviously been a great strain on him too. 'But why, Oliver? Why?'

Oliver felt suddenly sad for his father-in-law's obvious confusion. 'Well, I guess I haven't been much of a husband. Perhaps I should have been a bit more romantic – all that stuff. I'm the first to admit Sophia ran our house like clockwork, and I guess I took it all for granted. And with no kids it's been hard for her, a disappointment really. No hard feelings though, Ben, you realise?' he coughed, and found he felt quite emotional.

'You've been very generous, boy.'

This touching little talk ceased as the door opened and in walked the subject of it. Oliver jumped to his feet. They might be separated, they might be heading for divorce, but he could still acknowledge that Sophia Hawksmoor was a beautiful woman. And even now, fresh out of her bed, hurriedly dressed in slacks and silk shirt, with no make-up and the brush just raked quickly through her hair, she looked stunning and belied her thirty-five years.

'I couldn't believe it when I saw the car,' she said in the clipped voice which was the only thing that marred her. It was a little too abrupt, a little too sharp.

'I've come for Bandage.'

'Well, you can't have him,' she said, pouring herself coffee.

'What do you mean, I can't have him? Is he ill?'

'No, but you didn't expect to keep him, did you? How can I live alone in London without protection? I'll need the dog.'

'You've got the Filipinos.'

'I want Bandage.'

'But he's mine.'

'He's *ours*.'

'I thought he was a birthday present to me.'

'He was a present to both of us, and I've decided to keep him.'

At this, Oliver's heart lurched, and Ben interrupted. 'Sophia, come on, that's a bit hard. You can always get another dog.'

'I don't want another dog. I want Bandage,' she enunciated carefully.

Oliver banged the table. It was a tactical error, and as soon as he had done it, he realised it. But it was too late. 'No,' he said. 'You've got every other bloody thing I own – you're not having the dog.'

'We'll see about that,' she said and, pushing her coffee cup aside, she stalked from the room.

3

Thomasine woke just after eight and was immediately alert, which was unusual for her, for she was one of those people to whom waking, each morning, was a rebirth. The reason was obvious. There was a heavy weight in the crook of her elbow. In the night the dog had abandoned the floor and was not just on the bed, but in it with her. She stroked its soft coat, liking the feel of it against her bare arm, looked down at the sleeping bulldog and realised, with a start, that she had not felt this protective towards a small object since she had held her daughter, Nadine, when she had been born, sixteen years ago. Dangerous notions, stupid ones to pursue she told herself, and promptly thought of Robert. What would he think of this? She, lying in bed, cuddling the dog beneath the duvet. She was smiling, for, as she well knew, Robert would have been apoplectic with disgust.

Why, when she relaxed, did Robert always pop into her thoughts? It wasn't surprising, she supposed; after all, she had been married to him for twenty-two years, and for twenty of them she had thought that she was the be-all and end-all of his life, as he was of hers. She had loved him, she had tried to be a good wife to him – whatever that meant, she was none too sure any more. And in any case, being a satisfactory wife hadn't always been easy, not with Robert.

Thomasine remembered the conversation she'd had with her mother when she had first told her that she wanted to marry Robert.

'What birth sign is he?' her mother had asked immediately.

'Virgo, I think.'

'Dear God, Thomasine, you can't even consider it! Never *ever* marry a Virgo. I did, and look where it landed me.'

'So what's so very wrong with being a Virgo?' Thomasine asked.

'I'll tell you. They're pernickety, they're precise, they're exact, they're critical – hypercritical – and they're tidy. All the things you're not.' Di Haddon spoke in the bald, brutal way that some mothers have.

She had thought her mother wrong, of course she had – mothers were, in her youthful experience, always wrong, they knew nothing. But with the passing years she had had to acknowledge, grudgingly, that her mother possessed the gift, awkward and often inconvenient, of being invariably right.

The first sign that Robert might be the Virgo her mother had described occurred on their honeymoon night. He had been markedly irritated at finding one of her court shoes on one side of the bed and the other on the other side. Not that he'd said anything. It was the exaggerated way he had picked them up between thumb and forefinger, as if he was saying to her, 'Look what I'm doing, I'm putting your nasty, dirty shoes away. I'm putting your shoes away neatly and tidily as they should be.' She'd been irritated for a second or two, and thought of a smart-arse response, but had controlled it and, wanting to please him, she had thanked him instead and had never left her shoes like that again. Nor did she scatter her undies or talcum powder around the bathroom, or leave her clothes on the chair waiting to be hung up in the morning as had been her way. Overnight she began to tutor herself to be better, to be tidier, until their house was exactly as Robert wanted it. A model of efficiency. A place that anyone could come to at any hour of the day or night and not find it in a pickle.

It was because of her mother that she had embarked on this sea of compromise, for another of Di's wisdoms, trotted out blithely, completely ignoring the fact that she herself had failed in the institution, was that marriage was all about give and take. It had crossed her mind once or twice over the years that, discounting the money he gave her and the mortgage he paid, Robert was taking a lot more than he was giving. However, Thomasine had also learnt that life was a lot less stressful if she did as he wanted, and she regarded it as a small price to pay for happiness.

Thomasine, however, was not merely being a Goody Two-Shoes. In that first flush of determination to make her marriage work, she had discovered a wonderful thing. With order and system, everything ran far more smoothly than it had in the past. Housework, which she had always abhorred, could be sped through in a tidy house, whereas her jumbled-up flat had always taken a day, at least, to clean. This way she had more free time. She had used this time to attend cookery classes, and discovered she had a talent for it and that what could have been another chore was, in fact, a pleasure; she'd done an A level in History of Art; she helped a friend out in her boutique and did alterations for her; she'd resurrected a small painting talent and worked hard to make it a larger one.

While Robert congratulated himself on how well he'd trained her, Thomasine congratulated herself on the number of skills she was accumulating. Skills which, one day, might come in handy, and which gave her a welcome sense of security.

It was almost, she later realised, as if she subconsciously knew the marriage wasn't to last, that she would need to be able to do other things some time in the future.

Robert had been generous. He'd kept their London house for himself, but had given her the money to buy this converted school house in Middle Shilling. She had an adequate allowance for their daughter, Nadine. Thomasine, whilst accepting gratefully the money to buy the house, had refused all other assistance; she wanted to support herself. It was a point of honour with her – that door had closed, she must open another. It was not something her mother understood and she'd had long arguments with Di, who felt no inhibition in calling her 'stupid' – though what business it was of hers, or anyone else's, Thomasine could not understand.

Thomasine was confident she could support herself. Several years ago she'd illustrated a friend's children's book. She had enjoyed the challenge, but when the editor of the publishing house had told her to keep in touch in case they found other work for her, she hadn't. With her family to care for she did not have the time to become a professional. Everything was different now, she could start again. She was good, she knew she was. She had already been in touch with the self-same editor, who had promised to keep her in mind.

She shifted position and the dog snuffled, annoyed with the movement which disturbed her sleep. Sometimes she marvelled at the way she tried to fool herself. How could one hide the truth from oneself? Why, after all that had happened, did she still dream of the day he'd return – she'd even planned the meal she would cook. 'Fool!' she said aloud. 'Stop thinking that way.' Oh, she wished she could. Wished it was that simple.

Think positively, she told herself. Now she had a new house in a strange area, new friends to make and life was about to become an adventure. It was time for her to begin living her life. Her way.

The dog in her arms stretched languorously. Now this, this dog. She mustn't become attached to it, it would be gone soon, she was sure. For a second she allowed herself to think of keeping it, but smartly rejected the idea; she did not want the responsibility nor the restrictions that it would impose upon her. The dog's eyes opened and looked at her.

'I can't keep calling you Dog, that's for sure, too precious for words. How about ... how about Luna? I mean, if it hadn't been raining last night the moon would have been shining on you. Yes, Luna.' The little black tightly-curled tail twitched, as if acknowledging that such a name was to her liking. Or so Thomasine liked to think. 'I suppose you need a pee.'

She released the dog from her arms, slid off the bed, put on her dressing gown. 'Come on, Luna,' she said. But Luna didn't budge. Luna sat in the middle of the duvet and stared at her in a very disgruntled manner. 'Come on, Luna, what's the matter? Come on,' she said, encouragingly. Still the dog didn't move. Maybe she couldn't, maybe she'd stiffened up.

'Is that your problem? The old joints are stiff after last night's catastrophes? Come on then, I'll try and carry you.'

Try was the operative word. She didn't know how much the dog weighed but she guessed it must be fifty pounds or so. Gingerly she manoeuvred her way down the spiral staircase into the drawing room below, which had once been the main schoolroom. Now it was delightfully furnished in chintzes, a cliché, she knew, but then she didn't mind what others thought, it had been what she wanted. Cream Greek rugs were scattered on the highly polished plank floor. She opened the casement door into the garden and stepped outside, putting the dog down on the red-brick path. The dog stood and looked at her balefully. Thomasine stared back.

'Well, I've got all day. It's up to you,' she said.

There was a raw nip in the air, despite the early morning sunshine, but it looked as if it was going to be a lovely day. She took deep breaths of air, fresh from the downpour of last night, and felt very pleased with the world as she looked around.

Thomasine had not been alone in wondering if she was going to settle in the country, never having lived there before. A city girl she had been, born and bred. But something in her, deep down inside, had wanted to live in the country. She had promised herself that, when she had time, she was going to start delving into her own family history to find out where she had come from, why she had such a feeling almost of returning. Had her family once been of yeoman stock? Was that why she had this strong conviction that happiness would be found in the peace and solitude of the countryside?

Peace and solitude, she smiled to herself at that. Whoever said that didn't know much about the countryside. She only had to stand here now, at half past eight in the morning, listening to the racket which was the countryside. Birds, returning in droves now that spring was almost here, were making a twittering din. Cockerels were cockadoodling, cows mooing, two cats were fighting, dogs barking. She could hear the clatter of as yet unknown farm equipment, a tractor was whirring up, a plane was flying overhead. Had it not been a Saturday then the noise of children waiting outside for the school bus to take them into Shillingham would have been added to it all. She did hope that her living in what had once been the village school was not going to cause problems. She had heard that there had been a big petition to try and keep it open; she sincerely hoped that she wouldn't be blamed for its closure.

She looked down. Luna was still standing in the same place, looking angry, as if whatever was upsetting her were Thomasine's fault. 'Luna, my love, you do seem to be in a bad way. It's the vet for you after breakfast, I think. Come on, maybe the long grass will be more to your liking.' She manhandled the dog across the lawn to what she liked to call her wilderness patch – in truth it was one buddleia tree and a load of weeds that she planned to let run riot in the hopes that in the summer her garden would be full of butterflies. She placed the dog down on all four paws, but held onto its tummy.

'Luna, this isn't ideal, but it's the only way. You're going to have to pee. Come on, girl.' Maybe it was something in the tone of her voice, for the dog looked at her, lifted one leg elegantly into the air and piddled.

'That's odd. Why are you cocking your leg like that? You're a bitch!' She guided her back into the house and into the kitchen, mixed her some Weetabix and laughed at the folly of warming the milk for her. She didn't think she ought to add sugar, it couldn't be good for dogs if it wasn't good for humans, so she broke an egg on the top.

While she waited for the kettle to boil, Thomasine took out the Yellow Pages and looked up Veterinary Surgeons. She was in luck, there was one right here in Middle Shilling. She would call him after she had had breakfast.

4

Unusually for him, Jim Varley had overslept. He blamed it on the Scotch he'd drunk last night and made a mental note, admittedly one of many in the last two years, that he must control the amount he was drinking. It was an odd thing about such resolutions, he realised with a wry smile, that he only ever made them in the mornings, never in the evenings.

It was eight before he left the house, rejecting the enormous breakfast that Beth tried to press upon him, as she did every morning. With only coffee slurping about inside him, he climbed into his battered old Land Rover. He wanted to check Ben Luckett's filly before his morning surgery.

He regretted he was late because, in Jim's opinion, there were two times that were best to visit a stable. One was at twilight, as the horses were bedded down for the night and a sweet tranquillity descended upon the stables; the other, very early in the morning, as the horses and the grooms prepared for the new day and there was a briskness and excitement in the air. And now, by oversleeping, he'd missed it.

As he swung the Land Rover onto the forecourt of Ben Luckett's house the front door opened and a man dashed down the steps, climbed into a large

BMW, slamming the door angrily behind him. He crashed the car into gear and with a spray of gravel set off down the drive at a ferocious speed. Oliver Hawksmoor, Jim thought, and in a fine temper. The car had just started when a very angry-looking Sophia appeared on the steps also. Jim vaguely wondered what the fuss was about, but not wanting to get involved in other people's dramas, he thought it politic not to acknowledge her. Instead he continued round the corner of the house, past the kitchens and the kitchen garden to the fine red-brick stable block, and drove into the immaculately kept yard, complete with clock, stable cat and a few chickens pecking idly about.

He hoped that, intent on their own problems, no one in the house had noticed him arrive, for he really hadn't time to stay long. At the sight of him, Amanda, one of Ben Luckett's overworked but devoted girl grooms, came running towards him. Girls like Amanda always amazed him, the way they worked for a pittance just to be close to the creatures they adored. All was well, she told him. The mare was fine, the foal suckling well, both a picture of contentment. He was just about to get back into his vehicle when Ben Luckett himself appeared.

'I thought it was you I heard. I expected to see you earlier than this, Jim,' he said, rudely.

'Busy morning,' Jim lied.

'I suppose animals don't take weekends off,' Ben laughed.

Jim laughed back politely, even if he didn't think it much of a joke. 'Filly's fine, nothing to worry about there, and mum also. I'll pop back again this evening if you want, but I don't really think it's necessary.'

'Better to be safe than sorry, Jim. She's an expensive horse.'

'Fine, as you wish.' He put his bag of medical supplies on to the passenger seat and began to climb in.

'Doing anything tomorrow morning?' Ben Luckett asked.

'It's always difficult to say in my trade,' Jim replied cautiously, not wishing to commit himself.

'Just a few people in for pre-lunch drinks, if you fancy it?'

'Thanks for inviting me,' Jim said. He really didn't want to go, he hated drinks parties, or any party come to that, but perhaps he should accept Ben's invitation, the man was a good client and was always asking him, and he always turned him down. 'I'd like that,' he found himself saying.

'Well, that is nice,' said Ben, obviously as surprised as Jim by his acceptance.

Jim took the short cut back to Middle Shilling, which took him past the Oakleigh Kennels. He glanced at his watch. Had he got time to pop in and see Eveleigh? She was concerned, and with reason, about a St Bernard dog of hers. Visiting these kennels always gave him pleasure. They were immaculate. So many he'd seen were little more than a collection of sheds, dirty concrete runs, and God alone knew what was contained in the offal, stored in the fly-infested barrels, waiting to be stewed up later. But Eveleigh had neat rows of brick-built kennels, well fenced, with an outdoor run and an indoor sanctum.

The water bowls were always full of clean water – how was a mystery to him. She had heat lamps for poorly dogs, a special whelping room, and hanging baskets outside each kennel. Beyond was a large, securely fenced paddock where the dogs were exercised regularly. He wished all breeders could be made to inspect her set-up and improve their own. She was a caring breeder, and although successful in her chosen field, he very much doubted if she made a penny out of the enterprise, so great was her concern for the well-being of her dogs. Breeders were an odd breed, he smiled at his own lame joke. Money could be made, he knew, if one were ruthless and had no concern for the health of the dogs and overbred from a bitch, doctoring the forms to hoodwink the Kennel Club whose rules for registration stipulated, rightly, that a bitch must not be whelped over the edge of eight and then have only six litters in her lifetime. But there were still those who bred dogs because they loved them, and one breed in particular, rarely making a profit. Even the winner of Crufts, Eveleigh had told him, only won a small cheque, got a cup and, if they were lucky, some dog food for a year.

He beeped the horn of the Land Rover. There was no point in going to the front or back door, for by seven each morning Eveleigh was out tending to her dogs behind the house.

'Jim, have you come to see Siegfried?' Eveleigh asked as she appeared round the side of the house.

'Just passing,' he said. He liked to keep Eveleigh's bills down as much as possible. He would only charge her for any treatment today, no call-out fee. And, after all, it was true, he had been passing.

'This way,' she said, taking the lead. She was a tall woman whose body was lean and taut from hard work, though it would be hard to see today, dressed as she was in cords, tucked into her wellies, and a baggy jumper which reached almost down to her knees. She had a wide, open face, an honest face. Her blue eyes were surrounded now by a fine network of lines, and her nose, which when young, had been the bane of her life, was of a noble proportion which suited an older face. Her hair, once blonde but now greying, was invariably tied back into a pony tail – a mite incongruous in one of her middle years, but which, when socialising or judging, she wound into a neat bun or sometimes had set. She was a fine-looking woman who carried herself well and had several admirers, even if none of them had dared make an approach, for she had a natural reserve about her. Rumour was that even if they had spoken up, it was unlikely that they would have received a response for, it was said, Eveleigh still grieved too much for her dead husband, Reggie, killed five years ago by joy riders on the Morristown by-pass. Eveleigh was aware this was said, and felt sad, for she was lonely. Secretly she longed for someone to replace Reggie, but did not know how to let others know it.

'How many dogs have you got at the moment, Eveleigh?' Each time he came there seemed to be more than the last time.

Eveleigh paused as she counted silently in her head. 'Well, I suppose eighteen St Bernard adults, six puppies and my King Charles.'

Jim smiled. 'Still taking in the waifs and strays?' he asked kindly. He was aware that of the eighteen St Bernards, only four bitches were used for breeding; the others were her own retired dogs, and those that other people did not want. Eveleigh, it seemed, always had room for just one more.

'A new one arrived last week; a dear sweet year-old St Bernard bitch. One of her front paws twists in very slightly and the owners didn't want her any more as she wasn't perfect. As you know, I have a return-if-not-suited policy.'

'But after a year? I mean, didn't they notice this before?'

'I'm sure it was not there when I sold the puppy. I wouldn't have sold a puppy as being perfect if I'd noticed anything wrong with it, I would have reduced the price. I've my name and reputation to consider.'

'Of course, Eveleigh. And I've seen all your litters and I never noticed one with a twisted foot, it must have had an accident since.'

'That's what I think. But how filthy, how absolutely filthy – what a way to treat a dog! Just because it has the slightest of limps, it's rejected. It's disgusting.'

'You'll never eliminate irresponsible dog owners, Eveleigh. Sometimes I wish people had to apply for a licence and pass a test to be allowed to own a dog. Still, when you think what lousy parents humans can make, is it any wonder? Let's go and see that old brute of yours, check him over. And I'll look at the one with the bad paw.'

Champion Siegfried Nibelungen of Oakleigh was sleeping heavily, as old dogs do. He finally deigned to raise his head and peered at them from under the wrinkles that, in the way of St Bernards, sagged, giving him a mournful expression. A steady stream of slobber dribbled from his mouth and Jim, knowing St Bernards of old, hoped he wouldn't shake his head and cover him with it. The old dog stretched conveniently for Jim, as if inviting him to listen to his heart. It was slowing down, just a little bit more each time he came. He knew what Eveleigh was praying for, what every dog owner prays for; that the dog would die by himself, so that the awful decision to have him put down would not have to be made. Jim hoped especially with this one that Eveleigh could have her wish.

He checked the dog with the twisted paw. The malformation was barely detectable. Far more likely that, once the dog was fully grown, the owners had tired of its size – a common happening with the large breeds. Eveleigh invited him for a coffee, as she invariably did, but looking at his watch he reluctantly refused. He enjoyed nattering to Eveleigh, she always made him feel relaxed. They had known each other for nearly twenty years and so there was never any need to explain themselves to each other, to pretend. It was an honest relationship, similar, he presumed, to having a sister to talk to.

By the time he reached the surgery he was running seriously late, and as he rushed in Beth met him with his telephone messages.

'What's the surgery looking like?' he asked.

'Not too bad, four people, but there were lots of phone calls. Those hairdresser blokes called; their dog had puppies in the night.'

He glanced up. 'Really? And they managed OK?'

'They were so excited, it was lovely to hear. They were bubbling with happiness and sounded just like proud new parents.'

'Good. I'm glad all went well for them. Do you think I've got time for a cup of coffee?' He looked at her questioningly.

'I'll bring it in. But after surgery you're sitting down, Jim Varley, and you are going to eat some breakfast.'

'Please, Beth, not bacon and eggs. Something light.'

'Toast, with a scrambled egg.'

'Do I have to?'

'Yes you do.'

For the sake of a cup of coffee he agreed, and went into the surgery. On Saturdays he was on his own – his veterinary assistant only worked five days a week – so a light surgery was a relief, for it would mean less sterilising and general cleaning up afterwards. His first client was in and out in a matter of five minutes, a man who was planning to move to France and wanted to arrange for rabies vaccinations for his dog and cat. Then a cat with a nastily cut paw, which was soon bandaged and away. A pet rabbit which was off colour he hospitalised for observation; he was suspicious it might have an ulcer, caused by the stress of not being able to get to the doe in the next cage. He'd seen that before.

He was drying his hands on a paper towel as he turned to welcome the next patient with its owner. Standing rather shyly in the doorway was a woman who made Jim's heart lurch in a way it had not done for ages. She was tall, not too slim, with long brown shining hair, and she smiled a greeting with a generous mouth.

'Good morning,' he said, and suddenly felt as gauche as a schoolboy.

'Good morning. I'm Thomasine Lambert. I'm new around here. I moved into The School House in the village last week.' She said this in an attractive, low voice, but rather as if she spoke by rote, as if she were saying it a lot at the moment.

Jim introduced himself and they shook hands; he registered that hers was cool to the touch, with long, finely tapered fingers, like those of an artist. 'Ah, what have we here?' he said to cover up how flustered he felt, and knelt down to introduce himself to Luna. 'I like bulldogs. My grandad had one, you don't often see them these days.'

'I found her,' she said simply. 'She's not mine. I'm just looking after her till we find someone to take her on.'

'Found her? What, a stray?'

'Yes, on the by-pass. But she's not a real stray. Some ba –' She grinned. 'Bastard, yes, that's the word. He was a right bastard. He threw her out of his car in the storm last night. Abandoned her. She could have been killed. Fortunately for the dog, I was just coming along behind.'

'Did you inform the police? Perhaps she fell out of the car.'

'I don't think so, neither do the police. The kennel there was full and there was something about the dog, something appealing, so I said I'd take her home until somebody wanted her.'

'You don't?'

'Well, no, not really. I mean, I've enough to do at the moment without a dog as well.'

'Right, so what is it you want me to do? Examine her? Is she hurt?'

'Yes, her chin is grazed and she seems to have done something to her leg and it's stiffened up overnight because she's having awful trouble walking. In fact, when she peed this morning she cocked her leg like a dog and she's a bitch.'

'Have you got another dog?'

'No, I said I hadn't time for dogs.'

'Then she was marking her territory. A dog can pee high up and aim its scent further; so by not squatting she was spreading her scent, marking your garden as hers.'

'How clever of her,' she laughed. 'I just thought she was being fastidious.'

Jim picked Luna up and sat her on his examination table. 'You're a weight and a half, aren't you?' The dog looked at him, then at Thomasine, and then lay down. 'Well, she's not scared of vets. Either she hasn't seen too many vets or has been so often that she's resigned to us. Let's have a look.' He checked the graze on her chin, gently moved her legs. 'Nothing broken there, I think you're probably right, it's just a bad sprain. I'll put some antiseptic cream on that chin and we'll give her a jab just to be on the safe side and...' He stopped speaking as he ran his fingers down the dog's flank. 'Ah, I think here's the reason why she got thrown out of the car. Not obvious at first because she's naturally so stocky.'

Thomasine leant forward eagerly. 'Why?'

'I'm afraid she's pregnant and, since she's been abandoned, probably not by a bulldog, probably a little mistake.'

Thomasine looked at the dog. 'Oh, Luna. What were you up to?' As always when she spoke to the dog the little tail waggled excitedly, making her whole rump wriggle with apparent pleasurable anticipation. 'So the father could be anything, I suppose.'

'Exactly. I mean you wouldn't ditch a bulldog in pup to a bulldog, their puppies sell for a lot of money. They're probably mongrels, and the problem with bulldogs is they're very bad whelpers, the puppies' heads are big and can get stuck in the birth canal, which, of course, is dangerous and might lead to a Caesarean. Any operation is a risk to a bulldog, they are difficult to administer a general anaesthetic to, so there is always the possibility of complications. In other words, Miss Lambert, I think you've got a bit of a problem here. You could land up with a large litter of mongrel puppies – half bulldog, God knows what they'll look like. You may not be able to get rid of them and, I have to warn you now, there could be considerable veterinary expenses as well.'

'What do you recommend, then?'

'I know of a dog refuge near here, who will do their best to care for her and hopefully find homes for the puppies afterwards. The only other alternative I'm afraid is to spay her, but then, as you say, she isn't your dog.'

'No, and what about the risk from the anaesthetic you mentioned?' Thomasine leant against the examination table and stroked the dog protectively. 'How many dogs are at this refuge?' she asked.

'It varies. Close to Morristown, it gets its fair share of abandoned, unwanted dogs. She has a lot of greyhounds in, you know; when they can no longer win races, they're abandoned. There's a lot of irresponsible dog ownership around, so that on average she has two to three hundred dogs at a time. No matter how Betty tries, this dog wouldn't necessarily get the attention she's going to need.' He looked with sympathy at Luna and patted her; she licked his hand in response.

Thomasine looked at Luna too. If she was going to have a bad time, if it was all going to be difficult, no matter how kind the refuge owner, it wouldn't be the same as being just one dog being cared for. 'I think I'll keep her for the time being and look after her. I'll face the matter of the puppies when that arises.'

'The time being?' he queried.

'When she's had the puppies, then I'll find a home for her, it shouldn't be too difficult, a pedigree dog like this.'

'Maybe it'll be more difficult than you think.'

'Why?'

'Perhaps you'll love her too much.'

'Me? Not a chance.' Thomasine shook her head and he noticed how the overhead light shone on her hair. 'I don't even like dogs. It's just that I hate cruelty to any animal. I don't think a dog should be treated in this way.'

'Fine. I'd say she's halfway through her pregnancy. I can arrange for her to have a scan if you like, to see what's going on in there or, to keep the cost down, I could just keep an eye on her. I'll give you a diet sheet for her, some vitamin pills and a wormer. Do bring her back if you're at all worried. If she begins to whelp, give me a ring. It doesn't matter if it's in the middle of the night – it invariably is.'

'You're very kind, thank you so much.' Thomasine looked down at Luna, who was so relaxed she looked as if she had fallen asleep. 'You know, I think she's a witch. As soon as I decide one thing, she looks at me and I find I decide something else.'

He smiled. 'Some dogs have that effect. She's a good bulldog, though. Once back to normal she'll be one to be proud of.'

'You think so? There, did you hear what the man said?' Thomasine asked Luna as she bundled her into her arms.

As soon as she was out of his surgery and in the car she immediately regretted what she had taken on. It was the combination of the dog and the vet – it was all his fault. His 'poor bulldogs suffering' routine, plus Luna and those eyes, had made her lose her senses. And what if Nadine wanted her to keep it? No, that was unlikely, Nadine liked cats, not dogs, and was always nagging her to buy her a Siamese. Thomasine had read somewhere that a cat lover rarely became a dog lover.

'That's your lot, Luna. You can stay until you have your babies and then that's it – out into the big world with you after that.' Luna gently butted her with her large forehead. 'I mean it,' Thomasine said sternly as she put the car into gear.

5

Since Kimberley White's bedroom was over the kitchen at Primrose Acre it was warm, benefiting from the heat generated by the solid fuel Rayburn which was never allowed to go out. The small room was in need of decoration, and new curtains would not have gone amiss, but Kimberley was resigned to nothing ever being done to improve it. Tom, her father, was at pains to tell her what a lucky cow she was to have her own room and not to have to share as he had had to. She sighed inwardly whenever he said so, for it meant that he was about to embark on a long description of his own deprived childhood when, as the youngest of eight, he hadn't even had shoes. She knew the saga off by heart. After so many repetitions, she had acquired the ability to switch off and think of other things. In any case, she didn't believe a word of it. She had asked her Nan before she had died if what he related was true. 'Nothing of the sort,' the old lady had snorted indignantly. 'We weren't rich, but my hubby made sure we never went without. My Tom always was a bloody little fibber.'

The room looked over the fields of Chris Walters' farm at the back of the house. A pleasant view compared to the clutter of broken machinery, defunct fridges and washing machines, which cluttered the front and were part of her father's scrap dealings, one of his many sidelines. In winter the wind whipped over the flat field as if coming straight from Siberia, so she could not have her window open at night, for then it was too great a battle for the Rayburn to keep the room warm.

The wind had died from last night's storm. She pushed back the curtain, which was now just a faded memory of the riot of bright-coloured flowers it once had been. She saw the sun glinting on the furrows of the next-door field, registered that, despite that, it was cold, and dived back under her blankets. She had no idea of the time, she did not have a clock and wasn't wearing her watch. She did not need either; she could rely on her mother to call her. If she was unlucky then her father would be bellowing up the narrow stairs with its frayed runner, yelling for her to get up and give him a hand.

Kimberley had fantasies about the runner on the stairs; she hoped that one day her father would catch his foot in it, tumble down the stairs and hurt himself – a twisted ankle, or, when really annoyed, she'd dream of a broken leg. However, such thoughts tended to be treacherous, for sometimes she found herself hoping he would fall and break his neck. When that happened she shut her eyes tight, trying to shut the idea from her mind. It was wrong to think of a parent in such a way, wicked. Something bad would happen to her if she let such a thought escape. But for all that, it lingered there and, much as she scolded herself, it would never quite go away.

Kimberley had other dreams which she liked to unlock, polish and improve. One was of getting a job and having enough money to leave home. She dreamed of a nice flat with decent furniture, and how she would buy ready-made lined curtains like the ones she had seen in Marks and Spencer's in Morristown. She thought about it so often that if she closed her eyes she could almost see it, with its Habitat sofa-bed, the white shelves she'd seen in Texas for the books and CDs that she would one day buy. Yellow and white she wanted, with striped rugs in blue and cream on the floor which, of course, she would have stripped and polished.

The only way such a dream would ever become a reality was if she worked as hard as possible to get her A Levels. She was good at maths, but had rejected any idea of going on to university, for that would mean being dependent upon her father for too long. Her ambition was to work in a bank and one day become a manager. Not her father's bank in Shillingham, that would never do, for then he would come in, loud-mouthed and unwashed, and embarrass her.

Years ago, when still quite young, she had become aware of her mother's life – worn to a frazzle with hard work and never enough money, frightened to death of her husband and his moods, and seemingly with no mind, or opinions, of her own. Kimberley had no intention of ending up like her. That she was still at school was an example of the contrariness of her father's nature. He had so often told her how much he loathed her that she now did not even register it. Whatever she did was never right for him. He shouted abusively at her, occasionally hit her – and yet took a perverse pride in her achievements, and so her education continued.

The way her mother lived angered Kimberley, for she was certain that her father made far more money than he let on, that somewhere there was a stash of it hidden away. She had watched him doing deals often enough; he never accepted a cheque, always cash. Frequently he said to her, tapping the side of his nose with his finger, 'Mark my words, Kim, deal in notes whenever you can, then there's no proof of nothing.' If he did have money hidden away it was so unfair to her mother, and it would be one more reason to loathe her father.

After the treatment of her mother, she most hated him for the treatment of the dogs. It shamed her now, that it had taken her so long to wake up to what went on in the big sheds outside, and to realise it was cruel. The sheds and the dogs had been there all her life and since, in the way of children, she knew no better, she had not questioned anything. She had assumed that it was normal for dogs to be raised and kept in such conditions. Two years ago she had woken up to all the hideousness of it, and still despised herself for being so thick.

Until then she had helped with the dogs, cleaning them out, feeding them, playing with the puppies. But after the row, and what a row it had been, she had never been in the sheds again.

She could still remember every detail of that particular argument. It had started calmly enough. Rarely for her, she had stayed overnight with her only friend, Liz. Rarely, since her father did not like her going into other people's houses – she might see how other people lived and get dissatisfied. That visit to Liz's had been allowed because he knew Liz's father hadn't two halfpennies to rub together, and because Liz and her family were moving away to Durham. Liz, who loved animals, had insisted they watch a film on Channel 4 about puppy farming in Wales. At first she wasn't that interested, but as she listened to the impassioned commentary and saw the tears that Liz was shedding for the poor dogs, it was as if the scales had fallen from her eyes. She realised that that was exactly what was going on at Primrose Acre, and that it was wrong. Now she knew why she had never been allowed to bring any friends home. It was why her parents also had no friends. It was why any callers at the smallholding were promptly dealt with and sent packing.

She had been excited as she described the film to her parents. She explained how she felt as if, since she had discovered how wrong it was, they must also, and then they would agree that it must stop.

'Stop!' Tom had bellowed. 'Don't be such a stupid cow! Where the bloody hell do you think your keep comes from?' He banged the kitchen table with his fist, making the plates jump and jangle. 'Where the fuck do you think this food came from? Not from the veg we sell, not the eggs, from the fucking dogs. Wake up, you stupid bitch.'

'But it's cruel.'

'Of course it isn't – they know no better.'

'Perhaps if you had less, perhaps then we could care for them better. Improve the conditions. And this programme said that the bitches, like ours, are over-breeding and it kills them, and . . .'

She did not finish what she was saying; instead she saw stars as Tom's fist whammed into the side of her face.

'If I hear any more of this stupid claptrap, you don't get a penny more from me, and that's straight. You say another dicky bird and you can go and get yourself a fucking job and leave here, is that understood?'

'But Tom, her education . . .' Sue, her mother, began, but the fist landed square on her mouth and any further speech was lost in the spurt of blood from her loosened front tooth.

'Don't you hit my mum like that!' Kimberley was on her feet, but her mother waved a hand at her in weary resignation. 'You can bully me, and blackmail me, but I can promise you one thing, I'm not going to help you with the dogs ever again.'

'Watch it, miss.' Her father waved a forefinger menacingly at her.

'I mean it!'

To shut her up her father had hit her again and she had run from the room and up into her little bedroom, slamming the door noisily behind her, for she was determined not to let him see her cry.

By taking such a stand Kimberley had, inadvertently, made matters worse all round. Her mother, who was already overworked with her tasks in the house and on the smallholding, now had to do all the chores for the dogs that previously Kimberley had done. Her father, cantankerous as always, refused to allow Kimberley to help her mother with the chickens and the pigs – she worked, but only at what he told her to do, invariably on the vegetables, weeding, sowing, digging, harvesting – probably because he knew she loathed the job so much.

She had certainly made things worse for the dogs, for without her no one ever played with them, talked to them or gave them even a modicum of comfort and human contact. Kimberley had not realised that not only did her mother not like dogs – she was frightened of them, having been bitten as a young child. She did the minimum of work possible, and was out of the shed as quickly as she could.

As if things were not bad enough, worse was to come. Last year her father had been introduced to dog fighting, and had taken to the sport with zeal. He'd his own fighters now. These dogs were not neglected, but fed the best muscle-building food. One shed was set aside for them and there they were trained on a treadmill he'd devised from a conveyor belt he'd picked up at a clearance sale. Tied on to it, the two pit bulls he'd acquired ran for hours at a time to nowhere. They were trained to pull ever-increasing weights attached to a harness, building strength and muscle all the time.

And then, because of the isolation of the smallholding, Tom allowed the odd dog fight to take place there. Sunday lunchtime was quite a favoured time or, occasionally, late at night cars with no lights bumped up the drive from the main road. In the house, Kimberley and her mother could hear the shouting of the men, their blood lust up. These nights they turned the television up loud.

'I hate this, Mum, it's cruel.'

'It's what your father wants,' she answered.

And because of it all, Kimberley suffered pangs of guilt and self-loathing. Not just because of her mother's lot, but because she knew about the dogs and did nothing. Most of all she despised herself that she did not walk out but had hung on, living under his roof, eating his food, allowing it all to continue just so that she could work in a bank and have a pretty yellow Habitat sofa-bed. She felt she should go, but lacked the courage to do so.

'You getting up or do I have to come and turf you out?' her father shouted.

'I'm up,' she lied. 'Doing homework,' she compounded it, and hugged herself with glee beneath the covers.

'There's some early potatoes to be dug. And the last of the cabbages.'

'It's too soon for potatoes.'

'You do what I fucking tell you.'

'I've got to go into Shillingham.'

'Not until you've done that, you don't.'

She had planned today too, she thought as she quickly dressed in jeans and thick woolly jumper. She'd not had school yesterday and had, she thought, done all her chores so that she could get away this morning. She looked at her watch. Eight. She'd have to rush if she was to catch the bus as well as dig up his bloody potatoes. She flounced down the stairs and passed him without saying a word, flung a heavy winter coat over her shoulders, collected her boxes and marched out to the vegetable patch. To get there she had to pass the dog sheds; she could hear them barking and generally rustling about as her mother quickly tended them. At the rubbish pile, she stopped dead in her tracks. Her father had only half covered the body of the Old English Sheepdog with rubbish, its head was protruding. It was a head Kimberley recognised, it was Charlotte – she had christened them all, she always had. Now they were all nameless, she supposed.

'Oh Charlie, not you. I should never have left you to him.' Gently she stroked the dead, unfeeling head. She had to get away, she must; getting her A Levels wasn't worth having to see things like this.

Two hours later, Kimberley was in Shillingham. She shopped quickly for her mother. Her pocket money was on the meagre side, but she had an agreement with her mother, unknown to her father, that whatever she saved by judicious shopping she could keep. Rather than lug her bags about with her, she had an arrangement with one of the stallholders that she could put them safely under his stall. She would collect them when she caught the late afternoon bus home.

Just after eleven she was sitting on the rim of Cromwell's fountain in the middle of the market square, waiting for the gang to appear. It was a large and ornate fountain where, it was claimed, Cromwell had stopped and drunk the water which, it was also alleged, came from an underground spring thousands of feet below the town. The truth was somewhat more mundane in that the water came from the reservoir on the outskirts of town, and the fountain was Victorian rather than pre-Cromwellian. But the local council, aware of the revenue that any association with Cromwell attracted, happily allowed the legend to remain uncorrected.

As she waited for the others Kimberley knew that people were staring at her: the fountain gang had a reputation for hooliganism, and by sitting here, on a Saturday, she was proclaiming herself one of them. They were a lot of yobs, she was fully aware, but what else was she to do? She had to meet up with people her own age, and these boys and girls accepted her as she was, asking no questions. She knew she was cleverer than them, that they had little in common, but she was lonely at home and at school. After Liz had left, she had tried to make other friends, but without success. Friendships had been forged earlier in school careers, and because she had been content just with Liz, there was no room in the various groupings for her now.

She would have liked a boyfriend. Several of the fellows in the fountain gang fancied her, she knew that. But what they offered, clumsy fumblings and quick couplings, was not what she wanted or expected. She had seen the other girls handed from one gang member to the next and had kept herself aloof. It was surprising they put up with her, but they did – she was never sure why, but had a sneaky idea it might be because they felt sorry for her. She wore her poverty with dignity, and maybe they respected her for that.

Perhaps, one day, when she could smarten up, when she had a place of her own to invite him, then someone special would enter her life. Until then she sat waiting for the friends she had. Her blonde hair was tied back in an elastic band. Her old duffel coat, that had once been her mother's, was clutched firmly about her against the cold. Her jeans were tucked into black wellington boots instead of the Doc Martens she dreamed of. And she watched the bustle of market day swirling about her.

6

Oliver, eventually realising the danger of driving so fast, slowed down and pulled into a lay-by. He might be as furious as hell with Sophia, he might be upset about Bandage, but he did not want to kill himself. He sat for a while smoking. He did not want to return to London, he hated weekends in the city, with everyone he knew away in the country. It was an odd contradiction in Oliver that he could not abide being alone in London, and yet enjoyed it in the country. He was so near to his holiday home he might as well go and hole up there, lick his wounds and plan his strategy over his dog. 'My dog,' he said aloud and with emphasis. Cheeky bitch, how dare she think she could nick back a present just like that? She'd never liked the dog, in fact invariably ignored it, and Bandage loathed her too, so what was the point? Spite, sheer unadulterated spite, no more, no less. He was well shot of her, that was for sure, he told himself as he started the engine again.

He parked the car outside Bishop's End, something he had done so many times before that he had become blind to its familiarity. This time, when he got out of the car, he walked slowly round the entire property and looked at it in a different way. A house that he used purely as a weekend retreat was a different matter from a house in which he intended to live permanently. Minor inconveniences which might be overlooked in a holiday home could turn out to be insupportable in a main one.

He paused in his tour of inspection outside the bow-fronted dining-room window. It was a pretty window, tall and wide, with the panes reaching almost to ground level. The problem here was that a row of macrocarpa was shutting out too much light; they were not his most favourite trees, but he had been too idle to see to them. The dining room was rarely used since they preferred country kitchen eating on their weekends. But, this could change. He could just imagine Sunday lunch in the pretty room, with his best silver – if Sophia hadn't nicked it. If those trees came down there would not only be more light, but a clear view of the magnificent Cedar of Lebanon on the far lawn, which had been planted by Aunt Phoebe's Bishop grandfather, who had built the house and given it its name.

He looked up. The guttering on this side of the house was in need of repair, and, he thought, one of the chimneys was looking a bit dodgy. The house was watertight. However, the woodwork round the doors and windows, which had once been crisp and white, was now a flaking greyish-green from neglect.

He had worked his way around to the front again. The steps leading up to the extraordinary Gothic porch needed prompt attention; they were cracking and covered in moss, since the front door was never used. If he moved in, perhaps the front door would once more come into its own. These were all minor things to do, but they had their uses in that already they were calming him down, making him begin to think of his future and not his past.

In the porch was a wooden bench on which Aunt Phoebe's trug and gardening gloves had invariably sat. He wondered what had become of them and resolved to search for, or replace, them. He stood on the top step, surveying the front garden. Phoebe had been a manic gardener, and one of pure genius. She had made it appear as though the garden had evolved effortlessly and by accident, not design; whereas, of course, such gardens involved an enormous amount of work and money. Since her death the wondrous garden had become seriously wild. That anything still bloomed was a credit to the plants' tenacity, not Oliver's care. This was something he would have to attend to, and quickly.

He began to list the other things he had already seen that needed attention, adding that the house was in need of a coat of paint. It was just his luck, when every other house in the area was made of the pretty grey, local stone, he should end up with the Bishop's concept of a Strawberry Hill Gothic house rendered and painted pink. It was an unpleasant candyfloss sort of pink, from which he had always averted his eyes and tried to divert his friends' remarks. Perhaps if he could get the colour toned down a little it would look better.

It was odd what divorce did for you, he thought. Last night, he'd lain in his bed thinking long and hard about himself, a totally new experience for him. And then made the spot decision to move. And now this morning, just look at him, wandering about his garden, looking at his house dispassionately in the way a surveyor or an estate agent might do.

He put his hand up and felt along the rafter of the porch, wondering if the spare front-door key was still there. Covered in cobwebs and rusty, it was. The key turned reluctantly in the lock. He pushed at the door with his shoulder until, with one last heave and an agonising creaking sound, it swung open. He battled through the folds of a heavy brocade curtain which hung, against draughts, over the door on the inside in the hall. He would get the floors here sanded and polished, buy new rugs. He would ask Grace White if she would clean every day, and if not to find him someone who would, and then the hall furniture would be buffed and shine and smell of beeswax and lavender and he would have large vases overflowing with fresh flowers. It would be just as it was in Aunt Phoebe's day. He would bring the house back to life. He felt such excitement at the prospect, such pleasure in his incomplete plans. Goodness only knew what other ideas he would come up with – enough, no doubt, to fill his notebook. New curtains, chairs re-upholstered, books bought, his paintings up. Still – he stopped the frantic scribbling in his notepad – he must not overdo it, he didn't want the house to lose its slightly faded charm, most decidedly he did not want to end up with a house that shrieked of the tarting-up typical of Sophia's designer buddies. Perfection of her sort the house did not want; perfection of Phoebe's it would.

From the hall he wandered along the stone-flagged passageway with its original William Morris wallpaper, still more or less intact, to the kitchen, still in need of Grace White's attention. This was the only room he had renovated. It was doubtful if Phoebe had ever ventured as far as the kitchen, leaving the nether regions of her house to her servants. In consequence, it had been dark and forbidding. He had had the lot ripped out, an oil-fired Aga put in to replace the fearsome range that his aunt's cook had battled with, and had the furniture replaced with built-in oak units. The purists might shriek, but it was now a comfortable room to be in. Not that Oliver knew much about cooking; when they had guests, and Sophia had deigned to join them, she brought hampers of food from Fortnum's. When here alone he stocked up from the local Sainsbury's and Marks. If he moved here he would have to sort something out about food; Wimpole happily admitted she couldn't cook and had no intention of learning. Perhaps he could find a gem in the village.

He looked at his watch and found it was nearly noon. He crossed to the Mickey Mouse telephone he had given himself one Christmas and which had appalled Sophia so much she had banned it from the London house, dialled his number and listened as it rang and rang. That was odd, where was Wimpole? She so rarely went out. He replaced the receiver. 'You've earned yourself a pint and a pie, Oliver, my lad,' he told himself.

Ten minutes later he was in the Duck and Thistle, downing a pint. They knew him in the pub; they had respected his aunt enormously and because of her there had been a welcome, if on the tepid side, for him. They were always polite, but he realised early on that they were telling him, subtly, that he might own a house here, he might weekend, but he did not belong. Because of this attitude, understandable though it was, he rarely popped in.

This time, propping up the bar, listening to the chatter of the other drinkers, he decided to change all that. He took the bull by the horns and confided in the landlord that he was thinking of living here permanently.

The change in the landlord, and in the manner of the locals when he excitedly passed on what Oliver had said, was dramatic. No one grabbed him and hugged him physically, but it almost felt as if they had. That would be grand, the assembled company assured him. Bishop's End was a sorry sight, empty most of the time. No one liked second-home-owners here. As if to compound their approval the landlord offered him a drink, something that had never happened before. Things were looking up, life in the country would be an improvement on the city. He even found himself talking gardening and crops, putting out feelers for a permanent gardener – his friends would never recognise him.

7

It was no hardship for Kimberley to sit and wait for everyone. She liked Shillingham and had known it all her life. Compared to Morristown it was small and not so threatening, for Shillingham was a market town which had managed to escape the fate of others of a similar size when decisions had been made to enlarge them and to turn them into dormitory towns.

Each Saturday, and on quarter days, a thriving market was to be found in the main square – admittedly it tended to have more cheap clothes, handbags, and ethnic tat stalls than farm produce these days but, nevertheless, it gave the town cohesion. It was this market which attracted Kimberley's friends, less for the reasonable cost of what was on offer but for the ease with which they could nick the stuff.

Not that Shillingham was without shops. Because it had no giant hyper-market on the outskirts, shops still stood a chance of trading. And these shops worked like a magnet on the gang. Whatever could be stolen they took, and not necessarily covertly. The owner of the off-licence had been enraged when they had walked in one day, lifted a bottle of Scotch, and had the audacity to say 'ta' as they walked out. He had a large Alsatian behind the counter now; it had never been known to go for anyone, but the group were not giving it the chance to prove itself. They were more interested in the stealing than the goods. When the shoe shop had a display outside on the pavement – only one shoe of each pair – the urge to pinch was so strong that they lifted the lot. They had long been banned from the Spar mini-market, and the police were called if they as much as popped their heads in the door.

Kimberley was not part of the thieving. She had no desire to acquire a police record and mar her chances of working in a bank. But also, when she had got to know the gang about six months ago, it had been decided that she should not risk being caught, for then she might have to leave school. In fact it was Butch, their leader, who reached this conclusion, much to the annoyance of the others, especially the girls. When she had first joined them, Butch had made a pass at her, but it was a somewhat half-hearted attempt, as if he didn't really want to and when she had shoved him and told him to 'piss off' he'd seemed almost relieved. In an odd way she felt she had become their mascot. For some reason, which he never explained, Butch, a classic non-achiever, had enormous respect for Kimberley's intelligence and almost a pride in her achievements. She had often wondered why, and worried that it might have something to do with her ambitions to work in a bank, and his ambition to rob one.

Their presence every Saturday was a shame, for it marred the reputation of Shillingham as a law-abiding town. Not only did they steal, but they had targets which they considered legitimate – they particularly hated the homosexuals who ran the hairdressing salon and enjoyed hurling abuse at them. And they loathed the travelling people with even greater venom, and chased them away at every opportunity. Nor were they keen on the disabled or the old – so they terrorised a lot of the population. They were, however, careful never to aggravate anyone male, fit, and young.

One by one, the others joined Kimberley. They did not kiss each other, shake hands, or clap each other on the shoulder. Rather their greeting was a grunt, though occasionally one pushed another as if trying to shove them into the water at the base of the fountain. It was obvious to any observer that to show pleasure in each other's company was forbidden.

There were seven of them today, four boys, two other girls and Kimberley. It was probably the cold weather keeping everyone away, for on a good day there could be as many as twelve. The other girls were unemployed, and always had been, and had no desire to find work. They were both seventeen and, although she was a year older, Kimberley felt nervous of both of them, for they were loud-mouthed and tough and were best friends to the exclusion of any other females. Shelley was the girlfriend of Butch, who, though never elected, took the role of the leader, primarily because he was the biggest, he was eighteen, and he had a motorbike.

Kimberley did not envy Shelley her role as Butch's girl, for there seemed to be few advantages to the position. She rarely rode on the back of his bike, but took the bus with the others. It seemed Butch thought it made him look soft to have a girl on his pillion. There was no affection between them, no soft words or lingering looks; if anything, Butch was ruder to her than anyone else. Having a particular girlfriend did not stop Butch occasionally taking one of the other girls to the dark corner at the back of the Rialto Cinema where he could quickly screw her and be back at the fountain, all zipped up, in five minutes flat – Kimberley knew, because she had once timed him.

All the other boys were underage and all they possessed of the bikers' world were their leathers. In these they strutted around trying to give the impression that they had a Harley Davidson around the corner rather than a mountain bike, which was the case.

Most of them came from Morristown and had been to school there, or rather had played truant there. It was a mystery to the inhabitants of Shillingham why they plagued them each weekend. The truth would have cheered them immeasurably – they were too scared to swagger about in their own town, for there was a fearsome tooled-up gang on the Forest Glade Estate, who ruled the roost and had ordered them off their patch. So they were, in a way, serving their apprenticeship here in the smaller town. All, that is, except Butch. He liked it here, liked to be top dog and knew that if he joined the Forest Stags, as the Morristown gang was known, he would be a mere nobody. But the others lived in hope that they might be invited to join, which made Butch despise them all and treat them even worse than he would normally have done.

'Christ, it's bleeding cold, you all right, Kim?' Butch asked her while Shelley sulked.

'Fine thanks,' she said, hunkering further into her coat.

'Aren't you ever going to get some decent clothes? You let us down,' Shelley's friend Amber sneered, rubbing her hand up and down the fine black leather of her fringed jacket, which Kimberley envied her more than she would ever let on.

'Leave her alone, you don't know her circumstances.' Butch jumped to her defence.

'And you do?' Amber dared to ask.

'As a matter of fact, I do,' Butch said, but to Kimberley's relief did not elaborate.

They sat around for a bit smoking, joshing, being rude, being obstructive, and then Butch told the girls to go and get them something to eat.

'Your dad breeds dogs, don't he?' Butch asked her as soon as the girls were gone and the other boys, Snotty, Greaser and Ginger, were engrossed in their own conversation.

'Who told you that?' she asked, looking up sharply.

'I saw him at the service station the other side of Morristown, unloading a pile of puppies from his van into another bloke's. That's what they do, don't they? Puppy breeders sell 'em on to pet shop dealers, that sort of thing.'

'I don't know.'

'Course you do!'

'You saying I'm lying?' she demanded, with more spirit than he had ever seen before.

'Nah. It was just . . . I wondered if he bred any fighting dogs?'

'No,' she said.

'You sure?'

'I just said.'

'Only a mate told me he did – pit bulls, that sort of thing. He'd planned to take a bulldog bitch he'd nicked from someone's front garden to your dad's to be mated with a pit bull. But he never got there. Some bugger nicked the bloody dog from him.' He laughed. 'Tell you what, you can't trust no one these days, can you?'

'Not my dad.' She looked away from him and hoped she sounded convincing. After all, it was more than likely Butch was right. It was ages since she had been in the sheds to see what he was up to. In the time she had helped out it had always been the popular breeds her father had bred – King Charleses, Dulux dogs – he always claimed that advert had done wonders for his sales – Yorkies, poodles and whatever had won at Crufts that year for, sure as sure, there would suddenly be a demand for it.

'Why?' she asked Butch suddenly.

He looked to left and right and leant forward. 'Don't breathe a word or I'll fucking screw you witless, but there's a dog fight most Saturday evenings round about here. You can make a lot of money on bets. I just thought I might like a dog of my own. Might be interesting.'

'I'll ask him,' she said, not intending to do any such thing. What her father did was bad enough without this.

The girls returned with some chocolate and coke they had nicked, and the evidence was quickly devoured. For the rest of the day they loafed around, idling about the town, making themselves annoying, returning to their fountain and then wandering off again. A pretty useless day, as usual.

Kimberley was not happy here today and wanted to go, though when she said she was off, Butch stopped her, and said he'd lam her one if she went. She was pretty certain it was because of the dogs.

Gill was alone in the shop. He and Justin, unable to decide who should stay with Sadie, had, in the end and after much good-natured bickering, tossed for it and Justin had won. Without his partner it had been a ghastly day, as Gill had had to do the work of two. He had planned to try and rush home at lunchtime to see how they were all doing but had had to content himself with a phone call instead. He could have kissed his clients a dozen times over for, when he told them why there was such chaos and why he was all at sixes and sevens, no one made a fuss or complained. Even better, two clients had gone out and bought presents for the puppies – squeaky toys from one and a super padded basket on short legs from the other. Gill could not wait to get home and show them to Justin.

One of his last customers was Eveleigh Brenton, who had come in for a rare hairdo since, as she explained, she'd been invited out for drinks at the Lucketts' – what Gill would give to be invited there.

'Mixing with the smart set are we, then? Lucky you! But you're heaven sent and no mistake,' said Gill as he wielded brush and dryer. 'Our Sadie had her pups last night – no I tell a lie, this morning. Five little sweethearts.'

'That's a relief for you. It's always a worrying time with a bitch's first whelping. It could go either way.'

'We'll never let her go through that again, poor love. I tell you, Mrs Brenton, Justin and I felt every pang. It was awful.' He shuddered dramatically. 'We both looked at each other and guess what, we said it in unison, "Never again," we said. Isn't that extraordinary?'

'You will be careful when selling the pups, won't you? Make sure they go to good homes?'

'We shall inspect them ourselves, we've already decided. Mind you, three of them are spoken for already and we'll keep one, so that only leaves one. This time we're determined to win Best of Breed. And to think it's all thanks to you, we'd never have thought of showing or breeding from Sadie if it hadn't been for you. How do we choose the one we'll keep? I promised Justin I'd ask you.'

'Honestly, I can't help you there. At this age it's almost impossible. But even a few weeks on it's difficult. It's an instinct, I suppose. I look at a litter of my St Bernards and I just know which one it is, I feel it here.' She clutched her cardigan to her bosom.

'Bet you're never wrong.'

'No, never,' she answered, modesty making her bow her head.

His last client gone, the shop shut, Gill cashed up. He had seen the fountain gang lurking about during the day. He did not fancy walking alone across the market square to the bank's night safe with the day's takings. As a precaution he slipped the cheques, notes and cash into a handbag he had bought once in Italy, and which he had given up using here in Shillingham because of the comments it caused. He wound the strap three times round his wrist before locking up and setting off, loaded with the puppies' bed and toys.

The gang were just about to go; the last bus to Morristown was due in ten minutes.

'One of the poofters coming, on his own!' yelled Ginger.

'Get him,' called Butch.

'Too fucking right,' shrilled Amber.

Gill heard them and felt his guts turn to water. He put his head down and walked quickly, hugging the walls of the perimeter of the square. One jumped him from behind, two from the front and another tugged at the bag. He hung onto the strap for grim death. But the puppy bed got stamped on and the contents of the bag of squeaky toys were kicked all ways.

'Fucking let go or I'll kick your bleeding poofter head in,' Butch snarled, sounding his most ominous. To help, Ginger stood on Gill's hand and Snotty kicked him in the side. Gill let out a shout of pain.

'Go boil your balls,' he yelled with foolhardy courage, and then paused for a split second for dramatic effect. 'That is, if you've got any!' He was rewarded by another vicious kick in the side.

'Leave him alone, for God's sake!' a girl shouted and Gill, through the pain which was distorting his vision, saw a young blonde-haired girl in jeans and a duffel coat.

'Wet cow!' Shelley shouted.

'He's never done anything to you lot,' Kimberley retorted. She could turn a blind eye to the shoplifting, she couldn't watch this. They had never physically attacked anyone before, bar the odd shove and punch. This made her feel sick.

'He's a sodding queer,' Greaser sneered.

'You a fag hag?' Snotty asked.

'Gay, if you don't mind.' Even as he said it he knew it was stupid of him, but somehow it had just slipped out. Gill tried to curl himself up to protect himself against another kick. Instead Butch laughed. Not a small laugh, nor a sinister laugh, but a loud and happy laugh.

'You've got to hand it to the geezer – queer as he is, he's got guts. Leave off Ginger, Snotty, Greaser. Come on . . .'

Butch ran off and the others followed like lemmings. Only Snotty and the girl remained.

'I'll get you, don't worry, you disease-ridden shitbag,' Snotty spat at Gill before he, in turn, ran away.

'Thanks, miss,' said Gill, as he got painfully to his feet. 'You probably saved my life.' He picked up the broken bed; she helped him collect the squeaky toys.

'Don't be silly, they wouldn't have done that, they're not all bad, you know. They don't usually . . .'

'Beat up queers?' At least she had the grace to look embarrassed. 'Not bad? You could have fooled me,' Gill said with feeling, but grinning at her.

She smiled back, but she wasn't smiling later in the bus when both girls attacked her, pulling her hair, spitting great gobs of phlegm on her and splitting her lip into the bargain, telling her never to turn up at the fountain again, or they'd really dust her up. The other passengers sat huddled in their seats, studiously looking out of the windows at the dark night. The bus driver ignored the noise coming from behind. Kimberley stumbled off at her stop, the jeers of the two girls ringing in her ears. She limped along the road into the turning for Primrose Acre. At least she now knew how the homosexuals must feel. Although the square had been crowded with shoppers returning home, no one but she had come to his rescue, as no one had come to her aid on the bus.

When Gill eventually managed to hobble home, he tried to minimise what had happened to him.

'Don't fuss, Justin. I only walked into a bloody door.'

'You expect me to believe a door did this to you – just look at you, your jacket's torn and look at the state of your trousers!'

'I banged into the door and then fell down some stupid steps. Okay?'

'What door, what steps?'

Justin helped him out of his black coat, which was muddy and torn. 'I can do that,' Gill said sharply, having to fight the urge to cry out, for the pain was not being helped by Justin's tugging at the sleeves. All he wanted was to be left alone to soak for the rest of the evening in a hot bath.

'No, you can't. Whatever next? You didn't answer, you haven't said where you fell.'

'Christ, you sound like a nagging wife.'

'How would you know? Keeping something from me?' Justin looked at him, and then laughed with the confidence of one who knew all there was to know about his companion.

Gill's mind seemed not to be working. He tried to think of something to say to reassure Justin, but he felt as if his brains had turned to porridge. He felt dazed and muddled.

'There was no door or stair, was there?' Justin asked gently.

'Yes, there was – the store room . . .'

'Two tiny steps a mouse couldn't fall down – oh, my God, just look at those bruises!' Justin exclaimed as he removed Gill's Snippers T-shirt. Where he had been kicked showed bright angry red, already beginning to discolour from the engorged blood. 'Stay put, don't move an inch!' Justin raced from the room, up the stairs two at a time to the medicine cabinet, found the witch-hazel and was back in a minute, kneeling, tending the bruises.

'I think we should go to the hospital. What if something's broken?'

'I'm pretty sure nothing is. Honest. It's worse than it looks. You know me, how fragile I am, bruise like a peach.' Gill started to laugh but had to stop because it hurt too much, and he wondered if a rib was cracked, but decided not to say anything.

'Come on, Gill, love. You're telling me porky pies, aren't you? Protecting me. It was those filthy louts, wasn't it? You were alone, they jumped you, didn't they?'

'Something like.' Gill felt too weary to continue to try to cover up the truth.

'I'm going to call the police.' Justin jumped to his feet.

Gill put out a restraining hand. 'No, Justin, don't. What would be the point? You know the police, they'd probably reward the little sods with medals for doing it.'

'But this is Shillingham.' Justin looked distressed.

'What sympathy are we likely to get from the fuzz? I don't care where they're stationed, they're all homophobes. Forget it. The yobs didn't get the money, thank God. Sad thing is they broke the puppies' present from Mrs Greenslade.' He nodded at the now very battered cardboard box which he had managed with difficulty to lug home.

'Maybe it can be mended. I'll try – the wonders of Superglue,' Justin said. 'A right one you are, you haven't even seen the little ones yet.'

'I'll make it up to them, promise.' Gill grinned weakly, stood up shakily and, with Justin for support, made his way to Sadie's nest behind the sofa. Sadie wagged her tail, with its pompom on the end, glanced up at him, gave a gentle bark as if to say she was happy to see him but she hadn't time for him just yet, and went back to grooming her puppies. 'Beautiful sight,' Gill said softly, smiling at the blind, snuffling little bundles. 'They don't even look like dogs yet, do they?'

'What a thing to say!' Justin admonished. 'Jim Varley popped in this afternoon to check them out and said they were all perfect. In fact he said they were the best litter he had ever seen,' he reported proudly as he poured Gill a large brandy. This wasn't strictly true, Jim hadn't said that, but it didn't stop Justin saying he had, for he felt that was what Jim *should* have said.

Justin pulled two chairs up and they sat, side by side, nursing their brandies and telling Sadie at regular intervals what a clever girl she was. Later Justin cooked them an omelette which they also ate, sitting on the chairs, beside her.

8

Thomasine woke to the sound of church bells. She lay in bed feeling very satisfied with the noise, for wasn't this one of the very things which made the countryside attractive to her? This was England, this was what ex-pats dreamt about, and here it was, just up the lane, the bells ringing as if just for her. Ten minutes later, she was less sure and wished that there were a volume control button on the belfry. Further sleep was impossible, and even though she had planned a Sunday lie-in, she got up. Luna, who was moving more easily this morning, slid off the bed unaided and was able to negotiate the stairs herself.

Thomasine let the dog out on her own for the first time. While she waited for the kettle to boil she kept watch out of the window, afraid the dog might run off, but after a lengthy inspection of the garden, Luna returned and stared at the door imperiously. When Thomasine opened it she waddled past her and took up position beside her bowl, looking aggrieved that her breakfast was not yet prepared.

'So this is a dog's life, is it?' Thomasine smiled at the small creature as she mixed Weetabix and milk as if bidden. That done, she sat at the table with her tea and wished she'd something to read. She'd asked in the village shop if it was possible for the Sunday papers to be delivered and had been met with amused and somewhat condescending looks, as the woman behind the counter informed her she would have to go into Shillingham itself for those.

Later, in the bathroom, she studied herself intently in the mirror, wondering if the dramas of the past months were written on her face for all to see. She thought she looked much the same, but she was probably the last person to judge. She made a moue of her mouth to see if any lines had appeared since she had last checked, but there were none. She made her lips smile and was pleased that they were still well defined. The fine network of lines around her eyes she'd had for some time, and she accepted them, for what more could she expect at forty-three? But her eyes bothered her, for she was sure they sparkled less, had a wary look to them which had not been there before. In her misery she had eaten a mite too much and she knew she had put on two kilos, but did it show in her face? She turned this way and that, but couldn't decide. She relaxed; Nadine hadn't said anything, and she would be the first to comment if she thought her mother was getting fat.

Her appraisal finished, she decided that physically she had weathered the emotional storm reasonably well – then why did she feel so unattractive? She was aware she was still licking her wounds and that her self-confidence had taken a severe knock, but would she ever recover? On chat shows on television she'd often heard the expression 'lack of self-esteem' bandied about and had thought it meaningless. She didn't any more. Now she knew what it meant only too well; she felt as if she was nothing and of no interest to anyone – how could she be, when within her she knew she was a total failure? As a child she'd had a rag doll and one day, out of boredom, she'd removed the kapok stuffing – that's how she now saw herself, a husk of her former self.

'Find a lover,' her mother had advised glibly. It would be an impossible task for her – how could she search for a lover when, for a start, she was still in love with Robert and feeling about herself as she did, how could she expect anyone to be the least interested in her? It was an idea she did not even entertain.

She picked up a hank of her thick, dark-brown hair and wondered if perhaps the time had come to have it cut. There was nothing worse, she thought, than a woman hanging on to the past with a too-youthful length of hair and the same make-up she had worn when young. Maybe she'd find a hairdresser and have the lot off and restyled, maybe even have a fringe – after all, a new life required a new image. Yes, she'd do that next week. Meanwhile there was today to get through. She ran a bath.

With no husband to cook breakfast for, she could have a long leisurely soak in the bath. There were some advantages, she told herself as she soaped her arms. Positive thinking, that's what she must do a lot more of. The house was so quiet, she thought, as she lay back in the water and closed her eyes. She had wondered how she would feel with the quietness after the bustle of London, she had not dared hope she would find it as restful and calming as this, since everyone had said it would drive her mad – her daughter included. She smiled broadly at the thought of Nadine and her reaction to Thomasine's plans to move to the country. She had been adamantly against.

'You needn't expect to see me every holiday. I'd miss my friends.'

'Of course, darling,' Thomasine had said, but it did not stop her secretly hoping that after a visit or two Nadine would find new friends and interests here – that was a fond hope. In the way of such hopes lay problems – Chantal, Robert and the delights of London. Nadine and Chantal got on well. Thomasine knew that for Nadine's sake she should be pleased, but in reality she felt a jealousy which, no matter how much she reasoned with herself, refused to go away. One resolution she had made, and was determined to stick to, was that she was not going to make an issue over whether Nadine stayed with her or with *them* on her half-term and holidays from boarding school. That would be a recipe for disaster where a sixteen-year-old was concerned.

She'd never wanted her daughter to go to boarding school but had been defeated not just by Robert, but by Nadine herself. She had told her daughter it wasn't all fun and midnight feasts in the dorm and that she'd be homesick.

She couldn't have been more wrong – Nadine loved her school from day one. Thomasine had felt hurt that she didn't miss her; not that she'd told anyone, she knew it was childish and selfish of her, and that she should be pleased for the child. But now she was glad Nadine was so content at school – not only had she missed the worst of the trauma between her parents, but, more importantly to Thomasine, there was no tussle over where she was to live full-time. Thomasine had a sneaky idea that Nadine would have opted for life with Chantal and Robert, and the humiliation of that would have been intolerable. Then the world would have known that she had not only failed as a wife, but as a mother too.

Everyone she knew had urged her strongly not to move to the country. To hear some of them talk, one would have thought she was moving to another planet. But she had stuck to her plans; she had felt it would be wise to get away from the area she'd lived in with Robert, surrounded by their many friends. She didn't want any of those friends feeling they had to take sides, as she herself had done too often in the past with other couples. She knew what it was like to be torn between 'him' and 'her'. Far better not to be around, far better to be Thomasine in the country. Those who were true friends would make the effort and visit her, and the others would send her Christmas cards. That way, friendships that mattered to her were likely to be maintained.

These same people had told her how lonely and miserable she would be, how making friends in the country was an impossibility. Well, they were wrong. The very day she had moved there had been a telephone invitation to drinks, which boded well for the future.

Now that day had arrived and Thomasine felt as nervous as any debutante. She wished she hadn't accepted; she was certain it was too soon; that she wasn't ready to meet new people; that she would clam up and make a fool of herself. Still, she had said she'd go and manners forbade her not to turn up.

Thomasine took some time deciding what to wear, unsure what people in the country wore for pre-lunch drinks. She finally chose a long, biscuit-coloured cashmere skirt to wear with highly polished brown boots, matching waistcoat and a rust-coloured silk shirt with a high collar. This expensive outfit always gave her confidence. She pinned a small topaz brooch at the neck, and out of habit put her engagement and wedding rings on her finger, then spent some time looking at them, wondering whether she should or shouldn't wear them any more. The trouble was that if she didn't her hands looked completely naked, as if there were something wrong with them, since the rings had lived there for so long. She tried them on the other hand but that didn't look right either. She got out her small jewel box and delved into it. Somewhere she had a topaz dress ring; it was large and would easily cover her wedding band.

Downstairs she found a contentedly sleeping Luna. What was she to do with her? She could hardly take her to a stranger's house, but she didn't like leaving her. She might wake up and find herself alone and get frightened. She supposed she could put her in the back of the car and leave her in it, but then she might get cold and catch a chill. She put a blanket in the dog basket she had bought yesterday in Shillingham, and one eye looked at her and closed again. 'Luna, it's for your own good,' she said. 'It's not a good idea to be sleeping on the floor in the draught in your condition. You should be in the basket in the warm, by the fire here, now come on!'

Ten minutes later she left, pleased that Luna had finally condescended to use her new bed. What she did not know was that as soon as her car had left, Luna slid out of the basket, pattered through to the sitting room, hauled herself up into Thomasine's favourite armchair, turned round three times and then curled up in comfort and was quickly snoring noisily and contentedly.

Thomasine stopped at Shillingham on the way and bought her newspapers. The weather was holding crisp, sunny and dry; if it wasn't for the dog, she would have gone out for a pub lunch. What a pain, she thought. Still, it wouldn't be long and she'd be free to do such things; as it was she had some nice pâté in the fridge and some white Mâcon. As she drove along she grinned at the idea that now she was alone she could eat a whole tin of fruit salad all to herself if she wanted. Robert would never have allowed the tins into the house, he would have thought her childish to want it. But she loved the feel of the slippery maraschino cherries sliding down her throat, and one of the first things she'd done when he left was to go out and buy a supply of them.

She found the Luckett house easily but, at the sight of half a dozen cars parked on the forecourt, she had to stop herself from bolting. In London once or twice she'd forced herself to go out alone, and that had been difficult, but here, to venture out among strangers was a terrifying prospect. However, there was to be no escape for her as her car stopped.

Ben Luckett came out on to the steps to welcome her. She admired his house and he said 'thank you' in the laid-back way of someone who was used to having his house complimented and was perhaps finding it all a bit of a bore. His wife, Cora, tripped towards her in an immaculately pressed, turquoise silk trouser suit. Costume jewellery clanked around her neck and on her ears, but the real thing was on her hands. Thomasine would have bet that Cora's underwear matched – she looked the bandbox type. Robert would have approved of that, for try as she might, Thomasine always ended up with mismatches – her knickers always seemed to wear out long before her bras. What a bizarre thing to think, she thought as she took Cora's hand in greeting.

'Mrs Lambert, I'm so pleased you could come. It's never easy moving into a new area, and I said to Ben as soon as I'd heard you had moved in, we must have that poor woman over and introduce her to some local people,' she said kindly, though Thomasine could not imagine why she should be regarded as 'poor'. But she smiled nonetheless and thanked her. 'Now, come along in,' Cora said. Her high-heeled strapped sandals, scarlet toenails peeping out of the front, click-clacked across the ancient flagged floors of the Elizabethan house. 'They're all in here – everyone's slurping away, and they're dying to meet you.'

They entered a large, beautiful room. In the fireplace, the surround of which was ornately carved stone, Tudor roses in both spandrels, was a roaring log fire. Cora flitted about her guests like an exotic bird, busily introducing Thomasine, bracelets jangling, diamonds flashing. She introduced at such a rate, so quickly, with the confidence of someone who knew everybody there, that Thomasine feared that she would soon have everyone in a muddle – except of course for the vicar, whose collar was a useful means of identification. She had a flash of guilty embarrassment that she hadn't been to matins, and then wondered why – she never went to church. He was a quiet, rather ineffectual man, in stark contrast to his wife who, for some inexplicable reason, she had expected to be dowdy and plain, but who had an intense expression on her intelligent, rather attractive face. She was as smart as a button and ran a consultancy business in Morristown, she told Thomasine.

'Consultancy in what?' Thomasine asked.

'Man-management,' said the vicar's wife, Charlotte, with a snapping of jaws which would have put the fear of God into any man, Thomasine thought. Asked what she did, she 'Ahhd' and dithered a second too long and the vicar's wife, impatient with her uncertainty, swung smartly about and left Thomasine wondering if it would be presumptuous to say she was a book illustrator.

'I'm Fee Walters.' A woman about her own age, who had witnessed Thomasine's discomfort, approached. She explained she was a farmer's wife from the other side of Shillingham. 'Don't take any notice of Charlotte, she's an arrogant bitch. But her husband's rather a sweety, if terrified of her,' she said quietly. Thomasine introduced herself. Finding someone smiling, open, and apparently interested in her, she felt herself relaxing sufficiently to say she 'hoped' to illustrate children's books, even though she said it in a whisper so that the others couldn't hear. Fee, also whispering, confided that she'd written one.

'Just for my kids at bedtime, you understand,' she said, looking flustered.

'The best ones often are. I'd love to see it, if you wouldn't mind.'

'Mind . . .? I'll bring it over tomorrow before you change your mind,' Fee laughed as Cora grabbed hold of Thomasine's hand and dragged her away.

'This is my step-daughter, Sophia. You've pots in common, she's a Londoner too,' said Cora.

'I'm not a Londoner, Cora dearest, I happen to live there,' Sophia said, her teeth very slightly bared. Thomasine, who had started off for this drinks party feeling pleased with her outfit, began to feel not necessarily untidy, but not as smart as she had thought. Sophia was immaculately dressed from head to toe in muted grey. She was beautiful, with the fine-boned, fine-skinned, fine-haired litheness of some English beauties, and, glossy with confidence, made Thomasine feel immediately inadequate.

'I hear you've bought the old school house, absolutely charming *little* building, I do envy you it.' She smiled such a ravishing smile that Thomasine wondered if the emphasis on 'little' was deliberate or whether she was being a twinge paranoid. 'I do hope you are very, very happy here. My father, I know, will go out of his way to make your time here as pleasant as possible. It's a wonderful place, absolutely wonderful.'

Thomasine, though wondering if she wasn't over-selling the Shillings a little, was at the same time completely thrown by Sophia's high-wattage charm, and mumbled a sort of 'thank-you'.

Sophia introduced Thomasine to a tall woman who, at first sight, looked rather on the fat side, but in fact wasn't. It was her hairy tweeds that made her look far larger than she was; tweeds of an alarming mustard colour.

'Mrs Brenton,' said Sophia. 'Eveleigh is a bit of a celebrity around here, she's one of the dog world's most prestigious judges.'

'Oh really, Sophia, please. You go too far.' And the woman looked gauche and embarrassed, which did not marry well with her height, nor the tweeds.

'But it's true, Eveleigh.' Cora interrupted. 'If you've any problem with your dogs, phone Eveleigh – don't bother with old Jim Varley here, he's only the vet. Eveleigh knows far more than he does, don't you, Eveleigh?' And she playfully pushed Jim to show him it was just a joke.

'Oh for goodness' sake, Cora, what a thing to say,' said Eveleigh, looking bothered. Jim, standing beside her, laughed good-naturedly.

'Hello, Mrs Lambert, we meet again,' said Jim. 'And Cora's right, if you've got a St Bernard or a King Charles, Eveleigh is the person for you. Breeders tend to know the intricacies of their particular breed of dog, as much as the vets do.'

She didn't think he was being defensive, but she looked at him again to check. He smiled at her and she decided he was not, he was just being patient. 'How's the little bulldog?' he asked.

'Asleep. All she seems to do is sleep.'

'You have a bulldog?' Eveleigh's face became animated with a genuine interest. 'You don't see many of them about these days – I love a good bulldog, my grandfather had one, you know.'

'Really? Everyone's grandfather seems to have had one.' Thomasine laughed, looked at Jim and smiled. He longed to be able to grab the smile and take it home with him.

'Mrs Lambert acquired this one by accident, and it's pregnant, probably not by another bulldog.' Jim explained.

'Do you think that's going to be a problem for her?' Thomasine asked Eveleigh, just making conversation. And then realising how rude she must sound to Jim, apologised with a tentative smile towards him. He shrugged his shoulders as if he understood. She hoped he did – she liked him.

'Well, not necessarily,' Eveleigh paused, seemed to rock on the heels of her sensible shoes, took a deep breath, paused again and then launched herself into the explanation. 'If she mates with a Great Dane she's not going to produce Great-Dane-size dogs, she's a bulldog so nature would have to adjust the size of the puppies to fit a bulldog's uterus, or they would not go to full term. There's a problem once they're born, oh dear me, yes. How do you get rid of them? I do sincerely hope it hasn't been mated with one of the banned breeds. So reprehensible. You see, the original pit bulls were the result of a bulldog being mated with a terrier. With a bulldog you have enormous strength, tenacity and, above all, courage – you'll never hear a bulldog yelp or whine. But pit bulls, by law, are neutered so that they will eventually die out as a breed. What is to stop an unscrupulous breeder trying to create a new fighting dog? Say, breeding pit bulls back with bulldogs and then the result with another breed – an Alsatian, say, or a Staffordshire – to confuse the authorities. A dog which doesn't look anything like a pit bull, but has its characteristics – I mean, the consequences are quite terrifying, especially when you think of the damage already done in dog fights. A dreadful world we live in!' she said with deep feeling, and then put her hand over her mouth. 'Oh, dear me, I do apologise, but get me onto the subject of dogs and I do tend to go on.'

'We're quite used to you and the subject, Eveleigh dear.' Sophia, though smiling as she spoke, did not put sufficient warmth into it to remove the sting of her words. Thomasine felt sorry for the woman as she visibly blushed with confusion.

'But what will the puppies look like?' Eveleigh, concern for dogs overcoming confusion, looked anxious at the prospect. Not as anxious as me, thought Thomasine.

'Dog fighting? But not round here, surely?' Thomasine asked tentatively.

'Everywhere, I'm afraid. Wherever there's man there's cruelty,' said Jim. Sophia linked her arm in his in a proprietorial manner.

'Now please stop all this dog talk, Jim. I absolutely forbid it. I tell you, Mrs Lambert, whenever these two get together it's all they talk about.'

'I suppose Oliver took Bandage,' Eveleigh said, bluntly, unaware that she might be stepping on toes.

'No, of course not! I couldn't let darling Bandage go, he's like a child to me – it would break my heart to lose Bandage,' said Sophia, managing to look beautiful and tragic at the same time. Eveleigh looked up sharply.

'I'd have thought it would have broken *Oliver's* heart, more like. He adores that bull terrier.'

'The one thing you can say about Oliver is he's not selfish and he realises I need the dog more than he does, for protection you understand.'

'I didn't realise you even liked the dog, Sophia. I thought you said it was ugly,' Eveleigh persisted.

'Well, it is ugly, isn't it? You can hardly call a bull terrier a beautiful object.'

'Oh, I don't know,' said Eveleigh. 'He's got a fine head on him, and I particularly like Bandage's eye, a good set to the eye there, a cunning mischievous eye he has.' She laughed at the thought of the black dog, which she'd always rather liked. 'But what is ugly to some is beauty to others. Take Mrs Lambert's bulldog, now. I've heard people without number find a bulldog ugly, and I think they're one of the loveliest-faced dogs in the world. Don't you agree, Mrs Lambert?'

'I haven't given it any thought,' Thomasine said lamely.

'Oh, I couldn't agree with you, Eveleigh, bulldogs are monstrous compared to Bandage,' Sophia said blithely.

And Thomasine felt an illogical surge of anger with the woman, and wished she'd defended Luna's looks instead of sitting on the fence.

'Well, anyway, who owns Bandage is settled and that's it.' She clung harder to Jim's sleeve, and Thomasine found herself very confused about all this talk of an Oliver whilst she so obviously belonged to Jim.

'Well, you could knock me over with a feather, that's the last news I would have expected about Bandage,' said Eveleigh, apparently unprepared to drop the subject.

'It would have to be a very large feather, Eveleigh.' Sophia trilled a laugh, and quickly recovering the slip she had made, removed the very slightly spiteful expression from her face, and replaced it with her expert smile. 'Oh that was rude, Eveleigh, do forgive me.'

'Nothing to it. It's the truth,' said Eveleigh gruffly, though Thomasine was pretty sure she was a little upset.

'Anyone fancy seeing my new foal?' Ben had joined them.

Glasses were drained and coats retrieved as they obediently trooped out after their host into the yard. Thomasine was lagging behind; she had no interest in horses. Even less interest than she had in dogs, she told herself wryly. Jim waited for her to catch up.

'Don't like horses as well as dogs?' he asked, and the tone of his voice told her that he was teasing her.

'Not really. Years ago we went to stay on a farm of some friends of my mother and there was a Meet and I got kicked by a big brute, which then reared up, bolted, threw the rider, jumped a fence and fell over with a crash I'll never forget. I've never felt the same about them since. I don't mind watching them at a distance but I don't like to get too close.'

'I know exactly how you feel,' he said. 'There's no need to get too close, they're in their stables. It's a pretty little foal, you'll like her.'

They fell into step, dawdling behind the others, but they were not alone for long, for Sophia turned back and joined them, once again linking arms with Jim.

'Oh look, there's darling Bandage.' She pointed to the far end of the yard where a black bull terrier was on a lead held by a heavily-built man with grey hair and piercing blue eyes. The man was having to drag the reluctant dog towards them. 'Oh, Rudie, has he been naughty?'

'Not what you'd call co-operative, miss,' the man replied. Sophia did not introduce them.

'Darling Bandage,' she gushed, bending down to the dog who reversed smartly from her outstretched hand. 'Sulky thing,' she said, laughing.

'Bandage, here.' Jim patted the side of his leg and, with tail awag, the dog went to him gladly.

9

Gill lay under the goose-feather duvet and thanked God it was Sunday, because he felt he had been hit by an articulated lorry. Moving gingerly, he lifted his pyjama jacket and inspected his bruises, which were turning lurid purple and green.

'My, you look like a living Turner,' Justin said, also inspecting the gang's handiwork, as he placed Gill's breakfast tray on the bedside table. Justin had insisted Gill have breakfast in bed with the Sunday papers. In fact, they had lain arguing about where Gill was to eat for a good half an hour, and Justin had finally won. 'See,' he pointed to the tray. 'That's the first sprig of forsythia from the garden, blooming just for you. Poor dear.' And he patted the pillows up fat and comfortable. 'Now you take your time.'

'But I want to be downstairs.'

'You owe it to the puppies to get well quickly,' Justin insisted. 'Now rest!'

He didn't. As soon as he had eaten, he hauled himself out of bed. He'd have liked a bath, but quickly realised that that might be too difficult for him to climb into, so he took a shower instead. He dressed in his designer jeans and tasselled loafers, put on his Simpson's cashmere sweater in navy blue, a birthday present from Justin, and creaked his way down the stairs, hanging onto the banister for grim life.

After a quick inspection of the puppies, who were all asleep, Gill found Justin preparing lunch in the kitchen, and sat on a stool and watched him, offering too much advice, and being told so. It was to be a special lunch, a celebration lunch of smoked salmon, a cheese soufflé, which was Justin's *pièce de résistance*, a crisp green salad and a perfect Brie, to be washed down with chilled bottles of Tokay. It was a celebration because their friend Martin was coming with his new friend Stevie, whom neither of them had yet met and whom they were agog to know. It was Martin's dog, Bubblegum, who had mated with Sadie.

When Martin had brought Bubblegum to the house to mate it had been a shade touch and go at first. They had let the dogs out onto the patio to make friends, but they might have guessed that their classy Sadie wasn't going to give herself too easily. At first she had appeared not to be interested in Bubblegum.

'It isn't going to work,' Gill had said, not too sure if he wasn't rather pleased.

'Give them time. You get some bitches like this. After all she doesn't know what to do, does she?' Martin said confidently.

'Of course she does, she's not thick. She just doesn't fancy him – it's obvious,' Justin had blurted out without thinking. It was as well that Sadie chose that moment to raise her tail rigidly in the air and turn her rear end to Bubblegum in a gesture of invitation. Otherwise Martin, having a very short fuse, might have taken the huff and removed his dog forthwith.

As it was it was not to be easy, for every time Bubblegum got close to her,

Sadie snapped at him and stalked off, only to repeat the dance a moment later. It was frustrating – but then, both Justin and Gill later admitted to each other, they were rather proud of Sadie playing hard to get.

Then suddenly, there was a great flurry and it had happened – Bubblegum had mounted Sadie, they turned and were locked, and Justin couldn't watch and had to rush indoors and busy himself in the kitchen to take his mind off what was going on outside.

The mating successfully concluded, Martin had opted to take the pick of the litter in lieu of a stud fee. He did not normally do this, he told them, but he would in this case. For one, Justin and Gill were old friends from the London days. The other reason was he too had just missed Best of Breed with Bubblegum, at Crufts, the year after Sadie's failure. The three friends were now determined to breed the perfect miniature poodle puppy to win not only Best of Breed, but the championship too. Now the litter was here, and today, therefore, was a momentous celebration.

Their guests arrived. Stevie was not at all what they expected – he was on the lean side, when Martin normally liked them quite butch, and was taciturn, bordering on boring. Perhaps he was thick, Gill thought.

After the flurry of welcomes and a quick peep at the puppies, they sipped their Kir Royals as Justin set the table and Gill played down the events of the night before.

'Shall I get Dad in to see his puppies?' asked Martin.

'Should we?' asked Gill. 'Sadie might not like another dog too close – it's too soon.'

'She seems calm enough,' Martin said. 'And she's always struck me as being a placid sort.'

'Oh, let's!' Justin said. Martin went out to collect Bubblegum from his car.

While they waited for him to return, the contentment and happiness of the day became somewhat marred. Whereas Sadie had not minded Justin and Gill near her puppies and had been very polite to Martin as well, she took an instant dislike to Stevie when he bent down as if about to pick up one of the puppies. Sadie let out a low rumbling growl that grew in volume, like the sound of distant thunder getting nearer.

'What's your problem, old girl?' Stevie said cockily.

'I don't think you should try to touch the puppies,' Gill advised.

'I've been handling dogs all my life. And in any case . . .' But they were not to know what it was he intended to say for Sadie stood up, puppies tumbling from her nipples. Her hackles rose, her lips stretched back tight, her teeth bared as she stood guard over her family.

Stevie decided that he was not going to be beaten by a dog, and put his hand down again towards the pups. Sadie flew for him in a snarling, growling, spitting flash of white. Her teeth sank into his arm and although both Justin and Gill ordered her to let go, she was deaf to their calls. Stevie was screaming blue murder when Martin, all smiles, entered the room with Bubblegum – off the lead.

At sight of the male dog, Sadie let go of Stevie, who lashed out with a kick at the passing bitch. Enraged, Justin swiped him, hard. Martin bellowed with anger at Justin and Gill told him to shut up. It was at this point Sadie, a typhoon of fury now, made contact with Bubblegum. The two white dogs were a welter of flailing legs, snarling, spittle was flying and the noise of growling was awesome.

'But, Sadie, that's your husband!' Justin cried ineffectually. 'You'll get hurt!'

'Hurt? Hurt?' Martin shouted. 'What about my dog? Vicious bitch!'

'It's your fault, I told you not to bring that brute in here,' Gill said, raising his voice above the racket.

'Bugger the dogs. What about me?' Stevie wailed.

'Oh, shut up!' the other three said in unison.

The dogs rolled around the room. The men raised their feet to protect themselves. Tables were knocked over, lamps fell and short-circuited, pictures, nuts, knick-knacks rolled hither and thither. The jug of Kir went flying.

With the three men shouting in panic, Stevie howling, and the dogs fighting, it was difficult to say who was making the most noise. The racket did not stop until Bubblegum, larger by half than Sadie, rolled submissively onto his back, waving his legs in the air.

Sadie, a shade wet from Bubblegum's slobber, but without a mark on her, gave one more growl as if making certain he wasn't shamming. Then, with amazing dignity in the circumstances, she stalked back to her litter. There she nudged the puppies with her nose, making room for herself, lowered herself carefully amongst them, allowed them to suckle again and looked as if nothing untoward had happened.

The room was in chaos, the soufflé had collapsed, Martin was beside himself with rage and Stevie was crying after Martin had told him not to be such a wimp. Gill, limping, escorted them to the door.

'If my dog's damaged you'll pay the vet's bills, and you'll be hearing from my solicitor.'

'Don't talk such rubbish, Martin. You shouldn't have brought the dog in, I told you. He's not hurt,' Gill said.

'He's limping.'

'So am I, but I'm not croaking it.' Gill, exasperated, turned his back on the guests and exaggeratedly hobbled back into the house.

'What about that then?' said Gill as he entered the room. 'Wasn't Sadie magnificent – defending her family, that's what she was doing. He didn't even get to choose a puppy.'

'Too soon really,' said Justin, trying to create some order from the shambles which was their drawing room. 'Jim said it would be too early to choose, I asked him. A good month needs to go by, he reckoned. Oh, Gill, I feel all shaky.' He sat down with a bump. 'I was so frightened she would hurt herself.'

'Not our Sadie, she moves too fast. The way she flew at Stevie! I always said that dog had good taste, I didn't like the look of him one little bit.

Trouble with Martin, he always liked a bit of rough.' He laughed, trying to cheer the shivering Justin. 'Mind you, I've never been that keen on Martin either. I think he's out for all he can get.'

'You never said before.'

'Well, you know me, Justin. I don't like gossip or spite, but I reckon Sadie recognised him for what he is.'

'The lunch is ruined,' Justin said miserably.

'Nonsense, there's still the smoked salmon and cheese, and we've got another bottle of Tokay.' Gill bent down to touch one of the puppies. 'Just checking you still trust us, Sadie.' Sadie licked his hand in answer.

April

10

Alan Farmingham stood at the French doors of the semi-detached house on the edge of Morristown and looked at the overgrown garden with a sense of satisfaction. If the sale went through then putting it right would be the responsibility of somebody else, not him.

He turned and, still standing with hands in pocket, looked thoughtfully at the room he'd known all his life. It was shabby, even more than he remembered. In one corner the dado was detached and hung loose. On the far wall he could see the stain made by the coffee when his mother had hurled her cup at him in a drunken rage. He could remember the cup hurtling towards him and his ducking, but not what the argument had been about – how could he remember, there had been so many rows that they had melted into one great sense of unhappiness.

He crossed to the red-brick fireplace. The mantelpiece was stepped: on the bottom matching shelves stood two brass candlesticks, on the next shelves two china dogs, the head of one detached and lying beside it. On the top, in the clutter, his mother's pride and joy, the skeleton clock her husband had given her one birthday, stopped now and covered in dust. Behind it were stuffed a pile of envelopes. He carefully removed and glanced through them – mainly bills and circulars, and a couple of letters from him.

He looked at the furniture: an ugly bulbous table and matching sideboard; two armchairs, one either side of the fire, one barely used, the other worn and torn and with a grease mark where his mother's head had rested. He shuddered. He'd keep the clock, the rest could go.

He crossed the room and entered the kitchen, found himself some instant coffee and made a cup. He supposed he'd have to steel himself to go through her things, sort out her papers, her clothes, when his instinct was to burn the lot.

He sat at the tin-topped kitchen table and wondered where he'd find the energy to do any of it. He was still recovering from septicaemia, picked up while on undercover work in Spain – he'd been involved in a scuffle and had cut his hand deeply, allowing the invading bug to enter. While he was in hospital in London, his mother had suddenly died. He had made it to the funeral – the only mourner – and was now convalescent. Some convalescence! He was here because, unexpectedly in the current market, the house had quickly sold. He'd reasoned he could convalesce here just as easily as in his flat in Horsham while he packed up his mother's possessions.

What he hadn't been prepared for was how sad being here made him feel. Last night, when he'd arrived, it was odd not to hear his mother call out. Too many memories came flooding back, and not happy ones either – there'd never been many of them.

He'd go out today, no need to begin packing up immediately. It was a lovely April day, he could have a pub lunch, relax a bit.

Upstairs, he wandered into his old back bedroom. He looked down on the garden next door; neat and tidy, not a rabbit hutch in sight. He wondered where Mr Humphrey was now – dead probably. It was, he supposed, thanks to the old boy he was doing the work he did. He'd only been eleven when he had anonymously reported Mr Humphrey to the RSPCA for neglect of his rabbits. He'd watched, from this very window, when the inspector, who'd called in response to his tip-off, told the neighbour off in no uncertain terms, and then gently placed the rabbits into clean boxes and put them into the back of his van. 'You'll be hearing more about this,' the man had said to the neighbour, who was so frightened and guilty he'd not even bothered to protest at his rabbits being removed. And at that moment Alan had known what he wanted to be when he grew up – an RSPCA inspector.

There was no stopping Alan after that – any dog tied up and left howling; any cat up a tree; any badger at risk from baiting; any donkey with rotting feet: all had reason to be grateful to Alan's eagle eye as he toured the area on his bicycle, searching out animals in need.

'Bloody little St Francis of Assisi, aren't you?' his alcoholic mother had sneered at him. 'Pity you don't care as much for your poor old mum as you do for those sodding animals,' she added wistfully, as she invariably did when in her cups.

Alan, as always, ignored her. He felt no responsibility for what had happened to her, though she often tried to blame him.

'If it hadn't been for you I'd have been the one to leg it,' she often said. He often wished she had.

He was dutiful in that he shopped for her – she'd long ago given up venturing out to the shops in the local precinct. When he came home from school he cooked for them both – if he had not, he would have starved alongside her. He always checked at night to make certain her cigarette was out and she would not harm herself, and to prevent her burning the house down in the night he removed her lighter and matches and took them into his own room. So befuddled was her state that she never worked out where they'd gone if, in the small hours, she fancied a ciggy. Each morning he put them by the cooker, and she always presumed she'd left them there.

There had, in the past, been a succession of 'uncles', none of whom stayed long. When very young he'd fantasised that one of them might stay and be a real dad to him, but it had not happened and so he had resigned himself to being fatherless. But as his mother's looks had faded, and she had become more unkempt, even the 'uncles' ceased.

He often wondered about his father and where he was, what he was doing. Of course Doris blackened his name at every opportunity, but Alan had learnt to ignore her. Stuck as he was he could not blame his dad for one night saying he was going out to buy a packet of cigarettes and never returning. He'd been eight then, eighteen years ago, but he could still remember the hysteria of his mother when her husband didn't return. He'd begun to regard his father as a wise and lucky man, and held no grudges against him.

Wishing to escape did not stop him feeling sorry for his mother. Sometimes he'd worried about the future and what they'd do if he fell in love and wanted to marry. But this had all remained a worry only, since he'd not met the right woman yet.

What had changed everything was when his mother became obsessively jealous of him and began to interfere with his life outside the home, for all the world as if she were his wife. She didn't like his friends. She nagged if he was late home. She insisted on knowing where he was, who with, and had even begun to phone his local to check he was there. She was making his life intolerable.

Everything had come to a head one Saturday, when he had planned to go into the centre of Morristown to do some shopping.

'I'm off, Mum, anything you need from the shops?' he called out to his mother.

'Nothing,' she called back. He supposed she was about to settle down to watch the wrestling on television, which she did every Saturday afternoon.

As he stood on the pavement outside Bata, talking to Gina Angelino, he was unaware that his mother was on the other side of the street about to go into Boots. He made a date with Gina, a girl he'd long admired but who was always seriously involved with someone else. He hadn't been able to believe his luck when he'd chanced upon her between affairs.

He rushed home to put his new jeans inside out in the washing machine to shrink and to look less new. He then had a long bath and a careful shave, wanting to look his best for Gina. He hadn't registered that his mother was not in the house when he returned. He was lying on his bed anticipating the evening to come when the slamming of the front door made him jump.

'Is that you, Mum?' he shouted.

'Whose else would it be?' she called back.

'I didn't know you weren't here,' he said, surprised since she never went out.

'It's not as if we live in blooming Blenheim Palace, is it?'

'What's that mean?'

'You can hardly bloody lose me in this rabbit hutch, can you?'

He heard her clatter into the kitchen and bang something on to the tin-topped table. Now what had he done wrong? he thought. He ran down the stairs in stockinged feet, into the kitchen, and went over to kiss his mother on the cheek. Not that he particularly wanted to, but it was a ritual that she liked. But this time she jerked her head sharply away from him. 'Surprised you've got any kisses left for your mum,' she said icily.

'I was only trying to say hello,' he said.

'Been busy saying hello today, haven't we?'

'What's wrong, Mum?' he said patiently, knowing full well something had annoyed her and that she would not rest until they had it out. 'What have I done?'

'How am I to know what you've done? I can't keep an eye on you all the time, can I?'

He glanced at the bags. There was a Tesco carrier bag and another from Boots.

'You've been into town?'

'Evidently.' She too looked at the bags.

'So? Why didn't you say? I told you I was going in. I could have given you a lift, instead you carted all that lot back on the bus.'

'I don't like to ask. People should volunteer without being asked. I'm independent, I don't want to beg.'

Alan sighed inwardly. There was no point in sighing outwardly, for he knew his mother would pounce on that immediately as being a criticism of her. 'Mum, to ask your own son for a lift is hardly begging.'

She leant forward with a spiteful expression on her thin-lipped face. 'But you didn't ask me, did you? That's the whole point. It's always left to me to ask you, when all I want is for you to offer.'

'Sorry, Mum, I should have asked you.' He wasn't sorry, but what else was he to say? 'I just presumed –' But he was unable to finish the sentence.

'Presumed?' She leapt on the word. 'Well, maybe you shouldn't presume so much. Maybe *presuming* is the same as taking for granted.'

He sat down, took a cigarette out of the packet on the table and lit it slowly. 'Look, Mum, I don't want to row with you. I was thoughtless. I'll always ask you in future, I promise. Okay? I won't be in for tea, I'm going out.'

'Going out with that little wop tart, are you?'

'If you mean Gina, yes.'

'I hope you don't catch anything.'

'Oh for Christ's sake, Mum, I've known Gina since I was fourteen years old. We went to school together, remember? We're just going to the flicks.'

'Hm, and the rest no doubt.' She was busily and noisily unpacking her shopping, slamming the unit doors. 'I don't want you seeing that little whore.' She had stopped her task and stood looking at him defiantly, hands on hips as if daring him to disobey.

'Mum, don't push me,' he said slowly.

'You think you know it all, don't you?'

'No, Mum. But I know what I want and you can't stop me.'

'Oh yes I can. If you insist on whoring around, you needn't think you can stay here with me.'

He stood up, leant his hands on the table and looked her straight in the eyes. 'You don't mean that.'

She laughed. 'Oh yes I bloody well do. Test me.'

'There's no need, Mum. If that's how you feel, I'll go.'

'And where will you go?' Her voice was shrill but confident; she'd trapped him.

'To Horsham, if I'm lucky. There's a position in Special Operations open. I'd thought not to apply, that I shouldn't leave you, but thanks, Ma, you've made the decision for me – I'll go for it. If I get it, I'll move there. If not, I can ask for a transfer to another town.'

'No, Alan,' she shrieked his name, her voice hard with fear. He watched as the defiance changed to fright, her face seemed to sag, as if her flesh were melting. 'Don't leave me.'

'Sorry, Mum, you've gone too far this time. I choose my friends, not you.'

And he'd turned and walked out of the kitchen and out of the house. That which he had thought impossible had been made easy for him. Best would have been if, at the same time, he could have walked out of her life there and then. He couldn't. Nothing was ever as simple as that.

He'd applied for the job at Special Operations at the RSPCA headquarters in Horsham, had his interview, and then had to wait while other applicants were considered. Now he'd made the decision to go, the delay seemed to last for ever before he heard the position was his.

During this time his mother had waged a relentless campaign on his conscience, never for one day letting up. She cajoled, pleaded, screamed abuse at him. But his mind was made up.

'Just like your bloody father,' she screamed, her parting shot as he finally left.

He'd driven off and had had to stop the car a mile away from home for he was upset, far more than he had dared let her see. He was not like his father: for eighteen long and bitter years he'd cared for her, to the point of putting his own happiness second. At twenty-six, he'd looked at his future, seen how empty she could make it for him. Saw a lonely bachelorhood stretching ahead. No, he'd done not only the right thing, but the only thing. He'd restarted his car and moved on into his own future.

That had been over two years ago. After six years of conscientious work as one of the two hundred and eighty-seven local uniformed inspectors in England and Wales, daily investigating complaints of cruelty, enforcing the many laws relating to animals, sometimes successfully making the case that could bring the abuser to court, he had achieved his dream. He'd been selected to join the Special Operations Unit, a plain-clothes, often undercover group, regarded as the front line against cruelty to animals.

Set up in 1977 with four officers, it now had nine, and Alan was proud to be one of them. When he'd first joined he had enjoyed the seven-month training course, which had been hard and arduous. To all the learning and knowledge he'd acquired he had had to add new techniques. How to remain undetected, how to follow suspects and blend with the crowd, how to use all manner of modern surveillance equipment. He'd been taught subtle inter-viewing techniques; new legislation caused by entry into the EEC. His driving had, of necessity, to be more professional, more advanced, since often they were called upon to tail vehicles. He'd learnt to deal with boredom as, with a colleague, he pounded up and down the motorways chasing suspects. He'd learnt to control a slight feeling of claustrophobia when doing surveillance work in the cramped van with one-way windows they often used. He'd learnt to do without sleep and his stomach had become accustomed to getting food, and too often junk food, at irregular hours. Hardest of all, he had to learn to control, and to somehow distance his mind, when witnessing cruelty to the animals he loved. When working undercover they must not by a grimace show any disgust, anger or sadness at what they were seeing.

He'd trailed sheep to Spain, helped uncover a cock-fighting ring, worked with those trying to end the trade in exotic birds. More mundanely, in plain clothes, he'd patrolled markets the length and breadth of the country. Wherever there was a rumour of cruelty Alan and his unit would be hot on the trail. It was a bit like being a soldier, he reasoned: hours of planning, hours of boredom, and then a few minutes of exhilarating excitement when a raid was on.

The only change in him in the past two years was knowing that he wanted to settle down. Never having had a normal family upbringing, he wanted a family of his own. He wanted someone to love as well as to love him. He had a rented flat in Horsham, close to the RSPCA headquarters, which he'd never quite succeeded in making 'home'. He'd like a place of his own. He'd reached that age when he wanted to plant his own roots.

Now here he was in Morristown again. He didn't want to stay in the town, he'd made that decision easily. Still, in an odd way he liked being back in the area – it was pretty outside the town, especially the Shillings. Maybe, while here, he'd look for a cottage by the river Shill to buy from the proceeds of this house. He could always rent it and maybe retire to it. At this thought he laughed: at his age, the very idea of retirement seemed light years away. Still, he reasoned, it might be a good investment.

Despite being on sick leave, in a roundabout way he was working. There had been a spate of rumours of a new dog-fighting ring that had started up in the Morristown area.

Dog fights were numerous anywhere – in garages, farms, even in suburban back bedrooms. Normally only two dogs were brought to a venue to be matched. The size of the meeting depended on the ability and reputation of the dogs. Dogs who had proven their courage and skill could attract punters from as far afield as Ireland and Holland, with large sums of money changing hands in bets. The fights in the Morristown area were not, as yet, in this league and, as far as the inspectors could make out, it was a fairly amateur set-up, with several dogs being matched at one meeting. Given this, they had presumed it would be the easiest thing to uncover. The opposite had been the case. As soon as they'd received a good tip, then everyone, dogs included, seemed to disappear like morning mist.

Everything had gone quiet, and everyone hoped the ring had been disbanded. But just recently the rumour machine had begun to work again. As yet there was nothing sufficiently concrete to warrant the expense of the Special Operations Unit moving in.

'Still, Alan, since you'll be there anyway perhaps you could snoop around, see what you can find out,' Don, the Chief Superintendent and his boss, had suggested to him when, out of hospital, he'd popped into the office to check on his mail, and of course he had agreed. He'd said goodbye to Indy, the Jack Russell terrier who belonged to Jane, the Unit's intelligence collator, who was always in the cramped office at their headquarters. He wouldn't dream of going without patting the little dog like a talisman – it was superstitious of him, he supposed, but he still did it.

Alan looked at his watch. Most of the morning had passed with him lost in thought. He collected his keys and wallet. He'd go for a drive around the villages outside Morristown, he'd decided. Maybe he'd find the cottage of his dreams, rose-bowered and owned by a little apple-cheeked old lady who'd give it to him for nothing. 'Chance would be a fine thing,' he said as, whistling, he let himself out of the house and onto the unfriendly streets of Morristown.

11

It amazed Oliver that what at the outset seemed a simple solution could become such a complicated muddle.

What could be simpler than deciding to sell his house, give up his job and move to the country with his dog? Oh dear me no, he sighed to himself.

The past month had been a series of frustrations.

Wimpole had decided she wanted to go with him, then had second thoughts. Then decided again to go, and then went off the idea. Such vacillation would have tried anyone's patience to the limit, he told himself. When she changed her mind once more, Oliver flipped.

'For God's sake, Wimpole, you're like a bloody Yo-Yo. Make your mind up.'

'Do you have to be so bloody impatient? It's a big step I'm taking.'

'Impatient! Me? I've been positively saintlike with you, but even I'm reaching the point of having had enough. Either you come or no – it's make up your mind time.'

'Oh yes, and what happened to all that – *I won't go without you, Wimpole. Take your time. I love you*? Load of old cobblers, wasn't it? Just as I suspected. You only said it to bribe me.' She sniffed audibly.

'It wasn't. I meant it. But for heaven's sake, Wimpole, I've got to know one way or the other.'

'You're going then?'

'I'd like to.'

'I'll think about it,' she said, with infuriating smugness, and sailed out of the drawing room with head held high.

Oliver hadn't had much luck with estate agents either. It was an odd thing, but the house he'd bought from the self-same estate agent who had assured him what a highly marketable property it was had, in the five years he'd been here, become a difficult property to shift and not nearly as valuable as he had fondly hoped.

The worst hurdle, he'd anticipated, would be the one at work. He had spent many an hour in his bath, gin and tonic to hand, composing exactly what he'd say to his partners about wanting to opt out. He'd honed his speech to perfection.

Their reaction to his news came as a complete shock.

'We've been expecting it,' said partner number one.

'Amazed you've held on as long,' said partner number two.

'And of course you'll want your share at valuation paid out – no problem,' said partner number three, knocking the wind out of Oliver's sails.

'If you could give us a month of your valuable time before leaving, we'd appreciate it.' Partner number two swiftly dealt with what little wind was left.

His ego deflated, Oliver thought that at least his secretary would be sad to see him go. Instead she said it couldn't have come at a better time for her since, she announced with glowing pride, she was pregnant, and since she'd had a couple of miscarriages was taking no chances and was leaving immediately.

He'd not had any success over the return of Bandage either. The telephone rang and rang at Sophia's new house in London. Then he remembered she'd said she was staying with her father until the decorators had finished. But Ben said she wasn't there when he telephoned; he wasn't too sure whether to believe him or not. He'd tried to make an appointment to see his lawyer, but he was away and he had to make do with his junior partner, a chap he regarded as a total prat. He wanted to know if he could file for custody of a dog, or was it only children one was permitted to fight over in law? This lawyer irritated Oliver immediately by saying that unless Oliver had written proof that the dog was his then it might be a little difficult to prove. Since Sophia had paid for the dog with her own personal cheque and the receipt had been made out to her, the litigation could be lengthy and expensive. He had looked at Oliver as if he were barmy, and Oliver had decided it was pointless pursuing the problem with him, since he was obviously not a dog owner and would, therefore, never understand the anxiety and urgency Oliver felt.

This interview depressed Oliver more than anything else. The furniture, pictures and household goods she had taken could all be replaced; their removal had been an irritant more than anything. But Bandage was something else. And he had to face the fact that if he could feel this devastated over his dog it only pinpointed how empty their relationship had become. He'd loved Sophia once, and she him. So where had that love gone? And why had they allowed it to escape and die? It saddened him that his marriage should end in the importance of who'd written what cheque and who was in possession of which receipt.

Finally, today, frustrated by it all, and feeling he was no longer needed by anyone, he'd decided to go home.

Upon opening the front door it was to find that, with Wimpole away, he had been burgled. He stood in the even more denuded drawing room and lit a cigarette and found he wasn't in the least surprised; at this point in his life he should have expected it. What little Sophia had left the burglars had taken, except for the larger paintings. Suddenly a strange lethargy had taken over, and wearily he climbed the stairs to his bedroom knowing full well that his several pairs of gold cufflinks would have been lifted and, no doubt, his Patek Philippe watch. At least he had the satisfaction of knowing the watch had stopped and needed to go back to the makers. He entered his bedroom: it was in chaos, the contents of his drawers littering the floor. In the bathroom he found written in lipstick on the mirror, 'What's happened to you, mate? Hardly worth the bother. But thanks all the same. Your friendly thief.'

If it was meant as a joke, it fell on very barren ground. All it did was to underline how impotent he was in handling his life at the moment. Other forces had taken control of him; he was like the toy soldier standing in a paper boat, being swept along a gutter to a drain, as in the fairy story, which had frightened him rigid as a child. That's how he felt, bobbing along and everybody else messing his life up for him. He knew he should call the police, but he couldn't even be bothered to do that. What was the point, with their abysmal success rate with burglaries? He wanted to get right away. He quickly packed an overnight bag, left a note for Wimpole to tell her where he was, and drove to Bishop's End, wanting to put space between him and London, in the hope that he would find a measure of peace and equilibrium there.

Grace White, his cleaning lady, was in the kitchen when he arrived. 'Since you haven't been here for the past three weeks I was sure you'd turn up this weekend. I thought I'd best pop up and dust round a bit,' she said, putting the kettle on instead.

'Sorry to disturb you,' he said.

'I was just finishing. I always brew up when I've done.' She poured two cups of tea. 'They said at the pub as you're thinking of moving in, permanent like.'

'Well, yes and no. I'm not sure.'

'Ah, I see. I just wondered in the circumstances ... Your wife gone, like ...' Her voice trailed off. 'That'll be a pity if you don't. When the house is empty it looks sad – as if it's missing your Aunt Phoebe. How she loved this house. I can hear her now – "Grace," she would say, "when I'm dead and gone you look after this place for me. Oliver means well, but he's useless about the house, like them all." She didn't go much on men, your aunt.'

'Didn't she?'

'No. All, that is, except for you. Real soft spot she had for you. She told me – I can hear her now, "you mark my words, Grace, he'll be here. He'll come here to live one of these fine days." And there was me hoping her prophecy had come true.'

'I didn't say that I wasn't, just that I haven't completely made my mind up.'

'Ah well. That's different. If you're thinking of moving back and you're wondering how you'll manage, like, I could give you another two days a week. I couldn't do no more than that because I already do for the vet over at Middle Shilling.'

'Could you? That would be very kind indeed.'

'That's settled then,' she said, sipping her tea contentedly, and Oliver felt again he was being controlled by others. 'You look right down in the dumps, Mr Hawksmoor. Since I'm here, would you like me to make you a nice little casserole or something for your supper?' she asked kindly.

'Mrs White, you're a wonder. Is the village shop open today?' he asked.

'It's early closing day today, Thursday. You'll have to go into Shillingham itself if you want anything.'

'I'll do that. Get some supplies in. Anything you need, Mrs White?'

'Well, if you're doing a shop, I would really appreciate ...' Before he knew where he was, Oliver was armed with the longest shopping list it had ever been his responsibility to deal with.

Thomasine was running late. There was nothing unusual in this, Thomasine was often running late. In fact, if she thought about it, she seemed to spend most of her life chasing herself, never quite managing to catch up. She was in Shillingham a good two hours later than she had anticipated, doing a frantic last-minute shop, since Nadine was finally coming to stay for the run-up to Easter. It wasn't until she had opened the storecupboard door and looked into the fridge that she saw that she had let the catering side of her life slip rather. And what little she had Nadine would not deign to eat. A year ago Nadine had suddenly announced that she had become a vegetarian. Thomasine, sensibly, had not battled with her over this, hoping that it was just another teenage phase which would disappear with time. But it had not, and Nadine was at pains on the telephone last night to remind her mother that she was still vegetarian and not to try to *trick* her. Thomasine had thought it was an odd choice of verb, but had chosen to ignore it.

She was also in a panic because her husband was coming too. She knew she should think of him only as Robert or her ex, but she couldn't – he was her husband. She doubted if she would ever be able to think of him in another way. She wanted everything to be perfect, just in case he accepted her invitation to stay to dinner. After all, she told herself, if she was lucky and he decided to eat with them, anything could happen later.

In her hurried shop she had stocked up with fruit, vegetables, lentils, eggs and cheese, as well as a couple of steaks for Robert and herself. Now she was relaxing in the black leather swivel chair at Snippers.

'Here on holiday?' Gill asked, as he stood behind her.

'No, I've just moved here. I've bought the old school house in Middle Shilling.'

'Pretty, the Shillings, aren't they? I often think that with the river Shill meandering through them, the way it does, and each village straddling it, they're like pearls and the river's the string.'

'What a nice idea.'

'So, what do we want done here?' And he picked up a hank of hair and held it up to the light and scrutinised it. Thomasine felt herself go rigid, waiting for the criticism to come. Waiting for the question that all hairdressers invariably asked: 'And who cut this last?'

'Wonderful condition,' he said instead. 'Good cut, too. London?'

'Yes. Do you know Frederico's in Bond Street?'

'Know it? I was virtually born there, my dear. Everything I know Frederico taught me.'

'If you could trim the ends – just a little off the bottom. I think I'd like it cut and restyled, but I'm in a bit of a rush. Another day, perhaps.'

'It suits you like this.'

'I've been wondering if I'm not a bit too old for long hair.'

'You?' Gill laughed. 'You've got the face for it, love. Look, Gill here promises.' At this, he dramatically put his hand on heart. 'When I think you've gone over the top for long hair, on my life, I'll tell you.'

Gill had been working for a few minutes in silence, which in itself was unusual for an hairdresser, when another client came up, smiled apologetically at Thomasine and patted the deeply concentrating Gill on the sleeve. 'Gill, any chance of buying one of your puppies?'

'Well, Mrs Prentice, there could be, and there could not. Maybe yes, and maybe no.'

'Thank you, Gill, that's very, very clear,' Mrs Prentice laughed.

'We've got a bit of a problem; the man whose dog mated with our Sadie, well, she took an instant dislike to him and chased him out the house, and we've no idea now whether he wants to claim his pick of the litter or if we're going to get a whopping bill. Do you see? So, if he doesn't want the puppy, yes we could quite possibly have one for sale, but if he wants it, I don't think so. But I'll let you know as soon as possible.'

'How many puppies did she have?' Thomasine asked as Gill returned to cutting her hair.

'We had five. Lovely they are. We're taking it in turns, my partner and myself, to stay home and look after them. You know, just in this early period. We want to make sure each gets its own share of food and what have you and that nobody sits on somebody and kills them. That would be awful, wouldn't it?'

'How old are they?'

'A month – it's gone by in such a rush.'

'I've just acquired a dog,' she said.

'Acquired? That's a funny word to use.' He stopped cutting and stood with scissors poised.

'Not really.' And she explained how Luna had come into her life.

'And she's pregnant too?'

'Yes, but because of the circumstances the vet thinks that probably they're not bulldog puppies, that they're, well, we used to call them mongrels, didn't we? Now they're cross-breeds.'

'You keeping her?' He was wielding brush and drier expertly.

'I didn't mean to – it's difficult,' she replied. She'd had Luna for a month now and had reached the point – dangerous, she knew – of not being able to envisage what life would be like without her.

'I couldn't imagine being without our Sadie. Lovely girl, she is. Light of my life. We have such fun with her, especially after we found out about showing and the time to be had there. We've met some lovely people, you wouldn't believe how wonderful dog people are. Kind, helpful. We love the shows, we've missed them since Sadie's been pregnant, you know. Once or twice we went, just to look-see, but it wasn't the same as when we had Sadie competing. But we'll soon be back. You ought to come along one day, you know, you'd enjoy it. Meet a lot of nice people. Takes you out of yourself.' He held the mirror up so she could see the back of her head.

Five minutes later, her bill paid, packages in her hand, she opened the salon door, stepped onto the pavement and crashed into a man, dropping her shopping bag as she did so.

'I'm terribly sorry,' she said, bending down, chasing and scooping up the oranges she'd bought. 'I wasn't looking where I was going.'

'Please, neither was I,' Oliver replied, stooping down to retrieve the apples and carrots for her. 'I see you like fruit,' he grinned.

'It's mainly for my daughter, she's become a vegetarian.'

'I did that once, so I could face the cows in the morning without feeling guilty,' he said, thinking what a lovely smile she had.

'I know what you mean. I think emotionally I'm a vegetarian, it's just that I love meat so much . . .' She looked down at the pavement, thinking how odd he must think her nattering away to a complete stranger.

'Exactly!' And he handed her back the carrier bag.

'Thank you so much,' she said, and walked hurriedly towards the car park.

Oliver watched her. What an attractive woman, he thought. Beautiful hair.

12

Jim Varley had always thought of himself as a calm man, but he was finding great difficulty keeping so this evening. The subject of his irritation was standing the other side of his examination table, on which cowered a pretty Blenheim King Charles spaniel.

Jim had explained to the man that the discharge the dog was suffering from was because it had an infection of the uterus. 'It's more common when a bitch gets older and hasn't been spayed,' he continued. 'But it can occur in a young dog like this one.'

'Spayed? What's that mean? Taking it all out, I suppose.'

'Well, yes.'

'If that was done, then she wouldn't bleed and make a mess on the carpet a couple of times a year?'

'She is a bitch – bitches come into season.'

'Yes, but my missus doesn't like it, neither do I. I mean, it's not nice, is it, on the carpets and on the floor? I've locked her in the shed before, 'til it was over.'

'I see,' said Jim, anger beginning to seethe in him. Poor little bitch, living in the house and then banished to a cold shed, no doubt she thought she was being punished for something. No wonder she was so nervous, he probably hurt her too. 'Still, poor girl can't help it, it's only natural. We can treat this infection, but I do strongly recommend that she has a hysterectomy, then it won't recur, so then the carpets will be safe.' The irony in his voice was completely lost on his client.

'And how much would that cost, this here hysterectomy?'

'Well, she's a small dog. Seventy-five pounds, say somewhere between seventy-five and a hundred pounds.'

'You must be joking!' The man blustered.

'No I'm not. It's a major operation for a dog. Major operation for a woman.'

'Well, I'm not bloody paying that!'

'Then the infection will probably come back again and could lead to a very unpleasant death. Of course, the decision is yours, but if you take into account repeated visits to me and my fees, the cost of the antibiotics required to clear up the infection, you'll very soon be looking at the same sum of money,' he said as patiently as he could.

'Oh no, no I'm not. Put it down.'

'I beg your pardon?'

'Put it to sleep. I don't want it, neither does the missus. It's the last bloody bitch we have, I tell you that, the trouble it's been.'

'I don't like putting down healthy dogs,' Jim said.

The man stepped forward as if to pick the dog up. 'Then I'll find a vet who is a bit more obliging.'

'Hang on. Let's calm down here a minute.' Jim put a restraining hand on the man's arm.

'Calm down? I'm perfectly calm.'

'Would you have any objection to me taking the dog and rehousing it?'

'I don't give a damn what you do with it, I don't want it.'

At that, Jim scooped up the dog, carried it out of the surgery, placed it gently in a cage in what he referred to as his hospital ward. 'Don't worry, I'll be back.' He patted the small dog on its head, and noticed that it had stopped shaking with fear. So he had been right, it wasn't him, it was her owner she was afraid of.

He returned to the surgery, where the man was still standing. 'I forgot to ask you, what's she called?' Jim asked.

'Amy,' came the reply.

'Fine, thanks.' Jim turned, as if to conclude the interview.

'There's just one thing, if you're keeping her, I mean, like, it's my dog, it's a valuable pedigree dog that.'

'You needn't think . . .' Jim interrupted, his fists balled with angry frustration. 'You're not suggesting that I pay you for the dog?' he asked.

'I don't see why not, if you intend hanging on to it.'

'That's no problem then, Mr . . .' He glanced at the notes. 'Smith.' A likely story, he thought. 'I'll put her down tonight after surgery, if you'll just sign this consent form giving me the right to dispose of the dog. I'll send you the bill. I presume you've given my receptionist your address?'

'Yes, sure,' said the so-called Mr Smith, looking shifty, as he grabbed the pen. He paused, ever so slightly, before writing his name, as if he had to think what to write, Jim noticed with quiet satisfaction.

'Well, that's fine then, isn't it? No problem,' Jim said, willing the man to leave his surgery so that he didn't have to look at him. He had an almost uncontrollable urge to hit him hard in the face.

As soon as the man had gone, Tessa, Jim's assistant, came in.

'Who was that? He was so unpleasant.'

'Called himself Smith. Wanted me to put the dog down rather than pay for an operation.'

'Oh, I hate people like that. I want to kill them.'

Jim laughed. 'I know what you mean.'

'What're you going to do?'

'I told him I'm going to put the dog down.'

'Oh no!' she wailed.

'If you promise not to tell a living soul, I'm going to do a hysterectomy on her, once we've cleared up this infection. Highly unethical, probably.'

'I'd love to have her.'

'Tess, you've got five dogs already.'

'I know, but I often think there's room for one more.'

'No, Tess, it's not fair. You must spend all your wages on dog food.'

'My mum gets a bit fed up with it, but then she's an old softy too.'

'You needn't worry about this one, I might even keep her myself. I've always had a soft spot for King Charleses.'

13

Thomasine had promised herself that when Robert and Nadine arrived she would open the door after a decent pause and with a serene smile on her face. Instead, at the first ring of the bell she raced pell-mell towards it, skidding on the parquet.

'Nadine!' she said, opening her arms wide.

'Hi!' Nadine ducked under her arms, entered the hall and wandered off through the open door of the drawing room.

'Come in, do,' she said to Robert who was on the doorstep. 'Don't stand there. It's very kind of you to bring her, Robert.' She spoke in short, breathless bursts of excitement. Her heart pitter-pattered its betrayal. She wondered if she should proffer her cheek to be kissed, and wished he'd take the decision from her and kiss her himself. 'I'm sure she'd have been all right on the train, I'd have gone into Morristown to pick her up. It's no distance.' She knew she was prattling.

'I felt happier driving her. The trains aren't safe these days for young women,' Robert said, stepping into the hall, carefully removing his driving gloves and looking about him.

'But she's so sensible,' said Thomasine. She held out her hand for his coat, and mindful of the fuss he made of his clothes, hung it on a hanger in the small closet.

'I care about her,' Robert replied.

'And that means I don't?'

'You haven't made much contact with her,' he said accusingly.

'I've tried to. You know they don't like us phoning the school – I didn't want to make things difficult for her. But I've written.' She knew how defensive she sounded.

'You didn't call during her exeats.'

'She's welcome to come here any time – heavens, she's only had one weekend free of school.'

'That doesn't explain why you didn't telephone.'

'It was – I didn't –' She could not quite bring herself to tell him that she hadn't called because she could not face Chantal answering *her* telephone in *her* house. 'I didn't mind her going to you. She had things to do in London –

I understood.' Thomasine took a deep breath, needing to control herself; it would be silly to start fighting again.

'You don't ask, you insist with children.'

'With children, yes, teenagers – no.' She managed to laugh, if only a small one. 'Still, she's here now, at last.'

'I had to bring her. There was no guarantee she'd have stayed on the train.'

'What does that mean?' She had been leading the way into her sitting room, but swung round to face him.

'She didn't want to come. I had to force her.'

It was as if he had hit her. 'Did you have to tell me that?' she asked.

'You always were incapable of facing reality, Thomasine.'

'I don't know, I think I've been doing rather well at that,' she replied, aware of the familiar constriction at the back of her throat which was always a prelude to tears.

'What are you two talking about?' Nadine appeared in the doorway.

'Just saying hi!' Thomasine replied gaily, and knew it sounded hideously false. 'Would you like a drink before you go back? Or some supper?'

'No thanks.' He glanced at his watch; she noticed it wasn't the one she'd given him years ago, but an expensive-looking gold one. Aware of her glance, he quickly shot his cuffs to cover it. 'Chantal will be waiting for me. It'll be a good hour and a half before I'm home.' She knew that her disappointment was etched on her face, but it was no good, she couldn't pretend. 'I'll have a small Scotch, though,' he said, in a more kindly tone, as if he'd registered her expression.

They joined Nadine, who was prowling around the sitting room. 'It's a bit small, isn't it?' she said.

'It suits me well enough on my own.'

'But you won't be on your own when I come and stay, will you?' the girl said sharply.

'We're hardly the size of elephants, are we? I'm sure there's room for both of us to manoeuvre around in here.' She ended the sentence on an upward tone, trying to lighten her voice, trying not to sound too irritated.

'You've made it look nice,' Robert said.

'Thank you.' She went into the kitchen to get some ice. Luna lifted her heavy head, sniffed the air, registered that there were other people in the house, and with a weary sigh, hauled herself onto her legs and padded through to the drawing room. Thomasine followed with the ice.

'Good God! What on earth is that?' said Nadine.

'It's Luna. She's a bulldog.'

'She's gross!'

'She's pregnant, that's why.'

'What on earth induced you to get a dog.' Robert looked with displeasure as the dog lumbered towards him, moving his position sharply as soon as Luna reached him and began to sniff.

'I like dogs,' Thomasine said emphatically.

'Well, that's news to me. All the years we lived together, you never said you wanted a dog.'

'What would have been the point? You wouldn't have wanted one, too messy. Both partners have got to want a dog.' She realised that she was beginning to speak slowly, as if to a child, but was, in fact, controlling her temper. She laughed so that he wouldn't take offence, and then wondered why she bothered.

'Couldn't you have got something that's prettier than that?' Nadine said.

'I think she's lovely. She grows on you, you know.'

'It would take a long time for her to grow on me,' said Robert.

'I thought you liked animals, Nadine. That's why you're a vegetarian.'

'I respect animals. I don't have to share my space with them.'

Robert tipped his glass, finishing his drink. 'I'd better be going.' He kissed Nadine's forehead and stroked her hair affectionately. 'Now let me know what you decide, as soon as possible, young lady.'

'Yes, Dad,' she said, smiling sweetly at him. Robert did not kiss Thomasine goodbye, merely thanking her again for the whisky as she held the door open for him. Such coolness made her feel empty, almost as if she did not exist.

When she got back into the drawing room she meant to ask Nadine what her father wanted her to decide, but she didn't have time for she found Luna stalking her daughter around the room.

'Would you get her to stop doing that?' said Nadine, shoving the dog away.

'It looks as though she likes you.'

'I don't like her. I wish she'd stop it.'

'Oh, Nadine, don't be so silly. You're new, she just wants to get to know you. She's a very determined dog, you might just as well say "hello" to her and get it over with, then she'll leave you alone.' Quickly Nadine struck out with her foot, catching Luna on the underside of her large jaw. 'Nadine! Don't do that. Don't be cruel.'

'I didn't hurt her,' Nadine said.

'You wouldn't have to hurt her physically. You can hurt her feelings very easily, she's a very sensitive dog.'

'Oh, Mum, really!' said Nadine with exasperation. 'She's a dumb animal. What's for supper?' she asked abruptly, as if bored with the subject of Luna.

'I made a quiche. I thought you'd like that.'

'I don't eat eggs.'

'Oh, Nadine, you didn't say. It was supposed to be meat you didn't eat.'

'Well, I've stopped eating eggs, cheese and fish.'

Thomasine sighed with exasperation. 'What's left then?'

'Plenty. There's lentils, all the vegetables. Fruit. Nuts.'

'Quite honestly, Nadine, if you're going to be this difficult about what you eat, then I suggest that you get it for yourself.' Thomasine poured herself a large drink, her second, unusual for her this early.

Nadine sat down. 'What?' she asked, with an expression of surprise on her face.

'I didn't mind when I thought I could use cheese and eggs as well as fruit and vegetables. But now . . . I mean, I would have to buy a cookery book to do things for you, I'd have to learn how to create a balanced diet for you.'

'Chantal doesn't complain.'

'Chantal's new to the job and is still full of masses of enthusiasm. She'll learn,' Thomasine said with feeling, and immediately regretted it. 'I suppose I could knock up a ratatouille or something like that, would that do you? And some bread.'

'Fine. Where's my room?'

'That door over there.' Thomasine pointed and Nadine crossed the drawing room and opened her bedroom door.

'Ugh! Laura Ashley wallpaper.'

'But you like Laura Ashley. You room in London is done like this one.'

'Not any more, it isn't. Chantal agreed it was too twee. She said I should do what I want. I'm more sophisticated now. I don't like this sort of crap.' She waved at the pretty blue and white room dismissively. 'You should see my other room now, I've had it done in silver and black.'

'Sounds wonderful,' Thomasine said sarcastically. 'You might have told me you'd changed your taste so dramatically. Why does it have to be a state secret until you suddenly plonk it on me?'

'I didn't know you were going to decorate my bedroom all girly-girly, did I?'

'You might have guessed that I would, since that's what I thought you liked.' Thomasine could feel the anger welling up inside her again.

'This is a great new homecoming,' said Nadine, rolling her eyes to the ceiling.

'You can say that again. How do you think I feel?'

They looked at each other. Nadine looked petulant and now, removing her school duffel coat, Thomasine could see that the change in her daughter wasn't just in her taste in interior design. It was difficult to pin down, most of the clothes were the same as before – jeans perhaps a little more frayed; a cropped jumper well above her waist rather than a sloganned T-shirt; a backward-facing baseball cap. The biggest difference was that instead of the Doc Martens she had begged and pleaded for, she now wore the sort of tan coloured, heavy lace-up boots a forester would have happily paid for. But change there was, and Thomasine suddenly realised it was in attitude – there was a pouting defiance to her that had not been there before. Thomasine wearily pushed her hand through her hair, forgetting she'd had it done especially for this evening. Well, that was a waste of time, she thought and sighed audibly.

'I'm sorry, Mum. I'm being a bitch, aren't I?' Nadine said, as if the sigh had made her suddenly guilty. For a second she glimpsed the strong-minded but sweet daughter she had known.

'Yes, you are a bit. It's your room, and you must have it any way you want. I've always said that about your room, no need to change now. I'd be a bit iffy about silver and black though.'

'We could go to the local town tomorrow and get new stuff.'

'But I've just put it up.'

'You mean I've got to live with that until it needs replacing?' Any guilt she'd felt seemed completely negated, judging by her belligerent expression.

'I'd have thought that that would be the reasonable thing to do, yes.'

'I see,' said Nadine, in an ominously ill-humoured voice. 'I'll unpack, then, whilst you get supper.' She did not leave the room but flounced out of it, slamming her bedroom door.

Thomasine, in the kitchen, began the supper. She collected her cooking utensils, banging a saucepan down, snapping a door shut, the racket expressing how angry she felt. Why on earth had she hoped for Robert to stay? What for? To listen to him lecturing her? – she kicked a cupboard door shut. How smug he'd been, how censorious. And she'd let him. Why hadn't she let rip and told him the truth – she hadn't wanted to uproot, to change their lives. It was far more his doing than hers. So why had she been so mealy-mouthed with him? She ran the water in a gushing torrent into the sink. God, she despised herself, as no doubt he did too. Her reaction tonight had been humiliating – well, she thought as she lined up the vegetables on the chopping board, I won't be like that again, ever! With such a decision made she could feel herself calming. She pulled the kitchen stool towards her with one foot and sat herself on it.

As she worked it did cross her mind that having to prepare strict vegetarian food for the whole of the Easter holiday was going to be a pain, and how simple life had become *without* her daughter around.

'What a thing to think, Luna,' she said, looking down at the solid dog, who was, as always, sitting at her feet in the hope something interesting might fall from the worktop. 'What a way to think about my own daughter.' And Luna's small, black tail wiggled in reply.

14

Since it was Saturday, Kimberley was sitting with the others on the wall of the fountain in Shillingham. As usual the talk was of nothing in particular, mainly of the motorbikes they all dreamed of one day owning. She swung her legs back and forth. Why did she persist in coming here, what had she in common with the rest? As long as she hung around with them, how was she to meet anyone else? She knew what she meant by that – a boyfriend, that's what. A decent bloke, not one who nicked things and despised love.

Butch yelled with raucous laughter, a 'look at me' kind of laugh. She didn't dislike him, didn't despise him, in a way she supposed she felt sorry for him, for suddenly she saw how it would be for Butch in five years' time – he'd still be here, with another group around him he could control. The others would all have moved on.

'I'm going for a piss,' Butch said, loudly enough for the passers-by to hear and be shocked.

Yes, she thought, he was sad.

The market was busy with Easter week. The Council, or was it the stall-holders, had erected a large tableau of a cardboard chicken in an artificial garden. She had stopped Butch and the others from throwing stones at it. 'Leave it alone,' she'd said. 'Let the kiddies enjoy it.' And, give them their due, if there was one thing about the gang, they did like children and were nice to them. And so they had stopped.

Kimberley opened the bag she was holding and peered at the gaudy Easter egg she had bought for her mother. When she'd been little her mother had always bought her a chocolate egg, and some years had dyed hard-boiled eggs pretty colours and patterns, but she hadn't had one for several years now. She supposed her mother thought she was too old, but inside she still felt young enough for one. Maybe she should buy another and give it to herself.

'Mind if I sit here?' a man's voice asked.

Kimberley looked up to see a tall, broad-shouldered man with thick blond hair, dressed in jeans and a blazer – posh, she thought.

'Suit yourself,' said Kimberley, and swung her legs again, like a metronome, as if not caring, but she shifted slightly to give him room. She would have liked to sneak another look at him, to see if his eyes were as blue as she thought, but she didn't dare.

'It's a lovely day, isn't it?' he said politely. 'I hope it holds for Easter.'

'Yes,' she replied, and could not understand why she blushed slightly as she did so.

''Ere, you! Buzz off.' Ginger jumped up from his place two along from Kimberley. 'This 'ere's reserved,' he said, bristling with aggression as he took control of the situation in Butch's absence.

The man looked at Ginger – all five and a half feet of him – and slowly reached into his pocket for a packet of cigarettes.

'Pardon,' he said eventually. 'Did you just tell me to buzz off?'

'I did,' said Ginger, with a half embarrassed jerk of his head.

'Thought that's what you said.' He offered a cigarette to Kimberley.

'No thanks, I don't.'

'I'm trying to give up.' He lit the cigarette.

'You don't seem to be having much success.' She found the courage to smile.

'No, I'm not, am I?' He grinned and threw the remains of the cigarette on to the cobbles and ground it out with his heel.

'You shouldn't have done that.'

'Why not? You're right. Stupid habit.' He smiled again, turning to face her, and Kimberley could see his face full on. It was a square-shaped face, and yes, his eyes were blue, and with his blond hair she thought he looked like a Nordic warrior. He thought how pretty, how innocent she looked.

Butch, still zipping up his flies – again to shock – approached them, the buckles on his large boots clanging like the spurs of an ancient knight as he clomped across the cobblestones.

'Who are you?' He glared belligerently at the stranger.

'I told him to piss off, Butch,' Ginger said excitedly.

'Didn't you hear what my mate said?'

'I did.'

'And?' Butch asked in his most menacing way, hands on hips, standing with black-leather-clad thighs wide apart.

The man looked at Butch long and hard. 'And what?'

'Move when you're bleeding well told to.'

The man squared his shoulders and sat up straight, and Kimberley wasn't sure if she wanted him to move safely away or to make a stand; she feared he might be hurt if he did.

'No, I don't think so,' he said finally. 'I rather like it here. Pleasant, watching the crowds, isn't it?' He spoke to Kimberley.

'Yes, it is,' she said, looking nervously at Butch, and then down at the cobblestones.

'Well, this is our pitch, and we don't like you here, mate.'

'I'm sorry about that. I'd no idea that this was private property. I assumed the fountain belonged to the citizens of Shillingham.'

'Well, if you were a citizen of Shillingham, you'd know that every Saturday we sit here.'

'Every Saturday?' he said with exaggerated amazement, and Kimberley giggled.

Butch looked none too pleased. He saw Kimberley was giggling and smiling, and realised he didn't seem to be getting very far in this conversation. 'Off,' he barked, gesticulating with his thumb over his right shoulder, and then, for good measure, waggling it in the air.

'When I'm good and ready.'

Butch seemed to think about this for an inordinate length of time; if he allowed the man to stay he would lose face. 'I don't think so,' he said, glowering in his most menacing way. The man started to rise from the wall of the fountain. 'Ah, that's better. Seeing it my way, are we?' Butch looked smug. But as he stood to his full height the man towered over Butch by a good head. Butch made the tactical error of taking one step back.

'I'm sorry my presence bothers you so,' he said. 'But I intend sitting here awhile yet. So, why don't *you* buzz off.' He leant forward aggressively.

The members of the gang looked all ways but at each other, their eyes darting left to right, each taking a sneaky look at their leader's discomfort, each finding they rather enjoyed seeing him ousted.

'He's a big bugger, Butch, I wouldn't if I were you.'

'Shut up, Ginger,' said Butch. 'Leave this to me.'

The man had sat down again. From his pocket he took a brown paper bag. He offered it to Kimberley. 'Jelly baby, miss?' he asked pleasantly.

'Thank you,' she said. And even as she said the words, she knew that one small thank you was her resignation from the gang, that Butch would never forgive her now.

'Sod the lot of you,' said Butch, turning on his heel, and clomped off down the market. After a pause and a few startled whispers, the others ran behind him.

'Were you with them?' the young man asked.

'Yes and no,' she said, non-committally. 'I mean, I know them, but I'm not one of them, not any more.'

'I'm glad. A gang like that could mean trouble.'

'Yes. I know what you mean.' She looked at her hands and wished they weren't so rough. His glance followed hers.

'Are you cold?'

'No. It's my hands, they're always cold.'

'You know what they say – cold hands, warm heart.' She felt herself redden. 'I've got a pair of gloves, somewhere.' He felt in his pockets and produced a pair of leather gloves. She'd never touched leather that felt so soft.

'Thanks.' She put them on. The fingers flapped this way and that.

'My name's Alan Farmingham. And you're-?'

She looked nervously at the cobbles. 'Kimberley.' She dared to look up. 'Kimberley White.'

'Nice name. Are you from round here?'

'Yes. My father's got a smallholding out the other side of Lower Shilling, on the Conniestown road.'

'You came in on the bus?'

'Yes, that's right. There used to be one every couple of hours, but now there's just the one in the morning, then you have to wait until the afternoon to get back.'

'Long wait.'

'Oh, I don't mind. I like watching people.'

'Yes, I do too. I like to imagine what they do, what their houses are like inside, are they happy or sad, that sort of thing.'

'So do I,' she said, astonished. 'And sometimes I make stories up about them, silly things,' she laughed.

'Me too.'

'Do you live here in Shillingham?'

'No. I've been packing up my mother's house in Morristown. She died.'

'Oh, I am sorry.' Kimberley felt flustered, not sure what to say in such circumstances.

'We weren't close,' he said, as if sensing her confusion.

'Does that help?' she asked, thinking of her relationship with her own parents.

'It must do, I suppose. I didn't think I'd ever want to come back here but, funny thing is, I've been wondering whether to buy a cottage in the area.'

'Why not keep the house?'

'I prefer the country.'

'Me too. I'd hate to live in a town – too noisy and claustrophobic.'

'Exactly.' They both sat a moment in silence, liking how much they agreed. 'What do you do?'

'Nothing at the moment – I'm on sick leave,' he said, neatly skirting the question. When investigating, as he was now, even if only semi-officially, he didn't want strangers to know he worked for the RSPCA, you never knew who you were talking to. And yet, oddly, this girl didn't feel like a stranger to him. 'What do you do?'

'I help my parents,' she replied, pleased that she hadn't had to say she was still at school. She'd be mortified if he knew. She liked him and wanted to stay talking to him, and a man of his age – mid-twenties, she reckoned – might run a mile if he realised he was talking to a schoolgirl. 'Vegetables and things,' she added, non-committal.

'What do you do in your spare time?'

'Me? Not a lot. Best of all I like to walk up into the hills, up beyond the Shillings and hide in the copses, pretend I'm the only person left in the world.'

'I like to do that too. I like to get in the car and drive to the sea and walk miles along the beach, away from the bathers, then flop in the dunes and watch the birds and pretend the same.' He looked at her, his face alive with excitement. She felt it too. Oddly, she felt she knew him, that she liked him, that she would always know him. It was an almost overwhelming sensation.

She mustn't seem too forward, she would frighten him away.

'Do you mind if I sit here?' said a new voice. Kimberley turned to see a young girl dressed from head to toe in black.

'Please do.' And she laughed.

'What are you laughing at?' said the girl, somewhat aggressively.

'I'm sorry. I'm not laughing at you, but how odd things can be. I mean, I sit here every Saturday, come rain or shine, and I think this is the first time anybody else has ever come up and said, "Do you mind if I sit here," all polite, like. Now it's happened twice. It's funny. I'm Kimberley, this is Alan.'

'Nadine,' she replied, completely ignoring Alan and speaking to Kimberley. 'Does anything go on in this dump?'

'Not a lot. There's sometimes a disco on Saturday nights. There's more goes on in Morristown.'

'A disco! They went out with the ark. No clubs here? No raves? Do you go?'

'No, I can't, I live too far away. There's no late bus, and my mum won't let me hitch-hike,' Kimberley answered, puzzled about what the difference was between a disco and a club.

'I fancy trying a *disco*.' The girl giggled, as if finding the word funny. 'At least it gives a little glimmer of hope. My mum's just moved here, I don't know what she's thinking of, choosing a place like this.'

'Where does she come from?' asked Kimberley.

'London, Islington. Then she suddenly, without consulting *me*, decides to bury herself down here, it's madness. I told her, she'll go stark staring bonkers. If she expects me to keep coming down here, she's got another think coming.'

'Where does she live?' asked Alan, thinking the mother would probably be better off.

'One of those Shilling villages, I don't know which one. Stupid names, Upper, Middle and Lower.'

'They're lovely houses there, though,' said Kimberley dreamily. 'I do envy her. I'd love to live there one day.' She smiled at her own silly dreams.

'Maybe you will,' said Alan kindly.

'I doubt it, not now, they're too expensive. None of us locals can afford them.'

'But the problem is it's the locals who sell for the ridiculous prices in the first place,' said Alan.

'Well, how about this disco, let's go, shall we?' the girl interrupted, bored with the theme of the conversation; lack of money had never been a problem in her life.

Kimberley looked up at her. 'I'm sorry?'

'I'm inviting you. I'll pay. Come with me, you can stay the night at our place, we've got a spare room. Then you needn't worry about the buses and my mum can run you home in the morning.'

'Can anybody go?' asked Alan, leaning forward.

'Of course. Don't be stupid.'

'No, I meant with you two.'

'If you must,' Nadine said.

'I can't go. I've got nothing to wear, and I can't go home because that's the last bus and I wouldn't get back again.'

'Get your dad to run you in or something.'

Kimberley snorted with amusement at the very idea.

'It's not just that. I've got chores to do at home. And my mum will want her shopping. I don't think my parents would let me, actually. But thanks all the same. Maybe we could see each other some other time?'

'Fine! Okay by me. I'll give you my number. So it looks as if it's just you and me,' Nadine said to Alan.

'Perhaps another time. Take a rain-check, hey?' he said, standing up.

Nadine shrugged. 'Suit yourself. You might live to regret it,' she laughed.

'If you'll excuse me, I've got chores to do myself.' He smiled at Kimberley, and she felt her heart turn turtle. 'See you next week?' he queried tentatively.

Kimberley looked down again, taking great interest in her hands. 'That would be nice,' she said.

'Fine then, okay. Bye.' He waved and was gone.

'Oh my goodness,' said Kimberley. 'I've got his gloves. I must...' She jumped up. Nadine grabbed the sleeve of her coat and pulled her back down again.

'Don't be silly. He won't need those. Is he your bloke?'

'No, I said, we just met.'

'I'm starving, are you? Any chance of finding a hamburger joint?'

'No, but there's a mobile van over there, he does them. And hot dogs too. But count me out,' she said.

'What? Got no money?'

'Something like that.'

'I'll get them, I've got plenty.'

'Oh, I couldn't. I couldn't possibly.'

'Don't be so daft. Those that have should give to those that haven't, that's my philosophy. That and don't be cruel to animals, that's my most important philosophy.'

'And mine,' said Kimberley. 'I hate people who are cruel to animals,' she said, but looked away as into her mind's eye flashed an image of the dog sheds at her father's smallholding.

'Come on, then.'

Thomasine, shopping for yet more fruit for Nadine, fifteen minutes later, was more than perplexed to see her daughter sitting on the wall of the market-place fountain, happily chatting with a sweet-faced girl beside her, and munching, with relish, a large hamburger.

Thomasine sat at a table in the bow window of the Copper Kettle coffee shop waiting to be served. She looked about her, at the gingham table cloths, the polished copper pans hanging on the walls and the mainly middle-aged clientele chattering contentedly over their coffee and cakes. She thought, in the unlikely event of her owning such an enterprise, that she'd call it something more original, and she'd sling out the gingham for sure.

She moved the sugar bowl and pepper and salt pots into a huddle, and them moved them again, realigning them in a straight row like china soldiers. She drummed her fingers on the table and kept glancing at her watch, as if she were in a hurry. She wasn't. She had another half an hour before she was due to meet Nadine. She was restless because she was shaken.

Had anyone asked if her daughter was truthful, she'd have answered with confidence that Nadine would never lie to her. But now? Why tell her mother she was a vegetarian, why make all that fuss about food, why put her mother to so much extra trouble in the kitchen, when all the time it was just a game she was playing?

It was just that, a game, a joke. A joke she was finding difficult to understand. It couldn't be as simple as just another indication of how difficult and unpleasant her daughter had become.

And why had she changed?

The answer to that was inescapable – the divorce. The salt and pepper pots were moved around the table yet again.

Was claiming to be a vegetarian a way of getting attention? Too old now for temper tantrums, was she manipulating the adults in her life to take notice of her in this roundabout way?

If so, how sad. What had happened to their ability to communicate with each other? Had it ever existed? Had Thomasine, in the past, been kidding herself when she thought that she, Robert and their daughter were so close they could often guess what the others were thinking? Or did it just mean that Nadine was awkward and difficult? Perhaps it was a phase. Just because her daughter had reached sixteen was no reason to presume that the times of 'going through a phase' were over. Were they ever?

Still, even if it was not a cry for help but merely unpleasantness, who was to blame for that? There was no escaping the answer – her and Robert. She sighed, remarshalled the salt pot and inadvertently spilled some salt. She automatically picked up a pinch. What to wish? She looked out of the window at the shoppers milling about the market. She could wish for Nadine to be pleasanter; she smiled to herself as she thought that that was probably expecting too much of a pinch of salt. She could wish to get a good illustrating commission. Or she could wish for some romance in her life.

As if in answer to this, she suddenly saw Jim Varley striding along the pavement opposite. Ridiculously, she felt her heart quicken and she was half standing, about to rap on the window to attract his attention, when a young boy ran along the pavement towards him. He ruffled the child's hair in a practised way and swung him onto his shoulders. As he did so, a pretty, dark-haired woman appeared, and she was laughing at them both. Thomasine subsided into her seat feeling foolish, disappointed and, suddenly, very lonely. How foolish of her, of course he'd be married, an attractive fellow like him. But if he was, then where did that brittle Sophia woman fit in?

She realised she still held the pinch of salt. She flung it over her left shoulder and concentrated on wishing for a commission from a publisher instead.

'Do you mind?'

Thomasine looked up at the sound of the voice. 'Cora, how nice. Please do.'

Cora ordered her coffee and a plate of cakes. 'I shouldn't really.' She patted her very flat stomach. 'But what the hell?'

Thomasine smiled, but bleakly. Cora was as slim as a reed, probably never had to diet in her life, whereas Thomasine, to keep as slim as she was, had, out of necessity, to watch what she ate. She felt irritated by the Coras of this world.

'Hello, gorgeous.' The two women looked up, and Oliver bent to kiss Cora noisily on the cheek. 'Mind if I take a pew?' he asked, and sat down opposite Thomasine.

'Do you two know each other?' Cora asked.

'Not formally. We bumped into each other a couple of nights back, quite literally. Oliver Hawksmoor.' He held out his hand and smiled winningly.

'This is Thomasine Lambert,' Cora explained.

'Do people call you Tommy, or Tamsin?' Oliver asked.

'Neither,' replied Thomasine shortly. She had never liked people who asked if they could 'take a pew', and people who called her Tommy or Tamsin even less.

'Ah! Pity.' He smiled again and she felt he was the sort of man who was used to getting his way with that smile.

'So you've decided to move here?' asked Cora.

'If Wimpole approves.'

'Oh, really, Oliver. It's about time you got rid of that old crone. Honestly, a man of your age still clinging onto his nanny. It's wet.'

'That's right, that's me!' He shrugged his shoulders expressively and Thomasine was amazed at how unconcerned he appeared to be by the criticism, or was it an act? 'How did you know I was thinking of moving?' he asked, picking at the plate of fancy cakes Cora had ordered.

'Oliver, if you live in the country you can't burp without people knowing.'

'How's Bandage?' he asked suddenly, looking out of the window as he did so, as if he didn't want people to see his expression. But he hadn't been quite quick enough, Thomasine had caught it. She felt a quite illogical urge to make him less sad.

'Sophia's gone to visit friends in the Lakes,' Cora answered.

'Poor sods,' he said, with feeling. 'Fancy making up a party to rent a villa this summer? Tuscany, South of France, somewhere like that. You too,' he added to Thomasine. She wondered why he kept changing the conversation so abruptly, convinced it showed a very confused and floundering person. 'Do you know Sophia?' he swung round and asked Thomasine. 'Or are the saints preserving you?'

'I'm sorry?' Thomasine knew she sounded flustered. 'We met at Cora's.'

'Ah! Sad you weren't spared.'

'Oliver, you make her sound like an ogress.'

'As she is, Cora my love. As she is.'

Thomasine, seeing the time, got to her feet.

'Oh, you're not going already, I've only just got here.' And again, he flashed the practised smile.

'I must. I'm pleased to have met you, Mr Hawksmoor,' she said, formally. 'Bye, Cora.' And collecting her bags together she weaved her way across the coffee shop to the door.

'Pretty lady. What did I say to frighten her away?'

'Sometimes, Oliver, you're a little bit too smooth for your own good.'

'That's what Wimpole says. But what's a chap to do?' He grinned impishly at her.

'I like it myself,' Cora giggled, flirting lightly back.

Thomasine found Nadine still sitting on the wall of the fountain's basin.

'This is Kimberley, Mum.'

'Hello, Kimberley.'

'Can she come home with us, stay the night?'

'Of course, if she wants, but what about your parents, Kimberley?'

'You can ring them,' Nadine ordered.

'It's very kind of you, Mrs Lambert, but I must get home, my mother will be expecting me. The bus leaves in five minutes.' Kimberley smiled warmly at Nadine, who smiled equally warmly back, the first real smile Thomasine had seen since she had arrived. What a nice girl, she thought.

'Then we'll run you home, won't we, Mum?'

'Of course.'

'Then you can ask your mum if you can stay and you can pick up your toothbrush.'

'No, really. I'd best catch the bus.' Kimberley suddenly looked anxious, Thomasine thought.

'If Kimberley wants . . .' she began.

'I want to take her back,' Nadine said expansively. 'We've got plenty of time. Mum doesn't mind, do you, Mum? And I want to see where you live,' Nadine continued, with all the finesse of a Centurion tank.

They were soon bundled into the car and driving through the twisting lanes towards Primrose Acre.

'If you could drop me just along here.'

'But it's the middle of nowhere,' said Nadine, peering out of the window into the gathering dusk.

'No. My house is over there, see.' She pointed, and about a hundred yards off the road they could make out the outline of some buildings.

Thomasine halted the car and Kimberley climbed out.

'I'll come with you.' Nadine made to get out too.

'No, no. You stay here. It'll be better,' Kimberley said hurriedly.

'No, I'll come . . .'

'Nadine, stay here. Kimberley doesn't want you to go.' Thomasine intervened. They sat in the car and watched as Kimberley, carrying two shopping bags, entered a ramshackle gate and walked quickly up a driveway. They sat and waited. And waited.

'God, this is boring,' said Nadine, twiddling the knobs on the car radio.

'That radio was pre-set. It took me ages to do,' Thomasine said with exasperation.

'If you had some halfway decent cassettes, I needn't have tried . . .' Nadine said, with a smart Alec expression which, to Thomasine's horror, made her hand itch with longing to swipe her one. 'Let's go to the house and see what's going on.'

'She didn't seem to want us to.'

'Oh, come on, Mum. We can't sit here all night.'

'That's true.' Thomasine switched on the engine. They turned into the rutted lane and bounced uncomfortably along.

The front of the house looked like a junk yard, scattered with old fridges, cars and washing machines. To one side stood two large, closed sheds with corrugated roofs. Suddenly the front door of the house opened and Kimberley stood on the step, a white plastic carrier bag in her hand. A man, with equal suddenness, emerged from the shadows of the long, dark sheds. Thomasine wound down her window to greet him.

'Fuck off! We don't want your sort here,' he yelled.

'Charming,' said Thomasine.

'What a nerd!' Nadine added.

Kimberley ran down the steps. 'You shouldn't have come up here. He won't let me come, now. Please go,' she pleaded. 'Please.'

Thomasine put the car into gear and swung round, needing no second bidding.

'You're not going to leave her there?' Nadine protested.

'Too right, I am,' Thomasine said with feeling as she drove too quickly down the unmade drive.

'But she looked as if she was going to cry.'

'I know.'

'We've got to go back.'

'No way. Didn't you see? That creep was holding a shotgun!'

As they drove home, Thomasine still felt shaken up; it wasn't every day she was sent packing like that. But her paramount thought was – what had the man got to defend that needed a gun?

'Who the fuck was that?' Tom White lowered his gun, prodding his daughter into the house.

'A friend.' Kimberley wiped her feet on the doormat, trying to fight back her tears.

'You don't need friends.' Tom stepped over the mat.

'Who says?'

'I say.' He clattered across the living room in his heavy boots, leaving a trail of mud behind him, and locked his gun away in its case. Sue White hovered nervously at the table, carrying a dish in her hands, looking anxious and unsure if people wanted to eat or not.

'You can't decide my life like this. I've every right . . .'

'You've no bloody rights, not while you're living here under my roof, you haven't. I don't want no one snooping around here, isn't that clear enough? And stop that bloody snivelling.'

'They weren't snooping.' She wiped the tears from her face with the sleeve of her jumper. 'They invited me to stay the night. They were waiting for me,' Kimberley said, almost with pride, and placed the carrier bag she had been holding, containing her pyjamas and toothbrush, onto the chair.

'You don't stay with people, you know I don't allow it.'

'Allow it? I'm eighteen, I'll decide myself.' She swung round and faced her father.

'You'll do as I say.' Tom banged his large fist on the table.

'Oh, no,' sighed Sue, and collected her dish and put it back on top of the Rayburn. Her anxious expression deepened as she looked from her husband to her daughter, waiting for the row to really ignite.

'No, Dad. Not any more. It's time I began to lead my own life.' Somehow she spoke in a normal-sounding tone, but she sat down as she did. She had to for her legs would not support her.

'You what? You cheeky cow . . .' Tom leant menacingly across the table, his large face looming an inch or two away from hers.

'You're not scaring me, Dad. Not any more. I'm going to have friends, whatever you say. You needn't worry, I won't invite them here to find out your little secret.'

'What you mean, my secret?'

Kimberley jerked her head in the direction of the sheds. 'The dogs. If the authorities found out about the conditions of those dogs, you'd be closed down, fined, go to prison. And it's illegal not to have pit bulls spayed – you'd get done for that too.'

'Oh no! Don't talk like that, Kim,' Sue wailed.

'Shut up, you stupid slag,' Tom shouted at his wife. 'You threatening me?' he asked his daughter.

'No. Just stating facts.' Kimberley felt calmer now, surer of herself. So she was unprepared for the fist when it hit her on the side of the face, making her head whip from side to side, making her teeth rattle. She put her hand up. Tears of pain spurted into her eyes, tears she blinked away, determined not to give him the satisfaction of seeing her cry again. 'Don't you dare hit me!' She jumped to her feet.

'I will if I fucking well want, who the fuck do you think you are?' And he punched her again. Kimberley looked pleadingly at her mother, but Sue lowered her eyes and turned her back and put her hands over her ears so that she could not hear the sound of her husband's fist connecting with her daughter's flesh.

15

Was it cold in her room, or was it her? Kimberley felt ice cold. She lay fully clothed under the blankets and shivered. She ached from last night's beating, her head was sore, she knew her face must look an unholy mess. No room, no matter how pretty, how yellow and blue it would be, was worth this. She turned awkwardly and painfully and looked out of the window and across the flat field.

Gingerly she touched her face. It was as well it was Sunday and the Easter school holidays, so there was no chance of bumping into Alan in Morristown. He had told her where his house was and she had planned, despite there being no school, to think up some excuse to go into Morristown, to amble out that way, just on the off chance – not now, though, not looking like this. Her fingers gently explored her face; she felt the softness of the swelling, and winced with pain. She did not check herself in a mirror, she did not want to see the damage. But from what she felt, it was unlikely she could go out for several days.

A sense of isolation overwhelmed her. She could feel it behind her breastbone, a great aching lump of loneliness. Last night her mother had looked away from her agony. How often in the past had she done that? Times without number.

She lifted herself in the bed, doubled up her pillow for support, pulled the blanket up close to her chin and hugged her knees, making a ball of her body to conserve heat. She knew that it was her father's abuse of her, his assurances she'd never amount to anything, which made her work at school – to prove him wrong. But why should it matter so much to her to prove anything? He didn't love her, so why did she care? She owed him nothing – the work she did for him not only added to the abuse but negated the cost of keeping her, exonerated her from any feelings of gratitude. She should be working for herself, not for him. She should be proving to herself how good she was, and sod him.

And then there were the dogs. She inadvertently jerked her head at the thought of them, as if to remove it, but the pain of the movement merely made the thought more concrete. She had shouted at her father how cruel his neglect of the creatures was, but wasn't she just as bad? By ignoring them, pretending they weren't there, was she not just as guilty? They were there day in, day out, in their misery, and she could help them and didn't – she was as despicable as him.

Things would change. She swung her legs over the side of the bed and dug out some clean clothes from the chest of drawers. In the bathroom she switched on the infra-red heater on the wall, knowing that would annoy him into apoplexy if he knew. She washed and dressed, put witch-hazel on her bruises and avoided the mirror. She grabbed a cup of tea and then ventured out into the yard.

In the barn she found her mother. 'I'll see to the dogs,' she said.

'Would you?' Her mother smiled, but did not look at Kimberley, no doubt too ashamed to see her bruises. Kimberley ignored the smile as she took the large-headed broom from her.

'It stinks in here,' she said.

'The floor needs a good sluicing. I've been meaning to do it – but you know me and the dogs . . .' Sue's voice trailed off in apology.

'I'll see to it.' She leant over one of the concrete-floored enclosures and patted the head of a ginger-coloured corgi. 'You're new,' she said, and the dog, unsure how to respond to a kind tone, looked at her solemnly and then slowly allowed its tail to wag.

*

Thomasine had cooked scrambled eggs.

'I can't eat these. No eggs, I told you,' Nadine said.

'Eat toast then.' Thomasine scraped the egg into a bowl for an ever-expectant Luna. 'Who's a lucky girl, then, eggies for breakfast.' She placed the bowl on the floor, and Luna noisily began to lap them up.

'That dog is gross. Listen to it. It's making a disgusting noise.'

'She can't help it. If your face was squashed up like that you'd have trouble eating too. More tea?'

'And it's ludicrous, the way you talk to it – *eggies*. Really! Gross.'

'Is that the only word in your vocabulary? It's becoming tedious,' Thomasine said sharply. 'And what's wrong in talking to a dog?'

'You'll be talking to plants next.'

'I already do.' Thomasine began to scour the scrambled-egg saucepan.

'I hate it here,' Nadine said, morosely, staring out at the garden.

'So I gathered.'

'I make a friend, then her nerd of a father threatens us with a gun. I tell you, it's . . .'

'Gross! Yes, I know.' Thomasine grinned at her daughter, who did not respond. Oh, suit yourself, she thought, and would have liked to say it, but sense told her it would only make matters worse. 'What would you like to do today? I've got to drive into Shillingham to get the Sunday papers. We could have lunch at the Duck and Thistle.' Thomasine made herself sound bright and cheerful.

'Do they do vegetarian?'

'I expect so.' She turned away from her daughter, still confused at the game she was playing, the lie she was living. Perhaps she should have it out with her, tell her she'd seen her with a hamburger, but she decided against it. Nadine might be confusing and annoying her, but she loved the girl and did not want to embarrass her. 'Then we could go for a walk, take Luna across the fields, she could do with the exercise.'

Nadine looked down at Luna, who was now sitting beside her bowl in expectation that some other morsel might land there. 'No thanks. I wouldn't want to be seen dead with *that*.'

Thomasine sighed. 'Look, darling, is there something you want to discuss with me? Talk about? Is anything bothering you?'

'No.'

'Then why be like this?' Thomasine's face was screwed up with concern.

'Like what?'

'So unco-operative.'

'I'm not.'

'You are.' Thomasine shook herself: how easy it was to slip into childish tit-for-tat when arguing with her daughter. She sat down at the pine table. 'You're obviously bothered by something. It's not like you to be so offensive.'

'How would you know, you're never around to know what I'm like.'

'Nadine, don't be unfair. We discussed my moving here months ago. We talked about it ad nauseam. You agreed, you said it would be better for me to get right away from home.'

'Better for you, what about me?'

'You said you wanted to stay with your father if you had a free weekend, to be near your friends. That you wanted to stay at that school and not move to one nearer here. That you liked Chantal.' Thomasine condensed the weeks and months of discussion and worried debate into a few short sentences.

'I had no choice, did I?'

'That's not fair. Had I known you were going to be like this, I'd have stayed in London. I can move back, if you want?'

'I don't want.'

'Then what *do* you want?' Thomasine said with exasperation.

'I want to go to France with Dad and Chantal for Easter, that's what I want.'

Thomasine sat back in her chair, surprised at the sudden statement. Then the hurt came rushing in to take over from the surprise. 'You must do as you want,' she said, her voice shaky.

'I will.'

'That's all right then.'

'What will you do for Easter?' Nadine asked after a pause.

'I'll go to my sister's – as we planned,' she couldn't help adding.

'Good. You're welcome to it. I wouldn't want to go there, that's for sure, not to your sanctimonious sister's.'

'She's not that bad.'

'She is too. I shall have a lot more fun with Chantal – she's great. She understands me. After all, she's nearer to me in age.' On that parting shot, Nadine stood up and left the room, slamming the door behind her.

Thomasine felt she had just taken part in a conversation that had been pre-planned. That her responses had been part of a trap. That Nadine had purposely made herself unpleasant in the hope that Thomasine would happily let her go to France.

'Manipulative little bitch,' she said to Luna, who had been across the kitchen by her bowl at the beginning of the exchange, but had then moved and sat on Thomasine's feet, as if protecting her. 'Sorry, that's not very polite to you, is it?' She leant down and patted the dog. Oh, what of it, she thought, she'd probably be better off without her when she was like this. Perhaps her father's new set-up was all an exciting novelty. Perhaps if she fell in with Nadine's plans she would become disillusioned, that much sooner, with life with her stepmother.

It was best to think along those lines. After all, what alternative was there?

And she still had the rest of the day to get through with her recalcitrant daughter. 'Oh, hell!' she said aloud.

Jim Varley returned from the Duck and Thistle in Middle Shilling, where he had had his usual Sunday lunch. It upset Beth that he ate there, but he

ignored her objections. She already did too much for him, and he insisted
that from after lunch on Saturday until Monday morning, she was free to
come and go as she wanted. That was the theory, but soon after she had come
to work for him, he realised that she never went anywhere. Her time off was
always spent about the house – often alone, for her son was a gregarious child
who frequently stayed overnight with various little friends. These were the
times she caught up with her ironing and made the dried flower arrangements
which seemed to be her only interest, apart from her work. The sad fact
dawned on him that there was nowhere for her to go. He wondered what it
was in her past that had left her friendless. He didn't even know if she'd been
married to Harry's father. Was it something about young Harry's birth that
had caused problems ·in her life? After over a year of not asking, he felt he
was most unlikely to ask now; he had an abhorrence of people who pried.

He went in by the surgery door, through to his hospital ward, and checked
the little King Charles spaniel. The antibiotics were working well; the dog had
a more alert expression in her eyes and she scrabbled at the bars of the cage,
pleased to see a human being – another good sign.

'You're looking a lot better than you did the day before yesterday, young
woman. In fact, so much better, I think we can let you out of there and you
can come into the house. Would you like that?' He unlocked the cage and
lifted the dog out. He put her on the floor where she scratched her ears for a
moment or two, and then looked up at him expectantly. 'Come on then.'

Her claws clicking on the linoleum, she followed close at heel as he led her
through the door. In the kitchen, Beth was sitting at the table, her flower
arrangement paraphernalia spread out in front of her, and Harry was building
a Lego space station beside her.

'Nice lunch?' Beth looked up and smiled at him.

'Yes, thanks. Oliver Hawksmoor was there, he was on his own too. I nearly
suggested that we ate together, but didn't quite like to.'

'Why ever not?'

'I'm not sure. I don't know him well. I wondered, if by the time we'd had
the starter, I might find I'd made a mistake and we'd got nothing in common.
Then we'd have had to sit through the rest of the meal making polite
conversation.'

Beth laughed. 'That's logical, I suppose. Still, if everyone thought like that
no one would ever meet anyone new. I thought you knew him.'

'Oh, I know him – seen him about for years, but I don't actually *know*
him.'

Beth looked puzzled. 'What a dear little dog. What's she called?'

'This is Amy.'

'I think Amy's a silly name for a dog,' Harry ventured.

'You think of a name for her, Harry, and we'll call her that. Something
nice and short.'

Amy had climbed into the basket with Castille, Jim's old mongrel bitch, who was busily licking the new dog's face. How wonderful it would be if Amy gave her a reason for going on, he thought. He dreaded the day she was no more, for Castille had been chosen by Ann and was one of those links between the living and the dead that neither time, nor other people, can ever break.

'I hope you don't think I'm presuming . . .' Beth said diffidently, smiled, and paused as if marshalling her words. Jim felt himself stiffen fully aware that when people said that, they undoubtedly had presumed.

'What have you been up to?' He tried to sound interested rather than wary.

Beth rustled about in some papers in front of her. 'Here,' she said, handing him a sheet of his headed notepaper. 'I thought Tessa could type it up on Monday.' Neatly written was an advertisement for an assistant vet or partner. 'I put both, I wasn't sure what you wanted – a partner or not.'

He read the advert and then re-read it, not because he had not understood its content but to give him time to compose a response.

'You're cross with me, aren't you?' she asked, anxiously looking up at him.

'I'm quite capable of drafting an advert myself,' he replied shortly.

'I was only trying to help.'

'I'm aware of that.'

'You work too hard. You need some help. Ever since the vet in Shillingham retired you've been worked off your feet.' He laid the paper on the table, but did not reply. It was true, he worked too hard, but then he wanted the work, when he was busy from dawn to dusk he didn't have time to think, and that suited him – he'd learnt to be afraid of thinking too much.

'I'm sorry, Jim. You think it's none of my business, don't you?' She was standing now, working one hand in the other as if washing them with invisible soap. 'Please. I'm sorry,' she repeated. 'Do you fancy a cuppa? I've made a wonderful chocolate cake.'

'No thanks.' He turned to leave the room, not wanting to get angry with her.

'Are you cross with my mum?' asked Harry, looking up from his space station.

'Nope.' He had reached the door.

'I was only trying to help,' she said.

'Then don't,' he snapped, and walked out of the room, inadvertently slamming the door behind him, not seeing Beth slump at the table and put her head on her arms. Harry, leaving his toys, stood beside her, his small arm about her, trying to comfort her as best he could.

After Nadine's behaviour, Thomasine had no regrets about putting her on the train for London the following Wednesday. To be honest, she derived a certain amount of satisfaction from doing so; it might be spiteful and petty of her, but that was how she felt. At least she had the satisfaction of seeing that Nadine was obviously put out by this new resolve on her mother's part.

Thomasine let herself into her house, leant her back against the front door and let the peace of the empty rooms wash over her. Not for long, however, for there was an imperious banging upon the kitchen door – Luna demanding to be let out and disgruntled, no doubt, that she'd been left behind.

The welcome over, Thomasine picked up the telephone. In the night she'd realised that there was no way she could go to her sister Abigail for Easter – not with a pregnant dog who might soon go into labour.

As usual, when she telephoned, Luna sat almost on her feet. Thomasine accused her of being nosey, but all the same, she liked it and found it surprisingly comforting.

'Abigail? I've a bit of a problem. Well, a rather rotund problem actually.' Thomasine injected a carefree note into her voice whilst explaining about her new acquisition, Luna.

'So you're not coming? I must say, it's a bit late in the day,' her elder sister said in such an annoyed tone that Thomasine had no difficulty in imagining the cross face that would go with the voice.

'I'm sorry, I didn't think until last night. I'm not used to owning a dog. But I did wonder if you couldn't all come here?'

'We couldn't come. Not with the children. Not with dogs about.'

'Really, Abigail – I could understand that attitude when they were babies, but the girls are teenagers now and Fred's eight, for God's sake. I hardly think that they're going to go crawling about in the grass catching toxocariasis.'

'It's no laughing matter, Thomasine. Dogs are filthy creatures, God knows what they might pick up.'

'Did you know that you're more likely to pick up that eye infection from cat shit than from dogs?'

'Do you have to be so vulgar? I just don't want my children exposed, is that understood?'

'You know, Abigail, I feel sorry for your children. They haven't even had a normal upbringing, with your fanaticism about dirt.'

'And Nadine has? At least I've stayed with my husband.'

'That's a really bitchy thing to say.'

'Good, I meant it to be.' And not giving Thomasine the chance of another word she slammed the receiver down.

Thomasine, sighing, replaced her own. Luna put her head on her knee and looked at her sorrowfully.

'Oh, Luna. What a week I'm having. First Nadine, and now my sister. Still, I didn't really want to go anyway. How about you and I go for a – ' She did not say the word, merely thought it. This was her new game with the dog, and sure enough, Luna lifted her head from Thomasine's knee, waddled towards the cupboard where she knew her lead hung and looked expectantly at her, as if saying, 'Come on!'

Oliver had finally decided to let the house in London. In the present market he'd wait forever to move to the country, if he persisted in trying to sell it. He was surprised how quickly tenants were found, and after that the move from London went more smoothly than he had dared hope. He had to thank Sophia, and the burglar, in some part, since they had removed so much from the house that one small pantechnicon was quite sufficient for what was left.

He found sorting through his books and papers a sobering task. He sat cross-legged on the floor of Phoebe's Great Hall, the one he was turning into his own writing room, sorting through his life. From his baptismal certificate, school reports, old love letters from girls he could now barely remember, the order of his wedding service to a copy of Aunt Phoebe's will, there it all was – his life. Houses bought and sold. Cars pranged. Tailors' bills and bank statements galore. All rather boring really. Not what a member of the SAS would collect together, or a captain of industry, or a mass murderer even. He sat back, leaning on a sofa for support. It was all quite frightening; forty-five next birthday, over half his life gone almost without him noticing. He was physically fit, mentally alert, he'd a full head of hair, his own teeth, and so the years had slipped by without his body warning him that time was zapping past. He really must be a thoughtless prat, he decided, not to think about it before, and to need boxes of old papers to tell him.

It made what Sophia was up to easier to understand. Had she opened a box and viewed her life and thought this isn't right, I'm not as happy as I might be, I'm going out on my own to see what I can find?

If she had, it was brave of her. Would he have had the courage to do the same if she hadn't pushed him into a new existence? He felt in his pocket for his cigarettes. He looked at them – well, there was resolution number one, if he gave up the weed perhaps he'd have longer to enjoy this second chance. Yes, that was what it was he was being given, a second go at living.

He'd never liked making decisions, always preferred them to be made for him; on that score he was changing already. He'd decided to move, give up his job, start writing and give up smoking. He was quite proud of himself, if quite surprised also.

While in this mood, perhaps he'd better think of what other decisions he would like to make. He had all the material possessions he could possibly need, so what could he decide on? Success. He wanted to become well known as a writer so that he had something to leave behind when he died; since he had no children his books would take their place. He'd always been disciplined in his job, so working out a routine for writing would not be difficult.

It was sad he'd not had children. When with Sophia he had accepted the situation unquestioningly. It was odd that he should think about it now he was on his own. Odd after all this time that he should be saddened by it.

Did he want to get married again? No! He shuddered at the very idea. Imagine if it all went wrong again and he had to go through this sort of upheaval another time. He'd take things as they came; if a woman should happen into his life, he'd go for it, but he'd explain that he didn't want to get too involved and that marriage was not on his mind. And if someone came along he hoped she'd be disorganised and reasonable, instead of capable and bossy like Sophia.

'What on earth are you doing sitting in here in the dark?' Wimpole noisily entered the room.

'Thinking.'

'Dodgy thing to do – thinking. If you're not careful it'll give you the heebie-jeebies.'

'Maybe I haven't done enough of it in the past. Perhaps if I had I wouldn't be having to start over again at my age.'

'Your age? You're a spring chicken. Don't you go talking like that – you sound like a menopausal old crow. Where did you put the whisky?'

'Box – kitchen. I'd like one too.'

'It's too early for you.'

'You're as bossy as Sophia.'

'Do you have to be so rude?' She grinned at him before disappearing to get a drink.

He'd been surprised at how enthusiastically Wimpole, once she had finally taken the decision to move into the country, had thrown herself into the preparations. She'd even been to the local bookshop and bought a pile of gardening books, declaring she was going to grow her own vegetables, and he needn't laugh at the idea.

All he needed was to get Bandage back and all would be well. He'd try to get hold of Sophia later this evening, threaten her with legal action if she didn't return the dog. She'd had him nearly six weeks now, it was a ridiculous state of affairs. And then, for no apparent reason, he found himself thinking about that nice woman Thomasine, and if she was married and to whom and, if not, what her telephone number was?

Jim felt wary of Beth. Her wanting to organise his life had, in some strange way, changed everything. As he drove along he argued with himself, back and forth. It was kind of her to be concerned for his well-being and to suggest he needed a second vet – that was one argument. The other was that *he* would decide if he needed assistance, and it was none of her business.

He tried very hard to latch onto the first argument, but kept coming back to the second one and finding he felt happiest with that. Happy he might be, but not comfortable with it, for Jim was not an unkind man and would crawl a mile rather than hurt anyone.

He did what he often did when upset and needing peace and a chat. He drew up in front of Oakleigh kennels. Eveleigh invited him in, as always, with a welcoming smile, and the malt whisky bottle was produced from the sideboard without her even asking.

He sat in the wing chair, its seat comfortably sagging, its arm-rests worn bare from use, and looked about the untidy room and felt at home in it, as he always did. His own home was too tidy, he often thought. So tidy he could waste hours of precious time looking for things if Beth was out. When Ann had been alive they'd had a friendly clutter like this, they'd both been far too busy in their work to be houseproud.

'Thanks, Eveleigh, you always have a malt ready.'

'What sort of friend would I be if I ran out?' She raised her glass to him. 'What shall we drink to?'

He thought a while. 'Dogs and friendship,' he replied.

'The two most important things in the world.'

'Good Lord, that isn't – ' He pointed to the top of a corner cupboard.

'One of Beth's flower arrangements? Yes. She turned up here the other day with it. Rather sweet of her I thought.'

'I loathe them – dead things.' He shuddered.

Eveleigh's laugh was one of relief. 'I couldn't agree with you more, but what could I do? I had to accept it – but I put it right up there out of the way. She's a nice woman.'

Jim didn't answer.

'Is there something wrong, Jim?'

He looked at the whisky in his glass long and hard before speaking. 'Have you got over Reggie dying yet, Eveleigh?'

'I don't think I ever will. Does one? We were together for twenty years – I was only nineteen when we married, I'd grown up with him, you see – that is if one ever does, grow up I mean.'

'How long has it been?'

'Five long years, Jim. Does it get better? In a way, yes – you don't stop mourning or forgetting, but you get used to living with it. It's like a backdrop of sadness to my life, and I can't remember any longer what it was like to live without it. That, of course, is a blessing.'

'People say I should be over Ann by now.'

'Who are they to say? What do they know? It has to be different from person to person. It must depend on what your relationship was like. There can't be a chart that says your heart is mended this month in this year. What rubbish people say.'

'I just feel – well, if I met someone else at the moment I'd feel so guilty. I know I would.'

'I understand that, but such feelings pass,' she said, a shade wistfully, and looked up at him, but he was looking down, studying his hands.

'She was so young. Such a shock. I mean, one minute she was vibrant, alive, the next – ' He slammed one hand into the fist of the other.

'I think a sudden death, as we have both had to bear, has to be harder. The shock of it alone. I had always assumed Reggie would die before me – he was, after all, twenty-five years older. I'd imagined he would one day be ill and I would care for him and that I would be given time to adjust to the concept of being without him, and then the crash – I didn't expect that. So cruel.'

They sat either side of the fireplace, both deep in thought, both locked mentally into their own private sadness.

Then Eveleigh wondered if the 'people' he spoke about had been Beth. She had long ago sensed that Beth was in love with Jim; nothing had been said, but when she spoke about him Beth's face became more animated and she who rarely smiled did so. Others might think it a suitable match, but Eveleigh was not so sure. Beth, she believed, tolerated animals but would never be involved with them as Jim was. There was always the risk that as a one-parent family she was searching for security and not love. And lastly, Eveleigh thought her far too dim for Jim. At this she shook her head to stop such reasoning – it was not becoming.

'I'm glad you came by today, Jim. I've had the most extraordinary letters.' She stood up and from behind an ornament on the mantelshelf she took down a stack of papers. 'My filing system,' she said half laughing. 'Look, this is the first one, you see. It's from a firm of solicitors offering to buy this place.' Jim took the letter and quickly read it. 'Of course I replied saying it was not for sale. Then I received this one.' She thrust that forward too.

'They've upped the price by ten thousand pounds. Good God! And they don't say why they're interested? How odd.'

'Isn't it? I must say I'm a bit concerned – the land the other side of the fields behind was sold a couple of months back, I'm wondering if it's something to do with that, but I can't think what.'

'Have you replied to this one?'

'Not yet, I thought I'd talk to you first.'

'Then I suggest you write something along the lines of – you cannot proceed with any further correspondence unless you know firstly, who is offering, and secondly, why. At least then you'll know what it's about.'

'Bless you, Jim.' She accepted her letters back and smiled at him with deep affection, but he did not notice, since he was getting to his feet and saying he must be off.

And so he left without saying what it was he'd come for. He'd wanted Eveleigh's advice about Beth; was he imagining she was taking over his life? Should he get rid of her? If so, how? But when it came to it, for some odd reason, he found he couldn't raise the subject. As he drove home he wished he had.

16

On Easter Saturday Sadie sat upright in a large basket, watching her puppies frolicking on the floor around it. The imperious expression on her face would have made anyone think twice before touching them. Justin had erected a barricade of sorts around the area to keep them from wandering into the main part of the salon and, heaven forbid, getting trampled on.

'We're rushed off our feet with Easter bookings. There was no way we could leave them at home on their own and we both needed to be here,' Gill explained in a somewhat bored tone of voice. He had repeated the explanation at least a dozen times that day – so far.

'What are they called?' his client asked.

'We haven't named them – just numbers one, two, three, four … If we gave them names we'd never let them go to their new homes, for sure! Except for the one we're keeping, and that's Sukie.'

'Sweet.'

'Blissful, isn't it?' Gill waved his comb in the air, finished his teasing of her hair and with the dexterity of a magician, flashed a mirror to show her his handiwork at the back.

'Next,' he called as, with a click of his fingers, he indicated to their new assistant she should tidy up from the last client. 'Mrs Brenton. Just the person,' he said as Eveleigh, her hair already shampooed by Gill's assistant, took her seat.

'It's kind of you to fit me in. I know how busy you are, Gill. But I didn't know until yesterday I'd been invited out.'

'For an old friend, no problem.'

'Did you sort out the stud fee with the owner you were having problems with?' she asked.

'What, grumpy old Martin? We did exactly what you advised – wrote a cheque for the amount you suggested and popped in a covering letter saying that it was in full and final settlement – tickety boo. Worked like a charm. And we haven't heard a word from him – right scum bag.'

'That's a lovely pup you've chosen from the litter.'

'You think so? Honest?'

'That one especially. Have you thought about entering her for the Spillers Puppy of the Year?'

'No. Should we?'

'Why not?'

'You're our dogs' fairy godmother, Mrs Brenton, make no mistake. Of course we're aiming for Crufts again once the showing season gets going. Are you?'

'I've a good St Bernard bitch, Brünnhilde, and dear Lohengrin of course.'

'In with a chance?'

'One's always in with that, Gill. But you can never be sure. There's such a large element of luck involved. It all depends on the day and how the dog is feeling – the weather affects some dogs and makes them frisky or grumpy, just like humans. And then there's the judge – what side of the bed did he get out of and what's his preference.'

'Or who was he in bed with, you might ask?' Gill laughed. 'I thought judges weren't supposed to favour one breed over another. That they just judged best of.'

'Sometimes it's easier said than done. After all, we've all got soft spots for our own particular breeds. Would you swop your poodles for my St Bernards?'

'No offence, but – '

'Exactly.'

He worked a minute in silence. 'Just think if our Sadie or Sukie became Supreme Champion at Crufts!' he said.

'And why not?'

'Dreams, dreams! Justin says I'm a fool with my dreams.'

'We all need those,' Eveleigh said, rather sadly.

'Now don't you get all gloomy. Think positively, I always say, and it might just have a chance of happening.'

'Next,' he called, once he'd seen Eveleigh on her way. A tiny woman with red hair slipped into the seat she had vacated. 'New here?' he asked politely.

'We've just moved to Lower Shilling. We lived on the other side of Morristown but –' she paused, her expression seeming to crumble from the bright, smiling face she'd first presented him with. 'We had to move –' Her eyes filled with tears. Gill, sensing a confidence was about to be spilled, flicked his fingers and ordered the assistant to get them coffees.

'Tell Gill,' he said comfortingly, turning back to his new client.

What always annoyed Jim Varley was that on Friday nights, and the eve of any big holiday, the surgery was nearly always empty. Yet come Monday, or the day after a holiday, it would be crammed – just like a GP's surgery, he'd discovered when he'd confided this phenomenon to his doctor. No patients, canine or otherwise, were ill when it would be inconvenient, they decided. Of course that didn't mean that on Easter Sunday, Christmas Day, or the vet's birthday, just as they sat down to eat, they'd not be called out. He could even lay bets on what it would be – a dog sick from gorging. On Easter Sunday it was invariably chocolate eggs. They should carry a health warning that chocolate was bad for dogs. On Christmas day it was nearly always a turkey bone stuck in its gullet. And on his birthday – well, it could be anything.

Here it was, Easter Saturday, and Jim was driving back from Ben's. He wondered what the next two days would bring. He was also feeling disgruntled. Not because he'd been called out to the hunter Ben was worrying about – convinced it had colic, unnecessarily it transpired, all that was needed was a minor adjustment to the horse's diet. No, it was Sophia who had put Jim in this mood.

When she had appeared, he'd looked at her admiringly: she was certainly an attractive woman, especially in her riding gear. She was, however, the type of woman who made Jim feel uncomfortable. He was not used to dealing with women, he'd been married too long and too happily to maintain any skill at flirting. And he'd been in mourning too long even to want to. But he was not so stupid as to be unaware that Sophia was flirting with him; but was it just games she was playing, or did she mean it?

Jim was watching her leaning on the gate, her backside pertly outlined in the skin-tight jodhpurs she wore, rubbing herself against the gatepost very suggestively. He longed to tell her it reminded him of a cow scratching its rear against a hedge, but refrained. She ran her long-fingered hands slowly up and down her thigh. And her hand rested just a second too long against his on the top bar of the gate. Once she'd have been called a prick-tease; he supposed that was politically incorrect now.

'Penny for them?' She smiled at him.

'What? Oh, not a lot – just thinking about a cow.' He grinned.

'How bizarre.'

'Hardly. It's my job.'

Later he could not remember how, as they talked of this and that, the conversation had got on to the subject of Thomasine Lambert.

'Oh, that woman,' Sophie spat out. 'You know she's set her cap at Oliver? He can't move without her mooning about after him.' There was not so much to find attractive in her face now, spite had wiped it all away.

He felt anger at her for speaking of Thomasine in such a dismissive way, but it was swamped by disappointment that Oliver had got there first. He should have plucked up the courage to call on her, to invite her out for a drink, and now it would be too late.

This was not the only thing making him fed up. He was not looking forward to getting home. The atmosphere there had changed. He realised he had been short with Beth over the advertisement she had wanted to place in the journal, but he felt her reaction to his reaction was over the top. She did her work just as before, he had no complaints about that. It was the way she did it that bothered him; there was a lot of banging and crashing of pots, pans, brooms and Hoovers which reminded him of how his mother had indicated noisy displeasure with his father. Her work appeared to be done more quickly and, he noticed, some things were no longer done – his sock drawer, which she always arranged for him, was now a terrible muddle. She no longer cleaned his boots nor washed his hairbrushes. She was telling him something, but what? After all, it was finally his decision whether he took on a partner or not. And why was he so bothered? Was his reaction a sort of smoke screen? Was it, perhaps, he didn't want to share his practice with anyone now Ann was gone?

The last thing he expected to see as he walked into his kitchen was Beth in tears.

'What is it, Beth? Do you want to tell me?'

'I can't, I'm too ashamed.' She was sitting at the kitchen table, tears pouring down her cheeks. He'd never seen her cry before and suddenly felt awkward and clumsy, unsure what he should do or say. He didn't have the practice, he couldn't remember ever seeing Ann cry. So he stood, wondering if he should do something. Then a particularly loud sob made him put his arm about her, which only seemed to make matters worse as an even greater sob shook her body.

'Beth, it can't be as bad as all that,' he said kindly.

'It is, Jim. It's worse. I'm so afraid.'

'Then I think I should know why, don't you?' He crossed to the dresser and took down his bottle of malt and poured two large measures. 'Here, that is what you need.'

'I hate whisky,' she managed a watery smile.

'Then pinch your nose and pretend it's medicine – it'll calm you. Your friendly vet is telling you.' He sat down and placed his large, capable hand over her small but equally capable one. 'What's up, Beth?'

She took a deep breath and looked wildly about her, as if checking that no one else was listening. 'It's my husband.' She gulped. 'He's out of prison – been let out on parole, for good behaviour.' She snorted derisively at that. Jim sat stunned as he assimilated all these facts. He had not known Beth had been married, let alone to a jailbird.

'Is that bad?' he asked, and thought even as he spoke what an asinine question it was.

'Oh yes. He's vowed to kill me.' At this dramatic statement she began to weep again, but in earnest now. If Jim had thought she was crying before, he'd seen nothing compared with this. There seemed nothing he could do but let her cry, so he sat, patting her and stroking her hair until the storm had passed.

'Harry's not his, you see,' she finally said.

'Ah!' said Jim, for want of any other word, but reeling now and wondering how many more shocks Beth was about to deliver. She sat for some time gazing into space and then, almost with a jolt, launched herself into speech.

'He raped my best friend, you see, and to get back at him, I slept with his best friend. And got myself pregnant.'

'Are you sure Harry's not his?'

'Oh yes. I waited until he was inside.'

'Ah, well.' Jim looked wildly about the kitchen, hoping for inspiration.

'I had a letter from my aunt – she says he's going to find me and kill me.'

'Will he? I mean, people say stuff like that and don't mean it.'

'He does.'

'How does he know about Harry?'

'I told him. That was the whole point of sleeping with his friend, wasn't it?'

'I'm a bit out of my depth here, I'm afraid.' He tried laughing, not altogether successfully. How simple his own life with Ann had been, compared with a web like this. 'Can he find you? Would your aunt tell?'

'I don't think so.'

'Then don't worry. He'd have to get past me first.'

'Jim, you are a love.' Beth blew into a piece of handy kitchen paper. 'I know you've been angry with me. I know you think I went too far over organising you.'

'I wouldn't go so far – '

'Yes, you do. I've been so scared you'd ask me to go.'

'What on earth made you think that?' he said, having the grace to look embarrassed.

'I wouldn't have blamed you. I'd have understood – but now, with this hanging over my head . . .'

'Don't worry, Beth. It'll be all right. No one's going to hurt you,' he said, and as he did so he had the feeling that he was rapidly getting into problems he could well do without.

'Bless you, Jim. I'll do anything for you – anything.'

'That won't be necessary, Beth. Please!' He felt confused as he disentangled her arms from around him.

For the last few days Luna had had trouble climbing the spiral stairs to Thomasine's bedroom – her stomach was now so large she rolled like a drunken sailor when she walked. Not only was the effort too much for her, but it was too dangerous. So Thomasine had been sleeping on the sofa in her drawing room with Luna beside her in her basket – even getting to the comfort of the sofa was now too much for the bitch. It seemed as if she needed to be as close to Thomasine as possible at all times. She'd been told that when the time came Luna would become restless and would start to build herself a nest. Thomasine smiled as she looked down at the sleeping bitch. There was little activity there.

They were both in a small room that led off the kitchen, which, with its large windows, tiled floor and shelving had been intended as a conservatory, but which instead made an ideal workroom – Thomasine did not like to call it a studio, that seemed to be far too pretentious. The table beside her and the desk with its sloping top, like an architect's, were both covered in open books with illustrations of dogs. Thomasine was drawing a St Bernard. Or rather Thomasine was failing to draw a St Bernard. For several days she'd been occupied with this task, but each attempt looked wooden and insubstantial, and the wastepaper basket was full of this morning's rejects. She was trying to draw for Fee Walters' manuscript which, at her suggestion, she had sent to the one editor Thomasine knew. The woman had immediately shown interest in it and suggested Thomasine submit a couple of full-page colour illustrations. If she was successful, it could be the lucky break she needed, for this would be a lavishly illustrated children's book about a group of St Bernards. As she sketched she could not stop the dreams of becoming another E. H. Shephard to another A. A. Milne from floating about in her head. She'd enjoyed reading the book, and with her new-found interest in dogs, she felt she was in a better position to try to illustrate it than she might have been before Luna entered her life.

The latest effort was screwed up. This was hopeless, she could not get it right, perhaps it would be better to pack it in for this afternoon and try again tomorrow, she thought. She'd her household accounts to do, long overdue.

The paints set aside, she took down the shoebox in which she kept bills and receipts – how Robert would sneer at her filing system!

Luna moved onto her back so that her huge stomach rose like an inflated balloon. Thomasine watched her stomach, saw the rippling effect made by the puppies kicking inside.

'It must be hell in there, poor lady,' she said softly, and one large brown eye opened, regarded her for a second, and then closed. Luna had such a contented expression on her face that Thomasine could almost believe she was smiling.

Thomasine returned to her figures. An hour later she wished she hadn't begun. Maths had never been her strong point, but one did not have to be a mathematician to see that she was heading for a financial crisis.

Economise, but where? she asked herself. She did not live an extravagant life, rarely going out, only the odd pub lunch, and she'd bought no new clothes for ages. The move had been expensive, but still, where was the money going?

She began to break the figures down and made columns of sums – household, utilities, car and, at the last minute, she remembered to add a column for Luna's expenses.

Further into her calculations she reached the uncomfortable conclusion that she did not have enough money coming in to keep going as she was. She had written down an approximate figure of what she hoped to earn from her illustrations. The numbers jumped off the page as the realisation dawned that she would have to be producing illustrations like a conveyor belt, and far more than the market would ever demand of her, to make ends meet. It would take years for her to be recognised and be top notch – if she ever was. Maybe Robert had been right all along when he referred to her 'pin money'.

What other alternatives did she have? To get a job was the obvious, but doing what? She faced, bleakly, the prospect that there was little she could do – she had a minor painting talent, she could cook, sew, clean a house. That was all. She couldn't type, so office work was out; she had difficulty enough adding these figures up, so she wouldn't be much good in a shop. All she'd ever been was a housewife, she was trained for nothing else. She felt panic beginning to rise. Calm down, think logically, she told herself.

There was Robert, of course. She could pocket her pride and tell him she'd been mistaken and that she needed his help after all. But that meant confessing she'd been stupid in the first place, not working out a sensible budget – he would have. She looked up sharply – he no doubt already had! He'd have known exactly what her shares earned. He'd have asked publishing friends what she could earn with her illustrations. He'd already know she couldn't manage! The bastard! She mouthed the words. But why? To prove himself right yet again? To show he was still important to her? God knew. Well, she wouldn't give him the satisfaction. She'd find something to do. She was fit and strong – she'd do *anything* before she went begging to him.

And then she suddenly thought of the puppies. If she sold them, that would help. But what if they were ugly mongrels? Be optimistic, she thought, pray for bulldog pups.

The front door bell rang. Luna stirred, but showed no inclination to accompany her. Thomasine patted her head before walking from her work-room and through the kitchen, shutting the door behind her.

'Good afternoon?' she said enquiringly to the middle-aged couple on her doorstep. The woman was small of body, and features too; her face – which might have been pretty if her expression were not so strained – was surrounded by beautifully styled, naturally red hair. Her husband stood ramrod straight, white-haired and moustached, and so smartly turned out that Thomasine would have bet what little she had that he was ex-Army.

'Mrs Lambert?' he asked.

'Yes, I am,' she replied in the unsure way of one who, while knowing who she was, was unsettled as to why these strangers should enquire.

'I wonder if we might have a word?'

Thomasine stood holding the door, uncertain how to proceed. These people looked far too respectable to be burglars or mass murderers, she thought. The wife was far too nervous, the way she kept clutching and unclutching her gloved hands. But on the other hand, why was she so nervous? One could never be sure these days . . .

'I assure you we mean no harm,' the man said, as if reading her thoughts, and Thomasine felt ridiculously embarrassed at being caught out.

'I was thinking no such thing,' she laughed, perhaps a little too heartily. 'Come in, do.'

She ushered them into her drawing room and smilingly accepted their fulsome admiration of her house.

'Amazing what these architect chappies can do, isn't it?' her male visitor commented.

They all agreed, and Thomasine wondered if she should be offering them something to drink, but decided to wait to see what it was they wanted.

'Ronnie, you haven't introduced us. I'm Sally Tregidga, and this is my husband, Major Tregidga.' Sally spoke in a soft, pleasant voice.

'Cornish?' Thomasine asked. 'My sister lives near Penzance.' This was a mistake, for it encouraged the major, who was not as soft-spoken as his wife, to launch into an explanation of his Cornish antecedents. Thomasine could hear the clicking of Luna's claws on the kitchen quarry tiles.

'Ronnie, I think we should explain to Mrs Lambert . . .' Sally's voice trailed off, and she glanced at the kitchen door, at which Luna was now scratching.

'My dog,' Thomasine explained. 'She's dreadfully nosey.'

'It's like this, Mrs Lambert. It's difficult to know where to start, but . . .' He took a deep breath, as if in preparation of a long speech to come.

'Is the dog a bulldog?' Sally interrupted.

'Why, yes.'

'A fawn one?'

'Would you like to see her?' Thomasine asked, realisation dawning. No doubt they'd heard Luna was about to have puppies and perhaps they wanted one. She cheered up enormously at the prospect of a sale.

'No, Mrs Lambert. Not for the moment. I think it's best if we explain first.' The major held his hand up, palm towards her, like a traffic policeman. His voice rumbled on and Luna continued to batter at the door.

'We think, or rather we hope, you might have *our* bulldog,' Sally explained abruptly, interrupting her husband's flow.

Thomasine felt her stomach contract and had to sit down quickly. 'Yours? But I . . .' She wanted to say *I love her*, but stopped herself.

'You found her, we were told,' Sally continued anxiously. 'Abandoned on the by-pass by some brute.'

'That's right. But I'd need proof.'

'We have photographs.' Sally began to delve into her handbag, which she immediately dropped on the floor, the contents spilling everywhere. Flustered, she went down on all fours scooping up her possessions.

'Sally, darling, try to calm down, do. Let's explain a little more to Mrs Lambert, shall we? Our dog – a bitch – was stolen from our front garden in March.'

'It was all my fault. We never let her out the front unless one of us was watching her. We'd been warned by her breeder that bulldogs are so often stolen, they're so valuable and – oh, I can't even think about it, let alone say it.'

'Unscrupulous breeders,' the major explained for her.

'But the telephone rang and I left her – less than five minutes. But when I went back, she'd gone – '

'We posted rewards and put adverts in the papers – '

'We drove and drove around searching. It was such a desperately sad time – '

'But we had no luck, not one sighting, until this morning when my wife went to a new hairdresser – Snippers, I think it's called, and the young man said you had found one.'

'Gill,' Sally explained, nervously patting her hair. 'And he said it was about March time.'

'That's right.'

'Obviously you'd need proofs. Well, we've been listing them. She's got one crooked front tooth.'

'The vet said that was common in bulldogs,' Thomasine replied sharply.

'She's pregnant. The puppies are due Easter Monday,' Sally said. Thomasine was clutching her cardigan to her, for she felt suddenly cold in the heated room. Luna continued to scratch at the door in a demanding tattoo.

'Her nose, she's a little dip in the black pigment on the right nostril – a bit of skin fell off last summer. I always said it was sunburn,' Sally said, desperately trying to smile.

'I haven't noticed,' Thomasine answered honestly.

'She has an odd number of teats. Five pairs and then one on its own – eleven in all.'

Thomasine clutched the cardigan closer. She had noticed that. She often counted them to make sure she wasn't mistaken. Hadn't she counted them only this morning? Luna was, by now, hurling herself at the door. Thomasine stood and walked towards it, afraid Luna might harm herself, but aware what the battering meant.

'Here, I've found them, the photographs!' Sally was holding them out to her.

'Somehow I don't think they're necessary,' Thomasine said, opening the door and Luna, despite her size, despite her swollen stomach, raced into the room, scampering across the parquet, skidding this way and that, yelping, barking, and with frenzied leaps jumped onto the sofa and hurled herself onto Sally, who disappeared under a hail of long, pink-tongued licks of welcome.

Sally was in tears, the major found it necessary to blow his nose, and Thomasine watched the reunion as ice settled around her heart. There was no doubt, she did not need the photographs, but they proved conclusively that the Tregidgas were Luna's rightful owners.

Now Thomasine heard that she was two and a half, had been mated with another bulldog – no mongrels for Luna – and that her name was Fengie.

'Short for Fengari – the Greek for moon,' the major explained. 'It was a full moon the night she was born.'

'Isn't that extraordinary, I called her Luna – Latin for moon,' Thomasine managed to say, her throat aching with crushed tears.

Luna, having licked Sally, was now reintroducing herself to the major, who Thomasine noted with approval did not, despite his immaculate suit, seem to mind. From the shopping bag they had with them, he produced a threadbare cuddly toy which might once have been a bulldog, but which now was difficult to identify.

'Her comforter, she's had it since she was a puppy,' the major, with a hint of embarrassment, explained.

Now Thomasine learned that so great had been their sense of loss that they had had to move house to get away from the memories.

'Weren't you worried she might one day return? Don't dogs travel great distances to get home?'

'Our daughter and her husband took over the house so we knew there would be someone there. Sally could not stay, not with the memories.'

'We even had to sell the three-piece suite – I kept finding her hairs and every time I did . . .' Sally flapped her hand at the horrific memory, though now tears of happiness were rolling down her cheeks.

The major searched in his inside pocket and produced a cheque book. 'We were offering a reward,' he explained as he took the top off his pen.

'No, please, I couldn't.' Thomasine put her hand on his to stop him. 'It's been a pleasure, she was a joy to have with me.' She stopped speaking for the simple reason she was too choked to continue.

'There must have been expenses – the vet, baskets, food.' The major waited patiently as Thomasine took a deep breath before she could continue.

'I haven't had the vet's bill yet, he was waiting until she whelped. The rest was nothing.'

Luna now lay contentedly sprawled half across Sally and half on the sofa. Thomasine wanted them to go now, this was more than she could bear.

'She's got some toys she's used to and a lead.' She hurried into the kitchen and leant against the sink, taking deep breaths, trying to calm herself. You never wanted the dog, this is the perfect solution, she tried to tell herself, but with little success. She didn't want Luna to go, she loved her, she needed her. She wouldn't let her go, what was that saying? 'Possession is nine tenths of the law'. They might be nasty about it, but she'd say 'see you in court' – though how she was to afford that would remain to be seen.

She returned to the drawing room with resolution. Luna slid off the sofa and waddled towards her and, with difficulty, jumped on her hind legs and pawed her. Thomasine bent down and nuzzled the dog's massive head. Luna licked her ear, nudged her as she often did and turned and lumbered back to Sally and sat at her feet, resting her back against her shins and looking as if she was smiling.

Thomasine felt as if the dog had just said goodbye to her. She looked at Luna, at her obvious happiness, and knew she could not part her from her family again.

Sally, as if sensing her distress, got to her feet, crossed the room and put her hand on Thomasine's shoulder. 'Thank you so much for caring for her for us,' she said. 'We're only in Lower Shilling, you can come any time you want to see her and the puppies.'

'I don't think I could do that.' Thomasine stood rigid.

'Do you want us to go?'

'Please,' she said bleakly.

The major did not bother to clip on Luna's lead as Sally collected her belongings and they moved towards the front door. 'If you're sure . . .'

'I'm sure,' Thomasine said, knowing she was losing the battle with her tears.

The front door opened and shut. Thomasine, who had felt rooted to the spot, suddenly rushed to the door and opened it as the couple, with Luna waddling between them, walked down the path. They turned and waved, almost apologetically. Luna did not look back.

May–June

17

Sophia returned late one evening from her visit to Yorkshire and swept into her father's house in the proprietorial way which always irritated Cora.

'You will stay, won't you, Sophia dear?' Cora asked, all smiles, for Cora was an expert in covering up how she really felt.

'Thank you, Cora, but no,' she said, but her returning smile was a quick, slick, professional one, a mere twitch of the bright scarlet-glossed lips. A smile which anyone else but Cora would have realised was only a polite tic.

'Are you sure? Well, have some supper before you go.' Cora continued to beam as she invited her, and such apparent generosity of spirit made Sophia seethe.

'No thank you. I've just come to pick Bandage up and I'll get straight on,' she managed to say in a reasonable tone. 'You eat too much in this house,' she added, as if she couldn't help herself, allowing a little of her edginess to show.

'Do we?' said Cora, puzzled, since she ate like a bird and constantly watched Ben's diet, since there was little she could do about his alcohol intake.

'I don't like the idea of you out in that car on these roads late at night,' Ben said to his daughter benignly, totally unaware of the undercurrent of unpleasantness Sophia had managed to build up in five minutes.

'Don't be silly, Daddy. You fuss too much. As if anyone's going to do anything to me with Bandage on board! Isn't that so, Bandage?' Bandage, who was lying contentedly in front of the log fire, appeared to be asleep, but one eye was very slightly open, sufficient to monitor the scene, but not enough to be noticed. His white socked paws did not move. His black, shiny chest rose and fell rhythmically.

'That flaming dog does nothing but sleep,' said Sophia. 'I can't think why Oliver wants him so much. He's so boring. He could at least have a dog that does something interesting.'

'Sophia, what a thing to say! Bandage is an absolute sweetheart. I've grown very attached to him. I said to Ben, if Sophia or Oliver don't want him, we'll have him.'

Sophia swung round and looked at her stepmother with an exasperated expression. 'I explained to you both, I want the dog for my protection in London. There is no question of my giving him away. If I'd given him away to anybody, it would have been Oliver, wouldn't it?'

'But I thought you already had?' said Cora, the fount of all innocence.

'Cora!' Sophia said, teetering close to losing her temper. She resisted the urge; she was fully aware how besotted her father was with this stupid woman.

'You owe me one, Sophia. I lied to Oliver for you.'

'What lie, Cora?'

'I told him Bandage had gone to Yorkshire with you. That you'd be gone two weeks. He kept calling.'

'I didn't ask you to lie for me.'

'What else was I supposed to do?'

'What do you want from me? Eternal thanks?' Sophia asked. 'Come on, Bandage.' And she kicked Bandage on his rump with her boot. Bandage leapt up, turned, and seeing it was Sophia, sat down. 'Bandage, come along, we're going now. Where's its lead?'

Ben fetched Bandage's lead, which Sophia clipped on to the choke chain round his neck. 'Thanks, Dad. Bye, Cora, *dearest*.' Again they went through the ritual of the smiles and Sophia pulled at Bandage's lead. The dog, not wishing to leave the fire, pulled in the opposite direction. 'Bandage, do as I tell you,' she said, crossly. But Bandage had no intention of doing what she said. He pushed his front paws into the Turkey rug and resisted with all his might. And all his might was far too much for Sophia. 'Dad, help me, will you? Kick him up the backside, or something.'

'He doesn't want to go, he likes it here,' said Ben, with a degree of satisfaction.

'He's not staying here, Dad, is that understood? He's coming with me.' Whereupon she took a copy of the *News of the World*, which happened to be lying on the coffee table, rolled it up, waggled it under Bandage's nose, and Bandage, frightened of nothing in the world except a rolled-up newspaper, stood up and followed her like a little lamb, out to the hall, click, click, click, his nails echoing Cora's high-heeled shoes clicking on the stone floor. Bundled into the back of the car, he lay down and promptly went back to sleep.

An hour and a half later Sophia parked outside her new house. She prodded Bandage awake and dragged the reluctant and still sleepy dog inside the house. In the hallway she opened a side door which led into the garage, littered with the remains of Oliver's furniture, for which there was no room in the house.

'Your days of sleeping in the house are over,' she said. 'You sleep there, is that understood?' She pointed at his basket, which was already in situ in a corner. Bandage looked at it too, but did not move towards it. She filled his water bowl and shook a few biscuits into his other bowl, switched off the light, slammed the door shut and locked it.

Bandage sat for a while, then crossed through the dark and nudged the door with his nose and then hit it with his paw. It did not budge. So he scratched it, and then harder and harder until the door was rattling.

'Shut up! Settle down.' Sophia banged on the other side, making Bandage jump back with fear. He sat in the dark listening to the silence and then he raised his snout in the air and howled.

Sophia, preparing for bed, heard but chose to ignore him, putting in her ear plugs instead, blocking out the noise. Bandage howled on, but when no one came to fuss him, he slipped into his basket and collapsed on to his familiar-smelling blanket and was soon asleep.

The next morning Sophia was up early. After a healthy, but frugal breakfast, she began to unpack the tea chests stacked in the drawing room. She had an appointment at the *Design Today* office, but had planned to unpack two chests now and six in the evening. Methodical as always, she had worked out that in five days she should have the house organised to her meticulous standards. She would return after lunch, when a man from Sotheby's was coming to appraise the furniture in the garage.

Just as the first case was unpacked, and its contents unwrapped and sorted out on the sofa table, she remembered the dog. His hysterical welcome after his lonely night was not to her liking, and she spoke sharply to him before letting him out of the garage and into the small walled garden. She was even more put out when she noticed him crouching, and shuddered at the resultant pile of mess. She would need a dog walker, she made a mental note to phone an agency. There was no way she could allow the dog to defecate in her garden, it would have to be taken to the park. Bandage refused to come when she called, so she left him sniffing the small area. In her haste to get to her shower and dress she did not completely close the door to the garden, and was far from amused on her return to find Bandage contentedly asleep on the sofa in the drawing room.

'Off!' she ordered. Since there was no response, she grabbed some of the newspaper wrappings and waved them at the dog. Bandage jumped quickly to the floor, ran around the room as if in confusion until he found a corner and stood in it, facing the wall.

'Oh, for God's sake, don't start that stupid game. I haven't time.' She flicked the newspaper across his snout, grabbed hold of his collar and dragged him back through the hall into the garage, and slammed the door shut. After this exercise, she checked in the hall mirror that her make-up and hair were still intact.

In the kitchen she scribbled a note for her new cleaning lady. Unbeknown to Oliver, she had sacked the Filipinos. The house was far too small for live-in staff. She smiled in self-congratulation at her smartness – part of her separation agreement with Oliver was that he would pay the staff salaries. So with no staff she would pocket the money. She propped the note against the kettle; it told the woman what chores she wanted done and warned her that Bandage was in the garage. She added a PS, reassuring her that he was placid and wouldn't hurt a soul, but not to disturb him.

When the cleaning woman arrived the dog heard first the key in the door, then her footsteps in the hall. He was on his feet in a trice, pounding at the door, whining loudly. When it did not open immediately, he began to howl. The cleaning lady loved dogs. And the one thing she could not abide was to hear one cry, so she opened the garage door and let Bandage out.

'Aren't you a fine specimen, to be sure?' she said, and patted him as he welcomed her effusively. 'Do you want some milk, or something? Some Weetabix? My little Cassie loves a Weetabix for breakfast. You come with me.' And Bandage, secure in the tone of her voice and her smell, padded along behind her into the kitchen and waited patiently, tail wagging a tattoo on the tiled floor as she prepared the Weetabix. Liking the woman, he followed her round the house as she worked. He spent a busy hour sniffing and checking the furniture and objects in the rooms, recognising those familiar to him, having to inspect more closely anything that was new. That done, he sat in the hall and watched the door.

'You waiting for your mum?' she said as she passed him to answer a knock on the door. But when she opened it to the delivery man, Bandage was on his feet and through it in one swift movement. A mighty leap, his muscles rippling beneath his shining black coat, and he cleared the gate and was up the road in a flash.

'Bandage, come back,' the cleaning lady cried. 'Oh my God, what do I do now?' she pleaded with the delivery man. 'Will you chase him?'

'Not me, I've got work to do. Call the police,' he advised unhelpfully, and climbed back into his van. Bandage was already out of sight.

Bandage ran along the unfamiliar pavement, his nose close to the ground, nostrils splayed wide, allowing the air to flow freely up his long snout and across his sensitive olfactory organ. Several thousand different smells swirled about his nose. Amongst them he was searching for the one which was most important to him, the smell of security, the familiar smell of Oliver and home.

His four paws beat a rhythm on the pavement. Neatly skirting people, never lifting his nose, never deviating from his task – the instinct that led him home. He crossed Kensington High Street, not pausing for the traffic. A Volvo smashed into the back of a BMW, but he was long gone when the enormous row that he had caused erupted in his wake. With each step the scent he had searched for increased in strength. He moved faster until in the end he was running, swifter than he had ever done before, down his street, through his gate and to his door. He scratched at it and waited, but it did not open. He snuffled at the crack at the bottom of the door, whining, but still it did not open. He tired of trying and lay down. What was left of the morning passed, the afternoon slipped by, evening came. The dog, at intervals, whined and scratched the door. As night set in, and still no one came, Bandage pointed his black head to the sky, opened his large mouth and howled again.

A window next door opened sharply. 'Stop that bloody racket,' shouted a man. Bandage, frightened by the anger in the man's voice, crept back to the door, curled up on the basement step and finally went to sleep.

The arrival of the milkman woke him. It was not the usual milkman, but Bandage still stepped forward to welcome him as he clattered down the basement steps. 'That's odd, look at that. That's Saturday and Sunday's milk there, not touched. Have they gone out and left you? Poor dog.' Bandage wagged his tail in response. 'Gone away for the weekend, I expect. Forgot to take you with them, did they? Rotten buggers. Still, if that milk isn't taken in tomorrow, then I think I ought to call the police, don't you, boy?' He patted Bandage on the head, and carefully closed the gate behind him.

Bandage was very hungry. He sniffed at the milk bottles, licked with his tongue at the silver tops, but couldn't get them off. The postman arrived. 'Bandage? Is that you? What are you doing here? You don't live here no more,' he said, as he put the post through the letterbox. And, whistling through his teeth, was on his way, leaving the gate open. Bandage scratched at the door again. It remained firmly closed. He climbed the area steps, slipped through the open gate, and padded off in the direction of his favourite place, the park.

It was a large park, which Bandage had visited most days with Oliver, with a special dog area, where dogs were allowed off their leads. Bandage trotted through the gate and made straight for the other dogs. He spent a sociable hour playing; there was no aggression, since they all knew each other from their morning walks. Several people patted Bandage and asked him where Oliver was. These dogs were walked before their owners went to the office in the morning, and so by nine they had disappeared and Bandage was alone in the park, since the dogs that were walked by their mistresses after breakfast and before morning coffee had not yet appeared. Becoming restless, he moved into an area where he never normally went.

He was trotting along when a park keeper began to shout aggressively at him. Bandage stopped, flattened his ears and looked sideways at the man, who was waving a fork as he advanced upon him. With a sudden jump, Bandage was facing in the opposite direction and running quickly away from the shouting voice.

Ahead of him, sitting on a park bench, was a fat child eating an ice cream. Bandage was always attracted to children, and ice cream: the combination was irresistible. The dog bounded up, his tail wagging, jumped up at the child, at the same time as his long, pink tongue licked the ice cream. The child screamed, dropped the cone onto the dirty path, and Bandage immediately gobbled it down. The child's screams were augmented by those of a woman who rushed towards them and scooped the large child into her arms. The boy was now crying bitterly at the loss of his ice cream, but his mother, misinterpreting his cries, shouted and yelled for help. 'My child's been bitten! My child's been bitten.'

A group of people began running towards them. 'It's a pit bull,' one shouted. 'Get the police,' another called. Bandage sat on the path looking up at the people, his tongue lolling.

'Filthy dogs, I hate them.' A man spat in his direction.

'Where's that bloody policeman? Bloody dogs!' A man shook his fist at him.

'There, there, love. Should we call an ambulance for the little one?'

Bandage's tail ceased to wag; there was anger around him. A man, older than the others, approached him. He held his hand out to Bandage, palm upwards. 'There, boy, have a sniff of that,' he said, as he steathily lifted his other hand to grab at Bandage's collar. With a quick movement the dog stood up and crashed into the small crowd, passing between the legs of an elderly woman, who went flying, banging her head on the ground. Legging it across the grass, he sped towards the large gates which would take him to the road that ran parallel with his home.

The dog's ears were pinned back in terror. His eyes rolled in his head. This was a new experience. People did not normally shout at him when he was in the park with Oliver.

The large gates of the park were closed. Bandage trotted towards the small side one. As he reached it, two youths appeared, walking through the narrow gateway. One of them lunged at Bandage, grabbing him by his collar.

'Here, Guy, look at this. It's a pit bull.'

'Nah, it's not. Pit bulls are squatter than that and they're brown. He's black and white. And in any case, he hasn't got no muzzle on.'

'Maybe he took it off.'

'Don't be bloody silly. That's the whole point of a muzzle, a dog can't get it off, can it? Has he got an address there? Maybe he's valuable, maybe there's a reward for him.' Guy fumbled with Bandage's name tag. 'Cor, there's posh, those houses are very big and rich.'

'How about it, then? How about we take him back and get a reward?' asked Terry.

'There wouldn't be much point in that now, would there? I mean, he doesn't look as though he's been on the run long, maybe he just slipped out this morning. Better we take him with us, leave it a couple of days, then we'll go round and they'll be bloody desperate to get the dog back, won't they? Then they'll give us more money,' Guy said, proud of his own logic.

'Right then, mate. Come on then, let's get it home.'

Guy had to pull hard on the belt, since Bandage was reluctant to go with them, especially as it was in the opposite direction to home. He dug in his four paws firmly, and they slid across the paving stones as the two boys yanked and pulled at him. Terry, tiring of this, walked round to Bandage's rear and gave him a hard kick. He yelped.

'Serves you bloody right, get a move on,' Terry snarled.

They finally reached their objective, which was a Ford that had seen better days and was now held together by prayer and Superglue. They manhandled a reluctant Bandage onto the back seat, got in the front, and were soon hurtling off into the traffic. Bandage leant his nose against the window, sniffing desperately at the edge of the glass. The car was moving down a wide, busy road and was soon across the Chiswick flyover.

18

The sale of Alan's house in Morristown was seriously delayed. It was, it transpired, the last in a chain, and until the owners of the house two properties back sorted out their negative equity with the building society, no one else could budge.

In some ways, he decided, it was as well, since he'd not been exactly bursting with energy way back in April when he'd begun to pack up. Now he felt full of vim, so he'd taken a couple of days' leave to finalise the packing. He was surprised when the telephone rang.

'Alan? Sorry to bother you, but something's come up.' He heard the familiar voice of Don, his Chief Superintendent in the Special Operations Unit.

'No problem. What's to do?'

'It's probably nothing, but since you're in the area, it won't do any harm to check it out. The girlfriend of one of the uniformed inspectors was in a pub in Morristown, and she overheard somebody saying that if you wanted a good fight, you should go to The Locomotive. Now that could mean a punch-up fight, it could mean a bare-knuckle fight, or it could mean a dog fight. It's as vague as that. I wouldn't normally bother, but – '

'No, while I'm here. Mind you, I've been to The Locomotive and all I saw was a Siamese cat – not a pit bull in sight.'

'Another strange thing has happened. We've had a vet call from a good fifty miles from Morristown. He'd had to put a badly wounded dog to sleep. The owner said the dog had been in a fight with an Alsatian in the park. The thing is, the dog was a pit bull.'

'But these fighting types don't normally take their dogs to the vet. They treat them themselves.'

'I know. It's most unusual, and maybe the owner was being honest. He did say that since the dog was muzzled it didn't stand a chance against the other dog. Or maybe he was inordinately fond of the dog, or new to the game. Whichever, the vet didn't like the set-up. The man paid in cash – no name, no address. The vet says he doesn't know why, but he watched the bloke leave.'

'He got his car number?'

'No, not as good as that, but he did see a garage sticker in the back window. A Morristown garage, no less. It's a strange coincidence, isn't it? I suggest you link up with Andy and stake it out together.'

'Great.' Alan was pleased now he didn't have to rush back to Horsham. Maybe he'd even meet up with Kimberley again.

'I always feel safe with you,' Andy said to him as, a couple of days later, they walked through Morristown together. 'Big bloke like you, who's going to duff us up?'

'Famous last words.' Alan grinned and looked down at Andy, a good four inches shorter and three stone lighter. 'Just because I'm big doesn't mean I like to fight.'

The Locomotive had once been a seedy, run-down public house. A couple of years ago it had had a brewery face-lift, and was now awash with maroon buttoned plush, artful lighting, reproduction mirrors and extravagantly decorated frosted glass. No Victorian habitué in a time warp would ever have recognised his old hostelry. He might recognise the smell though, sour beer mixed with sour sweat, overlaid by stale nicotine.

The bar was heaving, which was good, for they could melt in with the crowd far better. They bought beers and, trying not to look conspicuous, moved amongst the customers and did what they were here for – they listened. It was at times like this Alan realised how boring most conversations were. He felt he could almost predict what people would say, whether it was football, the lottery, sex or the Government. And he was sure he'd heard every combination of every dirty joke there was to tell.

An hour and two pints later Andy was deep in conversation with an old man and Alan, his feet killing him, looked about for somewhere to sit and spied a space at one of the tables over in the corner.

'If you don't mind, Andy, I'm going to take the weight off my feet for a minute, okay?' He did not even wait for Andy's reply, but inched his way, carefully nursing his pint, to the table in the corner, asked the occupant if the seat was taken, and sat down, unaware that he sighed with relief.

'I know how you feel,' said the young, blonde woman with a startlingly red mouth, who was sitting on the plush banquette. 'I've been on my feet all day too.' The bright yellow curls bounced on her head as she spoke to him.

'Really?' said Alan. 'It's the standing still, I'm not used to it.' He rubbed the small of his back.

'Walk a lot, do you?' she asked.

'Quite a bit.'

'What, you a copper?' she asked suspiciously.

'No thanks,' he laughed.

'What do you do then?'

'I've been on sick leave,' he was able to answer truthfully. 'And you, what do you do?'

'I work in that big new Tesco the other side of town. I'm a supervisor,' she replied proudly.

'I haven't been there yet. I've been away.'

'Really? You staying for keeps now?'

'I haven't made my mind up yet.'

'I hope you stay.' She smiled at him in such a suggestive way he wished he hadn't chosen this table, she wasn't his type at all. 'Lots of people don't like Morristown. Me, I wouldn't live anywhere else. There's a lot to do, nice pubs, cinemas, good clubs. I like it here.'

'I went up the sports centre the other day, I was impressed.'

She looked him up and down with a bold expression. 'Bet you got a wonderful body under that there shirt.'

'Bet you say that to all the boys.'

She threw back her head to laugh and the curls bounced as if they had a life of their own. A man appeared at the table holding two glasses, a pint of beer for himself and a lager and lime for the girl. Alan stood up. 'Sorry, mate, did I take your seat?'

'No, of course you didn't, he's sitting the other side of me, aren't you, Vic? This is Vic.'

'I'm Alan,' he replied, glad that surnames were not necessary, but feeling animosity from Vic.

'And I'm Vicky. Vic and Vicky, funny, isn't it?' she laughed. 'Alan's been poorly.' Vic grunted in reply, and his bored expression showed he wasn't in the least bit interested in Alan's health.

'Vic drives a lorry, don't you, Vic? Delivering fertiliser to farms, that's what he does. It's good money.'

'I'm glad someone's doing all right.' Alan stretched his legs; from beneath the table came a soft growling noise, not an aggressive growl, but more a warning. Alan bent down. There, his lead twined round the table leg, securely muzzled, was a large pit bull terrier. 'Hello, what's your name?' He felt a surge of adrenalin at sight of the dog.

'Tyson,' said Vicky. 'It's a good name for him, isn't it?'

'Oh yes,' said Alan, lying through his teeth; how many poor dogs were called Tyson, he wondered. Whenever he heard that name in relation to a fighting breed of dog warning bells rang.

'You interested in dogs?' Vic asked.

'I like them, yes. I haven't got one at the moment. Had a Rottweiler at home,' he lied, in the hope of making Vic open up.

'Yeah, I had a Rottweiler. Didn't get on with the neighbours though, did it?' Vic laughed, and Vicky laughed with him.

'I don't know if I like the muzzle,' said Alan. 'Looks bloody uncomfortable. Stupid bloody politicians, stupid bloody act! A friend of mine's dog got done – no muzzle. He'd only taken it off for a minute, and they took the dog away and it's got to be destroyed. It's a mess of a law, if you ask me.'

'You only have to read in the papers about them dogs what have been locked up for years while their poor bloody owners try and explain that they're not even pit bulls.' Vicky was quite animated when she spoke. 'So when you've got one, a real one, like Tyson here, then you have to be very careful.'

'Very careful indeed,' Vic said, more friendly now.

'He looks pretty docile to me,' said Alan.

'He is. He's an old softy. Enjoys a bit of a scrap sometimes, though, don't you, Tyson darling?' Vicky patted him under the table and the dog's round rump waggled in appreciation. Alan did not see Vic's reaction, but sensed a tension returning.

'Well, if you'll excuse me, better get some shut-eye, I think. Busy day tomorrow.' Alan stood up. 'See you again, then.'

Because of his height he was able, easily, to look over the heads of the other people and indicate to Andy that he was leaving. They walked up the road and zigzagged through various back streets until they reached Andy's dark blue Ford saloon. Andy switched on the engine and they sped away from the area of The Locomotive.

'So?' said Andy.

'I'm not sure. It's pretty obvious, but I wonder if it isn't all *too* obvious. The bloke I was talking to had a pit bull with him, correctly muzzled, called Tyson, of course, what else?'

'Rambo,' laughed Andy.

'It was something the girl said. We were agreeing how docile the dog was and what a mess the Dangerous Dog Act is, and she said something about he liked to scrap occasionally, that's all. The mood changed. I don't know, I may have over-reacted or something.'

'Doesn't sound so to me. I got bogged down with that old boy, and all he wanted to talk about was flaming D-Day. I'd have been interested at any other time. Still, all in the line of duty – as he kept saying ad nauseam. Did they say anything to make you think they're regulars there?'

'No, but I think they are. They sat there as if they knew the pub well and every one in it.'

'Let's pray we're onto something. You coming back to Horsham?'

'No. I've got a few days off still. I thought I'd suss out fertiliser supply companies – our Vic back there works for one. You never know. But I'd better leave The Locomotive for a night or two.' Andy dropped Alan in front of his house with the sold sign. 'See you on Monday.' He banged the roof of the car in farewell.

Once he was in, he put the kettle on for a cuppa and had a pee. He plugged in the television set but, finding nothing of interest, flicked it off again. He went through the mail that had arrived that morning, but it was all boring circulars. He'd dismantled his bed and so made one up on his mother's old sofa, turned the light off and waited for sleep.

Sleep, however, was a long time coming. He had to calm down from the excitement of meeting the pit bull. Over and over again he re-ran the evening's conversation, trying to find a clue he might have overlooked.

Then he began to think of Kimberley. He couldn't get her out of his mind.

There was something about her, a sadness he wanted to take away; a loneliness, a bit like his own; a wariness he recognised in himself. The caution of one who has been hurt in the past and is afraid of the future.

19

'Who says the countryside's quiet?' Wimpole was noisily dusting the bookcases in Oliver's study.

'You're certainly adding to the sum of things.' Oliver frowned with concentration as he pushed another button on his computer, and what he expected to see did not turn up on the screen. 'Oh come on, don't bugger about,' he said sternly to the inanimate object.

'What does that mean?' Wimpole stood, hands on hips, her usual stance when spoiling for a fight.

'The computer won't do what I want it to,' he replied obtusely, knowing full well what Wimpole was about.

'You know what I mean – *the sum of things*.' She waved her bright yellow duster in the air.

'I was just commenting that if it wasn't quiet in here it was mainly because of you.' He said this with a broad grin.

'I'll have you know I was woken at flaming six this morning, with all those bloody birds yammering away.'

'Most people enjoy the dawn chorus.'

'I'm not most people.'

'Evidently,' he said under his breath.

'What was that?'

'Nothing.' His grin was not working this morning, that was for sure. 'You a bit grumpy, Wimpole? Something not to your liking?'

'I said. It's bloody noisy here. I hate birds.'

'You wanted to get me a budgie once, don't you remember?'

'That's different. I don't mind them in cages. No, it's those damn crows, and why do the planes fly so low? You don't get that in London, do you?'

'They fly low here because if they crash they kill fewer people. Logical, isn't it? We don't count.'

'Then why don't they fly higher?'

'They're practising, Wimpole, in case we have a war,' he said patiently.

'You needn't talk to me as if I was a five-year-old.'

He longed to tell her not to behave like one then, but he didn't. He might be trying to make a joke of this, but Wimpole was obviously bored and restless. He feared she was not adjusting as well as he had first hoped.

'What about doing some gardening?' he suggested.

'It's raining, but you haven't even noticed, stuck in here with that machine.'

'I thought I might go to London later today.'

'Where you going?' Curiosity, as usual, had got the better of her.

'I'm fed up getting Sophia's answerphone all the time – I'm going up to collect Bandage.'

'And the best of British!' She attacked the bookshelves with vigour. 'And don't forget you've got to interview that cook woman in an hour.'

'Can't you?'

'No, I can't. It's your house, you're paying the wages.'

'Well, sit in on it then.'

'I might.'

He smiled to himself – Wimpole would not miss the interview for worlds – and looked about the room with satisfaction. The house was coming together nicely. The builders and decorators had been beavering away under his supervision for over a month now. He'd been to Morristown, London and even Shillingham choosing wallpapers and paints, something he'd never imagined himself doing – Sophia had always attended to such matters – but had found immeasurably enjoyable. And doing so made him feel he was becoming a deeply domesticated animal.

The book, despite the many interruptions caused by his new-found domesticity, was coming along far better than he had dared hope. He worked on the long refectory table which Aunt Phoebe had used. He remembered how it had looked then. On one end of the table would be any reference books required for the particular novel she was working on. In the middle was work that had already been typed up by her secretary, and at the other end was Phoebe's large, black oak chair, intricately carved with reclining lions for arm rests, and the yellow legal pad and proper fountain pen that she always used in front of her. He sat on the chair, but the yellow pad was replaced by his Apple-Mac, and there were no reference books since everything was in his head. He felt enormous contentment at the end of each day as he switched off the machine. Wimpole was going to have to adjust, for Oliver had begun to think he could never live in the city again.

An hour later Grace knocked on the door to announce that her friend, Hazel Anderson, was waiting to be interviewed. Ten minutes after that, Oliver was aware that not only was it he who had been interviewed, not Hazel, but that somehow he'd failed to come up to scratch. It seemed that Hazel had not approved of his modern kitchen, artfully masquerading as rustic, and in keeping with the house. Nor had she liked his Aga, when he'd thought everyone loved them. And finally, he had to presume she hadn't liked him much either.

'Call that an interview?' Wimpole laughed when Hazel had swept grandly from the kitchen saying that she'd let him know.

'You weren't much help.'

'I didn't like her when she walked in. That hair's not natural – bottle blonde. She wouldn't have fitted in.'

'Problem is, Wimpole, what do we do? Cooks aren't exactly thick on the ground round here.'

'You'll think of something.'

'I'll go to Marks in Morristown and get some ready prepared meals.'

'There, solved already,' Wimpole grinned, which was an improvement on her sullen face so far today.

One of the painters stuck his head around the door to let him know the drawing room was finished. Oliver went happily to the task he loved – hanging his paintings.

The hanging completed, he changed and prepared to drive to London. He'd been too patient over his dog. Something had to be resolved. What had galvanised him today was a letter from his lawyer, back from his holidays, saying that Sophia's lawyer had said he didn't know what Oliver was talking about, his client had not consulted him about any dog.

The closer he drove to London, the more excited he became at the thought of seeing Bandage, and the more angry he became at the thought that they had been apart for so long. Her attitude over Bandage had been the pettiest thing of all. If she begged him on bended knee to take her back, he never would. Not now.

Sophia answered his knock on the door of her smart Kensington house in its equally smart square, which had cost him a king's ransom. The price would have bought her a mansion in the countryside.

'Oh, Oliver!' she said, almost as if she was informing him that that was his name.

'Yes, that's me,' he said cheerily.

'You needn't be so facetious,' she replied, and Oliver thought, Oh dear, here we go again. 'Why are you here?'

'Do I have to have a reason? Can't I just pop in like anybody else?' He smiled at her and hoped it looked halfway genuine.

'Hardly! Not you. Have you got the Hockney back yet?'

'I'm sorry?' he said as he followed her along the narrow hallway.

'The Hockney that used to hang on the stairwell, have you got it back yet?'

'I presumed you'd taken it.'

'Don't be silly, we'd agreed on the paintings. I sent it to be reframed for you as a birthday present.'

'Good Lor'.' The words were out too quickly and he couldn't retrieve them. By the stiffness of her back he realised that she had heard them too.

'You know something, Oliver?' she turned and stared at him. 'You know one of the things that irritated me more than anything else about you was your pathetic little attempts at sarcasm.'

'Sorry,' he said, and wondered whether she was going to add 'the lowest form of wit'. She didn't. Instead she opened the door of the small, elegantly furnished drawing room.

'Very nice, like a little doll's house.' He meant it as a compliment, and for once she smiled back, accepting it as such. He crossed the room to the doors which led to the garden. 'Shame they have to have these grilles on, isn't it,' he said. 'Still, no one would try to come in with Bandage here.' He half turned. 'I've been thinking about Bandage, Sophia.'

As he spoke, she sat down, not gracefully, but rapidly, all of a heap, not at all like Sophia. What was more, he couldn't quite analyse the expression on her face. Had it been anybody else, he would have said it was fear, but he knew that Sophia wasn't afraid of anything.

'Yes,' she said, in a small voice.

'I mean, everything else went so well. We agreed on virtually everything – that is, that you could have it.' He tried to laugh, found it didn't work, and stopped. For once, she didn't react. 'The truth is, Sophia, I don't want to fall out with you over anything, and that includes Bandage. But you know how I feel about the dog, and I wondered whether it wouldn't be fairer all around, if you need a dog here, and I understand you would feel happier with one, if I bought you another one and I had Bandage back.'

She did not reply. He had expected an instant no so, emboldened, he continued. 'Let's face it, you never were the best of friends, were you? And I've moved to Phoebe's house now, and Bandage would love to live in the country.'

From Sophia emerged a sob. Since Sophia was the last woman on earth one expected to cry, Oliver looked at her in amazement. 'Sophia? What's the matter?' She fumbled in her skirt pocket, produced a rather inadequate handkerchief and blew her nose, but tears continued to tumble down her perfectly made-up features.

He felt a rush of unease, a tightening in his own stomach. He sat down beside her and patted her hand. 'Come on, Sophia, what is it? You can tell me.'

She turned and looked at him with anguished eyes. 'You'll never forgive me,' she said.

'Try me.' He tried to sound encouraging, but was beginning to feel fear himself.

'It's Bandage. He's gone.'

'Bandage? Gone?' Oliver repeated inanely. 'What do you mean? Gone where?' But as he asked, instinct told him worse was to come.

'He ran away. The morning after I brought him back from my father's. I put him in the garage to sleep.'

'You did what?' said Oliver indignantly. 'You know Bandage feels the cold.'

'I know, I know.' She patted her eyes with the now sodden handkerchief. 'I had a new cleaning woman, I told her not to go in there, to leave him alone. But she didn't. He was crying, apparently, and she let him out, then a delivery came and he escaped.'

Even in a sitting position Oliver felt his legs weaken. 'What did you do?' he said, trying to sound reasonable, sympathetic and hopeful, all at the same time. Instead he was seething with fury, anger and distress, and more than anything, wanted to slap this careless, selfish woman's face.

'I went to the police, of course I did. I posted a reward notice in the local newsagents. I spoke to all the shopkeepers and I put an advertisement for one whole week in the local newspaper offering a reward. And, Oliver, I can't tell you how desperately sorry I am, but there hasn't been a word about him.'

Oliver stood, surprised to find that his legs did, after all, support him. 'I see.' He felt cold around his heart. 'I see,' he repeated. 'I suppose there's no point in my looking then.'

'No, not really. It's been several weeks now. That's why I've been avoiding you and not answering your phone calls. I didn't know how to tell you, Oliver. I'll buy you another one.'

At that Oliver swung round. 'Don't be so bloody stupid. You never understood, did you? You can't just buy another one. That was Bandage, he was unique, you can't suddenly go out to the pet shop and buy another Bandage. But you never grasped it, did you? Never realised how I felt about that dog. That misunderstanding sums up our relationship, our marriage, doesn't it? Bloody waste it's all been.' And for the first time, Oliver allowed her to see the bitterness he felt. He turned, walked out of the door and, as he slammed it shut, hoped he would never have to set eyes on her again.

20

Thomasine put down her pencil and gazed out of the window. She could not work today, she was too angry. She'd hoped that by working on her dog illustrations she would calm herself, but it hadn't worked. She wished Robert was here, for she wanted to hit him.

He had not even had the courtesy to phone or write himself, but had arranged for his lawyer to write to her. The letter, which had arrived yesterday, asked for the return of a ring she owned.

'What do you mean, you want it?' she asked over the telephone.

'For Chantal – it's a family heirloom.'

'But your mother gave it to me on my twenty-first birthday.'

'Only because she presumed you'd always be my wife.'

'I'm keeping it.'

'You can't do that.'

'Try me. I love that ring.' It was a pretty Georgian ring of opals and pearls and she did love it, despite her mother saying it would be unlucky.

'It's not the value of the ring. It's the fact that it's always been in my family.'

'I'll leave it to Nadine, then it will stay in your beloved family.' She could not keep the bitterness out of her voice.

'I'll pay you for it.'

'You creep!'

'You must need the money.'

'I'm fine, as a matter of fact. Don't bother.' And she slammed the telephone down, which was so unlike her that she could easily imagine the look of shock and surprise on Robert's face. Serves him right, she thought. She'd always done what he wanted. So often she had acquiesced. How many times, how many things?

She had started to feel angry with him back in April; now it was nearly June and she was furious. Not only had he humiliated her by choosing, over her, a woman young enough to be his daughter, but he'd insidiously worked on Nadine, alienating her too. She learnt in her weekly phone calls to Nadine what presents she was getting, the clothes, the holidays, the treats – none of which she could compete with. Was this the real reason he had not pointed out to her that she could not possibly manage? That he wanted Nadine all to himself?'

She *would* manage, and what was more, she'd insist Nadine come here more often. She was not going to just sit back, the dutiful little ex-wife, and let him have it all his own way. That role had got her nowhere, and she shuddered with anger that she'd ever allowed herself to be such a malleable wimp.

She looked down at her drawing and thought how bad it was. He was even affecting how she worked! She must pull herself together.

Luna going had been a blow she had not recovered from, and yet, today, she found herself wondering if she had used the loss of the dog to hide the misery over Robert. It would explain why she was still so disproportionately unhappy. Not that she intended to replace her; she had no intention of exposing herself to such misery ever again.

From behind the small bookcase she took a chart she had begun to compile earlier in the spring, when the garden had first began to sprout, but since Luna had gone she had not bothered with. Now she pencilled in where the primulas had flowered, shaded in the large bunch of Michaelmas daisies, and where she was almost sure there was to be a fine display of lilies later.

That done, she looked about for other tasks. She studied the illustrations again. She had to finish them, she only had one more week to present them. What she needed was to draw from life.

She pulled the directory towards her and looked up Eveleigh Brenton's number.

Eveleigh's Brenton's sitting room was a cluttered, cosy mess. Aromatherapy oils burned in two small earthenware pots, but the scent from half a dozen of them could not have competed with the all-pervading smell of dog. All the sofas were misshapen, squashed and covered in hairs. Thomasine was glad that she had worn jeans and a fawnish sweater so that Eveleigh need not be fussed about her clothes.

Eveleigh was shouting at her from the kitchen as she made them tea. A large St Bernard was draped over one sofa, and a small King Charles spaniel watched her balefully from a wing chair the opposite side of the fireplace. On the floor, a blanket covering it, was another St Bernard who appeared to be sleeping, though breathing in a rather laboured way.

Eveleigh appeared with the tray of tea.

'Do King Charleses always look as baleful as that one? She's looking at me really resentfully, as if I've no right to be here.' Thomasine laughed at the little dog's expression.

Eveleigh handed her a cup of tea. 'Ah, that's Coco. I'm afraid she was born middle-aged and depressed. I often think that she feels life has let her down, that really she should be living in a great mansion on a silk cushion with strawberries and cream for tea instead of landing up in my cottage with me!' Eveleigh chucked the little dog under the chin. The dog was apparently happy, since its tail was wagging, but it only managed to look more soulful. 'So, how can I help? A book, you say?'

'It's not definite. I have to submit two paintings. It's exciting. There aren't many illustrated novels these days, mainly picture books. But this is to be a novel for eight- to ten-year-olds with colour plates, so it's a big opportunity for me. I probably won't get it, but, of course, I've got to try.'

'Of course.' Eveleigh handed her a plate of sandwiches. 'How exciting, a novel about St Bernards, I shall certainly buy it. What's it about, or is it a secret?'

'I don't think so. Fee Walters wrote it. It's about a group of St Bernards in a monastery in Switzerland who have been made redundant as rescue dogs; replaced by helicopters and Alsatians. They run away and search for their own Shangri-la; of course they have lots of adventures on the way before finding a new home in Scotland, where they become rescue dogs again.'

'How delightful! Oh my darling Issy, maybe you're going to be a star.' Isolde, the St Bernard draped over the large sofa on the other side of the room, managed to lift her magnificent head in acknowledgement for a moment before it crashed back on the cushions. She then stretched her long white legs, ending in huge paws, before relaxing back into a deep sleep. 'The problem, as you see, might be finding them awake long enough to draw them,' Eveleigh laughed.

'Have you always had St Bernards?'

'Oh, yes. When I was a child we had one, Heidi. And when I married, my husband gave me one as a birthday present. Then my interest just grew – that's how most people get involved with the dog world, by stages. I loved the dog, and first I thought how lovely it would be if she had puppies. We mated her, Lorelei she was called, bless her. We had a very successful litter, and what started as a hobby grew. We went to the odd show, but as we became more successful the excitement got hold of us – you know, it gets into the blood. And my husband, he was interested in the King Charleses, and he bred those, and this little one's the last one of the last litter he bred.' She looked away, and Thomasine wondered if it was because she was close to tears.

'And this dog, why is it covered in a blanket?'

'Because he's dying,' said Eveleigh simply.

'I am sorry.' Thomasine was not sure what else to say in the circumstances.

'There's no need to be. He's had a good life. He's fourteen, which is a fine age for a St Bernard to reach. Jim said that my dogs live to such great ages because I love them so much and they want to live for me.' She delved into her pocket for a handkerchief, into which she blew loudly. 'That was a lovely thing for him to say, wasn't it?'

'Yes, but I'm sure he said it because it's the truth.'

'Siegfried is really a kennel dog, but when they're ill or poorly or depressed, or when the end is near, I like to bring them indoors. Fuss them that little bit more.'

'It must be awful. I mean – ' Thomasine's hand stroked her thigh. She hadn't thought of this aspect of dog owning. ' – fourteen years is a long time. I mean, to know a person and have them leave,' she said, clumsily, she felt.

'It is. And you're right to use the word "person"; they are to me. I tell myself constantly that I'm only to be privileged to have their friendship for a short time. I like to think it helps me when we reach this point. Though it rarely does, it always hurts.'

'How long . . .?' Thomasine did not like to ask the rest of the question, for in a strange way it seemed not very tactful to ask in front of the dog itself, even though he appeared to be deeply asleep.

'Tomorrow. I've already phoned Jim and asked him to come. I owe it to the dog, he can't go on much longer like this, it would be cruel.'

'The vet comes here?'

'Yes. I like them to die here, at home. All dogs are frightened of the vet's. And they know, you know, they always know.'

Thomasine felt a tear roll down her cheek. She brushed it away, feeling embarrassed.

'I'm sorry, my dear. I didn't mean to upset you. I'm so sorry. Siegfried here has had a wonderful life.'

'It just suddenly hit me that – I don't wish to intrude or anything – but you were saying your husband had died and you were alone, then the dogs must mean so much more to you. It's like me. The little bulldog I found, she rapidly became so important to me – helped me through a difficult time. I never intended to keep her, but when her owners claimed her – well, I thought my heart would break. But now seeing you like this, perhaps I'm lucky. She's gone, but she's alive. I couldn't have faced her dying.'

'You would have, you know. What I keep in mind is all the joy and all the happiness that my dogs give me in their short lives. That is what makes it all worthwhile. Shall you get another?'

'I don't think so. But, oh how I miss her, it's as if there's a big hole in my life.'

Eveleigh nodded wisely. 'That's what dogs do to you, my dear. They take over your entire life if you're not careful. Still, listen to me prattling on. But if you want to try and sketch my dogs, you're very welcome. Do come any time you want. I'm thrilled to think one of *my* St Bernards might be in a book.'

21

Jim Varley was walking down the lane, Castille padding along beside him. Back in March he'd almost given her up, had thought about putting her down, yet here she was, three months later, with a new lease of life. Trotting along behind him was the reason – the King Charles, totally recovered from her hysterectomy. Jim was pleased with the dog, now called Amtie, thanks to Harry, to which she responded.

He arrived at The Duck and Thistle and pushed open the door, smelled the comforting mix of cigarettes and beer and enjoyed the welcome he received as he ordered his whisky and leant against the bar, the dogs sitting patiently at his feet.

'How are you going to deal with the competition then, Jim?' the landlord asked him.

'What competition?'

'Haven't you heard? A new vet's opening up in Shillingham.'

'You're joking!' said Jim. 'When did you hear that?'

'Our Stephanie works in the estate agent's, she helped do the deal on the premises. They're taking over what used to be that old mill. Going to be a big health centre for animals.'

Jim laughed. 'Well, there's a relief.'

'You're not worried?'

'No. I'd like to think most of my clients will stay loyal to me. But there's a few I'd like to get rid of, I can push them in that direction.' He laughed again as he realised he'd been let off the hook, he needn't make any decisions after all, he thought happily. 'There's been a need for another practice around here for some time. Beth's been nagging me to take on an assistant, but, I don't know, I didn't really want to.'

'You ought to marry another vet, Jim,' the landlord said, not unkindly.

'I doubt whether I'd find another Ann, do you?'

'Well, you won't know if you don't look,' the landlord's wife interrupted, and Jim laughed good-humouredly.

The door opened and Oliver, dressed in jeans, sneakers and a large, shapeless sweater approached the bar.

'Hello, Jim,' he said.

'Oliver!' said Jim, unable to keep the surprise out of his voice.

'Surprised at seeing me still here?'

'Sorry. It sounds rude, but yes. I knew you said you were moving here permanently, but I didn't know if you'd stick it out – not with the lousy weather we've been having. Some summer!'

'I'll have you know I lived in the country all my childhood. I haven't always been a townie.' Oliver had had this conversation several times since he had moved. There was something about country folk that made them think they had a monopoly on living in and understanding the countryside; it always piqued him. 'Still, I know what you mean. I read an article in the paper the other day, written by some anti-dog cove saying he was moving to get away from the dog crap in the London parks. I had to laugh. As far as I can see, the whole countryside's awash with turds.'

'Guess he's in for a bit of a shock.' Jim smiled, warming to Oliver.

His country credentials out of the way, Oliver sipped at his pint.

'I was up at your father-in-law's a few weeks back and your wife was there. I'm sorry to hear about the . . .' Jim stopped, for he wasn't quite sure what to say. 'Problem' sounded rather tame in the circumstances.

'Oh, that. Well, probably for the best.' Oliver shrugged his shoulders good-naturedly. 'Only trouble is, I lost my dog over it.'

'Not the bull terrier?'

'Yeah,' said Oliver, biting his bottom lip; to talk of Bandage still hurt. 'He ran away. I scoured London. I went to every police station I could think of. He's a very distinctive dog, jet black with white markings on his feet, like bandages. No one had seen hide or hair of him, no traffic accidents reported at all. I'm beginning to wonder if he wasn't stolen.'

'Dog fighting, you mean?'

'Yes. Not that they'd get much change out of Bandage. He's the softest creature on two legs. He'd tiptoe round an ant rather than hurt it.' He smiled at the memory of his sloppy dog.

'Sometimes I get odd whiffs of a rumour of something like that going on – it's usually if a dog has been badly damaged. Oddly, these people are sometimes very fond of their dogs, even if they let them fight, and they'll bring a dog in to be patched up, but they lie and say it got into a scrap with a Rottweiler out on a Sunday walk, or something like that.'

'What do you do in a situation like that?'

'What can I do? Patch the dog up. I've no proof. Invariably they'll give me false addresses.'

'You've heard of nothing like that around here?'

'No, not for some time. Drink?' he asked, to change the subject. Just recently the local RSPCA inspector had asked him if he'd had any fighting breeds in. That meant something was afoot. He also knew that these days dog fights didn't just occur on isolated farms, but on run-down council estates in big towns – towns like Morristown. He was not prepared to tell Oliver, not yet, not unless he had some more concrete information. He didn't want Oliver crashing in and ruining some careful investigation which might have taken months to set up.

The door of the bar flew open, and Jim's heart lifted as he saw Thomasine come in. He waved across the bar. 'Mrs Lambert, care to join us for a drink?'

Thomasine's face was pink from the long walk she had just taken, and her hair glistened from the very faint mist of drizzle that had begun to fall. 'That would be so nice.'

'Of course, you know Oliver Hawksmoor,' he said, regretting that Oliver should happen to be with him at this precise moment. Thomasine smiled at Oliver and Jim felt a small frisson of jealousy at the warmth of the smile.

'I nearly knocked the poor man over some time back in Shillingham.'

'We don't often see you in here,' said Jim, keen to get her attention back.

'No, but I suddenly felt all four walls pressing in on me. I thought I needed some fresh air and to talk to fellow human beings.'

'Still missing – ' He began, and then stopped, cursing himself for being such a fool.

'The bulldog? Very much, but it's getting better.'

'There's a refuge about ten miles from here, she's always looking for good homes – especially for the greyhounds. They're no trouble – twenty minutes walking a day is all they need.' He had just returned from there and was always conscious, after a visit, of the need to find responsible homes for them.

'I don't think so. I'm better off without. I had tea with Eveleigh the other day. I wondered – her dog?' Thomasine asked.

'Siegfried? Gone, I'm afraid.' He looked at his feet, still distressed at having had to put the dog to sleep. 'Maybe you two can throw some light on this. Eveleigh had an offer for her kennels a while back which she turned down. They've since offered again, twice – each time more money than the last. What can be going on?'

'That land over at Cooper's Bottom's been sold, you know,' Oliver volunteered.

'Eveleigh said she thought it had.'

'It was all very hush-hush. I bet it's for building.'

'They'd never get planning permission there, surely?'

'My dear Jim. Have you not learnt anything's possible if you've got the right clout?'

'But it would be too close – '

'Exactly, to Eveleigh's kennels. She'd object most strongly. Hence buy her out at an offer she cannot refuse and wipe out the opposition.'

'Bit high-handed, isn't it? Those kennels have been there ever since I can remember. If they build it could become a real problem. These days it's not that uncommon. Kennels which were once way out in the sticks get caught up with urban sprawl. She'll never sell up though. Not Eveleigh.'

'Maybe she'll have to,' said Oliver.

'Why, if she doesn't want to?' asked Thomasine.

'Those interested might make her life too difficult. Do you think we should mention it to her?'

'She'd only worry unduly, Oliver. I'll keep an eye on the situation for her.'

Oliver suggested another round.

'Not for me, thanks. I must be going.' Thomasine smiled at Oliver, and he wished he'd seen that smile first, then he might have got there before Jim, who seemed to be lurking around in a very proprietorial manner.

That was odd, thought Jim, they didn't seem to be much of a couple to him.

Kimberley came out of the school grounds, her school bag laden with books, to find Greaser waiting for her.

'Where've you been? You haven't been to the market for weeks.'

'I had bronchitis. I've been home in bed, then the doc wouldn't let me go back to school for ages.'

'We missed you.'

Kimberley smiled, thinking she hadn't missed them. But being ill couldn't have come at a worse time, for she had had to resign herself to never seeing Alan again – he'd have long ago given up on her.

'I'll take that, it's heavy,' Greaser volunteered.

'What are you doing here?' she asked, more surprised by his unaccustomed courtesy than his presence.

Greaser fell into step beside her as she walked towards the large, noisy queue at the bus stop. 'I wondered if you'd like to come and see my new dog?' he said.

'Me? Why should you want me to do that?'

'Butch says you know about dogs.'

'Not a lot.'

'Well, you know more than I do, and more than Butch does probably. He says your dad breeds them, so you must know something.'

'Now?' she asked.

'Yeah, it's important.'

'But I'll miss my bus.'

'That's all right, Butch says he'll run you back on his bike.'

At that, Kimberley was torn. Butch rarely offered a female a lift, and she loved riding on the back of the motorbike, far more than she would ever admit to a living soul. When Butch went fast, and the wind stung at her face, she felt a freedom that was denied her at any other time.

'You sure he promised? Otherwise I can't get back this evening. And I've masses of revision to do, I'm in the middle of my A levels.'

'Sure I'm sure. We're going into partnership.'

She laughed. 'That sounds grand and official, not at all like you and Butch.'

They crossed the road, walked through a small labyrinth of the original artisans' cottages, past the Locomotive Inn and through a concrete archway into the hell that was the Forest Glade.

'Makes me feel like Theseus in the maze, this place,' she said.

'Who?'

'Oh, never mind.'

But as Greaser led her along one concrete walkway and down another, up one set of steps and down yet more into subterranean passages that interlinked with others, she decided she was right, she would have needed a ball of twine to find her way back to the entrance again. They entered a tower block. Greaser, more out of habit than expectation, kicked the lift, banged the button, and since nothing happened, said they had to leg it.

They climbed to the seventh storey. 'Keeps you fit,' Kimberley said.

'You can say that again.' He dug his hand into the letterbox and pulled out a string to which was attached a key. He popped it in the lock, and let Kimberley in.

Kimberley and her parents did not possess much, but what they did have was clean and well cared for by her mother. Nothing could have prepared her for the shambles which was Greaser's home. The swirling patterned carpet was littered with empty milk bottles, beer cans and piles of dirty washing. The air was full of the pervasive smell of fried food and stale cigarettes. Kimberley was not quick enough to remove the look of distaste on her face.

'It's a bit of a mess, but my mum's not well,' said Greaser defensively.

'I didn't mean . . .'

'No, no one does.'

A voice called out. 'Is that you, Graham?'

'Graham?' Kimberley giggled.

'Shut up,' said Greaser.

'Who you talking to?' the voice asked.

'Friend. Come on, you better meet her.' He pushed open the thin plywood door which led into the small, equally untidy sitting room. In a greasy-looking armchair, sat a scrawny-faced woman with lank hair hanging limply around her grey, defeated face. 'This is Kimberley, Mum, what I told you about.'

'The one that knows all about dogs?'

'That's right.'

Kimberley began to open her mouth to say that she didn't, but a glare from Greaser stopped her.

'Well, you'd best tell her to go and look at it. My *Neighbours* repeat's about to begin.'

'Okay, Mum.' He hustled Kimberley out of the room, they walked along the narrow corridor. Greaser stopped at a door, his hand on the handle. He turned and faced Kimberley. 'You needn't be scared, he's not vicious nor nothing.' He went in, and as he did so he switched on the light. Standing in the corner of the room, its back to them, its snout leaning on the wall, was a black, well-muscled dog with white markings on his legs, which looked as if he was wearing bandages.

'What's he doing?' Kimberley asked.

'I dunno, he does that all the time. He'll be friendly for a minute or two, you know. When I feed him he eats, then I say come on boy, come here, and he just looks at me and he goes in the corner of the room, puts his head on the wall like that and he'll stand there for hours, as if he's sulking.'

'Poor thing.'

'Why poor thing? I feed it.'

'It's hardly a nice way to spend your day, is it, in the corner of a room with nothing to look at?'

'I hadn't thought of that. I've taken it for walks, not that it wants to go, but it'll come if you pull hard enough.' He went over to the corner of the room. 'Sly,' he said, and kicked the dog in the rear. Warily, the dog turned round and looked at him.

'He's lovely, isn't he?' said Kimberley.

'Do you think so? I think he's an ugly bugger meself. What is it, that's what we want to know. Is it a pit bull?'

'No, don't be silly, they've got more squashed up faces than this. I think it's a bull terrier or something like that.'

'Bull?' Greaser jumped on the word. 'Like, they're related?'

'Yes, I suppose so.'

'Like it likes to fight, like a pit bull,' Greaser said, his head twitching almost in a nervous tic as he spoke.

Kimberley, who had been patting the dog, paused. 'Hang on a minute, you're not getting involved in that, are you? It's cruel and it's illegal.'

Greaser laughed, took a cigarette out of a packet, twirled it in the air and caught it in his mouth, a trick that had taken him many a week and many a ruined cigarette to perfect. 'Lots of things are, but it doesn't stop you doing them, does it?' He tapped his foot, stood straight and tall and looked cocky.

'But it's such a lovely dog. It would be a shame for it to get hurt.'

'But that's the whole point, isn't it? If you get a dog and you have the best dog, it won't get hurt. It'll hurt the other bugger.'

'I just don't like it, that's all.' Kimberley patted the dog. 'Are there dog fights round here? I'd have thought they were more likely to take place out in the country?' she asked with practised ease, as if she knew nothing about the filthy trade.

'Nah, here. There's one bloke, uses a room in his flat for it, covered in blood it is. People bet on them. It's good, you can make good money from a dog fight.'

'Where did you get him?' she asked, not wanting to think about the blood-stained walls nor the pain they indicated.

'I bought him from a geezer on the other side of the estate. He'd bought it from another geezer who came from London. Don't know how it landed up out here, but this kid I bought it from, his mum said he couldn't keep it, so I got it.'

'And your mum doesn't mind?'

'Nah, if she thinks we're going to make some money she won't bloody mind. What you think then?' And he kicked the dog.

'Stop it! Don't do that.'

'Got to toughen him up. I've been talking to a mate, he says that if you lock him up with another fighting dog, that'll toughen him up faster than anything – he'd have to defend himself to survive. And there's a bloke, what knows another bloke, what's got one of these treadmills, you put them on that, you know, they walk for hours and hours, all day long, going nowhere. Funny, isn't it? Then you got collar things you put on them and they drag these bricks around with them. It's to build the muscles up. This bloke's got a gym down there. You know, pit bull gym. Funny, isn't it?' Greaser laughed.

Kimberley was silent. She knew who he was talking about – her father, and the shed she never went into. The dog looked at her and she looked at it. It wagged its tail, almost imperceptibly, almost as if it was afraid to. It did it again, then the door swung open and Butch walked in.

'Right, then, what is it?' he asked, without preamble.

'She reckons it's a bull something or other, good for fighting anyway.'

'Great. Right, Kimberley, I said I'd run you home, and run you home I will. I'm in a bit of a rush, I've got to meet a man about this bloody dog. The sooner we get it bloodied the better.'

Kimberley patted the dog – she'd have liked to kiss it, she didn't know why, but she would. 'Good luck, boy,' she said instead, and followed Butch out of the door. They clattered down the stairs in silence. He gave her his spare crash helmet, stowed her book bag into a plastic pannier. She swung her leg over and sat on the pillion seat of the bike. He revved the engine, and they were soon skimming through the labyrinth of the Forest Glade estate, out of the centre of Morristown and on to the by-pass towards her home. Kimberley clung to Butch and felt the wind and felt clean and free and put the thought of the dog behind her.

The chain of house sales in which Alan had been stuck began to resolve, and he was back in his mother's house for the last time – the house-clearing people were coming tomorrow, the meters were to be read, he'd finally be shot of it. He cooked himself a couple of poached eggs on toast, ate a tin of baked beans from the tin, a can of peaches with evaporated milk, which was the last of his mother's supplies, and got ready for the night ahead. He'd been to The Locomotive several times on abortive trips – no dogs, no Vic. With nothing else to do, he'd decided to try one last time.

He could have wished for a better night to be out. Flaming June, he thought, as he pulled his anorak tight. It was cold and wet. He put his head down and trudged along the street to where his car was parked. He'd be glad to be shot of Morristown; the people had to be the unfriendliest he'd ever met, and at every turn were memories of his mother and his far from happy childhood. He'd yet to search out the one person he'd met and liked and who had shown a spark of interest in him.

He parked several streets away and it was eight by the time he got to The Locomotive, which was not as crowded as it had been on previous nights. He ordered his pint of beer and chatted with the barman. He glanced about the bar, and his heart leapt with excitement when he saw Vicky sitting in the same alcove as before, but alone. He nodded, and she nodded back.

Two lads walked in. One, he was convinced, was well under age; the other looked familiar, but then so many of these bikers did. He turned slightly so they wouldn't see him full face. They had a dog with them, a dog that apparently didn't want to be with them, for they had to drag it in. It was a beautiful bull terrier, black with white markings, and while he could admire the dog, he felt a wave of excitement. First a pit bull, now a bull terrier.

'Hello, come to see Vicky then?' She was at his elbow. He got a waft of very sweet perfume.

'Wasn't sure if you recognised me.'

'Big hulk like you, course I did,' she giggled, and he knew it was a come-on. He knew he shouldn't react, not when he was working, and not when he'd met her boyfriend.

'Where you been?'

'Oh, around.' He tried to sound nonchalant as the two boys approached them – then felt his heart lurch.

'Hello, Vicky,' said Butch, not even glancing at Alan. 'Where's Vic?'

'He's gone to see a man about a dog. Honest.'

'Only, I want to talk to him about this dog,' said Butch, tapping the bull terrier with his toe.

'Ugly looking thing.'

'We didn't buy it for its looks,' said Butch.

'He'll be here soon. Isn't one of you gentlemen going to buy a lady a drink?' she said, smiling coquettishly at Butch first and then Alan. Alan thought it best if he moved away, as if he wasn't interested in the talk of dogs. He began to throw darts at the board. Rather a futile occupation because he kept missing, he was too hyped up to aim properly.

'Don't play stupid old darts. Come and talk to me – I'm bored.' Vicky patted the banquette beside her.

'Where are your mates?' he asked, sliding in beside her.

'Taking that horrid dog round the block. Toughening it up, they said. They'll be back.'

Alan ordered them both more drinks and dug up some small talk to amuse Vicky while his mind reeled in anticipation. If the talk got round to dog fights, as he was sure it would, how could he get himself included? Two pints later Vic arrived, his pit bull, muzzled, in tow. He nodded at Alan, who smiled and said, 'Hello, Vic. Can I buy you a drink?'

'Well, thanks. A pint would be fine – the export special,' said Vic. Alan bought the round of drinks and carried them to the table where Vic had sat himself down beside Vicky. The pit bull had crept under the table and was curled up and already asleep. Alan put the drinks down.

'There were two kids looking for you. They got this horrible black thing with them, wanted to talk about you-know-what, I reckon,' said Vicky. 'Do you have to?' she snapped, bending down and rubbing her shin.

Vic said nothing, but started to sup his pint. Alan was racking his brains for something to say, but neither Vic nor Vicky seemed bothered to be drinking in silence. He tried mentioning football, but all Vic said was 'bloody football.' Talk of fertiliser didn't get much response either. He was rescued by the two youths reappearing, still with the bull terrier.

'You should get that bloody thing muzzled otherwise the fuzz will be on to you. They'll have arrested it before you know where the fuck you are, and then the thing will be put down,' said Vic, the longest speech Alan had heard him make.

'That's not necessary,' Alan said, without thinking.

'How would you know?'

'Because I know that that's a bull terrier and they're not included in the Dangerous Dog Act.' He felt his heart thudding, felt he was being far too knowledgeable for comfort, felt a tenseness about him that hadn't been there before.

'And how would you be such an expert?' Vic looked at him coldly.

'Because my dad's got a bull terrier,' Alan lied, and hoped that it was a successful lie.

'What? *And* a Rottweiler?'

'No, the Rottie was mine, it's dead now.' He picked up his beer and quickly sipped at it for something to do. He felt himself sweat at the stupid mistake he'd inadvertently made.

'Ah, I see,' said Vic.

'That's what Kim said, she's our friend,' said Greaser. 'She knows about dogs, her dad breeds them, said she reckoned that that's what it was. And I ain't got to muzzle it, mate?' He looked at Alan.

'No, you don't have to, but it's probably less hassle if you do. My dad's always getting into trouble with ours, people accusing him unnecessarily.' Alan rattled on now, wishing he hadn't set this conversation in motion. 'Do you live around here?' he asked.

'Forest Glade. You?' Greaser, who seemed more outgoing than Butch, asked.

'Wembley Way,' he answered.

'Nice,' said Vicky.

'You want to know a lot,' Vic added.

'Just curious.'

'That killed the cat.'

'Just asking.' Alan shrugged his shoulders as if he didn't give a damn. They drank without talking.

As the silence lengthened, it was evident he was not going to learn any more. Vic had obviously clammed up, whether out of discretion or suspicion of him, he could not tell. He felt he had lied himself out of the situation successfully, but it had been close – too close. It was so frustrating when he was sure they were getting that bit nearer the dog-fighting ring.

'If you'll excuse me. Busy day tomorrow.' Alan stood, buttoning up his coat ready to leave.

'Nice to see you, Alan. See you again next week? We're not here at the weekend.' She winced. Had Vic kicked her under the table?

'Right,' said Alan. 'See you.' Outside the pub, the rain slashed painfully at his face, which was warm from the bar and the beer. He pulled up the collar of his coat, dug his hands deep into his pockets, put his head down as he moved through the deserted streets of Morristown to his car.

As he walked, he went over the conversation, what there was of it. It wasn't so much what was said, but more the tense atmosphere. He paused in his step. He thought he heard a sound behind him. He swung round abruptly, but there was nothing there.

'Getting neuro,' he told himself, and strode on. He whistled between his teeth, trying to give himself courage, wishing Andy were with him and wishing he'd parked his car nearer.

Suddenly a fist was slammed into the back of his head and a strong arm grabbed him. He was swung round and, too quickly to be identified, a figure lunged, snarling at him, and smashed him with his clenched fist full in the face. He swayed, his knees buckled, he stumbled against the wall and then sank to the pavement. Alan had a split second of thought, wondering whether it was Vic hitting him and if so why – was it over the dogs or Vicky?

As he lay slumped on the pavement he was aware that someone else was kicking him viciously. He writhed, trying to get away from the boots, away from the pain, realising now that it was three men attacking him. Vic and the boys? Possible. He marvelled that he could still think.

A car appeared on the street, moving towards them, and only then did the beating stop and Alan heard his assailants running away into the dark, but not before one of them had slammed something into the side of Alan's head. Before unconsciousness swept over him, Alan's last thought was that he was glad that his mum couldn't see him now.

22

Kimberley sat on the bus, her shopping bags between her feet, and felt miserable. It had been stupid to expect Alan to be there. She had missed too many Saturdays at the fountain since she'd met him. First she'd been ashamed to turn up because of the bruises her father had inflicted upon her face, and then the wretched bronchitis. She'd met him in April, now it was June.

Of course that was presuming he'd meant it when he'd said 'see you'. Maybe he was just being polite, not wanting to hurt her feelings.

It was a shame too, for she'd made a real effort with herself. She'd persuaded her mother to buy her new jeans and a black T-shirt. She'd turned the cuffs of one of her father's old shirts, on which she had stuck a brooch of a panda, and over that she wore an old suit waistcoat of his. She'd washed her hair and wore it loose instead of in a ponytail, and had even bothered to put some mascara on, but nothing else, not liking the feel of make-up on her skin. She looked different from the last time he'd seen her bundled up in her old duffel coat. But now she was having to acknowledge that it had all been a waste of time.

She'd hung around for most of the afternoon on the off chance he might turn up, or that Nadine might be around. Even the gang weren't there.

From the floor of the bus she picked up the carrier bag and checked that the present she'd bought her mother for her birthday was still there. It was a basket of toilet water and soap, lying on blue satin, which was pretty and which she knew her mother would like. She wondered if her father had even remembered. She hoped so, for if not, Sue's feelings would be sorely hurt.

The bus lurched to a stop at a crossroads. Kimberley looked idly out of the window to see her father standing beside his van in deep conversation with a large man she did not know and, of all people, Butch. How odd, she thought as the bus started up and trundled on. The only time Butch had met her father that she knew of, Tom had been rude to him and it had caused a row. Now, to the casual eye, they looked like old friends.

If Butch and her father were in cahoots, then there was even more reason to see less of him. It had not bothered her that none of the gang had been in Shillingham. They bored her, and no doubt she bored them in return, for she said very little. She had never been comfortable with knowing that she was the most intelligent amongst them. She'd never wanted to be superior in that way. It was loneliness which had made her join up with them, and she had gained nothing from the association.

The bus pulled up at the stop by her lane. The driver helped her with the heavy bags as she alighted. She set off along the lane, turned in the gate and began the long hike up to the ugly little cottage, and wished she lived anywhere else but here.

Alan was still in hospital – unnecessarily, he thought, but the doctors had insisted he stay another forty-eight hours, since, at the end of the beating up, he'd been unconscious. There was concussion and, two days later, he still had a headache – not much, but enough to worry the doctor. He'd also suffered two cracked ribs, which bothered him far more than the head; he had twisted his ankle, presumably when he fell, and to top it all, was black and blue from where he had been kicked with heavy boots.

'Apart from that, I'm fine,' he joked to Andy, who was sitting on the end of the bed, leafing through the *Playboy* magazine he'd brought him.

'Do you mind if I nosh these?' Andy asked, opening the bag of grapes he'd brought in with him.

'Be my guest,' said Alan, and winced as he moved.

'You're a right bloody mess, aren't you?'

'Give me a day or two, I'll be back.' He managed to smile.

'Still, it's a pointer that we're looking in the right place. Was something said?'

'Not really. A couple of yobs came in with a bull terrier and the atmosphere changed. I'm worrying, if it was Vic who duffed me up, maybe it was because he was just jealous over the girl.'

'You didn't see who did it, then?'

'No, it was too quick – but there were three of them in the pub, and three set into me.'

'Just looking at him, Vic doesn't strike me as the sort of bloke who'd give up drinking at his local over a girl. Beat you up, yes, kill you even because of her, but give up his boozer – never.'

'Perhaps he's scared I'll be back wanting to give him a taste of the same?'

'Nah, I shouldn't think much frightens him.'

'What if he's worried I'll go to the police? He doesn't know I didn't see him.'

'It would boil down to his word against yours, and you can bet the whole clientele and the landlord would swear he never left the pub – not for a minute.'

'If it wasn't the girl then it's the dogs. I've been thinking, and I could have tipped him off inadvertently. The first time we met I said I had a Rottweiler at home. Then this last time I explained away being so bloody knowledgeable about the Dangerous Dogs Act by saying my father had a bull terrier. Stupid of me, I just wasn't thinking. But it would be enough to warn him.'

'If he remembered. I shouldn't let it worry you. It's done now.'

'I could kick myself. We were really on to something there. There is something else. The yobs who brought in the bull terrier have been bothering me. I'm sure I've seen them somewhere before, but I can't remember where.'

'What did they look like?'

'Short. Spotty. Cocky. One's about nineteen, the other's younger. Trouble is, they just look like any yobs you see lurking about the Forest Glade estate.'

'It's there, isn't it – in that bloody estate. It's so bloody big and every other bugger seems to have a Rottweiler, pit bull or breeds that look as though they could fight – and you can't arrest them all.'

'What's the boss say? Bet he's pissed off with me.'

'He's fairly philosophical. These things happen. He thinks we're on a hiding to nothing. That we don't have enough info to justify continuing – even on a semi-official basis. And he reckons if there's anything there then they've got the wind up and will lie low until they think we're off the scent.'

'I know what you're going to say,' Alan groaned. 'He's pulling the plug.'

'Don't upset yourself. It's not your fault.'

'It's not that so much, but I met this girl. I really liked her, then one thing and another, I've lost touch. I hoped I'd see her again. Now I've sold the house I've no reason to be here and if this case re-ignites he'll probably send two of the others – someone they haven't seen.'

'Not necessarily. I know I'm off to Yorkshire – same thing up there. And they're so busy with the live exporting hoo-ha – you never know, he's just as likely to send you because you know the area. After all, they're hardly likely to use The Locomotive again, are they?'

'That won't alter the fact that that Vic bastard will recognise me.'

'Cross that bridge when you reach it.'

'Thanks a bunch.'

'Right then. Anything you need? Smokes? Do they let you smoke in here?'

'You must be joking.'

'Well, that's your grapes gone, I'll be buzzing off then. Going out tonight with the missus to a particularly nice little restaurant we've just found.'

'Bastard!' said Alan as he sank back on the pillows, surprised to find that he felt completely drained.

Alan was not discharged until the following Wednesday. A taxi drove him back to his house. His car was safely parked in the street, no doubt arranged by Andy. He was still weak; just a few days in bed and he was quite wobbly on his pins. And when he bent to light the gas fire, shards of light floated in front of his eyes as he stood up.

What to do now? He had to contact the house-clearing people again and apologise for not being here last week. He wasn't up to work yet, that was obvious, but he didn't want to stay here a day more than necessary. He couldn't be rid of Morristown fast enough. Still, he felt quite sad at leaving the district; it was the town he hated. He began to sort through the mail that had accumulated. Amongst it was a couple of house details from the estate agent he'd been to last week.

Was it the prettiness of the local countryside that had made him decide to look for a place, or Kimberley? If he was honest, it was probably a combination of the two.

Yet if he found someone, would it be fair on her? His job, dangerous in some ways – as his bruises showed – was equally dangerous in other ways. It was like a drug, one could become enmeshed in it to the exclusion of everything else. He wasn't alone in going from one case to another longing for the adrenalin high that accompanied it. There was so much to do, so much cruelty to be dealt with, that one could become obsessed with it. He'd seen blokes in the society who cared only about the animals, and had shut people, and any concern for them, right out of their minds. He didn't want to be like that – there had to be a balance.

But since he'd met Kimberley at the fountain, he hadn't noticed any other girls. He didn't know her or anything about her. But for all that, she had hit him hard – a bit like Vic's boot, but nicer.

These thoughts galvanised him. He no longer felt tired and jaded. He stood up, reaching for his shoes with his feet, and slipped them on. He looked in the spotted mirror over the mantelpiece and studied his face. He couldn't go and find her if he looked like something that had crawled out of the swamp – he didn't want to frighten her away. The bruise on the left side of his face was fading and had turned a greeny-yellow colour that wasn't too bad. His split lip looked on the fat side, and kissing might prove difficult. He smiled at that thought, but quit when it hurt.

Abruptly he stopped studying his face. Of course, why hadn't he thought of it before? He could put an ad in the personal column of the local paper. He knew her Christian name, he didn't need her surname. 'Kimberley, meet you at the fountain Saturday noon. Alan.'

'Yes!' he shouted, punching the air with excitement and, grabbing his coat, forgot his aches and pains as he rushed out to drive into the centre of Morristown. God knows if she'd see it, but he'd give it a try. Maybe he'd be in time to get an ad in the Friday edition.

It was just Kimberley's luck that as she was about to finish her schooling the job market should be so difficult to break into. Although she was expected to do well in her A levels, half of which she had now sat, her interview with the careers teacher this afternoon had not been encouraging.

'The banks are cutting back on staff, Kimberley, that's part of the problem,' Miss Mitchell had said. 'Is there no chance of you going to university? It's not too late, you know.'

'No chance at all, Miss Mitchell.'

Miss Mitchell sighed. In Morristown she'd found that her most able pupils too often had the most unco-operative parents. 'Have you thought of any other possibilities? Insurance? Nursing? The police?'

'I'd always set my heart on a bank. I could still try,' she said, though smiling inwardly at the thought of her father's reaction if she even said the word 'police' to him.

'Of course, my dear. Don't worry too much, will you?'

That was a stupid thing for the teacher to have said, Kimberley thought as she later laid the table for supper. Miss Mitchell was safe in her job, she wasn't having to escape. She put the freesias she'd bought on the way home from school in a vase in the middle of the table. They were her mother's favourite flowers, though she never understood why since she couldn't smell them – the result of Tom's fist landing smack on her nose one winter night.

'What's the cloth for?' Her father eyed the table suspiciously as he clumped noisily into the room.

'It's Mum's birthday. I'm cooking supper for her.'

'You could have reminded me.'

'I'm sorry. I didn't think,' she replied, as she went into the kitchen to check the casserole. She could have reminded him, she was not sure what perversity had prevented her.

'You look nice. Happy birthday, Sue. Bet you thought I forgot.' She heard her father kiss her mother on the cheek – hypocrite, she thought. 'I know it's today, but I've planned a little surprise for tomorrow.'

'Tomorrow?' Her mother sounded uncertain.

'Yes, I thought I'd take you to that Chinese restaurant in Shillingham you said you liked the look of.'

'Oh, Tom. How lovely, but I thought – ' Her voice trailed off.

'No. Not tomorrow. Not around here for a bit. Vic reckons someone's been snitching. He had to put the frighteners on a copper who'd been snooping.'

'Oh, Tom, be careful.'

'Don't you worry about me. Next weekend we'll be off up north. Lie low for a bit. Only for a bit, though.'

And what did all that mean? Kimberley asked herself as she lit the gas under the potatoes.

'You seen my paper, Sue?'

'No. They sold out.'

'What you mean, sold out?' His voice was raised; her mother's had become fearful. That didn't last long, thought Kimberley as she collected three cans of beer from the old and dilapidated fridge in the pantry.

Once the meal was over Kimberley excused herself and went to her room. She spent a lot of time in this room, using school work as an excuse even when she'd done it all. From there she heard her father clatter into the yard, and a few minutes later her mother tapping at her door.

'Kim. You awake? Look at this.'

'What's that? But you said – '

'I know. But I didn't want your father to see this. Look.'

Kimberley followed her mother's pointing finger down the personal column. 'See.'

Kimberley, meet you at the fountain Saturday, Alan. She read and then re-read, in case she was hallucinating.

'Is it meant for you?'

'I think so,' she said, her voice sounding as strained and unsure as she was herself.

Kimberley could not sleep. She was frozen with fear that her father would somehow see the advert. And she couldn't sleep from the sheer excitement at the thought that tomorrow she would see Alan again.

When Kimberley looked into the yard the following morning, the yellow van stood with its back door open and her father was loading his two pit bull dogs into the back.

'Where's he taking them this early?' she asked her mother.

'He's going up north with them. Don't ask me, I don't want to know.' She flapped her hands as if brushing all knowledge away.

'But I thought he was taking you out?'

'Something came up.' She shrugged resignedly as if she'd half expected it.

'Would he give me a lift into Shillingham?' she asked. 'It'll save on the bus.'

'Probably, he's in a good mood.'

So Kimberley rode in silence beside her father into Shillingham, the two pit bulls slithering around in the back of the van behind a metal grid.

She saw him sitting on the wall of the fountain as she alighted from the van. She hoped he didn't see her, not with the dogs in the back. Carrying her shopping bag, she walked, heart racing uncomfortably, the palms of her hands damp with sweat, towards him. He was looking in the opposite direction.

'Hullo, Alan.'

'Kimberley! At last!' He jumped to his feet. 'Oh, am I glad to see you.' He put out his hand to touch her and then drew it back, embarrassed. She longed for him to do it again, but he didn't and she stood looking at the cobbles feeling awkward and wondering what was wrong with his face, but not liking to ask.

'Sorry about my mush,' he said, fingering his bruises. 'I walked into a door.'

'I see.' She sounded non-committal. She'd heard her mother use that line once too often to believe him.

'How long have you got?' he asked.

'I must do my mum's shopping, then I'm free,' she said, blushing to the roots of her hair.

'Great. Let's do that, and then what? Shall we go for a drive?'

'It's a lovely day for a drive,' she replied, for want of anything else to say, and she felt weirdly old as she said it.

The shopping finished in a trice, the bags loaded in Alan's car, she sat beside him feeling suddenly very grown up as, knowing the area, she directed him to her favourite beauty spots. He looked so smart in his blazer and jeans, she could hardly believe he wanted to be seen with her.

'I was worried you wouldn't see the advert.'

'My mum did.'

They had lunch at a pub called The Duck and Thistle. 'This village would be the place to buy a cottage.'

'No one can afford it – it's too expensive now. But I've an aunt lives here.'

'Want to pop in?'

'No thanks. I haven't seen her in years.'

In the afternoon they went to the cinema. Kimberley would have preferred to sit in his car and talk, but she hadn't liked to say. She hoped in the cinema he'd put his arm about her, kiss her even. But he didn't. So she sat through *Four Weddings and a Funeral* and must have been the only person in the whole audience who didn't laugh, since her mind was on other things. How to get him to kiss her being paramount.

'Fancy a Chinese?' he asked as they emerged from the cinema.

Over the dim sum he told her he was leaving. She felt as if the world was crowding in on her, as if the walls of the restaurant had suddenly shifted.

'Oh no,' she said, and immediately realised how obvious she sounded. 'Where to?'

'Horsham. I've a flat there.'

'Oh, I see. Why?'

'My job.'

'Oh, I see.'

'I'll be back. I promise.' He put his hand over hers and she felt a jolt and had to look away so he could not see the longing in her eyes.

'When?' She sounded desolate.

'I'm not sure. I'll let you know, though, if you give me your number.'

'We don't have a phone,' she lied, as she'd done so often in the past.

'Then give me your address. I'll drop you a line.'

'I can't.'

'What do you mean, you can't?'

'Just that.'

'Then how am I supposed to get in touch with you?'

'I don't know,' she said, feeling hopeless.

He looked at her long and hard. 'I'm sorry,' he suddenly said and waved to the waiter for the bill.

'You don't understand – '

'You can say that again.' His mouth was set in a hard line.

She walked in front of him out of the restaurant, misery clouding her mind, making her feel she could not think straight. 'It's my dad,' she eventually said as they drove along. 'He doesn't like me to have friends.'

'Then why didn't you say that back there?'

'I don't know.'

'If you want to see me again, then I suggest you come up with some idea of how we get in touch.'

'I don't know . . . I . . . Could you stop here?'

'But it's nowhere.' He looked about him at the emptiness.

'No, here's fine.' She already had the car door open.

'Suit yourself, then.' He leant over and slammed the door shut.

'I'll be by the fountain – ' she called, but she doubted if he'd heard as the car, sounding as angry as him, roared away from her.

She watched the rear lights disappearing into the distance, covered her face with her hands and ran crying along the lane towards her home.

July

23

Bandage, still known as Sly, had been in the hands of Butch and Greaser for well over a month. In that time they had not, oddly for them, been idle. To the relief of the inhabitants they had not once been to the Market Square in Shillingham, and without Butch the group had rapidly disintegrated. Butch had traded his motorbike for a van. The selling was not as traumatic as it might have been, for in Sly he was convinced he had the makings of a lot of money, and it would only be a matter of time until he could buy an even bigger and better motorbike.

The van was needed to transport Sly to his 'gymnasium', as they liked to call it, which always made them roll about laughing, and back to Greaser's mum's flat on the Forest Glade estate.

The gymnasium was a lock-up garage they'd rented down by the old railway station and Butch, quite a good mechanic when he put his mind to it, rigged up a treadmill using a small conveyor belt which had once been used in a mini-market, powered by an old motor mower. He'd seen a shot on TV of a pit bull on one, and had determined to make one for Sly. It only had one speed, but Butch was working on how to incorporate a three-speed drive. On this Bandage was placed in a harness so that he could not escape. At first he had trouble keeping his balance and often fell over, which they found funny, but he quickly got the hang of it and made no fuss when the harness was strapped on.

'You'd think the silly bugger would realise he wasn't going anywhere, wouldn't you?' said Butch as they watched him one day, tongue lolling, saliva dripping from the exertion.

'Perhaps he's trying to please us.'

'Don't be such a silly sod.' Butch pushed Greaser. But all the same, despite Butch's sneering at him for being a soft bugger, Greaser always patted the dog and said 'good boy' to him.

The garage was isolated, so they were not watched when they clipped cement blocks onto another harness they'd fashioned, and forced the dog to drag them, to make his shoulder muscles grow.

They'd hoped Vic would help them, but he did not want to know. 'It's like he don't trust us,' said Butch, affronted when Vic had been cagey with them one evening. 'Dog fights? What dog fights?' Vic had said. 'I don't know nothing about no dog fights.'

'Bloody liar,' Greaser complained. 'And I didn't like the way he laughed at old Sly here – said he'd never make a fighter. If he don't know nothing about any dog fights, then how's he know if our dog can fight or not? Tell me that.'

'Exactly. Bloody creep. Still, all's not lost. Do you know Tom White, Kim's dad?'

'Not likely!' Greaser laughed. 'He's an aggressive bastard. Didn't he tell you to fuck off one day when you took Kim home?'

'He did too. I've met him since though. He's a friend of my uncle – the one what does the MOTs . . . you know.' He winked exaggeratedly. 'I could tell you a thing or two about him, know what I mean?'

The opportunity arose when Butch's uncle Sid needed a package delivered to Tom White and Butch, who happened to be lurking about, much to his uncle's surprise volunteered to take it and raced around to collect Greaser and Bandage.

'What's in the package?' Greaser asked.

'Where my uncle's concerned it's best not to ask.'

Greaser had always fondly thought that there was nothing in the world that could frighten him; that was until he met Tom that first time. He hoped to God that Tom never found out that he and Butch knew Kimberley. He glanced nervously about the yard, hoping she would not suddenly appear. The package delivered, they stood smoking and talking about motors and horses, until Butch plucked up the courage to mention Sly and how they wanted to find out about dog fighting.

'Easier said than done, Butch. The pit bull fraternity is a closed shop, has to be.'

'Of necessity, Tom. They don't know who people are, do they? But you know my uncle Sid, so you know me – would I grass?' Butch looked stricken to his soul at the very idea.

'There's some as would grass on their grannies if there was a quid in it.' Tom stood, hands thrust into his trouser pockets, and looked at Butch with an amused expression.

'If you'd just look at our dog. You know about dogs.' Butch put on a wide-eyed, expectant look.

'No harm in that, to be sure,' said Tom, and turned to the van and watched while Greaser opened the back door and yanked Sly out onto the yard. Tom stood back, eyeing the dog, like a show judge. But as he stepped forward and began to run his hands down his sides, Sly began to tremble.

'Nice dog,' he said as he stood up. 'Bit of a wimp though, isn't he?'

'He's not used to being outside,' Butch explained.

'Agoraphobic, like my mum,' Greaser volunteered, but stopped when Butch glared at him.

'The thing about dogs is they don't naturally want to fight each other, they have to be "persuaded",' Tom said with a sinister laugh. 'If – and it's a big if – if I just happened to meet someone who might invite you along, that dog won't fight.' As if to demonstrate, he kicked at Sly, who whimpered and cowered on to the yard. 'See. You've got to strengthen the dog and build up its muscles before you could put him up against a good fighter and make any serious money.'

'We've begun to do that.' And Butch explained about the treadmill and the cement blocks.

'You mean business, then?'

'Too right, Tom.'

'Well, if I hear of anything.' He tapped the side of his nose.

'Right on, Tom,' said Butch.

'I hear you breed dogs,' Greaser said, while Butch glared even more angrily at him.

'And who told you that?' Tom asked.

'I can't remember . . .' Greaser said lamely. 'It's just, I like dogs . . .' His voice petered out.

'Oh what the hell. This way.'

Tom led the way to his breeding shed. At the door he paused. 'If you want to get anywhere with that dog you're going to have to make him nastier, you realise? Still, no doubt you'll manage that.' He laughed and unlocked the padlock on the wooden door.

At the sight of the dogs in their pens Greaser went all soft, and Butch had to kick him, but even then he bought a puppy – a German Shepherd – for his mum, and they took it home with them to Forest Glade.

To make Sly nastier, as Tom had told him, they devised various exercises of their own. They might be amateurs at this game, but their methods began to show results. The docile dog that they'd acquired was not as docile any more.

When they weren't training, the dog stood in the corner of the room in the small flat, resting his chin on the wall, his back to them.

'He's a moody bugger, isn't he?' said Butch, eyeing his rump, twirling the billiard cue he used to prod it.

'Not what you'd call a friendly dog,' said Ginger, who had recently been allowed in on the secret and had just turned up.

'I hate it when he does that, it's like he's sulking, like he's not going to talk to us,' Greaser said.

Butch whooped with laughter. 'Greaser, don't be so bloody daft, dogs can't talk.' He whacked the dog on the rump with the cue. 'Come on, boy, play.' The dog turned, grabbed at the stick, snarling. 'Cor, that's better. That's what we want to hear, my boy, nice bit of aggressive growling, bit of salivating, bit of slashing teeth. That's my boy.'

The telephone rang, and Greaser answered it. 'It's for you.' He handed the instrument to Butch.

There was nothing for Greaser or Ginger to listen to, since Butch's responses to the conversation were a few 'yeses' interspersed with the odd grunt and one 'right on, man'. They looked up expectantly as he replaced the receiver.

'Tonight. It's on!' he exclaimed, his eyes shining with a strange excitement.

'What's on?'

'The fight, Ginger, you dork.'

'No! When? Where?' asked Greaser.

'An hour, out at the old Berry factory.'

'Do you think he's going to be strong enough against Vic's pit bull?' asked Ginger.

'He's not fighting that. Not yet. Vic said we should regard tonight as Sly being blooded, letting him know what's what. Vic's arranged for an old has-been of a dog. Sly should soon make mincemeat of him, Vic said.'

They piled into the van, stopped for fish and chips, which they ate as they drove out of town along the by-pass until they turned off into a disused factory site. Half the roof had gone and there wasn't one unbroken window, but three parked cars and Tom's van told them they'd come to the right place.

'There's not many here,' Greaser said, surprised.

'This isn't a proper dog fight, stupid,' Butch said.

'Then what is it?' asked Ginger.

'A proper fight you'd only have a couple of dogs. This is as a favour to us – to test Sly out.'

'Why they doing us a favour?' Greaser asked.

'My uncle Sid had a talk with Tom and persuaded him, like. That's why –'

'What? Made him an offer he couldn't refuse?' Ginger laughed.

'Something like.'

Inside the building there were about ten men, none of whom acknowledged the friends, but there was a rustle of interest in Sly.

'Who's he?' Tom, who had sauntered up, asked.

'My mate Ginger.'

'You didn't say he was coming.'

'Didn't know I had to ask permission,' Butch said, trying to sound sarcastic, but only managing to sound scared.

'You always ask, Butch. It's healthy to remember that,' Tom said.

A pit bull was already being held in position in the ring. He was growling, snarling, snapping at anything or anyone, and ready to go. He was called Samson, and he was a veteran of a hundred fights, as witnessed by his ragged ears, many scars and the permanent limp in one back leg. Butch dragged Sly and held him, as he saw Samson's owner was holding him, on one side of a painted red line which showed which half of the ring was Sly's.

'He doesn't look as though he's going to fight,' shouted one bloke.

'You wait and see,' replied Butch, with a confident jerk of his head.

'When Samson attacks, he'll fight then,' said Vic.

'Right, seconds out,' the organiser shouted.

Butch took Sly's collar and lead off and gave him a shove towards the pit bull. At the same time the pit bull's owner let him loose; he ran silently towards Sly who, looking up with alarm, backed off. The pit bull raced round him in circles, every so often making a lunge at him with bared teeth. Sly stood in the middle of the ring shivering and with eyes lowered so that he made no eye contact with his adversary.

'What a waste of time this is going to be. Prod him up the arse,' someone shouted.

Butch leant forward and shoved Sly in the rump with the billiard cue. Sly shot to his feet as if stung. The pit bull, taking this as an aggressive action, jumped onto Sly's back and sank his teeth into his shoulder. Blood spurted in all directions. Sly tried to roll on his back in submission, but the pit bull was too big and heavy, and his teeth were still embedded in Sly's neck. Sly shook his powerful shoulders, then again, and again, until, with an almighty heave, the pit bull fell backwards.

Sly tried to reverse out of the ring, but the breeze blocks were in the way, and beyond them the men, who were all shouting and yelling at him. Shaking with fear he ran in circles, desperately looking for a way of escape. The pit bull, his teeth bared, stalked him. Suddenly it lunged at his throat. With a mighty heave Sly shook his head until the pit bull lost its grip and slid to the floor. Quickly Sly sank down and rolled over on his back, his paws in the air, in the time-honoured gesture of submission. The pit bull stood still, looked at the dog on its back, then up at his master expectantly.

'Kill the fucker!' A man screamed from the back.

'Nah. Mismatched. Shouldn't be allowed. This isn't sport,' his owner said, leaning forward. Grabbing his dog by the scruff of the neck, he yanked him away from the cowering Sly. Sly inadvertently and innocently had ended the fight. The pit bull had won on a submission. There was a muttering of discontent from the men around the ring, disgruntled and disgusted at such a short, one-sided fight. Greaser, on the other hand, had run outside and was being sick.

Butch jumped into the ring and pulled at Sly. 'Come on, you silly old bugger, you're not that hurt,' he said, feeling somewhat queasy himself. He'd thought he'd like the blood, but he wasn't so sure now.

Tom White approached Butch. 'Just as well we set up this trial run for you. A cock-up like that with real money on it, and things could get very nasty for you.'

'I can handle myself,' Butch said cockily, but his palms were wet with sweat.

'What made you think this brute was ready? It's got no bloody spunk at all. You've been stupid, putting it in the ring when it doesn't know how to fight. It's got to want to fight. They don't just naturally fight, you know, dogs. They're not like men, they quite like each other, you've got to make the things aggressive.'

'Lecture over?' Butch tapped his toe with simulated impatience. Sly, exhausted, sat at his feet panting and bleeding.

'How much did you pay for it?' Tom asked.

'Two hundred quid,' Butch said, his eyes flickering as he lied.

'Oh yeah?' Tom laughed. 'I'll give you twenty for him.'

'You've got to be joking! Twenty, twenty quid! That's a pedigree dog, that is.'

'How much do you want then?'

'A hundred.'

'When you paid two hundred for it?' Tom smiled sardonically.

Butch shrugged. 'I can stand the loss. In any case, it's a pain in the arse, that dog. The flat's too small for it.'

'Tell you what, I'll give you fifty, that's fair and square, I'll take it off your hands.'

'All right, then. You're on.' The money changed hands and Butch handed the lead over to Tom, who patted Sly, and the dog, oddly, trotted quite happily behind the man to his yellow van which was parked outside. He opened the door and hurled Sly in. There was a snarling and a growling from inside. 'That's my pit bull, Hannibal, he'll sort him out,' Tom laughed. 'Staying for the real fight?'

'Nah, I've got to get back – business, you know,' Butch said, trying to sound nonchalant, but still feeling sick. He swung round and sauntered off to look for Greaser, who was leaning wanly against the wall. Ginger, looking none too happy himself, was smoking.

'What's wrong with you two?' asked Butch.

'It was horrible,' Ginger stated.

'I like dogs,' said Greaser, tears running down his face. 'I didn't like that.'

'Go on, dog's all right.'

'He wasn't all right, he was hurt, and all that blood, I didn't know it was going to be like that,' said Greaser.

'What the fuck did you expect then?' Butch said belligerently. 'Come on, let's go and get a curry, I've sold him. Here you are.' And he gave twenty-five quid to Greaser.

'My mum won't like that, she liked that dog, she said she felt safe with it there.'

'You've got her the other one. The flat was too small for two,' said Butch logically.

24

Thomasine, like most people, accepted that there were times in life when everything appeared to go wrong, but she felt she'd had her quota without this.

Distilling its contents, she re-read the letter in her hand. It was from the publishing company thanking her for her *lovely* work, but *no thanks*. In the accompanying envelope were the three sample paintings she had sent them with such confidence.

She regretted how confident she'd been, so foolhardy of her, but then she'd had reason to hope. The sketches she'd done at Eveleigh's kennels had helped her enormously. Once she was able to use sketches from life rather than photographs, then the illustrations for the book came to life. It was the best work she had ever done. And it wasn't good enough.

She looked down at the work on her desk. She'd begun to paint watercolours of the locality in the hope she could sell them. The painting of the river Shill, which she'd been pleased with before the post came, now looked like rubbish. She stretched. Her shoulders were stiff, she'd been working since five this morning. It always amazed her how quickly time went when she was painting. Still, she wouldn't be doing much more of that, not now, not when it was such a waste of time and effort. She began to clean her brushes. She had grown to love this little room which she fondly thought looked more like a studio. Off the kitchen, it was warm from the heat of the wood burner which filtered through the door. It had a north-facing window, which gave good light when she was working at her drawing board, her paints neatly set on the table beside her. She resisted looking at the corner where Luna's basket used to be. She still missed the dog far more than she would have thought possible.

At least the publisher's rejection had solved one problem for her, whether she could afford to get her hair done – she couldn't, so, therefore, she would. She needed something to cheer her up. She phoned for an appointment later in the day and, deciding to do the other things she invariably did when fed up, ran herself a bath.

What on earth had she done for the gods to be so cross with her, she thought as she soaked in the oil-scented water – expense again, but hang it, she said to herself as she dripped the Hermès bath oil in.

The day stretched ahead. What should she do with it? She wanted to ease the disappointment by indulging herself. After her hair-do she could have lunch in Shillingham, then she'd browse in the shops, go to the library, buy herself some flowers. But what should she do with herself in the evening?

It had been over four months since she'd arrived here. She still liked it, was fond of this house. Why, she'd even adjusted to being alone, and there were advantages. She could watch shows like *Blind Date* if she wanted to. Robert would never watch such a programme, and neither had she, simply because he'd have made such a fuss. Now she could watch all night if she wished.

Socially, things hadn't worked out quite as well as she had first hoped. Available men seemed to be thin on the ground. She liked the vet, but he was obviously claimed, if not by that brittle Sophia Hawksmoor, by the very attractive housekeeper he employed. There was, of course, Oliver Hawksmoor, but she'd never really got over her initial dislike of him. He was too charming, too smooth – such types, she was sure, led only to disaster.

Still – she topped up the hot water – it would be nice if an unattached man moseyed into her life. Not for any great romance, she wasn't ready for that yet, not until all the bruises had faded. Just for company, that would be nice. But Nadine would not countenance another man in her life – even if it was only for friendship, she amended quickly.

Every time she thought about her daughter she felt uncomfortable and guilty. Nadine was hurting, it was obvious. Her much flaunted vegetarianism was a gesture to make people more conscious of her, an attention-seeking device. Still, what was understandable in a nine or ten-year-old was intensely irritating in a sixteen-year-old.

'And I thought you'd done a bunk. I said to Justin, where's that nice Mrs Lambert?'

'Holed up and feeling sorry for myself,' Thomasine replied, and wondered, not for the first time, why it was so easy to tell one's hairdresser what ailed one.

'Got a new dog yet?'

'No. I thought about it, but I don't think I'd want to be that miserable again if something happened to it.'

'What a doom you're in. We'll have to see about this. You're too young and attractive to hide away.'

'Well, hardly. I do go out sometimes.'

'Tell you what.' Gill stood, scissors poised like a weapon. 'Come to a dog show with us? Justin, what do you think?'

'You'd love it, Mrs Lambert. We have such fun! Gill's right, do you a treat.'

'Oh, I don't know . . .'

'I'm not going to listen. So there. We'll come and pick you up. No argument.'

'But what about the salon?'

'Oh, we shut it up. Haven't you seen all the dates we're shut in the window? Dogs come first. No doubt about it.'

'Well . . .'

'Then that's settled.' He clicked away with his scissors. 'Isn't it a joy? Those rough creatures have gone from the market square. One can walk about safe now, can't one? Right, that's you done. Out with the dryer.'

That night, alone with the TV and her bread and cheese, Thomasine decided she would, after all, go to the dog show. It would be something to do.

Oliver stood dejectedly looking out of the arched window of his great hall and wished it were raining – glorious sunshine and blue sky seemed an affront in his present mood. He turned away, a good measure of whisky in the tumbler in his hand and, thinking food might work, made for the kitchen. He opened the fridge, looked gloomily at the empty interior, and sighed at the prospect of yet another trip to the supermarket. He had to hand it to Sophia, when they lived together he could not remember ever finding an empty fridge. He wished Wimpole were here; she'd tell him what to buy.

Wimpole had gone to Whitstable, where she had a large extended family. She'd said she was going on holiday, but it wasn't really a holiday; she'd gone in a fit of pique. He hadn't meant to upset her, but in the way of rows, one thing had led to another.

It had started by him innocently asking her if she was bored. He thought he'd asked kindly enough, but she'd taken it as an accusation and had cloaked herself in umbrage and said he thought her shallow, which had reminded him of an argument with Sophia, so he'd told her to shut up and from there all hell had broken loose.

The problem was, row or not, he knew he was right – Wimpole was bored and, he believed, longed to go back to London. Whereas life for him had settled into a pleasant routine. He'd never been an early riser, but here he found an early start painless. Mind, Wimpole had said, wait until winter and he wouldn't be so keen to leap about early then. She might be right.

He'd given himself the task of alleviating Wimpole's boredom. She needed friends, he decided, but who? Whilst Grace White and she got on, he doubted if they'd ever make best friends.

It was when he was in Shillingham picking up some two-stroke for the mower that the solution drove onto the garage forecourt – Rudie Adams, Ben Luckett's chauffeur-handyman. Perhaps Wimpole needed a gentleman friend, he thought, grinning at the idea as he ambled over to the Range Rover.

'Rudie, just the fellow. I'm thinking of making a large pond in my meadow. Maybe attract some geese and ducks for the odd pot shot. I was wondering if you could advise me?' Oliver beamed as he lied through his teeth. He might enjoy eating duck; he couldn't abide shooting them.

'Sure thing, Mr Hawksmoor, when would be convenient?'

It had been so easy to arrange, and Rudie was nigh on perfect for Wimpole. Just sixty, a widower and, Oliver was pretty certain, attractive to women. With his thick mop of silver hair, rugged face and blue eyes, he'd always reminded Oliver of a Marlboro cigarette advert come to life.

The following day they had trudged over the meadow planning Oliver's pond, and what was more natural than for Oliver to invite him into the house for a drink?

After he'd made the introduction he sat back to watch developments. He was disappointed, for Wimpole showed no interest in Rudie and instead was quite brusque with him.

'If you don't mind taking your boots off, Mr Adams,' she'd said sharply. 'But some of us folks are partial to a clean floor.'

'I'm sorry, Wimpole, I didn't think,' he said, and despite his years looked flustered.

'Miss Wimpole, to you, if you don't mind.' Her voice, to Oliver, sounded full of steel. 'Tea or coffee, Mr Adams?'

'Tea would be nice.'

'I'm sure a whisky would be more appreciated,' Oliver interrupted.

'No thank you, tea would go down a treat.' Rudie attempted a smile and Wimpole looked insufferably smug. His attempts at matchmaking failing so completely Oliver excused himself, saying something about his book, and escaped to his writing. If there was one thing he couldn't stand it was Wimpole all starched and formal.

An old school friend who was a literary agent had shown interest in what he'd written so far, and only yesterday had phoned to ask when would it be finished? In a fit of enthusiasm he'd said four weeks, which, if he continued to row with Wimpole and fret about her being bored, was unlikely. He supposed he would always worry about her. 'You're too nice for your own good,' he said out loud. 'Bloody saint, that's what you are.' He drank a toast to himself in the whisky that Rudie had refused.

After this abortive attempt to help Wimpole he wondered if he might have been somewhat heavy-handed, for she began behaving oddly, almost secretively. She borrowed the car several times and then refused to say where she'd been. And that, of course, was the second reason for the row which was now upsetting him.

'At this rate I'll think you've got a fella,' he'd said, meaning it as a joke.

'And what if I have?' she replied, in a grotesquely arch manner.

'Wimpole, you don't mean-? You do! Who?' Such news had quite killed their row and he was jumping about with excitement.

'Rudolph, of course,' she replied, with a proud lift of her head.

'What, after the reindeer?' He chuckled at his own joke.

'No! As a matter of fact his mother was a romantic.'

'Sorry?'

'Valentino, clot,' Wimpole snapped back.

'Well, it's a very grand name,' he said, trying to make amends, but succeeding only in making matters worse.

She spun round on one heel to face him. 'What, too grand for the likes of me?'

'I didn't mean that,' he blustered.

'Then you should be more careful what you say to a body. Bloody insulting, if you ask me. I bet you thought I'd marry a Bert or a Fred; that such names suited me better. You're a nasty little snob, that's what you are, Oliver. I've always suspected it.'

'Wimpole, I'm sorry. Don't let's argue. It's just it's a bit of a surprise, that's all. Forgive?' He put his hand out to grab her because she looked as if she was about to rush out of the room.

'Well, if you're really sorry,' she said grudgingly.

'Oh, I am. I am. But when did you meet him?

'You had a stroke or something? Here of course.'

'Here? Rudolph? I don't know . . .' His voice wavered as the truth dawned. 'You don't mean *Rudie*? I didn't think. Of course his name must be Rudolph. Did you say marry? I'm going to have to sit down.'

'So? What's wrong with me getting married, or have you got something against him, then?' She stood, hands on hips, leaning towards him, her whole body aquiver with indignation.

'Nothing, it's just – ' he started, and then stopped, not knowing quite how to go on.

'You can't start a sentence and then stop and leave a body hanging in the air.'

'I wasn't accusing him or anything, it's just . . .'

'If you say "*just*" one more time, so help me I'll clock you one.'

'I didn't expect you to talk about getting married, that's all.' He felt quite stupid as he spoke, but it had been a shock, he hadn't had time to adjust. 'I mean, isn't this all happening too quickly. Aren't you rushing things a bit? You never ever said you wanted to get married, why now?'

'Maybe I never met the right bloke before. I'm getting on, there's no point in hanging about, is there?'

'No, but – hell, I never even knew you had any "*friends*" – you know what I mean?' He looked as confused as he felt.

'Crikey, you'll be calling them *gentleman callers* next.' At this she did manage to laugh, but it was not prolonged and she was serious again. 'You never asked, did you, Oliver? Too wrapped up in yourself – self, self, self – that's all you're any good for. Well, for your information, I do have a life of my own, even if you have never shown any interest in it,' she said sharply. 'Don't you want me to be happy? Frightened of having to cope by yourself?'

'That's not fair. How the hell was I to know if you never let on. I thought you were content as we were. I didn't think.'

'Then it's about time you started. When you suggested we moved out of London and into the sticks it came as one hell of a shock. Oh, you made your pretty speeches about not doing it if I wasn't happy with the idea. I wasn't born yesterday, Oliver, I know you better than you know yourself. You've always done what you want. I could vacillate until the cows came home – I knew what it was you wanted. What's next, that's what worries me? How long before you marry again, tell me that?'

'It's hardly likely – '

'Isn't it? What if your new wife doesn't like me, how long will I be welcome here then? I've got to look after meself. And getting married will ensure I'm all right.'

'Wimpole, please. I wouldn't desert you ever, I can't believe what I'm hearing. This is no reason to rush into marriage.'

'Isn't it? And I'm not *rushing* – I've thought about it, and I've made my mind up and that's that. It's time I had some security in my life.'

Despite that remark hurting him, he managed to stay silent even when Wimpole flounced from the room. The door reopened. 'I've got holiday due, I'm taking it now. All right?'

That had been two weeks ago, and she hadn't even sent him a postcard.

No food, no Wimpole, no Bandage. 'What doom!' he said aloud, and wondered how often these days he talked to himself, more than before, he was sure. He looked at the glass in his hand. Whisky at this time was not a good idea either. What the hell was happening to him, what was he *allowing* to happen? He poured the remains of the whisky down the sink and made himself a pot of coffee.

Wimpole had been wrong. It wasn't that he couldn't manage without her, that was too simplistic, of course he could. No, because of this row he faced losing the one person he knew, without doubt, had always loved him, despite all his faults. His parents had barely been aware of his existence, let alone loved him. Aunt Phoebe had, in her detached and mildly eccentric way, but she was dead and who was there now? Had Sophia ever loved him, or had he imagined she had because he'd wanted her to? If he was totally honest, the only creatures who'd ever loved him unconditionally had been his dogs. All his life there had been a dog trotting behind him, adoring him. Now he didn't even have Bandage.

He sighed deeply. Maybe he should buy another one. It was three months since he'd disappeared. Yet to get another dog would seem so disloyal – and how would Bandage feel if he came home and found another dog in his basket? He shook his head at that thought – it was stupid of him to cling onto such hopes. He had to mourn for Bandage as he had for other dogs in the past when they had died. His hoping that Bandage would return had been preventing the grieving process from beginning. And until it was over, another dog was out of the question.

He stood up. Sitting here wallowing in self-pity was not going to solve anything. He'd do some gardening, take over where Wimpole had got bored.

As he changed his shoes the telephone rang.

'Oliver duck, it's me, Cora.'

'Hullo there.' He forced a measure of cheerfulness into his voice.

'Ben's birthday lunch – next week. Of course you'll come?'

'But Cora . . .'

'I don't want to hear any buts. I know you're on your own, that Wimpole's gone off on holiday.'

'How do you know that?'

'I know everything.'

'I don't think I can face Sophia.'

'Don't be silly, just ignore her. You can't spend your life avoiding her. We'll be twenty for lunch.'

'Twenty? Who?' he asked, his curiosity getting the better of him.

'Odds and sods. Waifs and strays, you know me,' Cora laughed her attractive throaty chuckle.

'I don't know . . .'

'You don't have the number of that nice Thomasine Lambert, do you? I liked her, so did Ben. I thought I'd call her,' Cora said, with low cunning.

'Sorry, no. You'll have to try directory enquiries.' He tried to sound as nonchalant as possible.

'So, what about you, Oliver? We've got some Beluga – does that tempt you?'

'You know, Cora, it might just do that.' He couldn't care less about Beluga!

25

Kimberley had finished attending to the dogs and was returning to the house when she heard a whimpering noise coming from the shed where her father kept his pit bulls, Hannibal and Hector. She preferred not to enter: she'd only seen them once, and they looked so unpleasant they frightened her. Ignoring the noise she walked on, but the whimper seemed to follow her and grow louder, and compassion defeated fear.

She pushed the heavy door open and peered in. Compared to the puppy shed, this was a palace. It was clean, and filled with the comforting smell of good fresh straw; in the corner she saw a large gas heater, presumably for winter. The water bowls held clear water, and the two dogs looked up with interest and lolloped over to the fencing to welcome her.

Her father had acquired a third dog, and it was this one who must have been whimpering. He lay in a disconsolate black heap, and two eyes set almost on the sides of his head watched Kimberley's approach warily.

Kimberley leant on the gate to the pen. The dog sidled on its belly away from her, and she saw it was shaking. 'Is it you, Sly?' she asked, recognising the white fur on one of its front paws. 'Sly?' The dog did not respond. Kimberley wondered whether to approach further or not. But the pathetic way the dog held its head, the obvious fear, made her mind up for her.

Gingerly she opened the gate, talking to the dog all the time. She stepped nearer, holding out her hand, speaking encouragingly. She bent down and balanced herself with one hand in the straw and felt something wet and sticky. She looked at the palm of her hand and saw it was covered with blood.

'You poor old boy. Let me see.' She was on her knees now as she moved towards him. 'You're that dog that Butch had, aren't you? Not having much luck, are you, ending up with my dad.'

The dog lay still, his eyes watching her, but always looking away whenever her glance met his. Her hand was close to his face now. She let him sniff her, saw him relax. 'You know, I think you should really be called Bandage.' She enunciated the word clearly. He responded with a twitch of his rump, but this movement obviously hurt him, for he whined and then flopped back on the straw and stretched his neck. She saw the blood glistening on his fur. 'Bloody hell, what happened?' She knew it was a stupid question, she knew very well what had happened to the dog – he'd been fighting, or rather been made to.

She stood up and the dog looked at her appealingly, as if afraid she was leaving him. He started to whimper again. She crossed to a tap. She found a cloth which she wished could have been cleaner and rinsed it out. Bandage lay almost contentedly as, gently, she bathed his wound, yelping once when she pressed a little too hard. 'Sorry,' she said, and kissed the top of his head. The dog then turned, as if to show her the wound on the back of its neck. That was wider, as if the skin had been ripped. She needed several trips to the sink to rinse the blood from the cloth.

'You poor love,' she was saying when the door burst open and her father entered. At the sight of him, the dog began to shake.

'What're you up to?' he shouted.

'Dad, this dog's badly hurt.'

'So? It's its own bloody fault.'

'Can't we call the vet? It needs stitches, antibiotics.'

'Don't talk bloody stupid. A vet here – are you mad?'

'No, just fed up with what goes on here. It's not right.'

'Well, you know what you can do, don't you?' He glowered belligerently. 'You can piss off and leave your mother and me alone. Understand? Mind your own fucking business.'

'Right, if that's what you want, then I'll do just that,' she said with false confidence.

'Good. I've had enough of you. All this grand education and where's it going to get you? You're nothing but a bloody parasite. But I warn you.' He stepped menacingly towards her. 'You listen. You breathe a word about this to a living soul and, I warn you, I'll get you. Understood?'

'I won't say a word.' The look of fear and horror on her face was sufficient to reassure him that she meant what she said. She stepped back from her father, the dog cowering behind her.

Kimberley had been tired before she started. Now, trudging along, a case in one hand, a half-filled canvas holdall over her shoulder, Middle Shilling felt as if it was forty miles away. She had hoped to be able to hitch-hike, but she'd been walking for over an hour and had not seen one car.

She felt completely alone in the world, which in a way she was. But that was a thought she had no intention of lingering over. It was done now; she'd finally left.

It had been hard leaving, and she'd dallied too long and as a result had nearly bumped into her father – the last thing she needed. Last night, after the row and his ultimatum, she had gone to her room and packed her bags – everything she possessed in a case and the holdall. She had made two trips down the stairs, banging the case and bag, making what she was doing obvious. She wasn't sure why, almost certainly to make her mother come to see what all the noise was about – but she hadn't. Instead, this morning, when Kimberley had stood in the kitchen doorway, her mother was at the table making an apple pie.

'I'm going, Mum. Dad said I was to.'

'I know.' Her mother did not look up.

'Well, I'll be off then . . .' She lingered.

'Goodbye.'

Kimberley swung round and took a step into the warm, shabby room. 'Is that really all you've got to say?'

'What is there to say? What can I say?' Her mother paused in her task and looked up, and Kimberley saw how afraid she was, how sad.

'Oh, Mum!'

'It's probably for the best. You know what he's like.'

'Yes. I suppose so. But what about you?'

'I'll be fine. It might be better – less arguing, if you know what I mean.'

'No, Mum, I don't know. Are you blaming me for all the upsets? Is his filthy temper my fault?'

Her mother passed a weary hand over her eyes. 'Sometimes, yes. You answer back when it's best not to. You question what he does – no man likes that. You make him feel he's not master in his own house any more.'

Kimberley shook her head in disbelief. 'He's a bastard, Mum, rotten to the core. You know that.'

'He's my husband.'

'So? Does that excuse him? Does that make what he does right?'

Kimberley stood, her arms hanging awkwardly at her sides, not sure how to continue, how to end their conversation. Wanting her mother to fling her arms about her and beg her to stay, and knowing how unlikely that was.

'Here, take this.' From the pocket of her pinny, Sue took a small roll of folded notes. 'See you on your way.'

'You can't afford to give me that.'

'Yes I can. I've always got a little put by – just in case. He won't know about this.'

Kimberley wanted not to accept, but she had ten pounds in the world and since she had no clear idea what she was to do, she took it. She zipped it into her shoulder-bag, said thanks and, not sure if her voice would allow her to say more, put her head down so that her mother would not see the distress on her face as she ducked out of the back door.

She crossed to the barn where the fighting dogs were kennelled. She had planned to take the bull terrier with her. There was something about the dog, a lost look, a longing to be loved that found an echo in herself. But Sly, though she called him Bandage, was stiff and could barely move, let alone walk the distance she must travel. The cuts were congealed with blood. She wondered whether to bathe them again and decided against it, fearing further water on the wounds might open them again. Instead, she lay down on the straw beside the dog, scooped him into her arms and allowed her sense of isolation and betrayal to take over from the brave front which was so difficult to maintain. The dog whimpered and nuzzled her neck as if he understood her problem.

'I'm sorry, Bandage,' she whispered in the dog's ear. 'I've got to leave. I'll try and come back for you – that's a promise. One day when I'm settled.' She had to look away from the pleading expression in the dog's eyes, quickly left the barn and struck off across the field towards the road which would eventually take her to Middle Shilling and the house of her Aunt Grace.

Grace White was an aunt by marriage. Her husband had been Tom White's older brother who had died five years ago. Kimberley had met her aunt but did not know her. It was not in Tom's interests to be friendly with anyone, and that included family. But then the brothers had never got on, her mother had told her that. Kimberley had last seen this aunt three years ago when, on a rare shopping trip with her mother, they had bumped into her in Morris-town. They'd gone to MacDonalds for a hamburger and coffee. Kimberley had been fascinated to meet her, and decided she liked her. Now all she could hope was that the woman had liked her too.

Her bags slowed her progress dramatically. It was already afternoon, and her arms felt as if they had been stretched like elastic, when she finally found her aunt's house on the small council estate and knocked on the door.

Grace took one look at her weary niece and swept her into her arms. Kimberley felt she'd never known such a strong sense of comfort and security as she felt now, clasped to Grace's ample breasts.

'My Terry, your uncle, he often said "One day it'll get too much for that little one".'

'He knew?' she asked, as they sat at the small table in the tiny, cluttered kitchen. They were alone. Her cousins, after their initial curiosity had waned, were in the next room watching television.

'Chalk and cheese Tom and Terry were.'

Later, after Kimberley had told Grace what had happened, she said, 'And she let you go, don't forget that. They don't deserve you, that's for sure. So, what are your plans, or haven't you had time to make any?'

'I'd started to look for a job, but it's proving more difficult than I'd realised. I thought I wanted to work in a bank, but I'm not sure if I could stand being cooped up in an office.'

'What about school? I always heard you were the clever one.'

'That's finished. I've just got to wait for my results. I did wonder about getting a job as a nanny or something like that. I think I'd be good with kids, and I'll need a job where I can live in.'

'Do you like dogs?'

'Dogs?' Kimberley looked up sharply. 'What about dogs?' she asked cautiously, the years of training by her father still paramount. What did Grace know?

'Would you like to work with them?'

'I'd love that – provided it was proper . . . you know.' Her voice trailed off, not able to explain further, frightened she might let slip about the puppy farm and compromise her father.

'I sometimes help out a lady near here who's got a big kennels. When she goes away, I pop up and give the dogs their food. Her last kennel maid left and she's not found anyone suitable – very fussy she is. But she's rushed off her feet.'

'I'd like that.'

'I can't promise, you understand. You might not suit. But I can mention you to her next time I see her.'

Thomasine wondered if she was becoming a recluse. She'd always liked driving and normally enjoyed going to pick her daughter up from school, stopping for lunch on the way there and tea on the way back. However, this time was different. No sooner had she set off than she longed to be back home. It was as if the house had become her safe haven. To speed the process she did not bother to stop for lunch and chivvied Nadine into hurrying her goodbyes.

'We usually stop there,' Nadine said as they shot past the old coaching inn.

'I'd rather press on.'

'Why? What for?'

'I don't know. I just want to get home. Getting middle-aged, I suppose.'

'Getting!' Nadine snorted, but Thomasine decided not to rise to the bait. 'Have you changed my room?'

'Yes.'

'What's it like?'

'It's a secret.' Thomasine smiled, confident she would like this one. 'I expect you're excited about Tuscany. Quite the jet-setter, aren't you? France at Easter and Italy this summer,' she said lightly, which was quite an achievement since she was still upset that, yet again, she was to lose her daughter for the holidays. Nadine, reasonably enough, was seduced by the idea of a month in a villa with a swimming pool. She did not blame her, but rather Robert; chequebook power, which, in the circumstances, was a long way from fair.

'You don't mind me going, do you?' Nadine asked anxiously, to Thomasine's surprise. 'I mean, it does seem grossly unfair on you. That's presuming, of course, that you'd want me home with you.' She said this almost shyly.

Thomasine, while keeping her eyes on the road, felt for Nadine's hand and squeezed it. 'That goes without saying.'

'Then I'll stay if you want.' Thomasine smiled, for her daughter's voice was such a mixture of duty and disappointment, making her voice slip down only for hope to raise it again.

'Nadine, darling, I'm fine, really. I do understand, you know.'

'What?' she asked suspiciously.

'How difficult it is for you being pulled all ways. And of course you must go to Tuscany, it all sounds delicious. I'd go if it was offered to me.'

'I know Dad's trying to buy me. I'm not thick.'

'That's not fair. He loves you. Everything he does is because of that. Don't be hard on him,' she said, regretting that she had to be so reasonable, but with her heart singing that Nadine wasn't fooled.

'It is gross, though, isn't it? You're strapped for cash and can't bribe me in the same way. I wouldn't put it past him to have made sure you were short of money.'

'No, that's my stupidity. I'd never had to manage before, and I miscalculated.'

'What about the book illustrations?'

'They didn't like them – well, not enough.'

'What dorks.'

'Bless you for that.'

'The problem with Dad is he's not an objective person. He only sees things from his viewpoint. Not like me, I always take a balanced view of things. He hasn't got my tolerance,' Nadine said gravely, and Thomasine had to pop a Polo in her mouth to stop herself from shrieking with amusement. How wrong could one be? She smiled inwardly instead.

'I sometimes think I've been intolerant of you, though,' Nadine continued, and Thomasine received one of those shudders that one does when one's mind appears to have been read.

'In what way?' she asked innocently.

'I suppose I was angry with the split up, so I took it out on you. I just wanted to lash out. But I've changed all that. Tell you what, I'll make sure I spend Christmas with you – no matter what he offers?'

'What did he offer this time?'

'Driving lessons when I'm seventeen.'

'Did he now?' The creep, she thought, but said nothing and concentrated on her driving and relished the fact that her complicated daughter appeared to be less complex this time – or at least she hoped so.

At the school house, she was pleased to note Nadine prowling around the kitchen and sitting room as if checking if anything had changed, as she had invariably done at their home in London. 'Isn't it odd here without Luna?' she suddenly said, her tour of the sitting room complete.

'Horrible. I miss her dreadfully.'

'Get another like her, I say.' Nadine grinned at her broadly.

'Who could replace Luna?' she said as the telephone rang. Nadine wandered off as she answered it.

'Cora? How nice.' She listened as Cora explained about her lunch party for Ben's birthday. 'I would have loved to come, but unfortunately I can't. I have to drive my daughter to Heathrow that day – she's off to Italy.' And damn, she thought, the one day she'd received an invitation! 'Never mind, another time,' Cora said vaguely, and as the call was disconnected the door burst open and Nadine shot into the room.

'Mum! How could you! My room!'

'You don't like it?' Thomasine's heart sank.

'Like it? It's gross! Red! It's grim! I wanted black – I told you.'

'Wouldn't black be even grimmer?'

'You never listen to me do you? What I want never matters.'

Thomasine looked at her fuming daughter and marvelled that anyone could change mood so quickly. Still, the car ride home had been pleasant. 'Well, I'm not changing it again, and that's flat.'

Nadine opened her mouth, about, no doubt, to give a sharp reply, but was foiled by the front doorbell ringing. Even as she wondered who it could possibly be, Thomasine was grateful to them for interrupting what appeared to be a full-scale row in the making.

She opened the door to find the Tregidgas standing on the step. 'Mrs Tregidga!' She smiled politely, and then she saw Mrs Tregidga was cuddling a puppy to her. 'Oh, how sweet.' She patted the small head. 'Come in, do. How kind of you to call.'

She ushered them both through to the sitting room, where Mrs Tregidga gently placed the puppy on the rug. Thomasine was quickly on her knees. 'Oh, you sweet little thing.' The puppy, whose stomach appeared to be larger than its head, waddled over to her, clambering up onto her lap. Thomasine looked at Mrs Tregidga. 'One of Luna's?'

'Yes. It's a bit early to see, but the colouring will be exactly the same, and she's as stubborn as her mother.'

'You are *adorable*.' Thomasine nuzzled the small dog, who by now was removing her earrings with teeth as sharp as razors. 'Ouch,' she cried. The puppy stopped and, her head on one side, looked quizzically up at her. 'Look at that, just like Luna. It's so kind of you to bring her to show me. I did sometimes think of taking you up on your invitation to visit, but I didn't think I could cope with seeing Luna. Silly of me.'

'No, we understand, really. We're selling the pups now and, well, we didn't want them all to go without you being given a second chance to decide if you want one.'

'As a present, you understand, Mrs Lambert, for all you did for Luna,' Major Tregidga added.

'How kind of you. I don't know.' Thomasine shook her head. 'Only a moment ago I said to Nadine there wasn't a dog that could take Luna's place. But, she is sweet, isn't she?' The puppy licked her face excitedly. 'I'd love to keep her. I didn't know I'd want one – I thought I didn't – but now I know I do,' Thomasine said suddenly and laughed at her jumbled sentence. 'What's she called?'

'We left that to you. But let me know as soon as possible, I must know for the Kennel Club registration.'

'Nova. That's it. She's called Nova.'

In all the excitement she had not seen the major was awkwardly holding a box of puppy food and mineral supplements. 'Have you still got the baskets? If not, I've one in the car.'

'I've still got everything in the garage. Maybe deep down I always knew I'd succumb again.'

Drinks offered and drunk, the Tregidgas departed. 'Who was that?' Nadine asked sulkily, appearing in the doorway. 'Not another one! You said you didn't want one.'

'I changed my mind. Just look at her, isn't she sweet?' Thomasine fondly watched the puppy trying to chase her stubby tail and not succeeding. 'In any case, you just said I should get another.'

'That was then – '

'Before you saw your room?'

'Exactly.'

Thomasine sat back on her feet, the puppy playing with the folds of her skirt. 'Nadine, we can't go on like this,' she sighed. 'You must try to control your temper and learn to be a bit more reasonable.'

'I don't have to do anything I don't want!'

'Then you'll have a miserable life.'

'I realise that. Especially now you've got that mutt to love more than me.'

'Oh, Nadine!' she began, feeling sorrow and exasperation in equal doses, but Nadine had already slammed out of the room.

Nova suddenly collapsed on the rug. One moment she'd been playing, the next her legs gave way and she was asleep. 'I reckon you were asleep before you hit the rug, Nova.' Thomasine gently stroked the soft fur of the puppy, who was contentedly wiffling. Perhaps this was the wisest thing she could have done; she needed someone to love, and loving Nadine was becoming more difficult. She sighed, but then found herself thinking there was another plus factor – the puppy would give her an excuse to see that nice vet again. And then she resolved, no matter how hard it was, to ignore her daughter's tantrums and not let her pull her down.

26

Eveleigh felt happier than she had in weeks, ever since the letters from the solicitors had started to arrive. With a panache learnt from long experience of driving her battered Bentley, she negotiated the narrow lanes. Her style at the wheel of the enormous car frequently put fear into the stoutest heart. Many men who had faced the enemy in battle, bent the will of the wildest horses to theirs, and in one case stood firm in the face of a charging bull elephant, had emerged from Eveleigh's car white about the gills and in desperate need of a restorative.

Even the sun, which this summer had been a marked failure, had chosen to shine. The fields and hedgerows, because of the endless days of rain, were a healthy green, which, with the clear blue sky, seemed to lift Eveleigh's spirits even higher.

If she could sing, she would, she thought, for she was about to do what she loved most of all – to judge a dog show. When Reggie had been alive she had judged far more than she did these days. It had been easier then, with the two of them able to share their duties. She could travel to Edinburgh, one heady time even to Lyon, knowing that all was well at home in Reggie's capable hands. They'd had reliable kennel maids then – whether because standards were different or because Reggie was a better judge of character than she, she did not know. She'd certainly had more time then, with everything shared, than she did now that she ran the kennels alone.

She had been up since five this morning seeing to her dogs. She had typed out a long list of instructions for Grace White, who would only look after the dogs provided a list was left for her detailing their routines and needs. Rather unnecessary, Eveleigh thought, for she had every confidence in Grace – she would never leave her dogs with anyone she did not trust totally. So each dog's next feed had been measured out in bowls, and each bowl was labelled with the dog's name. For all her preparations, she knew Grace was afraid that she would do something wrong and harm the dogs, even though Eveleigh had pointed out to her that it was very difficult to hurt a St Bernard. Far more likely that Grace could be hurt by a friendly tap from one of their enormous paws.

Better still, this time Grace had an assistant, her niece Kimberley. Eveleigh had had a long talk with the girl and had liked her from the start. She appeared to have a genuine interest in dogs. However, from past experience, Eveleigh was wary of such claims. She had learnt that the inducement of the flat which went with the job had, on three previous occasions, made applicants declare a love for dogs which was painfully lacking when the hard work of helping to run a large kennels was faced. Kimberley presented another worry in that Eveleigh wondered if the job would be enough for her; she seemed very intelligent and an ideal candidate for university rather than a job as a kennel maid. Still, she'd agreed to take her on for a trial period and today would be her first day at work. But she was to stay at her aunt's until Eveleigh decided the post was permanent.

Yes, she thought as she tanked along, everything was most satisfactory, if only the persistent letters from the solicitors wanting to buy her out would cease.

It was all such a mystery. As Jim had said, normally their patience would have run out by now, but as far as she knew no application for planning had been made and nothing untoward had happened. It bothered her so that she could not sleep. Eveleigh felt as if she were waiting for something – what, she did not know, only that it was likely to be unpleasant when it came.

'It's probably someone you know who doesn't want to upset you,' Oliver had volunteered, and she had begun to wonder if this was so. It wasn't Oliver, that was for sure, and although she had several wealthy acquaintances, none among them were rich enough to buy the land and then let nothing happen for such a long time. She had thought of Ben, but when she'd asked him, he'd said it was never his practice to risk buying land with no planning permission – people lost money that way, he told her sagely.

The problem of the letters occupying her mind, the miles scudded by, and she was rather surprised to find she had arrived at the town two hours from Shillingham with no memory of getting there. Not the best way to drive, she lectured herself sternly, as she swung the heavy car round the streets in the direction of the large park where the show was to be held, in the open, provided this good weather continued.

She showed her judge's ticket to the man on the gate, which allowed her to park free. She placed the car neatly, despite its size, and rummaged around in her capacious handbag searching for both pairs of spectacles. She always carried two pairs for fear of losing one. She was, she realised, a strange mixture – anything to do with her dogs was ordered and meticulous; anything to do with herself was chaotic and muddled. She wondered if it was because she had been born a Gemini.

She sat for a while, as she always did, composing herself. But also she liked to spend these few minutes watching the people unloading their dogs. It was the first sight she would have of many of them, and in that first glance she could learn a lot. Several times she had sat in her car watching them and thought *that one will win*, and later, in the show ring, these dogs had proved her right. It gave her pleasure to see the affection and care most owners showered upon their charges: watching people as besotted with their particular breed as she was with her St Bernards always made her feel less alone.

She watched as dogs from the size of Yorkshire Terriers up to English Mastiffs were fussed towards the show ground. Poodles, terriers, spaniels, boxers, Great Danes, Chihuahuas, German Shepherds and Labradors – they were all there. This particular show was an important one in the calendar of shows; it was a county show, recognised by the Kennel Club, and there would be other judges here. Eveleigh's job today was to judge the St Bernard, Great Dane and Labrador entry.

She looked up with surprise as she saw Gill and Justin unloading Sadie and her new puppy, Sukie. She'd quite forgotten Gill had told her he'd be here. She was glad she hadn't been asked to judge the poodles. Judging a friend's dog was not easy, since she always dreaded offending a friend. Not that she could ever be accused of favouring a friend's dog over the rightful winner. It made things awkward, that was all.

'Thomasine too, this is a surprise,' she said, as she reached their car to find her new friend standing beside it.

'This is my daughter, Nadine.' Thomasine smiled broadly, but Eveleigh's sharp eyes saw her nudge the girl in the back and her equally sharp ears picked up the urgently whispered 'shake hands'.

'Hullo, Nadine. Do you like dogs?' Eveleigh asked.

'Some dogs,' the teenager answered sulkily. Not for the first time, Eveleigh wondered why was it that the pleasantest people always produced scowling children. Such encounters often reinforced Eveleigh's sense of relief that she had not been 'blessed' with any.

'Jim tells me you've another bulldog?' Eveleigh decided the safest course was to ignore the daughter and concentrate on the mother.

'Yes. Nova – Luna's pup. That's why we came in two cars – I don't want to leave her alone too long, or I won't have a home to go back to.'

'She's a chewer?'

'You can say that again. Any advice?'

'Well, don't give her an old shoe. So often people do, and then they wonder why, later on, the dog still chews their shoes when, of course, to the dog, it's the most reasonable thing to do. And avoid throwing sticks. It's so dangerous. Not only can they get splinters in their mouths, they can impale themselves and often it's fatal.' Out of the corner of her eye Eveleigh was aware that Nadine was yawning. 'Toys made specifically for dogs are best,' she finished in a rush, but Nadine had already wandered away. How rude, thought Eveleigh.

'Thanks for the warning, I wouldn't have thought of all that. She didn't really want to come.' Thomasine looked towards the humped figure of her daughter. 'But then she didn't want to be left behind. Confusing!' Thomasine said, laughing nervously in apology. She had an extra bundle of guilt this morning – she'd woken and found she was looking forward to next week, and Nadine's departure.

'Well, if you'll excuse me, I must be going,' Eveleigh said.

At the entrance to the marquee she was met by May Westmacott, an old friend of long standing, a breeder of whippets whose home town this was.

'You're looking in the pink,' said May.

'And you too. Good entry?'

'Very good, but I've a massive problem. Tom Grant was to judge the final line-up, but he's telephoned he's broken down and won't get here in time. Would you do it for us? You're the most experienced here.'

'I'd be honoured.'

They crossed the marquee, the heels of their sensible shoes sinking into the uneven surface. Eveleigh sniffed appreciatively: she loved that special warm smell of trapped heat and flowers so peculiar to an English marquee in the summer.

Eveleigh knew the other judges from countless shows. Some she liked enormously, others she was not so sure of, but they were all united on the one subject of dogs. Teacups were handed around and Eveleigh was soon enjoying a good old gossip. A heated discussion was soon under way about the merits, or not, of tail docking, on which as some thought, the Kennel Club was not making a strong enough stand for either case. For Eveleigh, there was no choice. A tail should not be docked; it was such an important means of expression for a dog, she argued. She was almost sorry that the discussion had to end but May said it was time, and ushered them through into the open where several rings, marked out with ropes, were laid out.

Open air shows were a joy, thought Eveleigh, as she walked towards her ring. There was a carefree, almost holiday-like atmosphere. She always thought the dogs enjoyed them especially too.

The day sped by happily. When not judging she watched the elimination process in other breeds, noting there was nothing she would not have done or chosen herself – it was always a comfort to know her judgment was shared by the others.

Today there was a particularly fine St Bernard – not bred from any of her own kennel's progeny, she was glad to see. That always made judging more difficult, even if it was several generations on. 'How on earth do you know, Eveleigh?' friends would ask her in amazement when, having eyed up a St Bernard she would say, 'I see Wotan in her.' Or Isolde, or Kundry or whoever the ancestor might be. She always gave the same answer, which in a way was no answer – 'I just know,' she would say, and smile modestly. But this St Bernard she recognised immediately. From the massive set of its shoulders she knew it must be one of Connie Cunningham's, and a prime candidate for success at Crufts next year.

She had taught herself to be totally scrupulous when judging the working dogs, which included St Bernards, but she always had to fight herself a little when St Bernards and King Charleses were in the final line-up, as today. It was hard to steel her heart and not automatically award first place to the St Bernard and second to the King Charles, which was the order in which they stood in her heart. But of course her integrity would not allow any such thing and she did question if, sometimes, she was not a little too hard on those two breeds in over-compensation.

There was little anyone could do to pull the wool over Eveleigh's eyes. She had learnt to recognise the silver shoes which were always worn by one particular breeder of Salukis. Most judges only looked at the dogs, so shoes were a good ploy to let a judge know who was at the other end of the dog's lead. Pink suede, silver, gold, tartan – she'd seen them all. She had seen women virtually throw themselves at male judges, and had heard that some gay breeders would only show to equally gay judges. One woman who bred Rottweilers drenched herself in Poison perfume to let whoever was judging know it was her. Eveleigh would never have anything to do with such subterfuge. It was the dog that mattered, not who bred them, or from where.

The tea break came prior to the final judging and Eveleigh, having downed her tea and nibbled at a sandwich, excused herself and went to the judges' loo. She went straight into one of the cabins, came out, crossed to the basin to wash her hands, and as she did so idly looked at the mirror above her. Then she stood stock still, water cascading over her hands, the basin filling dangerously full. She felt as if she were frozen. Finally she spoke. 'Oh no,' she said. 'Oh dear God, no.'

Above her on the mirror, written in scarlet lipstick was the message: 'E. Brenton is a cheat! Only her favourites win. Bitch!'

Slowly, Eveleigh removed her hands from the basin and began to dry them on a paper towel. What did it mean? She'd never cheated. Her honour as a judge was impeccable. There had never been a whisper against her.

She felt sick, and had to lean against the basin for a moment, taking deep breaths. There was a tap on the door. 'Are you ready, Eveleigh?' she heard May call.

'Just a moment, May, if you don't mind.' Her voice sounded weak. What should she do? 'No, come in,' she decided.

'Eveleigh, my dear, are you all right, you look as though you've seen a ghost?' May asked, her voice full of concern. Eveleigh did not reply, merely pointed at the mirror.

'Who the hell did that? My dear Eveleigh, I do apologise.'

'But what does it mean, May? I've never cheated in my life.'

'Of course you haven't. Somebody's disgruntled. Perhaps you didn't let their dog win in their class, so they're just being spiteful.'

'But it's true, I have almost made up my mind, the final selection will be the St Bernard.'

'And rightly so. It's obvious to anybody who knows anything about dogs that that one is a champion in the making – and I don't even like the breed,' said May comfortingly, and then, realising what she had said and to whom, clapped her hand over her mouth. But Eveleigh had not, apparently, even noticed.

'I can't now *not* award to that dog just because of this message,' said Eveleigh.

'But of course you can't, my dear. You've just got to put it out of your mind and ignore it.'

This was easier said than done as Eveleigh stood in the middle of the large ring and the final six dogs, one chosen from each class, circled her. The excitement of their owners transmitted itself to the dogs, as one by one they ran round the circle showing off their shape, their paces, showing her how pretty they were, how perfect. But Eveleigh was finding it very hard to concentrate – all she could think of was the bright scarlet slash across the mirror in the toilets. Was the person who had done it here, watching her? Although the afternoon was hot, Eveleigh felt cold, and in the middle of the ring hugged her woollen jacketed arms around her. One by one she inspected the line of dogs. She liked the American cocker spaniel, she had a special word for the basset, she enjoyed feeling, once again, down the massive flanks of the St Bernard. She was fair with the King Charles. She paused long and hard in front of a fine West Highland terrier, and admired, particularly, a very fine white poodle – she didn't look up, she knew it was Sadie. Down the line she walked again. The tension in the hall mounted as she stood back, deep in thought, looking at all the dogs.

She abruptly pointed at the St Bernard, unaware how dramatic the action appeared. Judging by the applause, her choice of the poodle as Reserve was popular. Next she chose the Westie, and finally the King Charles in Fourth. The St Bernard's owner was jumping up and down hysterically; the dog knew immediately that it had won and it too ran round in circles, twining its lead around the owner's legs until she was tied up, as if to a maypole, and everyone was laughing – except poor Eveleigh. She did not talk as long as the owner had expected her to, nor the audience, just long enough to check that she had been right and that it was from one of Connie Cunningham's litters.

'You've a future champion there,' she said to the excited young woman. 'Guard her well,' she smiled, nodded to May and said, 'I really have to be going.'

'Yes, of course, of course.'

She could not look at the faces of the people smiling and nodding at her as she made her way towards the car park, because she was so afraid that one of them was the person who had left the message for her. She virtually ran to her car and started the long drive home.

She felt a depression so intense it was a physical thing, as if it were sitting on her. Yet she had set out this morning in such good spirits, full of joy and lightness. That anyone could attack her integrity was alarming.

'Didn't you think that Eveleigh was a bit shaken up?' asked Gill of Justin as they loaded the dogs, Sadie sporting her rosette, and their equipment into the car.

'Well, she never does talk to us if she's judging.'

'No, it wasn't that. She seemed flustered.'

'Haven't you heard?' a big-breasted woman, who was helping her husband load their bassets into a Range Rover, said. 'Plastered all over the mirror in the ladies loo – accusations of cheating. Favouring the St Bernards. Probably did too.' She patted her basset as if to confirm her suspicions.

'Eveleigh Brenton would do no such thing,' Gill said staunchly.

'You want to watch who you're mouthing off,' Justin added for good measure.

'Oh, yeah, and what? You going to tell her? Who'd believe a couple of poofters?' the husband sneered. Justin put a restraining hand on Gill as he stepped forward.

'Leave it, Gill. Moth-eaten old bassets like that wouldn't win anyway.'

'You're right, Justin.' Gill climbed into his car, but wound down the window. 'Tell me,' he said to the woman. 'You know the theory that we all begin to look like our dogs? Are you as low slung as that basset of yours? Must be agony. Ta ra.' And in a triumphant flurry they were away.

27

Bolstered by alcohol, and the determination of everyone present to enjoy themselves, Ben's birthday lunch was beginning well. Cora had been over-optimistic that they would be twenty at table – or rather, Oliver thought as he looked around, she'd been exaggerating as usual.

As it was, they were ten in number – the family, Toby Watkins, a friend of Cora's, and Eveleigh, and four who were strangers to him. Two were women of a 'certain age' who, he quickly discovered, were both reeling from the traumatic effect of errant husbands making off with younger women. One was bitter and brittle, the other damaged and demoralised; both were trying too hard in Oliver's direction, which made him shy away with alarm. He'd have to have a quiet word with Cora about matchmaking for him. The other two were men: a totally humourless business associate of Ben's who, after a mere two minutes' conversation, obviously decided that Oliver was not worthy of his attention, and an Italian who, from the way he was paying court to Sophia, convinced Oliver that he must be a plant to make him jealous. He was too slick by far, and his suit matched. Oliver watched the play with amusement, since he couldn't for one moment imagine Sophia running her fingers through that pomaded hair.

He couldn't understand why Sophia wanted to make him jealous. Very odd. But had he ever understood her or what made her tick? Sophia could flirt away, he was not interested. Whatever affection might have remained from the marriage, she'd destroyed by so carelessly losing Bandage. Why, when he arrived this morning, he'd had the greatest difficulty being polite to her.

'Do you live here?' he asked, the minute he saw her.

'Of course I don't.'

'Then why do you spend more time here than in the house I bought you? I might as well have saved myself the moolah.'

'Where I live is nothing to do with you, Oliver,' Sophia replied, all dignity and ice.

'Thanks be to God!' Oliver enjoyed watching the dignified demeanour crumble into indignation.

Eveleigh, sitting opposite him, was, he registered, quite flushed, and in rather an attractive way. He could not recall ever thinking of Eveleigh in terms of attractiveness. In fact, she was one of those women whose gender was immaterial; a good sort, a friend, not a *woman*, not a feminine person. Suddenly he found he was seeing her as if for the first time. She had rather a fine face and exceptional eyes, and a good figure, he'd not noticed before. She was talking and laughing with Toby, who was sitting beside her, and then looking almost demurely down at her place setting. And then he suddenly realised she was drunk!

Oliver had never seen Eveleigh drunk, or so animated, before. Good God, he said to himself, she's flirting too! He looked at Toby Watkins with renewed interest; he did not know him well, he was one of Cora's friends, a widower in his fifties, ex-army by the look of him. From the end of the table he was aware of Cora grinning at him, and winking so obviously that her face was lopsided from the effort.

'Matchmaker,' he mouthed at her.

'And why not?' she replied.

'Why not what?' asked Ben.

'Nothing,' said Cora, smiling secretly at Oliver, and Ben looked at him sharply. Oliver hoped his father-in-law wasn't getting the wrong end of the stick. Although he quite liked Ben, he was never too sure about him – he'd seen him lose his temper once too often. He was an odd mixture, full of bonhomie one minute, a tyrant the next.

'Did you make Wimpole's match then, Cora?' he said, to distract Ben.

'With Rudie? It's good news, isn't it?' Ben beamed.

'I don't think Oliver's too sure,' Sophia piped up. 'He's probably jealous,' she added spitefully.

'No such thing.' Oliver glared at his wife; what a bitch she was. Still, she knew him so well that sometimes it was frightening. In this case he wouldn't go so far as to say he was jealous, that was a word which could too easily be misunderstood, but he was still adjusting to the idea of her leaving him, there was no doubt about that. 'I shall miss her, but I reckon she's found a good 'un in Rudie,' he said.

'It's nice for Wimpole, and she'll be less of a liability to you, Oliver.' Cora smiled benignly.

'Wimpole was never that.'

'You can say that again!' Sophia drawled.

The first-course plates were cleared away by, Oliver saw, his, or rather Sophia's, Filipino servants.

'I do hope they'll adjust,' said Cora, when the man and woman had left the room. 'They're absolute dears.' Sophia glared with such malevolence at Cora that a more sensitive soul would have wilted.

'Adjust to what?' the brittle woman asked.

'Life in the countryside. They're used to living and working in London.'

'I thought they still did,' Oliver said quietly. He saw that at least Sophia had the decency to look slightly embarrassed, and wondered whether to make some smart-arsed remark about his paying Ben's bills, but decided against it.

How tacky, he thought. How could Sophia be so petty as to lie over such sums, why hadn't she just asked for more maintenance? Still, in a rather comforting way he found her subterfuge gave him the moral high ground – that was, until she thought up some scheme to take it away from him again.

He'd stop thinking about her and concentrate on the pleasure of watching Eveleigh, of all people, being courted.

'Any news of dear Bandage?' Eveleigh asked, aware of his gaze upon her.

'Sadly, no. I've stopped putting adverts in the local papers and free sheets.'

'How sad for you.'

'Yes, it is rather.' Oliver noticed it made his throat ache when he talked of his dog. 'I still sometimes go up to London and drive around the streets, hoping – '

'One must never give up hope. A friend of mine moved to Scotland and her cat which, thinking it was kinder to leave it in its familiar environment, she'd left behind, followed her – it took three months, but it got there,' Eveleigh said kindly.

'That was a cat, not a stupid dog,' Sophia said sharply, with her customary insensitivity.

'Bandage is not stupid.'

'Then where is he?'

'Being held against his will,' Oliver said, feeling murderous towards Sophia.

'Dead, more like.'

'Do you have to be so bloody unfeeling?'

There was a perceptible rustling at the table as everyone changed position in their chairs and rearranged their knives and forks to cover their own discomfort at seeing others' battles being publicly aired, and everyone concentrated on the next course.

'I thought you said Thomasine Lambert was coming?' Sophia said to Cora some minutes later. She did not look at Oliver as she spoke. He was grateful to her, even if he didn't want to be, for asking the question uppermost in his mind.

'I phoned her, she said she couldn't. She sounded a bit odd to me, agitated, only half interested in what I was saying.'

'Maybe you interrupted her,' Sophia laughed, not a noticeably happy laugh.

'Doing what?' Cora asked.

'Oh, you know ... don't press me too far,' Sophia fluttered her lashes at the Italian who leered back.

'You don't mean?'

'What else?'

'But who with? I haven't heard a dicky-bird.'

'And you're usually the first,' Ben interjected.

'Why, Jim Varley of course. Who else?' said Sophia.

'Jim and Thomasine? Well, I never.' Cora flopped back in her chair. For some peculiar reason Oliver felt his stomach flip, his heart patter, and knew this was something he did not want to know.

'I think you've made a mistake there, Sophia. Jim has that nice Beth,' Eveleigh said innocently, unaware of the undertones of emotion swirling around the table between Sophia and Oliver.

At this Sophia threw her head back and really laughed. 'What, the dreary tragedy queen, Beth? You must be joking. He *employs* her.'

Oliver opened his mouth to speak, and then snapped it shut. Sophia was bored, she was stirring things up on purpose. He wasn't about to pander to her whim. 'Any further news from those solicitors, Eveleigh?' he asked, changing the subject.

'I write letters. They write letters. It's all so stupid.' She fluttered her hand across her face as if to remove the cobwebs of concern that were always with her, now augmented since the show.

'What's the problem?' Toby Watkins asked.

'I don't think we want to bother Toby with this if it's legal, Eveleigh, there's a good girl,' Ben said in an avuncular tone.

'Well, really!' If she had had hackles, they would have risen, for Eveleigh looked extremely indignant.

'Why not?' asked Oliver.

Ben slowly turned and looked at Oliver with a cold expression. 'Because I said not.'

'May I be the judge?' Toby asked.

'I'd rather not, if you don't mind, Toby. Some other time.'

'Toby's just retired from his law practice, haven't you, Toby? He's one of the best minds in the profession.' Cora smiled benevolently at her guest.

'Oh, I don't know about that.'

'So we don't want to bother him, do we, Eveleigh? Not at a social function.'

Ben, whose colour was normally high, now looked almost magenta, and his eyes were bulging dangerously. Suspicion flooded Oliver's mind like a flock of ravens. He wondered how he could ever have been so dumb.

'Unless, of course, you don't want Eveleigh to have Toby's advice?' Oliver said quietly.

'And what do you mean by that?'

'I mean I think you're behind the person offering to buy Eveleigh's kennels. I think you've been a bit hypocritical with our friend.'

'Watch what you say, Oliver.' Ben waved a forefinger at him.

'Do you mean that when I asked you, Ben, if you had bought that land, you lied to me?' Eveleigh asked.

'He did, Eveleigh. And why? Because if he put in for planning permission, you, of course, would object and, if he doesn't get rid of the kennels, who will buy the ticky-tacky boxes he intends to put up, pretending they are houses?'

'Oh no!' Eveleigh looked dejected.

'Ben, say it isn't true. Tell him.' Cora was standing, leaning forward on the table.

'You can't, can you, Ben? It doesn't matter, Cora. Eveleigh would have found out eventually.' Oliver got to his feet.

'You think so?' Ben sneered. Everyone turned to stare at him.

'Hidden, is it? One company inside another so she'd never find out who bought her? Is that what you mean?'

Ben sat silent. 'Oh, Ben! No!' Cora wailed. Eveleigh was standing now, and the rest of the guests looked confused and uncertain.

'For God's sake, it's all a storm in a teacup. Dad will compensate Eveleigh handsomely and she can open up somewhere else – no problem.'

'Sophia, you don't understand anything about human nature, do you?' Eveleigh bent to pick up her handbag. 'I'm sorry, Cora, but in the circumstances . . .' She pushed her chair back.

'Eveleigh, don't go, we can sort something out,' Cora wailed.

'I don't think so. I feel betrayed.' She turned and faced Ben. 'I thought you were my friend. I can't believe you'd act behind my back in this way. How could you?'

Ben looked up at her, his eyes darting from right to left as if looking for a way of escape. 'I sold my interest,' he finally said.

'Thank God for that,' Cora sighed.

'You did what?' Oliver shouted.

'But if he's sold it, it's nothing to do with us. The problem's solved.'

'Oh, Cora, don't be so dim. He could have kept the land and dropped the plans – he's rich enough. But no, he sells it. Now Eveleigh will have to fight God knows who. What a family!' Oliver now pushed his chair back. 'Sorry, Cora, I couldn't eat another morsel, not knowing this.' He began to follow Eveleigh out of the room.

'Creep!' Sophia shouted.

At the door Oliver paused and turned back to face her. 'Do me a favour, Sophia. Why don't you try, one of these days, to join the human race?'

28

Seeing Thomasine again, with her new puppy, had cheered Jim. Now she had a dog he'd be seeing her on a regular basis, and that pleased him greatly. He did not know what it was about her that attracted him – she was physically attractive, but then so were lots of other women and he didn't automatically fancy them. He thought about it a lot and reached the conclusion that it was something he'd never be able to explain – he wanted to look after her, pure and simple.

He was working in his surgery. A cat brought in by its distraught owners had been caught in a trap, and the skin on its leg was wrinkled up just like a sleeve pushed back up an arm. It must have fought for hours, if not days, to free itself; it was dehydrated and shocked. The owners had been convinced it would have to be put to sleep, but Jim had decided to operate and see if he could save the leg. He worked slowly, methodically repairing that which at first sight had looked irreparable.

Life was getting better, there was no doubt about that. Now the new veterinary practice had opened in Shillingham he had the time to devote to a cat like this: before, he might have been too rushed and busy. He swilled out the wound with sterile water and prepared to suture it up.

It was easier with Beth too. In an odd way his being annoyed with her had done her good. She was not quite so organising now, didn't witter at him, was less wife-like. Just as he wanted their relationship to be. Taking Harry out had helped too, he was sure. It had made her more relaxed, and he really enjoyed the child's company. He'd even taken him out on his rounds occasionally, and now Harry wanted to be a vet.

'Did it survive?' Beth looked up from her sewing, Harry from the radio-controlled car Jim had bought him for his birthday.

'Keep your fingers crossed, I think it's in with a chance.'

'Only you could do that, Jim,' Beth smiled at him with admiration.

'Thanks, but any vet would have done the same.'

'No. Only you.' And she looked at him intently, but not smiling this time, and there was a moment which he felt they were enjoying alone, and then Harry spoke. It was an odd thing, but just then, when they looked at each other, he felt a strong attraction towards her. He found himself looking at her properly, thinking what a pretty woman she was and how blind he'd been. But there was no future thinking along these lines, she'd never shown him she fancied him. But that look – he didn't think he'd imagined it – said she'd felt the same.

'Uncle Jim, can we go to the fair next week?' Harry asked.

'Don't bother Jim now, Harry.'

'If you want.' He ruffled the child's hair, glad he'd interrupted his chain of thought. He shouldn't be feeling like this: it was wrong, there was the child to consider ... 'Fancy a coffee?' he asked. 'I'll bring it through to the sitting room.' He put the kettle on as she left. He laid a brandy and a liqueur glass on the tray with the cups. 'Are you coming?' he asked Harry from the doorway.

'No, the car works better on the tiles.'

Jim shut the door.

Beth was sitting in the half-light, only the fading daylight illuminating the room. She sat, her legs tucked up under her, on the old, squishy sofa. A CD of Chris de Burgh was playing.

'That's not mine,' he said, as he placed the tray on the coffee table.

'No, it's mine, my favourite,' she smiled up at him, and there was the look again.

'I didn't think you'd want a brandy, so I brought a liqueur glass.'

'Drambuie's the best,' she said.

As he poured the drinks, he realised that despite having lived in close proximity to her for well over a year, there was so little he knew about her – what her favourite things were, what her opinions were. She'd always been just Beth. And yet something had happened. Was it her owning up, telling him of her past? Whatever had happened, he realised with a jolt, he was rather enjoying it.

He handed her her drink. 'Beth?'

'Yes?' she looked up at him and patted the cushion beside her, he sank down on it.

'It's really odd,' he began, and as he did so, the telephone rang. 'Damn it,' he said, as he crossed the room to answer it. He listened for a minute to the apologetic voice at the other end. 'No problem, I've eaten. I'll be with you in ten minutes.'

'What's up?'

'Bill Lyley from Merrybank Farm, he's got a cow in trouble calving.'

'Oh no,' she said, not bothering to hide the disappointment in her voice. 'But what about the Shillingham vets?'

'Both out on call,' he said, rather regretting having to go. 'I shouldn't be long.'

The house was in darkness when Jim returned. It had been a nightmare calving. Everything which could have gone wrong had. His body, but especially his shoulders, ached from the pulling on ropes – and all for nothing, both calf and cow had died. He hated such failures, and on the drive back had tortured himself over whether, had he done things differently, he could have saved them.

The one consolation, he had decided once he was away from the house, was that the call had got him away from Beth and the sudden temptation he had felt, after all this time. He'd have to watch himself with her in future; getting involved with Beth would solve nothing, only make for further complications, in her life as well as his own.

One thought cheered him. Since his wife had died, he could honestly say he had never felt anything quite like that for another woman. But things seemed to be changing. First he had reacted to Thomasine as a woman, and now this reaction towards Beth. Perhaps it meant he was emerging from the desert of mourning he'd been living in.

On the kitchen table was a plate of sandwiches left him by Beth which he pushed aside – he was too weary to eat. Instead he poured himself a large whisky and climbed the stairs with aching limbs. He would have preferred to collapse on his bed, but forced himself to take a shower and wash the sweat and the stench of death away. At long last he was in bed, and was asleep almost as his head touched the pillow, the glass of whisky untouched on his bedside table.

Thomasine came to Jim in his dreams. He felt as if he were lying on billowing clouds. Her thick, lustrous hair brushed his face and he could smell it. Her full breasts gently touched his body, exciting him, making him search for them to caress them. He felt in his dream her mouth kissing his body, moving further and further down him. And then he awoke, but the dream continued. He heard himself groaning from sheer pleasure as his penis stood erect, and he felt lips sucking at it, tugging gently, thrillingly. He lifted himself up on his elbows.

'Beth, no!' he cried out, seeing her and not Thomasine.

'Yes, my darling. Oh yes.' And Beth hauled herself onto him, her thighs clasping tight on either side as she lowered herself, and cried out with pleasure as she impaled herself upon him.

He bellowed 'No', but then abandoned himself to the joy of Beth riding him, her hands behind her head, thrusting her breasts at him. He was lost on a sea of lust and pleasure.

August

29

The summer arrived late and settled in. The Shillings shimmered in a heat haze to which there seemed no end. From morning to night mowers clattered over pampered lawns; weeds were annihilated; under cover of darkness hosepipe bans were broken; the pungent smells of barbecues were everywhere; the noise of radios, CD players, domestic racket and family rows filtered from ever-open windows. There was a loosening of reserve, a new friendliness in the air, as the inhabitants marvelled at this very un-English weather. And Thomasine, sunbathing on her lounger, a jug of freshly-squeezed lemonade beside her, with a good book and a new-found indolence, knew she should be ashamed of herself, but could not help relishing the weather reports that Italy was deluged by rain.

At Oakleigh kennels, the St Bernards suffered in the unusual heat. Eveleigh, every day, offered up a silent prayer of thanks that Kimberley had come to work for her; she would never have managed on her own. Each day they worked constantly to ease the dogs' distress, checking regularly that they were not dehydrating as they lay, tongues lolling, their great chests rising and falling rapidly as they panted for relief. They sponged them at intervals, changed water bowls endlessly, and in the background was the constant whirring of the electric fans Eveleigh had set up in the kennels. She was determined she would not lose one dog to the heat, as some had done in previous heatwaves.

Kimberley was almost happy, installed in her small flat over the stables which had once been full of horses, but were now an overflow for dogs and storage. She delighted in having her own home, a place to retreat to, where even Eveleigh knocked, respecting her privacy. She had volunteered to decorate it rather than wait for the painter to come, and so she had the blue, yellow and white decor she'd always planned. Her wage was more than adequate, with no rent or electricity to pay for, and already she was beginning to save money. The list of things she wanted to buy was long, but not impossible – she longed for a duvet set she had seen in Morristown, a blue-and-white vase in a shop in Shillingham, china she'd seen in Tesco, a wok, and new clothes.

If only the miracle would happen, then she would be totally happy. If only Alan would come back into her life, somehow contact her, find her. She'd several times gone to the Market Square and sat on the fountain and prayed he would turn up, but she did not bother any more. She tried to forget him. During the day when hard at work with the dogs this was fairly easy, but at night, in bed, treacherous dreams slipped unbidden into her mind.

Eveleigh tried to persuade her to go to a disco, join the Youth Club, but for the time being Kimberley could not see the point.

The dogs made her happy. She drew great comfort from their uncomplicated love and devotion. She had her favourites, Isolde and Brünnhilde, but she tried to hide from the others that this was the case. Surrounded by happy, indulged dogs, she often thought of the dogs in the hell she'd left behind, and of Bandage in particular.

During these weeks Eveleigh felt that if she had not had the support of this young girl she would have given up, for there was no one else. She rarely saw Jim these days, the one person she found it easy to talk to – whether he was busy or avoiding her, she did not know. It was silly of her to think she had offended him in some way, but reasoning did not stop her constantly worrying that, inadvertently, she had. So the strange things happening in her life she faced alone, with only Kimberley to turn to.

After the scrawled message on the mirror, Eveleigh had felt like cancelling all other appearances as a judge. 'But then the person who wrote on the mirror will have won!' Kimberley sensibly told her. When the heavy-breathing telephone calls started, it was Kimberley who suggested she buy a high-pitched whistle to deafen the caller, and she quite enjoyed that.

She began to think there were two campaigns against her. The company who had bought the land from Ben Luckett, whose identity she was no nearer discovering, were most likely behind the phone calls and the increase in junk mail which daily poured through her letter-box. And then there was the vicious campaign from some disgruntled dog owner. Both were frightening, both led to sleepless nights.

One night, soon after the show where the spite had started, with her increasing difficulty in sleeping she had tried everything – a whisky nightcap, hot chocolate, some Alka-Seltzer – and all that had happened was that she felt sick. She moved in the bed, searching for a more comfortable position. From next to her feet came a disgruntled sigh, to the left of her a deep uninterrupted snoring. Eveleigh leaned over and put on her light. In the debris on her bedside table she found her reading spectacles, from the floor picked up this month's copy of *The World of Dogs*, and she settled back to read, hoping to tire herself out.

'No, Coco, you do not want to pee now. Go to sleep,' she ordered the Blenheim King Charles Cavalier on the end of her bed. The dog, sensing the finality in her voice, stood up, did three circles and plopped back down in exactly the same position. Isolde, one of her favourite long-haired St Bernards, wearily lifted her head from the pillow beside her to see what was going on.

Finding it was nothing, she crashed her huge head down again, muttering her displeasure at being woken.

Eveleigh read for ten minutes, slumped back on her pillows, idly patting Isolde, but suddenly she sat up with a start. Smiling at her from the pages of the magazine was the face of Penelope Troughton. It was the accompanying caption which had startled Eveleigh, for Penelope had been billed as the country's leading expert on St Bernards! 'Who says?' she muttered, but she already knew – Liz Cooper, the editor of the magazine. It was slotting into place now – the smug smirk on Penelope's face when she'd last seen her at a show, huddled over a drink with Liz. She'd expected to be invited to join them; instead she'd felt distinctly in the way. No doubt they'd been planning this coverage. What really annoyed Eveleigh was that Liz was editor of that magazine largely because Eveleigh had recommended her so strongly for the job to the publisher, a personal friend of long standing.

She had weathered that slight, reasoning that Penelope had won a commendable number of Challenge Certificates and her pups, sold on, were doing well too. She must not regard her position as unassailable, think she was impregnable. If she was slipping, then it was her fault and she must not be paranoid.

Then a fortnight ago Pippa Cunning, one of her oldest friends in the dog world, had taken her on one side and told her that a rumour was going the rounds that at a West Country show she had favoured a dog which was from a litter sired by her Champion Siegfried Neibelung, and that the dog was well below par. Eveleigh could barely believe what Pippa was saying.

'But, Pippa, that was a fine pup – good colour, fine head, deep broad chest. It was the best there. I care too much about my reputation, let alone the dogs, to award to an inferior dog.'

'I know that, Eveleigh. It's jealousy, pure and simple. Try to forget it.'

But Eveleigh hadn't forgotten, and had returned to her home and her dogs and, too ashamed this time to confide even in her new kennel maid, she had fretted the problem until it had grown enormous. She knew it was not her imagination that people she had known for years had begun to avoid her. At the end of the last show she had found herself isolated instead of the centre of a crowd clustering around, discussing the whole show and the finer points – for Eveleigh, always the best time of all. She was convinced that nothing could get worse, but it had. Last week Pippa had called her.

'Eveleigh, there's only one way to tell you and that's straight out. The rumour is you're taking bribes.'

Eveleigh's legs felt as if they were made of rubber and she sat down with a bump on the stool by the telephone. 'You're not joking, are you?'

'I'm afraid not. I think you have to do something about this, it's so patently a lie.'

'But who would start such a lie?'

'Probably someone whose dog you overlooked in a show.'

'I find that so hard to believe. We've all had dogs we were convinced would win only to come nowhere – it happens. Maybe someone wants me banned as a judge.'

She had replaced the receiver and, unusual for her in the middle of the day, poured herself a large whisky.

'Anything wrong?' Kimberley asked as she passed through the kitchen.

'Nothing,' Eveleigh answered vaguely. This was far too serious a problem to confide in anyone. How she wished her husband was alive. Reggie would have known what to do.

Without even consulting Pippa she had taken out an advert in a magazine, which was read by most breeders, which declared her innocence. What a storm! The advert had been seen by the mainstream press and the story unfolded first in the tabloids and then, shame of shames, in the *Daily Telegraph* itself. The dog world erupted, some siding with Eveleigh but – and this hurt – many criticising her for her action. This morning she had received a letter from the Kennel Club which politely but firmly pointed out that such *little* problems were best sorted out within the structure of the Club and not in the national press. It was the use of the word *little* in relation to what was to her a catastrophe that had stung. She had replied immediately, in a letter which, she was now aware, had not been a model of tact and diplomacy, and had posted it this afternoon. She should have waited and calmed down. What if, by reacting so swiftly, she had fallen into her enemy's hands and blown her credentials as a judge?

She had stood on the scales in her bathroom before going to bed and had seen she'd lost more weight. She couldn't eat, that was the problem. She felt as if her life was imploding, and she did not know what to do to rescue it.

When Wimpole returned, to Oliver's relief she appeared to be devoid of rancour. In fact, he even wondered if he'd dreamed the row. He realised he hadn't when, with the slightest defiant lift of her chin, Wimpole announced the wedding would be in October.

'That's great. What do you want for a present?' he said. One good thing to come out of Wimpole's trip was that he'd adjusted to the idea of her leaving.

'Signed copy of your book when it's published.'

'Is that all? That'll be cheap.'

'Rudolph's got a lovely cottage at Ben Luckett's. Tucked away in the woods with a pretty garden,' she said as if boasting.

'That's nice. Is it furnished?'

'Oh yes. Rudolph's got everything we need. He's a widower, you know.'

'Yes. I know. So you're not going to call him Rudie?'

'Why should I? Everyone else calls him that,' said Wimpole, unable to keep the satisfaction of her new status out of her voice. 'It'll be nice to have dogs around again. I miss old Bandage more than I ever thought I would. Rudie looks after the kennels, you know.'

'Kennels? Ben's only got the labs and the Jack Russell.'

'No, he breeds dogs too. How odd you didn't know.'

'Ben's always been a bit of a mystery man. What sort of dogs?'

'You know me – all mutts are the same, except dear old Bandage. Terriers, hounds, that sort of thing. Not pets.'

Oliver, his relationship with Wimpole re-established, gave her a cheque to buy her wedding clothes and promised to pay for their honeymoon. Wimpole chose the Canaries. She spent half her time at Rudie's cottage, scouring it out – nothing would ever be clean enough for her – and redecorating the main bedroom, no doubt to expunge the presence of the first Mrs Rudolph Adams.

Oliver couldn't fault Rudie. He courted Wimpole in the manner of another age. He sent her flowers, brought her chocolates, arrived for their dates impeccably suited.

'Right gent, isn't he?' Wimpole glowed with pride.

'The tops.'

With such attention Wimpole blossomed, seemed to shed years and become softer, her tongue less sharp, more amenable. It crossed Oliver's mind that perhaps it was sex making this transformation but, hard as he tried, there was no way he could imagine Wimpole in bed with Rudie.

He was alone, writing, when he heard the sound of an unfamiliar car. He decided to ignore the doorbell in the hope that whoever it was would go away. He paused in his work to pour himself a drink. It was barely noon, but to hell with it.

'Bit early in the day, isn't it?'

The voice made him jump. He swung round to see his wife standing in the doorway to the hall, a picnic basket in her hand.

'How did you get in?' he asked, as icily as he could.

'I've still got a key, sweetheart. Don't you remember? Sweet of you not to change the locks.'

'There wouldn't be any point, would there? You've already nicked more than enough to fill your new house twice over.'

'Oh, Oliver, don't be so grumpy,' she pouted. 'I've a surprise for you. A couple of surprises, actually.' She bent down and pushed back the wooden peg holding the wicker basket closed. 'You didn't think I'd forget, did you?' The wicker creaked as she opened it. 'See. I went to Harrods this morning. All your favourite things – quails' eggs, that wonderful Austrian ham, cut so thin you can read a newspaper through it. Strawberries. Caviar. Chablis.'

'It's overcast, Sophia, the heatwave has passed – not picnic weather at all.' Oliver loved a picnic, but not with Sophia, not any more.

'So? We light a fire and eat on the hearth rug.' She laughed her deep-throated chuckle, and slowly stroked the side of her immaculately pressed jeans with a long-fingered hand on which glistened the large diamond rings he had bought her. Oliver was immediately on his guard. 'What do you say? Here in Aunt Phoebe's great hall, or the drawing room, or in our own rustic kitchen.'

'*My* rustic kitchen.'

'Oh come, Oliver, don't be such a bore, not today of all days.'

'What day?'

'Why, our wedding anniversary, of course. Don't tell me you've forgotten.'

'For Christ's sake, Sophia, we are in the throes of getting a divorce. We don't celebrate anniversaries like that any more.'

'Who says? Why can't we? We're friends, after all.'

'Are we? We've done nothing but snipe and carp at each other ever since we separated, or haven't you noticed?'

'There you go again, what has got into you, Oliver? You're usually such a sunny person.'

'It depends on the company I keep.'

'Oliver! How quick of you, just like a smart little sixth-former, aren't we?' She spoke and smiled with condescension. It was far safer to ask her to leave, he knew that, but natural good manners prevailed, or so he told himself. Or perhaps he was wary of the scene she might make if he did. 'Drawing room?' he chose. He couldn't explain, but he didn't want Sophia in his work room. It was his alone, safe from her presence, and he wanted it kept that way.

'All right then,' he acquiesced. 'I'll carry the basket, it's too heavy for you.'

'Bless you, darling,' she purred and led the way. 'You know, you really should redecorate Phoebe's hall – it's so grim. I see it in Etruscan red.' She waved a hand expansively at the pitch pine panelled walls, and he was glad he'd decided on another room.

Sophia had even brought a flower-sprigged tablecloth, which she carefully laid on the Persian rug in front of the fireplace, then she daintily set out the food while Oliver laid the fire.

'Woman's work, man's work,' she smiled as she spoke, and alarm bells were clanging even louder in Oliver's head. 'Sit you down,' she said, patting one of the cushions she had placed on the carpet. She produced two crystal glasses from the hamper and, shaking a silver cocktail shaker, poured a drink; from a small, silver box she took two olives, which she added to the alcohol. 'There you are. It's a bit early to eat, but you always said no one made a martini quite like mine.'

It was obvious very early into the meal that Sophia was pulling out all the stops to seduce him. It was an odd experience, for he was able to watch himself as if he were a stranger, knowing he felt no interest in the woman whatsoever. Why? She'd pushed for a divorce, not him. Left to his own devices he'd have muddled along with her. So why? She'd had such plans for herself. And then with a mental jolt he wondered if he'd been the fool of all time. Had she had a lover he knew nothing about, and that was what had prompted her to leave? If so, had life with this new man not lived up to her expectations? Was it over, perhaps? All mysterious, but of only partial interest since he was grateful to her now for showing him the way.

'I wish you'd stop, Sophia. You're not getting anywhere.'

'I don't know what you mean!'

'You're trying to seduce me, and I don't want to be seduced. And I can't help but wonder why you're bothering.'

'What a thing to say, Oliver.'

'It's the truth, isn't it? I thought you wanted to be shot of me. I thought . . .' But he did not finish, for Sophia began to cry.

Normally a total sucker where weeping women were concerned, Oliver sat in silence, aware she wanted him to ask her why she was crying, determined not to, and wishing she'd get it over with.

'You're so hard, Oliver,' she sniffed, patting her eyes with one of the ridiculous scraps of lace she called a handkerchief. He watched her warily, feeling they were playing some complicated game with their emotions, and fully aware he had not been given the rule book. 'I want to come back,' she said.

'Don't be silly,' he said bluntly, without thinking.

That only made her cry again. Oliver lit himself a cigarette, feeling he'd earned this one.

'I can't cope, Oliver.'

'What do you mean?'

'Smoking's so bad for you, Oliver. Please don't do it. I couldn't bear it if anything should happen to you.'

'You didn't think like that six, eight months ago.'

'I was a fool then. I see clearly now. We should never have parted. We had a good life together.'

'You *are* joking, aren't you? We did nothing but row.'

'Because we cared. Because we loved each other,' she cried dramatically, and Oliver quite expected her to beat her breast.

'Come off it, Sophia. You stopped loving me years ago. I was a bit slower, hung on to love a little bit longer. But it died. And then we were just a habit to each other. What is it?'

'I don't get invited anywhere – not like *we* used to be. Our friends have deserted me.'

'I'm glad there's some loyalty left in the world,' he said without a trace of irony. 'But a lack of social life is hardly reason to return to each other.'

She wrung her hands as if in distress, but he knew she wrung them for effect. 'I can't manage. I don't have enough money.' She blinked prettily through her tear-drenched eyes.

'Ask your father for more.'

'He won't give me any. He says he can't afford to.'

'Your father can't afford to? I don't believe it. He's as rich as Croesus.'

'He isn't. Not any more. He says it's the recession and Lloyd's.'

'I never knew he was a name.'

'He didn't tell anyone, said it was too showy.'

'And now?'

'He's paid oodles and still owes and says it's open-ended – whatever that means.'

'It means he's in dead schtuk. Poor old Ben.'

'What about poor old me?'

'Honestly, Sophia, I don't see how you can't manage on what I give you. Other people do – why, whole families get by on a percentage of what I give you.'

'I'm not other people,' she said with her old spirit.

'Then perhaps you'd better make a list of your best talents, and instead of playing at work, get a proper full-time job. How much do you need?'

'Oh, my darling, I knew you would help me out.' Sophia flung her arms about him, rubbing her thigh against his.

'It's all right, Sophia. You don't have to pay for it,' he said coldly.

Once the cheque was in her handbag, Oliver was amused at the speed with which she packed the remains of the picnic back into its basket. But he felt only relief that it had all been a trap just to get money. Everything was as it should be, and Sophia had not, as he feared, changed dramatically. He helped her carry the basket out to her car and loaded it in the boot.

'Oh, silly me. How stupid. Your present, with love, Oliver.' Dramatically she opened the car door and dived into the back, emerging holding a bull terrier puppy in her hands. 'For you, Oliver. My way of saying sorry for losing Bandage. Though it was an accident,' she added hurriedly.

Oliver looked at the all-white dog. His hands itched to hold it, but he controlled himself. 'And how long before you claim this one as your own? Your track record in giving animals as presents isn't that good.'

'Oh, Oliver. What a grumpy old man you're becoming. Of course I don't want it back. I'm not good with dogs, I realise now – they're too messy. Here.'

She thrust the puppy at Oliver, who took it, nestling his nose into its neck, smelling the warm smell of biscuits which puppies always had. Feeling the soft, pliant body trustingly moulding itself to him. 'Hullo, boy,' he said, knowing full well that within seconds he was in danger of falling seriously in love with it.

'It's a girl,' said Sophia. 'I thought a bitch was less likely to run away. What are you going to call her?'

'Slipper,' replied Oliver, not sure why.

30

After the show when Eveleigh had been so humiliated, Justin and Gill worried at the problem, just like Sadie with a bone.

'That dear lady, we've got to do something,' said Justin, wielding the brush on Sadie's elegant rump.

'But what? We don't have time to find out who the scumbag is who planted the message.'

'Whoever it was, they lied.'

'Too right.'

'Still, I'd like to cheer her up.' Justin continued with his grooming and Gill with the salon's books which he was neatly balancing.

'Sadie's birthday!' said Justin.

'Sadie's birthday!' said Gill at exactly the same time. This thrilled them to bits, for they relished these moments when they thought as one.

'A tea party for dogs.' Justin clapped scissors and comb together.

'With a cake.'

'And candles.'

'Bliss!'

Justin spent several evenings designing an invitation. He rejected every one until he was finally satisfied with a cut-out of a poodle with the date, time and RSVP inside in his best italic writing.

In the first flush of enthusiasm they planned to invite every dog they knew, but sense, or rather Justin's concern for the carpet, prevailed. 'But we can't just invite Eveleigh, it wouldn't be festive enough, would it, Justin?'

'On the other hand, would she want to be in a crowd when she's so fed up?'

'There's that nice Mrs Lambert and her bulldog puppy.'

'But how many dogs should Eveleigh bring?'

'You'd better invite just *one* dog! Imagine if she brought the lot!' Gill looked around the immaculate sitting room with a grin as he imagined Eveleigh's St Bernards packed in like sardines – it might be fun to try, he thought. 'No, best just the one,' he said aloud as sense once more came galloping to the rescue.

When Thomasine received the invitation she looked at it in amazement. A birthday tea party for dogs! Justin and Gill must be mad. Was this what happened to dog owners? Did she risk becoming like this? What could she possibly give a poodle who had everything?

Eveleigh smiled when she read her card. Dear men, she thought, how kind. It was not strange to Eveleigh that Sadie's birthday should be marked in this way. She might have a kennel full of dogs, but still she knew each dog's birthday and she always arranged a little treat on such occasions. She resolved to wrap, in pretty paper, a particular brand of canine toothpaste which her own brood liked enormously.

As Thomasine watched the dogs romping about Gill and Justin's sitting room, racing and chasing each other in and out of the patio garden, each dog with a different coloured bow attached to their collars, she found herself being reminded of Nadine's birthdays when she was very small and the youngsters had run wild, just like these puppies. Nova was almost hysterical with excitement and Thomasine feared she would soon be sick, as she had often worried over Nadine.

'You look a bit down, Mrs L,' Gill said, propping himself on the arm of her chair while he topped up her glass of Chardonnay.

'Thomasine, please. Do I? I don't feel it. This is such a happy idea.' She indicated the playing dogs. Nova and Sukie seemed bent on twisting each other's back legs off whilst their short tails wagged with sheer enjoyment; Coco and Sadie were chasing each other in ever-diminishing circles, yapping all the time.

'Heaven, isn't it? Just like kids, aren't they?'

'That was what I was thinking.'

'So was that why you looked sad – remembering the past?'

'Something like that.' She looked intently into her wine glass so as not to have to look at Gill.

'Are you lonely, Thomasine?' he asked suddenly.

'Me? Heavens, no. What a silly question. I've too much to do. My daughter visits, there's Nova – yes, I am,' she finished abruptly and returned to studying the swirling vortex of her wine.

'You needn't be, you know. We're always here. You can give us a bell any time – right little pair of counsellors we are.' He laughed.

'I'm not sure if it helps – you know, talking about things. Maybe talking only makes matters worse.' She'd never had a friend to confide in, had never needed one, she thought.

'How wrong you are. Talking things out is such a relief. Like a cleansing. Why, Justin and I couldn't exist without baring our souls to each other, having a good old purge.'

'I've never done anything like that, not even with my husband. In fact ...' She stopped, wondering if she was being disloyal, and then took a deep breath as she concluded she wasn't. 'It's only now I'm realising how little I knew him. We talked about the house, our daughter, friends, but I don't think we ever talked about ourselves. I suppose I'm as much of a stranger to him.'

'I don't think Justin and I could survive on that level. I want to know what he's thinking every minute of the day. I'd feel shut out otherwise.'

'You must love each other very much.'

'Totally. The day we met was the true beginning of our lives.'

'What a lovely thing to say. I'm beginning to believe that although I *thought* I loved my husband it wasn't really love – not love, love.'

'Once you've experienced it, there's no question in your mind. So many people settle for second best because they've never known the real McCoy. Like saying rump steak's your favourite because you've never eaten fillet.' He leant over and kissed her forehead. 'Just remember, we're always here. Oops!' He jumped up and quickly crossed the room to separate Coco and Sadie, who were disputing the ownership of a cushion from which, torn in the tussle, feathers were beginning to burst.

Thomasine smiled to herself. She had thought she was stuck with being Robert's sad ex-wife, still carting the baggage from that marriage with her, still the same old Thomasine. She wasn't. It might be slow, but she was actually moving along a path to becoming her own person, one with a clearer vision of herself. Why, she'd just talked to Gill in a way she had never talked to anyone before. Emotions, thoughts, were to be bottled up inside, never allowed to escape. Robert would be mortified to know who and what her first confidant was. She was having a last laugh after all. She looked up at the sound of a loud sob to see Eveleigh shaking out a large white handkerchief and disappearing behind it.

'Gracious! I must be going down with a cold, or there's something in my eye.'

'No, Eveleigh. You're upset. You must realise you can't shoulder all this alone. You've got to talk.' Justin had put his arm round her.

'There's Jim. I talk to him. He's a great help.' Eveleigh blew into her handkerchief.

'But have you told him about the message on the mirror?'

'No, I can't. I've been too ashamed.'

'What message?' Thomasine asked, and Gill exclaimed.

'Oh don't talk about it, please. I loathe to hear it, it makes it more real.'

'But why should someone do something like that to you? It must be tied up with this land thing.' Thomasine crossed the room and crouched on the carpet beside Eveleigh and patted her hand. Nova and Sukie joined them and snuffled noisily around.

'It's all such a great worry. I love judging – the dog world is my world. There's nothing else.' And she looked on the point of tears again, but bent forward and concentrated on patting the puppies instead.

'Now, Eveleigh, stop talking so silly. You're one of the best, the fairest judge in the whole country. You are not to let this get you down in this way. I won't have it.' Gill stamped his feet in their velvet embroidered slippers, and Eveleigh managed a laugh. 'Why, just think of the old Major and then think who's the best?'

'Who, why and what's the Major?' Thomasine asked.

'He was a menace, nothing in a skirt was safe from him and his marauding hands,' Gill explained.

'The problem was, Thomasine, he never awarded a prize to a dog shown by a man. Never! Too often he chose on the looks, and I'm afraid the age, of the handlers and not the dogs. And he always seemed to think he should be rewarded too.'

'A sort of droit de seigneur,' Gill suggested.

'Exactly. Apart from this little problem he was a dear man and had done much good for dogs generally. So we had to solve the problem somehow. You tell Thomasine, Gill.'

'Well, we had a friend who cross-dressed – '

'You didn't!' Thomasine sat with hand over mouth.

'We did. We popped him in the ring with an Afghan that complimented his blond wig to a tee. The Major gave him best in show. Chased our friend behind the judge's marquee, and we've never had any trouble from him since! Look at that!'

Both men dived across the room as Sukie and Nova appeared dragging Sadie's water bowl between them, water slopping over the lip. They were too late. Nova tugged too hard, the bowl tipped up and water drenched the carpet.

'I've always loved aqua follies!' Gill exclaimed.

Later, the mess cleared up, the dogs asleep, exhausted from all their playing, the four friends shared another bottle of wine and chatted. There was no doubt that Eveleigh looked happier now, and Thomasine felt more relaxed and content than she had in ages. Gill was right, she thought, to talk did help. She looked at the little group. She had friends, true friends, and the thought made her feel as if she were glowing.

Nova had rapidly eased the longing for Luna in Thomasine's heart. Her affection for Luna would never be totally supplanted, but she could think about her now and not be overwhelmed with sadness as before.

Even Nadine, upon her return from Italy, had been quite polite about the dog. As was normal now, Thomasine awaited her arrival with apprehension. She could never be sure how her daughter would be with her. She was, however, tolerable, even though she resented Thomasine's English tan, far deeper than her waterlogged Italian one.

Thomasine controlled herself and did not pry into the workings of her ex-husband's new life, but bit by bit she was shamefully pleased to gather that Chantal was a 'pain', Robert was a 'misery', and that they were constantly snarling at each other. She kept a straight face as her daughter told her, but she was singing with joy inside. Not, now, in the hope that these were signs that he might return to her but, rather, she was ashamed to admit, sheer spite that not everything was perfect for him.

Nadine returned to school, and a calm descended on the Old School House, a calm Thomasine was learning to relish. She quickly re-established her routine and, with Nova for company, needed no one.

'You should show that little one, she's precious,' Justin said. Today he, instead of Gill, was doing her hair.

'I enjoyed that show of yours, but I don't know if I could manage it myself.'

'We always make the time – it's like a drug.'

She hadn't meant time, but rather money, but let the remark go uncorrected. 'Nova, here,' she called, for Nova had slipped from under her chair and was padding across the salon in search of attention.

'You know who that dog reminds me of?' Justin asked. 'She walks like Mrs Thatcher – all boss and bustle.'

'But no handbag.'

'If only she had a handbag!' Justin laughed. 'But you know, Thomasine, seriously – I'm no expert on bulldogs, but she looks like a prizewinner in the making to me.'

'But this showing business seems so complicated. At the one I went to with you I was completely confused.' Nova settled down again under her chair.

'It's simple. There are six groups – gundogs, toy, terrier, hounds, working

– Eveleigh's St Bernards are in the working group. Mind you, it's difficult to see her sleepy old giants working at anything. And our Sadie and your Nova would be in the Utility group.'

'Why Utility?'

'Because they're not sure what else to call them, I reckon.' Justin wielded brush and hair dryer. 'Then each breed is divided into classes within its group. Some are age-related – Puppy, Junior, Yearling, Veteran. Then others are by the previous wins they've had. If it's an Open Class, then any dogs of the breed for which the class is provided can enter. See?'

'Sort of,' she said, even though she didn't.

'Then dogs are judged – always first.'

'Hardly fair.'

'It's sex rearing its ugly head. You have to do the dogs before the bitches' scent is in the arena, otherwise they might be a bit of a bother and not concentrate.'

'But what does CC mean – when you see it written after Sadie's name?'

'That's a Challenge Certificate – best dog or best bitch. When a dog has won three of those, then it's a Champion, and you'll see Ch in front of her name – that'll be the day! Then the best dog and best bitch compete and that one is a BOB – Best of Breed. Then all the BOBs in the group compete and we end up with Best in Group. Then those six all compete and from them is chosen the Best in Show. Simple really.'

'If you know how,' Thomasine laughed.

'Of course no dog can compete unless it's registered at the Kennel Club. Only pedigree dogs. But there is a show called Scruffts now – that's for cross-breeds. Sweet! Still, I digress. It's best to start with an Exemption Show – it's good training for the dog and it's all a bit of fun. Get the feel and then move on to the Sanction Shows – they're all novice dogs there, no champions allowed. Then you move on to the Open Shows – you don't win any CCs at those, but you're competing with dogs who already have them. You really learn then if your dog is going to make it. To get your CCs only Champion-ship Shows count. I know it sounds confusing, but honestly, it's as easy as pie once you start.'

'So to go to Crufts you have to qualify at one of these shows?'

'That's right.'

'It might be fun.'

'We and Eveleigh would help you with ringcraft, that sort of thing.'

'Ringcraft?'

'How to show – it's an art, you know. There, see the back, I've taken a couple of inches off, just as you said.' He held the mirror up for her to see.

'We must stop meeting like this,' Oliver laughed as he bent down to pick up Thomasine's handbag, which she had dropped upon bumping into him outside Snippers.

'Maybe I should get my eyes checked!'

'Since we have met, how about a coffee or something?'

'It'll have to be the something. Dogs are banned in the Copper Kettle.' She tugged at Nova's lead and the dog appeared and began to trot along beside her.

'Another bulldog,' he said, as they walked towards the White Hart.

'Yes, Luna's puppy. Sweet, isn't she?'

'Adorable. I've a new one too – Slipper. But she hasn't had all her injections yet, so I've left her sulking at home with a disapproving Wimpole.'

'I thought Wimpole liked dogs?'

'She does, but not this one apparently.'

'I heard she's getting married?'

'She is. Some time in October.' They settled at a table in the lounge bar, Nova happily sitting on Thomasine's feet. He ordered their drinks. 'This is nice,' he said, sounding satisfied. He looked across the table at her and thought again what an attractive woman she was; not beautiful, but with an alive, intelligent face which he liked more. Still, he told himself, this was the last sort of complication he needed at the moment – getting involved with Jim Varley's woman was not the best way to make friends.

'So, what's new?'

'Not a lot,' she smiled. 'Life in the Shillings is remarkably uneventful, I'm happy to say. Justin, the hairdresser, has been trying to persuade me to show Nova.'

'I thought about doing that with Bandage. Maybe I'll have a go with Slipper. We should do it together.' He smiled broadly.

'That would be fun,' she replied, but immediately registered that he did not mean it, it was just one of those things people said to be friendly. She accepted her gin and tonic.

'It will be strange for you without – Wimpole, I suppose.' She nearly slipped up and said 'Nanny' but stopped herself in time.

'What, how will I get on without my nanny?' He smiled as he spoke, but she knew she blushed, as if he had read her thoughts, how awful! And he thought how pretty she looked when she did. 'My wife was always teasing me about Wimpole. Said I was soft. But she's always been there, you understand. I didn't see an awful lot of my mother, she wasn't that interested in me, but I had Wimpole, so it didn't matter so much. And since she never left once I was an adult it'll be really strange without her.' She had an almost unbelievable longing to take hold of his hand, and felt quite shaken that she did.

'I do worry about her, too. I mean, I'm not sure why she's suddenly getting married.' He looked at her, puzzled, as if she might have the answer.

'Presumably because she's in love. That's most people's reason.' And she realised as she spoke that that had not been the case with her, she'd only *thought* herself in love.

'But I'm not sure she is. She's not behaving as if she is.'

'Maybe that's an age thing. Her generation are far more buttoned up about emotions, aren't they?'

'Do you think so? I hope you're right.'

'Why don't you ask Wimpole how she feels?'

'I'm not sure I could. She might bite my head off.'

She had only meant to have the one drink, but found herself accepting another. And when he invited her to have a bar snack with him, she looked at her watch.

'I don't know why I'm watching the time – I've nothing to go home for. Yes, that would be lovely,' she accepted, taking the menu.

'There are so many adjustments to make when a marriage ends, aren't there? Having time to oneself, for one.'

'Or too much of the stuff.' He wondered if he'd imagined that she sounded wistful, and Jim Varley or not, had a longing to stop her feeling so.

'Do you miss being married?' he asked tentatively, not sure, since he hardly knew her, if he should venture on to such territory.

'Yes and no. I miss having someone to care for, and yet I quite enjoy the freedom to do what I want. Problem is, I'm not sure what it is I want to do.' She laughed, but he was sure she was being brave. She was wishing he would not talk about marriage; it sounded as if he regretted the end of his.

They were both rescued by Nova who, smelling their toasted cheese sandwiches, chose this moment to investigate further and jumped up, trying to peer at the plates.

He smiled at the small dog. 'They cost an arm and a leg, don't they?'

'She was a present from the owners. There's no way I could have afforded to buy one, or any breed come to that. I'm just hoping the vet's bills won't be too horrendous.'

He looked up in surprise. If she was going out with Jim he was surprised she had to pay the bills for her pet – Jim didn't strike him as mean. But also, from her clothes and the expensive handbag on the seat beside her, she looked as if money was the least of her worries. Still, one could never tell. 'What's the problem?' he decided to ask.

'I've been incredibly stupid. I just thought I could make a career for myself as a book illustrator – no problem.'

'And there is?'

'The world is full of illustrators – proper ones, and the housewives like me who think how nice it would be to paint a bit.' She laughed, but somewhat tentatively as if, he thought, she was covering up a hurt. 'I did some paintings of Eveleigh's St Bernards. I *know* they were the best thing I'd ever done, but the publishers rejected them.'

'Then they're stupid,' he said, not liking to see her distressed and wishing there were something he could do about it.

'That's kind of you. No, they know exactly what they are looking for. My best isn't good enough. And the problem is I can't do better – I'm aware of that. I shouldn't have so blithely counted on making a living from it.'

'Is there nothing else you feel you can do?' He wondered what her ex-husband was about.

'At the moment, no.'

'You know what I'd do if I were you? Make a list – write down all your talents and see where you go from there.'

'What talents?' she laughed.

'You'd be surprised.' He was pleased to see she smiled. He liked her smile, and it flashed across his mind, why did he have to be so honourable where Jim Varley was concerned? He didn't owe him anything, and he already had that Beth woman he was shacked up with.

Thomasine looked at her watch. 'Help! Is that the time? I really must be going,' she said, just as Oliver had opened his mouth to ask her out to dinner.

'Must you?' he said, longing to ask her why time should suddenly have become important.

'I'm afraid so,' she replied, wondering what on earth made her think he sounded as if he didn't want her to go.

As she drove home Thomasine began to make a mental list of her talents, just as he had suggested. It was rather a meagre list, since all she had ever done was be a wife and mother. She could arrange flowers, keep a house clean, sew, drive a car and cook. These, and a small painting ability, were all she possessed.

Get a live-in housekeeping job and let out her house was the obvious solution, but out of the question now she had Nova to consider. And she would hate strangers in her house too. And where would Nadine stay when she condescended to visit? She could just imagine her reaction to such a career for her mother – fury, no doubt.

She wished she knew someone close by with a young daughter to talk to about Nadine and the trials and tribulations of living with a teenager. But she knew no one here who fitted the bill, and, as Nadine catapulted from one violent reaction to another, there was no comforting voice to reassure Thomasine that it was 'just a phase.'

Thinking about Nadine just piled on the worry. A letter from the bank this morning had not helped. She was overdrawn and sliding, at an alarming rate, into a debt which would quickly become serious.

She frowned deeply as she drove through the afternoon sunshine. What the hell was she to do? She knew what solution her mind was about to present her with, and saying 'no' out loud and firmly did not stop it. Robert. She would have to ask him for help.

This thought so upset her that she crashed the gears as she changed down to negotiate a tight corner. She could just imagine the smug smile on his face if she asked for financial help. There would be an 'I told you so' lecture, followed, no doubt, by one on the realities of life and the necessity to budget carefully.

She drove into her driveway, parked outside the small garage which had once been the school's latrine block, and sat for a while, her hands on the wheel even though the engine was silent. When had she begun to think of

Robert in such a way – in, if she was honest with herself, a totally realistic way? She had just thought about her husband as if she did not like him, and yet only four months ago she was planning how to get him back; dreaming of what she would say, how she would handle the situation when he asked her back into his life.

More had happened to her than she had at first realised. Despite the many worries there was a contentment in her life, a placidness. If he returned, such equilibrium as she had evolved would, she was now certain, be disrupted.

She did not want that. Nor, she realised suddenly, did she want him.

She opened the car door. She'd come a long way without even realising it.

31

Jim Varley had taken to staying out on calls for as long as possible. If he was offered a cup of tea or a drink he accepted. This surprised his clients who, in the past, had been used to Jim rushing in, dealing with their animals, and rushing out again as quickly as possible. Not any more – he lingered, talking of animals, crops, politics and, occasionally, local gossip. Of an evening he was, more often than not, in The Duck and Thistle, and when not there he'd isolate himself in the surgery and catch up on all the latest veterinary literature.

His explanation for this change in routine was quite simple – he had more time. The opening of the new, modern veterinary practice in Shillingham, called The Animal Hospital, had certainly relieved his workload considerably. He was not worried; he'd quite enough clients to keep the practice busy and profitable. It was pleasant not to have to work too hard and he was learning to enjoy not being tired all the time. The farmers in the main had stuck by him, as had Ben Luckett with his stable of horses, and the local riding school, and local pets were still brought to him. It was the Shillingham dogs, cats and gerbils he'd lost, and that did not bother him unduly.

These were all reasonable explanations for his new-found relaxed attitude and sociability. Except it wasn't the whole truth. He avoided going home because of Beth.

He was ashamed of himself; he was behaving badly, and was only too aware of how badly. Since the night Beth had climbed into his bed when he had thought he was dreaming, she had done the same another six or seven times – and he'd let her. But, worse, there were the nights he'd crept along the corridor and stealthily opened her bedroom door, conscious of the loud clanking noise the iron latches made, afraid of waking Harry, but driven by lust to ignore his conscience. And on these occasions, since he was the instigator, he could not pretend he'd been dreaming: there was no one to blame but himself. He was ashamed of himself, but it didn't stop him.

The only reaction he'd had before now was when he'd met Thomasine and his physical reaction to her had shaken him, since it had not happened for such a long time. Even that had come under control once he'd found out she was seeing Oliver. A pity, but just as well, he'd told himself. He'd no desire to find anyone, he was quite content, and when he needed a female slant on things, there was always Eveleigh to turn to.

And then Beth had crept into his bed. In one night she had awoken the buried desires and needs in him. And now he could not stop them, even though he knew he should. He didn't love her, he never would, he was certain. Therefore, he must stop the sex, get control of himself. He must tell her he did not love her and hope she was not too deeply hurt. He had to sack her, that was the bottom line.

He shuddered and shifted his hands on the steering wheel as he thought of that. It was such a brutal way to treat someone who had never hurt him and whose only fault was that she loved him.

He was relieved when he turned the corner in the lane that approached Oakleigh Kennels to see, in the fast falling dusk, his friend Eveleigh. She was standing with a shovel, one wellington-booted foot resting on a huge pile of gravel which was blocking her driveway. She looked as if she could do with some help; he would offer and then, hopefully, she would invite him to have a bite to eat and he wouldn't be home until late.

'Eveleigh, what on earth?' He was laughing as he got out of his car, safely parked well into the hedge behind Eveleigh's Bentley, in which two St Bernards were resting their heads on the backs of the seats, viewing the goings-on through the windscreen.

'Well may you ask. I'd been to a show and came back to find this – not ordered by me.' She kicked at the gravel with annoyance. 'I can't get the car in. It only needs a lorry to come along and with a car the size of mine the lane will be blocked.' She pushed back her hair from her face with an irritated gesture.

'Were you successful at the show?'

'Yes. Brünnhilde – another Challenge Certificate.'

'Brilliant.' He beamed, but Eveleigh was in no mood to join in. He walked round to the side of the Bentley. The name had such a fine ring to it, redolent of luxury and glamour. Not in this case. Eveleigh's Bentley was dented from her many encounters with gateposts and the like. The interior was wrecked, and Jim knew from experience that rather than the sweet smell of leather and polish, it whiffed potently of dog.

'Do you know who dumped it? Telephone them and insist they send someone round to clear it for you, that they've made a mistake.'

'No idea at all. No delivery note, nothing. Just this obstruction.' Angrily she wielded her shovel, filling it a couple of times and scattering the gravel on her front driveway.

'That's going to take for ever. Look, the main problem is your car. What say you drive it to my place? I'll follow and bring you back – my Land Rover's smaller.'

'Would you? What a dear you are, Jim. The main worry is I haven't fed the dogs their supper.'

Used to Eveleigh's dogs barking, he had not at first been aware of them, but now he realised they must all be calling, their huge black snouts skywards as they demanded their food.

'Where's Kimberley?'

'It's her day off – she's at her aunt's. I only went to this show because it was in Morristown.'

'One thing's for certain, your dogs may be put out, but they're so well fed, no harm is going to come to them if they have to wait an extra hour.'

He drove, glad to be in front of Eveleigh, for he was often reminded of Panzer troops in tanks when seeing Eveleigh behind the wheel.

Beth was puzzled when she heard them arrive and they did not come into the house. She looked out of the window to see Eveleigh getting into Jim's Land Rover. She relaxed – at least he was with the one woman she didn't have to fear. Jim was safe with good old Eveleigh.

From Eveleigh's Jim checked in for any urgent calls. There were none. 'When will you be home?' Beth asked in the wifely way which terrified him.

'I don't know. Don't wait supper for me, I'll grab a bite. Eveleigh's got a bit of a problem here.'

'A bit!' Eveleigh laughed as she passed him by. 'How about a large drink before we start?' she suggested, picking up a bottle of Macallan. Jim needed no second bidding.

'Then I'll start on the gravel and you feed your dogs – it sounds as if they're about to start chewing their kennels.'

Two hours later Jim was exhausted. The gravel had been moved from the gateway, even if the drive was going to need a good levelling off.

'It looks like a lumpy mattress,' said Eveleigh, surveying her undulating front drive. 'Would you care to stay to supper, Jim? It's the least I can do.'

They ate overcooked lamb chops, frozen chips and peas, which was washed down with a St Emilion so good that it compensated for the rather basic meal. But given Eveleigh's startling news, it was doubtful if Jim would have noticed what he was eating.

'Quite honestly, it's beginning to worry me sick. Whoever's playing games with me, it's beyond a joke. I've had mail-order catalogues a yard high, none ordered by me. I had a load of horse manure delivered – paid for, mind you, but not with my money. I've had I don't know how many insurance agents call, double-glazing salesmen – most of them got really irate when I said I didn't want anything, that I'd not asked them to call. Then there are book clubs I've not joined, and it's cost me a small fortune to send the books back, home study courses – you name it, I've received it. It's so time-consuming sending everything back and having to explain. I just hope whoever's doing this has paid for the gravel. The front drive needed it, but I couldn't afford it, not at the moment.'

'Have you told the police?'

'Told them what? What is there to tell?'

'How long has this been going on?'

'Since about June – I can't really remember.'

'Any more letters offering for the kennels?'

'Yes, but I've been in correspondence with new lawyers – presumably they changed after Ben sold his interest in the land.'

'Have you thought that, because you won't sell, they could be using these devious tactics?'

'Lawyers?'

'They probably don't know. No, the owners of that land. I don't want to depress you but it could get worse, you know.'

'In what way? I couldn't imagine anything worse.'

'I had a friend who wouldn't get out of his flat when the block was sold. He had dog crap posted through his letterbox. Endless nuisance phone calls. Then a wreath came with his name on it, followed by a firm of undertakers come to measure him for a coffin.'

'What lengths to go to!' Eveleigh laughed, but there was little humour in it. 'Thank goodness I've got my dogs or they might try to burgle me, or worse!'

'We cannot be alone in knowing that St Bernards will lick a burglar near to death in welcome.' Even as he joked, he wondered how best to say what was uppermost in his mind – that things could get really nasty. 'Have you thought of an alarm system?'

'I can't afford it.'

'Get a couple of geese. The best alarm in the world.'

'I could, couldn't I?' She looked frightened, but also indecisive, as if she hadn't told him everything.

'Eveleigh, is there something else?'

'I don't think I could tell you. I'm so ashamed.'

'Try me.'

It cost her dear to tell him she'd been accused of being unfair in her judging, of taking bribes, and that today at Morristown she'd heard another vicious rumour, that at a show she'd swapped dogs – entering an inferior bitch and then having her Champion Brünnhilde appear in her place.

'Whoever knows you would know that is totally impossible.' He took hold of her hand. 'The land thing can't be the only problem – we're getting paranoid. It must be someone in the dog world doing this to you. Someone jealous of your success, or someone whose dog you passed over.'

'But how do I prove that? How can I carry on?'

'You mustn't give in. This is a form of blackmail.'

'I almost hope it is the owner of the land, that would be easier to deal with than having to acknowledge that my fellow breeders could behave in this way.' Eveleigh never cried, not since her husband died, and even then she'd locked herself in the bathroom so that no one would see. But as Brünnhilde, in the house as a reward, put one enormous paw on her lap as if comforting her, her eyes brimmed with tears.

'Dear Eveleigh. Please don't cry. We'll get to the bottom of this.' He hated to see Eveleigh of all people in this state, she was such a dignified and private person that to see her so demoralised was, somehow, more shocking and painful. He felt useless as he passed her one of the Kleenex she always had handy to mop up her dogs' chins.

October

32

Kimberley never knew what to do with her days off work. With Alan gone, the gang broken up and only a bicycle for transport, her world was limited. She would have been quite happy to work, but Eveleigh refused, insisting she have free time. Mostly she spent it in her little flat, cleaning it spotless and making do, but sometimes she went to her aunt's. Aunt Grace had said she should come each week, but Kimberely did not want to impose – her aunt had enough work as it was, juggling home and job. But also she rationed her visits because she did not want to become too involved. Families, to Kimberley, were dangerous things. Better, she told herself with youthful wisdom, to stay clear of them.

Grace always welcomed her warmly. With two sons and no daughters it was nice to have another female to talk to. And Kimberley was such a help. Often when Grace came home from her charring she was too exhausted to do her own cleaning, for she was a large woman and the extra weight she carried made any task doubly hard for her. If Kimberley let herself in with the spare key, Grace would find her house spotless, food prepared and the kettle on for tea when she'd scarcely had time to put her own key in the lock.

'Do you think you ought to go and see your mum?' said Grace on such a day, over the lunch Kimberley had prepared.

'I can't see the point. I telephoned her again yesterday, she says she wants nothing to do with me. That I've hurt her and Dad too badly.'

'Well, there's a turn up!' Grace snorted with derision. 'Hurt your dad, have you – and a good thing too! Horrible man. Your uncle said to me on the very day they got married that your mother had seen the last happy day of her life, poor bitch.'

Kimberley shudddered. 'I wouldn't stay with a man, not if he made me as unhappy as Dad makes Mum.'

'Nor me.' Grace sipped at her sweet tea. 'It's those poor dogs bother me – after all your mother could walk, like you, but she chooses to stay there. But them poor dogs, what can they do – put up with it, that's what. Something should be done about them, I say.'

Kimberley looked up at her aunt, her heart thumping, her mind longing for her aunt to do that something.

'Still, he's family when all's said and done, and I couldn't welch on me own hubby's flesh and blood, now could I?'

'I suppose not.'

'That was lovely, Kimberley. You make a lovely omelette, but if you'll excuse me, I must be off.' She lumbered to her feet and picked up her coat.

'Haven't you finished for today?'

'No, I've got to give Mr Hawksmoor an extra day. They've got a wedding reception up there in two weeks – there's a lot to sort.'

'Would you like me to help?'

'On your day off?'

'I've got nothing else to do.' And so she'd joined her aunt on the walk to Bishop's End.

'Bless you for coming. I'd never have got it all done myself,' Grace thanked Kimberley as she stacked the last of the silver away, all polished, washed and dried ready for the reception. 'Would you dust the Great Hall for me? I'll hoover, but let's have a cuppa first.'

'Who is this Wimpole? Funny name, isn't it?'

'She's Mr Hawksmoor's old nanny.'

'His what?' Kimberley hooted with laughter. 'His nanny? You're joking, he's an old man himself.'

At this Grace trumpeted with laughter too. 'Don't let him hear you say that, he's only forty-five.'

'Forty-five! That old!' Kimberley said with youth's horror of age, which only made Grace chortle louder. 'Then how old is she?'

'Lord! That's a state secret. Sixty-something, I suppose.'

'And she's getting married. It hardly seems worth the bother, does it?'

'A late flowering, you might say,' Grace said with a grin. 'But she could go on into her eighties.'

'Who's her husband?'

'Rudie Adams – works out on the Luckett estate. I've never liked him much myself, but your uncle did. I think he's more of a man's man. I always find him a bit too charming, meself. Drat it! I forgot the silver photo frames in the Great Hall – would you bring them in here once you've done the dusting, there's a love.' And Grace collected together the silver-cleaning materials which she had already put away.

Kimberley stood in the doorway to Phoebe's Great Hall and looked about her with amazement. She'd never seen a room quite like this in her life. The sun was streaming through the high arched windows, dappling the blood-red Turkey carpet. The walls were covered in paintings – real ones, not prints – and where there were not pictures there were books, thousands of them, it seemed. A long refectory table stretched across the room, littered with books and papers, and Kimberley thought it was probably best not to disturb them. At the centre was a potted plant, and at the far end a collection of photographs in silver frames – the ones her aunt had forgotten. Her dusting finished, she began to collect them. As she reached out for one photograph and saw the subject she stood rooted to the spot, her stomach churning with anxiety. She jumped. There was a clicking noise and she turned, white-faced, to see a pink-eyed white bundle of a dog skidding across the oak floor towards her and falling on its snout as its paws tripped over the Turkey carpet.

'Slipper, if you pee in there I'll have your guts for garters,' the man in the doorway called out. 'Hullo, who are you? I'm Oliver Hawksmoor.' He held his hand out and smiled warmly at her. She looked at him and wondered why on earth she had presumed him old. He might be, but he didn't look it, not like her father. With a clatter she put down the photo frame she was holding.

'I'm Kimberley White. Grace's niece. I'm helping her out. She couldn't manage.' She spoke in short staccato sentences, from breathlessness and nerves.

'That's kind of you. Slipper, get down. Push her off.'

'No, no. I like dogs,' she said, bending down and letting the puppy lick her face.

'She likes you too. Dogs always know.'

'What is she?' she asked, but was pretty certain what his answer would be.

'A bull terrier. Sloppy old things they are. I get the odd person recoil in terror.'

'I think she's lovely. Who could be afraid of her?'

'You'd be surprised. I was catching a train to Scotland with my previous dog. We were strolling along the platform minding our own business, and this interfering old codger came roaring up to me, "Muzzle that brute!" he was shouting, jumping up and down, waving his fist at me. Quite a little exhibition. "Why?" I asked, knowing full well what was coming. "You're breaking the law. That dog should be muzzled – it's a pit bull." "Don't be such a silly arse," I said. But off he rushed and got a policeman, a fine song and dance I had explaining his antecedents to the majesty of the law. I always carried his pedigree with me after that – stupid act!' He grinned, which, Kimberley thought, only made him look younger. 'Sorry, but I do feel strongly about it, and I loved that dog.'

'What happened to him?'

'He ran away – nearly six months ago, but it's not something you get over.' He crossed to the half-dresser and picked up the photo frame Kimberley had been holding. 'Here he is. Lovely dog, he was.'

'What's his name?' she asked, but knew it was an unnecessary question.

'Bandage,' Oliver replied.

She was scared now, really scared, but when she looked up at him, to her astonishment, she saw his eyes were full of tears.

33

Whichever way she did her figures, Thomasine's problems were getting worse. A situation which was not improved when, unannounced, Nadine arrived home, white-faced and gaunt, carrying a suitcase.

'This is a nice surprise!' Thomasine managed to say upon seeing her forlorn daughter standing on her doorstep. 'You didn't mention you were coming when I phoned two days ago,' she said, more in puzzlement than reproof.

'I'm sorry to inconvenience you,' Nadine flounced, misinterpreting her mother.

'Don't be silly, Nadine. I'm pleased to see you.' Thomasine's mind was already racing over how she could cope with her daughter's diet – preparing vegetarian meals had always worked out more expensive, she'd found, since she was far from expert in doing them.

'I had nowhere else to go.' Nadine dropped her case on the floor with a clatter, turned abruptly and flung herself into Thomasine's arms with such force she nearly knocked her off balance. Thomasine began to laugh, but stopped immediately when she realised Nadine was crying. Patting her shoulder and saying 'There there,' repetitively, she guided her daughter into the sitting room and, easing her limpet-like hold, edged her into an easy chair.

'Darling, what's the matter?' she asked, kneeling down in front of her, having to push an inquisitive Nova away. She was worried for she had not seen Nadine in tears for years. She waited patiently, handing out Kleenex.

'No one likes me!' the girl eventually said, but in saying it she released many more tears and a good few minutes elapsed before they could start to talk again.

'What makes you say that?' Thomasine prodded in a gentle tone.

'It's true.' Nadine looked at her wildly. 'Dad's got no time for me – I just get in the way. He doesn't want me there.'

Thomasine patted her hand comfortingly, but abided by her rule to say nothing against Robert, lest it be construed as criticism.

'And I hate Chantal. She's a conceited, stuck-up bitch. She never stops nagging me. "Nadine, do this, don't do that. Oh, Nadine, Ooh la la."' Her daughter expertly imitated Chantal's pronounced French accent, making Thomasine smile.

'She's not my favourite person, either,' she said, since her vow of reasonableness did not cover the usurper of her husband and home. 'She's got a mean mouth, I always thought.'

'And she doesn't shave her armpits,' Nadine added, her face twisted with disgust. At this Thomasine could not suppress her laughter. Nadine at first looked with annoyance at her mother, but then, seeing the funny side, joined in.

'It wasn't *that* funny,' Nadine said when they had calmed down.

'No – but funny enough. Fancy a glass of wine?' Thomasine asked as she scrambled to her feet. Nadine followed, and Nova brought up the rear, as they went into the kitchen and settled at Thomasine's favourite place when a talk was in the offing – the pine table.

'Dear old table.' Nadine patted it. 'You've had it longer than you've had me, haven't you?' She accepted the glass of wine her mother had poured her. 'You know it's wrong to have a bulldog,' she continued abruptly as Nova fussed about her.

'I thought of getting her a companion. It must be a lonely business being an only dog. But I can't afford another one.'

'I didn't mean that – you getting more dogs. I meant bulldogs shouldn't be bred. It's cruel, they can't breathe. Man's manipulated them to look like that.'

'Nova doesn't have any breathing problems. Listen to her.'

'Bulldogs have over thirty defects.'

'Possible defects. In a well-bred bulldog it isn't necessarily so. Good breeders are trying to eliminate such problems,' Thomasine said defensively.

'Of course if you do get another dog, you're only perpetuating the wickedness, aren't you?' Nadine neatly moved away from an argument she was not sure she would win.

'What wickedness?'

'Of pet ownership. It's demeaning to dogs, you know. There's no difference between a lion in captivity and keeping a dog in the home. It should have the dignity of running wild.'

'I haven't noticed any dogs complaining.'

'You never take me seriously, do you?' Nadine flared. 'Whatever I have to say, you just grin and make some smart-arse reply.'

'Perhaps if you didn't make such asinine statements I wouldn't need to.' Thomasine could feel the old irritation with her daughter welling up inside her and made herself choke it back. 'Look, Nadine, I'm sorry. You're right. I should listen to you.'

'I should think so.' Nadine moved her shoulders back and forth, reminding Thomasine of a bird adjusting its feathers.

'Does your father know you're here?' she asked.

'He told me to come. I told him I'd been expelled, that I hated Chantal, and so he said "Well, piss off to your mother if you feel like that". So I came. You got any nuts or Twiglets or anything?'

'No, I haven't. Did you say expelled?' Thomasine shook her head in amazement at the way her daughter could flit from one subject to another.

'That's right, E-X-P-E-L-L-E-D.' She spelt out, as if proud of the fact.

'What on earth for?'

'If they hadn't, I'd have walked out anyway,' Nadine said defiantly.

'Why?'

'I went on a demonstration, and to do that I had to bunk out. It would have been all right, except the creeps saw us on TV.'

'Us? TV?'

'There were four of us. I wasn't alone,' she smiled, proud of the fact. 'We were demonstrating about the export of calves. You must have seen it?'

'Yes, yes, of course.'

'Poor little things. I had to do something. It was great, though. I met some wonderful people and everything. Real animal lovers, real concerned people.'

'I can imagine,' Thomasine said with irony, remembering the pictures she had seen, not just the concerned, ordinary women who had started the campaign, but the animal activists who had appeared to hijack the demonstrations. She supposed it was their view of dog ownership Nadine had been spouting.

'I bet you're going to say it doesn't matter where and how the calves are raised.' Nadine glared at her.

'No, I'm not. I agree with you.'

'But you eat meat.'

'Yes. Often I wish I didn't, but I know I couldn't give it up. But that doesn't mean you mustn't respect the animals and ensure they have a good life and a decent, quick death.'

'Oh, great. Sorry, you're only a few months old, but here's the blindfold and I'll aim for the heart. Don't you know what an abattoir is like?'

'No, but no doubt you are about to tell me.'

'Hypocrites like you make me sick,' Nadine shouted angrily at her.

'As do hypocrites like you who lecture people like me and bang the veggie drum and then eat hamburgers when they think no one is looking.' Thomasine watched as Nadine's face went bright red and her mouth hung slackly open with surprise. 'I saw you in Shillingham last time you were here.'

'You never said.'

'I wanted to save you embarrassment. But you've just annoyed me, really annoyed me, and I wonder why I bother.'

'I'm finding it hard to do – be a vegetarian I mean. Sometimes I slip, but then I hate myself so much. I love animals, Mum, I really do.'

'And so do I. You've just got to temper your reactions more, Nadine. You won't win any converts getting up people's noses like that. And if we are to live together again, I think we both have to make some compromises.'

'Like what?'

'Well, I won't nag you about animal activists and vegetarianism if you won't nag me about not agreeing with you one hundred per cent. It's called give and take.'

'I realise *that*.'

'And if you're to live here, I think you should watch your step. You're a town girl, as I am, and we can't crash into the country and shoot our mouths off and try to alter thousands of years' tradition in a matter of months. Things will be changed far faster with reason than with riots.'

Even as she spoke, Thomasine knew this was not what she believed entirely, but in the short time she had been here, she had seen how tempers were fraying, how antagonism to the townies was mounting. She did not want trouble, she did not want her daughter hurt.

'What about school, then? There's no chance of them taking you back?'

'I wouldn't go if they begged me.'

An unlikely scenario, Thomasine thought. 'I gather there's a high school in Morristown, but it's pretty rough.'

'I can handle it,' Nadine said with a brave flick of her hair. 'I might meet up with Kimberley – you remember, the girl with the dad with a gun.'

'What a nice idea,' Thomasine grimaced, but at least Nadine realised this time that she was joking. 'But Kimberley's left school. She's working near here, at a kennels.'

'A kennels!'

'Now come on, Nadine. Give and take. And I can assure you these kennels are run like a dogs' five-star hotel.'

'Breeders!' Nadine's face twisted with disgust, as if she were talking about mass murderers. If her daughter was here full time Thomasine could, she thought, ask her ex-husband to contribute more – teenagers were an expensive pastime, anyone could tell him that.

'They got married,' Nadine announced.

'Who?' Even as she asked, Thomasine knew it was a stupid question.

'Chantal and Dad.'

'When?'

'Last week.'

'They might have told me.' Thomasine realised that that was all that bothered her.

'And me!'

Thomasine looked at Nadine with shock etched on her face. 'They didn't tell *you*? That was unforgivable.'

'Oh, I don't care. Sod them. Why should I bother about them if they don't care about me?'

Thomasine edged her hand across the table and caught hold of Nadine's. 'Darling, I'm so sorry,' she said, everything now explained. Her daughter might be seventeen, but she still hurt as much as if she were ten years younger, probably more.

'How many puppies was it that Luna had?' Nadine asked in her strange, flitting way.

'Five – four bitches, one dog.'

'You'd rather have the puppies than me.' Nadine was laughing as she spoke, but it was a false laugh. And it was the intent way she looked at her as she said this that made Thomasine realise how desperately insecure her daughter was. That her lashing out was only a sign of this insecurity.

'Don't be silly. It'll be lovely, just the two of us.' And she held her arms wide open for Nadine to fall into. 'I love you, you know, even if we do row all the time,' she whispered into Nadine's hair as with one hand she stroked it, and with the other patted Nova, who was scrabbling to be picked up and to join in the hugging.

Thomasine was in Shillingham shopping. She could not remember when she had last felt so nervous. It was no matter that she kept berating herself for being so stupid – heavens above, she thought, if she could calculate how many meals she'd cooked in her married life; how many successful dinner parties she had given; if she kept that in mind, maybe she wouldn't be so scared. It didn't work, her stomach seemed to have acquired a life of its own. She realised there was an inescapable difference between food she had prepared before and what she was doing now. She was being paid, and that made all the difference in the world.

It was odd, almost as if their minds had been working on the same track. She had taken Oliver's advice and had made her list of talents, and cooking kept surfacing, but how to use it? In a way, she hadn't been surprised when Oliver had called and asked her about cooking.

'It was just an idea I had in the middle of the night. Why don't you set up as a caterer – you know, cooking dinner-party food for others? I know people who have made a fortune doing it in London. It might solve your problems.'

'But that was London. I hardly think one could make a success of it here in the Shillings.'

'Then I think you're wrong, Thomasine. I know quite a few people who can no longer afford to employ a full-time cook who'd jump at the chance of employing you to do their dinner parties for them. I reckon it's worth a try.'

'But what would I charge?'

'I'll find out for you from friends in London. Then knock a bit off because this is the country. I'd reckon on something like a hundred pounds a dinner.'

'You're joking! To do justice to a dinner, say of six to eight people, most of that would go on food and wine.'

'No, you've got it all wrong. They pay for the ingredients, not you. That'd be for you.'

'Oh, I'm not so sure. I'm not a professional, I've no training.'

'I bet you're an ace in the kitchen.'

Modesty prevented Thomasine from commenting.

'I'll book you first. Thursday evening for four.'

Now it was Thursday morning and Thomasine was shopping from a list that had taken her the intervening two days to compile. She'd consulted every cookbook she possessed and had wavered and dithered over menus until she had arrived at one she hoped would do.

She'd already made the vegetable terrine, which was chilling in her refrigerator; she'd still to buy the ingredients for its coulis. She had decided on duck, which she'd do with a honey and lemon sauce, and for pudding she'd opted for a light home-made ice cream to be served with her own crisp almond biscuits. That and a cheese board would be enough, she hoped.

Her problem, as she selected and rejected, was that she'd been alone too long and had not cooked dinner-party food for such a time that she was afraid she would not buy enough. On the other hand she worried that perhaps she was buying too much.

Turning out of the small grocer's in Shillingham, which had the best selection of cheese outside Harrods, she bumped into Gill.

'Thomasine! Long time no see,' he said, looking pointedly at her hair, which she touched with one gloved hand with nervous guilt.

'I know. I'm sorry.'

'It won't do, Thomasine. Hair has to be looked after. I've got a cancellation, why don't you pop in?'

Thomasine looked around wide-eyed, with the expression of one who felt trapped. Her new budget did not include trips to the hairdresser's.

'What's the matter? You look so startled. What on earth have I said?'

'Nothing, Gill. It's me. I'm in a bit of a tizz, you see. I'm just starting a new job and I'm a bit worked up about it.'

'Honest? Doing what? Painting?'

'No, that didn't work out. Cooking actually,' she said with a defiant shake of her head, daring him to comment or, by a flick of an eyelash, show any disapproval. She'd already had enough of that from Nadine who, she had been at pains to point out to her, was *mortified* at the prospect of a cook as a mother.

'Cooking? That sounds interesting. What, catering from home, that sort of thing?'

'No, dinner parties, lunches – I'm hoping people will let me into their kitchens to cook for them.' She laughed nervously.

'Shillingham's been crying out for someone like you for yonks. If I wasn't so successful as a crimper I'd have been doing it myself.'

'Really?' Thomasine, for the first time that day, felt relaxed enough to smile.

'Tell you what – I'll stick your card up in the salon, push customers your way.'

'I haven't got a card.'

'You must get some – essential. Thought of a good name?'

'Not yet. I wasn't sure . . .'

'Name's all important. Come into the salon, I'll do your hair and Justin and I will come up with a name for you.'

Thomasine stood on the pavement clutching her shopping and felt awkward with embarrassment. She took a deep breath.

'The truth is, Gill, I'd love to have my hair done, but I've had a bit of a setback, and well, I can't afford it.'

'Then have one on the house.' Gill grinned, liking her for her honesty; not like many of his customers, who'd rather die than admit they were short of cash.

'But that's no way to run a business, Gill.'

'I owe you one.'

'How come?'

'That bulldog of yours. Didn't I tell you? Stupid me. Those nice people came back to me and insisted on rewarding me for putting them on to you. They said you wouldn't take a penny, so they gave me five hundred pounds.'

'*How* much? Good heavens.'

'I reckon you could say they loved that dog. They were over the moon they'd found her. I'd been waiting for you to come in. I nearly clocked Justin for charging you last time you were here. So I think a shampoo and blow-dry is on the cards, don't you?'

Gill had almost finished her hair when he asked her if she'd thought about the dog ringcraft classes Justin had suggested.

'There you are again, Gill. I honestly don't think I could even contemplate the expense of dog classes and shows.'

'Pop along – just to see. Justin and I take one every week in the Community Centre here.'

An hour later Thomasine tripped out of the salon feeling the confidence that a decent hairstyle gives a woman. But she was also walking on air, boosted with reassurances that the home-catering venture was a great idea, plus a booking for dinner for six next week at Gill and Justin's, with the menu already worked out. Best of all, she had a name for her business: Thomasine's Treats, they'd suggested. She quite liked it, but wanted to ponder it a bit longer. They had also given her the phone number of their printer.

Once home, she prepared as much of the food as she could and cling-filmed the containers and put them in baskets which she covered with gingham tea towels. She had time for a hurried bath. She was doubtful what to wear, but eventually opted for jeans and a T-shirt, since she'd be hidden away in the kitchen. But then she flapped at the thought she might be expected to serve the food and instead changed into a black skirt with a white shirt and a silk paisley waistcoat. She made a mental note to buy some large white pinafores. Gill, thinking ahead, had pinned her long hair up in a full, but neat, French pleat.

'You don't want your hair dangling all over the food now, do you?' he'd said when she had told him she hated herself with her hair up. Now, looking in the mirror, she decided he was right. Done his way, it suited her, made her face look thinner, made her look more 'grown up' somehow.

34

Wimpole was all of a dither.

'I wish you'd consulted me about this, Oliver. What if she can't cook?'

'I'm sure she can. Thomasine looks like a woman who can.'

'What does that nonsense mean?'

'She has a sensual look about her, not a puritan one – people like that can usually cook,' Oliver explained.

'I've never heard such a load of old cobblers in my life. What's she doing?'

'I left it to her.'

'What if Rudolph doesn't like it? He's a fussy eater.'

'Then Rudie will have to go without. Remember what Nanny used to say.' He wagged his forefinger at her and smiled affectionately. She did not respond.

'It's not good enough at all! And I don't like her name. My aunt's cat was called Thomasine, and a nasty, spiteful creature she was.'

'Wimpole, why don't you go and lay the table and keep your mind off things,' he suggested patiently.

While Wimpole clattered about in the dining room, Oliver lit the fire in the drawing room. He stood at the window while he waited to see if it would draw. He looked out on the garden, where October was already making its mark with fallen leaves and fading, bruised roses. It was an odd thing, but he felt Wimpole was not only nervous, like any bride in the run-up to her wedding, but more than that, as if she was frightened of something. Wimpole was never scared of anything. It was distinctly strange.

The fire drawing satisfactorily, and Slipper like a shadow trotting along behind, he went into the kitchen to find Thomasine already at work.

'I hope you don't mind me letting myself in, but the back door was open,' she said. 'And I've brought my dog with me. Once she's explored she'll sleep. Is that all right?'

'That's fine by me. Hullo, old girl.' He bent down and patted the puppy. 'You know, my grandfather had one of these.'

'Everybody's grandfather did.' Thomasine was laughing and he liked the effect.

'I've been lighting a fire. It's really chilly this evening. Duck! Lovely.' He washed his hands at the sink. 'Anything I can do to help?'

'I hope everything's under control. I'll yell if I get into a muddle.'

'Don't be nervous. It'll be fine.' He patted her shoulder and she felt a rush of pleasure, and then told herself to pull herself together.

'Fancy a drink?'

'I'd better not. I don't want to ruin your dinner.'

'Just a little one,' he insisted.

He sat at the end of the pine table and watched her preparing the food. He liked watching her; despite her nervousness she moved in an assured, smooth way. He liked her hair pulled back from her face, he had not realised what fine bones she had, nor that her eyes were so large. How he'd love to unpin her hair and see it fall heavily onto her shoulders . . .

'You look deep in thought. Any problems?'

'I was thinking how very attractive you are.'

'Me?' She laughed, self-consciously touching her hair as if checking it was still in place.

'Sorry, that was rude of me.' He too felt embarrassed, astonished that he'd had the nerve to speak out.

'Don't be – sorry, I mean,' she said softly and almost held her breath at her own temerity. Then the telephone rang and the spell was broken.

When Oliver went to take his bath she was relieved, since she hated anyone watching her cook. But, at the same time, she was aware she wished he'd stayed. This was very odd – hadn't she disliked him when she first met him, thinking him too smooth for comfort? One lunch and she liked him, and even more so tonight. It was dangerous ground – ground which was likely to shift at any moment. He'd that predatory ex-wife whom she'd no desire to cross swords with, she'd a disapproving daughter – what on earth was she thinking about? Go back to your celibate life, Thomasine, you don't need the complications of a man. Still, she thought as she began to make her sauce, she liked his dog.

When everything was under control in the kitchen, she checked the dining room. It looked a picture. Oliver owned some spectacular silver, which reflected in the highly-polished surface of the long refectory table. She admired the fine set of Jacobean chairs, so right for this room. The napkins were finest damask, the candles were the creamiest-coloured wax and the flowers, button chrysanthemums in bronze and yellow, were prettily arranged, she wondered by whom.

'Checking my handiwork?'

Thomasine turned to see Wimpole, smartly dressed in a blue wool dress and a little light make-up, standing in the doorway. She wondered how long she'd been there.

'It's a lovely room. The table looks great. Did you do the flowers? They're gorgeous.'

'What you cooking?'

'Duck with – '

'Not greasy, I hope.'

'I hope not too. It shouldn't be. I always – '

'I should have been consulted.'

'I'm sorry? Oliver told me to do whatever I wanted.'

'Well, he never should have. And it's Mr Hawksmoor to you.' Wimpole marched from the room, leaving a perplexed Thomasine, who'd never been treated like a servant before. She'd only met Wimpole once before and she'd seemed pleasant enough then.

With everything checked again, and on time, she finally allowed herself to sit down at the kitchen table and enjoy the drink Oliver had poured her. She began to list in her head the order of cooking the vegetables, but the thoughts slid away to be replaced by wondering what it would feel like to kiss Oliver. She covered her face with her hands as if to blot out the image. If she put the potatoes on –

And yet . . . what would it be like to lie in a man's arms – Oliver's arms! If he made love to her, would it be the same as Robert or different? Different, she was almost sure. Almost, for that was the problem; having known only one man sexually in her life, she could not be totally sure.

Silly thoughts, silly ideas. He was flirting, that was all, and she was no better than a mooning teenager. From outside she was vaguely aware of the sound of a motor.

'He's here,' Oliver popped his head around the kitchen door.

'You don't want to eat yet, though?'

'No, I was telling you to come and join us.'

'You're inviting me?'

'Of course, who else? You're the fourth, didn't you realise?'

'Well, no.' She looked down at her skirt, smoothing her baggy blouse. 'I'm not dressed . . .'

'You look fine to me, and Wimpole's not sporting her tiara! Come on.' He held his hand out to her and half dragged her across the hall into the drawing room.

Rudolph Adams was a large man, and looked out of place in the pretty drawing room. He stood clutching his cap to him as if trying to make himself smaller, as if afraid of breaking things. He was very fit looking, tanned with piercing blue eyes, and although Thomasine found the eyes rather cold, she could understand Wimpole finding him attractive. As she shook his hand she was aware of Wimpole watching her suspiciously. She made Thomasine think of a small bird, with her sharp black eyes and tiny frame.

They all sat down while Oliver fussed over the drinks tray. Slipper advanced into the room, sniffing at their feet. Thomasine saw how Rudolph lifted his feet as the dog approached.

'Have you met our latest addition?' Wimpole asked, bending down and scooping up the puppy.

'Put that down, Wimpole, it's unhygienic,' Rudolph ordered, and to Oliver's astonishment Wimpole obeyed.

Despite the difficulty of being both guest and cook, the meal progressed well. In future, though, Thomasine vowed to be one or the other, it would be easier. The food was eaten with relish, and Rudolph had two helpings of everything. Wimpole had changed from the sharp virago Thomasine had met before the meal, and was pleasant again. Had something upset her, or had she been nervous about the evening and that had passed? Or perhaps it was the excellent wine that had softened her up.

There was a new phenomenon in Thomasine's life. Just as when she had been pregnant every other woman seemed to be too, now she'd acquired a dog, every conversation at some point or other turned to that subject.

'You let your dog *sleep* with you?' Rudolph asked her with a shocked expression.

'Why, yes. I like to hear her snoring in the night.' She felt she sounded as if she were making excuses, which was quite ridiculous since she could sleep with a puma if she wanted to. 'Where do your dogs sleep?'

'In the kennels, of course.'

'But they're gun dogs,' Oliver intervened. 'That's different. Bandage, even if he didn't sleep with me, was close by in the dressing room.'

'Sophia allowed that?'

'Sophia had to lump it. I could never marry a woman who wouldn't share me with a dog.' He laughed at this, but Thomasine noticed Rudolph didn't, and she found herself thinking how glad she was she'd admitted the truth about Nova.

'Have you told Thomasine about that great Newfoundland you nearly lumbered us with?' Wimpole asked. 'The one that lived in Baskerville Terrace.'

'Not much point now when you've let slip the punch line,' Oliver said, and proceeded to launch into a long, involved and funny story about the dog.

Everyone laughed except Rudolph, who sat po-faced and not amused at all.

Later, the dinner at an end, Wimpole offered to help clear up, but Thomasine would not hear of it.

'No, that's my job,' she insisted, collecting the glasses onto a tray as the others made their way to the drawing room for brandies. 'I'll bring the coffee in.'

'You ought to marry her, you know, Oliver, before someone else snaps her up,' said Wimpole, very tipsily.

Thomasine stood rooted to the spot. She knew she often blushed, but never like this!

When she took the coffee in she quickly put the tray on the table, bolted back into the safety of the kitchen and began to attack the washing up. Heavens! How awful! Wimpole had spoilt everything now. Spoilt what? What was there to spoil? A bit of flirtation, that was all, hadn't she decided anyhow not to get involved? Such a change in the woman – it was as if there were two of her. Or was there such a change? Maybe Wimpole had said it on purpose, one to embarrass her and two to make Oliver run to the hills as men invariably did when *marriage* was mentioned.

'Sorry you were so embarrassed.' Oliver had walked in so quietly she hadn't heard him. 'She was very drunk, you know.'

'I realised that.' She did not look up from scouring the pans.

'You could leave that for Grace to do in the morning.'

'And have her say I'm a slovenly cook – no thank you.'

'Would it matter what she said?'

'Yes, to me, if I'm to be a professional,' she said primly. On guard.

'I'll help you.'

'No. I can manage. You go back to your guests.'

'I felt like a gooseberry in there, I'd much rather wash up with you.'

'It's all done.'

'Then have a brandy with me, here.'

'I've got to drive, even if it's only a couple of miles.'

'Coffee then?' She looked at him now and saw he was pleading with her. Treacherously, she found her heart liked that.

'Just coffee and then I must be going. I've put Nova in the car.'

'You shouldn't have done that. It's cold out there.'

'She's got her blanket.' But already he was rushing out of the kitchen to return a moment later with a very appreciative bulldog, whom Slipper welcomed ecstatically, as if she'd never seen her before.

'I worry for Slipper. I think she might be thick.'

'Shush – not in front of her. It's not fair.' Thomasine put her finger to her lips and wondered if, perhaps, she wasn't a bit tipsy too.

They sat at the pine table with their coffee and, just as proud mothers watch their toddlers play, Thomasine and Oliver watched their puppies.

'Rudolph doesn't seem to like dogs very much, does he?' she ventured.

'No, and come to think, Bandage was never that keen on him. It's worrying. Normally I never take to people who don't like dogs, or whom my dogs don't like. I've tried telling myself it's stupid, but it's never worked out – they've always let me down. Yet I've always liked Rudie well enough. Odd.'

'Does Wimpole like them?'

'Very much.'

'Then maybe he'll take to them for her, or pretend he does.'

'Pretending doesn't work – my wife pretended for years, and look where that got us.'

Thomasine was surprised to be invited to Wimpole's wedding a week later. She rather hoped that Oliver had instigated it, but it was irrelevant since she could not go. She had Gill and Justin's dinner party to attend to, and sensing that they were both probably good cooks, she dared not risk taking the afternoon off.

So she missed seeing Wimpole and Rudie wed in the little church in Middle Shilling, Wimpole, dressed in a cream velvet suit, looking younger than anyone had ever seen before. And she missed the cool atmosphere between Ben and Oliver that no fluttering on Cora's part could mend. She did not see Eveleigh turn her back on the Lucketts, nor note her leaving early. She was spared seeing Beth cling to Jim like ivy, which caused much gossip. But best of all, she did not have to see Sophia vamping Oliver, which caused even more gossip.

She would have regretted not seeing Slipper, resplendent in a white satin bow.

November

35

'But, Alan, your cover's blown, it could be dangerous for you to return to that pub. They put you into hospital once. They'll do it again.' Alan listened politely to his superior officer.

'But that was five months ago. And we never knew for sure why they bashed me up, did we?'

'True.'

'I mean, we don't *know* it was them. Or that bloke Vic might have thought I was chatting up his girlfriend, Vicky. It might have had nothing to do with the dogs.'

'But it might have had everything to do with the dogs.'

'If he has suspicions, my turning up after all this time, like I've been away, will surely allay them. If I go back to The Locomotive, what am I saying to him? *No hard feelings, mate.* Now, *if* he thinks I'm from the police or the RSPCA – well, the last thing he'll expect is me showing my face again.'

The boss looked doubtful. Alan ploughed on, determined to return to Morristown. 'Isn't this the first whiff you've had about the fighting in ages? I know it's not enough to send someone in officially, but the point is I'm going there anyway, to look for a cottage. And who else have you got to send?'

Alan knew he'd got his boss there. The whole office, it seemed, was out on assignment. Alan himself had only just got back from a trip to Spain checking out Spanish abattoirs and the movement of British sheep – and neither had been a pleasant occupation. He stood, sending up a silent prayer that his boss would listen to him. In the months away he'd found that, although he'd tried, he couldn't shake the memory of Kimberley. He wanted to see her. He'd overreacted when she was cagey about giving him her phone number and address. Perhaps her parents were difficult. He'd been a fool. He should have understood, especially when his own mother had been so possessive. He'd be an even bigger fool not to try to find her, not when she occupied his dreams in a way no other girl ever had.

'All right. But no heroics. You promise?'

'Thanks, sir,' Alan grinned.

The consensus of opinion amongst his team was that he was brave, but bonkers. Alan just shrugged and smiled broadly. He wasn't going to explain about Kimberley, nor that whilst in Spain he thought often of the fighting dogs and felt he'd let them down. They were all in the RSPCA because of a love of animals, but it wasn't something they verbalised. It was not a good idea to get too emotionally involved, they'd been told, but how the hell not to was beyond Alan's understanding.

He booked into a pleasant B&B late Friday afternoon, leaving himself just enough time to visit a couple of estate agents and collect details on cottages for sale in the area. He browsed through them as he ate a hamburger in the local MacDonald's in the large shopping precinct in Morristown.

For all his brave talk, he felt his heart thudding as he walked towards The Locomotive. But it was too late now. He made himself push the door open, and stepped into the smoky fug of the public bar.

Alan smelled the heavy perfume she wore before he heard her speak. 'Long time no see.'

'Hullo, Vicky. How's you?' he said, trying to sound normal but afraid that his nervousness made him sound like a robot.

'Where have you been? I thought you'd got fed up with us.' Vicky smiled up at him; he wished she wouldn't look at him like that, so blatantly sexual. 'You're ever so brown.'

'I've been to Spain.'

'Lucky old you. We didn't go away this year. Oh look, there he is. Vic, over here. Look who's back.' Vicky waved at the looming figure of Vic standing in the doorway, seeming, to Alan, to have doubled in size.

'Thought you'd pissed off,' Vic said, as he slipped the money for his pint across the bar. Alan had, in the circumstances, to admire his composure.

'I went away on a job. And I've been in Spain. But before all that, I was mugged. Went to hospital.'

'You never were.' Vicky looked so concerned that if Alan had not known better, he'd have thought it was the first she'd heard of it. 'Was you badly hurt?'

'Bit of concussion. Bruising mainly.'

'Did you see the bleeders?'

'No, more's the pity. I'd have given them what for if I had.' Alan banged one first into the palm of the other.

'I bet you would too,' Vicky said admiringly, and Vic shuffled his feet, fingering his beer glass, but still managing to look remarkably controlled.

'How's things, Vic? Seen those kids with the bull terrier again?' Alan, feeling he had nothing to lose, came straight out with it.

'Why you ask?' Vic glared at Alan.

'I liked the look of the dog. Just curious.'

'Curiosity killed the cat.'

'Lucky I'm not a cat then, isn't it?' Alan laughed, though he shivered inside. Hadn't Vic said that to him once before? 'I just wondered if they wanted to sell it, I might be interested in buying.'

'They already have – sold it, I mean. Bloody useless mutt it was too. No balls.'

'Who to?'

'Don't know his name.' Vic looked deep into his beer glass and Alan knew he was lying. However, he could think of no way to prolong the conversation without being too suspicious. More alarmingly, no other topic of conversation presented itself to him either. The way Vicky was continuing to eye him, he was afraid she was going to start flirting with him again. The last thing he needed was another beating from Vic.

'You got wheels?' Vic suddenly asked.

'Yeah. Why?'

'Interested in changing them?'

'Not at the moment. You selling?'

'Might be.'

'What?'

'Whatever's your fancy.' Vic grinned. Now why would he do that, tantamount to admitting he stole cars to order? Was he being tested, was Vic watching his reaction?

'I'll keep that in mind – next time, perhaps.'

'Have you got a nice car then?' Vicky asked him, undulating her hips very suggestively as she spoke.

'It's all right.' He avoided giving the make.

'Vic's got a bike and a cruddy van, haven't you, Vic? I keep telling him he ought to get a nice warm car, but he won't give up on his bike, will you, Vic?'

Vic ignored her, and Alan thought, oh dear, she's coming on too strong. 'My bird wouldn't like me to have a bike. Says a helmet would mess up her hair.'

'You got a girl?' Vicky looked downhearted.

'You don't want to let a girl tell you what's what. I wouldn't.' Vic looked – Alan didn't think it was his imagination – pleased.

'Anything for a quiet life, that's me.' Alan smiled and looked sheepish all at the same time. 'Same again?'

Their drinks ordered, he carried them towards their table and saw another man had joined the group – older, tougher, not someone he'd care to meddle with, he thought, seeing the cold blue eyes which stared intently at him in an unfriendly way as he placed the glasses on the table. He strained to hear what Vic and the man were saying, but all he heard was the word 'acre', or it could have been 'baker'.

'I'm off then.'

'Don't go on my account,' Alan said politely, reluctantly getting to his feet to let the man pass.

'I'm not,' the stranger said coldly.

'He's a friendly cove.' He laughed to show he did not care as he watched him go.

'He's all right,' Vic said, non-committally.

'What did you say his name was?'

'I didn't,' Vic replied sharply, picked up his pint and slurped noisily at it. Instinct told Alan he'd just met one of the dog-fighting cartel. He could just imagine Don's reaction if he went into the office and claimed he'd met one of the ringleaders. 'What makes you so sure?' Don would be certain to ask. 'I feel it. It's instinctive,' would be all he could answer. Don would nearly die laughing. 'Instinct! Go and get me facts!' he'd order. But Alan knew, he didn't know why, he just did. He wasn't going to give up now; after all, he was doing this in his own time.

'Penny for them?' Vicky was smiling at him.

'Don't want to bore you.'

'You'd never bore me.' Vicky slyly glanced from Alan to her boyfriend. Vic was staring at him in such an aggressive way that Alan decided he'd best make himself scarce.

'I must be off.' He stood up. 'See you both around.' He emphasised the *both*, hoping Vic noticed.

'Don't hurry back,' Vic snarled in reply.

Once outside the pub, he decided he'd made his last visit here. Vicky and her flirting were too dangerous, and in any case, Vic was too cagey to let anything useful drop. He'd be better off following him discreetly and see where that led him; Vic was too nasty a bit of work to get buddy-buddy with. He must have been mad coming here again, maybe the bang on the head had given him a death wish or something.

He strode on through the cold night until he reached his car, parked behind Tesco, and got in. He gunned the engine, eased the car out of the car park, and doubled back to the street in which The Locomotive pub was. He parked four cars away, doused his lights, switched off the engine and sat and waited, hoping Vic hadn't left in the meanwhile. Hopefully he would be in his van, he'd never keep up with the bike.

His heart sank when, after he'd waited nearly an hour, Vic and Vicky appeared, both carrying crash helmets. Another night, he thought, as he watched Vicky hoist her long leg over the pannier and admired her rear as she did so. The engine of the bike roared, but rather than speeding away, Vic drove up the road at a sedate speed. Alan followed, keeping a safe distance. From the way he handled the motorbike, Vic must be smarting from a speeding ticket.

The bike stopped and Vicky got off, hurled the helmet at Vic and shouted something at him that Alan, stopped a good way back, could not catch. She flounced off into the labyrinth of the Forest Glade estate, pausing before she turned a corner to give Vic a V sign.

It was not so easy keeping up with him as they left the city, for Vic weaved his way in and out of the traffic. He seemed to have thrown his previous caution to the winds, and drove far too fast along the by-pass. But it was dark and once off the fast road and on the country lanes, with no other traffic about, Alan, even from some way behind, could still see his lights.

Then suddenly there was total blackness and Alan cursed that he'd missed him. Coming round a bend he nearly had a fit as he saw Vic waiting by a gate, looking menacing astride his bike, his large black visored helmet on, watching the road, obviously checking if he was being followed.

There was nothing for it but to press on and hope he did not see who was driving. Alan put his foot down and shot past the opening. He looked in his mirror once he was past to see Vic starting up his bike. Now what, Alan thought, heart sinking. But the lights did not follow him. Instead Vic seemed to be crossing a ploughed field judging by the beams of light bouncing up and down.

Alan went round the last bend and slowed down. He had not the foggiest idea where he was – some sleuth you are, he told himself. Fifty yards further on he came to a crossroads and a signpost. One arrow pointed to Shilling-ham, one to The Shillings and the road he had just come along was signed to Conniestown. He repeated the name several times to get it in to his head and made for Shillingham. He knew his way back to Morristown from there.

Jim was asleep, on his own, when the call came. It was a very distressed Eveleigh – one of her dogs was ill and in great pain. He was immediately awake for, of all his clients, Eveleigh was the least likely to call at such an ungodly hour unless it was critical.

It was a bitterly cold night, and as he often did when called out, Jim pulled his cords over his pyjama bottoms and a sweater over his top – it saved time when, and if, he eventually climbed back into bed. Within fifteen minutes he was pulling up outside Eveleigh's. He went straight round the back to where he could see a light shining in one of the kennels. As he walked, he could hear the restlessness of the other dogs as they moved agitatedly on their bedding, snuffling at the doors to be let out. A couple of them were barking; not the full, normal, deep-throated bark, but a more experimental, uncertain bark, as if the dogs were clearing their throats.

'What have we here then?'

Eveleigh, kneeling beside a large St Bernard bitch, looked up at Jim, her face streaked with tears, her long hair – uncoiled from its normal bun – spiked with straw. On her lap lay the dog's huge head. Its mouth was lathered with froth and Eveleigh's dressing gown was soaked with saliva. The dog's eyes were rolled up. She looked at Jim and shook her head sadly.

Nonetheless, Jim took out his stethoscope and listened hard, but there was nothing. 'Eveleigh, I'm sorry.' He put his hand out and took hold of hers and squeezed it, trying to comfort her. 'It isn't one of your champions, is it?' The dog looked so bedraggled, its hair damp with sweat, not like the normal spruce appearance of Eveleigh's dogs, that it was impossible to identify which one it was.

'No. Thank goodness – Lohengrin's kennel is further down – I padlocked it. You can never be too careful – not these days. Brünnhilde, well, she's a bit of a favourite and she was sleeping with me. This was Isolde – she was a brood bitch.'

'How old?'

'Seven. A sweet dog.'

'She's not pregnant?'

'No. She could have had one more litter. But I thought she's done me proud in the past, let her have an early retirement.' She managed to smile.

'What happened?'

'I heard intruders. My little King Charles woke me – the St Bernards never hear anything, they sleep too deeply. But Coco heard. By the time I got down here, they'd gone and poor Isolde had been poisoned.'

'Poison? You sure?'

'Just look at her, Jim.'

'But it could be something else. An epileptic fit. A seizure, heart . . .'

'No. She was screaming with pain when I found her. She was doubled up in agony.'

'The bastards! Have you called the police?'

'Just you. I had to get back to her.'

'Of course. I think you should phone them, you know. This is very serious. There's nothing more we can do for Isolde, and the less we disturb her the better. Come on, Evie, let's make some tea.' He held his hand out to her.

Gently, Eveleigh lowered Isolde's heavy head on the straw. She leaned over and kissed her before allowing Jim to haul her to her feet. 'The last person to call me Evie was my husband.'

'I'm sorry. I didn't think.'

'No, please. I like it.' She walked in front of him out into the open. 'It's all right, my darlings. Nothing to worry about, go back to sleep,' she called to her snuffling, agitated brood.

Jim was not a person who easily lost his temper, but he did an hour later. One of the investigating policemen had already upset Eveleigh by querying if she had put rat poison down which the dog had inadvertently eaten. But worse was to come when, although not saying it outright, the man's train of thought became all too obvious.

'I mean,' he said, sipping at the tea Eveleigh had given him, 'I should think it costs a bob or two to put down a big dog like that.'

Eveleigh stood speechless, clutching the teapot to her as if, if she let go, she might hit the officer.

'That's a diabolical accusation,' Jim shouted.

'I wasn't aware I was accusing Mrs Brenton of anything, sir.' The 'sir' was added after an almost imperceptible – and insolent – pause.

'I can assure you that there isn't a more caring breeder in the whole country than Mrs Brenton.'

'And you're her vet, I gather.'

'Yes. What's that got to do with it?'

'Quite a bit, I should think. For a start, you would say that of a client, wouldn't you? A valuable client, no doubt.'

'Are you trying to suggest that *I* had something to do with this?'

'I'm not implying anything – sir. Just doing my job.'

'I've a good mind to report you for insolence.'

'You must do as you wish – sir.'

Again that pause, which was so irritating, and yet impossible to prove intentional. Eveleigh caught hold of Jim's sleeve and tugged it, gaining his attention.

'The officer has to ask all manner of questions, Jim, if we're to get to the bottom of this.'

'Thank you, Mrs Brenton. Now, all these strange happenings – the unordered deliveries. You didn't think to call us in sooner? Now, why was that, Mrs Brenton?'

'I didn't want to make a fuss,' she answered lamely.

'I see. Is there anything else we should know?' The policeman sounded bored.

'There were the phone calls.'

'What phone calls?' Jim asked.

'Didn't Mrs Brenton think to tell you either – sir?'

'I knew you'd worry, Jim. There was nothing you could do about it, was there?'

'What sort of calls?' Jim demanded.

'They were threatening my dogs.'

'Oh, Eveleigh. Why didn't you tell someone? We could have mounted a watch system or something.'

'I hoped it would stop. I'd almost decided to take up the offer to sell.' Eveleigh lifted her chin and clenched her hands at her sides. She was obviously fighting back tears, and Jim could not but admire her courage.

'And let them win?'

'I couldn't put the dogs at risk.'

'And where would you have gone?'

'I thought about Scotland. In the Highlands, perhaps, an isolated croft somewhere.'

'Oh, poor Eveleigh.' He put his arm about her shoulder. She turned and, despite the presence of the policeman, buried her head in his chest, allowing herself the luxury of tears.

36

The news of the break-in at the kennels swept excitedly through the villages. Police cars were not often seen in the lanes thereabouts, so that the presence of two at the same time, parked outside Eveleigh's, fuelled the rumours to an hysterical degree.

In the village shop Thomasine heard a whispered tale that Eveleigh had been found by the postman in one of the dog kennels with her throat cut. She did not stop to do her shopping, but drove home, feeling sick with horror and close to tears at the thought that Eveleigh was dead.

The telephone was ringing as she entered the house. She heard Eveleigh's voice on the other end with such a sense of relief that her legs felt suddenly wobbly and she had to sit down quickly.

'I'm so happy to hear you,' she gabbled. 'They said in the shop you were dead!'

'Oh these villages! They're unbelievable. No, I'm fine; sadly my dog, Isolde, died in the night. We had intruders.'

Thomasine then realised how low Eveleigh sounded, and kicked herself for not picking up on it sooner. 'I really am so dreadfully sorry about poor Isolde. She was such a gentle dog. I wonder – ' She paused, not sure if she had enough nerve to offer.'I wonder, I've got my painting of Isolde if you would like it, I'd – '

'That's why I'm calling you. I wondered if I could buy it from you – a souvenir of a dear dog.'

'I don't want you to buy it! I'm happy for you to have it.'

An hour later Thomasine delivered the painting. Inevitably they argued about it, since Eveleigh was adamant she should pay and Thomasine was equally adamant she should not. Eveleigh looked grey with worry and exhausted.

'Are your other dogs all right? Is there anything I can do to help?' Thomasine asked, and as she did, she realised how much she had changed. There would have been a time when she would never have thought to help out with dogs. 'After all, it's only a question of size, isn't it?' she said, mirroring her thoughts.

'How kind, but Kimberley is coping well. I bless the day she came, she's so willing.'

'Then let me make you some coffee, Eveleigh. You look washed out.' When she returned from the kitchen with the tray, it was in time to let Oliver in. 'Hullo,' she said, feeling ridiculously shy.

'Is Eveleigh in . . .?'

'Oliver, in here,' Eveleigh called from the sitting room.

'Jim phoned. Eveleigh, why didn't you tell us? We might have been able to help.'

'It was my problem, Oliver. I've never seen the point in burdening people, and I've been on my own so long now that I don't think to turn to others.'

'It's called friendship, Eveleigh. That's what we're here for, surely, to help each other out at times like this.'

'That's kind, Oliver, that's just what dear Gill and Justin said to me. But, oh dear, who would have thought it would come to this?'

'Was it poison, as Jim fears?'

'We shall know later today. Jim normally would have done the post-mortem, but the police insisted poor Isolde was taken to the vet at Morristown.'

'Whatever for?'

'I think they suspect us – well, me, of killing the dog, and they're afraid Jim is covering up for me.'

'You are joking, aren't you?' Oliver said, and Thomasine realised it was the first time she'd seen him serious.

'Unfortunately, no.'

'Is it another breeder, jealous of your success?' Thomasine asked.

'I find that so difficult to grasp. Dog people love dogs, we live for them. Who could be so cruel?'

'There are nutters in all walks of life, Eveleigh.'

'I know, but I'd rather not think so. Jim thinks it's far more likely to do with the land – some big businessman trying to scare me.'

Eveleigh told her all about the letters, the strange deliveries and the phone calls. Thomasine in turn was distressed that Eveleigh hadn't told any of them the full story.

'I do hope it's no one you know. That, in a way, would make it doubly bad.'

'Well, at least it's not Ben. That would have been too awful.'

'Ben Luckett?' Thomasine asked with surprise.

'He owned the land originally, but he's sold it.'

'What's to be done now?' Oliver asked. 'You know, in some ways the police involvement might be the best thing – it might scare them off.' He was about to add 'for the time being', but managed to stop himself in time.

'I'm glad you've got Kimberley here,' Thomasine said. 'It would be worrying if you were completely alone.'

'You need better security.'

'I've arranged that already, Oliver. A locksmith is coming to fit mortice locks on all the kennel doors – they'll be safe at night. And Mr Gurton, the electrician, is out there now putting up those lights that switch on if something crosses their beam – or something like that!' Eveleigh waved her hand in the air vaguely, a sure indication of her fatigue. 'And Jim has been a tower of strength. He's offered to move in until all this blows over – he can get his calls re-routed.'

'That is kind.'

'Oh, I don't think I could possibly take him up on it. He's such a busy man.'

An hour later Oliver and Thomasine stood by their cars in the November chill.

'How's business?'

'It's unbelievable. I can't thank you enough for getting me started. I haven't even advertised yet, but already I've got two lunches booked and I've had a couple of enquiries about Christmas parties.'

'Brilliant. I think you should get a green van with *Thomasine's Treats* in gold lettering on the side.'

'I'm coming round to that name too. Why green?'

'Because it's my favourite colour. Why else?' He grinned. 'Who are the bookings?'

'Some people called Hetherington, they live over near Conniestown – I've my hairdresser to thank for them. And, oddly enough, your father-in-law. Cora phoned and asked if it was true I was doing it and could I do a lunch for ten tomorrow. Apparently the two Filipino servants he had walked out and left him in the lurch. Did you mention me? Do I have you to thank for that?' She smiled at him.

'Not guilty. Tell you what, though. You could do us all a favour. Try and manoeuvre it so that you tell Cora about the dog poisoning when Ben's in the room. Watch his reaction.'

'Oh, Oliver, surely not? Eveleigh said he'd sold the land, so it can't be him.'

'It's easy enough to say, isn't it? Doesn't mean he has.'

'I can't believe that. Ben is such a kind man and he adores dogs.'

'So did Hitler.'

'Oh, Oliver, you know what I mean.' She playfully pushed him and then felt bashful at displaying such familiarity.

'I don't mean Ben administered the poison himself. Good Lor' no – he would never do his own dirty work. And I'm not saying he ordered it. More likely he's told someone to get rid of the kennels and has left it up to them how they do it. That's why I want you to watch his expression.'

'But this land can't be *that* important to him. He's loaded, isn't he?'

'Was. My adorable wife – soon to be ex, hurrah,' he added hurriedly, in case Thomasine misinterpreted his use of 'adorable', 'let slip that Daddy was a wee bit stretched, thanks to the Lloyd's débâcle. If that's so, then he's got to raise money and fast. Planning permission on that land is of the utmost importance, therefore, and poor Eveleigh is in the way. I know Ben Luckett. He's ruthless. This could get even nastier.'

Despite the success of the dinner she had cooked for Oliver, Thomasine still felt the same degree of nervousness as she unpacked her car and carried the boxes into Cora's kitchen. She had more to unload this time, for working at Oliver's had taught her that strange kitchens were as hard to find one's way around as any maze. Then she had wasted valuable time searching for the right saucepan, a balloon whisk, a sharper knife, so this time she had brought more of her own equipment. She was early too, another lesson learnt – she wanted to check out how the cooker worked, if it was an Aga, what alternatives were available – she had put a Baby Belling in the boot, just in case there was no back-up; she'd been caught out cooking on Agas before. You had to know about Agas.

Of course Cora's kitchen was the one she need not have worried about – it was a cook's dream.

'Shame I don't do more in it then, isn't it?' Cora laughed as she responded to Thomasine's compliments on the immaculate, custom-built, colour co-ordinated, equipment-packed kitchen. Of course there *was* an Aga, but backed up by a double built-in oven, and both Halogen and gas hobs.

'You could rent this fridge out as a bedsit,' Thomasine said when Cora opened the double doors of the huge Whirlpool refrigerator. Saucepans, when not neatly stacked on their own pyramid-shaped stands, dangled from a large batterie de cuisine, and on the marble-topped work surface was a full set of Sabatier knives.

'My char will help you, and she'll do the washing up and the floors.' Cora's scarlet, thin-strapped sandals tapped at the faded antique terracotta tiled floor which alone looked as if it had cost more than most people's kitchens. If she hadn't known better, Thomasine might have thought that Cora was pointing out the floor on purpose.

'I didn't know I was to have help. I assumed I'd be doing the washing up. If so, I'm probably charging you too much,' Thomasine said, frowning with uncertainty.

'What a sweet thing you are! Of course I shall pay you what we agreed. My char would be here in any case.'

'Well, if you're sure.' Thomasine began to unpack her boxes of food. 'I do hope you'll like the menu I've chosen.'

'Of course we will.' Cora eyed the food. 'Oh dear, didn't I tell you? Ben loathes mushrooms, and the vicar's wife only eats feather or fish.'

'Well, no, you didn't. Sorry,' said Thomasine, her heart already racing. The mushrooms were no problem, she'd just leave them out, but a Beef Welling-ton was decidedly not from a feathered nor scaly creature. Yet she had no alternative to fall back on. She there and then made the resolve in future to clear all menus with her client, whatever the client said.

Thomasine looked at her watch with an agitated expression. 'I might have time to pop out to Shillingham and buy some chicken breasts and do one en croute just for the vicar's wife.'

'Why not do ten, then we'll have an either or?' Cora suggested, smiling brightly at such an ideal but simple solution. 'A far better idea. There's a whole box of chicken breasts in the freezer.' She swung open the freezer section of the fridge.

'Yes, of course,' Thomasine agreed reluctantly; she'd wanted only to use fresh food in her business. She was glad now, though, that, given the extra work, she had not insisted on lowering the price.

She was placing the meat in the microwave to defrost – against all her principles – when the door swung open and in stalked Sophia. 'My, my, Cora told me you were the new cook and I said it's just not possible,' Sophia said in her husky drawl, and, despite her smile, looking down her nose at her, or so it seemed to Thomasine.

'It's very possible. I'm here.' She managed to smile back, and wondered why on earth she always felt at such a disadvantage with Sophia. She should loathe her for her ability to make her feel like this; instead she found she felt a sneaking admiration.

'What on earth for?'

'I need the money,' Thomasine replied honestly.

'Your ex looked well enough heeled when I saw him last, and if his bride wasn't in a Versace jacket, I'll eat my hat. Even if she looked a mite ludicrous. Somehow the jacket and pregnancy didn't go together.'

'Really?' Thomasine said with as little interest as she could muster, while a lump appeared in her chest. Of what? Anger? Pain? She was not sure which; as small as a pea, it rapidly began to take on the dimensions of a sizeable rock. 'You know them, do you?' She could not reisist a smidgeon of self-congratulation at how cool she sounded, especially since her whole world seemed to have slanted off-kilter at the roundabout way she had learnt Robert's wife was pregnant.

'I've known Chantal for years. Absolute sweetie – divine château, but of course you know that.'

'No, I don't. I've never been there.'

'Well, take my word, it's ravishing. I mean who she doesn't know isn't worth bothering with.'

'Well, that cuts me out,' Cora said. Thomasine could have kissed her and instantly forgave her the mushrooms and the vicar's wife's preferences.

'Me too.' She even found herself laughing.

'I suppose you knew she was pregnant?' Sophia asked, sounding offhand, but hitting the spot with stiletto-like technique.

'Oh really, Sophia! I'm sure Thomasine knows all this, but it's the last thing she wants to talk about – ex-husbands and their wives are boring.'

'Thomasine's isn't, he's dishy as hell.'

'Yours isn't so bad either,' Thomasine said with spirit.

'There is a difference though – Oliver isn't my ex.' She picked up a stick of carrot and waved it in the air before popping it in her mouth. 'And, *entre nous*, I doubt if he ever will be – an ex, I mean.' And with that she smartly left the room, the swing door flapping open and shut long after she'd gone.

'She's got a hope!' said Cora. 'The last thing Oliver wants is that bitch back in his life.'

Thomasine looked at Cora in surprise, and, she realised, gratitude.

'She's a spoilt brat, always has been. I wish to God some idiot would come and take her on – she's spending far too much time here for my comfort. Still, I'm holding you up. I'd better be ...' But before she finished the sentence Ben entered through the noisy flapping door, a silver tray with three glasses and a bottle of champagne on it.

'I thought the cook might like a small life enhancer,' he boomed genially.

Thomasine glanced at her watch again. It was far too early, but she had no intention of offending her host by pointing this out to him, so she accepted with a smile.

'Have you met our prospective new MP, the guest of honour at this lunch?' he asked Thomasine.

'No. I didn't even know we were to have a new one.'

'Old Johns fell off his perch a couple of weeks back. This bloke's his replacement.'

'You hope he'll be. I think this by-election could be interesting,' Cora said.

'Look at her, Thomasine – designer clothes, diamonds, spends more on manicures than the average family spends on food, and she calls herself a socialist.'

'You are what you're born, no point in changing.'

'There's every point. With my taxes . . .' Ben was beginning to wind himself up, no doubt as Cora intended, as he angrily tore at the wire around the cork.

'Maybe I should talk to this new candidate about Eveleigh's poor dog.' Thomasine not only wanted to defuse the situation, but also to do Oliver's bidding, and this seemed a good opportunity.

'What poor dog?' Cora asked with interest.

'Didn't you know? One of Eveleigh's dogs has been poisoned . . .'

It was Thomasine's turn not to finish her sentence for at that point, on that word, Ben dropped the bottle of champagne, which exploded sending shards of glass and fountains of wine all over the kitchen. For a split second Thomasine saw horror on his face.

'Ben, you clumsy bugger, you can clear it up.'

'It slipped right out of my hand.'

'Poisoned? What, rat poison?' Cora asked.

'An accident, of course?' Ben looked more than anxious.

'No. The dog's been taken away for an autopsy, but it looks deliberate.'

'Who on earth could do a thing like that? Horrible. Ben, you must do something.'

'What the hell am I supposed to do?'

'Go and see her. Try and sort out this kennel business for her once and for all.'

'It could be anyone, anything. Eveleigh's very successful with her dogs – it's probably another jealous breeder,' Ben said as he swept the glass up.

'I can see another breeder wanting to hurt Eveleigh, but not her dogs, surely? They'd be dog lovers.'

'I suppose it's like anything else, you'll even find fanatics in the dog world, people who'd stop at nothing.' Thomasine said this to make Ben feel more relaxed, and observing him from the corner of her eye she saw that it had worked – his shoulders visibly lost the rigid set they'd had ever since Thomasine had dropped her bombshell. She was certain now that Ben knew far more than he was letting on, though she was pleased she could report back to Oliver that he'd obviously known nothing about the dog being killed; his shock was genuine.

'Spot on, Thomasine. I'll get another bottle.'

'If it's for me, Ben, please don't bother, I'm rapidly getting behind here, I must get on.'

'Yes, come on, Ben, let's leave Thomasine alone to do lunch – no cook likes to be watched.' Cora ushered Ben out through the flapping door. Before she could begin to work Thomasine had to mop the floor where the spilled champagne was already becoming tacky.

Once back into the soothing routine of peeling and chopping, she allowed herself to think. Not of Ben and the dog, she was certain in her mind about that. No, she thought about her husband. As she diced her onions and garlic the knife sliced rapidly through the crisp, white vegetables, its motion dictated by the anger she felt. How could he firstly up and marry and not even let her know, and secondly not warn her about the pregnancy, have her find out from others? How thoughtless, how unkind – how bloody rude! And the creep, she'd wanted other children, begged him for them, and he'd refused. Well, she was glad she had now – at least that was one less link with him.

The knife paused in mid-air. She liked this reaction. A couple of months back she'd have been wallowing in hurt feelings and dashed dreams. That had been an uncomfortable time, a useless, demeaning way to feel. This anger was far better. The cause of the anger was much more satisfactory – not that he was married, but because he had such filthy manners.

Her satisfaction, however, wouldn't help Nadine. She would be truly hurt, no doubt she would regard it as rejection. Oh, hell. She thought of the moods and dramas Nadine could make out of this news, and she did not fancy the prospect at all.

Still, she'd think about that later, good food never materialised from a worried, distracted cook. She'd think of other things.

Oliver. Just thinking his name made a smile appear on her face. But what had Sophia meant about him? Did she mean they were getting back together? Oh no! She would hate that. She felt her spirits drop like an express lift. She hadn't, up until now, really faced the truth – she was more than a little fond of Oliver. What she was feeling was, she was pretty sure, the beginnings of falling in love.

37

Despite Alan's snooping and two more garbled and muffled telephone calls, he and his colleagues were no further on in their search for the Morristown dog-fighting cartel. The informant had said nothing specific, regardless of the gentle coaxing of the inspector. They all agreed that both calls were from the same person. One only had to listen to the taped voice to hear the upset and, most thought, fear in it. They had worked out the scenario that Fred, as they had dubbed him, had probably just attended such a fight; was sickened by what he saw, wanted it stopped, but once in contact with the RSPCA, lost his bottle and could not quite bring himself to name names. Whether that was from the fear of being beaten up or from a misplaced sense of loyalty was anybody's guess.

Alan, like the others in the office, had listened to the tape over and over again in the hope that in a pub, in a shop, they might just hear the voice again. The only other clue was the background noise of a television playing and a bird, a budgerigar, chirping in the background. Noises which would be common in half the homes on the Forest Glade estate.

Alan was also frustrated that, although his house hunting had brought him to Shillingham on several Saturdays, he'd never again met Kimberley. His social life was looking up and he had even been on a couple of dates, but he hadn't been able to get involved; it was Kimberley he wanted. As he drove again, a Phil Collins tape playing, he liked to think about her and make up imaginary conversations of what he'd say to her if he ever found her again.

It was Friday and Alan was en route to Shillingham again, booked into his bed and breakfast for the weekend. His trip was twofold. He was to pick up, from an estate agent, the keys of a possible property situated in a wood above Middle Shilling. It was within his price range, and he was keen to buy. The money from the sale of his mother's house was in the bank, but it bothered him lying there. He did not trust himself not to raid it and buy himself an exotic holiday or an expensive car, and he knew the sum could so easily be chipped away.

For a while he sang along to *In The Air Tonight*, but soon fell back to thinking. If he bought this cottage, what would he do with it? If he let it the extra money would certainly come in handy, but would being a landlord prove to be a hassle? Could he afford to keep it just for weekends? Whichever way, he'd have somewhere to retire to. At that thought he laughed out loud. What a notion, it was something he couldn't even imagine.

He supposed a day might come when he'd want to leave the Special Branch. It was difficult to imagine, since being in the Special Branch rapidly became a way of life hard to give up, especially when hot on the trail of something important. Then, the adrenalin never stopped pumping and one lived on a perpetual high.

'You'll get too old for it one day,' he told himself. And one day you'll get married and have to settle down, he also said to himself, which brought his thoughts full circle back to Kimberley.

He would also use his time in Shillingham to visit the local vets. He was probably on a hiding to nothing. He knew that invariably the dog-fighting fraternity, afraid a vet might report them to the police, chose to treat any dogs hurt in a fight themselves.

Still, it was worth a try. He might learn if any vets in the area had been burgled – if saline solution and drips were taken as well as medicines it was often an indication that dog fighters were involved, he thought as he parked his car.

The new veterinary practice had nothing untoward to report. He liked the young couple running it on sight. It was a husband and wife team – it was surprising how often it was – and they were as proud as punch of the new facility they had created, sinking all their savings and a frightening bank loan into it. Still, they told him, business was good and word got put around. The other local vet, a Jim Varley, had been good enough to pop in and welcome them and had no hard feelings. He had even suggested they did a night-call and weekend roster between them.

Alan, though he liked them, thought he'd never get away and for a good fifteen minutes was backing towards the door. He emerged onto the pavement, looked up and saw Kimberley on the other side of the road. His heart seemed to somersault.

'Kimberley,' he shouted. And without looking,he plunged into the road and raced towards her.'Kimberley!'

'Hullo, Alan,' she said, not pausing.

'I never thought I'd see you again!' He fell into step beside her.

'Well, whose fault is that?' She stopped walking and stood rigid, her emotions a raging mixture of joy at seeing him, aching with longing for him, perplexity and hurt at his cavalier behaviour towards her.

'Kimberley. I'm sorry. I was a fool. You don't know how often I regretted losing my temper – I've paid for it.' He grabbed her hand and held it tight, as if fearing to lose her a second time. 'But it's not Saturday!'

'No. I don't come in on Saturdays any more.' She still sounded distant, but she did not pull her hand away.

'I know,' he said.

'How do you know?'

'Because I've come looking for you.'

'That's nice.' She looked away shyly, but was unable to stop a huge smile wreathing her face.

'Coffee?' he asked, hopeful now.

'Um . . . Nice.' They made for The Copper Kettle and the Conco machine.

Once settled at the table in the window, coffee and cake ordered, neither was quite sure what to say to each other. Alan thought she had been pleased he'd been looking for her, but on the other hand, he didn't want to move too fast and frighten her away. And Kimberley, unused to being searched for by young men, was unsure how to proceed. Showing too much interest in him might frighten him away, too little and he could lose interest. But where the middle ground lay, that elusive area which might, just might, lead to happiness, was a mystery to her. Kimberley was on new territory.

'You look very pretty,' Alan blurted out, and could have bitten his tongue off for rushing.

'So do you – ' she giggled. 'Handsome, I mean, not pretty.' And she giggled some more, and hated herself for being so gauche. She looked at the paper napkin on her lap with great interest, as if she'd never seen one before.

'Nothing bent about me,' Alan laughed and held his hand limply in the air and knew he wasn't being funny.

'What are you doing here on a Friday?' she asked, and he could have kissed her for moving on to safe ground.

'I'm looking at a house tomorrow.' Experience taught him not to mention the vet.

'You won't find many houses for sale at the vet's,' she said, quite pleased with her joke, but then blushing furiously as she realised she'd given the game away, that she'd seen him before he'd seen her.

'Oh that. I just popped in . . .' He purposely dropped his napkin on the floor and bent down to retrieve it, giving himself time to think of a reply. 'I wanted to know if they knew of any kittens wanting homes.' He congratulated himself on that response.

'And did they?'

'No.'

'Just as well. You shouldn't really get one until you're settled in your new home. Moving cats about confuses them.'

'That's true. I just need something to love.' He put his head on one side and smiled at her – he couldn't let such an opportunity slip by.

'Oh,' she mumbled, and began to pleat the gingham tablecloth into neat folds. Half of her hoped that remark was a sign to her, the other half telling her not to be so stupid.

'And what have you been doing?'

'I've got a job,' she said with the pride of the newly employed. 'In a kennels. St Bernards, they're wonderful. The owner's teaching me all she knows. And I've got a little flat, all my own. It's lovely. And I've been shopping and bought this lamp for it. It's the exact blue I wanted.' This was the longest speech that Kimberley had ever made to anyone in her life, and she was so surprised at herself that she did not notice Alan relax in his chair with an almost inaudible sigh of relief.

'Do you like the job?'

'Other than Isolde dying.' And Kimberley told him of the poisoned dog.

'Bastards! People like that should be hanged.'

'And drawn and quartered,' Kimberley agreed with him, and decided conversation wasn't so difficult after all.

'I'm glad you like dogs.'

'I'm glad you do too.' She smiled but this time she looked at him as she did so.

'You wouldn't fancy going to the cinema, maybe having a curry, say tonight?'

'There's no late bus to the Shillings. I don't know if I could.'

'I'll come and pick you up. Remember I've got a car. Then maybe you could show me the dogs – I'd like that,' he said, and the professional in him registered that he could check the kennels out at the same time, all on the q.t.

Alan gave her a lift back to the kennels, but she didn't invite him in, she didn't like to, not without checking with Mrs Brenton first. In the excitement of meeting Alan, she had completely forgotten to buy the instant coffee that Eveleigh had asked her to get, since it was much cheaper in Shillingham than in the corner shop.

'I'm so sorry. I don't know what got into me,' she apologised to a far from annoyed Eveleigh, remembering the scene there would have been with her mother if she had forgotten something.

'Oh, it's no matter.'

'I can pop to the village shop.'

'Would you? Perhaps you could get me a loaf too.'

Taking the old bicycle she'd seen in a shed, and which Eveleigh had given her permission to ride, she raced into Middle Shilling. She was seriously puzzled when she saw Alan emerge from Mr Varley's and stand talking to him for a moment in the lane. Why? What was he about? She ducked round the back of the shop so that he didn't see her. The last thing she wanted was to embarrass him. All the same, she thought, as she pedalled back to the kennels, two vets in one day when he'd agreed a kitten was a bad idea – very mysterious.

Her bicycle wobbled dangerously when, as she passed the Old School House, a window flew open and a voice shouted her name. She stopped in the lane, legs either side of the bicycle, and peered up at a bedroom window.

'Nadine!'

'Hang on, I'll come down.' And a few seconds later Nadine cannoned out of her front door. 'Am I pleased to see you! I hate everyone here. There's no one to talk to. I've been keeping a look out for you. What do you get up to?'

'I'm working. How long have you been here?'

'Too long!'

'Why didn't you look for me?'

'Too depressed, I suppose. I mean – that school is gross.'

'A bit different from what you're used to, I expect.' Kimberley smiled, imagining how the others would find Nadine not to their taste at all. 'I live just up the road from here, at the kennels.'

'No! That's brill. Come in. Let's talk.'

'I have to get back.'

'When then?'

'I've a date tonight,' she said, her face glowing with pride. 'How about tomorrow evening, after work?'

'Brill!' Nadine waved her away.

Kimberley grinned broadly for the rest of the ride back. She'd a job, a flat of her own, perhaps a boyfriend, and her friend back. She couldn't remember when she'd last been so happy.

Nadine was restless and bored. She wondered now if she'd made the right choice in coming to Middle Shilling. Perhaps she could have weathered her father's and Chantal's sloppiness, and her stepmother's relentless nagging. She missed London with a miserable, sodden ache. She needed her friends. Every night she went to bed fed up, and each morning woke with the situation uncured by sleep. She even missed her old school and longed to be back there.

She knew her mother was trying to make things better for her, but for some reason her concern made Nadine feel an almost uncontrollable rage towards Thomasine. She wanted to blame her for everything that was wrong, but hadn't yet worked out how to do so.

To make matters worse, although she wanted to be left alone, Nadine resented the time her mother devoted to her new career. Thomasine was obviously overjoyed with her new-found independence and success, which fuelled her daughter's resentment. Why should she be happy when Nadine wasn't? And her mother was so patient with her that there were days Nadine wanted to kick her.

She loved the little dog Nova, loved to hold her, smell her, kiss her broadening head. While at the same time hating the dog, wishing it was not there and wanting to crush it to death. To add insult to injury, her mother seemed, somehow, to be aware of this and always took the dog with her, which merely made Nadine feel she was not trusted. Which hurt even more.

Nadine was convinced she was totally unloved.

She'd been here well over a month, she'd tried to settle in, but the countryside was so boring. She'd sussed out the local kids and found she had nothing in common with them, and she knew she never would. Kimberley was her last hope, but she feared even she might only want to talk about her new fellow – boring.

Still, maybe things were about to get better. Last Saturday she'd been wandering listlessly about the Cromwell Cross – the huge indoor shopping centre in Morristown – when she'd spied a group demonstrating outside a pet shop. They did not look like the pink-cheeked, smiling, sweet-smelling, concerned mums and grannies she'd demonstrated with over the calves.

They were dirty, scruffy and lank-haired. They were earring and nose-studded. They were abusive. They smelt. But that did not matter, they had a cause. They were the FAA – Freedom for All Animals, as their banner proclaimed, even if the graphics were on the amateurish side.

She approached them and stated her credentials, with which they were not nearly as impressed as she hoped. 'Bunny huggers!' they spat out dismissively.

She apologised for the kindly women. Agreed they were useless. Said it was all a dead loss – and felt like St Peter with her denial of them. But she smothered that notion and asked if she could join them.

They were wary, said no decisions could be made that easily; they had security to think about and she might be a plant. She agreed and gave them her address, her phone number and fifty pounds she'd saved for new jeans and a sweater. They promised to set up a meeting for her with their leader, 'Cracker Barrel'. They promised he would phone.

All week she'd waited restlessly for the telephone call that would haul her out of this boredom. The call that would make her a crusader again. Tonight she just knew it would come.

'Hullo. Is this the Ruskie? I was given your number to ring by the Hopper.'

'The Ruskie? I'm sorry, there's no one here of that name.' She felt her spirits sink.

'Code names, idiot! I'm the Cracker Barrel. Lines could be bugged.'

'Oh, you are. Oh, how wonderful!' And at the idea of a telephone tap she felt so excited she could barely get the words out.

'I gather you want some action?'

'Please.'

'You got transport?'

'No.'

'Pity. Do you know Morristown? In the bowling alley, next Friday evening at eight.' The telephone went dead.

Nadine was bubbling with excitement as she replaced the receiver. She loved the drama, the use of code names, the carefully chosen words. The very thought that someone might be listening to the call thrilled her. She loved the sheer unexpectedness of it all. What would tomorrow be about? A hunt, factory farming, live export of animals, a handy laboratory to smash up?

Until now her activities had all been pretty amateurish stuff, but with the FAA she was moving into another league. The FAA were dedicated to any means, violent if need be, and the very thought of them made her feel sick with excitement. She'd feared they would think she was too young and might be a liability. But she'd known what she was doing in the Cromwell Cross when she'd handed over her money and had hinted there was plenty more where that came from. So what if she'd bought herself in? The how didn't matter at all. Now she had a real purpose in life.

'Who was that?' Thomasine appeared in the kitchen doorway holding her flour-covered hands high. 'Anyone for me?'

'No. It was a friend. We're going bowling next week.'

'That's nice.' Thomasine returned to her pastry making and did not see Nadine poke her tongue out at her before picking up the phone to ask Kimberley if she fancied going bowling next Friday – she didn't feel brave enough to go alone. Kimberley found her infuriatingly mysterious about who she was to meet there. 'It's to do with a good cause,' was all she would say.

'But how will we get there?' Kimberley asked.

'My mum will take us. If not, we'll get a taxi. I'll pay.' Then she raced to her room to choose her clothes for the meeting, even though it was nearly a week away.

She couldn't look like them. It took ages to get one's clothes as degraded as that. So she settled on black jeans, black sweater and her leather jacket, which wasn't really enough for this cold weather, but it would have to do. She wanted to look slick, mysterious. A bit like the *Black Magic* man.

*

Kimberley had read about cloud nine: tonight she had climbed upon it. Alan had arrived early to pick her up from the kennels.

'Sorry I'm early. I couldn't wait to see you again,' he said as he got into the driver's seat and she curled her toes inside her shoes from the sheer joy of hearing him say such things.

He looked so smart in his pressed jeans, she wondered if he always ironed them, she'd never met anyone who did that before. The lack of nice things to wear had never bothered her before, but it did now. She hoped he wouldn't realise how cheaply she was dressed. In the market she'd bought a loose-knit, fawn jumper for a tenner, and the new black leggings she wore had only cost a couple of pounds. She still hadn't been able to afford the Doc Martens she yearned for, and was making do with a pair of high-ankled black trainers from Bata. She'd pass, for the time being. But clothes would be high on her list of priorities now; the bits and bobs for the flat would have to wait.

'You sure you're warm enough? You've no coat,' he asked, turning the heater up higher.

'I don't feel the cold,' she lied, not wanting him to know she couldn't afford a new coat and was too ashamed to wear her old duffel.

'I've a Barbour in the back. You'd better wear that. You are a silly, you'll catch your death of cold at this rate.'

In the darkness of the car she smiled and enjoyed his concern for her – a new experience.

They drove to Morristown. 'Fancy a drink? We're too early for the second house.'

'Lovely.'

He parked the car in the multi-storey, as near to the exit as he could get. 'Less chance of being vandalised.'

'It's a super car.' She looked at the red Golf with admiration.

'I decided to treat myself.'

'My, my. A new car and a new house! You must be loaded.'

'My mother left me some loot,' he explained, and she felt dreadful, afraid he'd think she'd been prying.

'I shouldn't have said that, I'm sorry.'

'Don't be daft. I don't mind.'

Her heart jolted when he took hold of her hand and, as they walked along, she felt it was somehow the most natural thing in the world to be doing. He looked down at her and she smiled. He squeezed her hand.

'This pub's a bit rough, do you mind?' He had stopped in front of The Locomotive.

'Not when I'm with you,' she said, and he was almost overwhelmed with pride and his need to care for her.

It was like passing through a thick curtain of noise as they went into the saloon bar. At the far side, pint in hand, Alan saw Vic. He waved, and making way for her, pushed through the crowd and introduced her. Kimberley felt so proud he wanted her to meet his friends. Alan was hoping that by turning up with the girl he'd boasted about, he would make Vic less suspicious of him.

'What you fancy?' he asked.

'Malibu and pineapple juice would be lovely.'

'I'll get these, Alan,' said Vic, turning to the barman. 'How's tricks?'

'Oh, so-so. This and that. You know how it is,' he said nonsensically.

'Too bloody right I do. Swings and roundabouts, isn't it, mate?' Vic replied and Alan agreed.

'This is Kimberley.'

'How d'ya do,' Vic said.

Kimberley turned to speak to him and, with horror, saw Butch and Greaser grinning at her from a table where they sat with a very blonde girl. She nodded, but as imperceptibly as she could; she didn't want Alan to remember she knew them.

'Join us,' Vic offered.

'No, ta, mate. We're just off to the flicks. We don't want to get too comfortable,' Alan said. Letting them see him with a girl was one thing, he didn't want to get too involved.

'Suit yourself,' said Vic, moving back to the table with his drinks, and Alan wondered if he'd offended him.

'Those lads were with you the first time we met in Shillingham, weren't they?' God, he thought, his memory must be going – of course that's where he'd seen them. It had taken Kimberley to trigger his memory. 'Friends of yours?'

'No, I know them, that's all,' she said, colouring. 'From school,' she added hurriedly, and then wished she hadn't for she didn't want to remind him how young she was.

Alan quickly downed his drink as she sipped hers. 'Shall we get going?'

'Sure.' She quickly drank the rest of hers and to her mortification burped. She covered her mouth, horrified, but he only laughed.

'See you, Vic.' He waved.

'Bye, Kim,' Butch called out. 'Where do you get to these days? Aren't we good enough for you?'

'Don't be silly.' Her face was as red as a geranium as she let Alan lead the way.

'Don't you like them any more?' he asked as they began to walk towards the cinema.

'Who? Butch and Greaser? They're all right. I just got bored hanging about with them.'

'They don't seem your type. Too rough by far.'

'I didn't have many friends; I suppose I used them for lack of anyone else,' she said, realising that being offhand about them might be misinterpreted. 'I was lonely,' she added for good measure.

'I know all about that.' And he took hold of her hand and squeezed it, which made her feel all right again. 'Nice dog he had.'

'Did he?' she said, feeling flustered. 'What's the film?' she asked, to get away from the dangerous subject of Butch and Bandage, now languishing in her father's shed, scarred and battered. She shivered.

'You cold?'

'No, I'm fine.'

In the cinema he put his arm about her and kissed her, and then some more. She let him put his hand under the big, baggy jumper. She wriggled in her seat from the almost excruciating pleasure of his hand searching for her breast, which he gently caressed through her brassiere. She'd no idea what the film was about.

She was in a daze of sexual excitement and budding love as they walked out and he took her for a Chinese. Over the meal they talked non-stop about everything, it seemed. She'd lost all her shyness, and as she wanted to know all about him, she did not mind letting him know the little there was to tell about herself. She kept quiet about the dogs, of course, but how she longed to tell him, to confide in him and ask him what she should do. The mention of Bandage earlier had upset her, made her think about the poor dog, renewing her determination to rescue him. But how?

He kissed her in the car outside Eveleigh's, but to her disappointment he didn't fondle her. She hadn't wanted to come home. She wished there had been somewhere they could go and be alone, for she wanted them to 'do it'. She was sorely disappointed that they hadn't, but was too young and too shy to know how to suggest that they did.

38

The previous afternoon, when she had returned from the Lucketts', Thomasine had tried to telephone Oliver to tell him of her conclusions about Ben, but his telephone was out of order. Although she had reported it, it was still not ringing in the morning so, taking her courage in both hands, she drove round to his house. As she approached Bishop's End the excitement she felt was unsought, but appeared unstemmable. She parked around the back and rang the back-door bell, and was surprised when Wimpole answered it and, somewhat grudgingly, invited her into the kitchen.

'I love this room,' Thomasine said, sitting at the pine table while Wimpole made the coffee.

'Herself wasn't much good, but at least she knew how to do up a house.'

'Sophia you mean?'

'Who else? Still, you're right about this kitchen, like an illustration in that tarty magazine she works for – when she feels like it. Pity she couldn't cook.'

'I saw her yesterday. She hinted she and Oliver were getting back together.' Thomasine was pleased with the lack of interest she managed to put into her voice, making it sound like a passing comment.

Wimpole banged her cup down on the table. 'Over my dead body!' she declared. 'And that's just wishful thinking on her part. I reckon it hasn't worked out for her as well as she thought it would, being on her own, and she wants him back. But the best thing that ever happened to Oliver was the day she walked out – even if it did mean losing his dog. Which reminds me.' Wimpole leapt up from the table with an agility which belied her years. She quickly walked to the back door, put her head out and bellowed 'Slipper'. The puppy came scurrying in. 'He gets so neurotic about this mutt, he's so scared it'll run away like the other one. My hubbie's having to build a new fence to keep it in – at least that's what the idle bugger's supposed to be doing.'

Thomasine began to laugh at this, thinking she was joking, until she glanced up and saw the bitter expression on Wimpole's face. She realised she was not joking, and stopped the laughter immediately. Wimpole, fusssing with the dog's water bowl, did not appear to notice.

'Thomasine, what a wonderful surprise!' Oliver said the moment he entered the kitchen. 'I wondered where my coffee had got to, why didn't you tell me Thomasine was here, Wimpole?'

'Because you said you didn't want to be disturbed – getting precious about his writing is our Oliver, just like his Aunt Phoebe.'

'I meant don't bother me with boring things. Of course I want to be interrupted when it's Thomasine.' Oliver smiled at her and Thomasine, to her annoyance, felt embarrassed and very gauche and wished she didn't want him to mean it quite so much.

'I bet you say that to all the girls,' she retorted, and immediately regretted it, since it made her sound even more gauche, like some pick-up in a discotheque.

'He doesn't. He means it,' Wimpole added.

'How's the book going?' Thomasine asked, not just out of interest, but to get the conversation back on safer ground.

'A bit hit and miss.'

'It's wonderful. I couldn't put it down and can't wait to see what happens next,' Wimpole declared, sounding for all the world like his mother, her voice dripping with pride.

'I'd love to read it. That is if you don't mind. If you want.'

'I'd take that as an honour. I'd value your opinion.'

'I'm off to dust.' Wimpole stood up. 'See you later, Thomasine.'

'Grace came yesterday,' Oliver said.

'She's all right on floors, that woman, but she's blind to anything higher than a skirting board.'

'You never approve of anybody in my life, Wimpole.'

'Yes I do. She'll do.' Wimpole nodded in Thomasine's direction and smartly left the kitchen.

'Gracious. Whatever next!' Thomasine laughed nervously.

'I rather tend to agree,' Oliver said softly, so softly that Thomasine wasn't sure if she'd heard right.

'I came to tell you about Ben. I tried to call you. Did you know your telephone was out of order?' She spoke briskly, to cover her confusion and the moment, if moment there had been, slipped away.

'And?'

'He was shocked rigid about the dog, even dropped a full bottle of champagne. I'm sure he knew nothing about it, but . . . I think he's involved. Perhaps he told someone to make Eveleigh's life difficult and they've gone too far.'

'Like old Henry the something or other. "Who'll do the business on this wretched priest?" and poor Becket got bumped off.'

'Something like that.' She smiled. 'What do we do?'

'Ben's not a bad man – greedy maybe. We should be able to reason with him.'

'You sound rather doubtful.'

'I've never had any dealings with him over business and money. He might be different where the filthy lucre is concerned.'

'What if we blackmail him – tell him that we'll go to the tabloids if he doesn't lay off? His shareholders wouldn't like that sort of exposure,' Thomasine suggested.

'He hasn't got any – his companies are all his own, at least as far as I know. Of course, if we were right and the tabloids printed it, he could say goodbye to his knighthood. However, if we were wrong, I can tell you I wouldn't fancy being sued for libel by Ben – and he'd have every right to.'

'Would Sophia help?' She was shocked at how much she disliked even using her name in case it made him think of her.

'Sophia? You have to be joking. Sophia is only interested in one thing – herself. If she thought we were going to make Ben out of pocket, she'd work against us, not for us. In any case, she hates dogs.'

'Is Ben scared of anybody or anything?' Thomasine felt wonderfully pleased with his response. He apparently loathed Sophia. Wimpole had been right, any thought of reconciliation was obviously in Sophia's mind alone.

'Losing Cora – he's always been scared that because she's so much younger one day she'd do a flit. Bloody hell, yes – Cora! If we could get her to work for us . . . Brilliant thinking, Thomasine.'

'I didn't do anything – you thought it through.'

'How about you, me, Jim and Eveleigh talking to her, all together? That's the best way.' He poured them more coffee. 'How's the cooking going?'

'Better than I hoped. I had another enquiry this morning. In fact, I've written a bit of blurb to put in a brochure, I'd like you to look at it before I take it to the printers.' She opened her handbag and took out the piece of paper on which was the final draft of her idea – the wastepaper basket was full to overflowing with the rejected attempts.

Oliver felt in his pocket for a pair of spectacles which he slipped on in order to read her effort. She watched him as he concentrated on the paper and she thought how well the half-lenses suited him.

'That's very good. Excellent. And I see you've kept "Thomasine's Treats" – it's snappy, memorable. Have you thought about the van? I see it in dark racing green.' He sketched the shape of a van expansively in the air with his hand.

'It'll be some time before I can afford a van – I've masses of equipment to get first.'

'You need a partner.'

She looked away abruptly. He spoke in that soft, smooth tone again, and she wasn't sure if he meant it or was teasing her. She picked up her bag from the floor.

'I'm off to Shillingham. Anything you need?' she asked automatically. Life in the country had taught her one thing; whoever was making a journey into town always offered to shop for friends.

'Lunch,' he answered shortly.

'Lunch – you mean food?'

'No. I mean may I take you out to lunch?'

'How long is this going to go on?' Beth asked as Jim stood, his hand on the back door, looking as if he was longing to escape.

'What?' he asked, knowing full well what she meant.

'You know damn well. How long are you going to be shacked up at Eveleigh's?'

'Don't be ridiculous. I'm not shacked up. I'm helping her out. When this blows over I'll come back.'

'It's not very professional.'

'I don't understand.'

'Well – your messages and things,' Beth said lamely, clutching at straws.

'I don't see the problem. My night calls are re-routed. I'm here in time for surgery. You take the daytime messages just as before.'

'You're being a shit, Jim,' she spat out.

'I beg your pardon?' He stepped back into the kitchen with the weary expression of one who knows what is coming and is already tired of it.

'You know exactly what I mean. How could you treat me like this? One minute you're in bed with me, the next it's Eveleigh.'

'Eveleigh! Have you gone totally mad, Beth? What the hell are you going on about now?'

'You're as thick as thieves with her, you always have been. So why haven't you done something about her before? Why involve me and then do this to me?' She was shouting now, her normally pleasant face twisted with an anger he had never dreamt her capable of.

'Beth! I don't know what the hell you mean – Eveleigh's a friend. She's got a problem with intruders and I'm helping her sort it out.'

'Pull the other one. And in any case, don't I have problems? What do I do if my husband turns up? Why aren't you looking after me?'

'I'm sorry if you jumped to the wrong conclusion. You said yourself you'd stopped worrying about your husband. When you've come to your senses maybe you'll feel like saying sorry.' He turned to go.

'Sorry! Me say sorry? It's you who should be apologising. First you seduce me and then you treat me like this. How dare you do this to me!' And she leapt at him and began to pummel his back.

He turned slowly, deliberately, grabbed her hands and held them tight. 'Now, you listen to me, Beth. I did not seduce you. It was you who climbed into my bed, remember?'

'You didn't push me away.'

'No, I know, and now I regret I didn't.'

Beth's face seemed to dissolve in front of him. As she absorbed his words her mouth turned down, her eyes filled with tears which gushed down her cheeks, even her body slumped. 'Please don't say that.' She stepped back and held her hands up, palms turned towards him as if warding him off, or pushing the words away from her. 'Don't spoil it.'

'Oh, Beth, there's nothing to spoil.'

'Yes there is – you love me. I love you.'

'I don't, Beth. I'm sorry, but I don't love you.'

'You will. I'll make you love me.'

'It doesn't work that way. I wish I did love you, it would make everything so much easier. But I can't make myself, if it's not there. I should have made you leave me that first night, or got up and moved away myself. I should never have let it happen again and again after that. I've been wrong. I'm sorry, Beth. Deeply sorry.'

'But you enjoyed being in bed with me – you couldn't have faked that.'

'That's true. I did enjoy it. But it doesn't make it right.' He paused, looking at her, at the sadness in her face, and hated himself. He took a deep breath. 'It was sex, Beth. I'd hoped that was all it was for you too.' He loathed hurting her, but knew he had to.

'You used me – you fucking bastard!'

'Yes, I used you and I'm ashamed I did. I said I'm sorry. It won't happen again.' And he turned abruptly, walked out of the kitchen slamming the door shut behind him, not wanting to see her face, witness her distress and to know he was the cause of it.

Eveleigh was round the back of the kennels bedding the dogs down, with the kennel girl helping her. Solemnly Kimberley shook his hand, after wiping hers down the side of her trousers first.

'Can you see to the last two, Kimberley, while I get Mr Varley a drink?'

Kimberley was happy to be left on her own. In the time she had worked here the dogs had become her life, and the last two, Lohengrin and Brünnhilde, champions both, were her favourites. There was something about the evening routine that was different to the rest of the day. The dogs had been exercised and were tired. They'd been fed and there was a sleepy contentment about them with the daytime friskiness gone. They were more affectionate, more malleable. Each and every one enjoyed a good hug before they were bedded down for the night.

These two and Parsifal had been moved closer to the house to be in earshot, for on them were pinned Eveleigh's hopes for Crufts next March. It was still four months away but, as Eveleigh was fond of saying, the preparations for Crufts were ongoing and never-ending. Although there were new locks on all the night-time kennels, these three had even larger padlocks on their doors and Eveleigh had instructed Kimberley to string tin cans on a trip wire, hidden by sacking, across the opening of each kennel.

Content that all was safe and secure, Kimberley knocked on the sitting-room door to tell Eveleigh she was out for the evening. She took her bicycle and made for Nadine's house, where she had been invited to supper, thinking she was glad that Mr Varley had arrived early. She didn't like to leave Eveleigh on her own. She thought they made a nice couple. She didn't usually think like this, she supposed it was because she was in love herself and wanted everyone else to be.

Eveleigh, seeing the drawn expression on Jim's face, poured him an extra large whisky. 'Get that down you. You look as if you need it. Hard day?'

'You could say that. But I'm not on call – the Shillingham vets are on this weekend.'

'It must be odd for you, after all these years, to have free evenings.'

'It's bliss.' Jim stretched in the comfortable armchair and put his feet out and rested them on Parsifal, who was sprawled, all eighteen stone of him, on the rug in front of the fire. 'Is this a precaution?'

'Yes and no. It's his turn for a treat.' She looked sheepish. 'I've not completely made up my mind between Lohengrin and Parsifal for Crufts. Brünnhilde, yes, she's the best bitch I've ever had.'

'Lohengrin's a fine dog,' said Jim, who nursed a soft spot for him.

'I know, I know. But maybe he's too young. Parsifal here is that little bit steadier but still I have a feeling about Lohengein – here.' She put her hand on her breast.

'Didn't Lohengrin get best male last year?'

'No, that was Siegfried and it was several years ago. Of course I thought he should have been Best of Breed. I nearly pulled out of Crufts this year, with all the unpleasantness, and then I thought why? That would be silly – that would almost prove me guilty, wouldn't it? And Jill is judging. It should be interesting.'

'I'd like to come with you if I can arrange it. I've never been to Crufts.'

'Then you should go. It's quite a spectacle, you know. That would be fun.' And then, as if thinking she had shown too much pleasure, changed the subject. 'I got steak in for supper, if that will do you? I'm not much of a cook, but I can grill a steak without too much mishap.'

'It sounds wonderful. And I've got a bottle of wine in the car.'

Jim had not meant to say anything to Eveleigh about Beth, it wouldn't be fair. But he did. Maybe it was the wine, the warmth from the fire, the relaxed atmosphere, or a combination of them all that lulled him into a state where it seemed the most natural thing to be doing. Once he'd finished talking it seemed an age before Eveleigh spoke.

'You're an honest man, Jim. Perhaps too honest. You could have gone on indefinitely with her, couldn't you? It wasn't very clever of you, but we all know about men's weaknesses, don't we?'

Jim looked up with alarm, but when he saw the smile on her face he realised she was teasing him, that she understood. It had suddenly become very important to him that she of all people didn't think too badly of him.

39

There had been a time when Kimberley had daydreamed of what a whole day spent with someone she loved might be like. The reality was not to be a let-down.

Alan called for her on Saturday morning. Shyly, Kimberley introduced him to Eveleigh. 'Alan wondered if he could see the dogs, Mrs Brenton?'

'You like dogs, Mr Farmingham?'

'Yes, I do. But I work so I can't have one.'

'I wish more felt like you. A lonely dog becomes a troubled dog. But please do, Kimberley. Show your friend the kennels.'

They walked outside, Kimberley clutching her jumper to her, too proud still to put on her old coat.

'She seems very nice, but a bit distracted.'

'It's the worry over the dogs that's doing it.'

'I hope you're safe here.'

Her smile burst wide and full of happiness. 'Yes. The vet comes and sleeps over.'

'Lucky vet.'

'This is Brünnhilde.' She stopped in front of the bitch's kennel. 'They're named after characters in Wagner's operas. Mrs Brenton's husband loved his music and she's kept the tradition on.'

The dog lumbered to her feet and trotted over to the wire, curiosity conquering her urge to sleep. She placed one very large and dirty paw on the fence, as if in greeting.

'She likes you. She only does that to selected people. What have you been doing, Brünnhilde? Just look at your feet. And I washed them this morning. You have to watch their feet, make sure the fur doesn't bundle up hard between their toes.'

'She's a lovely dog.'

'She's a champion. Her puppies will sell for hundreds and hundreds. Champion Brünnhilde Rhinemaiden Starpoint of Oakleigh, that's her real name.'

'What makes her a champion?'

'Well, see her height, she's tall – the taller the better, but she hasn't lost her correct proportions. She's got a lovely short muzzle, nice and square at the end. And she holds her tail beautifully, not curled up over her back. And her head . . . it's right.' She trailed off here, for she could not remember what else Eveleigh had taught her.

'You know a lot!' He grinned at her.

'I don't. I know nothing. But Mrs Brenton's teaching me.'

'Do you want to do this for ever?'

'Yes. I love it. I thought I wanted to work in a bank – but after this, no thanks.'

'These kennels are a treat.'

'Lovely, aren't they. In summer the dogs have flower baskets – cute, isn't it? And their inside kennels are all heated, you know. It costs a fortune,' Kimberley informed him proudly. Alan wished all dogs were so lucky.

He drove across to a pub by the river the other side of Morristown. Alan had booked them a table by the window so she was able to watch the river and the swans. She wished she'd been smarter, everyone else was. She carefully noted what people were wearing so that next time she came here she could look like them. It was a casual smartness, she noticed; jeans were clean and pressed, as were the T-shirts, and she saw that lots of the women wore navy blazers and lovely scarves. She vowed she would look like that as soon as she could afford it.

She enjoyed the roast beef and the wine, even though she normally drank beer and had never tasted red wine before. But her greatest pleasure was finding out more about him. She had wondered if, the other night, they had talked themselves dry, but they hadn't. And today he seemed to want to tell her even more personal things.

'My dad left one night. He went out to buy some cigarettes and never came back.'

'He wasn't-?' She paused; it hardly seemed polite to ask if he was dead.

'Murdered? Killed? Not as far as we know. He just disappeared off the face of the earth.'

'Did you look for him?'

'The Salvation Army tried and, of course, the police, but he'd done a runner and that was that.'

'Poor you, and your poor mum.' Her sympathy for him was sharply balanced by thoughts of how wonderful it would have been if her own father had chosen to disappear.

'I think she might have been one of the reasons he went – she nagged, d'you know what I mean?'

'Not really.' It was an honest answer. She didn't; her mother would never have had the courage to nag anyone.

'So he went AWOL. I had to get out too, she was doing the same to me – nagging all day long, possessive, smothering me.'

'You mean with love?'

'Yes.'

'But that must be nice.'

'It can be destructive too. I thought it was best for both of us if I left – I hoped she would make friends, find new interests. But she never did. Then she died and we'd never made it up. I'll always regret that.'

'I've never been loved,' she said sadly, and he longed to take her in his arms there and then.

'I love you,' he said simply.

She looked at him nervously, her eyes full of tears which she brushed awkwardly away. 'Please don't say things you don't mean,' she said with dignity.

He put his hand quickly across the table and took hold of hers. 'But I do mean it.'

'You don't know me, or anything about me.'

'I don't need to. It's the truth. I knew it would be like this. I always felt that one day I'd meet someone and I would be certain. That first day I was pretty sure – now I'm completely. And I know why now. I want to protect you. I need you to need me.'

'I want to be loved so badly,' she said, so quietly that he had to lean forward to catch her words.

It was crowded and noisy in the popular pub, but where they sat it was as if there was an oasis of complete silence. He still held her hand as they looked at each other, and their expressions said more than any words.

Kimberley felt safe with him. For the first time in her life she knew she was with someone who really did love her. 'I can't believe this is happening to me,' she said.

'Me neither, but it is.' And then he leant over and kissed her gently on the lips.

They drove through the country lanes back to the Shillings, and with the aid of a map looked for the cottage he was to view.

The car bumped up an unmade and overgrown driveway with woodland on either side. Kimberley didn't want the journey to end, didn't want to get out of the safe cocoon of the car, didn't want to meet and have to talk to anyone.

The drive opened out into a clearing which was full of brambles and overgrown shrubs and trees. In the middle was a small, brick-built house.

'The agent calls it a cottage, doesn't look much like one to me. Come on, I picked up the keys.' He dug in his pocket and waved a bunch of keys at her.

'Is it all right?'

'It's empty.'

It was a two-bedroomed, two-living-roomed cottage with a built-on scullery for a kitchen. It was musty and damp with a lingering smell of cats.

'It's pretty grim, isn't it?' Alan said, disappointed by the estate agent's description.

'It's certainly been badly neglected. But – I don't know, I don't know anything about houses, but if it was painted and had some pretty wallpaper it could be nice.'

'Do you really think so?' He brightened up.

'And you could make this back room into a kitchen-living room – paint it white and yellow, a happy colour, with matching curtains. And then the old kitchen could be the bathroom.' Her face was flushed with excitement as she spoke.

'It's all I can afford without taking a mortgage. Everything round here is so expensive. You really think we could make it habitable?'

'Without a doubt,' she said, her heart having lurched when he said 'we'.

He wrenched open the front door with difficulty, since the hinges appeared to be rusted. 'If we cleared all this and planted a lawn – '

'It would be nigh on perfect.' She clasped her hands together to stop herself from waving them around. 'Absolutely perfect,' she repeated, and knew that her dreams were taking her over, ignoring sense and reason. But she couldn't control them.

They went up the stairs to inspect the bedrooms again.

'Which one should we have?'

'Oh, this one,' she said. 'It's bigger and it's got a built-in wardrobe and – ' But at that point Alan's arms were about her and his lips on her and all thoughts of interior decoration were forgotten in the thrill of his hands searching her body, finding her breasts, playing with her nipples, drawing her along with him as he hardened, as his body pressed close to hers. Without pausing in their kiss they both bent down and were kneeling on the floor, and then lying side by side. They removed their clothes with a desperation fuelled by longing. Alan bundled his jacket into a makeshift pillow for her head and she lay back upon it and opened her legs invitingly to him. 'I love you,' she mouthed as he lay on top of her and gently entered her. Her body rose slowly towards his and his bore down upon her until they were rocking in unison and the thrusts he made became more powerful and demanding and the two of them clawed at each other with relief.

'Kim? We've got it!' Alan's voice was bubbling with excitement over the telephone.

'Got what?' she asked, although she knew the answer, she just wanted to hear him say it.

'The house. The seller's accepted my offer. Oh, Kim, isn't it exciting? We've got our house! We can begin planning. I'll be back on Friday. We'll go and see it again.'

'Lovely!' she said, feeling she was moving in a dream; terrified she might at any moment awaken. She pulled herself together sufficiently to explain about going bowling with Nadine. 'We can all go,' he said before he disconnected the call. She stood leaning against the kitchen wall, cradling the telephone to her as if by holding the instrument she was holding him.

'You look as if you've had good news,' said Eveleigh as she bustled past, carrying a stack of stainless-steel feeding bowls.

'Oh, I have, I have.' And Kimberley followed her out to the kennels, and while they worked she told Eveleigh about the lunch and the house and the way he said 'we'. 'And he says he loves me,' she concluded.

'I'm so pleased for you.' Eveleigh smiled at the girl. Over the weeks, she had become fond of Kimberley. With no children of her own, and unsure how to deal with the young, she had worried whether they would get on. She need not have. Kimberley had responded to her kind concern for her, relaxing visibly, yet appearing to find it difficult to believe she was safe and cared for. Eveleigh never pried, but allowed Kimberley to tell her what she wanted her to know and when. She reminded Eveleigh of some rescued greyhounds who had virtually given up on ever finding kindness from man, and were acquiescent and stunned when they did.

'But do be careful, my dear,' she ventured.

'Of what?' Kimberley leant on the broom with which she had been sweeping out the kennel run.

'When you want very much to be loved it's possible to mistake other emotions for love,' Eveleigh said, hoping Kimberley would realise she spoke from concern for her.

Kimberley frowned. 'I thought of that, honestly, but I'm sure Alan's speaking the truth. He's so straight, he hasn't time for messing about, I'm certain.'

'Well, let's hope you're right. But forewarned is forearmed.' Eveleigh collected the last of the water bowls to soak and scrub clean.

'Can I use your phone when I've finished here – just a quick call?'

'I'm fully aware you *can* use the telephone, Kimberley. *May* you? Of course.'

Kimberley looked after Eveleigh as she walked back to the house and shrugged her shoulders, not understanding what she meant. When she had finished sweeping the kennels she called Nadine to tell her she and Alan would pick her up at seven thirty on Friday.

'I don't want to go bowling with *him*,' Nadine said. 'You said you'd come.'

'I'm sorry, but I didn't know.'

'Traitor! Well, just give me a lift. We'll meet up after.' Nadine thought Cracker Barrel would not mind her appearing with another girl, but another man might anger him. She couldn't take the risk.

On Friday evening in the back of the car Nadine could barely control her excitement, but she was infuriatingly mysterious. Kimberley, concerned for her, warned her how dangerous Morristown could be, especially at night.

'Don't fuss. You sound like my mother. Don't forget I'm used to London, this dump's nothing compared to that.' They dropped her outside the bowling alley and she waved them off as if impatient to see them gone.

'What's all the mystery?' Alan asked as they drew away. 'Drugs?'

'I don't think so. I think it might be something to do with animals.'

'Animals?' Alan crashed the gears with a grating noise.

'She's potty about them. She got expelled for demonstrating about the export of live calves. She was on TV,' Kimberley said proudly. 'I think she might be meeting up with some group of – ' She waved her fingers in the air, searching for the words. 'You know, what are they called?'

'Animal rights activists?'

'Yes, that's it! Bit of a mouthful, isn't it?'

'Do you know which one?'

'No idea. Heavens, I'm not even sure that's what she's doing. Why are you so interested?' she asked warily. She realised she was jealous – a new emotion, something she'd never felt before. That must mean she was in love. She smiled in the darkness of the car.

'I hope she wasn't carrying a bomb!' he joked, sidestepping her question, telling himself he must be more cautious. 'Curry do you?' He pulled up outside an Indian restaurant.

'Alan, you needn't keep spending money on me like this.'

'I like to.' He put his hand on the nape of her neck as he spoke, and she forgot all about Nadine and what she might be up to.

They waited a good fifteen minutes in the car outside the bowling alley, even though they'd arrived at ten on the dot as arranged. Not that they minded. They made good use of the time. A rapping on the window made them jump guiltily apart. It was Nadine, alone, and tense with anticipation.

'Nice time?' Kimberley looked over her shoulder and saw Nadine's eyes glistening with excitement, and momentarily wondered if Alan had been right about the drugs.

'Sure thing. I won.'

'You went bowling?' Alan asked.

'That's what one normally does at a bowling alley,' Nadine said sarcastically. She disliked Alan, but had refrained from saying so to Kimberley, not yet, not while she needed help with transport. 'I met a friend.'

'From school?' Kimberley asked.

'Not likely!' Nadine snorted and lit a cigarette.

'I didn't know you smoked.'

'You don't know everything about me,' Nadine replied, adopting an air of mystery, but she couldn't keep it up and giggled instead. 'Oh, it's no good, I've got to tell someone or I'll burst. You swear not to tell a living soul?' She refused to continue until the others had agreed. 'This group's the real thing. We're going to raid a dog fight, beat the bastards up.' She flopped back on the car seat, a triumphant expression on her face.

'How? When?' Alan asked quickly.

'Next week, on Saturday.'

'Where?'

'I don't know. I expect they move the venue – a different place each time. Why are you so interested? You're not one of *them*, are you?' She was worried now.

'Don't be silly.' For Alan the realisation that, through Nadine, they might, after all this time, be about to crack down on the local dog fighting was almost too much to contain.

'Dog fighting's for sickos,' said Kimberley, aware that her palms were damp from sweat, her heart racing. Would her father be involved? Would Bandage be one of the dogs? She shivered, even though the heater was on.

'You cold?' Alan asked.

'No – I was thinking about the poor dogs.'

Alan pulled the car into a lay-by and stopped the engine. He swung round in his seat. 'Do you think this is wise, Nadine? It could be rough. You could get hurt.'

'I don't mind. I don't mind if I get killed, if we stop the cruelty.'

'That wouldn't do much good,' Alan said reasonably. 'What would your mother have to say?'

'Oh, don't you start! I had enough trouble back there with Cracker Barrel, he said I was too young as well. Creep. I told him what's what.'

'Cracker Barrel? What a name!' Kimberley laughed.

'We have to have aliases – the fuzz you know. I'm Ruskie – Nadine/Ruskie, get it?'

'Doesn't sound Russian to me. It's French, isn't it?' asked Kimberley.

'From the Russian, of course,' Nadine snapped back, sounding affronted.

'How many will be going?' Alan relentlessly continued.

'I don't know. I've only just joined this group of the FAA.'

'What's that when it's home?'

'Freedom for All Animals,' Alan volunteered. 'Isn't it?' He hurriedly asked.

'You seem to know an awful lot, Alan.' Nadine leant forward, her arms on the back of the seat in front.

'I read an article about the FAA in one of the Sundays.'

'You're not the only one loves animals, Alan does too, don't you, darling?' Kimberley said defensively, but felt awkward using the endearment. She never had before, and it was strange to hear herself say it, as if she were using a word from a foreign language. 'Why don't you leave it to the RSPCA to deal with? Phone them up and tell them, Nadine.'

'You must be joking! What good would that load of wankers do?'

'That's hardly fair,' Alan said as calmly as he could.

'They get bogged down with trying to placate all sides. They don't take a strong enough stance.'

'Don't go around trying to kill people, you mean. What about that scientist whose car was blown up last month?' Alan could feel his anger growing.

'He deserved it, the way he treated animals – vivisectionist creep!'

'So that humans could live,' Kimberley said quietly.

'Not if it means creatures suffer. In any case, there's no proof. Maybe the car just happened to catch fire.'

'Or pigs might fly.' Kimberley heard Alan mutter under his breath.

'If you feel like this, Nadine, then you must never take any medicines, in case they've been tested on animals,' Kimberley reasoned.

'I can't undo what's been done. I'm talking about the future – no more testing.'

'So it's all right to let kids die of cancer, that's fine by you, is it?'

'Why you being so horrible to me?' Nadine said sulkily.

'It's true what Alan's saying, and why have you got make-up on?'

'I only wear stuff not tested on animals.'

'How convenient. How do you think it was ever decided that such and such an ingredient was safe to slap on your face? Somewhere along the line it was tested,' Alan argued logically.

'Not recently.' Nadine was beginning to feel deflated. 'Whose side are you on? I thought Kimberley said you loved animals too?'

'I do, but, in my personal opinion, there has to be a balance. If controlled experiments on animals means a kid can live, we have to do it, with as much humanity as possible.'

'You're a barbarian!' Nadine's voice exploded with anger.

'I don't go round planting bombs under people's cars. Burn buildings down, putting other lives at risk.'

'No, you're too much of a wimp to do anything like that, aren't you?'

Alan opened his mouth to defend himself, but stopped just in time. 'Oh, what's the use!' he said instead, and restarted the engine.

'I wish you two wouldn't row,' Kimberley said quietly. 'I'd like us all to be friends.' In response there was a loud snort from the seat behind her.

40

Because Cora was away, it was over a week before Oliver could arrange a meeting with her. After much debate, he and Thomasine had decided it would be better if Eveleigh and Jim weren't present, that too many of them might appear intimidating.

Oliver shaved with particular care this morning, not because he was off to meet Cora, but rather because he'd be seeing Thomasine.

'That dog's piddled again,' Wimpole greeted him as he entered the kitchen.

'She's only a puppy.'

'Well, I'm not clearing it up and that's flat. I'm not a lavatory attendant,' Wimpole huffed.

'Have I ever asked you to?' Oliver commented patiently, and would have liked to add that since this was no longer her home it wasn't any of her business. And come to that why, now she was married, was she spending so much time here? Often, like this morning, she let herself in and was pottering about before he was up. Still, what was the point, he didn't want to hurt her feelings and make her feel unwanted. He went to the laundry room, Slipper padding along behind him, to collect a mop and a bucket of disinfected water. 'You get us both into trouble, Slipper. You've got to pull your socks up and get this peeing sorted out. Garden, girl, that's your loo.' The small dog sat on the floor and listened to Oliver, her head first on one side then the other. Oliver chucked her under her chin and the dog rolled onto its back, kicking its four legs in the air with joy. 'Old Bandage used to do that, you know.' His voice was tinged with the sadness he always felt when thinking of his lost pet.

'It's the first sign of madness, talking to yourself,' Wimpole said as he returned.

'I was not talking to myself. I was in conversation with my pooch.'

'Even madder.' Wimpole sniffed dismissively. 'You ought to rub her nose in it, give her a slap. That'll stop it.'

'It would do no good whatsoever. If you can't discipline a dog without hitting it, you shouldn't have it in the first place.'

'Discipline! My arse.'

'What's got in to you, Wimpole? You're in a real grump this morning. Anything wrong?' Oliver asked, not criticising but concerned. When Wimpole burst into tears he wasn't prepared for it. 'Oh, Wimpole love, sit down, do. Are you tired? You shouldn't bother coming here, you must have enough to do at your own house. I can manage. Oh, good God!' He looked panic-stricken as Wimpole's wails became louder. He'd never seen her cry, ever, and was at a total loss. He stood beside her chair pouring her tea, patting her shoulder, running his hand through his hair and generally flapping.

'I wish it was like what it used to be!' Wimpole eventually said through her sobs.

'Wish what was like what it used to be?' he repeated inanely, and shook his head in bewilderment at his ungrammatical sentence.

'Like then. Not now.' Wimpole gulped for air.

'Aren't you happy, Wimpole?'

'Of course I'm not bloody happy. I wouldn't be wailing if I was, would I?'

'I suppose not. Is there anything I can do?'

'Not a lot. It's my own fault. As my mum used to say – you made your bed, now lie in it.'

'I've never understood what that means. I mean, if you make my bed, does that mean you have to lie on that one, or what?' he babbled from sheer embarrassment.

'Sometimes, Oliver, I think you're completely thick,' Wimpole said snappily, pushed her chair back and rushed from the room.

She's doing too much looking after me and Rudie, Oliver thought as he fetched the plate of scrambled eggs she had made him, sitting warm on the top of the Aga. He should have thought. He didn't know why she did, he hadn't asked her to. But the first morning back from her honeymoon she'd arrived long before he was up, and it had just sort of continued. She'd carried on as she had before the wedding, sorting him out generally. He'd been selfish not noticing how tired she must be with a husband to care and cook for. He must put a stop to it.

He jumped up at the sound of a knock on the back door and immediately kicked the bucket of sudsy water flying. 'Oh shit!' he exclaimed as the door was opened tentatively and Thomasine poked her head round.

'Morning,' she said, but immediately burst into laughter at the sight of Oliver standing in a spreading pool of water, the bottom of his trousers soaked and Slipper skidding around the puddles, rump waggling, wondering if this was some new game.

'Hi! Sorry!' He shrugged expressively, picked up the mop and began to limit the damage.

'I'll do that – you go and change,' she volunteered. When most of the water was back in its bucket she put the kettle on and cleared the table as she waited for it to boil.

'Can anything else go wrong?' Oliver said, grinning as he came back into the kitchen in dry trousers. 'What a start to the day! The dog peed, Wimpole bawled her eyes out, and I nearly drowned.'

'Wimpole? What's wrong?' she asked, as she set the teapot onto the pine table and got mugs from the dresser.

'She suddenly burst into tears and said she hated "now". All that had happened was the puppy had messed, and I cleared that up.'

'That doesn't sound like Wimpole.'

'We had a minor disagreement about house training dogs, that was all. Then I asked her if anything was wrong and hey presto – Niagara Falls had a competitor.'

'She's had a row with her husband.'

'No, it's more than that. I mean – she cried.'

'Women do.'

'Not Wimpole.' He was frowning as he spoke. He found he hated the idea of Thomasine crying.

'It must be one hell of an adjustment, getting married for the first time at her age. I've had it the other way around – sorting my life out after a divorce. It's hard. But then you know, don't you?' She looked at him enquiringly.

'No, I don't. If anything I can't remember when I was last so happy.' As he spoke he found he didn't like what her words implied. She must love her husband if she was finding it so hard to build a new life.

'You don't miss Sophia at all?'

'Missed my dog – never her. I suppose I didn't love her any more. You obviously loved your fellow, though.'

'Do you know, that's the odd thing. I thought I did, but now I'm sure I didn't. I was in love with what being with him meant – a family, security, my home. It took me time to realise, but I was grieving for a way of life, not for him.'

'Hell! You don't know how happy hearing that makes me. I thought you were still mooning over him.' He referred to Robert with loathing. Anybody, anything, which made Thomasine unhappy filled him full of hatred.

'You are sweet, Oliver.' She wished he would do something – take her hand, kiss her, not just say nice things and then not follow them up. She did not know where she stood with him and feared it was just his innate charm talking. 'I don't think I like Rudolph very much,' she said.

'Don't you? Why?' He wished she hadn't changed the subject. Whenever he plucked up the courage to let her know how he felt, she was off on another tack, like a startled doe.

'He looks a hard man to me, and he seems to have no sense of humour – and that's always a bad sign.'

'Like people not smoking or drinking. You find yourself wondering what their hidden vice is.'

She laughed. 'Yes, I suppose you do – but less with smoking these days. Have you given up yet?' She smiled at him.

'I thought I'd give it a whirl on Monday.'

'Oliver, it's always *Monday* with you.'

'It's a good day to start things.'

'Or not, as the case may be. Should we be going?'

'Yes, sure. I told Cora we'd be there around ten, so we've plenty of time. I'll just shut Slipper in the laundry room.'

'Will Ben be here?' Thomasine asked as they drew up outside the Lucketts' house.

'No. I asked Cora that. Quite intrigued, she is. Oh no!' he moaned as Sophia appeared at the front door.

'My, what a pleasant surprise. The two of you,' Sophia said pointedly as they approached her. 'Cora's all agog and so am I. Come in, do.'

'I've come to see Cora – privately, if you don't mind,' Oliver said as Sophia showed them into the drawing room.

'Then Thomasine can join me for coffee and a chat.'

'No, Thomasine's with me.'

'How cosy for you both.' Sophia smiled – dangerously, Thomasine thought. 'I'll tell Cora you're here.' She left the door ajar.

'I don't think she likes me,' Thomasine whispered, for she had the uncomfortable feeling that Sophia might be listening at the other side of the door.

'She'd loathe any woman who happened to be with me,' he said in a louder than normal tone, easily heard beyond the room.

'Does she want you back?'

'God forbid,' he said with feeling. 'It's more a case of she doesn't want anyone else to have me. I mean, have you been going out with Jim Varley?'

'Me? No.'

'There you go – proves my point. Sophia told me you were.'

'Why on earth should she say I was with Jim?'

'To put the kybosh on me trying anything on with you.'

'You're joking!'

'Oh no, I never joke where Sophia's concerned.'

'But Jim's got Beth – you should have known that.'

'No, because he'd told me there was nothing going on there, that she was his housekeeper pure and simple.' Jim hadn't at all, but what the hell, thought Oliver, all's fair . . .

'Poor Beth. She loves him.'

'Does she? Good God, I don't think Jim knows that. Cora – ' His face lit up with pleasure and he kissed his stepmother-in-law enthusiastically on the cheek.

The atmosphere in the room was not so pleasant five minutes later, after Oliver had explained why they were there.

'I can't believe you can accuse my Ben of having a dog killed. He loves dogs, you know he does. How dare you come here, spreading lies like this,' Cora said angrily, jumping up from her chair as if she had sat on a bee and standing, tiny but belligerent, on the hearthrug.

'I didn't say he did. You're not listening to me, Cora. I think it was a case of someone acting a little too enthusiastically.'

'It amounts to the same thing.'

'Hardly. Look, all I want you to do is to ask him to lay off Eveleigh and her dogs.'

'Why can't she move?'

'Why should she?'

'It would save a lot of hassle if she did.'

'Why can't Ben buy land elsewhere?'

'Land's not that easy to get around here, as well you know.'

'Tell him I'll buy it off him.'

'With planning permission?'

'Don't be daft, Cora. It would be worth a fortune with planning permission – if he gets it, which I seriously doubt. No, tell him I'll pay him what he paid plus all his legal expenses up to date. I can't do fairer than that.'

'Yes you can. You can mind your own sodding business.'

'Cora, love!'

'Don't Cora love me. Ben's my husband and I stand by him whatever he decides to do. And I don't go behind his back on anything. You might be a sneak, Oliver, but I'm not. I'm shocked by you. I never thought you were a devious bastard, but you are, just like the rest.'

'Cora, please. I don't want to fall out with you.'

'Then you should have thought this out. I'd be obliged if you left now. And preferably never came back – and that goes for you too, Thomasine. Even if you haven't said anything, you're obviously in cahoots.'

'Right, if that's how you want it to be, Cora. But you won't win, I'll promise you that.' And so saying, Oliver walked quickly across the room and Thomasine hurriedly followed him.

'Thanks for the coffee,' she said to Cora as she went, and decided that was about the silliest contribution she could have made.

As they crossed the hall they were greeted by a slow handclap from Sophia, sitting on the stairs.

'Well done, Oliver. Not quite the little diplomat you thought you were, are you?' They both chose to ignore her.

'Wow! That was tough,' said Thomasine, settling into Oliver's car.

'Not quite what we expected.'

'Bully for her though, he is her husband. Loyalty is important.'

'Even when he's wrong?'

'Probably even more so when he is,' she said sagely.

They drove along in silence for a while, both wondering what to do now for Eveleigh and her dogs.

'Now what do we do?' Oliver eventually said. 'I don't really fancy the tabloids.'

'Couldn't you talk to Ben?'

'I thought of that ages ago, but Business Ben is a totally different kettle of fish from Friend Ben. I doubt if he'd listen.'

'Not even to your generous offer?'

'Not coming from me. He might have done if it had been Cora.'

'I'd hoped to keep this from Nadine, my daughter. But if we went to the papers she'd learn about it from them. She'll end up picketing Ben somehow or other. She's heavily into animal causes. She even got expelled because of them.'

'Doing what?'

'Demonstrating. I'm not sure, but I think she's in with those FAA people.'

'I hope not, they're a load of loonies.'

'I can't be sure, but I was cleaning her room and found some literature of theirs.'

'Then I should try and wean her off them, if I were you. They're subversive and violent.' She shivered at his words. 'They are, no doubt, watched by the police – who have probably got huge files on them all. It could make life difficult for her when she grows up.'

'I don't think that's reason enough to ask her to stop. You can't talk to the young on those terms. She believes passionately in any animal group's causes; fear of the law and the future won't stop her.' She sighed deeply.

They lapsed into silence again as Oliver negotiated the narrow country lanes.

'How about getting her involved in the legitimate side of animal welfare?'

'How?'

'Talk to Eveleigh. Get her interested in that side of the dog world. Start showing your dog – get her to do the showing.'

'Nadine! You don't know her. She thinks all pet ownership should be banned. She thinks it's demeaning to the animals. She probably regards Crufts with as much loathing as a feminist regards the Miss World Competition.'

'Lord, you have got a problem then. Is it my imagination, or wasn't life a hell of a lot simpler once?'

'Much. And especially for parents.'

'Thank God I never was one,' he said with feeling.

With Jim definitely out of the picture, and Thomasine's explanations of her feelings for her ex-husband, Oliver felt free to ask Thomasine out to dinner that evening.

They drove to a quiet restaurant in Morristown, where they enjoyed a good meal. On the way back Oliver suggested they stop at his house for a coffee and brandy. Thomasine, who had left a sulking Nadine at home and Nova playing with Slipper at Oliver's, readily agreed.

One brandy became two as they explained themselves to each other. A kiss was the natural progression, and then another. Both of them, having lived without sex for so long, had mistakenly told themselves it was not necessary for them, that they could live without it – which they could, until those kisses released the pent-up feelings, freed the need lying fallow in both of them.

Oliver's mouth on her nipple shocked her body into remembered anticipation. Both of them felt they would explode from the frustrations that neither, until now, had been aware of. Frantically they tore at each other's clothes, desperate for the touch of skin on skin, for him to be inside her.

Their passion accelerated with a speed that overwhelmed them. As he began to enter her, she paused for a second and thought 'This is unwise', but need overcame reason in a millisecond and their bodies joined with abandon. As they came they both called out their love for each other.

They flopped back on the rug in front of the fire, exhausted, covered in their mingled sweat, and looked at each other with amazed expressions.

'I meant it. I love you,' he said, as he traced the outline of her mouth with a finger that smelt of her.

'I love you too,' she said softly, those words she'd never thought she'd say again.

Saying the words made them want each other again. To hold, to feel, to kiss, to explore. Quietly, sensuously this time, they made love. Joyous, languorous giving of love. And, this time, unbeknown to both of them, Oliver's heartfelt relief that he'd never been a parent had already come to an end.

December

41

Jim slept at Eveleigh's for almost two weeks. After the first, it was apparent that his presence was not entirely necessary; not a peep had been heard at night, apart from the odd prowling fox and startled rabbit. But he stayed on because he was enjoying himself, for Eveleigh was good company. Until he arrived at Oakleigh Kennels he had not been aware of how tired he was, or how tense. The stress of living with Beth, the consequences of his wrongdoing, were far greater than he had realised.

The evenings spent with Eveleigh were some of the most contented he'd enjoyed in ages. They had far more in common than either of them had known before. They both liked George Shearing and early Stan Kenton music. Together they did *The Times* crossword puzzle. Both were avid Dick Francis readers. They liked plain, wholesome food, especially steamed puddings with custard, were partial to a malt, and would rather have claret than burgundy. Neither could imagine living in a city, and would prefer to be dead than do so. And, above all, they had their passion for animals, especially dogs.

'We're like a couple of old slippers, aren't we?' said Jim one night, stretching comfortably in an easy chair in front of the large fire, which they were sharing tonight with Brünnhilde.

'Who'd somehow got separated.'

'Then found each other again.'

'Exactly.' Eveleigh felt contentment too, having resigned herself to never finding it again.

At night, in the spare room, Jim found he was conscious of Eveleigh in hers, just along the corridor, and her close proximity sometimes made it difficult for him to sleep – but he'd learnt his lesson and did nothing. He valued his friendship with her far too much to risk it over sex.

Eveleigh, in her room, often could not sleep either, and found herself thinking of Jim and what he was like without his clothes on. Often she wished she could be brazen as Beth had been and go along to his room and climb into bed beside him. She cuddled whichever St Bernard was sharing her bed instead.

He could not stay here indefinitely. With no intruders, they began to wonder if perhaps they had overreacted. And Jim knew he could not keep up his resolve not to touch her if he stayed much longer. If he was to build a relationship with Eveleigh, he had to do it properly and court her as she deserved. He respected her too much for anything else.

As she saw him off on the last morning, Eveleigh stood at her kitchen window and wondered what was wrong with her. Why hadn't he made love to her?

As soon as he entered his house, Jim wished he hadn't been so honourable and was back at the kennels. The atmosphere was heavy with indignation, hurt, and ruffled feelings. Even Harry had stopped speaking to him. He scurried into his surgery to escape the oppressive atmosphere. Sitting at his desk, he wondered how long he would have to lurk in there away from the main house. It was then that it struck him what a ludicrous situation his lack of control had landed him in.

As he berated himself for a bastard, a voice inside him, small at first but rapidly growing, clamoured to be heard. This was unfair. It wasn't *all* his fault. Beth had started the whole catastrophic sexual adventure – his sin was his weakness. They were not married, nor had the subject ever been addressed, and yet Beth was behaving like a disgruntled wife. And it was his house, after all, that he was being made to feel uncomfortable in. And to add insult to injury, although he was still paying her wages, she had to all intents gone on strike; his laundry remained undone and the house was uncleaned.

He had to tell her to go!

Each morning he resolved that he would talk to Beth that evening, tell her she must find somewhere else to work, that she could remain here until she did. Such resolutions were easy to make, but by evening he could not do it and would hole up in his study pretending nothing was going on. Since she no longer cooked for him, he ate at the pub and in the morning made himself coffee with the kettle in the surgery. He didn't even have to use the kitchen door, but let himself in by the patients' entrance. He hadn't set foot in his kitchen for days.

If relations in the house were at an impasse, Jim and the new veterinary practice in Shillingham had shaken down into a mutually beneficial relation-ship, where Jim had to be on night call one week in three and every third weekend. For the first time in his professional life he could plan ahead. He could even accept invitations to dinner in the knowledge that he wouldn't be interrupted and have to go rushing out into the night. How pleasant it would have been if he and Ann had had such freedom! Such thinking got him nowhere, he told himself as he drove along the winding road towards the Walters' farm, where a cow with mastitis awaited him. And Ann, if she could have, would have told him to stop being a fool, to stop thinking about what might have been, and to get on with his life without her.

As he approached the entrance to the farm he realised he was back to his normal good spirits. Nowadays, as soon as he left the house he felt slightly happier, and the further away he drove the better he felt.

Chris Walters was waiting for him in his immaculate yard. Coming here was always a pleasure, not just because he liked Chris and his wife Fee, but because it was all so ordered, the creatures well cared for. It was a mixed farm, part animal, part arable – not so common these days, with large-scale farming the norm. Chris's farm had a few of everything. Jim often said it was a dry-land ark. They'd cattle and pigs, goats and chickens, ducks and geese, horses, ponies, dogs and cats, and Chris's latest venture, a herd of deer for venison.

Chris was not that type of farmer who, resenting Jim's fee, called the vet out too late. Chris called at the first sign of trouble, and so the cow's mastitis, caught early, was soon treated and the cow happily settled.

'Time for a drink?' Chris offered.

Jim looked doubtfully at his watch. 'I'm running late.'

'There's something Fee and I want to talk to you about. It might be serious.'

'In that case – ' Jim followed Chris to the back door, where they slipped off their wellingtons, and stepped over a sleeping St Bernard blocking the passageway.

'It's something about St Bernards – they always have to obstruct your passage. Buttercup there is for ever sprawled across the doorway.'

'Protecting the pack, no doubt.'

'Really. You think so? Asleep!' Chris laughed as, in stockinged feet, they entered the chaotic, but welcoming, kitchen. Two golden retrievers sauntered over to inspect the visitor, but upon realising it was Jim, painful memories surfaced and they scurried quickly under the kitchen table and watched him with suspicious eyes, bodies taut and prepared for instant flight.

'It must be awful when you love dogs to have them run away from you,' Fee said as she put glasses and a bottle of whisky on the table for them.

'Not all dogs remember. Some have no recollection of me treating them at all and only react on the surgery doorstep.'

'But mine are the most intelligent dogs I've ever met,' Fee said proudly, and Jim smiled to himself. How many times had he heard that? 'How's Beth?'

'She's all right.' He realised he looked sheepish, as if his guilt was stamped on his face for all to see.

'I called her up the other day, she sounded a bit odd.'

'Did she?'

'Yes – I wanted some of her dried flowers and she was quite sharp with me.'

Jim could understand if Fee felt affronted, since it was she who'd found the job for Beth in the first place. 'It's her husband – he's out of prison and she's a bit windy about him finding her.' He congratulated himself at such a brilliant explanation.

'Beth? A husband? You're joking. Beth's never been married.'

'No? Are you sure?'

'Certain. I've known her since schooldays. My mum knows hers – she'd have said if there'd been a wedding.'

'I must have heard it wrong. So, what was it you wanted to tell me?' He had to change the subject, he felt so angry and so puzzled. Why should Beth have lied to him?

'You'd better tell him, Fee. It was you who heard it.'

'It's just a worry, Jim. We've got no proof – nothing like that. And this is strictly between us.' As Fee spoke she looked constantly at her husband, as if for encouragement. 'It's difficult. He's not the easiest of people.'

'Who isn't? Don't worry, I won't repeat anything said within these four walls.'

'Do you ever get called to the smallholding off Conniestown Lane? Primrose Acre, it's called.'

Jim thought a while before answering. 'No. I'm pretty sure I've never been there. They grow vegetables, don't they? Sometimes in summer you see a stall on the roadside with strawberries for sale.'

Jim sipped at the whisky Chris had handed him and wished they'd get on with it, he'd be late at Oliver's at this rate. 'What seems to be the problem?'

'On odd nights my dogs here have gone mad howling, and once in the daytime. They don't normally do that, they're very calm dogs, as you know. At first we thought it was a fox they could smell and we checked the chickens, but we've lost none. Then one night the dogs were down here howling and pacing and I was upstairs. I looked out of the window – and I noticed over at Primrose Acre – you can see it from the bedroom, it's too far away to see from the yard – well, I saw some cars parked, and that in itself is unusual. And when I opened the window I could hear men cheering and shouting. And in a lull, I don't think I imagined it, I'm sure I heard dogs growling and snarling.'

'Aren't you a bit far away to hear anything?'

'Fee's got ears like a bat. She hears my car when I'm still on the road. I admit when she called me I couldn't hear a bloody thing. But if Fee says she heard it, she did. And it would explain the weird behaviour of Romulus and Remus here.' He bent down and patted his retrievers who, evidently having decided that Jim hadn't come to see them, had inched forward on their bellies, tongues lolling, to be more part of the scene. 'Look at them, nosy buggers, can't bear to be left out of anything.'

'So, you think that there are organised dog fights going on over there?'

'I didn't say that, exactly, Jim,' Fee said quickly.

'No. But it's what you think?'

Miserably, Fee nodded her head.

'Would you mind if I mentioned this to the RSPCA?'

'Why Fee's so worried, Jim, about all this going further is, if she's right we want it stopped, who wouldn't? But if she's mistaken, what then? I wanted to go and look, but she begged me not to.'

'You don't know this man. He's evil. He'd kill you.'

Both men laughed at her concern. 'I mean it,' she said defiantly.

'We are both worried. If she's slandering him he could sue, and we can't afford that sort of hassle. Times are hard.'

'I understand, honestly,' Jim told Fee. 'I wouldn't even mention you by name to them. Just that someone had seen something suspicious and told me in passing. I've already had a visit from an inspector, asking if I've treated any dogs wounded in fights or had any equipment stolen. This could be the lead they're waiting for.'

'In that case I think you should, don't you, Fee?' She agreed. She was smiling now that the responsibility was shifting to someone else.

'Is there a pattern to it?'

'We've racked our brains on that. Not really. But it's nearly always a Saturday.'

As soon as he was back in the surgery Jim dialled the number the young RSPCA inspector had left him, but there was no reply. He dickered with calling the usual number but decided against. Perhaps the young man was part of the Special Branch, and it was a case of the utmost secrecy with one section not knowing what the other was up to.

He bathed and changed and was coming down the stairs as Beth came up them.

'Jim, I think Castille's ill.'

'How ill?'

'I think she must be dying.'

Jim bounded down the remaining stairs two at a time. As he approached her basket, Castille looked up with the blank look of a dog in pain. As soon as she realised who it was, her tail thumped against the side of her basket; not her normal tattoo of welcome but a rather weary, half-hearted thump or two.

'What is it, my old love?' Jim bent down beside her and ran his hand along her flank, then felt her bloated stomach. Her normal breathing was interrupted by a sharp intake of breath as his fingers felt a distinct lump. He hardly needed the thermometer to tell her temperature was far too high. She panted from dehydration; her breath smelt foetid.

'How long has she been like this?'

'Only a couple of days.'

'She couldn't get like this in a couple of days. Has she been eating, drinking?'

'Not much.'

'And you didn't tell me?'

'You're hardly ever here. And in any case, you've not shown any interest in the dog. Don't blame me.'

He looked up at her from the dog, his hand still absentmindedly stroking her, calming her. 'You did this on purpose, didn't you? You're punishing me through the dog.' He spoke in a calm way, almost emotionless, as if the shock had destroyed all feeling. But this very calmness made him sound more frightening.

'Don't be silly. I thought she'd get better. She's been ill before.'

Jim ran through all the possibilities – there was only one. The dog had a growth in its groin large enough to feel, tight as a ball. He could relieve the fluid that had built up. He could give her antibiotics for the fever. He could give analgesics for the pain. But for what? The tumour would continue to grow, the pain increase, the dosages with it. Jim knew what he had to do.

He walked stony-faced into his surgery. As he prepared the syringe his fingers trembled and he dropped it twice before he was able to fill it.

He returned to his dog. Once again the head lifted, the tail weakly thumped. He'd done what he despised in others – he'd cruelly neglected his own dog. He'd been so involved with his own problems he hadn't noticed her deteriorating. Beth should have told him sooner, but it did not alter the fact he himself should have been aware of it.

'I'm sorry, Castille,' he said, his voice thick with emotion as he took her paw gently in his hand and searched for a vein. The dog did not even whimper as he inserted the needle, but licked his hand as if knowing he was helping her. He pushed the plunger slowly. 'I love you, Castille. I couldn't let you suffer. Forgive me . . .' As he spoke, the fluid seeped into the dog and painlessly she drifted away; his only consolation was the relaxed expression on the dog's face as death claimed her.

Jim remained some time kneeling in front of the dog. He wished Beth would go. He wanted to be alone with Castille. Wanted to cry, to mourn for her. He looked up.

'Oh, Jim. I'm sorry. I'd no idea.' Beth stood looking with horror at the dead dog.

He ignored her. 'Amtie,' he called the little King Charles who was cowering under the table, sensing the events unfolding in front of her. 'Come on, Amtie. You must say goodbye too.' He put out his hand to encourage her. Jim believed that dogs should be allowed to acknowledge the death of their companions and grieve too. The little dog padded over to Jim and stood as close to him as she could. He put his arm round her. 'See. Nothing to be scared of. Castille's at rest now.' And the little King Charles sniffed at Castille, looked at Jim, and then padded back to her basket.

Jim bent down and lifted Castille, heavy in death. Beth opened the door into the hall and then into the surgery.

'Are you going to bury her now?'

'No. I'll do that in the morning.' He laid the dog on a bench and covered her with her blanket from the basket, pushing the material round her as if to keep her warm. He stood, his head bowed. He'd fought the tears long enough; as they seeped from his eyes, he acknowledged grief had won.

'Are you staying in now?' He thought he detected the sound of hope in her voice.

'No, I'm going out.'

'To Eveleigh's?'

He didn't bother to reply, couldn't find the energy to question her over her phantom husband. He got his handkerchief out from his pocket and wiped at his eyes.

'Of course dear Eveleigh will understand, won't she? You can cry on her shoulder, can't you?'

'What on earth are you going on about?' said Jim wearily.

'Look at you. A grown man crying your eyes out. It's only a dog.'

He swung round and looked at her, his expression passing quickly from sadness to anger. 'How little you know, Beth, how little.' Beth looked away from him, aware she'd said too much and now he never would forgive her.

42

Jim did not speak of Castille's death at Oliver's dinner party: he doubted he could have talked about it without breaking down, and did not feel he had the right to lumber them with his sorrow. But he was very quiet, and once or twice Oliver and Thomasine exchanged puzzled glances. Eveleigh blamed herself for his silence, certain he was annoyed at being so obviously paired off with her and wondering if, now he was back with Beth, he regretted confiding such intimate details to her as he had, and was now drawing away from her. Eveleigh had, in the past, often found this was the outcome when secrets were shared.

Oliver and Thomasine tried their hardest to rescue the evening. The plan had been to discuss where and what to do next over Eveleigh's kennels. But looking at his guests' sombre faces, Oliver doubted if this evening was the best time to make plans – Jim and Eveleigh's hearts did not seem to be in it. Maybe he'd made a mistake, maybe he should have invited Beth too. It was a puzzle, one never knew where one was with people.

Thomasine was so full of happiness she felt she would burst if she could not let some of it bubble free. She was amazed and stunned at how she felt and wanted to tell everyone, wanted the world to know. So far she had told her dog and had hinted to her mother, but Di hadn't been listening, or else the hint was too subtle, for she had nattered on with no comment. Instinct had told her to be wary of telling Nadine, for her daughter, she knew, would have to be made privy to this information in gentle doses.

Still, she thought, Jim and Eveleigh would soon become aware of the way she and Oliver looked at each other, constantly touching each other. But they didn't. The evening creaked on with silences becoming more frequent and longer each time. She had hoped to discuss the animal movement that Nadine was involved in with Jim, to try and find out more, but decided that this evening was not the best time for that either.

Jim was drinking heavily, which puzzled them all. Oliver had opened a third bottle of wine with serious misgivings, and had virtually decided to forgo the port, but Thomasine, after she had put the Stilton on the table, missed Oliver's signals and placed the port decanter and glasses beside it. When Oliver mumbled that perhaps they'd had enough without the port, Jim, for the first time that evening, showed animation as he strongly disagreed with his host.

'He shouldn't drive,' Thomasine said half an hour later when, to everyone's consternation, Jim fell asleep sitting bolt upright at the table.

'I do hope he's not on call,' Eveleigh fretted.

'How about some strong coffee?' Oliver suggested. 'Do you know what's wrong, Eveleigh? He seems to have been a bit off colour for the past few weeks.'

'I've no idea,' she replied, in such a tight-lipped manner that Oliver was pretty certain she knew something.

It was finally decided that Eveleigh would drive Jim home and Oliver would return Jim's car in the morning. Thomasine was relieved at this; if Oliver had driven him back she would have found it necessary to leave too. They were too early into their relationship to assume he'd want her to stay.

Oliver helped a stumbling Jim into the car and they both waved his guests away into the night.

'Phew – what a sticky evening, wasn't it?' Oliver said with feeling as the tail lights disappeared around the curve in the drive, and he put his arm about Thomasine.

'Do you know what was wrong? Was it us?'

'Something with Jim, and something Eveleigh knew about, I think.'

'She's potty about him, of course.'

'Who?' Oliver stopped dead in his tracks from surprise.

'Eveleigh, of course,' she laughed at his astonished expression.

'Well, I never. Old Eveleigh!'

'She's not *that* old. And she's rather attractive in an understated way. She's got a fab figure. Don't tell me you've never noticed?'

'To be honest, I hadn't. She's always bundled up in tweeds and Barbours.' He grinned at her. 'Where're you going?'

'To clear the table and load the dishwasher.'

'No you're not. Grace'll be in in the morning. Come here.'

'What are you paying me for then?' she said archly, but her heart was racing with anticipation.

The cold air revived Jim dramatically. He sat up, rubbed his face with his hands, looked around and saw Eveleigh beside him. 'Oh shit! I'm sorry.'

'That's all right, Jim. We thought it best you didn't drive, the police might be about.'

'I don't know what got into me. What must Oliver and Thomasine think?'

'Probably that you're overworked and stressed,' she said kindly. The car lurched as Eveleigh swung it around a sharp bend. It was as if the jolt made Jim's memory, until now damped down by alcohol, return in a rush.

They were soon at Jim's, and Eveleigh carefully negotiated the gateway and stopped in the yard.

'Here you are, safe as houses,' she said, turning to him with a bright smile. 'Jim! Oh, Jim, what is it?' He was sitting rigid, facing front, staring with unseeing eyes out of the windscreen, tears gushing down his cheeks. 'Is there something I can do? Do you want to tell me?'

'It's Castille – ' He stopped. Speech was hard, as if he had a rock in his throat.

'Your crossbreed? Has something happened? Is she ill? Is she – ' At this Jim covered his face with his hands and a sob escaped, an anguished, ugly sound for he had tried to choke it back. 'Oh, Jim. My poor Jim.' She put her arm around him and pulled him towards her so that his head lay on her breast. She stroked his hair gently. 'I understand. Grieve, Jim. Let it out,' she said softly.

It was as if her permission released him, for now he cried in earnest with no attempt to control it. For minutes he cried as she held him close.

The tears subsided. He lay still a second and then sat up, pushing his hair back from his forehead, fumbling for his handkerchief, blowing his nose, dabbing his eyes.

'What must you think of me? I'm sorry. Blubbing like that, whatever next!' He tried to laugh.

'I grieve with you, Jim. There's nothing so hard as losing an old companion like that. And doubly hard for you if you had to – ' She found she couldn't quite put into words 'destroy her'. Jim nodded bleakly. 'It's bad enough having to make the decision to call you to put one of my dogs to sleep, and still, every time it happens, no matter how ill the dog, I feel a murderess. I can't imagine how sad and guilty you must be feeling.'

'She'd had a good innings. She was fourteen.' He said this as if it could help, but it didn't.

'She was Ann's, wasn't she? So you've also lost a link with the past.'

'How did you understand that?' He looked at her with surprise.

'You forget Coco, my little King Charles – she was my husband's. I know he touched the furniture, sat on the chairs, but sometimes, when I stroke her, it's different. It's like, as my hands touch where he once touched, it's as if I can feel him.'

'Someone said to me "It's only a dog." That upset me more, somehow.'

'Only people who've never been loved by a dog can spout such rubbish. I've found that in some ways losing a dog is harder than losing a person. All that devotion, that undemanding love. I never cried when my mother died, but I mourned for months for a dog that died shortly afterwards. In some people's eyes that must make me a monster, I suppose. But I got more from my relationship with the dog than I ever got from my mother.' She patted his hand. 'Don't feel guilty about it, Jim. Grieve – it's a very real grief you are facing.'

Jim had never heard Eveleigh tell so much of herself. 'You're a friend in a million,' he said. 'Maybe Castille will be reincarnated as a nice person.'

'On no!' Eveleigh looked quite shocked. 'I've always thought the Buddhists got it seriously wrong presuming that the human form was the highest level of attainment. No, no. I think if a human lives a good life, then, with luck, they'll come back as a dog – far more suitable.'

Jim looked at her and saw she was smiling. He laughed a real laugh this time. 'Eveleigh, my darling, you're a tonic.' And he leant over and kissed her full on the mouth, and then opened the door quickly, leapt out and shot across the yard to the house so as not to see her face. The door slammed shut.

Eveleigh sat in the car for a moment, her fingers touching where his lips had been. Mixed emotions sped across her face; shock, disbelief and happiness succeeded one another in milli-seconds.

From an upstairs window, Beth, her face twisted with anger, watched.

When Alan returned to the office in Horsham he found a message from Jim. 'Ten-thirty, my place?' he read, and Jim's name; that was all. Such terseness and discretion must mean Jim had information so important he could not risk it over the phone. He set out immediately to drive to Middle Shilling.

'You do understand that the friend who told me about Primrose Acre has no proof?'

'You're not prepared to tell me who told you this?'

'I promised not to. You must understand, Tom White is an unpleasant character and many hereabouts are afraid of him.'

'White, you said?' Alan did not write the name down, since notebooks could get lost.

'You know him?'

'No,' he replied, but he wondered if Kimberley, with the same name, did.

'We'll look into it. Thanks, Mr Varley, for tipping us off.'

'It's not much, but it is the only thing I've heard.'

'Any lead, we're grateful.' He didn't like to ask Jim if he thought it was possible for a human to hear over that distance, even at night. He also refrained from pointing out that it was rare for a fight to be held on premises which were someone's home. Normally buildings used for fights were such that the owner could disassociate himself and claim he knew nothing – like very isolated barns or disused factories. Not someone's backyard. It seemed implausible, but on the other hand Nadine had been adamant a fight was to take place this coming Saturday . . .

After seeing him off, Jim reluctantly returned to the surgery and his waiting clients. His depression was worse this morning; he still had to bury Castille, he still hadn't seen Beth, and he had a murderous hangover.

Alan rang the doorbell of Eveleigh's house severaltimes, but no one answered. He walked around the side of the house with the diffident step of one who's not sure whether he should proceed further or not.

As he neared the back he heard the noise of chain link rattling, as if the dogs were hurling themselves at their fencing. He quickened his step, aware that he was hearing sounds of great agitation.

'Here you! Who are you?' he shouted loudly as, turning the corner into the yard, he saw a man huddled over the entrance to one of the kennels halfway along the building. The man looked up, grabbed the bag at his feet, and began to run. The dogs, hysterical by now, barked and growled and leapt, frustrated by the fence that prevented them reaching the intruder as he hurtled past them towards the open fields beyond.

Alan gave chase. The man had scrambled through the bushes which marked Eveleigh's boundary. When Alan reached it he leapt over. He was gaining ground easily: evidently the man was older and slower than him.

Alan was within an arm's length of grabbing him when his foot caught in a rabbit hole and he crashed face down, the wind forced out of him in an animal grunt. All he could do was lie there, fighting to catch his breath, as the intruder loped away across the field. As he got to his feet he heard a car door slam, a powerful engine start up, and saw a flash of a dark car, black or dark grey, he was not sure. But its make and number remained a mystery.

Gingerly, he tried his foot on the ground. It was sore, but no great damage had been done. He limped back across the field towards the kennels and arrived just as Eveleigh appeared, her expression anxious, alerted by the cacophony from her dogs. At the sight of him she looked warily to left and right and backed towards one of the kennels. 'Alan?' she said, puzzled, but with her hand resting on the bolt ready to spring Wotan, one of her largest dogs, if necessary.

'Mrs Brenton – please don't be afraid of me. I think I interrupted an intruder. At least, when I shouted, he scarpered. I don't even know why I yelled, there was something furtive about the way he moved that made me. And Kimberley had told me about your losing a dog.'

'Thank God you turned up, Alan.'

'I was in the area and I hoped you wouldn't mind me popping in on Kimberley.'

'Where was he? Which kennel?'

'This one.' Alan walked towards the middle of the run and stopped before one gate.

'That's Lo Lo. Oh my God.' From her pocket Eveleigh took a key and unlocked the padlock. 'I've had to put these on each kennel. Shocking!' Lohengrin jumped up in welcome, placing his front paws on her shoulders and enthusiastically licking her face. Alan stepped back smartly as the dog shook his head and a spray of slobber headed in his direction. Eveleigh pushed the dog down and opened his mouth, smelt his breath and ran her hands along his sides. 'He seems all right, but I'd better call Jim Varley.'

'Look at these.' Alan had tripped over a pair of wire-cutters which had fallen into the grass. 'I won't touch them, they could be evidence.'

'Then you think I should call the police? They were most unpleasant last time, and did bugger all. I've got to think. Leave the cutters for the moment. Can I offer you a coffee?' She began to walk back to the house.

'Hell! I've just thought. Do you think Kimberley is safe?' He began to quicken his pace.

'She'll be fine. One of my dogs has an ear infection, she's taken her to the vet's – I try to call him out as little as possible.' It would have been so easy this morning to call Jim in to see the dog. She'd wanted to, but sense had prevailed. After his outburst of grief last night it would be better if he chose when he came here, rather than be summoned by her and put in a difficult position.

'I've just come from there. I didn't see her.'

'That's odd.' Eveleigh looked even more worried as she unlocked the back door.

'This means I can never leave the kennels, not for a moment!' Eveleigh said as she put the kettle on the Rayburn. Angrily she spooned instant coffee into two mugs. 'I had to inspect the home of some people who want one of my puppies – see if it was suitable.'

'Do you always do that?'

'I've been caught out before. Years ago I sold a dog to a couple who claimed they'd got two acres. It transpired they lived in a flat in a high-rise – I ask you! Of course the dog was impossible, poor dear, cooped up and knocking things over – St Bernards need a lot of sea room. So they brought it back. Since then, whenever possible, I check them out. You can't be too sure.' The kettle boiled and she added water to the mugs and was fussing about with milk and sugar when the door opened.

'Alan! What are you doing here?' Kimberley looked anxiously at her employer, unsure how she'd react to boyfriends calling in the middle of the day.

'He saved yet another dog, my dear. Thank goodness he came when he did. Coffee?' She collected a mug as she filled Kimberley in on the latest events.

'How can people be so cruel?'

'That's not all. On my way back from inspecting the new people – they're fine by the way, Kimberley, the puppy will be safe with them – I met a friend of mine – Fee Walters, they farm over near Conniestown. She told me she's almost certain that dog fights take place near her, she feels certain there's to be another on Saturday. I wish I'd a machine gun, I'd go myself and kill the bastards.'

'Saturday?' Kimberley felt her stomach clench and her pulse race.

'I must phone Jim.' Eveleigh crossed the kitchen to the telephone. Alan took the opportunity to search for Kimberley's hand and squeeze it.

'I have to go,' he whispered so as not to disturb Eveleigh. His heart had lurched at her casual mention of the dog fight. So now he knew who was involved. He'd have to get back to the office, talk to his boss. Information was coming in too thick and fast to be ignored. He prayed this Fee woman didn't blab to many more people.

'See you tonight?' Kimberley whispered back.

Alan looked at his watch. If he drove like a bat out of hell he could see Don and still make it back. Hopefully he'd be put on the assignment, and then he wouldn't have to rush back and forth.

'Sure thing. What do you fancy, cinema? Hamburger?'

'Nice pub, I want to talk.' She wondered what had made her say that. He'd think it odd.

43

'I didn't come to live with you to be neglected like this,' Nadine said sulkily as she buttered some toast for an extraordinarily late breakfast. Thomasine was wiping Nova clean. They had been for an early morning walk and it had rained so hard in the night that Nova's underside was soaked from the grass and her paws were muddy. Thomasine rubbed the dog vigorously with a towel. As Nadine spoke she concentrated harder on the dog and chose to ignore her daughter, or rather to try to, for from past experience she knew the girl was trying to wind her up.

'Look at you. What a mess,' Thomasine talked to the dog as she fussed over her, obviously to Nova's satisfaction for every time she stopped rubbing, the dog head-butted her arm to start again. 'You'd never win at Crufts looking like this, would you?' She bent down and kissed the wide, flat top of the bulldog's skull.

'You think more of that dog than you do of me.' Nadine's lower lip protruded in a petulant pout.

'Don't be silly.' Thomasine still did not look up.

'I'm not. You are. Just listen to you – it's gross. To get your attention I'd have to turn into a flaming bulldog, wouldn't I?' Nadine pushed her chair back, its legs grating noisily on the quarry-tiled floor.

'No, that won't be necessary.' Thomasine laughed as she finally looked at her daughter, but judging by her sour expression the joke was completely lost on her. She stood up. 'What's the matter, Nadine? I can't believe you're jealous of a dog. That's ridiculous.'

'Is it? You're never here with me, but you take her with you everywhere. You talk to her and you never talk to me.'

'That's not true. I spent hours with you yesterday talking about your school work and your options. What else do you expect of me?'

'You just think of yourself. You don't worry about me – if you did you wouldn't be out until all hours, leaving me alone here.'

'For God's sake, Nadine, at your age! I didn't think you still needed a babysitter.'

'I get lonely. I need company too. If I had a car I could get out and about, meet my friends.'

'How often do I have to tell you I can't afford to buy you a car? It's all a struggle at the moment.'

'Ask Dad to help.'

'No.' Thomasine swung round, away from her.

'Why not?'

'Because I don't want to.'

'So I have to suffer because of your pride?'

'Look, Nadine, can't we talk this through like two sensible adults? What's the problem? Tell me and I'll see if I can do something. Come on.' Thomasine sat down at the table and took hold of her daughter's hand. Nadine looked fixedly at the table and said nothing. 'Please, Nadine. Talk to me. I don't want to go on with this endless carping.'

'No one loves me!' Nadine burst out, and began to cry.

'That's not true. I love you, so does your father – whatever you think.'

'No you don't. No one does. I've no friends.'

'There's that nice girl Kimberley. You said you liked her.'

'She's got a boyfriend. She's got no time for me any more.' She continued to sob.

'You'll meet someone, one day.'

'No I won't. How can I, living in a dump like this?' Nadine snapped back, the tears immediately stopped. 'It's all right for you to talk. You've got a bloke to screw you.'

Thomasine gasped. Her hand seemed to take on a life of its own. It flashed across the table and slapped Nadine across the face.

'How dare you hit me!' Nadine had jumped to her feet, holding her reddening cheek.

'I'm sorry, I shouldn't have done that.'

'Too right you shouldn't.'

In the basket Nova sat shivering from head to toe. Her large eyes watched the two women with an expression almost of terror. She panted noisily. Thomasine squatted down and scooped the dog into her arms, making soothing, mewing noises, holding her tightly.

'See. What have I said all along? It's the dog, not me.'

'Is it any wonder? She just wants to love me, she asks for nothing in return. It's simple, this love, uncomplicated, undemanding.'

'Oh, stuff you and that thing.' Nadine banged noisily out of the kitchen.

Nova began to lick Thomasine's face gently with her long, pink tongue. She buried her face in the soft, furry ruff at the dog's neck and allowed herself to cry.

All day Kimberley had been preoccupied. She kept forgetting things and dropping things. Worst of all, she failed to shut one of the kennel gates properly and allowed Wotan to escape. It took her ages to persuade the great brute to go back into his kennel.

'What is the matter?' Eveleigh finally asked her.

'Nothing. Honest. That intruder upset me.' She hoped this would placate her boss.

'Understandable. And all those questions from the police – such suspicious people. But let's hope they can trace where those wire-cutters came from and who bought them.'

'Probably Texas Homecare, and we'll never know.'

'We've got to hope, Kimberley.'

'Has Alan phoned?' she asked, in a tone which, she hoped, implied only minor interest.

'Yes. He went to the police direct and left them with a sketchy description of the man. He seems a nice young man.' Her smile was a small, sly one as she glanced at her kennel maid.

'Yes.' Kimberley blushed. She felt tongue-tied. 'There's just one thing – ' She paused. 'Alan invited me out tonight, but I won't go if you're frightened to be left alone.'

'Me, frightened? Good gracious, no. I've dug out my husband's old shotgun – just in case. I've also decided that I'm going to bring all the dogs into the house, to be on the safe side.'

'All of them?' Kimberley looked aghast.

'Yes. It'll be a bit of a squash, but at least we'll get some sleep.'

The rest of the day dragged by for Kimberley. She longed to see Alan again, for when she was with him she could forget the worry that was gnawing at her. The talk of dog fights made her concern for Bandage increase. She hated herself for her futile indecision so far. She wondered endlessly whether she should confide in Alan and tell him everything – about the fights, the puppy farm. How wonderful it would be to unburden herself. She tried to imagine how it would feel to be rid of the guilt which she seemed doomed to cart about with her.

But what could Alan do? Wouldn't she be lumbering him with her problems, and was that fair?

She tucked her new white shirt into the waistband of her equally new black skirt and studied herself in the mirror. She worried whether her legs were good enough for such a short skirt, at the same time wishing she'd had enough money to buy herself new shoes. Was it her imagination or did she look different, more assured? Was she standing straighter, prouder, or was it simply that, unused as she was to wearing skirts, of course she looked different. She pinched her cheeks to give them more colour – she hadn't any blusher. Perhaps she would confide in him after all. She couldn't go on like this, not sleeping, always this gnawing guilt. Yes, she'd already told him she wanted to talk to him; perhaps subconsciously she had been preparing the way.

*

'Love your legs!' Alan said the minute he saw her in the skirt. 'Sexy.'

They did not go to the pub. Instead they went to the new house.

'But it isn't yours yet.' She looked about her nervously.

'Soon will be, so does it matter if we jump the gun by a week or so?'

'How are we going to get in?'

'There's a broken pane of glass in the back door. I noticed it when we came before. Here, take this.' From the boot of his car he took two tartan rugs which he handed her. Then he delved back and came up with two Tesco carrier bags. 'Supper,' he explained.

The second carrier bag contained paper, wood and firelighters, not food. Kimberley stood clutching her coat tightly about her.

'Don't want you catching cold,' he said as he laid a fire in the small sitting-room grate. He put a match to it and was rewarded by a belch of acrid smoke. He flapped his hands in front of his face ineffectually.

'Here. Let me.' Kimberley took a piece of newspaper, scrunched it into a ball, lit it and stuffed it up the chimney.

'It'll catch fire.' He tried to stop her.

'No, it'll warm the chimney. It's cold, that's why it's smoking. See? That's better, isn't it?'

He'd thought of everything, even remembered the corkscrew for the wine, which they drank from paper cups. There was a knife to cut the quiche, and paper napkins to wipe their fingers, and candles to see each other.

'Strawberries? At this time of year. You're mad!' She pushed him affectionately.

'Only the best for you.'

'This is the most romantic night of my life,' she said, sighing with contentment, settling into his arms as they lay down on the rug he'd laid on the dusty floor.

As he began to make love to her, she discovered just how wonderful, how tender, how complete making real love could be. And she understood that when 'in love', lust changed, became a wondrous, tender thing. She was learning how wonderful it was to give as well as to receive. When Alan was inside her and she felt his weight upon her she wished it would never end. It made her feel lost when it did, and she felt such an intense loneliness that she had to fight hard not to cry and it puzzled her how, in the midst of such happiness, she could feel so sad.

'So, you wanted to talk. What about?' He was propped upon one elbow looking down at her, stroking the soft skin of her breasts.

'No. What gave you that idea?'

'You did.'

'Can't think what I meant.' She didn't want to lie to him and felt a twinge of guilt, but it was only the smallest of lies. She did not want the outside world with all its pain and nastiness to spoil this time with each other. She'd tell him another time, she promised herself.

But her wish was not to be granted. 'Have you seen anything of Nadine?' he asked.

'No. She phoned asking to see me tonight, but I said no. I felt bad about it since I think she was crying.'

'She struck me as too tough a nut for that. Odd, wasn't it? Two lots talking about a dog fight in such a short space of time.'

'I suppose so,' she said, reluctant for this line of conversation to continue.

'If you see her and she says anything, you'll let me know, won't you?'

'Why?' She sat up, clutching the rug around her. 'You interested in dog fights?'

'Might be,' he said nonchalantly.

'I'd hate that.'

'Then I'm not interested.' He grinned at her.

'I'm glad.' She settled back into the crook of his arm, but the mood had changed, she felt worried again. Restless.

'I suppose we should be going soon,' she heard him say.

'Would you do me a favour?' she asked abruptly. Knowing suddenly what she must do. 'I've got to pick something up and it's miles out in the sticks.'

'Sure. But isn't it a bit late? It's gone midnight.'

'No. They'll still be up,' she said vaguely.

As they approached Primrose Acre, Alan felt there was something familiar about the lane they were in. He couldn't be sure, but he thought he was close to where Vic had stood in a gateway the night he had followed him. Still, these lanes all looked the same in the dark.

'Where the hell are we? Is this near Conniestown?'

'It's miles over that way,' she answered quickly. 'Can you stop here?'

'But there's nothing here.'

'This is it.' As the car came to a halt she already had the door open. 'Wait here.'

'I'll come with you.'

'No, please. It wouldn't be a good idea. These people, they wouldn't approve. They wouldn't like the idea of me with a boyfriend.'

'Who?'

'Just people. I won't be long.' And she'd gone, and though he peered through the window he could not see her. He settled down to wait, a niggling worry at the back of his mind that something wasn't right.

It was as well she didn't have new shoes on, she thought, as she ran across the ploughed field that ran beside the rutted driveway. She stumbled several times and forced herself to slow down, otherwise she might fall and hurt herself and then she risked being found. There were no lights in the house, but she hadn't expected any.

At the yard, she tiptoed across the cobbles. She was hoping that the dogs, since they knew her, would not bark. So when a deep growling began, rising by the second towards a bark, she nearly jumped out of her skin.

'Shush, it's me. Don't be silly,' she whispered as she opened the shed door, but to no avail. The dog continued, but what was worse, the others joined in, making an unholy chorus. 'Bandage. It's me. I've come to get you.' She felt her way across the shed to Bandage's bed. She put her hand out to calm the growling creature. There was a noise like a trap shutting sharply, and Kimberley yelped with pain as the dog's teeth closed on her outstretched hand. Her yell made the dog release her. She put her hand between her legs, whistling with the pain. She couldn't believe that Bandage would do that to her.

Across the shed she found the bench where her father kept the dog bowls, and where she knew there should be a torch. She switched it on and swung the beam, and where Bandage should be she saw a strange dog, hackles up, his mouth in the rictus of a snarl, his teeth flashing ominously in the light. She walked down the other side of the barn checking each pen as she went. The two pit bulls she knew were barking noisily. There was another new dog, a Rottweiler, she thought. In the last pen, his back to her, standing in the corner, was Bandage, his head down, his shoulders hunched with dejection. Poor Bandage, she should not have delayed. She should have come for him weeks ago.

'What the fuck's going on!' The barn door banged open. Just in time, Kimberley threw herself down on the filthy floor and cowered behind a large sack of feed. As she dived she had the presence of mind to click the torch off.

'Stop that fucking racket, you filthy sods.' She heard her father kick the wooden partition, but the barking continued. Then she heard a sickening thud and the scream of a wounded animal. 'Shut your bloody mouths. Understood?' her father bellowed at the dogs, and from the ensuing silence she could imagine the dogs cowering with terror as she once had, as her mother still did.

She longed to have the courage to jump out and hit him herself, but reason prevailed. It wasn't until she heard the door slam again that she realised she had been holding her breath from sheer terror.

She stayed where she was for a good five minutes. She listened to the agitation of the dogs, willed them to calm down. She peered around the sack, and gingerly put on the torch. On the sack was a length of rope. She grabbed it, opened the barricade into Bandage's pen and before he had time to react, had the rope around his neck and was pulling it hard.

She had moved so swiftly, so silently, the other dogs had not recovered their senses. But now they had, and the barking and growling began again. Bandage wouldn't budge. She pulled, she pushed, but he stood in his despondent position as if he did not hear her.

'Forgive me, Bandage, it's the only way,' she said, and kicked him hard in the rump and then he moved, jerking her out of the barn, across the yard, into the field. She flopped down on the earth behind the hedge – just in time, as the kitchen door opened and, through the vegatation, she could see the silhouette of her father against the light. This time he had his gun in his hand.

She pulled Bandage to her, hugging him tight, whispering words to him, praying he wouldn't bark too.

She waited, crouched in the field, until her father had entered the barn again. Then she was on her feet, urging Bandage forward. She wanted to run as fast as she could back to the safety of the car before her father pursued her, but Bandage was limping and their progress was slow.

'Where the hell have you been? I was worried sick,' Alan said as she stumbled up to the car.

She opened the back door and with difficulty manhandled the heavy dog into the car and leapt in beside it. Alan swung round in the seat. 'What on earth – ? What the hell have you got there?'

'Drive, for Christ's sake, drive!'

From the side window she could see a light bobbing across the field towards them, she could hear her father shouting. 'Go! Go!' She banged the back of the seat with a clenched fist.

Alan, seeing the light himself, put the car into gear and they lurched forward. He drove in silence for a few minutes, and then, checking there was nothing behind him, pulled into a lay-by.

'What's going on, Kimberley? Who does the dog belong to?'

'Me,' she lied.

'But ...'

'Please,' she begged him. 'Get me home.'

He drove, not knowing what to say. His mind was in a turmoil. It was a bull terrier in the back. It had wounds – healed, but fighting wounds, he was sure. A moment later he stopped at the crossroads, saw the sign to Connies-town, and knew that was where Vic had lurked that night. Was that Primrose Acre? And if so, what was Kimberley's connection with it? It was her dog, she'd said. Did that mean she was involved? His hands held the wheel tight.

He pulled up outside the kennels, and turned round to see Kimberley, her arms about the dog, crying.

'Kim,' he said. 'Talk to me.'

'I can't.'

'Is it really your dog?'

'No. I lied. I was frightened you might make me take it back. I rescued it.'

Relief flowed through him as if his veins were full of molasses. 'Oh, Kimberley, I love you. You don't know how happy you've just made me.' And Kimberley looked at him, puzzled, not understanding his reaction one little bit.

44

Jim stopped his car on the hill behind the Shillings, climbed out and looked down at the villages still asleep beneath him. The houses were covered in a soft mist, as if in the night a cloud of chiffon had floated down and buried them. Only the roofs of the taller houses protruded, and here and there was the smoke from the newly-lit fires of the early risers. It was cold, but the air was sharp, not damp, and he looked up at the sky in the juvenile hope that snow might be threatening, but saw the sun breaking through. Jim leaned against the warm bonnet of his Land Rover, lit a cigarette, and waited for the village to wake from its night-time slumber.

Below him the mist peeled back, as if the villages were sloughing off a skin. The sun shone – it was going to be a wonderful day, one of those rare bonus days that winter occasionally presented. Ann would have loved a day like this.

As the thought entered his mind, he was already steeling himself for the sense of loss and longing which always followed. Only it didn't. He gingerly tried again; imagined Ann, on her horse, as he'd seen her that day ... He smiled to himself. He was thinking about Ann as he did about his father, his mother, his best friend killed in a car crash. 'Have you gone?' he said aloud to her spirit, and there was no reply. He waited for sadness and felt only a strange, calm happiness. 'Of course,' he said, as if he finally understood something.

He'd made a decision, he hoped wisely.

Bandage had lain all night, his head resting on his paws, his eyes wide open, alert to every sound, to any danger, in a miasma of scent – dog and bitch scent which overpowered everything else. When morning came, he stood. He walked the confines of the strange kennel he was in, sniffing at the smell of dog. Several times he inspected the perimeter, his nose snuffling, smelling. He stopped abruptly. He lifted his snout and stood rigid, his nostrils moving slowly like a miniature bellows. He ran to the end of the kennel, pounded up the length and, straining the muscles of his hind quarters, sprang powerfully up and soared over the wire mesh. He landed heavily the other side and lay quiet a moment. Then, his breath regained, he was running, his snout close to the ground, across the yard, along the side of the house, out into the lane, his concentration total.

Thomasine had been up since five. She doubted if she had had more than a couple of hours' sleep, and then it had been fitful slumber – tossing and turning, jolting awake several times, with her heart racing and an awful feeling of premonition.

She had finally given up trying and got up. Nova had not appreciated her rising so early and had looked at her resentfully before burrowing under the duvet and settling down for an uninterrupted snooze.

Maybe Nadine was right about the dog, perhaps she was being stupid about her, treating her, she supposed, rather like a child. But then, it was something she could not seem to help. She loved the dog with an intensity which had surprised her. She had fallen for Luna, but nothing could have prepared her for the way she now felt about Nova.

She sat at the kitchen table, a mug of tea in front of her, and felt depression pressing in on her from all sides. She thought she'd been fortunate and had found a new happiness with Oliver. But it was a happiness which could not be, not with Nadine as angry as she was. If she stayed with Oliver and kept the dog, her daughter's misery and sense of isolation would only increase. But if she gave Oliver up and sold Nova, then her own unhappiness would be incalculable.

She heard a familiar thumping noise – Nova negotiating the stairs. Nova did not walk down stairs like a sane dog, but instead slid down them by placing her front legs on the tread and letting the rest of her slide down behind her – quite terrifying when she'd first seen her do it, but she was used to it by now.

She let the dog out for a pee. She bent down to pick up her water bowl to refill it and found herself clutching the sink as a wave of dizziness hit her, followed sharply by a need to rush to the loo. She wasn't sick, she just felt it. She sat on the lavatory lid waiting for the feeling to subside. How odd. She was never ill. Perhaps it was stress, worrying about Nadine. Or perhaps it was the chicken that she'd only half eaten last night. That was probably it, she decided, and immediately felt better for finding a solution. She sluiced her face with cold water and felt better still.

By the time she returned to the kitchen, Nova was hurling herself at the back door to be let in. When the door opened she strutted in, angry discontent at being kept waiting in every movement. 'You're a tyrant, Nova.' Thomasine bent and patted the creature which had so quickly and cleverly dominated her. 'Biscuits?'

The dog settled with her breakfast, Thomasine made herself another mug of tea and realised that it was her fourth so far that morning. Still, she supposed it would do her less harm than coffee. She resumed her seat at the kitchen table and went back to fretting over what was best for her to do. She had to resolve something, that was for sure. Then with a jolt she sat upright. *She* had to resolve it. Why her? Why did it always have to be Thomasine who resolved things?

How many times in her life had she apologised when she hadn't been in the wrong? How often had she cooked one meal when she would have preferred another? How often had she done things she wasn't interested in, gone to places she didn't want to visit, just to keep the peace? How many times had she backed down for others?

She had never been allowed to be herself: first there was her domineering mother, then her selfish husband, now her tyrant daughter – at that she managed to smile – and tyrant dog. Why was she so weak? That was it, she'd conned herself over the years to believe that her acquiescence was a form of strength, when all along it had been a weakness.

It hadn't mattered so much before, and she hadn't needed to analyse it because she'd believed she was happy doing it. Now she had touched real happiness, and she was supposed to let it slip because her daughter wanted all her attention. For how long? One more year, and she'd see her only when it suited Nadine to come home from university, or whatever she was going to do. Years of aloneness stretched ahead if she allowed Nadine to have her way.

She knew now why Nadine was so anti the dog and Oliver – she didn't want Thomasine dissipating her energies on anyone or anything else. Probably it was Oliver she objected to the most, and Nova was being used as a substitute – she didn't want the inconvenience of her mother with a new man. It wasn't jealousy which was motivating her, as Thomasine had first presumed. No, she didn't want the disruption. Just as her own mother had never allowed her to bring friends home for tea, because of the mess and noise they might have made. Just as her husband had objected to her getting a job, in case he might have to fend for himself too much.

'Simple, when you can see the wood despite the trees, Nova.' The dog stood on its hind legs, using its pleading expression to be picked up. 'You're getting too fat,' she said as she did so, and Nova settled her rump contentedly on Thomasine's lap, her front paws on the table, and looked arrogantly about the kitchen, rather like a ship's figurehead.

Absent-mindedly Thomasine stroked the dog's pelt. She could feel herself calming down; she invariably did when she sat like this, stroking her pet.

She loved Nadine, nothing could ever take that away, and there were many things about her she liked. Her generosity. Her passionate concerns. Whether it was raising money for Romanian orphans, joining motorway protesters, tying herself to a tree which the local council had designated unsafe, or, as now, protesting against the export of live animals, Nadine's feelings were genuine.She was quite capable of sacrificing all she had for others.And yet – oh the moods, the tantrums, they made her so tired! Maybe later, maybe when she was older and less obsessed with herself, she'd be easier to know.

'Maybe,' Thomasine said sadly.

When one St Bernard stirred, they all stirred. Loud had been the snorting, farting and snuffling which had, Kimberley was sure, rocked the house during the night. She eased herself out of her bed – one dog lay across the bottom and one beside her – tiptoed into her small living room, where another lay on the sofa, and had to step over the sleeping form of a large male dog, who had chosen to sleep across the kitchen doorway as if guarding the contents.

Before she had finished dressing they were all awake and inquisitively inspecting their new surroundings. As she leapt to save an ornament sent flying by one swishing tail, she appreciated why Eveleigh insisted on inspecting any new homes to make sure they had a large enough turning circle for one of her dogs.

The St Bernards flounced down the stairs in front of her as she ushered them into the yard and across to their kennels. All the other kennels were occupied and swept, so Eveleigh must have been up for some time. She assumed she must have seen Bandage. She was not concerned. She had decided to tell Eveleigh she and Alan had found him straying on the road. She knew her employer well enough to know she would make no fuss.

She had, before sleeping, laid her plans. As soon as she'd finished her morning's work she was going to take Bandage where he belonged, back to Mr Hawksmoor and Bishop's End. She could let him free in the garden, then hide in a bush and watch and wait to make sure his owner found him. She couldn't give him to him direct, he might ask too many questions.

She made her way along to the end kennel where, last night, she had locked Bandage. It was empty.

In the kitchen she found Eveleigh making breakfast. 'Mrs Brenton, you haven't seen a bull terrier this morning?'

'No. Should I have?'

'It was a stray I found. I locked it up, it must have jumped out. It doesn't matter,' she said, not meaning it. It mattered a lot.

Alan's day was going to be a busy one. He had had to hare back to Horsham to consult with the Chief Inspector. After such a slow and frustrating start on this particular enquiry, everything seemed suddenly to be rushing to a conclusion. When the snippets of gossip, the little information they had gleaned, were jigsawed together and cemented with this latest information, including the dog Kimberley had rescued, they all agreed there was enough to justify Alan moving to the area for the run-up to Saturday. They had suspicions enough to approach the local police, who would decide whether to launch an operation against Primrose Acre.

The main problem they faced was lack of time. They hadn't been able to familiarise themselves with the premises, do recces, observe, at leisure from a distance, the comings and goings. They did not have time to work by the book. Instead, they were studying Ordnance Survey maps to decide who should be where and who would move in from which direction. Alan always loved this stage – this was when the excitement began, when the adrenalin began to pump.

Oliver had worked half the night on his book. He was glad he had it to concentrate on. He'd been put out last night when Thomasine had rung to cancel their date. She'd sounded odd on the telephone and when he'd asked her what was wrong she had, infuriatingly, replied 'nothing'. Oliver loathed it when women said that. He knew from experience with Sophia that, on the contrary, it meant that everything was wrong, or something catastrophic had happened, or was likely to happen.

'*Nothing*, my arse,' he'd muttered to himself as he'd replaced the receiver. He'd found some cheese skulking in the refrigerator and helped himself to a large wedge of Brie and, with a pile of Bath Oliver biscuits and a new Pinot Noir he wanted to try, he'd settled to work. As the fire crackled, as Slipper snoozed and farted, Oliver decided he was content with his life. Why complicate it with a woman who said 'nothing', he told himself.

What with the work, the bottle of wine and the brandy he'd drunk to reward himself for a good night's effort, Oliver woke late and in a sorry state. Thank God it wasn't one of Grace's mornings, he thought as he pulled his bedroom curtains and was blinded by the unexpected sunshine. 'Oh, no, it's a lovely day,' he moaned, for good weather always made him feel worse, as if he was being punished further. Hangovers were best nurtured by miserable, rainy days which were in tune with the pain of the sufferer, he thought as he let Slipper out the back door.

Filling the kettle was a head-splitting effort, and when it boiled and the whistle blew, Oliver thought his head had finally broken in two.

'Do you have to make so much bloody noise?' he said angrily as he opened the back door to Slipper's scratching. 'Shut up!' he said, for he dared not shout because of what it might do to what remained of his brain. The dog, of course, took no notice of a spoken command and continued to bark, jumping up and down on the spot like a demented jack-in-the-box. 'Come in, won't you, it's bloody cold.' He held the door wide, but the dog continued to bark, and then, sure it had Oliver's attention, ran up the yard, then back, and then up again. 'Slipper, will you come in, it's cold enough to freeze the balls off a brass monkey. *Slipper.*' He ventured a yell, and immediately regretted it. In answer the dog ran to him and then back again, barking furiously all the while. 'What is it? Have you found something?' Oliver stepped back into the kitchen and across to the passageway where his Barbour hung. He slipped on his wellies, not easy with bare feet, put the jacket over his dressing gown and hoped he wouldn't bump into anybody.

'Come on then, Slipper, what is it?' he said wearily, reaching the step. Slinking across the yard, its belly almost scraping the ground in an effort to ingratiate itself, was a black dog. Slipper ran round and round it in delirious, yapping, circles.

Oliver stepped down. He looked at the dog, which averted his eyes. Its tail was hidden between its legs. Half of an ear was ripped off, there was a gash on one front leg, its hackles were up, but from fear, not aggression. Oliver took another step, his heart racing. He could barely breathe. He wanted to believe; he didn't dare. He knelt down on the cobbled yard.

'Bandage,' he said softly. 'Bandage, is it you?' He put a hand out towards the battered dog. In his daydreams Bandage, should he ever return, always came back as the dog who'd left. He should have been bounding across the yard, flinging himself at Oliver, drowning him in licks for kisses. But this dog cringed when he put his hand out. This dog hung his head as if in shame. This dog was a cur.

'Bandage. It is you, isn't it? Oh my poor old boy, who's done this to you?' Oliver was sitting now, oblivious to the cold of the damp cobbles, his hangover miraculously cured on the instant. He talked gently, softly, encouraging the dog to slink closer to him. He grabbed hold of Slipper, whose antics were not helping the progress. 'Come on, old boy. I love you.'

The dog was close enough now that if he leaned right over he could stroke him. But it cowered from his touch as if stung, leapt back and stood away from him, head down, shivering, watching warily, prepared at any moment for flight. Oliver sat there for a good half hour, patiently talking, willing the dog to trust him, to move closer. Inch by inch, he shuffled nearer to him.

Finally, from somewhere, the dog found the courage to stand close to him. Gingerly he put his hand out. The dog sniffed it and momentarily, his tail twitched. Oliver touched him, all the time talking, welcoming him, telling him how much he'd been missed, how much he was loved. Oliver ached to hug him, but knew he must be patient and do nothing to startle him.

His patience was rewarded. The dog suddenly squatted on the floor, laid his head in Oliver's lap and howled. It was a chilling sound, for the howl spoke of loneliness, fear and pain – or so Oliver thought. He threw caution to the wind and bent down and bundled the dog into his arms and hugged him tight, as if he'd never let him go. 'If I find who did this to you, Bandage, I'll kill him, I'll bloody well kill him.'

45

'What do you think, Jim?' Oliver asked anxiously. He had been watching Jim for the last ten minutes painstakingly examining Bandage, who lay patient but scared on the newspaper which Oliver had laid on the kitchen table.

'You wouldn't know it was the same dog, would you? He's had all the stuffing knocked out of him, poor old dog.' Jim patted the dog's head. Bandage wagged his tail, but tentatively, as if he wasn't sure if he should.

'He's so frightened. Bandage wasn't scared of anything – well, almost, he hated thunder and rolled-up newspapers.' Bandage licked Oliver's hand. 'Sorry, Bandage, fancy talking about you in the past tense, it won't do, will it?'

Jim stood up and stepped back, surveying his patient. 'He's lousy, you realise. He's half starved. He's weak from a combination of that and exhaustion. He's got worms. And his front leg's a bit iffy – I don't like the smell of it at all.'

'What, gangrene?' Oliver said with mounting horror. 'What about his ear?'

'That's healed. Don't worry – I think we've probably caught the leg wound in time. Even if we hadn't, dogs get around amazingly well on three legs.'

'I'd hate that.'

'Better than putting him down, though. These are old dog bites, you realise. The sore on his leg is from a deep cut – probably made by something metal, a spade perhaps. It was obviously left untreated.'

'He's been used for fighting, hasn't he?' Oliver felt sick at the idea.

'He might have been at the beginning. But not recently. He's not been up to scratch for some time. Fighting dogs are kept as fit as fleas, they have to be to fight. The odd thing about the bastards who go in for this business is that they look after their dogs. There can be a lot of money tied up in bets and challenges, so they feed them well. He's just too starved and unfit to be any use in the ring and, as we can see, he lacks aggression.'

'If they tried to make him fight he wouldn't, he's the least aggressive dog I've ever had.'

'They have ways and means, you know. They make them aggressive, teasing the poor brutes. They get their blood up throwing live cats in with them – nice friendly actions like that.'

'What on earth for?'

'To get them to taste blood, the theory being once they have they'll want more.'

'If he wouldn't fight why did they keep him so long?'

'Stud, I should think. He was, and could be again, a fine dog. He didn't need to be well fed to mate.'

'So it hasn't been all bad then, Bandage?' He smiled at the dog who, as time ticked by, was becoming more and more relaxed with them.

From his bag Jim took a pile of bottles and packages. He injected the dog with antibiotics for the wounds. He had medicated shampoo for him, flea powder and worming pills. He produced a bottle of white liquid which, he promised Oliver, could clear up the patches of eczema he had.

'Eczema? Like a human?'

'Dogs can suffer stress too. Imagine what his life has been like for the past few months – first he's stolen, and he feels lost and homesick; then he's made to do something he doesn't want to do – fight; then, it appears, he runs away to find you. A human would have had a nervous breakdown with that lot. He's going to need a lot of TLC, and you'll have to watch him with Slipper. Territory and position are all that matter to dogs. We used to think that probably all they thought about all day long was food and sex. It isn't. It's guarding their territory and thinking, "I'm top dog and how do I stay so?" or "I want to be top dog, how can I push him out of the position?"'

'Restless life. I wonder where he's been.'

'Judging by his paws, not far away. If he'd walked a long way I'd have expected to see some damage, or at least hardening of the pads, but his are fine.' Jim began to repack his bag. 'He's more than likely to have been nearer than either of us know.' He paused. 'This is strictly between us, but do you know anything about a Tom White – has a smallholding over near Connies-town? No? Well, the rumour is he might have been staging dog fights over there.'

'Here? But . . .'

'I know, you presumed it was a pastime of inner city louts? You'd be surprised.'

'Bastards!'

'My feelings exactly. Still, must get going.' Jim hauled his heavy bag off the table and Oliver saw him out.

He returned to the kitchen. 'Bath first or breakfast, Bandage? Which do you think?'

The dog sat down, ignoring Slipper, and looked up at Oliver, his tail thudding on the kitchen floor, his eyes, for the first time, showing interest in Oliver and his surroundings. But just then an RAF plane flew over low, and Bandage scampered under the table, shaking and panting loudly.

'Let's do the bath later, old friend. Let's find you something to eat, get you settled.' Oliver continued to talk to the dog as he prepared him a bowl of food.

Kimberley bumped into Nadine in the post office. She was scared and depressed at losing Bandage and she didn't really want to talk to anyone, but Nadine persisted and she found herself accepting an invitation to go back to Nadine's for coffee, from where she telephoned Eveleigh to check she did not mind her being late back.

'Why did you do that?' Nadine asked.

'It seemed the polite thing to do.'

'Right Goody Two-Shoes, aren't you?' Nadine plonked the mug of coffee and a packet of Jaffa cakes onto the table and took a bottle of milk from the fridge. 'Help yourself,' she said to Kimberley as she selected a CD to put into the slick black player at the other side of the room. What it must be like to be so rich, Kimberley thought, for she knew from previous visits that there was another player in the sitting room and Nadine had her own in her room. All she possessed was a small radio which, since it had seen better days, was getting harder to tune.

'What's that?' she asked as loud music poured into the room.

'It's Marion's latest.'

'Oh yes?' She tried to sound knowledgeable.

'They're American punk – Orange County.' Nadine rattled off, tapping her heavy Timberland boots to the noise, and moving her mouth as if she were chewing gum, even though she wasn't. Kimberley eyed the boots and wanted them, wondering if they were 'it' now and Doc Martens passé.

'Nice,' said Kimberley, not understanding what Nadine was talking about and not liking to say she preferred Country and Western herself.

Nova, who had been snoozing on Thomasine's bed, managed to find the energy to come and investigate who the visitor might be. 'I love this dog. Just look at her face, it's almost human.' She patted Nova, whose rump swayed back and forth from pleasure.

'I hate it. It's ugly. Gross!'

'She's not ugly. She's beautiful. I thought you liked animals.'

'In their place. I don't think dogs should be owned. It's undignified. It's abusive. It should be banned.'

Kimberley laughed. 'What a daft idea. And what would you do with all the dogs? Kill them?'

'Of course not.' Nadine flicked her hair back with annoyance. 'We'd allow those in ownership to die out and ban any future ownership. Breeding would stop.'

'Oh yeah, and who's going to tell the dogs that?'

'You're being thick on purpose.'

'But what would be the point?'

'The point is you'd give the animals back their dignity.'

'Not much use if they're becoming extinct.'

'And the world would be a healthier place. Do you know how much urine and faeces dogs dump each day in this country?'

'No, but I'm sure you're going to tell me,' she grinned.

'You sound just like my mother!' As Nadine scowled in response, Kimberley wondered why she was bothering with her. She had Alan now, she didn't need anyone else. Then she stopped such thoughts, feeling ashamed of them. Maybe she didn't need Nadine, but maybe Nadine needed her. There was a restlessness, a vacancy in her expression, which struck an echo from her own past. She must try and be patient with her.

'You can laugh, it's serious. Why don't you come and meet my group? We need people like you. People who care about animals.'

'But I wouldn't want dogs banned. I like dogs.' As if to confirm this she fussed over Nova.

'There's masses of other things. We demonstrate against vivisection. And fur coats, and the horses, sheep and calves shipped abroad live. And dog fighting.' She breathlessly listed the group's causes.

'Yes, you mentioned the dog fighting the other day.' She studied her nails. It still bothered her that Alan was interested, but he had asked her to find out and she'd do anything for him.

'It's definitely on. This Saturday. Why don't you come? It's going to be wild.'

'Where is it?'

'We're meeting at the crossroads outside Conniestown, you know, that village between here and Morristown.'

'I meant where's the fight?' She was aware her heartbeat had quickened.

'I don't know. We're not told things like that until the last minute – security is very tight,' she said proudly. 'It's on some smallholding or something. Don't your parents live out that way? Didn't my mum drive you there?'

'That's right, but it's not a smallholding,' she said quickly, which was true – it might have been a smallholding once, but her father had not worked it as such for ages.

'You see, you should come. You could help us, you know the area.'

'I've got a date on Saturday.'

'With Alan?'

'Yes.' Kimberley smiled; she liked to hear his name being used by others.

'You slept with him yet?'

'None of your business!' She blushed furiously.

'Then you have.' Nadine giggled. 'What's it like? Did it hurt?'

Kimberley was saved from having to answer by Thomasine appearing through the back door, laden with Sainsbury's carrier bags. Nova threw herself into an hysterical, welcoming, hurling ball of fur.

'Hullo, Kimberley. How are you?' Thomasine smiled, pleased to see the girl, hoping that if the friendship was on again her daughter might prove easier to handle.

At sight of her mother Nadine's face set again into a scowl. Kimberley offered to help with the shopping, while Nadine sprawled, rather ostentatiously, on her chair.

'Come on, Kimberley. Let's go somewhere private where we're not being spied on.'

Kimberley glanced from daughter to mother and saw Thomasine's shoulders slump. 'I've got to be getting back to work,' she said, not wishing to get involved; she liked Thomasine too much to side with her daughter.

'Please yourself,' Nadine said sulkily, but she followed Kimberley out into the garden. 'Some friend you are, siding with the enemy.'

'I think your mother's lovely. I wish she was mine.'

'You're welcome to her.'

'Oh, Nadine, you don't mean that.'

'I do. She'd rather have that bloody dog than me.'

'If you're always like this, I don't blame her,' Kimberley said sharply, quickly mounted her bicycle and pedalled away before Nadine could even think of an answer.

She pedalled furiously down the main street and when she saw her aunt outside the shop began to wave, but when she saw she was talking to Oliver the bicycle wobbled as she almost lost control.

'I didn't realise I could have that sort of effect on a beautiful young woman,' Oliver smiled at her as she stopped. Kimberley looked at him blankly, not understanding Oliver was jokingly flirting with her.

'Guess what, Kimberley, Mr Hawksmoor's dog's returned. Isn't that wonderful?'

'Really? That's good. How?' She thought she'd better add.

'Turned up in the garden this morning,' Oliver explained, and wondered why she looked so shifty.

'You must be really happy . . . Got to go.' She got back on to her bicycle.

Oliver watched her cycle away.

'Tell me, Grace, do you know a Tom White?'

'And why would you be asking?'

'The same name – that's all.'

'He's my brother-in-law,' Grace replied, tight-lipped.

'Is that so?' Oliver, having elicited this information, didn't know quite how to proceed, and wished he'd thought it out before opening his big mouth. 'Does he keep dogs?' he blurted out, thinking he'd got nothing to lose.

'I wouldn't know. Mr White and me never socialised with that side of the family,' Grace said with dignity.

'Ah, yes. Well. I see,' he replied in the time-honoured way of one who didn't see anything. They parted, Oliver to drive into Shillingham to get some extra vitamins for Bandage, and Grace to her home where she immediately picked up the phone, called the kennels and asked to speak to Kimberley.

'It's just he looked really fishy when he asked me about the dogs, Kimberley. As you know, I've not much time for your dad and what he gets up to, but when all's said and done, he is blood, and so I thought I'd best mention it.'

'Thanks,' she said, replacing the receiver. She stood leaning against the table, feeling sick.

'Not bad news?' asked Eveleigh as she walked past.

'No, nothing,' she replied. It was all too close for comfort. First there had been Eveleigh's friend telling her about dog fights near Conniestown. Then Nadine and the way she talked, it could only be her father's place. Now Mr Hawksmoor asking questions. What on earth was she to do?

46

Thomasine had to get out of the house. The atmosphere which Nadine was creating was getting her down, despite her resolution to ride the storm.

Nova was leaping up and down with excitement, yapping her high-pitched bark, which always sounded so surprising, coming from a bulldog. 'How do you know? I haven't even said W.A.L.K!' She spelled it out, and Nova hurled herself on the floor, rolled onto her back and turned round and round on the carpet, four legs flailing the air. 'You're a witch, Nova.' She bent down to clip on the lead.

She walked on the hills behind Middle Shilling. Nova enjoyed rootling in the copse, putting up a rabbit, snuffling about in the leaves, getting covered in mud. Thomasine climbed to the summit of the hill and looked down at the villages below her.

Far away beyond the church tower, beyond Badger's Wood the other side of the river, she pinpointed where Oliver's house must be. Was the smoke rising from those trees his chimney's smoke? She wished he were here. In such a short time he had become all-important to her. Thoughts of him filled her waking hours, and her sleep was dotted with dreams of him. Her body now, just thinking about him, told her of its aching longing. She might have fine thoughts of giving him up, putting duty first, as she had yesterday, but she knew she deceived herself. So much for her new-found independence, her self-sufficiency.

She knew as she stood there, the breeze whipping at her jacket, her cheeks reddening from its sharpness, that she could never let him go. Knowing this made her feel elated, full of courage, able to deal with any problems. Somehow she would work it all out; somewhere she would find the patience to deal with her daughter.

As she descended the hill these feelings of euphoria escaped her, and she imagined them fleeing back up to the top of the hill like a huge bundle of tangleweed. And the nearer the village she got, the less resolute she felt.

With Nova safely back on the lead, they trudged along the road back to The Old School House.

'If ever I saw a depressed walk, yours is it.' Oliver had pulled up beside her. 'Problem?'

'Don't even ask, I might feel impelled to tell you.' Her heart flipped wondrously at the sight of him.

'Fancy cooking me an omelette?'

'It's about time you learnt.' She looked at him, at the fullness of his lips, the laughter lines at his eyes, and longed to touch him, to curl up in bed with him, to have him inside her. Just thinking about it, she felt aroused. She moved her body almost imperceptibly from one foot to the other. He looked up at her, recognised the desire in her eyes, and touched her hand, which leant on the open car window.

'Come home with me,' he said, his voice husky.

'I can't. Look at me, look at Nova.'

'I don't mind a bit of mud.'

'You will.'

He climbed out of the car, and as he leant over to open the back door his body pressed suggestively against hers. In unison they laughed with delight, knowing what the other was thinking.

'Up you get, Nova.' Oliver helped the short-legged bulldog into the car as Thomasine climbed into the front seat.

'You seem in a good mood,' she said as he joined her.

'I wasn't when I got up. I don't like being stood up.' He looked sternly at her.

'Oliver, I said I was sorry. I just couldn't make it.'

'Don't I deserve an explanation?'

'I didn't want to bother you, it's my problem and it's so predictable, I suppose. It's my daughter – it would seem she doesn't approve of us . . .'

They sat in the car in the middle of the village while she told him about Nadine.

'You don't sound too certain how you feel.'

'It's very confusing, that's why. I love her, and yet it gets so difficult at times. I want to throttle her and then I hate myself for my reaction. One thing, though, I'm determined that she's not going to dictate how I live my life.'

'Poor kid, she must be confused too. Look at the changes in her life so far. The divorce, a new stepmother, and a pregnant one too, a new home, a new school. And now us. One would be enough.'

'She *is* seventeen,' she said with a tinge of exasperation.

'So? What difference does age make? Seven, seventeen or twenty-seven – it must still hurt like hell to watch your parents split, deal with the confusion and have to face the sort of insecurity you're left with.'

'Please don't say that, Oliver. I feel bad enough about her as it is. And to be jealous of my dog!' She shook her head, still disbelieving.

'I doubt if she really is. She's too intelligent for that. More likely she's seen you dote on Nova and to get noticed by you she pretends to hate the dog.'

'How do you know all this? You talk like a parent.'

'No, a child. It happened to me too. I was a classic case, I blamed myself for my parents' divorce. I thought it was something I'd done, that they didn't like me any more. I was left with a great gaping hole in my life and I never felt safe again. Then we drifted apart, my mother and me – I suppose I hated her for a time and she, sensing that, withdrew from me. I guess it's something you never get over totally.'

She put out her hand and touched him. 'Thanks.'

'Now let's get this show on the road. I've got a big surprise for you.'

'What? I hate surprises.'

'You'll love this one.'

Five minutes later they entered his driveway. 'Oh no! I wanted an omelette and to take you to bed – look, bloody Wimpole and hubbie, what a time to choose.'

Thomasine began to laugh, but stopped abruptly, her face draining of colour. Standing on the driveway was a large, black Mercedes with a half-remembered number plate. The 'A' on it seemed to enlarge and jump out at her, so that she closed her eyes, as if to make it stop, overwhelmed by the certainty that this was the car from which Luna had been thrown back in March. But then sense took hold and asked her how she knew, and logic pointed out she could not accuse every black car with an 'A' in the number. But she hadn't, that was the point; in all those months she'd never once thought she had seen the car. Not until today.

Thomasine took a deep breath – so what if intuition thought this was the car? What could she do about it? Who'd believe her? And, in any case, did she want to mention it to Oliver? No. It would not be a good idea, he loved Wimpole. She might be driving a wedge between Oliver and his old nanny if she told him her suspicions.

'You all right, you've gone pale?'

'It's nothing,' she smiled wanly. There's that bloody word again, he thought as he opened the front door for her.

Wimpole appeared in the hall at the sound of their entry.

'What a happy day, Oliver. The vet was over to see one of Ben's nags and he told us. See, I always told you that old mutt would find you again. You can't keep a good dog down, don't they say?' She whooped with pleasure as she stood on tiptoe to kiss him. 'And Thomasine too, there's a nice surprise,' she said archly. They entered the kitchen, Thomasine and Nova last.

Nova, upon smelling dog, raced in front of Thomasine, but no sooner had she entered the kitchen than she stopped abruptly, skidding on the tiles. She stood rigid a second, then turned and cowered behind Thomasine's legs.

Rudolph was sitting at the kitchen table, a mug of coffee in front of him, grinning broadly at Bandage, who was standing in the corner of the room facing the wall, his tail curved between his legs, his flanks shaking.

'Look at that silly bugger.' He pointed at Bandage and laughed as he did so.

'What did you do to him?' Oliver demanded.

'Me? I ain't done nothing.'

'You must have. Just look at the poor creature.' Oliver looked angry.

'He just pissed off into the corner and sulked.' Rudolph looked put out, but more by Oliver's reaction than the dog's. He stood up and crossed to the kitchen sink. From beneath the kitchen table came a low growl. They all looked down – Slipper lay, head between her forepaws, teeth displayed, her body taut as if prepared for fight or flight.

'Bandage wasn't there when I was in here,' Wimpole said, looking anxiously from Oliver to her husband and back again. 'Oh, shut up, Slipper, do!'

'Bandage only does that when he's upset.' Oliver stalked across the kitchen to his dog and hunched down beside him. He began to stroke him, talking softly. The trembling stopped, his tail switched a minute degree.

Rudolph remained standing at the sink, staring impassively out of the kitchen window as if the whole business was of no interest to him. Thomasine stared at his back, willing him to turn and look at her, hoping she would be able to read in his eyes that it was he who had thrown Luna into the road.

Slowly Oliver coaxed the dog further into the room. Bandage walked stealthily, lifting one paw into the air and pausing, glancing nervously about him, before placing it down on the floor again. His ears were pinned back, his lips slightly curled up over his teeth in a rigid grimace. But at each step his confidence appeared to grow until he was in the middle of the room – and then Rudolph turned from the window and looked at him with an expression of distaste. The dog barked once, a high, frightened, sharp bark, and dived under the table and curled up, making himself as small as possible beside Slipper, who jumped to her feet and stood guard, her hackles up and growling louder – a slow, deep, rumbling growl.

'It would appear that my dogs don't like you very much, Rudie,' Oliver said, and Thomasine hoped he never had cause to speak to her like that, his tone was so chilling.

'Rudolph loves dogs,' Wimpole said staunchly.

'Quite honestly, Wimpole, I think it would be better for the dogs if Rudolph waited for you outside in the car.'

'Well, really, Oliver. Can't the dogs wait outside?'

'No. I don't want Bandage frightened further and Rudolph's obviously upsetting him.'

'Don't let my presence interfere with such an important dog. Bloody hell, whatever next,' Rudolph said, and without any farewells, he stamped from the room, which made the dogs jump.

'I never thought I'd hear you of all people being so rude, Oliver. You don't know where he's been, what's happened to him to make him like that. It's not Rudolph's fault.' She sounded angrily defensive.

'Look at him now.' Bandage had wriggled out from under the table on his stomach. He stood up and was busily sniffing at Wimpole's feet, his tail wagging and, reassured, moved on to Thomasine, his tail waving back and forth like a metronome, his hackles down, his face relaxed. He, Nova and Slipper had a good introductory sniff. 'See, he's not afraid of anyone else. But he was frightened witless when we came in. Odd, isn't it, that he was only afraid when Rudolph was present?'

'I don't think I like what you're implying, Oliver.'

'And I don't like what I'm thinking.'

Wimpole was looking with a concentrated expression at the floor, and Thomasine realised she had not seen her look anyone in the eye since they had entered the kitchen.

'What's going on, Wimpole?' Oliver asked in a gentle voice. 'Tell me.'

'I don't know what you're wittering on about.'

'I think you do, Wimpole,' he said, even softer.

'I'd better go.'

'If you change your mind – if you think you can talk – phone, I'll come and collect you.'

'I shouldn't hold your breath, then,' Wimpole replied, sounding sassy even though she looked oddly dejected. She slammed the door as she left.

'What on earth was that about?' Thomasine asked as she sat on a chair, as aware as the dogs that the atmosphere in the room had completely changed.

'Thomasine, it might sound daft, but I trust my dogs' judgement where people are concerned. Bandage here has never been wrong once. If he doesn't like someone, sooner or later they turn out to be duff. He never liked Rudie, for sure, but he didn't behave like this. What we've just witnessed in Bandage was sheer terror. Why? Has he been involved with Bandage's disappearance? Is he involved in the fighting . . .'

'I wonder . . .' she began, and debated whether to tell him about Rudolph's car, but decided not to. She'd no evidence, it wouldn't be fair. 'Still, Bandage is back, and you must be so happy,' she said instead. 'Will it put Slipper's nose out of joint?'

'Jim said to watch them. It might have been more difficult if she was a dog, but as a bitch – oh, I'm sure she'll be happy to cede him the position of pack leader. As it should be.' He was grinning now.

'So long as only dogs stay such male chauvinists.'

He grabbed hold of her and pulled her onto his lap. 'Don't you want me to dominate you? Lord it over you? Be brutal with you?'

'No thanks. Just equals suits me fine.' She laughed, happy that his mood had changed.

'Thank God for that; being macho is an exhausting occupation.'

They made love, not in bed as he had planned, but in the Great Hall, where he had lit the fire. They never got round to having the omelette.

'Alan? Jim Varley here. Thought I'd better report to you an odd thing. Do you know Oliver Hawksmoor? No? Well, it's by the by, but his dog, which has been missing for at least nine months, turned up this morning. Bull terrier, scars all over it, undernourished. It's been used for fighting or I'll eat my hat.'

'Any clues to where it's been?'

'No, except not far. His paws were in too good a condition for a marathon hike.'

'Thanks. Mr Varley, we might be needing you. We're sure now that there's a dog fight on Saturday evening.'

'Saturday you say? I'll keep that free then – for the wounded. Bit like *Casualty*, isn't it?' He replaced the receiver and turned round to find Beth standing at the bottom of the stairs, a sullen-faced Harry behind her.

'Hullo. You made me jump,' he said, feeling gauche. Had she overheard him? Still, the conversation would have meant nothing to her. This was it, he told himself, now. Do it – say it.

'Jim, I'm leaving.' Beth announced calmly.

'I don't want to go! Uncle Jim, stop her,' Harry wailed, and kicked at his mother, clipping her shin.

'You little bastard.' She swung round and pushed Harry back towards the stairs. 'Now shut up!'

'Look, Beth, don't carry on like this. We made a mistake . . .'

'No, you're wrong there, Jim. I made the mistake – I thought you were a gentleman, but you're as big a lying pig as the rest of them.'

'I've not lied to you. Not as you've lied to me.'

'Oh yes, and what does that mean?'

He paused, thinking what was the point, and then an image of Castille's fever-racked body flashed in front of him. 'The husband that doesn't exist, for one.'

She looked away from him for a split second, as if collecting her thoughts. 'I don't know what you mean,' she said.

'Why did you tell me that sob story – was it to soften me up? Were you scared I was angry with you and wanting me to feel sorry for you? Well, I did – more fool me. But it was a trap that didn't work, did it – come the end.'

'A trap? Me trap you? What for? Half the time you stink of animals and disinfectant – it gives me the shudders. And you're boring, Jim Varley, so bloody boring – in and out of bed,' she finished on a spiteful but triumphant note.

The doorbell rang.

'That's for me.' She pushed past him.

Ben Luckett stood on the doorstep.

'Hi, Ben. Can I help you?' Jim stepped forward, trying a smile on for size.

'Come to pick the little lady up,' Ben said over-heartily. 'Cora felt too embarrassed to come.'

'Sorry?' Jim said, nonplussed.

'Didn't she say? Oh, Beth's coming to work for us. Cora and she arranged it.'

'I didn't even know Beth knew you.'

'Yes, she's been coming to the house for yonks doing those dead flower thingummy-bobs. She burst into tears, told Cora what had happened, and here we are – we're taking her on. Cora's a bit ruffled about it, bit anti you – you know, female solidarity, that sort of crap. I can't say I blame you.'

Jim opened his mouth to defend himself, but shut it again.

'I'll give her a hand with her bags,' he said instead.

It was harder saying goodbye to Harry than he had realised it would be. He hugged the boy close and wiped Harry's damp face with his own hanky. 'I'll still see you, Harry – we'll work something out.'

'It won't be the same.'

'Harry, get into this Range Rover, now,' Beth ordered, thin-lipped with spite. Had he done this to her? The new job had certainly given her the confidence to show exactly what she thought of him.

The sound of the phone ringing gave him the perfect excuse to slip away. A cow with a prolapsed uterus, just the thing to get him out of the lonely house for the evening, and to keep his mind off his confused feelings of guilt.

47

On Saturday morning, Kimberley's face was wan from sleeplessness. Tossing and turning through the night hours had given her no solution to her problems. When she saw Alan this evening, what would she do? She could imagine herself confessing to him about her father, but would he be glad, want to meet him, become involved in the fighting? Or was it a front, and would he be disgusted with her for not acting sooner? Which was the real Alan? If he wanted to see the dogs fight, would she feel the same about him?

Eveleigh called her from the yard to the telephone.

'Kim, love, I'm sorry. I can't see you this evening, something's come up,' she heard Alan say.

The long 'oh' with which she responded was full of suspicion. Alan felt a heel; he knew how insecure she was and he loathed to hurt her.

'I wouldn't have done this in a million years – I wanted to see you so badly.'

His voice was sincere, and gave her the courage to ask what had come up.

'Work. I've got to work this evening.'

'Come round when you've finished.'

'I might be at it half the night.'

'Half the night?' The suspicion deepened.

'It's God's honest truth.' He paused a moment. 'Have you seen Nadine?'

'Yes.' Her heart felt as if it would burst.

'Did she tell you – you know – '

'What?' Her mouth was dry.

'Where her lot are meeting on Saturday.'

This was her chance, she could tell him now, all her fears, she could share them, make things better for herself.

'No, she didn't say,' she finally said. How could she tell a living soul her father's dreadful secret?

'Ah, well. I'll see you tomorrow.'

'Fine. Take care.' She hung onto the receiver, loath to lose contact with him, but also worried at how he kept on about Nadine. Why?

Alan was standing in front of the blackboards at Morristown Police Headquarters. He'd drawn the layout of Primrose Acre on one board. Maps of the region were pinned on the other. The room was crowded with members of the RSPCA as well as police.

He was edgy. He wasn't too happy at the lack of surveillance and knew the others would rapidly be agreeing with him.

'As you can see, given the exposed nature of the property, we've had to use these Ordnance Survey maps rather than staking it out. Using binoculars, we're pretty sure these outhouses are all there is. And this one – ' Alan used the wooden pointer ' – this long shed is the closest to the Walters' farm, the most likely place for the noise to have come from, so we think that's where the fight will be.'

'Why is the surveillance so poor?' one of the senior policemen demanded.

'Lack of time.'

'Then if it's so iffy, why don't we leave the raid this time? Use Saturday night to suss it out, take the car numbers, identify the punters and go in next time?' the same police inspector asked.

'There might not be a next time,' Alan's Chief Inspector patiently explained. 'These rings are not run by amateurs, you know. Their security is top notch. They only release the venue of the fight to their followers at the last possible moment. They're invariably one step ahead of us.'

'How do you know it's here?'

'We don't.'

'Then what the hell is all this laid on for?' the police inspector said in exasperation, looking round the crowded room.

'We've had odd rumours of dog fighting hereabouts for over a year. It started in a small way – garages, back rooms, that sort of thing – but then it got bigger. They got wind of us some time back and packed up for months – moved up to the Midlands, we think. We want, obviously, to catch as many as possible. As you know, it's an offence to attend a fight, let alone organise one. Our mole reckoned that a really big one, with punters coming from as far away as London and the Midlands, with big money involved, was about to take place. He didn't know where, just that it was soon. We'd suspicions about a couple of places, and then young Alan here got wind of Primrose Acre.' To Alan's acute embarrassment everyone looked at him.

'And who's your informant?'

'This is Alan's show,' Don said, waving his hand, deferring to Alan.

'I haven't met him, sir. But from his voice I'd say he's a young chap. My theory is he attended a fight once, hated it, and contacted us. The trouble is, whoever he is, he's pretty lowly in the hierarchy, so that although he knows when there's to be a fight, he's not one who's privy to it until the last minute. He sounds scared, really scared, and, unfortunately, this last call he sounded ratty with us, like he was ready to give up. Also, one of the local vets got onto us. A bull terrier which had been missing for months returned home: in his opinion it had been used for fighting, and in this vicinity. I have also been informed that the Freedom for All Animals brigade are on to something this weekend.'

'Oh bugger me – not that lot.'

'I'd hoped I might find out where they're meeting – to stop them. But unfortunately I haven't.'

'It's mad not having cased the farm. Surely you could have done more?'

'Not really.' Alan realised, from the attitude of this particular policeman, who would be blamed if it all went wrong. 'I drove around and walked a bit, but as you can see from this plan, it's impossible to size it up properly, the house is too exposed. It's ideal for their purposes, however. Flat fields surround it, you can see any cars on the road from the house, and no one could approach without being seen. Their lookouts will have it easy.'

'I think you should go in, Bob.' The Chief Superintendent, who had been quietly listening, stood up. They were in luck; unbeknown to them, this policeman bred boxers as a hobby. 'We don't want to prolong the dogs' suffering, do we?'

At these words from his senior officer, the police inspector acquiesced, even though he muttered to himself. The wheels were in motion, a search warrant application was being made, they had the necessary police back-up. The two teams would work in unison. They were almost home and dry.

When darkness fell they climbed into the horsebox, which they often used like a Trojan Horse on country operations. For who, in the country, would give a horsebox a second glance? Inside the vehicle the tension and excitement was relieved by some pretty lame jokes.

Alan had visited the Walters that morning, and persuaded them to allow their yard to be used as an ops centre. He assured them he'd learnt from sources other than Jim that Primrose Acre was involved. Chris and Fee had, as requested, pulled the curtains of the farmhouse. The yard light was out and their dogs firmly locked inside the house. One by one the men climbed out of the horsebox and moved across the ploughed field, hidden by the night, keeping to the cover of the hedgerows. Without incident they took up their pre-arranged positions and settled down to wait.

Alan peered about him in the darkness. It was perfect. It was a moonless night, and he could barely see Andy in position just twelve feet away from him. The whole smallholding was completely ringed by men. But he felt sick with worry. All this organisation, men and overtime, and if no one turned up, he'd be to blame, he was sure of that.

Kimberley paced up and down her room. Her agitation was twofold now. To the worry of what was possibly about to happen to her father, and Nadine's friends on their raid, was added the fear that Alan had met someone else, someone he preferred to her. Why else, after all he had said, would he cancel their date?

She couldn't cope with this burden of worry, which increased rather than diminished as time ticked by. She kissed goodbye to the St Bernards she'd moved, for safety, into her sitting room. She did not want to bother Eveleigh by telling her she was going out, and so she slipped unnoticed into the yard and pushed her bicycle to the road. In her haste, confused with her concerns, she had forgotten the light was broken. She wondered whether to turn back, but decided it did not matter; she knew the roads well, and there would be little traffic at night.

Despite Oliver's understanding attitude, inspiring Thomasine yesterday to try again and be more patient with her daughter, they had had another momentous row. She could not even remember what had triggered this one; they all seemed to be melting into one. The upshot was the same though: they were not speaking to each other. Thomasine decided that rather than risk being rebuffed if she tried to say goodbye, she would leave a note on the kitchen table to explain she was dining at Oliver's.

Nadine, skulking in her room, smiled to herself as she heard her mother's car leave. At least she needn't creep out now. Dressed from head to toe in black, her hair stuffed up under a black beret and with black sunglasses on, she paused in front of the mirror and admired how like an SAS soldier she looked. In the kitchen she raided the tea caddy where her mother kept spare cash, just in case she needed it. Soon she was on her bicycle, pedalling furiously towards her rendezvous with the other members of Freedom for All Animals. She was excited, not just because they were about to go into action, but also at the prospect of meeting new people, amongst whom might be someone who would like her, perhaps even love her.

Jim was at Oliver's when Thomasine arrived. Worried about the wound on Bandage's leg, he'd decided to call in to check it out.

'I think he'll be all right, Oliver. We caught the wound in time. I'll give him another shot. I must say, he looks better for his bath.' He patted Bandage.

'Smart rascal, aren't you?' Bandage responded to the fuss, tail wagging and gently head-butting Jim's leg. 'He's a great deal more relaxed. Looks as if he's going to trust us after all. Maybe it won't be the long haul I feared.'

'I was afraid he'd need *counselling*, like the rest of the world,' Oliver smiled. 'Stay for supper,' he invited reluctantly.

'No thanks. You don't need me around,' he teased. 'In any case, I've a dinner appointment at Eveleigh's.'

'Good on you. Seeing a lot of her, aren't you?' It was Oliver's turn to tease.

'Not that much,' Jim said, puzzled, as Oliver showed him to the door.

'See you tomorrow?'

'Maybe, I'm not making any promises. There's . . .' He stopped abruptly, remembering in time to be discreet. 'I might be very busy tonight and tomorrow, I'm expecting a load of casualties. I'd best be off,' he mumbled, and virtually bolted out of the door.

Oliver looked thoughtful as he returned to the kitchen, where Thomasine was cooking their dinner. He replenished his and Thomasine's drinks. Something devious was afoot. How could he know in advance he was going to have a load of casualties, unless . . . 'Here you are, sweetheart.' He handed the glass to Thomasine.

An hour later they got the closest they'd ever been to a row when he pushed his plate away, barely touched.

'What's the matter, don't you like it?'

'I'm not hungry.'

'You've barely spoken. I feel like the hired help, and a not very successful one at that.' She took his plate and threw his food into the trash can noisily, marking her displeasure.

'I'm sorry, Thomasine. It's just there's something at the back of my mind I can't shake off. Jim triggered it. He said he was expecting loads of casualties. How could he possibly know?'

'Perhaps he's psychic – ' She began to laugh and stopped. 'Nadine!' she said, clutching at her throat. 'Oh my God, what's she up to? She's been too secretive lately – more so than usual. She gets odd calls and never says who from. And that FAA business bothers me. What's there around here, any laboratories?'

'Not that I know of. I did wonder, what with Bandage and odd things Jim's let slip, if there was an illegal fight planned, something like that.'

'That's just the sort of thing they'd go for. Oh my God!'

'Give her a bell. Check she's safe.'

Thomasine's heart began to thud with foreboding as she listened to her telephone ringing and ringing unanswered. 'She's not there,' she said bleakly. 'Did Jim tell you where?'

'No. But the other day he was asking me about a Tom White, who lives over near some friends of mine – he asked if I knew him. I don't. But I asked Grace and she was very offhand. You don't think-?'

'At Primrose Acre? Kimberley's dad?' Thomasine's face was ashen. She grabbed at Oliver's sleeve. 'I've got to go there. He's dangerous, he threatened us with a gun. Oh my God, she could be killed!'

'I'll come with you. Leave Nova here with my two dogs. I'll get my torch,' he said, and wished he had a gun.

Nadine's legs felt like jelly by the time she reached the crossroads for Conniestown and a small waiting group of people. She might be only seventeen, but she was not particularly fit, for exercise and organised games were of no interest to her.

No one leapt forward to welcome her – not like the other groups she'd been with. Nor did she see the friendly faces of the middle-aged and elderly women, along with the gentle hippies, who had been so in evidence when she had been demonstrating against the export of live sheep and calves. This lot looked rough and aggressive. Like her, they were dressed in black from head to toe, but they wore leather and heavy buckled boots she'd die for. She smiled at them, but there was no response. She was already keyed up for the attack, it didn't help to find she was beginning to feel nervous of the others. She laid down her bicycle in the ditch.

'When do we get going?' she asked the man standing beside her in as friendly a tone as she could muster.

'I dunno,' he answered, flicking the blade of a Stanley knife open and shut menacingly as he did so.

'Seen Cracker Barrel around?'

'Don't be bleeding wet.'

'It's cold, isn't it?' she said to the man on her other side, hugging herself and jumping up and down.

'What did you fucking well expect?'

'Sorry I spoke,' she said, a spurt of anger at his rudeness giving her momentary courage. If it had not been too juvenile, she would have liked to poke her tongue out at him.

'You didn't say nothing about birds coming along, Gr – '

'Shut your bleeding mouth. No names, get it!' His lips were pink against the black of his knitted balaclava. Those and his brown eyes were all that were visible. 'She's got the camcorder, nitwit. We need her.'

Nadine stayed silent. Her stomach felt as if it was turning to water – she'd completely forgotten to bring the video camera. She decided to say nothing, it might be safer, her lapse would not endear her to them. She'd think up some excuse later. If there was a fight, and looking at this lot she thought it more likely, she could say it got broken.

48

'It's just along here.' Thomasine leant forward in her seat, peering into the deep darkness for the turning. 'Look there, see the lights.' She pointed excitedly over the fields.

'Shit! Stupid sod, no lights,' Oliver cursed as he swung the car violently to the right to overtake a cyclist. Ahead of him a minibus, without signalling, swung across the road, entered a driveway. It was going far too fast to turn and so it rocked dangerously. Oliver stood on his brakes. 'That driver's insane. We'll let it go.'

'But, Oliver, we don't have time.'

'You won't be much help to her dead, will you? A minute won't make much difference.' He spoke sharply, not cross with her, but with the lunatic driver ahead. As he stopped the car the cyclist with no lights overtook them and, also making no signals, turned into the same lane.

'Psst, Alan. Something's coming.'

The minibus hurtled at full throttle up the rutted drive, the passengers bouncing about like corks in a barrel. Nadine, lighter than the men, was thrown all ways until her head banged on the metal roof and she slumped back onto the seat, lights flashing before her eyes. She moaned, but the men were too excited to take any notice of her. She rubbed her head, beginning to wish she hadn't come, wishing she was at home with her mother. Seeing the coshes and the knuckledusters appearing in the hands of the others, she started to feel seriously afraid.

The members of the RSPCA and their police companions bent double as they raced across the furrowed field. Adrenalin flooding their systems made them move faster and be more alert. At the same time as the minibus juddered to a halt, the doors crashed open and the demonstrators tumbled out, they ran almost silently into the yard.

There was no point in stealth now. The demonstrators, swinging round, had seen them; knives, clubs and cans of mace were raised menacingly as, with an unholy roar, rage blinding them to the policemen's uniforms, they hurled themselves into action. There was the sickening sound of flesh meeting flesh, animal-like grunts, thuds as some fell onto the cobbles.

'Police!' a voice shouted, but no one took notice as the fight continued. Nadine stood, frozen with fear, in the doorway of the bus, and sharply stepped back.

'Alan, the shed! Over there – second along!' Above the racket he heard Andy yell.

Oliver's car screeched to a halt. At the sight of the mêlée he was out of his car in a flash, Thomasine beside him.

'Christ, women too! You cruel bitch!' screamed a man as he hurtled towards Thomasine. 'Call yourself a fucking woman!' Oliver jumped between them, his arms up, his body swaying in front of a terrified Thomasine. The man continued to run towards them. Oliver, fist clenched, swung his right arm and hit him square on the jaw. He sprawled at their feet. Oliver looked at his fist with astonishment, as if the hand, unaided by him, had done the dirty work.

Alan and the others in his team were running towards the shed. Alan grabbed hold of the door catch, pulled with all his might as the others raced past him into the darkened interior. A flashlight swept the walls. Andy flicked on the lights.

They stood rooted to the spot. The shed was empty.

There were no dogs. No spectators. No blood. No gore. No pain.

A few bales of straw were piled one on top of the other in tiers which might have been for spectators to sit on, but might also have been only a straw store.

'Shit! Shit! Shit!' Alan banged one huge fist into the palm of the other. 'He was tipped off. But how? By whom?'

He felt washed with despair at the failure of their efforts. The adrenalin was still pumping, flowing through his body, and the flight-or-fight surge was rapidly converted into anger, made worse by frustration at the outcome.

As one, he and his colleagues swung out into the yard. The fighting had ceased; a semblance of order was returning. The police had begun to take control of the demonstrators, who were now identified for what they were, and not participants in any dog fight.

Tom White stood on his doorstep, a smile on his face – a smile Alan longed to wipe off once and for all. 'Nothing there, sir,' Alan reported to his Chief Inspector. 'They must have been warned.'

'Get him. Arrest that bastard!' The man Oliver had knocked down was back on his feet. He waved a fist at Tom White, threatening. 'He has fighting dogs. I've seen them. I've seen him train them. There must be proof – some sign in there.'

'It's no use,' said Alan, almost certain that here was the informer, but for the man's safety he said nothing. 'We have to catch them with the dog fight in progress. The floor could be covered in canine blood, it wouldn't do us any good.'

Tom White stood impassive, his wife hovering behind him, the irritating smile still on his face.

'The puppies. He's a puppy farmer. You should see the conditions. This way.' The young man turned on his heel, the others followed. They opened the door of the second barn. The stench made them reel back. They covered their mouths with their hands.

'Where's the bloody light?' a voice called out.

'Gentlemen, let me be of assistance.' Tom White calmly walked through them and switched on the light.

The pens were in place, the cages piled one on top of the other. Of the dogs and puppies there was no sign.

'As you can see, I used to do a bit of breeding – no great amount. Puppy farming!' Tom snorted. 'What gave you that idea?' He laughed. 'I gave it up ages ago – not a good enough earner.' He smiled again, and Alan was not alone in wanting to hit him – hard.

From outside came a commotion. Oliver was angrily explaining, or trying to explain, that he was not interested in dog fights and never had been, and they had no right to arrest him, to a police constable who was more interested in picking his teeth than listening to Oliver's pleas.

'Please, will somebody listen. We were looking for my daughter,' Thomasine was nearly in tears from a combination of fear and frustration. 'Her name's Nadine.'

'I know Nadine.' Alan stepped forward.

'Is anyone a doctor?' a voice called from the darkness. 'There's an unconscious girl over here.'

'Nadine!' Thomasine cried, and was swept along by the others towards the bus.

Nadine was lying half in and half out of the bus. A police constable was slapping her hands, trying to rouse her. She groaned. Thomasine was quickly at her side. Slowly Nadine sat up, rubbing her head, looking around her with an exaggeratedly puzzled expression.

'What happened?' she said weakly. 'Where am I?'

'You were knocked unconscious,' the policeman explained.

'We must call an ambulance.' Thomasine looked about anxiously.

'Mum! What are you doing here?' Nadine spoke in a normal voice. But then, as if suddenly remembering, she put her hand back on her head and groaned again. 'Did we get them?' she asked, a pathetic catch in her voice.

Oliver, released by the police, watched her closely and wondered.

'Were you unconscious?' Thomasine asked anxiously.

'I don't know. I think I might have been.' Nadine looked away from her.

'You all right, Ruskie?' One of the demonstrators stepped forward.

'Cracker Barrel? Did we get them?'

'Nah. Bugger all here.'

'Oh no!' Nadine began to cry. She cried from pent-up fear, from disappointment, from all the confusion which beset her. She felt something trickle on her forehead. She brushed at it and looked at her hand. 'I'm bleeding!'

Thomasine dabbed at the blood.

'Let me. We're trained in first aid.' One of the policemen knelt down and looked at her head with the beam of his torch. 'I think it's only superficial – head wounds always bleed, they look far worse than they are, but I think we should radio for an ambulance.'

'I'll drive her, it'll be faster.' Oliver stepped forward.

'Mum, I'm scared.'

'She's under arrest.'

'Please, Officer.' Thomasine looked at the senior policeman with appeal.

'It would seem there have been some crossed wires here. We all had the same goal, even if your daughter and her friends went about it in the wrong way. Best get her seen to.'

Oliver picked Nadine up and carried her to his car, Thomasine in hot pursuit. The group around the minibus began to break up.

'I wish I could get my hands on the bastards who warned him. I'd kill them,' Andy muttered as they walked back towards the horsebox.

'Me too,' said Alan, falling into step beside him and suddenly feeling exhausted. A slight figure materialised from the shadow of the barn.

'Alan!'

'Kimberley. What on earth?' His face lit up with pleasure at the sight of her.

'Hullo, Kimberley. Long time no see.'

'Greaser?'

'I've been waiting to get your old man for ages – bastard!' He spat onto the ground with distaste. 'Ginger's here too.'

'Your father?' Alan looked at her with horror. 'Tom White's your father?' He stepped back from her – he had to, for fear he might hit her if he stepped towards her. What a fool he'd been! Of course it all fitted in now – the dog she'd rescued, her name. He'd allowed love to deaden reason. 'I thought you felt like me. That you loved animals too.'

'Alan, I do. What have I done?' She stepped forward, putting her hand out to touch him.

'Done? You've let that creep, your father, get away with murder. You warned him – it had to be you!' And Alan pushed her away from him and, feeling his heart was breaking, stalked off into the night.

The Casualty Officer insisted Nadine was kept in hospital overnight, a routine measure for cases of mild concussion, they reassured Thomasine. The cut on her head was superficial and required no stitches, only a plaster.

On the drive back Oliver said little, giving Thomasine time to think. She was shocked at how easily her equilibrium had taken a knock. How could she have thought she would forge ahead with her life, that Nadine would have to put up with it or go back to her father? It was impossible to separate oneself from one's child so simply. Nadine was part of her and always would be. Nadine could have died if things had been worse at Primrose Acre, and they would not even have said goodbye. Then how much happiness could she have had, with that legacy of guilt and pain?

Oliver drove the car into the driveway of Bishop's End. 'The dogs must think we've deserted them. Poor old things,' Oliver said as he unlocked the door and they heard the barking and scrabbling from the kitchen. 'Poor Thomasine, you look done in.'

'I am tired,' she said wearily, pushing back her hair from her face with a gesture which implied it was almost too much effort.

'Have a brandy.'

'No, I'd better not get too comfortable or I won't want to go.'

'Then don't,' he said softly. They opened the kitchen door and allowed the three dogs to welcome them back enthusiastically. Oliver put his arm about her. 'Stay here tonight.'

'I could, couldn't I? Even my dog's here,' she smiled through her exhaustion. How often she'd wished she could sleep with him for a whole night, wake in the morning to feel him close beside her. It hadn't been possible with Nadine at home, a Nadine who monitored her movements with the moral severity of a nun. And now she was so tired that the idea of making love was the last thing she wanted.

'Just to sleep, curled up like spoons. What do you think? You're too tired for anything else.' He kissed her cheek gently. She looked at him tenderly.

'It's almost as if you know what I'm thinking.'

'I wish I did – then I'd know.'

'Know what?'

He stroked her hair and leant his head against hers, and when he spoke it was so muffled that she told him she had not caught what he said.

'I'm frightened you might have made a bargain with God.' He looked at the floor as he spoke, as if afraid of what response he might see in her eyes. 'You know, before you knew that Nadine was all right, you might have promised God to ditch me if He saved her. And now you feel you're stuck with it.'

Thomasine clasped her hand over her mouth and looked at him with horror-filled eyes. 'What have I said?' he asked anxiously.

'The truth.' She sighed. 'Only, oh God, I'm so ashamed of myself, I couldn't do it! I reckoned I should. *Please God, if you let Nadine live I'll give up Oliver.* It was so simple, but when it came to it, I couldn't make the promise. I couldn't face losing you! I feel dreadful about it. What sort of mother am I?' And what must you think of me, she thought, but did not say it, afraid what his answer might be.

Gently he cradled her face in his hands and stood looking at her for what seemed an age.

'I love you, Thomasine. Like I've never loved anyone before. When I'm free – will you marry me?'

On top of everything else this was almost too much for Thomasine, who felt she was about to cry from happiness. 'Oh, please,' she said in a whisper, which wasn't exactly what she had intended; they were not the words she had practised, those times she'd fantasised when alone in bed and waiting for sleep.

'Oh, my darling, I'm sorry. You've had a bastard of a night and then I'm so stupid, I spring this on you.'

Afraid he hadn't heard her correctly, she pulled herself together with a shake of the head. 'I couldn't think of anyone I'd rather spend the rest of my life with,' she said, which she thought sounded a lot better. Evidently Oliver did too, for he hugged her so tight, as if afraid she was about to escape from him. Miraculously, Thomasine found that all her exhaustion had disappeared in a flash, and sleep was the last thing on her mind.

The dawn was fast approaching when, snuggled close in the crook of his arm, squashed close together in the narrow space that three deeply sleeping dogs occupying the rest of the bed allowed, he whispered in her ear. 'If you had made a promise to God, what would you have given up?'

She giggled. 'Don't be shocked. I did make a bargain – not much of one, but other than you, it was the only thing I could think of giving up which I didn't want to. Gin!' she replied.

Kimberley had hardly slept. Her pillow was damp from tears. She felt bereft, empty. She saw her dreams fading, as insubstantial as the morning mist. She cuddled up to Sieglinde, whose large head with its tender expression rose from the pillow they shared. With hooded eyes she looked at Kimberley, and then her long, pink tongue appeared and licked her face, as if licking her tears away.

'Sieglinde, what am I to do?' She nuzzled the ruff of hair at the dog's neck, the softest part of her, and drew comfort from the closeness and warmth of the huge dog.

If everyone believed as Alan did, that she had warned her father, how long could she expect to keep this job? How could she expect Eveleigh, with her passion for dogs, to retain her with suspicion like that hanging over her? And as if losing Alan wasn't enough, she would lose Nadine too – another one with passionate views about dogs. Alan, Nadine, Eveleigh, the dogs, it would be too much – she might just as well be dead.

Everything was so unfair. Last night her father, thinking her one of the demonstrators, had slapped her face so hard her head had rocked back and forth on her neck. He had accused her of informing on him and would not believe that she hadn't. Worse, her mother agreed with him and hit her too, and spat at her, telling her she never wanted to see her again.

Damp from her own tears, squashed by the huge dogs, Kimberley gave up. She might just as well be up and working as lying here feeling sorry for herself. If she was doing something, then maybe she could put her misery aside, if only for the time being.

Eveleigh found her scrubbing out the kennels. Not the normal daily cleaning, when the runs were sluiced and the kennels mopped, but on her knees with a scrubbing brush, frantically attacking every inch, the scent of disinfectant heavy in the air.

'My dear Kimberley, what are you doing?' Eveleigh stepped back with horror when Kimberley looked up at her, and she saw her swollen, discoloured face. 'Oh, my poor child, who's done this to you? Let me help.' She put out her hand and Kimberley grabbed at it. Eveleigh helped pull her to her feet. 'I think we've got to talk.'

'The dogs' feeds,' Kimberley said, with difficulty through swollen lips, stuttering her words between sobs, which Eveleigh's concern had reactivated.

'They can wait. It won't hurt them, just this once.' Eveleigh led Kimberley into the kitchen. She sat her down on a chair and, before asking her to explain anything, collected a bowl of warm water, cotton-wool balls and some witch-hazel. 'Such a pretty face,' she tutted as she worked, bathing the girl gently, soothing the bruises. Then she made a pot of tea and, despite the hour, added a large tot of whisky to it. 'Peps you up fast,' she explained to a doubtful Kimberley. 'Soothes the hurt inside. Now, I want to know, Kimberley. Did Alan do this to you?'

'Oh no. Not Alan. It was my father . . .'

Eveleigh sat silent as Kimberley, at first with difficulty, but eventually in a torrent of words, told of her father, the dogs, the puppies, her shame, and finally explained the events of the previous evening. 'I went there . . . I'm not even sure why . . . And Alan blames me . . .' Her voice finally trailed off, the sorry tale told.

Eveleigh sat for a moment looking with rapt attention at her hands, as if they held the key. Kimberley slumped in the chair, exhausted now, docilely awaiting her fate.

'I've never heard such a load of codswallop in my life! What a dreadful situation. The choices you faced would've taxed anyone! Look at the number of wives and mothers who know their man is a rapist or murderer, and can't bring themselves to phone the police. It's the same sort of dilemma.'

Kimberley managed a wan smile at the way Eveleigh equated murder with cruelty to dogs. She would, she thought.

'But I knew about his activities and I eventually knew they were wrong – the puppy farming, the dog fighting – and I did nothing. I'm guilty by association. I should have stopped him.'

'How? You were a child. Just one look at your face shows what a violent person you were having to deal with. As soon as you could escape, you did.'

'Yes, but I left the animals to their fate.'

'I don't think you could be expected to shop your own father.'

'But it's not as if I loved him.'

'Perhaps not, but one has a sense of duty, even if misplaced. And the poor dogs. There was nothing there, you said?'

'Not one dog. It was as if they'd never been, it was as if I'd imagined it all.'

'I wonder where they've been taken – does your father have a close friend who might have helped him out?'

'He knows no one – not in that way.'

'Still, it's put a nice, neat finish to his activities, hasn't it? The RSPCA are sure to keep a sharp eye on him now – he wouldn't dare start up again, would he?'

'What if he moves away? And what about the dogs and puppies?'

'Ah well, my dear, that doesn't bear thinking about.' Eveleigh shook her head sadly.

*

Alan had not slept either. He could not think of a time when he'd been so depressed. The nature of his work often led him to disappointment, but his failure was made worse by Kimberley's involvement.

He could never forgive her – never. Would he continue with buying the house now? If he didn't complete the purchase he'd lose his deposit, but could he ever live there with the memory of his happy times with Kimberley, and having to be constantly reminded of her duplicity? Could he face the house aware that the joy he'd known there was lost to him for ever?

He thought he had known her, he'd been convinced he'd found his soulmate. How wrong could one be? It was beyond his comprehension that anyone could behave as she had. He'd been trained not to get too involved; part of his job, when undercover, was to be able to witness cruelty to the animals he loved and not by a blink to show his distress, his anger at man's insensitivity to living creatures. But this time he was not dispassionate – his anger against Kimberley was total.

He had other painful memories too. The dressing-down he'd received from the police inspector was far worse than he'd anticipated. He was left feeling demoralised, unprofessional – a fool!

Lost as he was in these dark thoughts, he jumped when the telephone rang.

'It's on again.' He heard Andy say.

'You're joking!'

'Nah. Sorry to interrupt your Sunday lie-in, but I've just heard from Don. It's on this morning, so you'd best get your skates on.'

'You sure this isn't another wild goose chase?'

'No. Your Deep Throat friend has come clean. He's a Graham Garner – known as Greaser.'

'Why should he suddenly allow us to know who he is?' Alan asked suspiciously.

'He was one of the FAA people last night. Says he's pretty sure Tom White didn't see him and that when he met up with his mate last night he was falling about laughing at their cleverness in shifting the dogs. This mate – a creep called Butch – hasn't got a dog, but follows the fights. Greaser said he'd like to go next time and Butch told him where the dogs are and the venue. Just like that! If they cancel this fight they won't have time to move the puppies and bitches.'

'They had time enough last time.'

'The joint's already staked out. The fuzz have got it surrounded – anyone can get in, but no one gets out without their say so.'

'Even so –' Alan was still doubtful, his depression making sure he only saw the darkest side of things this morning.

'Don thinks it more than likely. He reckons the bastards have been lulled into a false sense of security. After last night's cock-up, they think we're off with our tails between our legs and the coast is clear. Clever, really, when you thing about it. And I suppose with creeps coming from London and the Midlands they've had to lay on something.'

'Devious sods. When and where's the briefing?'

'Morristown. Nine-thirty. I've put the vet on stand-by. Ta-ra.'

Alan quickly showered and changed. He was glad this had happened – he needed something to keep his mind off Kimberley.

49

Oliver offered to take Thomasine to the hospital to collect Nadine, but she declined. 'I need to talk to her by myself,' she said, her face set in a determined line.

'Don't be too hard on her.'

'She could have been killed.'

'But she wasn't, was she? Are you going to tell her about us getting married?' He smiled, somewhat sheepishly, as he spoke.

'I don't know – where Nadine's concerned, it's best to play it by ear.' She stood on tiptoe to kiss him goodbye. 'I still can't believe it's true. That you love me.'

'Join the club.' He kissed the tip of her nose and held the car door open for her.

In the kitchen he put the kettle on for coffee, and he wandered back into the hall, Bandage, Slipper and Nova padding along behind him with nails clicking like castanets on the wooden floor.

The telephone rang shrilly. He paused before picking up the receiver. It was an odd thing, but he knew it was bad news before he even picked it up.

'Hullo – ' he said, tentatively.

'Oliver – you said if I wanted to talk – you said you'd collect me. Oh, Oliver – come quick.'

'Wimpole, what is it?'

'I can't talk. Not now. He'll hear.' And the line went dead. Oliver was in his car in a flash and en route for Wimpole's cottage.

Nadine appeared to be no worse off for her ordeal. In fact she was more cheerful than she had been in months. She apparently liked the nurses, for Thomasine, as she entered the ward, found her sitting on her bed, fully dressed, laughing and joking with a circle of admiring young women. She stopped laughing at sight of her mother.

'I've come to take you home, Nadine,' she said, feeling suddenly awkward, as if she had walked in uninvited on someone's private party.

'Mrs Lambert, we think your daughter is so brave. Anything could have happened to her last night,' a plump nurse gushed.

'I'm proud of her too,' Thomasine replied. 'Very proud,' she emphasised. She looked at Nadine, who smiled slightly in response.

On the drive back to the house they talked of the weather, the nurses, the number of magpies they saw, all inconsequential matters, in silent accord to delay discussion of weightier subjects until they were home.

'Where's Nova?' Nadine asked immediately they entered the house and no dog came scurrying to meet them.

'Oliver's looking after her for me.' Immediately she wished she hadn't said that. She should have thought to cover up where she'd been all night, and returned the dog before going to the hospital.

'Oh yes!' Nadine said knowingly, and began picking over the fruit in the bowl in a desultory manner, as if not sure if she wanted to eat anything or not. 'Did you mean it?' She swung round and faced her mother.

'What?'

'That you're proud of me.'

'Yes. I am. *Very*.' Thomasine paused, unsure how to continue. 'But that doesn't mean that I'm happy about what you did. I thought I was going to pass out with fear.'

Nadine grinned broadly with pride. 'I didn't think you'd care what I did.'

'I can't imagine why. I really do love you, Nadine, whatever you think.'

'I've made it hard for you at times, haven't I? To love me, I mean.'

'Sometimes.' Thomasine felt that if she'd been standing she'd be reeling with shock.

'I don't know why I do it, you know. Half the time I don't want to – it just happens.'

'You know, I think it will be happening less now. Once you acknowledge something like that, then you're halfway to solving it. At least in my experience.'

'You've been very patient. I mean, what with Dad being such a shit – '

'Nadine!' Thomasine tried to look shocked, but instead failed and found she was laughing.

'It's true. We both have been. Mind you, Chantal was the biggest shit of all.'

'Just because I laughed you needn't think that gives you *carte blanche* to swear like that.'

'It's true though, isn't it? How's Oliver?'

Thomasine put her hand to her head, amazed. 'What's changed, Nadine? I'm almost afraid to believe this is happening – you'll be saying you love Nova next.'

'I do – well, a bit. I still think she's ugly. No, it was last night. I mean, if I had been killed – banging my head like that, the doc said I could have. Well, if I had, you'd have been left all alone. That's unreasonable, isn't it? And you'd be left with nothing resolved, just bad feelings. And I wouldn't want you to remember me like that – hateful, selfish – gross!' She grinned at her use of the last word.

'Don't even talk about dying!'

'And I was scared last night – it was different from any other demo I'd been on. It was a raid, and really violent. I didn't like most of those people, I think some of them were more interested in the chance of a fight than the dogs. And when I saw you and Oliver – it was the best moment I'd had in years. And I realised how much I loved you, and, well, that's it really.'

'Oliver is very nice you know, and he cares about you too. And, well – ' She paused, still uncertain this conversation was real, but Nadine had to be told. 'He's asked me to marry him, and I said yes.'

'That's brill! Where will we live?' Nadine said, with barely a pause.

'I don't know, we haven't talked about that, he only asked me last night.'

'Ah ha, I see – up to hanky-panky as soon as my back's turned,' Nadine grinned mischievously. Thomasine pretended to hit her.

'Cheeky! Which do you think you'd prefer?'

'His place. It's bigger than here. And I'm sorry I called you names – I was confused.'

'I understand. I'd forgotten already,' she fibbed. She stood up. 'That's settled, then. What do you fancy for lunch?' And she found herself marvelling that in the midst of such momentous discussions and decisions she should think of stomachs, but that, no doubt, was what being a mother was all about.

'Thing is, Mum, I really will try – to be better, I mean. I might not manage it all the time. I expect I'll have the odd gross day.'

'What a relief!' she laughed.

'What's funny?'

'You are, my darling. Oh, how I love you! Now I know you *really* mean it.' She ruffled Nadine's hair which, judging by the violent way she jerked her head away, did not go down well. And then, as if realising her reaction, she ruffled it herself and grinned broadly at her mother.

'What about Kimberley, Mum?' she asked abruptly.

'What about her?'

'I'm just so shocked. That was her father's place, you realise. She must have known what was going on there – and never told. I don't think I ever want to see her again – ever.'

'Don't decide anything until you've talked to her. You don't know what went on in her life – maybe she was terrified of her father. There's not a lot you can do about anything, no matter how you feel, if you're threatened by the sort of violence that we've never known. Be understanding, Nadine.'

'Oh hell! Haven't I been nice enough for one day!'

'Why, oh why didn't you come and tell me?' Oliver, sitting at the table in Rudolph's cottage, pushed his hand through his hair in a gesture of frustration.

'Tell you what? That I'd made the biggest mistake of my life?'

'I'll be honest, I was surprised when you said you were getting married – it wasn't just my own confusion. I wondered why, at – ' He stopped abruptly.

'At my age? Was that what you were going to say? Cheeky!'

'Well, yes. I should have asked you outright.'

'Would I have known the answer? Oh, I took a fancy to him – he can be very nice. But I think, at the back of my mind, I felt that it wasn't fair to you to have me as a liability for the rest of my life.'

'You were never that, Wimpole.'

'But you didn't know what was ahead of you, did you? You might have met someone who wouldn't put up with me – and then where would I be? I suppose I was trying to carve out my own security – and a right mess I've landed myself in.' She put her fingers up and gingerly experimented with touching her swollen lips. 'My old mum always used to say that my mouth would get me into trouble one day – all lip, she used to call me. She was right. It must look as fat as an elephant's.' And she laughed, but Oliver realised it was not from humour but to cover up the unimaginable pain she must be feeling.

'When did you realise it was not going to work?'

'If I'm honest, I had me doubts before we even waddled up the aisle. He could be right as rain and then suddenly – whoosh – he'd be in a temper for no apparent reason. He's a violent sod. Then on that honeymoon . . .' She shuddered. 'Well, it wasn't nice, not nice at all. I said to him, I'm not having none of this, and that's when he whopped me the first time.'

Oliver, presuming she was referring to sex, had to cover his mouth with a hand so that she could not see his half smile. Instead he accepted a second cup of tea, suggested she try drinking hers with a straw, and he promised to buy her some when she said she didn't have any. 'So where is he now?'

'Gone out, and I hope he never comes back.'

'You're coming home with me.'

'I hoped you'd say that.'

'See, Bandage was right again. He didn't like Rudolph one little bit, did he? So why did he hit you this time?'

'Because I said I'd go to the police and report him, and he said – ' She stopped, looked about the small cottage room as if afraid Rudolph was still there and would hear her, and then began again. 'And he said if I snitched on him he'd bloody kill me. And I said he hadn't got the balls to do that – which was stupid of me, but by then I was in a rare old temper – and then he hit me. Then I called you and then he came back and I rang off, and I'm so scared. You see, he could, I know now he's quite capable of killing me.' The words had tumbled out of her in a panic-stricken rush.

'What on earth has he done that he'd kill you rather than let you tell?'

'It's the dogs.'

'What dogs?'

'The fighting dogs. Out the back.' She gestured with her head in that direction. 'In the kennels, he breeds them.'

As the realisation of what she was saying dawned on him, his anger hardened and grew until he felt as if there was nothing in him but this fury. 'Bandage, did he have anything to do with Bandage's disappearance?'

'No, but a friend of his did. He laughed. He thought it was funny. He said the stupid dog remembered him. I should have told you, I know. I didn't know what to do, which way to turn.' Wimpole began to cry, silently, as she saw the expression on Oliver's face. 'Oliver, be careful – ' She put her hand out as if to restrain him but he shook her away.

'How long have you known?' he asked stiffly, not sure if he could control his fury with her either.

'Since I moved here.' She spoke barely louder than a whisper, as if that could minimise her shame.

'You have to tell me everything you know – *now*.'

The cold tone of his voice made her clutch her throat at the fear that she could lose him too. He sat opposite her, listening to her sorry tale, his face becoming stonier with every word. He had thought he was full of anger before, but that was nothing to the rage which was beginning to boil up within him at the appalling story she was relating. He stood up abruptly, pushing his chair back so that it fell with a clatter to the floor. He did not bend to pick it up, for he was deaf and blind to everything but his new and desperate need to avenge.

'Oliver, he's mad – ' Wimpole too was on her feet. But he did not hear her, did not see her hand outstretched to delay him, and forgot his promise to take her with him. He rushed from the room and out into his car.

The narrow roads which criss-crossed Ben Luckett's estate, of necessity, slowed Oliver's driving until he was banging the steering wheel with frustration at his speed. The stupid woman, she had wasted so much time, why could she not have told him the minute he arrived, he muttered to himself. Without stopping he swung the car through the gates and once on the main road was able to put his foot down. He drove fast, too fast.

He was delayed further by a large horsebox lumbering along in front of him. He hit his horn and flashed his lights, but the vehicle blocked him. He inched out and saw a short stretch of straight road where only a maniac would overtake. He pulled out, pushed his foot down hard, and prayed. A car was approaching, on collision course. He took a deep breath and forced an extra smidgeon of speed from his car, snaked in front of the horsebox at too acute an angle, almost clipping its fender and, fighting to control the car, careered towards his destination.

By the time he arrived at the house of his father-in-law, he was drenched in sweat, his heart was racing, he was dry-mouthed from nerves, his system flooded with adrenalin and his blood pressure sky high. He ran up the steps to the front door, not bothering to ring the bell but pushing the door open and stalking in. He called out, but nobody anwered. He searched in the drawing room, dining room, in the study, in the kitchen, but the house was deserted. He stood still, the only sound his beating heart. Now what? Suddenly he stiffened as he heard a roar of men's voices. He crossed to the den – a huge room with a full-size billiard table. At the far end was a double-glazed sliding door which led into the indoor swimming pool. He grabbed hold of the handle and slid it to one side.

The noise was deafening. A crowd of men, shouting and baying, were perched on the edge of the empty pool. They were so engrossed that they did not hear the door slide back, the sound of Oliver's footfall on the tiled surround, nor his exclamation of horror. They were totally oblivious to his shout of 'you cruel bastards!'

He stood on the edge of the pool and looked down on to a scene from hell. The bottom of the pool was covered in stained sawdust. A red line had been drawn dividing the arena into two halves. It was a suitable colour, given the amount of blood splattering the pale blue tiles of the pool. The men were screaming and shouting, some abuse and others encouragement. Standing at the deep end Ben Luckett momentarily looked up, his eyes ablaze with excitement, a dribble of saliva trickling down his chin as he salivated from pleasure at the spectacle of two dogs, terrifyingly silent compared to the men, tearing each other to shreds for the entertainment of their owners.

'Sport! You bloody call this sport! You sub-human bastards!' Oliver screamed at them as he leapt into what would normally be the shallow end of the pool. He ran, slithering and sliding on the blood and saliva, towards the dogs. His only thought was to separate them. He was a third of the way along when a man jumped down, landing heavily on top of him, and rolled him roughly on to the floor.

'Mind your own fucking business.' He recognised Rudolph's snarl. Oliver, despite Rudolph's considerable weight, scrabbled to his feet and, heaving with all his might, threw Rudolph onto his back. He had the satisfaction of hearing an animal-like grunt escape from Rudolph. He didn't stand a hope in hell, was his last conscious thought, as a pile of bodies, like a rugger scrum, fell on top of him. The wind whistled out of his crushed lungs and all he could feel was pain until, mercifully, everything turned to darkness.

He lost the darkness, and wanted the comfort of it back. Hot, searing pain arched through him, as if his whole body was broken. All there was in the universe was pain . . . In the distance, a long way from him, he began to hear a great roaring, drumming noise . . . As he tumbled through the tunnel from unconsciousness to consciousness, accompanied by the agony, the noises separated, became clearer. They were coming closer. And then they were all around him. Shouting, screaming, roaring. He heard the thud but could not yet see as men toppled over into the pool, slamming down onto the hard tiles, grunting, groaning. He heard the sound of dogs barking – ferocious, alarmed, violent dogs. He could not as yet tell that the barking was not from the dogs he had tried to save, for they were oblivious to everything but their fight, their laboured breathing adding to the general cacophony.

He felt the pressure on his body ease as one by one the men were removed from him. He lay flat, still winded, trying to breathe normally. His mouth was full of sawdust, the salt taste of blood on his tongue. Gingerly, he sat up, and winced as what felt like a dozen sharp knives stabbed inside his chest. He shook his head and looked around him. The swimming pool was a heaving mass of fighting men, human blood mingling with that of the dogs. They skidded and fell on the ever-spreading crimson pools. In their midst, teeth firmly rooted in each other's flesh, ignoring the mayhem around them, the dogs continued their ominously silent struggle as men fought and fell on all sides.

Oliver slumped against the side of the pool, for a moment enjoying the cool feeling of the tiles against his cheek. Two men in uniforms he did not recognise stealthily approached the dogs, holding wooden staves with wedged ends. Expertly they rammed the wedges into the dogs' mouths and, with muscles bulging at the strength needed to prise the determined jaws apart, freed them from their cruel dance of death.

Oliver yelled in agony as he was yanked to his feet, his arm painfully twisted behind his back. 'Hang on a minute, I'm bloody hurt,' he managed to say, but after that he did not seem to be able to hack through the muddle in his head to find the right words to stop them clipping on a pair of handcuffs. He was left standing, propped up against the side of the pool.

Now he could see Rudolph sprawled unconscious on his back on the bottom of the pool, covered in blood, his mouth open. Ben, purple with rage, his eyes bulging alarmingly, was in handcuffs too. The place was a mêlée of police, police dogs and RSPCA inspectors as they rounded up the spectators.

'This way.' A young policeman pulled at Oliver, another pushed him in the back and someone, he wasn't fast enough to see who, kicked him in the shins.

'Not again!' he sighed. 'I'm not one of them. I was trying to break the bloody fight up,' Oliver protested, but the effort of saying all that was almost too much for him. He felt himself sway as if his legs had been drained of blood and sinew.

'Oh yes, sir? That's what they all say.' And the policeman unceremoniously shoved Oliver up the steps of the pool. 'You're coming along with me.'

50

It was chaos at the police station. The duty sergeant had given up trying to keep his temper and was shouting for some semblance of order as he attempted to process the sudden influx of customers.

Oliver looked up. One large fair-haired man was swinging his fist at an only slightly smaller one.

'You fucking creep, I knew you were a plant! I bloody knew!' Vic shouted.

Alan put up his hand and grabbed hold of Vic's wrist. 'Sorry about that, mate. But animals come first in my book.'

'You slime. I should have fucking killed you when I had the chance,' Vic shouted as two burly coppers restrained him. 'How do you sleep at night being a ponce!'

'And how well do you sleep, Vic, after torturing defenceless animals? You're sub-human, you are.' And he swung on his heel and ducked into one of the interview rooms to prevent himself from smashing his fist into Vic's face. It would only give him momentary satisfaction and would be followed by a lot of problems he could do without.

Oliver had given up trying to explain he wasn't one of *them*, and sat philosophically on a bench awaiting his turn. He hugged his chest to ease the pain slightly. Conscious of someone sitting down beside him, he shuffled his rear along the seat, and looked up to see Ben Luckett, perspiring profusely.

'Hullo, Ben. Come here often?'

'Don't you ever take anything seriously? Do you always have to behave like a facetious twit?'

'If I didn't make a joke of it, perhaps I wouldn't be able to control myself. Then I'd do what I really want to do, and you wouldn't ever see the light of day again, Ben.'

'Who are you kidding? See me shaking in my boots?'

'You are in a bit of a spot now, though, aren't you? No knighthood – oh dear no, not the way the Queen feels about dogs.' Oliver laughed quietly. 'And think of all the money you invested dreaming of the old "Arise, Sir Benjamin" routine.'

'You shit!'

'No, Ben. You've got it wrong. You're the shit, you and that cruel bastard Rudie over there. What a nice pair you make. Got Rudie to do the dirty work, did you?' It was like casting a fly, he decided, getting Ben to spill the beans – not too fast, gently does it, he told himself.

'I don't know what you mean.'

'Don't you? If I say Eveleigh Brenton? Ring a bell?'

'Eveleigh? You know I know her.' Ben shrugged.

'Dogs. St Bernards in particular. One of them dead. Get my drift?'

'Oliver, I despair of you. No wonder Sophia wanted to ditch you.'

'Tell you what, Ben, I'm in a bit of a quandary here. I mean, I know you and Rudie did it. I'd just like to hear you say it.'

'You mean you've no proof. Bad luck, Oliver.' Ben threw back his head to laugh, and Oliver saw his back teeth were rotten and full of metal fillings whilst his front teeth shone white and perfect.

'Actually, Ben, I know an amazing amount. You should believe me.' Thanks to Wimpole, he was only lying a little.

'You don't fool me,' Ben counter-bluffed.

'That's a shame – for you, I mean. You see, I haven't been seen by our friendly coppers yet. It's not going to be that difficult to explain to them that I'm not one of your merry band. To show my appreciation of their courtesy and fulsome apologies – you know, to show I harbour no hard feelings – then I think I should drop in their shell-likes all I know about you, Rudie and the poisoned dog, don't you? Then you really would be looking at a prison sentence, Ben. On the other hand, if you tell me what I want to hear, if you do what I want you to – then I could be persuaded to forget it.' He touched his lips with his index finger.

'What do you want to know?' Ben asked with the resignation of the pragmatist.

'Well, for starters . . .'

An hour later Oliver accidentally compounded his problems in the interview room. The officer asked him if he minded a member of the RSPCA being present. He was not entirely sure, but he thought the man sitting opposite him was the same young man who, last night at Primrose Acre, had said he knew Nadine – Kimberley's boyfriend.

'I do know Kimberley White,' he said, cheerfully offering her name as his credentials. 'She'll vouch for me, I'm sure.'

Alan paled. He stood abruptly, pushed his chair back, mumbled an excuse to the policeman and stalked from the room. He was still so angry over Kimberley, and hurt too. He could not be certain that in the presence of that creep he could maintain the professional detachment that was expected of him. Better by far to leave the interview.

Without Alan to vouch for him, it took Oliver three long hours of frustration, controlled temper, cajoling and apology to be believed and to get out of the police station. To add insult to injury, he had to get a taxi home from Morristown, since his car was still at Ben's.

He had hoped Thomasine would be there, but only the dogs welcomed him. He decided to have a bath to soothe his aching limbs and get rid of the smell of blood and the police cells. He had just lowered himself into the tub when the telephone rang.

'Where have you been? I've been worried sick.'

'It's a long story. Got a week?'

'I thought I'd better let you know that Nadine is being angelic and approves of us – can you imagine!'

'Can I come round?'

'I think you should. I've got Wimpole here, she's in a dreadful state. Would you bring Nova with you, please?'

'Hullo, Oliver!' Nadine was grinning broadly as she opened the door.

'How's the head?' he smiled back at her.

'Better than your mush. What happened?'

'I had an argument with a man about a dog.' He bent down to unclip Nova's lead; the effort made him wince from the pain in his chest.

'Are you all right? You look funny,' Nadine enquired with unusual concern.

'I'm a bit sore – it's nothing,' he replied, thinking how brave he was.

'They're all through in the kitchen.'

'All' was Thomasine, Eveleigh and an agitated Wimpole who, from her red-rimmed eyes, had been crying hard, and at sight of Oliver looked as if she might quite easily start again.

'Wimpole, love, don't . . .' He realised that all his anger with her had evaporated.

'Don't even say it or I will,' she answered, blowing noisily into a man-sized handkerchief. 'I thought you'd never speak to me again.'

'Don't be silly.'

'What happened? We've been worried sick,' said Thomasine, standing on tiptoe for a kiss.

'Did you see Jim?' asked an equally anxious Eveleigh.

'Sorry, no. But it was such chaos.' He explained, at length, about the dog fight in the swimming pool, toning down the gory bits in deference to his audience.

'And Rudolph?' Wimpole asked, and Oliver wondered if he'd imagined it or was her voice tinged with sadness? If so, he hoped it was for what might have been and not for the man.

'He's in the clink with Ben. But knowing Ben's luck, they'll be out by nightfall.'

'Did you find out about, you know?' Wimpole asked, looking anxiously at the other women.

'What? That you'd overheard Rudie on the phone, presumably to Ben, saying he'd seen to the dog?' Oliver put it baldly, working on the principle that it would all have to come out eventually. It was probably better to do it straight away.

'Oh, no!' Eveleigh said.

'I managed to prise the lot out of Ben. It was as we suspected, Thomasine. He'd said to Rudie that he wished someone would get rid of Eveleigh and her dogs for him. Rudie obliged – just as well he didn't try to get rid of you, Eveleigh. Ben swears he didn't know anything about it until you told him, Thomasine, and I'm inclined to believe him. He did lie, he hasn't sold the land – that was to divert our suspicions, Eveleigh.'

'But did my Isolde have to die? Such inhumanity.'

'Do we know who tipped them off about the fight at Primrose Acre?' Thomasine asked to divert Eveleigh's trend of thought.

'Yes, Beth.'

'Beth!' Thomasine and Eveleigh chorused together.

'Inadvertently. Ben overheard her talking to Cora, something about she hadn't asked Jim for some money owing to her in her rush to get out. Cora said she would run her over to pick it up on Saturday evening and Beth said there was no point, that Jim was expecting to be busy. Ben put two and two together – hey presto, all the dogs were moved.'

'Cora knew nothing about this, did she?' Thomasine asked anxiously, worried that if she had then she would never trust her judgement of people ever again.

'Not a dicky bird. Ben packed Cora and Sophia off to Paris for a weekend of shopping armed with his credit cards. And what's more he shipped Beth out too, Harry as well. They were sent to Euro-Disney via the tunnel. Treats that he knew they were unlikely to refuse.'

'Did you tell the police all this?' Thomasine asked.

'No.'

'Why on earth not?'

'The snippet of conversation Wimpole heard was not proof, it said nothing really. What dog? It could be any dog. Wimpole didn't like the way Rudie said he'd "seen to" the dog. She said it made her go chilly inside, didn't you, Wimpole? But she might have been imagining it. He could have meant he'd sprayed it with flea powder, or changed its feed. So I did a deal with Ben – if he was straight with me then I wouldn't tell the police.'

'But I don't understand why you had to make the deal,' Thomasine said.

'If Oliver hadn't forced it out of him then I would never have been able to relax, not knowing if it was him or, as the police thought, a jealous breeder. I would have always been looking over my shoulder – never sure. Isn't that it, Oliver?' Eveleigh asked. Oliver nodded. 'And was absolutely everything him?'

'The lot. The rumours, the gravel, insurance people – everything. Rudie helped him again there but he also used other people who owed him favours – even from your dog world, Eveleigh. He was like a Chicago gangster calling in his markers. I jotted down their names, if you want them.'

Eveleigh shuddered. 'I'd rather not know.'

'Very wise of you. Don't forget, he might have coerced them. You'd never know with a character like him.'

'But of course, none of this helps me with the Kennel Club. If they continue to believe the rumour-mongers then I'm finished as a breeder.'

'All taken care of, Eveleigh. He's agreed to write to them explaining he did it as a joke that got out of hand. He's willing to grovel for you – on the understanding we never tell about Isolde.'

'But how do you know you can trust him to do this for Eveleigh?'

'Simple. Unless she gets an acknowledgement from the Kennel Club that all has been explained and that she is no longer under suspicion, my bargain with Ben is null and void and I toddle off to the nick and tell them all. We've got him tied in knots.' He started to laugh, but stopped abruptly since it hurt his chest too much.

'Oliver, you've gone white, are you sure there's nothing wrong?' Eveleigh fussed.

'It's only my ribs; they took a bit of a lambasting.'

'You're going to the hospital,' Thomasine insisted.

'I'll go and see the doc – '

'Hospital,' Thomasine said firmly.

'God, woman, you're so bossy – I love it.'

'Oliver, I don't know if I shall ever be able to repay you.'

'No need, Eveleigh, it was my pleasure.'

'I think you should still shaft him.' Nadine spoke for the first time.

'No. I gave my word.'

'I could,' she said defiantly.

'Nadine, no! You don't understand what you would be up against,' Thomasine admonished.

'But to kill a dog?'

'Nadine, it's dreadful, I know. After all, it was my dog, but please, you'd not be doing me a favour. If you break Oliver's promise Ben might return to the attack. The dogs are my only concern. I suggest that we tell no one outside this room – and that includes Jim. I think it might put him in an intolerable position professionally.'

Nadine was obviously thinking, weighing up the pros and cons. 'Well, all right then, but for the sake of the dogs only.' She was quite taken back by the adults' approval of her decision, unused as she was to it.

'What made you telephone Oliver this morning, Wimpole?' Thomasine asked, suddenly aware that the older woman had been sitting in the corner of the room, saying nothing.

'I – ' She looked over at Oliver as if asking for help.

'You'd seen some dogs about, hadn't you, Wimpole, and didn't like the look of them. She thought they were pit bulls.' Wimpole smiled at him, grateful that he was not about to tell them that she had known full well what dogs were bred in Ben Luckett's kennels and had an even shrewder idea about the dog fight, though even she hadn't known it was to be held in Ben's swimming pool.

'Why was the fight in the swimming pool? Imagine the expense of emptying and then having to fill it. That I don't understand,' said Eveleigh.

'It's an ideal place, easy to sluice the blood away when it's all over.'

'Oh never!' Eveleigh wished she hadn't asked.

'Ben'll be off to Spain, I bet you. He'll want to escape the scandal. No knighthood for him now.' Oliver once again felt a degree of satisfaction at that.

'There's just one thing, Oliver. How can you guarantee that the person who buys the land off Ben won't do the same to Eveleigh?'

'I can guarantee that totally, Thomasine. You see, I'm buying the land.'

'*I love you*,' Thomasine mouthed at him just as the telephone rang. 'It's for you, Eveleigh.' She handed over the instrument.

'Jim, what a lovely surprise.' As she spoke Oliver and Thomasine looked at each other knowingly. But the joke faded as they listened to Eveleigh's voice becoming serious, noted the absence of any smile. 'That's horrendous!' she said, replacing the telephone. 'I've got to go up to Ben's.'

Twenty minutes later they drove up to the back of Ben Luckett's house in convoy, Thomasine driving Oliver, with Eveleigh following in her cumbersome Bentley. Nadine had been persuaded to stay behind.

They found Jim and a gaggle of police and RSPCA men in a barn beyond the stables. As they approached, Jim looked up, his face set in a rigid expression. 'Bless you, Eveleigh, I thought we could rely on you.' He looked more tired than any of them had ever seen him before.

Thomasine grabbed hold of Oliver's hand for support at the sight that awaited them. In boxes, crates, behind wire netting, were dogs of every breed. Dogs, bitches, puppies – lice-ridden, with suppurating sores and no spirit shining in their eyes, no tails awag, like normal dogs. They cowered in fear, backing away from the hands that were trying to treat them, as though unused to anything but cruelty.

'Tom White?' Thomasine asked.

'We assume so.'

'The poor creatures.' Thomasine sank on one knee to pick up a puppy – a Yorkshire Terrier, she thought, but its hair was so encrusted with filth it was difficult to tell.

'How many?' Oliver asked.

'We've counted sixty so far, and then there are the pit bulls.' Jim nodded to a corner of the barn where five dogs sat in separate cages, one covered in blood from recent wounds. Four others, scarred but not bleeding, sat and watched them with wary eyes.

'The whole thing's odd. The RSPCA inspector told me that normally only two dogs are brought to a venue to be matched, but this time they presumably planned three fights. They'd obviously only had time for one. I had to destroy the other dog – it was past help. This one will mend, I hope. Those others must have been the next acts in the cabaret,' he said bitterly.

'Still, they bagged the lot,' Oliver said with satisfaction.

'Yes, we were lucky. Normally Ben would have been conveniently away for the day. They were obviously so confident that there would be no raid, he took the risk. And to think I liked him and thought he cared for animals. Unbelievable.' Jim shook his head.

'Man's best friend! That's a laugh, isn't it? When you see how we abuse them?' Eveleigh said. 'How many dogs do you want me to take?'

'The inspector will tell you. It's very good of you, Evie.' He put out his hand to touch her, and then, realising it was covered in blood, snatched it back. Eveleigh put up her own hand and touched his cheek.

'You look so tired,' she said softly.

Alan had been sent from the police station back to the Lucketts' to help the hard-pressed uniformed inspectors. 'Excuse me,' said Eveleigh to the others upon seeing him. 'Alan, may I have a word?'

'I heard you're helping, taking a load of the dogs until we can find homes for them. That's good of you, Mrs Brenton.'

'It's nothing of the sort. I feel privileged to be asked to help.'

'That's nice. Still, you might have them for some time – the puppies will be easy enough to rehouse, but the bitches – that's another story.'

'I doubt if some of them ever will be. They're too traumatised ever to settle in a normal family. But it's not the dogs I want to talk to you about. It's – '

'Kimberley? I'd rather not talk about her, if you don't mind, Mrs Brenton.'

'But you must, Alan. The poor child is distraught.'

'So she should be after what she's allowed to happen.'

'But, Alan, she's only a child. What could she have done? Have you no compassion?'

'For the dogs – yes. For her – not a scrap. Excuse me, Mrs Brenton, I've work to do.' And he turned and walked away from her.

January

51

Christmas came and went. As a forest takes time to recover from a great storm, so Shillingham and the Shillings took time to recover from the awful events at Ben Luckett's.

People divided neatly into two groups. The largest said they'd always had their suspicions about Ben, always knew he was up to no good. 'You only had to look at his eyes,' was a common phrase. They were not surprised. The other group, smaller by far, evinced astonishment that such a 'nice' man should have been involved in such appalling cruelty; some even said they were sure there must have been a mistake. Unfortunately for Ben, this group lacked both the weight of numbers and the verbosity of the majority, who appeared also to be rather enjoying Ben's downfall.

Ben did not face the fine of two thousand pounds, or six months in jail, that was the maximum punishment in law. (At this information, 'Pathetic,' or 'It should be life,' were frequently repeated.) Ben, as Oliver had predicted, had scarpered to Spain as soon as he was out of police custody. 'At least he can watch the bullfights,' Eveleigh was heard to say acidly.

Ben's financial affairs were in a more fragile state than anyone had realised. So Cora, left to deal with a mountain of debts and the forced sale of her home by the bank, received much sympathy and understanding. But Oliver remembered the stand she'd taken when he'd asked her to help over the kennels, and knew he would never feel the same about her again, and Eveleigh herself harboured serious doubts that Cora was entirely ignorant of her husband's activities. Eveleigh knew that if ever she had to choose between a husband and dogs, she would have no crisis of loyalty; she would not hesitate to turn him in.

Sophia was too mortified to return home, ever, which suited Thomasine very well.

The loss of Ben as an employer was felt deeply in the community. The receivers had pared the remaining employees down to a skeleton staff, just enough to keep the estate ticking over. It reflected in the local shops' takings, of course, so redundancies were inevitable. Both Grace White's sons faced being laid off from the home farm, unless a buyer could be found quickly –

unlikely, with the market in such a parlous state. Beth was looking for a new job, difficult with a young son. And Rudie had moved away, no one knew where.

Oliver had cracked two ribs in the fight, but there was no question of him lying on a sofa while Thomasine nursed him tenderly, especially as she had been with him when the doctor told him to 'carry on as before'. Instead he opted for a fine line in stoicism, and was rewarded with much admiration for his courage. His purchase of the land assured the safety of Eveleigh's kennels. She, in turn, hired the land back from him for more space to exercise her dogs.

Thomasine and Oliver, to the detriment of Thomasine's Treats, saw each other every day, their relationship intensifying until it seemed that they had no need of anyone or anything else. This was not strictly true: Thomasine was always conscious of Nadine, but since she had met a young RSPCA inspector who worked locally, her daughter was in love, happy and, most importantly, happy for her mother too. And without doubt both Thomasine and Oliver needed their dogs.

Tom White and his wife were ostracised. No stallholder would buy his vegetables, and when they wanted to shop they had to travel to the anonymity of Morristown. He had not only to face charges in relation to the dog fighting; the RSPCA were prosecuting him for causing unnecessary suffering to the dogs on his puppy farm. They hoped he would be banned for life from keeping animals, but knowing the unpredictability of the courts, they had prepared themselves for less.

Alan continued with his purchase of the house. He did not plan to live there but to rent it out instead. He was glad when he was assigned to a group monitoring the export of live sheep, trailing convoys across Europe to check the animals were rested and watered, as EEC laws required, on the long journey to their final destination. He was busy and deeply involved in the work, which was necessary, but could be dangerous. He thought often of Kimberley, but with anger and bitterness.

Kimberley had always worked hard but now, as if in atonement for her father's sins and her own cowardice, she laboured for the dogs' welfare in such a way that Eveleigh was concerned for her.

'You need time off, Kimberley.'

'I need to do it, Mrs Brenton. I won't rest until each dog that came from Primrose Acre has been loved back to health.'

Eveleigh did not say what she feared – that that day would never come. The puppies had been no problem, and good homes were easily found for them, especially when the media picked up on the horrifying tale. The mature bitches were another matter. Jim Varley could cure their ills and Kimberley and Eveleigh could nurse their poor, undernourished and skinny bodies back to health, but Eveleigh doubted if all of them would ever recover their spirits completely, if their fear of man would ever be replaced by trust.

Of these bitches, Eveleigh took a King Charles into her house as a companion for the ageing Coco; Oliver adopted an Old English Sheepdog and Thomasine a Yorkshire Terrier; Gill and Justin welcomed a miniature poodle. The RSPCA, Jim Varley and Eveleigh decided that the remaining eight, too nervous to risk placing with families, would be better off spayed and cared for by her in the kennels, until the day they died. The same decisions, hard though they were, had to be repeated at the dog refuge and at Fee Walters', where the other Tom White dogs had been taken.

Jim often dined at Eveleigh's and she had, on the odd occasion, dined at his house, albeit doing the cooking herself. Jim had also taken her out to dinner in Shillingham, and they had attended a couple of dog shows together. Their relationship had settled into a comfortable cosiness in which Jim thought he'd never been happier, but with which Eveleigh was less content.

Thomasine emerged from the doctor's surgery feeling stunned. It was not possible! She went straight to The Copper Kettle, and ordered a coffee.

She was pregnant!

She had gone to the doctor because she thought herself menopausal. She had been content with that idea. She wanted no more children, Nadine was enough for anyone! And how good to start this new life with Oliver with no concerns about contraception. So she had thought.

She ordered another cup of coffee and, to comfort herself, a large slab of chocolate cake. How to tell Oliver? She wanted to marry him, but how would she feel if, in the future, in the midst of a row, he should turn to her and say 'I only married you because of the baby'? She did not want that.

And Nadine! She blanched at the thought of having to tell her daughter she was pregnant. She could imagine how horrified she would be – what seventeen-year-old wanted to be seen with a pregnant forty-three-year-old – heavens no, she'd be forty-four in a month – mother?

She could, of course, as the doctor had hinted, get rid of it. Have an abortion. All neat and tidy, Oliver need not even know. A night in London – she was going shopping, she could tell him, staying with her mother – Oh dear God! Her mother. She could just imagine the furore when she told her. She ordered another cup of coffee and was halfway through it when she realised she was late for her hair appointment.

'Well, what a to-do it's all been, hasn't it?' Gill said as he fussed over her hair. 'Our poor little Sandie, she looks so scared all the time. Our Sadie's been a saint with her. She and Sukie are busy teaching her how to be a dog.'

'That's nice. Yes, my fiancé's dogs and mine are the same with the two we adopted. They're very protective too.'

'We could learn a lot from dogs, I always say. They're certainly kinder to each other than we are. What's awful is Justin and I didn't know it went on – puppy farming, I mean.'

'Me neither. Though I must admit that sometimes I'd see adverts for puppies listing half a dozen breeds and I thought, that's odd, one breeder breeding so many different dogs. I know now.'

'What, that they're a puppy farmer's?'

'That or an agent's. I tell everyone, beware of adverts like that.'

'At our class we're getting the message across. Thought any more about coming?'

'I might – we have five dogs between us now. They're quite a handful.'

'You come along. Bring your fiancé. I tell you, it's a laugh a minute.'

On the way back home Thomasine practised half a dozen scenarios of how to break the news to Oliver, and hadn't opted for the right one by the time she reached The Old School House.

'There's a message for you from Oliver. He wants you to pop over – soon as poss,' Nadine said, as she helped unload the bags from the car. Thomasine was still adjusting to having a helpful daughter. She always thanked her extravagantly, but she'd schooled herself not to be surprised if, overnight, the monster Nadine returned.

The groceries unpacked, she drove straight over to Oliver's to find an agitated Wimpole in the kitchen, cleaning silver. 'You made me jump!' She dropped a fork on to the floor.

'Sorry. Where's Oliver?'

'In Phoebe's Hall, where else?' Wimpole replied, and knocked the bottle of silver polish flying. Thomasine bent to pick it up.

'Wimpole, I've been meaning to ask you and I always forget – did Rudolph ever say anything to you about having a bulldog?'

'A bulldog? No, I can't say I remember him mentioning one. Why?'

'Oh, just a thought.' Thomasine would have loved to know if it had been from Rudolph's car that Luna had been slung all those months ago. And was it Rudolph, in a roundabout way, she had to thank for getting to know dogs – Luna and Nova in particular? But she supposed she'd never know now. As another fork clattered to the floor she thought perhaps the subject of Rudolph and dogs was upsetting Wimpole, so she went in search of Oliver.

'What's wrong with Wimpole?' Thomasine asked, kissing the top of Oliver's head as he bent over his work. 'She seems in a bit of a state.'

'She's been evicted.'

'She's what?'

'Well, not exactly, but the estate's been sold and she's got to get out of her cottage by the end of March.'

'Poor Wimpole. Then what?' she asked, but already knew the answer.

'That's what I wanted to talk to you about – '

'It's all right by me.'

'You don't know what I was going to suggest.'

'I imagine you were going to say she'd come here to live.'

'Well, you're wrong. I wouldn't presume such a thing, not when we're getting married. We are still, I hope?'

'Please.' She pursed her lips for a kiss, and then remembered. A shiver raced through her.

'What's the matter?'

'Nothing.'

'My darling Thomasine. Please, do me a favour. Please don't ever say "nothing". In my experience it always means all hell's about to break loose.'

'I'm pregnant,' she burst out, not at all in the way she had intended. She stood in the middle of the room, her arms limply at her side, looking at her shoes and realising she was slightly pigeon-toed, but not wanting to look at him, anything but that.

She heard him cross the room, felt him take hold of her face in his hands, but she kept her eyes closed.

'Look at me.'

'I can't.'

'Please.' He bent forward and kissed both eyelids gently.

'I didn't mean to tell you like this,' she mumbled.

'It's the most wonderful news I ever heard.'

'You don't have to say that.'

'I know. I'm just telling you it is. Look at me, my darling. See my face.'

Gingerly, she opened her eyes. His face was so close to hers that she had to step back before she could see his smile, his eyes which glinted with something suspiciously like tears. 'I never thought to hear wonderful news like this, ever. I'd resigned myself to never being a dad. Now this.' He spread his hands in jubilation.

'I can't marry you,' she said. 'At least, not yet.'

'You what?' He stepped towards her, and she reversed away from him. 'But you said – '

'I know, but this changes everything.' She placed her hands either side of her flat stomach. 'Now you feel you have to marry me, and I couldn't bear that.'

'I loved you enough half an hour ago to want to marry you. What's changed?'

'You probably think you love me more now.'

'I do.'

'But you don't. It's the thought of the baby that has made you say that.'

'God preserve me from women's logic.' He put his hand to his head.

'You needn't be so bloody patronising,' she flared up from confused emotions.

'Darling, I'm not. Believe me – I'm only a man, for God's sake.' He shrugged and experimented with a laugh, but she did not respond to it. 'Look, Thomasine, I can't help loving you more with this news. I can't say I'm sorry that I want to look after you even more – there'll be more to look after.' It was a weak joke and neither of them smiled.

'Don't you see? I want you to want *me*. To marry *me*.'

'Then what do we do? I was going to suggest Wimpole moved into your house and I rented it off you, and you and Nadine came here. So pat.'

'I have to have the baby first. Then if you want to marry me, we can.'

'What the hell's the difference?'

'It's simple. I'm not making you, you see. You'll never be able to say you only married me for the sake of the child.'

'But I never would!' he protested.

'Yes, you would. One day down the line. In a row it would be useful ammunition.'

'I do think, dear Thomasine, you're off your trolley.'

'I don't think so. I'm being very sane. I'm protecting our relationship.'

'I can't see it.'

'You will, one day.'

52

Kimberley was a constant source of worry to Eveleigh. She had always been a quiet girl, but now she rarely spoke. She did her work in the same conscientious way, and, if anything, appeared to love the dogs even more. It was just that as each week passed, and there was no note, no call from Alan, she slipped further into herself and deeper into depression, in the face of which Eveleigh felt helpless.

Snow had arrived with a vengeance. For two days the kennels had been cut off from the village by the bitter January storms. The new arrivals preferred the warmth of their night-time kennels, and burrowed into the clean straw. Not so the St Bernards. As the first snowflakes fell a mighty rustling and panting and excited agitation rippled from kennel to kennel.

'I do believe the snow triggers some deep buried memory of their ancestors in the Swiss mountains,' Eveleigh was convinced. 'You wait and see,' she said to a sombre-faced Kimberley as she prepared to release the dogs.

With a rush the great dogs were snuffling and sniffling through the snow, finding the deepest parts, hurling themselves shoulder-high into the drifts, rolling in it, eating it, creating snowstorms of their own, the snow flying from their paws as they dug holes in it for no apparent purpose. 'Come on, sweeties.' Eveleigh opened the gate into the pristine, snow-covered paddock, where the dogs went wild. 'Aren't they having fun?'

'They're all like puppies,' Kimberley replied, and for the first time in weeks she was smiling.

They followed the dogs into the field. It was Kimberley who threw the first snowball, which sent the St Bernards into paroxysms of joy as they tried to catch it in their large jaws.

'Sieglinde, no!' Eveleigh shouted, laughing, as the dog jumped up and knocked her to the ground, whereupon she started frantically burrowing in the snow and half burying her. 'Siggy, you've got it wrong. You silly dog, you're supposed to rescue me, not bury me.' Eveleigh was still laughing as she began to scramble to her feet, but Wotan, joining in the fun, pushed her from behind, and she shouted in pain as her ankle twisted beneath her.

'Are you all right?' Kimberley struggled through the deep snow towards her.

'It's my stupid ankle, it's doubled up. I can't get my boot off . . .' She stopped speaking as she and Kimberley watched the white snow turning red with alarming speed.

Kimberley brushed at the snow frantically, having to push the heavy, inquisitive dogs out of the way. Eveleigh's right foot was facing the wrong way. A bone protruded above the top of her ankle boot. Ashen-faced, she looked at Eveleigh.

'Does it hurt?'

'Oddly, no.' Eveleigh looked at her ankle with fascination. 'Perhaps we should stop the bleeding,' she suggested diffidently. Kimberley took off her belt and tied it tightly around Eveleigh's shin. It worked, the bleeding slowed.

'I'll go and phone for help.' She took off her anorak and put it round Eveleigh's shoulders, and ran. Half a dozen St Bernards, thinking it a game, joined her, but Sieglinde and Wotan stood guard over Eveleigh.

Kimberley dialled for an ambulance. She then tried Jim Varley, but got the answer machine, so she phoned the only other family she knew and Nadine answered.

'I'm not speaking to you,' she said immediately.

'Please, Nadine. This is an emergency. I need your mother . . .'

Grudgingly, Nadine called Thomasine.

Her calls finished, Kimberley grabbed a blanket, had the presence of mind to fill a hot-water bottle and raced back to Eveleigh, who was still sitting in the snow looking grey and shivering uncontrollably.

It took the ambulance and Thomasine nearly half an hour to battle through the snow to the kennels. There they found Eveleigh sitting up, wedged between two St Bernards and leaning on a third as if she were sitting in a living, furry, armchair. She was wrapped in blankets and, in the circumstances, reasonably cheerful and very calm about the situation.

'I couldn't stop her shivering, then I thought the warmth of the dogs might help.'

'Undoubtedly you and the dogs saved her. Shock can be a killer.'

'She'll be all right, won't she, Mrs Lambert?'

'Surely she will, but I doubt if she'll make Crufts this year.'

As soon as Jim Varley received the message that Eveleigh had been taken to the casualty department in Morristown, he was in his car and racing to see her. He had a long wait. Eveleigh's fracture was so severe that surgery was required. But eventually, when she recovered consciousness, it was to find Jim sitting beside her bed, holding her hand.

'Jim . . .' she croaked.

'Eveleigh! God, what a scare you gave me.'

'I've only broken my ankle,' she said with difficulty, still muzzy from the drugs in her system.

'Only? When I got here and they explained to me – God, if it hadn't been for Kimberley . . . I could have lost you! I've been so slow, so stupid. It was staring me in the face and I didn't see it.'

'See what?' She waved her hand vaguely at him.

'That I love you.'

'That's nice,' she said softly, before drifting back to sleep.

Eveleigh was the first to admit that she was not an easy patient. Apart from the odd cold, she had never known a day's illness. And now, feeling fit but immobilised by her broken ankle, the inactivity was almost too much for her to cope with.

Kimberley cared for her during the day with a patience Eveleigh thought she would never be able to repay, especially when half the time she was being irascible with her. Jim had moved back into the house so that Eveleigh should not be alone at night. His presence did not stop her short, sharp bursts of irritation, but he was patiently amused by them.

Her food was wrong, the house too hot or too cold, the weather annoying. Incapable of resting, she'd sit on a chair manoeuvring the hoover around a room Kimberley had already cleaned. Most of all she fretted about her dogs and the care they were getting.

'Eveleigh, honestly, you're working yourself into a state over nothing. Kimberley is managing beautifully. That girl's a godsend.'

Jim meant well, but this only gave Eveleigh another source of worry – she began to fear the dogs would switch allegiance to Kimberley, love her instead of herself. She worried that, unless she got moving quickly, she would never get back on to the old footing with them.

Everyone put this uncharacteristic behaviour down to her enforced immobility. Certainly she found this irksome, but if the truth were told, what was upsetting Eveleigh the most was Jim. At night, when she lay on the bed which Kimberley and Jim had carried downstairs and put up in the rarely used dining room, and she heard Jim above her moving about in the spare room, she could have cried from pent-up emotion and frustration. Why didn't he come to her? Why didn't he make love to her?

Eveleigh received a constant supply of visitors. Gill and Justin brought Sadie, Sukie and Sandie, and offered to do her hair. But Eveleigh brusquely rejected the offer. 'What does it matter how I look?'

'My, my, we're not our usual sunny self today, now are we?' When even the antics of their poodles failed to amuse her they opted to leave.

'We've got to do something, Jim. She's going to get stuck in this doom if not, people can, you know.' Fee Walters, who had come to visit her, spoke to Jim outside the house as she was getting into her car.

'Fee, I just don't know what to do. We just can't seem to chivvy her along.'

'Well, somehow or other she's going to have to go to Crufts – otherwise she'll be a crabby old so-and-so for ever,' Fee advised. 'That's our last hope with her.'

Friends from the dog world made the journey, far from easy given the atrocious weather, to see her. But Jim began to think they did more harm than good. Their endless chatter about Crufts was pushing Eveleigh further away from them all as the realisation that she would not be showing her dogs finally sank in.

Nadine, in her new role, ran errands and played canasta with her. She even, at Eveleigh's request to be understanding, re-made friends with Kimberley. Oliver made her laugh, but the person she most looked forward to seeing was Thomasine.

Eveleigh had never had a friend other than her Reggie, and certainly she had never sought a female one. But Thomasine was different. Thomasine was how Eveleigh would like to be. She was open and said what she thought, something Eveleigh found difficult to do. And while attractive, it was in an unconcerned way – how she looked and what she wore were of minor importance to Thomasine, for Eveleigh could never have made friends with a fashion plate. And, most importantly, Thomasine did not gossip, nor did she pry. Eveleigh could not have put up with either.

Eveleigh had never confided in a soul. There had been times when she had thought what a comfort it might be, but she was incapable of doing so. Until she got to know Thomasine and thought she might perhaps risk it, almost certain that Thomasine wouldn't say a word, not even to Oliver.

'. . . You see, Thomasine, he told me he loved me. At least I think he did, but I wasn't totally out of the anaesthetic, so I might have dreamt it,' she found herself saying one afternoon when the two of them were alone. She had been right, confiding was a great comfort.

'And you want him to have said it?'

'Well, yes. Very much so. But what do I do? I mean he's kissed me once, that's all.'

'Maybe he's scared to. Maybe that's why he only said it when he knew you'd be all woozy. Has he ever told you anything in the past that he might think stands in the way of you building a relationship?'

'Of course! Yes,' Eveleigh said, more animated than she had been in days. It had to be Beth. He'd confided in her his shame at sleeping with the woman; did he think she now despised him as much as he despised himself? 'Thomasine, you're so clever,' she said, but she did not explain further, and her assessment of Thomasine was correct. Thomasine did not ask but, sensing this particular conversation was at an end, asked her if she fancied more tea.

'I'd prefer a gin and tonic.'

'You're getting better.' Thomasine smiled at her as she stood up to prepare the drinks. 'I've something to tell you,' she said, resettling herself in the armchair and resting her feet on Brünnhilde's broad back.

'I thought several weeks ago that you had.'

'So? What?'

'I think you're going to tell me you're pregnant.'

Thomasine looked astonished. 'How do you know? I only found out myself last week.'

'I just knew – there was a look about you. I can't explain.'

'You're a witch, Eveleigh. Or is it being a breeder?' She laughed at this notion.

'Maybe it is.'

Despite Eveleigh's determination to get back on her feet, her ankle did not feel the same way. She could move on crutches now but, with the snow still lying, she was unable to venture outside. And there was no way she could put any weight on her foot. Using the crutches tired her and her frustration with herself as she pushed herself to the limit was enormous. The doctor patiently explained that there was no way she would be fit enough to trundle her dogs around Crufts – just over a month away.

'You could get someone else to do it for you,' Oliver suggested.

'Who?'

'Maybe Thomasine could help.'

'What if Brünnhilde pulls her over, in her condition?'

Oliver looked sharply at Thomasine. 'I didn't tell her, she guessed.'

'Thank goodness someone else knows. Talk to her, Eveleigh. Try and get her to see sense. She says she won't marry me.'

'Thomasine?' Eveleigh looked surprised.

'I will marry him. When it's born. Not before.'

'Eveleigh, I'm potty about her. Please persuade her.'

'I can't make her, Oliver. That's her decision.'

'You must have an opinion.'

'Yes, but I doubt if she wants to hear it.'

'Eveleigh, you can be the most frustrating person on this planet.' Oliver was virtually jumping up and down with annoyance.

'What about Crufts?' Thomasine asked, pointedly.

'There's Kimberley.'

'But she's so young.' Eveleigh frowned. 'It takes a long time to learn how to show a dog to the best advantage.'

'She's quick. She'd learn. She knows the dogs.'

'But, Oliver, she'd be up against the most professional handlers in the world.'

'Is there someone else you trust who would show for you?'

'No.'

'There you are then – it's Kimberley.'

The problem was that Kimberley did not share Oliver's confidence in her when he later put the proposition. 'I'd make a mess of it, and Mrs Brenton would be so angry with me.'

'There's no one else, Kimberley.'

'She did mention it. I said I'd think about it.'

'There's not a lot of time to think, Kimberley. Look, even if you don't manage to get up to Crufts standard, it'll give Mrs Brenton something to think about. You'll be doing us all a favour – this boredom of hers is getting a bit of a pain.' He spoke with so huge a grin that she did not feel disloyal when agreeing with him. 'And, after all, it's only like taking a dog for "walkies", isn't it?'

It wasn't. It was far more complicated than that.

February

53

Eveleigh had finally decided which two dogs to enter for Crufts, Brünnhilde and Lohengrin. Of the two, Kimberley liked Brünnhilde the most. But it was the male dog on which Eveleigh pinned her greatest hopes.

Kimberley had already attended a couple of Gill and Justin's ringcraft classes with a puppy Eveleigh had kept from her most recent litter. Despite all her experience of showing dogs, she still liked her puppies to gain the knowledge of how to perform in a show-ring, and get used to strange dogs at the classes which Gill had taken over.

Brünnhilde's session passed without incident as she behaved beautifully, but Lohengrin evidently sensed Kimberley's nervousness immediately, pulling on his lead, rolling on his back and finally tripping her up. Kimberley was quickly reduced to tears.

Thomasine had driven them to the community hall in Shillingham, and was sitting on the sidelines with Eveleigh. 'He's too much for her,' she said, as the large dog deftly walked in front of Kimberley, tripping the girl yet again.

'He's showing off. He knows he's in control. She's so nervous it's transmitting to him – down the lead like an electricity conductor,' Eveleigh said in a voice which sounded partly disappointed but also as if this was exactly what she had expected.

'What are you going to do?'

'If we're going to show at all, then I'm afraid it will have to be Brünnhilde. We'll never get Lohengrin to stop being so silly with her now – he's enjoying all the attention far too much.'

'They look the same to me. Brünnhilde's slightly smaller. So why do you think Lohengrin's better?'

'It's not so much that he's better formed than Brünnhilde, it's just he's got such a personality. She's very sweet, but she never shines in quite the same way. He loves the ring, people watching him – he performs. It makes him stand out – a judge can't ignore him. You're seeing the downside here – he just can't stop clowning. Gill, love, you'll never get him to shift that way – bribe him, it's all we can do,' she called to Gill, who was losing the battle of wills to get Lohengrin to move from the centre of the small ring they'd marked out with tape on the wooden floor. The dog was sprawled right across the walkway, preventing anyone else moving.

Gill dug in his pocket and produced a titbit, waving it at the dog. Like magic, Lohengrin rolled over and was up in a trice, trotting along behind Gill sniffing at his hand.

'What a bad boy!' said Gill, returning him. 'I'm surprised at one of yours, Eveleigh. I said to Justin, I thought all Eveleigh's dogs were perfect, I said.'

'Not always. Lohengrin is going through an adolescent phase. They often do, and on top of that it's having an inexperienced handler – he knows it, so he plays up.'

'Right big show-off, aren't you.' Gill tweaked Lohengrin's ear. 'But Brünnhilde's a dream. Kimberley can manage her.' He smiled kindly at Kimberley, who was trying not to show how useless she felt.

'But not well. She's all over the place with her. The dog doesn't stand a chance.'

Thomasine pulled a face at Gill over the top of Eveleigh's head and squeezed Kimberley's hand tight. 'Still, we've got two more of your classes, Gill.'

'I'm afraid not. The council's closing us down. Not tickety-boo at all.'

'But, Gill, why?' Thomasine asked.

'This hall is used by a play group – say no more!'

'The anti-dog lobby?'

'Exactly, Eveleigh. Someone complained it was unhygienic and Bob's your uncle – we're out.'

'But you clean it well, surely?'

'Justin and I scrub our little fingers to the bone after every session. I tell you, you wouldn't find a dog hair in here, with the gallons of disinfectant we use.'

'First the parks. Now this,' Eveleigh said.

'It'll be the streets next. They'll have flying squads zooming about arresting OAPs with their pooches on a lead. The prisons will be full!'

'I get so upset. It's irresponsible dog owners who have brought about this state of affairs.' Eveleigh looked so depressed that Thomasine could personally have killed all the anti-dog lobby, who probably all looked like her sister Abigail. 'Well, we can forget Crufts then. That's for sure.'

'Why, we've got this far? Tell you what. I'll come over after work and help Kimberley. Would you like that?' Gill volunteered.

'It's out of the question, Gill.'

'Yes please,' said Kimberley without thinking, and ignoring Eveleigh.

'There's no point . . .'

'See you Wednesday evening.' Gill rushed off before Eveleigh could object further.

*

Oliver was not at the disastrous class. He'd driven to London to see Sophia. He'd decided not to tell Thomasine, but Wimpole, a much subdued Wimpole, knew where he'd gone.

'What a pleasant surprise,' Sophia welcomed him. 'Come in, do. I've been meaning to call you. Drink?'

'Thanks.' Oliver appeared to be studying the paintings on the wall, but was, in fact, collecting his thoughts, trying to work out the best way to approach her. He'd practised all the way up in the car, but now, faced with her, all his plans and intentions seemed doomed to failure. He could have asked a reasonable woman straight out, but Sophia was unlikely ever to be open to reason. If he should ask for a divorce he'd guarantee she'd say 'no' on principle.

'How're Slipper and Bandage?'

'Marvellous. Thanks.' He took the whisky she handed him. 'They get on like a house on fire. Daft expression that, when you think about it, isn't it?'

'Sorry?'

'Who wants a house on fire? . . . Never mind. How's Ben?'

'Getting fat.'

'And Cora?'

'I haven't seen her for weeks. Learning Spanish. She joined Daddy. They've a divine villa.'

'How did he manage that?'

'Manage what?'

'Are you being obtuse on purpose? He's supposed to be bankrupt, remember?'

'Am I likely to forget? They bought it ten years ago and put it in Cora's name, so it's safe from the creditors.'

'I didn't know.'

'Neither did Cora.' She laughed, and, though he grinned, Oliver was convinced there was something dodgy about the transaction. 'It was great of you to buy that land. I never thanked you.'

'Anything for dear old Eveleigh.'

'Has she snared Jim yet?'

'I don't think that's quite the right word to use. Let's just say their relationship is moving along satisfactorily.'

'And you and the so *sweet* Thomasine?'

'I see her from time to time,' he said guardedly, afraid to tell her the truth.

'You should shack up with her,' Sophia interrupted. 'After all, you've *so* much in common – dogs, I mean. Perhaps you could breed – dogs, I mean. Still, I'm glad you came. I've been meaning to call you – talk about something important.'

'And what's that?'

'Darling, don't be upset, will you? Promise you won't be cross?' She pouted prettily at him.

'I can't promise till I know what it is.'

'Well ...' Sophia, with infuriating slowness, trailed her finger round the top of her glass, making it ring. 'Pretty noise, isn't it? I want a divorce, Oliver.'

Oliver choked on his drink, delving in his pocket for a handkerchief to mop up the whisky he'd spilt.

'There, I knew you'd be upset. Oh dear, I should have been more subtle about it. I'm sorry, Oliver, to tell you so brutally, but I've fallen in love – you have to know.'

'Who with?' He was glad he'd choked on the whisky, it disguised his voice so it was difficult to know if he was happy, sad or angry.

'He's sweet. You'll love him. Filthy rich.'

'That's nice for you.'

'So you won't have to give me so much money now.'

'That's nice for me.' He felt stunned. Was this Sophia? 'Well ... I can only wish you happiness, Sophia.'

'Oh, how sweet of you. How dear. Another drink?'

'No. I must be going. It's getting late.'

'Did you come for anything in particular?'

'Not really, I was just in the area,' he lied, as his heart sang.

Outside the house, at last, he could not resist doing a jig in the middle of the road to an audience of one stray, but very puzzled, dog.

Kimberley's patience with Eveleigh knew no bounds. Several times a day she pounded round the ring they had contrived from hay bales, thankful that the thaw was over and that the weather, for late February, was dry. Brünnhilde shared her patience as she good-naturedly padded round with her.

'Your stride's too long – '

'Too short – '

'Pull her head up – '

'Push her head down – '

'Don't crowd the dog – '

'Too fast – '

'Too slow – '

She took all the criticisms in good part, even managing to smile as she did, so determined not to let Eveleigh pull her down and take away the little confidence she was building. Away from Eveleigh, Jim, Thomasine and Nadine attempted to boost Kimberley's belief in herself.

For nearly a month Kimberley had been learning to show the dog, not only walking and running, but stationary too. How to show the dog to her best advantage, to note the line, to place the feet, to groom the all-important flowing tail, to ensure Brünnhilde's total confidence in her. All this besides her duties in the kennels.

Crufts was now two weeks away and tension was rising.

'There won't be a dog at Crufts who doesn't love to show. It's up to you,

Kimberley, to get that something extra out of Brünnhilde,' Eveleigh said for the umpteenth time.

Kimberley dropped Brünnhilde's lead and stood in the middle of the makeshift ring. 'What the hell do you think I'm trying to do!' she shouted, before running blindly to the house, leaving Nadine to catch Brünnhilde.

'Well! Really!' Eveleigh exclaimed.

'Really! Exactly! She's doing her best and what appreciation do you show her?' Nadine advanced on Eveleigh, who was sitting in the wheelchair she had reluctantly adopted. 'She's worked off her feet, and now this! You don't even say thank you to her. And I'll tell you something – she wants Brünnhilde to win more than anything else, just to repay you for all you've done for her. More fool her, I say.' Nadine stood glaring belligerently down at Eveleigh, the resin cast supporting her ankle propped up in front of her.

'Am I that impossible?'

'Gross.'

'It means so much.'

'To her too.'

'I must apologise.'

'I should jolly well think so.' Nadine pushed Eveleigh back to the house, Brünnhilde in tow.

Jim carried a tray, with a small silver bowl of snowdrops and Eveleigh's omelette, into the sitting room, where she sat in a chair by the fire, her ankle on a footstool in front of her, her other foot resting comfortably on Brünnhilde, whose large body covered most of the hearthrug.

'You are so kind to me,' she smiled up at him.

'It's my pleasure. Though you must be getting fed up with omelettes,' he joked as he uncorked a bottle of white wine and poured her a glass.

'My, this is good,' she said after she had tasted it. She looked across at Jim sitting in the chair opposite and felt how right they were together, how comfortable and content she felt with him. If only he would say something – if only she had the courage to act on Thomasine's advice. But then she was so afraid she had dreamt the tender scene in the hospital. How she loved him, how she longed for him. She pushed her hair back from her face and, without realising, sighed.

'Anything wrong?' Jim asked, looking up from his own food.

'Nothing –' she began. 'The dogs, Crufts, Kimberley, everything –' she sighed again. She drank a quick gulp of wine. 'No, that's not true. It's – Forgive me, Jim, but I have to speak.' She closed her eyes, shutting the sight of him away, afraid what she might see on his face. 'Jim, I love you!' Her hands were clenched now in tight fists. She felt mortified. What had got into her?

She felt her hand being lifted, was aware of his breath on her knuckles, felt his lips brush her skin.

'Eveleigh! My darling. I love you too. I've been afraid to say – '

'I thought you did once – in the hospital.' Still she sat with her eyes tightly closed.

'Look at me, Eveleigh, please.'

'I can't, I'm too embarrassed.'

'You must.'

Gingerly, she peeped out. He was so close to her, smiling so gently at her.

'You weren't fully *compos mentis* when I told you. It was a bit of a cheat. And I was afraid too. After Beth – I didn't know what you thought of me.'

'I admired you for telling me. I tried to understand how you'd got into such a pickle, but then, I'm a woman, so I couldn't grasp it totally. But in any case, after what that woman did over the dogs – well!'

'Dear Eveleigh,' he smiled. 'We'd make a good team, you and me.'

'And think of the vet's bills I'd save.'

Jim leaned over and kissed her. Brünnhilde opened one eye, lifted her head, watched them a moment, and then sank back into the serious business of sleeping. If Eveleigh had not been so occupied she would have been convinced her dog was smiling.

March

54

Four days before they left for the show Kimberley, with Nadine as assistant and Eveleigh supervising, began the long preparations for Brünnhilde to look her best.

They bathed her in the large footbath Eveleigh had had installed, soaping her and giggling furiously as the dog shook herself, spraying water from her thick pelt, soaking them to the skin. They rough-dried her with towels in front of the fire, and then with a hairdryer as they brushed out her long hair, which Brünnhilde particularly liked. They had to pay extra attention to the long fur around her paws and on her chin to get them as white as possible, though total whiteness would never be achieved. Jim had trimmed her toenails, since Kimberley was afraid to do them. They brushed her with a wire brush to remove all the loose hair, fluffing her tail up. Her ears were cleaned, her eyes, the folds of skin on her face, her teeth. Brünnhilde looked wonderful. Until it was time to leave for Crufts she would live in the house, fussed and cosseted.

Thomasine decided that without doubt she had been fortunate to meet Oliver. He cared about Nadine and felt a responsibility towards her, which she had barely dreamed was a possibility. She constantly told him how grateful and relieved she was.

'You don't have to keep thanking me, Thomasine. You're a package deal, you and your daughter. I wouldn't have asked you to marry me if I didn't want Nadine too.'

'She's not the easiest child – '

'She's not a child, sweety. She's a young woman.'

'Is that where I've gone wrong?'

'Maybe.'

He had involved Nadine in all their decisions. Where to live, which room she wanted, how she wanted it decorated.

'It's perfect as it is, Oliver,' Nadine said. Thomasine struggled to hide her astonishment as Nadine accepted the flower-sprigged wallpapered room with its looped and swagged matching chintz curtains.

He'd accompanied them to a parent-teacher evening at the school, where the reports on Nadine had made Thomasine's heart sink. But on the way home, when Oliver talked to her, her unbelieving ears heard Nadine agree she'd been a fool and would work harder in future.

No longer was there a problem over the dogs, her clothes, her untidy room. She'd even eaten meat. Before her eyes Nadine was changing.

The move from The School House to Bishop's End was accomplished in stages, but now the final boxes had gone and the furniture van had today moved the pieces of furniture Thomasine wanted to keep. Wimpole would be moving into their old home the following day.

By evening they were all tired. 'Let's go to the flicks and have a Chinese?' Oliver suggested. Thomasine, having reached the point where she was convinced they would never be straight again, happily agreed. As they drove home, half listening to Nadine and Oliver talking, she felt, strangely, that they were a complete family in a way she had never experienced with Robert.

'We've got to decide on music. After what to watch on TV families fall out over music more than anything else,' Oliver said wisely, as if he'd been a parent all his adult life.

They argued good-naturedly about what cassettes could be played in the car. The final agreement was that all classical and modern rock music were banned. They settled on the safe middle ground of Pink Floyd, Status Quo and the odd Beatle recording, which all three liked.

'It'll be compromise all the way now, I suppose,' Nadine said from the back.

'You can play whatever you want in your room, just don't inflict it on us,' Oliver answered.

'Some compromise!'

'It is. Your modern stuff in your room. Classical in my work room. Mix, as now, in the drawing room. What could be fairer?'

'What about the kitchen?'

'Country and Western.' Thomasine turned and smiled at her daughter.

'And in the nursery?' Nadine asked slyly.

Thomasine's and Oliver's jaws both dropped open, and eyes widened in unison, like a formation dance duo. Thomasine, who at four months still barely showed, had been putting off telling Nadine.

'You should have told me, then you needn't look so gob-smacked,' Nadine said, trying not to shriek with mirth at their expressions.

'How long have you known? Who told you?'

'I guessed. You've been whispering and secretive – I was right, wasn't I?'

'I didn't know how to tell you,' Thomasine confessed.

'Quite easy, you just do.'

'I didn't want to upset you.'

'Why should I be upset?'

'Well . . . you know . . .'

'You weren't afraid I'd be jealous, were you? Mum, that's gross! Of course I wouldn't be – jealous of a baby, whatever next? I'm grown up now.'

'Of course you are, and I was stupid. I'm sorry.' But Thomasine did not yet possess Oliver's confidence in a changed Nadine; she still remembered her jealousy over the dogs. Such a person could easily be jealous of a baby.

'When are you getting hitched?'

Oliver glanced sideways at Thomasine. 'After the baby's born.'

'You what?' Nadine leant forward. 'That's dreadful. Why? Your divorce will be through in time, Oliver. You've got to get married.'

'Don't lecture me, it's your mum who's the problem. You tell her.' And Oliver could have sung with happiness, knowing Nadine would be relentless in her onslaught on Thomasine's objections. He couldn't have hoped for a better ally.

'I do hope the dogs are all right – Nova and the puppies are quite capable of chewing the house down by now.'

'Don't change the subject,' Nadine and Oliver shouted in unison.

Nadine was in bed. The dogs, a snoring, twitching, scratching bunch, were sprawled in front of the fire. Thomasine and Oliver sat curled up together on the sofa, enjoying the peace and each other.

'Just look at Slipper.' Oliver pointed to where Slipper, lying close to Bandage, had one of her paws on him, as if she were holding him.

'They're wonderful, and to think a year ago I didn't give dogs a thought.'

'It was delayed development, that was all. You were so nice already, the dogs had to follow.'

Thomasine threw back her head and laughed with delight. Oliver leant over and took hold of her hand.

'I love you so much. Please, please marry me.'

She stopped laughing and gazed at him for what seemed an age. He had such a dear face, such a kind face, she thought. And how she loved his smile. How she loved him.

'Am I being stupid?'

'Very.'

'As if you weren't enough, now, I suppose, Nadine will never let up either. You wear me down.'

'I mean to. Is that a "yes"?'

'I think it must be.' She smiled at him as he sat, still holding her hand. 'What's the matter?' she asked, suddenly concerned, for it looked as if his eyes had filled with tears.

'Sorry!' Self-consciously he put up his hand to wipe his eyes. 'It's just, I've never wanted anything so badly in my whole life as I want to marry and love you.'

'My darling,' she sighed, and leant to kiss him as Oliver produced a ring from his pocket and quickly slipped it on Thomasine's finger before she changed her mind.

They set off for Crufts very early on a bleak March morning in convoy. Oliver, with Thomasine and Nadine, went first. Brünnhilde sat on a clean blanket in the back of Eveleigh's Bentley with Kimberley. The window, despite the cold was, of necessity, slightly open, for Brünnhilde was panting with excitement as if she knew where she was going. Without the fresh air the other windows of the car would quickly steam up. A far happier, non-irascible Eveleigh sat beside Jim, who was driving the large car.

'I do hope Grace and Wimpole manage,' Eveleigh said. 'I hope we haven't asked them to do too much.'

'Eveleigh! Stop worrying!'

'Oh, Mrs Brenton, I mixed the other dogs' feeds and made endless lists for them.'

'I'm being silly, aren't I?' Eveleigh smiled at them.

'Yes,' they replied in unison.

At sight of the huge Exhibition Centre and the crowds in Birmingham, Kimberley wanted to run. 'It's enormous!' she exclaimed, standing outside the car, the wind whipping across the open plaza, fluffing Brünnhilde's fur. Kimberley pulled her coat tight, and waited while Jim unloaded Eveleigh's wheelchair. Then, pushing Eveleigh and holding on to the dog, she moved towards the dogs' entrance where, having shown their exhibitors card, they were allowed in.

It was Sunday, the final day of Crufts, and the working dogs judging day. Their documents had been sent to them by post; now they had to match their number with those on the dogs' benches. An official of the Kennel Club, a friend of Eveleigh's, saw how difficult it was for Kimberley to manage both chair and dog, and stepped in and pushed Eveleigh.

'I was so glad that unfortunate business was cleared up, Eveleigh. Scandalous! That someone could pull it off,' he said.

'Ben Luckett had contacts everywhere, people who owed him a favour – even in our dog world.'

'I never believed any of it, you know. Nor did any member I spoke to, not of you, Eveleigh, you've done so much for dogs.'

'Thank you,' Eveleigh smiled modestly.

'You got the letter?'

'From the Chairman of the Disciplinary Sub-Committee? Oh, yes. I'm going to frame it,' she laughed, managing expertly to cover up the hurt she had felt and the intense relief when the letter came.

Kimberley was walking alongside them as they entered the first great hall, already crowded with people and dogs, even though the general public would not be allowed in until ten. From the ceiling above each ring hung its number: they were looking for ring number 19, for close by it would be the St Bernard benches. They crossed the first hall, past the stalls being set up where anything a dog would ever need could be bought, from food to blankets, from kennels to figurines, from oil paintings to jewellery in the shape of every dog represented, and even one for a pet crematorium. They passed the Guide Dogs for the Blind stall, the Retired Greyhound Trust, HM Customs and Excise with their search dogs. They kept stopping as they progressed through the second exhibition hall as people rushed up to speak to Eveleigh and wish her well.

At last they reached the St Bernard section. There were the rows of numbered wooden benches, each with a partition, and they finally found theirs. Brünnhilde had a good sniff and jumped up with no bidding, then sat down and with wise eyes surveyed the scene.

Eveleigh was being greeted on all sides by fellow St Bernard breeders, glad to see her here, happy that all the unpleasantness had been resolved. She tried not to think that it was a pity they had not spoken up for her when she needed them, but managed, instead, to smile her thanks and keep her counsel.

Dogs were being put on the benches. Some were placidly clambering up themselves, the more nervous or the novices having to be pushed, pulled and hauled onto their seats. Benching chains were clipped on to a holding ring for security but, looking at the number of St Bernards already overwhelmed by a great need for sleep, they seemed to be unnecessary. Brünnhilde greeted the dogs either side of her before curling up for a snooze herself. More than twenty thousand dogs were judged over the four days of Crufts, and today a good five thousand of them were settling into position. It was amazing, Kimberley thought, that the humans were making more noise than the dogs.

Jim arrived with the bags, and Kimberley was soon occupied unpacking Brünnhilde's grooming kit, filling her water bowl, shoving her blanket under her for comfort. She then sat beside her, as if guarding her, constantly brushing her just to keep busy and to keep her nerves at bay while Brünnhilde snored contentedly.

'It's unbelievably clean, especially when you think this is the last day. I thought it would whiff something awful of dog,' Oliver said, as he and Thomasine joined them at the St Bernard benches.

'And did you see the dog loos! Amazing!' Nadine was failing in her plan to look nonchalant, swept along like everyone else by the atmosphere of mounting excitement.

'And the dogs are all so good. Just look at them sitting there so patiently. Nova would have caused a riot by now.'

'They're used to it. Most of these dogs have been doing shows since they were puppies,' Eveleigh explained.

'Kimberley, here are your clothes.' Thomasine held out the zippered plastic dress bag she'd brought with her, since there had been too much risk of it being crushed in Eveleigh's Bentley.

'Should I put it on now?' Kimberley asked, incapable of making any decision herself.

'You might as well – we've an hour, but by the time you've titivated yourself...'

'I'll come with you, Kimberley,' Nadine offered, and they wandered off together.

'Any chance of seeing Gill and Justin?' Thomasine asked.

'Probably not. Poodles are in the Utility Group, and they were shown yesterday. We can find out if they won.'

'Then the bulldogs were yesterday too? Oh, what a shame, I hoped to see some.'

'You must go to the Kennel Club's Discover Dogs exhibition, Thomasine. You'll find examples of every breed of dog shown here over the four days of the competition.'

After her experiences the previous year, Eveleigh was determined that Brünnhilde should not be left for one minute alone on the bench, just in case. She and Jim took the first turn, and Thomasine and Oliver took the opportunity to see the dogs.

Each breed had its own section, and they walked up and down the aisles lined either side with the wooden benches on which sat the pick of every breed in the country.

'I want them all,' Thomasine said, as they ambled by admiring the boxers. In contrast to the St Bernards, none of these dogs slept, but sat bolt upright, eyes darting each and every way, excitedly alert. The Rottweilers sat as if on duty and watched them pass with wary eyes. Alsatians with beautiful expressions, pricked-up ears, tails pluming behind them, slunk by, obediently close to their masters. They met Alaskan Malamutes with intelligent eyes and coarse, oily coats, magnificent mastiffs and Newfoundlands. Norwegian, Finnish, Swedish and French dogs of whose existence they'd been, until now, ignorant. Desperate-to-please Dobermans, elegant Danes, spotted Dalmatians; sheep dogs, cattle dogs, water dogs; hairy dogs and strange, half-bald Portu-guese water dogs; push-me-pull-you dogs. Tall, short, thin, large – Thomasine thought she must be in paradise. In the Discovering Dogs section they found two bulldogs and, adorable as they were, Thomasine was convinced that Nova was better.

Kimberley changed in the ladies' into beige trousers, cotton blouse and matching flat suede pumps.

'God, that's so ugh! What on earth made you buy that!' Nadine said, without thinking, and then, since she was still in 'nice' mode, apologised.

'I quite like it. Mrs Brenton bought it for me, she insisted. She says smart dogs deserve smart handlers.' She was putting on a light make-up, concen-trating on brushing on her mascara. 'I don't usually wear this colour, but she wanted a colour for Brünnhilde to stand out against – give her a better outline. This works well with her reddish-brown bits.'

'You nervous?'

'Terrified.'

'You'll be fine. Bet you win. Hang on, you've got a bit of hair sticking out.' She reached up and pushed the offending strand back into the band which was holding Kimberley's blonde hair in a pony tail. 'You look great.' She hugged her friend.

'Thanks. Shall we get a coffee? Do you think we've got time?'

They dawdled on their way to one of the many cafés, looking at the things to buy. Kimberley bought a poster of a St Bernard and Nadine one of a bulldog – 'for my mum, not me,' she insisted. They were looking at costume jewellery, all dog-related.

'Kimberley?'

She swung round. She felt the blood rush from her face to be replaced rapidly and redly. 'Alan,' she spoke in a whisper. 'Ooops,' said Nadine.

'You look lovely.' He meant it, then wished he hadn't said it.

'And you look so smart.' She glanced quickly, but admiringly, at him. 'In uniform.'

'I'm on duty at the RSPCA stand.' He'd missed her, but until he saw her he had not realised how much. And upon seeing her again the old longing flooded back and, mysteriously, the bitterness had disappeared.

'No more Special Branch?'

'Got the sack?' asked Nadine, feeling remarkably left out of things. In any case, she'd never really liked him – too nosey by far.

'Can we talk, Kimberley?' He ignored Nadine.

'I can't . . .'

'I see. Sorry I asked.' She saw the anger in him flare. Why did they always have to have these misunderstandings?

'You don't understand. I'm showing a dog in fifteen minutes.'

'After?'

'If you like,' she said simply, and turned quickly on her heel, knowing she was blushing again and furious with herself for doing so.

'What a creep. Why do you give him the time of day after the way he treated you?'

'You didn't want to speak to me, either,' she said heatedly, not liking to hear him criticised.

'That's different. I changed my mind, didn't I?'

'But you were here, and God knows where he's been.' She said this with concern, for he had looked tired and much thinner than three months ago.

Kimberley stood at the entrance to the ring with the line of St Bernard bitches for the post-graduate class, Brünnhilde standing patiently beside her. Her heart was racing, her mouth was dry, she wanted to pee, she felt sick and she couldn't imagine what she was doing here.

Someone gave an order and the line moved forward as the dogs and their handlers entered the ring. Kimberley was aware of the crowd, several deep, clustered around the edge of the ring, but she did not look up. *Concentrate on your dog*, she remembered Eveleigh's instructions. She checked for the neatly folded Jiffy cloth she'd put in her waistband to mop up any slobber from Brünnhilde's generous mouth.

She patted Brünnhilde with short, sharp, nervous pats. The dog jerked her head and looked up to her, a puzzled expression on her large gentle face. 'Sorry, Brünnhilde. I'm fine. Don't worry about me. Who's a beautiful girl then . . .' She spoke gently, as instructed – *Talk to the dog*. She dared to glance about her, but something seemed to be wrong with her vision, for she could make out no individual face, everything was a blur.

Watch the judge. Where was the judge? Down the line, she need not check Brünnhilde's position yet. Or should she? Better. She bent down and aligned Brünnhilde's front legs, checking that her large, arched feet were neatly together.

'How old?'

The voice made her jump. 'Sorry? Um . . .' Her mind was a total blank as she looked at the woman judge with blind panic.

'How old is she?' the woman repeated patiently.

'Three,' Kimberley managed to say.

Brünnhilde stood stoically as the woman felt her body beneath the thick, long pelt. She checked her ears, her eyes, her tail, her teeth. Ran her hands down her thick legs. Checking for faults, for deformities, for what? Kimberley's mind shrieked and she saw that Brünnhilde's feet were not in line, and she bent down, worrying how long they'd been like this.

'If you would take her round, please.' The judge sketched in the air the route she was to follow.

'Good girl, Brünnhilde. Good girl . . .' She tugged gently on the lead as Eveleigh had taught her and Brünnhilde shook herself, but to her relief no slobber flew, and ponderously, then more easily, she began to move in an unhurried, smooth motion, Kimberley running alongside. Brünnhilde's tail flowed behind her, the feathered fur spreading as she moved faster. And it suddenly all felt so right as she ran in step with her and they appeared to move as one. Just as Eveleigh had said, *as if you're ballroom dancing.*

Five bitches were selected and Brünnhilde was one, though it took a whisper from another woman to tell her. Then all five were inspected and they stood in line again. Everything seemed to take an age as the judge paced up and down the row looking carefully at each dog, checking a second time, then a third and then a fourth.

The judge stood back, deep in concentration, looking up and down the line. Dramatically she lifted her arm and pointed straight at Brünnhilde. The crowd went wild. Brünnhilde jumped up at Kimberley. The only person who did not know that Brünnhilde was Best Bitch in her class was Kimberley. The woman beside her told her to go and stand by the board she had not even seen brought into the ring. People were congratulating her, kissing her and she had a rosette pinned on her.

The welcome from the others was tumultuous.

'I couldn't have done it better myself,' Eveleigh beamed at her, clutching her hand.

'You were great,' said Nadine.

'I couldn't breathe,' said Thomasine.

'You both brought a lump to my throat,' said Oliver.

'Well done,' said Jim.

'Hullo, Kimberley,' said Alan.

Kimberley sat with Alan having a coffee, still flushed with triumph, still so excited she could barely sit down.

'I missed you, Kim.'

'Me too.'

'I'm sorry.'

'Me too.'

'I should have believed in you.'

'There was a lot to believe.' She looked away from him, loathing to think of that time, the shame, of those poor dogs. Then she was aware of his hand searching for hers.

'Eveleigh told me you'd not gone to warn your father. That you'd gone to make sure it was stopped.'

'Something like that. I'm not even sure any more what I was doing. But why didn't you tell me what you did? That hurt me,' she found the courage to say.

'It's difficult, Kimberley. I wanted to tell you – often. But . . .'

'You didn't trust me.'

'In this job it's often best not to say anything. If I had told you what I was about you'd have been put in a spot – Be honest. What would you have done?'

'I don't know, that's the honest truth. I understand in a way. I nearly told you about my father. I don't know how many times.'

'But you didn't.'

'No, and I hated myself that I didn't. If I had, we'd never have had our falling out – all these lonely months.'

'It's been hell, hasn't it? When I saw you just now in the ring, I loved you so much, I wanted to tell everyone.'

'Please . . . I couldn't bear it if . . .'

'We won't this time. I promise. I bought the house, it's mine. There's the chance of a transfer to Morristown – uniform branch. I've looked into it, I can apply – if you want me to.'

'But won't you miss your work in the Special Branch?'

'I can adjust. I'd rather be with you.'

'I don't want you to stop doing what you like. It would be better if you waited to move.'

'But then the place will have gone.'

'There'll be other chances. Honest, it's better this way. I'll move to Horsham. I don't mind.' But she did, she felt a lump in her throat at the thought of not being with the St Bernards. 'You look tired, and thinner.'

'I've been tracking sheep being driven down through France to Spain. There was a bit of an altercation,' he grinned. 'My foot got in the way – got run over!'

'You might have been killed!' Her eyes were round with horror at the very idea.

'But I wasn't. And I'm back. My foot's fine. I only told you to make you feel sorry for me. I love you, Kimberley, will you marry me?'

She could not believe what was happening to her – drinking coffee from polystyrene mugs, here in this crowded hall, surrounded by people and dogs. She smiled; the dogs seemed appropriate. She was suddenly full of such delirious happiness – no bleak future, never again unloved, someone to care for her. 'I'd like that.'

'Kimberley!'

She looked up from their entwined hands. It was Oliver.

'Sorry to interrupt, but Eveleigh's throwing a wobbly, convinced you've done a runner. You're needed – it's time for the Best St Bernard Bitch to be chosen.'

'I'm going to faint. I know I am.' Thomasine was fanning herself with her programme. Brünnhilde had, after a gruelling session in the ring, been chosen Best Bitch. The wait for the selection of the Best of Breed, when she would compete against the Best Dog, seemed endless. If Thomasine had felt tense before, it was as nothing to now.

Brünnhilde won! She was chosen as the Best St Bernard and now had to move on to the selection of the Best of Group, which would be judged in the main ring and where she would be up against the best of each breed of working dog. If Brünnhilde emerged Best of Group, then she'd be in the final with the dogs from the other five groups.

Brünnhilde seemed to be aware that she'd done well, but this did not stop her catching up on some much needed sleep after so much excitement. Her great head lolled on her legs, her paws hung limply over the side of the bench and she wiffled contentedly.

'Wonderful, isn't it, the atmosphere here?' Oliver said to Thomasine as they sat on the folding chairs Jim had brought, guarding Brünnhilde while Eveleigh and Jim grabbed a bite to eat.

'Dog people are so nice. They must catch it from the dogs.'

'Shall we do this – show our brood?'

'I'd really like that – bet my Nova wins more than your Slipper.'

'Poor Bandage, he'll never be smart enough again.'

'But you've got him back, that's the most important thing.'

'And I've got you. Bliss!' He leant back in the chair and immediately toppled over, but the clatter didn't even wake Brünnhilde.

Brünnhilde was Best in Group!

The excitement in the St Bernard section had reached an uncontrollable level. Old rivalries were forgotten, ambitions were buried, everyone wanted Brünnhilde to become Best in Show – if she did, then she would be the first St Bernard to win the honour since 1974.

'It's all too much!' Eveleigh was frantically fanning her face. 'Where is the child?'

'Don't worry, she's with that nice RSPCA Inspector. They look as if they're floating on air – and I don't think it's all down to Brünnhilde.' Jim was having a great day. He'd met up with colleagues he'd not seen for years. He was already loaded down with samples from the animal-food manufacturers who wanted him to try their new products – for whelping bitches, for puppies, for adult dogs, old dogs, fat dogs. 'It's amazing! There's a diet for each and every dog, I wish I'd come here years ago.'

'I wish you had too.'

'Happy?' he asked.

'Totally,' she replied. She clutched the arms of her chair with her work-roughened hands. She felt a strange elation, the excitement she supposed. She suddenly realised that the fear had disappeared. Ahead of her stretched a happy future; she had a companion for life, loneliness was banished.

If Kimberley had thought everything tense before, it was as nothing compared to this. The huge hall was buzzing with excited anticipation. The atmosphere was charged as if with electricity. The stands around the main ring were packed, the tickets sold months ago – just for this, for her and Brünnhilde. She shivered. It didn't bear thinking about.

'Are you cold?' the woman beside her asked.

'Excited,' she replied, and hoped Eveleigh hadn't seen. *Speak to no one but the dog and the judge*, was another of her instructions.

Brünnhilde sat down, her tongue lolling. She was hot. Kimberley was hot. Thank goodness she'd taken Eveleigh's advice and dressed in cotton; already she could feel sweat trickling down her spine.

She wanted a drink. She looked around her at the blazing lights. Of course, television, but such a thought only made her stomach contract. I'm going to faint, she thought, and took deep breaths. Her throat was so dry she could barely swallow. Was she ill?

Brünnhilde nudged her. 'Sorry, sweety, I haven't been talking to you. It's all right. I'm all right.' Of course she was. Alan was out there somewhere watching, he'd begged, bribed, and cajoled his way in. She was going to be married. Have babies. Puppies. Oh God, she was so happy.

She tweaked at her waistband, suddenly remembering Eveleigh's warning that this judge liked *a neat dog and a neat handler*. She was aware the woman beside her was shaking. At least she wasn't doing that. Just look how she was transmitting her nervousness – her dog, a Weimaraner, sleek and grey-beige, was already pulling on the lead. At least she wasn't doing that!

The judge looked so severe. A bright red rose in his buttonhole. He was a famous breeder of Rottweilers, Eveleigh had told her, thank goodness there wasn't one in the ring. As she talked to Brünnhide, steadying her all the time, she watched him. He didn't once smile and he was working his mouth all the time, sucking in his cheeks, licking his lips as if he had toothache. 'Please God, don't let him have toothache,' she said aloud, as if to Brünnhilde.

'I beg your pardon?' said the finalist the other side, a white bull terrier attached to her lead.

'Nothing,' Kimberley said, feeling foolish and thinking that Bandage, but for his poor scars, was a finer dog than this one.

They lined up. The announcer called their names. The final six were the bull terrier, best from the Terrier Group, a beagle from the Hound Group, the gundog, the Weimaraner, a Pekinese in the Toy Group, a German Spitz for Utility, and Brünnhilde for the Working Dogs.

The judging finally began. The beagle performed perfectly, face alert as he trotted neatly and precisely around. The Weimaraner looked frightened and nearly tripped up his handler, but his gunmetal coat gleamed with health and excellence. The German Spitz was an exuberant happy pile of white fur, obviously having the time of its life. The terrier behaved impeccably, and then it was the turn of the Pekinese, which moved smartly like a hairy hovercraft on the green carpeted ring. So large for such a little dog.

Brünnhilde was last. After her examination, the longest, most thorough yet, she and Kimberley moved out into the ring. The roar from the audience soared to the rafters. Since Brünnhilde was representative of the working dogs, and this was their day, she had the unfair advantage of stands packed with working-dog enthusiasts, cheering, egging them on.

Round they went, Brünnhilde with head and tail held high, lolloping rhythmically along, taking control, showing Kimberley how it should be done. And Kimberley realised she was enjoying herself as she hadn't done before, she could have happily run round the ring for hours, she felt so at ease.

When they halted she hugged Brünnhilde with all her might, and dared to look into the crowd and saw them all – Eveleigh, Jim, Thomasine, Nadine and, best of all, Alan, waving, thumbs up, shouting encouragement at her.

Then she bent to the task in hand. Making Brünnhilde stand tall and straight, showing off her line to perfection. Talking constantly, sensing Brünnhilde had had enough, that she wanted to crash down and sleep, and knowing, if she did, she'd never get her back up again.

It took an age, an awful nail-biting, saliva-drying, heart-pumping age.

The judge waved for the stands to be brought in. The attendants, smart in black and white, strode in carrying the numbers, the all-important numbers one and two. And the cup was there, and Kimberley felt sick again, and she was sure she was going to fall.

The judge walked back and forth, reversed from the line, studied them unsmilingly – and then his left hand pointed dramatically, followed in a millisecond by his right and he was pointing at her. The roar of the crowd was deafening and she and Brünnhilde ran forward, Brünnhilde jumping up and down in excitement, knowing she'd done well. Rolling on the floor in a whirling mass of fur.

'Reserve Best in Show! It's beyond my wildest dreams,' Eveleigh was saying once the cups had been awarded, the congratulations made, the photographs taken, the kissing calmed down and the tears mopped up.

'I thought I'd won,' Kimberley was downcast. 'I thought he pointed at us first, not the Pekinese.'

'My dear girl, you don't know what you achieved today. People show all their lives with this dream and never attain it. I'm so proud of you both.'

'Honest?'

'Pleased as pleased can be.'

And Brünnhilde barked once, long and loud, as if she was too.